Reviews for The Dragon's Edge.

CU00493779

The Dragon's Edge is a weight
adventures, laced with profound
challenging times of today. You ..... ~~ ~~awn~~ into this colourful
world of dragons and magic, and into the Spirit of Nature. It is also a
story that seeks to answer some of life's eternal questions.
Peter Knight, author, Stone Seeker Publishing and Tours

Just buy this book!
Be prepared for the journey of a thousand lifetimes, thrilling reading.
Topcat

Best book I have ever read!
A brilliant book, compulsive reading, a great story, so relevant for our
times. Highly recommended.
Stephen Rooke

This is a deeply researched book and, whilst labelled a fantasy
story, it is really more than that as it offers an important, allegorical
message to the reader about the world we live in given we see human
and climatic catastrophes almost on an everyday basis. It is a story
about another world not dissimilar to our own that provokes the
reader into thought on determining an explanation to destructive
events, backed up with mystical insight on the events that caused it. It
does offer hope too, provided that we, as a race are prepared to do
something about it. A massive subject! From the start the author
writes with passion about the cause and the story unravels with
deeply researched visual scenarios about two young travellers, Okino
and Mariella in their journey and enlightenment throughout the
mystical land of Arimathea but also with conviction and knowledge
on the subject matter. It is worth making the effort to read 'The
Dragon's Edge' thoroughly, one chapter at a time, in order to
visualise, percolate and absorb. I found it to be a great escape to and a
story with resonance during these rather worrying times. A great first
novel!
David Gray

A wonderful, enthralling, spellbinding novel, written with heart
and style. The Dragon's Edge is a fascinating page turner filled with
wisdom, humour and hope for those who believe the world is worth
saving.. A delight to read.
Debbie Leslie

An indispensable book for anyone who decides to embark on a journey towards inner knowledge. The author holds out his hand to guide us into the invisible world .....of the fantasy that becomes reality......wonderful journey into ancestral memory....and that makes us forget who we are.....
Shannon Mcwise

A glorious read set in another place.
A book to lose yourself in. A world away from all the politics and posturing, this is a book that transports you to somewhere magical that is tinged with a frightening realism of what can be lost if we don't take stock of what we already have.
C. Brabham

Beautiful descriptions and magical dragons.
A most amazing book and so relevant to our current world. I resonated strongly with this book and am so pleased it had a happy ending. I feel everyone should read it and maybe our world will change.
Gladys Dinnacombe

I thoroughly enjoyed reading this book, a long read but it gripped me to the end. It's themes of good versus evil, habitat destruction, corporate greed, the concept of Arimathea being an evolving being in her own right, and the need to reconnect again with the land are all very relevant to us today.
Joyce Henry

Inspirational.
This is an absolutely magical book. From the first page you are drawn into the inspirational world of Arimathea where monks sit silently in prayer. A journey through this book is not to be missed, it takes you through mountains, forests & sacred places. Into the world of ancient dragon races & to connect again with their magical realms. We need to feel our sense of belonging again. This book inspires just that. Wonderful...
M. S. Broad

The Dragon's Edge

For Francesca.

Who gave me so much love
and support just when
I needed it most.

For Samah
Have a great journey!
Best wishes
Pete ...

" Originally they came out of the Light."

First Published in Great Britain in 2020 by Dragonhill Publications.

The Paperback edition first published in 2020.

A CIP catalogue record for this title is available from the British Library.

ISBN 978-1-9162925-0-5

Dragonhill Publications policy is to use papers that are natural, renewable and recyclable products and made from wood grown in sustainable forests. The logging and manufacturing processes are expected to conform to environmental regulations of the country of Origin.

Dragonhill Publications,
www.dragonhill1618.com.

Printed by
Cloc Printers.
Unit 10, Millmead Industrial Estate,
Tottenham,
London N17 9QU

The Dragon's Edge

By

Peter Royston Smith

One moment can change a day,
One day can change a life and
One life can change the world.

Gautama Buddha

Part Two   Land, Sea and Air.

Part Three   Spirits of the Desert

"We returned here from our lives whenever we could, to find it again, entered our magical realm where these magical creatures lived their momentary lives and where anything was possible…"

Introduction

Peter Royston Smith was born in Guildford in March 1961. Fifteen days later Yuri Gagarin flew into space for the first time and orbited the Earth ...

I had arrived in the Space Age and soon became fascinated with all it had to offer. We were the first generation who became used to seeing pictures of the Earth from space. The idea of travelling to other worlds moved from the realms of fantasy when Neil Armstrong stepped onto the Moon in 1969.

A creative streak emerged in those early years. I enrolled at Southbank Polytechnic to study Architecture. I found myself reading the writings of Frank Lloyd Wright and became interested in the fusion of Art and Engineering which arose in the medieval era in the form of Gothic cathedrals. I started to delve into the mysteries of Chartres. I found it had been built on the site of an old Sacred Grove established by the Celtic Druids. The phenomena of telluric currents and subsequently ley lines provided a link with a mystical world with which I found I had always resonated. I visited Chartres Cathedral and after walking the labyrinth, I felt an unusual excitement as I stood on the transept in the magical glow of the beautiful coloured glass.

I also became fascinated with the ideas of James Lovelock. He speculated our Planet was a goddess named Gaia. She was a complex self regulating organism with processes and systems which had allowed her to evolve to where we can contemplate the world we now live on in this way. I began to accept the idea we lived as part of a conscious world where everything was infinitely and profoundly interconnected.

All through these times and as soon as I was able I had wandered in the wooded hills around my home. Later these wanderings became journeys to the most distant and lonely parts of our beautiful islands. I made pilgrimages to the mysterious old Stone circles where they survived embedded in the Earth, aligned with the Sun, the Moon and the Stars, where their ancient builders had carefully placed them and where the energy flowing through our world came to her surface.

As the environmental crisis on Earth deepened and was generally ignored by the mainstream there seemed little being done to counter the gloomy predictions. I became a druid myself and found a Sacred Grove deep in the New Forest in Hampshire. We channelled the energy flowing from the Earth as we stood amongst the ancient Oaks and hoped Gaia would guide us.

I made a game called 'Dragonhill' to reflect my journeys through the mountains and forests to those ancient sacred places. I found in these places my inspiration flowed a little more intensely and as a result I became closer to Gaia.

The destination was always the summit of the Dragonhill where the winner would commune with the Dragon who was dreaming out the wisdom attained from the previous worlds he had inhabited. But it was too complicated and I started to write a guidebook.

It became 'The Dragon's Edge' and Gaia became Arimathea.

The Planet of Arimathea

The Dragon's Edge.

Chapter One
The Temple of the Dragon.

High in the mountains of the long-forgotten world of Arimathea, eleven monks sat silently on their prayer mats under the ancient timbers of their remote monastery. Smoke from their incense burners drifted sinuously into the air, weaving ghostly forms through beams of light penetrating from clerestory windows high in the walls of the octagonal hall. The stout doors had been opened to allow in the fresh mountain air, infused with delicate light reflected from the drifts of snow covering the slopes beyond. Perched on a fortuitous ledge, the monastery had been built by monks many generations before to exploit the vista it now commanded overlooking the towering snow mountains beyond.

The walls blended with the cliffs of a steep ravine falling to the valley below where a lively river tumbled amongst ancient boulders left long ago by melted glaciers. The sky reflected on its surface, revealing a silvery thread visible from high in this temple eerie. Sculpted by millennia of snow melt trickling from the slopes of the mountains on either side, its serpentine form snaked and swirled its way down and across the gentle slopes of the valley flood plain. The raging torrents of the early spring had now been transformed into forceful silent currents flowing down through the cultivated fields on either side of its banks.

Far beyond the mountains the stream would eventually merge with the ocean. Here a monk was able to expand his consciousness into some of the wildest and most uninhabited areas of his world. In those expanses he would meet all the fundamental questions and mysteries governing his existence. He could watch the serene white heaven of this remote icy world retreat, to again be replaced by the miracle of green life emerging from the fertile valley in the spring. From here he could wonder about all the myriad of life existing beyond the stark emptiness of the mountains and of the miraculous weave of cosmic circumstance that had brought it all into existence.

There was no date for the founding of this monastery. It was assumed this place had always been revered and sacred, always journeyed to and perhaps at some time possessed. However, the vast open beauty of eternity it revealed soon made the idea of possession irrelevant. So the monks had settled here. They had brought what timber and stone they needed up the winding mountain paths and carefully built a temple fitting for this majestic setting. The temple was built as if it had grown out of the mountain. Outside walls had been made continuous with the cliff face. Terraces were formed at every opportunity so any activity whether dining, meditating or simply conducting a conversation became inextricably linked and enhanced by the presence of the breath-taking landscapes of Arimathea stretching to the horizon beyond.

The accommodation was simple. Each monk had his own small room with a view looking out over the mountains. There was a bed and enough room for him to meditate in solitude if he so wished. There was a refectory where meals were eaten communally. Their food was grown on the lower slopes in their own terrace gardens or was brought from the village closer to the valley floor. Many of the monks would have been recruited from the village but occasionally one would arrive from outside and prove himself to be worthy of acceptance into their order. Occasionally there would be monks visiting the temple who stayed for weeks or months, in retreat from the lives they had found themselves leading in the more heavily populated parts of Arimathea. Invariably they would return with a greater understanding of the predicament which had brought them to seek out this remote outpost of humanity. In their time at the monastery they would have done little more than talk with the monks, contemplate and meditate in the spectacular landscapes.

However, these transformations were of no surprise to the monks who lead their lives here. In this isolated mountain retreat there was nothing to interfere with the monk's connection to his beloved world enabling him to seek a deeper understanding of his existence on all levels. Understanding there was a supernatural presence under lying this breath taking physical world was not difficult in this stunning location. However, debate as to its nature and the influence it may or may not have on planetary matters was often and fiercely debated. Once conversations about the general running of the community had been completed to a satisfactory end then the discussions about the nature of their world could resume. The questions were everywhere here. The monks had dedicated their lives to understanding how this wonder had come to be. Every aspect of their lives had become bound up with their quest to gain further insight into the nature of their world. As the monks had come for generations to think on these things so their thoughts had been recorded. Much had been written and many of their personal contributions to the nature of the mystery were stored in the temple library.

In one of the central teachings handed down through the generations was a legend with which the monks had never been able to wholly disagree. The legend although it had never become a 'truth', had always captured and focused the imagination of the monks in their work. It was the legend of the dragons who had given their name to the temple. This legend gave form to the spirits, the monks believed, who had come to inhabit Arimathea from far away in the stars. It was acceptance of this legend which gave structure to further explore the mystery which had always bound the monks together. It was reflected in the carvings of the timbers throughout the structure of the temple, in the artwork, tapestries and paintings adorning the spaces. Sculptures and even floor mosaics reflected this old legend which had been continually handed down through the generations. Today the legend would be handed down yet again in the unique way their tradition had demanded for many centuries.

The monks had gathered in the temple to initiate a new monk into the Order. He had been living in the monastery for a year in the company of the other monks. In this way the community was able to ascertain whether he had the temperament that would allow him to follow his calling and be beneficial to the continuation of the monastery's work. He was given little instruction in this year. However, the young monk was given access to all areas of the monastery. This included the library where the writings of the monks were stored. It was hoped he would gain some understanding of the nature of the work by absorbing what he saw and found around him. It was felt if the young monk was not in sympathy with the general atmosphere and ambience of his new home within the year, then it was assumed he would leave of his own accord.

The presence of Arimathea's spirit flooded in through every opening. The diversity and breadth of its manifestation in the physical world was lovingly portrayed on the walls throughout. Amongst the serpentine writhing of the dragons, were portrayed flocks of birds rising from lakes, herds of exotic animals grazing across the expansive open plains. Big cats prowled through jungles, dolphins and whales cruised blue oceans on the walls behind the columns down which the dragons slithered endlessly from the stars on the ceiling to the floors below.

The planet floor was represented by one huge eight pointed star aligned with the four cardinal points North, South, East and West and the ordinal points between. The dragons possessed the wings of birds or bats and the horns of deer, they had the aquiline features of dolphins and whales, the claws and teeth were of cats. Eyes were wild, fiery and possessed of an uncanny feeling of infinity soon apparent when any more than the briefest glance was given. They were frequently depicted in the clouds of sunsets, in waterfalls and rivers. Lightening was portrayed so as to leave no doubt what the monks thought lay behind the primal forces that had formed Arimathea.

Nothing was said about the actual legend to the initiate and when a similar subject was discussed then no importance was put upon it. The initiate was left to form his own opinion about what his work would be. This process had been the same for as long as could be remembered. The monks of the order knew in this way their monastery would have a continuous history enabling them to enhance their knowledge and understanding of Arimathea and their place upon her, with few breaks or disturbances certainly for many hundreds of years.

Somewhere out in the mountains a horn sounded. A deep sonorous note boomed and vibrated through the valley. The circle of monks was motionless. The sound gently rippled the air as it flowed through the hall. There were echoes and resonance's adding an otherworldly dimension to the sound until the note was finally allowed to fade back into the star shine. In the serenity of these moments the monks were once again separating their consciousness from their physical bodies.

The sensation of sitting began to fall away, arms resting gently on thighs, equilibrium transferred the weight of muscled frame and skull perfectly down through the skeletal structure into the structure of the temple. Where bones, muscle and flesh had been, the monks felt only light. Light emanating from the accentuated life force existing in each of the beings sitting in the circle. This light had no boundaries in any dimension, and now was merging with the life consciousness of Arimathea. As each spirit became elevated so the light in the hall started to change, almost imperceptibly, as if a thin mist had slowly cleared revealing a landscape flooded with the brightest star shine. The columns and beams, their connections, the plains of walls and screens were flooded with geometric information echoing through time, through the time of the legend, through the time of the first establishment of the monastery, through the time of all the lives and experience of the monks who had sat and meditated in this space. In this heightened state of consciousness, information unseen became profound meaning, shining from even the smallest details. The openings of the windows provided the final connection into the sublime shining beauty of the planet of Arimathea beyond.

The monks now held the higher connection amongst themselves and the spirit of their world. They were in suspension, unhooked from their moorings in time, untarnished by the history of what could have been or what might yet be; liberated from their perceptions of themselves as physical beings and the space they inhabited. The idea of themselves as individuals separate from the universe had fallen away. A subtle spherical aura was now glowing around the circle.

The oldest of the monks stood up and carefully walked through the space where the twelfth monk would have been and over to the large open doors leading out to the refectory. As he stood in the opening he was joined by a further younger monk. They greeted each other fondly and the older man indicated for the younger to enter the temple. Side by side they walked through the doors to where the circle of monks was now deep in meditation. The younger monk stood in amazement at the edge of the aura. The master walked in and with a smile beckoned him to sit in the empty space. There the young man settled down and looked around the circle. The monks who had already become like his brothers sat silently.

The meditation technique the monks had revealed to him would take him deep enough for the purposes of the initiation. He relaxed into the posture they had taught him, closed his eyes and concentrated on becoming aware of his own life force, of his breathing, of his heart beating and pumping his blood around his body. As he became aware of his own consciousness, he also became aware he was not limited in any way by his physical frame and was able to feel the combined and heightened consciousness of the other monks sat around him in the circle. Then he was aware of the star light and the cool mountain air, he heard an eagle call high over the ravine and the wind gently blowing in through the open shutters. He felt his whole self, soaring out into the wide open spaces. He encompassed mountains and seas and the winds as they circled his world. He felt the rich tapestry of life unravelling under the gentle warmth of Arimathea's star.

The old monk looked around, saw the sphere was complete and settled his gaze on the initiate.

"Okino, we welcome you. It is always a special day when we initiate a new brother into this circle. Now for the first time you are experiencing your consciousness connected with your brothers, who in turn have made their connection with the spirit of Arimathea. When you are ready, feel comfortable and as you experience these new levels of consciousness, in your own time perhaps, you could tell us the thoughts you are now having."

Okino drifted in the light forming in his mind. He could still feel the monastery around him, the atmosphere of the mountains beyond the open doors, the pungent smell of the incense calming him, deepening his state of relaxation. But the light was beckoning him to a deeper place. He felt no reason to resist as the reality from which he had come gradually started to fade into the deeper recesses of his mind. In the light, shadowy forms and movement started to arise. He found he was sitting on new ground under a new sky which was giving a new and more substantial solidity to the light around him. The shadows made by an invisible star were becoming more solid moment by moment.

Soon he was able to open his eyes and look out on this new world forming around him. It came in and out of focus as if there were more than one scene he was looking at. One moment there were people walking through parklands beside a lake but then there was only a baking desert. He saw buildings forming amongst tree lined streets but then everything changed again and the images of the buildings faded into soaring rock faces. It was as if this new world couldn't decide what it wanted to be or where or when. The heat fluctuated, a ferocious gust of wind became a gentle breeze, then he could feel moisture in the air as if he was enveloped in a dense mist. He became aware of space all around him as if he was on the summit of a hill and there was a distant horizon. A land into which he could travel and experience only connected tenuously to his own life and the world he had left.

As he started to feel this new density the atmosphere around him seemed to lock into place, to solidify as if it had remembered where it had to be and for what reason. For a few moments the light in the mist increased, glowed intensively with a gentle golden light. The mist started to recede below the rim of the elevated place where Okino could see he was sitting. He was surrounded by a circle of stones in a frozen winter landscape. The stones were twice his own height and appeared to be very old. Snow had drifted around them and had settled on their tops and on any ledges distorting their shape with frozen white additions. The surface of the frozen layer between the stones had been undisturbed by any movement. A star was rising between two of the largest stones. It rose like a blood red sphere out of the frozen mists still laying thinly across the land below. Okino's breath billowed in front of him and drifted across the circle in clouds like ghostly envoys. In his direct vicinity the hill fell steeply into the landscape below. There was a ring of carefully laid stone slabs surrounding the monoliths from where the snow, it seemed, had not been able to settle or had drifted away. Okino waded through the deep snow to this outer rim of the circle. There were steps, constructed from the same stone, leading to a path which then carried on out into the landscape beyond.

Okino walked around this circular path looking out across hills and plains. The mist now barely visible allowed the features of the land below to be seen more fully. At the bottom of the steps the path appeared to wind its way through the landscape, joining other paths as it progressed. The stone was white and had a mottled grey constituent. There were black veins running through it and shards of clear crystal reflected the low light from across its surface. Below his feet and beyond, the path sparkled enabling Okino to trace these shining pathways as they wound their way onward. He could see dwellings and small villages nestled in amongst the hills almost wholly buried in the deep covering of ice and frozen snow. The only signs of vegetation he could see were enormous trees which stood resiliently against the bitter cold. They appeared to be entirely dormant, showing little sign of life in what appeared to be the constant state of winter that had come upon this land. Long heavy icicles hung from their branches and glistened in the low half-light glow from a star which seemed to be moving in a very low transit just above the horizon.

The paths wound through the thick blanket of white towards larger buildings rising from the stillness like rocky islands from an ethereal white sea. He could see one close by and two much further away in the distance. Under the snow covered roofs, they appeared to be carefully crafted and built from the mottled grey stone with the solidity of castles able to withstand long passages of time. The crystalline quality of the stone shimmered in the cold misty atmosphere adding to their ghostly appearance. Everything else seemed to be chaotic and unformed. Ice covered rivers reflected the low Starshine as they threaded their way across the plains and through the hills into frozen lakes, now expanses of shining ice and drifting snow. There was a feeling of emptiness here Okino had never felt in even the starkest of the landscapes he had experienced and it was completely silent. There was no sound or movement of any kind beyond his breath freezing immediately in the icy air.

He carefully descended the icy steps down the side of the hill and started to make his way along one of the paths. In places it had been covered by large expanses of drifting snow. Still there was no vegetation of any kind other than the enormous trees. Any more delicate organic material had long since disappeared and there was no other sign of life. The deep snow covering was punctuated by exposed bedrock which appeared to have been pushed out from the rocky mantle below by whatever cataclysm had occurred here. Everywhere he felt as if some invisible process was sucking the atmosphere out of the land, leaving it covered only with the wintery white mantle on the ground and sealing it from the universe beyond with grey leaden skies above.

In the world where he lived there were always sights and sounds happening in stimulating combinations. This continual commentary would give him complex information about the processes or the other lives who lived there; allowing him insight into how it had all come to be. All the elements he found so fascinating about moving through a landscape were missing from here. All the worlds within worlds and the connections enabling them all to inhabit the land together, relying on all the distinct aspects of each other's existence; the intricate web of stories and evolutions which had created every feature they now possessed and enriched every turn into every new vista; all the fascinating detail was missing leaving his senses yearning for the rich textures and the depth of colour, the sound always present, filling and defining the space around him.

He was in an alien derelict world where something inexplicable had happened leaving a landscape frozen in time; it had quite literally stopped. There were no animals, no insects and no birds and barely any starlight. It was devoid of even a breeze or gusts of wind of any nature. It felt as if it had been left suddenly; as if the life force which had driven everything, the consciousness supporting the psyche of this place had strangely fallen out of the atmosphere and simply vanished. This was the only story here and more and more it felt like it had suffered a nightmarish ending.

As he moved nearer to the huddles of buildings, he could see many had collapsed leaving only low walls weathered for many years of exposure to whatever atmosphere had survived here. Many looked like they had been physically destroyed. The stonework lay chaotically scattered partially covered by snow and ice. In the eerie stillness Okino thought he could hear strange disembodied screams, they were panic stricken and terrified, provoked by a chaotic series of events as their homes began to fall apart and the solidity of the landscape became compromised. Desperate shadows continually slipped past him as they fled from whatever force had enveloped their land, momentarily exposed as if their terrified trace had scorched its mark on time to haunt this sad and unfortunate place. Other buildings had collapsed into icy crevices opened in the ground leaving them bizarrely leaning in rubble and surrounded by snow drifts forced up around them. All signs of life had been removed from them in the time that had elapsed and only the stone had resisted the disintegration which had occurred.

The shining stone path, where still exposed, had bridged relentlessly the ripples in the ground and atmosphere which had shaken the landscape into this perilous state. Okino decided it would be impossible to tell when all this had occurred. Only the path ahead was solid and unwavering, making its way through the silent trees wrapped in their icy gowns towards one of the temple castles in the distance. The paths and the castles, it seemed, had remained pristine throughout since whatever catastrophe had happened here. Through this stone he could feel only the remnant of an energy source rising up through his feet from a network spreading far out into this world and down into its depths. Just enough he deduced to hold it together and to prevent it completely disintegrating back to where it had come from. This he decided was true of all he had discovered here. It was being tenuously held as if someone or something was waiting for a time when the energy would flow back and life would return and everything could start again.

He was at the entrance to one of the temple castles. The solid timber door stood half open. Okino pushed away the snow that had accumulated on the landing. As he walked in he noticed he was already feeling tired and weary for the amount of walking he had done. Had this been why the beings who had lived here had left or disappeared? The energy levels were simply not high enough to sustain any kind of complex or sentient life. It would explain why animals and insects were also nowhere to be seen. He walked into a large stone hall. It was long and high above him. It had a series of high clerestory windows sending only dim light to the space below. Snow sat on the sills of the empty openings and the remnants from the last snowstorm lay in frozen drifts against the stone walls. There was an enormous bowl towards the centre of the space partially filled with snow and still blackened by whatever had been burnt there when last it had been used.

Okino imagined the effect of such a fire in this dramatic space; an image of the inferno flickered around him for a few moments; there were hooded figures standing around the bowl. He knew it had always been kept burning at the heart of this place. This is where the inhabitants had come in reverence to celebrate the life force. This is where they had come to contemplate the miracle at the heart of their existence, the warmth from the flickering flames, the nuclear fusion in the centre of their Star always shining down on them filling their atmosphere with vibrancy and the etheric womb from which life had emerged. They had known and assimilated the mystery into the fabric of their lives but like their ghostly figures he had briefly seen standing around the fire it had faded back into the structures of the Universe.

He walked past the fire bowl and moved deeper into the hall. There were many torches of all description lining the walls, but it had been a long time since they had been alight. The atmosphere of the entire hall was similar to the land beyond its walls; one of the cold and wintery places which had been deserted under some sinister circumstances. At the back of the hall under the largest window high in the wall, there was a long table made from a single smooth slab of the sparkling grey stone supported on stout stone legs. The stonework appeared always to be connected; perhaps to channel the energy Okino was still feeling, continuously and softly pulsing as if from some powerful invisible generator deep in this bleak frozen world. As he came closer, he saw there was a line of words badly or quickly carved into the table. There was a thin layer of frosty snow obscuring the entire sentence. He brushed it off and then read.

"The dragons have deserted us."

There were stone benches along the table and Okino collapsed exhausted and confused across the table. The words seared through his thoughts. Who had the dragons deserted and why? Had they left this dimension or had they left the whole of Arimathea and if so for what reason and when had all this happened? There never had been any historical record of the dragons, so he presumed this had all happened a very long time ago. Had there ever been a connection with the monastery and his order? He found he could hardly move and he was now feeling a dark unfathomable emptiness around him. He felt he was losing consciousness and fading into the emptiness. The words carved on the table were now urgently being spoken, echoing through the space around him. He lifted his head and looked down the hall. He could see a chaotic dark aura hovering over the fire bowl. As he watched he saw the blue skies and the sparkling rivers and all the life it had consumed; the people, their children, everything they had created and lived for, all which had inspired them in their world was trapped inside the maelstrom, feeding it's dark chaos; and now it was sucking the remaining energy out of the surrounding atmosphere.

Okino watched as the last of the ghostly flames died down. He felt as if he was falling into a deep and endless emptiness and if he didn't find his way back, he could easily evaporate into its dark oblivion. He searched around himself and reached out for the light. He knew it was somewhere out in front of him. Gradually he was able to bring it back into his being.

Slowly he started to feel himself back in the circle of monks and safe in the monastery with the mountains all around him. He gasped, exhaling the dark fetid emptiness from the hall, inhaled deeply the sparkling fresh mountain air and relished the brightness as it filled his lungs and the rest of his being. He opened his eyes and immediately saw the concerned faces of the eleven monks looking over at him. They were relieved when they saw him open his eyes. He smiled around the circle at them and they smiled back expectantly. They eagerly listened to what he had to say. Then they were silent and concerned for his wellbeing and for their world. Then it was traditional for the master to welcome the initiate.

"It is clear you have not experienced a traditional initiation!"

A gentle ripple of laughter ran around the circle of monks,

"However, we know the times in which you have come to us are far from normal. There seems to be an element of communication from within the deeper dimensions in what you have experienced. It may carry some warnings or explanations. I think there is much to be discussed and debated in the coming days. But there can be no doubt, however, you have successfully taken your place here. So, I welcome you as our brother Okino, on behalf of all in this circle to The Order of Dragon, may your service be long and for the benefit of all who live on Arimathea."

Chapter Two.
Okino's vision.

Okino had come to the monastery in the true tradition. He was born in the town of Lamai situated in the province of Jahallala. It nestled on the lower slopes of a valley in a range of mountains in the far north of one of the six continents forming the land masses of Arimathea.

The nature and the most prevalent geological history of the planet now dictating the climatic conditions of Jahallala had been the gradual separation of the two land masses. They had split and moved apart leaving six continents with additional islands broken off from them. They were separated by the large oceans surrounding Arimathea. The continental plates had pushed and grated against each other at various different times in Arimathea's turbulent evolution. These processes continued to push up spinal mountain ranges on each of the continents. These spectacular mountain ranges and in many places their snow capped peaks dominated the surrounding lands. Their long spines had benefited greatly the lands lying in their shadow.

Arimathea was in a miraculously beneficial orbit around her Star. Her land masses and her seas were warmed by its radiation to perfectly regulate and create her atmosphere. Her lands and seas were warmed and cooled as she spun creating the fluctuations in pressure which drove her winds around and over the surface of the planet. These weather systems had created diverse climatic conditions across the landmasses of the planet. Heat and rainfall around the equators had made tropical zones where jungles and rain forests proliferated. Areas of desert, where the rocks of Arimathea's exterior covering had been reduced to huge areas of drifting sand and were continually exposed to the most ferocious heat the star could throw down upon them. Here only the driest winds emptied of moisture on their journey across the land closer to the seas formed and reformed the vast landscapes of ever-changing dunes. The arid areas where intermittent rainfall and moisture within the atmosphere allowed only specially adapted plant and animal life to exist.

In all these areas humans had learnt to live with the knowledge of countless generations. They had developed abilities to find the limited food and water in these extreme places. It was the temperate zones of the planet where most of the human populations had gravitated towards and eventually settled. They had spread out and roamed the planet after the great ice sheets had receded and found these areas where the gentle changes from winter to summer gave optimum rainfall and temperature for their species. It was in these areas where the great farming revolution had taken place. The warm convection currents collected water from the oceans and carried it over the warm lands. The winds coming up against the mountain ranges were either compressed high in the cold atmosphere to become snow and ice or were deposited as rainfall in the lands between the seas and the spine mountain ranges. The fertile lands were ideal for farming and so early settlements became villages and eventually towns and cities.

All the connecting networks spreading out across the planet were started in these fertile areas. Jahallala lay in one of these temperate zones. The plains between the coast where the land started to rise into the mountains had been populated from early times. There was an abundance of clear fresh water from the melting glaciers flowing down the many rivers from the mountains creating rich fertile flood plains. There had been rich forests full of wildlife and abundant flora and fauna. Towns had grown alongside the rivers allowing trade to the coasts from the earliest times.

As humans learnt to effectively cross the oceans and trade with other countries across the seas, so influences came to Jahallala from all corners of the planet. It was rich for its beneficial position like so many of the temperate lands conducive to the new farming way of life humans had developed. But these riches meant Jahallala had been fought over continuously by the rise and fall of the many empires who had attempted to dominate Arimathea and its people. The people who now lived in these plains below the mountains were a race as mixed as the many peoples who had flowed over them through the ages. Towns and cities were rich with the reminder of the cultures who had come and been assimilated by the land and the people who had lived there. The remains and ruins of many of these races and cultures also lay in the fields and on the fertile river plains dominating those low lying areas as a reminder of her turbulent history.

The mountains however had avoided much of the turmoil the lower lands had been subjected to. The traditions and the ways of the people who lived there had been little disturbed for as long as their stories had been passed down through the generations. The passes were impenetrable for most of the year. The winters were severe and unforgiving to any who disrespected their icy power. In the brief Summer when a force could entertain the idea of some invasion the vast expanses beyond were almost entirely impenetrable as a result of extreme heat and were eerily uninhabited. It was only in the higher isolated valleys where the more sheltered conditions had allowed the mountain people to maintain a lifestyle little changed for thousands of years, free from the continual invasions hampering the lands below.

Okino and his friends were taught the history of their country in their village school. The journey through the mountain passes across the plains to the richer lands beyond was treacherous and was rarely made. Okino had been curious about his world from an early age and seemed to understand the nature of his planet and its place in the universe, surprising to many of the adults in his community. His parents noticed from any early age he seemed different from the other children of his generation. Even when very young he would often be found sitting under the stars and was soon able to recount to anyone with only the scant knowledge of the atlas available, the position of Arimathea within the cosmos in relation to the stars and galaxies many hundreds of light years away.

As he grew older, he would make regular visits to the monastery to help the monks in their gardens and listen to their stories. As he became more independent he would spend long days wandering the mountains in search of the wildlife inhabiting the slopes. He would sit quietly for many hours, waiting for mountain leopards and even bears to wander past. He would climb high into the mountains, for as well as his affinity with the land on the lower slopes he also had a great love for the mountain air. He relished its moods and changes and when the wind dropped he would often be found on one of his beloved peaks looking over the lower hills and plains of Jahallala.

Okino always did well at the little school. He absorbed information quickly and learned his lessons fast. He became fascinated by everything the monks who taught at the school could teach him. He relished especially the lessons about the geography and wildlife of Arimathea. But he excelled in all his work and was always quick to help his classmates who found the lessons more difficult.

His parents and the wider community soon realized he was destined for the monastery. His father who was a farmer had also become a gifted tailor. He farmed on the flood plains of the river tending the herds of goats and growing crops of vegetables, corn and rice planted and harvested by the community as a whole. Often Okino would follow him in the fields and help with watching or milking the goats if he was not at school or playing with his friends in the town.

Life in these mountainous areas of Arimathea was tenuous and was held in great respect. Mistakes could not be made. The people went to great effort to find what role their offspring would play in the community. Nothing, least of all talent could be wasted. The energy of a child who had the ability to be a farmer would be wasted as a baker or a blacksmith. However, a monk who also had knowledge of farming was a great asset to the monastery. The children generally had a good knowledge of their parent's trade. They were drawn in to help at times when they were needed. During their childhoods they were given the opportunity to work in all areas of the community. If a new building was needed then everyone able was found a task to perform. Likewise, when the terraces needed ploughing or harvesting anyone who was able would help out. The harvest was an important time for the community and even schoolwork would be allowed to drift if extra hands were needed; much to the delight of the children.

It was a great honour for a family in the community to realize they had a child destined for the monastery. The monks became the teachers. In this responsibility lay the future wellbeing of the entire town. Through their lessons, the children were taught how to become responsible members of their community. As well as being taught reading, writing and mathematics they were taught the stories, myths and legends containing the history and philosophy of their people. In their mathematics and science lessons, practical ideas connected with the crops and the animals were brought in from an early age. They were taught about the physical world in their geography lessons, about their direct mountain environment but also of the wider world. The children sat wide eyed as the monks told them stories of satellite broadcasting, of aero-planes, supermarkets and the mass media dominating cultures on other parts of the planet. Here the monks offered strong justification for the continuation of their own cultures, knowing many of the children sitting in front of them may be tempted by the ideas they were hearing and a few would eventually leave to find their way to the cities beyond the mountains.

As well as educating the children, the monks guided the people in all areas of their lives. Their own intuitive connection with the world, so important to the community's way of life, was strengthened by their training in the monastery. A certain amount of mystery surrounded the period between when a young man was taken to the monastery and when he appeared again in the community. When a father was found to have a priest on his hands his friends would make humorous commiserations. They joked that while their sons who became, builders, farmers and blacksmiths would help the older generations with the back-breaking work which still had to be undertaken, the monks would be meditating on what it all meant for the spiritual health of the community.

However, when the joking was over and the farmers and the builders sat in their meetings they knew the monks were the very bedrock of their community. For when the mountain winds howled through and froze their crops in the ground or an unknown disease was sickening their animals, the monks once again showed them why it was they strived so and were at times let down. They had a way of reassuring a man or woman who had become isolated and alone in some catastrophe about the true nature of his or her existence. They pointed to the mountain flowers blooming only every three years or the mountain leopards who ate only every three or four days. They reminded them they had a precious and privileged place in their world. While there was disaster today there would be triumph tomorrow. They showed them the strength of support they had in the community. They could be relied upon to demonstrate sound understanding of the problems facing their existence derived from generations of experience, common-sense and wisdom handed down and preserved in the monasteries.

So, it had been decided, Okino had the ability and potential to join the monks. When he was eighteen years old his father was bound to ask him if he wanted to go to the monastery, explaining he would not see his parents for a whole year while his initial training was undertaken. Okino had been waiting for the day and showed no hesitation in his reply. He could not wait any longer for his training to begin.

The next day Okino and his father made the long climb up the narrow paths to the mountain retreat. His father was surprised when he was greeted by the monks as if he were already one of their own. He had known for many years this moment would come. As they said their goodbyes and he made his way back down the stony mountain track he knew everything was as it should be. Okino had always shown wisdom and competence in whatever he had set his hand to. A wisdom he felt would eventually outgrow the little mountain community. There had always been something special about the boy and he had always wondered what destiny had in store for him.

Okino settled in to his first year in the monastery as if he had returned after a long journey. At this stage he found he was able to direct even more of his time into his wanderings and contemplations. His teachers actively encouraged him as the results of his solitude soon brought fresh insight into the monastery. The teachings handed down were reinterpreted by every generation. The monks knew the world beyond the mountains was changing rapidly. Values and traditions held by previous generations were rapidly falling away. Seen as repressive, the old ways were replaced by a freedom unrestricted by the moral guidance of more respectful generations. The wise old monks knew what had happened in their own communities when groups of people had started to reject the customs that had kept the mountain communities thriving for hundreds of years. Where one group of people were gaining where they had not before, invariably there was another who was losing out.

It had always been easy to see in the mountain communities where resources were so delicately balanced. Unconsidered changes nearly always brought difficulty. They encouraged the young monk as he explored his way into the future to consider all they could teach him about the past. Much of the training was to keep the monks firmly focused in the present. They were given disciplined exercises encouraging them to consider every angle in all their decisions and actions. It was one of the hardest aspects faced in the early stages of their training.

When the young monk had been in the monastery for a year he was given the traditional initiation ceremony and fully welcomed into the brotherhood. Okino's ceremony had been unusual for one so young and had caused much debate and controversy. The dragons were at the heart of the teachings of the order and yet Okino had revealed at some stage they had deserted the world they had come to inhabit and guide. It was full of symbols which were much discussed and their imagery was dissected from every angle. Eventually it was decided the meditation had been sent to further illustrate the beneficial nature of the dragons and the consequences for the world if ever they left. Although there were those who harboured the suspicion the dragons had already left Arimathea or something had happened to suspend their influence.

The monks soon recognized, although Okino's wild and natural ability as an intuitive spiritual being, was endearing and obviously advantageous, it would have to be channelled so he could become a beneficial member of the monastery and the wider community. At the appropriate times, and not necessarily to Okino's approval, his own activities had been deliberately restrained. It was stressed on more than one occasion that although, of course, he was still an individual, his ability to become an unselfish member of the brotherhood was imperative to the advanced meditation work he was being taught. Although he was wise in many ways, he was young and headstrong and the older monks prayed silently to themselves the lesson they felt was due to him would not be too harsh.

One morning Okino announced after their morning meditation he was going to take a long walk up to one of the mountain peaks on the other side of the valley. This would have caused no worry amongst his brother monks other than the fact there was a very slight but persistent breeze. Many of them knew this to be a sign there may well be a storm on the way. However, although they lived very much as a family, to keep their personal identity was deemed to be extremely important for each of the individual monks. They were also encouraged to be personally responsible and on that morning some of the older monks may have said in their experience it did not seem to be a good day to go climbing in the mountains. But they did not. Here in the monastery each one of them was free to make their own mistakes. They knew sometimes mistakes had to be made for growth to occur. So they watched as the intrepid Okino headed off down into the valley with a light meal. He did reluctantly take an extra blanket roll when one of the monks remarked casually, he thought the breeze seemed a little stronger than earlier in the morning.

Okino had convinced himself the wind would gather no more intensity and actually it was a very beautiful day to go walking in the hills. He liked the fresh breezes. He could hear the gentle voice of the mountain in the trees as it swirled around the rocks. He liked to watch the falcons and the eagles who would soar out high above him. He savoured the different smells reaching him. Essences of pine and the profusion of wildflowers drifted through the clear mountain air from the rocky slopes down into the lush valleys. He filled his mind continuously with the experience of his world. Crossing the busy mountain stream running through the valley he admired the colour of the sky across the surface as it washed over boulders rounded from their journey in the mountains. Looking downstream through the valley and into the far distance he wondered of the continuing journey of the water now passing beneath him as it made its way down to the sea. He thought one day he would like to make that journey. Follow the river to the sea. Sit on the beach and look out across the ocean and wonder of the lands beyond. His attention settled on a wider part of the stream where a pool had formed. The breeze gusted gently, distorting the reflection of clouds now scurrying in a purposeful manner across the sky. Okino thought they were starting to look larger and more interesting. He often thought he could see dragons in the clouds and often wondered whether this was the way they now travelled when they wanted to become physical and so travel anonymously through the world.

He walked across the grassy meadows forming the plain at the bottom of the valley. The early spring star shone brightly. Flowers stretched themselves out of the grass up into the star shine. As he started up the low slopes of the mountain, Okino stood for a few moments, admiring the beauty of his surroundings. Breathed it in so he felt there was no difference between himself and the shimmering vision around him. As he continued the slopes became steeper. He concentrated on his climbing as his heart and lungs started to work harder.

Occasionally he would stop and cast a glance back as the valley started to recede into the distance. The stream which he had crossed, glinted in its meanderings now more obvious from above. The wind had again become stronger. Strong enough to ruffle the mountain grass around him. He strained his eyes in an attempt to see the little monastery on the far hillside. But he had come too far. It was midday. Again, he continued his climb eager to reach the top of the mountain. He had to become more wary of his footfall as the ground started to change from earth and grass, to looser stones, rocks and boulders. He made for the slope with the least gradient.

After a strenuous climb carefully watching each footfall, the top of the mountain was at last in sight and with one last effort, heart pounding and legs aching from the intense climb, he finally reached the summit. Breathing heavily, he sat himself down. It was by no means the highest of the mountains in the range, but it commanded a spectacular view over the hills, valleys and distant ranges. Okino again allowed the beauty of his world to infiltrate deep into his being. His insignificance when compared to the vast wilderness before him faded as gradually he blended his own spirit with the mountains. As his body stilled, he once again started to feel at one with his world and the universe through which it relentlessly spun. The true miracle of his existence always filled him with awe. Alone on these summits for a few moments he was able to leave the life of Okino the monk and join the supreme peace of space and time underlying his physical existence. In defiance of the wonder he was feeling, the snow chose those very moments to start falling.

He watched as snowflakes began settling innocently on his robes. A cold shiver snapped him back to reality. He was on top of a mountain and it had started to snow. His robes were thick and there were many layers beneath developed over many centuries by his people for their life in the mountains. But now he could see the weather conditions deteriorating quite rapidly. He unrolled the thick blanket, thankful for the concern of the monks and wrapped it around himself. Rapidly a few flakes had multiplied and within minutes the snow was falling heavily.

Okino gathered his thoughts. Standing on the summit, the magnificent view he had been admiring only minutes before had all but vanished in the snowstorm now developing around him. He found his bearings and started to descend the mountain the way he had come. The snow again intensified and the wind was gusting momentarily strong enough to knock him off his balance. He was now in a blizzard and it was hard for him to keep his eyes open to see where he was going. He knew he was going down the mountain but soon realized he had no way of knowing which way. He cast his mind back to the morning as he left the monastery. He remembered and then acknowledged, for the first time the concerned look on the faces of his fellow monks.

He was now in an extremely dangerous position. If he wandered too far away from his route, he knew he could easily become lost. He decided the safest thing to do was to find some shelter from the blizzard and wait for the storm to end. He would make his way around the mountain to where the wind might be less intense. Hopefully he would be able to shelter in the lee of some rocks.

He struggled on through the blizzard, now so intense he could hardly see the ground beneath his feet. He hurried on, battling against the cold he knew would overcome him in a few minutes if he stopped. Desperately searching for some shelter from the wind he stumbled on around the mountain for what seemed like hours. He felt sure he should already have been frozen to death. He remembered the feelings he had experienced perhaps only an hour before. The quiet peaceful beauty of the mountain had now transformed itself into this raging demon. Then for a moment as he separated himself from the extreme danger, he again experienced the underlying peace, present even in these extreme conditions. Leaning into the wind to keep his balance he became aware of a shadowy mass on the slope slightly above him.

He changed his direction. Movement now was becoming difficult. His feet and legs barely seemed to be part of him as he struggled step by step towards the shadow. The loose stone and shale had been replaced by drifts of snow. He was losing all sense of himself and felt the soft frozen ice crystals suddenly crashing into his face as he fell. He forced himself to crawl onwards through the freezing snow to the solid face of what turned out to be an outcrop of rock. He made his way blindly around the base. He felt the intensity of the wind drop. Again, his world had become peaceful. Instead of the vicious frozen white there was soft warmth. The rage of the storm had receded and become the distant howl of an angry animal cheated of its prey. Okino somewhere acknowledged to himself he was safe and lost consciousness.

He fell into a troubled dream as he lay there on the mountain. Frozen unconscious he had come to the borders separating his life from his death. He drifted in the dream through episodes of his life. They had brought him to this place where it seemed he could leave at any moment. He was watching his parents, his brothers and sisters; but he was apart from them. His parents beckoned him over to join in the fun they were having. But they were only fading into the distance and he was alone again in the meadows looking after the goats. He laughed at their strange antics as they became dancers in one of the festivals he remembered seeing as a child. He heard the intense beating of drums as if some vast heartbeat was pervading everything and everywhere.

He saw his teachers in awe of his unusual abilities and he understood them now for what they were. He remembered being with the monks, watching them making their mandalas in the sand. They had given him building blocks and watched as he built them into carefully balanced structures. He watched the smoke from the incense as it drifted through the candlelight of the temple, across the murals generations of monks had carefully painted. He saw tigers and lions hunting their prey, found himself soaring high over the mountains as an eagle and cruising the oceans of the world with whales and dolphins following the colonies of life which had sustained them through the years. He crawled out onto a beach. It was dirty and polluted. He could see a city had formed behind it. Walking amongst the debris of redundant and forgotten machinery he saw a little girl. She was crying inconsolably. He felt enormous sadness for the little girl and went over to her. He asked why she was crying so. She was surprised to see him but ran up to him and flung herself around him continuing to cry. He tried to comfort her and asked her what had made her so unhappy. She turned and pointed at the beach.

"Look at what they have done to my beautiful beach where I have played so happily all my life. They have turned it into a dirty junkyard. Why have they done this Okino? All the animals and fish I used to see have gone away. The sand I used to build sandcastles in is full of oil and chemicals and the sea brings in more junk every day. That is why I am so sad."

Okino was unable to speak to her but found himself looking deep into her sad little eyes. The beach around her and eventually her young body started to disappear. Her eyes held his gaze. In his periphery vision the world had fallen away. The deep turquoise of her eyes implored him to hold her gaze as they tumbled through space. When they eventually came to rest Okino found himself to be in a large cave. Fires were lit. He was warm and comfortable and able to relax in the flickering light washing over the walls. The eyes of the little girl were now those of a mature woman who sat watching him on the other side of the fire. Okino looked nervously around the cave.

"What is happening to me and where am I?" asked Okino,

"You are safe," said the woman, "You have put yourself in incredible danger and your physical body is sheltering in an old wolf's lair."

"...and who are you?"

"I am in your dream, Okino; a dream that will stay with you for many years and possibly shape your life from this point, perhaps even the lives of many others. Of course, you will never know whether it ever really happened. But in your waking life you have come so close to me it will be hard for you to deny what I am going to tell you. This very afternoon while you were sitting on the mountain before the storm you came as close to understanding my nature as any being that has ever evolved on this world."

"So are you a spirit?"

"I am the life force, the consciousness of Arimathea, Okino, and yes a spirit as your race has come to understand beings such as myself, I have grown slowly as this cold dark rock has formed and transformed through the nature of who I am into everything you understand to be this living world. You and everything around you on this world has come from me."

Okino looked deep into the eyes of this woman. He knew he was dreaming. He knew his body still lay asleep on the mountain and if he now trusted his ability to look into a soul and see the true being dwelling there then he had to believe what she was saying. He was now feeling the same deep connectedness with the consciousness of the planet he had experienced in his meditations. The essence of creatures from land, sea and air had started to flood his mind. He saw her origin; felt the peace he was feeling in this cave with her now at the heart of all their beings. In this dream he knew her to be the consciousness he had striven to become closer to all his waking and dreaming life.

"I know my dreams to be deceptive. What I know to be true in my dreams has often proved to be fantasy when I reawaken in the morning. This meeting could be something I have brought into my dreams through my yearning to learn about the mystery at the root of our life here."

Arimathea smiled.

"Okino, you have described exactly what has happened. Whether or not you choose to believe what I have told you or the conversation we are about to have will be for you to decide when you wake on the side of the mountain."

"Are you going to explain to me why and how everything is how it is?"

Arimathea laughed.

The fire glowed a little brighter and Okino's fear receded a little further.

"Such inquisitive creatures you are. Perhaps, in time you may come to such an understanding, if indeed it is there to be found. But you may have to live many more lifetimes. Before such a time there will always be much for you to do as you walk your path.

Firstly, I want to talk to you about how you came to be on this mountain in a blizzard with inadequate clothing and no way of finding your way down if a disaster such as this befell you. Why you hadn't given any thought to what might happen if you were caught up in a blizzard and how long you might be out here. You haven't brought any extra food or protection from the wild animals living out here. You are so aware and clever in so many ways but you have made a fundamental mistake that would have killed you. I have realized some parallels with your entire race in this episode. In your impatience to satisfy the yearnings you woke up with this morning you have neglected to think about the fundamentals of your own life. Convert this to the continual actions of an entire species, the dominant species at that and a life-threatening situation starts to have all the ingredients of a catastrophic planetary disaster."

"I think you are being dramatic. I have managed to find shelter, soon the storm will pass and I will make my way back to the monastery. Next time will be different. I will be better prepared."

"There would not have been a next time, Okino. If I had not stopped you in your tracks and made you look up to the cave you are now in, you would have carried on hoping something would miraculously turn up. You would have managed to struggle further around the mountain before collapsing and freezing to death in a snow drift. Probably never to be seen again. By the time the other monks came to find you, your bones would have been scattered across the mountainside by the animals who would have thanked me for the meal you provided for them."

"In that case I am obviously very grateful for this kindness you have shown to me."

"You should be. I very rarely intervene in this manner but you are an unusually gifted human being and I have a problem you may be able to help me with.

If everything continues as it is, life on this planet will cease to exist in the next one hundred turnings around the Star. You belong to a very clever race, Okino. You have developed survival strategies unlike any other creature that has evolved on Arimathea. These have made your race strong and successful. The result has been a great proportion of you have forgotten the true nature of my being and think my life has no consequence for your existence. The rate at which your species is expanding and using up my energy is putting the planet of Arimathea into terrible jeopardy.

However, there are many different forces which bring a world into life and to its death and they are all subject to the greater forces flowing through the universe. Now, a string of circumstances which could avert this catastrophe is gathering strength. A group of gifted individuals such as yourself have again been born on this world. Together they may have influence on the situation I have described. There is little more I can tell you other than the ability you have acquired for me to bring you here, may well be instrumental in the survival of our world into the distant future."

Okino looked deep into the eyes of the spirit who had appeared in his dream. He had always suspected he had some greater destiny other than living out his life in the sleepy mountain town. Now Arimathea was telling him his life was bound up with her own survival. But as she sat with him in the warmth of the fire there seemed to be nothing unrealistic in what she was saying. She could have just told him he would continue his life living as a monk in the remote mountain settlement. But then something in the flames had wound its way into his thoughts and touched a place in his being where he had not been before. He recognized himself, but he was much older and seemed to have travelled long distances through time and perhaps in many different lives. He knew this was not the first time he had met such a being or had been told there were matters of planetary importance in which he must engage.

"So, what is it I must do?" Okino asked casually as he raised his gaze from the fire to look directly into the brilliant turquoise eyes before him.

The spirit of Arimathea looked deeply back into Okino's eyes.

"I cannot tell you anymore. You must come to your own conclusion and then take action when you think it to be appropriate, when circumstances present themselves. For inevitably they will. You must always trust yourself and think deeply on what I have said to you and know I will help you. You have always known where to look for my wisdom and guidance. I will never be far away!!"

Arimathea and the cave started to fade. Okino started to wake in the lair on the mountainside. He realized he was curled up with an enormous wolf. As he again became fully conscious, he realized he could feel the rise and fall of the wolf's body as the breath passed in and out of her lungs. He thought he should be afraid; curled up with this wild animal having passed out from the freezing cold in the storm. But strangely he was feeling no fear. He felt as warm and secure in the small lair in the side of the mountain as he ever had done. He could hear the last of the winds whistling around the boulders outside the cave and felt no urge to move.

Instead he cast his mind back to his dream. It was fresh in his mind. He clearly remembered the words of the woman in the cave. Could it really have been the spirit of Arimathea who had spoken to him? He decided it didn't matter to him either way. The words she had spoken were clear in his mind. She said she had saved his life and here he was sharing the body heat of a wolf. Again, he drifted back to their conversation. His journey to the mountain had been reckless. He thought of the monks back in the monastery. They would be out of their minds with worry. He felt deeply ashamed for his stupidity. He had been so intent on fulfilling his dream he had not focused on the consequences of not fully considering how he was going to achieve his goal. He would have died and wasted everything that had happened so far in his life to bring him to a point of such awareness. He had let his parents down and everyone who loved him through his inability to consider his actions. She had spoken of the planet as one entity. Again, he had the feeling, the same deep connectedness with the consciousness of the planet he had felt on two separate occasions that day. She had told him it was in one of these she had changed his fate. Now in these moments lying next to the wolf in the tail end of the blizzard which would have killed him, Okino's life was starting to take on a very different meaning.

Chapter Three

The Fishmonger and the Meteor Stone

The next day, Okino had found his way back to the temple. He had been extremely weakened by his loss of consciousness in the storm and was not completely sure how long he had been lying in the wolf's lair. As the star sank once again behind the mountains, he staggered up the last steps to where two of the monks were tending herbs on one of the terraces. They were greatly relieved to see him and helped him through the temple to his room. The word of his return spread quickly.

He was visited by the master of the temple who asked him about his experience. Okino told him about the journey to the summit. How he had been caught in the snowstorm and how he had found shelter in a cave on the side of the mountain. He chose not to tell his master there had been a wolf in the cave. Also, he chose not to tell his master he had been visited by the spirit of Arimathea as he lay safe in the body heat of the wolf. His master and the rest of the community were relieved he had suffered no great harm as a result of this lesson which they had, after all, seen was imminent. The episode caused great interest over the next few days and Okino found himself telling the story in greater detail to the monks who were closer to him. However soon life returned to normal.

In his thoughts and meditations, he continually attempted to unravel the meaning of the dream he had had in the wolf's cave. Arimathea had asked him to think deeply about the words she had spoken and come to his own conclusions about what he should do. As he considered the magnitude of the problem Arimathea had confided in him, he felt helpless in this distant outpost to contribute anything to the resolution of the problem. But he remembered she had said she would help him. Coming to the conclusion this was the only way anything could happen, he decided he would carry on his life in the monastery as if nothing had happened. If the dream had been a fantasy generated purely in his own imagination then nothing further would come of it. He decided he would remain open to the experience and if the dream had been real then everything would unfold in his life in the fullness of time.

The months went by. The mountain incident started to fade as Okino started to take up his true role in the monastery. As his confidence started to grow the master recognized it was time he began to teach at the school in the town. He would start to teach the younger children. The master and all the other monks knew his true love was in the nature surrounding the monastery and the town. On returning from his wanderings he would always recount some tale about some special encounter he had had with a creature or a plant. It was decided the younger children would benefit from his stories and possibly some of their own encounters.

Okino was delighted with the decision and appeared so enthusiastic the master worried he may put the children in danger. So before Okino started to plan his lessons the master gave him a serious warning and strict parameters about the distance the children were to be taken and the animals they were to be shown. It seemed the size of the animal coincided directly with the distance the children could be taken from the town. The master seemed happiest if Okino concentrated with small insects on the ground and under stones very near to the school. When he became more confident with the classes perhaps he would be able to take them further into the surrounding countryside.

The classes were a great success from the beginning. The majority of the small class was captivated by Okino's gentle manner. Any who felt they could take advantage of the quiet young monk soon found he was as firm as he was gentle. He told them on the first day any of them who caused any trouble would simply not be allowed to come on the walks. Then he started to explain the kind of things they would be seeing.

Okino had always had a special interest in spiders and beetles. He started almost immediately to give the children a special insight into a world into which they had only caught out of the corner of their eyes. They shrunk back in terror as detailed drawings of traps and webs appeared on the old blackboard in front of them. They soon became spellbound and as they made their way home they often disrupted the silent and undisturbed lives of many of the town's tiniest inhabitants. Okino watched with delight as they delved into crevices and cracks and uplifted stones to reveal the scurrying creatures below. He noticed the girls were not as enthusiastic as the boys with the idea of spiders and beetles, but he assured them many of the creatures lived in areas where there were plenty of flowers and herbs.

As the children drifted off home after one of the afternoon lessons Okino decided to wander through the town. The adult population greeted and chatted to him enthusiastically. Many of them had not seen him since he had left for the monastery the previous year. Now they had a greater respect for him. They knew soon he may be sitting in front of them listening to their problems. They told him briefly about how their lives had been and went on their way.

As he made his way through the streets of the little mountain town he relished the sights, sounds and smells of his home. Everything seemed more vivid to him. The market, with its stalls loaded with bread and vegetables now seemed to have a deeper meaning for him. The training the monks had given him in their meditations and lessons had always spoken of the interconnectedness of all things. Fresh vegetables from the mountain terraces represented the wisdom of generations of farmers, the abundance of the soil and the interdependence of the little community on both.

One of his mother's friends greeted him, smoothing and brushing some dust off his new robe with such affection he could have been her own son. She offered him a loaf of fresh bread, rapidly disappearing from the table outside her house. He lifted the small white loaf to his nose and shut his eyes. He inhaled the smell deep into his whole being. He laughed aloud with the joy of it and his mother's friend laughed with him. Soon other men and women came around to smell the bread and soon the street was full of laughter. The people were pleased and proud to see their latest monk back amongst them. When they were again able to regain their composure, many of them came up and gave him a brief hug. Others gave a respectful bob of their heads and offered a blessing. They drifted off happily with the laughing bread leaving Okino with his mother's friend. She had sold all the bread.

Okino said his goodbyes and wandered off down the cobbled street, happy to be back in the town amongst his people. Every one of the timber buildings fronting onto the street had some memory for him. He even remembered a few of them being rebuilt. The town had grown over the centuries huddled on the side of the mountain. The timber frames of the dwellings were linked one to the other. Carefully laid stone walls infilled the stout oak frames. The heavy construction of the buildings, although time consuming to build, gave protection from the severest winter conditions. If a house ever needed to be rebuilt the whole community would be involved in some way or another. Any of the old timbers or stone suitable would be re used. New timber had to be brought from the Oak woods in the forests further up the valley and stone from the quarry higher up the mountain.

For a community still completely unmechanized the felling, and processing of a number of trees into beams and planks was a time consuming process and was not undertaken lightly. Great care was taken over each individual building. This was reflected in the exterior. The joints of posts and beams, trusses and rafters were all carefully crafted. Stonewalls were protected by over sailing roofs supported on stout purlins. In some of the streets only a narrow band of sky was visible above. Small openings in the walls were filled with thick slabs of glass allowing only small amounts of natural light to glow through the houses. There were large rooms on the ground floor and perhaps three rooms above. All the buildings had large stone chimneys. The fire was at the centre of family life.

Memories of his friends and family holding hammers, carefully constructing a roof looking out over the valley to the mountains beyond drifted through Okino's mind. He remembered how cosy those houses had always felt. He remembered the dancing light from the fire as his mother kept an eye on the old cooking pot which invariably contained a vegetable stew. He remembered how he would curl up in the old skins passed down through the generations as some ferocious storm howled around the town outside. He had loved to listen to his father telling stories about his life in the mountains as the timbers creaked in defiance of the wind.

He remembered the monk who was doing the cooking for the week had asked him to collect a fish for their evening meal. The monks rarely ate the flesh of animals but this was true of many of the people in the town of Lamai. The amount of food they could grow in the harsh mountain environment did not warrant feeding it to animals so they could in turn eat the animals. An old goat or chicken who could no longer provide milk or eggs may with great regret be slaughtered. The fish in the lakes had always been a natural and valuable resource and careful thought was always given to their consumption.

When the decision had been made and before the animal was eaten, prayers would be said, in respect for the spirit of the unfortunate creature, now free to again resume its journey back into the Great Spirit; before being reincarnated into its next existence. Then everyone would enjoy the feast the animal had provided while debating the karmic nature of the food chain and the place of the humble chicken and goat upon it. The tenuous nature of their existence in Jahallala meant the boundaries between the life they lived and the life beyond were much debated. The return and the progression of the soul through continual reincarnation was at the heart of these debates which often would include much speculation on the nature of consciousness and so the nature of their entire world.

In the monastery the choice was left to the conscience of the individual priests as eating or not eating meat had never been seen as a hindrance to the spiritual development of the monks. However, to take part in the killing of animals was forbidden and it was preferred if the animals had not been killed specifically for the monks. Any superiority shown by those choosing not to eat meat over those who chose to was seen as a failing in the spiritual development of the offending priest as was any competitive behaviour.

So Okino made his way down the hill, still being greeted by his old friends and neighbours to where the fishmonger lived. When he arrived at the house it was closed up. Okino knew he had the right day. As he was standing in front of the shop wondering what might have happened, an old friend of his father's came up and greeted him. They chatted briefly of each other's fortunes before Okino asked whether he knew what, if anything, had happened to the fishmonger.

"Oh, that is not a happy tale. It seems the fish in the lakes have started to become ill. Many have died. Fine large fish which would make a good meal for you and the monks tonight. It is breaking old Sareki's heart. He has been down at the lakes for many days trying to work out what is wrong."

"That does not sound good at all. We would certainly miss the fish." Okino remarked and added thoughtfully. "I think I might take a walk out there and see if there is anything I can do."

"I'm sure he'd be very grateful for the clever perspective you monks seem to bring to problems like this. You always were a clever lad, Okino. It's good to see you where you ought to be."

The two friends said their goodbyes and Okino set off again down the hill. It was not long before he came to the edge of the town. A solid wall had been constructed which had come to shelter many dwellings behind it. The cobbled road then continued down the hill. Winding down through large outcrops of rock and into the pastureland, Okino could see the valley stretched out before him. It was early spring in the mountains and the grass was growing strong and green. In the distance he could see the herd of yaks grazing. Herds of goats were coming down from the mountain on their way down to the river to drink, carefully watched by their young herders. Clouds gave reminder of the gentle showers that could occur at any moment. They scudded in hectic formation across the predominantly blue sky. The mountain air now had the promise of the warmer months ahead.

He looked up to the mountain where he had nearly died a few months before. It stood majestically amongst its subordinate hills. Okino briefly flew in his mind to the peak. With the knowledge and memory he had, he was able to look down at the land surrounding the mountain and into the distance to the far off horizon. Down here in the valley he was able to see the subtle colours of the wildflowers as they nuzzled their way out of the grass. He could see the detail of their newly opened heads as they bobbed in the wind. He could see the little track ways made by rabbits as they scampered between their burrows. The larger tracks would have been made by the mountain deer also probably on their way to the river to drink. The goat herders' track he was on led directly into the distance where he could see the lakes glistening in the Star shine.

On the mountain however, he would be seeing the vastness of the landscape. He would be looking at the long ridges of the mountain ranges and wondering of the millennia in which they had been formed. He would be in awe of the planetary forces continuing to force them ever higher, knowing similar forces were acting upon the crust of Arimathea at any moment in time shifting and shaping his world. Here on the ground the river was a fragmented slither of glistening light. On the mountain he would see the silver thread running across the plain, through the valley into the distance and towards the sea. He would be able to see the scouring the glacial ice had left. In more recent history he could remember the torrents of snow melt water passing through the wider channels of the river, adding to the fertile alluvial soil the town relied on for its living.

As he walked briskly down the track he wondered at the forces so delicately and yet solidly balanced in his world. He sucked in a great lungful of clean mountain air, bent down and took a handful of dark earth from the diggings of a new burrow and squeezed it through his fingers. He acknowledged the miraculous carpet of vegetation springing from it. There was a darker rain cloud moving down the valley and as it started to pass overhead a shower began to fall.

He lifted his face into the rain to feel the cool mountain water wash over his skin. His outstretched hands collected small pools of water in his palms. The raindrops were big enough to cause splashes. Tiny droplets jumped back into the air causing a mist of water vapor around his body. The Star pierced the cloud and shone through the falling water. Okino watched with delight as a rainbow started to form in the valley. Denser and denser the colours became. Then a second rainbow formed under the first, until it seemed a considerable section of the sky was now gleaming with all the colours of the spectrum.

Okino walked on towards the lakes watching as the rainbow faded and the Star shone down on the valley floor now gleaming with water droplets. Suspended from the blades of grass, each droplet carrying a replica Star shining from it. Okino was stopped in his tracks. He stood in awe of the sight now confronting him. Arimathea beneath his feet, the air all around him, the rain and the star conspired together to create an ethereal scene, distracting him for a few moments, suspending time and reality, he felt a deep sense of awe for his world. Again, he experienced the reverence he so often felt when confronted with such beauty. But now within the reverence there was the deeper, all pervasive peace he had felt in the presence of the spirit in his dream. He knew she had touched him perhaps as a sign to show him soon his work was to begin and she was there beside him.

As he started once again down the path the Star flashed across something substantial, partially covered by sand and stones in the grass. Okino thought nothing of it and walked on. However, a few paces down the path he was compelled to turn back and investigate the object. The flash had come from a coloured stone, half buried in amongst a small accumulation of gravel and sand left in the grass. These deposits were often brought by the strong currents from the mountains in the spring when they flooded the water meadows and were left when the flood receded. Okino carefully removed it from the ground and wiped away the sand. The surface was almost glassily smooth but there was a sharpness as he closed the palm of his hand around it. As he turned it in the star shine he found it had a transparency giving a sense of deep space within it. There were hues of greens, purples and dark reds swirling and occasionally flashing within the centre of the stone. He had never seen anything like it and wondered whether after the rainbow he had just seen, there could be any significance to finding such an unusual stone. Intrigued, he put the stone in the pocket of the thick cotton trousers he wore under his robe for a more thorough examination later on.

He walked on across the sparkling meadow until he came to the edge of the large lakes. The breeze was sending ripples across the surface of the water. Each wave top glistened as it directed the Starlight into Okino's eyes. Occasionally a fin would rise from the lake causing a further disturbance. Okino knew them to belong to the large fish who lived in the lakes. Sareki's family had carefully managed the lake for many generations so the fish stocks would never fall below a level where they could replenish themselves. The lakes were a valuable and fortunate resource for the town and so were greatly treasured. The fish were ordered from the fishmonger by the towns people for celebrations or special occasions. But now something was interfering with this pristine habitat. As Okino walked around the lake towards the little hut along the shore, he saw several dead fish. Their scales had been disfigured by disease, giving the handsome silver fish a disturbing dark ochre hue.

Sareki had noticed Okino and walked along the bank to meet him. Sareki's old face told of his life observing and working with the environment around the lakes. His bright eyes now tinged with worry shone from his dark wrinkled face. He was pleased to see Okino and they chattered about the town and Okino's monkhood as he led him back to the front of his hut. A fire smouldered in a small ring of stones. One of the fish he had retrieved from the lake that morning lay gutted and sliced lengthways on one of the stones.

"So, there it is, Okino," he pointed down at the fish, "Their flesh is discoloured all the way through their bodies. Also, there is a distinctive fraying around their gills."

"Have you noticed anything strange about the water in the lakes."

"Come with me."

Okino followed Sareki down the bank to the far end of the lake where the water exited back into the river and then continued on its course down the valley. Sareki pointed to a build-up of green and brown algae being blown across the surface, now collecting in the far corner of the lake.

"You have never seen anything like this in the lakes before?"

"Not in all the years I've been looking after them, and look,"

He pointed to the entrance of the river. Foam was floating from the fast flow of the river into the calmer water of the lake and was gathering in the large accumulation at the other end of the lake.

"Something has changed the purity of the water in the river. These fish have evolved in pure mountain water. I would say that whatever is causing this foam and this algae is also killing the fish."

"How can the water have changed? Everything around us has been farmed in the same way for centuries."

The two men looked thoughtfully out across the lake. Okino knew the land around the lakes had been farmed in the traditional manner for generations. Any waste from what was taken out was put back in the next years and the land was drained and irrigated with ditches running into mainstream of the river.

"Do you think this will affect the crops we are growing, Sareki."

"I have been asking myself the same question. The water is very rarely used to irrigate the barley and the root vegetables grown higher up around the lakes because at the times we grow them there is sufficient rain. But lower, further down the valley, as you know, this water is channelled down through the irrigation ditches into the terraces where the rice is grown. Whatever it is will be absorbed by the rice plants growing in the water."

"So, we know the fish and the rice will definitely be affected."

Okino looked thoughtfully up stream to where the river was flowing down the valley

"Do we know what is happening further up the valley perhaps beyond the forests. Didn't there used to be a community and pastureland up there?"

"I've not been up there for some time. It is too high up for the crops we grow here. Certainly, there used to be some small villages. But as far as I know they have been deserted for some time. It was hard to make a living up there and I think the people gradually drifted down into the towns in the valleys beyond wherever they are."

"So, have you ever been to the town Sareki?"

Sareki smiles up at Okino.

"Never had the need, son. But maybe someone needs to take a look along the river and perhaps go up into those hills to see if there is something going on up there."

"I think you're right. I will go myself, perhaps tomorrow. There must something or someone up there which is effecting this water so strangely."

Okino was looking upstream towards the Oak forests he knew covered the higher land beyond the valley. The forest was largely wild and unexplored. Timber was often taken from the edges but people rarely ventured much deeper. The canopy was thick and it was easy to become disorientated. There were people who could tell stories of being lost in the forest for many days. They came back with stories of the leopards and wolves who roamed without threat amongst the ancient trees. The result of this was the people from Lamai rarely had contact with the villages or the people who lived beyond.

As he contemplated the journey and the dangers involved, he smiled to himself as he remembered the night he had spent curled up with the wolf in her lair. He had taken out the stone he had found earlier and was rolling it around in his palm. He tossed it from hand to hand in gentle arcs, barely aware of what he was doing. Sareki was showing great interest in the stone watching carefully, trying to get a glimpse of the detail as it flew back and forth between Okino's hands.

"So are there any fish which aren't contaminated, I still haven't purchased any dinner for the monks tonight."

"Since you've asked, and between you and me. There is another pond around the lake which is supplied by another stream which doesn't seem to be affected. If you walk with me, I have one over I caught this morning. You can take it if you like. It's the least I can do if you are going up through the forest to investigate all this tomorrow."

They started to walk around the lake. "Where did you find your stone, Okino?" Sareki asked with a fascinated smile.

"I found it on the way over here sitting in the grass. I'd just seen the most amazing rainbow as the rain started to fall in the valley." He handed the stone to Sareki who examined it carefully and then looked up at Okino excitedly.

"There is a story which came down through the generations. It was told to me by my father. The story goes, one night a meteorite exploded over these mountains. Apparently, there was an enormous explosion possibly before it hit the ground. Some of the fragments were said to have landed higher up in the valley. Several people said they saw it and they searched for pieces the next day, but no-one ever found one single shard. The story goes most of the meteor landed high in the mountains and the fragments were washed down into the river and then some were carried downstream. There have been those who have sworn on the full Moon you can see some of the fragments glinting on the bottom of the lakes where they have been left. I assumed it was just one those stories expanded in the telling over the years. Until now!!"

He was holding the stone up to the Star mesmerized by what he was seeing in the stone. "I've never seen anything like this in or on the ground around here, it looks different, feels different and there definitely is a glint, a little flash coming from deep within it, I would have actually said far beyond it like you are actually looking deep into space."

The fishmonger and the monk had come to the edge of the lake and were standing, staring into the water. Sareki was still holding the stone.

"This is quite amazing," he whispered, "I can see all the fish in the lake almost as if there is no water in the pond at all."

He handed it back to Okino who also found he could see below the surface of the lake to where the fish swam in the shallows near to the bank.

"It is an extraordinary stone you've found. I think you may have found a piece of the old meteorite." He looked up into the sky, "You never know, it may have been circling the universe for billions of years before it finally landed here. It could have been part of another world or even several. There is definitely something about it. I should look after it very carefully and don't tell too many people you've got it."

Okino smiled reliving the sight of the rainbow. It had seemed like a special moment when he had found the stone and now it seemed it had some supernatural power. If Sareki was right and it was a fragment of the meteorite then the fabric of this stone, he thought, may contain and connect him into memories far beyond any knowledge existing on this world. The two men walked back around the lake to Sareki's hut. He retrieved the fish from the lake and gave it to Okino to take back to the monastery.

"I hope it gives you strength and brings you good luck on the journey you are about to make."

"I'm not entirely sure where all this is leading but I will let you know as soon as I can, Sareki. There must be a reason and I am determined to find it."

"Thank you Okino, I am sure you will become an excellent monk. Send my best wishes to all your brothers and I hope you all enjoy your dinner."

With these farewells Okino and the fish made their way through the valley and the town, up and along the steep paths to the monastery of the dragon high on the side of the mountain.

Chapter Four.
Dinner at the Monastery.

In the evening Okino sat down with the monks to eat the pie made from the fish he had brought back from the lakes. They ate quietly, contemplating the food they were eating. Many of them worked in the fields in the valley and closer to home in the gardens where most of their vegetables were grown. They were aware of the energy many generations had put into their cultivation to make them continually productive. Their training encouraged them to be conscious of the energy as it was released from the food into their bodies. They knew it to be an unbroken cycle and a fundamental part of their existence. Here in this remote region, far from the fuel hungry cities, energy was still held in high esteem and nothing was wasted. The awareness of the transference of nutrients absorbed into roots and warm Starshine falling on large green leaves, of the yaks in front of the ploughs and people picking and sorting the freshly grown vegetables, flooded the minds of the hungry monks.

The fish had been carefully prepared and mixed into those vegetables. This was a special treat relished by the monks. Added to reminiscences of their connection with the soil, there were also thoughts of the fish and the clear mountain water in which it had lived. They knew fish to be ancient creatures who had evolved over many millions of years. Breathing water, the life blood of Arimathea as humans and other mammals breathed the air, they had a unique relationship with their world. The monks visualized the pure white melting snow streaming down the mountains into the lakes as clear bubbling water as the flavour of the fish flooded their senses. They also became aware of the water realms connecting out across the oceans and the multitude of ancient creatures living there. They were silent with respect for this creature. It had given its life not only to prolong their own life but to enhance it.

As they finished their food, conversation slowly turned to the happenings of the day. As the warmer weather approached there were conversations about the new growing season and the gestation of seeds in the vegetable gardens. They had all experienced the starshine and showers in the afternoon and discussed at length the wonder of the multiple rainbows. As Okino told them about the lakes and the plight of the fish they became silent. Even though they lived so remotely they knew the planet of Arimathea was developing at a phenomenal rate in the distant lands beyond the mountains. However, their lives had been little changed by these advances. So when Okino related the story of the dying fish in the lake, a ripple of concern ran through the monks sitting around the refectory table.

They were increasingly vigilant for signs the outside world was encroaching upon their unique community. As yet, none of the trappings of the advancing technology proliferating elsewhere had reached them. Younger men had left and travelled the mountain passes to the roads leading to the larger towns beyond. Those who had returned, told stories of relentless industrialization spreading across the planet. They told of crops being farmed on industrial scales with the indiscriminate use of synthesized chemicals. They told of mountains of food being stored unused while in other areas of the planet people were starving. They told of animals being reared with the use of intensified chemicals enabling them to become fully grown in less than a year. Forests were being cut down, habitats and their unique animals being lost forever. The oceans were being plundered of the rich and diverse creatures living in them and the surface of the planet itself was being relentlessly mined for everything and anything that could be melted, refined or processed into the material goods the inhabitants of the wealthier nations of Arimathea craved and would briefly use before they were buried in the enormous craters being excavated for their waste.

"I have decided to make a journey tomorrow" Okino announced. "I'm going to follow the river up to the hills to see if there is anything obvious causing the change in the river's water. There may be something very simple at the root of it all."

"It could take you a few days to walk up into the foothills of the mountains to where the river rises. Make sure you are well prepared, Okino." One of the monks advised. There were a few chuckles of laughter around the table.

"And supposing the trouble is farther away, my young friend." The master asked. All heads turned towards Okino.

"Then I may find myself going further than I first anticipated, master." Okino replied.

His master looked calmly down the table towards him. He suspected a special purpose for this young monk as he had watched him undertake his training over the previous year. Although he had settled into the life of the monastery very successfully, the master had a feeling there was more for him to learn in the outside world. The nature of his initiation seemed to have held significance for the work of the monastery in the future. The old monk knew rapid change was taking place in the outside world and the work of the Order of the Dragon had always been to preserve the sacred connection with the spirit of Arimathea.

He was aware of the possibility Okino had been called by Arimathea to travel into the world from their mountain retreat. He himself had made such a journey in his younger years. He knew even then it had been hard to maintain the high standards of physical and spiritual discipline accorded to a monk of this order. But he knew Okino as a young man who had shown signs of living these ways even before he had come to the monastery and he was not worried about this aspect of Okino's announcement.

However, he was concerned during the journey Okino would meet the darker forces now stalking the planet of Arimathea. He could not be sure how Okino would react to the disinterest he would find in her ultimate welfare. He looked over at the young monk. He was strong and fit. His episode on the mountain those months before had brought a further depth to his understanding. He also suspected something else had happened on the mountain Okino had not told him about. But he had great respect for the integrity of this young man and hoped he had not told him for the right reasons.

"You take all of our blessings with you, Okino. There may be difficult times ahead for you; difficult decisions to make and you can be sure even as we speak there will be those who will be preparing to meet you. Be sure to remember the peace you can always find within yourself. Always take time to find your connection with us here wherever you find yourself. May the blessings of the Dragon Spirits and the Great Mother always be with you."

The old monk then rose from his chair and left the refectory. The other monks started to clear away their dinner. They had sensed from the tone of the master's voice this may be more than a walk up the valley for Okino. They had all grown extremely fond of this bright young man. When they had finished, they gathered in the great hall and sat in their circle in the ancient temple. They decided to dedicate their evening meditation to Okino's journey. They asked the Spirit of the Dragons to guide him. They sank deep into their meditation and visualized Okino protected and unhindered, carrying the strength of the mountains and the security of their unique brotherhood at all times. Then in the silence of the temple with the candles flickering and the powerful incense swirling into the rafters above they each gave him their individual blessing and wished him well for the days ahead.

Chapter Five.
The Forest.
The next morning Okino left the temple, made his way down the mountain track and across the pasturelands to the lakes. He wandered over to see Sareki who was sitting outside his hut mending some large nets. Okino told him he was starting his journey to follow the river.

"I wish you luck son. I'm going to try and rescue as many fish as I can from the polluted lake and put them in the two supplied by the other stream. It seems to be the older fish are the worst affected."

He stood up and they both turned their gaze to where the river flowed out from the mountains in the distance.

"The more I think about it there must something going on up at the old settlement. I see you've got some provisions," pointing to the rucksack the other Monks had made him prepare. Sareki disappeared into his hut and came out with a large slab of food.

"Here take this. There's fish and goats cheese mixed with vegetables. It will keep you going for days if things get desperate."

Okino looked at the dried cake and winced as he smelt it. Sareki produced some cloth and they wrapped the evil smelling fish pie. Okino found a place for it in his ruck sack. He thanked Sareki and started off up the valley following the banks of the river.

He found the terrain alongside the river varied enormously. Soon he had left the cultivated lands of the valley. As he walked through the rocky, stony scrub land he became more aware of the phenomenal work carried out by generation after generation to change the land into the fertile and drained pasturelands now so natural to his own generation. However, it was the river he was concentrating on. He carefully scanned every stretch and bend, alert for anything unusual. He found more evidence of the mysterious froth in the pools where it had formed as the result of rocks or impediments in the river.

He became fascinated by the steady flow as he walked up against the current. The shallows became racing, jumping, sparkling sheets of gleaming rocks and pebbles as the deeper stretches suddenly flowed into them. There were cascading weirs and small waterfalls, often formed by some obstruction sending undulating ripples of reflected clouds into chaotic swirling tapestries of interwoven waves and spiralling eddies. He became entranced by the beauty and diversity of life living along the banks. He had already spotted many other varieties of fish. He watched birds diving deep into the depths to catch the life swimming below. He saw rodents diving from their carefully constructed lodges just above the water line. Occasionally he would catch site of one swimming valiantly across the powerful current hurrying it would seem to carry out some pressing task on the other side. As the river raced past, he found little sign of the pollution. Only when the river slowed to stillness did he find the foam collecting.

Later in the afternoon he started to become aware of the forest. It started to appear as if a fine line of purple mist had been drawn in the far distance between the slopes of the valley. The shadows started to lengthen and as he gradually moved closer, he started to appreciate the scale of the forest before him. As he approached the outskirts, he could see the stumps of the trees cut down and removed for construction. He remembered the occasions when he had seen houses being built. He looked down at the great circular stumps and remembered slender beams and posts. He marvelled at the ability of his people to take such a tree and convert it into a building frame which would eventually become an enclosed and cosy home lived in for hundreds of years.

After the quiet gentle swishing of the river, the edge of the forest in the early evening at the end of this spring day was a cacophony of sound. The trees were full of the territorial songs of a multitude birds. Individuals and colonies were nesting high in the slowly greening canopies. Larger birds were returning from their days foraging while the smaller varieties flitted from branch to branch pecking at the newly forming leaf buds. Deeper in the forest Okino could hear the calls and howls of larger animals.

The Star of Arimathea was sinking down behind the mountains. Okino looked back down the valley from where he had come. He could no longer see the gleaming slithers of the lakes. He decided to make his camp here amongst the thinned trees. Not far away he could still hear the river as it made its' exit from the forest. He made a fire easily with the flint lighter given to him by one of the monks, setting light to some dry moss and twigs. As the fire grew he was able to use larger pieces of wood and soon the fire was large enough for him to cook some of the beans and vegetables in the small metal bowl he had brought. As he ate, he watched the stars slowly glitter into view in the darkening skies and the Moon rise over the mountains.

When he had finished his meal, he lay down next to the fire. He was weary after his first day of walking. He felt the vastness of the land around him, the ground was hard but he was warm under the blanket especially made for the shepherds guarding for wolves at night. He wondered at the sanity of what he was doing and thought about the monastery and the monks settling down for their evening meditation. He thought of the night before and their meditation in the great hall as an owl called from in the tree above him. He sat up, crossed his legs straightened his back and closed his eyes. The sounds of the surrounding forest quickly enveloped him.

He imagined his brother monks sitting there with him amongst the trees, the dancing flames of the fire lighting their peaceful smiling faces. He looked up into the clear night sky where he could see the familiar constellations for the time of year. The strange feeling of familiarity he always had, came over him. Whenever he looked into the stars, he felt a long way from home. Sitting on the outskirts of the wood in the old blanket a parallel insight started to emerge. He felt as if he had now started his journey back towards wherever he had come from. It was a strange thought and he wasn't quite sure what it meant.

Almost immediately he realized the feeling he had had was far more complex. He knew from the teachings of the monastery he may have been incarnated many times on many different worlds. It was a part of himself he acknowledged as the mystery of his existence. Perhaps now the mystery was starting to unravel. He just had time to wish all his nights would be this peaceful before his tiredness overcame him. He stretched out under the blanket and went to sleep.

The next morning, he woke after a fitful night's sleep on the hard ground as the Star rose over the mountains. He stood up and stretched thankful for the warmth on his face. As he rolled up his blanket and found his way back to the river, he contemplated a dream from the night before. He'd been back in school in the little mountain town teaching the children about the animals of the forest when one of the children had arrived with a mountain leopard. He had led it into the classroom on a chain. The children were able to stroke and play with the leopard until one of the boys got hold of its' long tail and gave it a pull. The leopard reacted badly and struck out at the child knocking him across the classroom with a huge paw. The children had run out screaming leaving only Okino and the leopard. Okino remembered staring into the huge beautiful eyes knowing he was totally at the creature's mercy. It snarled baring a scary array of large teeth as if irritated by such inferior beings, slunk out of the classroom and disappeared back into the mountains.

Wondering about the meaning of the dream, he continued his journey up the river. As he made his way deeper into the forest it became progressively more difficult to follow and observe. He found himself clambering over fallen trees and outcrops of rocks jutting out over the banks. There were large stretches of waterlogged bog where other watercourses drained into the river. The trees now were ancient, far out of the reach of axe or saw and the means to transport them. Their great trunks forked into huge gnarled limbs winding their way skyward through the tangle of undergrowth with dense ivy clinging to them.

The forest had become darker, shadows were deeper. Huge roots seemed to crawl over the exposed rocks. A shiver ran through Okino as he realized he was in dangerous untamed territory. The old trees creaked as the wind rustled through the canopy as if some invisible creature was traveling through the forest. As he examined bark rivened into deep crevices spiralling into the limbs above, he remembered the look in the leopard's eyes. Calm and beautiful; a very different kind of being with a very different kind of consciousness; but both very much alive and adapted to survive in their own way, in their own environment.

Okino noticed how the branches grew from the heavy trunks in direct proportion to their size and height in their relentless effort to access as much light from above the canopy as possible. If there was a gap there was always a branch or a whole new tree heading towards the precious life-giving light above. Here was a life in a community of lives. Unlike the community he had come from but life all the same reacting to its environment as best it could, ultimately to reproduce and continue its' species. Although these trees did not have nervous systems ending in a controlling nerve centre, he became convinced he could feel their old spirits as he clambered in and out and over their extraordinary forms. So deeply connected into the ground, growing so much as a part of it, almost like a skin. Okino came to feel this forest was a living extension of the ground and so of the life and spirit of Arimathea. It was wild, free and uncontrolled. Every tree, creeper, shrub and flower was competing for space and light. At times Okino thought he may not be able to get through the tangled maze before him and on several occasions he made an ungainly combination of slide, slip and fall as he climbed down the banks into the river to negotiate a particularly uncompromising area of undergrowth.

On one of these detours around a large outcrop of rock surrounded by a thicket of thorns with razor like qualities he came upon a waterfall. The river plunged over a small ledge of rock. Although only waist high, the affect was dramatic. The falling water had made a pool surrounded by smaller rocks. The water seemed to fall in slow motion as the full river shot out over the ledge into the bubbling cauldron below. A mist of water droplets was constantly forming in the air. Large rippling waves spread out and lapped on sandy shores on either side of the entrance to the river. The overhanging tree limbs had made an almost cavern like space. Moss had covered many of the rocks and lichens hung from the limbs of the old trees reaching for the airborne vapor. Okino gasped with delight as he took in the scene before him.

He waded across the river to a spot where he could sit and absorb the spectacular feature before him. He was weary and felt like he could do with a rest after the day's exertions. The skin on his hands had been torn by his battles with the undergrowth. As he neared the beach on the other side of the river, he took off his coat and loosely fitting shirt and flung it onto the bank. He stretched into the Star shine, bent down, cupped his hands together, scooped up some of the cool clear water and splashed it over his face and body. The water was cold but his body soon dried when he eventually sat on the side of the pool in the warmth of the midday star.

He broke off a piece of Sareki's fish pie and took some bread from his rations and ate contentedly examining every aspect of the pool. His eye was drawn to the beach below as the water with its energy spent, covered and then was absorbed into the sand. He noticed a flash of golden light as a Star ray landed on something amongst the sand and pebbles. He jumped down from the bank and carefully delved into the place where he had seen the glint. There he found a golden ring half covered by sand. It was surrounded by symbols he didn't recognize, was pure gold and as clean and as bright as the day it had been made. Again, the Star caught the golden surface as Okino moved it in front of his eyes.

He climbed back onto the bank and sat down. He judged the ring to be a good fit and could think of no reason why he should not put it on. So, he slipped it onto his finger. The ring was a perfect fit. Okino was delighted and marvelled at this amazing find. Then he remembered the stone he had found on the way up to the lakes the day before. He reached into his pocket and felt for the sharp edges of the meteor stone. For a moment he feared it had gone but when he delved further with relief he retrieved the stone. He admired his two finds and wondered of their significance. His gaze again settled on the waterfall and he felt it's beautiful elemental qualities beginning to infuse his being.

As he watched, the water vapor appeared to be spiralling towards a specific point over the pool. He started to become aware of a sphere starting to form. The vapor was forming into clouds. A deep blue was being drawn out of the water below forming a layer of colour below the clouds. Then solid green and sienna browns were being drawn from the forest forming solid layers on the forming sphere. A ray of bright starlight fell upon the sphere and it began to glow intensively beneath the ancient branches in the pool's cavern. Okino watched in stunned amazement as the sphere then started to revolve. He recognized the patterns on the sphere as familiar landmasses and oceans. A tiny replica of Arimathea was forming in front of him from the vapor in the pool, the surrounding forest and the ray of star light.

The light around the small planet started to increase spreading out to the surrounding forest. Okino watched as the buds of early spring started to grow rapidly. Simultaneously the water of the river started to slow. The pool below became shadier as the rapidly forming leaves blocked out the star light. The air became warmer as the Star rose higher in the sky, the pool was suddenly surrounded by flowers and lilies growing on the fringes of the now still water. Okino could see fish clearly, lazily swimming in the clear still water. There was a quiet buzz in the surrounding forest… butterflies danced from flower to flower and dragonflies circled. A fish surfaced from the water and consumed an insect skating across the smooth surface. No sooner had Okino absorbed this scene, the Star was lowering in the sky and the leaves started to fade to the bright orange, gold and yellow of autumn. Then leaves started to fall and were absorbed back into the earth. Rain started to fall. Flowers disappeared. Again, the flow of the river increased and as the Star again lowered in the sky, snow began to fall covering the trees and ground. The waterfall became a sparkling display of dripping stalactite shaped icicles and the pool iced over completely. Okino shivered with cold and pulled his blanket over him.

He was relieved when the Star once again moved higher into the sky and the snow and ice started to melt. The river became a torrent as the melted snow came smashing down from the mountains carrying silt and debris in the flood. Then as the river slowed again, the Star resumed its correct position and the buds started to grow on the trees. For a few moments Okino watched in fascination as the planet slowly revolved before him. It felt as if Arimathea had revealed her true nature to him. He watched the glow fade back into the cloudy world as it continued to spin slowly over the pool. Again, Okino felt the remarkable serenity he had felt when the spirit had appeared to him on the mountain. It occurred to him he knew about the cycles of the seasons and how ancient lore told how Arimathea had been formed from the Elements of Earth, Air, Fire and Water. However, somewhere in the stillness he knew the spirit of Arimathea had instilled this wisdom more deeply into him. The quality of these visions, he knew, were undoubtedly changing the fabric of his being in some way. The planet started to turn back into vapor. The solidity and colour flowed back from where it had come into the surrounding forest and pool.

He sat for a while contemplating his own life in the light of what he had seen. He saw every part of his life had been like the passing of one of those seasons. His life, his journey had started and would eventually end and according to the teachings of his order would resume again in a new incarnation. He realized there could be no still point in any aspect of any life. He and his world were in a constant state of transformation. The parallels were plain to see. He lived in a world that could be hot and cold, wet and dry; it could be so still the lightest feather could rest undisturbed on the polished face of stone and yet it could rage with a ferocity which could make grown men fear for their lives. He could see how these cycles and rhythms fundamental to the life force of Arimathea had been crucial in his own development.

The transformative power of renewal and decline had permeated through all his memories in the same way he had seen in the trees around him. He remembered the times he had spent throughout his early life in the security of his family; how they had loved him and nurtured his fresh new being with love and attention. He remembered how they had encouraged him to be independent and strong in his own right so when he found himself in the little school having to hold his own amongst the other children, he had felt confident and safe. There had also been times when difficulties had arisen, when something or someone had upset him. He recalled even now the pain caused by an inconsiderate action or harshly spoken word and there had been times when he had thought his life seemed too difficult.

He remembered how these times had passed almost unnoticed to be replaced by times of enormous pleasure; playing in the meadows and woods with his friends or working with his father in the fields; thinking how clever he was to know what to plant and when; the ease with which he handled the animals and his great strength as he lifted Okino up, put him on his broad shoulders and carried him home when he was tired to his mother who was waiting with a hug and a plate of her wonderful food. Yes, here the young tree had started to grow strong and healthy alongside the other young trees in the forest. His roots were deep in this fertile ground and supplied with the nurturing rains of love he had been inspired to grow into the energy giving light. He had been allowed to grow through these seasons to stand high in the forest where he had started to take his place amongst the other fully-grown trees. He was still young enough to remember those carefree days when his parents had taken so much care of him. He was aware this cycle of his life was over, and a new cycle was beginning.

Sitting by the side of the pool in the forest many miles from home he was as daunted as when he had set out for his first day at school or the first night, he had watched the herds. The fear of the unknown. But also, he felt exhilarated by these confirmations. Suddenly he was gripped by a great excitement for this new time. He was confident it would lead to even more being revealed to him about his life on Arimathea. He stepped down onto the beach of the little pool, bent down scooped up some water in the cup of his hands and splashed it over his face letting it drain down over his body. He felt a flash of sunlight as it washed over his eyes again filling him with strength and enthusiasm for the next part of his journey.

Chapter Six
The Clearing.

As he collected up his belongings and packed them into his rucksack Okino assessed the best way forward. He had noticed the large outcrop of rock partly forming the waterfall rose quite considerably into the canopy and above the top of the trees. He decided it was a fairly steep climb but not impossible and he thought he might be able to see the extent of the forest from the top. Eventually after some exertion he was able to pull himself onto a small level platform conveniently formed to view across the forest canopy. Okino sensed at some stage it may have been fashioned by some of his ancestors, for now he had the most astonishing view over the trees below. He could see in the distance where he had entered the evening before but could see no end to the forest in the direction he would be traveling.

He took a few moments to admire the incredible spectacle before him. He was immediately aware of the abundance of chaotic vibrant life rising from above the treetops in the songs of thousands of songbirds. At any one time there were many journeys being purposefully made across the tree canopy. Groups of smaller birds flew from tree to tree while high above the canopy larger birds were flying into the distance where the mountains rose dramatically. He could now watch the breezes he had noticed from below sweeping across the canopy ruffling the treetops. As he looked more closely, he could see the individual trees; he could see the gaps where the older trees had fallen and younger ones were taking their place. Again, he wondered about the existence of these extraordinary beings and thought as he became more deeply entranced by the canopy he could sense their silent energy supporting all this teeming life thriving in amongst them.

While contemplating this fascinating web of interconnected life unravelling before him he noticed a gathering of crows wheeling in great numbers over the forest in the distance. His attention had been drawn to the urgent cries of the dark spiralling mass. He wondered what might be causing the crows to act in such an excited way. He let his mind wander as the birds continued to arrive. He had never found or be given a satisfactory explanation for this behaviour and so he had no way of knowing why the crows were acting in this manner. The only insight he had ever had when observing such a gathering was that these creatures maybe experiencing some level of existence he as a human could not possibly be aware. As he watched, he wondered whether there could be invisible energies only the crows were able to see or feel. Perhaps by gathering together in this way, they were able to raise some ability amongst themselves to make it visible. Their strange, eerie and persistent calls suggested they were communicating with each other; transferring information perhaps into a collective forum of knowledge, gleaned by each individual since their last gathering.

As he contemplated this communal frenzy, he began to wonder whether it may have some significance for his own journey. The crows continued to wheel ever more frantically as if the intensity of this strange ritual may affect its place in their historical memory. It occurred to him, for some reason, this may become one of their most memorable crow myths. Its power increasing as it was remembered in their collective consciousness down through the ages. If so, what could be its significance out here in this ancient forest? Perhaps the crows were simply singing and passing on legends to their young who were learning who their race had come to be. In this cacophony all would be stored in their collective memory.

He wondered whether there could be some old forgotten legend at the root of his own journey. After all, since he had set out, he had found a mysterious stone, a ring and he had been shown visions of Arimathea's life cycles. As he concentrated on the gathering, he increasingly felt there was some connection between him and the actions of the crows. Had he become involved with a legend which had made his journey necessary? Had it brought him here so he could also be somewhere in the future? He thought again about the great interconnectedness of the forest. How the lives of the trees were bound intricately with the life of everything living amongst them. There was no separation. Oxygen made by the trees was breathed in by all the creatures around them making their lives possible. A legend then, a strand of truth or lore running through all of time, re-generating itself, whose strength had and would survive in the telling to inform future generations and benefit the whole web of life. Perhaps the old legend of the dragons the monks had always held sacred and that had guided their teachings was surfacing here. A great surge of enthusiasm welled up in Okino. He suddenly sensed he had become involved in something far larger than anything he could have possibly imagined. He allowed himself a few moments to absorb these possibilities and at the same time as a way of confirming his intuition he decided he would investigate what had inspired this frenzy amongst the crows.

So, he slithered down the rock and started to make his way into the forest in the direction of the gathering. Okino could see and hear the crows flying over the trees. The nature of the forest had changed. Huge ancient oak trees had cut out so much light there was very little under growth on the forest floor. Okino enjoyed the walk through what seemed like the great halls of some vast construction. He soon found he was within sight of the place where the crows were circling. Their calling now directly overhead had reached an almost deafening crescendo. Okino hesitated. The endless calls of the crows now had an eerie supernatural sound and had reached a magnitude he had never experienced. There was undoubtedly something here and he considered walking away immediately. But he could see nothing suggesting there was anything sinister. He moved warily closer until he was at the edge of a clearing in the trees. He quietly sat down leaning up against one of the old Oaks and began observing. The crows appeared to have completed whatever ritual they had performed and began to disperse as noisily as they had arrived. Soon all was quiet.

The clearing was almost entirely circular and surrounded by Oaks. There were younger trees growing in the spaces between. The space within was covered with grass, flowers of many varieties and fallen limbs from the trees above. The ground was predominantly flat. However, there were undulations running partly across the width of the clearing, small mounds of grass occasionally formed ridges and low slopes in what appeared no particular pattern. The trees were huge and ancient and this was clearly a very special part of the forest. There were long gouges on two of the Oak trees where deer had been scraping their antlers. High in the tops of the trees he could see evidence of large nests. Then for the first time he noticed the atmosphere of the place. Okino decided this place must have been formed amongst the trees a very long time ago. The Oaks seemed as solid as the ground itself. Their limbs were gnarled and wizened making them appear as fantastical creatures survived from a long-forgotten world. He swore he could hear them whispering their disapproval for his violation of this sacred space.

Everywhere he looked there was new life bursting from the ground and the trees. The vast trunks and huge twisting limbs had almost filled the space above and the sky was only visible through the delicate tapestry of branches and leaves. It certainly seemed a mysterious and auspicious setting for the legend to be continued; possibly it had been waiting here dormant for many, many years. Awaiting his arrival? Okino stood quietly amongst the Oaks savouring his discovery. The star was starting to sink behind the mountains. Without hesitation he decided he would stay here for the night. Rays of starshine penetrated through the lower branches laying long strips of golden light on the grass. The birds were starting to roost and again the forest was becoming still. Okino started to gather wood for his fire. He decided he would make it at the centre of the clearing.

Later in the evening, Okino's small fire had served its purpose and he had eaten a moderate meal from his rations of vegetables and fish pie. He started to build up the fire. He carefully selected branches from the surrounding forest and considered where each may take its place on the growing conflagration. As branches turned to small logs the fire had begun to significantly light the entire clearing. The great trunks and surrounding foliage shimmered in the dancing light of the flames. Beyond the darkness of the forest seemed to be even more impenetrable. The calls of wild animals occasionally interrupted the fierce crackle of combusting wood. The high pitched shrieks of the deer seemed to come from all around him. Okino turned his thoughts back to where he had been in the afternoon.

Standing here deep in the forest with the fire he had built reaching high towards the canopy he began to reminisce about his life and how he had come to be here. He thought about the mountain community in which he had grown; how he had guided his life from an early age towards joining the order of the dragon. The teachings of the order acknowledged Arimathea as the resting place of an ancient universal spirit. He had become fascinated when they had told him of their calling to keep the connection with the spirit alive. The spirit he imagined he had always felt in his lonely walks in the mountains and in the skies and the infinity of the stars and galaxies shining there.

But what of the legend. How or where had it been born? Was it forming again around him in the heat and energy of the flames as they flew momentarily out of the fiery caverns into the darkness of the night? As the heat became more intense on his face he felt as if the primal forces of creation and destruction, now concentrated before him, were binding him ever deeper into the destiny of Arimathea. He closed his eyes as a strange excitement rose in his being. He relished the powerful feelings swirling through his imaginings.

The old myths he had been told and learnt were full of trials and hardship. The dark forces encountered always seemed to have the advantage. There was little to which they would not resort to trick and defeat a vulnerable hero. It was only through the strength of resolve, tenacity and an unswerving belief in the original quest, the hero had eventually been able to win through. Okino wondered whether he would be able to find such strength. Again, he felt the flood of excitement growing almost in answer to his doubt. He realized his love for Arimathea had grown since the vision he had seen in the waterfall.

The memory of the spirit he had encountered in his dream flashed through his mind. She was coming closer to him in this waking dream she had entrusted to him. He felt she was alive in the flames before him searing through the night air; sensed her in the trees around him, flowing from the deep soft earth beneath his feet; in the soft calls of the owls and the breezes crossing the clearing and cooling his face as the intensity of the flames started to fade.

Although in the passing days there had never been any question as to whether he would follow this path to wherever it may take him, a new determination was being born in the flames. He suddenly felt someone much older in himself. Felt an old weight not there before. It was like he was having a new reinforcing structure built into his frame. He looked through the lattice work of branches above. He could see the stars shining through. As far as he knew he was still only investigating the strange disease of the fish. He smiled to himself and shook his head. As the fire died down Okino made himself comfortable, covered himself with his blanket and in the warmth of the glowing embers amongst the soft grasses of the forest he drifted off to sleep.

Okino dreamt he was in the forest in deepest winter. He was walking towards the clearing. His breath froze in the air in front of him. Thick snow laid across the ground and weighed down the branches of the trees. The forest was silent. The star was low, barely above the tree line and cast unending shadows across the forest floor.

Okino could see the clearing in the near distance. He moved carefully through the trees, crunching his way through the deep virgin snow. When he arrived not a footprint or any snowfall had blemished the purity of the circular space. The rises and undulations in the clearing were now accentuated by the layer of snow lying upon them. In the centre there was what seemed like the stump of a tree also covered in snow. On closer observation Okino noticed there was ivy growing over the stump. He started to walk over to the centre.

As he walked, he momentarily felt something solid beneath his feet. He scraped away the snow and noticed it seemed to be covering over something. He pushed away further snow with his boots to find what appeared to be a large expanse of flat stone. He scraped away and continued to reveal a smooth surface. It was starting to take on a strangely organic bone like form. He started back suddenly, nervous about what may be lying here. Tentatively he started to scrape away more snow. Okino stood back in astonishment as he suddenly realized what he had uncovered. There before him was a giant stone wing. It stretched out almost twice his own size. He could see veins and claws perfectly formed in the stone. Excitedly Okino started to scrape off more snow. He found another wing and uncovered a torso with a large tail at one end and a huge head at the other. Excitedly the young monk cleared the remainder of the snow from the surface of the stone. Then he stood back in amazement as he looked down at the body of an enormous stone dragon lying flat on its back, wings outstretched and filling the clearing. Removing the snow had revealed thick ivy still covering the stump protruding from the chest of the dragon. Okino pulled away at it until it finally relinquished its hold.

There embedded in the chest of the dragon was a beautiful but wicked looking sword glinting in the low sunlight.

Okino contemplated the scene before him for a few moments. Who had driven the sword into the dragon and why? There were some symbols on the blade similar to the ones on the ring but they were nothing Okino recognized as of that time or even from Arimathea. The dragon had a look of disappointment rather than pain as if everything had depended on him and he had been unable to secure the outcome he had imagined. Okino again felt his excitement rising. He wanted to pull the sword out of the dragon. Cautiously he made his way through the glistening piles of snow and climbed onto its wing.

He could not grasp the sword to get enough of his strength behind it, so he climbed up onto the body of the dragon. The stone was already icy and he had trouble keeping his balance. He contemplated the scene for a few moments. Here was the legend. He knew he was still deep in his dream, but it felt so real; as if he had returned to the frozen land in his initiation. Standing on the petrified body he had uncovered he had a feeling everything would change for him and perhaps for his world if he pulled the sword out of the dragon. A new version of an old truth registered sharply in his mind. "Let sleeping dragons lie." But this dragon was clearly not sleeping. He had been brutally killed and perhaps for good reason.

He remembered the old stories the monks had told him portraying the dragons as the beneficial Spirits who resided deep in Arimathea. He knew in those moments beyond any doubt, he had been brought here to remove the sword. He cautiously took a firm grip on the icy handle. He paused and looked into the sky above the clearing and asked for Arimathea's blessing. The Star shone brilliantly through the ancient trees, illuminating the clearing in a pool of pure white light. He felt her close; felt the reassurance she had given him before he awoke from the dream in the cave.

"Remember I will never be far away." She had said to him. Now again he felt her at his shoulder. Felt her pleasure in what he intended to do. Closed his eyes and acknowledged the love she had for him.

He tentatively gave a pull on the sword. It slipped easily out of the dragon as if he had released it from recently killed flesh. Somewhere in the distant mountains there was a rumble. A wind brushed through the trees, fallen snow swirled around the clearing. Okino could feel it spiralling inwards approaching where he was standing. It entered the dragon where the sword had left an open incision. The nature of the stone immediately started to transform progressing out from the wound; almost imperceptibly it was starting to shine. The body of the dragon started. Okino lost his balance and jumped back to the ground. More and more light seemed to be saturating the rapidly disappearing stone. Its lungs were filling with air and the great body started to rise and fall. Waves of light raced across the surface of the enormous creature. In the surrounding clearing the snow was melting.

Everywhere throughout the forest, melted snow was dripping from the trees. In every drip the low Star shone and the grass was already starting to grow underneath. The forest was coming back to life. Across the dragon's enormous flanks and down through his wings and tail, up into his enormous skull, the light again intensified sending further pulses of energy down through the neural network of the supernatural creature. It was slowly awakening. Now the light which had been predominantly white took on a green glow and became of a more solid quality. Okino started to notice a skeletal structure forming within the translucence. He could see the great spine running from skull to tail and the finer fanlike bones of the dragon's wings, powerful bones within legs and arms were materializing within the now solidifying body. A hard protective armour plated shell was forming around its body, arms and legs. Sharp claws on hind legs and arms glistened again as the sharpest ivory.

As he watched, the dragon who now appeared to have been sleeping, started to stretch his wings, legs and tail. Then slowly the dragon's eyes started to open. Nothing in Okino's short life had prepared him for this moment. The universe suddenly opened up before him. A great wave of unbridled potential flooded through his being. Potential lost from worlds that had been formed and destroyed. The possibility of life on future worlds filled his being with uncontainable excitement. It seemed like he would explode with the wonder flooding from the eye of the dragon. A great surge of energy raced through the clearing. Okino threw up his arms and leapt into the air. He let out a scream of joy unable to contain the vision enveloping him.

The dragon finally energized, flipped over and leapt onto his hind legs. Still glowing with the supernatural light racing through his semi-solid form, he stretched himself high into the air, re-inhabiting his body, re-igniting muscles in arms and wings, flicked his powerful tail, lifted his huge head and roared. Air as hot as the centre of any Star was blown from his nostrils vaporizing newly forming leaves and branches at the tops of the trees where his breath touched. Every tree in the forest seemed to bend under the force of the sound issued from the awakened dragon. There was a crack of lightening overhead and thunder rumbled around the valley. When the echo and the winds caused by the roar died down there was complete silence in the forest.

The dragon turned to see Okino, observed him for a few moments, particularly interested in the sword he was still holding. It moved with great agility towards him, looking deep into his eyes. Okino sensed he was looking far deeper than even he knew existed in his being. It was searching through the millennia of lifetimes existing in his soul for some recognition of this boy. The dragon then turned and walked back to the centre of the clearing. He crouched on his powerful hind legs stretched out his wings to their full extent and with one enormous downward sweep he shot up into the air above the clearing. Okino watched as the dragon dived and swooped through the air before eventually disappearing towards the mountains. He stood in the clearing with the trees in full leaf, the Star shining down and the forest full of the sound of vibrant life.

Okino awoke next to the smouldering fire as the star once again crept out from behind the mountains. He looked around the clearing. Everything was as it had been when he had fallen asleep the night before. His dream had been so real. He could still feel the cold of the winter's day on which he had revealed and freed the dragon from whatever dreadful magic had been cast over him. Okino moved over to one of the Oak trees and wrapped himself in his blanket. He nestled into one of the buttresses created by the roots at the base of the enormous trunk to contemplate the dream. Okino and his brother monks had dedicated themselves to the order of the dragon. They lived and accepted the idea of dragons as spirits living as energy in the world. They believed dragon was the name humans had given to the supernatural beings whose life force had flowed through Arimathea and eventually brought into being all the creatures who were now living upon her. He knew the energy to be real for he had seen dragons drifting across the sky on moonlit nights. But they had been only clouds. When he had asked his master about the dragon clouds he had smiled and told Okino how the dreams of dragons were strong and knew no dimensional boundaries. He gestured around him and into the distance and said quietly,

"Such clouds would suggest they can project their form from their spirit dimension into our own through which ever element they choose."

"But did the dragons ever actually live?" Okino had asked.

His master replied there were tales such mythical creatures had existed but they had faded from the world when men became separated from and lost their connection with the world of spirit. Now there were only legends from different and varying cultures in which the dragons had been both beneficial and destructive murderous creatures. The latter view was generally found where the indigenous philosophy had been adapted by men to assimilate the old tales. Energy and lifeforce described in the old folklore became powerful all seeing, all knowing gods in religions whose laws and entreaties were used to enslave their people. Okino remembered thinking surely religion was meant to free the people. When he voiced this observation, his master had said

"Human beings are predominantly strange mixed up creatures who have far too much power for their own good."

Okino sat watching the light from the rising Star gradually fill the clearing and started to go over the events of the night before. This latest dream certainly had the same quality of reality as his dream on the mountain. Now he had released a dragon from what seemed like an ancient spell or curse. He smiled to himself remembering his thoughts about the threads of the legend starting to emerge in his own life from the evening before. It was becoming more difficult to deny as his visions became more connected in his waking and dreaming lives.

During their training the monks were made aware of the different levels of consciousness and the possibility of many dimensions layered over the top of one another. Each dimension they had been taught could inform and so influence invisibly outcomes in other dimensions. If this was so and the primal energy of the dragon had truly been released back into some other dimension of this world then the consequences were not entirely predictable. Okino shuddered but in the same moment remembered the blessing he had had from Arimathea before he had pulled out the sword.

As he contemplated the consequences of the dream Okino noticed a movement in the forest beyond the edge of the clearing. He watched as a family of deer, unaware of his presence moved slowly towards the clearing. There was a fully-grown stag with magnificent antlers, two does and three youngsters who clearly had been born possibly in the last few weeks. Okino froze as the deer entered the circle of ancient trees. The stag walked steadily over to one of the Oaks and again gouged his great antlers into the bark. The two females had started to feed on the lush grass. The three youngsters followed their mothers lead and started to munch happily away at the nutritious food. The stag also started to eat. He raised his great head continually as he tore away at the grass. Okino knew from his previous encounters with wild animals that if he stayed perfectly still this animal would not register his presence as a threat. However, the stag was slightly on edge having probably caught Okino's scent. He must have decided there was no imminent danger as the small family continued to graze unbothered by the figure of the silent monk crouched in the buttress of the Oak tree. The deer were so close, Okino could smell their potent scent.

He could clearly see and feel the powerful nature of the stag. He was in his prime. His every movement exuded the confidence of a being who at this moment, was unchallenged in his territory. His huge muscular frame splendidly covered with a thick shining coat, seemed to glow with a supernatural quality. There was a strength of light around him. Everything about the surrounding forest was concentrated within his aura. He stood as much a part of the forest as the trees embedded in the ground around him.

As he watched these creatures Okino became even more conscious of the sounds of the surrounding forest. Every tiny movement of even the tiniest mouse seemed to be registering somewhere. Ears twitching constantly, the stag searched the airwaves for a change in sound or vibration signalling a threat to his precious family. The genetic pass for his species into the future. Here he stood at the peak of his evolutionary pyramid. Okino could only wonder at the twists and turns of fate that had brought this magnificent creature to be standing here before him. Perfectly adapted for life in the forest and the surrounding hills, Okino sensed the deer lived as one of the truly old spirits of Arimathea.

In those moments as he watched the family calmly going about their life, surviving in this wild place unknown to other human beings, he recognized something of the energy he had seen in the dragon the night before in his dream. Something he had seen in the dragon's eye was here in the family of deer. They were wild and untamed with the ability to roam wherever the stag was prepared to take them, wherever they could live in the surroundings they had become adapted to. They had no fences or boundaries; they were not held like the goats and yaks, bound by their owners to roam only where they were allowed. They had no house or dwelling to which they had to return or defend. They slept here on the forest floor amongst the trees tonight but on the hill sides tomorrow in the moonlight.

In his dream he remembered the dragon as being physical but mostly pure energy. Here in reality, the deer were more physical but Okino recognized the pure energy of the dragon in their stance, in their relationship to the forest. Here these creatures were continuous with the forest, able to live and be completely at one with it. There never had been any separation, everything they needed was here because they had evolved generation after generation in this environment. Suddenly Okino felt very out of place. His home was far back down the valley. His race had evolved in a very different way. He had come from a small mountain community living in the same place for perhaps many thousands of years. They had built shelters, made clothes and adapted to their environment. Humans had survived by their ability to live despite their natural surroundings.

Now Okino felt the separation. What twist of evolutionary fate had brought his species to where it was? Some freak weather condition, some geological upset leaving his race, furless, clawless, badly adapted for speed in a battle for survival without the continuity that had provided the deer with his thick fur coat and the ability to survive on grass alone; that had given the mountain cats the ability to hunt down their prey with silent stealth and the eagle the ability to dive from the sky where they were invisible to their prey up until the moment it died. His race had survived through their ability to think and assimilate the information available, come to conclusions on the best course of action, make decisions and act on them. If they had not always made decisions fully considering the wellbeing of Arimathea perhaps it was because she had not given them the advantages they saw in other creatures.

As Okino acknowledged the differences between himself and the creatures before him he felt himself once again sink deeper into the reverence for the complexity of Arimathea. The deer were supernatural creatures and now he relished the space and time he was spending with them. He breathed their scent and the air he shared with them deep into his being; absorbed every detail of their form into his mind and connected with their life force and the aura making them so inseparable from the forest. He wanted to become them, feel their heartbeat in his; know what it was like for them to stand on this world.

He briefly closed his eyes and imagined he could see and feel through the senses of the great stag. In the next few moments, it seemed there was no part of the forest of which he could not become instantly aware. All the creatures he had seen in the distance now became part of his close vision. He bounded from tree to tree as a squirrel and lay sleeping deep in the ground in a badger's set. There were nests full of young birds and parents in their desperate struggle to feed them. He felt the river and the fish swimming deep in the currents. Here he was able for the first time to sense the pollution flowing through the water. It was slight but entirely alien and enough to cause imbalance in the ecology of the river and underlying everything were the trees, the solidity of their silent lives was of a continual beneficial nourishment pervading throughout the lives of all the creatures living in their shelter.

Okino breathed deeply and felt the solid ground beneath him. He sensed currents of life light flowing from below and around him into the clearing around him. He felt them coming up through his body filling him with rejuvenating energy and feelings of wellbeing. He felt the warmth of the Star as ecstasy upon his face and in the moments before he opened his eyes, he saw Arimathea standing before him, shining and radiant, her hands outstretched as if proudly showing him what she had created. He had never felt so much love. As he opened his eyes, he found tears of joy had welled up and run down his cheeks. The deer were continuing to graze but were gradually moving out of the clearing back into the forest. As quickly as they had appeared, they now drifted away without a sound and were gone. Had they been revitalized by the grass fed by the life light Okino had sensed? He wondered whether they intuitively knew of these places able to preserve and restore their vitality.

As he collected up his belongings, he thought he felt some of this intuition rising in his being. His journey must continue and so he should find his way back to the river. But now he knew the source of the problem with the river was almost certainly not in the forest but beyond. He knew now his way lay through the forest. His gaze fell to the place where the deer had entered the clearing. On examination he noticed there was a small pathway. He decided to follow it. As he reached the edge of the clearing, he turned and remembered all that had happened to him there. His journey had expanded. Now he was looking at far more than a beautiful circle of trees. He could see the deeper layers through which he had somehow connected back into the soul of his world. He bowed in respect to the spirit of the place, turned and continued down the track made by the deer.

Chapter Seven
The Canyon.

In the next days Okino continued his walk through the deep forest. His senses had become keenly alive. Colours of plants, trees and foliage appeared more vibrant. He felt the space of the forest even more acutely. The trees had now become islands through which everything else seemed to flow. Starlight shining down through the canopy fell to the forest floor in golden pools of warmth and nourishment. He watched how insects, birds and animals had their own integral role in the continuing life of the forest. Everywhere he looked a different and essential task was being conducted. Alongside the deer path there were many further paths used by any number of smaller animals. As he walked, he examined, observed and listened. He became more aware of his footfall, knowing he was now broadcasting his presence to anything he might like to become closer to.

He was always aware of the deer as he made his way through the forest. Occasionally catching sight of them, frozen in the near distance, observing and assessing before disappearing deeper into their forest at the first and slightest movement. Never far from his mind were the dreams of the dragon and Arimathea. He continued to assimilate their meaning. He imagined he heard her whispering on the breezes around him.

"Over long periods of time successful species will adapt as they find their own place on the web of life."

These words echoed through his thoughts as he watched bees and all manner of insects flying or crawling their way through the forest; through the grasses and up the vast tree trunks into their labyrinthine canopies, all inhabiting the environment into which they had evolved. There seemed no end to the detail he could find. He was able to examine small plants on which there were two or three species of insect each living and exploiting a different part. As he observed the detail of these the smallest of creatures and watched as occasionally he caught sight of a bird flying through or over the wood he thought of the dragon and the power with which it had swept up into the skies.

He was continually reminded of the supernatural creature. It seemed the memory had lost none of the quality of the original dream, which in his experience always started to fade. The dream of the dragon however, seemed to grow ever more vivid in his mind. He remembered with ever increasing clarity the crispness of the cold winter air, the colours and the sound of the dragon as he reawakened. The moment expanding most in his mind was the sensation he had experienced when he had looked into the dragon's eye. It seemed to be growing in conjunction with his ability to observe and comprehend the intricate wonder of everything going on around him. He saw reflections of the dragon in the detail of all the creatures surrounding him and the moment he realized what the detail was, the deep connection and his comprehension of the complexity of life on Arimathea once again increased.

His wanderings eventually led him back to the river. For a while he had forgotten his mission and become lost in his explorations. On the riverbanks again he continued to look for the signs of the pollution he had been following. Sure enough the foam he had first observed in the lakes was still forming in the swirls and eddies on the surface of the river. However, he thought the foam was starting to look thicker, slightly less diluted.

He looked up and down the course of the river. Downstream the current slunk off under the trees standing densely on both banks. Upstream Okino noticed the river was being forced between the sides of a valley. In the distance he could see the river had become faster. In the same moment he noticed the sky now framed by the steep slopes of the valley beyond had become considerably darker. He felt his hand instinctively reach for the stone he had found earlier. He felt the slightly rough texture as he contemplated the dark clouds at the head of the valley.

What seemed like a distant memory surfaced in his thoughts. There was a heavy rainstorm high up in the mountains. Sheet water was racing down the face of the loose rocks and scree into the river channel at such a rate the river was swelling faster than the normal channel of the river could carry. He remembered how people had been caught in these flash currents when the normally benign river, with no warning, suddenly became a dangerous torrent washing everything before it. Okino rapidly assessed an alternative route around the canyon. It would involve a substantial climb up the side of the hill encroaching on the normally wide valley bottom. The sky beyond had again become darker. He thought he could see flashes of lightening. It would be an arduous climb, but he had become sure the river was going to flood and disaster would follow if he followed the river up through the canyon. Before he could allow himself any more temptation he set off on the climb over the hill.

The slope was steep and the grass hung loosely on the scree. Okino had to consider every step, making sure the grass was firmly connected to the slope before he put his full weight down on it. On more than one occasion his feet slipped out from beneath him and he slithered in an undignified manner until he was able to get a firm grip on a rock or some vegetation that had managed to find a crevice of soil to inject some deeper roots. Okino made slow progress but soon the ridge of the hill was in sight. However, Okino became overconfident and neglected to assess the ground on the last few steps. Again, he crashed down and started the familiar slide down the hill. He was able to grab a small dead tree which had been unable to maintain its growth as it increased in size. It was able to halt his downward descent but it was clearly being uprooted by this increased strain on its tenuous hold of the mountainside. This brief slow down gave Okino just enough time to find a rock on which to get a foothold before the tree gave up its hold. He used the uprooted tree to push himself back onto his feet and once again continue his upward journey. He knocked the dead roots from the bottom of the tree and used it to gain a better balance as he assessed the ground below. He broke off a further dead branch as it brushed across his face and he eventually reached the ridge of the hill.

He stood victoriously leaning against the small tree he had plucked out of the hillside and looked down the steep face of the canyon to the river below. There was no evident increase in flow. He could also see from this elevated position where the river was disappearing into the distance. It crossed a small flood plain nestling in the foothills of the mountains. Okino could see a little group of dwellings and felt sure he could see a rising plume of smoke. Instantly he realized he had not eaten properly for days. He imagined a pot of bubbling stew and freshly stone baked bread. He briefly assessed the strength of the unfortunate tree. It was a good size and weight to be carried. Rot had not yet set in. He ran his hands up and down it, removing further small twiggy branches and took hold of it at the place he felt he would naturally carry it. The fledgling tree that had had such a short life in the rocky scree of the ridge now felt good in his hand and he gave the ground on top of the ridge a play full tap. He then grasped it with both hands, leant on this newly formed staff and looked out across the valley.

Now he had his breath back and the shock of his fall had subsided, he was able to take in the lie of the land around him. The thick forest lay behind him and the destination for which he had set out lay ahead. He felt a glimmer of satisfaction as he looked beyond the forest to where he had started out almost three days before. High on the ridge he held up the tree staff in salute and greeting to the people of his village and his brother monks whom he sensed would be wondering how his journey was developing. He smiled as he connected with them, sitting in meditation in the temple and acknowledging the star shining in through the doors and windows. He let his thoughts and theirs mingle in the light and the incense as it drifted into the crisp light. He remembered he was near his destination and turned again to the little huddle of buildings he could see in the distance. He could see the storm in the mountains beyond had not moved any closer, but an occasional bright flash lit up the low dark clouds indicating it was continuing. Okino started his descent, excited and slightly apprehensive of who or what he might find ahead.

Soon he had left the slopes of the hill and was making his way across flatter ground running adjacent to the river. He could see the river had become wider and shallower as it flowed across the broad plain. He could see beaches of shingle and sand at the edges. He could see a crop of some description. He could just make out two people as they worked in amongst the plants. They were engrossed in their task and had not noticed him as he walked along the riverbank. There were two children playing further up on one of the sandy beaches. As he came closer, he could see how they were going to the water's edge, selecting stones and placing them in growing patterns. He continued to look for the signs of the pollution.

Their parents noticed Okino as they checked on the children from a distance in the field. He waved with his largest most friendly smile which seemed to allay any fears and they both went back to work. As Okino watched the children playing happily he contemplated the idyllic scene he had discovered. Could this be the origin of the pollution in the lakes? The crop seemed extensive and contained a plant he did not recognize. Instinctively he felt for the stone lying deep in his pocket and turned it between his fingers. There was something wrong here, not yet apparent to him. He turned his attention again upstream to where he had seen the storm. The dark clouds seemed to have dispersed. The star sparkled on the river as it ran over the stones, mingling with the happy sounds of the children as they played.

However, now just above the sound of the gently flowing river there was a more powerful sound. A deeper hissing rumble, barely audible in the background. Okino noticed an almost imperceptible change in the speed of the flow. Then everything started to change. The gentle rumble was coming rapidly nearer and the current of the river became quicker. Okino realized in an instant what was happening. He looked around to where the parents were in the crops. They were too far away to comprehend and act in response to the situation arising. He ran down towards the river and jumped down onto the shingle bank where the children were playing. The two children looked up in alarm at the sudden appearance of this stranger. The river, rising rapidly, was already starting to wash away the patterns in the sand. One of the children staggered under the force of the current and teetered on the point of falling into the water. Okino lunged for her and caught her. Unceremoniously he grabbed her around her waist and held her with one arm. She started to scream in panic. Okino then grabbed the little boy under his other arm. Both children screamed and struggled.

The rivers' depth had increased rapidly and Okino realized the full force of the flood was approaching. He calmly made the last few steps to the bank of the river holding the struggling children. The beaches had disappeared. He launched the two children into the air. They landed stunned on the bank above. Okino then scrambled up the bank as the flood water came up to his waist. The children were screaming uncontrollably and now their parents were running down to the river. They gathered the children up into their arms, faces white with terror as they watched the peaceful river where there beloved offspring had recently been playing, now transformed into a raging torrent barely contained within its banks. As the astonished parents calmed the children down, they watched Okino with tears of delight and relief in their eyes. When they were able to put the children back on the ground, they thanked him profusely, they bowed, bobbing their heads continuously while clasping his hands. They all stood relieved looking down at the river. Vegetation, branches and logs were being washed down in the torrent.

"They would have been gone. We would never have seen them again. It is a miracle that has happened. We have never had a visitor here who has come on foot before….and yet you arrive at this moment to save our children."

The mother in her early twenties reached over and touched Okino,

"Are you an Angel to have come here at this time."

"I am not an Angel" replied Okino, "I am very much a mortal and now an extremely damp one."

"We are indebted to you for all eternity" said the man, bowing again "I am Haran and this is my wife Serilla. My children are Kefna and Larisen."

"I am Okino, a priest of the Ancient Dragon Order."

The two parents grabbed him simultaneously and hurried him with their two children up towards the buildings. Inside Haran organised some dry clothes for Okino to wear and hung his own soaking garments around the fire.

Outside the crude low stone and timber dwelling the little family and Okino sat at a broad solid table on benches stretched out along one of the long sides. True to Okino's earlier vision Serilla brought out fresh stone baked bread. Okino broke it carefully and blessed it quietly before carefully placing it in his mouth. Haran watched and noticed the blessing the young monk had given.

"So you are a priest. What has brought you to our humble farm at such a time, Okino?"

Okino looked at Haran and his family. He chewed on the bread and silently took a mouthful from the bowl of rice, chicken and beans which had also been given to him. He chose not to answer the question for the moment.

"You are a long way from just about anywhere up here." Okino remarked,

"We have an old truck. It takes us the good part of a day to get to the nearest town, Aharri, where we sell our crop and buy provisions."

"Have you been here long?" Okino inquired.

"This was my grandfather's farm. He died many years ago. We all grew up near the town, my father was also a farmer. This old place lay derelict for many years before we decided to move back up here."

Okino was watching the chickens pecking around on the ground. There were yaks in a pasture beyond and goats in a smaller enclosure. There was another larger building Okino assumed must be the barn. Both the house and the barn looked as if they had been recently and effectively repaired with new timber and roof slates. The buildings had been well built perhaps many generations before and now had been effectively adapted by this latest family.

"My Grandfather mainly kept Yaks, a few of which we found roaming wild when we first came up here. They have become part of the family. They give us milk and we have sold some of the male calves."

"...And what are you growing up here?"

Okino was looking over to the green bushes. They seemed to be flourishing. Serilla had reappeared from the house with more bowls containing Yogurt and Honey. Haran seemed reluctant to explain about his crop. The two men looked over to the mountains and silently ate the yogurt. The farmer was wondering what had brought this priest on his journey many days from the monastery.

"So what?…".

"So what?"

Both men had started to speak at the same time. They grinned at each other. Kefna had recovered and was chasing one of the chickens. For now, the chicken was faster. His sister laughed gleefully as the chicken outran her little brother. The two men laughed, glad for a relief from the tension building between them. Okino shifted his weight on the bench as if starting to speak.

"You first, I guess." Haran said tentatively.

"Look, I'm sure it is something really simple we can sort out. But I've made the journey up from the village and the monastery where I live because something has changed with the water flowing down the river into the lakes where we keep the fish we have been farming for generations. Something is affecting their skins and as a result of this they are dying in great numbers. We have never known this to happen before. So I decided to follow the river to see what I could find. This is the first place where there is any activity between here and the village. I may be wrong but I don't imagine there is much going on further up into the hills. So, you see Haran, there may be something you have started quite recently which is effecting the biology of the river."

Haran looked at Okino in disbelief. He then looked over at the crop which Okino had found him and his wife lovingly tending.

"So, what are you growing Haran" Okino asked slightly more insistently this time. "We may be able to help you. We have generations of experience of growing crops up in these mountains."

Haran sighed.

"I suppose it was all too good to be true. There just had to be some sort of hitch sooner or later. Anyway, yes, we have just started to grow this crop fairly intensively. It's an herb that grows wild in these mountains. Apparently, it needs very specific conditions. Altitude being the main one. It's called Keraika. My grandfather supposedly discovered it. However, I'm sure the people who lived in these mountains must have known about it, he just happened to be one of the last. The thing about it is that it suppresses appetite. It allowed them to live up here with virtually nothing to eat. They never spoke to anyone about it mainly because they never really spoke to anyone. But my grandfather told my father about it just before he died. Nobody really knew how old he was. He certainly never told anyone. So, when he died the old place went to rack and ruin.

We were living down in the town. More people started to come from the outside world and one night my father was talking to this hugely overweight guy. They were drinking heavily and they got talking about his weight and how he couldn't stop eating. My father told me he nearly laughed himself to death. Here we are all our lives on the point of starvation doing everything we can to feed our children in desperate fear they are not getting enough to eat. Then here was someone from another part of the world telling him there was an epidemic of ill health in which people are literally eating themselves to death because there is so much food."

"I have heard things have got pretty mad in other parts of Arimathea but that really does sound ironic."

Okino certainly saw the irony but was slightly apprehensive about what he was about to be told.

"Anyway, my dad told him about Keraika and they drove up in this guy's vehicle the next day and found some. They put it into the food they made that night and sure enough the guy didn't need to eat for days. He stayed for a few weeks and went back a shadow of his former self. The whole thing was a huge joke in town until one day the guy came back and contacted my dad. There was some company back in his country who reckoned they could sell it to all the people who were eating themselves to death. Our farm just so happens to have enough flat ground at the right altitude to grow the stuff in the kind of quantities they could use. So, we entered into a contract. It was agreed

I would come up here and grow the Keraika plants and it would be collected twice a year after the growing season from the town.

Everything was fine for the first year. But we found the ground was not rich enough in nutrients to supply two crops a year to meet the demands of the contract, and so," he paused,

"Follow me."

Haran beckoned Okino to follow him over to the barn where he threw open the huge timber doors. There in the gloomy light, next to an ancient truck, piled high to the eaves was a stack of large white plastic sacks. The only immediately identifiable word was **WADE.** The logo was clearly written in bold letters amongst other further information about the specifications of the chemicals contained within it; now almost certainly causing the problems with the fish downstream in the lakes.

"It's synthetic fertilizer!!"

Suddenly everything became clear for Okino. Here was the root of the problem piled high in front of him. The chemicals Haran was putting on the herbs to make them grow faster to meet the terms of his contract were leaching through the thin mountain soil into the river. The water had been pure for so long the fish had no tolerance to even the smallest concentration of these chemicals when they had reached and gradually accumulated in the lakes. The degradation the Human race had brought upon the planet of Arimathea had now reached even their isolated mountain home.

Later that evening Okino, Haran and Serilla were sitting around the fire in the little stone house. The children had been put to bed. The adults were quietly watching the flames in the stone hearth. Okino remembered these times in his own home with his mother and father. He thought how little had changed in these remote areas of Arimathea. He wondered how long these mountains could hold back the flood which appeared to be coming? Now they had something the world beyond felt it needed to continue as it always had done. Surely it would not be long before the whole valley was cultivating the amazing Keraika plant. He had seen magazines left by the few travellers who had come to the monastery in search of enlightenment for their lost and damaged souls. He had seen a world of beauty and perfection where everyone had enough to eat and a place to live, money to spend on cars and jewellery, exotic perfumes and clothes fitting perfectly around their perfectly shaped bodies. He half smiled and half shuddered to himself as he remembered why he was here. The full extent of the lies between those pages was becoming apparent.

He looked over at Haran. His face had the look of a man who was having deep and conflicting thoughts. They were easy thoughts to read. Haran had been given a break; a means to bring his family out of the poverty of their mountain existence and into the way of life promised by the magazines. How long would he stay in this mountain home when the potential of the Keraika plants began to be truly realized. Would he leave his roots here to live the dream in the "Otherworld" lying beyond? Okino had suspected there would be some man-made reason for the pollution. But now there were personalities involved he could understand the dilemmas facing Haran and his wife and so many of the poorer people on Arimathea. Wasn't it their responsibility as parents to aspire to a higher standard of living for their children?

Haran was emerging from his thoughts. He looked over at Okino stretching in the warmth of the fire.

"So, we have a problem my young monk friend,"

"Indeed, we do. However, I do not believe it is our problem alone. The dilemma we are faced with is ultimately confronting the whole of Arimathea."

Okino looked over to Haran and his wife to see if there was any response. They looked back at him with confused and questioning expressions.

"It seems there are parts of Arimathea which have developed standards of living for their people which are not sustainable for the whole planet. As they use up their own resources, they will have to increasingly take from those countries surrounding them. They will promise their wealth to communities like our own as this vast ravenous machine continues to ravage the planet. Now they are demanding more than your land can supply to satisfy their greed and the insatiable demand fuelling it. As a result, you have used this fertilizer and the delicate balance of the fragile mountain environment has been damaged."

Haran and Serilla were silent and then asked despairingly...

"What can we do?"

"The way I see it there are a number of possibilities. You can stop using the fertilizer. Your yield won't be as high and you would have to find some way of putting nutrients back into the soil. Have you ever thought about getting some more yaks"?

"You'd have to a have fairly large herd of yaks to generate enough dung to naturally fertilise all those plants. They are not particularly easy creatures to have around. I struggle with the few we have. No that definitely wouldn't work." Haran was shaking his head vigorously.

"If you wanted to continue to grow intensively, I suppose you could grow the plants in containers so they are isolated from the ground connected to the river. This would mean a lot of work to start with, but you would be able to experiment with quantities and types of fertilizer to get possibly an even higher yield."

"Now that is not such a bad idea," Haran's mood lightened immediately, "The plants are bushes. We take the new growth twice a year. If we carefully transferred the bushes to some sort of container maybe two or three to each container we could rig up some sort of continuous watering regime. We could experiment with the amount of nutrients added through the same system. It would take a fairly large initial outlay, but we may be able to fund it with the sale of this next crop, which incidentally we are about to harvest and should be our most profitable so far."

"So, when would you start your harvest?" Okino inquired...

"We were getting ready to start pretty much as you arrived. So, we could be starting in the next couple of days. Why? Are you thinking you might like to help?…I could pay you once the crop has been sold in Aharri. We would welcome another pair of hands. It is hard work for the two of us and as you saw today it's hard to keep an eye on the children when we are both working."

Okino looked into the fire. He smiled to himself. He seemed to have solved the problem with the water and now his journey was unravelling further. Also, he was amused by the idea of having money!!

"It would be an honour to help you bring in your harvest. I could also be tempted to go with you to Aharri. I think it is about time I visited a town. I really only came here to find out about the pollution in the lakes but I have a feeling there may be something further for me to do. I might find out what it is when we get to Aharri."

"Excellent!!"

Haran and Serilla were pleased to have another pair of hands to help. "It's good to have you on board. We are so indebted to you for saving the children this afternoon and now this…there was something we were going to offer you. We think you may appreciate it more than us.." Haran reached into the pocket of his thick mountain coat and pulled out a string of beads and handed them to Okino.

Okino leant forward to take the necklace of polished stones. He examined the stones carefully in the firelight.

"It was made by my Grandfather who as I said lived up here all his life. Each bead is a different kind of stone and apparently, so he always told me, there is one bead for every kind of stone found in these mountains. You'll be able to see them better in the daylight."

Okino continued to examine the necklace. The nature of the rock would be much the same as in his own valley. He recognized many of the different coloured stones. It occurred to him they represented a complete record of the fabric of his land for him to carry wherever his journey was to take him. They had been lovingly chosen, smoothed, polished and carefully strung together.

"This is beautiful. I'm not sure I should be taking such a precious object as this from you."

He started to offer them back to Haran who immediately gestured the necklace back towards him"

"No, this is a very small token of our gratitude for what you have done for us. My grandfather wore them for many years. He always said it was like being embedded in the very strata of the rock itself, go on, try them on."

Okino examined and opened the clasp. He carefully put the necklace around his neck and flicked the solid clasp shut. The weight of the stones fell on his neck and shoulders and he closed his eyes. He let all his memories of the mountain lands in which he had always lived flood into his mind. They gradually and vividly intensified. The high peaks and valleys, the gurgling streams as they raced down the hills, waterfalls crashing over precipices and filling the air with rainbow sprays. The low fertile plains in the alluvial valleys and the high desolate scree covered slopes, all the paths he had ever roamed now vividly were present in his mind as one beautifully interconnected whole where every stone, crevasse and cliff face had its place in the vast construction of the mountains.

Underlying all these physical features were the vast planetary forces at work forming each and every feature Okino had come to know and love. He felt the unfathomable tracts of time as the forces of the vast continental plates pushed together and thrust the mountain ranges skywards over millions and millions of years. Here was insight into the physical workings of the planet of Arimathea. Okino opened his eyes in amazement to see Haran and Serilla watching him with enormous grins on their faces. They had glimpsed themselves the wonder held in the beads their grandfather had made but had always felt they would be of more use to someone else. Now such a person had arrived and they were able to pass on this wonder.

"I thank you, for this beautiful gift you have bestowed upon me. Your grandfather undoubtedly had a great and true understanding of his world to have made such an amazing thing."

"Then we have passed it to one who has equal with him. May his wisdom be always with you."

Chapter Eight
The Harvest.

Okino slept close to the fire. As he contemplated the day, for the first time he acknowledged to himself his initial mission had been accomplished. The source of the pollution had been found and a solution had been discussed and agreed with Haran and Serilla. Okino lay back on the comfortable mattress. The little house had several small windows high up in the walls. The thick glass allowed moonlight to invade the living area. Shafts of light fell in pools on the thick woollen mats lying on the stone floor. He remembered the previous nights lying on the forest floor being slightly unnerved by the sounds of the animals who were sharing the forest around him. Here he felt safe in the house Haran's grandfather had built and he drifted off to sleep wondering whether he would meet the dragon he had awakened previously.

He opened his eyes to see Haran nudging the fire back into life. He turned to see Okino was awake. He smiled and the day of the harvest began. The children and Serilla emerged. They were excited and hurried their breakfast of steaming tea, bread and dried fruit. It was agreed after the previous days potential tragedy the children would have to help as best they could with the operation at hand. Haran was stern with them in his warm good-natured way and the children responded well to his offer of being involved with the operation so important to their lives.

Breakfast consumed and suitable clothing agreed the little group emerged from the stone house out into the warming mountain air. Haran showed Okino how the Keraika plants were to be harvested. The bushes were waist high and planted in neat rows wide enough for someone to move between. They were solid evergreen bushes. Haran pointed out the shoots of new growth on the top shoots of the plant. These were the leaves to be taken. He showed an expertise in nipping the leaves off with the sharp knife telling of many hours carrying out the procedure. The leaves would be put into the baskets sitting on the ground beside them and the children would follow the adults and empty the baskets when they were full into large sacks in the barn.

Soon the little family and their newly acquired labour force were hard at work. The children watched intently as the baskets started to fill up, but after only a few minutes they had become restless and Haran started to tell them a story.

"One day a farmer went out to his herd of yaks grazing happily down by the riverbank. But when he counted them, he found there was one missing…The farmer looked to and fro up the riverbank but the missing yak was nowhere to be seen.…"

Okino watched as the children became instantly entranced by their father's story, he listened as other mountain animals became involved. The children shrank back as their father impersonated the sly old mountain lion and giggled as he strutted like the nervous deer. Okino drifted back into his own thoughts. He was now becoming an accomplice to the tragedy happening down in the lakes. He had harvested before many times down in his own valley. If a large crop had to be brought in quickly the whole community was always mobilized. He had happy memories of these times and drifted through them as the task of cutting the little green leaves quickly became second nature. Haran was now crossing a river to where he could see the missing yak.

Okino remembered their own animals. He remembered them as important members of the village with their own specific characters and names. He had ridden the yaks back from the fields astride their broad powerful backs and remembered fondly the gentle rhythm of their stride back into the town. The baskets would be full of root vegetables from the fields or fruit from the trees in the orchards. It would be stored or distributed to the folk of the town in the next few days. He remembered there had always been good and bad years. Some years they were hungrier than others. But there had always been enough and here he was, strong and healthy, a tribute to the farmers who had developed the ability to continually supply just enough food in the harsh mountain environment for the little settlement to survive from generation to generation.

He remembered seeing the farmers delving down into the ground and running their fingers through the soil. They would always look into the sky and shake their heads, cursing which ever gods had let them down that year. The rains would either be too heavy or too light. The Star shone too hard or not enough and never in the right combination. When the snows came in the winter the land was left until the melt.

Okino vividly remembered as a young child the miracle that appeared to happen next. As the first warmth from the Star shone down onto the valley, the crops planted before the snows descended began to sprout from the ground and slowly over the next few weeks the fields would again turn to green. No time was wasted by these magicians tending the land. If the farmers cursed either land, Star or rain they would sure to be up at the temple the next day making some small offering in recompense for their carelessness. For at the root of all their tending and nurturing of the soil, all their manuring and ploughing, all the love they lavished upon it was really the deep respect they had for the planet of Arimathea instilled in them by their fathers. Okino had always been surprised how these grown men would sit out in their fields long after the work had been done silently conferring with the space around them. They would offer their respect on little altars built beside the fields many generations before. Bowls of water were always present and a particularly splendid specimen of vegetable from the last harvest. The women would leave flowers and the occasional loaf of bread once the wheat had been cut, ground and baked.

If the farmers were the magicians who tempted the magic out of the ground, then the priests in the temple were the intermediaries between the farmers and their spirit gods. This is how it had always been. Even with their knowledge and experience of generations, the farmers would always go to the priests when they had a problem they thought was with their connection to the land. For they were the ones whose gift had been spotted from an early age. They had been trained in the temple not only to perform the rites publicly at specific times of the year, but also to maintain the connection with the spirit of Arimathea in their daily lives. Through this observance everyone was hopeful Arimathea would maintain her benevolent provision of their livelihood in the mountains.

They had also come to understand how there was some further alchemy between Arimathea and the life force she contained, the mystical energy which brought the crops from the ground every year. This, in their myths and stories, had always been referred to as the Dragon Light. Both farmers and priests had access to modern information on farming which had filtered through to them from the modern world outside. They were under no illusion the growth of plants in the soil was a complicated set of organic and chemical reactions. However, nothing they had ever read had ever really convinced them the relationship between the dragon and the spirit of Arimathea was not behind those processes and ultimately brought them into being. So, although now they knew why their ancestors had always mixed the dung of their animals into the soil to increase the microbial action they were still deeply respectful of this ancient spirit bond whenever they had any decision to make about the working of the land.

Okino played all this through his thoughts as he helped with the harvest of the Keraika plants. In his contemplation it was not long before the gravity underlying the problem his community had faced from Haran's use of the synthetic fertilizers started to become clear in his mind. If the use of these fertilizers had become widespread throughout the rest of Arimathea so production from the ground could be increased, he could see how any belief Arimathea was anything more than just a medium for the production of food would become redundant. If harvests could be boosted by the addition of chemicals which aided growth then the idea of a supernatural being underlying the process finally became irrelevant. The process had been demystified and Okino could see how the respect for Arimathea and her dragon or whatever beautiful energy or force lay behind this amazing world had fallen away so quickly. But now farmed land was continually producing more than it was naturally able and was left full of chemicals which were gradually upsetting the balance of the entire world. The process was creating an ever-expanding population who became ever more dependent on these increased levels of production. So, what would happen when the ground was so degraded not even the chemicals would grow anything?

The paradox was complete. The human obsession to control their environment and so ultimately control their destiny would eventually destroy them. Okino sensed somewhere in all this lay the key to the next part of his journey. He dropped another handful of the bright green leaves into his basket. It was full. Haran had engineered his story for his children perfectly. The farmer had finally caught the crafty old yak with the help of an entire cast of animals and his intimate knowledge of the mountains. The children cheered. Okino saw Haran in another light. He had entertained his children and at the same time had given them a valuable lesson about life in the mountains. The children hurried to collect up the baskets and took them to the barn where Serilla helped them transfer the leaves into the sacks.

Gradually as the day went on the little workforce worked its' way through the rows of Keraika. The spring weather high in the mountains had the ability to change frequently. Bright Starshine could be quickly replaced by heavy showers of rain. It seemed they were all far too busy to notice the slight dampness the brief showers brought about. Okino frequently looked around at the surrounding mountains as he stretched his back. He looked up fondly at the high summits and ridges in the distance. This had been his home for all of his short life.

He was thankful as he quietly contemplated what he might do next. Haran had asked him whether he would like to travel in the truck to deliver the Keraika crop. The idea of travelling to the town in the lorry where he would have money to buy things in a market excited him. There was little money in the village where he had lived. Any money gained through trade with the outside world was kept by the community for when essential provisions were needed. The villagers traded amongst themselves with chickens or whatever they had to offer each other. There were frequent disagreements and some sort of currency had often been talked about but here in this remote area of Arimathea the value of a chicken, the provision of a table or a roof, a sack of potatoes or a sack of grain had never been agreed.

Okino smiled to himself as he remembered how these disagreements would ultimately end up at the "high council". As in any vibrant economy the value of products would constantly fluctuate. If it had been a good year for goats and the population had risen substantially but there had been a bad harvest, then the value of one goat against a sack of grain would fall. However, the deliberations of the "high council" although serious were always good natured and decisions were never reached without taking the interest of all parties in relation to previous years and future years into consideration. He decided he would go to the town with Haran and became more excited by the prospect.

The bushes were still low and the ache in his back soon became part of the operation. Slowly the divide of the bushes that had been stripped and those that had not started to become more apparent. Hour by hour Okino watched as the proportion changed. By the time the bright green bushes were in the minority the mood had changed amongst adults and children. A mood of silent determination had fallen over the little group of harvesters. Their routine had become seamless and the pile of sacks grew relentlessly outside the barn. In the late afternoon as the Star was again lowering over the surrounding mountains the last of the bright green leaves had been stripped from the bushes. Everybody congratulated each other as they stood in front of the pile of sacks now ready to be loaded onto the truck.

Haran and Okino looked at each other and decided the task could wait until the following morning. In the last of the Starlight they all went down to the river which was now back to its normal level. Okino, Haran and Serilla watched as the children resumed the game that had ended so abruptly the day before. Haran and Serilla were happy and relaxed and chattered away to Okino about the plans they had. Okino listened as he watched the children making their patterns in the sand. How oblivious they were to the concerns of their parents as they again became embroiled in whatever world they had constructed in their imaginations.

"Thanks again Okino for the help you have given us today...it has made everything so much easier. I'm sure we would not have done it in two days without your help."

"In many ways I have enjoyed the whole experience. In other ways..."

He reached for his back and gave a pained expression,

"I have not enjoyed quite as much. But if the offer to go into Aharri is still open I would like to take you up on it. I have never travelled to such a town before and certainly not in a truck!!"

Haran claps him on the back and says...

"Of course, you must come my friend!! Where else will you spend the wages you have earned. How could you come all this way, turn back and return to your monastery? There is a whole world waiting for you out there."

"That is what worries me... I have a feeling the whole world is waiting for me!!"

That night there was very little eaten. The active ingredients of the Keraika had been absorbed into all their systems. Everyone was tired and weary from their exertions in the fresh mountain air and soon they crawled aching between the blankets on the soft woollen mattresses and fell immediately to sleep.

Okino had slept lightly on his first night in the home of the farmer but now fully relaxed and exhausted he fell into a deep sleep. He dreamt he was flying high above Arimathea in a slipstream. He was above a thin layer of misty cloud and through the gaps he could see he was flying over an ocean. A coastline was rapidly approaching and a thick jungle stretched to the distant horizon. There were mountains and smaller hills emerging from the jungle as it swept out over the planet. He was cold and insubstantial. He had no body or form just thought and recognition of where and how he was. Then there was a shadow.

The light from the Star was briefly taken away as a dragon flew over. It was still glowing with the immense energy Okino had witnessed at its awakening. He strained to catch a glimpse of the dragon's eye but he was as yet too far away. It flew with an occasional powerful down beat of its wings allowing a continuous glide on the slipstream. Okino noticed the dragon had combined his own energy with the powerful current of air on which it was riding. It seemed they had both become part of one of the weather systems flowing around Arimathea. Through the consciousness of the dragon he sensed an endless flow of air and moisture, of hot and cold, high and low pressure forming and driving the vast engine of atmospheric change around the planet. He could feel the cold winds from the poles and the hot winds from the deserts. He could feel those winds meeting over the oceans where the moist rising air was forming the beginnings of storms or the gentle breezes that would distribute the rains over the temperate areas.

Okino moved closer to the dragon until he was almost under the wings of the creature. Closer now the dragon seemed even less formed. The glowing pulsating energy was more apparition with little defined edge. Light from his aura flowed behind him and was left hanging in the surrounding air. Its entire energetic frame was constantly readjusting to maintain a perfect trajectory across the ocean. As the dragon crossed over the coastline and beaches below he started to fly lower. Okino felt the dragon scanning the atmosphere, far across the landscape to the horizons beyond for some sign, a change, for an inconsistency in the fabric of the planet floor. His great head and eyes moved constantly, precisely surveying each feature of the jungle below. Deeper and deeper, for hour after hour they flew, passing over great rivers that disappeared over vast cliffs and fell hundreds of feet in a cascade of rainbows and billowing cloud mists to where the river once again continued on its sinuous way. They stretched like great ribbons of light curving and carving their way through the never ending jungle.

Suddenly there was a change in the energy of the dragon. He flew even lower, just above the canopy of the trees. Okino could again hear a multitude of frenzied life rising from the jungle. His great wings beat more rapidly as he slowed his speed almost to a hover. It seemed to Okino the dragon had found what he was looking for. They were above dense jungle. Trees soared up from the forest floor grown from centuries of competition for light with their neighbours.

The dragon started to carefully lower himself down through the trees but soon was confronted with a dense tangle of vegetation which was preventing him from landing. Okino felt his lungs expand as he sucked in a quantity of air. Then with the familiar roar he expelled a jet of fire from his nostrils with such ferocity that everything coming into contact with it and much beyond was instantly vaporized. The trunks of the trees were scorched and set alight but remained standing. Now only the scorched jungle floor could be seen below. Okino remembered the silence following the roar when he had awoken the dragon. Now the jungle was silent as the dragon lowered himself into the space he had created.

There before them lay another brutally murdered stone dragon. It appeared this dragon had crashed from a great height into the jungle. A sword was still embedded in its' neck. The dragon stood still and silent, his great head lowered in respect for another of his kind. Okino felt anger welling up inside the supernatural creature. He moved with great agility around the stone body and took hold of the hilt of the sword. Then with a roar in defiance of every known power in the Universe, he pulled out the sword. As in his previous dream, Okino watched as light started to flow from the surrounding circle of trees into the wound left by the sword. The dense stone began to shine. Pulses of light were transferring life to limbs and the tips of wings; claws again began to shine. The stone had been replaced by the mysterious glow and from in the glow another dragon began to materialize. The great chest started to rise and fall and as further signs of life started to appear it began to stretch its limbs and wings.

Okino saw remnants of the surrounding jungle starting to regenerate. Plants burst through the charred remains of the vegetation previously inhabiting the space. Climbers and ferns were seeking out the light emanating from the dragon. Creepers and vines grew up into the trees at an accelerated speed and branches scorched by the dragon's fire regenerated back to where they had been seconds before the holocaust had struck. The dragon's eyes opened. Again, Okino's dream flooded with possibility and potential. Brightly coloured birds in mid-flight when the inferno had struck, burst back into the air to continue their flight across the clearing. The jungle floor once again became a seething mass of life as the dragon rolled over and unsteadily climbed to its feet. Okino noticed its bones were finer and its features were altogether more delicate. As it adjusted its' wings and tail to finally stand upright across the clearing from the original dragon, Okino noticed its movements were less muscular and certainly more graceful. He decided in all his amazement this was almost certainly a female dragon.

The surrounding jungle had regenerated itself entirely. The two dragons moved closer to each other, spread their wings and stretched their long necks, they moved to each side of the others head and finally bowed reverentially. A surprised family of monkeys that had materialized leaping out of the ground now ran in panic across the clearing and bounded up one of the surrounding trees. They sat on a high branch chattering hysterically as the two dragons continued their reacquaintance. They crouched down on their hind quarters, looking directly into each other's eyes. Both dragons now appeared to be transferring light and energy between each other. Okino knew they were transferring the memories and knowledge they had gained since their last meeting. He sensed there was great sadness between them but then he felt a great surge of determination as the dragons rose to their full height. Then with one great downward thrust of their powerful wings they flew effortlessly up into the skies above the jungle and disappeared.

Chapter Nine
Transition.

The next morning Okino helped Haran to load the Keraika into the back of his old truck. As he worked, he contemplated the appearance of the female dragon in his dreams. The similarity to the first dragon and the continuity of events within his dreams were now starting to convince him there was an overwhelming possibility something extraordinary was happening. Exactly where remained a mystery. It seemed by chance or by some design he had been given access through his dreams to a set of events possibly happening in another spirit dimension the priests had always alluded to, just underneath or parallel in some way to the reality of his waking hours. Okino, even in the few hours since he had had the last dream was beginning to think this was almost certainly an extension of the life he was leading on Arimathea. Perhaps these dream layers had always been projected into the human mind as a way of representing force or energy in the layers of existence beyond human understanding.

Certainly to the primitive human mind where perhaps the dragon had first emerged, the idea of a creature combining attributes of the animals they saw around them with the ability to breathe fire so connecting them powerfully to the life giving power of the Star would have been a powerful image. Now, here they were in his dreams. Apparently reawakened or resurrected after some conflict. He thought of the clearing the crows had presumably directed him to. Perhaps his imaginings and mystical abilities, finding the mysterious meteor stone and the ring combined with the power of the ancient trees and the fire had enabled him to break through into the dimension where the dragon could again be re-awakened. Huge unending chains of thought were exploding through his mind.

Arimathea had undoubtedly been present in the moment he had pulled the sword from the dragon in his dream. Based on his last experience in the slip stream he had released an extremely powerful spirit able to tune into and probably manipulate the very forces of nature governing the planet. It was all too late to worry about now. Whatever chain of events had been initiated by his action were now well under way. He remembered her words in the cave. It seemed almost beyond doubt now she was guiding him into and through these dreams.

Haran and Okino finished loading the Keraika sacks onto the truck. Haran emerged from the back of the barn with an enormous handle which he proceeded to lodge into the front of the ancient vehicle. Okino watched with fascination as Haran turned the handle until he could turn it no further. He then closed his eyes braced himself and with an enormous effort pulled the handle towards him and out of the truck. A small puff of smoke emerged from the back of the vehicle. Then silence. Haran repeated the procedure but still nothing happened.

"Usually takes a few turns" he assured Okino. By now the children had emerged to witness the starting of the truck.

Haran once again placed the handle in the engine and pulled back with all the strength he could summon. This time the great engine turned slowly of its own accord and then burst into life with a tremendous explosion from the exhaust. Okino immediately thought he had fallen into another dream and yet another dragon was waking. Great clouds of blue smoke came billowing from the back of the truck filling the barn, much to the hilarity of the children who ran through the barn laughing and coughing uncontrollably. As the smoke started to clear Serilla appeared with a basket.

"You'll be needing this for the journey". Haran looked inside,

"Thank you, my Angel."

"Now you be careful in that truck and look after Okino in Aharri."

Then she turned to Okino.

"There are some terrible and treacherous bandits living there. Most of them friends of Haran!!"

Okino gave her a little bow and ruffled the hair of the children who were now close by her side.

"I hope to see you on the return journey, but the way things are going I'm not sure how long it will be before I come back this way."

"It has been a pleasure to meet you, Okino. I wish you success and good luck wherever you find yourself"

The little family said their goodbyes with hugs and kisses. The children looked distraught now after the hilarity of the truck starting up as their father and Okino climbed up into the truck and slowly drove off down the track towards the town.

The "track" was just wide enough for two yaks to travel downside by side and was not really suitable for a vehicle. The ancient wheels and large tires ran along the extreme edge most of the time. On occasions the track would fall away completely due to some subsidence or a heavy rainfall which had washed away a new gully. Rock falls from the sides of the steep hills had left their debris partially or entirely blocking the way. The early part of the journey was slow and extremely bumpy. Okino having never been in such a vehicle clung on nervously to whatever he could as Haran drove as fast as the track and his idea of safety would allow. This was not a great speed and after a while the journey found a rhythm of its own.

Okino started to relax and enjoy the sensation of traveling without any effort whatsoever. Okino had read about cars and vehicles in the books and magazines that had found their way to the village but was fascinated to hear Haran's explanation as to how the internal combustion engine actually worked. He was amused this new creature in which he was traveling was being propelled by the resultant forces of fiery explosions. He thought of the great plume of fire expelled from the dragon which had caused the inferno in the jungle the night before. Now, here he was in a machine his own race had invented, being propelled across the landscape by a series of tiny fiery explosions. In the flatter parts of the journey it almost gave him the sensation of flight.

As the solid old truck trundled through the mountains the two men talked of their lives in this remote part of Arimathea. Periodically they would have to stop the truck and remove a particularly bad rock fall or fill in a gully. These were parts of his country Okino had never seen. As they moved from valley to valley and a different set of vistas arose, Okino would ask Haran to stop so he could absorb this new part of his land. They took advantage of these stops to eat and drink from the basket Serilla had given them.

It was a fine day and they had clear views of the soaring snow-capped peaks across the plains as they stretched far away into the distance. These were distances that would have taken Okino on foot or even with yaks many days to traverse. Now they could get back in the truck and within an hour they would be through the next range of mountains and looking across an entirely new vista. Okino was amazed. He forgot about his journey and the dragons and the pollution and fell under the spell of the machine and its ability to show him these unexplored areas of his beloved Arimathea.

Harran watched his innocent delight with amusement. He knew his delight would end when the full impact of these machines on the atmosphere of Arimathea fully dawned on the young monk. He knew the further Okino travelled away from these pristine landscapes and the nearer he came to the industrialised metropolis, the horror of what was happening on his world would soon become apparent. For now, he allowed the monk his joy.

It was late afternoon before they reached the highest point of the pass through the last range of mountains and were able to see the town of Aharri stretched out in the valley below them. Haran stopped the truck. He was relieved the old vehicle had completed the journey once again and tapped the dash and murmured a blessing under his breath. He opened the basket and took out the remaining bread and offered half to Okino and they sat back to take in the view.

From here on the pass they could see the pattern of the town below them. It appeared to have grown as the need and opportunity had occurred. Larger buildings in the centre gave way to the smaller dwelling houses which in turn gave way to an outer ring of what appeared to be tents and other such temporary accommodation. The town was surrounded by fields in various states of cultivation. Even from high on the pass it was clear there was a great deal of activity in and around the little town. Animals were tethered around the tents. There appeared to be some horse racing underway judging by the trails of dust being created in one of the uncultivated fields. Haran seemed suddenly excited at the prospect of going down into the town and grinned over at Okino as he started up the truck, now with a fully charged battery.

"It's the big Spring market, Okino. The first since the passes have been clear of snow. Everyone has come down to the town to trade whatever they have for the first time in four or five months. They will be buying food and grain, now running low back in the mountain communities. The traders from the lands in the South will have brought their surplus supplies of grain and rice they stored specifically for this market. They will trade it for merchandise the mountain folk have been making over the winter. It is a great spectacle and there is always the meeting of many old friends!!"

As he drove the truck carefully down the crude track towards the town Okino was also becoming excited. With every passing minute new details of the town came into view. The height and construction of the buildings, then where the road entered into the town; then he was able to see individual tents and the people tending their animals or sitting talking in the late afternoon Star shine.

"They will be relieved the winter is over, which as you well know can be hard up in these mountains. There will be great celebrations tonight and sore heads in the morning."

Haran held his head with a grimace and then laughed aloud. Tents and yurts had been erected close to the road. Haran drove the truck carefully through. The people smiled and waved at the truck as they passed. Some seeing Okino's robes on the arm draped out of the window did a little bow as they acknowledged the presence of the monk. This was Okino's first experience outside his own community of the reverence with which the monks were held throughout these mountain communities. He felt proud to be here representing his own people who rarely ventured far from their village and was looking forward to meeting people from the many surrounding villages gathered here..

Men and women made their way up and down the dusty central street. Okino could now see they were heading or returning from the central market lying ahead in the centre of the town. Some hurried, others wandered while others stood passing the time of day, perhaps with a friend or relative they had not seen since the previous summer. Okino wondered of what they might be talking; of what news they had. He suspected they would be talking about their crops and the weather, the sons and daughters who had been born to them. They would be talking about their experience of the harsh winter and they would be telling the stories passed on to them of joy and heartbreak, of victory and defeat. There would be stories of those who had not lived to see the spring. The youngest children and the old ones who were particularly susceptible to the desperate cold in these mountains.

Haran turned the truck into a gap between two timber and stone constructed buildings.

"So here we are, my friend, Welcome to Aharri." He smiled over at Okino as he opened the door of the truck and jumped down to the ground.

"We will stay at my old friend's Quairim's house tonight."

He gestured to one of the buildings. He walked over to the house and banged on the door. Okino had jumped down from the truck and sauntered to the edge of the street. He could still feel the last warmth of the afternoon star as it shone down on the wide street buzzing with the sounds of chatter and movement. He took in the detail of the carefully crafted buildings for the first time. Stone carefully laid within the timber frames echoed how his own village had been constructed but with subtle individuality. Differences making this town unique in the same way as the clothes were distinguishing the people from their different villages. Dogs, chickens, goats and even the occasional yak wandered amongst the procession to and from the market. Haran's friend had come from around the building. They greeted each other with warm hugs. Haran turned to Okino.

"This is my new and dear friend Okino. He is a monk from the temple of the dragon high in the mountains. He has already saved the lives of my children and helped to bring my harvest in!!"

Quairim turned to Okino and smiled warmly. He placed his hands together and bowed lowering his head for a few moments before taking both of Okino's hands....

"You are most welcome my holy friend, I hope you enjoy your stay with us"

"I thank you. I am already entranced by your town and this wonderful occasion."

Quairim laughed and turned again to Haran

"He's a monk alright, people do say they have a strange way of looking at the world."

The two men laughed and led Okino up the street towards the market. As they walked ahead Okino went back to his contemplation. After the isolation of the last days he was happy to be back in this bustling lively gathering. He was surprised to observe he was feeling a similar energy around him as he had experienced in the forest where he had recently wandered. In all the activity going on around him he recognized the underlying peacefulness he had found amongst the trees. This busy hive of activity was giving him similar feelings as he had experienced after the rainstorm on the way out to the lakes and in the forest. She was here in the soft warm light and the shadows, amongst the merchants and the farmers, amongst the goats and the chickens.

He felt a flood of emotion rising inside him. In the glow of the afternoon Star, he felt her joy and love for the intricate and diverse nature of the life which had arisen on Arimathea. He watched the people walking alongside him in the street as if he was having an entirely new experience. Their complex expressions and gesticulations, the tones of their voices as they conversed with each other, the intelligent sensitive life force shining from their eyes. As he wandered through the market and in amongst the stalls he became completely astounded by their incredible ability to see and assess their world and then create so precisely and in such profusion such a beautiful array of products.

The market had created a maze of narrow temporary streets created and lined by the stalls now filling the central square of the town. Without exception each stall was ingeniously stacked with as many goods as was physically possible. Okino observed silently as he gently nudged and pushed his way through the crowded little streets. Those merchants who were not involved in some transaction would accost him and show him their products. Although cautious and respectful of the monk nothing at this stage could detract from the frenzy in which they all were involved. They were here to sell everything and they only had a few days before they would have to return home. No opportunity could be lost.

Okino looked in amazement at the variety of goods he was offered. Anything it seemed that could be carved, sewn stitched or woven, thrown on a potter's wheel or grown amongst these mountains was now being sold. The array of beautifully woven fabrics and the rich earthy colours of the kiln fired pottery, the smells of herbs and spices, the breath taking curves of hand carvings all assaulted Okino's senses. He was particularly drawn to the garments. The jacket he wore over his robe was adequate but it had seen wear from at least two generations of mountain folk. It had been well made and had kept the frost off his father and his grandfather as they watched their goats on the cold evenings.

The garments Okino was being shown had the same craftsmanship and the same stout construction. The fabrics were woven from the fine wool of the mountain goats and dyed with the bright colours the people of the mountains blended together so well. Finely quilted, inlaid with further layers of the fine yak's wool and lined with stout cotton, jackets like this had been constructed for generations in response to the harsh mountain environments. In the next hour Okino circled the market. He went from stall to stall trying on the jackets he particularly admired. He compared prices; very conscious he would have to find a very good bargain with the amount of money Haran had given him. However, on his way he was unable to avoid being shown and persuaded of the benefit he would gain from all the other products as he drifted amongst the lively crowds.

He was particularly taken by the carvings of one particular man. He sat quietly at the back of his stall carefully watching as the river of people flowed past him. Although his white beard and deep wrinkles determined the time he had lived, Okino was amazed by the youthful light shining from his eyes. They acknowledged each other as Okino spotted a beautiful leopard. The stature of the beast was remarkably lifelike. Low slung and muscular, the cat seemed to have been frozen as he prowled the endless wastes of the mountains in search of prey. Okino also noticed the carving of a dragon. Her wings were just slightly unfurled from her body, she stood proudly, eyes fixed, gazing deep into the future. The leopard and the dragon had both featured in his dreams. He saw the dream images reflected in these inanimate carvings and for a moment he thought he saw their life shine through from the layers of his dream. The old man watched Okino carefully and noticed his wrists as he lifted the dragon and admired the intricacy of the carving.

"I see you are a monk from the temple of the Order of the Dragon."

The old man with the beard had spoken softly from his position at the back of his stall. He had seen the small tattoos all the monks were given just above their wrists.

"Yes, that is true I am."

"You are far from home, for one of your kind. We rarely meet since I have been too old to make the journey to the temple. I often wonder if the old monastery still exists up there. So, separate from the world you have always been. There is much deep wisdom held there. I went there once when I was younger and spoke to a master. His words have always guided me."

"The teachings have been handed down through many generations and it is true our community is very close. We rarely travel far from the valley where the town below is situated."

"It is knowledge that needs to be kept close to its source, my son. There are those who would take what is stored between those ears and use it to further proliferate the chaos which has come upon this world."

Okino was slightly taken aback by the words of the old man who was now looking deeply into his eyes. He recognized the understanding in what he had said.

"I have been warned of these things in my dreams."

"Aah, So you have had dreams, young monk. Have these dreams come to you since you have been on your journey."

Okino had not mentioned he was on a journey. Although his dishevelled appearance may have given away the fact he had been living rough.

"I was having dreams before I left the monastery and subsequently since I have left."

Okino continued to study the dragon carving intently. It seemed to be very old and the beauty of the carving gave it an uncannily lifelike quality. He was reminded of the energetic nature of the dragon with which he had flown the previous night. The old man noticed the intensity with which he was observing the carving. He watched the flickering remembrance in Okino's eyes. The old man raised himself wearily from his seat. He carefully made his way out to the front of the stall. He was a tall man, taller than was characteristic for these mountains.

"I think there is someone you should meet or put it another way someone who would like to meet you. I think perhaps we should go and find her. I am afraid you will have to trust me my young friend. She has travelled a long way to find you."

He signalled to the man on the adjacent stall who nodded without question. Okino obviously looked slightly concerned because the old man smiled and put a hand on his shoulder.

"Don't worry Okino, my name is Niala and I have been waiting for your arrival and today it seems someone else has been looking for you!"

Now Okino was concerned. He had definitely not told this man his name and how could there be somebody here who was looking for him. However, he could see no immediate threat, so he gestured to the old man to lead the way.

Niala led him through the crowds. As they passed one of the stalls where Okino had been looking at one of the splendid and most expensive quilted jackets, he stopped and turned to Okino.

"I thought I saw you trying on one of these fine garments earlier,"

"You are right, I did try on one of these."

Okino had admired and tried on a particularly beautiful and finely woven woollen jacket. A deeply varied spectrum of dark red to crimson lines had been woven through it. The old man picked it up and offered it to Okino who slipped it on over his robe and the shirt he was wearing. It fitted perfectly falling almost to Okino's knees.

"But this one was far too expensive for the money I have."

He had taken out the little wad of notes Haran had given him. The old man laughed and said something Okino did not understand to the man behind the stall and pulled the hood over Okino's head. He stood back, laughed again and admired the result.

"Put your money away young Okino, I am honoured for you to have one of our jackets and any way, you need to look your best."

He smiled from his twinkling, knowing eyes and patted Okino affectionately on his back.

"Everything is changing for you now!"

Then he turned and again started to make his way through the crowds. He was clearly well known on the market. Regularly people would wave or greet him personally. Okino although mystified by this attention walked proudly in his new jacket with his new friend. Okino told him briefly about the reason for his journey and how he had come to be here. Niala listened intently. It did not take them long to find their way out of the market into the outskirts of the little town and then on to where the tents were pitched. The old man paused and viewed the scene to find his bearings. Then he headed off, winding his way through the array of temporary shelters where, in some cases entire families would be living for the duration of the market.

Eventually he stopped outside an unusually light and brightly coloured tent the like of which Okino had never seen before. There were panels and zips in fine synthetic material where normally there would be flaps of hide threaded together with leather. There were two horses tethered outside. Such fine horses were rarely seen in these mountains. They were not considered strong enough for the rocky terrains in the mountain passes. Yaks although stubborn and sometimes unpredictable were generally quiet and gentle creatures. They were well accustomed to the rigors of the mountain altitudes and were the preferred animal. Their fine fur could also be combed out and woven into almost any other animals. However, Okino noticed these horses were clearly well bred and sturdy enough for the journey they had clearly undertaken to get here. He was curious at once to see who owned such expensive animals.

"Mariella, are you in there?" The old man called into the tent. There was a short silence and then a slightly sleepy female voice came from within.

"Yeah, I'm in here, give me two seconds to get a bit organized."

Okino looked at the old man who smiled back at him. They waited in silence outside intrigued by the shuffling going on inside the tent. A few moments later one of the zips slid down around the entrance and Mariella emerged and stood in front of Okino and Niala.

"Hi Niala, who's your friend?"

She stood almost as tall as Okino and immediately was looking straight into his eyes. Okino met her gaze. As their eyes met Okino could not decide whether they were the deepest blue or the deepest green he had ever seen. Her long dark hair was ragged but probably wasn't accustomed to being so and the thick blue robe she wore nearly covered her ankles and was tied loosely at the waist. This was traditional dress for women in the mountains and was often supplemented with further cloaks and blankets.

"Yes, hello again, Mariella, this is Okino he was showing an interest in the carved dragon you yourself were interested in. I noticed he had the tattoo of the dragon order monastery you were asking about this morning when you were telling me about your journey and the reason for your visit."

Mariella looked over at Okino studying him more intensely.

"Hello Okino, I am deeply honoured," Okino offered her his hands in greeting and she took them respectfully looking continually deeply into his eyes.

"Do you mind if I .."

She signalled to his wrists.

"Of course not."

She gently turned his wrists displaying the intricate dragons carefully tattooed on every new monk of the order.

"So, you are a Monk of the Legendary Dragon Order,"

"I was only recently initiated into the Order but I have been living in the monastery for perhaps two turnings of the Star, my period of initial training will continue when I return….but recently something has been effecting the fish in our lakes so I set out to investigate."

Okino realized both Niala and Mariella were already listening intently to what he was saying. He paused as he remembered all that had happened so far and wondered how much he could or would tell them.

"As with all journeys it is hard to tell where it all began….and how about you? It seems to me you have travelled a long way to be here in these mountains."

"I am from a long way from here Okino. I have come from one of the major cities of Arimathea in the South. I have travelled across the ocean and through all the plains and foothills of your country with my horses to be here at this time."

She paused and again looked deeply into Okino's eyes. He was slightly startled by how deeply she was delving. She saw his discomfort and broke her gaze.

"Come, let us sit in the evening sunshine. I will make some tea and perhaps we can talk of our world and how we have come to be here together."

She again disappeared into the tent and came out with a large blanket which she spread out on the ground. She assembled a small stove and poured some water from a container into an old kettle. She indicated to the two men to settle down as she busied herself with boiling the water.

"I notice you said very specifically "at this time." When you were talking about your journey"

Okino ventured curiously,

"I did. But there is a lot I have to tell you before I get to that I think."

The mountains from which Okino had travelled that afternoon stood behind them in all their majestic beauty. Mariella looked wistfully out across the plains running through the circumstances resulting in her being there. Okino thought he detected a slight grimace as if some painful event had passed through her thoughts. She glanced up at Okino and knew he had seen her pain. She smiled reassuringly back at him.

"I needed to get away, perhaps have an adventure. Its crazy back there. But most of all, I think, it was Arimathea, who has brought me here. Aaargh. I've rehearsed this speech so many times it may sound crazy out loud. If this all sounds too weird to you guys stop me at any time and I'll leave you alone, but since I have come all this way and you are here I may as well just spit it all out."

"You see, I live in Straam one of the largest cities in the South. In the last year or so I have begun to find it intolerable. I have spent more and more time in the countryside and in the wilderness, out in the mountains and forests.

I started to see and really feel and experience in some profound way how incredible it all was and it started to change how I thought about everything…in a strange way it was like the planet started speaking to me, but not speaking like I'm speaking to you guys.. ."

She looked up at Okino hesitantly as if to gauge his reaction. He met her eyes at that moment, nodded and smiled back in recognition of what she was saying; relieved she continued.

"Then I would go back to the city and see the lives the people were living there…. and there is just as much weather in Straam, but you have to spot it up through the skyscrapers, and there are trees and parks which dedicated people look after. They keep them beautifully so there is some reminder of the natural world in the heart of that immense city. But it occurred to me the majority of people there are in complete denial of their connection beyond the futuristic manufactured environment in which they exist. Even to the extent I'm not sure a lot of people consider we are actually living on a planet anymore."

Okino and Niala smiled.

"There are many in these mountains who would still laugh if you told them they were living on one of many planets spinning through space around another burning sphere."

Niala nodded in agreement.

"Oh yes there are still some very strange ideas floating about… the difference between here and your city is your people are now mostly free from the damaging and quite ruthless effects our beautiful planet can exert on their existence. You live in your air-conditioned towers and so it does not matter what season it is. Here the winter can still kill you fairly quickly. Ideas about the supernatural are far more prevalent if you have little control over your direct circumstances. I know many who believe the humble yak is a holy animal and is revered and respected for its abilities to withstand all the evil spirits the mountains can throw at it!!"

Mariella smiled,

"I can believe from what I have seen of yaks they are directly related to the gods,"

She poured the heated water carefully into the cups she had prepared.

"…but there is an acknowledgement in what you say that we humans are not all-powerful superior beings, with the right to take from this world anything and in whatever quantity we can get our hands on."

There was a passion in Mariella which was already surprising Okino. As he listened to her his view of the world beyond the mountains was already starting to change. He had not acknowledged to himself there would also be people who lived in cities who were also passionate about their world. Now the first person he had met from a city was someone who was every bit as aware of Arimathea as he was. She was also a beautiful confident girl moving towards her womanhood. While she talked, he couldn't help casting his mind back to the spirit he had met in his dream. The image of her was becoming increasingly vague but he had not forgotten the colour of her eyes or the effect they had had on him. It also appeared from what he had heard so far similar forces had inspired their respective journeys.

Mariella passed the brewed tea to her guests.

"It is strange," Okino said as he thoughtfully took sips of his tea, "My journey from the monastery has been because of the very attitude of which you are talking!"

"You mean you have been seeing the effects even up here!?"

"Indirectly…but as a result of what you have been talking about!!"

"Which bit was that, Okino?"

"…When you were talking about taking whatever and in whatever quantity. It is particularly astonishing to many of us who live on what we can produce in our fields that people in your part of the world have health problems from overeating!!"

"…You're right. So, you know more about what is going on than I had imagined."

"Your magazines reach us. Sometimes from people who have returned and sometimes with people who have sort us out and reached our town. From these we have some idea about your side of the world."

Mariella grimaced,

"So, you'll know it's all completely insane, although the level of the insanity you will understand depends on what magazines you are reading!"

"Oh, we have a wide range. Motoring magazines and fashion, all sorts. They have given us insight into your lifestyles."

"More like selling lifestyles which very few actually have."

"So, your people do not all live in mansions with fishponds outside!"

"No, they do not. Mostly the magazines sanitize the world for all the people I was talking about. They divert their minds away from what is really happening. Really, I could sit here all night and tell you about the horrors of the world, many of which I am sure you know about.

The question is…Is there anything that can be done about it!? The reason I'm up here is because I have come to believe from what I have been told, you guys, although you may not have a complete solution to this predicament, may have some insight into the situation in which we find ourselves!!

The question Mariella had posed had turned the conversation around entirely. She had revealed herself as far more than just a rich tourist from the developed world. Okino was suddenly very curious as to what she might be looking for.

"We are a little-known monastery. Few people from your world have ventured as far up into the mountains to find us. There may be traditions and practices we have developed independently from the rest of the world. The mountains are ancient beyond our imagining and we have allowed them to infiltrate and shape our philosophy and our way of life on many levels for many hundreds of years. How have you come to hear we may have insight into the problems of our world?"

Okino was looking directly into Mariella's blue green eyes. He was attempting to be stern but he was fascinated already by the twist of fate which had brought this young woman to the mountains. She again broke his gaze and looked out into the distance. She smiled as she remembered and looked back towards him. She started to talk by gesturing out towards the mountains in the distance.

"As I started to experience the wild natural beauty I was talking about I started to have insight into the nature around me. Everywhere I looked I saw how everything seemed to be connected and regulated and dictated very precisely by what I was coming to fully appreciate as the precise movement of Arimathea around her Star. As I looked deeper, I started to feel a profound sense of some all-pervasive magical force behind this movement…not like it had waved a magic wand…but a sense the rhythm of its existence could only have resulted in all this eventually appearing.

Once I had realized this, everywhere I looked I saw the results of this realization in everything around me. The trees, the animals, the landscapes…even when I went back to the cities and saw people acting the way they did, in the light of this fundamental principle everything started to make sense!"

"I know you know all this…You can do it for anything…if you had time you could eventually find a reason for even the most ruthless city banker…and so you will say everything has evolved as to the circumstances surrounding it, but still I sense it all exists in something which decided there needed to be an atmosphere…to find some expression for itself; some vast etheric womb which held the possibility of just about anything or a very specific something because all the ingredients were somehow floating around in it. If the rhythm was held for long enough then the ingredients would all join up and a few billion years later here we are trying to figure it all out and maybe one day we will."

She paused looking at the two men to gauge their reactions. She could see from their thoughtful expressions she had their full attention and so she went on.

"So, no big deal you might say I had come to my own realization of some power or force in the Universe. Obviously not an original idea!! But isn't that the beauty of it though: somehow it feels as if it is. Perhaps for only a split second it feels like you have had some profound insight into the true nature of things. You can't really understand where it has come from, but it really feels like there is something magnificent and truly, out there amazing behind all this. But of course, the truth is we as a species have always wondered about this power, this force. God or the gods as they have come to be known have always mystified us. We have revered them, worshipped them, tried to communicate with them, made terrible sacrifice to them in the hope they will be merciful to us but really we still don't know what or who it is or whether it really is just something else we need to believe in to survive!!

I wanted to know more. I thought if I looked at many different cultures and how they regarded their gods I may be able to find some common thread which was common to all these ideas. I started to read texts from all the major religions of Arimathea, past and present. As I went on these texts I was directed to became older and rarer. I was soon journeying to libraries in far off parts of the country where I had discovered there were original or copies of the oldest religious writings. Strangely enough, the common thread was in fact the rhythm. It seemed most religions had originally grown up in response to the rhythms of their environment. People had found a way to exist within the rhythms of Arimathea which they found were constant and on the whole dependable. The worship, reverence or sacrifice all occurred in the hope their environment, the result of the rhythms, which at some point became their gods, would act beneficially towards them.

One morning I found myself in this little museum where I had heard there were some beautifully translated old texts supposedly from an Ancient nomadic people of my country. These are very rare for few of the nomadic peoples have ever written anything down. The librarian was a lovely old fellow and was clearly pleased to see me for whatever reason. He was surprised when I asked to see the translation, but he was happy to fetch it and soon I was settled down on one of the tables delving into this marvellous work.

Unsurprisingly this transient people found their supernatural power in the nature of the world around them, the ground beneath their feet, the star and the rain but particularly in the wind which seemed to bring the change of climate and so the change of the year. It appeared to bring them everything they needed for survival on their continual journeys around the country. The librarian hovered around and I sensed he wanted to talk so after an hour or so reading, I remarked on the beauty of the text. There was no-one else in the library so we able to talk.

I told him really what I have told you. He told me he had travelled extensively as a young man and seen many parts of our world and absorbed many of the religions in those places. He told me wherever he had travelled he had experienced feelings of awe and wonder for what he described as "The spirit of Arimathea" whether in the jungles, in the deserts or high in the mountains. He described it as an underlying peace he had found in the noisiest of cities. This he had found in many different cultures, was directly connected into an idea of an underlying spirit! He turned the pages of the book in front of me, pointed to some text and started reading."

She paused and looked to the skies and closed her eyes.

Arimathea, Star Mother,
You who are called by a thousand names,
May all remember we are cells in your body
And dance together.
You are the Grain and the Loaf
Sustaining us each day.
And as you are patient with our struggles to learn
So, shall we be patient with ourselves and each other.
We are radiant light and sacred dark -the balance-
You are the embrace which Heartens
And the Freedom beyond fear.
Within you we are born, we grow,
Live and die-
You bring us around the Circle of Rebirth
Within us you dance,
Forever."

Mariella opened her eyes. The prayer from the text she had recited had changed the nature of the atmosphere around them. Okino noticed the Star was finally slipping behind the mountains. He closed his own eyes to relish the moment in which he found himself. The truth at the heart of the teachings he had so revered and the monastery had held so close had been recited to him in a verse by someone from a city on the other side of his world. It directly connected him to another race in another time in another place, expanded his awareness through the millennia back to where the prayer had been written, to where a race had come to similar conclusions about their existence as his own little tribe high in the mountains.

For a moment he wondered of the person who had written the prayer, perhaps sitting on the ground outside his home. He may have been watching his animals feeding on the grass grown from Arimathea, warmed by Star shine and watered by the rain. There had been difficult times when the snows had stayed longer, or the rain had not come as soon as it might have but he had lived these sixty turnings and he had strong sons and daughters. Now he had forgotten the struggles he had had as he watched the smiling faces of his grand children playing with the dogs around their camp. He may have been looking back on his life, knowing soon he would again pass over the rainbow bridge. He had clearly seen how he had become inseparable from all he saw around him. For these few years he had spent on Arimathea he had taken part in the mystery and had glimpses of what lay behind it. He was not afraid of death. He had seen it as an inextricable part of the mystery and the continuation of his world. Then he may have written his prayer.

But how did she know about the monastery and the wisdom held there. He looked quizzically over at Mariella. She saw the question on his lips.

"Then the old librarian said he had heard from another traveller there was a small tribe, possibly legendary, high in the mountains of the North who had held knowledge about the Spirit of Arimathea they had never been able or willing to share with the outside world for fear it would fall into the wrong hands.

He said that they were called, "The Order of The Dragon!"

Chapter Ten
Two worlds collide.

Twilight had fallen on the little town in the valley. As the strongest of the Stars in the evening sky were starting to appear, Okino decided he should return to the market to find Haran. Niala also wanted to return to the market but Mariella was now keen to question Okino further about the monastery and his life there.

So, they all walked together back towards the marketplace. Okino was amazed to see the square had been completely lit up. Several generators howled somewhere in the background and trading seemed to be taking place at the same frantic level. Niala returned to his stall leaving Okino and Mariella to stroll around the market. Mariella had clearly already made many friends among the market traders who clearly were aware she was a traveller from one of the cities in the South. They would indicate a rug or a piece of jewellery and shout out a price and when she smiled and waved at them, they would laugh and shout out something lower.

As Okino moved through the market with her he could not help but admire her unshakeable confidence. She was thousands of miles from her home in the city where she came from. He wondered how she had travelled many hundreds of miles from the coast with her horses, alone and possibly with other bands of travellers seemingly with no harm having come to her. He knew the mountains to be full of thieves and robbers who would have soon known there was a woman traveling alone. They would have known she was carrying an amount if not a large amount of money. The computerized banking systems had not reached this part of Arimathea. She glanced up at him while examining a piece of fabric a trader had offered her and caught his wondering look. She smiled back at him.

"So Okino by that look it would seem you haven't come across many like me!"

"Well no, I haven't…well once!!"

"So where was that?!"

"It was in a dream actually!"

"So, what kind of dreams do monks of the Holy Dragon Order have Okino?" she smiled.

He grabbed another piece of fabric and started to examine it and after a few moments having collected himself he quietly remarked

"Many different kinds of dreams. Probably much the same as anyone else."

"What kind of dream was it when you dreamed about someone like me, Okino!?"

Okino was amazed again. Within a few remarks she had once again come to exactly where she wanted to be. Surely, he could not tell her about the incident on the mountain. He himself was not completely convinced it had been anything other than a wild hallucination at the height of the shock his body must have been in as a result of the freezing cold. On the other hand, how long would he be able to withhold from Mariella everything that had happened to him. After all she seemed to have come to find him. She must have been traveling for many weeks to be here in this remote part of Arimathea and here was he perhaps a hundred miles from where he had started at the monastery.

As he watched her sorting through and examining the various different materials on the stall he thought of the alternatives. If he were to tell her nothing he would have to walk away and continue on whatever path he chose. However, he had no other plans beyond escorting Haran to Aharri. Would he return to the monastery having kept his secret wondering what would have happened between them for the rest of his life. From what she had said her concerns for Arimathea were similar to his own and to any monk of his order.

He was not accustomed to making such decisions. His life in the town and monastery was not open to such unknowns. The structure of his life was geared specifically for service to his people through his devotion to Arimathea. He may find himself in unfamiliar territory as different situations arose. But at the end of the day he knew he would be sleeping in the monastery and so, life would go on.

He suddenly realized he now had a significant choice to make. Two paths on which to go forward. Return to the monastery or reveal the nature of his own journey to Mariella and open up all the possibilities arising from their knowledge being combined. She looked up at him and smiled. He knew in that moment what he was going to do. Monk or no monk, the importance of his vows of secrecy to his beloved order were rapidly starting to evaporate. He sensed a future like a great wide open plain before him which in turn would lead him to the rest of Arimathea, known only to him in his dreams. Great oceans and jungles were in such a future, towering cities and all the wonders which had been developing on his world while the order of the dragon had quietly hidden itself away in the mountains. He thought of the original dragon he had awoken and subsequently the female dragon in the jungle. The dream now had a possibility. The dragon was active in the world and could no more go back to the clearing to spend the rest of eternity waiting to be discovered than Okino could suppress the potential now opening before him.

He shuddered with excitement as he remembered the feeling he had had when he saw the eyes of the dragon open. He laughed aloud with the joy of the memory and looked up into the clear night sky. There were the stars bright and magnificent stretching out into the infinity and locating him perfectly within it as always. He stretched his arms and his whole body out to their full extent as he acknowledged his place in this eternity. Now taller he looked down to see a puzzled Mariella looking up at him. Had she come to him? Had she sent her envoy with those turquoise eyes knowing he would recognize them. He was almost breathless with excitement, daring to think how deeply he might now be bound up with the future of Arimathea.

Again, he felt the old soul he had first revealed standing by the fire in the forest. A spirit that had travelled for eons observing and building on its knowledge as it dwelt in the vast diversity of life and vibrational form. Okino the apprentice monk was nearly gone. There was not time and there would be no point for his return to the monastery. His training was over. He remembered the look on the face of his old master as they had said their goodbyes. At the time it had mystified him. But now he had an insight into what it may have been. It was respect. The master had looked at him as if he were the apprentice and Okino had been the master. Okino shook his head, suddenly stunned by these thoughts. He looked around at the market, at the energy and life on display there amongst his people; their creativity and optimism as they bartered and joked amongst one another. The dangers confronting their world would be far in the back of their minds. Their duty was to their families and their tribes, towns and villages. Their ultimate fate as always was far out of their hands as the great evolutionary battle of the Universe raged on. As Okino watched them taking responsibility out on the edge of their lives he started to feel himself moving up towards the front lines of the war.

He and Mariella had walked almost the full length of the market square. They were passing an open fronted tavern. There were a number of tables surrounded by an assortment of chairs on which further business was being discussed by many traders. Towards the front there was a table free. Okino decided this would be a good place to settle down and have the next part of their conversation.

"Perhaps we should settle down, have something to drink and talk. Also, I could do with something to eat!"

They sat down at the empty table. The owner of the tavern descended on them directly. He stood in front of the monk and performed the bow Okino was now becoming accustomed to. He also turned to Mariella and repeated his action.

"How might my humble establishment be of service to you, my young friends?"

"Thank you for your kind greeting, we are honoured to be your guests." Mariella beamed at the owner, "I think we will start by having two large bottles of beer and I for one will have goat or chicken stew, whatever is on the menu today."

"Goat, Chicken or Vegetable all blended with a fine array of spices and herbs fresh from this magnificent market this very afternoon."

"A marvellous selection, Sir, Okino what are you going to have."

"Oh, Vegetable stew for me and some water if that's all right"

"So that is a Chicken and a Vegetable stew, and two beers, good sir."

Okino looked surprised but Mariella spoke before he had time to respond.

"You are not in the monastery now and I want you to loosen up a bit. Let some of that austere dragon monk discipline relax for a while."

Okino grinned, leant back in his chair and looked around the tavern. There was an excited buzz of conversation into which they would blend comfortably. The owner of the tavern returned with the beers and placed them down in front of the two young people.

"Enjoy my friends, your meals will soon be ready"

He hurried away leaving Okino and Mariella to their beers.

"So, I'm all ears. Are you going to tell me about these dreams?" Mariella lifted the bottle to her lips watching Okino intently.

Okino also sampled his beer. It was bitter and sweet at the same time, the bubbles fizzed on his tongue and the inside of his mouth. He would always remember this as perhaps the moment when he started his transition into the modern world. He placed the bottle carefully in front of him wondering where to start. He explained about his childhood in the village and about his frequent visits to the monastery to talk to the monks. He told how he had started his apprenticeship. Mariella was enthralled and occasionally asked him to expand on some detail. To Okino's delight she was particularly interested in his encounters with the wild animals as he had sat in meditation on the mountains. They were able to share experiences of encounters with leopards and bears, finding their admiration for these creatures was second only to the mountains in which they lived.

Okino talked of the deep connection he had always felt with the landscapes around him, how he had loved to help his father with the goats and how he had watched them when he was older at night in the corrals to scare off the wolves when they came sniffing around looking for any easy meal. Mariella had remarked how different this all seemed to where she had grown up in the suburbs of Straam where wolves had long since disappeared. She explained she had seen them on her visits to the wilderness and heard them howling in the hills around her; how on one occasion one had come and sat all night at the edge of the clearing where she had made her fire. How it had seemed so much like a domestic dog which they had all grown up with. Then they were both quiet. He could feel the beer working into his mind, lowering his inhibitions and removing the doubts he had about telling his story to Mariella.

He explained how he had been initiated into the order and the strange dream he had had in his first meditation with the other monks. Okino then began to explain about his journey up into the mountains, the fateful storm and his meeting with Arimathea in his dream. As he explained the events of the next few months Okino realized this was the first time he had spoken any of this out loud. Until these moments this had only been in his own head. Now with the strong beer taking effect he let it all flow out. He explained about how he had set off to investigate the problem with the lakes, how he had awakened the dragon who had subsequently awakened the other in his dreams and about Haran and the Keraika plants. The setting of the tavern only seemed to make the whole tale even more fantastic but suddenly all the more real. He leant back and took the last mouthful from his beer.

"So that is the story so far. It seems I have been drawn out of my life in the monastery to take up this journey based on dreams and coincidental happenings. The whole episode seems so improbable. I would have put it down to a wild hallucination except for the fact, and this is the clever part, I woke up alive on the mountain next to an enormous wolf!! The dragon dreams have particularly mystified me. I cannot decide if they are spirits from another dimension, from my imagination as archetype for some unknown yearning or metaphors for what is happening to me on Arimathea. All I know is the two dreams continued on from each other. The first dragon knew where the female was and when they met they definitely knew each other. Also, they do not seem to fade like normal dreams but everything around me seems to make them more real!"

Another beer had arrived. Okino sat forward with his elbows on the table clasping the bottle with both hands as he watched the bubbles rising from the bottom adding to the froth on the top.

"But do you know what the really, really spooky thing is!?"

"You mean this story gets spookier!"

"Well yes I am afraid so, you see the only thing I really remember about Arimathea was her eyes were the same colour as yours!!"

Mariella smiled and looked away to watch their dinner arriving. They started to eat and she again looked over at him.

"I'll tell you what amuses me."

"You're going to aren't you"

"I am and it's this… I have researched and been delving into some of the most ancient texts on Arimathea for many years. Many of the oldest from different parts of the planet talk of a similar spirit which you have described, often accessed high in the most remote mountains. Described in most accounts as the spirit of the planet, it is generally associated with the forces of creation which have come or are inherent in this world. But also commonly mentioned are the more localized spirits. They are also described in a number of accounts as containing the wisdom and knowledge relating to a particular area. These are in some of the oldest texts I have found. In the newer texts these accounts have disappeared and deities have been introduced who seem to bear no relation to the region whatsoever.

I presumed the knowledge of these original spirits had been lost. Of course, to the world generally they have been. Then I spoke to the librarian who had travelled to this part of Arimathea in his youth. When he told me about your Order, he told me how you guys would hold this information until such a time it could emerge again to benefit the world. Also, through my research I had found accounts in old folk tales and songs where a loss had been felt. Almost like the spirit containing the knowledge relating to the area who had previously been able to guide and advise had disappeared or faded away."

Okino remembered back to his initiation into the order and the strange emptiness he had felt in the landscape into which he had emerged and the desperation of the people he had felt there. In his dream on the mountain Arimathea had told him she had a problem she needed resolving and then he had found the murdered or sleeping dragon in the clearing where he had been led by the crows. Now this girl from a city on the other side of the world had found evidence that certain spirits had disappeared from the memory of the people who wrote the history of their land. To his amazement their stories were actually starting to tie together. Mariella had continued to talk.

"Then there were predictions these spirits would again return. The time predicted showed no particular correlation other than they could only return when there was sufficient imbalance in the world to draw them back from wherever they have been to once more join the battle between light and dark. So something happened!! Something to do with those swords I shouldn't wonder!!

Well Okino, I have seen what is happening on this world and I can assure you the forces of destruction are in the ascendancy. But recently there have been alignments of stars and planets that might indicate a change on our world is underway!! But of course, much of this you will know. So what I find amusing is that you, a monk from this legendary order, holding all this precious wisdom, is surprised all this supernatural stuff with spirits from other dimensions and dragons being reawakened is actually happening and you need me to come half way round the world from a city to tell you it actually is!!"

"There is a certain irony in what you say and it has crossed my mind that if this knowledge has been carried down through the generations it is serving no useful purpose to Arimathea if it is held in an isolated outpost like our little monastery!!"

"Absolutely not, Okino. It sounds to me like perhaps the founders of your monastery had some connection with these dragons when they were here in the world. If you wanted something to be kept secret and slightly mysterious, your village with its monastery on the side of a mountain, almost totally inaccessible to the rest of the world would seem like the right place to leave such a legacy."

"It is starting to look more and more convincing. But all this is still based on these strange dreams I have had. I know you think perhaps I am being overly sceptical but we are trained to be rigorous in our thought when it comes to making decisions and coming to hypothesis and in reality what are the actual facts suggesting the spirits of this world are intending to reassert their influence over its evolution?"

"As far as I can see there is one overriding fact. Your monastery has undoubtedly maintained a unique connection with the spirit of this planet for many generations uncorrupted by power and dogma. Now in her hour of need Arimathea has communicated in the only way she knows how; through your consciousness, through your dreams and visions, that she wants you, a talented and naturally intuitive young monk, who has had been given the ability through the legacy the dragons probably left, to be a channel for her into the world!"

Okino, looked into the confident steady eyes of the young woman across the table from him. She was absolutely certain in what she was saying. It was almost as if Arimathea was speaking to him here in the tavern as he ate his stew and stared into her blue green eyes. Somewhere inside, Okino knew she was right. It was the old soul who had been awoken by the fire in the forest she was speaking to. The soul who had travelled to this life across the eons to fulfil some ancient vow, a debt, a prophecy, some destiny; he had no way of telling the nature of what it was but he felt something or someone was prompting his memory.

He felt no inclination to delve any further at this point. However, Mariella's insight was spreading a new air of acceptance into everything that had happened to him. Whatever happened next however, more than anything else he hoped Mariella was going to be involved. A smile developed and he tentatively asked,

"Our separate journeys do seem to have become intriguingly entwined. If they were to merge what do you think we should next?"

Mariella looked at him thoughtfully and then she answered,

"I think we should encourage your dreams. There is definitely something going on in some parallel dimension with the dragons. We need to find out what that is and how we fit into it."

She continued without letting Okino comment at this stage.

"You remember I was telling you about the old manuscripts I had been reading, Well, one gave a list of places where these original spirits were thought to have been particularly revered and acknowledged. There appears to have been one about three days traveling south west of here. There is no longer any kind of settlement on the actual site, only a village nearby. However, there is evidence the old town still exists in some old ruins. I thought it might be useful to go there to see if we could find some evidence of what happened for those old spirits to disappear. It might be worth you coming along; you may have some more dreams down there. In my experience old ruins usually have interesting psychic traces left hanging around; particularly if there were people connecting into different dimensions over long periods of time…what do you think!!"

"I think we should go there, immediately!!"

Okino was surprised at how quickly he had agreed. He had not thought of any of the practicalities of how he would travel with Mariella because he really was not concerned. The idea of the ruins had focused quickly in his mind. Layers of unexplored history which possibly could shed some light on these mysteries enshrouding him, were beckoning to him irresistibly. There appeared to be no obstacles in his mind and he could see the path taking them to the ruins clearly set out before them. However now he had made the decision it suddenly seemed like a very long path.

"How will we get there, Mariella?"

"We will have to get you a horse. There are a few for sale in Aharri at the moment. I was watching them race this afternoon. In fact, I have one in mind that will suit you very well. Look don't worry about all that; it can all be taken care of. Just start concentrating on what you might find at the ruins. Start to home in on them in your mind, the preparation will help us once we get there."

She looked over at Okino who at the mention of horses had started to show signs of panic.

"Don't worry Okino everything will be fine!!" She laughed and touched his hand across the table reassuringly.

This show of affection was immediately interrupted by Haran, his friend and three other men.

"Aaah Okino, we were wondering what had happened to you."

Haran looked down at Mariella and felt the fabric of the new coat Niala had given to him.

"Well, I see I shouldn't have worried. You seem to have everything very well sorted out!! Sitting here in a new coat and with one of the most beautiful women I have ever seen in this town!!"

Okino came back to reality. So much had happened since he had been separated from Haran in the marketplace.

"Yes, I am fine. everything seems to be…well, yes, I am enjoying every minute…and by the way this is my friend Mariella! Sit down with us, get yourself a drink and some stew, I'd recommend it."

"I am honoured to meet you Mariella."

Haran gave a little bow. He and the other men pulled up chairs to the table and sat down. The other two men were clearly from one of the more industrialized areas of Arimathea. They were wearing, what seemed to Okino, like tailored clothes that fitted them precisely, detailed with zips and pockets and buttons. They wore stout boots which were heavily laced. They looked dishevelled and tired in a way the other men in the bar who had been possibly living in their tents for weeks did not. They looked like they had come from another world. However, they sat down confidently looking around and acknowledging the tribesman who were looking across at them curiously.

"This is the fellow I was telling you about, Okino, Jas Tillina, he has brought his colleagues up here to see the Keraika. Ben and Zeph, this is Okino. He is a monk from a monastery further up in the mountains."

The three men reluctantly turned their attention away from Mariella.

"Good to meet you Okino. We hear you helped harvest the Keraika."

Jas addressed Okino just a little louder than was appropriate for the bar and so invading the conversations happening on other tables. There was a brief silence before conversation was resumed.

"I did…there were problems with the purity of the water in our lakes. I had left the monastery to investigate and followed the river running in to it upstream and eventually arrived at Haran's farmstead."

"Yeah Haran was telling me the fertilizer from the plants was causing problems with your fish. He's asked me to investigate getting some containers up there. That'll sort the problem out. Some hard work for Haran to start with but he may be more efficient in the long run. Very public spirited of him to co-operate!!"

"Haran is a good man who was immediately concerned about the wellbeing of his neighbours and was keen to find a solution as soon as possible regardless of the work it would mean for him!"

"Hey Sure, Haran one of the best. All I mean is you would have difficulty up here getting someone to make the changes if he felt the problem might have been exaggerated!!"

Okino looked over at the three men so far away from their home. Now he had heard for the first time the difference existing between his world and theirs.

"I have heard about the system of law enforcement operating in your country. I understand in any organized society there has to be a set of laws and a judiciary to administer them but does not an over dependence on such a system take away individual responsibility. Up here in the mountains everybody still relies on everybody else. You may think that Haran would be wise to defy our town for his short-term gain and continue to use the fertilizer. But one day he may need some fish for his dinner."

"Take your point, son, but where I come from you would just buy your fish from the next shop!"

"And which shop will you go to when all the fish have been poisoned?

There was an uncomfortable silence around the table.

"Look son, I don't want to cause any trouble… but we've found an opportunity here and if we push it in the right direction everyone is going to benefit. Ben and Zeph have come to see the product. They have been helping me with the marketing. The companies we have approached so far are very interested."

"Yeah, Jas turned up three stone lighter after his first visit and we thought there must have been a miracle…if he can lose that sort of weight with Keraika then anyone can!! There is just no knowing how far this could go!"

Okino looked around the bar at the tribesman doing their deals, drinking and telling their stories. He had read about marketing and distribution. He wondered how long Haran's little farm could produce enough Keraika to meet the demands that would inevitably arise. He thought back to the harvest and how much he had enjoyed helping the little family bring in the crop. He also suspected with the technology now available on Arimathea anyone with a Keraika plant or seeds, a soil sample and a large industrial growing facility would probably be able to produce limitless amounts of Keraika without having to use the tiny amounts Haran could put on his old truck and move across the planet twice a year…. and what could they do? The lawyers would say it was a wild plant and how could someone have ownership of it? Then the lawyers would argue the conversion process was what made the product saleable and then they would put a patent on it. In a few years the whole episode would just be another tale told around these tables.

"The thing is the Keraika has been used in the mountains to stave off the pangs of hunger when there hasn't been enough food. If you take it to a place where people are eating too much, do you think there might be a temptation for people to use it to just stop them eating too much all the time. It has never been used in such a way before, who knows what problems it might cause!!"

The three Southern men grinned across at each other. Jas looked across at Okino. His amusement had rapidly transformed to an emotionless grin. Okino sensed from this expression there was almost certainly some alternative plan which Haran would never be a part.

"Obviously the product will have to be tested before it goes on the mass market but we are not claiming this to be medicine…oh no this will be sold as a new exotic herb from the far North that can be used primarily to flavour cooking."

"But isn't the meal meant to stop you feeling hungry." Okino had immediately spotted this further amusing irony as had Haran, Mariella and Quairim. They looked over intently at the three men.

"Well, it's not going to work in the same way as it does up here, is it? It could be used to stave off hunger to the next meal. There are many different ways this could be used. Obviously primarily for losing weight but that is the beautiful flexibility which is going to make it so successful!!"

Zeph was now looking uncomfortable with the way the conversation was developing and turned his attention to Okino.

"So, you are a monk, Okino. You say from a monastery further up in the mountains…so is that like a priest …look after the church…sorry, monastery and make a speech on Star days about how bad everyone has been?"

Again the question was just a little too loud for the level of sound in the bar. Conversations on the other tables stopped in mid flow and there was silence once again in the tavern as the tribesman waited to hear how the young monk would answer the question which appeared to have a slightly mocking tone to it.

"Monks play a part in the community just like everyone else. Primarily through our practice we maintain a connection…more like an understanding, with the layers of consciousness, you may call them spirits, we believe to exist just below this everyday existence. The people of the village will often come to us for advice on matters they feel are a result of some disharmony with their connection to these spirits."

"So, all that kind of stuff still goes on up here does it!! Man, we did away with all that spirit stuff years ago."

He laughed,

"You're fooling yourself, son. There aren't spirits or levels of consciousness it's all been proved.... unless you are talking about the spirit of hard cash!!"

The three men laughed amongst themselves.

"If you people are going to join the modern world, you'll have to start thinking in a modern way and give up all this superstitious voodoo stuff…"

Mariella had been watching the three tribes' men on the table behind. They all appeared used to the rigors of life in the mountains. They had clearly travelled many miles to be here. Their clothes and faces told of the hard and unforgiving lives in which the people generally lived at the mercy of the elements. She had watched as they listened to the visitors from the city. Now she watched as they very silently stood up from their table in the shadows and then slipping silently behind the foreigners, withdrew their long sharp knives and placed them very precisely at their throats. Their laughter stopped immediately and was exchanged for expressions of sheer terror. The knife at Zeph's throat had been held a little too hard. A small drop of blood ran down his neck and disappeared into his clothing.

"You people, whoever you are, are a long way from home to be telling us about how things should be in our own country."

The tribesman paused and allowed his words to linger in the silence.

"So now you are going to apologize to our holy brother monk and everyone in here. Then you are going to leave so we can continue our evening without any further offence to the spirits of our land!"

The tribesman took their knives away from the throats of the foreigners. Clearly shaken, the three men apologized to Okino and everybody else in the tavern. They then left and disappeared into the still lively activity of the market beyond.

Chapter Eleven
The Cauldron.

Okino drifted slowly back into consciousness as the first beams of Starlight sneaked in through the small windows of Quairim's living room. There were many new sensations that simply had not been there before. He remembered a warning he would feel like this as he had indulged his new found delight for beer. After Zeph and Ben had departed they had talked and drunk well into the night. Many of the traveling tribes' people had wanted to talk to Okino, ask him questions or simply pay their respects to the young monk. They were amused to see him drinking beer. The monks generally did not drink beer but they did make their own brews from the hops cultivated in the gardens around the monastery. This was mostly drunk on special occasions. They were never seen in the local taverns drinking out of bottles. When they asked he told them about his town and inevitably questions about the work of his monastery had been raised. Okino had felt his mind flooding with memories of his home and excitedly explained about the life of his community.

Those who listened did not need him to explain about the work of the monastery. As he talked about the brothers, the people of the town and the mountainside on which they all lived they heard the understanding he was always seeking and the devotion he held for them all. As he talked, he had realized he was moving further away from everything and everyone he loved and for a few moments he had fallen silent. When he looked up, he saw the concerned faces of Haran and Mariella looking across the table at him. He was surrounded by the smiling throng of marketeers and traders and all his worry fell away. He took another swig from his bottle of beer and chuckled to himself as somewhere in the back of his mind he realized for the first time the full implications of continuing his journey.

Now, as he lay in the comfortable bed another thought closely followed, quickly overriding the first. His traveling companion on this further leg of the journey would be his new friend Mariella. Although during the evening a provisional arrangement seemed to have been made with some of the other tribe's people who were traveling in the direction of the ruins Mariella wanted to investigate, this new alliance raised a number of further questions.

The monks lived in the monastery without wives or girlfriends. Their relationship was with the spirit of Arimathea. Nothing was supposed to interfere with the bond forged through their training. This connection must remain as clear and uninterrupted as was humanly possible. As the wonder of this relationship started to reveal itself over those initial years the considerable sacrifice made by their denial seemed predominantly worthwhile. However, when temptation overcame an individual monk and a relationship had been initiated, a disciplinary procedure was introduced.

The monk in question was denied access to the temple meditations, so important to his life in the community and fundamental to his connection with Arimathea. For a period, he would become separated while deciding which path he wanted his life to follow. Monks who had strayed from their path as priests had found these decisions almost impossibly difficult to make. On the one hand they had tasted the serene and awe-inspiring connection with the spirit essence of their world which in turn brought considerable contentedness and wellbeing. On the other they had tasted the ecstasy that comes with falling in love and all the pleasure that inevitably follows.

Eventually a decision would have to be reached. If the monk decided to come back to the monastery he would eventually be allowed back into the temple once the affair was deemed to be thoroughly out of his system. He would never be allowed another indiscretion of this kind. If he left the monastery he would never be able to return as a monk. On occasions monks had been unable to make the decision and had wandered off into the mountains preferring the untold physical hardship and possibly eventual death from exposure to the denial of one of these pleasures over the other.

Okino closed his eyes and groaned as for the first time he saw these further implications. He could not deny Mariella was an attractive and desirable girl and he could see how temptation may well arise. He opened his eyes to the sound of Quairim busying himself preparing breakfast on the other side of the room. Both he and Haran were also showing signs of their excessive drinking the night before. All three sat around eating bread and drinking strong coffee with only a very brief discussion about what had happened. The conclusion was that Haran's arrangement with Jas was probably not in jeopardy even after the aggressive act of the tribesmen because they were so desperate for the deal to go ahead. Their brief laughter ended in further moaning.

So, the morning progressed. The relative silence only broken when conversation was unavoidable. Okino decided if he ever had to decide between beer and the monastery he would gladly choose the monastery just so he didn't have to feel like this again. The effects of this overindulgence had not receded when Mariella arrived. She displayed none of the symptoms of the three young men and had no regard for their beleaguered state. Also, she had made a long list of things needing to be done before she and Okino could set off on their journey. The first was to buy a horse. Okino looked at the other two in disbelief as he was hurried out of the door onto the street beyond.

Mariella strode off as Okino staggered under the effects of the bright Starshine. Suddenly there seemed no protection in the sockets of his eyes as bright light seared into the most sensitive parts of his neural cortex. He briefly wondered aghast at the contents of the concoction he had so eagerly consumed. Ghostly figures walked towards and around him. He heard continual laughter in the distance. By the time they had reached the plains stretching far across to the mountains in the distance some normality of sight had returned. He was standing in front of twenty or so horses. They were all tethered and everyone seemed to be eyeing him with interest. Okino's view of horses was they were lively and unpredictable creatures having neither the strength or composure of the yak which he was more familiar with. Mariella grabbed his hand and led him through the group to a large brown and white horse standing in the centre. She gestured at the horse,

"So, what do you think?"

"What do I think about what?"

"This horse, do you like him?"

Okino looked up at the horse who was now looking directly at him while carefully chewing through a large mouthful of hay. He was looking into eyes which were clear, bright and intelligent. However, in this intelligence Okino also detected mischievous intent. The horse flicked his ears forward and gave a little murmuring whinny, took half a step forward and nuzzled into Okino's shoulder, nudging him slightly off balance. He then stood back and waited for a reaction. Once he had regained his balance, Okino again looked at the horse. However, now he was looking at an entirely different creature. It seemed through this gentle nudge the horse had transmitted an offer of friendship which Okino had received without any misinterpretation. Now the horse was waiting for his reply. Okino lifted a hand and stroked down the neck of the horse who responded by taking another mouthful of hay from the ground and continued to eat.

"I do like this horse; I think we would get on very well…but he is huge…will I have to…you know get on him?"

Mariella looked at Okino in disbelief grabbed his shoulder and pushed him towards the back of the horse. She signalled to the owner and between them they manhandled Okino protesting onto the horse where he sat nervously gripping onto the mane as if it would keep him there if the horse decided to bolt off towards the mountains.

"Just relax, there is nothing to it really. Just sit up straight and go with his movements."

"What movement, we are not going to…"

Mariella grinned, untethered the horse and gently encouraged him to walk forward. Okino froze in terror. He was moving on a huge horse with his first mind numbing hangover. How could things get any worse! The horse walked steadily forward. Mariella lead him carefully around speaking to him softly all the while as Okino confronted all his fears about being on a horse, one by one, until there was no more fear to confront and there was nothing else to do but to relax and start to enjoy the steady rhythmical sensation.

Once he had relaxed Mariella threw the leading rope over the neck of the horse and signalled to Okino to grab hold of it. Again, he froze. Now he was in charge of the horse without having had any instruction on what to do in any event. Mariella stood back with the owner giving instructions on how to change direction and words of encouragement. Sure, enough the horse was doing exactly what he asked him to do. Again, Okino relaxed and started to enjoy this whole new experience all be it, still far too high off the ground. Mariella had turned to the owner and out of the corner of his eye saw her hand over a large bundle of notes. It seemed she had bought the horse.

In the next hour Okino followed Mariella amongst the traveling community as she set themselves up for the journey ahead. There was food to buy for them and the horses to top up what they could eat on the way. In the market she bought bags of rice and vegetables, spices and dried fruit, fuel for her small cooking stove, some blankets and another tent. Okino didn't ask and felt sure all would be revealed in the fullness of time. All this was bought with a seemingly unending supply of cash. Occasionally she would return to Niala's stall where her dwindling supply would be replenished. She told Okino she would have to buy enough to keep them all fed for about three weeks traveling.

Depending on what happened at the ruins she had intended to make her way to one of the large ports on the coast further South and head towards the warmer climate across the ocean. A voyage of this nature would eventually take her to one of the city ports in the developed South. She told Okino not to worry about all this and insisted he kept focusing on the ruins. She had brought maps and showed him where the ruins were in relation to the position of Aharii. So he did what she said, tried not to worry and on occasions he was able he returned to his contemplations.

Mariella introduced Okino to the other people they would be traveling with. There would be two families. Their business in the town was nearly complete and three large trailers were being filled with the provisions they had bought as a result of their trading in the market. The trailers were each pulled by two yaks. They now stood quietly, tethered near to where two fathers and their sons were loading grain and rice from one trailer onto their own. They recognized Okino from the night before and laughed at his delicate state.

Once the formalities were over a huge sack of grain was launched over at Okino. In the last few moments of its flight, he realized what he was meant to do and braced himself. He staggered under the weight of the sack as it thumped into his body. In these moments he felt the next part of his journey begin. The other men smiled and clapped him on the back as he slung the sack onto the back of the wagon where it was carefully placed in position. The tribesmen grateful to have another pair of shoulders, made him part of the chain transferring grain from the wagon that had come from the central store onto their own wagons. Once he had adjusted to the loads he was carrying, Okino fell easily into the rhythm of the physical work. Exchanging conversation with the other men, he established they would be leaving early the next morning and the journey would take three days to where they would part company with Mariella and himself.

Their journey would take them across an expansive area of plains and hills lying between the sea and the mountains from which he had come. The tracks were well established but the journey was slow due to the enormous weight the yaks would be pulling. They talked enviously of the old truck Haran had managed to purchase but explained they had never been anywhere near being able to afford one. The grain they had bought would be planted for their next crop and substitute their harvest until they returned again to the market in a months' time. Like most of the people in these mountains they were only making a subsistence living. However, their village was at a lower altitude so their crops were more prolific than for his own town and as the weather was less extreme the harvests were more reliable.

He was told there had always been a village there, but mystery surrounded the connection with the ruins to which Okino and Mariella would be traveling. There were legends which had arisen over time and passed down the generations. A variety of these legends began to be outlined. It seemed there were many theories as to the demise of the former settlement. They ranged between supernatural haunting and curses laid by offended spirits, warfare between neighbouring tribes and disease and illness brought on by either of the former. Okino thought it would not be a good idea to hear these stories in detail before he arrived. The men laughed and respected the opinion of the young monk, saying it would be interesting to have new insight into what had happened to the old place.

When the wagons were loaded Okino excused himself and wandered off through the camp to find Mariella. He noticed there were entire families camped in spaces around the town. Children ran between the tents playing at some invented game that sometimes involved annoying one of the grazing animals. They appeared healthy and happy, oblivious of the constant battle for survival they themselves would eventually inherit. Their mothers kept a careful eye on them while carrying out their own preparations for the journey ahead. When he occasionally caught their eye, they smiled confidently back at him. He saw the strong resilience so necessary for the struggle in the tenuous existence they had always led. He thought of how the southern men had mocked their belief in the spirits the night before.

Many of these women he could see wore charms. They believed they would protect them and their families from the ravages of ill fortune. They would have stocked up on their stores of herbs for the salves used for generations to ease their husbands damaged muscles from the heavy work they performed year in and year out in the fields; the medicines and concoctions they would make for their children when they became ill through lack of nourishment from an early age. The tonics they would mix for their old people who having worked and provided for the previous generations would be nursed through their final years to be consulted about the many problems which arose consistently in such a precarious existence.

Who could blame them for reciting some incantation, asking for some blessing or performing some ritual in the production of these concoctions? Everywhere they looked they saw themselves at the mercy of the natural world. They knew their plants grew stronger and had greater potency when they were growing in the waxing of the moon. The potency that Star shine, the rains and the winds brought to them were known to be truths in their lives so who could say to give these elemental forces the names of spirits or gods was somehow unsophisticated or primitive.

The strength of their beliefs had been reflected in the reaction of the tribesmen who had held knives to the throats of Ben and Zeph. No chance could be taken if there was a choice between upsetting these forces or not. For even if your experience meant you had no particular reason for believing in them, you would always know someone who did. Okino smiled to himself as he remembered his own doubts about the dragon dreams.

He noticed two women sitting on the ground outside their tents cutting up vegetables. They looked up at Okino as he passed and acknowledged him as usual. He was still on his search for Mariella and sensed somewhere she would be needing a hand with the preparations. But as he moved past the two women chatting quietly to themselves, he noticed the large pot the vegetables were being thrown into. It was suspended over what would later become the fire and was now filled with water that splashed as the sliced vegetables were thrown in. However, there was a difference between this cooking pot and those normally used. The metal looked lighter and the construction finer as if it had been made by someone who had a greater knowledge of the alchemy of combining metals. Even from this distance he could see there was some artwork either engraved or moulded into the pot. The pictures were finely drawn and he was unable to make them out from where he was standing. He stooped to have a closer look and the women stopped talking as they noticed his curiosity.

"I was just admiring the design on the side of your cooking pot. It doesn't look like it is from this land."

The women looked at each other and laughed.

"No, it is not and there is quite a story behind this old pot. I take it for granted since I use it so much when we are at home and because it is so light I always bring it on these expeditions as well!"

"It looks strangely foreign, and not even of this time. Is it very old?"

"If you are interested, I will tell you the story. Here look, settle down. You can cut up some vegetables. "

The woman smiling signalled at her friend to give Okino a pile of vegetables, a knife and a chopping board. The two women demonstrated what needed to be done. Okino started to cut up the vegetables and when they were happy he was doing what was necessary the woman started her story.

"The pot is very old and came from a land far away from here. The story goes my great, great grandfather got into some terrible trouble in the town. He was still a young man but he had been married to a girl from the next village and they had young children. The story goes he was discovered to be having affairs at various different times of the year around the villages with at least three other women. It all came to light when one of these women became pregnant and gave birth to a child. The baby had been conceived when her husband had been looking after the goats in the high pastures during the summer months. She revealed the identity of the father when put under extreme pressure by her furious husband and family.

Of course, there was a terrible scandal and outrage from the village where the girl had originated. The whole episode brought terrible shame on our village and of course our family. Two of the other women were the wives of prominent members of the council. To make matters worse all the women were very good friends and their secrets ruined their friendships and caused a terrible split between the villages. It was the worst kind of betrayal that could happen among friends and between communities where everyone was so close. We need to be able to trust each other for when some disaster strikes, which it frequently does.

Anyway, my great, great grandfather was made to appear before the high council and explain himself. What was there to explain? Circumstances had led him to befriend all these women and one thing had led to another. He was a likeable fellow and had managed to lead them astray. Of course, he tried to shift the blame away from himself saying the women had seduced him and previously he had led a good and blame free life. This was not altogether true because by all accounts he was a bit of a rogue generally. However, this was the first time any hard evidence had come to light.

The high council heavily influenced by the aggrieved husbands of the adulterous wives told him there could be no alternative but for him to leave the village; of course, he protested. But his wife had thrown him out of their home with only the clothes on his back and things in the village were made so difficult for him he really had no alternative. So, he left quietly and was not heard of for over twenty years. He travelled down to the coast and was hired to a trading ship in which he sailed the oceans of Arimathea. The ship was eventually hired by a wealthy group of men from the South to sail to a distant shore where they had discovered an ancient civilization in a jungle on the coast.

There was talk of treasure and so great rewards for all involved. But the oceans in that part of the world were treacherous and the jungles unexplored. The captain decided if everything worked out and all went to plan he would be able to settle down and end his dangerous life on the oceans. So off they went and found the lost city by the ocean. They hacked the ancient buildings out of the jungle and stripped the place of everything they could find. Most of the actual treasure came from tombs sealed for many thousands of years in which there were depicted scenes from this ancient civilization's mythology. Supernatural beings perhaps, their gods were shown as both benevolent and terrifying, holding the fate of the people in their hands."

The woman paused for a moment and smiled at Okino. She clutched the charm around her neck.

"…. My great, great grandfather found this pot there. He had seen the engravings on the side. He saw the cycles of the land and the harvest depicted in the carvings. You see…".

She turned the pot so Okino could see the various scenes. There were pictures carved of people working the soil with ploughs and animals. There were clouds in the sky, and rain was falling, surf crashed at the shore, further round there were crops growing under the Star and fishermen throwing nets into calm seas. The next scene was the harvest with the Star again lower in the sky, there were people eating and drinking while giving thanks to their gods who had yet again provided for them. Lastly or firstly for there was no beginning or end, the men were sowing the seeds back into the land.

As Okino turned the pot and looked closer he noticed the patterns used to depict the weather in the sky and below flowing through the ground. He noticed eyes and teeth and claws were hinted at; undulating landscapes were described by serpentine bodies rising through the hills, wings of the cloud creatures soaring through the air, and great heads were clearly visible as the waves broke upon the shore. He realized dragons of land, sea and air had been carefully illustrated on the side of this cooking pot made by a civilization perhaps many thousands of years before.

"So, my great, great grandfather brought this very pot from around the world after all his time away and came back to the village. He told my ancestors about his travels and the wonders he had seen. He was able to tell them there had always been people living on Arimathea like them. Wherever he had been he had found people who had learnt how to survive in their environment, how to grow their crops with the knowledge handed down to them. The weather although inconsistent, like the continually changing patterns on the surface of a river, was always flowing in the same direction. There was a familiar rhythm to this irregularity they were always able to recognize. The weather at certain times of the year would often give them insight into what might happen in subsequent seasons. Old sayings and proverbs rattled down the generations. Animal hibernation patterns, the flight of birds, the flowering of plants had all become involved with the prophesy of certain kinds of weather. Everywhere he went he had found people who believed animals were older than human beings, more attuned to their world who were able to sense when the weather or the seasons would change. They were treated like oracles who had specific knowledge of the powers governing the world and they had become revered and respected in the belief systems of many different races.

He had travelled so extensively he had been able to compare stories of weather patterns from people around the world. He found correlations in these patterns across countries and continents from one year to the next. If certain severe conditions were prevalent in one place a parallel condition or compensation would almost certainly be apparent on another part of the world. As if Arimathea had her own self-regulating atmosphere!"

The cooking pot was now full of vegetables. The women turned their hands to making the fire underneath with their newly replenished supply of charcoal. They lit the fire and soon the water was starting to boil, softening and extracting the life-giving energy from the vegetables so carefully coaxed from the soil of Arimathea.

The fire was again present in the final transformation. Engraved around the cauldron, was the wisdom which had enabled it all to be. Here were the dragons showing themselves once again. Here they were portrayed as the everyday forces another civilization had recognized as a fundamental part of their world and although they were wild and could never be tamed ultimately, they appeared to work for the benefit of Arimathea. Life had grown and evolved as a result of their influence on the world. The human beings who had become accustomed to them had embedded them into their folklore and legends; here on the old cooking pot they had portrayed them in a beautiful work of art which portrayed the seasonal rhythms of their lives.

"Did they allow him to stay in the village after all that?"

"They did. In fact, he became something of a respected elder. The understanding of the world he had gathered and the stories he had to tell gave the village great stability. The knowledge they were part of a great race who had lived as part of this world for many millennia gave them greater confidence. Their little group of villages had become quite isolated in this remote region of the mountains but with this new confidence he inspired they started to trade with Aharri which had grown up as one of the market towns for this region.

That confidence has grown over the generations to the point where the goods and products we make in our village are keenly sought after by other traders. Many of our traditional skills instigated or revived in my great, great grandfather's time had been handed down through the generations and have become successful enterprises. We have a famous pottery and we sell our tapestries and the clothing we make. The fine new coat you are wearing was made in our village. All of which help our children with their own transition into adulthood. We lose a few to the outside world but very often they return with fresh new ideas and knowledge in the same way my great, great grandfather did, but with a greater respect for our way of life, the richness of our culture and tradition they had not found in the places they had been!"

Okino sat for a few minutes silently watching the bubbling cauldron. So often he had watched these stews being made, anticipating the thought of eating the thick rich food he knew would instantly satisfy his hunger. He knew of the processes involved with bringing it to this point. But now in this story he again had come to a deeper understanding of the nature of his world. There was a beautiful ending to what had appeared a disastrous beginning. Life in the great cauldron of Arimathea continually transforming itself.

Again, he had come closer to her and to understanding the concerns she had. Appearing for so many years to be robust and all powerful now it seemed she was as vulnerable as any independent organism. He saw the responsibility his race had now taken on as they came to have more influence and played an ever more powerful part in the health of her systems. So much of what he saw and understood of the engravings on the side of the cauldron was about a mutual understanding being passed on through the generations by cooks and farmers who had contemplated those images. He shuddered when he remembered the words of the Southerners the night before. For these were the people who now held this beautiful gift in their hands.

Chapter Twelve.

The Awakening

The next morning Okino rode beside Mariella on the new horse out of Aharrii as the small caravan left the town. The wives and children from the three families were riding on the carts being pulled by the yaks. The men rode horses alongside and out in front. Two of the carts were piled high with grain and one further cart carried the yurts and the provisions the families had brought for the journey. The children were excited and shouted at the yaks to pull. The yaks pulled, leaning their enormous weight and power into their highly decorated harnesses. Steadily they all moved off into the plains that would take them back to their village in the hills beyond. The Star was warmer now and a gentle breeze made for exceptional traveling conditions. As the Yaks governed the speed with their peaceful dogged determination they also governed the rhythm of the journey.

The younger children sat up next to their mothers who were steering the yaks. The older children sat behind on the sacks of grain. They were well prepared and settled down earnestly to a game. It involved throwing carved figures which could land at a variety of different angles and dealing from a pack of cards. They were quiet for some minutes as play commenced then erupted into screams of laughter and recrimination. There then seemed to be a period where cards were traded. At this point it was clear to see who the winner of the round had been. Apparently, there was great glory to be had. The winner would raise his arms in victory while his fellow combatants would hold their heads in their hands. The children would then resume the game.

Okino was intrigued. He had not seen this game. Perhaps it was traditional to their village. He decided he would at some point in the journey ask the children if they could show him how it was played. For now, they were totally absorbed and he did not want to disturb the world they had clearly created. He remembered back to the days and long nights of winter huddled around the fire with his friends or family. They would regularly enter one of these other game worlds where they could pit their wits against each other. He knew how time could become distorted or somehow compressed as everyday life was forgotten as the rules of the game took over. As he watched the little entourage settle into their journey, the Star pleasantly warming his face, he realized he had started to enjoy the steady rhythm of his horse.

He looked over at Mariella. She too was enjoying the Starshine. She had the slightest smile betraying her quiet contented mood. She was looking far ahead into the distance across to the mountains. Deep in thought. He wondered whether her thoughts were back in Straam or out in the future searching through the ruins. He had tried to imagine how her life in Straam would have been. She had the quiet confidence he had noticed in the children of his own village who had mostly grown up in loving supportive families. She was obviously determined. Whatever was driving her brought an energy to her entire being. He had watched in the haze of his hangover as she had organized the provisions for their trip. Moving between the various traders to purchase exactly what she wanted only at the price she was prepared to pay.

He had noticed how these deals had always ended in laughter as the traders realised how craftily they had been manipulated by this beautiful stranger from the world beyond their own, where she would have lived in a mansion with a smooth road running up to it. Where a number of expensive automobiles were parked outside. He imagined it to be set amongst carefully manicured lawns punctuated by pools of crystal-clear water fed by fountains and stocked with graceful golden fish swimming idly amongst the carefully positioned plants. All this he had seen in the magazines brought by the strange mix of characters who had stumbled into the village over the years. He imagined her as one of the glamorous models floating amongst all this extravagance. She would have worn jewellery and probably driven one of the expensive cars. He looked over at her again as she swayed with the rhythm of her horse. She had told him of her love for their world and the revelations that had brought her here. But of her life she had said very little. There must have been some catalyst for this enormous passion she now held for her world. She turned and caught his eye. He sensed again she had seen the wondering look in his eyes. She smiled and turned back to the landscape avoiding the questions she knew Okino must have been about to ask.

"You want to know more about me, don't you?"

Okino was surprised and intrigued by the question. He contemplated his answer as he caught sight of an eagle gliding far above them. He imagined looking down through the eagle's eyes to the caravan below. He saw himself next to Mariella in the vastness of this landscape and the world beyond. He could feel the mountain air warmed by the Star under his carefully evolved wings holding him there as he watched the ground below. Watching for his next meal. Unscheduled with no guarantees he hung there waiting for some unfortunate creature to make his last move.

"Look Mariella, an eagle."

She turned her gaze searching the sky to where he pointed and caught sight of the huge bird. They watched as the eagle wheeled over them. They had to look away as it instinctively put itself between them and the Star.

"Do you think she is curious?" Okino asked, "Do you think she wonders what wonderful beings could organize such an expedition, with several different kinds of animal other than themselves. Animals who are allowing themselves to be ridden and are willingly pulling their contraptions filled with their food. So as we admire her ability to soar and spot her prey with eyesight effective from high in the sky, will she be admiring our ability to live as ground based beings having no need for hanging in the endlessness of the skies day in and day out."

"Is that your reply to my question or just a general observation about the eagles? Because if it was just an observation about the eagles….

"I think it is both. We cannot know the thoughts of the eagle and yet the difference between the sky dweller and the ground dweller is apparent. In the same way the two of us have our origins in two very different worlds and so we have lived very different lives. Now we are sharing the same world and as I look at the eagle and imagine myself in her place to try to gain some insight into my world so I will benefit from the perspective you have of your world."

"So that is the monk's answer! What is the twenty something man's answer?"

Okino couldn't help but smile. He quickly scanned the skies and then the landscape for inspiration to answer this further question. He found none. Why did he want to know more about her? Such an obvious question…but deeply penetrating. He could see this was going to be an interesting trip.

"I was just wondering…. you see the only real knowledge of your world we have is from the magazines. The Star is always shining and the people always look relaxed, happy and well fed. But never too well fed. In fact, I always think the people look a little thin. From what I have heard these pictures do not reflect your world only some ideal used to sell material products. I was just trying to imagine how you would fit into that world."

"Into the world in the magazines or the world it is supposedly portraying?"

"Surely they are the same. However, one is a fantasy of the other. I am interested in how you came to be who you are in all of that."

"Mmm, I suppose we have some time...let me think…where to start!?"

Okino looked over expecting Mariella to start her story but she was again gazing off into the landscape and clearly drifting back into her thoughts. There was a victorious shriek from one of the children. Simultaneously he leapt excitedly into the air, as he landed, he lost his footing on the grain sacks and toppled in an ungainly fashion off the low cart and into the dust. Okino winced as he leapt up, brushed the dust from his shirt and continued his celebrations running around the cart. The yaks lumbered on unimpressed.

"My dad is a successful lawyer in Straam. He has his own law firm. But it's because he's clever and knows stuff. He always says it came from sitting around on park benches watching people when he was meant to be reading his law books. But he must have read them eventually to do what he does. He does prosecution and defence law. Now he picks and chooses what cases he takes and employs some of the best lawyers in Straam. So, he's done well. Then he says his success is because of my mother is so totally amazing. So yes, I have had a privileged background but we weren't always wealthy. We live in a big house now but when dad was establishing himself our lives were certainly less extravagant.

We always lived outside the city and so I was always out in the countryside surrounding the house. We played in the woods amongst the mysterious old trees and in the streams running like pure enchantment through them. There were fields and meadows with cattle, sheep and corn. These were our playgrounds where it seemed we ran and climbed relentlessly. There were schools of course, where we learnt about what was happening on the rest of Arimathea and how we would make our way into the future. It all seemed very detached to be honest. I did fairly well in school without any great effort and always relished the thought of coming back home and being out in the wild again. This did fall away somewhat as I grew into my teenage years but I always managed to escape back whenever I could. Of course, there were boys and dating and the whole social thing started to completely dominate my life.

My yearnings to escape into the countryside gradually started to be forgotten as I became immersed in the social circles of Straam. My mum came from an established family and was always sought after for all the most exclusive social gatherings. Something that obviously never did my dad's business any harm. I started to mix with some of the wealthiest people in the city of Straam where a lot of these gatherings would take place. I enjoyed it I would have to say. I always had a string of wealthy boys and men vying for my attention. I wasn't entirely sure which way I wanted my life to go so I just kind of went with the flow for a while. I knew my folks wanted me to go to college and get a career but as I say, I wasn't convinced and had a feeling something would turn up sooner or later.

I moved into an apartment in Straam with two of my girlfriends and took a job as a personal assistant for one of my dad's competitors and the social whirl continued. However, I did start to notice how immersed I had become in all of this. I always kept an ear open to the news and became more aware and concerned about the environmental problems being more frequently reported but at that point I didn't get involved. I was concerned but there was so much fun to be had! The lifestyle I and all those around me were living would seem outrageous to most people on Arimathea. We were spending more money in an evening than some villages, perhaps your own would spend in a year. But we were young, and it was who we were and perhaps it was our rebellion. It went on for a while and mum and dad were pretty good about the whole time. They always asked questions when I went home about when I was going to start doing something serious and gradually it started to sink in.

All this wildness was starting to wear a bit thin. I even started to think about things I might like to do. But not quite in time. Because then Remi turned up in our club one night. I saw this man and looked at the boys around me and just lost interest. This man was a predator and his jungle was the city. I wasn't completely sure about him, he wasn't the type of man I would normally go for, but I was completely fascinated. He wasn't even much older than my friends but he had a ruthless confidence and breath-taking good looks. There were girls around him but I had decided I wanted him. I kept him within distance so he would see me sooner or later and we made eye contact a few times. He eventually came over to where I was sitting and asked if we had met before…I seemed familiar…not brilliant but when I said "no" he apologized for intruding and offered to buy me a drink for the trouble. So it all began. My relationship with Remi!"

So, it really was like he had seen in the magazines. Wealthy, beautiful young couples driving up to hotels and clubs in expensive cars. They were immaculately dressed and greeted a group of similarly wealthy, sophisticated young people. Then they swept into the foyer and were greeted by a manager who obviously knew them personally. Always laughing, always happy. He could see her there. He had seen the untouchable confidence he imagined only the very rich and powerful could command. He had recognized all the sophistication under the crude ill-fitting robe she was wearing. Recognized it only, for it was not on show. The loud brash arrogance of the men in the bar the night before was nowhere to be seen. But he had not seen the fear in Mariella's eyes. She had no idea of how badly things could go wrong up here. In a bad storm, an earthquake or an avalanche.

"He was fine to start with; we fell hopelessly in love. Well perhaps I did. I always felt there was some dark corner I would never be able to penetrate. We did all the things you do!" She looked over at Okino, who had a questioning look in his eyes. She laughed.

"We came to know each other pretty well, suffice to say and after a few weeks I moved into his apartment. Well, I was there pretty much all the time anyway!! My father looked darkly at me when I told him. It puzzled me at the time."

"So do you think your father had recognized something in this man you had not seen?"

"I think he had recognized the part of Remi I was attracted to and saw where it was all going and possibly how it would end. But they were always good at letting us make our own mistakes!!

So, life continued, sometimes he would work late: he was an investment banker. He never talked much about his business but I could tell when he was making money….and when he wasn't. There were mood swings. If he had pulled off some deal he would come home high as a kite. He would tell me, how quickly and craftily he had acted. He knew the markets. Always knew what stocks were going up, which were going down and all the characters involved. I realized quite early on he probably was not the best human being walking the face of Arimathea but I thought then heh…who's perfect?

I continued to work with the law firm and I was starting to see another side of the business community. It was uncanny. Suddenly from my very sheltered up bringing I was swimming with the sharks. It amazed me immediately, how suddenly I was at parties with gangsters and known criminals. Desperate, destructive people who were known to spread misery amongst the ordinary folk of Arimathea, defended and protected by the brightest cleverest legal brains of a generation.

At first, I was in awe of it. I had been welcomed into the elite areas of our society. But I began to see how lies and corruption were holding it all together. I could see how the vast machine of wealth and privilege was cocooned in air-conditioned skyscrapers and limousines away from the destruction of the natural world it was proliferating.

Then one night, I came out of a restaurant to one of those limousines waiting on the street. It was raining hard. We sheltered under the canopy not really knowing what to do. I suddenly realized what was happening to me. The wild little girl who had relished being at the tops of Oak trees and splashing around in streams had been sucked into their illusion and I was being cut off from all the beauty I had so relished. I walked out into the rain in my silk dress, turned my face to the sky and felt the rain falling down all over me. There was an enormous gust of wind. I swear it came down the street for me. I felt the enormous force almost knocking me off my feet but at the same time something very gentle whispering around me. Then I was being bundled into the back of the limo. Remi fussing over me. But I was awake. I had been awoken and I felt alive again.

I watched the world from different eyes on the way home and stood out on the balcony of his 19th floor apartment well into the night, feeling the wind and the rain, listening to Arimathea and all her spirits as they swirled and gusted like wild animals around the towers of the city. Remi went to bed slightly puzzled; this was a side he had not seen. It was a part of me I had not entirely felt. It had been a long time since I had been so connected into…. into it all!! I had grown from an adolescent girl into a fully grown woman. There was a new power and new anger! I wasn't sure whether it was my anger or an anger being transmitted to me from the storm.

I could see Arimathea from the balcony and what she had become. Towers of steel and glass set in fields of concrete and tarmac, ablaze with light; Humming, buzzing, hissing, whirring full of people I could not see. I knew they were down there in their cars and the restaurants and up there all around in the towers. I looked around to see if I could see anyone else on a balcony. But there was no-one. I could not see another soul!! But in those hours I knew I had felt the whole soul, the soul of this entire world. What it is, how it is, why it is. I could not tell you how these things came to me because the transmission was not in words; They just came in my thoughts. It was the first time I came across the premise. It did not solidify into an idea until later, but it was there. How could all this have been any other way?

Somehow you expect the world to look different when you wake up in the morning after these revelations. But of course, it doesn't and life goes on pretty much as normal. But my perception had shifted. I looked at everything as part of the 'soul'. Cars, planes, skyscrapers where did they all fit in. And you know what, they all do. But what happened next with Remi made me realize what was really happening and what was happening to our world."

Mariella had paused and looked out towards the mountains. Okino thought he saw the start of a tear but was unable to see her eyes entirely. The little cavalcade had settled into the silent monotony of slowly moving through a vast landscape. Even the children had settled back into the bags of rice and grain, dozing or staring out into space looking for some change to contemplate. But the sky was clear and deep blue and outlined by the mountain ranges on the edges of the plain and was mostly empty.

"As time went on we spent less time together. We had our own worlds. They would cross over but not as much and I started to know less and less about what was going on in his world. He would say he was working on some deal and I had no reason to disbelieve him. The cycle always continued. He would pull off one of his deals and we would party for a week then he would disappear again. He never told me in any detail what he was doing. Then he started to go abroad. Sometimes for a week or two, out to the tropics. He always came back very well-tanned. When I asked, he said he was doing business in Raihsa City. You know down on the coast in the rainforests or what is left of them. I don't know how much you hear up in the monastery but the rainforests are disappearing at an alarming rate. And guess what Remi wasn't involved in a conservation program.

Like I said he would always be combing the papers for some clue, some lead he could make a killing on. A headline on the smallest of paragraphs at the bottom of a page would sometimes set him off. Something like "Protests at the headquarters of a mining company." This was what had set him off on his next venture. In his visits he had located the mining company and eventually found out they had found a deep seam of coal close to the surface in the jungle. In protected jungle. The protestors were local tribes' people whose hunting grounds would be desecrated and representatives from international environmental organizations drawing attention to the potential loss of another swathe of rainforest. I knew nothing of all this until I saw it all on the news. The price of coal is going through the roof as sources are becoming more and more difficult to extract.

He went down there as a representative of the bank, found out the extent of the seam from the engineers and then approached the mining company. He told them the bank would invest in the mine in return for 60% of the shares in the company. This company was practically bust but had located this amazing asset and had no choice but to accept. Just the problem of the protected forest. Remi had a meeting with the governor of Raihsa.

"So Mr. Governor which part of your city isn't working too well at the moment. Oh, the public drainage system is antiquated and needs up grading; well consider it sorted out. Oh, and there is just the little matter of a license to mine the coal in the protected forest. It would be so good for your debt laden economy!!"

Within months they had driven a road through the jungle out to the site of the seam and started mining the coal. The shares of the company bought for virtually nothing went through the roof. Remi sold his 10% of the company he had personally bought within twenty minutes of the new mine being announced at an astronomic profit. By the end of the first day of trading the mining company had been bought by a global mining corporation at a huge profit for the bank with Remi taking his 7% for setting it all up. I never actually found out how much he made that day but it must have been a lot…a huge unimaginable pile of cash!!

I was watching the whole thing on the news when he came in. There was of course international outrage. He was as happy as I had ever seen him. He told me we were going out to celebrate because he had pulled off the deal of the century. I looked at his tanned face and then back at the TV. It suddenly all dawned on me. This is where he had been going on his visits abroad. Then it all came out. How he had arranged the whole thing; quietly without anyone knowing he had made himself a fortune and arranged the destruction of another swathe of Arimathea's rainforest.

I was so shocked and absolutely beside myself with rage. This whole disgusting episode had been perpetrated by the man I was living with!! I knew he was pretty ruthless when it came to making money but this was just too much. There was an enormous row. He said if he hadn't done it then someone else would have done. All I could hear as he tried to justify himself was the chaos as the forest was being ripped down. I felt a terrible sense of panic and hopelessness as I imagined the huge tress crashing through the undergrowth and the screeching panic of the animals as their home was destroyed. Any feeling I had for this man had now disappeared. When we had shouted all that could be shouted, I collected up my belongings and I went back to my parent's home where I felt safe now this bulldozer had been driven through my own world."

Mariella became silent. She turned away from Okino who had had regular eye contact with her throughout her story. She looked out across the plains to the hills. Okino had felt her pain and knew she was reliving the ferocity of this experience. So, here was the true life behind the pictures. Lifestyles being fuelled by the ruthless exploitation of Arimathea's natural world. The complexity of the economic processes briefly described to him were quite astounding to Okino. His town was small. Everyone knew each other and each other's business. There was very little crime because there was very little to be gained from any kind of deception. If a crisis struck, which it often did, everybody had to trust and be able to depend on each other to get through.

Okino now had an image of this vast city where relationships were based purely on what could be gained by both parties. In Mariella's world criminals mixed openly with lawyers. In fact, it seemed they were mutually dependent on each other. A parasitic relationship in which he could not be sure who was benefiting who the most. Remi's behaviour showed it was possible to act within the law while having no concern for the wellbeing of Arimathea's people or her threatened jungles. Okino could see why the delicate support systems still in place in these mountains were so important. Where people generally understood they were reliant on the environmental systems being healthy then the community would act responsibly towards each other. In this new world of cities and intercontinental travel the responsibilities to neighbours had become blurred. The park would always be looked after and clean water would still be coming out of the taps. A complacency had arisen in the minds of men such as Remi. He had no concern for the consequences of his actions in other parts of the world. In his city of steel and glass, operating from the protection of his global corporation he had become untouchable.

The monster had given him the power and its' approval to exploit and ravage Arimathea by whatever means necessary to feed the ever expanding and voracious appetites of the corporate machines battling over her dwindling resources. Okino had seen the consequences reaching his own town. He had seen how the fish that had fed his people so delightfully and sustainably for generations had been poisoned by the monster. It was indeed a depressing thought. How could such power ever be confronted and overcome when the most powerful and ruthless people had become its servants and allies.

Then he smiled to himself as he acknowledged how the story so far had come to him. How this picture of Arimathea was unravelling for him and Mariella. He saw how the trauma she had suffered when the revelation her lover was involved in some of the worst accesses of environmental degradation. The terrible shock had finally broken through the cynical attitude built around her by the society in which she lived. A shiver ran through his being as he acknowledged yet another possibility. He wondered whether these circumstances had been carefully directed towards Mariella by the spirit who had visited him in the cave.

"So, you see how I was taken out of the city and it's breathtakingly false illusion and put firmly back in contact with the reality of what is happening on this world."

"What did you see as the illusion" asked Okino curiously. There appeared to be no illusion in the way he had heard the story.

"The illusion, my dear Okino, is that we as a race can pursue endlessly our goals of material wealth and so our personal happiness without even considering the natural balance of the world which is undoubtedly suffering as a result of our thoughtless excess."

"So presumably, you then made the cross over from being involved in the illusion to separating yourself from it completely."

"I told you yesterday what happened next. I started wandering deeper and deeper into the countryside around our home and in the light of the realization I had in the city gradually started to see the world in a very different way. But it was only when I went further afield into the hills and mountains I really started to feel that underneath all the abundance of life there was something, a presence."

"Like spirit?" Okino questioned,

"Yes, now I would say spirit." Mariella looked dreamily around her. "How can you describe it's presence. I look around me and see a glow."

She gestured to the ground where the grass and trees were growing.

"There is a kind of buzz to it, even though you cannot see it all, you know at a microscopic level everywhere you look is teeming with living creatures going about the lives they have evolved into; even in the most barren of places where life does not exist so prodigiously it is still there suspended in the atmospheric light. I came to think everything I could see had become an extension of my own consciousness because of my own ability to comprehend it. Then it seemed because there was no limit to my ability to comprehend it then perhaps this consciousness and my part in it somehow embraced the entire planet."

Okino could not help but smile at Mariella's enthusiasm. The circumstances which had brought her to this point had been intense and undoubtedly life changing. As a result, she had put her life on hold and decided to travel across the world to find his order. What was he able to offer her now she was here he wondered? He thought briefly back to his initiation and subsequent training. He had deepened his ability 'to be' in the greater consciousness every waking and so it would follow sleeping moment of his life. Separation would seem unthinkable now, even too many of the adults in his community. The importance of this awareness in their lives was alluded to in the lessons the monks taught to the children. The monks would always make them wonder. Push their minds into the realms where the consciousness was operating beyond but also as a part of their immediate surroundings. They would ask them.

"How do you think we are all able to see and experience the same world?"

Then the monks would sit them down in the star shine in the fields for a few minutes and then ask them how they felt. Rarely would they say they had felt connected into an infinite consciousness which encompassed the entire universe but they generally said they had felt something outside themselves that was physical which had made them feel quiet and content. This was the start of the sense of respect and belonging to Arimathea the monks attempted to inspire in all the children in the hope it would foster an unselfish attitude to everything and everyone around them. There seemed to be little sign of this in the upbringing of children on the other side of his world. Any kind of connection with the natural world seemed to have been lost as life gravitated progressively towards the city and everything that came out of it.

Now the children of rich lawyers were being guided to cross to the distant reaches of Arimathea to find the people who had not lost their ability to connect with this consciousness in the hope something could be done to reverse the degradation.

"Did your father and mother know that you were coming halfway around the world to find the Ancient Order of the Dragon? Did you explain to them why?

"I have explained exactly what I am doing? They of course hope I will eventually regain my sanity and in the meantime have given me as much support as they can in these distant places. My father does have an enormous network of connections across Arimathea which has been convenient for transferring money."

This explained immediately how Mariella had been able to travel so effectively. She clearly had also brought protection at the highest level throughout the entire journey. Okino had to admit to himself circumstances were starting to look very interesting. His thoughts returned to their destination. A ruined settlement nestling amongst the foothills of the mountains which could have some enormous significance for the outcome of their quest. She would tell him almost nothing about this place he had previously been unaware of. She had found it in one of the libraries in her own country while delving into the mystery she had started to uncover. Again, Okino could see how their two worlds had started to blend together.

"So, there is nothing more you can tell me about where we are going!"

"I've told you I don't want you turning up there with any preconceived ideas. You will just have to be patient."

They fell back into silence and the rhythm of their journey, slowly moving through the timeless and beautiful landscape of the higher mountainous regions of Arimathea. Later in the afternoon as they approached their first campsite two of the southern men Ben and Zeph roared past in their powerful off-road vehicle making hand signals from the windows. Mariella made it quite clear she would not tell any of the tribesmen what the meaning of the signals were. Everyone suspected they must have been controversial and there was much muttering and cursing. The vehicle created an enormous cloud of dust that had the entire caravan coughing and waving their hands for many minutes. The yaks however did not seem to notice and continued pulling relentlessly. The children laughed hysterically amongst their spluttering as they tried to escape the cloud by running out of it. When the dust had settled everyone was the colour of the landscape. Strangely ghostlike they wandered on until the Star was low on the horizon. The women pulled up the yaks and they stopped for the night.

Chapter Thirteen.
The Dragon Cloud.

The next hour saw frantic activity as the overnight camp was planned and constructed. It seemed this place was regularly used as a campsite as the fire pit had been recently used. The ground was flat and there seemed little chance of any significant wind during the night. A circle of yurts would be built with all the entrances facing towards the fire area. Once positions had been agreed the yurts were unloaded from the wagon and the process of construction began. Okino saw Mariella produce another one of the light brightly coloured tents. She showed no sign the arrangement could have been any different and the subject was not discussed or even acknowledged as a problem.

Okino lifted the two tents down from the third horse and carefully placed them in the position agreed. There were knowing smiles and quiet discussion amongst the other adults as they watched Mariella and Okino putting up their temporary dwellings. Okino watched intently as the traditional yurts were carefully built. A cleverly jointed lattice of diagonal slats was first extended and placed in a circle to form the walls. A gap was left for the entrance and the lattice wall was secured to the ground. Timber slats were positioned into a circular rim at the apex and secured on the walls to form a conical roof. Carefully sewn and jointed skins were unravelled and placed over the structures.

Okino assumed these were the skins of yaks which had been in the families for many years before they had died. Now they were fondly remembered as the tents were once again put up. The fur side of the hardy mountain creatures were put on the inside of the structures. Permanent dyes had been used to decorate the outside of the skins and much pride was taken in the intricacy of the patterns. Further skins were placed inside the tents for ground cover and to sleep under. These traditional tents proved to be effective in even the most severe mountain conditions owing to the superb insulating properties of the fine yak fur.

Okino looked over at the enormous creatures who had been pulling the wagons tirelessly all day. He wondered whether they were completely unaware of the use the hides their most recent ancestors had been put to. As he battled with a bewildering set of slender interconnecting poles and intricately sewn synthetic material, he was struck by how this continuity was both practical and beautiful. Practical in the sense that hides such as these were valuable and careful thought would have been given to their usefulness before being discarded or sold. Beautiful because the memory of the animal which had struggled for them during its entire life was now honoured by having a permanent place in the life of the community and in the journeys in which it had played such an enormous role for so many years.

The buzz of activity was soon mixed with the aromas of cooking food. The dragon cauldron was soon bubbling busily over the fire. The yurt builders having finished their work gradually took their places around the fire with the women and children. The Star had timed it's setting obediently leaving a flaming aura around the mountains in the distance. The first stars were flickering into the deepest blue of the evening skies and as the moon started to rise adjacent to one of the larger peaks a delicious stew was served on battered metal plates. Again, there was quiet as Mariella, Okino and their travelling companions hungrily consumed their evening meal. One of the men brought out a crate of the wicked local beer that had made Okino feel so ill the previous morning. Remembering the difficulty he had had with his sight Okino declined as a bottle was passed to him. There was much laughter and

Okino reluctantly took the bottle and sipped at the liquid tentatively to the happy cheers of the assembled gathering.

Quiet conversations were soon initiated around the circle and attention drifted away from the monk and his new companion. There was a silence between them as they drank the beers whilst looking into the flames. Mariella smiled…

"I have a surprise for you Okino the monk."

Mariella had spoken softly and nudged him affectionately,

"As you will have noticed much to do with this journey is traditional for these folks. They have no idea when these journeys down to the town first started but it would have been a very long time ago. This place has been where they stop for a very good reason."

"So what reason is that?" Okino was now very curious. He had already become aware of the settled nature of this site.

"Follow me."

Mariella had finished her food, she stood up and started to wander away from the fire and looked over her shoulder to make sure Okino was following. She was making her way towards an outcrop of rocks on a rise some distance from the track. Okino hurriedly caught up with her, now intensely curious as to the nature of this surprise. As he walked over the cooling sand, under the cloudless canopy of the universe with the moon rising, at the side of this mysterious girl again he felt the strange sense he was leaving his old life behind. The old being he had felt in the marketplace was here with purpose at this time. There was an eagerness not entirely his own propelling him up the gentle rise. There had been some trick of the light playing in the dusk. The rise was longer and higher than he had perceived when he had left the fire. It had appeared to have been no larger than a collection of boulders but in fact was a sizeable rocky outcrop. The ground started to flatten out and the two figures walked onto the level area on top of the rise.

Mariella and Okino had walked into a ring of standing stones. Each stone was only slightly higher than a man and the diameter of the ring was twenty of Okino's long paces across. The slender stones stood eerily piercing the surrounding horizon, mixing their imposing stature with the gentle slopes of the mountains beyond. Roughly hewn faces glowed in the gentle light of the rising moon. Okino turned to Mariella in delight as he stepped into the centre of the circle and turned to give each stone a brief inspection.

"So, this is where it is. I have heard of this old circle but never realized it was this close!!"

"They told me about it when I inquired about the route we would be taking to the old ruins." Mariella had joined Okino in the centre.

The stones were of varying sizes. Immediately it was possible to see how their height correlated with the outline of the mountains in the distance. Okino wandered from stone to stone admiring the geological formations and running his hands just above their surface.

"This is a wonderful surprise." Okino came back into the centre next to Mariella "There is a bit of a story here. Perhaps we should settle down here for a while."

Okino and Mariella settled down in the moonlight in the centre of the old circle looking out towards where the mountains crouched on the horizon as if they were unearthly predators waiting for a star to fall. For now, they hung far out of reach in the moonlit sky. Okino savoured this moment before he began.

"One of the monks, Lastri, spent some time looking into these old monuments. He wrote a detailed account of his research. I came across it when I was looking through the library in the monastery. It is an extraordinary place. Built literally on the side of a mountain. I would love you to see it one day. Obviously, it is legendary because the knowledge of it has filtered out and you have arrived here looking for us. I haven't told you much about it so far. But as this journey progresses the more I think there must be a link to the work that has been going on there."

Okino looked thoughtfully into the Stars and muttered to himself,

"I should have told them about what happened up there!"

"So, any way, for as long as there have been records the monks have been working on techniques to connect and so ultimately maintain and deepen their contact with the consciousness of Arimathea. This they have always done by developing and refining the meditation techniques handed down through the centuries. They have taught me many of these techniques and I have been involved since my initiation in many of these meditations. The connection with the consciousness is profound although I am not sure anyone had actually spoken to the planet before she rescued me on the mountain. But it would seem they did all the groundwork for the connection to be made. Part of the groundwork was the work of the monk who looked into these circles.

It had come to his attention the use of stone circles could intensify further the experience of the consciousness. As you can imagine we don't have instant access to information as you do so the acquisition of the books needed for his research took some years. But every now and again one of the folks from the village would decide they had to make the journey to the world beyond the mountains. These times always seemed to be somewhat defining moments for the village. The traveller would always come to the temple to ask for a blessing from the monks. Invariably small items such as books were ordered to be sent if the traveller ever reached the places where such books could be purchased.

Months would go by and the order may even be forgotten about. Then as if from nowhere the item would appear when somebody arrived from the nearest town of Aharrii. So, you understand extensive research in the mountain town of Lamai is generally a long drawn out affair. This never deterred the monks as they believed they were able to receive much of the information they needed from their meditations. Any knowledge gained in this manner however was more likely to be inspirational and as a result old Lastri, built a series of stone circles on the lower shallower slopes with assorted varieties of stone. He documented the results of his meditations. In themselves these initial findings were remarkable. He found as the years went by and the Stones became more 'rooted' to the ground so his experiences became more profound. He talked of silence and stillness within the stones which enabled his mind to become quieter for longer periods of time without distraction. He was finding as a result of this he could connect with the surrounding landscape in a deeper and more profound way.

Then just when he had completely forgotten about the book he had sent for and was becoming satisfied with his own intuitive research, it arrived. The arrival of such a book was greeted with much excitement. The moment of arrival was seen as momentous and the precise circumstances under which it had appeared were carefully analysed. In this case it was seen as significant Lastri had almost decided his research was at an end. It was how the monks liked things to be and they always took great pleasure when such coincidences became apparent. They celebrated by bringing one of his smaller stone circles into the temple where it resides to this day.

Now he was able to examine layouts of the twenty circles surveyed in the book. They had been found consistently across the temperate areas of Arimathea and had displayed many similar characteristics. He found as expected the stones often recorded significant events in the astronomical calendar; so, star rises and moon rises at solstices and equinoxes and other festivals or significant dates for the tribe who made them. Then there were star and constellation rises significant to the particular culture. Scientific analysis of the rock had shown many of the circles consisted of predominantly piezo quartz. Typically Granite, a composite of quartz mica and feldspar possesses a specific vibratory frequency which heightens the human sensory system and its ability to pick up sensory information otherwise undetectable.

This circle, much to his delight, was documented in his book. It was the nearest to the monastery so Lastri made the journey here and there is an account of his visit in a journal.

He came here for a Summer solstice. He recorded the star rose over the stone in the north east, which would be that one. Also there were stones aligned to our most visible stars, Aralasir, which would probably be the central stone of that group. As far as his actual experience, he wrote of the profound beauty he had found here. It had undoubtedly deepened his conviction Arimathea was a sentient being and whoever built these circles had found a way of coming closer to her within them. He had ventured that positioning the stones so specifically in relation to astronomic events, which of course happen so precisely in time and space year after year, would eventually tune the quartz of the stones into the cycles of the universe. With the meditation techniques he had, he wrote, been able to amplify his experience or connection with the universe as his sensory systems were modified to become harmonious with the frequency of the circle."

"So, this is a carefully constructed instrument for tuning into the universe!"

"On one level. But in the book Lastri eventually received, there was a hypothesis these old stone circles were built by ancient people who knew about the network of energy lines in which the life force of the planet flows. The stones are also drawing energy out of the ground straight from the planets life force to release it into the air around them. So not only would you be tuning into the universe but also into the concentrated consciousness of the Planet of Arimathea!"

"And you know how to do that?"

Mariella had been listening carefully to the young monk while she contemplated and absorbed the quiet atmosphere within the stone circle.

"Seems like perfect conditions to me. Perhaps we could try now!!"

Okino was quiet for a few moments. It was a beautiful night and the camp would need to be packed up for an early start so there would be little time the next morning. He was weary after his first day in the saddle but he sensed Mariella's infectious eagerness and a wave of enthusiasm started to run through his being. It was a magnificent opportunity.

"Ok let's do it."

He pulled himself up slightly stiffly,

"Find a place on the outside of the circle, but just inside the stones where you feel comfortable and can relax, I'll do the rest. Just treat it like one of your normal meditations for the moment. So, concentrate on your breathing, feel the life force within your body and your connection with the ground and everything around you. If you feel a concentration in your forehead let it flow out as if it were helping to fill a sphere of light engulfing the circle."

Then Okino the monk, initiate of the most sacred Order of the Dragon, started to walk slowly around the circle, stopping to acknowledge the landscape beyond the standing stones. Mariella wondered of the prayers and the incantations he was reciting handed down through generations of monks, what invocations was he offering to initiate this holy rite? She had been right to come, follow this strange dream, bringing her from the madness of her life with Remi, all the lawyers and the gangsters; all the way round the world to find this holy boy and take part in the destiny unfolding for them both. As he completed his circuit, he came and settled down next to her at the edge of the circle. He turned and smiled at her. She smiled back. She knew in those moments that this was what she had really come for.

Okino straightened his spine, steadied his breath and started to concentrate on the consciousness within his own body, now contained and slowly becoming part of the surrounding atmosphere of the stone circle. He felt the age of the old stones and felt the stillness within their enclosure. He became conscious of the mountain ranges in the distance and the empty spaces in between bathed in moonlight. A great sense of ease rose within his being as he remembered everything that had happened to him in those last few days;

how he had set out from the monastery to follow the river; his nights in the forest and the dragons, his time at the farm and in the town, meeting Mariella. He turned again to see how she was. She had become still and silent as this special place slowly became part of her being. Her eyes were now closed and a look of blissful happiness had come over her face. He turned back to face the centre and noticed how the moonlight was falling on the standing stone directly in his gaze. Then he closed his eyes as all the comforts of the Universal consciousness started to flood his soul.

Mariella had drifted deep into the consciousness of Arimathea. She had moved out to the edges of her atmosphere, at the edges of her light, signalling the existence of this oasis out into the deep blue of endless space. Before her was the simple, yet infinite complexity of the world on which she lived. She could see the oceans and the land masses, the clouds flowing over them, between and above them. She could see the great ranges of mountains in which she knew she was sitting. She felt Arimathea's light dawning through her, was moved with a deep love for her, as deep as any she had previously experienced as the comprehension that everything she had ever known had happened on the beautiful magical blue green sphere floating in the starlight before her. Any explanation, any reason or theory faded into insignificance and irrelevance as childish nonsense in relation to what she was seeing. There could be no explanation they would ever understand. There would always be some layer beneath such an explanation to defy any crude hypothesis.

But she knew without any doubt whatsoever, it was part of her. She knew she was carrying in the person she had become, the magical power that had brought all this into being. In the same way she knew everything she could see down there carried its' own fraction of the miracle; each individual tiny life, as part of the vast teeming explosion of variety and beauty it had become, each plant, each wave, each gust of wind, every mountain range or scorching desert, every cascading river flowing into the vast unending oceans had its place and had become a part of Arimathea and her ability to continually recreate herself infinitely through the millennia.

Mariella was overwhelmed with such compassion and such a profound depth of empathy for all she could see, she wondered if Arimathea had allowed her to experience her creation as if it had been her own. She began to feel tears running uncontrollably down her face falling into the space around her and down towards Arimathea. Felt them exploding into the planet below, vaporizing and mixing and finally being absorbed into the thin layer of vaporous air surrounding her, into the breath of the world. The infinite pulsation, the rhythm of a million billion lives breathing her in and breathing her out and drawing her closer and deeper into the life force of Arimathea.

She drifted back down to the stone circle where she knew she was in a deep meditation with Okino. The moon had only moved fractionally across the sky and he was standing on the edge of the circle, his hands slightly outstretched, palms and face bathing in the moonlight. He turned as he felt her return and she smiled and beckoned over for him to join her. He walked across the circle and sat down next to her. There was no need to talk. They closed their eyes and absorbed themselves into the atmosphere of this place in which they had come to be.

The stone circle was now in a large clearing of trees. The edge of the trees was fifty paces from the perimeter of the stones just beyond the bottom of the rise on which the stone circle sat. It was a semi-arid landscape and the large healthy trees seemed to be evenly spaced with sparse vegetation growing through the sandy ground flowing around them. Beyond the trees the mountains in the distance had not changed from the undulating silhouette over which they had recently watched the Star set. The circle itself seemed unchanged, perhaps the edges seemed more angular and sharper suggesting Okino and Mariella had surfaced somewhere in the distant past where the continual abrasion of the wind around them had yet to wear away their sharpened surfaces.

As they silently absorbed the scene a meteorite skimmed through the atmosphere crossing from one horizon to the other. A trail of burning cosmic debris was left in its' wake as it momentarily flashed brightly across the sky. It was an exciting moment for now the skies seemed to have marked this moment and possibly the significance of what was to come. The roars and screeches of the nocturnal creatures living on the wooded plains beyond punctuated the silence reminding Okino and Mariella underlying this peaceful scene as ever was a teeming variety of life engaged fully in their battle for survival.

Then somewhere in the near distance they heard the sounds of a large group of human beings moving through the trees. As the sounds grew louder the group appeared to be approaching the stone circle. They chattered quietly amongst themselves. Occasional laughter indicated to Mariella and Okino they were in good spirits and so hopefully posed no threat to their safety. Soon the movement of the group could be detected as it moved towards them and out from the trees into the moonlight. The full extent of the group was fully revealed.

There seemed to be approximately thirty or forty individuals. There were men, women and children. They appeared strong and vigorous in their movements. They wore skins carefully sewn and decorated with sections of fur. They wore fur boots bound with further leather straps. Many of the men carried large spears or bows slung across their backs with quivers full of arrows. They were well built, heavily muscled, swarthy and unshaven; the women wore longer garments and wore necklaces of beads draped around their necks. Their hair was long and dark and the children ran freely amongst the advancing group. Two of the men at the head of the group were carrying the body of a large deer tied at the ankles and suspended over a pole. The antlers of the unfortunate creature narrowly avoided the ground and swung freely as blood dripped from its mouth and nostrils demonstrating it had only recently been killed. The tribe climbed the rise easily and soon were entering the circle.

The first men to enter the stone circle were momentarily surprised to see Okino and Mariella sitting up against the stones. However, this did not seem to be a strange occurrence and they immediately came across the circle as Mariella and Okino got to their feet. The two men approached warily as they offered a greeting of outstretched and bloody hands. Mariella and Okino both clasped the outstretched hands vigorously. The four human beings from very different times now greeted each other with the universal gestures of human friendship. The taller of the two men then pointed to the deer now lying in the centre of the circle. With a number of hand signals he clearly indicated he would like the two travellers to join them at their feast to celebrate with them. Mariella and Okino accepted and sat back down against the stones as the tribe began to prepare for the evening ahead. Some of the children came over to Mariella and Okino clearly curious about the two strangers. They felt the fine weave of their cotton and woollen clothes; the girls ran their fingers through Mariella's long dark hair. Despite her months on the road it remained un-matted and remarkably clean. The children had never seen a haircut like Okino's and delightedly ran their fingers over his closely cropped head giggling happily at the feeling it gave.

Then they were called back by their elders and were soon running out into the wooded landscape and returning with the bundles of wood they had collected. A large pile was made and soon one of the women started to build the fire. The men were preparing the deer. It appeared it had been killed by one of the young adults. It had been the first time he had killed such an animal and so for the first time had been able to make a significant contribution to the health and survival of the tribe.

The skin and head were cut in one piece from the animal and placed reverentially over one of the stones. The legs were trussed up with strips of hide around the creature and a pole was unceremoniously driven through the centre of the deer. The fire now was starting to take hold in the dried timber and the corpse of the deer was lifted onto supports at either side of the fire where the flesh soon started to hiss and spit in the intense heat. The tribe then settled down on the ground around the fire. The atmosphere had become rapidly cooler and additional furs were brought out from the piles of belongings each member of the tribe was carrying. One of the women noticed Mariella and Okino in the clothes more suited to the warmer climate from where they had come and brought over what appeared to be wolf hides stitched together to make two cloaks. They gratefully wrapped themselves into the thick fur.

The tall man who had greeted Mariella and Okino now stood up and addressed the rest of the tribe. He indicated to the young man who had killed the deer and explained this rite of passage was in honour of his first deer kill. The younger man now moved towards the stone where the hide of the recently killed deer still hung. The bloody hide was then draped over him so the head of the creature complete with antlers now sat on his own with the enormous hide covering his body. In the flickering firelight man and beast appeared to become one and a great cheer arose from the tribe as they acknowledged the latest hunter to emerge from the tribe.

He stood silently as four large drums were produced. Then a silence descended on the gathering as a drumbeat was quietly started. The drums created a deep resonance of sound in the finely hollowed tree trunks over which animal skins had been stretched and bound. The ancient sound reverberated in amongst the stones. As the drumbeat gathered in intensity the tribe began a murmuring chant. In response the drums became louder. In turn the chant gathered in strength. Deeper and louder the drums and the voices competed and then gradually they became part of the same sound. The rhythm had increased in pace and the chants had gathered in intensity. The sound now was vibrating out across the plains into the distant mountain valleys. All the land containing the rhythms that responded and thrived upon the cycles of the Star was being awoken by the sound of the tribe in their celebration of their continued survival. The tribe now rose to their feet and started to dance stamping their feet upon the ground and swaying to the increasing tempo being produced by the drummers. Louder and faster they chanted. The fire was stoked with the larger dryer wood and the flames leapt higher around the cooking deer.

Mariella and Okino had been compelled to join in with the chant and as it became louder and more intense and the dancing of the tribes' people became more and more frenzied the nature of the light being produced by the fire was starting to change. It had become whiter with threads of green and it was more concentrated around each of the stones. Slowly it was starting to move. Almost imperceptibly at first, the light from each stone was spiralling in towards the fire. As it spiralled inwards it was passing through each of the chanting tribes' people. Each shuddered with delight as the light passed through their being. Again, it would gather in intensity. Eventually each spiral of light from each stone was arriving in the intensifying light just above the flames. Brighter it became as each strand combined and strengthened; filled with the planetary and universal force from the stones, the intensified life force from the energy of the drums and the chanting of the tribes' people.

Then the nature of the light over the fire began to change entirely. No longer constant, it began to swirl and eddy and patterns were starting to emerge. As the patterns fluctuated, images started to form. The light was condensing in the swirling light into a disparate torso and a huge skull, claws and wings. As the various forms came together and they became fully focused in the now steadily flowing light, Okino recognised the infinitely burning eyes of the dragon staring down into the circle. As the dragon light hovered over the circle the drums again intensified. The tribe was roaring together in the mayhem of the huge drums and the chanting as the dragon light spiralled outwards from the fire. It moved slowly around the circle passing through every member of the tribe.

Finally, it arrived to where Okino and Mariella were dancing ecstatically, wrapped in their wolfskins. Okino felt it acknowledge their difference from the rest of the tribes' people and again he felt the dragon's recognition as he had done before. The dragon light then enveloped them both, seared through them, engulfing them in the knowledge and understanding it had, enlivening every part of each and every level of the consciousness they possessed and invisibly and unknowingly to them expanded their ability to interact with their world, the worlds beyond and all the corridors and passageways of the labyrinths joining them through time and space. Only then they knew they would be able to travel with the dragons to wherever it was necessary to illuminate the nature of their conflict on Arimathea in the hope it could in some way be resolved. They settled in the knowledge for a few moments, in the certainty their journey would unravel towards this end.

The dragon light then moved on around the circle where finally it settled over the young hunter. The tribe roared their approval as the young man raised his arms to the stars in the hope that now they would acknowledge him into their universe. The dragon light spiralled back through the space between the stones and gradually merged again into the fire. The tribe surrounded the young hunter congratulating him and eventually the bloody skin of the deer was removed. They surrounded the cooking deer which due to the intensity of the fire on the outside was now ready to eat. Okino and Mariella were drawn in and were offered the meat from the deer. But as they ate the dream began to fade. They both knew they were moving back and slowly they were able to open their eyes back in the stone circle in their own time.

Okino acknowledged Mariella before again walking around the circle and offering his prayers to the stones and thanks to the powers he had previously summoned. Then he walked back to Mariella who leapt to her feet and took both his hands and looked deeply into his eyes.

"Okino, that was amazing. I had absolutely no idea that could be possible. I know now what you mean about the worries you were having. It seems we both travelled…, you were there weren't you!"

"…. In this circle, in prehistoric times with hunters that raised a dragon?"

"Yes, well that's a relief; we were both there together to witness those people bringing the dragon out of the land with the drums and the chanting and as a result it seems we now have had some profound contact with the dragon, of which strangely I seem to have no recollection whatsoever."

Mariella paused as she realised she was still wrapped in the wolfskin cloak the woman had given to her. She wrapped it closely around herself…

"…And look Okino we still have the wolfskin cloaks. What on Arimathea must those poor people think?"

"Perhaps they are used to having strange visitors in this circle from other times…So it can't have been both our imaginations if we were both in the same place. But you see what I mean. These episodes are so extraordinary. It all seems to be happening in some other time but in the same place."

"You really are going to have to try and accept everything the monks have been handed down all these years and have subsequently taught you is really how things actually are. These dragons are operating across time and space in ways we can have only imagined but really have had no evidence it could really happen. But now it has been shown to us, you can't still be having doubts this is actually happening."

Okino looked over at Mariella. Again, she was trying to convince him when here they had incontrovertible evidence the dragon he had released was now working in the world and more specifically through his and Mariella's world.

Mariella observed with frustration.

"I wish I could remember.... something happened when the dragon light passed over us! It's like one of those facts you know is in your memory but you just can't quite drag it out...then you remember it later in the day when the moment has passed for it to be of any use."

"It'll surface when it's needed, I should imagine. They'll be a good reason why you can't remember immediately. Possibly the same reason as I have this strange doubt. I think my original strategy was correct!"

"Just remind me what that was, Okino!"

"Well, just carry on and see what happens next!"

"I'll go a long with that!"

"Oh, and by the way, have you seen what is up there!!" Mariella was pointing into the stars

Okino looked up. A solitary cloud was drifting across the moonlit sky. An angular skull framed the deep night sky with cavernous eyes, a streamlined torso drifting on delicately crenulated wings made it unmistakably a Dragon cloud. Okino laughed.

"I can see this is going to be quite some journey!!"

Chapter Fourteen
Rhythm of the world.

Far across the planet on the other side of Arimathea four men and two women in their late twenties had walked for three days deep into the sacred Akaloma mountains. The mountain range joined the two continents of Eremoya and its' lower southern neighbour Arralan. The Oceans lapped the long sandy beaches on either side of the range sacred to the indigenous peoples who lived on both continents. Spectacular flora and fauna had evolved as a result of its proximity to their weather systems. At lower altitudes tropical jungles had grown undisturbed for thousands of years and although the vegetation became sparser at higher altitudes the winds blowing across them from the oceans still provided enough warmth and precipitation even at high altitude for a luxurious covering of grasses, shrubs and less dense jungle.

It was late spring as the small band of pilgrims had trudged the little used paths to the place high in the mountains so sacred to their ancestors. Formed as a flood plain in a wide valley sheltered by the towering ridges on either side, the fertile soil left by flood waters had washed from higher in the mountains and settled to fom a uniquely sheltered environment which animals and plants alike had found beneficial. The indigenous peoples of the adjacent lands had always come here and one such group of visitors had decided to build a circle of stones. There were twenty-three stones still standing. They varied in height from the waist of a man to just higher than the head of their tallest. They stood in a bow of the stream; preserved by an outcrop of low rock at the higher end of the plain. The story of the building was long since forgotten; only the carefully placed stones displaying the preserved geology of a hundred million years of planetary evolution silently whispered of the care they had taken in their construction. It was a beautifully unique and remote site. It could only be reached on foot by the most determined pilgrims and so had remained un-spoilt by the hordes of tourists who would otherwise have descended upon it in coaches and sports utility vehicles. However, the construction of a road through these mountains had never been attempted.

These stone monuments had often been regarded as easy sources of quarried stone in more populated areas and had been demolished when local villages needed to expand. If they had survived this destruction, the sanctity of these ancient sites was often invaded by visitor centres and gift shops as local governments in partnership with preservation societies had realized they attracted a continual stream of visitors. They were an interesting destination to drive to from the cities where the opportunity to consume cheap food and buy the souvenirs provided was combined conveniently with the intriguing mystery left by their distant ancestors.

The six visitors now sat quietly remembering their tribal roots and ancestry in these mountains. Their tribe, the ancient Amahano people had long since been absorbed into the culture of successive invaders who had brought their houses and their machinery, who had cut themselves off from the land once they had divided it up amongst themselves, had killed all the animals they feared or could profit from and then divided it with their roads and railways. They had over run and mined the sacred places and treated the peoples who had lived in harmony with their land as if they had been animals themselves. Now they lived within the boundary fences the invaders had built along the lines they had drawn on their maps. All this the young people remembered and even further back into their tribal history as they sat quietly amongst the Sacred Stones.

They had come for the very reason they imagined these stones had been erected; to the place where the rites of their people had been celebrated and where they had been joined with the spirits of the mountains and the animals and their sky gods to come closer to their world and the harmony they knew to exist within it. As well as their proximity to this luxurious valley the stones shared an acoustic relationship caused by the natural amphi-theatre made by the surrounding mountainsides. They sat with the large light alloy and timber drums they had brought along with their camping equipment, the bare minimum of food and survival apparatus, to play amongst the stones and this valley where the unique sound generated would give the quality they desired for the recording of their next piece of music. With the hi-tech recording equipment waiting around the stones the six musicians were re-inventing the music of their ancestors in the recording studio they had built and where their journey had started five days before. Their chants and drum rhythms had captured the imagination of a generation of young people. In redundant buildings hollowed out to form vast dance halls, the sounds reminiscent of ancient tribal gatherings mixed with synthesized technology and amplification had created a dance craze that had spread rapidly through the industrialized cities of Arimathea.

One night they had decided this success was no fleeting whim of the next generation attempting to find its' own identity but an impulse stimulated by genetic memories deep in their human psyche. They had become inspired by the idea the young people had found their way back to the ancient rhythms, the sounds of the great universal turning running through their lives and the lives of everything around them. They had decided to recreate the rhythms the ancient peoples had invented to concentrate those processes into their rites. They added the embellishments technology allowed them and then overlaid them with the chants of their people to create a rich soundscape and so reach deeper into those genetic memories, deeper into the history of who they were and perhaps who they could be.

The feathers they had bound into their hair from along the pathways were caught in the gentle breeze as it whispered around the silent stones. The depth of the silence increased. An eagle calling high amongst the summits was fading into the distance of the realm they were beginning to leave behind. Deep in the planet the channels carrying the dragon light were again stirring. Across time, this light had flooded through Arimathea. Now again she shuddered with delight as her returning dragons concentrated their light through the boy priest Okino. He had travelled deep into the fabric of time and space into the labyrinths of Arimathea's planetary memory and now the light was surfacing in many of her sacred places found in those early years before the human race had lost their ability or inclination to connect with their world. Now the light flooded up through the circle in which the young people of the ancient Amahano race were sitting, invading their minds and engulfing their beings.

In their silence, in the bond they had between each other and the stones, they felt a startling change in their state of being as the dragon light reconnected with the ability they had previously retained and subsequently forgotten. Now they had started to remember the codes and the vibrations, the impulses sending information through Arimathea's infinite matrix. Another scene started to emerge in the blazing white light, in another land in another circle. Here they were sitting with an ancient people in the moonlight, in the searing heat of a fire and the smell of a deer's roasting. There was a rite in process and they had become part of it. There were enormous drums in front of them, the drumheads were made of thick hide and the bodies hollowed from tree trunks. They had substantial rounded pieces of wood with which they had started to play the drums very softly. Enormous anticipation was building amongst the people surrounding them. They started to hum very softly. As the drums increased in tempo the chanting became louder. These sounds increased as each took cues from the other and the soft murmuring became louder, more intense and an excitement flashed through the people around them.

The intensity of the chanting increased and they drummed harder and harder until the thunder of it all suddenly startled them, as if they had awoken from a long sleep into some higher state joining them with the hills and the sky and the ground on which they sat; opened them again to the connections they had retained deep in their ancestral memory spreading out through the starlight to the eagles silently listening high in their eeries to the thunder of the crazy humans, and the deer and wolves howling in the hills and the salmon swimming up the streaming river currents to their spawning grounds, the great whales singing their echoing songs from the beginning of all time, floating through the oceans of their luminous moonlit world.

The rest of the tribe was now dancing wildly, joyously almost deliriously as the thunder removed them from themselves and transferred them to where they needed to be as the dragon light burst out from the ground and the fire and the stones, circled through the rapturous tribe and finally surrounded the initiate who had the deer's skin draped over him, it's life blood running in dark rivulets like veins down his body. They could see he was out in the stars, out beyond the frontiers of the mind in which he had dwelt or even dwelt now, out in the infinity of the vast exploding, spiralling Universe.

All around them and through them so there was no separation, they experienced Arimathea and the forces of rhythmic life continually flowing through her, guiding her processes, activating her responses and providing the frameworks in which each evolving being and creature had found their place day after day, night after night, from the early stages of their initiation into molecular development through to complex beings. Now they were acknowledging her consciousness through the music they had come to sense; it had been from early times their response to the life force in which they had become an intricate part, shared with everything around them in all the activity of their lives.

Now they were enlivened into this new realm of understanding by the rhythms reflected in the vast movements of the universe around them; in the rite of these ancient people long since extinct or forgotten and dismissed as primitive by the sophisticated machine age theoreticians; although they were guided through their own days by the same responses and instincts, by the Star they barely acknowledged through the canyons of the skyscrapers or the moonlight subtly working through their world in ways they had forgotten to feel or understand.

The young Amahanos were experiencing something of the secret lying dormant in their souls passed down through the generations. It almost certainly had some genetic or bio molecular reaction, some response provoked by the release of a series or combination of hormones; a mere state explained by a new breed of human who demanded rational explanation, who had become lost to the pure exhilaration and joy of being alive in a world that then and even in these days when the rites of their people were long forgotten, mostly defied explanation.

These thoughts and experiences the young people of the ancient Amahanos took back with them to their home and the recording studio they had made high in the hills. They took the recording they had made as they sat in the trance induced by the dragon light. Strangely, the recording had captured perfectly the thunderous sound of the drums and the roar of the chants amongst the twenty-three stones of the old circle in the sacred valley. When they had adjusted the sound levels, layered, balanced and manipulated the spectrums of sound so accurately collected by their recording equipment; when they had highlighted in the opening bars the calls of the eagle who had inadvertently or not added her own voice to the recording, they sat back and listened to what they had made. When they closed their eyes, they thought they could the feel the dragon light wrapping itself around them, moving through their minds re-activating those old memories of deep connection to Arimathea and filling them with the joy they had experienced that afternoon in the stone circle.

When the track they had made was finished they opened their eyes and looked over at each other before breaking into uncontrollable laughter. When this initial reaction had subsided and they had played the track over and over again during the next few days they decided they had more than achieved what they had set out to do and started to discuss how and when they could best deliver this latest work to the young people in the cities who would be eagerly waiting to immerse themselves into it.

Chapter Fifteen
The Valley.

Once he had returned to his new tent and buried himself under the Yak hides Mariella had generously provided for him, Okino fell into a deep sleep. He had no time to contemplate what had happened in the stone circle. It had taken all the rest of his waking energy to move his body back to the tent. His body weight had seemed many multiples more than what it should have been. Although somewhere he knew something very important had happened his need for sleep had overridden all his attempts to stay even briefly awake.

So, to the gentle murmur of the men and women who still were swapping stories around the fire he drifted into a vivid dreamscape that lay waiting for him as he rapidly lost his waking consciousness.

Okino was walking in a thick mist. He could barely see the ground beneath his feet. He could feel it was uneven and strewn with loose rock. There was a gentle breeze which occasionally created a pocket of thinner mist around him. In these moments Okino was able to ascertain he was in a valley whose sides were becoming increasingly steep. They were funnelling him towards what seemed to be a thin vertical opening. He entered a thin crevice just wide enough for him to walk comfortably without touching the sides. They were running with water and intermittently strewn with layers of algae and moss. He could see Starshine glinting on water through a narrow opening at the end. Drawn on by fascination for what lay beyond he warily left the crevice.

The mist had cleared so Okino was able to see this new space was dominated by a small lake defined on all sides by low slopes. They rapidly graduated into steeper low cliff edges forming a bowl which appeared to be holding the lake. At first the mist was moving over the ridges forming a ceiling to the space obscuring the surrounding ridge. However, as the mist was propelled by the breeze it began to bring substantial openings. Okino was able to see the ridge was punctuated by a series of peaks. On many of the peaks, entirely motionless and seeming to Okino at first to be further rocky outcrops, crouched a dragon. They were all of a similar size to the dragons he had seen in his previous dreams. As he observed more fully, he recognized the first dragon he had awakened. He was able to walk around the lake on a narrow pebbly beach. He decided he would try to get closer to one of these sleeping dragons. The surface of the lake rippled gently from the breeze and lapped very gently at the waterline defined by smaller and rounder stones. As he moved around close to the water's edge, he could see the dragons were reflected on the surface of the lake.

In his previous encounters the awakened dragons had seemed to consist mainly of energy. As he scrambled as high as he dared up the low slopes the dragons were only a stone's throw away, he observed they had become merged with the rock around the pool. The shimmering pulsating energetic creatures he had awakened appeared to have reverted again to solid stone. The shale beneath his feet was slippery in the extreme and he found it difficult to maintain a steady view of the creatures above him. He tried to see whether he could find any sign of breathing. However, it seemed they were completely still.

Okino slid back down the slope and walked to the edge of the lake. As he slowly turned on his heels observing them there were sounds of rapid air displacement and two further dragons landed on two of the unoccupied peaks. After a brief scan around the ridge and taking particular interest in Okino for a few moments they settled down into a similar state as the earlier arrivals.

He counted fifteen dragons, evenly spaced along the ridge. There was one unoccupied peak. Okino remembered how, when he had seen the male and female dragons meet in the jungle, they appeared to transferring thoughts to one another. It started to occur to him the dragons may again be preparing to share their recent thoughts and experiences. Okino assumed they had all met with a similar fate and been petrified in some uninhabited part of the planet by similar mysterious swords. Okino remembered the writing so alien to Arimathea. He wondered whether he would be able to intercept any of these telepathic communications and wondered whether it would be dangerous. If these were infinite universal beings, there may be a possibility their thoughts would be too expansive for his human mind to cope with.

He carefully observed their reflections on the surface of the lake. He noticed a very fine ripple was starting to spread across the pool as if tiny stones were being dropped at consistent intervals into the centre of the pool. The power of the ripples seemed to be perfectly spent as they reached the shores of the lake. There was no rebound to spoil the ripples emanating from the centre. Okino could see nothing causing such a precise ripple. However, as he concentrated, he realized the ripples were not disappearing at the edge but were in fact transferring into and through the air. This felt like a breeze delicately whispering over his face and into his mind.

As he concentrated on this sensation, he realized the frequencies that at first had seemed constant were continually changing. Once he began to observe these changes, Okino became aware he was concentrating more acutely to pick up the variations as they occurred. He then started to recognize simple patterns and rhythms. Easily recognizable at first, these patterns soon started to develop into more complex wave forms. As soon as he understood a particular form its' complexity rapidly developed. As they developed further and further, although the wave lengths became less recognizable as patterns and rhythms into an infinite variation, Okino was able to perceive the symmetry taking him deeper and deeper into this world of vibration; until it developed beyond complexity into pure and simple light and images were slowly starting to form.

Okino started to see images of a pristine world where most of the forests were still standing. Amongst this untamed world there were human beings eking out a primitive living on the land they had managed to tame. By draining flood plains with ditches and felling small areas of forest, they had developed small field systems where they were planting and successfully harvesting early crops of wheat and corn. Originally nomadic tribes they had now anchored themselves to the land. They were now transforming it and occupying it with small clusters of dwellings, protecting themselves from the weather and wild animals.

Again, the complexity of the scene increased. Okino was sitting amongst their dwellings watching as the women ground up corn between great revolving circular stones and carefully collected up the precious flour. Other women were adding water to the flour kneading it into doe. They all watched the fire under the crude stone oven, checking the temperature with a light touch and adding an appropriate log if the fire was cooling. He could see out in the distance further people harvesting one of the fields and others were separating the grain from the ears they had gathered. They worked silently and effectively, occasionally questioning or discussing their actions.

The underlying light of the original vibration was always present. It was part of them, Okino became aware they had developed as part of it, almost as a result of it. As he recognized it in the people, he was observing he started to recognize it in himself as a feeling he had had only with the monks in their deepest meditations. The deep connection with the spirit of Arimathea he had experienced earlier in the stone circle was achieved using techniques developed and handed down over generations of monks. Yet here were a primitive people going about their everyday lives immersed in a similar experience. He watched the children playing next to their mothers. They were strong and well fed, interacting calmly and meaningfully with each other. The dwellings were well constructed showing signs of considerable structural and environmental understanding. There was a peaceful purposefulness running through this little settlement. For a time that night they accepted him as one of their own. He sat around their central fire and listened to the stories and legends they chose to tell him.

They told tales of the wandering times; of the great journeys their ancestors had made as they spread out across the land, exploring their world, surviving as best they could amongst the dangers they encountered; moving over the hills and mountains, across the great plains and following the rivers. They came to know the changing moods of the seasons; the migratory routes of the creatures who moved through and lived within them. They adapted their lives to the movements of the animals they were able to hunt and the growth of the seasonal fruit they were able to harvest. They lived by the movements of the Star through the sky and the changing direction of the winds. They came to recognize how these movements coincided with their food supply and carried this knowledge and the skills they had learned closely within their tribes.

They observed their world with a great curiosity as beings who could come to conclusions about what they saw and experienced. They found themselves living in a world where patterns were predictable and were able to be followed. They suspected there were invisible forces behind these patterns which they would come to call spirits and gods just beyond their own physical existence. As they travelled through the lands, they observed there were areas where these forces were more beneficial at different times of their year and so they migrated between these areas as the seasons and the winds changed and the animals moved. They evolved names for the spirits in these different lands. They referred to them in their stories and legends which eventually became an entire imaginary construction of the supernatural forces they came to believe surrounded them and gave explanation for their lives. These stories and legends they passed on to their children.

Why they had eventually decided to settle in this area could not be entirely explained. But from what they knew of their lives here, their ancestors may have decided the spirits in this land were as kind as they had encountered and so they had been reluctant to leave. Much of the knowledge they had learnt and refined about the patterns of the seasons they now were able to apply to this area where they started to adapt and grow the foods they had previously migrated constantly to find. They came to domesticate the wild animals they had followed and expended so much energy hunting. They developed fixed dwellings from the knowledge of the temporary shelters they had previously constructed and the size of their communities were slowly growing. In the early times populations had been sparse and confrontations with other humans were always avoided as injury of almost any kind would always lead to a painful death for the injured person and a traumatic experience for the rest of the tribe.

They were proud of what their tribe had achieved, even within their own lifetimes. Their houses were always better than the ones previously constructed. They had improved the amount of corn they could grow and the numbers in the herds of goats and sheep had increased. Their children survived more often than they died. They were grateful the spirits had eventually brought them to this place where they had been able to thrive and make their lives better.

As they walked through the trees, they had led him to an ancient circle of Oaks standing deep in the forest. They imagined their distant ancestors had always come here. They stood mysteriously, each gnarled and twisted limb reaching for the sky recording the history of their growth, where they felt was the very centre of the forest and the world in which they lived. They told him the forces flowing through their land seemed to be concentrated in this place and their connection between the ground and the stars was enhanced by the life and time which had flowed through here and was now bound up in the ancient trees. Here they celebrated the important times of their lives and gave thanks to the spirits for all they had brought.

They told Okino that at some time probably around fires like this; they had decided there was no separation between people, the landscapes and everything living around them. It had become clear to them the rivers, the mountains, the plains and the forests were a continuation of the spirit world which flowed through their lives. They reflected the cycles of life and death as they changed through the year. They were sustained and nourished by these cycles and the knowledge and wisdom previous generations had gained of them were held within their tribe. They suspected this spirit world to be the continuation of a greater spirit flowing through the stars they saw in the night skies.

They saw animals, as a further continuation of their wider spirit family who could also teach them further of the challenges they would face throughout their lives. They often seemed ill equipped to cope with the conditions and trials they faced. They would often come to this place and ask to be blessed by the spirits of these ancient creatures in their battle for survival. They had found the relationships the old trees had with the star systems, with the Star rises and the moon rises, as they were held for a moment between the ancient branches. So, they would align themselves with the cycles of the skies and their world. When they came to these sacred groves to give thanks and celebrate, they would ask the old spirits to share their ceremonial space. The cycles of life and death were most apparent here as they flowed through both their worlds when the leaves fell from the trees in winter and grew again in the spring as if they had died and been reborn.

In the wider landscapes, horses, buffalo and deer ate the grass and would be hunted by the wolves or the mountain leopards. Like a great river rising and falling as the year went on, the spirit flowed through their lives and the land; strongly one day and slower the next depending on the rain that had fallen or the starshine that had warmed; gentle rain would turn their fields green again in the spring and starshine would turn them golden in the summer. The winds sweeping in from the East bringing ice and snow in the winter were less welcome than the warm summer winds from the South in the summer. All came to have their own place in the cycle. For when winter spread it's icy hold across the land and all their preparations for those times had been made, they lit the fires in the long nights and told the old tales of the great wanderings; the great feats of endurance and bravery that had brought their ancestors, the heroes of their tribes to these sacred lands where they had been able to find such peace.

They remembered their own accomplishments which had brought in harvests, their successful hunts always celebrating their own skill and bravery. The children would listen and learn the wisdom; know where to find it in the forests and meadows, in the rivers and on the mysterious old beaches. They would see the correlation of the rising tides with the waxing and waning of the moon and start to understand how the Universe moved as one. They would feel the change in their minds and bodies in the landscapes of the full Moon on a warm summer's night; feel the thrill and the magic of the Star light as they watched it return and the trees again produce their leafy gowns and the crops their mothers and fathers had planted, burst from the ground.

As they made their way through their lives so the understanding of their world would grow and in turn they would pass it on to their children. For every boy and girl was encouraged to nurture their own connection with their land and the great mystery. When they saw the speed of the deer, and the craft of the wolf, the stealth of the mountain leopards and the ability of the fish to return to their streams year after year, the speed with which an eagle could pluck the fattest of them from just below the surface of a lake, they in turn became in awe of the strange and wonderful dreamlike world in which they found themselves.

The awe they felt soon became the respect they would need for their survival. Then in reverence they would return and celebrate in the old circle of ancient trees. They felt here, they had some cross over, an overlap with the spirit worlds; the invisible realms from which they suspected their own spirits had emerged at the beginning of their lives and to where they would return when they died. In these special places they felt their ancestor's, human and animal were always close and so they returned here to celebrate births and deaths as the passing of their own spirits between those realms beyond. They came to regard their lives as a privileged journey on which their spirits were formed and were able to grow in the wonder of the physical existence they experienced on Arimathea. It was her life as well as their own they celebrated, here in the old Sacred Groves.

They wandered back to the space between the houses and settled again. The men fell silent staring deep into the flames searching for the wisdom they knew to reside there that could guide them into the future. The light emanating from the flames showed the peaceful calm in their eyes as very gradually it increased and slowly engulfed the scene. Okino found himself again sitting by the lake. The ripples on the water had subsided and the mirror like surface still reflected the silent dragons under the drifting clouds above.

Now it seemed he had been given access to some of the collective memories of the dragons. This had been a history, a specific point in time. He recognized the early beginnings of the complex society that had subsequently developed across Arimathea; perhaps just before the time when the natural lore his early ancestors had lived by was soon to end. As if the dragons needed him to have this insight so he could understand what was to come. The scene around the lake started to fade and Okino woke briefly amongst the warmth and comfort of the great yak fur hides and the silence of the night, before falling into a deep and undisturbed sleep.

Chapter Sixteen
Entry to the Ruins.

Okino emerged from the cosy womb of his tent into a frantic hive of activity. The camp was being speedily dismantled and loaded onto the wagons. Mariella greeted him with a bowl of warm porridge. There was a selection of dried fruit scattered across its' surface. She asked him how he was before scurrying back to whatever she was doing, saying something about taking his tent down before everyone left. She seemed happy and relaxed. Okino in truth had never seen her any other way. Then he remembered they both had had a profound experience in the stone circle the night before. Perhaps at last she had felt justification for leaving her life to travel to this distant land on a tenuous errand to find his mysterious brotherhood of monks.

Since then he had dreamed about the fifteen dragons in what appeared to be a specific and organized gathering. He remembered seeing their winged energetic spirits flying in and settling down on the ridge, acknowledging each other's arrival. Had they all been woken in the last few days since he had woken the first dragon in the forest? It would appear so. Now they sat in council, remembering and conferring, perhaps reassuring each other after their long absence from the world. Perhaps they were regenerating their powers, gradually feeling their way back into conscious being in whatever parallel state they existed. He had felt the nature of their blended concentration as he sat on the banks of the lake. They clearly had the ability to project their own collective consciousness into his own. The abilities he had recently learnt and expanded in the monastery appeared to have allowed him to make a channel into the dimension in which they existed.

Then he was on his horse, surrounded by the little caravan advancing towards the mountains. Okino thought they looked larger as if they may reach them by the end of the day. He thought of his journey with Haran in the truck and how fast they had moved through the mountain ranges. How slow the yaks were and how hot the Star had become. Mariella rode up beside him.

"We should be at our destination by evening."

"That is a great relief."

"Did you sleep well, I looked in to see if you were all right, you were out cold." Mariella pushed her horse forward to get a better look into Okino's eyes.

"I'm sorry I've not spoken to you this morning. One of the children has been ill and I have been helping his mother look after her."

"Don't worry. Although it perhaps would be a good idea to come and have a conversation with me every now again just so that I know which dimension I am in."

"Is this to do with what happened in the stone circle?"

"Partly, but I dreamt again last night. The dragon's showed me another tribe slightly more advanced than the one we saw last night!"

Mariella reached over and stroked his shoulder affectionately. He began to tell her about the fifteen dragons as their journey towards the mountains slowly continued.

Hours passed drifting through the dust and the rising heat of the day before the little group came to a fork in the road. It was marked by two large boulders. One road would take the families to their village. Mariella and Okino would continue onward to where the ruined settlement Mariella had found in the memory banks of her library on the other side of their world, awaited them. There were hugs and tears and promises to visit the little town before she returned to her life on the other side of Arimathea. She had grown fond of this little group of mountain people. She had been surprised there was so little difference between them. Hopes and dreams though played out in their different worlds, were the same. They wanted security and love, safety for their children to grow up fit and strong. They feared the approaching technological world, distrusting the men who came to sell this new dream into their lives. They watched as their husbands were slowly tempted, intoxicated by the promise of what these self-assured confident men were offering them.

Mariella feared the advance of this machine for the same reason as her mountain sisters. She and they feared what was coming was pushing away something precious which had taken many generations to build. If it was lost it would be lost forever. Mariella had seen their concerns for their village happening on a global level as traditions and rituals were pushed aside for the shiny and the new. For now, however, it was the yaks who dictated the pace as the families slowly started the last leg of their journey towards their homes.

They did not have to ride much further before the ruins finally came into view nestled in amongst the lower slopes of the mountains as they came through a small outcrop of hills.

"There they are,"

Mariella exclaimed,

"At last!"

She flashed a grin over her shoulder at Okino before urging her horse rapidly into a gallop. Okino's horse was in no mood to hang behind. Although he had been riding the horse for some days and had become used to the different movements with which the animal moved at various speeds, nothing had prepared him for this new experience. Once he had decided there was little he could do to stop his own horse bolting off after Mariella's now disappearing rapidly in a cloud of dust, he became resigned to this new adrenalin filled sensation. From a carefully coordinated collection of muscles and bone, the horse had transformed its movement, as muscle and sinew tightened, into a single strand of raw and continuous power. Okino could not distinguish between the end of one movement and the start of the next as the horse galloped flat out into the cloud of dust.

He was able to gently steer the horse out of the cloud so he could see Mariella ahead. She looked back and urged her horse on faster as she saw Okino approaching. Now they were racing. Okino felt a flood of exhilaration coursing through his being. Wind and dust flew into his face as he surrendered to the powerful creature beneath him, felt its power flowing through his own body, adjusting to this new rhythm, he let the horse run, urging him on as he gradually gained on Mariella. Her long blue robe and dark hair flying out behind her as the two horses raced each other across the plain. He looked over at her and caught her eye. She grinned back at him and urged her horse on faster. All thoughts and anticipation of what lay ahead disappeared in the sheer exhilaration of speed, of thundering hooves and the rushing wind as they hurtled towards whatever discoveries awaited them. They were as close now as they ever had been in the days since their meeting. Sharing the experience of these beautiful animals and their awesome abilities far away amongst the deserted mountains, their friendship became complete. They both sensed the moments as the transition occurred, acknowledged it within themselves and to each other as their delight filled what they knew to be precious moments.

Soon the dusty ground became uneven and strewn with stone and the horses had started to tire. They pulled up the panting creatures and dismounted, patting their sweating, steaming flanks. As they waited for the horses to catch their breaths, they dismounted and observed the little settlement nestled between the converging lower slopes of two hills for the first time. The icy peaks of the mountains beyond towered above them. Silently they led the horses into the old stone ruins.

It was now late afternoon and the ruins were bathed in the soft light of the Star as it began its downward descent behind the mountains. The first buildings they encountered were small dwellings the inhabitants had made for themselves. There seemed to have been little overall planning and they seemed to vary in size. Only the remnants of walls, stoutly built from crudely formed stone now remained. Trees and shrubs had invaded the entire settlement seeded from the sparse population on the lower slopes of the hills. They were growing randomly in amongst the buildings and added a wild magical atmosphere to the deserted settlement. They also told of the return nature had made once the humans had for whatever reason decided to move on.

Okino and Mariella wandered silently leading the horses through the dilapidated structures. Mostly they appeared to have one or two rooms. They decided they had been made for one or two people. Possibly in the case of the larger ones a small family. There seemed to be no sign of recent human activity. The walls were sporadic and large sections had probably been plundered for building work elsewhere. As they moved through the buildings Okino and Mariella started to imagine how the occupants might have lived here. In the quiet of the ruined settlement Okino was already imagining a lively community. He could see them in their houses and in the spaces between, joking and telling their stories.

As the dwellings came to an end, they walked into a larger open space surrounded by more substantial buildings. Beams of Star shine fell through tall pine trees creating further areas of shade in early evening light bringing a mystical timeless quality to this larger area. Large solid walls were constructed from deeper, wider pieces of stone which appeared to have ensured their survival. Many still retained doorways with heavy lintels supporting stonework above. Through the doorways there were empty open spaces varying in height. All the roofs had long since disappeared often leaving the tree canopy above giving a feeling of open airy enclosure. The late afternoon Star light filtered gently through the spiky branches of the pine trees bringing soft cool light to the spaces below. Solid stone floors had obviously proved more difficult to plunder. Nature had invaded many of these spaces without any consideration for the built forms. Creepers and vines had wound their way through openings and up through open roofs and into the trees above. Birdsong floated down and echoed through the stone shells. The contrast of stark bright light and the deepening shadows gave a contrast and dramatic three-dimensional impact to the ancient structures resisting and blending with the forces of nature.

It was hard for Mariella and Okino even to make a guess at the function of these larger spaces. However, they were able to imagine large numbers of the community gathered together within them. Perhaps eating under the same roof or gathered to perform their rituals; perhaps there was a library or workshops where they made or repaired the things they needed for their life here. There was no sign of any of this activity and these long deserted buildings had become blended with Arimathea in a way those who had conceived and built them could never have imagined.

Mosses had clung and spread their luscious green, ferns had unfurled and ivy draped over the old stone walls inside and out. The interiors and exterior of the larger central space beyond ran seamlessly together over the old stone thresholds. The buildings stood like old sentinels in some ancient pact made with the spirit of the mountains to contain and gently hold whatever had inspired the people who had built them. Okino and Mariella stood smiling, silently absorbing what had been revealed to them after their long journey. They were already wondering how and why it had all come to be, but for the moment they stood in awe of how breathtakingly beautiful it all had become in its' own journey down through the centuries to where it had now met them here.

On the far side, central to the open space, there remained a partially collapsed wall. Remarkably an archway had resisted the forces of disintegration and was clearly an important point in the procession through the little settlement. Beyond this wall there were more trees amongst an unpaved stretch of grass where a herd of mountain goats were grazing peacefully. Mariella was drawn to the sounds of falling water. Eager to go through she looked round to find Okino surveying the space between the larger buildings. He had noticed a fragmented circle of flat paving. Although many stones had been removed there was unmistakably a pattern of radiating lines emanating from the centre. A circle of trees had grown around the remaining stones. They seemed to be older and taller, generally more substantial than their surrounding family. Okino walked around the circle and stood in the centre, closed his eyes and drank in the atmosphere. The trace of human activity was faint now but there was undoubtedly something special underlying the atmosphere here.

He thought for a moment he recognized a sharpened frequency in the light as his mind flooded with imaginings and ideas about all he was seeing around him. He remembered the emptiness of his initiation vision. This place seemed to be reassuring him however, that nature would always recover and eventually engulf the temporary constructions of the human race. This had all happened a long time ago and yet still the bones of these crude buildings were standing. There was a similar sense of desertion here. Yet nature had survived, whereas in his vision whatever held it had disappeared entirely. Again questions about what lay behind the fabric of his world were arising. It was indeed a strange and mysterious place.

Mariella walked over to him and stood with him for a few moments allowing him to drift slowly out of his contemplation. Then beckoning him to follow her with a smile, she took his hand and lead him towards the arch. They led the horses through into the space beyond and simultaneously gasped in amazement. Where the slopes of the hills and the mountains had met, they had formed a rocky valley. It was higher than the grassy plain on which they stood, by the height of one of the single storey buildings. In the valley between, the melt water flowed from the peaks above and cascaded over a rocky lip into a pool below.

Entranced Okino and Mariella walked towards the waterfall. A gentle mist hung over the pool. The surface fizzed softly and continuously as bubbles of air burst across the surface from the depths of the pool below. Multiple rainbows formed and faded in the low rays of the rapidly descending Star. The pool was formed amongst large boulders now shining with the moisture fallen from the air to rest upon them. Intricate ferns projected out over the water and mosses clung onto the stones wherever conditions allowed. Three gnarled pine trees grew out of the gaps in the rocks, their twisted stunted, clearly ancient appearance, further added to the enchanting scene lying before them.

They sat down on the closely cropped grass, eyed suspiciously by the goats who had moved to what they had decided was a safe distance and silently enjoyed the serenity now surrounding them. The fatigue from their long journey in the mountains rapidly fell away as the heat and dust was replaced with the crystal-clear atmosphere of the cool mountain waterfall. The horses grazed hungrily. Her own horse nuzzled Mariella as if she was sitting on the last piece of edible grass. She laughed and stroked his soft muzzle playfully. Smiling quietly and talking softly to them, she started to remove the saddles and the packs strapped onto the horses. Soon the pile of tents and travelling paraphernalia untidily occupied a patch of the formerly pristine riverbank. The light was fading and the two travellers in one last effort wearily pitched their camp amongst the boulders. The soft sound of the waterfall punctuated only by the occasional splash of a jumping fish returning to the icy depths below.

Okino remembered back to the day when he had gone down to meet old Sareki and how they had first noticed the mystical abilities of his stone. He dug down into one of his pockets where it was carefully stored, took it out and held it up to the dying rays of the Star. The flash from the depths of the Universe it contained blinked reassuringly out to him. He held it carefully, further contemplating the river and the waterfall before him. Slowly the glare on the river started to fade and he was able to see the fish below the surface of the river as they wavered their muscular bodies to hold their place in the strong currents. As he watched he started to see the individual currents as they flowed through and out of the pool and started their journey down the channel of the river. He watched as they wound together under, over and through each other forming what appeared to be several continuous spiralling muscles carrying the energy of the river. He felt how that energy was carried through the banks and into the ground beyond and how he himself could feel their coils lightly entering the soles of his feet and dispersing through the rest of his body.

So, here was the source of the lightness he had felt as he had walked up to the river and noticed generally in the ruins. His acknowledgment of this sensation then brought further wonders to the landscape around him. He noticed colours had become more vivid, physical space had become deeper and more solid but at the same time had a transparency in which he could see the underlying vibrational quality unique to each object and life. He felt this new wonder transferring through his senses into his consciousness, filling him with a new ability to look on the structures of his world and see the underlying mechanisms in the layers of time and space.

Mariella who had been struggling with one of the Yak skins, looked over to where Okino was standing. She noticed his presence had changed, it seemed as if his aura was very slightly glowing. He held his hands with open palms to the world around him, head and eyes raised to the last of the stars' rays in a stillness she had rarely witnessed in another human being.

She gave up with the yak skin, quietly walked up beside him and sank into the peace of the moment. One of the fishes jumped from beyond the watery currents to capture some unfortunate creature before splashing back to disappear back into the depths. The sudden noise brought Okino back from his reverie. He turned, smiled at Mariella and handed her the stone. She examined it carefully, started as she saw the flash and looked at Okino in wonder. She noticed immediately how her perception of the space around her had changed.

"This is amazing, Okino, where did you get it? You didn't tell me about this!"

"No, I didn't. I mean I didn't mean not to tell you, but what with everything else I've put it to the back of my mind. Can you see the fish?"

"Yes, I can see the fish and the energy in the currents, in fact the energy flowing through everything!"

What she was seeing took her breath away. The stone he had given her had sharpened and adapted all her senses. She had immediately been able to clearly see the fish swimming in the crystal-clear water.

"The spirit energy is very strong. No doubt why this little community was built here."

"...and why there are so many beautiful fish...so perfectly suspended, floating in this pristine clear water. Almost like the spirits would be in such a place,"

"I think they are the guardians of this place perhaps the embodied spirits of the energy flowing through it, swimming in the currents they know them intimately as they change from day to day. It will be they who know the secrets that it holds. The only beings with direct and unbroken lineage to the spirits who survived what happened here. If only we could talk to them."

Mariella smiled.

"Perhaps we will. Who can possibly tell what is in store for us here?"

"If not these spirit fish I have a feeling there are many other spirits close to us already who will be willing to help us."

Mariella recognized why he had been chosen to become a priest in this land where everybody saw the world as a magical realm full of spirits flowing through the consciousness of Arimathea as humans or trees, leopards or chickens and now the fish swimming just below the surface of their own watery world. Now he was here and probably before he had arrived, he was searching for the spirits who had always inhabited this place who would enable him to further understand and so unravel the mystery he had become involved in.

She put her hand on his shoulder, looked out over the river herself, as the last of the Star disappeared behind the distant mountains. She had been right to bring him here.

Chapter Seventeen
The Origin.

Later in the evening Okino and Mariella sat in their new camp leaning up against one of the larger boulders wrapped in a yak hide and watching the glowing embers of their fire. They had cooked a vegetable stew made from their supplies and now were as close as they had ever been, intimately sharing the confines of the hide binding them together, sharing their body heat as the temperature started to drop. The Moon bathed the gardens in her silvery light. The river and waterfall shone with a supernatural quality amongst the shadows cast by the surrounding trees. The two travellers relaxed in each other's company.

"So, what do you think of this place I have brought you to, Okino?"

They were so close. In the serenity he had found in this place the young monk had also found his fondness for his young travelling companion was growing. How much longer could he deny his feelings for Mariella were growing stronger? If he relented what would be the consequences of his actions? His connection with Arimathea was deep now and becoming deeper. The life of the celibate monk was for the purpose of keeping this relationship sacred. Deep in those turquoise eyes he saw Arimathea as she spoke to him on the mountain in the snowstorm. Perhaps she had come to him incarnated in the form of this spirited young woman so they could be fully united. It was a tempting thought denying the wisdom of his order. He wrenched himself away from thoughts of this further enchantment now slowly but surely weaving its way through his being and turned his gaze back to the scene on the banks of the river.

"It is an amazing place. But something has happened leaving this beautiful place unsettled for perhaps many hundreds of years."

Okino felt the light he had first noticed in the circle of trees growing in his mind. He continued.

"It feels old but strangely timeless. This settlement almost certainly indicates someone recognised it's special quality"

An almost imperceptible breeze blew through the trees. The embers in the fire glowed brighter for a few moments. Images and whispers of the people who had come before alighted vividly into Okino's mind.

"I think people have often discovered this beautiful place full of pristine natural energy. The water is pure and will always be flowing from where the mountain snows at some altitude are always melting. I think there is something here which makes people want to return. I say that because I think there is something more to this place than just the river. I feel perhaps there may be some healing presence here.

"This all seems very vivid, Okino!!"

"It's incredible, I think a story is surfacing through into my thoughts."

"Ok I'll shut up then!!" She snuggled into Okino a bit closer settling in for the story unravelling in the mind of the young monk. Whatever or whoever was feeding into his consciousness had obviously made a link and it seemed to be getting progressively stronger with every connection made. She allowed herself to drift back to the time Okino was uncovering. There seemed to be no separation. She could see no sign of the settlement that had subsequently grown. She was only aware of the ghostly shadows of the buildings behind her. But they could have been a part of her past or her future. There was just the eternal flow of time. One moment now shimmered before her in the moonlight. Okino had paused. She looked up towards him. He had again closed his eyes and appeared to be concentrating. There was the face of a strong, sensitive, good looking young adult dedicated but as yet unsure of the role he was playing and would play in the evolution of his world.

Their meeting and all that had subsequently happened had left no doubt in her mind. Her experience in the stone circle the previous night had laid to rest any doubts haunting her. All the memories she had of Arimathea had been carefully run past her. All the beauty and variety of her lands and seas, all the creatures living in amongst the powerful forces that had brought her to this point, the power and ingenuity of her own species and the wonder and tragedy it had brought upon her world. The overwhelming love she had felt had brought tears to her eyes. Was she also being compelled to play her part in the next chapter of Arimathea's evolution? For these moments she relaxed in new certainty and waited for the young monk to continue with the story...

"We are still in ancient times, but the nature of Arimathea and the landscapes the humans were inhabiting have been fundamentally changed. Many of the wildernesses in the temperate zones have been deforested or drained. People no longer wander from place to place but have settled down to farm in the reclaimed areas. The structure of the land has changed and the constraint of territory and boundaries has transformed the way they live. Villages have been established as they have come together in areas where their labour and skills were most needed. Larger towns have grown up centrally to the villages and have become the sites for the markets where the products from the surrounding villages and farms are traded. Many of the towns have also become home to towering castles, looming over the poorly built habitations of the rest of the population.

Many trades have grown up amongst the people. Craftsmen of all kinds, who would have provided expertise in their community, while also working in the fields, now specialised in their chosen craft. So the smiths made their forges, the carpenters and potters set up their workshops; The butchers, bakers and green grocers all set up their business in whatever centres could provide enough trade for them to make a living from the service they were providing. As these centres grew and their products flowed out from the villages and towns into the cities and down to the ports, a new tradesman had emerged. The merchants moved through this network carefully assessing the products they could trade, buying in one place and selling for a profit in another. Travel and the movement of goods was time consuming and often a dangerous business. The farmers and other tradesman had been willing and eager to surrender a small part of their profit to the merchants who could move and sell their products in the other towns or villages where they were needed.

During this time there was a young merchant, called Rabir, who had been travelling between the towns, villages and down to the ports. He was working in the business his father had built, trading the glass and pottery being made in his village on a route his father had built up over the years. He had grown up with the craftsman and had a great respect for the beautiful products they made. He had always enjoyed their company and had often watched them working when he was younger. His father was pleased he had joined his business and as he grew older, he was less able to travel long distances and liked less and less to be away from his home and family for long periods of time. Rabir had taken over and added to his old trading route travelling further and further through the land.

He relished the long journeys with the horses and the old wagon his father had always carefully maintained. He would set off with his cargo of delicate glass and pottery products to the towns and villages along the route where he would exchange them for the currency of the region or any small items he knew he could sell to the traders in his own town. He would try to arrive in a destination when he knew there was to be a market and set up a stall amongst the other traders.

On the most distant point of his journeys he would reach the old seaport of Zedocha, where ships brought products from across the seas of Arimathea. Here he would buy fine materials, spices, carefully crafted jewellery, unusual everyday items he knew he would be able to sell for a good profit in the towns and villages on the journey home and indeed back in his home village.

As people travelled across the seas between countries the risk of disease spreading had increased and on one of his journeys Rabir came down with a fever. He was ill for a few weeks it seemed but was eventually able to fight off the worst of the illness. As soon as he felt he was strong enough he started his journeys again.

However, one night the weariness he had experienced since he had recovered again overwhelmed him. He had to rest for a few days in a small tavern where a local healer came to see him. In their ensuing conversations, the healer mentioned she had heard of a place in the foothills of the northern mountains where the nature of the land and air was so good, people who had gone there suffering in the same way as Rabir had returned greatly revitalised if not entirely cured.

So, in the next months he guided his life so he would be able to travel to this place. He had travelled through the wider lands for many days. They had remained uninhabited so he followed only the crude instructions he had been given by people along the way. He found in many of the villages there was always at least one person who had visited or had a story they had heard from someone else who had benefited from the qualities of this mysterious place. As his journey continued, he became increasingly intrigued by the reputation of his destination.

Eventually he arrived here, at this waterfall nestling in the valley between the hills and the mountains. He had brought supplies for a few days and he rested here against this very rock. He let the wonder flow through him. He became entranced and enchanted by this beautiful place. His strength began to return, helped he was sure by the ambience he found here. He left and returned to the village and his trading. But Rabir remained haunted by his experience and again guided his life to return. On his travels he heard further stories of people who had recovered here and decided he would return and stay for a longer period. He organised his business carefully so he would be able to stay for longer. He investigated the nearest towns which were two days travelling away. He found they were rarely visited by traders from the coast. He found there were a number of high value items he could sell in these towns to make him enough profit to have one of his traders visit them regularly. With a small detour provisions could then be brought here if it ever became his new home.

Slowly in the coming year he established a place where he felt he would be able to live for longer periods of time. He built a solid timber house from trees he had found on a wooded hillside further up the valley. He floated the trunks down the river and hauled them into place with the help of his horses. He used scree which had tumbled from the upper slopes of the mountains to build walls and split the stone with his chisels to make the tiles to cover his roof. He built his house solidly with a hearth and a chimney so he would stay as warm as these hills would allow in the severe winters. He experimented with planting vegetables in the springtime and brought up some domesticated goats. He soon found he could leave them to their own devices when he went back to trading his route. In his travels he occasionally mentioned to one of his customers this new project. They would listen with interest to his story but then would be sceptical about his ability to live so far away from the economic system they had come to depend on so closely.

There were those however, who became fascinated by his idea and eventually travelled to this enchanted place where he was slowly building a home. A small group of pioneers who had been captivated by the place, perhaps because they had come with their own illness and been revitalised by their stay, started to share Rabir's dream and changed their own lives with the aim of eventually moving here. They built their own dwellings and in prolonged stays began to plan their new lives.

They all had become fascinated in the ability of this place to heal them from the tiredness and disillusion they had come to feel under the increasingly rigorous administrative regimes being adopted by the leaders of their country. Many people had thought for some time the power of their rulers was becoming far too closely entwined with the power of the priesthood. For many generations now, the old spirits of their ancestral lands had been demonised and exchanged for new gods from beyond their world. Communication with these new gods, apparently, was possible only through the priests. Now their rulers were able to control, with fear of retribution in the next world, the growing populations from whom they frequently demanded heavier and more ridiculous taxes. These taxes were cruel and oppressive and were draining the population of its vitality and creativity.

They talked at great length as they spent more and more time in the settlement about their experiences. Away from the spies of the priests, they soon started to talk about the surviving myths which told of the old spirits of light living within Arimathea. They started to become convinced it was they who were affecting their entire experience of being here. They decided this energy was flowing through everything and decided the plants and trees could contain revitalising properties. They started to build a knowledge of the plants they found and tested their theories. They decided early on they would never be physicians and would not claim to be. However, they became confident they could reduce the weariness contributing to the illness they had felt recede in themselves. They concluded after more experimentation, if their bodies were stronger, they would have a better chance to fight any illness they were faced with.

They continued their work by infusing particular plants into water from the springs on the hillsides to make plant tonics and after considerable success with the people who visited, they decided they would start to trade the tonics throughout the land. In their travels the tonics they sold did prove successful. They told the people who they thought might benefit from their discoveries and often discussed the many possibilities in their new venture. They were quietly excited and around their fire one night, while discussing the implications for their brothers and sisters trapped in the grinding monotony of their lives, they decided they would call their little settlement Asima.

Inevitably as the success of the tonics became more widely known, people started to visit the newly founded settlement of Asima. Initially they were nervous of such beneficial claims. But they were soon won over by the explanations Rabir and his friends gave and they almost always benefited from their visit. Respect for the little group spread and soon a steady flow of people began to arrive. People started to give donations to the settlement as they noticed a real improvement in their health. Rabir always insisted donations made were to be as practical as possible. So, farmers brought grain to be planted in a field transformed by the donation of an old plough. Building materials and the skills of the builders themselves were traded when lives blighted by illness were transformed enabling life and so business to resume. If nothing practical could be given, then currency was accepted and was used to buy essential items as numbers in the community started to grow.

Winter in these hills as always would cause the most challenges. Many who came to live here during the Summer would return to their communities as the winter months approached. Rabir and his closest friends would stay and administer to whoever ventured into these frosty regions and catch up with any work they had not had time to complete during the busy summer months. Rabir noticed the energy he had felt running through this place also began to run through the lives of the people who had come to live here and subsequently through the life of the whole community.

He was able to watch the settlement of Asima evolve in the beautiful energy he had initially felt. Slowly but surely everything was arriving; on the carts and wagons of the people who returned or through the will of the little band of people who had chosen to stay. Helped by the skills offered, several larger buildings were carefully thought out and built to enhance the natural beauty of their surroundings. Fields started to yield the food they needed and animals started to thrive and produce much valued milk and eggs. At first Rabir saw only the singular energy he had first recognised at work as the settlement grew. But soon he started to realise the energy though undoubtedly local to Asima was inextricably linked into perhaps it's fortunate position on the planet of Arimathea. He began to recognise other aspects contributing to the overall well-being he saw growing around him.

It soon had become apparent Asima was well placed to take advantage of the best of the Star throughout the year. She nestled in front of the hills and mountains making a natural Star trap but also sheltered her from the ferocious winds coming from the North. This gave a prolonged growing season and with guidance and careful thought the surrounding land was irrigated from the river. Soon a good variety of vegetables, wheat and corn crops were being grown. Perhaps as a result of this relationship with the Star, Rabir noticed time seemed to have a very special quality here. He noticed this when they started to build the first dwellings to house visiting families. Very few mistakes were made with the construction of the stone structures they were making. He found strategies arose easily and were generally carried through decisively and with very little argument. The ability to think creatively here, combined with the enormous will and drive for the settlement to succeed continuously brought about successful outcomes. Similarly, in the fields, an understanding of the nature and balance of the climate and its relationship with the soil arrived relatively quickly and enabled the optimum crops to be grown from an early stage. In both these activities Rabir saw and felt the love was growing for this place and so the care being lavished on every activity.

They agreed on plans for the future they thought they would be able to carry out in the light of their successes. With the establishment of the dwellings and as harvests were successful, the birth of the first children became landmarks in the establishment of little Asima. The children were born and grew strong and healthy and soon their gurgles became laughter as they played happily beside the river watched carefully by their adoring mothers and fathers.

With all this success, the failures or disasters were always met with surprise. Although the Star brought life and fruition to Asima, she was not exempt from the darker aspects of life in these mountains. The winter snows brought bitter cold and preparations in those first years were inadequate. Timber for the fires and food had become short and more animals were slaughtered than had been thought necessary. Children had suffered from the cold and hunger. Journeys through the icy conditions to the outside world had to be made. Careful preparations looking into every possible situation likely to arise had led to a successful return of the little band who had ventured out for provisions when the worst of the snows had melted.

But to buy provisions needed in the winter was expensive and left less money for buying further seed to plant in the late spring when the crops planted before the winter were harvested. Despite these setbacks Rabir always had a feeling the spirit of Asima wanted them to succeed with their venture. Every now and again something unexpected would happen to transform a situation that under normal circumstances would have turned out very differently. Particular paths of action were often blocked or came to light for no good reason. Whether it was building a roof on a house or rebuilding the irrigation to a field, the strategy would have to be rethought before it could be continued.

Visitors were amazed at the speed at which the settlement had been established. But Rabir and his little group knew it was because many of the tasks they had carried out, although always physically demanding had been made easier when the building materials, the method and strategies all seemed to have been provided perfectly in time as circumstances had arisen. Every now and again the settlers noticed what was almost certainly an intervention from Asima. When they came to assess the probability of such a coincidence occurring and the chances were found to be almost impossible, a magical intervention was suspected rather than ever proved. They became used to the occurrence of these coincidences and decided they were only what had always happened in their previous lives. Although they did seem to be more prevalent here in Asima.

Rabir became progressively more curious about the nature of the spirit allowing them to continue in this manner. The coincidences and timely arrivals became so frequent and opportune they started to wonder whether it would ever be possible to communicate with what appeared to be the beneficial spirit of this place. They began to devise sophisticated meditation techniques, allowing them to travel deeply into the presence they felt all around them. In the same way they explored the surrounding countryside. They found the presence was strong on the surrounding hills and in time came to realise the waterfall was only one of a number of special places all with their own particular characteristics.

As they made these discoveries the settlers debated long and hard as to the nature of these characteristics. In time they decided each one of these places was a different aspect of a whole entity. Each place made them feel very different. Almost as if an aspect of their own beings became more pronounced. It wasn't long before they started making links with the enhanced quality of their performance, creativity, ingenuity, their will to succeed, the care they felt they were able to lavish on everything they undertook and everyone with whom they came into contact. They came to understand the presence as a consciousness that had become part of them and everything around them. They started to wonder whether their own animals and the wild animals living in the surrounding countryside were also part of this consciousness. They soon became convinced after various encounters this was true. Once this had been accepted the consciousness started to give startling insight into the nature of the world around them.

Rabir had noticed this particularly amongst the predators and the wild goats living on the surrounding hills and mountains. In his wanderings, every once in a while, he would come across a snow leopard. Generally, it would be in the distance and the leopard would be stalking his favourite prey the mountain goats. They were silent stealthy creatures, enveloped in thick furs and equipped with bone crushing teeth, long claws and astounding agility more than enough it would seem to outwit the goats, inferior it would seem in every way. Rabir soon learnt this was not the case.

He watched on several occasions as a leopard slunk invisibly towards a goat feeding unaware on the steep mountain slope. He watched as finally the leopard with no cover left, would have to reveal herself as she bounded the last few strides towards the seemingly doomed goat. In a fraction of a second the goat would launch himself from where he was feeding, into the air and hurtle off down the mountainside. The pursuit would continue from rocky crag to rocky crag down through the gullies and across the loose scree. Two creatures, the hunter and the hunted flying down the mountainside. Bound after bound, twisting and turning, every sense and sinew operating to maximum efficiency, adjusting balance in all this momentum, as forces shifted from one foot to the three others over continually changing surfaces, reassessing velocity split second by split second, in their almost vertical descent, driven by one thought only; their survival.

The goat to live another day, to graze with her young on the tough mountain grass and the leopard to feed herself and her own young who now lay asleep curled up safely in their den. In this death-defying chase down the mountainside Rabir suddenly began to understand how this spirit he had noticed at work as he built his community, was working through the whole of Arimathea. It had always provided a means for evolution by providing opportunities to progress in the race for survival. If a goat became too fast for a leopard to catch, leopards would starve, and goats would become too prolific for the sparse amounts of grass and vegetation existing on the mountain. The goats then would starve also. If the leopard became too good at catching the goats, then gradually their food would be eradicated and the leopards would die out. Each creature then, had to become more complex to stay in the race while a careful balance was held to allow both to survive.

Deeper and deeper they delved. There seemed to be no end to the possibilities of their discovery as they realised the full potential of such a consciousness. From this point they started to see the planet of Arimathea in a very different light. She was the potential fulfilled of an amazing…an amazing what…. what was this thing, was is it a spirit? They had felt its continuation through their own lives, so perhaps it was one huge life force inhabiting the entire world. If this was so then there would be others who had had these experiences and almost certainly come to similar conclusions.

If anyone in their own land had this knowledge, then they were keeping it very quiet. Ideas about supernatural forces were now restricted to external all-powerful deities who demanded rigorous standards of conduct. These were upheld by the priests in their temples. Absolute allegiance to their kings now connected to these new deities in the same way they had been linked previously to the land, was rigidly bound into the law. However, here was a way of understanding the world which fundamentally threatened these ideas. On nights when they were able sit out beside the river and look up at the clear night skies, they started to wonder whether something so magical and inexplicable, so outside their own ability to provide explanation had perhaps come from the stars, from a different world.

On one fine Summer's morning Rabir was moving their herd of goats up into one of the cooler mountain pastures. The heat of the Star had baked the landscape and everything in it; an extreme the settlers had come to relish. Fires could be lit for cooking and the struggle against the relentless cold of the winter months was for a time forgotten. The Summer months brought out another inhabitant who mysteriously disappeared during the winter months. Rabir delighted in their reappearance. As he rounded a twist in the path or came over a rise, he would see them briefly, basking in the Starshine on a rock before they scurried away at lightning speed. They were the stone coloured lizards who were best suited to the severe heat typical at the height of summer in these hills.

On the rare occasion he spotted one before it spotted him, Rabir would quietly sneak up on the lizard to admire the intricacy of what appeared the carefully orchestrated designs of their tiny coloured scales, the detail around their bright intelligent eyes, legs and claws, the sinuous nature of their long tails and their calm dignity. Rabir supposed they had come from another age. Their poise of superiority came from the knowledge and wisdom they held from many millennia past, long before humans had inhabited Arimathea. He imagined all their intricate detail may once have belonged to a far larger creature; that some evolutionary twist had brought them to this smaller size destined now to scuttle away to hide under a rock at the slightest sign of danger. This is how his encounters would end as he came too close for the lizard's comfort.

He reached the high pasture that morning in good time. He waited for the goats to settle, eating the lush new grass thriving in the cooler temperature of the higher hills. Then he climbed to the top of a small rise above the pasture with an excellent view over the valley below. He could see the little settlement in the distance and the river emerging from behind the hills and snaking off into the distance. It was a marvellous position for the contemplation of his new world; the vast open sky disappearing into infinity beyond the far distant horizon. Now the valley was dry and dusty, but in a few months' time it would be again covered in the pristine white of the winter snows.

On such a day he was often able to watch the eagles soaring high above the hills and plains scouring the ground below for some vulnerable creature to make a meal for the rapidly growing eaglets back at their eyrie high on a mountain ledge. Rabir always wondered how it would feel to soar with only the warm wind under those feathered wings; to float in the vast expanse of blue ethereal sky and then silently plunge back to Arimathea at unimaginable speeds to execute some unfortunate creature possibly unaware until the last second of its life, of the peril about to come upon it. He was in awe of these creatures, as he was of the snow leopards and the lizards. His admiration was less for the goats but he had great respect for their tenacity and the agility that could test the craft of even the wiliest mountain leopard.

He let these thoughts drift through his mind as he wondered of his own race and his own skills to reason and process information, make decisions, act on them, to bring about some specific outcome. Was this power more or less next to the eagle or the leopard? A comparison seemed irrelevant and he settled back to enjoy the peace and tranquillity of the hill. As he quietened his mind, he felt the familiar presence rising from the hill and merging into his consciousness. The peaceful wonder it brought never ceased to surprise him. The world around him would take on a new dimension, more than it had been even in the minutes before when he had soared high into the skies with the eagle. Now he saw the leopards and the eagles, the lizards, the goats and even himself with a common origin, one spirit being possessing the potential for all the qualities and attributes of all these fabulous creatures. Slowly from the depths of the consciousness came a stream of vivid imaginings.

Later he described whatever came spiralling up out of the hill on which he was sitting as a magical stream of catalytic light. It wove its way through all the ideas and thoughts he had had in those last few months lighting them up with new understanding and realization. Now he could see and feel all the places he had discovered and creatures he had encountered almost simultaneously. The waterfall and the hills, his favourite trees, his time in the fields now resonated with knowledge previously he had not understood.

The wise gleam in the sandy lizard's eye became everything their race had contemplated while sitting on their rocks. The icy cold in the wind ruffled fur on the snow leopards back became all the winters her species had survived. He felt the air under the wings of the eagle as the vast interconnected system of winds and breezes whispering around his world. He felt their will to survive over the forces of death in the same way he himself had been driven to continue his own life. His thoughts were woven into those of the lizards and the leopard and the eagle. He was able to see how in their own ways they must share similar ideas about the phenomena of time and space as he, to care for themselves and their young day after day, year after year, to understand threat and safety, to decide what would be beneficial and destructive for their lives.

As he sat on the ground on top of the hill, he had a sense of the whole of Arimathea as one infinite consciousness. He could clearly see how all these creatures, plants and landscapes had grown as part of her and so in turn had come to possess her qualities, her shortcomings and characteristics and reflected her infinite potential. He realised his striving to understand and improve his life came directly from this consciousness and now in these moments, these realizations were being relished by this conscious planetary being, here in his thoughts and in his life, in the life of this astounding world he found himself to be a part of. He himself with his intelligence and ability to sense and reason; to understand his place within it, with the leopards and the lizards and the eagles all having their own role in the intricate tapestry of life. It had all come to be in this harmony with just enough imbalance to slowly but surely continue its' own survival and develop towards its own ends.

Rabir sat there on the hill as one thought unravelled in the spiralling light now engulfing his mind. The leopards, the lizards and the eagles, indeed himself and all the life on Arimathea could be recognised as one infinitely diverse energetic light filled being. It had mastered the elements of the physical universe to ultimately walk and talk, fly and swim, with claws, teeth and wings and yet also had become a great philosopher able to fathom out the inconsistencies between the immaterial and material and strive to resolve the differences in all it was able to bring into existence. This being of spirit light and energy had travelled through the vast emptiness of time and space carrying the knowledge and dreams it had accumulated on its' journey down the eons and found Arimathea, alone in an orbit around her Star. An ancient spirit soul who had also come alive in this world. They had come together in this continually forming Universe and blended all they could share and a new spark of consciousness had been born and had grown into this fabulous world.

The name for this light eventually given and which has reached us here in our mountains, was dragon, subsequently depicted in many different cultures in many different regions of Arimathea as a blend of spirit and consciousness. This understanding Rabir came to must have been revealed to many others before. It may have been an image this being felt humans could understand, or an image they themselves made as they came to know it and fetl it working through their lives as Rabir had done. But he is important in our story because of how he and his people re-established a connection and how he subsequently worked with this spirit in the community growing around him."

Okino became quiet. The moon had passed its highest point and now was sinking towards the mountains in the distance. Mariella was still beside him. He moved carefully to ascertain whether she was still awake. She grinned up at him as he looked down. Moonlight shone from her deep blue eyes.

"That was amazing, Okino!! You told it like you knew the story and had been telling it for years."

"It felt exactly like that. Like I knew the whole story, almost as if I had been there right up to the point where the dragon revealed himself to Rabir; Almost like I had lived his whole life. The detail that I knew, that I could actually see happening in front of me was incredible."

"Did you recognise the dragon as the one you first encountered in your own dreams?"

"The image wasn't really a dragon. Rabir was given the idea of a consciousness from which all the life on Arimathea had emerged. I have become used to the idea of the dragon being associated with such a consciousness and so it has clearly taken on that familiar form in my dreams"

"So, the image of dragon is something we have projected on to a spirit being, who arrived from somewhere out across the universe, which combined with Arimathea to complete her and bring this entire world out of their combined consciousness"

"It would appear so!"

Okino and Mariella were silent. They looked around them as if they were truly seeing their world for the first time. Mariella whispered

"...and so, do you think we are all part of this one extraordinary being?

"It does seem to make sense of how it has all come to be and it appears the dragon, for whatever reason, chose then to share this knowledge with Rabir. Perhaps more importantly he has chosen to share all this with us now."

Again, they were silent. Then Mariella turned to Okino,

"We were right to come to this place, we've only been here a few hours and well, it quite literally speaks for itself!!"

"...In more ways than one! Tomorrow I want to investigate the remains of the circle I found in the square. I have a feeling it may reveal the next part of our mystery!!"

They both fell silent, thinking through what they had heard in the cosy warmth of the great yak hide. As the Moon started to sink behind the mountain, Mariella carefully extricated herself from Okino gave him a brief kiss on the cheek and retreated into her tent. Okino crawled into his own tent, with the memory of Mariella's warm body imprinted on his. Although again he battled with his feelings for her, soon, when he was wrapped again in the warm hides he fell into a deep sleep and dreamt of a normal day with his fellow monks back at the monastery.

Chapter Eighteen
Revolution.

Okino awoke the next morning after a sound sleep enveloped in the warmth of the great hides. He had been tending vegetables and picking herbs with one of his brother monks. He had known all he had been told in the story the night before as they had debated the various life giving and beneficial properties of the vegetables the monks grew in their gardens. It had been stressed to Okino, the monks should always maintain a healthy physical state, so important for their meditative life. The rest of the community had always benefited from the knowledge the monks had gained and generally managed to remain healthy on what were often inadequate food supplies. Okino remembered the starshine on his face and the vervent green of the strong vigorous vegetables so carefully nurtured in the thin mountain soil, filled and fertilised with the waste of monk and animal alike.

The synthetic material of his tent glowed brightly around him telling him he had slept well past Star rise. He thought of his day ahead and the explorations he intended to make within the ruins. He wondered what might be revealed to him next. His connection with Arimathea was strong here. Perhaps stronger than ever. It seemed he was being given the history behind the mystery in which he had become involved. How this had all come to be. Now he felt a new resonance. The possibility this mystery and the temple of the dragon were connected had become even more likely. Immediately he could see the continuity as he compared the two communities. The similarity between Rabir's dedication to communicating with the spirit of this place and the work of the monastery to maintain a relationship with Arimathea could almost have been continuous. The idea of the link intrigued him.

He also remembered how there had been a sinister underlying menace to the growing human activity. Perhaps here were the first signs of how the strange need of certain humans to amass power for themselves over their fellows at the expense of everything around them would eventually cause the separation and disinterest in their world. There were clear links with these developments and his friend Haran who had been seduced by the offers of the businessmen from the South to grow the Keraika more intensively and the resulting pollution of the lakes. Creative and productive people who worked honestly and tirelessly to make their lives better for themselves and their families were being ruthlessly exploited by men who had no interest in growing crops or even the amazing properties of the Keraika plants.

Suddenly inspired to delve deeper into the mystery, he unravelled himself from his hides and crawled out of the cosy warmth of his tent. Mariella had not yet woken. All was quiet. The birdsong infused the sounds of falling water permeating the cool morning air. Okino stretched happily into the blue skies as he cast his eye again over the beautiful scene before him. He noticed there were embers still glowing in the fire. He set about bringing them back to life and sat back watching a brightly coloured bird hop from rock to rock as he heated the water remaining in the pot. He made a hot drink, mixing herbs Mariella had purchased in the town with the boiling water.

He turned his attention to the ruined buildings lying behind their camp. He was easily able to imagine the little community going about its daily routine. People moved from building to building with food and water, somebody was fixing one of the roofs. The continual chiming of the goat's bells mixed with an ethereal chant drifting out from one of the larger buildings, echoes of the beautiful notes lingered on the mountain breezes, so real in his mind, Okino listened again more intently to determine whether it was really there. He smiled to himself. Echoes were breaking through in so many ways. Arimathea had opened his mind, his entire consciousness to her and now he was willing to listen to what she had to say.

This new thought startled him. He felt a new certainty which until now had eluded him. The story was unravelling and from somewhere in the shells of the ruined buildings behind him she was beckoning to him. He finished the last of his drink and made his way excitedly towards the square beyond. He paused at the threshold represented by the archway in the stone wall. He was drawn to the centre of the square circumscribed by the ring of trees and flat stone slabs in its centre. He walked over the grass and stepped onto the slabs. The circle was twenty paces across and he counted sixteen radial lines, now fragmented, originating from the centre. Immediately he became aware of the Star and its movement though the sky, the orientation of the whole settlement and the surrounding countryside in relation to it. He started to walk around the circle. As he moved, he found the focus of his thoughts was subtly changing. Again, he felt the old being he had discovered surfacing within him and recognition of the unending flow of time that had come to a very specific point in this moment.

How pure and uncomplicated his world and the Universe around him could become. In all its infinite complexity it chose the soft breeze and the warmth of the rising Star to speak to him. His racing thoughts of mysteries and intrigue down the ages were calmed. How easily and perfectly this journey had entwined into his life and his world; no longer static or linear it was spreading out and delving into the very deepest roots of Arimathea and the dimensions of consciousness running through her. As the forms around him became further enhanced by the strengthening light he saw the possibility of dialogue with them all and most importantly with the secrets they held. Powerful feelings of elation flooded through his mind. He had slowly circumnavigated the circle of stones lying in the square. He was back where he had entered facing the morning Star.

He settled down on the grass just within the stones and after a while closed his eyes to feel the bliss of the warm light energy filling his body. The light shimmered and again began to fluctuate at different frequencies. Out of this light the buildings around him were slowly forming but not in their ruined state but in the pristine condition they had enjoyed in the earliest part of their existence. He was in the breeze, in the chiming of the bells, embedded in the green auras of the plants and in the soft warm earth from which they had grown; he was in the stone forming the buildings in which the settlement was flourishing; He was in the light and so in the essence of the enchantment embedded within it. He remembered the swirling light sensation Rabir had experienced as it had flooded out of the hill and how his imaginings had become solid and experiential. There was no movement from one space or time to another. Everything just began to materialise from the dawn of a fine early morning all those years ago.

People started to emerge from the buildings, stretching luxuriously in the beautiful Starshine. A tall man noticed him and raised his hand in greeting, grinned in recognition and headed towards the circle where Okino was sitting. He sat down on the circle, quietly whispering,

"Good morning Rabir, I trust you slept well."

"Indeed, I did, Erilan."

He laughed,

"Stranger dreams than normal I am afraid. I don't think this place will ever cease to surprise me. It seems to have layers of time through which I am constantly being moved. Last night it was as if I had become a traveller who had come here from the far distant future when all this had been forgotten and the world had moved on."

"Have you any idea why he came"

Erilan replied and Rabir continued,

"Sometimes I have strange flashes when I am carrying out my everyday tasks. As if there is more importance to everything we are doing here than we can possible imagine."

"I have the same feeling. The question I suppose is… What could we possibly be doing that will reverberate so far into the future and have implication enough for someone to want to find out what it is?"

The two men are silent again and raise their faces to the early morning Star. Okino feels the light swirling around them feeding into them, enlivening their minds with the realisations they had found enabling them to make decisions in their respective times. Erilan looked over at Rabir.

"Let's go back to the beginning. Unravel it all from there. This wouldn't have all started for no reason and the ends may well have their eventual outcome in the time of the traveller. We cannot possibly know when an idea or the consequences of an idea have run their course."

Rabir turns to him thoughtfully.

"…and so often we carry on because our lives have presented us with circumstances which take us where we think we should go. If our goals are to be met, then why would we question the way being shown to us?"

"If we could see disastrous consequences for the world around us?"

"Would we? Do we always think of every outcome when we change our course? Maybe we think of the obvious ones but there will always be the consequences of the consequences as the world goes on. We can never know all the outcomes of our decisions. Circumstances stack up all around us and provide possibilities and sometimes we choose to go with one because there is just no other way open to us!"

Erilan laughed and then,

"So why did you start all this, Rabir?"

"Originally I became ill and someone told me about the healing properties of this place."

"But there was something about your illness and the illness of everyone who comes here to engage with this place. I think there we will find the root."

"I came here and most of the people come here because they are exhausted. Their bodies are tired, their minds are tired and they never have the opportunity to recover."

"I think you are right. It seems many have never been allowed to recover because their bodies are not strong enough to fight off the illness which is becoming more prevalent in our land. The reason they cannot recover is because they are enslaved in a system governed by mean and ruthless men who have no conscience and who will not let them rest. They will literally work their people to death to follow the perverse ideas of entitlement they appear to think they have. They hold their positions of power by terrorising our countrymen and women with their ghastly punishments; if we don't pay their wretched taxes, if we don't drop everything and go to fight in their senseless wars or when we dare to raise why they have the right to do these things to us.

They have taken away everything about our lives which we held sacred, our connection to the lands in which we have grown and for generations have worked in the old clans and tribes. In a few generations they have taken everything they want from us to pay for their castles in which they lead their ridiculous lifestyles."

Rabir nodded in agreement. He sat quietly listening with his face to the Star thinking about all he had created around him. He could feel the life enhancing energy so many people now were coming to experience working through his mind initiating the questions he needed to ask.

"So how did they become like that, these fearful monsters stalking our lands. They do seem to want more of everything. More land, more armies, more people to work for them as if they are frightened something terrible will come for them and what…what are they frightened of."

"I think they are terrified of the world their kind originally made. I think perhaps at one time we knew about our world and the place we had in it.

Like a wolf or a mountain leopard. We knew what to do, because we had been doing it for millions of years. Following the animals and the seasons we were part of the world. We moved through it without fear. We told stories to our children which explained their world, so they knew what to do. We followed the rhythms of the world because they were also our rhythms, so we slept and ate when we needed to.

Somewhere the chain was broken, we stopped telling the stories. Then a new story started to emerge when we stayed in one place. This new story needed rulers who decided they needed armies and castles to defend themselves from the other monsters who had grown up in other tribes and were terrorising their own people in the same way. Ultimately they feared the world they didn't understand and they wanted to dominate it, control the uncertainty they saw in it; they want power over it because they fear it will come for them one day and consume them and take away all that holds it at bay for them."

Rabir knew now and Okino felt the moment as it came to him. He relaxed deeper into the light, into the knowledge as it rose in his mind. This is what the time traveller had come for. To feel this moment and its possibility to change the world. His next words flowed out of the light and into the minds of the others who had come to listen to their conversation in the circle.

"But here we have found the old ways again. The light living in the world, always known by our ancestors who roamed the land as their ally and guide. Not something to be afraid of or hide away from. But something to embrace in all their journeys as part of themselves and equally as part of the land and the stars in the night sky. All of us who have come here have been denied our ability as spirits of Arimathea to fully experience this light. Now it only comes to us from the priests of the new religions. They serve the frightened rulers and threaten us with their lies of the terror awaiting us if we should disobey their decrees, step outside their systems of control which starve us and our children and leave us no time to enjoy the lives we have on this beautiful world. Now the light they have denied us has been found again and it is coming for them because we have found the truth and have been invigorated and inspired to live again in the old ways as best we can in this world we are making."

"If ever such an idea as you have spoken took hold amongst the people of Arimathea then certainly our future and so our history would be changed forever. I think this is what our traveller came to hear."

A young woman who had joined the circle and had listened to the conversation, then started to speak.

"I have recently arrived but already I have felt the wonder of the light here. What you have said is true Erilan. It is what our rulers have always feared. Already many people who came here have returned to their own lands where they have rediscovered the wonder embedded in the old sites found by their ancestors. They are starting to reject the fear imposed upon them by the priests of the new religions. The benefits are easy to see and feel. As their ability to commune again with the spirits or the dragons of Arimathea, as they have come to be known, so their influence on the material planes is again proliferating and becoming more obvious.

The connections and coincidences are becoming more widespread as the dragons grateful for this new found interest are dreaming out even harder their wisdom into the light. The illusion of fear is starting to fall away as the true wonder of their existence is being fully realised. In the towns and the villages people are again watching the Star rising with a new awe they have not felt before in their lives. A great surge of enthusiasm is welling up, Rabir, as the people connect back into the wonders their world can offer. Your ideas and the feeling of injustice the people are experiencing is beginning to spread like wildfire around the populated areas of Arimathea."

The circle of people and the buildings of Asima faded, the light swirled and changed as a new aspect of the dream took hold. Okino now found himself in the cool elegant gardens of a temple deep in the heart of one of the larger cities. It was surrounded by a large wall. The noise of the city beyond could be likened to the annoying drone of a large insect. Starlight sparkled on the water of the lily filled ponds. Carefully arranged stone paths wound their way through the carefully tended trees and shrubs filling the extensive walled area. Two priests sat on an arbour deep in discussion. The peace and tranquillity were maintained by the wall separating the gardens from the city. Here, separated from the grime and struggle of everyday existence endured by most people, was where the priests received the communications from their gods.

On the other side of the wall a small group of people had inhabited a building with a substantial garden. They had deduced the temple gardens would have been where the city was originally founded; where the spirit of this place would have been strongest. Today they had decided they would attempt to reclaim the old site back from the temple in the name of the dragons of Arimathea. Okino watched as three men and two women walked unopposed into the temple garden and settled down to start meditating and preparing to once again initiate their connection with the dragon. The priests watched as all this transpired and then made their way over to where the people were sitting on the grass.

"I am sure you realise these gardens are for the exclusive use of the priests of the temple." The first priest ventures tentatively.

One of the young women opened her eyes and smiled at the old priest.

"We no longer recognise you have the authority for sole use of this land and so in the name of the dragons of Arimathea we now reclaim it on behalf of all the people of this world."

The old priest appeared slightly unnerved, turned and smiled nervously at his fellow priest.

"Aah yes, the dragons of Arimathea we have been hearing so much about. A short-lived cult no doubt; it will perhaps have some influence but like so many ideas that have no basis in reality or law it will disappear rapidly!"

He emphasised the word 'law' as he summoned another priest and whispered to him aside from the five protestors.

"We will need to have these young people removed as quickly and as smoothly as possible"

The priest turned back to the young people.

"So young lady, how do these dragons give you the authority to claim these gardens back in their name?"

"They are the original spirits who transformed it from cold dark rock into the paradise you see around you. I think they have a better claim on ownership than you, Sir!"

".and you are certain of this!!"

"I am, the evidence is all around us."

The priest looks around at the beautiful gardens he has spent the best part of his life maintaining. He had instructed gardeners and landscapers for most of that time to best preserve the refined beauty that had become his responsibility.

"I see the evidence of hard work and years of dedication to preserve this beauty"

"It is not your pretty plants we have come for, sir. It is the spirit living in this ground we have come to liberate."

Suddenly there was a shout behind them. The girl continued to watch the old priest carefully. He turned to see a large section of the wall to his garden had started to collapse. A great cloud of dust rose and rolled out across the gardens. His mouth fell open, his hand went up to the top of his head and smoothed the little hair he still had. He watched aghast, as people emerged from the cloud of dust and climbed over the rubble, walked calmly into the garden and found a space to sit down amongst the butterflies unaware of the momentous events unravelling around them as they flitted from flower to flower.

Okino felt the outrage of Arimathea's people as the nature of the deception wrought upon them was fully grasped. He sensed a revolutionary wave steadily gathering momentum in the populated areas of Arimathea. People started to tear down walls and fences wherever they found them and re inhabit the lands taken away from them. Inevitably violence broke out as the landowning rulers tried to control the revolution. But the situation had spiralled out of their control. Okino watched their desperation and fear as more and more of the population flooded onto the stolen land. He watched as a group of soldiers on horseback, armed with swords and lances rode onto a field being occupied. An assortment of temporary solid structures were being built by the men. Women were cooking around the fires, children played with their animals amongst the trees. The soldiers systematically killed everyone and everything alive on the field and left the bodies hideously butchered where they had fallen to be eaten by the crows.

So, a great war broke out on Arimathea. The people massed together under their chosen leaders. Men and women who rose out of the circumstances they found themselves in, strangely inspired to stand up and lead their people against the fundamental injustice wrought upon them. They fought fiercely and passionately against the armies raised to quell their rebellion; the people terribly aggrieved against their leaders who faced the possibility of losing all their power; neither side would back down and thousands were slaughtered on both sides.

As the conflict raged for a turning around Arimathea's star, communities and families were split by the practicality of the revolution. As more and more men and women were maimed or died agonisingly painful deaths from their injuries the will of the general population for the rebellion inevitably started to weaken. The disillusioned population started to defect to the stronger armies of their oppressors where they fought with guilt and regret against their brothers and sisters with crafted weapons rather than the adapted tools of the rebellion. The conflict was seen to become hopeless to more and more of the population, so the ranks of the ruler's armies began to swell. Again, the balance of power was turned in favour of the armies loyal to the kings.

Those who still found the domination of the rulers unacceptable and who had less to lose than their brothers and sisters, became outlaws, retreating to live in the forests and mountains. They continued a guerrilla war attacking the forces of the rulers whenever they could. They fought under the emblem of the dragon and in their camps continued to development their relationship with the spirits of Arimathea whom they found to exist strongly in the wild places they now had rediscovered. They started to live closer to the trees in the forests and near the mountain streams in the high places where the larger armies of their enemies were vulnerable and dared not go.

They continued to forge stronger relationships with the dragons, guided by the stories they had heard from their fellow fighters who had met Rabir or his followers. They learnt how to live from what they could find in the landscapes and were helped by the unmistakable coincidences that slowly but increasingly started to happen around them. Without the mass support of most of the population their resistance became less and less effective to the point it became little more than an annoyance and the repression of the revolution by their overlords was seemingly complete.

However, in these ragged communities a closer relationship was being formed between the outlaws and their world. Unwittingly they had become involved in the age-old struggle that would always arise between the forces of creation and destruction. Their connections with the dragons became more consistent and unequivocal. There was urgency to these new communications that could not be resisted giving the outlaws new hope in their struggle.

Chapter Nineteen
The Council of the Dragon.

Okino now found himself in a column of men making their way quietly up the side of a mountain valley, along a path three or four paces across. He was clearly in the consciousness of another man. Already they were high above the valley floor and he could see the flickering of fires in the distance. There was a full moon shining brilliantly in the night sky. It was a warm evening and his fellow travellers chatted openly as they continued to climb. They were a rugged collection of characters all dressed to withstand the rigours of their existence apparently living in these hills. There was an excited edge to their conversations. Okino knew where they were going and the purpose of their mission. It seemed the dragons had asked to meet the outlaw forces face to face in this dimension. Their sympathy for the cause was obvious but the outlaws always had assumed the dragons would be unable to help them. This now appeared not to be the case. Now trusted leaders and the mystics who had made the connections with the dragons were heading for a designated peak high in the mountains where they would find out what the dragons had in mind for their struggle against the ruling lords.

"How do you think this is all going to happen?" inquired the man who was walking next to Okino,

"These dragons, do you think they can be trusted? After all they are only like the forces of nature don't you think and we know how unpredictable they can be!!"

Okino found he could carry on the conversation. He remembered his last meeting with Arimathea in the cave way off in the future at this point. He wondered briefly whether the problem she had explained about then had originated in this time.

"Something must be going very badly wrong for them to reveal themselves I should imagine!"

There seemed little else to say at this stage and the two men went back to their silent ascent of the mountain. Okino found himself fully absorbed in the nature of the land around him and how it appeared to him in the Moon light. Every step he took he felt the changing, ebb and flow of energy beneath his feet. The rock face directly to his side glowed in the gentle light. In the distance the wolves howled their delight as the moon rose again illuminating their precious night world. It seemed like they were walking into the very stars themselves as they approached the summit of the hill.

Climbing the last steep and slippery path, they emerged on a level expanse stretching perhaps thirty or forty strides across. They gathered around a pile of timber previously prepared in the centre. One of the men produced some fine kindling and a flint strike. He lit the fire and it crackled into existence. There were murmurings of approval as the men turned and took their places seated on the ground in a circle around the fire.

Okino felt the man's apprehension as the flames gathered strength. He felt all he had learnt from Rabir flash through his being. His own experience of the world became concentrated somewhere in the front of his mind. Images of his little town perched in the mountains, memories of the revelations he had received as a child that had set him on his path, his encounters with the wild animals on the mountains and some of the most profound conversations he had had with the monks, his meeting with Arimathea, all whirled through his mind into the concentration now becoming a gentle light shining through his being. For a moment he remembered he was sitting in the broken circle in front of the old ruins, but this thought was quickly extinguished as again he began to concentrate on the flames now roaring thunderously up into the night sky.

Then, the gentle light building in his consciousness started to move out of his body and towards the fire. This was happening all around the circle. Glowing spheres of light were slowly but deliberately and purposefully moving towards a place just above the top of the flames. As they joined the light expanded and began to engulf the entire circle. The energy from the fire appeared to be feeding itself into the light. Just before it became completely impossible to look into, the light stopped growing in intensity. In the centre something was starting to form. Something like a shadow spreading itself through the Light.

Okino recognised the form starting to emerge. In the now fluctuating green light, a sinuous form was developing wings, legs, arms and a massive head containing the familiar green eyes. The green light ran through the steadily forming limbs as the energetic form of the dragon started to absorb the light from the etheric womb of the surrounding universe. It roared in defiance up into the stars as its form began to fluctuate. Other animals started to appear. There was the powerful form of a great stallion rearing up on its hind legs, it had the wings of an enormous eagle attached to its back, the horse transformed completely into an eagle but then a stag appeared rearing up gouging the air with its hooves. Again, the image changed into a huge and terrifying bear. The circle of men shrank back at this the most terrifying apparition as the great paws struck out and reached up into the stars.

Okino thought the stars seemed to be glowing momentarily brighter as the dragon started its final transformation. The bear shrank and its great ragged body and limbs slowly changed into the more diminutive but no less imposing form of a tall male human being. In the last stance of the bear he was reaching for the stars his eyes closed in deep concentration. The fire had been completely absorbed into the creatures as they had formed in turn and now the dragon stood as a man in the glowing ashes of the conflagration. Slowly he lowered his arms and opened his eyes. He looked slowly around the circle of men who peered apprehensively back. He was head and shoulders taller than any man in the circle. He was wearing a long coat made from the stout material worn by many of the men in those mountains. His dark hair hung shoulder length framing a rugged face. Okino noticed immediately the faint green glow in his eyes. Confirming to him this was a dragon but now in human form.

"Greetings my friends, freedom fighters of the planet of Arimathea, it is good to be amongst you at last!!"

The outlaws were astonished by what had just happened and sat very quietly, curious as to what would happen next. The dragon signalled for them to get up and walked over towards them. They rose cautiously as he approached and shook all their hands warmly. Their initial hesitant response to this new being receded quickly and they greeted him enthusiastically and all introduced themselves to him.

Once all their introductions were complete the dragon walked over to the pile of wood, picked up an armful and placed it in the centre. Some of the men helped him and soon the fire was rebuilt. The dragon inhaled deeply and breathed out a jet of flame which instantly ignited the pile of wood. The crowd of men grinned and nodded to each other in recognition of the power the dragon had demonstrated. He waited until they were quiet and he had their full attention.

"I am Merilon, I have come as a representative of the ancient race, you have come to know as dragon. We settled in this world after a long flight across the Universe many thousands of years ago. We carry the dreams and memories of the many worlds we have known. When we release them into a planet where a creation spirit such as your Arimathea has come to dwell the potential for a new world to come into existence is once again created. In our union all the life you know and see around you has gradually evolved. However, in the dispute you are having with your leaders the seeds of the death of this planet are being sown.

This world and every other world is surrounded by the deep wastes of space. The tiny sparks of life able to miraculously form are continually subjected to the enormous forces acting upon them; many of these forces carry only the urge to return to the original peace, the dark emptiness of Oblivion. All life battles against this urge. In every species born upon this world the urge to continue the spark of life from one generation to the next is paramount above all else. However, as the expanses are unfathomable so are the forces dwelling within them, even to us. They will take advantage of any weakness they can find in the web of life and work their way into any vulnerability to bring about its destruction. The fundamental disagreement you have with the rulers of your world which you have failed to resolve, allows them unknowingly, to continue in their dark service of Oblivion. As they enslave and exploit you and Arimathea with their lust for control and power, they are sowing the seeds for the inevitable destruction of this world."

There was a stunned silence amongst the outlawed freedom fighters. They had known what they were fighting for and against was fundamentally wrong, but never in their wildest dreams had they equated their struggle with the eventual destruction of Arimathea. Okino was the only one in the group who knew what Merilon was saying. Living in the future Merilon had described, he knew where the exploitation would lead.

"We have always had very specific laws governing any interference or help we are prepared to give as a world is developing. But there is an important destiny for Arimathea. It lies far off in the future beyond these primitive battles you are now fighting. But Arimathea will never reach such a future unless this destructive path is somehow altered. So, we have decided we will intervene to help you at this point in your struggle. The powers we have at our disposal will soon give you an advantage and the majority of the oppressed people of the world will re-join the struggle when they realise this cause is no longer hopeless. Myself and other dragons will join in an alliance with you. With our ability to manipulate the atmospheres in which circumstances and outcomes are determined and our ability to influence the elemental forces, we will divert Arimathea's path away from her destruction and towards her freedom and health!"

Okino then watched as the strategy of the dragons to undermine the power of the ruling lords began to surface across the face of Arimathea. He had learnt from Rabir how his community had benefited from the support the dragons had at the time unknowingly given. It had operated like a tide of good fortune running through their whole operation and all who became involved with it. The plans they made had come to fruition with very little to divert them along the way. Fair and seasonal weather and a good supply of fresh water had enabled crops and human beings to flourish alike. The health of the community had remained strong and had been threatened only by minor ailments but they had been easily cured with the plants they had been directed towards.

The livestock they had raised also remained strong and healthy and few had been lost to the leopards who for the most part had enough wild goats to satisfy their sparse populations. Perhaps most importantly they had the support of the traders and the people who had come to be visitors to the community. A regular trickle of supplies had arrived from the merchants who were prepared to go a little out of their way but who always benefited themselves from a good night's rest in Asima. It had soon gained the reputation of being able to restore calm to even the most hectic life. It had become known as a beneficial place where lives could flourish again as they began to embrace the beautiful natural energy they had been shown and found all around them.

However now, the tides of good fortune soon started to turn on the ruling lords. As the dragon's manifest in the world they made sure everyone knew the nature of their presence. Fifteen dragons, flew from the wild places where they had been brought back into the world, over their countries, over the towns and villages so there could be no mistake they had returned to the surface of Arimathea. They visited each of the rulers in their human form who had taken an authoritarian and repressive attitude to the rule of their countries. Each was introduced to the history the freedom fighters had been given and each was told the implications of their present actions for the future of their world.

Carefully the dragons explained how the acquisition and the holding of the lands around them with violence and the threat of violence, enslaving the people and amassing further power and wealth through the indiscriminate exploitation of the people and the resources inherent in the land, would cause the eventual destruction of Arimathea as this strategy gained momentum over the next millennia. The dragons then recommended the land and any the wealth amassed through any strategy of fear and intimidation be given back to the people. In this way the entire population would benefit from the gifts and productivity Arimathea had given to them. A time frame for all this was then explained. Evidence of the changes were to be seen within at least one year from that day. If no evidence of the changes were seen after this time then action would be taken by the dragons.

The ruling lords listened in stunned silence as these tall green-eyed men and women who had somehow managed to walk through all the defences of their fortified castles delivered their 'recommendations', which also sounded like threats and ultimatums. They found it immediately worrying when they ordered the guards to throw them out of the castles, they were unable to get anywhere near them and they had been able to leave peacefully without any further trouble. It was strange how the uninvited visitors had left an atmosphere of peaceful calm amongst both the military and domestic residents of the castle and a distant dreamy look in the eyes of their wives, daughters and sons.

The recommendations and stipulations of the dragons were totally ignored and for the next year the exploitation of the general population was increased as the defences of the castles were improved and extended. Decrees were issued in all the towns making it clear anyone who was found to be associated with the dragon lords, as they came to be known, would be executed in a painful manner. As the year went on rumours circulated as to the nature of the imminent rebellion.

Greatly favoured amongst the general populations was that the dragon lords would bring their legions up from the caverns in the depths of Arimathea to wipe out their oppressors. In the armies of the ruling lords a creeping fear was undermining morale as stories circulated of entire battlefields ablaze with burning corpses, incinerated from the heat of dragon's breath. Anyone who was not previously contracted into trading or providing service with the landlords now declined despite the promise of even greater rewards and those who came to the end of their contracts did not renew them. Even by the end of the year the lives of the ruling lords were becoming more difficult as rumours abounded as to the nature of their fates.

So, the action of the dragon lords had begun long before the year was up. At the end of the year with the defences greatly enhanced, the landlords waited for the attack for which they had prepared. They were surprised after some weeks nothing had happened. But very distinctive changes had come over their fortresses.

The food supplied to the castles had been intermittent although the soldiers had been working harder on the fortifications and many were showing signs of under nourishment and were falling ill. At the same time the crude drainage systems taking the waste out of the castles began to collapse. Unable to find a workforce who were willing to enter the castles and repair the drains the water supplies soon became polluted. Many of the soldiers began to fall ill as the waterborne diseases spread like wildfire amongst the garrisons and the populations of the castles. They realised the dragons were effectively besieging the castles with their powerful magic and the soldiers suffering from illness and starvation started to leave the castles. This process began furtively but once everyone knew what was happening mass desertion began openly. The ruling lords were now locked in their huge castles without their armies who returned home to their families.

As the tide of good fortune had swept over Rabir and his community, ill winds now blew over the power bases of the ruling lords and they rapidly started to fall apart. Any kind of relationship they had with their tenants, merchants, servants even their direct families started to disintegrate in the strange circumstances arising in the world around them. They were simply deserted as their power bases fell away. The soldiers were slowly nursed back to health by the local populations with effective cures which also mysteriously appeared. Their weapons and armour were hidden and soon they were able to resume their former lives. With the structure of power the landlords had exerted over the general populations of Arimathea dissipated, the people of Arimathea started to reclaim the land that had been taken from them.

An organisational system to replace the ruling lords was debated and discussed at great length. It was decided it should be allowed to evolve over the coming years with respected members of the community voted onto the councils. They would preside over meetings where decisions effecting the development of the community would be taken. Everyone who chose to would be able to attend. Slowly the lives of the newly freed citizens of Arimathea were able to find their new paths into the future. Land was released and everyone was given enough to grow their own food and perform whatever skill they could provide. A sense that a new era was starting as a wave of optimism flooded across the lands of Arimathea. Never again would a small number of people be allowed to command so much power over so many. The ruling lords virtually imprisoned in their collapsing, disease ridden castles with only their family members who chose to stay, were now seldom seen.

Chapter Twenty
The Return of Oblivion

Okino had watched this whole process unfold in his state of deep meditation in the courtyard of the ruins. As he watched the farmers returning to their farms and resuming their businesses he started to drift through the atmosphere as if on the winds being blown out across the lands of Arimathea. Everywhere he could see the results of the revolution. The great fortifications stood silent and brooding, like vast sulking monsters whose sharp teeth and claws had been removed leaving them unable to catch or consume their prey. Higher and higher he drifted up into the furthest reaches of the atmosphere until eventually he was far out into space where he was able to see the entire blue green planet of Arimathea floating amongst the infinity of space surrounding her. A shiver ran through his being as he remembered Merilon's words.

"As the expanses existing are unfathomable so are the forces that exist within them."

The darkness then seemed to thicken and envelop his little world as if preparing to suck out the newly found energy it was enjoying. The echo of the chilling truth reverberated through the stars and played over and over in his mind. Far beyond even the emptiness between the galaxies, star belts and nebulas, beyond the fabric of his own dimension, he grappled to find some solidity in the laws governing the struggle between life and death and the great ebb and flow of this mysterious Universe.

As he delved into the depths of the vast expanses of space to find some certainty, some contract which described the ultimate rules of engagement between these age-old enemies he could find none. He felt only the vigour and the power of the stars burning in their nuclear ferocity transmitting their light and heat out across the darkness in the sure knowledge that eventually it would fall upon some darkened world. There it would once again nurture the miracle of life; but it was clear from the moment of inception it would feel the urge to return to oblivion as it again struggled to gain its tenuous hold.

He struggled to find some conscious spirit, some essence behind this urge, that also, like the dragons had its origin in the collapse of some previous Universe. Some notion of destruction that had been born, so powerful it's residue would always remain in every molecule of its re-incarnation. His human instincts told him he should find a race of ruthless spirits who were in eternal battle with their adversaries in life. He wanted to find the evil twisted monsters his race had invented to explain their misfortune or acts that seemed beyond natural occurrence. He wanted to find the malevolent spirit that could turn men into the devils who were capable of depravity beyond the limits of their angelic origins.

As he searched to the edges of the darkness, as men had always searched for some excuse for their vile actions against their fellow men, against the creatures with whom they shared their world and against their very world itself, he found only the vast emptiness of space and billions upon billions of tiny bursts of light at different stages of their existence. The very youngest, tender and fragile, but growing slowly and surely, stronger and stronger, until once again that strength would slowly be overcome by the emptiness. Its vigour would begin to fade and eventually die as the force of light held in its molecular structures passed into the realms where it would await its eventual reincarnation into some further body.

This urge for emptiness would creep in naturally as the life force began to weaken. Okino wondered how it was the darkness was gathering strength now the dragons had exerted their other worldly abilities giving them so much power on Arimathea. The dragons had manipulated the forces of life to combat those forces of emptiness which had found a hold in the human race. As he contemplated his blue green world and how life had come to be there he remembered the goats and the snow leopards and their tenuous existence together on the mountain, and how the evolutionary systems of life, depended on the processes of death and renewal to be in balance for their continuation.

If there ever was an imbalance in this process, then it would become a systemic weakness which in turn would have to be redressed. The ebb and flow, the built-in failsafe system ensuring the continual existence of the Universe was now in operation on Arimathea. The powerful dragon race had taken a calculated risk by challenging this equilibrium. By using their magical powers, they had taken the war for Arimathea onto another far more dangerous level.

Chapter Twenty-One
The Dragon Light.

Mariella had awoken from her sleep. She lay in the warm glow of her tent contemplating the revelations of the night before. It seemed she had been brought here to the birthplace of a mystery that had originated on Arimathea many centuries ago. Her dreams had fluctuated between the life she had led in Straam and then strangely reinforced what she had heard of the rise of the little settlement. She recognised the connections Rabir had made with his world. She recognised how it could have been possible for him to learn the fundamental truths of life on Arimathea by sitting quietly and contemplating his world from the hours she had spent in the wildernesses around her home and the longer journeys she had taken which had ultimately given her the confidence to travel to Jahallala.

She smiled to herself as she remembered the conversation she had had with her father when she had told him this was what she wanted to do; his silence as he stared deeply and inquiringly into her eyes as if for the last time. How he had smiled as he was remembering all the special moments, many of which she would have no memory, as he told her he would give her all the support she needed if it would bring her back to him safely.

All the way through her journey, his influence, the power he had come to hold on Arimathea had helped her on her way. In the ports and in the towns through which she had travelled, she had felt the warmth and security he was able to command. The careful planning he had insisted she make, she had carried out meticulously, so ensuring she never travelled alone or unprotected. At each new destination she had met up with a new guide who had been recommended and rigorously vetted. The routes she would travel had been carefully agreed to avoid any unnecessary danger. She had hated this aspect of the journey but it was what she had agreed for him to allow her to carry it out.

Now she was out here in some of the wildest parts of Arimathea with the monk she had travelled so far to find, on what seemed now only a strange whim. She had found him more easily than she had anticipated. She had been scheduled to travel deeper into the mountains to find the Temple of the Dragon. To find Okino in the market had merely reinforced her belief her journey had been entirely justified. Again she smiled to herself as she remembered leaving the little museum and driving through the mountains back towards Straam.

She had stopped her car on one of the passes, climbed a little way to a promontory which gave fabulous views over the plains below to the mountains in the distance. The idea that there may be a mystical community of monks who had managed to preserve some ancient connection, long lost by the rest of the world, with a spirit underlying all this beauty had already completely fascinated her. It was then she had decided she had to find them. In the wake of all the degradation she had seen in her world, now it would seem appropriate such a connection should be brought out from its distant mountain hideaway into this complex industrialised world. Then hopefully it would be able to weave whatever magic it may possess into the future destiny of Arimathea.

Then she had become strangely enthralled by the idea of these ruins so distant from any other settlements, at the foot of these hills and mountains. They had given focus to her journey and for the lack of any other obvious destination this is where she had decided to come to. Certainly, so far she had not been disappointed. Her connection to Arimathea had deepened since the visit to the stone circle. The revelations in the story the previous night had told how this place contained something of the magic she had come to find and had initiated a similar curiosity in her as it had in Rabir the merchant.

For a moment she wondered about the authenticity of the stories Okino had told. Could this place really be so powerful it could transmit the memories it held to Okino. She tried to think of some everyday episode which even in a very basic sense was transmitting information in a similar way. The nearest she was able to get was the ability of some people to read into the physical phenomena which may lead to the development of a particular weather situation. But it seemed there was something far deeper at work here.

Suddenly she was gripped by an incredible excitement. Everything she had planned had come to fruition and she was here in this incredible place with a monk from the Temple of the Dragon who it seemed was receiving messages and communications straight from the consciousness of her world. She wanted to be out experiencing it. She disengaged herself from the complex weave of yak skins she had constructed around herself to keep warm in the cold mountain night, hauled her blue robe over her head, unzipped the doors of her tent and crawled out into the early morning Starlight.

Already she could feel the imminent warmth of the day in the rays of the steadily rising Star. She stretched herself up towards the sky and shook out her long dark hair. She looked round to see if there was any sign of Okino. There was none.

She turned her attention to the small river and the pool into which the waterfall consistently fell. Now in the fresh early Starshine it seemed even more beautiful. A soft mist had formed, as the first warming rays hit the colder water. The rainbows constantly forming and reforming seemed brighter and more vivid than in the evening light when she had first seen them. The delicious nature of the water played through all her senses reminding her she had not been completely immersed in water for several weeks.

She leant down and dipped her hand in the water. It wasn't quite icy. She tried to persuade herself she could detect something approaching a bearable temperature. The temptation had become too much and she ran back to her tent, dived in, rummaged around and emerged with the huge fluffy towel which she carried as her one luxury and walked back down to the edge of the pool.

Mariella watched the waterfall for a few moments. She knew that it, or something there was beckoning to her and she was becoming powerless to resist. She let the blue robe fall from her shoulders and down onto the ground. Now deeply exhilarated by the subtle mix of warmth from the morning star and cold mountain air on her body she put her foot into the shallow water at the edge of the pool. It deepened quickly as she walked in and the water was soon over her hips. She decided it was very cold but perhaps not as cold as some of the rivers she had swum in the wildernesses of her own land. In her experience she knew the pain would pass as her body became used to the temperature. Then she would have a few minutes to enjoy the water before her body heat was sucked completely from her by the cold. She had no time to waste and plunged into the pool towards the waterfall. She surfaced gasping as for a few moments the cold water prevented her from drawing breath. The cold was excruciating but slowly she forced herself to breath and she half swum half pushed herself towards the waterfall.

When she reached the falling water, she found she was able to stand on the bottom of the pool. Now the bubbling, fizzing water lapped around her hips. The depth of the pool seemed to be constant and solid rock below gave

Mariella a solid base on which to stand up in the flowing water as it cascaded over the lip of the waterfall down over her. She felt the weight of it as it crashed down onto her head and shoulders. She had to alter her stance to withstand the weight on her slight frame. In a few moments she had made the shift necessary to overcome the extreme temperature and started to enjoy the sensation of the water flowing down over her body.

All her senses registered at the peak of all their experience as water, coloured rainbows and mist mixed with Starshine. She felt the warmth in her body somewhere in the back of her mind, but for the most part her being had become part of the river. She felt herself become only a continuation of the life it held. The colour of the rainbows seared deep into the cortex of her mind, water splashing over her shoulders, back and breasts pulled her deeper into the physicality of her world, it thundered past her ears filling her mind with the primeval roar of the fundamental forces existing on Arimathea that had allowed life to be initiated and continue. In amongst all this powerful sensation Mariella felt herself grow into the experience the waterfall was giving to her. In the mountain water that would flow down through the plains, gathering strength on its journey before irrigating the lands which would feed thousands of people, she began to feel the creative, nurturing essence of her world reflected and rising in her own feminine nature; the profound truth that the birth whether of worlds, or eventually the birth of her own children, creation of any kind came from this womb of nature and the yearning to be one with her counterpart in the Universe, the fertilising spirit of the male, of the dragon light that could and would again instigate the inception of life.

Powerful emotion was spreading through her mind and body in anticipation of the completed union that would once again bring Arimathea to life. She felt her ecstasy as the dragons flowed into her and through her being after the interminable emptiness, filling her with their dreams, flooding through her cold dark rock warming her, completing her, fulfilling the potential she had always known lay deep in her womb. She felt the universe shudder with joy as the life force was again born inside her. Life that would again explore, enlighten and expand, that would reach out and discover deeper and more profound methods and ways to experience its wonders. A life force that would find new ways to grow as it adapted to new circumstances on this new world guided only by the combined spirit wisdom that had brought it into being.

Although lost in her experience, somewhere in Mariella's mind warnings had started to ring. The vital warmth keeping her alive was starting to wane. Her own consciousness returned and she opened her eyes and she knew immediately she had to get out of the pool. She had started to shiver and her limbs already felt slightly stiff from the cold. She forced herself to the bank and clambered out and wrapped herself in the warmth of the towel she had left on the grass. She sat shivering with her arms clasped around her up lifted legs and started to absorb the warmth from the Star. She lost track of time as she drifted through her experience, letting the shock of the cold be gradually absorbed by the warmth of the rising Star.

Okino had returned from his meditation in the courtyard and had wandered back to the camp through the gateway. Vivid images of the darkness thickening around his world all those years ago were suddenly expelled when he saw Mariella curled up in the Starshine on the riverbank. He ran over to where she lay and realised she was barely conscious. He saw her blue robe beside her. Her hair was still damp and he realised she had probably been in the water. He ran to her tent and grabbed one of the yak hides. He had seen the results of this cold when his fellow villagers had been caught out in the snows. He wrapped the yaks hide around her, sat her up and vigorously rubbed down her neck and back, shoulders and arms. He made sure that she was fully awake before running back to the fire which he rapidly brought back to life. He carefully heated some water, mixed in some of the herbs, took it over to Mariella and insisted she drink the hot liquid immediately. Slowly she returned to full consciousness. She smiled to herself as she sipped the hot tea, looking over towards the waterfall.

"Are you Ok Mariella, what were you thinking, swimming in this water?"

"It was the waterfall, it seemed to give me no option. I weighed up all the danger but in the end it just pulled me in. I had the most amazing experience Okino. It was like I became Arimathea; I felt the dragons moving through me and all that potential…"

"It must have been very cold, this will be melt water from the glaciers further up in the mountains!!"

"It was very, very cold, but I seemed to adapt to it quite quickly, probably with a little help from Arimathea, and any way it was worth it, an amazing experience."

She looked over at Okino and shook her hair out in the Sunshine.

"What have you been up to, have you just got up!!"

Looking inquiringly over at Okino.

His concern evaporated when he saw the glint back in her eye and he laughed…

"It seems we have some catching up to do! You should come over by the fire."

Mariella followed him over to the fire. He had been genuinely shocked to see Mariella in such a critical state. It had been a terrible risk for her to have taken out here with no help available. It did seem out of character for her. He had never been given any impression she was the kind of person to take risks. It certainly seemed conceivable she had been mesmerised, even enchanted, possibly in the same away Rabir had been entranced by the spiritual qualities of this place. The little pan boiled and he poured out two more steaming cups of water and added the tea. He grabbed a loaf of bread broke a piece off and handed it over to Mariella who was still wrapped up in her yak hide.

As Mariella absorbed the warmth of the tea and the fire, they started to exchange their experiences of the morning. Okino told how the little settlement had started to attract more and more people, how Rabir's work had expanded and how the settlements reputation had grown. He explained how people had started to stay longer and eventually left, so connected into Arimathea that on their return to their own communities they started to find their own holy sites that had been taken over by the alien religions. He explained how they had overlaid the indigenous spirituality and how the priests and the landlords had seen their mutual advantage and come to control these sites and the people. He told Mariella about the revolution and the civil war that had ensued; how it had ground to a halt as the greater power of the landlords had stamped out all but a small band of revolutionaries. He told how the dragons had made contact, intervened in the power struggle and how eventually the populations had been able to return to their lands. Finally, he told of the apparent thickening of darkness he had seen around Arimathea and the feeling of foreboding telling him that the struggle was not yet entirely over.

"These dragons are obviously powerful spirits. Certainly, from what I have experienced, their union with the original female spirit of Arimathea resulted in everything that has happened since."

"It certainly would appear so."

Okino had caught Mariella's eye. He thought he saw a slight change in the way she was looking at him. He chose not to acknowledge it and turned his attention back to the tree he was observing on the other side of the pool. But her expression had registered deep in his male psyche and he knew instinctively what it was.

"So now all we have to figure out is, how, these all powerful spirit beings that managed to travel from a distant galaxy, inhabit and initiate life on this planet, ended up flat on their backs and turned to stone with those mysterious swords plunged into them for possibly hundreds of years before being discovered and released by your good self in a dream!!"

"Something must have happened; something went wrong with their plan!"

Okino was shaken. He was trying to ignore the ongoing attraction continuing to develop between his travelling companion. Mariella looked over at him briefly surprised at the stress in his voice. Then went on,

"…and if the evolution of Arimathea is somehow guided by the dragon dreams and suddenly they were turned to stone, then everything would have changed from that point on."

Okino and Mariella sat quietly contemplating the thoughts and experiences of the last few days allowing them to drift through their minds; back to the days in the distant past when the dragons had made the decision to alter the fate of their world.

"The ruling lords must have somehow turned everything around again, but how?"

Mariella ventured.

"All the power they had built up had been stripped away. The land they had governed had been given back to the original owners and respect for the priests and their alien gods had been completely dissipated. They were sitting in their enormous irrelevant castles brooding over these strange tall beings who had suddenly arrived from nowhere and changed the balance of power with no apparent effort; almost overnight.

Plans being hatched for even greater control, enabling them to raise even greater tax revenues had been well and truly wrecked. All this had been snatched from their grasping hands. They must have been angrily brooding in their empty castles looking out over the lands they had previously controlled, trying to find some way to undermine the power of the dragons. However, it seemed things were not all going the dragon's way. Although the harvests had been adequate the farmers started to notice a slight decline in yields even from the most productive farms. It seemed these were easily explained by one of Arimathea's notorious 'weather' cycles. The dragons were able to explain how to adapt their planting patterns to counter the changing weather. But there were also problems with the livestock.

They had noticed a slight rise in the number of animals being born with deformities and yields of milk and eggs were down on what they would normally be. The farmers would have normally suspected something was worrying or unsettling their animals. Something they themselves were not immediately aware of like a new pack of wolves prowling around the farm at night. But on the whole the people went happily about their new lives free from the grinding taxation the landlords had imposed on them and free from the fear of retribution from the alien gods."

Mariella now had closed her eyes and raised her face to the Star. She seemed recovered from her experience and now seemed energised by it. Okino had listened as the words had started to flow, as they had for him the night before. He remembered the sensation as the pictures, feelings and explanations flooded into his mind. Now Mariella, it appeared had made a similar connection with the spirit that had become so important to the development of this settlement and the fate of Arimathea. Her experience in the waterfall had obviously affected her even more deeply than she had realised. He relaxed back against one of the rocks and listened as the story again began to unfold.

"The dragons in their human form continued to live amongst the people of Arimathea. After initial scepticism and having considered the ease with which they had overthrown their rulers the dragons soon came to be accepted by the general population, as the incarnated representatives of the supernatural force that dwelt upon their world. Their Love for Arimathea flowed out in their stories and wisdom, rippling out through the populations who came to have a greater understanding about the nature of the spirit living in their planet, of which the dragons assured them, they were an integral and important part. They were told all the many aspects of their lives were an inseparable part of the entire spirit. They started to find the experience of their lives had begun to deepen as they accepted this extraordinary revelation.

Their families, their animals how they went about their work, the cycles of the Star, the turning of the stars above them, how everything moving through the present moment became something to be relished. All they remembered about their past or anticipated in the future had or would become an integral moment in the development of their world; everything was inseparable from the continuing evolution of the spirit of Arimathea. A time of great enlightenment started to spread across the face of Arimathea as artists, poets, engineers and architects raced to express this new understanding of their world. Occasionally the dragons reverted to their energetic form and made flights across the countryside, enjoying their new freedom, just to leave no doubt in any minds as to their true identity."

"In evolutionary terms the human race on Arimathea suddenly took an enormous leap forward and it was being enjoyed by everyone accept the previously ruling lords who watched these developments with distaste, cynicism and anger. They felt they had been cheated out of what they had built by these apparently supernatural creatures. They held meetings in their castles, in their great empty stone banqueting halls. Even their families had deserted them now to be a part of the extraordinary events taking place on Arimathea.

They went over and over the injustice that had befallen them, talked amongst themselves and analysed everything they knew about the dragon's strategy in the hope they would find some weakness that would allow them to take back their control. But on every one of these meetings they came to the same conclusion. Unless some weakness in the armoury of these supernatural monsters revealed itself, they may as well become resigned to things as they were. They would then fall into silence and drink deeper and deeper into the reserves of wine and beer stockpiled in the castles for the sieges that had never happened. They would stay in each other's castles for days, sinking lower and lower into inebriated self-pity and often could be seen on the battlements of the castles staring listlessly over the lands they had lost. They were for the most part ignored but their frustration and anger was much celebrated by the people they had previously enslaved.

However, there were those who were not quite as elated with the new order of things as their fellow countrymen. Some traders had been able to secure great wealth and status as a result of the landowner's patronage. The merchants and traders who had benefited from this found the new trading conditions intolerable as they had to compete with other traders in the markets. There were others used to the old monopolies supported by the power held by the lords who had started to feel their lives becoming increasingly difficult. Farmers who had been thrown off the land granted to them as good will from their lord for services they had provided; owners of the mills given exclusive rights to the corn in the region; anyone who had been given patronage of the landlords at the expense of their fellows found now they were bypassed in this new autonomous world.

There were those who were convinced it would not be long before the dragons showed some sign of weakness. Careful observations were being made. They watched the places and establishments they visited and with whom they were spending time; took careful notice of all their movements. It was many months before one of the traders became aware of something that eventually might be to their advantage. He noticed at regular intervals of a few weeks, the dragons would disappear completely and reappear a few days later. Where they went, however, remained a complete mystery.

The dragons had been careful no-one did see where they went at these times. They would extricate themselves from any company and slowly drifted away from the town or village in which they were staying. Then they would melt inconspicuously into the surrounding countryside. There again they would enjoy the quiet of their world. They found the continual noise of the towns and villages eventually began to unsettle them. Beyond the continual clatter of human activity, they could hear the sounds and sensations which could sustain them in their physical state, separated as they now were from their dragon souls. They would walk across the plains and through the woodlands relishing the sunshine, the winds or the rain on their faces. In the sounds of these places, in the birdsong, the whisper of the wind through the trees, the fall of starshine and cloudy shadow, they found echoes of the memories of the worlds they had carried with them on their journey to Arimathea through the vast emptiness of space. Features of these worlds had again emerged with subtle and mysterious changes making it even more beautiful than the world enveloped in the terrible cataclysm they had left. The landscapes and everything in them seem to have become more intricate, more developed in this new world. A complexity had arisen in the life here that had surprised even the dragons.

But they had known the little planet they had found was special. How easily she had accepted them into her being. How comforting they had found her embrace after their lonely journey, how readily the solidity of her being had responded as they had become one. Slowly the result of their union started to become apparent as the streams of their now combined consciousness started to flow through the network of channels being formed in this sleeping world. Complex chains of events were initiated at this time. Gradually fabric and energy would be brought together allowing circumstances to arise, that in turn, would again start the precious life force on its journey towards the new and incredible variety of life that would eventually be manifest on Arimathea.

Then, their dragon spirits embedded in the crystalline structures at the centre of their new home would sleep. As they slept, they dreamt of the eons of time through which they had existed and mixed the memories of all they had seen and experienced into their dreamscapes. Their dreams would then flow through this new world slowly guiding it towards its destiny in the distant future.

But for all their analysis, the conclusions they drew and for all the parameters they planned, they knew again they would be powerless as the mystery of time and space to which even they were subject would weave in its random and unpredictable spell. Resigned perhaps, to the nature of their own struggle with the forces of life and death they remembered why they had come and wearily headed for their beloved hills.

As always in the history of worlds, there were those who felt uneasy with the proliferation of any kind of innovative new life. As the mood of the people of Arimathea swung irresistibly towards freedom and growth there were those who would have held back this new progression at any cost. They were of course in the service of the lords. Contrary to their fellow beings, who rarely questioned why they felt so fulfilled to be free and able to explore their lives so creatively, there were those who hardly gave any thought to why it seemed only sensible to suppress this freedom at any cost. They saw only the waste of precious energy being frittered into the thin air of indulgence where there seemed to be no consequence other than joy and happiness. These they had come to regard as wasteful luxuries serving neither, the individual or the society in any other way than to create satisfaction and laziness. They held the firm belief that this was not how civilisation ever would advance. These were the scribes, the bookkeepers who worked for the landlords ruthlessly advising them on the best way to expand the assets they had built up by using terror and a total lack of any conscience.

Their world and so all they had influence over consisted of numbers and calculations. Where there were boundaries and fences there were exact areas. Within those areas there were exact amounts of produce, whether corn or potatoes, they could be grown and harvested by a number of people. The concern and obsession of the scribes was the cost of the growing and the cost of the selling. If there was profit, then the landlord could pay more people to be in his control. If need be, he would equip them with the weapons of conquest and acquire more land. The greater the amount of land he had in his control the more profit he made and the more people he would have in his control to be making even more profit. The scribes continually made the calculations, analysed the processes involved and made any efficiencies to increase the profit.

An easy adjustment frequently made was the amount of people they had in the process and the amount they paid them; to keep the cost of making a sack of grain low compared to what they could sell it for. They were obsessed with this calculation, cared for little else in their miserable lives and their obsession increasingly had come to dominate the lives of the people of Arimathea.

Now, the fences and walls, the symbols of their ruthless domination had been torn down and the scribes looked at the empty columns in their books. The ruling lords were frustrated, angry and powerless in the face of the mass desertion of their armies and workforces. They saw the productivity they had achieved in the surrounding land falling away as the people became used to, in their eyes, their profligate lifestyles. This of course meant everybody had enough to eat, time to enjoy their lives and possibly buy some of the other products now being made. The plans for conquest were being put on hold as their power and wealth ebbed away. The loyal merchants and trades people who had been in their patronage had long since deserted them. Only the most faithful of scribes remained with them in their empty castles, considering the predicament the dragons had brought upon them.

There was one amongst them, Samir, who, when not keeping the books for his master, had documented and so contemplated a great deal of Arimathea's history up until the point of the revolution. His history had started with the population movement as trading routes had expanded across the face of Arimathea and how the systems of government had arisen as economic activity had grown.

He had found many influential settlements had grown up around the sites that had become sacred to the people of Arimathea. Many had grown up beside rivers, trading routes in themselves to the great ports on the coasts. People had initially visited on pilgrimage to ask for blessings from the spirits who resided there. Eventually the roads between these sites became the routes connecting the trading countries across the great continents of Arimathea. Many of these settlements had seen the rise and fall of great kingdoms and empires as a new race of conquerors streamed across their lands. After the initial carnage when the old regime had been defeated and a new leader had taken over, things went back to how they had always been for the general population.

The newly conquering king would franchise the old lords to instate their oppression and dominance much as they had done under the previous tyrant by enslaving and taxing as was necessary to fund further conquest. However, there was only so much land they could conquer on one continent. No one tyrant had ever succeeded in conquering the whole of Arimathea as the oceans were wide and too dangerous for large armies to cross. So, an empire would have to be consolidated. The speed the new empire went into decline would often depend on the governing lord's ability to extort enough money from the surrounding population to maintain the armies needed to keep everything under control. It was this fine balance Samir had always explored and was continually reflected in his great ledgers.

The control of the sacred sites had always been seen as important to maintaining ultimate control. Here was held the power of the priests of the alien religions. They held the connection to the supernatural world which still held considerable influence in the lives and minds of the people. They in turn, to maintain their own power became 'advised' and 'influenced' by sects and organisations who gathered large networks of people together all in some way trying to assure some benefit and advantage in the desperate struggle human life had become.

Religious ideas had been expanded and adapted and more complicated philosophies, rules and creeds evolved to suit the ideas of these new organisations exploring the best ways of gaining and maintaining their advantage. They in turn were courted by the emperors, kings and overlords as these new ideas became effective at gaining more influence amongst the people who generated the wealth they needed. So, the power flowed around and around. As empires and kingdoms rose and fell the power to control the people for their allegiance and the wealth that could be extracted from them was lost or consolidated.

Now this control, which had evolved across Arimathea for many centuries had been dissolved. These creatures that had now emerged may or may not be the spirits who had originally dwelt in those sacred places but their influence and whatever power they were able to wield had severely affected what Samir was writing in his ledgers. Their enthusiasm for life on this world was flowing out of the planet and spreading amongst the 'carefully managed' populations giving them ideas that freedom and creativity would again enable them to fulfil their lives on Arimathea.

It seemed as if out of exasperation with the continual suppression of her beautiful children, Arimathea had allowed the appearance of her dragons. Samir acknowledged they were certainly powerful adversaries appearing at first to be indomitable. He smiled as his knowledge and experience of conflict with powerful enemies of the past had convinced him there was always some weakness he would be able to exploit. The writings he had been able to access through the city libraries within the region told him little of the true nature of the creatures he was dealing with. The myths and here say revealed more about the fears the temples and their priests had mostly successfully managed to instil in the general population to denigrate their influence in the past. The most recent writings he had found, those of Rabir which had started to spread rapidly, gave him most insight into the true nature of what was happening. He wrote about the importance of the specific sites that had been revealed and rediscovered. Rabir had detailed how these sites were able to provide for the people who came into contact with them a deep connection with all aspects of themselves and their world.

Chapter Twenty-Two
The Dragonhill

Mariella had become quiet. Again, only the gentle rushing of the water, the sound of the small birds and the occasional tinkling of the goats' bells could be heard. Okino looked over at Mariella still wrapped in her yak hide despite the warming of the morning star. She did not restart the story. She turned and reached for her blue robe and let the great hide fall from her shoulders. Okino diverted his glance from Mariella who without warning had suddenly revealed more of her body than he had been prepared for. He turned his mind quickly back to the story left hanging so tantalisingly. The image of old Samir hunched over his books high in the tower of the empty castle hung in his mind.

Mariella had replaced her blue robe and had leapt up. She came over to him and offered her his hand. He looked up at her. The dust and grime that had become invisible had been washed away and revealed her radiant youthful complexion, glowing with healthy vitality. She was even more beautiful. Her deep blue green eyes sparkled full of wonder pulling him deeper into the spell threading its way into his being. He smiled shaking his head as he took her hand. She pulled him up.

"Come on Okino I want to go and explore this fabulous place. Whatever came next is over there in the ruins, I am sure of it. It wasn't in the story so far but something has been left lingering."

They walked barefoot across the springy turf and through the stone arch into the main square of the complex of ruined buildings. Mariella walked to the centre of the circle in which Okino had meditated that morning and slowly turned examining the buildings surrounding them. Okino's mind was awash with the happenings revealed to him as he stood now on the rim of the circle. He contemplated the atmosphere that must have been generated by the dragons revealing themselves and all they had known. Had they come here to this little outpost to visit, stood here amongst these buildings and enchanted the people who lived here with their creation tales. Had they felt the power of the river and breathed this clear mountain air scented with the enlivening perfume of the pine trees? Was it they who lived here now amongst these old stones laid so long ago with the passion dedicated to all they had brought to Arimathea?

So many possibilities had now been presented to him through his dreams and meditations; now they seemed to exist just under the surface of his world. He felt the dragons could materialise here before him at any time. But also, he knew they would not and this was, of course why he was here. He felt the star on his face and delighted in the pure joyful simplicity lying behind all this complexity. Again, he heard Arimathea's voice whispering through the trees and across the ruined stonework.

"I have so much yet to be fulfilled from this time and all that has come to be. It must not be lost forever!!"

A wave of desperate emotion flooded through Okino. He felt she had experienced the pain of separation. As if she had lost something she had dearly loved.

He glanced around the ruins for some sign of Mariella. There was none, so he wandered over to where he had seen her last and found her drifting through the silent Star filled ruins. They wandered through the empty shells admiring the embellishments Arimathea had chosen for the ruined walls.

They arrived at one of the larger buildings into which they had not yet ventured. A large arched opening had long since given up its door to the elements, opened into what almost certainly would have been a large hall. The ceiling would have been high and lit from windows high in the flanking walls. The stone floors again had survived. Creeping plants had invaded and hung in continual curtains of vegetation over large areas of the high walls. Mariella sat in one of the low alcoves created in the substantial stonework. She was absorbing the atmosphere, carefully studying each detail, taking herself back to the time when it would have been inhabited.

Okino stood and absorbed the tall space. There was a fine proportion here he felt was not accidental and he wondered of the alignment of the building in relation to the movements of Arimathea's star. He casually started to work the alignment through his mind in relation to the position of the star now rising above the walls. He looked up to see where the light coming through the gabled end wall was falling from the window high in the hall. He noticed the depth of the reveals of the window seemed deeper than the windows in the other walls. He decided he may learn more of this discrepancy from outside the building. As he left, he noted the depth of the other walls and then stood back to get a good view of the gable wall containing the high window.

The sloping wall of the gable certainly seemed to be considerably thicker than it's flanking walls for apparently no good reason. When the roof was in place, he decided this discrepancy would have been entirely invisible unless a detailed survey was carried out. He wandered back into the hall and went to the end gable wall. It was thickly covered with creepers and ivy. He pulled away at the plants. Mariella started to help and soon the wall behind was entirely uncovered. In the corner of the wall they found a ragged opening in the stonework. It had been opened quickly and probably violently. There was space in the darkness beyond.

"So, there is the extra depth to the wall."

They peered into the space beyond and found a narrow stone staircase leading into the darkness below.

"So, what are you like with spiders, Mariella?"

"I'm OK with them but I think you should go down there first just in case!"

"Just in case what?"

"…Just in case there is something really grim down there you should see first!"

"We'll need some light."

Mariella delved deep into the woven cloth bag she continually carried. Okino tried to see what it contained but she glared at him as she pulled out a small torch and handed it to him. Okino scrambled over the loose masonry at the head of the stair and flicked on the torch. It gave a deceptively powerful light and he started carefully down the steps clearing the copious amounts of cobwebs as he went, followed closely by Mariella.

At the bottom of the steps Okino turned through another opening which took him underneath the space above. He played the torch into a low room that appeared on first inspection to be empty. He gingerly moved into the space and played the torch over the walls. Now they could see there were markings and reliefs carefully carved over large slabs of stonework built into the walls. They started to examine each of the slabs in more detail.

"This appears to be a flattened-out map of Arimathea,"

Ventured Mariella,

"Slightly distorted, but you can make out the layout of all the continents. There appears to be some sort of grid laid over it."

"...and here a spherical diagram with the grid wrapped around it. In fact, there are three views presumably so you can see the whole planet." Okino was moving between the three and looking over at the larger projection.

"...the grid seems to wrap surprisingly geometrically around Arimathea and appears to fit over the landmasses very conveniently. I never noticed it before but with the grid applied the land masses do look remarkably balanced. I wonder what is happening on these intersections!"

They moved further down the wall and began studying a further map.

"I think this may give us some idea!!"

They were now looking at what appeared to be a larger scale map.

"This looks like a map of this direct area. Look there are the mountains and the river running down through the valley. The buildings are shown around the square and isn't that the circle."

The road on which they had entered the ruins was shown and, certainly not to scale, the stone circle where they had spent the night. The village to where their fellow travellers had returned was not shown on the map. There appeared to be further paths leading away from where further places had been marked. Many of these paths seemed to lead to a central site clearly shown as a large hill rising out of the lower foothills of the mountains beyond. It would have a clear view over the valley and down to the ruined settlement. They quietly moved between the different diagrammatic maps comparing and assessing all this information so carefully set out before them.

"This is all very intriguing. The hill in the centre looks like it could be the hill Rabir described the morning the dragon first revealed itself. Also, it is on the intersection of these the two grid lines shown on the larger map over here."

Okino was now pointing to their region on the larger map of Arimathea. "I wonder if each of these intersections has a hill... in which case..."

He started counting across the map.

"There would be sixteen of these hills across the landmasses of Arimathea. If the hills are associated with the dragons you would think there would be sixteen dragons but there are only ever fifteen. So, what happened to the last dragon. This is all very intriguing. Clearly this is information the community did not want discovered, but probably was."

"mmm so one hill for each dragon, set out across the face of Arimathea.... I wonder, could these places be where their presence was most felt on the surface and perhaps where they were able to move from in the planet into the world above. Do you think this was the hill you were on when the dragon materialised for the first time for the rebels?"

"Could well have been, it was dark and I couldn't be certain."

"Well look, it can't be far. Perhaps we should take the horses and ride up there."

"I agree, there may well be something up there to shed some light on what happened next!"

Okino and Mariella left the hidden cellar and the ruined hall and drifted back to the river and their camp. They prepared some provisions from their supplies and soon were riding out of the ruins. The Star was again getting hot as they deliberated over the direction they should be heading. They decided they could see the hill they should be heading towards in the distance and struck out at a leisurely walk. The horses were able to pick their way through the landscape without much help from their riders so Okino and Mariella were able to resume the conversation they had started while examining the map in the cellar.

"It was interesting to see the whole map of Arimathea. Up until then I had been thinking quite locally about this whole thing. There was one of those intersections not far from where I used to visit back in my country." Mariella looked over inquiringly at Okino. He was looking intently down at the rocks and beyond to the low slopes of the hills.

"It seems like I have been here in Rabir's story. The lizards he talked about are bound to still be around here!"

"...and the snow leopards...although I should imagine they hunt at night at this time of the year." Mariella searched into the distance, imagining she might see one of the elusive cats.

"...Then there were all those other places marked on the map. I wonder if they are all as beautiful as the waterfall."

"Perhaps we should visit each one...how long do you think we will stay here. Have you planned the next leg of the journey yet?"

"I haven't really but kind of assumed we would stay her a few days then head down to the coast, depending on what we find here of course. But if we go to one of the ports, I can communicate with home make sure everything is Ok. Then Okino, monk of the mysterious Dragon Order perhaps you will have your first taste of the modern world."

Then she turned her attention back to observing the hills. Okino laughed. They had talked briefly about him travelling to Eremoya and Straam city.

"As you know I have no plans. Increasingly it seems plans are being made for me!"

"But you need to go to the city to track down the source of the pollution, don't you?"

Okino laughed again,

"Oh no, Mariella I didn't necessarily mean you are making all my plans for me...what I mean is as soon as I stepped out of the monastery I seem to have been propelled onward towards whatever lies out here for me and I am compelled it seems to just follow along; or to watch as this whole story appears to unravel, particularly at the moment as the spirit of Arimathea is choosing to reveal the nature of her relationship with the dragons!!

"So, what about these sixteen hills!?!"

"I think there is a good chance they are specifically to do with the dragons; possibly their entry and exit points from their spirit realm, where they can become part of Arimathea, in the atmosphere above where they are free to exist in immaterial form."

"…but then they decided they had to become material to alter the course of human history and so of Arimathea…which of course they didn't because the crisis they hoped to avoid does seem to have materialised!!"

"I think they may have miscalculated, or possibly underestimated the darker forces on this world and took a risk that may have gone catastrophically wrong!!"

The path had become narrower and twisted amongst large boulders. Eventually it became steeper as they started to ascend the Dragon hill. The horses picked their way steadily up the rocky path made by the herds of goats as they migrated around and through these hills. Soon they were looking down over the valley and across to where the hills beyond continued towards the sea. Heat now shimmered across the stones and the occasional flash revealed the position of a lizard as it disappeared into safety under a nearby rock. Okino smiled as he acknowledged these would be the descendants of the lizards that had disappeared in the same manner from Rabir all those hundreds of years before.

He wondered if their lives had changed at all. Had they made any adaptations? Some twist of fate bringing them even nearer to their perfect lizard state or had generation after generation sat on these rocks only to scuttle into a crevice at the slightest sign of a large hovering shadow above or the crackling of undergrowth in their direct vicinity. Deep in the cortex of their tiny stone coloured heads, alongside survival techniques honed over millions of years would be their reaction to their world; how they looked out on it and what they saw, how they existed as part of the web of life. In their stillness, the envy of any monk striving for such peace, had they come to an understanding making unnecessary movement irrelevant as the vast beauty of Arimathea and the infinite universe beyond glowed endlessly through their intricately precise little beings?

The goat paths were steeper now and soon they had arrived on what would appear to be the lower plateau where Rabir had left his goats before ascending to the summit of the hill. They decided to dismount and secured the three horses on one of the pine trees scattered across the hillside. Mariella turned to Okino, smiled and took his hand.

"So now we will meet the dragon!"

Okino smiled back at her and they started to climb the final part of the hill. The Star was now high in the sky and the air was still and alive with the low hum of the insect life around them. It did not take them long to cover the short distance to the summit. Soon they were standing on the very top slowly turning to admire the landscape now stretching across to the distant horizon of Arimathea. Mariella was entranced and moved dreamily around the summit carefully absorbing this new perspective. Okino had to agree it was spectacular but quickly became more interested in the surface of the ground below his feet. He had noticed immediately how unnaturally flat the surface seemed to be. There were no rocks or protuberances of any kind. The sparse mountain grass had been grazed as normal. Also the edge, where the hill started to fall away seemed to be very precise.

Okino idly scuffed at the surface where the grass was no longer growing allowing the sand to be exposed. He pushed the toe of his boot deeper into the sand and scraped it away. There was solid stone almost immediately under a thick layer of sand. His mind flashed back to the dream when he had discovered the dragon under the snow in the forest. He scraped away more and soon had exposed an area of solid level rock lying just below the surface of the hill. The surface was not natural and appeared to be smooth as if it had been carefully cut.

"Mariella, I think you should come and have a look at this."

Mariella broke away from the ecstatic dream into which she had imagined herself to be one of the eagles floating through the vast space around her, higher and higher on the uplifting thermals, fused into the silent Starlit air. Back at ground level, she was surprised to see Okino was already tearing into the top of the hill. She wandered over to where he was on his hands and knees, scraping away at the sand and grass. He had exposed an area of some five paces across of perfectly smooth stone. There was one straight joint bringing two separate stones perfectly together.

"Well that is very surprising."

Mariella observed almost under her breath as she also started to push away the sand at the edges of the stonework Okino had already exposed. They worked silently and uncovered four steps, each as high as his hand to his elbow but as wide as his foot. They stopped digging and stood back, looking at the hill. What at first had seemed so naturally perfect now appeared to have been very carefully constructed. The extent they had exposed suggested this construction was covering the entire hill.

"Yes, it is very surprising," Okino wandered thoughtfully over the stonework so precisely laid over the top of the hill.

"So was this how Samir came to curb the power of the dragons?"

"...because somehow he found out they maintained their connection with Arimathea through the channels which came to the surface on these hills. If we assume his strategy worked, they may have eventually lost their ability to influence what they had instigated here on the surface!"

"...it would also explain the terrible loss she expressed to me this morning."

They were silent as the full gravity of the situation took hold.

"...it would have been quite an operation to drag all this up here!!" Mariella broke the silence,

"….and build it so intricately and precisely. But there was a lot at stake!! There appears to have been no attempt to destroy or remove it."

"Assuming there are fifteen other similar hills, Samir must have organised similar constructions over every single one to take the influence of the dragons out of the world completely!!"

"So, what happened to the dragons if they were unable to return into Arimathea; and what has been happening to the planet?!" Mariella now seemed genuinely shocked.

"It's hard to tell what has happened to the dragons but we know what has been happening to Arimathea!! If the dragons were unable to dream into Arimathea, then all human development in the hundreds of years since that time will not have benefited from the wisdom they would have otherwise instilled through their dreams"

"There would have been a lot written down." Mariella was trying to regain some hope from what appeared to be a deliberate act of destructive sabotage.

".. but it could have easily been destroyed in those days. The true loss would have been the wonder the dragons had for their world. It just would not have been present in those first inspirational moments of every idea since this was perpetrated. When this strategy was decided upon very little consideration for the well-being of Arimathea would have been given!!"

"…which certainly would account for the degradation and destruction carried out by the human race but would not have affected other animal species who had already found their way to exist on Arimathea a long time before any of this happened!"

"Exactly. We have transformed Arimathea during this time by using our minds, having our own ideas and thinking through problems. But it seems we have been missing a vital ingredient in those thoughts!!"

"…The one that contains the information about the true nature of Arimathea!!"

"It would seem so."

Mariella and Okino were silent as they looked down at the enormous slab of stone built across the Dragon hill.

"It seems strange the stone alone could cause such a problem for such powerful supernatural beings. It is a natural material so they must have travelled through it as they flowed through the planet!"

"In your dream, the dragon was turned to stone by the steel of the sword!!"

"I have a feeling the dream is somehow symbolic of what has happened here. They couldn't have put steel down there; it would have rusted away after twenty years?"

"…then what do you think is down there?"

She shivered as a cold dark shadow passed momentarily through her thoughts. Mariella moved hurriedly to face Okino, took both his hands and looked deeply into his eyes and spoke urgently!

"She has brought us here, Okino. This is why we have come." She gestured to the stonework covering the hill.

"We are going to have to remove this stone and whatever there is under or within it. Only then will the dragons be able to return to Arimathea."

Chapter Twenty-Three
Dragon Wisdom

The sound of the crickets, continuing their lives oblivious to the planet changing events occurring on their hill, filled the air. Okino and Mariella had found what they had been looking for. They stood silently bound into their quest and their increasing closeness on the impenetrable slab of stone Samir had laid across the summit of the Dragon hill. The quest on which they had embarked had now revealed its next element, its' new direction. Through their dreams and intuitions they had been led to this place, high in the hills of Arimathea. They had trusted and followed the faint echoes they had heard in their spirit souls; the souls they shared with their beloved world; perhaps triggered by some unease in their lives into which they had grown in very different parts of their world, carefully guided by all those around them; Okino in the isolation of his mountain village and Mariella in direct contrast in the wealthy developed city and suburbs of Straam.

They had made their own first tentative steps for independence and made the mistakes and had the misinterpretations a new being, with a new array of thoughts and ideas would always encounter. At what point in their journey from their creation at molecular level to these adult human beings had this unease been engendered in their souls? Here perhaps they had found some answer. As they stood on the solid barrier, they felt close to the origin of the empty feeling they had discovered in the deep recesses of the people they had become. It felt like some malevolent thought or idea that had come to stalk the constructs of their lives; an episode left unexplained and unresolved slowly releasing its malignant legacy into all in its wake. It had left this unease caused by an absence brought unnaturally upon their world. Here was the solid evidence. The stories given to them had told of the suppression and cruelty of the most ruthless of the human race over their fellow beings. Perhaps here was evidence a vital connection to the planetary consciousness had been cut off allowing the destructive reign of terror to continue.

Okino and Mariella stayed on the hill as the Star started again on its downward descent. They quietened their minds, embedded themselves in the atmosphere of the place in an attempt to find some residue of the connection Rabir had felt when the dragon had finally chosen to reveal itself. They only fell further under the enchantment of the spectacular position above the plains. As the Star shone through the soft warm air shimmering around them, it created a stark contrast to the solid barrier laid so purposefully between them and the portal the dragons had used for so long to their crystalline realm below and their beloved Arimathea. Softly she whispered around them. Cajoling their young minds, tempting them to intercept some memory to further explain what had happened here.

Okino drifted back in the starshine to his village deep in the mountains. He caught a glint out on the lakes. Perhaps a rising fish so carefully raised and nurtured. He was near the bank watching the water lazily lapping in against the bank. He could see old Sareki mending one of the long nets that would stretch across the whole lake. All the lakes were drained at least every three years and he would move the entire stock of fish into an adjacent lake. With a system of locks and weirs he could divert the water from the river into one of the other lakes and the lake would slowly empty. Once a lake had been drained the messy business of extracting the silt built up on the bottom would begin. Okino remembered looking over the expanse of rich dark sediment full of nutrients from the waste of the fish exposed again after the previous years under the cold mountain waters.

As he watched, a strange array of machines would appear from the small building where Sareki lived in the summer months. It was a regular event, every two or three turnings, for the village, so the men and boys would drift out to the lakes. Amongst smiles and grumbling about the initial disgust at having to again wade into the foul-smelling lake bottom, a system of timber rails was carefully constructed across the mud on posts driven down to the firmer sediment below. Large boxlike sleds were hauled out of the building, slipped down onto the rails and pushed out across the lake. The rails converged on a series of tripods and soon became animated as a complicated system of ropes and pulleys raised and lowered them into the lake.

Okino smiled to himself as he remembered the great teams of yaks lumbering over the plain dragging the enormous carts that would transport the silt over to the fields and kitchen gardens. There were four teams and six yaks in each team carefully driven and led by two men. They were a splendid sight with their individually coloured harnesses liberally adorned with small bells. Sareki greeted each team of yaks like they were his old friends and then continued to run ceaselessly between the constructions: checking the stability of posts, the taught-ness of ropes and the arrangement of his pulleys to give the maximum lift for minimum effort. Then he would stand back and assess the whole operation and make any adjustments he thought necessary.

Then everything would become quiet. The old master monk would appear as if out of thin air and give a blessing to the operation. Okino acknowledged how steeped in tradition and ritual this operation had become. It was part of the cycle of their lives. Everyone who took part, which by the end of the day amounted to a large proportion of the village, was light-hearted, laughed and joked as they waded out and started to shovel the foul smelling silt into the sleds. They reminisced about previous years as they dragged the sleds back to the banks and hauled them up to be emptied into the great carts. But everyone who lived in those mountains knew the serious nature of their task and gradually a silence fell over the proceedings as the back-breaking work found its' rhythm. The village came together under the necessity of squeezing every last grain of productivity out of their land. They knew this operation would mean, all being well in the other areas of the process, they would have enough food to get them through the winter. It was symbolic of their collective will to give their crops the best chance they had.

The next time they would come together in such a way would be at the harvest when the fruit of this laborious task would again be manifest in the fields as fat grains of corn. Grown men passed on this message to their sons as they toiled in the stench of the mud and as they silently ate the bread and drank the beer brought for their dinners they were initiated into the brotherhood of the generations who had chosen to take their place in the communal struggle to survive. They had become a thread in the rich tapestry of their people and when they went back to work they shovelled harder.

When the last cart was full and Sareki was happy the right proportion of silt had been taken for the ecological balance of the pond and the health of the precious fish, they would throw down their tools and collapse exhausted, but with a strange, almost ecstatic sense of wellbeing they had directly taken some part in assuring the well-fare of the village for another year. Then they ran over to the clean lake and threw themselves in and happily splashed the sparkling water over themselves and each other until they were once again revealed from under the filthy grime.

Okino watched as the entourage of people and yaks slowly drifted away. Sareki opened the locks and the water flowed back into the lake before following the rest of the village, now happily united to take part in the ensuing feast. In the coming days the fertile silt would be spread across the fields and would be absorbed into the humus in the coming months. Okino remembered the cycle as it progressed through the year. He watched as the farmer left his house and decided this was the day and as a result the grain remaining from the year before had been sown into the soil. He had been present and helped with the harvest when he became big enough to wield the smallest scythes used to cut the corn. He had been shown how to use the baskets to separate the grains from the chaff and thrown the resultant mix into the wind to have only the grain come back down as the chaff drifted into its own pile later to be fed to the animals. He had been to the mill where the streams tumbling down the mountain had been carefully diverted into one powerful channel to turn the great water wheel. He had watched fascinated by the system of cogs and wheels that made the great stones inside the mill slowly turn. He had guided a stream of grain into the centre of the stones and watched as the ground flour had flowed from the edges of the great stones. The miller had shown him how he separated the bran of the outer hulls from the white middle and shown him the difference between the floor with and without the bran. He had given Okino a sack of the wholemeal flour with the bran and a sack of the purest white flour to take to the baker who in turn baked the flour into two loaves. It was a day Okino had never forgotten.

He smiled now, high on the Dragon hill, as the aroma of those two loaves being taken out of the oven surfaced in his thoughts. He had taken those special of loaves home that afternoon and shared them with his family at dinner. The process was complete. At every stage of his journey there had been someone to show him what had to be done next in the process that brought his food out of the fields, enabling him to eat and ultimately survive. Knowledge refined, added to and passed from generation to generation for as long as humans had discovered this was what they were able to do.

Here on the Dragon hill the significance of his thoughts wove seamlessly into the stories he had been shown in his meditations in those last days. He had not been born into this world alone having to discover everything about how to survive. There had been a continual thread of wisdom and knowledge that had brought him to where he was today. He had chosen to ignore this wisdom on occasions but had come to realise wisdom was exactly what the word offered to him. The Kingdom of the Wise. It was a strange ethereal place threaded with a network of paths where any number of situations, occurrences and experiences, good or bad, had been overlaid with the vast stream of beneficial knowledge accrued by previous generations.

Now as he sat on the sealed entrance to what may have been a primary source of planetary wisdom he suddenly realised the implications for his world if this source had been suddenly denied to a race such as his own who had so much ability to transform it. Unguided, the experiment would continue relentlessly, eventually resulting in an undefined, perhaps dangerous outcome. In the same way as if the collected knowledge of the village had suddenly been lost.

Okino looked around to where Mariella was still in deep thought. However, as if she had sensed Okino's attention she turned to face him. She smiled lazily, stood up and stretched into the cloudless blue skies.

"I thought perhaps we could ride down to the village; it can't be far from here. I would like to see it and see Farina. We became quite close during those few days on the road."

They started to walk down the hill to where the horses were grazing peacefully on the lush mountain grass. Okino noticed a wider path descending down the opposite side of the hill.

"It will be interesting to see how their village compares with ours and also to see what tricky deal Ben and Zeph have been trying to entangle them into. They admired my new coat and I saw them talking to the guys on the stall. They all seemed to be getting on very well. The next thing was we saw them fly past us on their way here. This path does seem familiar to the one we climbed, the plains are on the right side and it seems at the right gradient."

The path followed the hillside and was taking them down into a valley where the village soon came into view.

"Did you have any further thoughts earlier?" Okino asked Mariella who was now able to walk beside him on the widened path.

"Obvious things I suppose, mainly questions. That hill for instance seems set away from the hills we have now entered; it just doesn't seem part of the local geology. I kept thinking of worm casts and the little piles they leave when they take leaves and debris down into the soil. Eventually they develop into what seem like miniature hills if they are left for long enough. It would follow that if our dragons have these channels flowing through Arimathea these hills would be forming independently of any geological structures...which makes me want to go immediately and see how all the other hills have developed and how they fit into the local geology."

"I still can't understand how the stone alone could prevent the dragons from going in and out of their channels."

"I felt something Okino, when I was thinking the very same thing. It was something very dark and cold. I have never felt anything like it before. Then it was gone. It was like I had stumbled upon something I shouldn't have and almost as if it really wasn't entirely there."

Okino had been particularly interested in this loose end of the story. In the part of the story that was missing, Samir must have been given or found some information leading him to the conclusion building over the hills would disable the dragons. Who on Arimathea could have found out the dragon's vulnerability and almost certainly the key to the power they were holding? They may never know or perhaps it would arise at another time in different circumstances. He wondered briefly what those circumstances may be and where this mystery would take him next. After all there were fifteen further hills across the face of Arimathea!

"...Also" Mariella continued, "I was thinking again about the implications of all of this."

She paused and looked over to see if she had Okino's full attention. When she saw she had, she continued.

"It has occurred to me perhaps this is all part of the destiny of our world and everything has happened exactly as it was meant to. Or put another way, all the advances we have made may never have come to be if the dragon wisdom had been flooding through Arimathea and become part of our every decision. Think of all the miraculous things that have ultimately helped us to become independent rather than at the mercy of Arimathea, the dragons and their vision of the future."

"Of course, the great mystery is surrounding us all, the dragons and Arimathea; the battle between Life and Death, Light and Dark. Arimathea did mention it and you may well be right. But if all these discoveries ultimately do mean the death of all this again and billions of years of evolution will again be lost, then surely some intervention, in which we are now involved becomes part of the cycle of survival. We have advanced in this incarnation, in other ways than aeroplanes and computers. Arimathea has been able to communicate directly to us, you and me, and maybe others across Arimathea to hopefully prevent the approaching disaster and carry on towards the next part of our destiny!!"

"…Which does assume some preordained path, an outcome planned by what you refer to as the great mystery."

"It certainly cannot have been planned. I suppose in the same way as we have aspirations or ambitions for achievements in the future, there may be a place ultimately aimed for and as we well know there are situations that occur along the way attempting to prevent us from achieving our goals."

"So really you have come to think of the mystery in the same way the crickets and the lizards may or may not contemplate us. They could never understand how we have such an influence on their world in the same way we will never understand how the mystery ultimately works through our world."

"I am entirely sure the crickets and lizards have a much better understanding of the world than we do for the very reason they became fully evolved when the dragon wisdom was flooding through the world. But who knows whether they understand our role in it? But I see the point of your analogy."

"...but it must be part of our consciousness also. It would have been there when we were evolving."

"...I think this is why we feel this sense of unease and why we have delved so deeply into the mysteries of our physical world and have made the enormous technical advances we have achieved. As complex sensitive beings we have been unable to feel fully connected to the consciousness of our world in the way we would have done for millions of years. The nearest we can come is by gradually becoming accustomed to the idea through a spiritual training or continual absorption into the wonders of the natural world. I think this is the connection we have always held with Arimathea. She has always been with us as life continues all around us. You know, as you start to observe the complexity of her processes, it becomes increasingly difficult to see how there could not be some sentient consciousness behind it all."

"...but then this ability to observe her processes has led to the enormous understanding we have and the technical advances we have made. So, the big question I suppose is where would we have been if we had always had the dragon wisdom flowing through the world? Would we have striven in the same way to transform Arimathea in the way we have?"

"We may never know the answer to that….but maybe if you think of some of the developments so instrumental to the situation we find ourselves; then perhaps overlay the knowledge the dragons could have brought to say the development of carbon based fuels to power the industrial world. Wouldn't the dragons have not given us some understanding of the potency of such a material stored deep in the planet, existing as part of her history and her physicality in the same way we have layers of skin or blood pumping through our veins.

With their knowledge of planetary mechanics would they not have given us a sense of foreboding as to the consequences of using such a powerful substance so recklessly. Maybe the dragon wisdom would have given us a better understanding of the incredible powers lying within our world. I think we would have developed them unselfishly, considering ourselves and all our discoveries as part of the entire community of Arimathea rather than disconnected and oblivious to the natural world."

"Could we really have had that kind of understanding?"

"I am thinking from the point of view of where things are now…our influence has increased to such an extent there are few parts of Arimathea not touched by the activities of the human race. I have a feeling it just would not have happened in the same way if we had grown with the dragon wisdom flowing through our thoughts and dreams. I think we would have developed, made discoveries and breakthroughs that would have transformed our lives but the criteria for our development would have been different. We would have been more concerned for our planet home and I think Arimathea would be in a happier state generally!"

Chapter Twenty-Four
Farina's village

Okino and Mariella were now entering the new village of Asima. It had been built in a further valley which cut deeper into the mountains beyond. The dusty track soon turned into a familiar cobbled street so prevalent in the mountain villages. There was one main street and there appeared to be smaller streets running off forming intersections at various points. The village appeared busy. It was smaller than his own, but men and women hurried down the main street in and out of the houses and what Okino assumed were also small shops. Children, some of whom Okino recognised from the journey back from Aharri, ran through the street. When they saw Okino and Mariella they diverted their attention from whatever game they were playing and ran up to their two new friends, greeting them with a stream of excited laughter and welcome.

They stroked and patted the horses with great enthusiasm while explaining the exploits of the previous days. Before either Mariella or Okino could reply they had run off as fast as they had appeared into one of the side streets. The energy they had so happily formed around them hung in the street as they disappeared into the huddle of dwellings and larger buildings forming the centre of the village. Okino and Mariella dismounted the horses and let them drink from a great stone trough at the side of the street. One of the yaks stood silently in the star shine oblivious it would seem to the tall sleek invaders who were now drinking thirstily.

Okino began to notice the buildings. They seemed to be of a superior quality than he was used to seeing in these little mountain villages. There appeared to be fewer timber frames. The stonework in many of the buildings had been accurately dressed and laid in accurate courses. Immediately he remembered the precision with which the stone on the hill above had been cut.

The roofs however had reverted to their normal style and Okino suspected the original roofs had not survived the walls on which they had been built. Mariella pointed to the vehicle they had last seen disappearing into a cloud of dust in the days before. Okino was not pleased to see the sleek metal all-purpose jeep that could so shrink travelling time through these rough terrains but smiled to himself when he remembered the old truck starting up in Haran's barn and his own journey through the mountains. There was no sign of the two southerners for the moment.

Farina emerged from the side street down which the children had disappeared. She carried her baby daughter who had become so distressed on their journey. She was obviously relieved to be home and gurgled and waved her tiny hands happily as Mariella said hello to her.

"It is lovely to see you again, my friends, the beautiful girl from the city who travels with the mysterious monk from the hidden valley!"

She smiled knowingly at Mariella as if some conversation had taken place in which Okino had not been involved. She turned to the monk and bowed happily.

"Come down to our house and I will make you some tea. I want to hear all you have found out in the old ruins. They are so beautiful now you never could have imagined the tragedy rumoured to have happened there."

Okino had put to the back of his mind these people had their own stories about the ruins. In the light of what had transpired and the intriguing loose ends, Okino and Mariella were keen to hear the fate of the ruined community from the locals. The side street became considerably narrower between two terraces of houses. Farina turned when she came to her own house and opened a solid timber door. She smiled as she ushered her guests into her front room.

An assortment of timber chairs were arranged on the stone floor around the great hearth of the fire which stood in the centre of the wall adjacent to the doorway. The stone floor was mostly covered with heavy woven rugs. Okino recognised some of the intricate patterns from rugs he had seen at the market in Aharri. The cushions which had been made to fit the chairs had been constructed from a similar material. On the walls hung further larger rugs. The patterns had been replaced by panoramic mountain views painstakingly reproduced with breath taking effect. On one of the walls there were cupboards and shelves where brightly coloured pottery was displayed. Okino recognised the unique designs and marvelled at plates, cups, dishes and vases.

Hanging over the fire was the old dragon cauldron. A stew bubbled quietly away next to a further pot where the water for the tea had started to simmer. Farina ladled the steaming liquid into some cups she had previously doused with an ample portion of aromatic herbs. She invited her two visitors to sit down. The effect of the room had completely captivated her guests. Textures and the coherent patterns, the rich colours that shone from the expertly finished glazes, brought layers of mesmerising complexity to the simple room. As each intricate detail expanded into the whole ingenious pattern Okino and Mariella were drawn deeper into their thoughts and the mystery surrounding them. Geometries of which they were unaware flooded through their minds as cortex was stimulated by the rich juxtaposition and reflection. Okino remembered the lessons he had been taught while watching the monks creating their beautiful mandalas. They had told him there were flows and patterns in the whole of creation. It would take him many years to see these patterns as he became accustomed to watching with the wisdom he was beginning to understand. They would point to a tiny swirl in the pattern of sand.

"Is that my swirl in the pattern?" Okino had asked.

"You may have to move a little closer, my friend!!"

Okino did get closer to the little mound to which the monk had pointed. Nothing had changed until he suddenly realised he was looking at one grain of sand in a pile of thousands and thousands making up a tiny piece of the mandala.

He smiled to himself as he realised the lesson had new resonance. He had been given special and privileged insight into how the pattern of time and space on his world had been woven. He had thought it had perhaps moved around into the next swirl, when in fact it spread out into the enormous layout carefully engineered to spread across the floor of the temple!

Farina interrupted Okino's thoughts by handing him a steaming cup of tea. The rich scent of the powerful herbs invaded his thoughts. He took a sip. His mind returned from its wandering to the Starlit room. Unanswered questions that would possibly give him insight into the deeper pattern began to surface.

"Your house is beautiful, Farina. It reminds me of the temple I have left deep in the mountains. I sense a very old tradition in the weaving of your rugs. I sense a connection with the discoveries we have made in the ruins. You are so near. There must have been a connection with this village and what has happened over there? In our meditations we have been able to ascertain a community was formed and from the discoveries of that community a revolution against the rulers of Arimathea ensued! We also have gathered there were powerful supernatural forces involved."

Okino and Mariella told Farina about the meditations and stories that had arisen out of the ruins in the last few hours and how they had come to discover the Dragon hill. As they spoke, Farina looked wistfully over at the old cauldron simmering away on the fire. She had always felt if she looked long enough at the dragons portrayed on the sides in the dancing light of the fire they seemed to come to life. She had often wondered whether this had been the intention of its creator or some strange coincidental magic that had arisen to portray and remind people of the nature of the dragon spirits they knew to live in Arimathea. Now this young monk and his beautiful travelling companion had come to visit her.

She listened enthralled by the story she was now being told. They were accurate portrayals of the legends passed down through the generations of her tribe. But these were not portrayals. These gifted young people told the stories as if they had been involved, as if they had been sitting amongst the people when the extent of the pretence exerted over them had been revealed as if they had felt the outrage as it rippled out across Arimathea. As Okino described the moments the dragon had revealed himself she could hear the crackle of the flames and the amazed murmurs of the tribesmen as Merilon emerged from the light in the stars high on the hill she had known and visited all through her life. The hill where her father had told her the story of the dragon that had visited their land from deep in the very fabric of their planet and once again opened the people's minds to the wonders of their world. All these stories her people had passed on and held sacred all these hundreds of years from when the history of Arimathea and possibly the Universe had been changed.

Such knowledge would be rare; it would have faded in the memories of many whose ancestors had witnessed the events; all Rabir's writings from those times would have been tracked down and eradicated by the rulers as once again they established their authority. It may now be her knowledge alone that explained how the dragons had become so vulnerable to the darker forces who had schemed and planned for their destruction. For these were the places the dragon had returned to commune with his beloved Arimathea. He had visited the community of Asima and confided further knowledge with Rabir and the other mystics who had surrounded him. Asima had been rebuilt, away from the original site, when her ancestors had returned, near to the Dragon hill and the strange mystery surrounding it.

Interference by such a powerful supernatural force had been unprecedented on Arimathea and the repercussions would be felt from those moments down through time into these very moments in this remote mountain village. The priests and the holy men across Arimathea sympathetic to the dragon's task had become enthused and confident with the knowledge made known to them. As the dragons made themselves known in the regions in which they had emerged, so the momentum of change and optimism had gathered. For now, the dragons passed on in their many interactions with the priests and mystics the knowledge of the primal forces they represented. The forces of creation had brought them to where they now sat, in their temples high in the mountains or in the quiet backstreets of the cities, in the sacred places rediscovered by the gifted ones who, perhaps had not been trained as priests or seers but had, perhaps due to some unexpected twist of fate in their lives, stumbled upon the understanding that had led them to play their part in the revolution that had occurred on Arimathea.

The dragons had always made clear they had no way of predicting the outcome of their interference but explained they had felt compelled to gently steer this little world away from a future ending in its catastrophic destruction. So, the holy men and the priests had thrown their charms and consulted their oracles. They delved far into the past of previous worlds and examined the paths of the stars far into the distant future to see if they could find a successful outcome for such an undertaking. They journeyed in trances to the many levels of existence the dragons had revealed to them. They asked them for help in the task that would eventually take the human race to a place where they may eventually understand these forces, become one with them, work with them in their lives rather than being oblivious to them, ignorant and in denial of them. Here was the destination the dragons had always had for the worlds they had inhabited and nurtured, in the hope some extraordinary as yet untapped potential might be released into the Universe.

They diligently recorded the wisdom they had received. Quietly they embedded the knowledge they had been given into their temples. In carefully constructed manuscripts that would be read by generations of initiates. They carved the old animal spirits into the spiralling columns that had come to Arimathea to hold the stability governing the ebb and flow of space and time. The dragons taught them new abilities giving them more effective and constructive connection with the spirits of their world and directly with the spirit of Arimathea. There was little arcane or secretive about what the dragons taught them and much relied on the recipient being in the full realization of the miracle and the wonder inherent in his or her existence.

The priests in their temples and monasteries in the remoter parts of Arimathea whose philosophies and practice had not been corrupted by the rulers to subjugate their populations, quietly and unobtrusively became possessed of the most sacred knowledge that had ever come to be known on Arimathea. This knowledge, irrelevant to any mind which had not fully accepted the nature of his or her world, would be held as wisdom, protected and handed down through the ages to surface again should it ever be lost to the wider world.

Okino and Mariella had finished their account of the events they had been shown in their dreams and visions. Farina was quiet as she contemplated her two visitors. The legends of the dragons she had carried telling of their wisdom being embedded into the world had been accurate. Okino was living proof the abilities the dragons had passed on to the temples had indeed survived and served its purpose. But now there was vital knowledge only she could pass on.

The two young people watched expectantly. A gentle breeze whispered its way through the open window and ruffled some of the wall hangings. The flames in the fire responded by dancing a little more vigorously. Mariella had handed back Farina's baby and now she was feeding hungrily. Farina was smiling contentedly down at her, hoping one day she would retell the story to this tiny soul, unaware now of how it was shaping her world. Farina briefly looked over towards her two visitors and closed her eyes.

ChapterTwenty-five.
Farina's Tale.

"There is a lot you have been told it would seem. But not, for some reason, how the whole saga whatever you like to call it, came to an end. Perhaps Arimathea thought there was specific insight into the next episodes only our legends can offer. Perhaps she found this part of the story too hurtful, for the situation has never been completely resolved. To understand what finally happened, well not finally it would seem because perhaps you will become the next part of this tragic tale, you will have to understand how the dragons were in the world. How they lived as supernatural planetary life force or energy incarnated as human beings, all be it very gifted human beings.

For all the aeons of space time they had lived, they had flowed. Flowed through the worlds they inhabited, flowed again into the stars when a world inevitably came to end and flowed into and through the fabric of the next world in which they came to dwell. They flowed through the channels in Arimathea as light and vibration, through the molecular and sub-atomic structures present in this area of the universe. The life force they carried would react with the bedrock and slowly they would dream this new world into being. As you know, for the good of Arimathea, eventually they flowed out of their underworld channels out of the Dragon hills onto the surface as human beings. They flowed across the surface of the world as they had done through the rock below. Free in a world evolved from their memories, they wandered continually from place to place, always totally absorbed and surprisingly entranced by this new world.

They roamed the lands into which they had chosen to inhabit initially to help the freedom fighters to redress the balance between the people and their rulers. Once the armies had been rendered incapable and the revolution had been successful the dragons were able to continue their travels.

Incarnated as strong men and women they were able to cover enormous distances. Across the plains, through the vast forests and high into the mountain ranges they wandered, deeper and deeper relishing this new world which had evolved since the catastrophic failure they had left behind all those eons before on the other side of the universe. They marvelled again at the sophisticated systems that had again come to life. They smiled to themselves as they stood on the highest peaks and acknowledged the sophistication of the atmospheric balance. After so long drifting in the cold wastes of space, the gentle warmth of the Star on their faces never ceased to bring enormous joy. A profound sense of belonging and responsibility arose when they contemplated all that had come into being as a result of their union with Arimathea. It was then they confirmed their determination to prevent all this ending in the cataclysm they had witnessed and fled from before.

In their travels they studied, meditated upon and soaked up the wonder of the processes in everything growing, flying or wandering alongside them on their journeys. They swum deep in the rivers and found the ancient beings living under totally different circumstances within the same laws in the rivers and oceans. They recognised these ancient spirits as the energies that had inhabited their dreams. They had held specific roles and held the structure of the dream in place. Now they saw them roaming in their physicality, struggling to survive, chasing down their fellow creatures, killing, eating, sleeping, mating, giving birth and dying.

Always they could see the proud spirit of the desperate beast. They watched the wolves and the cats in the wildernesses standing proudly contemplating the lands in which they had grown, searching the horizon for their prey. The powerful mother bear carefully tending her precious cubs as they frolicked unaware of the dangers they continually faced. How they all would stand and fight to the death to protect their offspring as if they knew all life on Arimathea depended on the survival of each one of these precious bundles; as if they had been in the dragon's dream when all the great spirits had slowly started to disappear.

A dream in which the world had slowly faded, as each life force holding its place had lost its foothold and drifted into extinction. The dragons saw their dream truly alive in these creatures, in the life force they possessed, in the ancient spirit wisdom they each carried and used in their daily battle for survival. They recognised the ancient wisdom in these creatures as they survived in the high mountain ranges or deep in the tropical forests.

Wisdom they always had to rediscover as they followed their mothers and fathers on hunting trips, as they played with their siblings toughening up muscle and tendons, sharpening reactions and thought processes leading them back to the memories lying dormant in their new bodies. Here they would find the instructions on how to operate these sharpened teeth or claws, how to use these wings to soar high into the breeze, how to use this stamina to run to exhaustion or outwit another creature who would be using all his or her own embedded wisdom to escape sudden death. As they found the wisdom carried by this ancient spirit who had found its way into this new being so the path for the survival of the next generation was assured.

Like an artist or poet who has rediscovered an old painting or a poem when the memory of the struggle to bring it into existence has faded; when the imperfections have long since been forgotten and he or she is able to look at his work with unimaginable pride, so the dragons looked upon this world of Arimathea.

At this time their thoughts were all entwined. The dragons soon built a very comprehensive overview of the world as it really was. Contemplations of environments across the planet were processed into the combined consciousness of their existing memories. So, trees contemplated in forests North, South, East, and West, gave the dragons precise knowledge and insight into the processes, their strengths and weaknesses in relation to their position and so the planet as a whole.

The dragons without exception had a special love for trees. They had always felt they were more directly connected to these ancient beings than any other. Their roots delved deep into the soil on the surface of their world. Delving directly into the energy of the dragons as their channels flowed close to the surface. Like no other creature trees were constantly in contact with the processes of the atmosphere throughout their long stable lives. They reached up into Star and Moon light combining energy borrowed from the ground to form the protective layer around the fragile surface of Arimathea.

Strong Starlight would be absorbed through branches and leaves allowing them to grow higher and stronger. Flood waters capable of washing away delicate topsoil were absorbed and held stable by their extensive root systems; holding in place the soil fertilised possibly for thousands of years by their fallen leaves, in turn providing all the nutrients needed for the trees to grow. The complex array of gases involved in these processes created the air in which every creature on the planet lived and breathed. Here, embedded in these beautiful living structures, these elegant beings, was embedded the wisdom holding the balance for all the other ancient spirits now inhabiting the world.

In their great families, the great forests covering vast swathes of the planet, also supported a myriad of exotic life. The dragons found a wonder even they found hard to comprehend. They would often walk far out of their way to walk through one of these ancient forests. They would frequently climb high into their leafy branches where they could bask in the refined and peaceful essence of their great love, Arimathea.

Amongst the branches they found the smaller birds, no lesser spirits for their stature, living out their lives searching out the tiny creatures living on and under the extensive bark skins of the trees and amongst the fallen leaves and limbs being gradually broken down by the forces of decay and the weirdly shaped moulds and fungi. In this layer of Arimathea's surface, the dragons were able to watch the age old adversaries of Life and Death carrying on silently and mysteriously. These processes of generation and regeneration gave them immense satisfaction.

At these times however they had to acknowledge they had broken with the ancient lore by becoming incarnated. High in the tree tops they could observe the hawks, daring and skilful hunters, diving and weaving at lightning speed through the wooded glades in search of sustenance. They also watched the great gatherings of black crows on their migrations through the skies. These were the creatures the dragons feared most. Their chilling cries filled the air with a foreboding they could not ignore. These were the spirits which had always aided the dark forces of decay as they relentlessly attempted to break down any system showing any kind of weakness. The crows would seek out these weaknesses and call in the destructive forces of disease and disintegration hurrying in the spectre of death. Then again, the carrion crows would inevitably feed.

All these creatures and all the other millions of species holding their place on the vast web of life had become the physical manifestation of accumulated wisdom the dragons had gathered through the aeons of their existence. Now they were experiencing this physicality in a way they rarely had before. Their enthusiasm for all that had transpired was boundless. When they eventually came out of the wilderness and entered the towns, they were soon to be found with a crowd of people gathered around them, explaining the intricacies of the beautiful world they inhabited.

At this time in human history what the dragons were telling them was incredible beyond belief. The idea their planet was spherical and spinning around a star came as a great surprise to most. They found it almost impossible to believe it was a huge organism living in its own right as an entity comprised of millions and millions of other spirit creatures, each with their own specific role to play in maintaining its health and success. However, everyone who listened walked back to their homes looking at their world in an entirely different way.

The learned scholars also came to listen to the dragons. There were those who found these new revelations hard to accept within the parameters of what they understood about their world. Many refused to accept what the dragons were telling them. But there were those who engaged and delved deeper into what they were being told. They found the dragons had detailed knowledge of the processes of life at a molecular level. They listened as they were told of whole layers of cellular activity remaining completely invisible to their eyes, threaded with the dreams the dragons had bought from the stars and which had guided the steady evolution of their world.

The scholars would continually ask, even though they had no sensible theory themselves about how all this life had come to be on their world...

"How will we ever be able to know what you are telling us is true if we cannot see the evidence of what you are saying?"

The dragons might answer.

"How would you make anything?"

...and watch their puzzled faces.

"Look at any of the tools you use in your everyday lives, a good example would be, say the scythes you use to harvest your fields. Initially you have a need, in this case to cut the corn as quickly and as efficiently as possible before the rains come and ruin the crop. That is the principle, the initial thought guiding the evolution of the tool. At first it maybe too heavy or too small so the next one you make would have a larger but lighter blade taking less energy to wield in the heat of the summer Starlight; and so, it would cut more corn. If the short handle causes you a crippling aching back by the end of the day the next one may have a longer handle. So, although the scythe is evolving through the necessity of its purpose it is guided by the fundamental requirement of its creation.

The fundamental requirement on Arimathea or any world has always been to allow another world to develop to its maximum potential. Every life and process is refined through its evolution to that ends. Whether to control animal populations or to regulate the climate, the initial dream continually guides every separation and reconstruction of every body of cells. So, we now find ourselves with a self-regulating planet, for the most part stable and allowing life to be refined and develop into the future. Of course, there is no telling what the humble scythe will eventually evolve into!"

The scholars would then ask.

"So, it would follow presumably, each and every life has an importance within the life of Arimathea as she strives towards her evolutionary potential? But how can one life have significance in such a creature such as this?"

Depending on who they were talking to at the time the dragons would use some simple analogy for how the tiniest fragment could influence the whole. When replying to the scholars they would pick up one of their carefully crafted books.

"Take each one of your books. You will know how many chapters there are. If you took out a chapter, the thread of the story or the idea behind the book would be lost. You almost certainly would not know how many letters make up the book and if a few were missing here and there, the sense of the book would not be lost. But the whole book is only truly complete when all the individual letters have been carefully arranged so the initial idea has been successfully conveyed to everyone who comes to read it. Every tiny letter becomes part of the work. Take a painting or a sculpture. A million brush strokes or carefully executed cuts to create the final work of art. Your buildings constructed of thousands of bricks and tiles, carefully crafted pieces of timber all brought together, by hundreds of carefully executed actions by many craftsmen to create the one final construction. This is the truth behind any creation. But before any work starts there has to be an idea, a thought, an intention running through the whole process to hopefully bring a successful outcome to the endeavour!"

This was how the dragons explained the intricacies involved in the creation of Arimathea. Their ideas were easily transferable from one person to another and they spread easily amongst the population. The wonder rapidly became respect as people began to understand they lived on a complex world, understandable in terms of simple principles, similar to those governing their own lives and everything around them. These ideas spread rapidly until they had encompassed the entire planet and been absorbed by many of the people who heard them.

However, there were the questions even the dragons could not answer. Every now and again when these fundamental principles had been understood inevitably someone would ask.

"So, who or what is behind the initial principle? If you have carried this knowledge from previous worlds which has again been able to evolve, where did the knowledge originate. Do not the priests of the new alien religions acknowledge the higher power beyond Arimathea, out in the stars where you yourselves originate!"

The dragons could not argue against this observation. They tried to explain the mystery in terms of the laws of the country or the common sense every parent tried to instil in their children. It became an invisible but constant influence as it flowed throughout their lives. It was wisdom gathered over many generations which enabled everyone to live sensibly within their community if they chose to do so. Ultimately, it was a state in which the universe was held and in which the possibilities were infinite. In the probability of those possibilities coming to fruition in the diverse nature of each world as it came into existence, lay the mystery.

Ultimately their home was in the stars and they knew themselves to be an intrinsic part of the greater mystery working through the forces of creation and destruction. These energies had worked and were working through everything that had ever come to be. They knew there was no real separation in this physical world; just this flowing energy, fluctuating from one state to another in a vast reaction between time, space and potential seemingly driven by the intention to maximise the probability of every possibility eventually coming into being.

This, they indicated to the scholars, who had so much understanding and misunderstanding about their world, was where the mystery had brought them to. To this fabulous world with all the wonder and beauty it contained, with all the terror and the misery, the brutality that had taken the mystery so far from the pure love in its ethereal yearning for harmony.

The dragons had been on the journey since those early times and had watched those forces surface in the mystery as consciousness on many worlds. When the dragons discovered a planet where the great mystery had been able to concentrate its fertile potential, they had rapturously joined with it. Again, they had slept and dreamed, merged all they had seen and experienced through the eons into this new consciousness as it began again to form a world.

This is what the dragons told the humans who had noticed the relationship they shared with the mystery was similar to the relationship they had now formed with the dragons. The difference was the dragons had now revealed themselves. They were making them aware that in every part of their lives, the ordinary and the uneventful, were circumstances connecting them into the incredible miracle that had come to exist in the Universe.

The dragons were able to explain to the people, the miracle was in the deeper levels of complexity underlying all the life on Arimathea. Accepting these deeper levels and how they worked in everyday occurrences would inevitably enhance all of their lives. As these revelations became accepted, slowly it dawned on the people of Arimathea they had all become part of an incredible, unexplained miracle that had revealed itself on Arimathea. This knowledge, although at first almost impossible to comprehend, found resonance deep in the souls of the people of Arimathea where the dragons had hoped to reach.

Meanwhile, the power and influence of the landlords was being invisibly and continuously stifled by the abilities of the dragons to disable the systems of fear that had allowed them to exert such enormous control. This fear had been easy to instil in the human race. They had become so aware of their lives and how they were maintained. This had made them vulnerable to their ruthless brothers and sisters who had found the cruel ability to threaten the fabric of their lives could give them the power they craved. With the eradication of this debilitating fear, they were left with a new enthusiasm to live more fulfilling lives. The dragons watched with great satisfaction and relief as they observed a new course of events beginning to unfold. They hoped this action would ultimately lead Arimathea away from the disaster they had foreseen.

As this new understanding of the relationship they held with Arimathea started to grow all areas of life for the people of Arimathea started to develop. A new respect for their world and their place in it began to grow. As they realised the implications of what the dragons had told them and the oppression fell away, they found they had new responsibilities for themselves and the world around them. Most of the farmers decided they could best contribute with the skills they already had. Handed down through the generations and with the insights the dragons had given them they were soon producing bigger and better harvests. This instantly made life less perilous for all who now benefited from a better more substantial diet.

There was also a bigger surplus of crops being traded with their neighbouring communities. With greater trading capacity, they again began to develop their skills to make new products. The skills of the smiths, the carpenters and the builders and all the other craftsmen and women were again in high demand. As they traded amongst themselves communities began to strengthen and began to make decisions about how they could improve. New schools were established with the new understanding and appreciation of Arimathea and the mystery carefully laced into the lessons. All the children's special individual skills were noticed, encouraged and developed from an early age enabling them to reach potential they would never have reached working in the fields to maximise the profits of the landlords.

In those years huge leaps were made in many areas ultimately important for their wellbeing. Their health began to improve as their healers started to think holistically about the human body and the way it now had become regarded as an integral part of the world. The law was transformed, as ideas about relationships between material possessions, people, animals and the lands in which they all existed dramatically changed. A great resurgence in the interest in science resulted from the idea of the continual evolution of the planet as one entity while possessing an almost infinite multiplicity of individuals upon it. As trade thrived between regions and countries so these new ideas along with the products, they were producing spread around Arimathea.

The dragons began to notice, the similarities they shared with the human beings. As their confidence grew, they became more creative and were more able to direct and take responsibility for their own lives. They were continually identifying new strategies as different circumstances arose. Whether making basic essentials such as pots and pans or entire buildings the result would not only depend on the specific conditions to be overcome but on the creator's individual perspective.

The dragons observed these strategies would arise from quiet meditative thought, a state they recognised from their own dream processes and similar to their connection with the great mystery in the Universe beyond. The dragons wondered whether these human beings had a similar link to the mystery as they themselves. They had become sophisticated creatures with enormous creativity connecting them directly to the forces of light and creation.

But for such a powerful race to have become so disconnected from the underlying consciousness which contained so much wisdom for successful life on their planet, the dragons identified as a serious threat to the safety of Arimathea and a weakness easily exploited by the forces of darkness and destruction. For as long as they held influence here, they would continue to bring Arimathea's people closer to her wonders. But the dragons had started to realise there may be more they needed to do to ensure the safety of their beloved Arimathea.

These observations and their subsequent thoughts permeated through the combined consciousness of the dragons living as human beings on Arimathea. They had all recognised the creative forces the humans undeniably possessed and which seemed to work in an uncannily similar way to their own. As they travelled, they saw how the human dreams and their resultant creations were changing and could powerfully change Arimathea in the future. Many of these dreams enhanced their lives and Arimathea was evolving into a more beautiful world as a result.

However, never far from the dragon's minds was the reason they were here. They had come to undermine the inclination of a minority to suppress and exploit the majority of the people on Arimathea. They knew the threat had not gone away and it may only be a matter of time before it would surface once again to set Arimathea back on her path towards annihilation.

Chapter Twenty-Six
The Dragon's Meeting.

So, the dragons decided they would meet in the presence of their beloved Arimathea in a place unknown to the human beings. At this stage of its development there were large areas of the planet still undiscovered. The regions always beloved to the dragons were the high mountainous regions of the North. They remained for the most part inaccessible. It was important they were undisturbed. Arimathea was a beautiful world and any of the high plains, gorges, wild rocky coastlines or jungles teeming with strange wildlife would have made spectacular meeting places.

However, it transpired all the dragons were missing being in their dark caves deep inside Arimathea. They remembered the great caves of the outer regions, carved by the powerful endless tides and currents when these regions had been submerged below the oceans in earlier times. The most spectacular of these caves had been formed and subsequently raised to one of the highest peaks in a mountain range as yet untouched by human interference. The dragons collectively longed to be there and so it was agreed they would travel and meet to discuss their latest dilemma. They would travel in their original energetic form so avoiding the time spans it would inevitably take to reach such a remote region. To make this transition they would have to travel to the dragon hills and combine with their dragon souls.

Transformed once again into the primal energy that had brought them from the stars, no longer limited by flesh and bone that had provided so much insight into life on Arimathea, they flew into the skies that had beckoned to them. Now they could soar effortlessly amongst the cloudscapes that had so tantalised them. They swooped down through hills, followed the courses of rivers and skimmed the tops of their beloved woods where the rooks would rise croaking their protests at the dragons as they flew effortlessly by.

They swooped over villages and towns, where anyone who happened to be looking up would wonder how the air seemed to ripple and sizzle in their wake or why the trees seemed to stretch just a little higher to feel their fabulous energy. They watched as birds flew higher to be in their path, clouds mysteriously parted before them, paying no heed to the weather conditions and flinging Starshine down onto the land ahead of them. Further and further they flew, out into the remotest parts of Arimathea where the great mountain peaks rose like great battlements protecting some mythical land where only those with such supernatural credentials could access.

As they flew closer to their final destination, the consciousness of the dragons became ever more closely entwined as they anticipated their arrival. One by one, floating high on the great weather systems flowing up from the ocean they came into sight of Karama-sarai, the holy mountain. They stooped down from the high air currents that had carried them around Arimathea and joined with their brothers and sisters as they circled and spiralled through the air. Ecstatic again to be in each other's company they screeched through the cold mountain air defying all the laws of the physical universe over and through the majestic snow mountains of Arimathea.

The Star was still high in the sky as they glided back towards the holy mountain and one by one set themselves down upon a wide rocky ledge. Here was the entrance to the cavern. One by one the magnificent creatures gracefully landed, until fifteen dragons, seven male and eight females had arrived and had undergone their transformation back into human form. They had travelled through many different worlds throughout the aeons of time as one creature from the stars. Now they saw the human beings they had become, tall and statuesque, each with the soft glow of green in their eyes. They smiled and laughed, admired lean muscles and pleasing curves. They greeted each other, hugged and caressed, delighting in the familiarity they felt in the strange and beautiful creatures they now inhabited. As they talked, they took the torches from the walls, all of which ignited instantly and started to make their way down a wide tunnel leading through the mountain. Their excited conversations tailed off and they became quiet as they made their way deeper into the darkness.

As they neared the heart of the mountain, they began to feel Arimathea as she flowed through the strata of the rock all around them. They relished her closeness in the nurturing darkness now illuminated with the warmth of the flames dancing on the walls. Here was where the life with which they had become so involved in the previous months had begun. They relived the memories of aeons sleeping in the endless darkness, dreaming out their memories and the knowledge that would eventually bring those first sparks of life to some distant corner of this new world. These memories now steadied their resolve to do everything in their power to protect the miracle that had evolved here despite the risk they knew they could be taking. They thought of the beautiful children they had so entranced with their stories, of their fathers and mothers who watched them with such love in their eyes, settled now and free in the towns and villages they had built nestled amongst the hills and forests. As they made their way into the mountain tunnel, they thought of the warmth of the Star and all the life they had seen enjoying its beneficial touch upon Arimathea. There could be no other risk more worth taking than to protect this miraculous corner of the Universe!!

The end of their journey through the darkness, eerily timeless and now strangely symbolic of the journey they had made to this world, was eventually signalled by the appearance of a dim light in the distance. They forgot their thoughts and hurried towards the light which steadily grew until they emerged into the enormous cavern in the centre of the mountain. High in the roof there was an opening providing a shaft of light that fell onto the cavern floor illuminating a circle of sixteen large and upright stones. Each stone had been carefully sculpted to provide a seat allowing its occupant to face the centre of the circle. At the centre of the circle there was a pile of what appeared to be large boulders. The dragons briefly explored the further regions of the caves where a stream fell from high on one of the walls and provided a series of still pools. However, the light was starting to fade and the dragons returned to the circle and took their places one on each of the stone seats in the circle.

When they all were seated there was one seat left empty. This was acknowledged only with a number of knowing glances amongst the dragons. They were silent again for a while as the last light from the shaft faded. They savoured the darkness as it became complete. When they all were ready, each dragon drew a great lungful of air and simultaneously directed jets of flame towards the rocks in the centre of the circle. As the flames subsided the rocks were left glowing under the intense heat directed at them and after a few moments burst into flames illuminating the dragons and the spacious cavern. They sat in silence contemplating the flames and the recent time they had spent on Arimathea. Images and impressions of their most memorable experiences flooded through their collective consciousness. They had shared similar pleasures as they had observed Arimathea but they all had become aware of the flaw they had discovered in the human beings. Eventually Merilon stood up and started to speak.

"It is good to be here with you under these new circumstances incarnate as human beings. A strange and wonderful group we make. But I fear there is little time for becoming re-acquainted. I think we have all sensed the forces of destruction searching for a way to undo what we have done for the people of Arimathea. It seems we need to discuss how we can continue the transformation without us becoming even more deeply involved. If all this starts to escalate, we could find ourselves in a terrible war of our own making with unthinkable consequences for Arimathea."

Merilon returned to his seat. There was a further silence before Alamistra, one of the female dragons arose to address the circle. She was tall and her long fair hair flowed down her back. The green glow of her eyes shone from the soft curves of her face as she walked confidently around the circle acknowledging her fellow dragons. She stopped as near to the fire as she dared clearly luxuriating in the heat. Then she began to speak.

"It is true we dare not become any more involved than we already are. But now I have lived on Arimathea and become involved with the human beings, I have seen how they live for the most part in complete turmoil. Their moods swing daily or even hourly from happiness to sadness, from loving to hating, their insecurity and need for acceptance amongst their fellows plagues much of everything they do, their fulfilment has been in the past or will be in the future, an attitude which threatens their ability to achieve either because they cannot understand it is in the present success in both of these places are achieved. They occupy their minds with destructive habits which only worsen their situation and cause even more conflict. This conflict within themselves continually threatens almost every aspect of their lives. They can easily misunderstand and misjudge what is happening to them and most dangerously of all completely disregard not only the relationships with their fellow humans but the entire world around them. These are dangerous traits for such a powerful species. I think we need to find a strategy to somehow reduce their turmoil. It seems as if there is a continual war raging inside them which they appear to have no ability or will to resolve."

Alamistra returned to her seat and another one of the male dragons, Aralstir now stood up.

"I think we have all realised where the conflict originates. They are a young race compared to many of the more ancient spirits who have come to dwell on Arimathea. However, they have become sophisticated, intelligent and creative far beyond their years. I think we all have recognised the similarities they share with us."

He raises his hands,

"...and look how easily we fit into their form. However, although they have developed an ability to channel the creative forces of the Universe extremely proficiently, it seems they have lost their ability to connect with the consciousness underlying and sustaining life on this planet. The turmoil has arisen because they originally evolved in this relationship and its loss has resulted in an emptiness and confusion they have been unable to understand or fill.

The situation is made more dangerous because now the most misguided amongst them have formed their own ideas about the nature of their world based on the emptiness they feel. They have proclaimed this emptiness as an inevitable and necessary part of their existence. The separation will only increase and the turmoil deepen as these ideas take them further and further away from their ability to connect with the consciousness. This conveniently serves a minority and the most deluded of them to use this new proclamation as a vindication to exploit and at worst enslave the people of Arimathea for their own benefit. I saw and felt the direct influence of Oblivion in the fear being instilled and could see the seeds of destruction being carefully sown. This could, proliferated into the future, bring about a catastrophic end to this world. Our interference I fear has only temporarily restored their confidence. However, the underlying problem is not resolved."

Aralstir himself then sat as a murmur of concern ran around the circle. Zaralahn then stood up and started to speak.

"This would be a tragic end to such a beautiful world but I agree there is little more direct action we dare undertake. If Oblivion has been involved in this separation and the subsequent oppression, it will continue to escalate it's influence if it finds a way to defeat our strategy. This would only lead to a hopeless future for the people of Arimathea and the rest of this world. However, we can do what we have always done and that is to dream out further wisdom into Arimathea. This will be absorbed and gradually it will become specifically part of the human consciousness. Hopefully this will begin to guide them to find their way back into a deeper understanding of their world."

There were murmurs of approval. Another female dragon, Teron, stood to speak.

"So, what form will these new dreams take? They are complex creatures with highly developed senses, they can be highly perceptive and intuitive, potentially giving them the ability to make very accurate assumptions about all aspects of their world? We have seen with the revolution how their experience of the world and their intuition can connect them quickly back into the consciousness.

However they are easily influenced to distrust this connection; which is hardly surprising when you consider the priests of the alien gods have persuaded them over the years to believe that acting upon or even having such a connection with their world will send them straight to the fires of their burning eternity in the next life; often after they have been burned to death. This cruelty to their fellow beings, I find the most disturbing. But perhaps it does go some way to illustrate the depths of the confusion they are in and the lengths they are prepared to go to quell their own personal turmoil.

I think we should help them to develop their perception, their intuitive powers of reflection so they can see how everything happening around them connects them into the wider consciousness. Maybe then, as they feel those connections and understand how they have become an intricate part of a beautiful and complex web of life their respect and their understanding for the wonders of Arimathea will then become the wisdom they develop and carry through their lives."

Teron sat as the dragons showed their approval for her thoughts with gentle applause. Zaramir now stood.

"These are indeed wise words I am hearing. We will have to decide the nature of these new dreams we are going to direct towards the human beings. Do we agree, they must be able to somehow intensify their understanding of the underlying complexities and beauty of Arimathea by deepening the experiences in their everyday lives? Their senses and perceptions are well developed and will soon pick up on any additional dreams we send if only in their sub-conscious. Perhaps we should join into our one consciousness and concentrate on how these dreams might be."

The dragons whole heartedly agreed with more excited murmurings and Zaramir returned to his chair. The dragons became quiet, looking deep into the fire burning in the centre of their circle. They concentrated on the fire. It began to return them to the central, still point at the start of the universe from which all things were initiated and where everything was possible as pure potential. Their minds combined as the one spirit being also born at that point forged from the implosion of a million concentric dimensions. With all the knowledge and wisdom they had learnt since those first moments and all they had learnt in the time they had spent with the human beings on Arimathea, they would search for a new dream in the combined layers of dragon and planetary consciousness

In their vision the extraordinary and diverse nature of Arimathea soon became prevalent. In their journeys and flights they had never been in any doubt this was the most beautiful world they had brought into being. As their thoughts and impressions formed, each becoming a unique strand forming in the one consciousness, it was undoubtedly the nature of Starlight as it filtered down through the protective atmosphere from the blackness of space that had most surprised the dragons when they had first experienced it through their Human eyes.

Under the blue skies, at times completely invisible from the dense clouds covering them and the infinite range of conditions caused by the varying cover in between, it seemed every version of life that ever could have been had suddenly burst onto the land and into the oceans where the Starlight had fallen. All the dragons it seemed had travelled and marvelled in admiration of the spectacular scenery they had experienced as they had journeyed around Arimathea. From the crystal-clear mountain peaks, pure and white, untouched in their frozen atmospheres, to the dense tropical jungles where a variety of life had burgeoned well in excess of anything in the dreams the dragons had brought from other worlds.

Arimathea had become something entirely unique as she revolved constantly around her distant star. She had provided all these environments for all this life to unfold. The dragons knew how unlikely this all was. As they looked out into the dark skies at night and remembered their journeys in the lifeless wastes of space they yearned for the morning and the first rays of Starlight to again illuminate and feed this incredible world. Although they knew it was the complexity and constancy of the vast physical Universe beyond, holding Arimathea in a great web of astrophysical phenomena, which perhaps had made her creation inevitable at some place and point in time, they remained in awe of the unexplained mystery lying at the heart of her creation.

Inevitably as they experienced these environments in their dreams, the life flourishing within it started to surface in their thoughts. Specifically, they remembered that although they were perceiving Arimathea through human senses, they realised the human beings living on Arimathea had none of the insight into the wonders and the terrors of the Universe they had gained as beings who had travelled extensively through it. However, in their observations they had found the human beings were not incapable of experiencing the wonders available to them on Arimathea. They had seen the elation they experienced with successful creative achievement or in moments of profound and loving connection with their fellows. It was at these times they were able to look out on their world as if the mystery had momentarily been revealed to them in the incredible nature of what lay all around them.

This, the dragons recognised, was the state in which the human beings became more compassionate, and as a result they developed a deeper respect for themselves and their world. It was in these moments when they recognised how all their actions were directly affecting the world around them. They concluded if the human beings could achieve this state more often perhaps they would start to adjust their actions and Arimathea would be a safer place now and would be in less danger in the future.

So, the dragons decided they would try to reach the human beings through their emotions and their ability to think creatively and come to solutions beneficial to their situation. They also knew them to be reflective. This was where the dragons decided they would attempt to intensify their connection. Perhaps if the human beings began to realise the thoughts and feelings they were having were part of the wider consciousness of Arimathea, so linking them incontrovertibly with her they would start to consider her in all their plans and decisions in the same way as they would for anyone who was close to them.

Deeper into their dream they drifted through the consciousness of Arimathea, allowing her to guide them into the deepest recesses of her wonder. She brought them to a quiet field surrounded by deep hedges and ancient trees where a farmer was ploughing his field with an enormous shire horse. The great plough churned the earth and the man walked in the furrow it left behind. The star was low in the sky and it was late autumn.

The dragons were able to hear his thoughts as he came to the end of his working day. He and his horse have ploughed only part of the field and he will return tomorrow and possibly the next. The dragons can hear he has much on his mind. He is pleased he has been able to bring in his harvest on time but worried he will not sell the grain for enough money to sow next year's crop and feed his family without having to sell some of his cows. Then the roof to his cottage will need mending before winter. His children, his wife and indeed he himself all needed new clothes. He was also worried that if when his family and his business had taken their share of the income, he would not have enough money to pay the taxman when he came around in the spring.

He was angry and resentful to be working so hard and still struggling to hold his place in the world. He could not understand what was given in return for all the tax he had to pay. He gives the horse a pat on the neck and then reaches up and affectionately runs the huge ears through his hands. The horse responds with a low contented whinny and turns and nuzzles his owner with his huge head. The farmer smiles and for a few seconds forgets his worries as he transfers his attention onto the animal he spends so much time with working these fields.

They knew each other well enough to know it was time for them to call it a day. The farmer looks for a moment over the newly turned soil. The birds who have been following him all day are still pecking out the worms from the soft brown earth. He watches as a black bird tugs out a huge worm and flies off into the wood at the bottom of the field. The low evening Star is settling on the tops of the canopies and a few rays have escaped from the edge of the wood creating pools of light in the shaded side of the field. Again, he grimaces as he detaches the horse's harness from the plough and starts to lead her back along the track towards the farm buildings.

The track leads him down a gentle slope and through the stretch of Oak woods nestling in the intersection of his five fields. As he enters the extensive woodland he stops, pulls up the horse and looks around in awe. The Oaks were planted many generations before and now are three hundred years old. Starlight falls down through the high branches filling the space with soft evening light. He slowly moves the horse forward down the track which also intersects with a footpath leading from the village.

He, his family and all walking through them treasured the trees that provided cover for many species of large and small animals. He often saw deer and foxes, and there were badger sets in the banks deeper into the wood. The high branches were always full of a large variety of native birds. They were now filling the wood with their final dusk songs.

But he looks up into the canopy with dread. The trees and the land on which they stand are a valuable resource. If they were felled and sold they would very quickly solve his financial problems. The land which amounted to the size of one of his larger fields would give him more grain to sell and would make the harvest considerably more profitable. When like this year, the price of grain was low the corn would barely support the farm. The price he would receive for the felled Oaks would certainly transform his family's lives. But he loved these woods!!

There was sanctuary here and continuity with the generations who had planted them. Also, here he felt he held a piece of the world which wasn't just about the struggle he had in it. He felt he entered this other world whenever he came here. He knew if he relinquished the struggle for its' existence then something terrible would be lost for himself. There were so many memories of his childhood. This was where he had brought his friends to play. Then in his transition to adulthood there were the sweet moments in the courtship of his wife laying by the little stream, listening to the bees and the wind whispering through the giant Oaks and now, here was the place he always visited for some respite.

It was inconceivable he was even contemplating the idea. But he had been and it was because things had become very difficult, almost impossible and he just could not bear to lose his farm. If he did lose it someone else would come and fell the wood anyway. He had put off making the decision for far too long and now things were critical. He shook his head, gently tugged the horses lead rein and the two walked deeper into the wood.

As he walked, he saw a figure in the distance walking towards him. He could see from the stature it was a man but it appeared as though he was walking out of the Star, so low it had become now, he could not make out who it was. The wood now became strangely silent, almost as if it had been hearing his thoughts and it knew these moments had become a turning point in its destiny. The figure was approaching now and the farmer recognised who it was. How strange to meet him now like this? With all he had on his mind. The two men now walked up to each other and greeted each other respectfully. It was old Silas the grain merchant. He was dressed unsuitably for a walk in the countryside as if he had been diverted from some more urgent matter in the town. He himself seemed surprised and a little uncomfortable to see the farmer. But it seemed they were both compelled to stop and exchange some conversation before they went on their way.

"Beautiful evening, Jeremiah."

"It is that Silas, in fact it has been a very beautiful day. Of course, I would have preferred not to have been ploughing that bloody field all day, but there you go."

He stretches and rubs his hand over his shoulder which is painful from guiding the plough.

"I haven't seen much of it myself. I seem to have had my head in the books all day!!"

There is now a silence between them. Jeremiah knows he will be assessing the market to decide what price he is going to offer the farmers in the area for their grain. After a few moments awkward silence Silas looked around him and appeared to be admiring the wood.

"This old wood must have been here a few years, Jeremiah! I often make a diversion down here at the end of the working day in the town on my way home, gives me a feeling of serenity after all the wheeling and dealing. I hope you don't mind but sometimes I go into the wood and sit by the stream."

The farmer turns to look at him and pats the horse on the neck, ruffles its long mane. So, here is the man who indirectly is deciding the very destiny of the wood, telling him it has become a valued part of his life. Silas sees the astounded look Jeremiah is giving him. The great orange sphere of the Star has settled on the horizon at the end of the lane silhouetting the farm buildings. The two men stand silently on the shores of the world unaware that all around them, in the trees and the air and the ground beneath their feet, in the time and space that has brought them to this place, in all the dealings they have had between each other and the lives each has lead up until that very point was held a possibility.

The dragons had dreamt a situation that could happen in the future as their influence was slowly forgotten. When they had returned home, deep into the psyche of Arimathea and men would again resist her charms, casting the memory of her sacred beauty aside for their short-sighted greed and physical gain. But now as they flowed again through their beloved Arimathea they would dream a little harder the essence of creative light, the power to bring about some transformation as the entwining of a new set of diverse possibilities initiated a new uncharted outcome and a new pathway, with even greater potential spiralling into the future.

Old Jeremiah in that moment felt the possibility rising like the dawn of a new day in his mind.

"So, you enjoy using my woods, do you Silas?"

"Very much, Sir. And I know a few others who would say the same. Quite a talking point in fact amongst those of us who enjoy this path; so many of the woods have been felled along these ancient old paths." He looked at Jeremiah curiously expecting some rebuke.

"So it probably might be of some surprise to you that, a very short time before we met tonight and in fact for some time, I have been considering felling these woods, because frankly the farm is just not making enough money and I could do with the extra field and the money for the Oak would make everything a lot easier."

Jeremiah stops to judge the reaction he is getting from Silas.

"That would be a great shame, my old friend. There would be those who would be greatly upset by such a loss to our town."

"So, what value would you put on these woods, Silas. Since it is the grain prices you are giving making things so hard for me. Perhaps you should think what would be lost here for the whole community if this wood came down!"

Silas smiled at the old farmer. He looked around him as the Star disappeared behind the horizon and a deeper dusky glow came to the wood. There were bats now flitting in the spaces between the trees hunting down the moths on their crazed trajectories through the warm evening air. It would be a terrible loss he thought impoverishing his and the lives of many others.

"Well, you better come and see me in the morning at my offices and we will talk again."

With this the two men shake hands vigorously and each continues on his way.

The dragons drifted back to their cavern in the mountains. As they woke from their dream, and sat quietly around their fire, collectively they discussed what they had experienced. They were all agreed as always, in a strange and magical way, their intentions had blended with those of Arimathea and the Great Spirit mystery and a new possibility had been born. Now at its birth the interaction between Silas and Jeremiah seemed inconsequential. But in those few moments the dragons had recognised the powerful combination of universal force and will they had previously witnessed behind the birth of momentous and transformational planetary events. They settled into further discussion as to the nature of the dreams they would release into Arimathea's future."

Chapter Twenty-Seven
Samir's journey.

Farina paused. She relaxed into her chair. She closed her eyes and became very still. It seemed to Okino she had used considerable energy to relate the occurrences of those previous centuries. He was concerned and moved into the chair next to her. Mariella lifted the baby who was sound asleep and put her in the wooden cradle standing a safe distance from the fire. Okino took her hand gently and feeling her energy was low, gently combined his life force with hers. She slowly opened her eyes as if she had been in a long sleep and sat up again in her chair. She seemed at first to be surprised by her surroundings. Mariella had poured some of the herbal tea for her and she sipped at it calmly as she again became fully conscious. Mariella and Okino watched anxiously as she finally settled back into her chair and smiled back in complete recognition.

"I have never been able to tell the story like this before. It seems as if Arimathea is also choosing to tell her story through me. Her memories of these times are strong, almost overwhelming. This thread we have held is acting like a stream down which the entire reality is flowing; it is like I am there, as if I know the dragons, their holy mountain and their determination to steer this world away from disaster. However, the story is not over yet. There is more to come.

"In the time the dragons travelled to the high mountains, the castles of the disenfranchised rulers were falling rapidly into advanced states of disrepair as the masons who usually maintained them, deserted their previous masters to build schools and houses. In the great surge of creativity resulting from the dragon's intervention, the thickening of the darkness now occurring was hardly being noticed.

In the castles the forces of decay began to crumble the vulnerable mortar and so the masonry in the massive stone walls was deteriorating at an accelerated rate. Nails in the rooves started to rust more quickly, resulting in slates becoming dislodged leaving gaps in the roof coverings. As water trickled through and found its way into the roof timbers, rotting roofs soon started to collapse leaving whole areas of the castles uninhabitable. The lords and their most faithful servants were therefore confined to small areas, where they continued to debate endlessly how they could bring an end to the power the dragons had exerted over their lands.

In one such castle, the scribe Samir had been forced to leave his tower in a remote part of his master's castle when a section of wall had collapsed leaving his quarters exposed to the cooling autumnal air. There was much talk of injustice amongst those who remained. Afraid, but mostly embarrassed to venture beyond the walls of their crumbling domains, the lords would travel to each other's lands in darkness to hear and disseminate their latest plans.

The priests of the alien gods were frequently summoned to debate the nature of the dragon's power. However, they had nothing to offer and their ignorance and impotency in the face of the supposedly inferior powers dwelling within Arimathea had caused derision amongst the rulers and caused many of the priests to reject their beliefs and leave anonymously to live in areas of the planet where they were not known. Again, and again, after debating complicated and ever more ridiculous schemes for the capture and eradication of the dragons, they came to the same conclusion. If there was a weakness in the armour of the dragons then it would have to be found before any thought of re-establishment of their empires could be contemplated. The general population remained stubbornly fearless, ignoring the progressively infrequent decrees their previous masters issued regarding their governance. As focus moved away from the goals of personal gain and advantage of the few, to maximising the potential to be found in themselves and their world, the people were evolving new methods of government amongst their communities based on consent and mutual trust. This immediately made the previous fear-based regimes irrelevant and redundant.

Samir started to travel through the countryside out into the towns and villages. He wanted to assess how the lives of the people had changed as a result of the changes the dragons had brought about. He felt sure he would come across some insight that would eventually lead to the downfall of the dragons. He stubbornly believed there would be some weakness he would be able to exploit. He just had to find it. He would keep his eyes and ears open on these tours for anything, worldly or otherwise which would give him some advantage in this disastrous state of affairs.

He rode out from the castle where his master had become resigned to the fact he would have to pay for builders if he was to prevent the collapse of his castle. Once he had made this decision he became reconciled to the many areas in the life of the castle he needed to reinstate if he himself was not going to sink into oblivion. There was a steady flow of people from the surrounding villages who came to offer their products and services with the satisfaction their landlord would have to pay them respectably for anything they offered to do for him.

As the castle was repaired and cleaned, stocks of food were replenished and the kitchen gardens restored and again cultivated, his family returned and life resumed almost as before. Samir however knew the implications for his master's fortune which was not being replenished at the rate at which it was being expended. As he rode past the fields now being harvested by the farmers who had reclaimed their land, he shuddered when he thought of the losses his master was suffering. He only scowled at one of the hardworking farmers who gave him a good-natured wave as he rode past and became even more determined to return things to how they had been before, when this man had been a tenant on his master's land.

Everywhere he went he saw this resignation amongst the landowners and the wealthy merchants. As a result, the fortunes they had made from exploiting their people were now flowing out into this newly evolving market. As more people benefited from this sudden surge of money flowing into their communities, more was being made and so more was being sold. Everywhere he went, Samir saw the result of this lively trading situation. The markets were full of the new products grown or manufactured and now were being freely traded amongst the people. Tables and chairs, rugs, paintings, pottery, glassware, corn and herbs and livestock, all found their new value as people bartered and haggled over their new worth.

There seemed no limit to their expression and creativity. They learnt new skills and developed abilities far in excess of what they would have imagined they were capable. They were often surprised how easily their new found skills enabled them to create such profoundly beautiful objects so quickly. But then they had been surprised at how remarkably their whole outlook had changed since the dragons had been moving amongst them. The wonder they saw in the world around them seemed to transfer itself easily from their experience and their minds through their hands and into the object they were making, the scene they were painting or the situation or idea they were attempting to express. In much of the work being made at this time, the wonder the artist had first seen seemed to have become embedded in the actual work of art almost as if the essence of the moment in which it had been conceived was shining from it. The qualities of these objects became especially relished. They were found to imbue any home with the mysterious wonder the dragons continually communicated and had so captured the imaginations of her inhabitants.

One morning in one such market, Samir came across a stall which was selling an assortment of beautifully carved wooden animals. He had to admire the way the sculpture had so caught the essence of each creature. He felt himself transported to a quiet riverbank as he contemplated the silent stance of a heron. Higher in the mountains he surveyed the bears territory stretched out before him. There were a number of mountain cats, so elusive, but now he prowled the steep mountain paths with the graceful, muscled creatures as they stalked some unsuspecting creature; perhaps one of the fine mountain goats proudly displaying his splendid horns, alert on some precipice for any sign of his deadly nemesis now standing so intriguingly beside him.

In amongst all these creatures, the sculptor had taken it upon himself to carve the likeness of a dragon. Standing upright on powerful legs, wings unfurled perhaps roaring in defiance at the darkness he or she was holding at bay on Arimathea. He obviously felt antagonism towards the dragon but felt a strange fascination for the object before him. He leant forward and examined it without actually touching it. He noticed the life seeming to emanate from the flowing wooden torso and particularly from the hollows carefully left for its eyes. Before the occurrence of recent events when he had no concept of how these creatures were to effect his life by so upsetting the balance of power on Arimathea, he had always been enthralled by legends and myths in which a being, could have an ability to change the course of events.

Here was a creature not living in the same way he or the other creatures on Arimathea existed; apart from her and for the most part at the mercy of her. These supernatural creatures were Arimathea. There had been no apocalypse, no catastrophe that had changed the flow of events; they had made no obvious declaration of their power or exerted any particular physical force. The power base of their masters, the ruling lords had simply ebbed away. Now life was going on around him in a very different way. They had steered the course of events, manipulated space and time towards a different outcome in the far distant future. These were indeed, the beings that up until now had inhabited only the myths and legends of his world. Samir decided he would buy the carving of the dragon.

As he rode quietly out into the countryside, contemplating these thoughts he was constantly aware of the dragon he was carrying in his saddle bag. There was a presence that seemed to emanate from it. Of course, the dragons were paramount in his mind but now this preoccupation had grown. He found himself studying the surrounding countryside with greater interest rather than staring into the middle distance while contemplating some unconnected thought. It seemed as if his surroundings had suddenly come into focus and were screaming out to him to acknowledge and re access them. There was no doubt he was riding through a particularly pleasing part of the landscape.

But it would have looked even better if it was back in control of his master and the grain being harvested was heading for the castle granaries. But the sky did look wider and bluer. The ground over which he rode, the fields and the distant hills did seem to have a glow, a mysterious luminescence he had never noticed before; and there was so much sound. The calling and intermittent laughter of the people in the fields, the sound of his horse's feet rhythmically, striking the ground, there was a breeze which rustled and dislodged the turning leaves on the trees on the side of the track; the birdsong seemed to wash over the entire sound scape to complete the symphony through which he now rode. Then he heard a new sound: a sound that resonated more harmoniously with his own being.

High above him a large murder of crows was making its way across the sky. Their incessant calling was now eerily filling and dominating the landscape. As he watched the seemingly endless stream of the black birds purposefully travelling across the sky to what appeared to be some pre-ordained destination, one of the large black creatures dropped out of the sky, spiralled down and landed on the dead branch of a tree directly above Samir's path. The large crow then proceeded to screech down at Samir as if delivering some ghastly portent it had brought from its dark and distant domain. It seemed to be repeating the same cry over and over again so there was no possibility he would forget it.

Samir calmed his frightened horse. He was familiar with these birds, who frequented the roof tops and chimneys around his quarters in the castle and watched in astonishment as the scene before him unravelled. Once the crow had decided he had effectively delivered his message he leapt from the branch and flew off to join the rest of the murder leaving Samir wondering what had just happened to him. He pushed his horse on and continued down the road. The crows continued to fly over. There was now a continuous black line of the creatures disappearing into the distance and Samir thought, quite specifically towards an outcrop of hills rising from the plains slightly apart from the other higher ground outlined on the horizon.

The crow, he thought was either warning him to stop and go no further or to follow the murder to the outcrop of hills. He was curious as to what the crow could be warning him away from which was attracting so many of its own kind in such numbers. They were mysterious creatures and this was an enormous gathering. He sensed something must be providing some reason for the crows to travel together in such enormous numbers. It was mid-afternoon so he had a few hours of Starlight left. He was not concerned about returning to the castle and the crow had been very insistent so he decided to ride out to the outcrop of hills.

He underestimated the distance and the time it would take him to reach this new destination. The fields soon fell away and were replaced by rougher countryside and the road finally disappeared completely. In the twilight hours he and his horse were picking their way through a boulder strewn landscape leading up to the hills now looming higher and more threateningly than they had when he had decided to visit them. The crows were still arriving. Sporadically another wave would arrive to fly over the lower hills towards the interior. When Samir came close enough to assess a way into the hills he made his way towards a valley where he discovered a path which would allow him and his horse to travel towards where the crows appeared to be heading.

The path was well used by other people or by the animals living here and although it was now becoming quite dark he was able to travel safely up the valley. The steep sides to the path soon became lined with dense undergrowth and tall straight trees soaring into the darkening skies. A little light from the newly risen moon and the stars filtered down to light the path and Samir tentatively pushed the horse hoping he was able to see what lay a head better than he himself. Despite the darkness he knew he was climbing higher into the hills. The calls from the crows were again becoming more pronounced so he deduced they must have reached their and possibly his destination. Then he noticed a flickering light at what appeared to be the summit of the path he was climbing. He hurried the horse on very curious now to find out what or who was over the rise.

He dismounted and led his horse up to a ridge and peered over. There was a fire burning on a level piece of ground in what appeared to be a bowl surrounded by trees. Light from the flames danced amongst the ghostly trees now filled with the crows. Their plaintive calls had now been replaced by what seemed to Samir like an expectant chatter; as if they were waiting for the show or performance to start. A figure appeared carrying wood. He threw it down onto a pile he had previously collected. He sorted through the pile, carefully selected some branches and threw them onto the fire before settling down, warming his hands in the flames. Samir could make out very little about the figure. Despite the bulk of clothing and the long straggly hair, Samir could tell from his stature he was male. The crows, it seemed had become aware of some change in the atmosphere around them and the crescendo was raised as they started to call again. Samir sensed this may have been something to do with his appearance and slowly prepared to return from where he had come. But the figure had raised himself to his feet quickly scanned the ridge which surrounded his camp and caught sight of Samir lit up in the flames as he started to make his retreat.

"Don't be so fast to disappear now you have arrived. I have been expecting you or one of your kind."

The figure below had shouted up to Samir and stopped him in his tracks. The crows were silent. The show it appeared had begun.

"Who are you and how did you know I was coming?"

"I knew you would arrive with all these other crows…for some time you have had something you needed to discuss with me!"

He now had Samir's attention. The old scribe paused. He must be referring to the situation with the dragons. What else would two men discuss in such an arena surrounded by such a dark audience? But this was not to be a discussion only about how his masters felt so aggrieved. No, this he sensed, would be about something far more serious that something or someone, somewhere had decided he needed to have. Samir after all was unequalled for always being able to assess both sides of every story. How else would he always know the most profitable route to go forwards? He made his way down the incline and joined the stranger in front of the fire.

"So, who did you say you were and where have you come from?"

Samir ventured, uncertain as to whether he really wanted to know the answer. The stranger was very tall and entirely covered from head to foot in ragged clothing. A deep monks hood covered his head so Samir was unable to see his face or even the form of the stranger as he looked straight ahead concentrating on the fire. Samir slightly concerned by this purposeful anonymity, wondered who could have attracted so much attention from the crows.

"Oh Samir, so caught up in the world you and your kind have constructed around yourselves. Everyone and everything must have a place in or outside it. Isn't that what you have come to talk to me about? How the world you and your masters have constructed has been brought to its knees by something outside all that you thought was in your control?"

"It had crossed my mind; I have to admit it would be useful to find someone who knew a little more about these dragons so we might have a better chance of re-establishing the way things used to be."

"The way things used to be." He shook his head. "So, you think you have a right to enslave your fellows for your own benefit!"

"It is the way things are, the system. How we organise ourselves. Human beings are radically different creatures. Some will lead gently, others ferociously but there will always be those that will follow without question because they are afraid…of the consequences."

"There are those who scare their fellow beings into obedience is what you are saying and while we are talking honestly, Samir, you are one of them!"

"I act in the interests of my employer it is true."

The stranger went over to his pile of wood and selected two large logs and threw them onto the fire. A great plume of sparks and flames issued from the conflagration. The crows called down their approval as he turned back to Samir.

"Samir, you and your employer are proliferating a flaw in the human race that could eventually initiate a planetary catastrophe. I know this cannot have crossed your narrow mind which is surprising as you do seem to study the history of your race. Have you never wondered why as a species you find it so easy to exploit so cruelly your fellows when you have great edifices founded on the premise you should treat your neighbour as you would yourself? Have you not wondered, Samir, why the priesthood of these religions live in luxurious palaces next to your kings and rulers while your people fester in poverty barely able to feed themselves?

Do you think it is right the people of your land are threatened with eternal damnation if they so much as utter a word against any of the actions of their king who taxes them to starvation and with the money he takes from them regularly sends them to their death in wars against equally tyrannical leaders over some squabble over a scrap of land which in truth neither of them ever had any right over in the first place? Don't you ever wonder how things came to be like this amongst your race?"

Samir was surprised by the questions now being put to him. He looked deeper into the fire as if he could find the answer there.

"When you put it like that I suppose the situation is not ideal. But as I said it is the system we have…."

"But you don't have it because the dragons have decided it just can't be allowed to go on; another world destroyed by selfish greedy human beings….and you have to admit everything is more productive and everybody is happier without your regimes of terror scaring everybody into submission."

"The markets certainly seem very buoyant at the moment it has to be said."

The old scribe exasperated the dark stranger with his uncommitted answers. He knew the rise and fall of the human race would be caused by people who were following orders from their superiors.

"The thing is Samir and you will remember I told you this, whatever happens from this point on. It is all about Love."

Samir was surprised and looked over at this stranger curiously.

"Everything started with Love, the Universe, eventually this planet, everything; on a vast wave spreading out across the emptiness of space at the beginning of time. It is what your priests call the god and what your people used to call the goddess, it is the great mystery and all the other names your race has for the supposedly supreme beings who live beyond this world. It is warmth and light, a strange magical and infinite vibration, it is the essence that has brought this world into being. The dragons operate within this vibration. They have brought the essence of previous creations to Arimathea from the stars. They are not the creators of this world they only carry the memories of those previous worlds that bring a new world into being with their dreams. Everything,"

He signals around him to the trees and the crows and the fire.

"Everything, Samir, comes out of those dreams, the love that made those dreams has interacted with all the fabric of the Universe and gradually, very gradually it has turned into you."

He nudges Samir's arm.

"Yes, Samir, you! You have been made from Love. You and all your kings and rulers have been made from Love. So why do you think, since you are made from Love you treat your brothers and sisters so badly."

Then he asked insistently.

"Tell me Samir, why. Why when you live on such a beautiful world do you think you have the right to enslave and violate it so dreadfully?

Samir is clearly out of his depth now and offers no reply and looks deeper into the fire.

"I'll tell you why. It is because you have separated yourselves from the Love flowing through this world with your economics and your trading systems, with your boundaries separating and dividing the people, setting them against each other. You deny her people the ability to live in the Love that has made the rivers, the mountains, the plains, all the animals and everything this beautiful world has to offer.

As your race has adapted and come to depend on these new systems for survival, slowly the ability to feel the Love flowing through this world has fallen away... then what is left? Emptiness is left Samir, empty souls, empty spirits existing only to serve your wicked lords...and what is it the darkness stalking this world craves? Emptiness: emptiness to suck out any life emerging out of the Universe! Your race has not only replaced the way it naturally exists in Love and so in harmony with their world but it has actually demonised it with religion, craftily based on a god who espouses Love, but on your terms so that it can control the system made to fill the emptiness that has taken it away!

The further you draw away from this Love which could feed your soul as a being who exists on this planet the further you draw away from the consideration and compassion you feel for your world and everything on it! Even you can see what will happen next!"

"It's eventual destruction!"

Samir had suddenly realised what the stranger was telling him. There was silence between them. Then the stranger turned to him. Samir thought he saw the faintest green glow from underneath the hood covering the strangers head.

"The dragons want to correct it now before, well...Surely better to swat one little fly before it transforms into a vast swarm, wouldn't you say?"

Samir remembered the day when the dragon came to the castle and explained the consequences of the system taking hold upon Arimathea. He wondered at the time whether things really could be any other way. Now he was silent as he remembered his experience earlier in the day when he had seen people working so contentedly and so effectively in their fields. He remembered the confident wave the farmer had given him.

"The thing is Samir, rightly or wrongly this anomaly has become part of the evolution of our species and the world we inhabit. Somehow, we will have to evolve beyond it, without help from the dragons or the Great Spirit mystery in which they operate or anything else. Terrible unimaginable things will happen but also incredibly beautiful beneficial things will come about as a result of it. However, the wisdom your race will hopefully eventually find and act upon is actually bound up in the struggle; you will have to come to terms with the light and the dark; live at peace with them, with yourselves and your world. Never before has such wisdom been attained.

All the other creatures living with you on Arimathea learn to live at the mercy of these powers. Your race must learn, is destined to understand them, the tension formed between them, in yourselves and all living things. They are the most powerful of energies and they drive this universe. Your nature and your great intelligence will enable you to define them and understand them. You can find their meaning and their true significance only in your deep experience of them, in the adversity, in the love and the horror you will meet: and yes, your race will grow powerful and will be as destructive a force as one species has ever become and there will be wars that rage around this world and many will die.

The life systems will become compromised and extinction will threaten this planet. However, the evolutionary path of this world has often been changed by a series of otherwise arbitrary circumstances coming together; there is a possibility the understanding will come to you. Through all that you have seen and brought about there may come the realisation you will need for this world to survive. You will have to find a way to live in consideration of your planet home. If you do there will be a vast unleashing of potential for the entire planet; but not because a vast section of the human race is being unnaturally suppressed. There is no power in the Great Spirit Mystery who knows how this could come about or whether it ever will."

The crows called down their approval in a great crescendo as if they had recognised some great prophecy uttered into the flames. They had felt the resonance of its pronouncement echo through the trees and out into the stars above.

"I have great sympathy for the dragons. They are a noble race who have again brought about an incredible miracle amongst these stars and it will be hard for them to watch it again being gradually destroyed. But they have made a catastrophic mistake in what they have done. They have caused an unnatural shift in the balance between the powers of creation and destruction and inevitably it will have to be corrected."

"So, you are saying everything the dragons have put in place will evaporate and we will go back to where we left off!"

"This will not happen because it in any way justifies the way you and your masters have been treating your brothers and sisters; it will happen because it must happen to maintain the harmony the dragons have presided over. All that has come to be so far is a result of the wisdom they have dreamed finding its place in the tension between life and death, creation and decay: not because any particular species has been given some special advantage."

"How will it happen? Is there something we will have to do?"

The stranger became quiet as he continued to look into the flames. Samir sensed great concern in the dark stranger's silence as if much of what had to happen next would be his responsibility. How had he come by these visions of the future? Such knowledge of this world and the human race made no sense to Samir who found himself and his species very much at the mercy of his world. But here this bedraggled fellow was talking about his race bringing about its destruction. The fire crackled and spat out an ember throwing an arc of light out into the woods, the crows shrieked out in surprise but then settled again seemingly aware there was further mystery to be unravelled before the night was over.

"Who are you, Sir?"

Samir asked directly,

"...and all these things you say about the future from where do they come? Are you a madman roaming Arimathea on the fringes unable to make your way in normal society or have I fallen into a dream lying unconscious beside the road?"

The stranger shifted his weight and looked up through the trees.

"There is no need for you to know who I am, but since you ask you are not asleep or dreaming and I am no madman, but I do live out here "on the fringes" watching the world. I have become part of her again like these crows and these trees, I have come to know her, hear her whispers all her moods and the way she changes and the nature of her change. My name has no consequence here, but I have been called Mithrael, though not many have remembered that name, it is from the stars. Come sir, sit with me, I have food we can share."

Mithrael sat on a large fallen trunk on the other side of the fire and indicated for Samir to join him. He reached into the darkness and a large leather bag appeared. He delved in and pulled out two large rabbits which he quickly skinned and gutted. He ran a long straight stick through both and handed one to Samir before putting the one he had retained near to the heat of the fire. He signalled to Samir to do the same. Soon the raw flesh was sizzling as the lean meat gave up what fat it retained.

"So where was I. Oh yes, The whisperings of our beloved Arimathea. Do you here her Samir?"

Samir shook his head, intent now on the cooking rabbit.

"No, I thought not. There are few who do. It's because you have to be out here, live with her, feel the Love I was talking about and recognise when she is talking to you. Not like you would expect. She does not use words or even meanings in the sense you would term as communication. She uses all she is. Everything happening around us contains her words. How the rain falls on the river or bounces off the trees, how the Starlight falls in a clearing for a moment before a cloud comes, the appearance of an animal or the flight of a bird across your path. Patterns, movements, occurrences; everything happening during the day becomes her words, her messages.

Many days she will only remind me, another day she will give me an insight into her wonder, make me smile with some riddle or confound me with some contradiction I will have to work out for myself. Until I work it out and it all makes perfect sense. These become like sentences flowing through the day. I know that I am learning or have come to know that gradually she is gifting me with her love and wisdom. This is how Arimathea has communicated with me and how I know the things that I have told you. But of course, Arimathea also lives within the greater mystery and is subject to those higher laws. Now the actions of the dragons have caused disparity and the will of oblivion to return the equilibrium has become apparent.."

The stranger became silent as he withdrew the rabbit from the heat of the fire and examined it carefully. He carefully pulled off a piece of the cooked flesh and put it into his mouth. Samir watched expectantly and repeated the action when a look of satisfaction came over Mithraels face. They became absorbed for a while in the taste of the succulent freshly cooked meat.

"I started to notice the crows more and more." The stranger continued. "They were always around but suddenly they were more abundant. I noticed their gatherings everywhere I went. On several occasions a single crow or some multiple would be in my path screeching their strange calls. Gradually this feeling of foreboding started to work its way into my thoughts. I was living far away from your towns and cities but as I came closer to your communities I heard of the revolution and eventually of the appearance of the dragons. The appearance of greater numbers of crows seemed to coincide as the effects of their interference started to take effect. The carrion crows were gathering to serve their dark master, Oblivion, driven by it's hunger for chaos and death, they were spreading through the land in search of any weakness they could exploit and so bring to an end the lives the dragons were leading on the surface of Arimathea!"

The stranger now had Samir's full attention. He had only half absorbed the theories about the quarrels between the powers of light and dark and the place human beings were taking in this struggle. He had been far more interested at the time in satisfying his ravenous hunger. But now he heard the words 'death' and 'dragons' in relatively quick succession and his curiosity for what this outlandish character was telling him suddenly had become far more interesting. He wiped some of the consumed rabbit fat from around his mouth.

"So, have you found out how to take away their power!"

"Well yes I think I have. You see the crows now gathered in their enormous numbers across the land were able to observe the dragons at all times, even when they disappeared off into the countryside, something we humans could not do because the dragons have the ability to sense our presence for miles around. The crows like a number of species of birds who flock together, have a way of communicating with each other. It has developed as a way of informing other birds for considerable distances if a beneficial feeding opportunity arises. So if one bird finds a field where their insect food has become particularly prevalent or there has been a large amount of grain left after a harvest then the other members of the murder' as it has come to be known will instantly know from the individual who has found it. They have what would seem to us like a kind of communal mind which then has the ability to store information gathered so the best feeding areas will always be remembered. The dragons of course know about this ability. However, what they have not realised yet is just recently, perhaps as a result of the use of the power they have used to disrupt your master's despicable activity, I have gained an ability to access the mass mind of the crows. As I have told you, as a result of the life that I lead out here, I have learnt to pick up the messages it seems that are left for me.

One morning I was sitting in contemplation when I noticed three crows had landed in the branches of the trees above me. They started screeching down at me as they often do but now something different was happening. I started to have vivid imaginings of flying over the landscape and a strong sense of searching. Occasionally I would land in what seemed to be a familiar field and assess the feeding potential. I had also become aware of what seemed like a mass consciousness assessing each site for its worth to the whole murder. This was the surface information being passed and circulated to all the crows in those moments.

I became aware a good field had been found and a decision had been made. I found myself flying over the landscape again, meeting up with more and more crows heading in the same direction until eventually we spiralled down into a field where a mass gathering was taking place. Hundreds and hundreds of crows converged on that field where the worms had come very close to the surface. All around me there was a feeding frenzy going on as the worms were wrenched out of the ground. They squabbled and fought each other and for a while the sense of the one mind fell away.

I lost track of time as I almost lost track of myself in the mind of the crow I was now experiencing. I felt my hunger gradually disappearing with every successive worm disappearing down my throat. The other crows also seemingly satisfied were starting to fly out of the field and into the treetops where they proceeded to clean their feathers and chatter away to each other. Now I became aware of the mass consciousness again. But now they seemed to be sharing the experiences they had had since they had last all been together. Mostly the places they had visited; so great flights across landscapes and hills drifted through my mind. But in amongst all this I sensed and was able to watch something altogether different.

A small group of crows it seemed had been sitting on an outcrop of rock having feasted on an unfortunate colony of succulent beetles. Now they were enjoying the afternoon sunshine, only half awake, when they noticed a large human very wearily making his way up the hill directly in front of them. When he reached the top, he stood still as any rock on the hill for a number of minutes absorbing the strong midday Starshine only occasionally wavering in the breeze.

Eventually he sat cross legged on the ground, his spine straightened and with his eyes closed. Again, very still, the breeze only occasionally ruffling his long dark hair. Then a remarkable thing started to happen. The breeze stopped and all around the hill became very quiet. Everything around the man and in the vicinity of the top of the hill seemed to be intensified. The green of the grass, the sandy colour of the rocks and the very nature of the air started to glow. It almost seemed as if the colour, even the strong Starlight was being sucked out of the surrounding area, into the direct vicinity of the still and silent man. Then I noticed the colour from the grass had started to slowly spiral in a green mist around his body.

The man slowly became enveloped as the spiral combined with further Starlight and then became lost as his form melded into this bright and intensely colourful glow rising from the hilltop. The light started to fluctuate, slowly to start with but with increasing speed until the fluctuations became so fast they again became unnoticeable. Then creatures started to be forming in the glowing body of the light. There was no one creature it would seem but I noticed many different animals as the process continued. I noticed a horse rearing up on its back legs defiantly punching the air with its front hooves, but then there seemed to be an eagle sharing the light, then a deer and the mountain cats, then I noticed the reptilian form of the geckos living in the hills, a great bear and the more fluid forms of sea creatures all seemed to be sharing this light. The creatures gradually merged their forms into one creature; the creature we have come to know as dragon, constructed now from light and energy, of ancient thought and dreams of realised potential was emerging from the hillside and engulfing the human who I now realised must have been one of the human dragons that had come to perform some sort of re-unification with an aspect of its' being remaining within the fabric of Arimathea.

I could see the man becoming more transparent within the light. He stood up and I watched as his form started to merge into the creature. I saw him stretch out into the light and as his arms appeared to become one with the wings he became completely immersed and disappeared into the form of the dragon. Then this light being, this creature formed from energy flowing out of the hill with one great downward motion of his wings flew with incredible speed up into the sky. I soon lost sight of it as it flew high into the clouds and beyond.

The surprised crows sat on the rock until the dragon returned from its flight later that day. It landed in the same place from where it had taken off. It settled for a while clearly contemplating the landscape below. Then it lowered its head and gradually the light and so its form started to spiral back into the hill from where it had emerged, leaving the human sitting motionless in the same position as when the process had started. However, he was not motionless for very long. A few seconds after the light had finally disappeared he leapt to his feet and laughing with joy, strode off down the hill completely revitalised it would seem by the whole experience!!"

Mithrael now was silent. He looked over to Samir to gauge his reaction. The scribe was looking deep into the fire unable to conceal the joy this new information had given him. An enormous grin had spread across his face. He couldn't remember when he had last felt so happy. Here was the information everyone had wondered about but no one had been able to obtain.

"So, you think this is how they are able to stay on the surface; by visiting these hills to become somehow revitalised?" Samir asked

Mithrael again became quiet, looking deep into the flames.

"I have thought long and hard about this. I have no way of knowing for sure but it seems their visits to these specific places are fundamental to the dragon's existence on the surface of Arimathea. It seems to me it may be their true dragon essence perhaps their souls still dwelling within Arimathea with which they have to re unite, make the connection so they can maintain their ability to influence the flow of events in the way they have."

"So, if I am following this correctly, if we were able to prevent their ability to connect with their dragon souls then they would no longer have their power and fairly quickly they would become ordinary men."

"As I say nothing is certain here."

"…But a barrier across the tops of those hills, a layer making it impossible for their souls to enter the world may be the answer to all our problems!"

The solution to the problems the dragons had caused to the rulers of Arimathea had suddenly and mysteriously arisen. In those few days after Samir's meeting with Mithrael in the wood, the words of the mysterious stranger embedded themselves into the history of Arimathea. Samir had spent the night by the fire contemplating everything he had heard in isolation after Mithrael had disappeared without warning or explanation. The crows had become quiet when Mithrael vanished. He had placed the carving of the dragon on a large stone he had found nearby and drifted in and out of sleep thinking about the implications of what he had heard.

He was surprised to find at one point he had started to have sympathy for the dragons. He had been touched by the beauty of the land he had travelled through the afternoon before in a way he had not before. Arimathea and his direct surroundings had never been any more than a backdrop for everything in which he had been involved. He was a practical man and the estates of his master had meant little more than columns of figures. Now this system had collapsed and the figures had become unimportant, he had perhaps for the first time seen his world as it truly was. The ground, the sky and everything in between had actually become quite miraculous to him. He had watched the people in the fields working as hard as ever. But they worked with a new vigour he had not seen before. All this of course would be threatened by what he had been told.

He had been unaware the next morning he would be awoken by the great dark gathering which had remained amongst the branches above him throughout the night. They had started their relentless chattering as the first rays of the star gently filtered through the trees and then had simultaneously risen in a deafening cacophony like a vast black whirlwind directly over him. From there they called down to him insistently to act upon what he had been told. He had watched as much of the gathering had dispersed leaving only a still considerable contingent of the crows circling over the wood; then remembering the inference of the night before, he began to follow the remainder of the crows as they flew off towards the North and the mountains beyond.

Chapter Twenty-Eight
The Dragon's Dreamland.

Farina had again paused. She rose from her chair, went over to the cot and checked the sleeping baby. She was sleeping soundly. Okino prodded the fire back into life and added a log from the pile on the hearth. Mariella poured some hot water into the colourful ceramic mugs and handed them round as Farina and Okino again settled down in their seats.

"So, who was the mysterious stranger? He certainly didn't sound like a normal inhabitant of Arimathea. For all the world he sounded like the missing sixteenth dragon." Mariella ventured.

"It would explain how he knew so much about the history and the distant future of Arimathea and his ability to connect with the crows." Okino offered and then continued.

"The crows seem to be important here. They seem to have sensed the inevitable destructive urge had been initiated and they were hoping to feed from the final result. Mithrael, our mysterious stranger, possibly the sixteenth dragon, for the reasons he explained wanted to end the rebellion. He must have instructed the crows to lead Samir to where Merilon had regenerated, to the Dragon hill, just outside the village. The dragons must have known the crows were under the influence of a force at least as powerful as themselves which is why they feared them so much." Okino said thoughtfully.

"Yes, my friends, Samir came here, so the story goes..." Farina took a deep breath and continued with her story.

"The crows arrived first. Large numbers of them, enough to shatter the peace of the little community with their disturbing cacophony. There were crows in the mountains but never in such numbers and knowing their reputation everyone prepared for the worst. Samir eventually did arrive escorted by heavily armed mercenaries. They walked around examining the layout of the settlement and inspected inside the buildings. They questioned Rabir in the main hall. He was relaxed and helpful. He seemed surprised such interest had been given to his little community and insisted he had just written a book about the old spirits which may have once inhabited Jahallala. It was a legend he had found. It had only been a strange coincidence his writing had fuelled the revolution which had spread like supernatural wildfire and had resulted in the Arimatheans overthrowing their rulers.

Samir was suspicious. He knew this was the centre of the rebellion and somehow Rabir was involved with the dragons and yet there was no sign they had even been here. What signs might they have left you may well ask? But Samir had expected to find a sinister central lair from where these creatures were guiding the rebel activities. But there was little except a small farming community in a very beautiful location.

More crows were arriving and the majority of them were gathering on the roof of the hall where they were gathered. Their screeching became so loud it became difficult to hear what was being said. Samir knew the crows were central to all that had been revealed so far. He became convinced that whatever it was he needed to find was there in the hall. So, he ordered the mercenaries to tear it to pieces, raise it to the ground stone by stone if necessary. He would not leave until he found what he was looking for. So, they stripped the room of everything, all the wall hangings and all the furniture and flung it out into the square until the place was a bare shell. Samir noticed a render surface had been applied to all four walls at a level just below the high clerestory windows. This he had not seen in the other buildings. He ordered the render to be stripped. They found the entrance to the cellar where the maps had been carved into the walls so future generations would always know the location of the dragon hills.

He left a good deal more cheerful than when he had arrived with Rabir in chains. He returned later with more mercenaries and set up an entire encampment at the bottom of the Dragon hill. They came with a large number of covered wagons pulled by huge powerful horses which looked as if they may have come from some far distant land. It seemed Samir had entered into a pact with a foreign king who had been wealthy enough to retain his carpenters and masons by paying them lavishly when the revolution had started. After his meeting with Mithrael in the hills, the crows had never been far away. The huge numbers he had originally followed had dispersed again across the planet to disseminate the information they now had and also to continue their observations. Much of what happened next was the result of their own appetite for destruction.

They spread Samir's plan through their networks and in the coming weeks they reached all who needed to hear what he proposed to do. The psychics and the magicians loyal to the rulers in the lands, in which the sixteen Dragon hills were situated, gleefully recounted the details of the dreams and visions the crows had given them. The kings of course listened with great interest. Finally, a way had been found to end this outrageous state of affairs and soon everything would be back to normal. Masons and carpenters were summoned and offered large sums of money for the work they were to undertake before being dispatched off with a large entourage to the foot of each of the Dragon hills. Once they arrived, they set up their camps completely independent from the surrounding towns or villages.

Outside Asima, Samir and his workforce carved a smooth path up the side of the hill. They removed anything obstructing their way. At the same time they started to assemble a number of large machines. They went into the hills and started to quarry stone using explosives rarely used in Jahallala at the time. They dragged huge stones from the quarries with a team of the enormous horses. They harnessed the horses into machines with a series of long booms. The horses walked continually in circles and turned, with the help of an array of pulleys and interconnecting cogs, the huge metal cutting disks which had been unloaded from the covered wagons. Each stone took many days to complete. They chose the shallowest gradient and then slowly the horses dragged the finished stones up to the top of the hill. The masons and carpenters had built further timber constructions allowing them to manipulate and lower the stones into place and cover the entire summit of the hill.

The whole process was guarded at all times by the foreign mercenaries. They watched the perimeter making it impossible for anyone who was curious to find out more about the nature of the strange new addition to the hill. Light from the fires on the summit could be seen burning through the night. However, the strange sulphurous smell drifting out over the surrounding countryside could be smelt at all times of night and day and gave rise to much conjecture as to the nature of the activity. Although the whole operation was cloaked in secrecy the inhabitants of the community suspected the dragon's secret had somehow been discovered.

There was little to be done for the mercenaries were hardened warriors and little of the misfortune that had hampered the rulers' forces at the height of the dragon's influence seemed to affect the progress of the construction. Samir's activities became progressively more mysterious with the arrival of a further entourage of foreign visitors. They arrived one afternoon on fine black horses. They wore black robes and were assumed to be of some foreign priest hood. They made their way immediately to the top of the hill.

That night unworldly chanting was heard emanating from the top of the hill and eerily drifted out across the silent land. In amongst the chanting, enormous sparks flew off into the night sky and out into the stars. There was a frenzied clanging and crashing of what sounded like a demented blacksmith working metal at his demonic forge. The sinister nature of all this activity led the people of Asima to fear the worst for the survival of the dragons and possibly their own community.

During this period no one saw or heard from the dragons. Deep in their mountain retreat they had remained. They had retreated temporarily from their quest to free Arimathea from the tyranny of the ruling landlords and had sunken deeper into their collective council; relieved to have joined together in the security of their isolated mountain cave deep in the rocky environs of their beloved Arimathea. Unaware of the conspiracy unfolding in their absence, they were slowly considering a fabulous system of experiential inspiration they would eventually release into the fabric of Arimathea. They had become lost in their enthusiasm and excitement as they wove together and realised the power of this entirely new dream based on the entwining of circumstance and consciousness. The dragons, who had slept in planets for millennia without stirring, now had drifted into a deep and undisturbed dreamtime.

They had examined at great length the possibilities of this new idea after they had first combined their consciousnesses. This had allowed the meeting of Silas and Jeremiah and their subsequent discussion about the fate of the Oak woods. They had been encouraged when the opposing interests of the two men had flowed together. They had easily found common ground in their heightened experience and the two men had found no difficulty in coming to an agreement the wood must be kept as they became overwhelmed by the synchronous beauty of the Star setting around them. The sublime moment had served to re-establish the special nature of their previous memories and the profound effects they had had in those previous times. In the dream the consciousness of Arimathea had played her part in the successful outcome. As a result of the feelings of compassion provoked in the two men standing in the wood with the light from the star illuminating the wood, the trees in their dream had been saved.

So, the dragons explored through the aeons of memories they shared, how this consciousness had come to be and become so crucial in the development of all life and the many paths it had taken. They explored the knowledge they had acquired of the many dimensional labyrinths in which they had existed as they had travelled across the universe.

A new state had evolved out of a previous catastrophe; as had the previous and the previous. No beginning no end. All physicality had been erased or sucked back into some deeper dimension. It floated within the Great Mystery as it transformed itself again through the living of the dream and floated through the infinity as refugee energies from the previous universe.

All the old energies merged into the one Love, the only true surviving state, and they began to live as one through the Eons...But even the power of Love could not hold back the machinations of the Great Mystery and pressure to transform again gathered intensity. They could only stay in a state of inertia while the memory of the horror was held and only then by diffusing the energy through the new state. So, it was held and the pressure built and built within the One until the point was reached where the energy could not be held any longer.

So, a new cataclysm came about. Such was the density which had built within this new state, it exploded so violently and the detonation was so severe it ruptured many of the surrounding dimensions. This caused a lack of stability and many collapsed, merged into a new dimension and found a new position in the labyrinth. Here the old energies found themselves instantly defined by a newly formed atomic state. They also found they had become aware in this new state and for the first time they were conscious of the characteristics their energy contained. As this new consciousness moved through the universe it combined with the Light being formed by the energy of newly formed stars. Here the dragons had found their origin.

They remembered the shattered stunned silence. The new Universe was no more than a random dust of atomic material drifting through the layers of this newly formed dimension in the vast dark emptiness. The dragons flowed into the debris, into the darkness. Lacking at first any understanding of this new state they drifted, searching aimlessly. They found themselves spiralling towards a central point as they explored the meaning of this new awareness; the characteristics of the energies they had inherited and what it meant for the beginning of this new dimension. The energies again filled this new state. The dragons became their central nucleus, the mind of each energy as they merged into the consciousness. Eventually, the dragons came together at the centre of a vast spiralling vortex. The fusing of these new energetic beings sent a powerful wave of potential energy pulsing out across the universe. This potential became embedded in the fabric of this new state ready and waiting for a dream to signal the start of a new evolution.

The dragons had found within this consciousness they had the will to survive and determine a future. They found they had the ability to understand progression and the transition from one time to the next. They found for the first time they had the ability to think creatively and make decisions to enhance the path they took into the future.

The dragons understood the states of Light and Dark within themselves, how they were acting in the universe beyond, how they were bound into the tension these energies caused and how they were working continually to transform this new universe. They understood they could make decisions about the future based on their experience of the past and the present.

They realised the consciousness existed in three-dimensional space and they could move freely through it in any direction. They found they were able to hold an overall picture of the entire consciousness and understand how it operated as an integrated system where all these aspects could allow new possibilities to arise and flow together as they became ever more infinitely entwined. In their knowledge of the whole they found they could comprehend the greater cycles, of the newly evolving stars, as material and spirit began to gravitate towards their growing light.

They found they could experience this new light as it began to shine and evolve in the peaceful dawn of this new time as the Love, that had for so long drifted unsupported and vulnerable in the emptiness, now found it's place in the gentle new Light radiating through the darkness. They found this was the most powerful of the new aspects and could influence everything allowed to come under its spell.

They found they had knowledge of the Elemental spirits, Earth, Air, Fire, and Water which they also found were re appearing. They became aware how their spirits could also transform and influence the consciousness with their subtle supernatural powers. They found they were also possessed by the nature of the countless spirits who had fled and now had returned from the older universe as it receded. They would ultimately determine their physical form from these spirits when the time arose. They found they had an instinct to protect this fragile newly evolving consciousness from external threat and how they had the ability, at this stage, to ultimately change its outward state in order to avoid detection and confrontation with the more ruthless powers who would stalk and consume its special quality.

They found they could understand how gentle rhythms flowed through this new state influencing all these different aspects and how the possibilities and outcomes fluctuated and changed as all these new energies started to find their place together in this new Space and Time.

Slowly they began to understand how they could act, be, feel and experience within this new consciousness as the old energies merged and overlaid each other. It felt like a vast womb with the ability to nurture…something!! The dragons remembered how they had discovered the abilities they had; All these aspects, which would prove so instrumental in the progression from this state of disconnected space dust into complex planets where intelligent life, aware of itself and its environment would eventually evolve, were now swirling through the wastes of space trying to find identity.

They found they could dream futures from the memories the energies carried. They could dream of what might be, explore all the possibilities held in this new state by all this wonder emerging out of the darkness. They started to weave their way through the emptiness, dreaming fabulous combinations of these aspects of the consciousness into the glow of molecules and atoms and the infinity of spaces lying between.

The dragons had become part of the mechanism into which the one Love had transformed itself to exist in this new Universe. It shone through the glowing light. It would always be opposed and drained at every opportunity by the darkness in which it existed but it could gather strength and always shone brighter and stronger than before.

Arimathea had eventually evolved out of this new wonder. In the isolated cave high in the mountains the dragons wondered if they could separate out the aspects, so the entire nature of the consciousness could be better understood within the psyche of the human race. They hoped the experience of this wonder might bring them closer and connect them again into the nature and origins of their world.

They became deeply and especially enthusiastic and inspired with this memory. Joined in their ancient spirit bond, they began to weave their thoughts into a magical dream to soothe their beloved Arimathea and bring her closer to the reckless humans as they decided how they were going to be with her and live upon her. Now the dragons would send the age-old wisdom of the consciousness they had carried through the stars deeper into their dreams. It was the intention of the dragons that the wisdom lost to the people of Arimathea as a result of fear and slavery, would eventually be made available to them through these dreams.

So, they projected their knowledge of these aspects of consciousness into a dream space where a new matrix was forming. The consciousness moved invisibly through the silence exchanging emptiness with potential. Light from a distant Star began to shine down through the mists spreading warmth across the forming land. From in their thoughts a beginning had been made, an elemental world moving through the stars, emerging in a dream.

This world had been given the will to grow and evolve and so as the dragon's memories and the consciousness started to flow through the empty lands they were transformed with hills and mountains, lakes and seas, plains and savannahs and great jungles and forests leapt from the ground. In this dreamscape there was process and the rhythms of night and day, of cool and hot, dark and light governed by the Star acting on the whole. Winds carried weather systems from the seas feeding the burgeoning forests and keeping the southern deserts dry. As the rains came so the water flowed into trickling streams and wide new rivers drained the flooding land. So, this dreamscape formed, only in the minds of the sleeping dragons, a mirror it became of Arimathea and in amongst the sacred hills the dragons would hold and maintain the dream.

As the higher aspects of this consciousness came and warmth, love and life came to flow through this dreamscape there came to live amongst the hills, a race of people who had grown to know the wisdom of the consciousness surrounding them. They had grown with and never been separated from the wisdom it contained. They had always been aware of the dragons who were part of this consciousness and accepted them as part of their own existence in the landscapes of their world.

They knew of all its aspects and facets and became so enthralled by the wonder of its creation they devised a magical system that would always express its presence for all who might come to discover it for themselves; A system they spread throughout their land in amongst the mountains and the forests, the seas and rivers and far across the plains, deep down into the southern deserts and jungles. They found the knowledge and wisdom to be found within the consciousness flowed out into their lands from certain hills and surfaced in certain special places around them. In each one of these places could be revealed the nature of one aspect of the consciousness. Here they came to be with the consciousness and the dragon beings at the heart of their world.

Fine craftsman they had become with great knowledge of the stone of which their land was comprised. They carefully conceived for each of these special places a beautiful temple crafted from the sparkling crystal laden stone so prevalent across their world. They built the temples and pathways to connect them into the crystal stone bedrock below the ground. They interconnected this system of paths and temples so they all led back to the dragon hills. Here was where the dragons would sleep and dream. They carefully crafted all the walls so all the spaces were filled with the dreams of the sleeping dragons.

The dragons then were able to project into this dreamscape an environment entirely dedicated to a deep understanding of the consciousness that had come to dwell on Arimathea. Each temple would contain a different aspect of the consciousness. It would flow together in the dreamscape and blend the relationships existing between the different aspects. The people of Arimathea would eventually access this dreamscape and experience all the aspects of the consciousness as they journeyed through it in their own dreams.

In this early time of its' conception, the dreamscape was nurtured and maintained solely within the dream of the dragons. They were careful not to allow the nature of this new creation to seep out into the wider consciousness beyond their remote mountain hideaway. They had become increasingly aware, almost day by day the darker forces were gathering. But they were absolutely determined not to reveal their dream world before it could be accessed successfully by the entire human race. However, in this isolation they had created around themselves they had become so deeply preoccupied with this new dream, they had become unaware of how rapidly those plans were advancing."

Farina became silent. The spell of her story telling had again entranced the young monk and his travelling companion, engulfing their thoughts in the tale, further unravelling the mystery in which they had become involved and back into the time from whence it had sprung. She sat quietly for a moment and eventually turned to Okino and Mariella smiling tiredly. They sat in silence in the fading light. Farina lifted herself wearily up from her chair and lit an array of oil lamps placed carefully around the room. The soft glow now combined and enhanced the light emanating from the small windows as the star lowered again towards the horizon. She checked the baby who was now sleeping deeply and put another log on the fire before sitting thoughtfully in her seat.

"I think perhaps that is all I can tell you for now. I suddenly felt the stream of images and well, the amazing conversation going on in my head coming to a conclusion and starting to fade."

Okino was deep in his thoughts staring up at the mural of the mountain scene occupying one entire wall of Farina's room. The rich colours now seemed to become more pronounced in the soft light of the oil lamps.

"So, the dragons created an entire landscape in their consciousness which would convey to all the people how to live with and reach their full potential on Arimathea. I recognise this dreamscape from the meditation I had at my initiation. But it was dead and deserted and seemed like something terrible had happened there. I remember "The dragons have deserted us" had been hurriedly carved in a stone table and these words echoed through the atmosphere. Something must have happened in this new dreamscape. It sounded like it would have come through our dreams. Of these dreamscapes there are no memory in our tradition. If they had succeeded in embedding them into the consciousness of Arimathea, surely, we would have found a way to access them with the skills we have developed in the monastery. Perhaps the dragons sent me one of their dreams as a warning of a terrible darkness we are yet to encounter at the centre of this mystery."

He looked over at Mariella and Farina. They both looked concerned by this new revelation.

Chapter Twenty-Nine
Legacy, Magic and Technology.

Farina was clearly exhausted after her long concentration. The dragons in their communion around the lake had projected their memories from which ever dimension they now existed into Farina's own memory streams. They had expanded in detail everything that had been passed on to her by her father. She in turn had narrated this important passage of events to Okino and Mariella. Now she had fallen asleep in her chair. The late afternoon Star shone down through the small windows and together with the lighted oil lamps, the rich colours of the carefully crafted tapestries and pottery were deepened. The two young people decided it would be safe to leave Farina and her sleeping child while they made some further explorations of the village while some light remained.

They left the house and returned to the main street where they found the horses waiting patiently. They briefly reassured the animals before making their way further into the little village. They were greeted with smiles and gestures of welcome from everyone they passed. Frequently the villagers would hurry back in through their open doors and return offering freshly made bread or cakes. Mariella and Okino accepted these snacks gratefully and told the contributors anything they wished to know about their journey.

All were intrigued by the ruins and many of the people to whom they spoke volunteered their own opinions as to the fate of the community. Many assumed their village had been founded by the people who had left when it was abandoned and had continued many of the ideals of self-sufficiency founded all those years before. They had always assumed many of the traditional ways they still used in the production of their pottery, tapestries and clothing had been initiated in those times.

They were aware of the contribution Rabir's community had made to the turbulent time Arimathea had gone through and were now intrigued by the purpose of the visit from this sophisticated young southern woman and the monk of such a legendary order. Okino could only tell them what had happened there could still be having repercussions for the whole of Arimathea. This of course intrigued and puzzled the villagers. Many of whom had little concept of life even beyond the mountains around them. But he found an acceptance there was a remarkable history associated with the quality of the atmosphere surrounding their village. They all had stories of enchantment originating at the waterfall. It was, it now transpired much visited by the villagers. It had always been associated with the good fortune Rabir had found when he first established the community. However, the uncertain history and possibly its brutal destruction had discouraged any of the villagers from ever resettling the ruins.

As they turned a corner at the end of the narrow street, they saw the jeep that had brought the two southern city dwellers to the village. Okino enquired as to their whereabouts and asked how they had reacted to the village. The villagers said they had been quietly talking to them about their lives up here in the mountains, swapping stories about their lives in the cities. They had been quite shocked by the reaction they had provoked in the bar in Aharri and so far, had not offended anyone. Mariella smiled to herself and gave Okino a knowing look he assumed came from her experience of the attitudes of the people who had surrounded her in the city. These men had spotted a business opportunity in the beautiful things being made here. Now they would be trying to find out whether this possibility could be turned into profit for themselves and their corporations back in the cities. They were attempting to win the confidence of the villagers with their open friendly approach; gradually allowing them to believe they had their best interests at heart and how their lives could be transformed with just a few adjustments.

Okino wondered what the adjustments would mean for the village and the benefits they would really bring. He saw happy contented people showing the signs of struggle with the hard realities of life in the mountains. But he knew from the knowledge of his own town the beautiful things they produced came out of knowledge and tradition possibly unchanged for many generations. Those traditions provided a lifestyle just sustainable within the economies of these mountains.

He had started his journey as a result of an intrusion from the developed areas of Arimathea. These businessmen had been sent by their corporations in search of the originality and authenticity lost from their own world. But Okino suspected from what he had seen and read in the magazines this authenticity could only provide the profit they needed from mass production and the 'economies of scale' the huge financial machinery of the developed world overwhelmingly demanded. He wondered whether it was possible for these two worlds to merge healthily together without the fragile beauty surviving in the lives of these gentle people being lost amongst the dictates from the boardrooms of technocrats coming from the floors high up in the skyscrapers of Straam.

They had arrived at two large stone buildings. Double doors were thrown open and inside Okino instantly recognised the fabrics and material from which his own jacket had been made. Long rolls of the material hung on frames lining the long wall at the back of the large room ready to be cut. There were eight tables spread evenly throughout the room with space between allowing easy movement between each. At each table sat one of the villagers. There were two further large tables where the fabric was being cut to a number of patterns.

There were women of all ages and two men sitting at the tables expertly operating the manually driven sewing machines. They were sewing together the jackets that had stood out so strikingly in the market. They were comprised of two materials; a thick white cotton lining and a closely woven woollen fabric forming the outside. They turned the machines expertly with a foot pedal determining the speed of the needle as the fabric was expertly pushed through the guides. They looked up briefly from their work when Okino and Mariella came into their workshop. They gave a brief nod and smiled broadly and fondly before returning to their work. There were younger girls who seemed to be assisting, fetching and carrying material and carefully studying the machinists as the garments were carefully sewn up. They chattered away to each other as they worked and the pile of jackets destined for the next market regularly increased.

Okino and Mariella felt comfortable wandering through the tables, observing and admiring the work being carried out in this happy atmosphere. There was a continual murmur of conversation and laughter as the garments took shape. Mariella it seemed was especially interested at this stage. She had greatly admired Okino's jacket in the past few days and now faced with the whole range she carefully considered each colour pattern.

Okino watched her moving through the workshop. She instantly charmed the villagers with her open warmth and friendliness. She asked them which colours they would recommend and placed the different lengths of jacket up against herself to check for size. Okino knew immediately the colour scheme he would choose for her. He felt it was only a matter of time before she came to the same opinion.

As she tried it on, he saw the subtle turquoise stripes set in the very deep blue and green background material could have been made for her. She looked over smiling at him for approval. The old lady standing next to her, playfully pulled the hood up over her dark hair as Niala had done for Okino in the marketplace. The new jacket gave shape to the old blue robe she continually wore and the turquoise stripe now accentuated her deep blue green eyes shining out from under the hood. Okino was slightly overwhelmed for a few moments at what appeared to him almost complete perfection. She turned completely around for him. He smiled calmly across at her, carefully disguising the strong emotion he was feeling. Now as the memory of the woman who had appeared in the cave as Arimathea had faded, Mariella had now, he realised taken her place.

"The jacket is perfect for you, Mariella."

He quietly ventured.

She held his gaze affectionately for a few moments while wrapping the jacket happily around herself in indication of the comfort she now felt before turning back to the smiling lady who watched with interest and amusement the interaction between the two young people. She delved deeply into her blue robe and pulled out the woven bag where she kept her money and pulled out a note which she handed to the smiling lady. Her eyes lit up and she pushed it back. Mariella folded the note and pushed into a pocket in the side of the ladies' coat and danced off through the open doors leading to the next workshop. There was much laughter amongst the workforce and knowing nods towards Okino before everyone returned to their work. Okino ignored the inference he knew was behind this attention and followed Mariella through the open doors.

In a similar sized workshop, there were six hand operated looms. Further villagers were weaving rugs and the fine woollen material being used in the construction of the jackets. Mariella was already admiring the weaving underway on one of the larger looms. This was being carried out by a young man who was carefully manipulating eight different colours at the edge of his weave into a complex geometric pattern. The colours were deep and rich.

They were clearly colours used in the jacket she had just purchased; others she recognised from Okino's jacket.

"Do you do all the dying and spinning of the wool here as well." She inquired

"We do actually, but that all happens in a building father away from here. Some of the dyes can really stink so we keep the whole process out of smelling range. Most of the wool comes from our own animals. We use sheep and goats' wool mixed with the wool we get from the yaks. We do buy some wool in from the other villages who do not have such a thriving weaving operation. We spin it all and dye it all, so yes, the whole operation is carried out here and has been for many generations.

Many of the dyes we use are unique to these mountains. We use plant dyes mainly which are easily harvested and regularly occur from year to year and create the deepest and most beautiful colours. Everybody learns how the whole operation works. All the children start to learn the skills alongside their normal lessons at the school. So, we can all make carpets and fabric and know all about the dyes, we know how to make the pottery and all the pigments that make up the glazes. Then we can decide whether we want to specialise in one thing or move from one to another. I personally like to make these rugs. It is a complicated task and I can get lost in it for hours and find completing them incredibly satisfying. Then when I take them to the market, I like to hear the gasps of wonder from the other weavers who know the complexity of the weaves I am making. They are much admired and often we will have five or six people bidding for each rug in the markets of Aharri!"

As Okino surveyed this further workshop he noticed the two southerners, Ben and Zeph. They were deep in conversation with two of the older villagers, a man and a woman who were examining documents spread out on one of the tables. He made his way down the workshop to try to overhear the conversation underway. Okino tried to keep one of the larger looms between himself and the city entrepreneurs who he knew would instantly recognise him. At this point he wasn't sure if they had noticed Mariella who was still watching the work being carried out on the looms at the other end of the workshop.

"...the thing is you have a good product we can sell in the fashionable shops in Straam city. If we bring in the power looms you will be able to produce even more of these amazing rugs and fabric to make the jackets. In no time, trust me, we will all be doing very well I can assure you."

"When you say, 'bring in the power looms' what does that mean exactly?!"

"What happens is we assess the kind of production levels you might be able to achieve. We have a lot of experience of this. We've taken these machines to villages in many of the remote areas of Arimathea. We look at things like your optimum workforce at any one time and how much wool you are able to buy and process and so how many rugs and jackets you could make. Then we can do the sums, work out the money we could all make and then we take a small part of your profit for the machines."

"So, will we buy the machines or is there some kind of lease."

"You will eventually own the machines. The length of time it takes for you to buy them will obviously depend on how much product we can move. But hey, look, think of how this village is going to benefit. We have villages we have helped who have fresh water being pumped from the ground into filtration plants straight into people's homes, pipes laid for sewers, the schools have got new books and computers. Hell, we can even put a windmill up on one of these hills and rig some hydro-electric up in that stream to power it all. You could have a truck to get you to Aharri in an afternoon, so no more trudging around in the heat and dust with those little oxen you got."

"They're yaks"

"They're from the Stone Age, man. Things are moving forward fast on Arimathea and we want you to be a part of it. There is just no need for you guys to be struggling away out here. This is a chance for you to join the technological community. The beauty of it is that you can still live out here. Your life doesn't have to change that much. We can connect you up to satellites; you can watch the big games, hear what's going on, and take part with what is happening on this planet. All you have to do is do what you are doing with a few machines that will make the whole operation easier any way. Do you hear what I am saying?"

"We do hear you, and of course we are interested. Still our children are dying from what lurks invisibly in the water; they need educating even if they stay here, which they are more likely to if we can pull all this off. But if they go out there they will have a better chance of survival if they know more about it. The whole idea of not being so isolated and benefiting from the connection with the rest of the world resonates deeply with us. Perhaps this is an opportunity we cannot afford to miss. After all what could happen if, as you say, there is a limitless supply of money amongst the fashionable people of Straam who would be queuing up to buy our beautiful jackets and rugs.!"

Okino shuddered as he listened to the southerners. There was a hollow sound to their promises and the benefits all sounded far too good to be true. Even with his basic knowledge of the world that existed beyond these mountains, he knew any ideas about an endless supply of money were not strictly true. He had studied enough about the global economic markets to know they were subject to rises and falls when they became too dependent on any one factor. If for whatever reason the factor was to meet with some misfortune, or a mistake was made in the calculation of its true value then the entire market could be shaken near to collapse. Suddenly he could see the vulnerability of this little village. If they exchanged their place in the local economy, where they made a modest but regular income trading what food and necessities they needed within the region, for a place in the global economy they could soon find themselves at the mercy of one of these global market collapses.

Okino quietly started to leave the workshop. Mariella joined him as he left the building.

"Those guys are going to stitch this village up. They're going to bring in machines and technology so that everyone will have to work twice as hard to pay for it. I suspect they will write their contract craftily so they will get the majority of the profit before the village start making enough money to pay for everything they are promising. It could all get very nasty if they don't. It won't be charming Ben and Zeph who come to collect the debt. Some of these guys may end up working in Straam to pay it all off. It sounds like the old story Mariella, possibly the ultimate result of what the dragons attempted and failed to do. Now the whole world has become enslaved by a vast dark all-consuming economic power that arose as their wisdom faded from the world. Ironically, in the light of what we have discovered, it would seem this is one of the last corners of Arimathea which has escaped being dragged into it! I think it is important to warn the villagers to be very careful. Perhaps your Dad could recommend a good lawyer!"

"Sounds like they are going to need one."

"I like your new jacket by the way. I would look after it. It may be one of the last things made on Arimathea without a machine!"

After their visit to the workshops they wandered down to the river at the bottom of the valley flowing around the hill and down to the settlement and the waterfall. They talked of the convergence that appeared to be happening. Still however they had not learnt of how the intervention the dragons had made had turned out. Although the appearance of the stone cover over the hill had given them a good idea.

The outside world had yet again found the distant out post of Asima. Would it now leave some new legacy to upset the delicate balance of its existence? Unsympathetic to the subtle flow of energy Rabir had found here, Samir had come to turn off the wonder it was bringing to the world. Now the Southerners had come to take advantage of the creativity it had nurtured. But as they changed and manipulated the people of Asima with their promises of wealth and comfort they were almost certainly sowing the seeds of destruction for the little community. For when the fashions in the transient markets beyond their mountains inevitably moved on to their next distraction the loans for the machinery would remain only partly repaid.

The currents in the river were strong and flowed over the boulders on the riverbed giving the appearance of carefully interwoven muscles attached to a rocky limb below. For now, the river remained untamed, flexing, curling and spitting on its journey past the village. Would it provide enough power to turn the turbines to power the new machines; or would the channel have to be engineered with steel and concrete to provide the correct rates of flow. Okino suddenly saw the irony more clearly.

"So has this process completely taken over Arimathea!?"

"Okino, these must be some of the last places unshaped, manipulated and computerised. This river and village and much of these mountainous regions do remain pretty much off the grid. But look how fast it is arriving!"

"Everything the dragons had foreseen ultimately came to be. We are watching it happening here. Take Ben and Zeph. They recognise the wild beauty as something their world needs. It has been lost in their manufactured world, but it seems they have no understanding at all how it comes about. I have a feeling they just don't care. They will try to reproduce the wild originality with the process they understand by simplifying it, making it quicker and more profitable. Of course, they will exclude the magic ingredient of Love, intuitive care and the knowledge continuous with this whole way of life, these people and this place."

They made their way back up the street towards Farina's house pursued as usual by the little band of admiring children.

Chapter Thirty
The Discovery

Farina invited Mariella to stay over for the night once they had returned from their exploration of the village. Okino and Mariella were pleased for the invitation to sleep in the solid cosy little house. Okino went out to move the horses into the safety of the overnight paddock while Mariella helped Farina preparing the food for their meal. He wondered of his own town as he wandered alone down the stone street. He knew the monks would be wondering of his progress. He would like to be able to discuss what had happened so far but the telecommunications he knew to have covered and connected most of Arimathea had not as yet reached these remote regions. He smiled to himself as again he saw the advantage of the technological advances that had come about through the natural urges of his race. He had been won over by the ability to travel vast distances in the truck in a fraction of the time it would normally take. Now he found himself yearning for the ability to talk to his fellow monks who were perhaps hundreds of miles away. This technology undoubtedly had its own brand of magic. This magic though had been prised out of the mysterious nature of the world and turned it into cold hard reality. The human ability to perform the tasks they would otherwise perform naturally had been increased exponentially across the face of Arimathea with all the threatening danger it was causing to her survival.

Okino arrived back as the Star sank behind the mountains and dusk was starting to fall over the village. The preparations for dinner were well underway and Farina's husband, Tarak had now returned. He greeted Okino warmly and welcomed him to his home. Soon they were all enjoying the stew that had been slowly cooking on the fire since they had arrived. When the news from the higher pastures had been reported the dilemmas facing the whole of Arimathea were soon being discussed in the light of the afternoon's development.

"So were the dragons wrong to interfere with the natural flow of evolution on this world." Mariella asked as the debate started to slow. There was a thoughtful silence before Okino volunteered an answer.

"I am starting to think the dragon's intervention has become part of the evolution of this world. Perhaps it was unprecedented but I have a feeling perhaps the stakes became higher and the dragons were forced to take the battle between the spirits of creation and destruction on to the next level. We can easily make judgements about what is wrong and right from the perspective of our lives lasting perhaps eighty years. But we can have little grasp of the concept and the machinations of time involved with the creation of worlds spanning billions of years. As these forces engage with each other over the millennia, could there be any rules? I think we are seeing what Rabir observed with the leopards and the goats. If one side briefly gets the upper hand before long the other finds or is given a way to redress the balance. So, the Universe goes on!!"

Later that night as the questions became far too complex for the tired minds from which they had arisen, the four young people decided perhaps they would find the answers in their dreams. Mariella looked across at Okino with a smile as he arranged the assortment of hides and blankets on the floor on the other side of the room. She knew Okino's connection with the dragons and indeed her own was becoming stronger as their involvement deepened. Would the dragons reveal the final part of the mystery tonight she wondered as she stretched out happily on the luxurious woollen mattress Farina had provided for her to sleep on?

Merilon had been flying for many days. He was returning from the dragon's council when he was intercepted by Okino now deep in his dream. He had emerged from light filled clouds into the incandescent blue and was sucked directly into the stream of energy and consciousness Merilon had become. In the ethereal place between the surface of Arimathea and the Universe beyond, Okino the young monk and Merilon the dragon were now sharing the same consciousness. Okino felt entirely comfortable with this new development. Whereas before he had always been a passenger and an observer, he had now become the dragon.

He noticed immediately how his awareness had enormously expanded. He was high above the clouds, but he was sensing the planet floor below. He sensed a temperate climate; a land of rolling hills and valleys and flood plains with rivers flowing gently through fertile, carefully maintained agricultural land. He knew there were people and animals; he felt the woods and forests as networks of solidified life force processing light, transmitting their gentle soothing auras and continually filling the atmosphere with clouds of their life sustaining breath. He felt how they maintained and protected the delicate layer of fertility where all this life was nourished just above the solid bedrock of the planet below. He yearned deep in his being to be there and knew soon he would return and be reunited with Arimathea, to rest and sleep, dream the fabulous new dream the dragons had initiated living deep in the recesses of his memory. He remembered briefly, the wonder of its construction. For a moment his memory and the landscape below the clouds shared a similarity and overlapped into one thought. He was curious as to the nature of the land over which he was flying and dipped his wings and dived down into the white clouds. Momentarily he was plunging through the misty vapour before suddenly the rolling green hills of the land below were gloriously revealed to him.

The dragon hill was still far away. There was an ocean and a gradually ascending landmass between him and his rest. As he descended, he could see he was flying over a beautiful land. The Star speckled the green fields as it was strained by the clouds above. There was a network of track ways connecting small settlements in every direction. He was low enough to see people working with their animals in the fields. The ripening corn rippled as he flew over. Startled people looked up and horses spooked sideways as they felt force over their heads they normally only felt in their veins. The atmosphere rippled as he passed, wings, torso and head, almost, but not entirely there, over the fields, but just enough to confirm they had not been dreaming or had some wild heat induced hallucination.

This was the true nature of the dragons and Okino now felt the duality with which they inhabited Arimathea. They had become an inextricable part of this world but still they belonged in some other realm, now long extinct. They had become its final remnant, making their new life, in this new realm where conditions would always frustrate the purity of their form. To these realms though they had brought the ways by which they had always lived. Where they found emptiness, they filled it with their infinite dreams of potential, transformed the cold emptiness into warmth and light. But always the curse of Oblivion had followed them, disturbed by the shining bustling oasis of life light they could create at the heart of any emptiness. Still it found ways to project its terrifying legacy into the living souls of the creatures who had grown there.

But the dragons had found the human creatures could learn and interact with them, they could feel the wonder they felt for all they had created. There was enough wisdom buried deep in their souls that remembered their origin in the stars, in the distant realms where for so long Oblivion had become exiled; Where life had no agonising uncertain end, only a time to naturally sleep again within the Great Spirit and dream of all that had been learnt; new wisdom, new understanding and new forms in which to manifest the infinite beauty they had found within those dreams. Then a glorious rebirth refreshed and empowered to live and breathe again.

Okino swooped, and climbed, soared and dived with the dragon in this new understanding of how this had all come to be. Mountains, hills and the lowlands sped past and soon he was over the sea again. He knew now, as he and generations of monks had suspected, this existence and its underlying mystery had its origin in some other realm. At some stage they had decided to dedicate their practice to learning the truth behind their world. Now it seemed, as he joyfully inhabited the energy of this being who had originated in another dimension, their efforts through the generations had not been in vain. Would it be enough this understanding had finally been transferred?

As he flew low over the waves, a pod of dolphins rose to the surface. He felt their joy at his presence and flew even lower until he was skimming the waves. The dolphins sped from just below the surface and leapt high into the air screeching their ecstatic greetings to their distant ancestor. Merilon and Okino merged with the pod; into the fluidity of the silent blue, a few downward thrusts of powerful tail fins through the mirror like surf and again, briefly floating through the warm Star filled air before diving back into their silent blue world below. In the silence, Okino could hear communications from other creatures being clearly transmitted as complex vibration connecting them to many different pods in other areas of the ocean. He was able to understand these were very different beings. Their minds were clear and untroubled, fully focused on the sensation of travelling through the surf, possibly to meet up with their larger extended family. He was surprised to feel what his race would call joyfulness, even happiness, to be pursued when the miserable grind of existence was completed, was continuous amongst these creatures. They were at one with each other and their world and they appeared to be in no doubt as they raced across the ocean this was the most wonderful thing any one of them could be doing.

This state of mind, it appeared, was where these creatures had evolved to live and as the pod, now constantly growing in numbers, streamed across the surface of their watery world, Okino wondered how long, if ever it would take his own race to reach this place of complete joyfulness and continuation with their world. He was tempted for a few moments to think they were far too complex to have such a simplistic breadth of emotions; until he again felt the complexity of connection the dolphins had with their environment.

It seemed to Okino as if they were continually monitoring a three-dimensional image of the entire ocean, above and below the surface as they were flowing through it. He knew where the nearest land masses were, he could see the contours of the ocean floor, he knew where all the other creatures were and whether they were a threat to him or his family. Above the surface he knew whether the Star was shining and the weather conditions and how they were changing. He even appeared to know the water temperature at any point in this model, how this would affect the chances of a storm forming and so the implications for the pursuit of his prey in such an area.

Here was a mind that had developed complexity far beyond the angst-ridden confusion his own race seemed to flounder around in. Okino recognised this mind had long escaped the confines of thought and comprehension alone. He was now in a mind with the ability to link its neural network into the vast expanses of its surrounding environment and into the consciousness of Arimathea.

Okino momentarily felt the dragon deciding he needed to continue his journey. They left the pod and soared high over the waves. Merilon had sensed land and knowing this would be the last part of his journey he was eager to continue.

Okino could see the ocean crashing into a rugged coastline in the distance. As they flew nearer, he could see the powerful waves end abruptly as they pounded into a towering cliff face. The coast was strewn with mountainous fragments excised from the exposed rock face, now left to fend for themselves in the continual onslaught of wind and waves. Merilon the dragon circled. Okino felt him sampling and sucking great quantities of salt filled air into his lungs. He lowered his trajectory again and flew along the coastline below the cliff tops. Okino knew he was savouring the atmosphere of this transitory place where the land met the ocean in its ferocious never-ending war of attrition.

Merilon chose one of the outlying crags and carefully glided down on the buffeting winds, landing easily on the summit. He carefully folded his wings and stilled himself as he opened all his senses to the atmosphere of the place surrounding him.

The rock where Okino and Merilon were now perched was steeply formed, an almost conical out crop. Waves broke violently around it before they continued on to the foot of the boulder strewn cliffs. As they re-bounded, they met further incoming waves. The result was a seething, rushing cauldron of exploding pounding surf. The larger waves sent the surf flying high, filling the air with misty residues. In turn they were caught by the wind and blown back over the cliffs. The impact of the waves caused deep thunderous booms in amongst the deep dark caves. The retreating surf hissed violently as it rushed back out of the crevices and inlets created over the millennia.

The dragon was savouring this wild tumultuous place. Okino sensed he had returned here on many occasions to relish the elemental forces of Arimathea interacting together. Their primeval origin was powerfully manifest under these cliffs. Here the dragon was reminded of the forces continuing to shape the edges of his world. In amongst the thunder of the waves, crashing against the solidity of the cliffs he sensed the power of the mystery in which he had become involved. If he had become one of the sentient powers in the Universe, then here he was reminded of the powers to whom he was subjected. He had lived for so long at their mercy, accepting he was subject to the unyielding struggle in which they were engaged.

In his act of rebellion against this ancient lore how much had he been able to change? He could not hold the complex magic he had woven through this world indefinitely. The dragons though, had opened up the humans again to the incredible nature of their world; they had shown them the abilities they possessed to fully involve themselves more deeply into the wonder. He knew them to be powerful creatures who could take control of their own destiny.

However, they could be easily influenced and controlled by their more ruthless brothers and sisters. Here was where the dark forces of Oblivion would be concentrating their efforts. Infiltrating power-hungry minds with schemes to regain the control they had lost. Control, which once regained, would ruthlessly eradicate the newly found creativity transforming the lives of the previously enslaved people of Arimathea.

Okino felt the powerful senses of the dragon deliberately scanning every detail of the scene around him. The warm Starlight mixed with wind and crashing surf seared the experience into Okino's own thoughts. He felt those ancient elemental spirits, heard them calling to him in the plaintive cries of the gulls.

"We will continue, on this world and all worlds despite the rise and fall of fragile life; despite the knowledge of us they will gain and use to manipulate us for their short sighted ends, we will be here in the rays of the Star and the misty surf; always defying them, always mystifying them."

Then Merilon decided it was time to continue his journey back to the dragon hill. Again, he unfurled his great wings and with the one downward sweep he leapt into the air and climbed high above the land over which they now would be flying. The cries of the elemental gulls soon fell away; he flew faster now with a greater sense of urgency. Okino sensed the reserves of energy he had to move through the world in this way were severely depleted. Higher he flew, leaving the fields and towns below the clouds as he joined again the powerful streams of air in the upper atmosphere.

As they flew onward the detail on the land mass below became less distinctive. Eventually, Merilon sensed the approaching mountains, his final destination and started to make his descent. Lazy rivers wound their way downward over flood plains and into the valleys of the low foothills before finally, in the hazy distance the high snow mountains came into view. Again, Okino felt Merilons' excitement as he banked steeply to the left, flying purposefully now, skimming the summits of the higher hills. Lazy rivers were now replaced by fast flowing torrents cutting their way through steep sided canyons. The landscape seemed familiar to Okino but he had no specific memories of the mountains and plains he would come to inhabit in the distant future. They were only ghosts he was unable to comprehend or understand inhabiting the outer reaches of his mind.

Merilon had found the hilltop on which he intended to land and was excitedly circling in anticipation. Finally, with a series of quickening beats of his wings he lowered himself on to the summit of the hill. In the next few moments Okino knew all was not as it should be. He had felt Merilon relax his being on his descent as if he was about to indulge a comfort he had been denied for a prolonged period of time. However, when the dragon landed Okino instantly felt a sense of panic and incredulity. The dragon looked quickly around to make sure he had the right hill. Convinced he had, he immediately turned his attention to the surface. He began to scrape away the soil displaying signs of recent interference and discovered to his horror, the layers of stone Samir had laid across the entire summit. Okino felt dread coursing through the dragon's being as he realised what had happened. Immediately the furious dragon started to dissolve and transform into the tall green eyed human. He knew he only had enough energy to maintain himself as a human being. He had of course anticipated being again re-united with his dragon soul and being recharged with the supernatural power held within the body of Arimathea.

As Merilon registered his disbelief and despair at this sinister development he also was showing signs of exhaustion. He had sunk to his knees staring down at the smooth continuous surface of stone separating him from his life-giving essence. He tried to force his thoughts through the barrier before him. But he sensed there was more than had been at first apparent. Somewhere in the layers of stone there was a darkness, a destructive energy he did not recognise. As he connected with it, the mysterious layer began sucking out even more of his precious remaining energy; it was something he knew could have only come from the far distant and darkest reaches of the universe. He was forced to disengage his concentration. Before the dragon Merilon and the priest Okino finally lost consciousness, they knew all the dragons had or would be subjected to a similar fate as they returned to their hills. They had been rendered powerless both as dragon and human being.

Okino and Merilon drifted in and out of consciousness. As they slept, they drifted through the darkest outposts of the Universe, silent and cold, where stars had long since ceased to exist. They floated in the endless wastes, occasionally surfacing on the Dragon hill amongst the luxurious star filled skies of Arimathea only to fade again into hopelessness and desperation, unable to summon the ability or the will to rectify the predicament in which they now found themselves. In one such waking episode, the Star must have risen for there was warmth and light. Then there was the familiar sound of bells in the distance. They seemed to be coming closer and in the darkness, they took on the form of blazing comets signalling some revival, a new age bringing safety, comfort and enlightenment to the dark wastes. Warmth and light filled their eyes, voices echoed across the void theorising about the mysteries of the universe. There was debate about the nature of the situation they had found here and how best to remedy it?

Then there was movement, from the stillness, from the inability and helplessness that had frozen everything, some exterior force chose a new course into the future. In those moments the dragon heard and understood voices across the void. There was urgency in the voice which could not be ignored. It invaded the eons of consciousness now surrounding him. The voice travelled in through invisible pathways he had carefully left if ever such a time arose when he became overpowered and lost in the labyrinth in which he had grown. He could be dwelling in any one of the multitude of realities he had brought into being or be riding on the shock waves of some cataclysm, ever further and more unreachable from this point. Yet now he heard the voice that could save him.

"If you can hear us Merilon, you must tell us what we should do to help you."

Merilon craved the comfort of Arimathea; the solidity of her all around him where the part of him he had left within her could complete him again. Then he would sleep and dream until he was strong enough to resume his struggle with Oblivion. From the emptiness in which he was enveloped he instructed the distant voice.

"Take me into Arimathea, as deep and dark a place as you can find and leave me there, forget I ever came to your world and tell no one where you have left me. This is all you can do for me. I am now in the power of the Great Mystery governing us all."

Chapter Thirty-one.
The Dragon Lands.

Okino and the dragon were tumbling through the darkness. He was now in a situation in which he was most definitely not accustomed to or comfortable with. All the knowledge and wisdom, the infinite dreams the dragon had accrued through vast spans of his life suddenly seemed empty and without meaning; without his connection to Arimathea there was nothing through which any of his previous thoughts could maintain any kind of grip. He was falling deeper and deeper into the labyrinth. The reference points he had left started to have little meaning. The shadows existing there, memories of long forgotten experience, of battles and confrontations, of past errors and calamity, of circumstances that should have remained buried in those outer recesses were finding their way into the terror he was now feeling. They were magnified and seemed to intensify the turmoil in which he now found himself.

So, as Merilon and Okino fell through the darkness terrible images of famines, of prolonged droughts and floods, outbreaks of disease and plague played through their unhinged nightmare. This mayhem had always broken out as a result of the collision of unforeseen circumstances in the evolution of the worlds they had dreamt. In these times there had been terrible suffering for humans and animals. There had been the loss of profound and beautiful wonders as Oblivion had again brought destruction and annihilation to Arimathea. Memories of such times and the terrible aberrations they had brought, their entire influence on all affected by them, were erased from the face of the world, but not from the memory of the dragons. The context in which these disasters had occurred had lost all meaning. He saw only the suffering caused as a result of some paradoxical causality he should have seen which had subsequently found its way into his complex dream.

Any mitigation for these upsets had become irrelevant. They fell through burnt cracked ground where entire regions where starving to death through lack of food and water; through regions where entire habitats had been swallowed up by an earthquake or devastated by floods. The agony and distress on the faces of the most vulnerable, animal and human alike and the devastation of their beautiful world was torturing the dragon as he fell. They were uncertain how long they were drifting through these catalogues of the destructive horror Arimathea had experienced as she had forged her way into the future. There had been and always would be terrible suffering and now the dragon could feel no justification for it as he fell through the endless chasms of darkness devoid of all the wonder he had found on Arimathea.

Eventually, in this hopelessness and in the memory of the efforts when they had attempted to steer the fate of their world, light started to appear in amongst these apocalyptic visions. He remembered the dragons had met deep in the holy mountain. He concentrated on the beautiful brother and sisterhood they had felt together. Warmth began to return. They had come together to discuss a new possibility. In their thoughts and the meditations there had arisen a new strategy. It had been gained from the knowledge they had gained as humans and subsequently shared as they had come together. They had dreamed a landscape where they would sleep in a Dragon hill. From there they would fill this land with their dreams just below the waking consciousness of Arimathea and where they could be accessed by the humans.

He reached out into the darkness to find the other dragons. Perhaps they could come together in this new layer of consciousness. He had no idea what had happened to them but felt sure they would come to the same conclusion if they picked up this new thought projected towards them in whatever catastrophe they found themselves.

So, the falling began to stop and the darkness slowly started to transform into the misty light of a new dawn. One by one the dragons connected together. Alerted by the beacon Merilon had sent into the wastes of their dark dream space where he had hoped they would eventually find his message. Their physical forms had apparently suffered various fates after the discovery their own hills had also been covered with stone and embedded with the dark spirit essence from the Stars which had left them exhausted and unconscious. The majority had been found by the freedom fighters who had been alerted by the mysterious work being carried out on the hills and dreams of the mystics that may have come directly from panic-stricken Arimathea.

Merilon and Okino had surfaced from their unconsciousness on a number of occasions. Initially they found themselves being carried up a mountain track on the back of a wagon being pulled by yaks. Freedom fighters male and female watched over them and spoke calmly to them when they briefly awoke. They were being taken to the deepest caves known in the region as the dragon had requested and they would be there the next day. Merilon immediately lost consciousness relieved at least he would be safe. The next time he awoke he and Okino had been in a cave. He was able to ascertain it was in the high mountains overlooking a considerable range of lower mountains and hills. Then he fell back into his dreams where many of the dragons were beginning to join in their new dreamscape

Okino found the quality of the darkness slowly began to change. It was no longer cold and endless. Now it had become finite and there was a warmth and comfort to the feelings around him. He felt as if he was being gently held in this new darkness. It was at last a familiar feeling he recognised. It felt as if it was Arimathea who was holding him and the warmth he felt was her Star warming the earth above him. For a time he lay still, unprepared to leave this place of safety and peace he and Merilon had reached. He felt the dragon recovering, relieved he had managed to find this new connection with Arimathea. They both knew it was distant and not entirely real but in some passageway of the labyrinth of time and space a connection had been made.

As the dragons concentrated on bringing this new world into focus it became progressively more solid. They could feel the changes occurring in the atmosphere above them, night and day came and went and occasionally an animal would run over them, sniffing the ground curiously wondering about the strange new scent emerging from the top of the hill. Having become accustomed to the lifeless emptiness it was easy for Okino and Merilon to detect the myriad of spirit life starting to fill this new world. The spirits of trees and animals, streams and rivers, a great ocean all of which the dragons had brought from their own memories were now again coming together. As these spirits began to flow and interact together and mix their precious essence new possibilities were born: potential for new wisdom to evolve came to this world. Okino and Merilon felt it flowing down through the earth surrounding them, infusing their hungry empty spirits with new hope and the realisation it was time to continue their journey.

So, it was as the land became fully formed above them the urge to finally break their bonds became irresistible. As the dragons simultaneously made the decision to live again, the light bound up in their fabulous potential spread through the spirit lands enlivening this new world. Okino and Merilon rose from their dark resting place out into the rising light of the early morning. They were high on the top of a hill from where they were immediately able to see the new world they had created spread out before them. They were surrounded by a ring of enormous standing stones holding the solid energy of the land from which they had come all around them. The soft light of the rising Star softly coloured the veil of mist blanketing the land. From the mist, a gentle cacophony of sound emanated from the myriad of songbirds filling the trees below them.

Okino in awe of the scene before him settled silently on the hill. He felt the continuity the dragon had with everything he saw around him, out to the distant horizons, out into the farthest reaches of space and to where the new Moon had risen over the Eastern horizon. For a few moments he, the dragon and the Universe beyond were complete. Truce reigned over the lands and in the stars now fading in the early morning light.

Okino still deep in his dream on Farina's floor and now in the dream the dragons had created, thought of his brother monks and the tiny monastery perched on the side of the steep mountain overlooking the real Arimathea. He smiled as he thought of the centuries of learning and discipline that had enabled him to arrive here to be one with the dragon. He wanted to bring them here to this hilltop, to see their gentle faces smiling back at him as they felt the peace he was now experiencing.

He thought of Mariella, his beautiful new friend who had sought him out and brought him to the sacred place where he had become so deliciously haunted by the spirits of his world. He wanted to immediately awaken her, shake her out of her own sleepy dreams and tell her he knew what it was to be a creator spirit of Arimathea. He wanted to tell her what it was like to be a tree or an owl living in one or a cat climbing up into it. He wanted to tell her the thrill of being a river in full flood, racing down its channel before flowing out into the ocean. As he explored this seemingly infinite set of new memories he had inherited, he realised he knew what it was to have been a mountain slowly being pushed out of the surface of the planet over millions of years and actually, how the body of Arimathea had shifted to bring her to the place she was in this time.

As he concentrated on the whole planet he became aware again of the thin layer of consciousness he was now a part of. As its full diversity and sheer wonder filled his being for the first time he thought its power could overwhelm him, Okino the monk. But now he realised he had the consciousness of Merilon the dragon. Here was where he dwelt; had always dwelt in many different worlds holding this wonder with all the other dragons as best they could. Dreaming, the warm creative forces proliferating through the world as the forces of oblivion continually circled, looking for any opportunity to silence the precious life arisen there.

As these thoughts passed through his mind he noticed one of the crystal stone paths leading down the hill. It was beckoning him to finish his speculations on the nature of his connection with the dragons and follow it down into the landscape below. He climbed unsteadily to his feet and started down the path. He passed over a bridge crossing over a lively river running around the foot of the hill and into the grasslands beyond.

The path meandered its way across the land amongst woodlands of ancient trees. There were meadowlands rich with wildflowers and the sound of bees labouring as they relentlessly extracted their life-giving nectar. The scent of the flowers drifted through the air beckoning to the winged pollinators to come and sample their wares and enlivening Okino's mind with their delicate fragrance. He had not been aware of any sense of destination only that he was to follow the shining path. But now slowly, he became aware there was a place for him to reach somewhere up ahead. Still he knew nothing about what he would find there but it seemed his will had been engaged.

The path stretched away into the distance through the open meadows. This allowed his mind to wander back to the long walks he used to take in his boyhood. In the high mountains above his town he had often strayed further than he safely should have. He had tested himself in these challenging environments in ways his parents and those around him had never fully comprehended. He had scaled mountains just a little bit too dangerous to be attempted alone or crossed the fast-flowing mountain rivers in temperatures too low to be completely safe.

The distances and the heights to which he had climbed to see the next valley or experience a new and unique vista had taken him into places where he was not completely in control. He knew the feeling of fear and anxiety as some new situation depended on him to exert every last fibre of his will and determination. He had gathered considerable knowledge about the nature of the mountains in his early walks closer to the town and these lengthier forays into the wilderness were natural progressions. Invariably, however he would find himself in situations that would test his nerve to the full. He had taken the strength he had found in those times into everything he subsequently attempted in the many aspects of his life from his schoolwork to the tasks and chores he had been given by his father or the wider community.

However, beyond all the strength he had found, he had noticed, in these moments of danger when it seemed he was not fully in control of his own destiny, he felt more fully alive than at any other time. Here he had come to feel he was in contact with the greater forces operating in his world. As he exerted his will and determination to bring about a safe outcome he had become more deeply involved with those forces. The forces of light and creation would allow him to climb to the top of a cliff, keep his feet and hands firmly in the holds he had chosen. He always knew the forces of destruction would allow him to slip from them, fall possibly to his death or to sustain some injury preventing him from making his way home and then starving to death on the mountain because invariably no-one knew where he was.

He often maintained these were the times that had eventually taken him to the monastery. He found he could express these insights to the monks. They would smile knowingly as the boy came with his conjecture about the forces with whom they continually struggled and then scolded him relentlessly for putting himself in such danger. This awareness which had proliferated through his life meant his training for the monastery had started a long time before he was eventually initiated into the brotherhood.

Now he recognised those feelings of anxiety as he moved through this landscape the dragons had dreamed for his race to again find their connection with the consciousness of their world. He had detected a change in the atmosphere. Clouds had darkened and a cool breeze was stirring the tops of the trees. Now there were cracks of lightening over the hills in the distance followed after a brief interval by a huge thunderous explosion that seemed to shake the ground beneath his feet and all the bones in his young body.

After the thunder Okino detected a chill in the air. It could not only be explained by the change in the atmospheric conditions. His anxiety heightened. The dragon had felt a new presence in the dream. It could not be a human as the dragons had not opened the channels allowing the humans access from their own dreams. It felt like something larger and considerably more sinister was in the atmosphere that only a few minutes before had felt so conducive to positive experience.

Now, however a malevolence seemed to hang in the air and it seemed to be spreading through the structures forming the dream. The buzzing of the insects and birdsong so pervasive minutes before, had been silenced. The trees, the grass and all the vegetation had lost its vibrancy and seemed to slump under some new gravitational force. Okino winced as hailstones suddenly started to rain from the sky stinging his face with their icy velocity. He pulled his hood up over his head and zipped up his jacket and battled his way onward through the rapidly deteriorating conditions wondering whether there was shelter ahead.

The hail became heavier and the hailstones larger, the interval between the lightning strikes became almost non-existent as they came nearer and nearer to the path on which Okino was walking. He could hear the cracking of tree limbs as the speed of the ferocious wind increased now directly hampering his ability to move forward. He now realised he was in a dangerous situation. As he forced himself onward, he projected his thoughts into the spaces beyond the weather around him. He was searching for one of the temples he knew he should eventually find if he followed the path. He searched for solid order, protected space within the maelstrom.

He found it increasingly difficult to force his thoughts through the howling storm surrounding him but there was a destination coming into view. It seemed at first like a cliff face in the distance. He realised this must be one of the temples. As he moved closer, he could appreciate the finely dressed stonework of the walls intersecting with the ground in which they sat. Vegetation had already grown around the walls as if they had been in existence for many hundreds of years. He could make out small windows and levels and distinct separations in the form of the buildings which were predominantly circular towers. As he searched for an entrance, now anxious to get out of the storm and avoid the increasing amount of debris flying around him, he found a large wooden door approached by a number of steps. He nervously climbed the steps and on the landing at the top pushed at the large solid door. It offered no resistance and fell open revealing a large stone hall interior where a fire was burning in a large hearth. He closed the door behind him, relieved the ferocity of the storm was almost completely silenced.

A large banqueting table in the centre of the hall sat on a stone floor. There was no sign of habitation other than the fire was lit and appeared to have been recently tended. Torches carefully placed high in their holders lit the space with a warm dancing light providing Okino instant relief from the threatening conditions prevailing outside those solid walls. Okino walked up to the fire. He felt instantly warm. He moved two of the solid chairs from the table, removed his coat and hung it over the back of one and sat on the other in a position where he could observe the rest of the hall. There was a stone spiral staircase projecting half of its form from one of the four walls and ascending to levels above. Balustraded handrails indicated the landings leading to the spaces beyond. The windows were long and thin and provided little light.

However, the feature of the room which Okino had become particularly interested in was the large collection of swords displayed on the walls. They were carefully hung on brackets fixed into the stonework. They were unfixed and many were able to be reached and could be removed from their settings. Okino observed these swords must have been gathered from many different civilisations and cultures. They ranged extensively between long heavy broadswords to the lightest most slender rapiers.

He contemplated the weapons, took some down, swished them back and forth as he began to dry beside the fire. Each of these weapons he decided suggested a quite specific kind of combat. The long broadswords suggested knights in full armour while the shorter swords suggested great shield walls where longer swords would have only been an unwieldy disadvantage. Overwhelmingly it seemed to Okino, it was not how these weapons had been used now intriguing him, if indeed they had been, but why they had been used.

He imagined a battlefield glinting in the warm Star shine with all the weaponry of war. There were two opposing forces with some difference of opinion about who should rule them or how they should be ruled; perhaps some indiscretion or slight between regions, a trade dispute between countries; perhaps one race had gathered enough power to attempt a global conquest and so rule the world. He imagined two armies standing in front of each other perhaps because of the difference in the ideologies of their rulers. One supposedly going to war to defeat the blasphemous opinion of the other. The other to defend the right to have their own belief which had grown up over the centuries in their own part of the world. He imagined the men standing in their armies. Soon they would be attempting to kill or horribly maim their fellows for one of these ideologies or squabbles they did not understand or perhaps did not even know about. They stood there in fear of what lay in front of them if they fought or if they did not. Then after the battle he saw the horror the two armies had inflicted upon each other.

The swords hung eerily on the walls, harmless without a reason to be wielded, each with the wicked potential for death and destruction held on its sharpened edges. Could their use ever be truly justified? An evil despotic regime torturing and murdering its own population, denying them their human rights deserved the justice of the more responsible members of the community brought down upon it; The will of one community being brought to bear on another. In the early stages of negotiation the sword stayed undrawn in the scabbard as a representation of the ability of one to ultimately exert power over the other.

Okino then drifted back to his earlier thoughts and the struggle he had had to make it through the storm and into the warmth of the castle. He had exerted his own power over the situation to bring about a satisfactory outcome. He smiled as he thought of his town and everyone there.

"Isn't that we do?" he thought.

In our struggle to stay alive, to carry on our existence as individuals and as a race. We continually exert our will over everything standing in our way, whether for our own good, the good of our family or the wider community. He thought of the wolves and their efforts to steal the goats and his own determination to prevent them after his father had given him the responsibility of looking after them. But didn't the wolf have as much right to his life as they themselves. So then, this power must be carefully used. Careful thought to assess the consequences of such actions would always have to be undertaken to justify such action, consequences for the balance of the world in our direct vicinity, but also for the wider world beyond.

If his town for instance decided they would kill as many wolves as it would take to keep their sheep safe what then would be the changes in the surrounding area. The natural prey of the wolves would certainly increase. Perhaps the actions of the wolf were the result of their earlier actions of domesticating the goats and leaving less pastureland for the wild goats. He recognised in his own community how carefully these decisions about intervention were taken after perhaps long debate with all concerned. In the wider world, in the future world he imagined such precautionary debate had long since disappeared.

He thought of the times when he had watched the houses being built and the extreme determination it took to bring the trees from the woods, cut them to shape and eventually lift the resulting beams into place; or to bring the stone from the quarries to build the heavy stone walls. Every year the harvest was brought in thanks to the determined effort of everyone in the town because they knew they depended on the harvest for their existence.

Even in the monastery, the will to preserve and improve the connection generations of monks had built with Arimathea would have been tested down the years. New ideas or possibilities for such a community would always have been raised. But if the stringent discipline for the attainment of such wisdom had been compromised, his final initiation into the order may never have taken place and his acquisition of the knowledge would never have been passed onto to him. He would never have survived the storm on the mountain without Arimathea's ability to communicate through his heightened consciousness and this quest would never have been initiated.

So, the swords around him, the sword as a concept came into Okino's mind to represent the will of not only his own race, but of perhaps every living thing in existence on Arimathea as they defied the forces attempting to take their life away. He saw the will threaded through the consciousness of all life as a fundamental necessity for its continuation and evolution. Ultimately if a life was threatened then the claws, the teeth, the sword would have to be drawn.

He looked around the walls of the castle and smiled. So, this is how it would happen; experience, dreams and thoughts gradually melded together to explain an aspect of the consciousness that had come to be for the preservation and continuation of Arimathea. The dragon who now had become Okino smiled with deep satisfaction. Surely this was a legitimate way of guiding the humans to a deeper understanding of their world. Here they were able to come to their own understanding through the knowledge they really already had.

Okino left the fireside, curious to see the upper levels. He walked across the hall and entered the spiral staircase. He climbed to the top around the narrow winders where he found a small door. He pushed it open and found himself on the top of one of the circular towers. There was a timber roof, allowing the occupants to visit the platform during any weather conditions. Now the storm had eased and Star shine predominantly filled the landscape in front of him. Any sign of the new presence had for now it seemed dissipated. He could see the new Dragon lands spread out before him and the Dragon hill from where he had come in the distance. The great stones embedded in the top, even from here were clearly visible. He could also see other castles nestled, glistening in the landscape where the ancient tribe of masons had chosen to situate them, connected into the wisdom flowing from the dragon hill. The paths occasionally sparkled as the crystal filled stone was exposed. Woods and smaller stone circles stretched out tantalisingly before him. He immediately felt the urge to leave this castle of swords and make his way out to visit the other castles.

He wondered how long he could stay in this dream. It seemed like an eternity since he had seen Mariella. But he knew there was something else he had to do before he returned. He descended the spiral staircase and collected his coat from in front of the fire, lazily put it on and once again contemplated the collection of swords. He shuddered as he remembered the terrible emptiness he had felt after the crack of thunder. He smiled to himself and went over to the racks of swords. He assessed each one and eventually took one down and ran his thumb down the blade. It was almost invisibly sharp. He took it over his head into what he remembered to be an attack position. It felt like it had instantly become part of him. He lowered it and made a few cuts through the air. He felt the balance gave a fine swing for little effort. For some reason, he decided he needed the sword and so he took down the scabbard, buckled it up around his waist and left the castle.

The path he had followed to the castle now continued, winding its way through a thickening forest. Star shine able to find its way through the thick canopy fell in pools of golden light on the path around him. Okino was aware of the weight of the sword hanging on the belt around his waist. He realised he had not questioned whether or not it was right for him to take the sword. It now felt as if the whole experience had been engineered so he would understand why he needed to take the sword. He had given no thought to the circumstances in which he would have to use it other than the fact he had felt something in the storm he might have to defend himself against. A chill ran through his being. Okino knew Merilon was a skilled swords man and had little doubt he would be able to defend himself.

The wood had become considerably cooler as the canopy became thicker. He felt the temperature drop again, but there had been no corresponding thickening of the canopy. Apprehension of his surroundings was rapidly turning to distinct unease. The breeze in the top of the canopy had increased. In his musings he had not contemplated the winning and the losing and all the factors bringing about the result. Perhaps not always about power and brute force. Sometimes it was about craft and intelligent tactics, perhaps a little luck and having the wind behind you, the shining road rising up before you.

Here was where the future of the world was continually decided. Thankfully none of the arguments he had witnessed in his town had resulted in a fight to the death. But there were frequently disagreements that often resulted in a visit to the monastery for a talk with the monks. Their advice was respected and mostly adhered to. In a small community such as theirs which depended on everyone being able to cooperate, a feud or conflict of any kind could have disastrous consequences.

Again, the atmosphere had changed, the air had become thicker, charged with uncertainty and ambiguity. Okino tried to rationalise the fear now arisen in his combined being. As he finally managed to persuade himself his fear was unfounded, a figure appeared in the distance. He could see even from this distance he was as tall as Merilon with long dark ragged hair falling around his shoulders onto the large bulk of his ragged clothing. His complexion was Star burnt and weather beaten. As he came closer Okino could see a thickset determined face reflecting the darkened atmosphere amongst the trees. The two men eventually came within ten paces, each now blocking the others path. The wind had dropped. Okino noticed a silence he thought could destroy any sound before it even arose. They stood for a few moments contemplating each other before Okino heard Merilon speaking through him for the first time.

"Is it you, Mithrael, my brother?" the dragon asked, "I thought you were lost to this world."

"After Allai-garan, as you know I did become almost hopelessly lost delving deeper and deeper into the farthest outreaches of those endless corridors of time, trying to find some way back to the days before those terrible moments."

It seemed as if the strength in which he initially stood in front of Merilon might have left him. Merilon could have struck in this moment but compassion for his lost brother and bemusement he should appear now, prevented him from taking this advantage

"There is no way back, not that I could find. Not to those places we want, we need to relive and alter. They are changed by our search and our craving and what has happened. Our misery, the pain Merilon, has transformed us forever and it prevents us perhaps, cannot allow us to have the possibility of re-enacting what would not only kill us but scatter us through the endless realms. But I did return.

I have become part of this land, Merilon, as much as you, the sky and the trees. On Arimathea, I am a shaman. You will not know but I have been given the ability to travel between worlds and dimensions. Possibly because of the upset you have caused, possibly because of my own journeys. You weren't difficult to find in here once you started connecting with the other dragons. A new very specific wave of consciousness, carefully buried in the other layers I grant you, but in the end it has to be easily accessible to the humans doesn't it, so you can continue with your hopeless manipulations."

He grinned at Merilon openly. His strength and defiant stance had returned.

"How did you think you could ever influence this hopeless species so intent on its' own destruction?"

"Surely you wouldn't allow it all to happen again, Mithrael," Merilon was pleading and continued.

"They are complex creatures, highly developed beings. They always respond and are changed by everything that happens to them. Somewhere at some time some distrust arose and they lost their way; lost or gave up their connection with the thought form that had guided them and brought them to what they had become. Now they are lost seemingly in a merciless world in which they feel they have been stranded, unprepared for all they find they have to endure. They are led by the cruellest of them. They take advantage of their vulnerability to enslave them and drive them further from the Love freely flowing through this world. The result has been the callous regimes who think nothing for the beauty of this world. Their wounded souls have been left empty by their craving for power and unaware they continue the dark work that will bring an end to this world."

"You know this is how it must be, Merilon. The way will have to be found by them. If there is any possibility it ever can be. If not the spirit will return to the peace from which all this originated and the process will eventually begin again on another world!"

Mithrael taunted Merilon.

"But so much of the potential we hoped for has already been fulfilled and these forces you will again allow to dominate this world are only interested in the ultimate Death of all worlds where any kind of life is developing."

".... As you are interested in purely the proliferation of Life which you know can only evolve into the future as a result of Death! I am here Merilon in the interest of the balance that operates between the two."

"Oh yes, the balance!! The balance allowing billions of years of complex evolution within a carefully held dream to be again destroyed by one species. But strangely not by an ignorant unintelligent species but by the most creative and exceptionally talented species ever developed on any world."

"But this evolution must in some way be flawed if it is leading to the death of another planet. These creatures have become so complex the world on which they have grown cannot sustain them."

"They have evolved on Arimathea as have every other species in response to the challenges their journey through time has given to them. Their minds have developed as a result of living and breathing her consciousness. They have learnt to construct strategies to survive in the form they have taken to suit the many situations arising in their day to day existence. Ultimately, they are using these strategies to change the nature of their world to suit their own characteristics. However, as they change the nature of their world to suit themselves they are drifting away from their unique connection with Arimathea."

"…And you think by helping them to understand more about the nature of their world this impending catastrophe will be avoided?!"

"Isn't that what we have always done, sent our dreams into the worlds we have inhabited to gently guide them into the future!"

"…But not like this, in this reconstructed dream world. The wisdom you talk of must be gained by themselves, when they come to understand their power and when they see the results of its misuse.

It is their inability to appreciate the power they have which has resulted in their destructiveness. They will only realise how they have misused this power when and if they start to tackle the consequences and then begin to act more responsibly; If they do not, they will have to watch their world disintegrate around them."

Mithrael had started to draw the sword he carried on his side.

"But this may take another thousand years. There will be wars resulting in millions being killed, Arimathea will be stripped of all her wonders and another catastrophic planetary extinction may be the result. So much of what they need to help them through this stage could be learnt resulting from their experience in this landscape through their dreams. They have had this knowledge. It has just become buried in their memories. It just needs bringing to the surface before it recedes even deeper. Think how much suffering could be prevented…"

Merilon seeing Mithrael was now on the point of attacking him drew his own sword and held it out in front of him ready to defend himself.

"These time spans are irrelevant. They must be allowed to evolve through experience and the circumstances resulting from their own shortcomings, then be able to develop their strategies to cope with and understand the destruction they are causing. Unless this is felt through the whole consciousness of Arimathea then nothing is being changed in her evolution as a whole. This you know is almost as critical when moving towards the ultimate destiny as her survival. Unless it is changed here and now it will just keep on happening; destroying world after world."

Mithrael took a swing directly at neck height towards Merilon. Merilon parried the blow. Okino felt the strength of the impact of the steel on his own sword. He knew immediately who between the two combatants was stronger. Merilon swung back, but Mithrael easily deflected his attack taunting him continually…

"…All the reactions, all the relationships crossing over, all the conjunctions noticed in the adversity, every single thought and memory enacted and re-enacted will become part of the evolution of your dream. Somewhere, at some point there is always a chance a group or a race of people will realise; some corner will be turned, some insight, some action will make the change and inspire a whole new branch of human evolution. It is the only way to bring the understanding you are talking about and it will all be in the consciousness potentially to be experienced by everyone."

Merilon was struggling physically from the blows crashing around him and mentally as he knew Mithrael was ultimately right. This was how the evolution of the world came about, on the edge of crisis and adaptation through wonderful chance, strange improbability and coincidence coming together to produce an even more beautiful outcome than could possibly have been thought or manufactured by any creator.

He felt the determination and the justification for Mithraels action in every crash of their swords. He was strong and prepared for the task he had come to do. Merilon however was weakened and his will to fight had been undermined by his loss of connection to his beloved Arimathea and the knowledge this new world they had created was possibly untimely. He looked briefly into the distant future to when the lessons to which Mithrael now referred had been learnt; when the consequences of their ruthless exploitation could be seen and they would seek and find the planetary wisdom they had lost. Then it would be combined again into the overall consciousness of the world. He saw the vehemence in the face in front of him: he felt the strength and confidence in the blows, everyone rattling the frailty coming over him. His dragon fire, the limitless life force he could draw from this world was now all but gone.

"So, dragon, it is time for a long sleep. In this world you have made you will be forgotten, separated and fragmented and Arimathea will grow for better or for worse without your misguided meddling."

Okino felt Merilon's will finally drain away. He looked around him. He was deep in the woodland. He was surrounded by ancient Oak trees. He heard the song of a thousand songbirds and somewhere in the distance he acknowledged the powerful roar of a stag consolidating his territory. The sword fell from his hand and as he finally relaxed, he looked deep into the Star high above the trees. He closed his eyes and felt its' warm light flood his body, he thought he heard the welcoming voices of Arimathea's ancestral spirits as Mithraels sword drove through his heart. The dragon fell heavily and lay as if pinned to the ground by the sword. He felt the searing pain somewhere in the distance as he looked up through the trees. He thought he could see two eagles wheeling in the deep blue sky above. They called down to him summoning him again. He knew that heavenly place and smiled as he remembered the uplifting air under his wings soaring through infinity over his beloved Arimathea. He felt her now beneath him but as hard as he tried he could not join her; the separation was now complete and seeped relentlessly into his being. A lifeless stone dragon slowly appeared; his wings stretched out across the clearing as his eyes slowly closed; the sword still buried deeply in his chest. A breeze circled three times through the tree canopies and left the grove.

Part Two.
Land, Sea and Air.

Chapter Thirty-Two
The Recovery.

In Farina's home back in the village of Asima the Star had risen over the mountains. Mariella knelt on the floor next to Okino's basic mattress where he lay. She had woken earlier in the morning to find he was in a deep and troubled sleep. This was unusual as he would normally be awake before her. She let him be and busied herself with prompting the fire back into life and walking down to the well for some water. Still it amazed her this was what had to be done. She cast her mind to Straam where an entire city would be waking to breakfast stored in refrigerators, water running from taps high in the multiple floors of the skyscraper city and hot water from their showers.

She smiled as she took a minute to take some water in her cupped hands and splash it over her face. The water droplets caught the early morning Star. Intense light flashed into her mind and combined with the cool mountain water instantly reviving her. She was surprised how natural this had all started to feel. The faraway world from which she had come would seem all the more unnecessary now she knew how many people in her world were surviving without its luxuries

She stared out to the distant snow-covered peaks towering over the little stone street and she wondered of the pristine untouched slopes and valleys of the wilderness beyond. She imagined the snow leopards, padding through the crisp white snow, sniffing the air, their thick fur coats shining with health as they continued their struggle in their harsh mountainous home. Her fascination with these beautiful cats, which in fact so far, she had not seen here in the mountains, had come from Okino. She had of course seen them in films made by people who had sat out on the sides of mountains for months on end risking frost bite and so loss of fingers for a siting of the elusive creatures. But Okino had seen many on his silent journeys through the mountains and on several occasions before they had seen him.

On their journey here she had listened in awe as he described the first time he had seen one of the ghost cats moving through a fall of rocks, close enough to see the detail in her fur, the steady gaze in her eyes and the superb balance in her poise. It was clear from this point Okino probably would have preferred to have been a snow leopard. Both were suited to their existence out here. Her fondness for both she now realised was bound up together with this extraordinary world she had uncovered for herself. Her fondness suddenly turned to concern as she remembered Okino had still been sleeping when she left. She hurried back down the street to Farina's house.

She immediately checked on Okino. He was still asleep but it seemed the nature of his sleep had changed. He was now increasingly restless, his eyes moved rapidly under their lids and he murmured under his breath. His head and limbs were moving sporadically. As she watched, these movements began to intensify and she noticed beads of sweat had started to break out and run down his forehead. She found a small hand towel and dampened it with water from the well and placed it carefully on his brow.

However, now Okino had become progressively agitated and there seemed little she could do to quieten whatever he was going through. Without warning he became very calm. Then, after a few moments he opened his eyes, sat bolt upright as if suddenly panic stricken and drew in a huge breath of air. The speed of this awakening startled Mariella. Then the two young people looked across at each other in stunned silence. As soon as he realised he had awoken, Okino slumped back onto his bed. He stared in shock up at the ceiling, remembering the vivid contents of the dreams before they flashed from his mind and the reality of the day again took over. Then he turned his head to Mariella who was now poised fascinated to see what would happen next. He reached out for her hand and said.

"It's good to be back!"

"Are you alright? Was it the dragons again…? you seemed to be in some kind of struggle at the end and then deeply peaceful as if…"

"…as if I had died!"

"Well yes. But don't they say if you die in a dream…Now Okino just you relax and take it easy for a few moments, I'm going to make you a cup of tea. Then you can tell me all about it."

Mariella went over to where the kettle was sizzling away and poured some hot water onto a mix of Farina's herbs in one of the brightly coloured pots, strained the tea into a mug and took it over to Okino. He sat up leaning his pillow up against the wall at the head of his bed and silently sipped the tea. Mariella could see he had to run some big thoughts through his head before he spoke to her. Then he turned to her grinning and said…

"The dragons are still alive Mariella. They are still sleeping somewhere, well only one in these mountains, but yes they are all still sleeping in caves where they were hidden all those centuries ago by the freedom fighters.... This is going to be difficult to explain."

"Just explain as best you can and what you can remember…as long as we know what we have got to do next…. if anything!!"

So Okino then did the best he could to recall the dream. His memory was clear so he was easily able to describe what had happened. However, as the words to describe the images flowed, his understanding and comprehension about what had happened to him was continually fluctuating. He had travelled as energy and although the energy had been considerably diluted, he had finally gained insight into how the dragons flowed through the world. He knew now how Mithrael had eventually acted to deny the people of Arimathea a permanent reconnection to the dragons at an important time in their development. There were unanswered questions. If the dragons had not directly intervened would the situation on Arimathea be better or worse? The human race had become disconnected from the wisdom embedded in the consciousness long before the dragons finally lay sleeping, separated from Arimathea and so powerless in their caves. Would they have eventually found a more permanent connection without the dragon's interference as Mithrael had suggested?

Now he had been responsible for waking them when he had been mysteriously guided to Merilon where he had lain in the forest for a thousand years and removed Mithraels' sword. Their subsequent meetings and their flight together explained why Merilon had appeared to recognise Okino once the sword had been withdrawn. He now appeared to have been brought back to life if only in the layer of consciousness the dragons had created for themselves. It did not appear, so far, to have been used for its' prescribed purpose.

His ability to intercept the dreams the dragons had created appeared to have arisen as a result of his order developing his natural ability to communicate with the consciousness of his world. Then Mariella had also made her deep connection with Arimathea and Farina appeared to have been connected through the generations of people who had lived in Asima. All their dreams and visions presumably transmitted from the dragon council around the lake would appear to suggest a time had now arisen where a continuation of the process curtailed by Mithrael could now be made possible.

When Okino finished the recollections of his dream a thoughtful silence briefly descended on the room. Farina and her husband had joined them. Further tea was made and as they sat quietly sipping the richly aromatic liquid Farina spoke first.

"Still there is no explanation of what happened to Asima and all the people who were living there; and the freedom fighters who rescued the dragons who would have known about the dragon hill."

"Don't we really know though?" Mariella ventured. "I should imagine once the dragons had been dealt with then anyone who had had any connection with them or knowledge about what had happened on the Dragon hill would also have been dealt with….probably painfully and fairly publicly just in case there was any temptation to try to remove the stone from the hills."

"It must have been a frightening time for everyone," Okino said quietly. "It is hard to imagine what it would have been like to have all that persecution and slavery taken a way to be replaced by the hope and inspiration the dragons had offered, only for it to be stripped away again and replaced with all the terror that then would have ensued."

There was silence again as dreadful imaginings seeped through their minds.

"The Lords and rulers had been seriously humiliated and the cost to their operations had been severe." Farina spoke quietly reflecting on this new era that had come to Arimathea

"They would have had no problem recruiting for their armies as the lands were again confiscated. The priests of the alien gods had been discredited and so the control they had exerted over the people would no longer be there to assist in this latest subjugation. The fear they would have had to raise in the minds of their people so the accumulation of profit and power could resume all over again, would have to be all the more terrible. Oblivion had returned to fill the minds of the power hungry with the promise of uninterrupted and unlimited exploitation of human and planetary resources."

"The result of which is that in a thousand years,"

Mariella spoke now,

"Arimathea has progressed from a collection of countries and domains with predominantly rural economies trading with each other across seas with the use of sails and across land with the use of animals into a fully industrialised, mechanised, computerised global community without any of the planetary wisdom which had held it all in place and guided it for the first five billion years!"

There were a few moments of silence as this thought sank in. Then Okino began to speak.

"I liked what Mithrael said to Samir. He seemed to have concluded the dragons were the carriers, almost like vast cosmic bees flying around the universe intent on finding a planet to complete and nurture them; an offshoot of which was they were fertilising the planets with their dreams. The dreams then contained the original urge, he calls it Love or God, a vast ethereal being or state, physically manifest in warmth and light in which consciousness can exist as the bridge between such a state and physical life..."

He indicated to everyone sitting around the table.

"...the ends of which was something approaching the potential this being had foreseen in its original ethereal state. But to arrive at such a state it would have to evolve into something altogether different. It would have to allow an expansion to allow this new world and ultimately the human race to develop at one with the original spirit. Eventually however they would have to make their own way, make their own decisions about how they wanted to live, have their own ideas and their own disasters; to find a way of living physically with the ever present threat of Oblivion and ultimately to find the bridge between themselves and the original ethereal state. Perhaps the dragons had to fade from influence to allow this new physicality to reach its full potential. When they interfered, they interfered too soon and a rift was made. Now with a premature end to Arimathea in sight and with Oblivion dangerously in the ascendant, perhaps all the debts have been paid and it would seem a way for the dragon to return has been allowed or become necessary for the survival of the dream into the future."

"So have the monks of the Dragon Order, hidden away in the hills for all those centuries found the bridge allowing it all to surface again from their dimension into ours?" Mariella had grasped the implication of what he was saying.

"It would seem so!"

Okino could suddenly feel the weight of this new time approaching. The battle lines between creation and destruction again were being drawn up. The great mystery had determined all was not done and a new episode was to be unravelled. There was always a turning point it would seem. How and where such a moment was decided could perhaps never be foreseen, but in the histories written of the great flow of events that had transpired in the world, these were the moments that would be poured over and analysed. The moment one force had transcended their subordinate position and once again became dominant over their oppressor.

There were factors that would always be attributed to the frustrated rebellious fervour of entire populations rising against their oppressors. Perhaps the over confidence that came with great power had allowed a lowering of a guard, an ill-disciplined decision, an overly optimistic view of the degree of supremacy able to be held. It seemed in whatever advantage had arisen therein lay the seeds of an eventual downfall. The nature of power would always deny this inevitability and perhaps here was its' true weakness. No matter how heavy the hold or tight the grip as the days and years rolled on the time of readjustment would be approaching.

Okino had noticed in the natural world these factors could be finely balanced and could swing comparatively quickly. A harsh winter or a lack of rainfall could dramatically affect a generation of plants or animals. The great tectonic plates and volcanic activity which had made Arimathea into what she was, were still moving and the next earthquake or eruption always threatened. So, the affairs of humans were still tenuously bound up with natural events.

The fortifications the humans had built in the world beyond his own had been built higher and stronger. They had become expert in those years when the dragons had been asleep in their mountains at shoring up the power they had accumulated. The ability of organisations and governments, even entire countries to dominate the less powerful, had been carefully developed through the passing of law, of governmental regimes and political dogma binding the populations of Arimathea into their systems of control.

In this position of power there was little to prevent them ravaging and plundering Arimathea of her precious resources. Now this plunder was endangering everything that had evolved here. Okino and Mariella had felt the time approaching; perhaps they had felt the rising tides of change in the consciousness they shared with their world, perhaps in the voices they had heard echoing through the labyrinth connecting them to the point where all this had been initiated, transferred through messages from those energies mixing infinitely into the weave of the mystery. This destruction must again be opposed. Okino spoke.

"So how are we going to remove the stone from the top of the Dragon hill?"

"Samir didn't leave us a lot of options really," Farina replied quietly.

"It seems we have only two choices."

Tarak spoke up enthusiastically. He had listened quietly, fascinated by all he had heard. Although he knew of the legends, up until now he had paid little concern to the mystery lying on the top of the hill. Like many of the men in Asima he was mostly preoccupied with the day to day survival of his family. Now it seemed his survival had become bound up with whatever lay on top of the hill.

"I have not seen these slabs of stone, but from what you are saying they are probably still there because up until now, with the resources we have at our disposal they have been impossible to move. So the first option would be to get some heavy lifting machinery up there, but I don't know of anything like that anywhere nearer than one of the coastal towns so it would take some time and resources to get something up here, or…"

He waited until he was sure everybody was listening.

"We blow the whole lot off with dynamite!"

There were a few seconds of silence as the other three looked at Tarak in amazement. It seemed such a violent solution to what seemed like a peaceful problem. Okino quickly played the explosion through in his mind. He watched great lumps of the rock rising into the air and tumbling down the hill to find their place with all the other rocks that laid there. It seemed a dramatic but a fitting way of solving the problem.

"I like it," he said with a mischievous smile on his face.

"But where will we get enough dynamite up in these mountains to cause that sort of explosion!"

"I know people in Aharri who work in the quarries at Reaka. I think we would have to bring them over here to do it, because that is going to be a serious explosion and they will want paying.."

"Money will not be a problem," Mariella interjected firmly, "The problem is getting over there and back, I don't really want to go all the way on the horses!"

Again, there was silence as they contemplated this new problem.

"What about the guys from the southern city, with their land cruiser we could be down there in one day, sort the explosives out maybe a day and then be back the next day. So, could be as little as three days!"

"Which is all very well, but we aren't really on good terms with those guys. We were pretty much allied to the men who nearly cut their throats!"

"Don't worry about that!" Mariella said with a smile, "I will deal with them. I think we should leave as soon as possible!"

Chapter Thirty-three
Return

Mariella left the house as soon as she felt Okino was settled after his ordeal the night before. She needn't have been concerned for the young monk. He was it seemed as skilled at travelling through the layers of consciousness to blend his soul with energy and spirits as she would have been at one of the cocktail parties, she had regularly frequented back in Straam. How different their lives had been up until they had blended them on this strange journey. She had felt a change in herself since she had been travelling with him and through his land. After her meditation in the circle of standing stones and her swim in the waterfall her perception of her world had deepened and become more vivid.

She had identified with the shaman dragon Mithrael in Farina's story when he had said Arimathea talked to him throughout the day. She had started to recognise this dialogue immediately. She heard it now as she had earlier from the mountains rising above the little stone houses. Their power and enormity spoke slowly to her of the true nature of her world and made her race seem transient. As she had these thoughts the little band of children ran up to her, faces beaming with their delightfully innocent intelligence, ragged around her, gently pulling at her arms and hands imploring her to come and play with them. How beautiful they were: how they shone with the natural vigour of their unspoiled environment. Having been reminded of the worst her race had brought to bear on Arimathea now she was reminded of their capacity for joy and Love; in these children she glimpsed for a moment the ancient race that had sent their wonder safely down the millennia to these future days.

They followed her down the street; the smallest children, two little girls held her hands happily while the older boys ran relentlessly around them. They walked down to the little corral where the three horses were waiting patiently, gently chomping on some variety of local vegetation. They had become used to the strange changes in their diet as they moved through the land. They were pleased to see Mariella. They whinnied gently, flicked their ears forward and nuzzled up to her when she came to the fence.

She had thought of them that morning when Okino was talking about the dragons and how they had brought life to her world. She had come so close to them during her own life and refused to believe they were not equally as sentient and conscious in their own way as she and the rest of the human race. Such intelligence in their eyes: always watching her, reading her emotional state. If she was calm and contented so were they. They allowed the children to clamber over them as Mariella led them around their temporary home, patiently tolerating the noisy wriggling things that had been hoisted onto them.

The large sleek land cruiser Ben and Zeph had arrived in was parked alongside the fence. The two southerners emerged from the deserted house in which they had been staying and noticed Mariella with the children and the horses. They grinned to each other and leant up against the fence to watch. She glanced over at them and acknowledged them with a friendly smile. The children soon began to tire of the horse game and launched themselves back into the environs of the village to continue whatever game they had been playing. Mariella freed the horses again and walked over to the two men.

"You guys are up and about early!"

"Yeah well, I don't think they gave us the most comfortable beds in the village!"

"Oh no, that was the one I had." Mariella beamed. She had slept very well on the woollen mattress Farina had given her to sleep on.

"We want to make an early start any way. We are starting to make our way back to civilisation today!"

"Are you sure it's more civilised back there? I have begun to wonder!"

"I speak euphemistically of course. I should have said perhaps; back to the unholy catastrophe that our civilisation has now become!"

So, they did have a sense of humour.

"I suppose you will be going back via Aharri?"

"That is not the most direct route but it is the way the road goes. Yeah we'll be going that way!"

"I wonder if you could give us a lift over there, I have some business to take care of before I head down to the sea. In fact, I would make it worth your while if you brought us back."

The two men looked eagerly over at Mariella. Now she knew they would do anything she asked of them.

"So how much would make it worth your while?"

"What are we talking, the best part of two days there and back, A few thousand should cover it! Will the monk be coming; I don't think he was impressed with us? It was unfortunate what happened in the bar and we really didn't mean to upset anyone: it's just all this spirit stuff out here it's hard to believe they are so serious about it. You know what it's like back in the city!"

"I do know and that is why I'm here; we've lost something and they still have it here."

"…and what is that Mariella?"

"I think they have a kind of awe for their world. I started to find it back there and wondered if it still existed amongst a whole people. I heard about the monks and so here I am….and I find they live in their world, in their physical world and yes, they see and feel the supernatural behind it. It's not an issue because it is just how their world is, like our world is how it is....and you have to admit our world is mostly a fantasy considerably more far-fetched than anything you will find out here!"

"You'll go back to it though when this is all over!"

"Maybe. Maybe not!"

Mariella smiled as she started back up the street to Farina's house.

"But I reckon things are going to start to change…there is nothing a little bit of supernatural won't sort out! See you down here later."

Back at the house Okino had fully recovered from his near-death experience between his dream and the waking world. He was sitting outside the house enjoying the early morning star shine when Mariella returned. She sat next to him on the timber bench skilfully fashioned from driftwood rescued from the river in the valley. He watched her as she settled quietly, closing her eyes to feel the warming Star on her skin, now darker and well acclimatised to the rigours of the weather she had experienced since she had left her home. The fascination he now held for her had grown as they experienced together and individually the strange mystery in which they had become involved. She had relaxed in his company and perhaps a little more into her journey. He knew Arimathea had come close to her. Possibly they had shared their own creation mystery. She had been as calm as anyone he had ever known from the first moment he had met her but now there was something even more substantial. He sat back and closed his eyes basking in the warmth, pleased and thankful he was here with her. Then after a few moments…

"I've organised Ben and Zeph to give us a lift over to Aharri. I think perhaps I will go with Tarak to buy the dynamite; you don't really need to come. I have a feeling you should spend some time on your own in old Asima; There may be some final insights you need to absorb before we leave."

In the wake of his previous thoughts he was surprised to register a slight apprehension at the thought of this separation. He acknowledged it and put it aside as he thought of the days he would spend exploring the area in and around the ruined settlement and wondered what new delights awaited him.

"Just be careful not to get too involved with Merilon while I'm away. I don't want to come back to find you have disappeared completely!"

"I don't think that will be a problem. I think I have been through the worst with him but I think you are right there may well be some further knowledge that needs to be transferred before we embark on the next stage of the journey; Whatever that is."

Chapter Thirty-four
Separation

Later in the morning Ben and Zeph loaded up the land cruiser and drove up the street to Farina's house. The sleek silver machine stood idling;

engine barely audible as if it had landed from some other world amongst the stone houses. Tarak's attention was distracted as he said his goodbyes to his wife and child. He was excited by this wild tale that had emerged in his life and the tall monk and his beautiful travelling companion who was now whisking him off in this amazing machine to Aharri. He was excited he would be there in time for dinner in the bar with his friends; A journey that would normally take him two or three days with the terrible discomfort of the cart and the excruciatingly slow speed of the yaks. Now he would travel in the air-conditioned luxury of the southern land cruiser. Okino noticed how distracted he was. He remembered how seductive the prospect of such a journey could be and smiled to himself as he remembered Haran's old lorry explosively coming to life in his barn. Mariella gave him a gentle hug and said a brief goodbye before reiterating firmly he should try and avoid too much trouble while she was a way. He watched them climb into the back of the land cruiser and disappear behind the lightly tinted windows, one of which immediately lowered revealing Mariella waving to him as the vehicle pulled silently away and disappeared into the valley between the hills.

Okino decided he would take his horse from the corral and soon found himself riding up to the top of the dragon hill in time to see the land cruiser, now just a tell-tale cloud of dust in the distance heading towards the horizon. Then he was alone again in the vast landscapes of Arimathea. Of course, they had not changed in any way but again he felt fully part of them, there was no part of his attention elsewhere. He did not think this was any reflection on how close he had become to Mariella but merely when she was around there was definitely a part of him distracted by her. Now although the full majesty of Arimathea was again revealed to him, he noticed the emptiness where she had been. He enjoyed her company and had never felt she was detrimental to his connection with his world and was beginning to think she was starting to enhance it. She was and always had been quietly respectful of his deep connection. She knew in a sense the success of her mission depended on this aspect of his being and he had recognised a great understanding in her ability to observe how best this could be achieved.

He reined the horse's head almost instinctively now, back towards the path heading down the hill. Instead of taking the path back to the ruins he decided to take an alternative path which lead to a stoutly constructed bridge. This allowed him and the horse, although nervously at first, to cross the river. He started to realise as he made this transition back into the landscape that clearly Mariella would never be far from his thoughts.

So, he started to drift through the day. He became accustomed again to the gentle rhythm of the horse as they left the wider track and carefully negotiated the narrower paths leading out into new unexplored land. He relished this feeling. He felt his senses fully opening to all the new experience as it unfolded before him. The boulder strewn slopes leading out into new vistas strewn with the indigenous pine trees filling the air with their sweet aroma; each twisted shape of their ancient trunks and branches spoke to him of their life and the circumstances in which they had grown.

He wondered whether his experience of the landscape had deepened since the dream when he and Merilon had merged their beings. He decided there was definitely an enhancement but in a distant way he could not fully comprehend. He concentrated on this feeling as he watched the landscape around him. There were clouds sending their shadows racing across the land as he had observed countless times before. He could hear the crickets and they're constant sound effects filling every scene much as they had always done. He would see the occasional mountain rabbit bob up from a patch of vegetation and make a dash for the safety of his nearby burrow. The lizards lay basking on their rocks unconcerned until the slightest attention was paid to them at which time they too would disappear into their rocky safety.

However, he felt there was more he was experiencing in these everyday occurrences, in each of these movements. He remembered the feeling as he had emerged out of the Dragon hill in the dream. He wondered whether he had carried that state with him into his waking life. As he watched the rabbits dive into their burrows or the noisy crows rise into the air, he felt sinew tightening, air being reacted against by carefully evolved feathers and the eddy's and drafts they produced. Tiny kicks of dust arose behind the lizards, revealing star lit patterns unseen before, as nerve motions instructed by electronic impulses from deep in their ancient minds fuelled by energy from the Star falling on their world, moved their tiny limbs. Everything continuous; no breaks or separation, a flow of energy towards all the mechanisms playing their part in the complex web of life she had become. Everywhere he looked he saw Arimathea shining back at him. But now there was something else he suddenly realised. A thought resounding so immensely through his being he felt he must stop the horse and sit quietly for a while in the shade of a small glade of ancient pine trees.

Mariella had become entwined in all of these thoughts almost as if a part of her consciousness had become part of his. He felt he had the sensation of looking through her eyes. He had no doubt the experience with Merilon's dragon consciousness had enhanced his thoughts but now he wondered, somewhat incredibly, whether Mariella had become so deeply connected to Arimathea he too was experiencing the planet through her deeper connection.

Ultimately, he was now contemplating the astonishing prospect that Merilon and Arimathea had somehow contrived to merge their two separated spirits into the beings of Mariella and himself so they could be reunited after their long separation; so experience themselves as mortals together. It certainly was an alluring thought. These energies had chosen to work through himself and Mariella; but not so strange in a sense. They had both sought to connect with their world in their different ways and dedicated a significant part of their life's path to delve into its' mysteries as Rabir had done all those years before. The energies inherent in their world had perhaps responded to their dedicated interest in the same way as they had to Rabir.

He smiled at the thought of her roaming the wilderness, embedding herself so deeply into her world she had managed to intuitively change the nature of her being and allowed Arimathea to become part of her consciousness. Still aching with the loss of her beloved dragons and deeply wounded by the human activity since they had been gone, she had also chosen to speak to him, guided them to meet, these two people who had reached her through the layers of misunderstanding and confusion that had arisen over the centuries. Now these two lives were gradually entwining; being carefully merged together by these ancient spirits, who had come to inhabit Arimathea and so bring themselves into human awareness.

As he was absorbing these thoughts, he became steadily more aware of the trees surrounding him. He suspected they may have been older than he first imagined. He relaxed back to lean against the solid tree trunk. The valley and the mountains beyond were framed by the other trees. As the wind blew gently through the upper branches he remembered how the dragons would go out of their way to walk amongst the forests and regularly climbed to the top of trees. He wondered whether Merilon had sat amongst the ancestors of these very trees, whether some of his dragon consciousness had become embedded here.

He remembered going to the woods at the edge of the forest with a great entourage comprising of builders, carpenters and anyone who could help to cut down and convert the trees for use in a new building. The monks would also come along to bless the tree before it was finally felled. There was always great curiosity amongst those gathered to find out how old the tree actually was. The rings were counted and much discussion then took place amongst the assembled towns people of their ancestors, whose lives the tree would have spanned. In this way it was invariably mentioned by the monk that both the life of the tree and the lives of their ancestors were celebrated in this ritual.

Okino knew there were those who were able to identify the patterns of the weather through the years from the width of the rings. The monks had always told him the trees were conscious beings, all be it very different from humans and animals, but they were closer to the consciousness of their world than any other creature alive, making them crucial to the flow of the spirit forces of Arimathea. They had always maintained by merging with one tree, everyone a part of the great family of trees, the environmental health of the entire planet could be assessed.

So much of what he had grown to know about the dragons was mirrored in the teachings and philosophies of the monastery. The idea of a direct connection between them was tantalising. Could there have been survivors from the community at Asima who had travelled deeper into the mountains to Lamai and founded the Order of the Dragon. There must have been those who had avoided whatever happened after the hill was built over because the new Asima had been built and Farina held the tales which subsequently had been carefully passed down through the generations. He observed his thoughts were flowing particularly beautifully here and wondered whether this might be one of the places carefully carved into the walls of the cellar below the hall.

He relaxed completely against the old tree and closed his eyes. He drifted into the spaces around himself, felt for the life force of the tree, feeling it deeply rooted into the ground and allowed his being to flow into the solid trunk, down into the roots and up into the limbs, reaching for the sky through every one of the coniferous needles as they processed their connection with their environment and the planet beyond. Here he was able to drift in the warmth where it had glowed in this atmosphere for the many eons Arimathea had been turning around her star. Okino noticed time here was becoming irrelevant; he was in one time, one moment of shimmering Starlight shining amongst the vast cold empty darkness.

In this moment he knew he was deeply connected into the consciousness of Arimathea in the very earliest of times when life had first started to emerge upon her. A crude atmosphere had formed, enough for the first set of chemical reactions to change Arimathea from a seething hissing molten mass of rock into a stable world able to support the diversity of life destined to eventually emerge. The gentle consciousness of trees was silently emerging as the dragon's dream flowed through and onto the surface of Arimathea.

The original micro-organisms forged in the primordial soup had grown into the soaring giants so important in forming the nourishing layer of gases all life would eventually breathe. In their great families they stood in the Starlight warming their world. Arimathea had first become a world of trees. In their union with Arimathea the dragons had first dreamed the great forests allowing her to breathe in the warm light shining from her consort, her nearest star. Through this garment the dragons were again able to feel the stars from which they had come; it filtered the light down through the green protecting her from the ravages of the harsh and violent electric storms, winds and torrential rains racing around her as her atmosphere formed and developed.

In the glades where the remaining starlight was falling, the Love that had formed between the dragons and Arimathea steadily grew. The ravages of the unstable exploding world the dragons had found slowly began to subside. Replaced with a peaceful tranquillity populated only by the gentle race of trees, it was then the romance between Arimathea and the ancient race of star travellers started to weave its spell across the face of Arimathea.

In amongst the trees and across the silent warming waters they drifted, forming between them a union so strong and pure it soon became reflected in the fresh new atmosphere. The harmony formed between them in the dark depths of her rocky womb now emanated in a beautiful glowing aura around her surface. Okino saw pools sparkling in the Star shine where basic molecular life forms had started their ascent; where the basic urge to survive became the ability of cells to absorb and ingest nutrients and reproduce themselves. Even then he found there was always more to this urge. The love formed between Arimathea and the dragons swept through everything in an invisible wave and resonated in every moment, in every transaction of energy taking place. Okino was able to see how the memories of the dragons were able to flow like an essence into the fertile spirit of Arimathea informing everything as it started to evolve out of the wonder.

There was little understanding of this wonder within the forming world. For the most part lives were crude and mostly short. But there was a very distant awareness of the original dream and that this had to happen in any way it possibly could to reach where it needed to be in the far distant future. Even in the tiniest set of cells sparkling in rays of Starshine, this awareness had filtered through the dragon's memories and became the motivation being laced inextricably into the life force and driving the survival of this pristine new world.

Simple organisms eventually became complex life forms. Their evolution occurred despite the myriad of planetary disasters that had befallen Arimathea. Okino saw how those surviving had been able to formulate strategies to survive droughts and floods. They had made choices at crucial moments. They had chosen the correct path when others had not and so had survived as their part of the world became frozen or a parched waterless desert. He felt how this awareness could have guided a gifted individual at any one of those crucial moments to make the right choices and take its species into the future.

He knew how this could happen. There were times he had had to make his own choices between one path and another. He had had to follow his own intuition, perhaps the sense connecting him into the awareness and which allowed him to decide his path into the future.

For the most part changes had happened slowly. They had grown fur or feathers, grown sharper teeth or returned to the oceans. They had found new foods to eat when the food they were accustomed to had disappeared, or through necessity devised new ways of catching it. They had moved over Arimathea on the winds, through the seas and across the lands. They had lived deep in the ground and high in the trees to avoid whatever may be preying on them in all their separate but parallel races for survival.

As these thoughts raced through his mind, the creatures he knew to inhabit Arimathea were passing through his vision and mixed with the dreams the dragons had shared in the previous days. He remembered the dolphins scanning the oceans for shoals of fish to provide the pod with their next meal. He felt how the dragon memories had accumulated on those previous worlds and fed through the awareness they inherently possessed; how they had become the muscular bodies providing speed and the complex brains generating the sonar allowing them to develop into a successful species.

He could only wonder of the complexity of the journeys, the twists and turns, disaster and triumph that had bought about the myriad of life now inhabiting Arimathea. Every species from the tiniest to the largest had found its own special set of survival strategies in its own part of the world with the set of attributes and characteristics it had developed to undertake them; each though, with the distant awareness of intention to develop towards a more efficient way of existing in their environment. Stronger than ever, Okino felt Arimathea as one being; Each creature reliant and relied upon to produce their own part of the vast process of life now forming a tiny part of this fabulous being.

In his vision he felt for the awareness in his own being. His thoughts went back to his village. He thought of his mother and father, how close they had been and how the Love between them had been reflected in the home he had grown up in. He tried to form an impression of the feeling in which his own life had evolved. He remembered how they had held their family together through their childhood. His mother softly nurturing them in the home she kept so beautifully. He had always relished the beautiful food she made for them while always taking her own special place in the work of the community.

He remembered going to the workshop of his father where he made the garments that clothed the community. Intricate and beautiful designs would always bedeck the simplest of his shirts and trousers. His coats were thick and solid, and over one of the fine sweaters knitted by his mother they could withstand the harshest of winter snows. He had been loved and cared for within his home by both his parents and also by the wider community. He and all the children with whom he had grown up had benefitted from the wider responsibility the town felt for their young people. He remembered for the most part happy times in which he had always been encouraged to continue this mutual consideration. He could think of few in the village who did not set a good example to all the children.

Occasionally some crisis had punctuated the general flow of wellbeing either of his own making or something that had occurred within the confines of his family or in the wider community. There was always the struggle to feed everyone and many of the arguments that had happened within the community had been as a result of a disagreement with somebodies' strategy to produce their part of the stock for the year or the resources used to produce it. Arguments were always sorted out at the council one way or another and grudges were rarely kept for very long; For when an unseasonable or particularly severe weather situation arose the tiny community would have to pull together closer than ever.

He stood at the edge of a lake surrounded by the endless primordial forest. The water in the lake lapped gently at his feet. The sound of the insubstantial waves fizzed as they sank into the sand on their return to the lake. He looked out across the water. The Star sparkled on every wave as it made its way towards him and ended on the beach. A million stars he thought lighting this container from which the first life might have crawled out onto land.

He bent down and cupped a handful of the sparkling water. He held it up to the sky. In his dream the cup he had formed with his hands now became a simple but elegant chalice. There were complex rhythmical carvings running continually around the outside suggesting the landscapes of Arimathea entwined with the energy of the dragons. The exceptional quality of light and peace in the atmosphere indicated to Okino Arimathea was close.

"Drink deep of my waters, Okino. For they have been condensed from Starlight and so have brought the wonders of Love and the Great Mystery to this world!"

Okino lowered the chalice and looked down into it. He saw a galaxy swirling and glistening full of stars and depths he could not comprehend. Then he raised the cup to his lips and took a sip of the liquid. He could see deeper into the galaxy into a tiny fragment where Arimathea's solar system turned invisibly amongst billions of other stars; each transmitting their light and swirling towards a vast furnace of light at the centre. He knew in those moments everything had come from there or from the end and the beginning of a similar process.

Arimathea, the dragons, the snow leopards, the lizards and all the other beings and spirits lying undiscovered amongst this galaxy had appeared as a result of the vast mass of space swirling before him. Perhaps, here was the engine, the powerhouse that had pushed the physical boundaries of mass, acceleration and momentum onto a crazy unstoppable ride spinning out across those astrophysical horizons, to the gateways where the phenomena of this space and this time were able to overlap with deeper undiscovered dimensions. Containing an ethereal realm remaining only as parameters; with the ability to form into a physicality only if and when the right circumstances could come into existence; where a dream had been slowly nurtured and fostered; an escape from its spirit state of pure Love had been sought and longed for. Now it had found its way to the burning mass at the centre of this limitless potential just before the pressure became too great. Okino watched as the moment came and the vast detonation that had followed, sent the dream flooding out across the Universe on a vast wave searching for a home and a place to exist.

Okino looked out over the scene before him. Water shimmered and lapped around the rocks at his feet. His eyes were now pulled down into the detail he could see below the clear water. Infinite colours had formed in the rounded stones. They had been rolling up and down on this beach for hundreds if not thousands of years forming them into smooth almost geometrically perfect objects. In amongst the stones he could see shells, now discarded, made by the tiny creatures to protect their soft vulnerable bodies from the voracious predators who would welcome such an easy meal. Drawn to one in particular he put his hand down into the water and drew out the large snail's shell. Its surface glistened in the starlight from the remaining water covering it.

The water soon dispersed and Okino recognised the pattern created by the snail in the manufacture of its humble home. Here was the galactic spiral that had appeared in the chalice. Did this humble, but most ancient of creatures retain the memory, possibly a record or even a reminder of how everything began, allowing it to produce the exact geometry at the heart of this mysterious existence. Okino reflected the detail on the shell seemed impossibly complex for even his own sophisticated mind to reproduce with such accuracy. So how did the snail produce such complexity. Unless this was the manifestation of the mathematics, the continuing dream running through the combined consciousness of the dragons and Arimathea as it had swirled and spun and driven this entire creation with its vast ethereal magical power. The snail had never become separated from the dream, so the symbol was continuous with it as it was continuous through the universe which had created it.

The light on the lake started to become brighter. The definition of surfaces started to disappear and blend into the strong Starlight as the vision started to fade. He was sitting up against the tree looking out over the plain. The star was hotter, the breeze still whispered through the tops of the trees and the horse was dozing, head lowered, eyes half open and ears laid back. Okino smiled to himself and wondered whether his race had misinterpreted the whole order of things on Arimathea. They had enslaved, killed and continued to eat other species because they had assumed they were superior and yet it seemed the humble snail had a greater knowledge of its existence flowing through its being than many of his own race. He wondered what dreams the horse was having and felt slightly guilty he would now wake him from those dreams to ride him back to the camp in the ruins.

As it was, he led the horse back down the track, again it seemed with a deeper insight into his existence and a greater respect for the horse. His mind wandered back and forth through the memories of the previous days looking for the thread running through it all. Continually his mind would wander back to Mariella, probably still in the land cruiser heading for Aharri.

He played in his mind with the power those thoughts were having over him. He undoubtedly was falling in love with her and he was missing her far more than he ever thought he would when she announced the plan to separate. Ultimately, he started to realise if he was not a monk or decided to renounce his calling these were the thoughts or desires that would, perhaps lead to him and Mariella having their own children. He would then have fulfilled his role in the dream as an inhabitant of Arimathea. He would pass on his life force and hopefully become the solid figure his father had been to his mother allowing his children to grow and flourish in a loving relationship so they could, in turn, take their place in the dream.

So, the spiral was the sign, the configuration of the dream manifesting itself throughout the Universe and the nature of Arimathea as it had willed itself into being, spreading itself on a vast cosmic wave from that initial explosion. Was this the force the human race had come to know as Love and perhaps even as God? A force that would eventually nurture life, guide it through an evolution in parameters in which it could survive and represented in the pure mathematics of the spiral. The dragons it would seem had bought the possibility of an evolution within those parameters to Arimathea.

He was grateful to arrive back at the ruins. They seemed strangely familiar and he spent some time drifting through the delightfully dilapidated old buildings. He again contemplated the maps on the basement walls of the hall and wondered if any of this was going on around any of the other dragon hills.

He found it hard to believe he had been the only human being Arimathea and her dragons had chosen to communicate with. Surely there were outposts in other remote regions of Arimathea where other dragons would be orchestrating their return. For now, he could not know and for the moment he felt he had absorbed enough about the mechanisms of the universe and the fate of Arimathea, so he busied himself making the fire and cooking the remains of the stew Farina had given him. As he ate, looking out over the pool to the waterfall, he contemplated Mariella's return with the explosives and perhaps a meeting with Merilon the dragon.

Chapter Thirty-five
Elementals.

The small fire Okino had made turned to smouldering embers as a spectacular Star set blazed across the sky. The sky had slowly transformed itself as he had eaten his evening meal. The wispy clouds had been forming during the late afternoon and had grown in stature. He knew they signalled a change in atmospheric conditions. The wind at least from the south, was warm and showed no signs at this stage of developing into anything more ferocious than a stiff wind during the night. The Starlight now played out a breath-taking lightshow on the underside of the clouds. Okino settled at the edge of the river to observe the beautiful natural phenomenon unfolding before him in the sky and reflected across the water of the pool in front of him. The clouds were drifting over at a sedate pace. As ever Okino watched with interest the shapes and forms appearing before him. He thought back to the beautiful dragon that had appeared in the clouds after the time they had spent in the stone circle.

Then he had still been mystified by the meaning of the dragon connections in his dreams. But he was used to their appearance in the clouds. He smiled now as he remembered his experience of the last few days. How these supernatural spirits from the stars had gradually revealed themselves to Mariella and himself; how their love for Arimathea had led them to break the ancient universal lore which had possibly put her under greater threat than the original danger they had fore seen. It seemed such a human response from beings that clearly had such power to influence the flow of events; certainly, rash and almost desperate. Then how could he possibly understand how it would be to watch billions of years of evolution wiped out in a few centuries. He smiled as he started to conceive in the clouds great wings spanning the sky now ablaze with orange and red, great heads with their all seeing eyes and the great torsos containing such energy deep in their bellies, carried since the beginning of time across the vast tracts of space.

A fish jumped suddenly from the sky water in a calculated lunge for prey, hanging in the air for a moment between the worlds, glinting red and gold and so full of primeval energy, before unceremoniously splashing back into the pool to leave the ebb of its disturbance to wash out to the sandy banks. Back down into its' watery world to contemplate again the sky and all therein through the currents flowing all around it. Did the tiny insects it was observing glint like the stars now appearing amongst the darkening skies? Stars to which it could travel in a flash of its muscular body!

As the light died into the dusk, the phosphorescence of the waterfall now spread out across the surface of the pool. The moon was yet to rise and an eerie quiet came over the river. Okino was very conscious of the ruined walls of the settlement looming over him. He cast his consciousness deep into the spaces he knew lay beyond the wall. He had never felt for a moment any sinister trace of what was reputed to have happened here. There was no sign of violent destruction the story of the sinister Samir had inferred. He had found only the dilapidation a thousand years of decay would bring to such constructions. There were signs stone had been removed to the new village and possibly reworked by those who had returned in later generations. Perhaps Samir had given the village an ultimatum they could not argue with and they had chosen to move away. They would have known where the dragon was hidden and really would have wanted to get far away from Samir and his mercenaries as quickly as possible in the knowledge they could return when the focus had gone elsewhere.

Maybe some never returned once they had founded other settlements or merged themselves into the surrounding towns and villages where they carried on the traditions they had founded here. Certainly, he had found the utmost respect for his order in Aharri and the old spirits living in these hills. He smiled as he thought of the little group of travellers moving away from their beloved Asima, perhaps silently in the cover of darkness, evaporating into the surrounding mountains having debated long and hard what they should do. There may have been threats of violence and somewhere there had been a realisation the knowledge they had found should not be lost and indeed must grow.

In the towns and villages where they settled, they told their stories and the ways they had found had continued in the rudimentary aspects of their lives from that point on. He thought of the bustling market he and Mariella had walked around. He remembered how alive and vibrant he had found the people. Their work was rich with colour and tradition and the atmosphere they brought from their harsh but fulfilled creative lives had filled the town with an optimism as they came together again despite the hardships they had endured. He saw the resilience of those traditions in the monastery and amongst the people of his own village. Life was precious and was a gift needing to be savoured and appreciated at every opportunity. All the processes involved in its preservation and continuation were sacred and carried out in reverence for they became the sum of that life. But when they sat around their fires and told their stories of victory and defeat they howled with laughter with equal ferocity, for they found these spirits it seemed had a terrible sense of humour.

His fire had finally died down and he decided he would go around to the circle in the square in the light of these thoughts. He drifted out through the arch and into the wide square now providing a perfect frame for the cloudless starlit sky above. He contemplated the sixteen stones in the circle of pine trees and his earlier experience within it. He remembered the fire he had made in the forest that perhaps had provided the connection with the dragon. He cast his eyes around half contemplating a similar conflagration. He knew there would not be enough wood to make such a fire but decided he would collect up what he could and build a fire in the centre of the stones.

He made his way through the ruins. Always the stars shone down through the walls as he collected the wood to add to the pile in the circle of stones. When he had made a significant pile, he set about lighting the dried twigs and grasses with the flint lighter. First the familiar smell of sparks igniting on flint, a tiny plume of smoke as the delicate dried material responded to the sparks and then the first miraculous licks of flame as they burnt through the dried grass and started to consume the small and then the larger twigs. Soon the fire was crackling away happily gently consuming the branches of the old pine trees that had fallen but had not yet returned their energy back to the Earth.

Okino relaxed into the warmth of the fire, the stars and the stones. He wondered how Mariella was coping and smiled. She would be coping just fine. She would have the whole of Aharri running around trying to get the best deal on 'explosives' and probably would have negotiated the best room in the best house to stay in while they were doing it. He ran through some of their conversations and the stories that had unravelled for them as he merged himself into the warm energy of the fire. He watched its energy rise and fall, gauged its life force and the flammability of the wood so he knew when, how and where to add the next piece.

The flames rose higher and their light fell upon the flat stones in the circle. Deeper and deeper he became entranced by the fire, the heat and the occasional sparks thrown out when a knot exploded under the intense heat of the central furnace; The heat on his face reminded him of the heat of the midday Star further marking its imprint into his already star burnt face. He remembered the fires he had sat around with his friends on summer nights like this out in the fields. He could see their faces, hear their words and their laughter as they related the story. They never tired of it and he laughed as he remembered the sight of the wolf being chased out of the village by the two old women, tail between his legs still carrying the loaf of bread he had stolen.

The flames danced on their faces in his memories and merged with the flames in the fire before him. In the surrounding darkness the Universe and all therein shifted as the dragon monk cast his consciousness deep into the flames and so beyond. The heat he felt on his face fell into insignificance as the fire projected out the essence it shared with the nuclear inferno burning at the core of every star. The warm transforming energy wound its' way into his visions and into his projected consciousness.

The dragons had been waiting. Only now, with all they had told him did he have the understanding to generate the thought patterns to make a connection through the layers of the dimensional labyrinth in which they existed. Slowly they appeared, one by one from wherever they were dwelling, around his fire. The fifteen spirits born from the fiery cataclysm at the beginning of physical time to carry the dream of harmonious unification of the Great Spirit into the physical realms now appeared around Okino's fire in the ruined circle. They were insubstantial and transparent making little impression in the darkness. Merilon had merged directly with Okino who noticed immediately the additional breadth of space and time suddenly added to his awareness. He was able to see the human characteristics of the dragons for the first time. He was amazed how close they were to the imagined images he had generated for himself primarily from their meeting in the mountain cave. They were all tall, sinuous, with dark and fair hair. The green light glowed strangely from their eyes betraying the supernatural life force from the time they had emerged. They concentrated on Okino and Merilon. Their lack of physicality did not allow them to be heard. Okino, at first, only heard the combined voice of all the dragons in his mind as they started to speak.

"Greetings Okino, you have done astoundingly well to get to this point so quickly!"

"I can't remember doing very much."

"The ability you have always had, the additional training you have taken on with the monks all of which you take for granted has enabled you to travel and absorb all we have told and shown you so far. There is a little more you need to know, before…"

"Before what?"

"…Before whatever transpires next. You will have gathered enough from the story so far that we can have little further involvement. There is a complex weave of detrimental circumstance building up in the world. It has become unbalanced and too much in the favour of Oblivion. It has taken all this time to make this connection we needed with your race!"

"So, where have you been, I can't believe you've been sleeping in the mountains for a thousand years!"

He felt a ripple of laughter run through the dragon spirits. Zaramir then spoke as an individual.

"We have slept for all those years. But as you know we have dreamed for so long we have the ability to access all the underlying dimensions making up this existence. When we were still one with Arimathea our dreams flooded through the planet and gradually, she became this world. But since we tried to alter the course humanity was taking we have existed only in the caves in which we were left, essentially dormant, nourished only by what she was able to send us through the air; her essence has kept us alive.

But we dreamed deeper again in this new state. We initially endlessly explored, hoping to find new pathways through the realms of the labyrinth, desperately trying to find our way back into Arimathea. Eventually, we became prepared to accept the dragon hills, carefully evolved as they were over millions of years, were the only way back. But we did find we could access other dimensions existing on the surface of the planet where other powerful creation spirits have come to exist. They exist throughout the universe and slowly emerge as a planet starts to evolve. As the planet refines so their physical and spiritual essence becomes more and more present and becomes part of the fabric of all that comes into existence. They also came out of the original mystery as we did. They provide the crossover between the spirit realms and the physicality by transferring their essence into the fabric of the world.

"So, who are these spirits?"

"You know them well Okino, they are the elemental sprits. As powerful as any you will find on the surface of Arimathea. In our travels we noticed how close your spirits were able to come to them. As we felt the Starlight on our faces, walked through the vast and magical landscapes of Arimathea, as we swam deep in the rivers and the seas, as we walked and ran through the scented air, as we breathed it, as we sat around the fires we made, we felt we could have easily drifted back to where we had come from.

But when we were separated from our souls deep in Arimathea we were bound to remain wholly in this state until we could find a way to return, which of course hopefully you now have found. But whether dragon, human, tree, wolf or dolphin we all share the greater consciousness and we can all dream wherever we want to be within it.

The understanding and experience the elemental spirits have brought through our dreams and into this world brings it closer to the original dream. They are embedded in every molecular combination existing and the influence of their traits and characteristics have influence over everything happening on Arimathea."

Okino felt a glimmer in his mind.

"So, you found the dimensions through your dreams where the elemental spirits exist?"

"In essence that is precisely what we did," Eremoya, a female dragon spoke,

"Oblivion again took a firm hold on Arimathea and the human race was again stagnating under the oppression and slavery of its leaders. With the dreams of the dragons driven from their subconscious, a terrible dark age had begun for the people of Arimathea. Poverty and so disease were spreading rapidly as human populations increased and lived in densely populated areas of the growing cities. The religions of the alien gods had been quickly reinstated and the search for the leaders of the revolution lead to terrible fear spreading through the lands as people who were guilty or not of ever taking part were publicly burned alive in their villages and towns all over Arimathea.

Even more oppressive economic systems were implemented by their rulers and their servants the priests, who controlled the lives of the growing populations by threatening and implementing terrible tortures if even the mention of a dragon was reported to have been heard. Control over most people's lives became so great they could barely feed themselves. Death and misery now stalked the lands where people only a generation before had thrived and flourished."

"So, the scales had been tipped the other way!" Okino ventured.

"Indeed, they had."

Zaramistra spoke now,

"Things had gone very badly wrong for us and it seemed the whole thing had been orchestrated by one of our own, Mithrael, who we thought had been lost in his explorations of the Universe but it seems had been living here on Arimathea as a human. I am afraid the situation is not altogether resolved."

There was a stony silence amongst the fifteen dragons around the fire. They were clearly disturbed by the enormous trouble Mithrael had caused for them. Then Zaramistra continued.

"As we slept undisturbed in our remote caves, we eventually found our way into the world through the elemental spirits. They are attracted to a world when it is developing. They sense where an evolution has potential in the labyrinth and seek it out so they can again emerge. They bring physicality from the dimensions of consciousness. So the original urge came out of the Fire, and the debris was amalgamated into stability with Earth, the fluid psychic flow of the yearning to be eventually arises again as Water; Air is created as a result of these three combining, Life and Love and all the new wisdom they bring is then able to emerge. They moved through our dreams as we flooded into Arimathea and sensed an opportunity to convert all they found into a new world. Dreams that would live and breathe, where life could proliferate under its own momentum, carry it towards a future they had sensed could be possible.

Now we found our way into their dream consciousness. Not dissimilar from ours you can understand because we come from the same urge. We came to understand how they lived in the spirit realms and how they could thread their magic into our own blend of memories, experience and imaginings. We learnt how they could infuse their essence through Arimathea, moment by moment bringing her closer to the ends of the original dream. Now in this new time with this new set of circumstances we immersed ourselves into their energy as they flowed through the world so we could at least experience the evolution outside the labyrinth; unable as we were to return to our souls in the heart of Arimathea.

We had considerable understanding of their nature as we had often travelled in the combinations of physicality they had brought to Arimathea. We had always travelled in clouds and rivers, and on the winds as they flowed around the planet. We can live in mountains or forests or in a lake or in a fiery volcano. We are in the soft breezes or the howling storms. We love to experience the worlds we have grown and we collect memories of all the emerging phenomena, so if necessary, we can dream it all again into a new world. So, we can live as elemental creatures when we need to experience a world as it has evolved through our own consciousness. We were always able to move into the consciousness of the other spirits who have evolved from out of the elements and inhabit the creatures they have become. So, we love to fly in the consciousness of eagles high in the air over the mountains or swim as dolphins and whales deep in the watery depths of the oceans or live as an entire pack of wolves or a herd of deer.

There is great delight in experiencing the world through the creatures whose senses have evolved so acutely. Each one is having unique experiences adding to the experience of the entire dream and the dreams we will eventually send into the fabric of the world. Only we can truly inhabit the element of fire. Fire is the element of transformation. Out of control it destroys the old, accelerating its' replacement with the new and fresh. In control it is the ability to dream. It is the ability to bring about transformation by careful and calculated actions. We share this ability with you for the simple reason you became particularly adept at picking up our dreams as they flowed from the ground when you were a young and primitive species.

For this reason, your minds developed slightly differently than other creatures so you could process and understand the dreams you began to have. So, as we combined with the elemental spirits, we hoped you would be able to intercept the intensified inspiration and start to turn those dreams into reality.

We knew from our experience and the special connections we had discovered, the elemental spirits were fundamental to the experience of this planetary existence. You as a human, born into this physical world with the wonderful array of senses you have evolved, and one who has become adept at immersion into those other dimensions, will be fully aware of their presence in every aspect of your life. They have blended infinitely at the intersections between this and the invisible dimensions underlying the stability and beauty of Arimathea. You take for granted the atmosphere that has formed around Arimathea because you have grown as part of it and have no comprehension of the vile and poisonous conditions operating in the rest of the universe. If you know and have experienced those conditions then to walk through this Star lit world, on the warm ground with a gentle breeze on your face, is to believe the harmony imagined by the great mystery has been achieved on beautiful Arimathea.

Here is where we concentrated our efforts. We immersed ourselves even more deeply into our dreams which allowed us to interact with their energy; into the conditions bringing these sensations as they regulated, balanced and altered the climates of Arimathea; We flowed into the starlight, into the breezes and the cool rivers flowing through the lands; deep into the variations that could turn them into savage and inhospitable environments, turning the land into sweltering deserts and howling relentless storms reeking destruction amongst even the most robust habitats. We came to experience all these environments as they changed and adapted as a result of the movement of Arimathea around and through the stars. We came to experience Arimathea physically, as a planet where all these interconnected influences are always adjusting one to another, acting as one across her entire surface to create the optimal conditions for Life to continue. We felt her living and breathing, as never before, as one beautifully infinitely complex being and our love for her deepened and made our resolve to save her stronger.

So slowly and lightly at first we had found a way to flow again through Arimathea, in amongst those ancient spirits. As time went on and the tyranny on Arimathea continued, we were able to develop our place within this new emerging alliance. We expected there would be some further repercussions to the coming together of two significant planetary influences. But we felt we had to do something. Also, now, our wisdom was flowing in a very different manner to how the occupants of Arimathea were accustomed, for it had been over one hundred years since we had been separated from Arimathea.

Legends and myths had been passed secretly amongst the people of Arimathea of those days when the strange mystery of their world had been briefly revealed. But as those who had seen and met us and been alive at the time started to disappear, the truth of the old tales started to fade in the general populations now so impoverished in their battle for existence. However, the revelations we had given about the true nature of Arimathea and were subsequently passed on in the folklore, reignited the memory of the deep connection retained in many human souls. They were the sensitive ones who without training or the knowledge continued in your monastery unknowingly maintained an ability to connect with the mystery flowing through their world.

They were always the inquisitive ones; the ones who would not accept what they were told to believe; they were the ones who always suspected something so complex and rich in diversity could never be as simple as they were constantly persuaded to believe by the followers and priests of the alien religions. They walked through the world with their senses open to all surrounding them. Senses that would have brought them success in hunting and the survival of their tribe now would bring them closer to the creation spirits of their world.

For as our bond with the elemental spirits became stronger so the intensity with which they could be experienced in the world increased; the wisdom we carried now combined with those ancient elemental spirits and flowed freely through Arimathea in everything from a simple hearth fire to a whispering breeze in the tops of the trees. To those inquisitive ones suddenly every one of these experiences had the potential to explain to them a little more about their world, to reveal a little more about the mystery they had always felt and now were compelled to delve into. In their curiosity they began to observe all the phenomena surrounding them, sustaining themselves and all of

Arimathea. They looked more closely at the patterns they saw and acted on the resonances they had with the knowledge already available to them. The closer they looked at plants and the creatures the more intricate those patterns appeared to become. They experimented with lenses and magnification which enabled them to observe the detail beyond the reach of the unassisted human eye. In these observations they uncovered the layers of existence under the surface of skins and membranes and micro-organisms of which they all appeared to be comprised.

They discovered eventually by their experimentation many of the processes sustaining the lives of plants and animals happening at this microscopic level; membranes allowing air to be absorbed through lungs and then into the bloodstreams to carry air to muscles and organs providing fuel for life to continue. In plants they found the processes converting Starlight to create the energy giving sugars allowing them to grow and reproduce. Their world was suddenly a seething mass of life sustaining chemical reactions and calculation. They found the mathematics and geometry underlying the structures which were commonplace around them. As they worked deeper into the glimmers of inspiration we were able to give to them, as they hypothesised and experimented, the deeper their understanding of these processes became. Whereas before there had been only been their supernatural suspicions and conjecture, the propaganda of the priests of the alien gods, now a solid understanding of their world was being formed. It was at this time we decided to fade again from the world.

In these moments of inspiration the humans were finding for themselves the paths that would lead them out of the darkness imposed upon them to a time when knowledge and reason would generally arise and it would become more powerful than the tyranny their damaged rulers had imposed upon them. So, we receded back to the dragon lands where we continued to develop the new dream we had conceived at the council in the mountains. We were confident then the humans would eventually come to this place, with an ability born through their own endeavour, to recognise and once again absorb the old wisdom."

There was silence around the fire. Okino had been listening to the dragons intently while carefully keeping his fire alight. Now he had heard the whole story. The dragons had again left Arimathea confident everything would now be able to return to a more beneficial path as the humans came to understand more about their world. Again, it seemed they had underestimated the ability of the human race. The knowledge they had gained had been exploited mercilessly to further feed their greedy ambition. Arimathea was now struggling under the enormous strain of the resulting wasteful activity and there seemed little sign their addiction for consumption could ever be satisfied. But then he thought of Mariella travelling halfway around the planet to find him in the hope something could be done. He felt there would certainly be others who had also been contacted by the dragons, or felt their presence again starting to flow through Arimathea.

He thought of Arimathea and the conversation he had had with her and he thought of the dragons themselves. Although at this point, in their struggles they had not prevailed, there were things even they had been able to learn. The landscapes they had developed would be waiting to be accessed when they were able to return again to their hills and infiltrate the dreams of the humans. They had merged themselves into the elemental spirits and directly inspired the humans to delve into and discover for themselves the fundamental laws of their world.

Most remarkable however he reflected, he was sitting around a fire talking to or at least listening to these ancient universal spirits who had become so concerned about the future of their world. He smiled, shook his head and looked up expecting to see the powerful eyes of the dragons staring back at him. But they had faded back into the darkness leaving him alone with the fire.

Chapter Thirty-six.
The Surface.

The next morning Mariella was travelling out of Aharri with Ben and Tarak heading towards the quarries at Reaka. It was a well-used road and the land cruiser was able to move at a good speed through the parched arid landscape. She had been told it would take the best part of the morning to reach the quarries. They had all visited the tavern the night before. Ben and Tarak had drunk large quantities of the local beer and so were silent. Mariella had spent the evening talking to Niala. She told him about what she and Okino had learnt while they had been at the ruins and from Farina. He had listened silently as the story unravelled. When it was complete, he smiled and shook his grey old head,

"It certainly has turned into a bit of a struggle. I would like to have met one of them, looked into those green eyes and felt their ancient origin, know the feeling from those times in the mountains and the plains. I suppose what seems most surprising is they seem to be in the same struggle as the rest of us; trying to do what they think to be for the best. But by putting energy into a situation no matter what the intention everything changes and not even the dragons could have predicted how such an intervention could have turned out!"

Mariella settled back into the luxury of the expensive technology now speeding her through the countryside. Ben had put some music on. The songs took her back to her life on the other side of Arimathea. As she drifted through the landscape of her memories, a stark contrast arose between the impressions passing through her mind and what she was seeing beyond the land cruiser as it sped through the rural villages.

Cities of glass with acres of concrete and tarmac flashed through her mind. Thousands of de-sensitised, programmed individuals filled the streets on their journey to work and the journey through their lives. Oddly there were some faces in amongst the sea of faces she had passed she would never forget. She knew from her wanderings alone in the city how easy it was to have some idea, just in a glance, where a soul was on their journey, where it was taking them as they walked through the park with the Starshine on their faces, or as they stood in the subway seemingly intent only on their destination.

In those constructions the governments and the councils and the corporations had brought into being, they were in the struggle Niala had spoken about. Perhaps in those streets the evidence of their struggle was most apparent. The people who weren't doing so well sat on the pavements, heads and glances lowered, with a cap or a cup in front of them hopeful in each moment they may perhaps extract some charity from the wealthy city dwellers passing by. But it was easy for them to dismiss or deny the problems of the folk at their feet, hurrying between the minefield of their business lives and the pressure cooker of their domestic situations. It was easy to fall victim to circumstances in either or both, entwined and mutually dependent on each other as they now were. Everything there depended on the ability to pay and continue to pay for the lifestyle chosen or not. If the ability was for some reason taken away, then the lifestyle could fall away surprisingly easily.

She caught the eye of a small boy walking down the main street with a small herd of goats. He waved at her with a huge grin on his face. His goats had shown little interest other than being slightly spooked by the growl and the momentum of their vehicle. She looked back to where the boy stood watching, perhaps wondering who he had seen and how and why they had come to be in his quiet dusty part of Arimathea. His village was solidly and traditionally constructed. There was still little glass in the timber and stone buildings. They were built to withstand the ferocity of the winter and stay cool in the summer. They had been built with a practical design and style reflecting the evolution of their construction and solidity of their purpose.

There was no tarmac between or even pavements with beggars sitting upon them. Everyone she saw was herding or carrying, selling or buying. She had travelled through so many of these little towns each with a special relationship to the hills or the rivers, each with their own simple originality which would flow out in even the slightest gesture of any one of its inhabitants; perhaps some of the poorest people in the world always smiling, always polite, greeted one warmly and would often offer dinner in their house. Yet they would be struggling as hard as any of the inhabitants of Straam and the consequences of their struggles were more likely to be life threatening.

She felt dismay for a moment, as she sped through the village, that she would not spend time with the boy and his goats, perhaps be proudly led into his house to meet his father and mother, perhaps his brothers and sisters where they would tell her of their history, all their gossip, tell her of the spirits and their activities amongst the people of the town, how their harvests had been and their hopes and fears for the future. Everything, all at once!

She remembered her father and how he had instigated this urge to travel to new places: experience and savour atmospheres to which they were unaccustomed. She could always tell when the time was about to come. He would start to look diligently at maps and guidebooks. Invariably if he was planning a local exploration her mother would accompany them. But there were occasions when they would go further afield to a town in a different county.

Generally, then they would stay in a hotel perhaps for a few nights while they explored the surrounding area. He would take great delight in extracting the uniqueness of the place, she would watch him standing on some spot, recording every tiny detail, then he would close his eyes as if storing everything he was feeling for some future reference that may or may not ever come. They would walk through the endless days talking about the world and how beautiful it was and sometimes how ugly it was. He rarely took her to his office in Straam for this he maintained contained some of the uglier aspects that had surfaced on Arimathea. He always told her he hoped in some of his work he could shine some beauty into the ugliness. Then he would go quiet for some minutes before enthusing again about this collection of buildings or that vista over to the hills. These had always been the happiest days of her life and many of the memories merged and perhaps had become a little misty. However, there was one day she would always remember for being particularly memorable.

She remembered her father had developed a love for sailing. Now he combined his love for finding new places with a fascination for drifting through them on water. There were visits to large inland lakes and there had been surprising amounts to learn about this new craft. She had been eight years old. He had been taught and she had learnt with him about the wind and how to sail with it and against it, how to capture it and hold it, as well as terminology and all the etiquette that came with sharing water with other boats. Some of which she had retained and some of which she hadn't. They used the boats generally supplied by the school until one day he had decided he would like to have one of his own.

There were long discussions as to what kind of boat he would buy. In the end he had decided he wanted something big enough they all could go out on for the day or perhaps two and so big enough for them all to sleep on. He wanted to be able take it out on the sea where he had decided the breeze was more consistent and so he supposed there would be less 'turning'. He acquired a great pile of magazines through which he searched relentlessly for the boat he would eventually buy. He eventually found one which he thought would be perfect down on the coast. The photograph showed a sleek well-maintained timber craft in easily accessible surroundings. Inevitably a journey was immediately planned to go and see it.

The journey to the coast would take half a day in their car so they decided they would leave early. The day had been bright though a little cloudy but they had been in good spirits and the journey had passed quickly. At the end of the journey however once they had passed through the last town on the map everything started to become considerably less straight forward. Suddenly the roads began to be less easy to follow on the map and they had ended up at a crossroads they had previously negotiated. They were clearly near the coast because there appeared to be tidal inlets which had to be frequently crossed on rickety old timber bridges.

Mariella remembered the thick woods lining the sides of the road. The trees were as old as any she had ever seen hung with great fronds of hanging lichens. There were strange animal calls which she later found out to be the large variety of frogs inhabiting those watery glades. She and her father became quiet as they gradually deduced from maps where they had been and where they should be going. Eventually they had arrived at a pair of rusty metal gates. They were as high as a man and had shed much of the white paint that would have covered them in previous decades. Once they had worked out they had to open the gates themselves they tentatively made their way up the long drive to the old mansion at the end of it.

The large timber house seemed to be in the same time period of dilapidation as the gates. Creepers had found their way over much of the two-storey exterior and over many of the windows on the rectilinear façade. There were long steps up to a long-covered veranda which crossed to the front door. She smiled as she remembered the look on her father's face as they started to climb those steps and sounded the great door knocker. The place seemed utterly deserted so they were both surprised and slightly startled when the door opened to reveal an unkempt man in his late thirties. He was tall, pale and a little underweight. Much of his face was covered by his beard and shoulder length hair was greying consistently. She remembered very clearly his bright blue eyes. Much to the relief of Mariella and her father he was smiling broadly.

"Good afternoon, Sir. My name is Aaron Keating and this is my daughter Mariella and we have come to see your boat!" Her father announced formerly.

"Of course you have Sir, pleased to meet you, Richard Wellbeck. Thank you for coming. I hope you didn't have too much trouble finding us! Come in, Come in!"

The inside of the house was consistent with everything else they had seen. But it was clean and homely and Richard made them instantly welcome and hurried them through to a large living room. Double doors were thrown open revealing a large garden beyond. Richard disappeared to make them drinks. Her Father and Mariella surveyed the room. Many large paintings of ocean-going craft decorated the walls; from galleons in ferocious fire fights right the way through to modern racing yachts under full sail flying across ferocious Oceans. Her father was clearly fascinated by these works so that when Richard came back with the drinks they started to talk about their origins and soon were deep in conversation.

Mariella had already become entranced by the garden. She drifted through the open doors onto a paved terrace. The air of dilapidation again was pervasive. Weeds were forcing their way through mortar joints in the paving and beyond what she could see had probably been a formal garden, now was completely overgrown. There was a circular patch in the lawn which had been crudely cut. Four adjustable chairs were arranged around a table; there was an empty bottle and empty glasses sitting on it. Paths had been cut from this circle out to the further reaches of the garden.

The grass had grown high and was mostly on the point of shedding its seed. She wandered down the paths to where carefully arranged ornamental trees and shrubs had now grown tall, broken free of their pruned discipline and spread themselves luxuriously into the spaces they were able to find around them. Insects hummed and buzzed everywhere in the mid-afternoon Starlight and the garden was filled with birdsong. The webs of spiders seemed to glisten everywhere now undisturbed by the meddling of gardeners.

She had never seen anything like it. She pushed through what would have been an entrance in a hedge but now had almost resealed itself through neglect. The hedge was entirely circular and had been clearly grown to circum-navigate a large stone ornamental pool raised at the sides and stretched across the large space formed by the hedge. Lilies had entirely overgrown the surface of the water and now filled the pool with their beautiful white flowers. There was a fountain in the centre. There was a statue of a girl sitting on a small outcrop of rock. Crystal clear water gushed from the rock splashing into the pond. Mariella became particularly interested in the girl. Additional vegetation had grown in the natural crevices making the scene eerily realistic; Her clothes, the way her stone hair fell around her shoulders, the flowers she held created a delightfully innocent and peaceful scene.

However, on closer examination Mariella could see the stone from which the little girl had been carved had deteriorated considerably. A cold winter had allowed a hairline crack to form in the stonework. During the winter months water had turned to ice and widened the crack. It had worked its' way deeper and deeper into the unfortunate fault. Then one frosty night, the crack had finally split the skull leaving the little girl with little more than half of her face resulting in a hideous disfigurement. The result was grotesque and Mariella had started back as she realised what she was now seeing. Suddenly this serene, almost angelic scene had the overtones of a more sinister nature. The statue had lost the qualities of stone it had possessed and seemed to come to life. The little girl, suddenly distressed, stared accusingly out at her murderer. Her stare had transferred the trace of something terrible that had happened, possibly a violent death never discovered or solved. It had touched Mariella deeply, almost as if she had uncovered some terrible brutal event buried deep in her own being.

She had tried to hurriedly leave the pool but, in her panic had been unable to find the entrance through the hedge. She had run around the hedge several times. As her panic grew the horror that had been projected momentarily seemed to fill the space around the pool and she started to scream uncontrollably and eventually became paralysed by fear. It took several minutes for Richard and her Father to find her and extract her from the space around the pool. They took her back to the house and managed to calm her down. It was a feeling Mariella would never forget. She would never know whether there was any more substance in the feeling other than that it had felt so real. They had left quickly with promises there would be further contact but her father never went back. She had told him what had happened on the way home and he had been quiet.

"All the atmospheres we feel in these places, Mariella," he spoke softly, "I think contain the echoes and the vibrations of what has happened there in the same way as we carry everything that happens to us through our own lives. There are events that will not merge into our peaceful memories. They will always stand out and will make us shudder in the same way as a terrible happening may never settle into the generally peaceful nature of a certain place. If we become sensitive to the beauty flowing through the world, we may also feel ugliness when we stumble upon it. I am sorry you have had this frightening and painful experience today, who can tell where it has originated and you may feel this hurt well into the future and with time it's impact will fade. How you act on the feelings you have will always be up to you, of course."

It had been the single most important thing anybody had ever said to her and it had grown in significance as she had grown up into her world and become aware of what was happening around her. Now she was acting on the profound ugliness she had found. The echoes of the terror she was feeling and seeing on Arimathea would not die down, would not merge into the peaceful memory of her planet's life or her own. She had found it intolerable and she had decided to act. Now she and Okino had uncovered the struggle lying at the root of the terror she had felt. She thought of the ancient dragon spirits asleep in their caves high in the Northern mountains. She smiled. How would the scientists of Arimathea explain their presence or even their influence upon their world? If one flowed through their laboratory would they recognise it with all their subatomic machinery? Would they be able to detect the fabulous universal wisdom as it flowed through the sub space around them?

They had searched so hard in their equations and their particle colliding experiments for the illusive energy that could bring matter and life out of the emptiness but it had taken a boy in his late teens from these isolated mountains who had never even seen a computer to finally bring the reality into this world. There were older phenomenon in the world and the Universe requiring an understanding beyond what could be computed in a human brain or even in one of the machines they had constructed to increase its' power. They would have to make a very different leap sooner or later because it seemed with the laws of physics as they stood she imagined, they would be at a loss to explain Merilon and his mystical band!

The villages had receded as the land cruiser travelled deeper into the arid plain lying to the west of Aharri. She glanced through the front windscreen over Ben's shoulder. Hills were appearing in the far distance. She hoped they were their destination. She wanted to be back by the waterfall with Okino. She had felt strangely unsafe without him and was nervous about this whole trip. Ben was a confident man who despite his earlier mistake in the tavern had a way of winning the confidence and surprisingly the trust of these people. Ultimately she thought, of course that was why he was here! But as the tribesman had said 'they were a long way from home'.

By late morning they had entered the hills where the quarry was located. Mariella had not fully appreciated the scale of the operation she was visiting until they were confronted by one of the lorries carrying the stone down the dusty mountain road towards them. The sleek and luxurious land cruiser was dwarfed suddenly in every way by the vast vehicle as it thundered past them. Wheels towered over them; a vast pipe belched a great cloud of throbbing black exhaust fumes. Mariella tried to see the cab and its driver but it was high on the side and caked in dust. Ben, Tarak and Mariella were immediately shaken from the pre-industrial impression they had previously held of this far flung out post of Arimathea.

Somewhere up ahead there was something very much connected into the industrial technological era that had remained so elusive in this land where yaks were thought to be supernatural beings and dragons slept for hundreds of years in their mountain caves. Mariella steeled herself as she suddenly had to shift her idea of what the quarry might be. They continued climbing up through the mountains on a wide twisting road. Occasionally they were again passed by one of the huge mechanical monsters as they rumbled down the mountain road with the cargo of precious minerals starting their journey across the plains down to the city port of Zedocha.

They rounded a long bend flanked by the steep sides of the mountain. It had been crudely widened to give enough room for two of the trucks to pass each other. The quarry stretched into the distance before them. A vast crater had been excavated in the hills. The trucks appearing like a stream of brightly coloured insects, trundling down the terraces to where the earth movers would load them once again with their cargo of exploded mountain. Ben stopped the land cruiser and they contemplated the scene in silent disbelief. As they watched a siren cut through the roar of machinery and the insects started to evacuate the crater. An urgent scene ensued as tiny figures leapt from earthmovers or scrambled from whatever task they were undertaking onto the trucks which now sped upwards to the edge of the crater. When the crater was emptied and the siren had stopped, silence hung over the deserted quarry. Then initially in this silence at the far end of the quarry a section of the crater erupted. It took a few moments before the sound reached the far end of the quarry. Great plumes of dust and fine debris flew into the air as the bulk of a mountainside slumped to the bottom and disappeared under the great falling cloud of material.

Mariella shuddered as a wave of nausea flashed through her body. She flung open the door of the land cruiser, ran to the side of the road where she fell to her knees and ejected what remained of the bread, fruit and coffee she had eaten for breakfast onto the rocks. She was unable to get to her feet. As her head continued to spin she collapsed completely onto her side, her long dark hair flailing over her face and falling into the dust. She lay there still as the explosion echoed again and again, ripping through her, shattering and fragmenting all sense of who she was. Ben and Tarak ran over to where she lay motionless in the dust. Ben gently removed the hair from her face and called to her.

"Mariella are you Ok. Speak to me, can you hear me?"

She could hear him out in the distance, in the heat of the dust and rock. From that distance she knew she could move her hand upward and mumble....

"Yeah I'm Ok, but I don't think I'm too good with explosions!"

"Can you move? We should get you into the car."

She pushed herself up with both her hands until she was half kneeling half sitting but found she did not have the will or any strength to move any further and slipped back onto the surface of the road. She could hear Ben and Tarak debating what they should do. She felt them gently lifting her under her arms and heard the doors of the land cruiser opening, moving from the intense Starshine to the cool soft interior. She was able to sit up but still the sense everything was somehow happening in another room persisted. Tarak climbed in next to her and offered her some water from a plastic bottle to drink. The cool liquid in her mouth seemed to connect her again with that next room and she felt her strength starting to return but still she drifted in a strange uncertain state not allowing her to entirely participate in what was going on around her. Again, she heard the two men talking and the land cruiser growling into life. Outside the landscape started to move blurrily by; she decided she was comfortable and was able to let her mind drift through the intense blue sky where she seemed to be able to relax. She was tired and wanted to sleep but there was something she needed to do before she slept.

The doors were then opening again, harsh metallic, crashing sounds then the voice of Ben.

"We are here Mariella. How are you feeling. We have to go in and do this deal...for the dynamite remember...c'mon darling you gotta pull out of this now. Okino and his dragon friends are depending on you!"

The dragons she thought and Okino, that beautiful boy depending on me. She remembered standing on the Dragon hill watching him scraping off the layer of sand from the vast stone slab. She remembered how she had felt when she had heard of the heart-breaking separation of the dragons from Arimathea and the tragedy that had ensued on her world. Now she had come here...

"I remember. I'll be fine."

The strength had come back to her body, but the distance she felt had not entirely disappeared. There was more heat and dust and doors opening from a large temporary building.

"Greetings, my old friend Tarak. It has been a long time since we sat in that old tavern and talked of the old days. I see you have made some new friends. Travellers from the South perhaps and greetings to you. Come inside, Come inside."

It was light inside; the windows were dusty but gave an excellent view of the whole quarry. The trucks and earth movers had descended on the exploded area of the quarry like a flock of hungry scavengers. She was introduced by Tarak to his friend, Murran, a tall broad fellow with calm dark eyes who greeted them enthusiastically.

"I will make some tea before we talk."

Murran poured some water from a recently boiled kettle into cups he had prepared. Mariella and her travelling companions sat in the old leather armchairs positioned in front of the desk. It was covered in a large array of paperwork arranged in orderly piles. The windows were open and occasionally one of the monstrous trucks would roar past and a small cloud of dust would drift in, then be suspended and illuminated in the rays of Star shine.

Murran brought the tea over and sat down behind his desk. He talked and laughed with Tarak. Ben clearly was able to share some of the jokes; Mariella however remained quiet and found some peace as she watched the dust settling across the room adding to the thick layer that clearly had been gathering for some days. Forming new landscapes she thought, out of the ones that had been destroyed in the crater below; new landscapes amongst the figures and charts describing the extent of the destruction; the enormous weight of sediment crushed down and forced up as a continent heaved forming these hills over millions of years now floated microscopically through her mind and settled on her hands and in her hair and all around her.

"So Tarak, what has bought you and your friends out here to see me today."

"Well we do have a bit of a favour to ask you. Quite a large favour actually. I had hoped Mariella would be able to explain but she has reacted badly to the explosion that happened as we came in. Hey, Mariella you back with us. Tell Murran about your dragons. You are going to love this."

Mariella heard her name called through the shining particles of fine sand floating amongst them. Had she seen the shapes of the dragons in the draughts caused by gesturing hands and breath expelled from mouths animated by conversation? She moved her hand through the ray of Starshine. Yes, they were here, twisting and convoluting, flowing and swirling as their return to Arimathea was about to be discussed.

"If you are Taraks' friend you will know about the spirits living in these hills."

"Indeed, I was born and have always lived here. Have grown up and lived always with the idea the supernatural is all around us."

"….and yet you do this job. But that is another discussion, and anyway thankfully you do because we need some of your explosives."

Tarak and Ben smiled as they looked over to gauge the reaction of the man across the desk. Murran's broad smile was seeping away. Now she had his attention….

"All this Murran," she started, "What you are doing here, reducing these ancient hills to rubble so they can be turned into Cars and Aeroplanes, washing machines and fridges, computers and cell phones for people on the other side of the world many of whom have all those things already but just want new ones; Does that feel right to you?

"Well no, but the job came up and the money was gonna help."

"I'm not judging you; this is the way the world is now. Initiated by a strange twist in the struggle between the spirits who have always lived in these hills and in Arimathea, brought her to life, and the darker forces initiated on this world by Oblivion."

"So, the struggle between light and dark."

"Fundamentally yes. I came here to find the old Dragon order I heard was still living deep in the hills and was reputed to have always kept a connection with the Spirit of Arimathea…"

She told the story as briefly as she could to Murran who listened as intently to this beautiful stranger from across the world as he ever had done to anyone. He knew what he was doing here but like he said he would have been insane to have turned the job down. But he had lived with the old legends living within these hills. The old ones still told of the struggle when those old spirits had fought each other openly across Arimathea and it always was told their conflict had not been resolved.

Many theories had been debated as to the end of the legend and the mystery surrounding it. But no conclusion could ever be truthfully known, other than the dragons had again disappeared from the world and until they returned the world would not be at peace. Could this be the next part of the struggle unfolding? She spoke sincerely with wisdom that surely could have only come from the spirits who had brought it into the world. She was clearly taken with the monk. It seemed as if his monastery had carried a thread from those old legends down through the generations.

"…and so you see if Arimathea has any chance of coming through this catastrophic time…"

"You can have your explosives with my blessings, Mariella, wise and beautiful traveller mystic from the Southlands. Return your dragons to their beloved Arimathea and bring some peace and wisdom back to the surface of this troubled world. I am glad you have come to me and I am honoured to help you and the monk, Okino in this sacred task."

Chapter Thirty-seven
Re-United.

Okino was up in the hills above Asima with the horses when he saw the land cruiser in the far distance. It was speeding across the plain with its' dust trail rising up behind it. He was relieved and more than a little excited to see its' return and immediately started to make his way down the slopes towards Asima, hoping everything had gone to plan and Mariella was safe. The horses stubbornly resisted his attempts to speed their downward progress through the treacherous terrain.

In the quiet emptiness of the slopes infrequently populated by the old pine trees he had been contemplating what the dragons had said. He felt sure his journey must now take him across the ocean to Straam with Mariella. For it was there Oblivion had taken hold of his world. He knew this next part of the journey would offer him further challenges. He wondered how he would react to the city and everything it had to offer. After all it was part of the evolution of his world. The dragons ironically, had perhaps inspired this further development in their effort to free the people of Arimathea from their callous rulers.

He wondered if there was anything they still had not told him. They were strange and magical creatures and were still determined to prevent Arimathea's further degradation and possible destruction. However, one thing appeared certain, once they had safely returned into the depths of Arimathea, he couldn't imagine anything tempting them out for a very long time. They would not be walking the streets of Straam charming the streetwise city dwellers with their mesmerising green eyes and their wise insights into life on their planet. Any action now would have to be undertaken through the influence of the dreams they could send through the fabric of Arimathea.

The dragons had proved they could have continual access to his thoughts and dreams, even through those around him when there was something he needed to know. Farina remarkably had been able to access far deeper into the legends of her town than she had ever been told. The dreams he himself had been sent from the newly inhabited dragon lands appeared to be entirely separate realities for the sole purpose of guiding anyone who could receive them.

So how capable would the brainwashed materialistic populations of industrialised Arimathea be of receiving their dreams and would the experience be powerful enough to change their attitude towards their suffering world before it went beyond the point of no return. The dream he had been sent in his initiation to the order had never been far from his thoughts in the previous days. He could now see how it fitted with everything Arimathea had told him and echoed eerily through everything which had subsequently been revealed.

The frozen winter land had been deserted and was haunted by its previous inhabitants. It seemed there had been an invasion which had left the stark emptiness he had felt and in which the spirit people were unable to exist.

He remembered the terrifying intensity of the thunder in the storm he had experienced before Mithrael had fought Merilon and driven the sword through the weakened dragon. When Merilon and the other dragons were turned to stone the dark force he had seen in the temple must have entirely infiltrated the dragon land, draining its' ability to hold the magic the dragons had created there. It had remained held under this dark spell, uninhabited devoid of energy until he had been guided by Arimathea into the frozen winter forest to awaken the dragon. Merilon then had woken the other dragons and reclaimed, re-energised and began to redream their new dimension, sending their dreams to him and possibly to others in a new attempt to divert the world away from the peril it was now in.

The land cruiser had now passed the foot of the hill and suddenly skidded to a halt in a cloud of dust. The door was flung open and Mariella had jumped out of the air-conditioned environment back into the heat of the Arimathean Star. She waved up to Okino who she must have spotted on his journey down the hill and started to make her way hurriedly up the lower slopes through the rocks and pine trees towards Okino and the horses. In the last few paces she shouted up at Okino as she negotiated the last part of rocky slope.

"I hope you have been looking after my horses and not riding them to exhaustion all around these mountains!"

Okino smiled and leapt down from the horse. Mariella walked the last few paces towards them, briefly greeted the horses and then turned to Okino, took both his hands and looking deep into his eyes and beyond said…

"I missed you Okino!"

Then she wrapped hers arms around him and they hugged affectionately. They were both relieved and delighted to be back together. Their embrace lingered as they savoured the moment which they had both been anticipating in those previous days. As they eventually parted Mariella delicately pressed one of her slightly longer kisses on to Okino's cheek. The young monk looked down at her and smiled back…

"I missed you too, Mariella!"

He paused as he momentarily became absorbed deep into her turquoise eyes. They seemed to have become even lovelier in those last few days. He was reminded of the light just below the surface of the ocean where he had briefly swum with the pod of dolphins in his dream with Merilon. He managed to bring himself again to the surface and told her,

"…but I have made another connection with the dragons."

"No near-death stuff this time hopefully!"

"No, I think we are done with all that now. I have the feeling they are looking towards what might be possible after we have opened this hill…So how did it all go? Did you get the dynamite?!"

"Come on, I'll show you."

They walked back down the hill while chattering about the events of the previous days. When they reached the land cruiser Ben, Zeph and Tarak were waiting, leaning on the front with cold beers from the on-board refrigerator. They threw one to both Okino and Mariella who immediately snapped the ring pulls…

"Here's to a mission successfully completed!"

They drank thirstily from the chilled beer cans and Mariella lead Okino around to the back of the land cruiser where she opened the rear door to reveal two large wooden crates. She pulled off one of the lids to reveal the crude sticks of dynamite. There were rolls of wire and detonators carefully stored amongst a variety of drills, excavating tools and a small generator. Okino removed the lid from the other crate revealing a similar amount of explosive.

"So, they reckoned we are going to need that much. I see they didn't come back with you so presumably somebody knows how this is all going to work." The three men grinned at each other...

"Yeah they told us exactly what we have to do to blow a nice clean hole straight through the stone without damaging the top of the hill too much."

"Should be quite dramatic…. and loud!"

Okino contemplated what they were now actually going to do.

"There is a bit of preparation to do first."

Zeph ventured.

"It seems the nature of the stone slab means we will have to burrow into the hill so we can drill holes into the underside of the slab to plant the explosives. So that should be fun!"

Okino acknowledged Ben and Zeph were now happy and quite excited to be involved as the prospect of creating such a large explosion had obviously captured their imagination. Mariella then spoke seriously to the four men!

"Now listen guys, we are going to do this exactly how we have been told. We are going to make a proper tunnel under the stone and nothing is going to explode until everything is exactly as it should be, OK!!"

The tribesman, the two executives from the Southern city of Straam and the monk from the Temple of the Dragon then all agreed to proceed carefully with this new and dangerous venture.

Chapter Thirty-eight
Merge.

Early the next morning the small party made their way up to the top of the Dragon hill. With the help of the horses they carried the equipment they had brought from Aharri to tunnel into the side of the hill and under the slab. When they reached the summit, they admired the view over the plains and discussed a strategy, circling the edge of the stone slab trying to decide at which point it would be easiest to start the tunnel. They found the least rocky position and quickly organised their operation. When everything was set out and everybody knew what they were doing they started to burrow into the side of the hill. It was decided the tunnel should be just wide enough for two people to crawl down. Ben and Tarak started digging.

They vigorously tore into the stony soil with the spades and the small picks they had decided would be best to tackle the task. They were continually confronted with large rocks which had to be dug around and dragged out before the tunnel could proceed. The ceiling to the excavation would be the stone covering the hill. They had decided to slope the sides on each side of the tunnel to prevent any collapse. This meant larger amounts of soil would have to be removed but meant shoring vertical sides could be avoided.

As the tunnel became longer there were less of the larger stones they had encountered in the early stages. The challenge as with any such crude tunnel was removing the soil from the advancing face. Pushing the large amounts of soil back to the entrance soon became ineffectual and Mariella rode down to the village to find a solution. By mid-morning she had returned, by which time the tunnel had advanced under the stone at least the length of two men and was high enough for them to crawl down on their hands and knees. Mariella had persuaded the children to part with a small cart which they used in their games. It could be filled with soil and dragged back down the tunnel by rope and emptied down the side of the hill at the entrance to the tunnel. The cart could then be dragged back to the face of the tunnel ready to be filled again.

So, the work proceeded. Each member of the group took their turn digging painstakingly under the great stone covering. Lanterns were lit as the light from the entrance became ineffectual where the digging was taking place. As the Star rose higher in the sky the end of the tunnel became the coolest place to be. Dragging the cart out of the tunnel and emptying it, rapidly became the most favoured task.

As the tunnel advanced towards the centre of the hill, Okino started to notice a thickening of the atmosphere in the air around him as he was digging. He started to feel anxiety. The flickering light of the lamps in the darkness started to play tricks in his mind and he noticed fear beginning to rise. The optimism he had for this action was falling away and was being replaced by the doubt and the fear of reprisal. Once he had acknowledged this state of mind he decided to immediately exit the tunnel and return to the daylight. He was greeted by the grimy faces of his fellow miners.

"I think I will have to do the remainder of the digging. There is something else embedded under the stone in the hill, I have experienced it before in my dream with Merilon. There is no reason for any of you to be subjected to it for the moment."

His eyes fell on Mariella who looked decidedly worried by Okino's announcement.

"So are you going to be all right to do that. How much more do you think we have to do?"

"I think I will start to make the circular chamber at the end of the tunnel now."

Okino disappeared back into the tunnel dragging the cart behind him. He cleared his mind as he continued his work; filled his thoughts continually with the memory of the Starlight directly above him as the dark emptiness again began to infiltrate his thoughts. He battled away feverishly to construct the circular chamber from where they would embed a ring of explosives into the stone slab above. He thought of all the love he had felt in his life; of his mother and father and the people of the town who had been important and influential guides; who had nurtured his special gifts with their understanding and knowledge; he thought of their faces shining with happiness in some special moment where love had been passed unconditionally between them; filled himself with those memories as he dug through the dark earth.

Deep in these thoughts he knew he could feel Arimathea. He remembered her in the cave and all she had said to him about the dark forces that would pursue him if he should ever discover the destiny of the world. He called out to her but she could not breakthrough whatever curse had been laid into the Dragon hill by Samir and the chanting of the dark magicians all those hundreds of years before. He remembered the mountains he had climbed, bathed in starshine and the exhaustion and sometimes the fear he had fought to reach their shining summits so he could look down again on his beautiful world. He struck deeper and harder into the soil losing all track of time as he filled the cart, saw it disappear and dragged it back repeatedly; eventually he couldn't help but give way to the darkness. He let it envelope him and he lay drifting into the silence in the chamber he had carved under the stone.

Mariella noticed everything had gone very quiet within the tunnel. She couldn't see the candlelight.

"Something's happened!"

She dived into the darkness scrambling along the crudely formed passageway. In the chamber at the end she could see very little, so she felt her way around and eventually found Okino who now was unconscious. By now Tarak had also entered the chamber. They grabbed whatever they could and dragged Okino out into the Starlight.

"Wake up, Okino, wake up!"

She threw some water over his face and his eyes suddenly opened and he slowly sat up!

"It was taking everything…everything I tried to fill the emptiness was just drifting away from me."

Okino closed his eyes again as if to sleep.

"We've got to keep him awake and he definitely can't go back in there…maybe he is just too sensitive perhaps if.."

"One of us less priestly beings went in to drill the holes."

Zeph grinned and walked over to the generator and primed the fuel lines. He pulled the starter cord and the generator spluttered into action, filling the air with the coarse sound of the racing mechanical engine and blue exhaust smoke. He pulled one of the power drills out of the box of tools and connected it up to the generator. He gave the large industrial drill an experimental burst. The drill added to the cacophony now engulfing the top of the hill as the operation to expel its demon continued.

"If this stops for any length of time come in and get me."

He then disappeared into the tunnel with the wire of the drill trailing behind him. Inside he quickly orientated himself inside the chamber Okino had dug. He quickly assessed the size of the circle of holes he would drill. He gave no thought to whatever was lurking there and focused entirely on the task he had taken on.

Time after time he placed the point of the spiralling steel drill bit up against the stone above his head. The powerful drill drove effectively into the dense stonework filling the chamber with dust and screeching sound. He grinned to himself as he remembered his conversation in the tavern when he had nearly had his throat cut for doubting the existence of the spirits in these hills. But he could not deny there was something about these two young people and their talk of a planetary power that had been somehow removed from its place in the scheme of things. No one on Arimathea could argue effectively she was on a healthy course into the future but no one was going to admit it while there was still money to be made and the vast economies and infrastructures supporting the developed world had to be continually maintained and added to. He questioned his own motives as he started to drill the last hole. If he was honest, Mariella had enticed him into her plan with her startling blue eyes and clearly, she or at least her father must be well connected back in Straam which may be an advantage on their return. There may or may not be dragons involved.

He scrambled out of the tunnel into the fading light on the side of the hill.

"So, we've just got to set the explosives, wire it all up, retreat to a safe distance, blow the top of the hill off and wait for the dragon to return!"

He looked around at the activity surrounding him. Okino was now standing on the top of the hill contemplating the view over the plain below, clearly having recovered from his ordeal. Ben and Mariella had set out the sticks of explosive and organised the connection to the detonator.

"So how was it, Zeph?"

"Just got on with it, it's weird in there…. but what isn't about this country?"

Ben laughed and nodded in agreement, bundled the explosives together and disappeared into the tunnel. He wasted no time, pushing each of the sticks of explosive into the holes Zeph had prepared, carefully wiring the charges in a loop from one to another and securing the final wire so there was no possibility it could become dislodged. He sat back for a few moments admiring their work in the light from the lamps remaining in the chamber. He carefully checked each connection again to ensure the current would flow around the entire circuit and so ignite each one of the explosives.

It was a strange sight; one that he would remember and recount around the dining tables of Straam for many years to come. He had come here with Zeph to find ideas for new products to excite the voracious appetite of the fickle markets in his world across the sea. If the monk and Mariella were to be believed it seemed he had become involved in some supernatural plot to bring about some adjustments to that world. He remained sceptical and looked forward to seeing the explosion now so carefully engineered. He scrambled out of the tunnel careful not to disturb any of the detonation wire.

It was early evening before everything was in place. The Star now hung over the mountains in the far distance when the five of them, stood a safe distance from the dragon hill in front of the detonator. A murder of crows had gathered in the trees surrounding the old ruins in expectation of the forthcoming event. They screeched and chattered excitedly of the past events leading to this crucial point in the history of their world and speculated their collective prophecies of the events it would bring into being.

"So, who is going to do it?" inquired Zeph, "Surely, it has to be either Okino or Mariella."

Okino and Mariella looked at each other. They were both responsible for bringing events to this point; inspired on opposite sides of their world by the spirit of Arimathea. They had each brought invaluable resources from those separate places so this old dispute between the ancient powers residing here could be finally resolved. Maybe resolution would not be found but perhaps the story would again continue with a new equilibrium allowing the age-old adversaries to engage again; ensuring one could not bring about the end of the other. It seemed some aspect of the old dispute had been settled in the mists of time and the lore of the great mystery had seen fit to construct a flow of circumstance to bring about a new era in the light of all that had been learned; the breath of the world it seemed, was held in great expectation.

The crows became silent as Okino and Mariella knelt and placed one hand each on the detonator, looked deep into the other's eyes and beyond into each other's souls where they again found the undertaking that had brought them together. They then looked up to the summit of the Dragon hill. Okino felt the last rays of Starlight on his face; perhaps of the old era. He felt her around him again in the quiet of these remote mountains, giving her blessing, willing him to continue the task she had given to him. He started the chant and the four others joined him.

"Five …Four…Three…Two…One…"

He and Mariella plunged the detonator back into the casing. For a moment the silence continued. Then there was an enormous flash of fiery light as the force of the explosion cracked open and forced its way through the stone slab on the top of the hill. As the thunderous boom of the detonation reached them, stone from the shattered slab was flung high into the air above. Such was the force of the ring of explosives that much of the stone around and above was turned to dust and was now rising high in a cloud into the air. Smaller fragments the size of large pebbles shot into the evening skies and soon were raining down on the surrounding ground, some within twenty or thirty paces from where the small group were standing. Larger pieces of stone were thrown over the edge of the hill and had started their descent down the slope. They gathered enough momentum to roll some way down the hill before they finally slumped to a halt. The great dusty cloud drifted out across the plains on the light evening breeze where it would eventually fall to the ground and again continue its' journey through the fabric of Arimathea.

For a few seconds a stunned silence hung over the land before the crows as if in celebration rose as one shrieking their approval. They flew high from their roosts and began to circle above the shattered hill in anticipation of the dragon's return. Okino remembered the circling crows over the forest before he had awakened Merilon. He started to make his way up the slope picking his way through the new debris lying amongst the old stones. He knew as he neared the summit all was not entirely as he had hoped.

The explosion had blown the stone cover almost entirely off. Stone now clung precariously forming an almost continuous ledge on the perimeter of the hill. Below this ledge and across the entire summit a large crater had been formed by the explosion. However, it was not this scene of devastation concerning Okino as he stood on the jagged edge. The dark emptiness he had experienced earlier in the day had now been released from its' sanctuary in the layers of stone and hung like a dense mist over the top of the hill. The others were arriving at the summit. He signalled to them to go back.

"The explosion has released the curse from in the stone but it seems reluctant to leave. But I think I can deal with it now."

He somehow managed to sound convincing and Mariella and the three men turned and started back down the slope, shouting warnings up to him. He knew his tactic earlier had been right as he had managed to hold the darkness at bay before he had become overwhelmed by it. Also, he knew Merilon and Arimathea would probably be near, keen to be reunited but still frustrated by the emptiness they were unable to penetrate in this dimension. So again, as he stood on the ledge, he gradually took himself into the space where he could engage with the consciousness existing in those dimensions other than his own.

He forced the emptiness into the periphery of his concentration. Then he reached out into the frequencies of vibrating light where he knew Merilon could find him, to merge with him and ascertain what knowledge and powers he needed to draw out from the higher consciousness of Arimathea through his own to finally destroy the emptiness. It was happening, Merilon was there. He felt the dragon's energy move into his own; through his molecular structure like a wave of emotion fine music or kind encouraging words from a good friend could inspire. Again, he felt his consciousness expand as it had in the stone circle on the hill when he and Merilon had first emerged in the dragon lands. Earlier he had projected all the wonder he felt had been created in his own life and in his own consciousness. It had not been enough and he had become overwhelmed. Now he found he was being given access to all the wonder ever created and now existing in the entire consciousness of Arimathea.

The light of unlimited creation that had formed, threaded its way through the web of interconnected consciousness and blended with spirit to evolve into the enormous diversity of life on Arimathea, now flooded through his being. The understandings and realisations that had arisen within the consciousness as a result of continual adversity with Oblivion as every movement took Arimathea one step nearer to perfection, now shone through his mind as one pure infinite thought. In its' light he could see the snow leopards, the eagles and the dolphins, the lizards and wolves, the spiders, the beetles and the pure white swans all with their integral place, bound infinitely together within the one thought; every life time feeding into the knowledge the great spirit had yearned to know; to feel how it would be to slice through the oceans with a thousand brothers and sisters, or slink through the mountains across the sparkling snow with senses processing and experiencing every detail and aspect of those environments.

How it would it be to stand silently breathing in the Starlight in a forest for a thousand years or be a meadow sustaining and being sustained by the lives of a million bees. To grow and adapt and change over millions and millions of years, becoming more complex to create an experience of every nuance, shade and distinction it knew could be brought into being. In that light he felt the currents of will, of love and the nurturing qualities of time and space, the rhythms and cycles and the origins of memory contained within the fabric of the stars, urges of progression leading to movement into and ultimately through all these states of being.

Okino started to feel the solidity of his material form falling away. A torrent of the purest light was flowing from Arimathea into him, through him and out into the dark emptiness lingering around the hill. It had been weakened by its expulsion from its stony lair. He felt its' diminished ability as it attempted to devour the concentrated light being directed towards it. Arimathea and Merilon were leaving nothing to chance. Now, after all these centuries of separation they had found a conduit with the capability to channel all this light out from the underlying consciousness through into the physical realm to finally destroy the barrier that had kept them apart for so long. Okino felt the emptiness breaking down and evaporating as it became unable to resist further, as all the light and love in the consciousness of Arimathea was able to flow relentlessly through it, so freeing the Dragon hill from the curse Samir and his magicians had placed on it all those centuries before.

Okino beckoned down to Mariella who was watching anxiously from the saddle of the hill. She climbed the final slope to join him on the remains of the stone cover and came up beside Okino, slipping an arm around his waist and looked down into the crater.

"Is it over, Okino? Can they be reunited now?"

"Thankfully yes we can be reunited again."

Merilon had materialised and was standing behind them on the jagged edge. The tall human figure of the dragon loomed over them in the golden light of the Star set. Okino and Mariella turned in surprise to see the legendary creature that had filled their dreams and the stories that had so enchanted them in those last days. He seemed depleted from the strong vigorous being who had stalked the world all those centuries before. Mariella had wondered so much if this moment would come. There had always been the possibility he would just evaporate back into the hill. But here he was standing beside them contemplating the devastation.

There was of course so much she wanted to ask him. He turned and she looked directly into the strange glow emanating from his eyes as he peered down at her. It had been described as green in so many of the tales but now she could see or knew it was the life force he carried that glowed in the same way a tree with its new array of leaves would glow in early springtime. All the answers were in those eyes or would be when she needed to know them. He grinned down at her and put his arms around both of their shoulders.

"You have done well; all these centuries to find two people who could finally make the leap in the way you two have. It has been a long wait."

"Sorry about the mess Merilon, but it did seem the quickest way of sorting out the problem." Okino felt like he had finally met a friend he had known for a thousand years."

The dragon threw back his head and laughed up into the evening sky. The sound of his joy echoed around the valleys and mountains.

"A few thousand years and no-one will know the difference. The important thing is the channel is open again. Already I can feel the entire network spreading through the planet…beckoning me to come home. So, if you don't mind there is work to be done, dreams to dream, a planet to save and no doubt you will be giving me some help."

"No doubt…just let us know…"

"Make your way towards the city, my friends. You have unfinished business there Okino, and Mariella your mum and dad are missing you. Thank you for all you have done for us. You know this changes everything and nothing will ever be the same again."

He took their hands individually and then clasped each of them to him. Even in his depleted state this left both Okino and Mariella feeling like they had been on a long restful holiday. He then leapt down into the crater and stood with his hands outstretched, his face smiling and raised to the stars. At first the air seemed to shimmer as his aura became pronounced around him. The ground beneath his feet began to shine. The light from the hill after all those many centuries began to rise and move through him. His human form started to fade leaving only the energetic form of the dragon hovering briefly over the Dragon hill, wings outstretched, before the light engulfed him and he dived silently back into the hill.

There was a golden Star set spreading across the sky, perhaps transforming the Northern mountains of Arimathea a little nearer to one of those other realms from which the dragon had dreamed his new world. The first of the evening stars again made their appearance, perhaps sparkling a little brighter and somewhere in the distance a family of wolves howled in defiance out across the world for they had lived another spectacular day. If their howls were louder and filled with a new vigour and determination or they echoed a little more powerfully through the valleys and out across the plains it was because Arimathea was again in rapturous love and far across her oceans in all her distant lands everyone and everything living in her miraculous gentle light silently gave thanks and celebrated the return of the dragon to her depths.

Chapter Thirty-nine.
Networks.

The dragon flowed back down into the channels forged in those early times when he first merged with the creation spirit of Arimathea. They had carried his dreams from deep in her heart, from where he had come to sleep, through her fabric and up to the surface where they would flood into the world from the Dragon hills. They had been dormant since the dragon had been stranded on the surface. Now, as he passed through the magically enhanced channels, they came immediately back to life, enlivened again by the Dragon light as it travelled towards its destination. Deep in the caverns they met again where her concentrated essence emanated from the multitudes of geometric crystals formed as a result of the searing heat and pressure in the depths of her being in the earliest years of her evolution. They came together again in the ecstatic weave of energy, attraction and universal bond sending a wave of love light flooding up through the fabric of the planet.

Here at the heart, the soul of the dragon had slept powerless to convey the dreams needed to heal the terrible rift bringing so much danger to Arimathea. Without his spirit to carry those dreams to the surface, the dragon's soul had drifted, unguided through the depths of Arimathea's consciousness; deeper than he had ever been before. Into the soul of the universal being he had travelled, where he found the legends of the worlds she had known, long since faded into the darkness.

There he had found the broken silent worlds. The rocky parched and burnt out landscapes or the frozen ice fields where atmospheres had failed and everything evolved there had been lost. Some circumstance had arisen outside the new or old world's ability to cope. Something tiny multiplying to fast or something huge and fast falling from the sky to a world in a vast Universe continually bombarded by radiation and meteorites from the stars and only protected by a delicate atmosphere. An imbalance created instantly or interminably slowly in finely balanced ecosystems, unable to cope, suddenly out of control and nothing powerful enough to transform it, devouring the world. No miracles or will yet to save it, just disintegration.

In these evolving worlds inevitably anomalies would always be gradually changing its' environments. Perhaps an ocean cooled as a glacier melted a little faster when a volcano erupted or filled the skies with ash as a result of the tectonic plates of the world shifting. The sea became colder on the ocean shore. On the lower rungs of the food chain a once prolific food source was unable to adapt. Its predators initially competed a little harder to catch the food source they had been living on for millennia but as it disappeared, they did not have the ability to adapt or move and so another species went into decline and disappeared. These predators were predated on by larger animals and so the consequences were felt all the way through the food chain. Migration routes changed as the fish numbers declined so further ecosystems were affected as predators moved and invaded other predators hunting grounds. In most worlds in this universe the big fish always need a humbler food source to feed on.

Everything was constantly shifting and adapting in these vibrant living worlds the dragon dreams could bring into being. At any time an outcome could be changed if one creature or the mass consciousness of a species was able to gain some advantage as a result of some knowledge they had gleaned from the dragon's magical dreams. Whichever way circumstances developed the consequences were always felt throughout the entire web of life. As the consequences of this new anomaly eventually rippled through each and every environment and species near or far everything would have to adapt. If a new balance could be found it would inevitably continue to grow and again the entire world would be move into the future perhaps stronger and more resilient.

However, if a resolution and the ability to eventually find the equilibrium needed for continuation had been impossible to find, and this anomaly was unable to be resolved then the conflict would eventually consume the world and everything on it leaving only a silent husk. Many evolutionary lines perhaps millions of years in the making would come to an end with no knowledge as to how or why their stable world had suddenly disintegrated.

Again, the dream would be confounded. The enlivening and expanding magic emanating through the consciousness, unable to prevent the disintegration. The dragon dreams held the memories of all these evolutions, their origin and their most successful aspects, the new complexity of experience, the beautiful landscapes and processes that had arisen and how they had come to an end. Then, if all was entirely lost, in great distress and with regret, they would fly out again into the Universe to find a new world to inhabit.

However, now, there was only ecstasy. As the dragon reunited with his soul and Arimathea both of their beings began to be revitalised by the enormous joy they felt. Although he had found new connections with the elemental spirits who had supported his ability to exist, his power had been seriously diminished in those years of separation. The influence of the two separate entities had almost faded from existence leaving a dangerous weakening of the threads connecting the planet to the many dimensions maintaining its stability. Subsequently the powers of emptiness and oblivion had risen into ascendancy and the equilibrium within the structure of consciousness was being eroded like an island that had risen out of an ocean and now was being slowly washed away by a powerful new tide. In the moments the dragon's spirit and his soul again came together the conduits to the great universal consciousness across all the dimensions were again re-established.

Energy from all these dimensions flowed into the reunited dragon. The dragon beings had become in the great evolutionary flow of time interpreters. They had evolved as transformers of the energy of consciousness as it had evolved through the aeons. They had pursued it through many previous states in many different dimensions. So, an idea or a story, a construct of values having a specific meaning in a previous world may have no meaning in a new world. The underlying premise however performed a similar role in both but may not be recognised within the new dimension. The dragon had gained the ability to redefine the structure of the energy and bring it into focus so it could again come to life within a new set of parameters.

They existed in as many of these dimensions as they had discovered in the great labyrinths of the Universe. The possibilities for such dimensions were infinite and by no means all were familiar to the dragons. However, those most accessible to them were those dimensions running closest to the fabric of the space and time in which they currently had come to exist. It was possible for them to transfer ideas and conceptual constructs from one dimension to another. In this way they had been able to bring new worlds into existence utilising many of the most effective constructs of the previous worlds they had known. Each world then became a pinnacle and a new attempt to bring physicality closer to the harmony that had existed before the cataclysm. The construct carefully woven by the dragons on Arimathea had been as daring and as complex as they had previously attempted.

There could of course be no certainty as to how any world would evolve. The dragons could only dream a construct of the premise, in their experience, they now thought would be the most advantageous atmosphere in which the new dream could grow and flourish within the great mystery. So, the new world would lurch unpredictably towards its destiny as the inevitable cycles of growth and decline became part of its process.

The dragon sensed Arimathea had been damaged and weakened as they merged again deep within the rocky fabric of her being and joined with the consciousness existing in the thin layer of habitable atmosphere surrounding the surface of Arimathea. Fearing their first visits to the sprawling human cities they decided first to visit the forests where they had enjoyed so much time wandering as men and women.

In the frozen north they drifted through endless pine forests in the snow-covered expanses where still there was minimal human intervention. As they dwelt in the quiet glistening landscapes of mountain ranges and ice covered lakes, they felt for the creatures they knew to live there. The white snow foxes and the stealthy snow leopards, the powerful bears and the white owls who would glide silent as ghosts between the ancient trees in search of their unfortunate prey.

Here immediately they noticed the changes that had come over Arimathea. The animals were undoubtedly here in the same way as they always had been but their numbers had declined enormously and so the strength of their spirit families was considerably weaker within the consciousness of those areas and so Arimathea. The fabulous fur of the leopards and the foxes was prized by the mountain people for their ability to stave off the life-threatening cold of the winters in these inhospitable places. But they had been hard to track and kill. Leopards often would turn the tables on the hunters in the environment to which they were so perfectly suited and take advantage of an easy meal. Now as hunters came with their high-powered rifles able to kill over long distances the leopards' only advantage was her invisibility. She was hunted relentlessly by the determined humans who could sell her pelt for as much as much as five years wages working in the factories of their overlords in the cities. So, the dragon found her numbers were dwindling and her spirit was slowly fading from the mountains and forests with those of the foxes and the bears. The owls remained invisible to all and continued their silent ghostly lives hunting amongst the snowy glades watching from high in the ancient trees as their fellow creatures were murderously pursued.

With each creature they would merge. Into complex cortex, muscle flesh and fur: Into nervous systems where sensory information was transmitted at the speed of light down nerves to the complex lenses within eyes, as they stared out over the pristine sparkling snow scene and ears as they listened for the breath of a hare or a rabbit or an unsuspecting goat or deer. The dragon became the creature again as she scanned her world for some tiny movement. He was with her as she stalked the white mountain hare so preoccupied with his own search for food, he had become unaware of the danger soon to come upon him.

The dragon felt the life force drain from the animal as the teeth of the snow leopard sank into the neck of the hare, cutting and puncturing: he tasted the warm blood and felt the urge of this hungry mother to eat the fresh lifeless meat to satiate her own hunger. The dragon travelled with her back to her den to where the cubs waited patiently for the return of their mother and stayed with them as they consumed the hare ravenously. He then curled together with them in their extreme mountain home relishing the Love they shared amongst each other as they slept together.

As he lay in the undisturbed isolated mountain layer, he cast his thoughts out to the habitats of the world where Arimathea's Star was at its' strongest. In these thoughts he allowed his consciousness to drift into the tropical regions. Here the heat on the adjacent oceans and the continually circulating winds brought the deluge of water which had allowed the vast rain forests to form. Now in an environment dominated by misty humidity he drifted through the infinite variety of vegetation continuously battling its way towards the light above the canopy. The towering ancient trees had become the framework for every climbing and creeping plant craving the life-giving light. Smaller trees, spawned by their parents or near neighbours, sped swiftly upwards into an opening allowing them to thrive amongst their older relatives. Their seeds had been germinated amongst the fungi and moulds of the decaying forest floor, possibly thrown down by the monkeys living permanently amongst the tangle of branches and creepers.

The dragon now merged his consciousness into one of these colonies as they moved through the canopy, jumping and swinging themselves from tree to tree in their search for the fruit from which they entirely lived. High up amongst the towering giants he settled with an extended family as they stripped the fruit from the tender outer branches and systematically devoured the succulent flesh. He felt the close ties and the hierarchy which was continually asserted as the family watched for any threats from any approaching colony. They chattered amongst themselves and screeched warnings occasionally to broadcast their proximity to any who may be planning an invasion. Then when they had eaten their fill, they relaxed in their tree top home. The older monkeys would carefully weave platforms from surrounding vegetation where they were able to sleep and doze.

The dragon noticed how they absorbed and analysed the sounds of the jungle surrounding them. Firstly, they were searching for any threat that may be approaching but then he sensed they were relaxing into the sounds around them. From every direction sound gave a three-dimensional orchestral quality to the spaces surrounding them. The rhythmical call of birds calling out their territory, overlapping almost uniformly and in time against a backdrop of the incessant hum of insects seemed to sooth the monkeys as they dozed at one with their jungle home.

The younger monkeys uninterested by these more adult delights chased, teased and fought their siblings playfully as they explored their treetop home. They observed curiously the other creatures they came across and occasionally used small sticks to prise them from crevices in the tree bark when they were reluctant to play. Other individuals sat in quiet contemplation, as a relative studiously searched for insects in their fur. Each insect found was carefully removed and disposed of before the process resumed.

In the depths of the jungle the dragon found none of the threats he sensed these habitats were under. But as he passed time with the family of primates relaxing in their pristine jungle environment, he felt a horrifying memory in the collective consciousness of the trees; all connected as they were in this jungle and beyond in their one great family.

He felt the panic as the loggers could be heard approaching with their chainsaws and bulldozers. The monkeys were alerted by the terrifying noise as the destruction advanced towards them, fleeing deeper into the jungle as the territory their family had roamed and colonised for as long as the forest had grown there was systematically destroyed and burnt. The trees in which they had lived and slept and eaten, unceremoniously felled; removed to be sold and cut up to perform some new role in the mechanised world of the monkey's distant cousins.

They heard the crashing thud as the gigantic trees so familiar to them fell through the surrounding jungle destroying the landscapes and so the lives of the smaller creatures who could not escape. They could smell the smoke as the jungle was mercilessly and callously burnt; it stung their eyes as they made their way through a new unfamiliar part of the jungle into the territories of their rivals with whom previously they had shared only a boundary and the occasional warning display. Now they would have to fight for their fruit and the space in the trees to make their platforms where they could again listen to the rhythms of the jungle.

But it would not end. As far as they escaped the destruction would advance towards them wherever they settled. Every creature in the jungle became a migrant; the birds, the cats, the deer, the elephants, the sloths, everyone was on the run separated, unsettled and under threat as the ecosystems and all the extraordinary relationships between animals and plants existing within them for all those years, amongst all these conditions, disappeared for ever. Something of this terrifying memory was transmitted through the dragon to the monkeys. The adults started to wake. They looked around anxiously for the threat. They instinctively felt and called their family in closer. The dragon decided to leave and the family of monkeys relaxed again in the heat of the afternoon.

He rose up through the canopy. Here in this part of the world, inhabited only by the indigenous Indians he assumed his energetic dragon form for the first time in those many centuries since he had been away. The Indians would think of his manifestation as a blessing and an omen for their safety and good fortune if they chanced to glance up and see him flying over the trees. He flew low enough to hear the sounds of all the life dwelling there emanating from the trees below.

He felt his anger rising, the fire in his dragons' belly, as he felt the plight of the animals and the trees and the beautiful world he had dreamed and watched and been a part of for so long. Could Oblivion have really gained such an advantage during the time he had been banished from Arimathea. He could not dare to make another conscious intervention. Such action on his part would certainly seal the planets fate; if it wasn't already. Perhaps there was a chance the balance had shifted back towards life and creation and the powers of light and warmth were finding a way to divert the planet away from what seemed a catastrophic end. The humans were a paradoxical species capable of such despicable, thoughtless destructiveness even to their own. Yet also they had come closer to the enlightened state, to the spiritual and physical harmony dreamed all those eons ago than any other species in the cosmos.

He owed his return to those old souls, now returned as the two young adults wandering in the distant mountains of Jahallala. The connection the young monk had made was almost certainly because of the work initiated by Rabir and continued after Samir disbanded his colony, in the remote mountain temple at Lamai. Perhaps the price had been paid and now a new more positive time could unravel for Arimathea and her people without his interference. His mood lightened again and the fire growing in his belly began to subside. It was time he decided to continue his exploration. He gained altitude and soon he was flying high above the ever-moving layer of cloud vapour skimming through the lower atmosphere.

As he soared higher into the atmosphere the dragon again remembered what it was he so relished about the energetic sensation of flying. The air under his wings and across his body became colder as he flew higher, the sky above him a deeper blue, the stream of air on which he could ride became faster, through the cold he could feel the heat of the Star minimal in this thin air and it's movement slowly descending, towards the layer of clouds below him replacing the pure white with purple, pink and red undulations. He decided to chase the Star around the planet: kept it on the horizon as it moved into the West. He sped through the never-ending setting of the star always underway at some point on the sphere.

Again he marvelled at the infinite nature of the beauty this world held as it spun on its axis while revolving around it's only Star creating this eternal planetary dance and the endless drama continuing on its surface as a result of it coming to be. He had always delighted in these solitary flights high above the clouds. Arimathea evolving far below him had almost seemed inconsequential to him here as he contemplated the steady and precise rotation of these enormous bodies holding the same precise position amongst the star systems in which he had found them all those billions of years before.

Now however there was a new sensation. The dragon sensed a new vibration in the air, a new explosive roar. Far below him the lowering Star had glinted on a surface he had noticed as a tiny flash above the clouds. He adjusted his trajectory swooping downwards and as he neared the cloud system in which he had seen the flash of light, the pristine metallic shell and swept back wings of the airliner came into view. The dragon adjusted his speed so he could fly alongside; now in his purely energetic form he could fully observe his first experience of the technology that had emerged in this new age.

He found himself admiring the sleek streamlined machine. It appeared to float motionless above the clouds: the only sign of movement being the continual stream of condensed gas and vapour being blasted from the combustion chambers of the four jet engines where he sensed, what amounted to continuously controlled high pressure explosions being fed by considerable reserves of refined carbon fuel stored within the structure of the wings.

He sensed the fuel being forced down metallic veins by pumps, controlled by a computerised nervous system which also continually monitored all the aircrafts directional systems as it flew through and across the continually changing winds. He sensed this nervous system was connected into a further communications system stretching far around the planet. It was continually monitoring every electrical impulse being generated.

He sensed the hundreds of souls sitting in the carefully pressurised environment as if in their living rooms at home. They appeared to be sedated by music and films, food and drink as they hurtled through the atmosphere of their world to their holiday resorts, their business destinations or their family reunions.

He contemplated the many constant laws of the universe adhered to for such an object to travel through the atmosphere at such speed and height. There was a simplicity and a beauty to the outward appearance which defied the complexity of its achievement. Had this not always been the strength of all that had evolved on this world? For so long the humans had looked at Arimathea and sensed these laws, put them down to supernatural forces underlying everything they saw. Now they had conquered their crudest assumptions and discovered some of the rules governing the phenomena they saw around them and had used their extraordinary ingenuity to solve one of the problems always facing them.

The urge to move and to travel had always fascinated and driven them; It had spread them around the planet from their humble beginnings on the arid savannah lands. Now they had embodied many of the laws they had discovered on their incredible journey into this flying machine to carry them to any part of their world quickly and safely. If they had come this far, he wondered how deeply, they would eventually understand the true nature of their world.

They had been closer to that truth in their ignorance as they wandered in awe of the world in those early times, intuitively sensing how deeply those laws must run, and how infinitely complex they must have become for all this to have come into being. Supernatural energetic beings had explained the complexity in the stories they had passed down through the generations. In these last centuries in their arrogance of their place in the universe they had forgotten the stories and come to deny the possibility of their existence.

He wondered whether in the distant future they would discover the deeper inter dimensional laws and the fortuitous collision that had resulted in the appearance of consciousness and eventually their own intelligence? They had come to understand the most basic of these physical laws, enabling them to create these airliners and everything else they had achieved. But would they ever discover this consciousness had evolved their world as a transition to a higher destiny? If they made and accepted this discovery in enough time, then perhaps they would move onto the next stage of their evolution beyond these wasteful tricks.

The dragon had become interested in the communications system radiating from the aeroplane. He sensed continual and intense frequency changes flooding out into the uninterrupted space around the aircraft. His first thought as he started to acknowledge this phenomenon, was that the aeroplane was dreaming information out into the world. He suddenly recognised a strange parallel here with how he had transferred his own knowledge into the consciousness of Arimathea. Fascinated by this new discovery he concentrated his consciousness around and into the structures of these vibrations.

He found navigational information continually being transmitted to presumably other aircraft and destinations in the lands to which it was flying. He found information about the mechanical status of the aircraft and communications from the pilots to the air traffic controllers in the countries over which and to which they were flying, reporting progress and conferring about weather conditions in the places they would eventually be landing. He sensed also incoming frequencies feeding into the passenger systems. He was able to detect the frequencies bringing visual and audio entertainment and the news from where the passengers had left and from where they were going. He detected personal communications between individuals in all parts of Arimathea: far from being apart from what was happening as they flew high above the clouds, all these individuals were continuing their influence on events in their lives much as if they had been on the ground.

As his own consciousness was able to expand as far as any of these frequencies could travel, he was soon able to experience how the humans had built their global communication system. Satellites hung invisibly in their geo stationary orbits far above the surface of Arimathea enabling a never-ending tide of transmissions to flood through the atmosphere to any place where some device could receive, interpret and convert whatever information they held.

This was far from the silent place in which the dragon had flown in those days before his long sleep in the mountains. Every available frequency he could imagine was being used for some kind of transmission. Physically he only detected the frequencies silently but in his consciousness, there was the white noise cacophony of infinitely scrambled information. He soon became aware he was able to isolate individual frequencies and so interpret the information it held.

He thought of how his own dreams had flooded the world before these frequencies had been adopted by the humans. It seemed now they had created this crude but effective system of their own, feeding their desire for information and communication. Even in the days since their connection had started to fall away and they had begun to make their own way, in their sub conscious they would always have been picking up and processing the information he was dreaming. However, since he had been banished from Arimathea, they had filled the silence with their own dreams it seemed. He searched through the cacophony to find and isolate the frequencies he thought might reflect this idea.

He soon became aware of the network where they had stored and processed all their information. This network gave him instant access to the immense body of knowledge that had brought the human race to where it was. As the dragon merged his own consciousness into this network he found he was able to isolate knowledge on every aspect of Arimathea. All the science, religion and all their movements through the ages, cultures of all races, the built and natural environment and how both had evolved, how everything had always been entwined in the politics, the battles and wars constantly fought over land and sea. He found what was beautiful and what was ugly; he found what was profound and moving; all the wonder the human race had instigated for themselves and their world. But he also found far too regularly what was shameful and was clearly degrading and destroying this beautiful world. He wanted to find that Arimathea, was a world evolving towards a better time providing a stable home for all her inhabitants until the end of her natural life.

The dragon delved deeper into the web of knowledge the networks had formed around the world of Arimathea. He soon began to find the continuation of the path he had predicted would take Arimathea towards a catastrophic future. Silently he sifted through the electronic web assessing all that had developed from those early beginnings.

In those early times he had seen the rise of local economies developed through trade between villages and towns. This trading was controlled by powerful and ruthless individuals through taxation in life and fear of the terrible consequences of upsetting the alien gods in the afterlife. He had attempted to change this situation by taking the power from these individuals and the structures of fear they were building amongst the people and later by joining with the elemental spirits to inspire the gifted individuals who had maintained the ability to connect and become inspired by their world.

Now he was observing the consequences of those actions. His good intentions had not been entirely thwarted. The people of Arimathea had through their struggles, perhaps inspired by the people who had enjoyed a brief time in their history when they had been truly free, eventually evolved systems of law giving them the ability to control the activities of the most ruthless individuals.

In many parts of Arimathea governments had arisen to debate the best course of action when any major changes to their way of life was being considered. However, economies had expanded exponentially in recent times when scientific discoveries had unveiled the remarkable potential the planet of Arimathea possessed for the development of human activity. As a result, the dragon found the mechanisms of trade that had been crudely at work amongst towns and villages and very occasionally across borders and seas into other lands, now had proliferated across the entire surface of the planet.

He found in amongst the networks the evolution of cultures and political systems had allowed entirely different outlooks and ideas about their governance to emerge amongst the people of Arimathea. Crucially, he found they were all at different stages of their development towards being fully industrialised societies. This was the common thread running through all the nations of Arimathea at this time. Here was where the path had led to.

However, now it was no longer a grassy track meandering across the countryside through flower strewn meadows; occasionally passing a sparkling trout filled stream and ending in a market where everyone knew each other and for the most part had the same goals. Now the path had developed into a vast superhighway leading to a market containing all the countries of Arimathea. It was governed, monitored and manipulated the dragon found through these electronic cyber-networks.

Complex industrialised societies that had evolved over many centuries traded with countries that were only just emerging from agriculturally based economies. Countries with legal and governmental systems were trading with countries who were still governed by crude dictatorships. Their people were afforded very few of the human rights taken for granted by their fellow citizens. These varying cultures had been formed by a varied range of differing religions and philosophies. The dragon found the remnants of the religions dedicated to the alien gods survived in some of the most industrialised societies however in the remotest areas of the planet he found memories of his own race were still held. These differences often caused problems to arise in the relationships between countries and so the smooth running of the market. However, there was one common thread uniting and dividing them all; a thread all countries understood despite their culture, political system or their place in the global market.

Since the humans had first ignited the fires in the centre of their nomadic camps their fascination with the potential of the element that had shaped the universe had continued unabated. Now the dragon saw the ability to control its potential had reshaped Arimathea. Over many thousands of turnings, the humans had come to fully understand the ability of fire to transform the ores found just below the surface of Arimathea.

They had found infinite use for metals as their ability to forge and mould them had transformed much of their existence. Iron and eventually steel had transformed the world. Metal bolts in buildings were more effective than timber joints so they could be built wider and higher. Ships could be built larger and more safely and so could travel further across the oceans and so carry more men and more products. Iron sliced through flesh more effectively and warfare became more deadly. For those who possessed the knowledge and the ability to make metal, enormous advantage had been gained in trade and conquest as the humans raced for power over their fellow men and the tribes who surrounded them. But nothing in the advance of the human race had compared to the discovery and the transformations unleashed upon the planet with the discovery of the miraculous qualities of Coal and Oil.

The remains of the vast primeval forests which had covered Arimathea so extensively compressed over millions of years had created the miraculous dark fluid and the black rocks, the fossil fuels. With the explosive force of Fire at the heart of the machinery they had invented to harness its power, the humans had propelled themselves into a new era where there appeared to be no limit to what they could make, conquer and destroy.

Great mills had belched out palls of the thick black smoke fuelling and choking their expanding cites as products previously made painstakingly with human endeavour now began to be mass produced in their thousands by machines. People moved from the countryside where machines had taken over their work in the fields and were given work in the mills; A process which was even now continuing across the face of Arimathea. For the rich and already powerful who came to be in control of these new and fabulous resources the potential for exploitation of their fellow man rose out of all proportion. Populations had risen dramatically as improvements in basic medicine and sanitation improved life expectancy. There was unlimited opportunity for investment as the infrastructure of this new industrial age was being put into place and there were huge profits to be made.

Governments wanted railways and factories, power stations, power and water supply systems and eventually roads. Their countries became richer as resources were moved freely from countries where they had been bought cheaply, to countries where the products they had made could be sold expensively. Taxes again would increase on all those transactions and their armies became stronger with more and more destructive weapons. As a result, they were more able to defend the interests they had acquired before this time when states had been less sensitive about who owned or controlled their resources. In this frenzy of excitement and greed this new world had been forged. It had spread to as many countries and economies that had the resources to pay or be paid for the privileges afforded to it when joining this new industrial community.

This global market had arisen when the pressures for entire countries had become similar to those existing for the traders who had moved from town to town to sell their wares. If the person with the money wanted a better deal he could always go to the next trader. So, fortunes were won and lost. This premise, as previously in its earlier manifestation, set the structure for the entire global market and all the products and resources to make them, being bought and sold within it.

The dragon found the markets around Arimathea were dominated by the need to feed the machinery at the heart of this revolution. Now it was being run with the dwindling supplies and so the spiralling cost of the Oil still remaining. At first supplies seemed limitless when only a few countries had the ability to transform and put it to use. However, now it was fuelling the entire ravenous industrial machine fuelling the tireless global market surrounding Arimathea. Every country had to keep their own machine fuelled to keep their place within the market and generate the wealth their people now craved. For with the dream of wealth came the promise of security and happiness that would satisfy the emptiness continually gnawing away at the people of Arimathea since they had been separated from the consciousness of their world.

The emptiness they felt was continually exploited by their ruthless governments. It generated the wealth they depended on to generate the taxes they extorted from their populations they used to maintain the infrastructure of control over their countries. Now, it seemed the descendants of the power hungry individuals, the ruthless strand of the human race who had been in those earlier times the ruthless lords served by their servants the obedient scribes were now again in control of this altogether more sinister marketplace.

They could maintain the illusion amongst the ever increasing populations as long as enough of them could be provided with sufficient income to buy the endless chain of new products and entertainments offered to them; so distracting them from the suspicion they had become enslaved in an unfulfilling and meaningless existence. To provide this endless stream of products made the importance of securing the dwindling supplies of coal and oil absolutely paramount.

The consequences for Arimathea and her people as her resources had become exploited on such a vast scale was evident as climatic conditions around the entire planet were being changed. As the ravenous self-perpetuating machine parasite hungrily devoured its host it released immense volumes of gas which were gathering in the upper layers of the atmosphere where the temperature of the world was regulated. As a result, Arimathea's temperature was rising.

This was resulting in extreme weather conditions. Catastrophic droughts, ferocious storms, devastating fires and floods had become more prevalent often effecting the poorest of the planets people and the areas where large proportions of the planet's food was grown. As deserts expanded and starvation threatened, entire populations started to move into their neighbouring countries where resources were also under pressure.

The resulting conflict was already causing terrible wars between previously hospitable neighbours. As rainfall patterns changed, the supply of fresh water had become unpredictable and in addition many of Arimathea's rivers had become so polluted, as other by products from increasing levels of industrial activity were flushed without concern into them, they were of little use to the growing populations who had previously depended on them. Temperate and tropical zones were affected, jungles and woodlands, grasslands and savannahs all were under stress as were all the wild creatures who inhabited them. He had always known; the beauty of Arimathea's interconnectedness was limitless. But now it seemed what had previously made her so beautiful and had been her strength now appeared to be slowly killing her.

As he searched through the vast concentrations of information in the giant communication networks, the dragon found little evidence of the optimism he had hoped to find. However, he could not believe the revolutionary spirit of the human race who had made contact and been awakened all those years before had been completely dissipated. So, he searched deeper feeling for the gentle courageous spirits who had risked everything and fought for all the beauty and wonder they had found. He searched for their legacy, the trace they had left in the world to continue the struggle through the centuries. He searched where he thought he might find them, standing up to the injustice they saw was ravaging their world.

Where would they be making their feelings known at this time he wondered in the light of all he had discovered? He imagined they would be most concerned about the overall health of the planetary environment so under threat from the pollution of the machine age. So, he delved into the networks where information was stored about the indiscriminate mining and the destruction of the great forests. There of course he found them and to his surprise and delight he started to unravel a remarkable development in the history of Arimathea.

At first, they had existed only in their protest movements as they had begun to understand the threats. Then as the years went by their protest movements had become legitimate organisations. They became funded by the wider populations who also had become increasingly worried about the degradation of their world. Their worries had become backed up by the scientists who ran computer models predicting what would happen to the climate if levels of pollution were not reduced. They worked at new ways of harnessing Arimathea's natural resources and dreamed of a world which would be run by the power of the wind and the radiation from the Star which they knew to be infinite. But as they worked on their theories and their dreams the machine world continued to fill the atmosphere with pollution and to use ever increasing amounts of the fuels which had become increasingly difficult to find and expensive to extricate from the depths of Arimathea.

Meanwhile the scientists became ever more vocal backed up by ever more powerful computer models and the increasing power of the environmental organisations. Slowly a shift had started to take place amongst the political structures of Arimathea. The threat to the well-being of the delicately balanced developed economies intricately entwined with developing countries suddenly had become apparent. The shrinking of fertile land mass and the changing of weather conditions across the planet together with dwindling and more expensive supplies of the traditional fossil-based fuels seemed like a threat to just about everything including world peace. So, all the nations of Arimathea started to meet and soon everyone was blaming everyone else for what was happening. Clearly some were more to blame than others but then after years of argument and meaningless treaties, the nations of Arimathea finally agreed to reduce the amounts of their pollution.

Still the pollution increased and they all met again and slowly they realised if there was no consequence to any one nation ignoring the agreement nothing would ever happen. So, the council of Arimathea introduced enormous fines and sanctions for the nations who refused to play their part in this global effort. In turn, in the most polluting countries, laws were introduced and legislation for corporations unwilling to help in their country's efforts. They started to specify the amount of fuel burnt in the creation of everything from automobiles and aeroplanes to power stations and the efficiency they had to achieve to reduce the overall pollution of their country. Still the amounts of pollution rose.

It was at this time, it seemed the politicians of the world suddenly understood what the idea of renewable energy meant. It was readily available and it could reduce the pollution enough to avoid paying the crippling fines. So they went to the small companies who were making a few windmills here and putting a few solar panels on a large house somewhere else and asked them...

"How much energy can you produce using this technology?"

The answer they received and which they wanted to hear was of course...

'UNLIMITED!'.

Governments suddenly realised what this meant. Across the planet they brought in subsidies for organisations to start building as many windmills as they could and gave tax breaks for anyone who would put solar panels on their roofs or in their fields or across the deserts. They would pay them for the energy they did not use because the amount they would pay towards the subsidies and tax breaks was inconsequential compared to the fines they would incur if their pollution levels did not come down. All this had resulted in a huge explosion in the renewable energy industry.

Solar arrays started to be built across deserts and other wildernesses of Arimathea producing the power equivalent to several power stations. Wind turbines were planted in their hundreds across the seas shallow and stable enough to stand them in the wind streams of the world which were rarely still. Eventually the subsidies and the tax breaks evaporated as the costs of mass production brought the costs of all the machinery down. But a new stream of energy had been born on Arimathea. It was the ray of light the dragon had been looking for. In all the darkness of the strengthening grip of Oblivion, the initiative and the ingenuity of the human race and the love they had for their world had found a way of surfacing at this critical time.

The beautifully regulated world that had slowly come to be amidst the gentle dreams he had brought from across the universe was in chaos it seemed. But the humans had found a way and were attempting for whatever reason to change the destiny of their world. It was what he had hoped to find and he was greatly relieved. With this finding he decided he would leave the electronic networks the humans had created to lock in everything they knew. He would return to the natural world to which he was better accustomed and further explore Arimathea and the creatures the humans had become in the world they had dreamed for themselves.

Chapter Forty.

The Human race.

He found them first in their fields toiling in conditions changed little since those last days when he had last flown back to the Dragon hill. Fathers and mothers worked with sons and daughters tirelessly through the days tempting whatever they could out of the ground to support their meagre existence. They tended their livestock in the grasslands where they had not been taken over by the industrialised farms creeping deeper and deeper into the wildernesses of Arimathea. They ploughed their fields with ancient ploughs unchanged for generations and planted the seeds left over from the previous years' harvest. In the heat of the midday star they would settle in the shade of the trees gently talking or dozing. Their children stayed close and quietly played as their parents re-gathered their strength for their evening toil. Mothers carried their youngest offspring continually, tenderly administering to their needs as they indicated their hunger or their thirst. At the end of the day they went home to their crude houses where they would eat the minimal meals their labours could provide. Many days there would not be enough to satiate their hunger and they would go to sleep hungry.

The dragon had come to one of the last great savannah wildernesses surviving on Arimathea. These ancient tribes, some of the oldest on Arimathea, shared these lands with wild animals they would have previously hunted for their livelihood. Now the animals were protected by organisations in the industrialised world whose previous generations had relentlessly hunted them to near extinction. Now the children and grandchildren of the hunters travelled from these countries on their holidays and paid to see these rare creatures. The hungry families watched as the well fed, well dressed families rode across their wildernesses in sophisticated land cruisers. They were told the foreign tourists brought money to the country and it was in their interest not to kill the animals despite the hunger they frequently suffered. The dragon found there was little evidence any of the money had reached the hungry families and he witnessed the confusion amongst the families in the land cruisers as they passed through the villages and wondered of the plight of their brothers and sisters living in such poverty.

They had been assured at least a percentage of the profits from their visit would benefit the tribe's people as well as helping in the protection of the animals. The farmers looked on as they passed and could only dream and yearn for the lives they presumed these privileged folks must lead. Many of their brothers had decided to make the journey to the industrialised cities attempting to find some share of this wealth. They were rarely heard of again. Others had migrated across the continent to lawless states where they would be recruited as soldiers into the latest revolutionary militia preparing to overthrow it's legitimate but corrupt government. Here he found for the first time the strange paradoxical nature of the predicament in which the human race now found itself as he moved through the consciousness of both families.

From the luxury of the land cruiser Frank, looked out at the families who were tending their land. He saw them happily working together with their animals. They looked a little underfed but he assumed they were fit and healthy. He saw they would be rewarded by the effort they put in and presumably had knowledge that had been used to farm their land for many generations. As he passed through the villages, he sensed smaller families had merged into larger families struggling together through whatever difficulty their community might face and he was surprised to find he rarely saw an unhappy person. There appeared to be no resentment as they drifted past in the clouds of dust the large expensive vehicles created. On the contrary the people seemed delighted to see them and always waved ecstatically as they passed.

He thought of his own life from which he had briefly and expensively escaped. He winced when he thought of the pressures he constantly endured to maintain the life he had built around himself and he was expected to maintain in the world he and his family lived. Or was it existed? The costs had escalated as his family had grown and so the responsibilities he had undertaken to command a higher salary had also expanded. Deadlines had become tighter and there was little room for mistakes of any kind. He knew there were younger men who would always be attempting to move into his position if a slip up should ever occur. The debt he had accumulated to pay for the house and this life, his family now inhabited could only be serviced by the large salary he was earning. He felt he lived on the edge of a precipice where he was forced to stand and balance with the threat the ground could crumble at any time.

He looked down at his eldest son who was playing a computer game on one of the more expensive devices it seemed their lives now demanded. Without it he had been assured he would have been an outcast amongst his schoolmates. Now the wildlife they had been promised seemed sparse, he had taken to playing it to fend off the boredom of travelling through the endless landscapes as the land cruiser chased after the elusive animals. His wife was deep in conversation on her cell phone probably to one of her friends back in the city. He shuddered to think what it might be costing to bounce her conversation from the middle of nowhere here, up to a state of the art satellite silently hanging high in space and then down to a house or another vehicle cruising through the suburbs on the other side of the planet. He hoped the conversation was of some critical importance but suspected it was not. The simple life of the farmer therefore started to look very enticing.

There was an incomprehensible crackle through the on-board radio. The driver changed direction immediately and increased his speed as he sped over the rough terrain. He turned to the family in the back of the land cruiser and excitedly shouted.

"Lions have been spotted at a kill."

He was also pointing out into the distance. His passengers scanned the horizon but could see nothing yet as they crashed through the dusty bush. Their driver gleefully it appeared seemed to be taking the most pitted and undulating route and the family spent most of this period in mid-air between the comfortable seats and the ceiling. Remarkably the land cruiser stayed upright despite the drivers every attempt to roll it over. Eventually much to everybody's relief they were able to see another dusty trail converging on a pride of lions in the distance.

As they drew up to a safe distance, binoculars were trained on the feasting animals. Nine lions were tearing into, what in the recent past, would have been an old water buffalo. The lions were attacking the corpse of the massive beast ravenously. There may have been some hierarchy at play within the pride but now each one of the lions tore and ripped into the corpse as if this was the last meal they would ever have. The older lions spat and growled at their younger offspring who depending on their size and confidence growled back and resumed their feast. There was no time for prolonged argument at this stage as the flesh of the buffalo was rapidly disappearing.

Vultures were also starting to arrive in greater numbers wheeling down from the thermals on their enormous wings. The lions swiped and hissed at them and the vultures retreated for now and waited as their numbers increased to pick over the bones when the lions had removed the bulk of the meat. This was the first kill the family had witnessed since their arrival. They watched in stunned silence as the lions now covered in the blood being pumped at pressure from the severed arteries of the unfortunate beast systematically devoured its lifeless carcass. As the numbers of the vultures were increasing rapidly and with the bulk of the meat safely in their now distended stomachs, reluctantly the lions left the scattered pile of bones and retreated to the shade of a nearby thorn tree. The vultures immediately descended on the remains in a chaotic screeching cacophony and fought over the last scraps of the corpse.

The lions collapsed in the shade under the weight of the raw meat they were now carrying. They appeared to make a half-hearted attempt to clean the blood and remains from their coats before gradually succumbing to sleep in the mid-afternoon Starshine. There were exclamations of approval from the family as the land cruiser again resumed its journey across the savannah at a more sedate speed. Each reflected on what they had seen as they flashed through the photographs they had taken on their cameras. It was the first glimpse of the raw uncompromising brutality of wildlife they had seen since they had arrived and everyone had been suitably impressed. Frank was relieved not only because at last some enthusiasm was being shown for this expensive holiday but also that the spectacle had provided some respite from the endless bleeping of the computer game and the long-distance call to Straam had been terminated.

He himself had been shocked to register his own reaction. As he watched the wild animals tearing into the water buffalo and the subsequent squabbles erupting amongst the pride, he saw a strange reflection of his own life as an employee in the global corporation in which he worked. He decided the water buffalo could represent any one of the contracts allocated to his department each year to be secured. As a relatively small part of a corporation that had absorbed companies of every description, Frank's department was continually involved in the business of finding and purchasing land from which their mining subsidiary would then extract whatever wealth lay beneath the soil. These opportunities had become fewer and further apart over the years and so the legal transactions became ever harder to secure. The relationship he had with his colleagues had become ever more competitive as a result and once the possibility of a potential site had been identified the feeding frenzy began.

If a country or state was involved, every politician, councillor or minor dignitary was sought out and approached to find the precious influence that would secure the deal, the commission and ultimately the possibility of gaining favour with Harri Wade, the Chief executive and majority share-holder of the Wade International Trading Corporation. A signature on a contract securing profitable mining rights to WITC for perhaps half a century would take Frank or any of his colleagues into the next layer of comfort they and their wives had dreamt of and had made it their goal to achieve.

So, while supposedly acting as a team, the level of deceit, betrayal and disloyalty escalated out of all control as the ultimate prize of a life free from the worry of paying the bills came within their grasp. The lions suddenly seemed almost tame as some of the most infamous incidents passed through his mind. Luckily Frank himself had not been abandoned in a war-torn country without identity or money for the bribes that would often make the difference between life and death. Blackmail was common and some inappropriate incident, if discovered in a past life could be resurrected and used in exchange for access to the pen that would sign the contract.

The dragon felt Frank shudder as he imagined Harri Wade standing in his office overlooking Central Avenue in Straam. He would be considering possibilities for his empire as throughout the organisation his employees tore mercilessly into each other's lives for a place at the table stretching expansively down the plate glass office frontage. Frank's shift in consciousness was all the dragon needed to transfer his own consciousness across the measureless interconnected light filled sea of molecules, atoms and quarks separating the wild savannah plains and the office high in the glass clad Wade corporation skyscraper.

Harri was indeed standing looking out over Straam. The steel towers competing greedily for space all around him showed no sign of life behind the smoked glass facades. Harri's paranoia told him however, all his competitors were over there plotting to replace his market share with cheaper coal or cheaper ores and so undercut the sizeable monopoly he held in the steel industry.

He was a tall, grey haired man with steely blue eyes, his strong lean frame was dressed immaculately in a dark blue suit from the finest tailor in the city. He held much of the information he needed to run the Wade corporation in his own mind. He had come to trust no one. The computers in which his employees stored information and did much of their business he trusted even less. He had decided the only way to gain his employees loyalty was to pay them above whatever his competitors could offer them. To maintain this privilege, he knew there was little they would not do for him. He knew all their strengths and weaknesses and frequently covertly exploited them as he shrewdly manipulated circumstances to his advantage in all areas of their lives. He would also sack them at the first sign of any insubordination to protect his complete control.

The dragon sifted through the information in the chief executive's consciousness. So, this was the state-of-the-art human predator. His empire seemed to spread entirely around the planet of Arimathea and involved mining and drilling operations in some of the poorest countries. He owned refineries and smelting plants processing raw materials that in turn would be used in his factories to make products ranging from cars to the smallest of household appliances.

The dragon delved through Harri's consciousness to find how his corporation operated in the wider global economy. He found a network of influences and connections which enabled incredible sums of money to flow around the world fuelling the almost infinitely interconnected marketplace which now had arisen on Arimathea. It flowed through countries and governments, it was held by investors and banks intent on seeing their power grow. Governments in every country wanted to attract business and development to their country or trading block so they controlled and legislated as much as they dared to become more attractive to the generators of the power and wealth they craved for themselves and the people who voted them into power. Near the top of their list were the global corporations: Harri Wade and his competitors in the global market. The corporations in turn needed to attract the investors and the banks who would supply the money for the operations which would enable them to expand and so grow their influence.

Once they had invested, they put pressure on the corporation to maximise their profits and so the returns on their investment. This put pressure on the corporations to produce more for less and less. They used their power and wealth to set up their factories in the countries where the approach to human rights was less rigorous enabling them to manufacture for considerably less than they could in their own countries. The governments of these countries encouraged these enterprises despite the exploitation of their own people so the money and the power would continue to flow into their own banks. They then could maintain power for themselves.

The international geopolitical community had become a complex web of diplomacy, interrelated interest, power mongering, deceit and thinly disguised blackmail. As the reserves of the essential fuel driving the whole machine became scarcer, the countries who possessed the declining supplies found themselves with the power to manipulate the fuel hungry nations. In previous times they had been ruthlessly exploited for resources which now had become less important. They were often the most vulnerable and ill equipped to defend themselves or prevent uprising within their own people. Their subsequent domestic vulnerability might often mean they had decided they wanted to keep these valuable resources for themselves and the benefit of their own people.

So regional wars and skirmishes to depose uncooperative governments backed by the larger opposing power blocks to preserve their own interest in the fuel supplies had become another unsavoury factor in the struggle to keep the machine trundling on. This of course increased the chances of a serious confrontation between the major powers in the world. The dragon felt the pressure of this delicate balance across the face of Arimathea in the head and consciousness of Harri Wade as he considered the fortunes of his own corporation.

The dragon felt the calculation in his head and the risks he took every day to maintain his edge. It seemed this man knew what his company was making in terms of money and the business it was doing globally in each and every moment. As he made his assessment, he was continually formulating strategies to optimise the overall performance. As he stood looking over the avenue, he decided he would close two factories in one country and expand a larger factory in another. His overheads again were reduced and so his profits rose. The dragon observed as Harri journeyed in his mind making the connections through the network of his company so he could rationalise or adjust any aspect he thought could be improved and be made more profitable.

The dragon was reminded of his own powers to dream into and through the world. Dreams that could gently guide a world through its evolution; dreams that could infiltrate sensitive minds so the optimum decision could be made in the right set of circumstances. Here was a human who was evolving his own dream; Although destructive and detrimental to Arimathea he had significant power and the dragon realised the influence this single man could have on events all around the planet.

The dragon watched the executive as he turned to his table, pressed a button on his telephone. He greeted his secretary who had just arrived and rattled off a list of the executives he wanted to see immediately in his office. Then he returned to the window to resume his observations of the city, relishing the panic he had initiated amongst the highest rank of his organisation. The rush hour was at its height as the residents of Straam and the surrounding suburbs battled their way through the streets to get to their places of work. However now a battle of a more deadly kind was about to resume.

Harri heard the loud unmistakable cracks of gunfire echoing up through the canyon of steel and glass. It was hard to see what had happened from the forty-second floor although it seemed commuters were running chaotically away from the scene. The dragon now curious for further insight into city life disconnected from Harri and moved his consciousness down the vertical face of the skyscraper to the street below.

The dragon expanded his consciousness into the scene before him. The scale of the street and the towering buildings lining it on both sides had unsurprisingly, left none of the features the dragon remembered from his previous visit. He felt the resonance of the millions of years left by trees and hills and streams that once had existed here. Even the animals that had walked through here were still present as echoes from that previous era. He could sense the bears who had fished in the river now running beneath the street in a concrete tunnel, felt their intense concentration as they watched for the protein rich fish that would feed them through their winter hibernation. He felt the deer as they wandered silently through the towering pine trees now replaced by the towers of steel and glass and he heard the growls of the cats and the distant cries of the eagles as they hunted through the land. He felt the people who had lived here, travelling the river in their canoes, trading with their neighbouring settlements living harmoniously with all they found around them. He sensed how all he was feeling had been deeply ingrained into their culture and how it had been continued in the lessons they had been taught and which they would teach their children as it had been through generations and generations.

Now the dragon could see nothing of that world. It had been lost for ever and remained only in the sad memories of Arimathea. The dragon felt her loss as he surveyed the scene she now had become. In amongst the concrete and glass almost devoid of life other than the multitude of humans, rats, feral pigeons and the smaller insect life that had been able to adapt to this new environment, a tragedy had unravelled. In the trace left in the molecules of the light filled street the dragon sensed an argument had ensued. A deal had been made and broken; terms misunderstood. The money owed in turn was owed and as was the way of the world and of human business was owed and owed and owed, was unable to be paid breaking a chain of transactions that perhaps would end in further tragedy later in the day. Yet here was the tragedy at the very beginning of the chain.

Two desperate immigrants, from a distant land where their brothers may still have been working in the fields with their families, had argued. Both had been carrying firearms. They had both hoped they would be able to shoot their combatant before they themselves became victim to the endless cycle of violence proliferating through the strata of life in which they now existed. The dragon could sense the paths of the three bullets as they had travelled across the street. One passed harmlessly through the window of a coffee shop on the other side of the street narrowly missing all the customers as they consumed the final boost enabling them to return to their pressurised servitude high in the towers. Another tragically passed through the skull of the immigrant who had owed the money and who in his final moment of life on Arimathea had released another bullet which had then travelled across the street and passed through the lower abdomen of a young woman called Grace, who had been thinking she had not seen her mother and father for far too long.

The street was now deserted as most people had fled in terror of being caught in further crossfire. The immigrant lay lifelessly across the kerb amongst the grey cortex that had contained all his life had been, all the memories he had held. His soul was now continuing its journey deeper into the mystery. The dragon sensed the young woman was alive. He moved into her consciousness. She was far away from the tragedy that had engulfed her. Her mother had prepared a wonderful meal. Her father, brothers and sisters sat around a table greedily eyeing the feast. She was pleased they were all here and wished they could be together more often. She smiled over at her father who proudly sat amongst the family he had successfully raised. He opened a bottle and moved around the table pouring the wine into each one of their glasses. He sat at the head of the table and proposed a toast.

"To being together!"

They cheered and clinked their glasses together and the love between them flowed freely through the light around them and the smells of the cooked food and the sweet tasting liquid. But the light of their love was engulfing her. Beyond the room the young woman could hear sirens rapidly approaching and there was someone else in the room holding her there, holding back the light. She turned to see who it was but there was no one. She felt only her life; life she had not sensed or been aware of in a similar way before, being supported by everything beyond her and that was contained within the light. She decided she could settle into the warmth she felt at the table and she remembered all the times she had spent with the people who sat around her. Here was where 'beyond' started. Here was where her connection with the infinity holding her life force began, feeding her with unknown energies from the heart of star fields and galaxies that had been brought and were held in this world. She knew she was safe and continued to drift through the memories that had bought her to this moment. She felt her memories had led her here and would not end here and they would lead her into her future. There was too much she had not resolved; she had not completed her own journey into everything contained within this strange comforting light.

The paramedics arrived in the street. The dragon felt her life force strengthening as they stabilised Grace's vital bodily functions. He felt the boost from the infusion of chemicals they injected into her blood stream and the oxygen they passed into her body from the respirator. He felt how they were able to stem the flow of blood from the wound the bullet had left as it had torn through her body. He felt how they worked tirelessly in the cramped conditions of the vehicle in which they sped through the streets of Straam to keep her alive. He sensed the knowledge they held was the result of centuries of discovery and understanding of human physiology condensed into their education giving them this ability to hold her life in their hands.

For the first time the dragon felt the remnants of the indigenous peoples who had hunted here with the mountain lions and the bears. They had learnt new sophisticated skills to keep themselves alive in this new environment. The danger from the natural threats of their world had been entirely replaced by the dangerous pressures the marketplace was now exerting on the city. The bullets had been fired from the guns of immigrants who were ill equipped to cope with those pressures. They had been fighting for their lives just as if they had been confronted by an angry bear in the woods and the result all these centuries later was the same. Someone would have to die for the other to live.

Now Grace and the dragon were racing down wide artificially lit corridors. They were administered to by a new set of individuals who continually observed and reacted to the array of machinery which was now monitoring Grace's dwindling life. They crashed through another set of doors out of the chaos of the overstretched city hospital into the calm and sterile environment of the operating theatre. Grace was carefully positioned underneath the bright white lights. Tubes carefully inserted by the paramedics in the ambulance now connected her into a further array of machinery. The surgeons arrived, sterilised and covered with face masks. They briefly discussed the scene now confronting them and then quickly went to work to save Grace's life. They cut boldly through her skin exposing the damaged organs. They inserted further tubes into veins and arteries rerouting her remaining blood stream away from the injury.

The dragon felt her life force continually fluctuating as the leading surgeon delved amongst her internal organs assessing the full extent of the damage to her body. The dragon sensed his presence and authority, moved through into this new consciousness where he found the combined knowledge of many generations. He sensed the years of dedication and training this individual had applied to his chosen profession giving him the experience enabling him to make the decisions that would save Grace's life. The dragon sensed the calm urgency and expertise as he worked and guided his team of nurses, technicians and anaesthetists.

"The bullet has passed fairly cleanly through her liver which is why she has lost so much blood. It has not been destroyed so has continued to function at a low level. She has been lucky it has not hit any large blood vessels. But the liver has been damaged severely and I think we will have to replace it if she has any chance of survival. Somebody call through to see if we have a suitable donor liver in the city ready to transplant in the next couple of hours. Much more and I think we may lose her."

A junior surgeon hurried away from the operating table and made a call to another part of the hospital. He explained the situation concisely and then explained the search had begun. The surgeon looked up at the clock. He looked down at Grace's face. The dragon sensed his emotion for the first time as he connected with the life of this young woman who had been caught up in the series of events resulting in her lying here unconscious rather than beginning another dull and laborious day at the desk in her office.

He looked up at the monitors. He had managed to stabilise her and she would not be in pain and oblivious to the trauma she was undergoing. Then he looked down at the cavity where the damaged liver had been removed. Her blood was now flowing through a machine which would perform the processes of the damaged liver for only so long. The race was on to find the new liver. The surgeon knew this relied on another tragic situation in which another unfortunate soul may have already lost their life. He examined the clamps and the connections to the tubes diverting her blood. They were holding well; he had done a good job. He and his team had become used to these operations as the use of firearms had resulted in a proliferation of gunshot wounds in the city. He had lost many lives as he had battled to remedy the savage consequences of bullets passing through human bodies. There was little resistance until they hit bones when everything became a lot more complicated. Grace's bullet had narrowly missed her spine and so she had avoided certain paralysis. Would her luck hold now as the computers searched the hospitals for a suitable liver to match her blood type?

The dragon searched also. He sent a powerful transformative thought out through the city in search of a resolution to this distressing predicament. He did not want Grace to die. In the time he had shared her consciousness he knew her to be a kind soul who was loved by her friends and her family. Her tragic death would reverberate through the city but would soon be forgotten by all except those who were closest to her and who possibly may never fully recover from losing her.

The irony was not lost on the dragon. The immigrant who had accidentally shot Grace had travelled from the squalor of his existence in the city slum of his struggling country to improve his own family's chances of escaping from the dreadful poverty which surrounded them. Now there was a possibility he had destroyed another life, another family as in his desperation he had fallen victim to the dark forces of Oblivion operating within the city. The dragon thought of his beloved Arimathea as he dwelt in Grace's drifting consciousness. Was there some cosmic surgeon, perhaps the alien gods, able and willing to save her with their knowledge of planetary physiology if the damage to her life forces became critical?

The soft but urgent ring tone of the telephone immediately grabbed everyone's attention in the theatre. The junior surgeon answered the phone and listened to the voice attentively. A smile came over his face and he looked back at the team with a delighted look on his face.

"You are not going to believe this but the guy who was killed in the same incident by some mad and beautiful coincidence has the same blood group as Grace. His body was on the way to the city morgue but now has been diverted and is on its way here and should arrive very shortly!"

The team cheered and exclaimed with delight and disbelief. The surgeon looked down at Grace and smiled to himself.

"There is someone looking after you to today, Gracie!"

Chapter Forty-One.
Service.

Okino and Mariella had made their way back to the ruins after the dragon's return to the hill. They had immediately realised their time to be there had passed as they sat by the waterfall. They had exchanged their reminiscences of the previous days and relived the brief meeting with the dragon on the top of the shattered hill. They had both been disappointed the dragon had been unable to spend some more time with them but agreed after such a separation it was probably understandable he wanted to return to Arimathea without any further delay. They decided he also probably imagined any further time on the surface of Arimathea might be interpreted by the forces of Oblivion as further interference in planetary affairs which had previously brought so much trouble upon him and his world.

However, he had indicated how their journey should proceed. He had said Okino had unfinished business in the city which seemed strange since as he had never been there and that Mariella's father was missing her. Okino could only think he had meant he would find some resolution to the poisoning of the river flowing into the lake while Mariella knew her father would be missing her as she was desperately missing him.

Then there had been silence between them. The moon had risen higher that night and its bright reflection left the atmosphere shimmering as light from the surface of the rippling pool washed over the surrounding rocks and trees. Okino had been leaning on the rock against which they had settled the night they had arrived. Mariella had gone over to her tent. She pulled one of the yak skins out and indicated to Okino to move over so she could sit next to him. She wrapped the great skin around them both and snuggled into him lifting his arm over her so she could get as close to his body as she could. For a few moments they shared the extraordinary beauty of the scene before them.

"So, did you miss me, Okino."

Okino was not surprised by her question. As they had been discussing the previous days the tension between them to avoid talking about or acting upon what they were clearly both thinking had become increasingly difficult.

"I did miss you Mariella. Actually, far more than I thought I would and of course it raises all sorts of questions…"

"So, what sort of questions are those Okino?"

"Well, it crossed my mind perhaps Merilon and Arimathea had somehow engineered this situation so they could experience their world and each other through us as we became closer. I felt in the hills after you left as if I was seeing the world through your eyes and perhaps Arimathea's as well as my own."

"Do you think that was their only intention?"

Mariella wriggled even closer to Okino.

"I'm not sure I will ever understand or guess the intentions of Merilon and Arimathea as far as we are concerned. It just felt like a possibility since we have both become close to them. Judging from the mess we find on this planet it seems they have never had a clear plan as to what might or might not happen as a result of their actions"

"So, do you think they play with outcomes. Perhaps they put impossible circumstances together when the opportunity arises to see what wonders might eventually emerge. Look at all the fabulous animals on this world. Haven't they gradually evolved as a result of the challenges presented to them or do you think the dragons have just dreamed out the leopards and the lizards and the dolphins as they have been before on another doomed world?"

"The precise mechanics of evolution may always be a mystery to us but when all is said and done, I am not a leopard, Mariella, I am a simple monk of the most Sacred Dragon Order, dedicated to the service of Arimathea. At the root of all that has happened so far are the practices we have adopted over many centuries. The deep connection with Arimathea she has guided us to maintain. But do not think I dismiss for an instant the part you have played. I think in your own life you have made your own deep connection with her. Even though you haven't been living in a remote village in the mountains."

"I had always felt something. Even when we were splashing around in streams and climbing trees, I never felt I was alone and I don't think you analyse stuff too much when you are a child, you just accept everything as if everything is as it should be."

"Your world seems to drag you out of all that, dismisses your experience and plunges you into the machine world so you become part of it and subsequently completely enveloped, almost consumed by it. But Arimathea called and you recognized her voice speaking to you. She has brought you here so we can combine these gifts she has given us to help her."

"The feeling has become more intense and closer almost as if she is inside me, has become a part of me as perhaps you and Merilon have and now we are all acting together as one as we start this new part of our journey."

They are quiet for a few moments. In all the excitement the fabulous connection they had found had not been fully assimilated. Now in the moonlight they allowed it to settle and they felt the enormous pleasure of this new state of being together with the supernatural powers of their world. They wriggled in a little closer together. Then Okino continued

"'That is what l meant when I said they are experiencing and acting through us and now the dragon has again been allowed to return to Arimathea I am certain our mission is not over."

Okino was quiet again. He felt the moment and all the magic and wonder flowing around them. He looked down into Mariella's startling turquoise eyes shining in the moonlight. He felt the wise old time-traveller shaman who had never been far away since the night by the fire in the forest when they had awoken the dragon together.

"And don't think I haven't thought about what I presume you are alluding to; perhaps even what the dragon and Arimathea have desired for themselves. But you will have to trust my instincts here. When I met Arimathea in the snowstorm, I felt an older person than I am now who had possibly lived through similar times possibly on other worlds and as you said when we first met in Aharri there are many energies and forces concentrating on this world. Arimathea warned me about them and they will know about us now. They will be here with us watching and waiting for us to take some action they can take advantage of, either now or in the future.

You are a beautiful girl, Mariella, and I am entirely with you on this now, well I hope I am anyway. What could be more beautiful than us being together, now, in this beautiful place? But you know as well as I do everything would change from that point on. Our lives would take a different course perhaps not conducive to our original intention which was, although we never said it out loud, to attempt to in some way change the course of events on this world which are bringing about its destruction. We have been brought together as individuals with the power we carry between us and look what we have already achieved. We dare not risk future events for our own pleasure now. After all we can always be together when all this is over if that is what is meant to be."

There had been quiet again between them. All the magic they and the myriad of pilgrims had found in this place left the Water and the Mountain grasses and the boulders, the fish as they swayed gently, invisibly in the pool before them, possibly even from the peaks of the magnificent mountains surrounding them, spiralled around them, through and around them, filling them with the infinite Love which had originated in some far distant ethereal time, long before the stars shining down on them had come into being. Now it was here between them holding them together, forging bonds that would never be fully severed despite all that would come between them in their future lives. Mariella moved closer to Okino and kissed him on the cheek; lingered slightly longer than she had done before.

"Of course, you are right, my beautiful wise monk. Not that I was wrong of course. I just wanted to see if I could, well, have the conversation and I am glad we have because, well you know any way."

Okino laughed and kissed her on the forehead and she playfully hit him on the chest and they laughed and told their stories together in the moonlight until they fell asleep in the hide of the old yak.

Chapter Forty-two
Diversion in the Mountains.

As the dragon moved through the layers of consciousness underlying the world of Arimathea and began to explore all she had become, all the multi-dimensional forces of the universe concentrated there, sensed his return. The state of balance existing on the planet had already shifted as the strength of light and creation held in his own being was registered and respectfully acknowledged. This change had been noticed in areas of the consciousness with the ability to detect such subtle changes. Many of the most ancient species both plant and animal that had travelled down through time had the ability to sense the change as it occurred. Deep in their ancient cells, reproduced and copied down millions of generations since those early times when the Love between the dragon and Arimathea had brought the first stirrings of life to their world, there was an awareness the power of their alliance had returned.

Again, the yearning for the deep future beckoned; a future demanding it should be reached, for there was held the fabulous wonders as yet undreamed by those who had carried the legacy of the early instigation. Now the wonder was being knowingly squandered by humanity. All feeling the echo of the ancient dream reverberating down through time became enlivened as the chemistry carrying those complex primordial codes was again being reactivated. In those whispers was heard the potential that would remain undiscovered if the current path was adhered to. The ripple caused by this silent ignition in those cellular structures spread silently and irreversibly and was absorbed once again into the living fabric of Arimathea.

By morning the full effect of the creative forces released with the reunification of the dragon and Arimathea was being felt throughout the planet. As a result, Okino and Mariella now found they had no time to prolong their stay beside the river in the ruins. There were places certainly in the near future to which they had to travel as quickly as the horses would carry them. With little ceremony they packed up their camp in the knowledge they had unravelled the legend held in the decaying fabric of Asima.

They had left the ruins almost compelled by the need to leave that part of the story behind so the new chapter could start to unravel as quickly as possible. They talked little after the decision had been made other than to consult each other on the practicalities of packing their belongings onto the three horses. They both had wondered as they rode out through the dilapidated buildings so delightfully reclaimed by nature whether they would ever return. Then they became silent as they joined the dusty road which would take them eventually down to the coast and the old sea town of Zedocha. The journey would take many days and through further deserted mountainous regions. They would follow the course of the river down to the sea across the flood plains it had created through increasingly populated areas.

They soon fell into a steady travelling routine. Still the weather was hot and dusty. However large black clouds had been gathering over the distant mountains. As yet, they had not been bothered by substantial rainfall other than light showers on the fringes of the storms as they circulated around the mountain valleys. They rarely hurried the horses who seemed happy enough to continue at the sedate pace Mariella saw fit to continue. Progress seemed at times painfully slow and could have been tedious and monotonous had Mariella not introduced Okino to one of the travelling games she had picked up from one of her previous fellow travellers. It relied on the premise each traveller would have an unlimited collection of stories and information built up during their lifetime. Of course, many of these topics would arise in the normal run of conversation but each set of stories was subject to the continual edit of each storyteller. In the game however the previous storyteller would have to name the next subject which in turn would relate to the previous story. Mariella and Okino were still curious about each other's lives and so they named subjects about where and how they had lived. As the hours went on they were systematically gathering a fuller picture of each other's lives as the horses plodded on through the landscape.

They were two days into this new part of their journey and Mariella had started to tell a story, at Okino's request, about her brother who had joined her Father's law firm once he had graduated from his expensive college.

"My father made him start at the bottom of the office hierarchy. He became a pupil to one of the senior defence lawyers. He had moved out of our family home and was living with some of his friends in a house in a district adjacent to the office. All he had to do was turn up for work every morning and stay out of trouble while he did his apprenticeship so he could prove to my father and more importantly the other partners in the firm he could be a sensible member of the company; for a while all seemed to be going well. Nick was turning up for work on time and seemed to be responding well to his training. Increasingly, though he was unable to be contacted at the weekends, which was fine for a while and no one seemed to think much of it. But it was going on and on and he had not been home for months and my mother was becoming increasingly worried. However, at the beginning of the week he would start at the office as if everything was just as it should be.

On the insistence of my mother, father had called him up to his office one morning and confronted him with the facts and why he had not been home for so long. Nick had said he and his friends had started a band. They were going out to one of his friend's houses to rehearse every weekend. They had become deeply involved in this new work and felt if they worked hard enough before long they would be playing in the clubs of Straam. Nick was a competent guitarist, so nobody thought any more about it other than my mother who was not at all convinced by this story.

She hired a detective she knew on the Straam police force. She asked him to follow Nick on one of these weekends. The truth was very different as it turned out; although there was a band involved. Well, several bands actually. The detective followed him as he drove way across the country to the next city. Nick had driven deep into a rundown area and parked next to a club into which he disappeared. He came out ten minutes later with a carrier bag which he then put in the back of his car. The detective followed him back across the country, this time to a remote country house up in the wooded hills. There were steel gates and a telecom system on the gate. The detective had to wait as Nick disappeared inside. However, within an hour more people started turning up. A continual stream of young people in fact and a number of huge sound systems had started up. The detective, who was not much older than many of these new visitors, managed to buy a ticket and got in with the crowds who were now arriving. He soon found out a gathering had been organised and was starting to evolve amongst three sound stages in the grounds of this enormous country house.

As the party progressed bands played on alternating stages entertaining the increasing numbers of young people continuing to arrive. On one stage he noticed a female singer, whom he later described as 'a very talented young woman' who was the singer for what seemed to be one of the better bands. He found Nick standing in the front row enjoying the music with the rest of the revellers. He also noticed there were a number of shadowy figures moving through the crowd selling pills. They were having no problem selling them as they seemed to further enhance the experience of the music and the atmosphere generally.

Unfortunately, when one of the shadowy figures approached the detective, he instantly recognised him from a previous incident in which he had become involved with the Straam police force. The detective was then rapidly surrounded by a number of these distributers. They proceeded to manhandle him up to the large country house. I'm not sure anyone got to the bottom of what happened next entirely. But it seemed the entire event had been arranged to distribute the pills. Everything became very intense and one of the gang members put a gun up to the detective's head to find out how he had known about the gathering which had only been announced that afternoon into a known and secure network. He had no choice but to tell them about Nick and his mother's attempt to find out what he was doing at the weekends. Panic broke out and Nick was dragged away from the stage and also brought up to the house. With multiple guns pointed at his head Nick told the gangsters how he had come to be there.

It seemed the suitcase he had collected from the club and delivered to the house was full of the pills currently in fashion and now being distributed amongst the young people. It seemed a well-known gangster was the secret owner of the house and also a client of my father's law firm. His girlfriend was the talented singer in the band who it turned out had struck up a conversation with Nick at one of the cocktail parties regularly held for the clients of dad's firm. One thing had a lead to another as they say and Nick ended up having an intimate liaison with the singer during the party; he always claimed he did not know whose girlfriend she was.

Unfortunately, the gangster boyfriend mysteriously discovered the incident and threatened Nick with his life but realizing he was the son of the lawyer who was responsible for his extended freedom was prepared to let Nick live in one piece as long as he regularly delivered narcotics to the parties he was organizing for the young people of Straam every weekend out in the hills.

Nick told me everyone went very quiet when they realized their boss was responsible for this detective being at this lucrative event planned for many months and under every radar possible. Meanwhile the detective had taken the precaution of wiring himself up with a covert device which could transmit an alarm and any conversations happening around him directly to police station in Straam. He had triggered the device when the guns had emerged and the police had been avidly listening as the entire scenario of a drugs problem they had been trying to come to grips with in the city was described to them. They subsequently had immediately dispatched as many officers as were available on a Saturday afternoon to the country house location bringing the carefully planned event to a chaotic end.

Amongst those who were arrested that night was my brother Nick. The lawyer whose pupil he had been was sent to bail him out the next morning. Luckily the entire gang chose to remain silent about his part in the movement of the drugs and he was released without charges being brought. Needless to say, my father was very disappointed with Nick. As it turned out the company had been looking for a reason to get rid of the gangster as a client and despite an expensive trial that went on for many months, they were unfortunately unable to secure his release. He is now in a maximum-security penitentiary with little chance of seeing the streets of Straam in the near or distant future which now are considerably less filled with the drugs he was supplying there. My father forgave Nick and told him to put it down to experience. I am sure they became closer and the story is much told around the Keating dinner table. When I left Nick had in fact formed a band and who do you think was the lead singer?"

Okino laughed. He laughed at the story and the twist of events that had brought father and son closer together in such strange circumstances and he laughed at the way Mariella had further illuminated the strange distant future world he was now heading towards. He then looked apprehensively over at Mariella for now she could demand a story from him. She was grinning over at him wickedly.

"So, have you ever been in trouble, Okino"

Okino again scanned through his memories. In his remote hills thoughtless action by any member of the community could endanger everyone and this was always stressed from an early age. The town survived on a knife edge relying on everyone being aware at all times of their actions. There was little room for any kind of irresponsibility even amongst the young people. Inevitably there had been incidents in which he had been involved; many remained untold and involved his journeys through the mountains. If actual trouble arose amongst the young people, it was often to do with some neglect of the tasks they were continually given to support the life of the town where no one was idle for long.

"There was one incident!" Okino began. He shuddered and a dark worried look had come over his face as the memory resurfaced fully.

"Oh, just One!" Mariella retorted grinning over at the serious look on Okino's face.

"Well, obviously there were more than one but this was about as much trouble as anyone could get into in our town and it is still talked about in the same way as your brothers unfortunate incident I should imagine; with a great deal of pleasure and more than a bit of pain.

It all started up in the Summer pastures above the town where the grass is always slightly lusher than down in the valley at that time of the year. Many families have a herd of goats. We don't have money in the town so many of the transactions take place with the transference of livestock. Most people have goats or chickens and of course there are the families who have always owned the yaks. Yaks being holy creatures in Jahallala go pretty much wherever they want and actually take very little looking after and will not stray very far from the direct vicinity of the town. So, you pretty much know where they are. The chickens are at the backs of the houses so we can collect the eggs and in the same way they rarely stray far away from the hen houses in which they go into at night.

The goats however are more troublesome creatures. When they are down in the valley near to the town they have to be kept in corrals at night. This is to stop them being preyed upon by the wolves. Also, goats are notorious for wandering off, so much of our childhood was spent watching them. If you keep an eye on them and keep them all together, they are fine but unattended they will wander off, get lost or get into some kind of mischief in the search of the variety of food they continually crave.

So, one Summer there were five goat herds up in the summer pasture all being looked after by five ten-year olds, that was us, from their respective families. We were all friends and eventually as this particular day went on the goats although they would stay in their own particular group had become merged into one large herd. We were all able to watch them from the group of trees we were sitting under and took turns in walking around them to let them know we were all still around. Towards the end of the day we would take the goats down to the lakes for a drink before returning them to the corrals for the night.

The weather had been warm and fine all day but there had always been a threat of a downpour. Normally we would take the herds down the track going past the village. This was the long way around avoiding the steeper rocky slopes on the other side of the village. But as the weather was closing in and a storm seemed imminent, we decided we would take the herd down through the central street. We would keep the goats moving and it would take half the time and hopefully the goats would be safely in their corrals when the storm eventually came over.

All went pretty much to plan to start with. We managed to direct the goats to the top of the village and they were happily walking down through the street. There were some slightly nervous looks from some of the older inhabitants seeing so many goats on the move through the village but most looked at the sky and waved to us and gave us encouragement. We came to the central square which was mostly cobbled and populated with a single large Pine tree under which there was a stout old table where people often stopped to chat.

It was surrounded by houses, little food and workshops. It had been a warm day so all the doors and windows were open and some of the shops had the customary benches outside. As we came into the square we noticed another group of our friends sitting at the table playing the dice and card game we were all hideously addicted to at the time. We gathered round and instantly became involved with the run of play between the competitors and soon became involved ourselves.

The goats patiently wandered around eating any vegetation they could find. As we willed the dice to fall our way so the appropriate cards could be gathered, we failed to notice the storm was approaching until it was virtually overhead. A deluge of rain fell instantaneously as is common in these mountains closely followed by an enormous crack of lightening which we all swear to this day landed in the next street. We were jolted suddenly from the spell the game had already exerted on us to watch a full-scale disaster unfolding before our eyes. You may or may not know that goats hate rain. They can just about put up with a light down pour but they hate these sudden deluges. It's because they have evolved primarily in semi-arid regions and haven't got oily enough coat to deflect so much water. Throw in a bolt of lightning in a fairly enclosed space such as the square and a complete panic sets in.

The goats bolted for whatever shelter they could find. In the mountains they would huddle in caves and under ledges. Down in the village they headed straight for the open doors of the shops and houses. We watched as the goats clattered into the rooms opening directly onto the streets. In the houses these rooms were generally living rooms carefully arranged with rugs and the accoutrements for living the family had gathered. We winced as the frightening sight of fully-grown goats disappearing into people's houses was swiftly followed by the crashing of falling crockery and glassware.

Of course, the shops contained food! In the next few minutes we ran through the houses trying to chase the goats back out into the street. But the goats saw no reason to deny themselves a snack in the predicament they found themselves and were running out into the street with loaves of bread and vegetables greedily clasped in their jaws. In many houses we were confronted by angry house owners who having chased a goat around their living room were now standing in the wreckage of their home.

The deluge only lasted a short time and having managed to persuade the most reluctant goats to return to the square we made a head count. There were two missing. We resumed the search and it was a whole degree of the Arimathean Star's turning before we found the last two goats standing in the vegetable garden of the irritable, cantankerous, bad tempered, child hating, goat hating member of the village council, old Mr. Korani, munching their way through his prized vegetables.

Well you can imagine! The whole incident tested relationships between families that had reputedly not fallen out in centuries. Of course, it was raised by Mr. Korani at the next town council meeting and we had to go with our fathers to explain ourselves under the full glare of the villagers who had been involved. We had to make personal apologies to each person who had sustained damage and we were made to offer our services to help all the aggrieved homeowners in whatever way we could."

Mariella had been giggling since the goats had disappeared into the houses. But now was laughing uncontrollably.

"Were you ever allowed to look after the wretched goats again?" she managed to ask through the tears.

"Eventually. But a new law was passed so no more than five goats should ever be brought through the village at any one time and so it remains to this day."

"It's a lovely story Okino and I only wished I could have been there to see it."

Lost in the telling of their worlds the two travellers were unaware they were being followed. The rain clouds were slipping further from their retreat high in the mountains. Large droplets of water had started to fall. Mariella grimaced over at Okino and in some attempt to assess the movement of the storm she glanced back over her shoulder into the sky and then down the track. There she noticed the two travellers. They were also on horses and heavily masked by head gear wrapped around their heads.

"Okino we are being followed!"

Okino turned and carefully observed the two figures who now appeared to be speeding up.

"There is nothing we can do. We certainly won't outrun them with the three horses. It's probably nothing to worry about."

He tried to sound convincing and confident but this had always been his fear for this part of the journey. In the back of his mind he had always been worried Mariella could have been noticed in Aharri by some of the less law-abiding members of the mountain community. She had spent money freely and however much she had tried to underplay her foreign origins there was no mistaking she had travelled from the rich South.

They rode nervously on in silence as the rain gathered in intensity. They could hear the sounds of the riders approaching through the water already gathering on the parched solid track. They heard the panting of the horses as the two travellers rode up beside them. Their faces were mostly covered leaving only their dark eyes exposed. They said nothing coolly observing Okino and Mariella and their horses and all they carried. They looked to the ridges of the hills that had guided the river from the high mountains and never were more than a few minutes ride away. The horses became nervous of the proximity of these new creatures and the tension that now had arisen in their riders.

Okino noticed a gap in the hills. Through the rain he could see a substantial bridge that would take them straight into the mountains beyond. Perhaps this was why they had chosen now to make their move. What could be their intention? No sooner had the thought passed through Okino's mind had the masked traveller who was now riding next to him removed a handgun from inside his coat and waved it towards the bridge. They said nothing for nothing needed to be said. Okino's worst fears were now materializing. He now realized he had fully passed over into the future world where all the values held amongst his people had suddenly become irrelevant in the striving for advantage and profit. Now there appeared to be some sort of kidnap attempt underway. The other rider had also taken out a handgun. He tried to remember why they had not travelled down to the sea with Ben and Zeph in the safety of the land cruiser. He looked questioningly over to Mariella. She was showing no sign of fear. Her confidence even in this dangerous situation seemed unshakeable.

"Don't worry Okino, just do what they say." She calmly and firmly whispered under her breath and gently turned her horse towards the bridge.

Okino could see it was wide and well-made and there was a well-used track snaking up through a pass with steep sides in the near distance. The two men rode silently attentive now to each move Okino and Mariella made. The rain was increasing in intensity. The weather conditions certainly couldn't have been in their plan and couldn't be making the execution of it any easier. But they had every advantage. Okino assessed any kind of struggle would almost certainly end in disaster with the result he would be shot. Mariella, he assumed was most valuable to them and so he himself was extremely vulnerable. The silence of the riders was sinister and had allowed them to show no weakness in any of their actions. There was nothing for him to do except continue on.

They soon were crossing the bridge. The river was already filling and flowing close to flood level with the water that had been falling higher in the mountains earlier in the day. They continued up the steep path into the hills. The dried ground had now become treacherously slippery and the progress of all the animals became precarious and had slowed. The path became progressively narrower as they rode higher. The kidnappers had ridden side by side with Mariella and Okino. As the paths became steeper and narrower this became impossible and soon the path only allowed the horses to follow each other deeper into the mountains.

The sides of the valley began to rise steeply on either side. The horses at one point were walking through a stream being channelled down through the narrow pass further hampering there advance up the hill. Eventually they appeared to reach the summit and the path opened out before them. Okino was able to look up to the ridges around him for the first time in some hours. As he turned his glance back down to the track, he thought he had noticed a tiny movement on one of the ridges. He played the trace of the image over and over in his mind. It certainly had not been a bird but could it have been some animal? But what animal would leave the silhouette of such a shape against the sky. He looked over at Mariella. She still remained calm and he detected no sign of worry or stress whatsoever. Again, he looked casually up to the ridge where he thought he had seen the movement. There was nothing and he went back to the contemplation of the situation in which he found himself.

He had sensed the night the dragon had returned to the hill their journey may become more dangerous. He had had no contact with the dragon either in his dreams or through the intense insights he had become used to having. He assumed some readjustment to the world would be underway after the many centuries the dragon had been parted from Arimathea. No doubt the great mechanisms of the Universe were also adjusting to this new flow of events and perhaps had now manifest this new scenario. His monkish scepticism reminded him this was the inevitable outcome of two young people, one of whom had openly displayed real wealth in a land where many people simply did not have money, travelling unarmed through the wilderness. He tried to persuade himself it was nothing to do with the forces of Oblivion turning on him because he had freed their greatest adversary on Arimathea to take up the struggle against them once again.

But then he could not deny all that had happened to him with the dragon in the previous days. He had learnt about the struggle and how it would always go on relentlessly through the millennia. Until what…until all this beauty was gone or it had transcended into some unimaginable higher state of being and one or other of the forces was defeated forever. If any of this was true, then what power had they now drawn into their unholy struggle to so quickly bring on this new situation in which they now found themselves? He was curious although nervous to meet the person who had planned and engineered this plot; and who possibly intended to hold them captive in the mountains until Aaron paid the ransom for the return of his beloved daughter whom he had so dangerously allowed to travel through this land about which he knew so little.

The little convoy continued on the path which now could be seen winding its way over this higher level of the mountains into the distance. The rain stopped and the Star came out briefly and glistened on the smooth faces of the rain covered rocks. How different everything looked now he was proceeding into the uncertainty of what lay ahead. Their captors continued to say nothing and did not reveal their faces as they continued to ride through the mountains. Okino had kept his eye on the ridges in the distance curious to see whether the movement he thought he had seen would reoccur, but he saw nothing further.

In the late afternoon without any warning as they passed through a further narrowing of the path the two gunmen indicated to their two captives to turn up a narrow gully just wide enough for the horses to squeeze through. The path between again rose steeply. The horses struggled on over the uneven surface of what would have rapidly changed into a torrential waterfall in a storm. As Okino and Mariella gently encouraged their horses on, their captors brutally whipped their underfed mounts up the narrow path. Okino looked over at Mariella and for the first time he saw hatred for her captors. Up until that moment they had been unfortunate weak men who had been caught up in some warlord's plan to raise funds for his delusional revolutionary struggle against the superpowers of Arimathea. Now they had become her enemies.

Okino decided he would rather be her friend having seen the look in those eyes which had never given any impression she was at all the underdog in this situation.

The gully opened out onto a wide flat ledge that fell away sharply to the path they had turned off. On the mountain side of the ledge there was the open mouth of a large cave from out of which were now walking further men also with their faces covered. They greeted their comrades and approached the horses of Mariella and Okino. They signalled for them to dismount and follow them into the cave. Okino made a conscious effort to evaluate the landscape before he went in, scanning the mountains for any identifying features.

One of the men guided Mariella by putting his hand on her shoulder. She shook it off defiantly and strode into the cave, as if she was keen to get this whole matter sorted out as soon as possible so she could get on with her journey. She paused to examine the specification printed on the large satellite dish at the entrance to the cave. Okino grinned at his captor shook his head and followed her into the cave. The interior was large and well lit. There were rudimentary wooden chairs covered with goat skins set around a wide circular table on which there were empty cans of the beer that had nearly blinded Okino in Aharri and an ashtray full of cigar ends, many of which also littered the floor of the cave. There was a large bench in one corner on which sat a gas cooker with three rings clearly fed by a large gas cylinder sitting under the bench. There were sacks of food from which vegetables had been carelessly allowed to escape. Large bottles of water sat on the other end of the bench and metal plates and cutlery were piled unwashed over the remaining surface.

Around the cave a large array of weapons leant up against the walls. Okino recognized large calibre automatic rifles and rocket propelled grenade launchers from the books on warfare that had mysteriously found their way into the monastery. There also appeared to be a considerable amount of electronic equipment. There were screens and keyboards wired to a rack of battered computer boxes which in turn connected a tangle of cables into a large generator. Another cable ran out to the dish at the entrance to the cave. Okino peered deeper into the gloom at the back of the cave where he could see beds and piles of clothes and blankets scattered randomly across the floor.

Mariella had sat herself down at the table, crossed her arms and looked defiantly across at her captors. Okino sat next to her on another of the chairs.

"Well…. aren't you going to tell us what this is all about!"

The men settled on the edges of the cave. They relaxed now their part of the operation had been successfully completed and removed their head scarves to reveal their faces. They were not much older than Okino. One crossed the cave and revealed a pile of beer cans under a blanket. He took off a six pack threw one over to each of his friends and offered one to Okino and Mariella who looked at them quizzically for a moment before accepting one each without any further question. They all drank thirstily, allowing the relaxing effects of the strong beer to work through their tense systems. They sat siilently drinking for some time. The Star had lowered in the sky so the light crept deeper into the cave before they eventually heard further voices apparently arriving. A figure appeared silhouetted in the mouth of the cave. He was tall and lithe, older perhaps by ten years than the other men. He wore a headdress which framed his face. His eyes shone brightly out from the darkly suntanned skin as he moved into the cave with a grin on his face and towards Mariella as if she were a long-lost friend.

"You stay away from me, whoever you are!" Mariella ordered him coldly.

"Aaah, so unfriendly for one so far away from home Mariella Keating, daughter and heiress to the lawyer Aaron Keating, lawyer to the President of Straam and all the other gangsters who live there. Let me introduce myself, I am Azeera..."

"Look, I don't want to know who you are, but if you are the leader of all these little creeps then I just want to explain exactly what kind of trouble you are in so we can straighten out this stunt you've attempted and you can tell all your friends out there we do not want to have any more of this kind of shit for the rest of our journey down to Zedocha!"

There was a surprised silence for a few moments before the tall man laughed loudly and took a cigar from a pocket in his jacket, lit it and puffed great clouds of acrid smelling tobacco smoke into the cave.

"Have I missed something here, is it not I who is in charge?"

"You are damn right you have...that pile of worthless rubbish stacked in the corner, presumably it has some kind of computing capacity." Mariella was pointing over at the rack of computers.

"Oh yes, they are up to the minute in every sense they look a bit battered because, well it is not an ideal environment for computers."

"Well, turn them on then, it's getting late."

The smile on Azeera's face was weakening and a bead of sweat had emerged from his brow. This was not how this was meant to be going at all. He signalled to one his accomplices to turn on the computers. Initially this meant turning on the generator. They fumbled trying to start it before they realized they needed to put some petrol into the empty tank. Eventually the generator spluttered into life adding further fumes to the already smoky cave. When the generator was running constantly one of the men turned on the computer system which started to run through it's opening procedures.

"Oh, look a Southern Star computer system...what would you do without us?" She smiled over at Azeera as she got up and went over to one of the keyboards. She rattled across the ancient keys. Screens emerged onto which she typed further information. Then one by one, six pictures opened on the screen. Each had a specific feature. There were stunted trees and misshapen rocks, unmistakable vistas in the background.

"Do you recognize these places, Azeera. You should do because they are all out there, Oh, and who are these guys in the picture?"

The cameras zoom steadily in on a snipers' rifles with large telescopic sights in each picture, previously invisible but now clearly held by a shadowy figure crouched invisibly in the landscape.

"Give us a wave, guys!"

Each one of the six snipers raised a hand and waved back.

"Oh and I expect one of you has a shot directly into the cave, perhaps you could send one over and careful not to hit anyone at this stage."

Mariella was looking straight into her astounded captor's eyes. The bullet whistled through the cave and thudded into the back wall. Long before his reflexes allowed him to lower his head from slightly lower than where the bullet had flown. Everyone in the cave huddled closer into the walls unsure anywhere was now safe from the sniper who must have been on the ridge on the other side of the valley, a good five-minute flight for even an Arimathean crow. Okino found himself grinning again at the cowering kidnappers and shaking his head. So, he had seen someone on the ridge. This is how she had managed it. Old Aaron hadn't taken any chances after all. He'd sent a small army to shadow her all the way just in case someone like Azeera had been tempted to spirit her away into these mountains.

"Ok, nice shooting whoever that was. So now what I want you to do is to put all those guns you have on the table here. Come on each one of you."

One by one they put the handguns on the table and hurried back to their places at the edges of the cave. Mariella came and sat back down at the table.

"Oh, and you Azeeka, get me and my friend another beer and come over here... I want to talk to you."

Azeera takes the beers from the pile and passes them to Mariella and Okino before sitting down opposite them.

"Look I don't know what your cause is or what you are trying to achieve but you are not going to achieve it by extorting money out of my family. But to show there are no hard feelings we'll put a million Dezari's in your account for the trouble you are going to go to make sure this does not happen again! If you put your account up on the screen we will get that sorted out for you."

Azeera signals to one of the men to get up the account and sure enough within seconds of it being on the screen a million Dezaris had been added to the balance.

"So, have we got a deal? ...because if we haven't and something goes wrong my boys out there will have to come and find you!"

Azeera looks across at Mariella. Already he has been completely humiliated by this rich girl from Straam. All the injustice on his world brought about by these industrial countries with their mining to fuel their economies and their exploitation of his people to make the products they pay so little for and sell for so much, the scouring of the seas for their cheap food, the desecration of their beautiful countries with their investment in the vicious regimes so ready to welcome their bribery and corruption; How long would it go on and how would his country ever be able to fight back against the technology they command with the wealth they have at their disposal?

"I know what you are thinking Azeera… I see the way you are looking at me. I've seen it a thousand times since I have been out here and I am sorry I was so abrupt with you …but let me assure you, we are on the same side and things are going to change on this planet for everybody…. Just make sure I get down to Zedocha safely with my friend Okino here, so we can carry on what we have started up here!"

"It is a fine gesture you have made Mariella Keating and you have entirely 'hoodwinked' me I think you say. Perhaps you would do me the honour of staying here tonight and sharing some dinner with us so you can explain more about how you will change this world from what it has become."

"I think perhaps we will; have you got enough for my boys out there?"

Later in the evening the long tables had been separated from the walls of the cave, pushed together and lined with benches. The six men employed by Mariella's father to watch over her during her journey had emerged from the surrounding landscape soon after it had been agreed they should all eat together. They greeted Mariella as if they had not seen her for some months. She introduced them to Okino who had been unable to talk to her to discuss this unexpected development. They were deeply suntanned wearing beards and the local attire of long shirts, cotton trousers and the customary patterned head dresses were wrapped around their heads.

They had clearly been living rough for a considerable time but greeted Okino as if they had been reunited with an old friend. The sophisticated sniper's rifles, one of which had delivered the bullet so effectively to the back of the cave, were now slung casually over their shoulders and were inspected enviously by Azeera and his crew. Further beer from the pile was immediately distributed and the two parties settled down together as the Moon rose bathing the mountains in her beautiful light. Once she was certain all was calm Mariella took Okino by the arm and led him out of the cave. Their horses had been tethered next to those of their captors and now their hosts. Like their human owners they all seemed to be getting on as they lazily ground their way through some of the freshest hay they had had for some time. Mariella stroked down their necks lovingly and the horses responded with low contented sounds of appreciation.

"You really are full of surprises, aren't you?!" Okino broke the uncomfortable silence that had arisen between them.

"When did you think you were going to tell me about the band of mercenaries that have obviously been shadowing our every move since we met. They are good I have to admit and the stuff with the computers and the money that is just like pure magic to me."

Mariella looked over to him and smiled affectionately, reached up and ruffled his hair like the children in the stone circle had done only days before.

"There was no need to tell you Okino. Most of the time I forget about their existence. They are just out there in the hills watching over me and now us. They have been given exact parameters to follow so the experience or the independence of my journey will not be infringed upon. My father made me agree to it for the very reason that has come about today….and the technology keeping them in immediate contact with me if the need arises is expensive but is not unusual where I live."

"I am surprised though you didn't tell me but I suppose there are going to be differences between our worlds and what is acceptable in each of them. I have a feeling there will be a few more surprises uncovered by the time this trip is over!"

"You better believe it, Okino. You are going to see things beyond even your wildest dreams and heh don't think you won't upset my world with a few surprises of your own."

"I have been wondering about that.."

"I am sure the dragon knows what he is doing…well no, that is not strictly true; he does seem to be making it up as he goes along like the rest of us!"

Okino grinned as he stroked the head of his own horse. He had warmed to the creature he had reluctantly been thrown into a relationship with. He had been surprised by the intelligence he saw in those dark eyes. He always knew when another human being was looking past the outside veneer of his personality, reaching deeper into his soul, searching for the secrets held there for some revelation; to understand his true being. This horse it seemed never did anything else. He instinctively looked for the signals to alert him to any threat about to come upon him and if he found none in the soul in which he had delved he felt safe and responded accordingly. Good clean hay, not too dusty was the key to his happiness. In his dreams the gnawing hunger would be continually satiated as he drifted through sunlit meadows tearing away at the freshly grown grass, flavoured occasionally by the taste of the wildflowers always growing there.

These beautiful surprising creatures he had become involved with on this journey, had perhaps taken him deeper, into the soul of his world, of Arimathea who had initially surprised him, gradually revealing herself and these gentle spirits who so reflected her. He and Mariella had made her whole again and as their journey continued they would attempt to help her with the challenges she now faced.

Okino drifted through the evening with Mariella at his side. They admired the beauty of the Moonlight as she reclaimed the silvery mountains as if they were her own. He had come closer to her as he discovered this new layer of her mystery and the true and tangible sense of the power surrounding her, which she had come with and supported her here. It was held in the steel tower in which her father, perhaps even now sat deciding a strategy for the defence of some worthy or unworthy individual. It mattered not to him as he finely and cleverly interpreted the law developed by men to make their world just and fair, to secure and reinforce the funds needed to keep his company solvent and his daughter safe on her pilgrimage to "Save the World".

He savoured the smells of the cooking spices as they drifted from the cave and mingled with the warm evening breezes and the sounds of her voice as she joked with her soldiers. They were all tall and wiry. They spoke and expressed themselves well and asked him about his life in his town and the work of the priests. They listened in fascination as he told them about how he had become a monk. He wondered if they understood at all what they had become involved in. He realized they must have seen the explosion on the dragon hill. He asked them how they were able to survive so invisibly in the landscape. When they told him, he recognized the skills he had always used when he was in the wilderness. They savoured together the sense of awareness they shared of the entire landscape giving them the ability they needed to manoeuvre invisibly and he had needed when he was out stalking the snow leopards through the high mountain passes.

Now they each sat with a steaming plate of freshly cooked stew expertly prepared by one of Azeera's men. More beers were opened and a grateful silence fell over the little group as they hungrily devoured the delicious food. Mariella had positioned herself opposite to Azeera on the table. He was aware she was observing him and for the moment ignored her attention as he enjoyed his food. When he had finished he took a long drink of his beer and placed the can down in front of him.

"So young lady, you were going to tell me how you are going to change the world!"

Mariella smiled back at him and mischievously over at Okino who was sitting next to him.

"The truth is Azeera we have no idea how we or anyone else can alter the events that have brought this planet to where it is at this time. However, we have been gaining some huge insight into the nature of the problem!"

Mariella looked over to Okino. He saw the prompt in her eyes. The problem she could explain but she knew Okino had lived with what might be the cure all his conscious life. He had been able to explore with the monks the wisdom carried through to the present day but now he had merged with the dragon and felt the extent and true nature of the urge running through the world. Silence had fallen over the diners. He started to speak.

"When Mariella says we have been finding out about the nature of the problem we mean by going back to early times, really early times to find out the consequences of the fundamental choices early humans made and the motivations they had for setting our species on the path to where we are now. Underlying the evolution of this world is a vast universal struggle that has been going on since the beginning of, certainly this physical Universe and perhaps originates in an ethereal Universe that predates our own. The powers shaping the religions we always have 'believed in', of Creation and Destruction, of Gods and Goddesses we suspect have been manipulating our world somehow, remotely beyond us, are deeply embedded in every molecule and atom we are made up of. Not only in us though, every plant, animal, stone, river and sea, every cloud and storm possesses the knowledge, call it wisdom that somehow transforms this world into the future. It seems somewhere in our own transformation we have lost the ability to be influenced by this wisdom and so we have made decisions with no consideration for our world. Now we find ourselves on the edge of a precipice, we all know what that is and one way or another we will have to find a way for the wisdom to rise again in the human race."

Azeera looked quietly over at the monk who had unveiled a theory he had suspected in the back of his mind for a good part of his adult life. Okino paused. He saw Azeera was absorbing what he had said. He could feel him searching for the pathways up to the lofty heights of the distant monastery from the world he now inhabited where he had seen so much fear and injustice. Azeera lifted his head and stared up into the dark sky, infinitely filled with the tiny intense bursts of light signalling galaxies filled with solar systems perhaps similar to his own millions of light years away.

He had joined the growing ranks of the disenfranchised revolutionaries whose networks were gradually surrounding Arimathea because of the circumstances he had seen unravel in his own life. He had seen the results of global expansion and domination of the poorer countries by the richer and the exploitation as it had continued. He had chosen to become involved because the injustice appeared to be growing unchallenged and was threatening the world he had hoped his children would inherit.

But there had been violence and the atrocities committed he would have distanced himself from if he had been able. He himself had had to ask what other action would keep the anger of the people of Arimathea fresh in the minds of the rich politicians in their peaceful mechanized, well fed and subdued countries. His organization was well aware the media networks in their countries craved high drama that persuaded the rich populations to turn on their televisions, switch to their channels to attract the advertising revenues to pay for their flamboyant lifestyles.

So, the devastation of a bomb attack not only caused unfathomable misery in the lives of families and cities, but it could also be contributing to the sales of cars and fast foods; both of which were involved in the destruction they were protesting about. Clearly the strategy was misguided and Azeera had been looking for possibilities and searching through the connections and knowledge he had for a new way to help his world to find its' way more successfully into the future.

Now he had brought Mariella and Okino here by force at the suggestion and eventual persuasion of his 'organization' with the intent of extorting money from her father primarily for her return. It was not going to his or their plan. Now what Okino had said had set lights flashing on in his mind. He was as yet uncertain as to why, but some connection had been made with the narrative of his own life and now he searched for its expression. Mariella and Okino watched expectantly as if they sensed the thought gestating in Azeera's mind; bringing together the threads to bring expression from his own life to Okino's theory. He turned to them and smiled.

"I was brought up in a small fishing village on the coast you are now heading for. The village was not far from the beach and most of the men were involved with fishing or other activities associated with making a living from the sea. We harvested shellfish and different species of fish would arrive at our shore as the seasons went on. We had small holdings and small farms and we traded with neighbouring villages. I was always aware there was a city along the coast and occasionally the villagers would make the journey for some piece of equipment. We lived in meagre timber houses that were on occasion destroyed by a storm but they were easily rebuilt and we did not have too much of value inside them.

I have spoken to my parents about these times and they have told me they were always struggling to feed us. Fishing was never as easy as is often thought and even in little communities such as ours there were market forces governing the price of fish when they had eventually been caught. But of course, in those days I was immune to all their struggles. I lived beside the ocean with my friends and my memories of my growing there are full of warmth and beauty. I remember the old timber boats and watching my father and his friends dragging them up the beach and the boxes of flashing silver fish being loaded into the back of the old pick-up truck. Nobody it seemed knew the exact age of the boats or how many generations had set off into the ocean on them.

There was always the beach of soft white sand, the Star rises and Star sets and splashing through the surf and coconuts. Their soft flesh and its fresh taste was and is an experience I will never tire of. There were places where we would all go as a community at our special times, there were tales and legends we shared of the ocean and the creatures there which had been caught and would never be caught. We eagerly awaited the arrival of the turtles at the beginning of the summer. We watched in awe of the vast creatures as they hauled themselves up the beach and dropped their eggs into their nest holes from which would eventually emerge the tiny baby turtles destined to perhaps return, we were told in those times, for another hundred years to lay their eggs on our beach.

All the creatures and even each tree had some story to be told, something contained in the rich tapestry of knowledge and history of our village and all the families who lived there, the triumphs and catastrophes we had endured in the past, memories of our identity, our place in the world carrying us into the future. We were all taught about fishing and diving for the clams in the deeper water because it is what our people had always done. This knowledge contained information about the ocean and the weather affecting it passed from parent to offspring for who knows how many generations. When we swam down or crashed through the breakers out into the open sea, we again became part of it with all we knew about it, held it as part of ourselves so we were a continuous part of the world surrounding us. The wisdom you talked about we found was embedded in everything. The ocean itself was like a vast living creature to me with moods and tantrums that could be as soft and calm as a sleeping baby but as violent and unpredictable as any demon you could possibly imagine. Because of what and who we are and what we are able to hold within our minds we became this knowledge and our village reaped the benefits for many countless generations.

It breaks my heart really to tell you what happened. It is happening all over this world as the old pastoral world has to make way for the new, governed by oil and machines. The city had slowly expanded and as I grew, I was aware the buildings were advancing towards us, coming nearer and nearer up the coast. We heard stories and gasped hoping no such thing could happen to us here. After all, why would anyone want our stretch of old beach in the middle of nowhere with nothing but ocean in front of us? But of course, that was exactly what they wanted. We had no rights or ownership; the village had just been there forever. The government it seemed owned the land and of course it was worth considerably more with hotels built on it than with what amounted to a ramshackle old village which owned a few fishing boats. We had no worth and so we had to be moved.

They moved us to a suburb of the rapidly expanding urban sprawl. They put each family in a house constructed crudely and impersonally from concrete blocks in neighbourhoods which were wide apart. Our community was destroyed with all the other communities, dislocated and scattered through this new maze of concrete and tarmac. Inevitably things started to fall apart very quickly. There was not enough work for us all to make an adequate living in the new hotels and tourist complexes. But you can imagine fishermen who have been negotiating the rigors of the ocean all their lives now carrying the bags of the rich tourists from your country who would lie idly around on their beaches getting hopelessly drunk in the bars where our houses used to be.

The drug dealers soon moved in selling cheap but highly addictive drugs which at first gave some relief from this torture and misery brought upon us. But soon the cost was rising as we became addicted and soon we were mugging and robbing each other for the cost of the drugs we now needed to stop the cravings the drugs now left. It wasn't long before gangs patrolled their own areas and inevitably there were deaths as the hopelessly addicted ventured into the wrong neighbourhood while trying to secure some deal to quell the raging pain now racking their minds and bodies. We became an easy recruiting ground for the terrorist organizations who were now starting to emerge and I eventually decided I would join when my best friend who I had swam and dived and fished with in the warm turquoise paradise we had inhabited was caught in the crossfire of a gun fight between two gangs that had erupted as he walked down our street one night.

So, you see everything was lost. Knowledge, people, their livelihoods on the sea, the beaches; I don't know whether the turtles could ever survive what happened to their beaches; a world destroyed and another link with your wisdom gone forever or certainly until circumstances again prevail when it could again be found. It is where your wisdom is rapidly disappearing. It has no use in the world of thirty-storey hotels and new factory fishing boats tracking the fish down with sonar. Wisdom that comes with the closeness we felt with our world; it terrified us, gave us joy and comfort and belonging. But now it seems we have to replace it with all the stuff, which the TVs they sold us, tell us day in and day out we need to be happy and fulfilled in this modern world. But if we do not have money to buy those things, with what and where are we left my friends!?"

"…So, you became a member of a terrorist organization!" Mariella observed laconically.

Azeera raised his voice in frustration.

"Yes, I became a terrorist because Mariella Keating I think you would have become a terrorist. To see such beauty destroyed by this senseless new way of living is devastating."

"So, blowing up cities and people, because there have been people killed in these attacks, is the answer you think?"

Azeera quietly looked into the confident turquoise eyes, well educated, carefully raised by her rich parents at the heart of all he despised and hated about what was happening to his world. Perhaps there was hope. She had realized and understood what was happening. Perhaps they had finally reached someone who had the power to help them and she had come here, sat at his table with the monk who talked of the deep magic he had felt at the heart of his world.

"I am not proud of what has been done but when you are treated so badly by people you knew who have become lost in the power and the greed of this destruction and then your friends start dying around you! Wouldn't you fight Mariella?

She did wonder. Wondered about the countryside she herself had grown up in with all her friends and how special these places and people had become in the story of her life. What level of desperation would it take to explode a bomb in a city if it was threatened? She knew the effects terrorist action had had in her own country and others in the southern world. Enormous bombs had been detonated, calculated to destroy as much of the centre of the city as possible. As far as she knew warnings had been given in enough time for people to be evacuated but there had been many deaths. As the cities effectively ground to a halt the consequences had been catastrophic and entirely justified in the eyes of the perpetrators as she understood because the rich southern cities remained oblivious to the degradation being caused in the rest of the world to maintain their profligate lifestyle.

"We have to make the people of your country understand what is happening to Arimathea. You say you are helpless to do anything but still you buy the products and services from the corporations who are responsible for the destruction."

There was a note of desperation in Azeera's voice.

"The only time our voices are heard is when we dominate the world media with some dreadful atrocity and then of course we are branded as sub-human destroyers of lives who must be hunted down and imprisoned at least or mercilessly hung at worst. So, nothing will ever change and beautiful Arimathea will be turned into a polluted desert. It amazes me how you think you will escape all this as if your money will be able to make the rain fall."

"You seem like a sensitive man Azeera so presumably you have not actually been involved in one of these bomb attacks." Mariella inquired tentatively.

"I have not as yet. Well I haven't actually put a bomb in place but I have been involved in fundraising, and remember we always give plenty of warning so hopefully nobody gets killed!"

He laughs nervously as he looks over at Mariella and Okino. Their faces show no emotion at this stage.

"...But mainly I operate from in these hills with all this equipment. When an attack is planned they tell me when and where and I am responsible for the message that goes out in the wake of the event. As you have seen I have access to the information networks surrounding Arimathea. The message goes straight to the newsroom of every TV, cable and satellite channel on the planet. You may have heard them. As the cameras pan through the wreckage of another city centre, we ask for the devastation happening out of sight in the remotest and most beautiful parts of Arimathea to be immediately stopped. We stay on the move so the spy satellites have difficulty locating us."

He pauses and looks around at the faces who are staring back in disbelief. They are looking at him differently now. Even after all he has said they are remembering some of the destruction created by his organization in some of the most beautiful of Arimathea's cities.

"...But if you could come up with an action to focus the attention of the Southern world without blowing the hearts out of their cities and gain some sympathy for the plight of Arimathea then presumably you would put similar energy into supporting it." Okino suggested thoughtfully.

"Yes of course I would. So, what have you got in mind?"

Mariella spoke directly now. She had been casting her eye over the technology lying haphazardly around the crude stone age living accommodation. She got up from the table and wandered over to a table where she had recognised a sophisticated high-resolution camera capable of broadcasting directly into the web, forgotten and gathering dust. An idea came shining into her mind, not fully formed but an echo she recognized from somewhere, perhaps the future. She picked the camera up and started to speak.

"I am afraid we are dealing with forces who do not have schedules and plans they can share with us. So, we have very little idea how all this will take place and my guess is we will hardly notice at first when it actually does. But I am now convinced there are powers on this planet who want the degradation you are talking about to stop before all the wonder you have described is lost forever. We have had direct contact with them. So perhaps if you trust us you should give us a link to your network,"

She held the camera up before them,

"..perhaps a camera like this one with which we could stay in contact, load anything we find into your network and if something that could further your cause, our cause, started to unfold around us we could beam it straight into the networks you are connected into. Then certainly we would have the people of Arimathea's attention!"

Chapter Forty-three
Sherana.

Early the next morning, Okino and Mariella left Azeera's mountain hideout and by midday the horses were noisily crossing the stout wooden bridge they had crossed the day before. As they joined the road, they began to contemplate the strange alliance they had made the night before. Clearly Azeera's ability to flood the information networks of the world was a tempting prospect. Okino and Mariella were already wondering whether the dragon was aware of such a possibility. She remembered the powerful light which had come on inside her head when she saw the camera and she imagined he probably had. Powerful marketing ideas were regularly projected into the populations of Arimathea attempting to persuade them to buy competing and mostly identical products and services. They were promised their lives would be changed in as many ways as could be conceived around the tables of the stylish advertising agencies where the campaigns were conceived. Unbridled creativity unleashed to saturate media and minds so that when they came to buy their new car or select a new supermarket to visit there would be only one brand name held in their mind.

They were becoming aware this was not dissimilar to the method used by the dragon to slowly guide the world through its early evolution and beyond. Perhaps it was unsurprising the human race had inherited this ability from the dragon and now they were filling the world with their own dreams; dreams shaping ever more of the surface for the people of Arimathea. Beautiful and ugly, inspired and absurd, practical and ridiculous, far thinking and short sighted, Arimathea had been flooded with the constructions and ideas started as a dream in someone's head. Okino was accustomed to this idea as it was as true in the mountain communities as anywhere else. Now he would see the sheer audacity of the human race to transform their dreams into reality as he journeyed further from these remote places high in the mountains.

Even in the next few days as they came to the furthest influences of the city of Zedocha he saw for the first time the transformation to the landscapes made for as far as the eye could see. The river had grown from the clear fast flowing torrent which they had sat beside in Asima to a vast sluggish brown mass slipping through the land. They saw it now only in the distance as they were guided through broad expanses of irrigated fields lying adjacent to its banks on the flood plain it had formed. Now they would walk for whole days through a single crop being grown systematically in one enterprise. Isolated groups of people would be working their way down or across rows and rows of identical plants. Mariella started to give explanations as the sights Okino began to see became less and less familiar and more extraordinary to him.

Here for the first time he was seeing the mass cultivation of a single plant being harvested, processed and flown straight to the supermarkets in the Southern cities. Mariella smiled at his surprise and continued her explanations as huge lorries trundled past with the recently harvested crops or they rode past a line of tired workers waiting at the side of the road for a bus to take them back to the city. One more night and they would be in the city port of Zedocha. Everything from the moment they entered the city would then change.

Eventually, late one afternoon, they arrived at a group of rundown buildings. They may have been typical of the timber frame and stone variety but it seemed they had been patched up over the years with an assortment of materials. They noticed there was a tavern beside the road. Two of the workers they had seen earlier were sitting outside getting drunk and deeply engrossed in an argument. When they failed to notice the two dusty travellers in front of them, Mariella called down to them from her horse.

They looked up in surprise and despite their inebriation were able to inform the travellers a meal could be provided for them. They put one of the tents up in a group of trees just away from the road. They had become accustomed now to sleeping in the same tent since their conversation in Asima. They were generally too tired and in too much pain from the days riding to contemplate anything more than a meagre meal as their provisions had started to run low and sleep. This evening was no exception and once the tent was up they stiffly walked, leading the horses up to the tavern as the Star sank into the landscape of the flood plain, severed by the gleaming golden strip created by the Star reflecting off the river in the distance.

There was water and hay for the horses and they sat down at one of the tables in a lean to shelter built adjacent to a larger room which probably housed the bar and restaurant in less hospitable weather. The two workers carried on their argument oblivious to the new customers. Mariella and Okino were listening, deeply engrossed by the time an elegantly dressed woman with youthful brown eyes came out to ask them what they would like to eat and drink. The workers it seemed had an issue with the management of the farm on which they were working. Wages had been short and when one of their fellows had protested he was told to go home and not come back. One was trying to persuade the other they should take some action even though they were hopelessly drunk and would regret everything when they were sober and even more so if they were identified as the culprits. They were amusing themselves by contemplating the various actions open to them and the degree of upset it would cause to the company. Mariella and Okino ordered beers and stew with as many vegetables as could be provided. The diet of dried meat and rice they had been enduring since their rations had started to run low had now entirely halted their digestive systems.

The two workers were laughing wickedly as they discussed some aspect of their employer's lifestyle which they could exploit to their advantage by the time their food arrived. Both Mariella and Okino savoured the steaming plate of stew and vegetables by deeply inhaling the aromas as it sat before them. Their hostess indicated to the spare chair at the table and asked if they minded if she sat with them for a while. She silently watched them as they hungrily devoured the food she had so expertly made for them. As their initial hunger was satiated her two guests started to pay her attention as she sat silently observing them. Mariella caught her eye as she looked up from her dinner.

"This is absolutely delicious! Thank you so much; we haven't really eaten properly for days!"

Mariella told her as another mouthful of stew and vegetables was loaded onto her fork for consumption.

"Oh, and this is my friend Okino and I am Mariella, we're very pleased to meet you and to be eating your wonderful food."

Thank you, Mariella, I am Sherana, and I am honoured to meet you. I am glad you are enjoying your food. Have you been running short on your journey?"

"Yeah I think we would have been fighting over the last handfuls of rice had we not arrived here tonight." Okino indicated with a forkful of food over at Mariella. Sherana smiled,

"So, you have been travelling in the mountains?"

"Yes, we have. We have come from Aharri and spent some time at the old ruins of Asima. Do you know them?"

Mariella held her gaze as she gauged the reaction of their host.

"I did go there some time ago as a matter of fact. I found it to be one of those places you carry with you as the years go past. Even the memories are strangely refreshing!"

"So, do you remember the waterfall by the river?"

"I do young lady." She looked curiously across at Mariella. "It is a strangely mysterious place and there were many legends about it when we were young. But I think they will fade away as this new world coming upon us continues to consume everything that cannot be bought or sold!"

Mariella looked over at Okino who was paying attention to little other than his stew.

"We went there purposefully to find out about one of those old legends. Apparently, a rebellion was started there, way back in very early times. It was inspired by a mythical race of supernatural beings who were reputed to have been guardians of Arimathea. Was this one of the legends you heard?"

Mariella told her vaguely. Sherana instantly became more interested.

She creased up her eyes and examined Okino and Mariella in more detail. She gently lifted Okino's idle hand resting on the table, turned it over and saw the tattoo of the dragon on the inside of his wrist. A look of understanding seemed to come over her face and she smiled warmly at her dusty visitors.

"I have heard of such a legend and I know it occurs in many of the ancient cultures of Arimathea. However, I think it remains only in these remote areas. I travelled extensively as a young woman with my husband not unlike the two of you. At the root of those remote ancient cultures there was often a supernatural spirit being or beings who slept in the high mountains of the planet as guardians who would return if ever the life of the world should be threatened."

Okino had now finished his food. He looked over at Sherana who now was looking intently back at him.

"So Okino, you are a priest of the Old Dragon Order. There has not been one of your kind past here for many, many years. I wonder what you have found on your journey…"

Okino opened his mouth as if to talk. He suddenly felt the urge to tell her everything…

Sherana cut him short.

"First of all, do not be tempted to tell anyone what you have heard or been told or experienced. If you do it may become tangled into everyday nonsense which will dissipate the energy it has created. To work in the world, it will have to be strong and untainted. In my travels I saw and spoke to many of the oldest people in those remote communities and their stories had much the same conclusion. If the dragon was to return, the energetic flow running through the fabric of our world would have to be at its strongest for any action to change its future destiny."

She smiles at Mariella and Okino.

"Wait there a minute. There is something I would like to try if I may."

She gets up from her chair and disappears into the tavern. Mariella and Okino smile at each other. They look over at the two drunks who have been joined by a woman. They are trying to speak to her soberly and she is trying to suppress her laughter. Sherana returns and lights the old oil lamps before she sits once more at the table. She places a small ornately decorated bag on the table before them.

"These were given to me by a shaman from a tribe in a remote wilderness of Aralania."

She empties the contents of the bag onto the table in front of her. Approximately twenty-five bones from a small animal fall beguilingly across the table.

"Do you mind if we look?" Okino inquires with fascination.

"Of course not. Go ahead. I want you to get well acquainted with them."

Mariella and Okino both picked up one of the bones that made up part of the small animal that had lived and breathed as part of the life and consciousness of Arimathea.

"Are they all part of the same animal?" Okino was examining the small skull of the creature that had held the nerve centre, the brain of the creature processing it's every thought and action from the moment it had been born to the day it died.

"All the bones come from the same creature, a large rabbit apparently. The Shaman told me and then taught me how they could judge the state of the energy flowing in any given situation by reading the patterns the bones made when they were thrown. The theory being the bones are so imbued with the spirit of Arimathea they will fall into a pattern displaying the current and prevalent cycles projected into them."

"It does sound interesting. What do you think they can tell us and what will we have to do?" Mariella was examining each of the bones in great detail.

"Collect up the bones and close them into your two hands. Concentrate and remember all that has happened on your journey then hand them over to Okino and then he must do the same. When you are both happy the process is complete you can throw the bones."

Sherana sits back in her chair as Mariella collects up the bones and closes her eyes. She is silent for a few moments as the extraordinary journey she has taken floods into her mind. She opens her eyes and passes the bones to Okino. The circumstances and the intense chain of events that had brought him there flashed through his memory. Arimathea and Merilon had both woven their magical energies into his being. He felt this energy flow through his hands into the bones. He opened his eyes looked over at Mariella and let the bones roll out onto the table. They clattered to a standstill over the worn surface and slowly the pattern in which they had fallen started to become discernible. Sherana examined it silently.

"There seem to be two streams of bones running through and intersecting in the main body. The distances separating the bones vary before and after the intersection. You see how the emphasis has changed on the two streams. This one has fewer bones on the lower leg and more after the intersection. The other seems stronger before the intersection and weaker after. There are two further streams it seems feeding into the weaker before the Intersection. From this I would say you have been involved in a shift that has occurred in whatever energies these streams represent. I think they represent the anabolic and catabolic forces of the universe. Put in simpler terms the forces of Creation and Destruction. These other streams may represent the parts you have personally played or even the energy you have been responsible for bringing into the struggle. They appear to have given strength to the weaker stream resulting in the shift after this intersection." She looks up at Okino and Mariella.

"Can you identify which are the creative and destructive forces?" Okino asks.

".... I think that is something only you will know?"

"I would say the higher stronger branch represents the forces of light judging by all that has happened and..."

"Now remember what I have told you about recounting your tale, but I would find it hard to imagine a monk of such an order as yours setting out to assist the forces of darkness in the world." Sherana smiles knowingly.

"...and judging by the remainder of the bones clustered around the end of the stronger stream I would say there will be people in the journey ahead who are waiting and will be able to help you!"

"So, you think we have somehow become involved in a shift in the struggle between the forces of light and darkness on this world and there is further work for us to do wherever we are going!" Mariella was now as serious as Okino had ever seen her.

"...That is pretty much what I see before me."

"How will we know these people and what will we have to do... we are heading back to Eremoya. I thought perhaps our work was done. It really is different there. Anything natural has been buried under great slabs of concrete...how can we take what we have found in these beautiful places and hope they can work amongst all that; all that disinterest."

Sherana smiled over to Mariella and then at Okino. Mariella had shown the first signs of doubt as she began to confront the idea of returning to Straam with her story about the dragons and the Spirit of Arimathea.

"Did either of you know the people you would meet when you set out or know how all this would turn out?"

"I knew I had to find The Monastery of The Dragon Order!"

"...and you Okino?"

"I thought I was on a walk to the next valley to find out why our lakes were being polluted."

Sherana reached across the table and took the hands of both the young people sitting across the table from her.

"...But you both had concerns for the well-being of your world?"

Okino and Mariella turned and smiled as they remembered the first conversations they had when they met in Aharri. It seemed they had been driven by the same thought, the same inspiration. They both remembered the strange elation that had arisen between them as they shared their lives up to that time and the first days of their journey together.

"We did have uncannily similar concerns but from the different perspectives of our separate worlds which have strangely complimented each other as the story has unravelled!"

"…and has that surprised you?" she had addressed the question to Okino. He now felt the intensity with which Sherana was delving without seeming to ask anything very specific.

"I have been in two minds since I set out. There seems to be Okino the monk who has recently joined the Dragon Order whose humanity and monkish scepticism must question what is happening. But somewhere deeper there is an older character who I still recognise as me but seems to be very accustomed to the higher consciousness running through my dreams. This appears to have surfaced in the reality of our waking lives. There can be no doubt we have both experienced what can only be described as planetary forces acting through us."

"It seems ordinary to him what they do up in their monastery. But I have seen, felt and benefited from the deep connection they have built with Arimathea on my own journey, through my own consciousness. I have become accustomed to the experience but when I remember how things are back in Eremoya and how people have become utterly separated from any idea their world is anything but raw materials for their materialistic dreams it makes me shudder. As I think of our return I cannot imagine how even the forces we have encountered could change the state of mind underlying the entire economy, the state, the law, the way all those people live and work and are connected all over the world; everything would have to change. I just cannot conceive how that could happen!"

Mariella now had her face in her hands looking across the table blankly.

"…and yet you started out on your journey because something inside of you, and I stress inside of you said there had to be a way for it to change and it must change or all this will be lost for ever or again depending on what you believe to be true!"

"Yes, I did… it became a path that seemed entirely inescapable. But I think this is where Okino and I found a cross over. Everything had been gradually steering me towards the decision for years and eventually when I came upon the knowledge about the monastery I was convinced there would have to be some otherworldly, supernatural intervention on some as yet unrevealed level that perhaps these guys, hidden away in their mountains were keeping to themselves. Somehow, by some strange twist of fate, it had become my responsibility to drag the secret out of them."

"From what you have said I gather Okino has taken you to places where you have had some unusual experiences!"

"Well yes, at the stone circle on the way to Asima. I had an incredible feeling of being contained within oceans and mountains, rivers and animals, stones, currents, winds, waves; everything making the planet what it was. But then when I was in the waterfall, I felt the actual feminine presence of Arimathea and her birth, the flood of life and the nourishing and protective instincts she has for her creation just before I nearly froze to death!"

"Mariella, she has blessed you with an insight into the most sacred part of her being and this world she has become. No doubt you will now understand how every one of us women reflects those aspects of her in the same way her physicality reflects the being of whom she is a manifestation and so in turn we are all a part of….We are talking of course of the Great Mother, the Universe in which everything is born, lives and eventually dies. So, on this world where she has chosen for life again to emerge, we are all subject to her great cycle. We are born we live and we die and during that time we may pass on the information stored within the cells of our physical beings to the next generation who will further add to the information as we evolve into the future.

But as we well know, within the cycle of our lives we as women have our own cycles. We have to grow to maturity before motherhood can begin and then there will be a time in our life we are able to give birth and even within that time we have specific times during our personal cycles where we have the ability to conceive another human being. When born he or she can be guided during childhood but soon will reach adulthood and begin an adventure through their own life guided by all the wisdom we have been able to pass on and they accumulate through their own experience.

Could it be so different in the life of our world, Arimathea, who we reflect in so many ways? She has reached maturity and has given birth to a new consciousness on this world: a consciousness that has evolved and grown within the cycles of life and death. In planetary terms her cycles may last many thousands of years. But eventually and inevitably a new cycle will begin when the potential she holds, the direct link with the initial fundamental urge to create new life enabling her spirit to travel deeper into the future, will surface so strongly within her she cannot help but act upon it. As we are part of her the feeling will be surfacing in all of us. Many of our race of course will not recognise her call and it will be lost in the general confusion already felt as the result of the loss of identity with the consciousness. But those of us who have made the connection, who have nurtured the connection, will have felt it strongly and may have even be directly moved by it…"

She paused for a moment and looked carefully into the eyes of both Mariella and Okino.

"So, do you see the similarity with our own cycles? They produce a small window of a few days when we have the potential to again conceive life in our bodies and all the potential that can be unleashed into the world. Perhaps Arimathea has come to such a time when she feels she has felt the potential of new life within her she can now bring into the world. Perhaps she has felt the darker forces in her being have become too dominant. After all she will feel maternal towards her creation and if she feels it is within her power to offer some assistance to her young adult in its struggles then perhaps, she feels such a time has arrived.

So if you feel you have a destiny or your time has come and maybe you have been singled out for this path, because all these marvellous synchronistic events have been happening in your life, it means you have heard her call and decided to become involved: to take up the challenge Arimathea is offering to the entire human race. What do you think she would say?

"I am sick because of what you are doing to me through your lack of concern for me. All my wonder and beauty I offer is now under threat!"

The decision is open to everybody on this world and is the challenge facing all the people of Arimathea.

So, what I am saying to you both is; in a world in such deep denial and unaware of all this, the era you have experienced in your lives has been predominantly driven by the forces of destruction. The paradox of course is it has been the most creative time in human terms Arimathea has ever seen. But unguided by wisdom, she has been weakened. We have had so little understanding of the forces around us, so we have carried on building our industrialised world regardless of the consequences, unaware of the dangerous alliance we have unwittingly formed. Now the environmental systems of Arimathea are showing signs of serious stress. Droughts have meant crop failures on both the largest grain growing continents this year and are even threatening the standards of living in countries such as yours, Mariella. Strategies will have to be rethought if rising food prices spread unease amongst populations already under stress from the pressure their governments and financial institutions have put them under to maintain the stability of the economic systems. So, you see the time for change has arrived.

Those of us who have understood this crisis would eventually come, have been making the preparations, increasing our understanding of all we see around us, as we have waited for the shift to occur. Now as we suspect, the flow has changed, the hopelessness you feel will start to fade away as the creative forces of Life and Love start to make themselves felt throughout the entire consciousness of Arimathea. The dependence on the material dreams human beings have been fed for so long will be difficult to shift but their sub-conscious is still and always has been continuous with the consciousness of Arimathea. I think you will find they will be searching for a way to once again engage with their world and all her wonders so she can carry them and their children into the future!"

Chapter Forty-Four.
Zedocha.

By mid-morning, the next day, they had ridden through the out skirts of Zedocha and were now leading the horses through the heart of the city towards the port. The density of the buildings had continually increased during the morning and the traditional timber frame constructions had given way to more recent concrete buildings. The nature of their surroundings had changed inexorably. They had set off early as the Star climbed into the cool air of the morning and watched as the inhabitants had dispatched themselves and their families into the coming day. Okino observed these settlements on the outskirts of the city were not unlike the villages and larger towns deeper in the countryside. He suspected there were specific areas which had grown as a result of the influx of people who had made their way to the city to find work in and around the thriving city port. They had not given up their rural lives entirely and many clearly still kept goats and chickens in the small areas they had managed to secure around their houses.

As the children made their way to their schools, their parents walked in groups out towards the fields or in towards the industrial areas where they would work in the factories and warehouses. Yet again Okino felt the influence of the vast industrial machine growing before his eyes. He thought how life might be unravelling in his own village. Everyone would have their task to perform in a similar way as the people who now drifted past him and Mariella. The scale here was entirely different and he wondered how far the influence of the work these people carried out today would spread across the world. He knew in his own village anyone who went to work in the fields would directly see the fruit of their labours as the food they grew would be distributed throughout the community. Here he was observing an infinitely larger operation as lorries carrying produce back from the fields had to make their way gingerly through groups of unattended goats and entirely unconcerned chickens who strutted and pecked their way across the dusty roads; carrying crops that would eventually be carefully guided and monitored on every step of their journey to the plates of the wealthy inhabitants of the cities in the South.

He remembered the moment he had seen the fertiliser in Haran's barn and how alien the large white plastic sacks had seemed to him. Now he was beginning to have some insight into the scale of the world that had brought those sacks to the remote mountain farm. He became increasingly conscious of the roar of the city lying ahead and the frequency of the lorries increased as did the plumes of blue smoke they left in their wake. For many days they had been travelling through the pristine landscapes in which little had changed for hours perhaps an entire day. They had smelt little but the fragrances of the pollen clouds from the herbs growing on the mountainsides as they drifted down the slopes on the warm afternoon breezes. The hills or a village in the distance would then only approach as fast as their horses could carry them. Now it seemed increasingly everything was continually moving. The smell of burnt fuel had barely dispersed before the next vehicle passed adding to what had been left. Okino noticed for the first time the taste it left in his mouth and became used to the sound of the outraged chickens as they dived for the cover of their dusty yards as the frequency of the lorries became almost continuous. The horses were nervous but soon adjusted to a steady pace as they trustingly followed their dusty owners into the strangely organised confusion of a modern city on the planet of Arimathea.

It was the ghostlike dust that made the appearance of the little group so extraordinary as it made its way along the streets of Zedocha. The priest, the tall dark-haired girl and their three horses walked from the ancient world of towering mountains and their ancient spirits into the ephemeral cacophony of this port on the edge of the industrial world. There was little room on the crowded pavements for them to walk. However, the bewildered inhabitants gave them as much room as they needed as they rushed through the frantic struggle their city demanded for their survival. Mariella had told Okino about the phenomenon of eyes in the city and now he realised what she had meant. He noticed the distant self-absorbed look she had described as they rushed past on their journey. Many were so unconcerned or oblivious to the dusty apparitions confronting them they merely gave a disgruntled scowl as they hurried past perhaps for a few paces in the road which now, it seemed was shared by every kind of vehicle imaginable. Some would look up and catch his or Mariella's eye. Then they would observe the whole scene, possibly stop to stroke one of the horses and ask their owners where they had come from. They would forget the urgency of their task for a few moments and share the extraordinary nature of Okino and Mariella's appearance in their city. Perhaps they would tell of their own origins and when and how they had been seduced by the opportunities they had heard were to be had here. Then the distant look would come back into their eye and they would hurry on their way, disappearing into the noise and chaos.

Chaos was all Okino could see in the streets in front of him. Many of the men and women wore the traditional dress but now the influence of the southern countries was apparent. Both men and women wore fashionable tightly fitting trousers and cotton T-shirts, shirts and loose-fitting jackets. A smaller number wore carefully tailored suits, the women wore skirts of varying lengths immaculately finished with expensive sunglasses. They exited and entered the scene from their long sleek silver limousines floating coolly in amongst the melee of automobiles and scooters, of small carts drawn by humans, motorbikes and the occasional yak or horse. Both ancient and new forms of transport, coughed and snorted, purred and roared their contribution to the fog of fumes as they jostled for the little space their proliferation had now left on the narrow street. Inside the drivers screamed and used their horns frequently directing their frustration towards any and all the obstructions preventing them from moving forward perhaps for many minutes.

The limousines seemed to provoke the most anger. As he watched one of the sleekly dressed occupants disembarked to buy some item from a street trader and then disappeared into a shop blocking the only part of the road free from the drainage works underway further up the street. Okino was witnessing levels of anger which he had never seen in any situation. As the street became one endless melee of horns, he wondered whether this scene would end in some incident of violence. His question was answered as two helmeted individuals walked onto the scene. They appeared to be wearing body armour and carrying automatic rifles similar to those Okino had last seen in Azeera's cave.

The street quietened down as the policeman walked around to the driver of the limousine and inquired as to the reason for the obstruction. Meanwhile the driver of a yak cart had seen and moved surprisingly swiftly into an opening in front of the limousine. Now as the immaculately dressed passenger of the limousine returned and wished to carry on her journey the yak decided he would take a rest from his morning's activity. Even here the yak was a sacred animal so no form of persuasion that was legal could persuade him to move. The yak stood unconcerned as the street palpably shivered with rage, entirely at a standstill.

Okino smiled as he watched the scene. He knew the yaks as creatures who would continually perplex the impatient or the ignorant. Ultimately his people had presumed this was why they had been proclaimed sacred. They naturally handed out their wisdom to anyone who would bring about an end to a journey before it was truly over or continue at the pace ordained by the Great Mystery. He smiled at Mariella and handed the rein of his horse over to her. He made his way carefully through the strange collection of vehicles and irate drivers and over to the yak. He greeted the yak by affectionately ruffling its long forelock before bending down and whispering in its ear. To the surprise of everyone who was watching, the yak became instantly animated as if he himself now had somewhere important to be and started to move forward. There was a brief silence in the street before all those who had witnessed the event cheered and clapped out of their windows and along the street. Okino acknowledged the applause with a small bow and a blessing and walked back to his horse where Mariella handed back the reigns.

"So, what did you say to the yak, Okino, just in case I need to move one in the street when you are not around!"

"It's a sound they make to each other, you have to hear it really!" He smiled and started to lead the horse on up the street as the traffic again started to crawl its way onward to wherever it would eventually be.

Again, they continued with their journey through the layers that had grown over the life of the city. The fragrance of spices from the open cooking of street traders who called out relentlessly in the hope of enticing passers-by to sample their food, openly flooded the street and mixed with the smell of the manufacturing processes continuing behind or above the shop front facades, the odour of animals and the fumes of the engines continually running despite their lack of progress. Raw vibrant colour of traditional colour clashed with the shiny metallic surfaces of vehicles and grimy plate glass windows, the potholed disintegrating surfaces of the roads carrying the river of unbridled humanity flowing through and amongst the dilapidated modern buildings with their tracery of wires and cables draped like a haphazard web spun by some undiscovered arachnid dwelling secretly below the pavements waiting for some ghastly entanglement from which she would hungrily feed.

Okino found the continual noise surrounding him rose and fell as if it had gained its own low throbbing rhythm, a heartbeat in which each individual sound had its place. He observed the ever-changing scenes as intricate assemblies within this rhythm as he thought about all Sherana had told them the night before. The dragons had become so prevalent in the story, it seemed now as if Arimathea had once again made her presence known. She had spoken through the soft knowledgeable tones of Sherana who with little explanation had gathered the reason for their journey.

It had been clear from the stories they had heard, Arimathea had fallen out of favour with the Human race. She had become their adversary since they had left their wandering existence. Then she had become disconnected from her dragons and the humans had begun to forge their own path in parallel with the rest of her creation. The forces of destruction had found the weakness in her armour and had clearly exploited it to the full.

She continued to emanate her life force from deep within her being. But found she was becoming weakened as more of her spirits started to lose their foothold on the surface and began their retreat back into her consciousness. The light was starting to fade as humanity rampaged on, so powerful, so wrapped up in their conquest, so pleased with their dominance and the ingenuity they had found to change her, subdue her and bring her under their control.

Perhaps she had seen the power of Oblivion, recognised its emptiness in their behaviour; perhaps for a time she had become resigned to her decline. But it was all so beautiful and surely this could not all be lost.

Then again, she had remembered the little out post high in the northern Mountains. She had wondered whether she would ever be able to connect directly to them and she waited. Perhaps her story here was not over quite yet. Then she had found Mariella, felt her reaching out and she had sent her messengers in the wind and the rain. She had felt her roar in the thunder high in the tower that night. She had heard the call of her goddess and she had had no choice but to respond. Had this been the turning point Sherana had identified in her Shaman's bones?

The return of her dragons had then become her primary intent. Presumably she had realised the rest would follow. She had rescued him, pulled him into her plan and his strange journey had begun. Now her enthusiasm had returned as a new creative urge rose once again in her being. Now her dragons were freed, she would bring her world back from the brink. She would win over the humans or a significant number who could work her magic, harness their power to her dragon and they would take on the powers of darkness. Okino smiled as he felt her delight, filled with new excitement as she absorbed the mystical cosmic power of the dragon. So far, her plan had been realised and his part in it as he trudged through the polluted backstreets of Zedocha heading towards the greatest city on Arimathea.

He turned to see the dusty Mariella also deep in her thoughts. She caught his eye. There was a concerned shadow in her deep blue eyes. She immediately tried to disguise whatever was worrying her with the flashing grin he had become so accustomed to. A new phase of their journey was about to begin. Perhaps she was worried about taking him to her world which she had found so distressing. He smiled back at her reassuringly and asked.

"How much further have we got to go in this mad city?"

The buildings lining the streets had started to change. They had become more ordered and looked as if they had been continually maintained over some considerable time. They were not laced with the strange web of cables and wires running across and over the flaking paintwork predominant up until now. There were less yaks and scooters and more of the silver and black limousines. The street traders only scuttled hurriedly past the high steel gates as if they might be drawn into whatever lay behind and never seen again. The throbbing roar of the city had retreated into the background. Mariella had now taken the lead and eventually Okino found himself standing in front of the largest steel gates flanked by the highest walls. Through the gates Okino could see a large paved square flanked by further grand and well-maintained buildings. In the centre there stood a sleek black helicopter.

Mariella announced herself through an intercom on the wall and the gates swung slowly opened. Here were the gates to the otherworld and he was about to enter. A world that would dismiss all he had held to be true in his distant mountain home and would replace it with a manufactured vision that would astound, appal and shock him. As he stood in front of the sleek infinitely shiny black flying machine, he saw his dusty reflection with the three horses standing obediently behind him. How would a monk of the most sacred Order of the Dragon greet such a machine or ask a blessing for entry into its technological world.

For now, he wanted one, felt he needed one! In a strange way he had understood the chaos of the back streets. They had maintained and held their humanity and all it's strange craziness so prevalent in the market in Aharri on the night he had met Mariella. Now he stood in front of this silent black machine and they were being greeted by these men dressed in black. They seemed to know Mariella and after their initial greetings and a short account of their journey and about how they had travelled the men in black appeared to be breaking some bad news. Mariella then ran over to him clearly distressed.

"Something has happened back at home. This helicopter has come for me. They will take me to the nearest airport and I will fly straight home. I need you to take the horses on the boat. Everything is organised and booked. Here's where to go, and this will pay for everything. I think you will remember the number. It's 1616!"

She thrust a wallet full of papers and a plastic card into his hand. He opened the wallet looked at it briefly. There was a map indicating the route he would have to take to the docks.

You will have to make your own way to the docks. The boat sails tonight so I was planning on getting us all on board this afternoon. I am so sorry about this, but it's my mum she is really ill and I just have got to be there if…well anything happens…Take care Okino and look after our horses won't you and I will meet you in Straam."

She gave him a hug and an extra-long kiss. The helicopter had roared into life and the rapidly accelerating rotor blades threw up what little dust was left in the square. They reluctantly broke away from each other and Mariella ran towards the helicopter and carefully climbed into its howling body. The horses started backwards nervously, wide eyed as the thundering black machine rose into the air and hovered briefly over the square. Mariella still in the dusty blue robe he had first seen her wearing outside her brightly coloured tent, waved down to him frantically before she disappeared into the darkening sky over the city.

Again, he was alone but now he was even further away from home. He looked down at the map and carefully slipped the plastic card into his most secure pocket. The men in black had disappeared back into their building. They had left the gates open.

"Not very friendly."

He remarked to the horses as he led them out of the gate and looked briefly down at the map. He looked up and down the street before deciding the way to proceed. But now he had noticed a new smell on the air and he headed towards it excitedly as the seagulls called down their ancient song to him.

Chapter Forty-five
Ocean.

Okino wandered through the remainder of the city following the map that would take him to the docks. Now leading the three horses he again attracted great curiosity from the dwindling numbers of people who inhabited these broad streets. Their presence seemed to become progressively more incongruous as their surroundings became increasingly mechanised. Buildings huddled together in small groups strategically placed amongst the road networks and steel fenced enclosures holding goods that either had been unloaded or were about to be loaded onto the ships at the quays. Okino watched as the steady stream of juggernauts arriving at the docks added to the great stacks of shipping containers piled in every direction amongst mountainous piles of raw materials. He presumed the further stream of lorries removing the containers were bound for distribution depots and factories where the products inside would be further converted into whatever form they would take on their journey towards their final destination. A considerable network of cranes were continually lifting the containers backwards and forwards from or to their ocean-going hosts in what seemed to Okino like some endless carefully choreographed dance continually turning and whirling and flowing against the darkening evening sky.

As he arrived at the dock gate the entire area had become prematurely floodlit. The bright electronic light mixed with the soft evening Starlight. Okino felt the natural world he had known and was accustomed to, was fading around him. All references to his world were now disappearing as he stood in front of the plate glass window behind which a security guard was grinning down at him and the three horses. When he saw the puzzled gaze of the dusty monk and the three horses staring intently up at him the guard decided he would have to leave the comfort of his office to investigate. Okino gave a small bow as he approached.

'Now there is a sight I have rarely witnessed in all the years I have worked here."

He stroked down the neck of one of the horses who gave a low appreciative whinny.

"My name is Okino, I have come from a monastery far up in the mountains. These horses belong to my friend Mariella who has had to fly back to Straam in a helicopter. She has given me these papers presumably to show to persons such as yourself. We are to board one of these ships tonight."

He handed the papers to the guard who opened the wallet and read through them intently despite friendly nudges from the horses.

"That's fine son." He handed back the papers to Okino and noticed the tattoos on his wrist. He stood back and looked carefully at the tall dusty young monk.

"This all must be a little strange for you. It is still a fair way to the quay where you will board. I had a message earlier you would be arriving. I'll just give a call to the ship and tell them you are on your way. Just wait there a minute."

He disappeared back into his office. Okino watched the guard make a phone call while looking down at him and the horses. He then came back out.

"It seems your friend Mariella has some very influential connections. The Captain is coming down here personally to take you and the horses to his ship, The Osira."

As he waited Okino watched the guard check a number of the lorries in and out of the docks. Now with the windows rolled down he could see the faces of the drivers as they laughed and joked with the guard; before they had been concealed behind the glare on the glass of their cabs. He found himself surprised they were the faces previously he would have seen in the market at Aharri or in the streets of Asima. He found himself acknowledging perhaps he had expected a strange alternative race who had developed a mindset accustomed to operating and driving these technological machines which hissed and purred as they glided to a standstill or slid away into the night.

Yet here were his fellow countrymen who had perhaps decided their lives in their small mountain towns was too precarious or unpredictable or predictable and they had found their way successfully into this new world. They had mastered all it had demanded of them as they had made the transition from farmer or baker or blacksmith and now inhabited it and had become a part of it. He doubted whether they had questioned the new world they had entered or the part they would play as they allied themselves with the destruction it was causing.

In those moments as he stood waiting for the captain of the Osira he felt himself moving deeper into that other world. He was aware and was responsible for his actions and he began to question whether he really wanted to become more deeply involved in this world where his actions would start to have implications far outside the sphere of influence he had previously understood. He looked into the eyes of the horses. They looked trustingly back unaware of the ordeal unfolding around them. He wanted to go home; ride the horses back to Lamai where they would help his community continue in the way of life he knew to be so important; a way of life increasingly disappearing as a result of this new world humans had made for themselves. The horses looked at him their ears pricked forward as if they had read his thoughts. Were they urging him to turn back now? Take Mariella's card and travel back to his brothers at the monastery where he could spend his days wondering and debating about the mystery in which he had become so deeply involved and what the outcome may have been if he had boarded the boat. Then the silver limousine pulled up beside him and the window slid smoothly down.

"Hi, you must be Okino, I'm the captain of the Osira. Mariella said you might be struggling so I thought I would come down and give you a hand!"

Okino was then swept by the captain into the next part of his journey. The thoughts of doubt faded from his head as he watched the horses being led up a ramp into a transporter tempted by the thick layer of straw on the floor and the smell of fresh hay packed into the nets hanging on the walls. The horses never looked back. The smell of fresh hay had already passed through their nostrils and into the parts of their brains where they may have thought about resistance. Okino was happy to see them tearing the fresh hay out of the nets as the ramp was closed behind them.

He climbed into the back of the silver limousine similar to the one he had seen delayed by the Yak earlier that afternoon. The captain politely asked Okino about his journey and somewhere a part of him was answering. But now he was floating through the docks past the quays where the vast ocean liners and container ships stood silently, broodingly at their births. The cranes were continually loading the cargo ships with containers filled with recently constructed items destined now for the shops in Straam. The sleeker Ocean liners boasted the sweeping curves of luxury and expense containing multiple storeys of passenger cabins, swimming pools and helicopter landing pads. Containers full of food and provisions were swung into service areas where they would await their role in maintaining the luxury the passengers would expect during their long sea voyage to the other side of Arimathea.

Okino could see the crews guiding the containers into place giving him an idea of the incredible scale of these vessels. He could see the passengers strolling along the decks adjacent to their cabins, perhaps admiring the views of the mountains in the moonlight in the far distance beyond Zedocha detached as they were from their true beauty; or perhaps admiring the tranquil views over the city as the moonlight romantically reflected on the old stone buildings.

The limousine came to a halt where the transporter had stopped next to one of the cruise liners. The horses were then led down the ramp towards the gantry that would take them into their home for the coming days in the hold of the liner. Okino briefly intercepted and reassured them with gentle words of encouragement and solemn promises he would visit them as soon as he found out where they were. Apparently confident they were not being abandoned or sold they obediently followed a member of the crew up the ramp and disappeared into the cavernous cargo bay.

Okino remembered that Mariella's horses would have been through all this before on their incoming journey. His own horse then sensing no alarm was apparently happy to go along with them. Okino was left standing on the expansive quay with the captain. He was taller than Okino immaculately dressed in a uniform befitting the responsibility he held. He was calm and cheerful and curious about this new passenger who had arrived from the wilderness beyond Zedocha with Mariella Keating, who now stood in front of his ship wide eyed and obviously silently absorbing every detail of the scene before him. "Quite something isn't she, these ships are some of the largest objects ever built here on Arimathea?!"

Okino looked around at him smiling.

"I have seen pictures of such vessels but of course I just had no idea they would be so enormous and so brightly lit. If those are the doors and windows to the cabins where people are staying there must be thousands of people on board. Perhaps the number living in a good sized town where I live….and that noise…. the sound that it makes!"

The sound emanating from the cruise ship had suddenly registered with Okino. The sheer scale of the visual stimulus before him had briefly it seemed blocked his other senses. Now the deep low throb of the huge engines powering the ships around him even as they stood here on the dock, filled and even seemed to physically and rhythmically move the cooling night air; Okino was feeling the sound in his own body, an experience he had previously only felt with thunder and most recently the explosion on the dragon hill. Then in amongst the all-pervasive smell of the ships and the exhaust fumes surrounding him, a gentle breeze blew the smell of the sea across to him. He turned expectantly hoping to see the ocean spread out before him having momentarily forgotten these huge artifices before him were floating. He then quickly started to walk down the length of the entire ship to catch a glimpse of the ocean between the liner and the neighbouring cargo ship.

Then he was standing looking out across the bay where beneficial currents had allowed the port of Zedocha to naturally evolve. The moon was high in the cloudless night sky and spread a carpet of glittering moonlight across the gently undulating surface to where the water gently lapped on the sea wall below him. He could see a headland silhouetted out in the distance; a lighthouse intermittently flashed its warning to the ships approaching from the distant horizon.

So here at last was the edge of his world bathed in the light of the Star reflected down from Arimathea's only Moon. He had imagined when he had thought of his journey to the sea, he would find waves lapping on sandy beaches, freshwater outlets, sand dunes and breezes filled only with the smell of fresh salty air. However now he stood between these two monstrous machines, the ceaseless sound of their engines filled the atmosphere around them as if somehow they had become the sound of the world accompanying the Moonlight dancing on the water before him; a sound that had taken over from the peace and the whispering silence predominantly associated with such a sight on the shores of Arimathea. Here the silence had been eerily replaced by this new sound as if it's low throbbing intensity announced the arrival of a new supremacy in the natural order of the world.

Okino, alarmingly did not feel it was out of place with the movement of the stars and the moon and the rhythm of the surrounding Universe as if this power had come to dwell here as part of its own evolution. The great engines after all were driven by Fire at their heart. The Great Spirit had brought the urge for solidity out of its ethereal state and now his races fascination with Fire and its transformative properties had made it the dominant force on this world. Perhaps as soon as his ancestors had sat in the warm glow of their fires the separation from Arimathea had begun. As they became mesmerised by the flames, experimented with its properties and built their homes around it, the skills which had previously secured their survival had become less and less relevant and were eventually entirely forgotten.

Okino shuddered to himself as he remembered the dismay of the dragons as they realised their world had fallen again into disarray. Their attempts to turn the humans away from their path and its inevitable destination had ended in their unprecedented abilities taking an even firmer grip on the world. They were after all creatures of fire and ultimately of light. Had they not dwelt in the nuclear heat of the Stars and the dancing flames; had it been their own obsession with this element that had inspired the humans and brought them to this point in their history? Perhaps they had even instigated the discovery and their ability to use the heat within the flames as they had emerged from them. Clearly, they were torn between their love for Arimathea, the leopards, the eagles and all her other wonders and the clever ruthless independent beings that had evolved out of their dreams. Surely, they must have known the dreamer aspect of themselves would have to emerge as a bright unruly creature in no way bound by thoughts of planetary survival.

Somewhere behind him the Captain spoke.

"Okino I need to get back to my duties. You will understand it is a busy time for us. If you come with me now, I can give you a quick tour and show you to your suite!"

So Okino boarded the cruise liner. It would take him and the horses across the ocean to Straam and back to Mariella. He wished she were here to show him and explain the intricacies of this new world. As it was the captain whisked him through the carpeted hallways where the crew were busy preparing for this further leg of the cruise. He passed the smartly dressed passengers who looked with horror at the dusty traveller now being escorted by their esteemed captain through all the most exclusive areas of their holiday home.

The captain showed him where he would come for dinner at the centre of the largest banqueting hall next to him at the Captains table. Okino was shown the bars and nightclubs where many of his fellow passengers were already lounging in large numbers. He walked along the decks to the helm of the ship where he could look up at the bridge and out across the bay. Back inside there were cinemas and casinos, sports halls and gymnasiums where other passengers were working off the effects of their expensive holidays.

Deeper in the ship the captain showed him through the kitchens where the preparations for a banquet were underway. What seemed like hundreds of cooks worked cutting, boiling, frying and stirring the ingredients in the frantic steaming environment. They would provide three courses for more than a thousand meals in the space of a few hours. Okino caught the eye of some of the young cooks who worked at their positions as he walked through. They smiled at him through their panic and stress as they manipulated flames on their gas stoves attempting to prepare every kind of meat and vegetable, sauce and sweet imaginable to a delicious artistic perfection. Okino however was not able to see where the vegetable stew was being prepared and wondered how he would be able to choose what to eat from all the amazing food he could see being prepared.

Finally, they arrived at a door in one of the wider corridors. The captain smiled as he pushed open the door to where Mariella had secured for them to stay while they were on the ship. A spacious room was revealed, as luxurious as any Okino had seen in any of the magazines. He walked through in silence followed briefly by the captain, who then said,

"I hope you enjoy your journey with us. You are an honoured guest and I hope I will see you later on for dinner,"

He led Okino through to a large bedroom where three tuxedo dinner suits lay on the expansive bed.

"It is our custom to dress for dinner. Of course, I would in no way object to you wearing your robes but judging by the state of them we thought we could clean them for you ready for tomorrow morning. I think there should be one here that fits."

Okino felt the fine material of the lapels.

"I will follow the customs of your ship at all times and look forward to wearing these beautiful clothes."

He noticed the long dark blue silk evening dress. Mariella would still be on her plane to Eremoya and he wished she were here as he imagined her standing before him in the dress laid out next to his tuxedo.

"I must go now. Everything you could possibly need will be in here somewhere, so enjoy and I look forward to talking with you over dinner."

The Captain disappeared and left Okino standing in his home for the coming week. There was just long enough for him to have a brief exploration of the suite before he would have to get ready for dinner. He pushed open the sliding doors to the large balcony. He wandered over to the railing and looked out over the sea to where the lighthouse was still intermittently flashing. He thought really he would have liked to have settled down on the lounger looking out at the Stars with some food from the well-stocked refrigerator and maybe later on gone to find the horses but he felt obliged to eat that night with his important host who after all had helped him through this difficult transition.

After suffering extremes of temperature as he battled with and finally mastered the controls, he discovered for the first time the delights of a hot shower. The cascade of clean hot water was he decided one of the true wonders of the world as it seared through the layers of mountain residue caking his skin. He did not have time to question or deliberate why or how this had all had become so suddenly available to him but stood in the shower as if a part of some invisible quest had been fulfilled and he had reached a destination where at least physical ecstasy had been attained.

Reluctantly he left the shower and tried on the various tuxedos until he found the one he felt most comfortable in. He decided Mariella had judged his bodily statistics extremely well as he closed the door to his suite and started to make his way to the banqueting hall. Now there was nothing to distinguish him from the other male guests as they made their way through the ship in their identical attire. He reflected there would soon be protocols and customs in this strange new world he would question and would provoke thoughts and perhaps shed light on the predicament in which Arimathea now found herself. For now, he decided he would join his fellow passengers in the enjoyment of the evening ahead.

He arrived in the hall as it was steadily filling and the diners were making their way to the table places allotted to them. Despite his busy schedule the captain had already arrived at his table and was chatting to other passengers. Okino watched him and listened attentively as he exchanged polite conversation about the wonders to be found in the market in Zedocha and how they compared with other such destinations around Arimathea. He was clearly adept at distinguishing all being said in such conversations. Okino admired how he so expertly side stepped any discussion that might allow him to show favour in his response to one guest over another and how he carefully brought the quieter guests into the discussions. Soon the meals that had been selected earlier in the day were being delivered to the passengers. Before he had time to wonder what or how his own food had been ordered a waiter placed a carefully prepared fish with a large plate of vegetables to one side. Okino was surprised the kitchen seemed to have read his mind. He looked quizzically up at his host. The captain laughed.

"Mariella told me what you would like for dinner; Fresh fish and plenty of vegetables. So, there you are my friend, Sea Trout cooked to perfection with a pile of steamed vegetables!"

"Thank you, Sir, it looks wonderful!"

He put his hands together, closed his eyes, gently tilted his brow forward and silently gave a blessing to the spirit of the fish and thanks to Arimathea for her generosity. The prayer took him momentarily back to the monastery as if he was sitting with his brothers about to consume a fillet or some fraction of a fish in a pie from the lakes. His gesture was noticed and there was a respectful silence amongst his fellow diners. When he opened his eyes they were watching him with friendly curiosity. Soon everyone was again enjoying their dinner and lively conversation had resumed. This was Okino's first opportunity to observe his fellow passengers as a whole. The captain had for a moment been disconnected from the conversation happening around him and watched Okino as he carefully dissected the fish and assessed everything happening around him. Okino caught his eye.

"So many gathered together. You must meet so many people and hear so many different stories and hear about what is going on in their lives and in their countries."

"You're right I do meet a lot of my passengers; not only at dinner but all around the ship under different circumstances. Maybe if they become sick or something has happened they need to talk to me about. If I meet them when I am moving around the ship, they may ask how fast we are going or what the weather situation is. But it is always surprising how quickly some people can come around to telling me all that is troubling them or indeed their whole life story.

I have come to realise in the years I have been a captain they feel they can put their trust in me possibly more than in anyone else they know. I think perhaps it is because I am responsible for each and every one of them while they are on this ship. If anything goes wrong, then it will be me who will be answerable for whatever it is. You would not believe the things they tell me. It never ceases to amaze me the diversity of the lives people who come on these ships have led or are leading or hope to lead; most of them though I would say are the lucky ones.

One way or another someone or a couple who come on one of these cruises has been able to spend a lot of money. Even in terms of the lifestyles people are leading in the South. These are the people who have been in the right place, at the right time, had the right set of skills, had the right state of mind and all the right circumstances to give them the opportunity to be able to come on this ship. They make their money in all sorts of ways. By some methods perhaps I would not entirely agree with, but I cannot judge them and until someone in a court of law denies them their freedom, then I must accept them just like any other passenger.

Many will tell me they have started with nothing and worked hard all their lives to afford their lifestyle. If they have financial stability for themselves and their families that counts for a lot in any part of the world as it stands. They say to me 'I have put all this energy in and now I am reaping the rewards'. There are those for whom I have great respect; they have contributed enormously to the community in which they live. But there are many who would have had little concern for the well-being of their fellow humans who contributed to the making of their fortune along the way.

This ship pulls in at some of the most under privileged places on Arimathea. I have seen how the majority of people live in this world with a hand to mouth existence, worrying from day to day whether they will feed their children even down in the South. You will see all this where you are going Okino. Be sure to get Mariella to take you to the poor parts of town where they are shooting each other for the price of their next drug hit. I don't get many people on here who are trying to clear up the mess all that leaves behind; the surgeons perhaps who are taking the bullets out of people.

There is a lot of justification for extreme wealth where you are going, Okino, and you will have to make up your own mind about that. On this ship however we don't have to deal with the problems it creates. The worst that can happen is they lose all their money in the casino." The Captain has a wry smile as he waits for Okino's response

"It sounds like you have or are starting to have a problem with your own conscience."

"Of course, I wonder, anyone would who knew the cost of one of the suites that incidentally you are staying in. I am no politician or economist and have no idea how such inequality could ever be rectified so I do what I do and the world goes on."

"The nature of our world it seems is that some balance will always return to an unequal situation."

"Certainly, that may be true in the natural world but where you are going, Okino, there are people who are making up the rules as they go along in defiance of everything and anything to do with nature!"

The guest opposite Okino had turned his attention from the woman sitting next to him and now was concentrating on the captain.

"Now, now Captain we cannot allow this young man to dominate you throughout the whole meal!"

Okino listened for a while but soon found his attention wandering to the scene he saw around him. He watched in the light of what the captain had told him as course after course of the highly prepared food was consumed almost it seemed to Okino unnoticed amongst the continual roar of laughter and chattering conversation. The waiters and waitresses rushed from the doors into and out of the kitchen with further sumptuous creations only to be ignored as they placed them before the passengers. Okino was surprised there seemed to be little or no interaction between the two sets of people. One who appeared to be ecstatically happy revelling amongst all that was on offer to them and the other who had obviously been trained to show no sign of emotion as they delivered the food.

Here it seemed everyone knew their place for the moment. Okino watched in fascination as all these relationships unfolded before him as the evening went on amongst these people from the other side of his world.

Clearly there were those who were making less of an outward show of enjoying themselves than others. They conducted themselves in a more refined manner and these were the people Okino thought he might like to meet at some stage on his voyage. There were many however he decided that he would avoid at all costs.

The feasting was only interrupted when the captain stood up and asked for silence. He welcomed everybody in a brief speech and announced the ship would be getting underway in the next few minutes. A cheer went up amongst the passengers and sure enough as glasses were again filled from the numerous bottles of champagne that festooned the tables, the ship did move away from its moorings in Zedocha to continue its journey back to Straam.

Okino had answered all the questions addressed to him and consumed as much of the food placed before him as he felt necessary. When he noticed other passengers were starting to leave, he told the captain he was tired from his day of travelling and he would like to return to his suite. The captain stood up and shook his hand as he left the table before resuming his conversation with the rest of his table.

Okino retraced his steps back to his suite on the upper decks towards the front of the ship. He went straight through the living room, slid the windows aside and walked out onto his balcony. The ship was now leaving the bay and heading out into the open sea. The moon was high in the sky and was surrounded by only the brightest of the stars that could compete with its light. Okino leaned up against the railings closed his eyes. He felt the gentle head wind whispering across his face and through his hair. He could hear the noise of the bars and the nightclubs in the distance somewhere below him but for now there was predominantly only the low hum of the ships engines as it forged its way into the ocean. The land, his land was rapidly disappearing behind him.

He was to briefly inhabit this strange new environment which Mariella had decided was the best way for them to travel back to her own land; this vast machine on which he now stood floating across the moonlit sea as if out amongst the stars and the rest of the universe. A new world hewn, forged and moulded from the raw ores taken from the mines of Arimathea. It had been designed and crafted to epitomise luxury, privilege and status and now provided an escape for the thousands of passengers who could travel the world free from the inconvenient problems of pollution and crime now so prevalent in even the most exclusive holiday destinations. A massive floating hotel filled with the most exclusive food and drink and fitted with all the most up to the minute technology, enabling the passengers to completely escape from the reality of life on Arimathea.

Okino decided from what he had seen so far it appeared to be working. The passengers would not have to walk back through the streets to their hotels where perhaps they would be exposed to beggars or even thieves. They would not have to negotiate their journeys with taxi drivers determined to extort as much from their bank accounts on circuitous routes back to their hotels. He could see how this new world had been carefully conceived so all the cold harsh reality of deprivation could be completely avoided. A perfect world created within an imperfect world where every physical need and desire could now within reason and standards of decency be provided to those who were prepared to pay the high price of entry.

He smiled to himself as he wondered how the price of entry to this original world had been fixed. There clearly had been no assessment made of the passengers on this 'cruise ship' world other than being able to accumulate enough wealth to pay for the fare. There had been no consideration of the contribution they could make to this new world. There would have been no analysis of their previous cruises or even the life they were leading on Arimathea that could have been important for the development of this new world. Then again there was no evolutionary force to contend with on a cruise ship. The only skill needed was the ability not to run out of money while on board.

Then he thought of the staff and the captain and all his crew. They would have very specific skills to allow the smooth running of the ship. Presumably their relationships would blend and merge as time went on under the careful management of the captain and his senior officers, so the experience of the passengers was able to remain constant if not continually improve. If the performance of the crew was improving then almost certainly their relationship with the complex running of the ship would be constantly evolving. The engines, the environmental systems, the navigational equipment all would be subject to the ability of the crew to effectively and efficiently manage these systems. If any member of the crew was seen to be hampering the evolution then they could be helped or further instructed so the overall performance would be raised. Continually improving the experience of the passengers was the purpose of the evolution.

Okino wondered whether there could be passengers and crew on Arimathea? The idea of his planet as a ship cruising through the stars was a comparison easily made as he stood there on the balcony of this enormous floating machine. The universe stretched out into the infinity of space above and perfectly reflected on the surface of the ocean, surrounding him with stars.

The idea there may be a different and specific role for every being on such a star ship was intriguing. Perhaps when the dragon joined with Arimathea and was able to call in an almost infinite combination of souls and spirits the world had begun to evolve out of the consciousness. Their former abilities complimented and developed this new world as it struggled into existence. Okino could see how the dreams of the dragon could have flowed through the consciousness informing such a process. He thought of all the billions of souls who might have inhabited not only the lives of humans but the lives of every living thing on Arimathea. Each having been carefully chosen from the vast sea of souls or even instinctively knowing when to return and contribute to the great journey as it refined and honed the growing web of life.

Perhaps as the human beings became gradually more disconnected from Arimathea the loss and emptiness they had felt was because they had lost the ability to connect with the path chosen for them in the evolution of the consciousness. They had literally lost their way and only through intense work delving into the person they had become, could they again find their way back to their true selves and the mission they had been incarnated to carry out.

Okino remembered the conversation with Sherana the night before in her bar. She had talked of the paths and cycles running through the timelines and how the dominance of creation and destruction would fluctuate but ultimately would have to balance each other out for the life force to survive. Now he could see how if the abilities in the reservoir of souls could be called upon at a specific or critical time in the evolution so the development of the world could be enhanced or guided; it could even be strengthened to cope with a particular set of adverse circumstances. If this was continually happening throughout the whole of the consciousness, then the life force would evolve with a greater ability to cope as the millennia went past and the ongoing struggle between Creation and Destruction continued.

A beautiful system explaining so much about all he had heard and seen. He suspected there would have to be an almost infinite complexity of connections in a network such as he had imagined. Such a system may always be beyond human comprehension to fully understand and he supposed the only explanation would ever be magic.

While he stood on the balcony and looked out at the stars and the infinity which seemed so still, he knew it was all moving and expanding, contracting and rotating at speeds equally as hard to comprehend. Somewhere he was able to understand how it was all as possible and likely as his situation now as he floated under the power of the cruise ships engines out into the oceans of Arimathea.

Chapter Forty-Six
The Pool.

The complexity he had imagined stayed with him through the night as he sank into a deep sleep on the luxurious mattress of the suites expansive bed. Much of the deprivation he had seen earlier in the day on the outskirts of Zedocha became mixed with scenes he had seen later in the day at the captain's banquet. In a restaurant stretching out on a platform across the ocean, food was served from limousines and trucks, from dusty roads running between the tables. Itinerant workers moved from table to table choosing food to take from the plates of well-heeled diners. Intent on their conversations about how they had managed to secure a position on the ship they hardly seemed to notice as their expensive dinners were stolen from under their noses. Chickens and goats ran freely between the tables and were occasionally chased, caught and unceremoniously bundled into the back of vehicles by waiters and waitresses. On the edges of the platform fish were being caught and instantly cooked by chefs on open fires. Larger animals, previously slaughtered, perhaps the goats and chickens also were finding their way onto spits. Increasingly the tables were broken up to stoke the fires as they died down and the cooking of the meat slowed.

Well-dressed passengers and the itinerant workers had started to mingle. They stood watching the fires as they discussed the politics and philosophy about the roles they were playing in their world. As heated discussions ensued, they swapped immediately interchangeable items of their clothing. Tuxedos were swapped for thread bare black cotton quilted coats and silk evening dresses were exchanged for long black skirts and buttoned coats. Champagne and beer flowed freely amongst everyone and slowly the two groups of people became entirely indistinguishable. Groups of musicians entertained with a multitude of stringed and percussion instruments producing rousing music. Groups of people began to dance crazily and this inevitably was leading to more lewd behaviour.

Okino was able to move amongst the fieldworkers and the surgeons, the production operatives and the lawyers as they danced and argued and discussed, as they found and acknowledged the truths and the lies underlying their existences. They began to lose the pretence governing their previous station in the fields or in their grand offices. Gradually each soul began to realise the role with which they had been entrusted when he or she had been called from the Great Spirit consciousness. As each soul reached this realisation they began to shine, almost imperceptibly and very lightly as if a gentle mist was flowing over the surface of a world at dawn.

It then became clear the light emanating from their souls was shining down from the stars. As the people interacted in this new true form of themselves their light began to flow, from one person to the next at first but then as the numbers of shining souls increased it started to flow in waves through the crowd. Eventually all the souls at the party were connected as the light flowed infinitely through and in amongst them. They knew the light carried everything they needed to know about the role their soul would play in their new life. As they talked and felt and became that soul, they began to experience a feeling of unique potential complimentary with all the other souls around them as the party continued into the night.

Okino slept for the rest of the night in the peace this experience had brought to the dissolute group of diners and awoke with a sense Merilon had again visited him in his dreamscape. The bright light of the fully risen Star shone through a crack in the thick curtains drawn across the sliding doors to his balcony. Okino marvelled at the effortless comfort in which he now found himself after the weeks he had spent in the cramped tent with Mariella. He drifted through the memories of those previous days. The rigours of those experiences were far removed from this cocoon of luxury now surrounding him.

He decided the first thing he would do would be to find the horses and reassure them he was still with them. Mariella would be home by now and he hoped she had found her mother in better health than she had feared she would be when she had left on the helicopter.

The Star shine beckoned and he rolled out of the bed, pulled open the curtains and walked out onto the balcony. The turquoise ocean stretched miraculously to the horizon in all the directions. On the decks below he could see other passengers were already beginning to enjoy the activities on offer. There was a swimming pool surrounded by star loungers, a few of which were already occupied by people reading newspapers and others who were starting to enjoy the warm starlight. Okino noticed to his amusement a waterfall tumbling over carefully placed boulders had been incorporated into the design of the pool; large palm trees and smaller plants had been placed around the edges and further larger boulders appeared to incorporate low seats. The entire scene had presumably been designed and constructed to give the passengers some reference to a natural oasis. Okino was intrigued by this idea and decided he would visit the pool after visiting the horses. He would lay in the shade of one of the umbrellas, swim in the pool and perhaps talk to some of his fellow passengers. There were areas of his body aching considerably from the long ride and the relaxation a day or even a few days by the pool offered was extremely enticing.

He shuddered as he remembered reviving Mariella after she had ventured into the icy cold mountain water at Asima. Here in their manufactured paradise the designers had opted for the natural image of the waterfall to create their illusion. Here amongst all this state-of-the-art engineering and technology it was the simple nature of Arimathea they reproduced at the heart of the experience for the sophisticated city dwellers as they sought to escape from the reality of their lives.

Okino dressed, left the suite and made his way down through the corridors and the lower levels of the ship. He followed maps guiding him through the varying accommodation. The width of the corridors he decided would govern the size of the suites and cabins behind the lines of identical doors. He followed the maps to where larger blank areas illustrated the lowest service decks of the ship and by asking a number of crew members, he eventually found his way down to where the horses were settling into their voyage.

They were standing in a thick bed of new straw. Their nets were full of fresh hay in large stabled areas giving them the ability to move freely. Mariella had obviously specified precisely how she wanted her horses to travel home. They recognised him immediately despite the fact he had exchanged his dusty robes for knee length swimming shorts and the broadly striped bath robe he had chosen for his day by the pool. Okino stroked down each of their necks and fed them individually with hay. They nuzzled him and whinnied contentedly, clearly pleased and reassured to see him, before returning to the serious business of consuming the hay with which they had been provided.

Okino reassured they were happy resumed his journey through the ship to the pool. The passengers whom he encountered no longer viewed him suspiciously as they had the night before. Now they smiled politely and offered him some greeting. Okino was surprised at this point how they would walk on without any further contact. In his own land now far behind him, these encounters would have been opportunities for both parties to begin new friendships and so to learn further about the nature of their world. However, the customs of this other world appeared to differ and he would have to become used to them in the next weeks or months.

As the journey had progressed from one stage to the next, he had thought little about the time scales involved with his journey to Straam or if indeed he would ever return to the monastery in the hills. He knew of course he would have to return and briefly toyed with the idea of landing in the fields next to the village in the sleek black helicopter in which Mariella had been whisked away to the airport. However, he saw the stern look of his master in the crowd staring deep into his soul. What would he be searching for? He would be searching for the humble serene nature he knew to be instilled in the young monk who had left his monastery those years before. He would be searching for the signs of pride and self-importance so detrimental to the connection with their world his monks maintained away from the distractions and comforts of the modern world. Okino decided he would not arrive in the helicopter but on foot in the robes in which he had left.

He found his way to the restaurant bar adjacent to the pool. He had not eaten and decided to buy the bread and cereal and the rich black coffee listed on one of the display boards above the bar with the plastic card Mariella had given to him. He tentatively tapped 1-6-1-6 into the machine when it was offered to him. The young female crew member looking after the bar smiled and offered the receipt sensing perhaps he had never before performed this action. Okino bowed and offered blessings excitedly; for now, he had made his first transaction and so with the miraculous plastic he was able to feed himself. He carried his meal proudly over to one of the loungers where an umbrella had already been put up and settled down to eat his breakfast.

He relaxed into the morning, relishing the star shine on his skin and the enlivening feeling of the strong coffee in his body. He closed his eyes behind the Star glasses left for him and started to drift again through the days before. He knew there were places he should revisit and eventually felt he was being guided by Merilon to the top of the dragon hill amongst the ancient Star stones where they had emerged from their dark journey through the deepest regions of the universe. He was able to look out across the landscape to the distant horizons of the dragon's dream world. It now seemed to be more detailed and fully formed. The woods spreading across from the foot of the hill were alive with the sound of birdsong rising from it, the great Oaks were in full leaf.

He could see one of the castle temples projecting up through the canopy, the turrets created perfect viewing platforms for observing the surrounding landscape. He decided this was not the castle of Swords he had visited in the dream when he and Merilon had confronted Mithrael. However, there were two more castles he could see clearly. In the distance beyond the coast on a small island in the sea a castle rose from a rock left to fend for itself as the battle of erosion continued around it.

The other castle, in the near distance, glistened on an island in the centre of a lake. Waves gently lapped onto sandy shores leading up to walls rising straight and high to the towers above. There was a jetty leading to a large door. Then Okino was in a boat drifting across the lake. A mist had rolled down from the surrounding hills and covered the lake obscuring the castle, the shores of the lake and the surrounding hills. The thick mist and the silence it created was disturbed only by the presence of breezes occasionally whispering across the lake causing the mist to rise and dive and swirl into eddies. Okino lost all idea of space in the mist and how long he had been on the boat when the jetty loomed momentarily before it collided with the ancient woodwork.

He climbed from the boat, gingerly walked across the walkway leading to the door. He pushed at the stout construction and as before the door slowly swung open. The hall was of similar dimensions to the castle he had visited in the wood but the windows were larger and more numerous. These openings gave a greater connection with outside and the opportunity for more starlight to flow in from the surrounding countryside. Again, Okino noticed a timeless quality to the space. His own era or any time leading up to it seemed to have little importance. He felt he could have been taken back into the far distant past or way forward into the future.

The large banqueting table had been recently used. There were the remainders of a meal spread across it. It seemed as if whoever had been eating there had left in a hurry. Okino could deduce nothing further. A strong burst of Starlight through one of the higher windows sent strong refracted rainbow images across the high stone walls. In each of the openings arrays of large crystals had been placed to purposefully create this dazzling effect of spectral light in the interior of the hall. With the reflected light from the surface of the lake shimmering through the low-level windows the effect became entirely entrancing. Okino marvelled at the atmosphere resulting from the manipulation of pure refracted light. The scene emphasised the moment in which he found himself in crystal clarity. A moment condensed from all the time he had ever passed or would pass.

He made his way over to the spiral staircase in the corner of the hall and started to climb the narrow stone treads. He climbed until he reached the opening to a room at the top of the turret. It was circular with a timber roof carefully cut to provide a symmetrical timber underside consisting of eight segments of rafters and in filled with further boards. The walls below the eaves of the roof were continuously punctuated with square openings. There were magnificent views through each opening around the entire cylinder. In the centre there was a large crystal sphere. Okino wandered around the tower looking out over the landscape beyond. The coastline was closer now and he wondered of the mysterious temple on the outcrop of rock.

Eventually he settled down on one of the large comfortable cushions provided to contemplate the space. Pure white light radiating from the crystal's structure was intensifying. Okino remembered back to the valley where he had experienced the vibrations caused by the presence of the dragons gradually forming the vision of the settlement he had subsequently been able to visit. Now he experienced a similar sensation as the pure white light shimmered around him gradually absorbing walls, floors and ceilings into the ground, sky and the surrounding features of a new landscape forming around him.

Okino awoke in warmth and darkness. He had been sleeping on the ground and was covered by the fur of a large animal. When he pushed back the fur, he found he was amongst a large group of humans on the banks of a small river. They were huddled together sleeping on and under what appeared to be one huge blanket of fur sharing their body heat to combat the growing cold of the night as the days shortened. There were steep cliffs behind them and the opening of a large cave disappeared into the darkness. He sat up and shuffled with his fur over to a large rock where he was able to lean and assimilate this new dream. The rest of the humans were still asleep.

The Star was imminently to rise. Okino immediately noticed his senses were more acute and highly tuned. As the Star approached the horizon, he could feel minute changes in temperature as the direct rays became closer to the surface of his world. Already the tops of the tall trees on the other side of the river and the upper faces of the cliffs were shining with an intensity of golden light Okino had not experienced before. He watched as the light slowly began to move down through the trees. He knew it was moving because it was changing position but hard as he tried, he could not see the movement. He smiled to himself as he acknowledged the phenomena he had noticed on so many previous occasions when observing the movement of his world. However, now he absorbed this information with a flood of other information about his surroundings he previously had never experienced. The sounds and smells around him were forming a complete image in his minds' eye of his near and distant landscape.

From the sound of the river he could detect there was a bend where a shallow stony area was partially filling the inside course of the riverbed. The deeper channel of the river flowed around the outside creating still areas beyond. Under the bank he sensed the life force of several large fish. The scent on the breeze told him the species of trees inhabiting the forest. The intensity of the scent told him how dense the forest was. He knew there were fruiting trees somewhere within easy reach. He could detect strands of animal scent along the paths running through the forest, through this place and across the river. He knew deer and wolves passed along these paths and the frequency of their passing. He knew the weather conditions for the time of year and the coming day from the strength, temperature and direction of the breeze. He could identify the birds in the direct vicinity from their calls and whether this was their own territory or whether they were challenging for another's. He could hear their flight patterns and the seeds from which trees they were breaking open.

Further in the distance the scent of heather and grasslands told him the nature and extent of the landscape lying beyond. He also knew there was a large herd of deer grazing within easy walking distance. This sophisticated image was continually forming and reforming in his mind. It was giving him all the information he needed to survive the coming day. His search for food as always would be his primary concern. These were the days of Autumn. Fruit was at its height and his little group of travellers would have to gather and store as much as they could carry for the journey as they followed the deer herds South.

As the Star started to fall on his family and they began to notice the warmth they began to stir. Okino sat back gradually accustoming himself to the mass of information he was receiving about his environment. He remembered his journey with Merilon when they had joined the pod of dolphins. He had marvelled at the information the dolphins were processing as they swam through the Ocean. Now it seemed his own race had at one time possessed the ability to process such information about their own environment. He looked around there was no sign of a fire. He was wearing the skins and furs of animals. He and his family were living at the mercy of their direct environment and their senses were developed to enable their survival.

Not just survival, Okino was noticing, also for their enjoyment. All around him the world was alive. At first the crowded soundscape had seemed like a rush of unnecessary noise and information but now it became his connection with a world clearly alive and living all around him. He first noticed the vibration from the mass of the cliffs but soon noticed it was resonating from and through everything. Barely noticeable but once acknowledged it gave further insight into much of the natural phenomena happening around him. As vegetation, trees and birds responded to the growing starlight so the intensity of the vibration increased. This in turn provoked a wave of excitement to arise in Okino's being. He recognised this experience and realised the remnants of this phenomena must have survived through the countless generations to his own time.

The ancient experience of feeling Starlight returning to the world after the long night had continued to fascinate and enchant his race and here it seemed was its' origin. Senses with the ability to detect the frequencies of nature responding to the Starlight had long since been dulled along with the ability to form this moment by moment picture of the world. But the joy of the Star rise had remained locked into DNA as a remnant of these early times. For now, Okino felt inextricably integrated into his world, as part of its make-up, it's vibration, like never before. His being had responded to the Starlight and as excitement had arisen so his vigour and the optimism he would need to tackle all the coming day might present had also returned.

Now his close and extended family had woken and were sitting up also enjoying the first rays of the star and the warmth it gave to them. He felt each one of their spirits, unique souls who he had travelled with and cared for, had fought and killed for. A sensation he had felt moments before in the excitement his world had provoked in him, now returned intensely as he watched in awe of his wife and children, brothers and uncles and all the rest who had joined their tribe as they moved through the land. In those moments Okino found an overwhelming Love in a life he knew was often brutal and mercy less: where he would see the life force frequently disappear from animals and occasionally from members of his tribe as if it had left one state to be in another; where he knew he himself could die suddenly from disease or an injury at any time. Here though, Okino the monk, knew the Love and the vibration he felt, was the consciousness that had come to be when the dragon had joined with Arimathea. At this stage of human development, it was running continuously through their experience of each other and their world.

He saw it as they sat in the Star light as they hugged and touched each other affectionately cared for each other and murmured quiet conversation as they shared food and started the tasks of the day. A great happiness came over Okino as he sat wrapped in his fur blanket. He closed his eyes and turned to the warmth of the rising star. Here in this bliss he seemed to dwell for many eons until….

"Good morning, Sir. I hope you don't mind but didn't I see you coming onto the ship last night? It was a strange sight to say the least with you as dusty as I have ever seen anyone being escorted by our esteemed captain through the first-class accommodation. I just thought I would come and say hello."

Okino started from the dream. Clearly the dark Star glasses had disguised the fact his eyes were closed and he was deep in a dream. Okino looked up to see his fellow passenger standing at the end of his lounger. He was wearing long white shorts and a shirt entirely open revealing an expanse of tanned torso and well within the average age of most of the passengers Okino had assessed to be the age of his grandparents.

"Good Morning. Yes, I did come aboard last night. I have been travelling through the country on horseback for many weeks which is the reason I was so dusty. My name is Okino I am pleased to meet you. My friend made the arrangements for me to travel on this ship. I am to meet her in Straam. I know absolutely no-one so it will be good to talk to some people on the voyage. Please sit if you like."

Okino indicated to the unused lounger next to him. The man sat down and offered Okino his hand.

"My name is James Malin, call me Jim everyone does."

Okino shakes his hand and the two men settle back onto the loungers to enjoy the Star for a few moments. Okino was immediately full of curiosity. He remembered the words of the captain the night before when he had mentioned how his passengers were willing to tell him their life stories with almost no prompting whatsoever. This may have been an inconvenience for a man with the responsibility of such a vessel but Okino had decided he would listen to as many stories as there were willing to be told. What better way of getting a perspective on this world so rapidly approaching. Okino decided to prompt him before he was asked to explain his own story which he suddenly realised would be a little awkward.

"So, have you been on many of these cruises, Jim."

"Tell you the truth, Son, I come on maybe three or four a year these days. Sometimes they last for a month at a time. I used to look forward to getting home but as time has gone by these ships have become like home. Life in the cities just isn't what it used to be especially as I've got older and really, cruising this beautiful world through the warmest parts has many advantages over a conventional life. I've been to the polar regions as well. The scenery changes while everything I need is continually organised for me. I continually meet amazing people who without exception, all have a remarkable story to tell. I seem to have a knack of spotting the people with the really incredible stories so when I saw you arrive on the ship last night, I decided you were one of those people. I hoped I would be able to speak to you at some stage."

Jim peered over at Okino. Okino smiled back. His story certainly was incredible but he was unsure at this stage how much he would be able to tell Jim. However, even now he wondered whether the dragon might be carefully directing him towards the people he needed to speak to. If it turned out Jim could help him on his quest then he would have to reassess Sherana's advice.

"You must have done well in your life, Jim, to be able to spend so much time cruising Arimathea on these boats."

Jim laid his head back on the headrest of the lounger and laughed.

"I have done all right, son. I am one of the lucky ones you might say. I just have always done what I do. I never made a decision to do this or that. I just did what came along."

"So, what is it that you do?"

"I am a businessman, Okino, what in the old times would have been called a merchant. We are a special breed and you will have seen us amongst your own peers wherever you grew up. We are the people who will respond to a need as it arises amongst a group of people. It seems we have a state of mind which can see how to turn such a need into advantage for ourselves.

Some of my earliest memories were watching what the other kids needed and eventually what they would buy. At first, I found trading was a way of interacting with them but I soon realised I could gain much more. They would buy their sweets and the bits and pieces they used for their lessons like pencils and notepads from the shops on the way to school. I would notice how much they paid the shopkeepers. Then I worked out how I could sell this stuff cheaper to the kids by buying large quantities. The kids realised very quickly the advantage I was giving them and before long in a very minor and playful way I had started my first business.

I felt the advantage, even then; held my profit to buy more sweets or pencils, perhaps stuff the kids couldn't get on the way home. Kids talk and pretty soon I was spending more time running this business than I was on my schoolwork. But I was learning what I have used all my life ever since; how to satisfy a need and how to eventually turn it into profit for myself. Everyone is happy and it is how I have been able to come on these cruise holidays.

As I grew older and left school there were prosperous times. There was a boom, Okino, there had been a war. A war that had raged around our world and everyone had needed money to fight it. Unimaginable debts had accrued. God only knows somebody must have made some money selling planes, tanks and guns, bombs and shells to keep it all going year after year. The whole economy was being manipulated so the debts could be paid off. Interest rates were kept low and so money was cheap.

People returning from the war could buy houses and the suburbs were expanding. Mass production techniques had improved when creative minds were engaged to turn out weapons, bombs and planes as fast as possible. There was a great surge in the amount of household items available. Everyone wanted washing machines and fridges. A new era was starting and everyone wanted to forget about the terrible war whatever part they had played in it. Mass production was coming of age and it was making everything cheap to make and so cheap to buy.

So, I got a loan and started buying washing machines and fridges from the factory; sold them cheaper than the shops to everyone in the neighbourhood and eventually the city and then the next city. Then the companies would sell me the machines even cheaper because I was selling so many and by this time I had a service to install them as well. Then it was vacuum cleaners and the whole idea of cooking in the home was transformed. Everyone wanted the new compact easy to use oven cookers.

So, it went on. I never worried what I should or should not be doing. Eventually companies asked me to go and head up their marketing departments, sit on their boards and committees but it didn't last long because I had seen the next big thing, Okino. TV, everyone wanted a television. People had been flocking to the great movie houses for years to watch the movie stars. But now television beamed it all into people's houses and a visit to the movie houses became something of a special treat when the big new films came out. So yeah, I did all right.

Everyone was finding their way to the money as the world rapidly began to expand. While I did what came naturally there were other kids around me who were finding out what came naturally to them. The kids who were making things in their back gardens or in their dad's sheds, who became interested in the systems they saw all around them gradually started to move towards engineering in their education. The kids who felt they wanted to look after the other kids who fell over in the playground or felt enough compassion to offer some advice when they became ill steered their lives towards medicine and being doctors. Others would stick up for the kids who were being hounded by their peers and of course they became the lawyers. The inquisitive and curious became the scientists researching and developing the technology that would made this new world we have inherited possible. Of course, not everyone was able to find a calling or something that had gripped them for whatever reason from an early age. So, they got themselves jobs in the cities and the factories working for the companies making the planes and the cars and all the household stuff.

There were administration and organisational challenges and so the natural born leaders stepped in; and the creative art school generation were sucked into the expansion by the design and marketing companies to beguile the population into buying all the stuff being made; then the enormous expansion of the food supply chains to feed the people who had settled around the cities. They all absorbed a workforce hungry for the money to pay for their houses and all the products they could put in them. It all continued to expand to where we are today with global communication systems allowing us to spread our markets around the world. We have all found skills we just did not know we had a few generations ago.

But then there was another group of people who never were able to share this fervour for this relentless technological expansion of the human race. I think they were the intuitive ones, the artists, musicians and the poets, the visionaries. They watched us all as we were carried by this enormous wave into the future but showed little interest in the world growing around them. But they were interested in what lay behind it or beneath it.

They expressed their discontent and suspicion in any way they could. In their paintings and their poetry, in screen plays and novels they wrote, in the films they eventually made; they wrote songs and formed bands. It seemed something in their intuition was leaving an unease as it all unfolded. They claimed they could see the future and how it was always affected by the past. They said we were heading towards an uncertain future rather than the certain one which we were being promised. They spoke out against the economic system slowly engulfing Arimathea; it was still sending our children to war to defend our interests in other countries and allowed indiscriminate use of Arimathea's resources at the expense of her natural beauty and her indigenous peoples.

Now I'm talking fuel, son. Coal, Gas and Oil. The world is run on the stuff and they say it's running out. But I wonder whether they tell us that so they can keep the price high. Corporations hold monopolies over the supply. Everybody wants, hell needs a car and to fill it with petrol, they want central heating in their buildings in the winter and air conditioning in the summer. But like it or not the climate has started to change across the planet. Cleaner sources of energy production were found. Although they all have remained mysteriously underdeveloped and the reliance of the planet on Oil keeps on rising. The Oil companies aren't going to give up their goose without a fight."

Okino looked puzzled.

"A goose that laid golden eggs, son. An old fairy tale about a boy who plants some magic beans he traded for his mum's old cow. They grow into an enormous beanstalk and he climbs it up into the sky. There's a castle in the clouds and he ends up stealing a goose laying golden eggs for a giant. It ends happily in the fairy tale. The giant is killed but frankly I'm not sure this story will end so well.

We know somewhere in the back of our minds they are right but when we need to put food on the table and pay the bills we just get on with our lives; after all we've always been told by the politicians we could trust and rely on them to run the country and regulate all the corporate business activity in the best interest of our freedom and stability.'

Jim seemed to pause. There were clearly conflicts in his mind which he now was coming close to airing with Okino. He shook his head and sighed as he looked up into the cloudless blue sky.

'We never made any choice in our lives to turn the world into what it has become. It just all happened in the race for profit and wealth. The urge was always there as far as I can see. We wanted control over our destiny. But they have always been there with their predictions and their unsettling taunts. The human race would take the world to the brink of destruction.

Most of the human race of course has always denied this because the market had come to operate across Arimathea. Our destiny was transformed as we eradicated the uncertainty we have always felt in the face of the natural world. Now, we thought we could dismiss the power it had held over us. Superstitions about supernatural powers working through the world for our well-being or otherwise had no place in this new mechanised industrial world. Now we were in control of our own destiny. They invented all sorts of crazy stuff to try to slow things down but everything just kept on growing regardless.

But you know the strange thing about all this is that many of us subconsciously uphold those strange superstitions. Some of the most scientific people I know have little rituals they go through before they perform certain tasks or operations. Strange things like putting their left sock on first or some specific order in which to turn the lights out. They won't drive on certain routes on certain days or mention certain people in connection with certain activities. Presumably to avoid upsetting the supernatural spirits governing the successful flow of our lives.

Without thinking of the origin of such practices we call upon those ancient powers when we get ourselves into trouble. We like to be in control there can be no denying but when things go wrong, we want to know there is someone or something to sort the mess out for us. We deny so much of what those mystical poets are telling us but many of us act as if these powers and energies are living all around us. I don't think we really let go of them and we constantly appease them with our sayings and actions and yet still we defy them!!"

Jim became quiet. Okino had been listening attentively as he became used to the sensation of relaxing in the Starshine. Jim's words had drifted through his mind. He had explained the technological expansion in terms of the people who had been behind it. He thought of the similar characters in his own community. There were the healers and the farmers, leaders and organisers, musicians and artists and although there were no lawyers there were the members of the town who were particularly interested in the maintenance of justice on the town council. He could see the builders who had learned many of their skills from previous generations, enabling them to build the traditional houses, had similar talents to the engineers who were building the steel and glass skyscrapers in Straam. In both communities they were the people who had risen to the challenges their environment and their age had presented to them.

In the industrialised societies their achievements had been celebrated and marvelled at as the structures and systems they created had transformed the face of Arimathea. Yet even here amongst all this technology and growth, there had always been it seemed, the mystics who had retained a connection with their world and the beauty that had arisen upon it. They had spoken up for the fragility they had sensed in the face of the mechanised onslaught the human race had brought. But the idea of co-dependence had yet to be established on a world where the rise of humanity was unassailable and as yet unchallenged.

"So Okino it's been great talking to you. We should catch up soon maybe have some dinner and you can meet my wife who for some reason is now urgently signalling to me from the restaurant. So, I'll leave you in peace!"

"Yeah definitely I would like to meet her and thanks for your story this will all be an enormous help to me!"

Jim hurriedly made his way around the pool to the restaurant. Okino drifted back into the visions Merilon was sending him. The dragon's dreamscape formed before Jim had arrived had never been far from his mind. He had seen many of the scenarios Jim had been explaining materialise in the landscapes of the dream world. In the city he could see far off in the distance, the future world Jim had described had already been formed in the dragon's dream.

He saw the suburbs rapidly expanding, filling with people happy to be able to afford their own homes and all the products being turned out from the factories at ever increasing speed. People drove in their new cars from the suburbs to the expanding cities where the vast skyscrapers were bolted and welded higher and higher into the skies above their streets; now filling with air liners manufactured in the factories where only a few years before fighter planes had been constructed to fight the war which had engulfed the planet. Everywhere in this vision Okino saw the unbridled creativity of the Human race mastering new technologies as their understanding of the world grew.

Deeper and deeper the layers of this new era were revealed to him until he watched over Arimathea as she had become; weakened and degraded by this outbreak of industrial activity. Minerals extracted from her which had taken millions of years to accumulate and days to turn into products or the bi products of the processes to fuel this new dream being released upon her. They had discovered the horrifying and destructive power lying hidden in the tiniest structures making up the world. A succession of nuclear explosions had ripped deeply through the fabric of her consciousness. The threat of the war to end all wars arose between the nations of Arimathea. Now a terrible destiny hung over the world as the human race entered the Nuclear age. His vision of the city with its suburbs, factories and skyscrapers and all the people living and working within them disappeared in a flash of light. The dragon it seemed had made his point quickly and effectively. Okino shuddered at the speed with which the final transition had occurred; how fast his race had suddenly unleashed such a destructive force on Arimathea.

He awoke again with a very different feeling. Even before he opened his eyes he felt the strength of the star burning his skin. His life force was in an entirely less vigorous state than it had been with his tribe beside the river. It seemed as he opened his eyes, he was assessing whether he could afford the energy this simple action would use. As he once again looked over his world he knew why.

He was leaning against the stump of a long dead tree. He was wearing the remains of sophisticated well-tailored clothes clearly purchased when he was considerably heavier. Okino realised the reason for his lack of vigour was that he was starving to death. As he looked around, he could see his family asleep or possibly already dead. They were sitting under a crude canopy giving little shade from the Star. There was little sound other than the incessant buzzing of flies. Occasionally there was a moan from somewhere in the distance. Okino tried to see beyond the encampment his family had made. His view was obscured by other shelters made where other people were sitting silently, unmoving on the hot sand. He knew he would have to stand up to see beyond the shelters surrounding him but he had little will to perform such a task.

Okino had to concentrate hard to summon up enough energy to pull his body to his feet and when he finally stood shakily and looked out over the surrounding landscape, he wished he hadn't. The scene in his direct vicinity was repeated as far as his eyes could see out to the far horizon. Thousands upon thousands of people sitting silently in the midday Star light waiting to die. Some sat next to the vehicles that had brought them to this place in hope of salvation now redundant as the last available fuel had been used. This however was their final destination. There was nowhere else to go now.

Okino turned to see the reason for this enormous gathering of people. In the shimmering heat haze he could make out a huge wall stretched in both directions far into the distance. It towered over the dead burnt trees in front of it and Okino could see there were people walking along the top. A vast steel gate had been constructed over a six-lane highway leading beyond the wall. Okino could see buildings behind. Initially not much higher than the wall but beyond skyscrapers towered over the interior of what Okino concluded must be a city full of the last privileged human beings. Okino wondered momentarily whether conditions could be any better within the wall.

Human beings had always been ruthless and ingenious when their survival was at stake. Now it seemed these instincts had surpassed all that had gone before. Those within must have anticipated the catastrophe now overtaking whatever world this was and constructed an environment providing a food and water source for as many people as could be contained within the walls. It appeared a complete breakdown of the wider technological society and a catastrophic drought in a previously well-developed country had occurred. Now the last city in a land rapidly turning to desert had closed its gates on the people who had nowhere else to go and nothing to do except sit and die.

Okino collapsed into the dust aghast such a decision could have been made by his own race. He noticed his wife who was leaning against what would have been their family car. She opened her eyes and smiled weakly over at him. He crawled over and sat next to her, put his arm around her and she laid her head on his shoulder. She had been there in the hides with him next to the river. She had stroked his face in the early warmth of the rising Star. He could still feel the love that had flowed between them with her gentle touch. Perhaps their souls had travelled through all the millennia together, always found each other pulled together by some cosmic rite conducted in the stars to carry them through all they would face down through time. He had always known he had recognised those beautiful turquoise eyes when he had first looked into them. Now the light was fading from them and he sadly pulled her closer to him as he felt the life force depart from her body and he himself lapsed into unconsciousness.

So again the soul of an extinct world came to be floating across the universe; Okino had joined the dragon's soul for a moment as it drifted through the wastes of space hoping to find a new home in the galactic star fields; joined with all the other souls who had been born to continue the journey towards perfection in another time, but for now continued in the chaos of the uncertain and the undetermined, of the infinitely fluid, continued in the undefined state where everything contained in a carefully arranged structure and organisation was now uncontained and banished again to chaos. The tendrils of fate and destiny reached out, scanned the emptiness for some hold, in the hope of a chance meeting, some occurrence to guide some beneficial episode into its path. A tiny spark to again ignite the pathways of cause and effect, of light and dark, so the great soul could again progress onward with all it had learned.

Okino became conscious again, in the chaos of a stormy ocean. He spluttered out the water he had inhaled into his lungs with his first gasp in this new physicality. He rose and fell on the waves driven by the wind howling its defiance around him. Stinging rain bit into the exposed flesh of his face. At the top of a wave he recognised the castle he had seen away from the coastline looming above him; he instinctively concentrated his energy on swimming towards the dark and jagged rocks from which the castle arose. The swell and the currents swirling around the rock meant Okino had very little ability to control the direction in which he was able to swim. He seemed to be pulled further away from the rock. But no sooner had he acknowledged his despair had a further powerful wave flung him at great speed straight back towards the rock.

Again he was thrust back into the darkness and chaotic instability of the journey through the stars he had previously escaped, only to resurface once again to find himself adrift in the surf, with little strength to resist he was being pounded again and again into the rocks. Then at last he felt stability. He felt a strong hand grasp the clothing around his neck, drag him from the merciless battering he was taking from the waves and deposit him on a water-soaked timber decking. When he had coughed and spluttered out the remainder of the water he had swallowed, he passed out again.

He again became conscious sitting, with his upper body sprawled across a broad solid table. He was in the main hall of the castle it appeared with a ferocious fire in a large hearth behind him. His clothing was entirely dried. His head stung from a crack on the rocks as he sat up to take in the hall where he had come to rest. He started momentarily when he realised that staring down at him from high on each of the walls were the skulls of many large animals. He recognised immediately the skull of the deer with its enormous antlers spreading into the room lit only by the flickering of the flames. Other skulls were less recognisable but Okino thought he recognised a horse and an enormous bear possibly and an elephant. What else could have been so enormous? A rhinoceros with its two horns still intact and the cats recognisable from their vicious array of murderous carnivorous flesh ripping teeth. Others he could not directly place to the animal they had once belonged to but unmistakably high on the wall over the fire was the skull of a dragon.

No creature had ever evolved such elaborate horns emerging so symmetrically from the both sides of the long upper jaws and the cranium of the skull. Even empty of the eyes they once would have contained, Okino recognised in the eye sockets the depth of eternity he had briefly seen in his encounters with these creatures. This skull must have been miraculously preserved from a time when the dragons had lived in whatever part of the universe they had physically emerged; before they had been compelled to return to their spirit state able only to make visits to the surface from the realms in which they slept in their crystal caves deep below the surface. There were skulls of many other animals carefully mounted on the walls. As a result, this hall must have contained much of the ancient spirit knowledge amassed by these creatures and their species in their long evolution on Arimathea. From the plains of the savannah and the tropical jungles, to deep in the oceans and high in the mountains, from the temperate woodlands and the rivers winding their way down to the seas, the spirit memories stored in the old skulls flooded through the atmosphere of the hall.

This surge of information from the memories of so many of these ancient beings at first began to overwhelm him. The techniques these creatures had evolved to survive seemed to be as infinite as the creatures that had evolved on Arimathea and now they were flooding through his mind. He watched the great herds of grazing creatures making the initial transfer of energy from the grasses and vegetation they continually fed to sustain their lives as they drifted across the vast savannah and grasslands as the seasons dictated. He saw how they were continually pursued by the predatory power, stealth and agility of the big cats or the dogged determination of packs of wolves. Energy once again transferred to continue their life.

He saw how plants and insects had developed their sugary temptations to lure their victims into their invisible and sticky traps where they would be mercilessly devoured or dissolved by the poisonous juices enveloping them or injected into them. He saw how the anatomy of lizards and frogs flicked out their extended tongues to catch insects that had flown tantalisingly out of reach and the beaks of birds developed to crack the seeds previously unbreakable. He saw how bats had developed the ability to hunt their flying prey by pinpointing their exact position in the darkness by bouncing sound they themselves made off their victims and their surrounding environment. He saw how the eagles and hawks had developed such powerful sight by developing additional lenses in their eyes to detect the tiniest movements in the landscapes below. Across the surface he saw how fish and whales had developed membranous filters to harvest the vast colonies of sea creatures existing across the oceans of Arimathea.

In all of these visions of dust or frozen ice and snow, of icy winds or sweltering solid heat of the midday star, of the Star filled glades of the temperate forests or the dank gloom on the floors of the tropical jungles, high in the tree tops and in the depths and on the surface of the ocean, in all these places life had come to be. The life force had found a way to adapt and proliferate itself in every environment it had found on Arimathea. Okino felt the time scales responsible for these adaptations may have taken millions of turnings to become apparent; to change some behaviour or some sense or bodily improvement making it more likely a species would survive and so proliferate life as it had come to be on Arimathea.

He saw how all these lives had come to be an intricate and beautiful expression of the Love that had formed between the dragon and the planet of Arimathea already bathed in the warming nuclear light of her Star. The dragon had come to be the channel for the spirit consciousness when it had first flooded into the physical realms formed at the beginning of time. New life had then slowly emerged as his dreams filled Arimathea. As the form of life became more complex so the dream of the spirit consciousness to experience itself and its potential started to come to fruition in the harmonious love and light forming around Arimathea.

Okino drifted deeper into the dream. He found himself in a woodland full of birdsong. He scratched deep into his fire red fur to expel some annoying visitor before looking over to see where the four fox cubs were playing with the remains of the meal he had caught for them earlier. Their mother slept close to them with one eye on their antics as they tested each other's strength. For now, he can rest and goes back to dozing in the Starshine. He relives the days and nights hunting through these woods in amongst the bracken and the Oak trees. He had returned to one of his favourite sites. He had crept carefully to the fallen tree where he could observe the young rabbits as they emerged from their burrow. He would allow them to relax as they started to nibble through the grass surrounding the entrances. Then he would start to stalk them.

He remembered the exhilaration he always felt as he moved, careful to avoid making any sound to alert the rabbits of his presence. The cubs were growing fast and every moment of his day had to be an opportunity to feed them. He could not afford a mistake so they would go without food. He was nervous and yet he always felt excitement as his senses, fully alive, registered and monitored every sound and smell from the surrounding woodland. He had to be invisible. He had to become part of the wood, part of its ground and the breezes flowing through it. Any recognition of fox in their direct vicinity and the rabbits would be back into their burrow in a flash and his time would be wasted.

He seemed to lose his solidity in those moments: he felt the energy building that would allow him to make his final dash, the final spring when he would capture the rabbit he knew was so desperately awaited. In this state, in these times he had always experienced a strange euphoria coming over him. He would become more than this creature in the wood. He expanded into the trees and the breezes and the scent of the flowers around him, he felt the ground was softer and warmer and spread far beyond the woodland or even beyond where he had travelled. He felt even those lands had some familiarity. Above all he must make this kill; for the cubs it was critical but something told him his hunting was important for the wider expansive feeling at the root of his exhilaration. Then the moment would come, the preparation he had made, all the experience he had gained through countless hunts, all the tricks he had learned now came to fruition as he sprang and pounced on the rabbit who until that moment had known nothing of his existence.

He had only taken the edge off his own gnawing hunger on the way back to the den before leaving the dead rabbit for his mate and the cubs. He would hunt again later in the light of the rising moon. Now he would doze in the gentle hum of the summer woodland. His exhilaration had turned to the deep satisfying peace he felt when his family had eaten. Again his solidity fell away as he drifted out through his own memories and into the dreams he often had of wide plains stretching to the far distant horizons, where herds of beasts of every description grazed across fertile lands, where he hunted with a pack of strong brothers and sisters where he would never be hungry again. The Star was higher and stronger. This was undoubtedly his world but another very different land where a similar struggle to his own was going on. He felt a deep satisfaction and pride his own life was mirrored here by these magnificent creatures and the many other creatures whose lives and lands he was able to share in his deeper dreams.

Okino became aware of the hall dancing with the warm flames of the fire burning constantly in the great hearth. All he had seen turned in his mind. Again, the understanding of his world had been deepened. For all the sophistication people had taken on, in their denial and separation of their true nature they remained creatures who shared Arimathea with the countless other creatures who had grown and evolved into the life the dragon and Arimathea had brought about. They had merely grown into and exploited the opportunities and potential they had found as had all the other creatures inhabiting Arimathea. At some time, their unprecedented expansion had led them to believe they could separate themselves from the primitive beginnings they retained deep in their souls. Although they still had an ability to experience and respond to the beauty of their world and be moved by it.

Okino looked up with admiration at the dragon skull over the fireplace. Life on Arimathea existed on the edge he had created with dimensional possibilities he had blended from those previous worlds flowing through the consciousness. No outcomes were presumed or certain as the complexity of those forces flowed together in the wider consciousness of the Great Spirit Mystery. He noticed there were corbelled stone steps protruding from the wall leading to an extended mantel piece easily wide enough for him to stand on. He carefully negotiated the steps and the stone slab over the hearth. This brought him directly beneath the enormous skull of the dragon. He placed his hands on the skull of the spirit creature. So much of the history of his world had originated and passed through here, the nerve centre of this extraordinary supernatural creature.

Deep within the dream the dragon had sent him as he lay in the starshine, Okino's understanding was able to reach deeper into the consciousness of Arimathea and in turn he became fully connected into all her life force and all the spirit beings who had evolved there. For a few moments he felt the wonder of his life within it and his ability to be a part of it and understand its immense and astounding nature.

There were those, in those moments, who received his thoughts and his reverence. They recognised his understanding once again surfacing as the wisdom and ability long since disappeared and absent from the human race. As it had reappeared and was acknowledged, a ripple of delight ran through the ancient spirit races of Arimathea.

Chapter Forty-Seven
The Ocean Gathering.

When he surfaced from his dream, he was beginning to fully realise the powerful capabilities the dragon was now able utilise. The new dreamscapes he was able to construct were as close as his own imagination and could even access his daydreams as they ran parallel with his own waking world. The actual dreams he presumed were amalgamations of the dragon's own memories, dreams and visions. Feeding through into his thoughts they were now powerful experiential episodes. He had been in the temple dedicated to a crystal sphere where he had flowed into moments refracted from light travelling infinitely through time and space. It seemed, from here the dragon was able to create almost any time situation from where he needed wisdom to flow and where it would enable further understanding to grow; for this had always been the true and primary purpose of light as it had continued from the previous ethereal universe. The ability to recognise and to receive the information it contained within its pure form had never been lost. The dragon had always guided his dreams through the light to illuminate the lives of all beings who lived within the consciousness. The solid transparency of the crystals in the depths of Arimathea's deepest and most extreme elemental sanctuaries had always been fundamental in maintaining the nature of the consciousness around her.

All that had come to be and continued in this solid world came from the vibration of the light captured and held in the solid transparency of her crystal caverns. As she had formed and found herself in the orbit around her Star the vibrations of the light had embedded themselves within the crystals filling her with the Love and wisdom that had survived from the previous ethereal universe. They also sent a signal that had always flooded into the dark space around her. There was nothing to dilute or interfere with her gentle vibration as it travelled uninterrupted through the stars. The dragon on his hopeless flight through infinity had felt the gentle waves emanating across the star fields and followed them to their origin within Arimathea.

As Arimathea had evolved the vibrations had combined infinitely within the dragon dreams to form the consciousness. Each life came to have its' own individual vibrational signature within the consciousness of the life force. Many of the ancient animal spirits Okino had subsequently come into contact within the dragon skull castle had never lost the ability to detect and distinguish the vibration of their fellow spirits flowing through Arimathea. The oldest spirits surviving on Arimathea had become animals such as the elephants and the reptiles, the deer and the eagles, the cats, bears and wolves, in the seas the whales, sharks and the dolphins. All were descended from the most ancient spirits. They had survived through all the extinctions that had befallen Arimathea. Their senses were acutely developed in minds that had always been enveloped and deeply connected into the dream consciousness. The knowledge and wisdom contained within each of their dreams allowed each new generation to make its way in the world as it came upon the knowledge of previous generations.

The human species with the skills it had acquired through the twists and turns of its own journey had gradually become separated from the dream consciousness. The human mind at one time so connected had not changed in the small stretch of planetary time it had taken for the human species to undergo this separation. The abilities allowing the connection to the dream consciousness still existed in every mind. However, the pathways leading to those areas now lay mostly unused and forgotten.

The monks of the Dragon Order had preserved their ability to negotiate these pathways and had been able to maintain their connection with Arimathea. Others had found their way into the consciousness through deep spiritual practice and they remained the Shamans within the communities. However there had been such great abuse of the power by the priests of the alien gods, the idea or belief in any supernatural connection had largely fallen away as the people of Arimathea looked towards the new industrial materialism to satisfy the loss they felt as a result of their separation. Anyone who claimed to have a connection with Arimathea was now unable to persuade their fellow humans they were involved in anything other than an elaborate hoax to gain the remnants of the power held over them by the old priests in more innocent times.

Okino's belief in his own connection was unequivocal. It had been reinforced by all the dragon had shown to him. As he had connected with the ancient skull of the dragon, he had projected the strength of his reverence and understanding, deep into the consciousness of Arimathea. The nature of the vibration he had transmitted was as pure and as clear as any human had made since the early times before they had drifted away from Arimathea. Her ancient spirits constantly listened to the dream songs of the spirits with whom they shared their world as they crossed the land, swum the seas and flew through the air. The joy and wonder as well as the terror and the vulnerability they experienced continually flooded the consciousness and so they lived as one.

Now there was a new dream song they remembered but were not entirely familiar with. They cast back through the halls of memory in which even the calls of long extinct spirits would always echo. There they found and recognised the ancient song of the humans. After all this time it was crude compared with the complexity of their forbearers; it felt small and insignificant. But every spirit hearing the song felt great joy for it meant the humans had again found a way to join with the consciousness of Arimathea. It was always in the nature of Arimathea to have a great celebration at any birth. Each birth gave hope for new life, an expansion into a new time and a chance to find a way to abandon the old destructive ways holding back the ultimate purpose of the dream.

The ancient spirits sang their songs of celebration. They told of a spirit lost on the paths to Oblivion, unguided and alone it had wandered and taken comfort from only the material rewards the emptiness of oblivion could offer. But now a way back had been found. Soon there would be many more and the danger in which Arimathea had found herself would end and the journey towards the great harmony would again continue. This song then, rolled like a great wave around Arimathea. Through the frozen wastes and mountaintops, though the great jungles, across the plains and through the deep oceans its joy and wonder grew and the message echoed through minds who had waited but thought they would never here the song again. Although the song of the human was faint many of these spirits decided they would seek out its origin. Then they would multiply its power so it could delve deep into the slumbering recesses of the human mind; awaken the human race again to hear the joy and the wisdom of Arimathea once more.

In the early evening Okino made his way back to his suite. He smiled when he found his crimson robes had already been laundered and laid out carefully on the bed. Now a new dilemma presented itself. He had enjoyed the degree of anonymity wearing the southern clothes had given him. So, would he wear his priestly robes now they had been cleaned so immaculately? He decided to wear them only on special occasions. Generally, he would wear the southern clothes Mariella had so carefully chosen for him.

He wandered out of the plate glass sliding doors onto his balcony pleased with his decision and leant up against the balustrade. The Star was now on its downward descent towards the horizon and the breeze had dropped. A number of high fragmented clouds drifted across for the most part an entirely blue sky. The ocean was ruffled only by a gentle breeze. He tried to assess the height of the waves but the distance down to sea level made the dimension deceptive.

Mariella passed into his mind as so often she did in these times of contemplation. He wanted to tell her about the visions the dragon had sent him and ask her what she thought about them. He remembered she had been with him beside the river and then she had died in his arms in the desert. He felt they had been together in many lifetimes. How was this significant for him and them? He wanted to ask how she was and what was happening in her world back in Straam. He had become used to her company. He was missing her and he wished she was here with him. He wondered whether there was any way of communicating with her. Clearly the captain must have spoken to her at some stage. He resolved he would ask him at the first opportunity.

His gaze took him out to the horizon as he contemplated the seascape around him. But now there was a difference in the expansive rhythm of the sea spread out all around him. There was something breaking the surface. At first, he noticed this new disturbance in the far distance. It was hard to see what the cause could be. As he watched however, the breaks in the surface became more frequent and nearer to the ship. Enormous spine backs rolled out of the waves closely followed by the unmistakable tail fins of the largest creatures ever to exist on Arimathea. A number of blue whales had converged on and now seemed to be following the course of the ship.

As Okino looked around in every direction more seemed to be arriving and the earlier arrivals seemed to be coming as near to the ship as they dared. Okino could hear the sound of water being evacuated from their blowholes. He tried to count the whales now cruising alongside the ship but as he counted more were arriving. He also noticed in amongst the whales, dolphins had started to arrive. Individuals, larger groups and whole pods were now racing in amongst the whales. As they came closer, he could see their aquiline forms swimming beneath the waves. Then once again they flew into the air, streaming with ocean before they plunged back beneath the surface. Everywhere he looked the ocean was now teaming with the great rolling creatures, some of whom were also flying completely out of the water seemingly in competition with the smaller dolphins.

Now the full power of these vast creatures could truly be appreciated as their huge fluid forms rose as if in slow motion fully from the surface of the Ocean, hanging in all their majesty before crashing again into the ocean below. Okino knew enough about the oceans to understand these creatures must have come from many miles around to intercept the ship in such numbers. He remembered swimming in the pod with Merilon and the ability the dolphins could employ to stay in continual contact with their families and pods in the surrounding area of ocean. He had felt the connection between the pods and how they had been able to transmit information between each other. It seemed now they had heard or felt something in their communal mind to make them converge on and surround the ship.

In these moments he felt Arimathea close to him and all around the ship in amongst the great flowing mass of life as far as he could see coming together here. He felt her joy as the great mass of creatures surged through the ocean in celebration of some special happening they had chosen to mark with this extraordinary gathering. Before all he had been through with Merilon he would have suspected some strange freak of nature had brought these creatures together. Now he had little doubt this was part of the new cycle Sherana had talked about in her restaurant, brought about by all that had happened on his journey and his interaction with the dragon.

His fellow passengers had noticed what was happening around them. They stood in amazement leaning on the balustrades of the walkways surrounding the ship exclaiming and calling out in amazement at the miraculous phenomenon unfolding before them. Okino noticed many were already excitedly filming the dolphins and whales and he suddenly remembered the camera Azeera had given him when they had left the cave in the mountains. Just in case anything extraordinary started to happen around him.

He hurried through the sliding doors of the suite and went over to the material bag which he had carried over his shoulder and in which he had dropped the camera a week before. He took it out, unzipped the small leather container and slipped out the small black camera. Okino examined the controls carefully. Azeera told him he had 'set it up' so all he had to do was turn it on. Okino had no experience of using such hi-tech electronic gadgets and panicked for a few moments before deciding to think calmly about what he was faced with. He pushed the most prominent button on the side of the camera and to his amazement a screen immediately lit up displaying graphic icons telling him exactly what he had to do. He touched the screen with the icon portraying a movie camera and another icon flashed telling him the camera was in operation.

He moved onto the balcony and pointed it out towards where the whales and dolphins were still swimming along with the ship. He could see the image on the screen. Another icon appeared as a satellite dish beaming out waves of information into the great beyond. He pressed this icon and in another part of the screen a scene from the cave in the mountains came up. Azeera and his fellow conspirators were sitting at the table drinking beer. As soon as the picture came onto Okino's screen a notification must have told them a broadcast was being made to them. Azeera decided he would take the broadcast himself and walked over to the computer screen in the corner of the cave.

"Hey Okino, it's great to see you, I wasn't sure whether we would hear from you guys again after all that happened. Is Mariella there with you!"

"Hi Azeera. Mariella had to fly home. There was some problem with her family. But we talked about the ability you had and we both thought it would be an amazing opportunity if the right circumstances arose….and now I don't know if you can see but something amazing is happening!"

"Sorry to hear about Mariella's family…but yes I can see what is happening. So it seems you are on a cruise ship possibly travelling back to Straam I presume and correct me if I'm wrong but as far as I can see you are being followed by every whale and dolphin on the planet….use the zoom Okino…get closer into some of those whales…this is quite extraordinary!"

Okino found the zoom icon and started to zoom in on areas of the gathering. It was a deceptively powerful camera for its size and soon he was beaming close up pictures of the whales and dolphins now being joined by further pods of manta rays over to Azeera in his mountain hideaway.

"So, what do you think is happening here Okino. I know you said things were going to change but this…do you think it is some sort of message to us … surely this cannot be a normal event…or some sort of giant coincidence. There must have been some sort of mass communication for so many animals to come together at one time. It almost implies some pre-meditated thought and organised action. Are they trying to tell us something? Thinking from the point of view of our cause, Okino, if we were going to broadcast this…perhaps they are saying

"This is our planet too. You are not the only species on this world who can communicate with each other and make things happen."

"It certainly would look that way…I've had some strange dreams today; things have suddenly become clearer about the consciousness we are all sharing …the life force, everything… but we have lost our ability to connect into it…maybe they are showing us it is time we started to find our way back to where we belong in the true nature of things."

"So, what would you say the true nature is, Okino."

"Arimathea is a fully sentient being and everything on her contributes in some way to her health and well-being. Her spirit, her soul dwells in every living thing and she experiences the beauty and the wonder she has grown here through the senses of all those lives….Every one of us is our own world with infinite cells and molecules and atoms making our world work, allowing us to breath, allowing us to digest our food and ultimately reproduce, allowing us to experience our lives through the senses we have evolved.

Arimathea is all of this and far more than we can possibly understand without the ability we have lost. We are drifting blindly through our lives cut off from the incredible miracle into which we have grown. We have a privileged place on the web of life she supports. We do have the intelligence to understand our place here and that gives us a responsibility to the being of whom we are an integral part….I think the time has come when we are going to start to find our abilities again and I think this is Arimathea showing us how beautiful and powerful she is. She will wake us up by finding her way into whatever part of us we have neglected…and when you see this, what is happening here, you can't help wondering whether there is something going on here we haven't yet discovered or accounted for in our scientific theories."

Chapter Forty-Eight
The Broadcast.

As Azeera had promised he started to broadcast everything Okino was sending him from the Osira. As Okino filmed the events from his balcony, zooming in and out, the ocean creatures continued to supply for their captive audience ever more breath-taking images, further displaying their abilities to act together. Azeera beamed his pictures with Okino's commentary on a loop playing at regular intervals into the television networks of Arimathea. As the broadcast continued it directly cut, without warning, into the prime viewing time of the people of Arimathea. It immediately interrupted international and local news, sports events, drama and films, game and reality TV shows, awards ceremonies and documentaries.

The people of Arimathea had become shocked and disgusted by the terrorist's ability to beam their atrocities straight into their homes without warning and their politicians had continually lobbied their governments to prevent them from doing so. However, the nature of the airwaves meant it had only been a matter of time before such piracy could be performed by engineers who had knowledge of how to achieve such transmissions. After all, they had been badly treated and badly paid since the dawn of the broadcasting era and now were willing to offer their skills to the highest bidders. In living rooms and bedrooms, in pool halls and bars, in offices and factories outrage and anger was expressed as plots were being lost, goals being missed and the expectation of seeing further carnage and destruction in one of Arimathea's beautiful cities seemed imminent. However, they found a very different story was now unfolding on their television screens.

Okino's skill at manipulating the powerful camera increased rapidly. Azeera had given him as sophisticated a piece of handheld equipment as ever had been conceived and manufactured in the factories of Arimathea. It had been a gamble for him. Okino and Mariella would always be able to locate him with the information he had put into the memory. But he had seen and heard something he liked and trusted in them. He had regretted immediately his attempt to extort money from her father and felt his humiliation at the hands of her security force had been entirely justified. Now his intuitive gamble and his hope these two travelling companions could transform his organisation's campaign was paying off.

The images Okino was sending were without question stunning. As the whales rose from the surface in unison, the scale of ocean being disrupted by the enormous creatures was incredibly captured by the high definition zoom lens. As the dolphins streamed through and across the surface, over the waves and the surf created by the whales, as they dived back into the ocean their grace and intelligence was clear for everyone to acknowledge. Okino moved through the scene trying to capture the diversity of life now appearing. The great manta rays seemed to hang in the air on their outstretched wings that would normally carry them through the depths like strange futuristic spacecraft. Now their numbers gave the effect they were continuously flying over the waves. The black and white streaks of the orcas now had appeared, powerfully rising one after the other in amongst the immense gathering.

After the disappointment of having their entertainment yet again interrupted, the people of Arimathea either went back to what they were doing while half watching what was going on in TV land or became completely fascinated with what was unravelling before them. Those who became engrossed in the scene above all could not help to feel a deep sense of pleasure as they watched this latest offering from the broadcasting pirates. The pictures themselves beamed from the tropics were full of strong sparkling light reflected from water as it streamed from the racing, sinuous, streamlined bodies. The warm turquoise seas looked deeply inviting as they were continuously pierced from above and below. But there was something else gripping all those who took the trouble to notice. There was an unmistakeable sense of joy in the actions of these creatures as if something or someone within their realm had announced a huge celebration to which they all had been invited. There was nothing short of an exultant mood it seemed with every leap they made over and back into the waves. It was touching the people who saw it in a remarkable way as they became mesmerised by the unprecedented scenes they were witnessing. Okino's haunting words seemed to come directly from that other realm.

In the scientific community there had been much discussion about the degradation happening on Arimathea and it had become widely accepted her environmental systems were being severely damaged. The idea Arimathea was a sentient being or had a soul was only acknowledged by a very few scientist philosophers whose intuition had taken them deeper and further beyond the current state of planetary science. In the wider society the idea rarely surfaced and was seen by most as ridiculous; such was the power of the conditioning imposed on generation after generation of people in the industrialised areas of Arimathea.

But now these pictures they were seeing live in their homes, at the places where they worked and relaxed seemed to talk to them of something much deeper than they had been prepared to acknowledge about their world. They were used to seeing creatures such as these trained to perform in captivity for rewards to relieve the boredom of the crushingly bland environments they were kept in. But these were free creatures of many different species coming together for some reason. The word puzzled over most and which caused so much debate in the tide of subsequent discussion that took place was 'reason'. For such a number of creatures to come together for any other reason than to travel as fast and effectively to the next food source was unsettling for many. The fact so many people across Arimathea had seen the phenomenon had prevented any governmental powers who previously may have been able to deny it ever happened and conceal the evidence in a secret vault, made it all the more intriguing.

In the days following, the gathering around the Osira was played and replayed throughout the communication networks of the world on news and documentary channels. It was discussed endlessly. Experts in animal behaviour expounded theory after theory trying to explain what had provoked such a mass gathering. This extraordinary coverage resulted in a very large proportion of the entire population of Arimathea, who now had access to some sort of televisual media, seeing this historic event.

Chapter Forty-Nine.
Yaan's Story.

On the misty island of Eron, Yaan Fairweather was returning from the old stone circle on the moorland hilltop. He had sat quietly in meditation in the early morning starshine surrounded by the solidity of the granite mantle that had bubbled up from the crust of Arimathea 450million years before. The soft waterlogged cover of the moor formed over the mantle had left only the prominent tors, scoured by elemental ferocity to protrude from the tops of the highest hills. The fierce winds racing across the desolation scouring the ancient rock had made their changes. But the folds left as the liquid rock that had slurped from its subterranean fissure still remained as a reminder of its origin.

The tors remained unchanged amongst the racing clouds and the rising and falling of the streams running at the bottom of the low boulder strewn slopes. In the mists frequently occurring here, they appeared like strange ghostly sentinels watching over the land as a reminder to all who may wish to change it. There was a solidity to the wild landscapes dominating these moors that had come to be at the heart of all the journeys Yaan had made over the years he had lived on the edge of this wilderness. He had learned the ancient granite had the ability to transform the energy he had found flowing through Arimathea and over time he had discovered the old stones in the circle he frequented had unexplained qualities able to give him insight into the world on which he lived.

Beth and he had lived on the edge of the moor for fifteen turnings of the star and so were well used to the quick mood swings dominating its climate. There was little between this high ground and the Ocean bringing warm air currents up from the tropics and the ferocious winds often accompanying them. The moorland had high rainfall for the island and because the land was predominantly soaked in rain and warmed by tropical winds it was often shrouded in the mysterious mists.

They had fallen for these mysterious qualities on visits they had made early in their time together. Yaan had studied Ancient History and Philosophy at his University and had met Beth when she had visited for a lecture by one of his tutors one morning. She had shared his fascination with the early people who had lived on these islands and they had spent much of their early years together travelling to the many ancient sites remaining in the more isolated parts of their land. Eventually they had come to this moor. The numerous communities of ancient hut circles, stone avenues and the stone circles provided a perfect setting for the work they had both decided to engage. Here they felt they would be able to explore better than anywhere how those ancient people lived. They embedded themselves in a dilapidated old farmhouse they had managed to buy and transformed it into a cosy home. They had both read and researched extensively during the long evenings and so had become experts in their subjects. They both became confident lecturers and were often invited to speak at universities across Eron.

However, all the research they had found and all the reading they had ever done could not reveal the mystery lying behind the lives of the humans who must have lived in these desolate areas. Much of what had been written was based on the facts revealed by the advanced forensic examination of the remains unearthed from the bogs near to the settlements. A number of bodies had been uniquely preserved with the crude tools, weapons and belongings they had been given to take on to their next life. Apart from the small rings of stones representing their dwellings, the ruins of the further constructions they had made had always caused argument and mostly consternation.

Many of the stones from the stone circles had been removed by the generations who had followed as they had provided an easy supply of quarried stone. If the results of the facts were to be believed these early people lived short and desperately hard lives; from the perspective of the modern comforts of 'civilised' humans who stared back through the millennia to gain some insight into their early beginnings. It seemed to Yaan and Beth however that all the information able to dispel these suppositions was lost in the mists of time enshrouding these moors.

From their earliest visits they romantically imagined the secrets hanging in the light of the streams, in the gentle breezes ruffling the tough moor land grasses and in the mysterious mists. Somehow, they had been haunted and held by the eternal nature of the old tors. They frivolously at first reconstructed the lives of the people who had placed the old stone circle carefully on the rise so central to the surrounding hills. But as the complexity of the task began to reveal itself their attitude had started to change.

There had always been much speculation about how the larger stones had been moved from the quarries found on the other side of the moor. But it had always been assumed a large and determined workforce motivated by fear or some promised gain would have been able to eventually bring the stones to this place. What was more difficult to maintain was how these people came to the complex astronomic alignments that appeared to have been made to position the stones. The study of the stars in a place where the skies were predominantly cloudy often lead to speculation that travel between the ancient lands of Arimathea where skies were clearer and so the transfer of this astronomic information was more prevalent than previous generations had judged.

Still the mystery of why the Stone circles had been built had remained and gradually it became central to the work Yaan was undertaking. As they became more and more deeply involved with the moor, they came to know it through the constant experience of moving across and through it. When the weather allowed they would spend days living in it and so absorbing all the sights and sounds it offered. They started to realise their frivolous reconstructions may have been more realistic than they had first imagined. The juxtaposition of the solid tors, their isolation from mechanised Arimathea, the winds filling the air with their insistent whispering, the water continually gurgling and chuckling through the weirs and falls carving out the rock through the millennia, the varying intensity of the mists, the calls of the deer and the buzzards all appeared to imbue this landscape with such atmosphere and personality that on many levels it appeared to be alive, and possessed of a consciousness unspoilt and whole and more importantly for the work of Yaan and Beth still very tangible.

As they became more immersed in this idea of a living landscape they wondered if their previous imaginings had in fact been the traces of the people who had lived and become part of this being they were now discovering. The idea the moor contained the memory of all that had come before became so intriguing to the couple they concentrated on improving their abilities to interact with this consciousness. In much of their research the ability of the ancient peoples to connect with the spirits of their world was often hinted at but since nothing factual could ever be presented for criticism very little evidence for these practices existed. However, the large stone edifices constructed for mysterious and unexplained purposes existed consistently across much of Arimathea. They had continued to be built into quite recent history if the vast stone skeletal edifices constructed in honour of the alien gods were taken into account.

The misty island of Eron and the moor was no exception. Yaan and Beth started to look at the stone circle in the centre of the hills in a very different light. If the missing information unable to be proved was that these edifices had been communication devices with the being or spirits existing within the land in which they were built then it was time these relationships were reactivated.

In the next years Yaan and Beth had undertaken to gain the ability to submerge their own consciousness into the surrounding landscape. Advice on how this could be achieved differed widely. There were a multitude of books and courses on personal transformation compiled by the many authorities on the knowledge they sort to acquire. Many offered fast track solutions and were often the most expensive and clearly ineffective for what Yaan needed to achieve. There had been a resurgence in the provision of techniques for meditation in the southern industrial areas as life for the population in general became more and more stressful. The demands made on the people who were having to survive in the vast financial machine their society had become were becoming almost unbearable.

Many of the costs of even the basic essentials were starting to spiral out of control. The cost of fuel particularly as the dwindling resources were taken from ever more dangerous and isolated deposits had started to influence the costs associated with primarily powering energy dependent economies. This in turn influenced the cost of all aspects of the average person's life, complicating them beyond all imagining as the margins where profits could be achieved became ever narrower. The efficiency now having to be achieved for the growth marking the success and so the financial strength of the smallest companies to the largest national economies, was exerting new unseen pressures on the human psyche causing psychological illness on unprecedented scales.

Health professionals remained certain the best way of tackling such illness were the numerous anti-depressant drugs developed by eager pharmaceutical corporations as this epidemic of the modern era took hold of the population. However a healthy scepticism about all forms of involvement with such corporations and their interest in their balance sheets which took no account for planet or person had led to the steady growth of an alternative movement promising a brighter future for all on Arimathea growing amongst the increasingly disillusioned populations. However, this movement although seeming to assure people action was being taken, on analysis offered no sensible solutions to the long term problems facing Arimathea. The most sceptical suspected it had even been started by the institutions themselves to divert attention away from the worst injustices they were instigating to keep the machine on track.

Any involvement with this movement seemed to be destructive to Yaan and a diversion from their aim. So, they started down a path which they considered would gradually ease them through the wall of barriers and conditioning their society had instilled within them. They were surprised to find for two people apparently quite disconnected from mainstream 'society' there was deep seated fear that would have to be released before any meaningful connection could be made. The fear ran deep through generations and generations, governed the effectiveness of their service to the machine and depended on them following the paths set out for their lives. At every stage of their life path they paid into and served the machine world while they believed they were free and they had choice to act as individuals. These paths were reinforced by parents who in turn had been brought up within a system and educational environment which had been carefully adapted to hold the artifice of deceit in place; any deconstruction must bring the illusion to an end by constructing a new personal connection to the wider planetary consciousness while living with a healthy disregard within the machine, aware and unfearful of all it represented.

Yaan delved deeply into all he would have to do to break down the conditioning built into his sub conscious. Fairly soon he came across the idea of the bubble. Once aware of the concept it was not long before he was able to experience it for himself. When he noticed it for the first time he was surprised at how deeply the conditioning had become. He had started along this new path because he felt there was a wider consciousness in the world and he wanted to be able to tap into it. But whenever he made an effort to expand into it by first of all 'emptying' his mind he found distracting everyday thoughts immediately jumped into his mind's eye and demanded attention. He noticed most of these distracting thoughts were to do with the many layers the machine world had built into his life. Every aspect, it seemed had its own set of problems demanding his attention. There seemed no end to the time he needed to dedicate to sorting through these problems.

Dominant throughout it seemed was how he paid for his place as a cog in the machine. This he soon found was also bound up with how he saw himself within the hierarchy of his peers and everyone else in the machine. Here it seemed was the first point of separation; the start of the construction of the bubble. His education and his parents had expected him to rise above his fellows. There was an expectation he should have a bigger house and a bigger salary; children doing well in their schools….and here was where he saw how the whole deceit was proliferated. His status was judged within the 'society' continually by all he had gained whether it was a house, a new car or a family and all the products they in turn demanded. All this reflected on how he and everyone else thought he was performing as a member of the machine world. Here was where he was judged and where he judged himself. How could anyone ever win on these terms? There would always be something more to have for himself or his family and so here he found himself trapped in his own bubble along with everyone else, unable to think of anything outside the demands it and the machine was putting on him.

He and Beth had discussed this trap previously unaware of how deeply it had become threaded through their lives. He could not deny he wanted to appear successful for the sake of all the people around him and he could not deny it made him feel good amongst them when he announced his lecturing successes. Beth and he assumed they would start their family and they had managed to acquire the cottage in the countryside many would envy. All these thoughts were forming how he saw the construction he had made of himself in relation to the machine world. He started to realise they were preventing the expansion out of and beyond his bubble enabling him to merge into the consciousness of the moor. The continual worry and fear about how to hold his life together and pay for his place in the machine world was preventing him from finding out something fundamental about his and his races origins. Perhaps preventing him from revealing how destructive this comparatively new way of living was for his generation.

The bubble was fully constructed around him as he walked through his world. The only thing that mattered to him were the threats to the security of the apparition he had become. Anything else he just did not have time to think about. He had become a ghost in the machine.

He gasped in horror when he was struck by this terrible realisation. All the things he did not have time to worry about were the issues tearing his world apart. His imprisonment was complete along with all his fellows; all fighting like rats to keep their place in the carefully constructed maze they could never escape while their masters outside the maze continued with their destructive addiction to gathering more and more wealth and power. He knew much of the destruction they had brought to Arimathea was in the places out of sight of anyone who could bring it to a halt. The vast open cast mines delving deeper into the crust of their world were not in the back yards of his people here on the misty island. They were in the remaining wildernesses where only a few of the poorest indigenous people clung onto their ancient ways of life. Now it seemed the quest to expand his own consciousness brought with it a new responsibility.

So, he and Beth continued with their quest. He had more time to himself as Beth had taken a full-time teaching post at the local University. As his lectures became more and more sort after he was able to charge more for each one allowing him time for this new research. Once he had made the decision, the correct advice and information started to flow towards him. It was the wider natural world he needed to connect with, break down the bubble separating him from the levels where the elusive old spirits were still roaming.

He had come across information about the revival of the old religion that had despite the Alien Gods, never really gone away for the very reason Yaan was now seeking them. He selected a number of books which he judged to be the most instructive for his purpose and started to read. Some of what he read crossed over with his own field. The peoples he had researched had their gods and goddesses, the spirits of the lands who were celebrated in the old festivals, now taken over by the alien gods. As he went deeper he discovered the system of festivals overlaid the cycle of the year and informed an entire branch of wisdom relating to the people's lives and the very fabric of the land itself.

He made a deeper connection with the old stone circles almost immediately. Everything in the old religion proceeded through the cycles of the year and so the circle was at the centre of much of the wisdom. The seasons proceeded through from Winter, Spring, Summer to Autumn and had their festivals celebrating the beginning of each phase. The seasons were distinctive in the misty island. Various goddesses reflected the fertility and productivity of the land as the power of the Star god waxed and waned through the year. The wisdom reflected their relationship throughout the cycle. The Star god died in the depths of winter at the Winter Solstice but at the same moment was reborn and increased his strength through to the Summer Solstice. The young maiden appeared in the Spring tempted by the gathering strength of the Star God risen from his wintery death. Summer would begin as they consummated their love amongst the leafy bowers and the heady fragrances of the burgeoning land. In the Autumn she would give birth to the fruit which was growing on the trees and hedges.

Further celebrations then marked the harvesting of the crops grown in the fields to support the communities through the rest of the year. The goddess changed again into the withered old crone as the Star god receded from the world. She came on the East winds and presided over the time of darkness coming over the land and was appeased at the festivals held around fires with offerings and blessings in the hope she would not be too severe in the winter months. She was the goddess of Arimathea who gave life and took life as the cycles of the year and the cycles of each person's life progressed.

In the circle, these times had their place and so the seasons and the life progressed around the circle. The North where the Star never ventured was the place of winter and the place of Arimathea and her creativity and powers of nurture to where all life returned at the end of its life. The East was the place of the Star rise and the Spring, of new life and initiation. It was the place of the most powerful winds so was the place of the breath of life and Air. The South was the place of summer, of strong and vigorous life at the height of its power, of the Fire and vigour of light and life flowing through the land; it was the place of will and sustained power and enablement. The West became the place of Autumn and Water, of the setting Star, of Love and the currents of emotion flowing deep in the rivers of the human psyche and the world.

When he had absorbed this information Yaan excitedly went to the old Stone circle and found these places and felt the correspondences informing this entire system. When he stood on the ancient ground with the sound of the bubbling streams behind him he looked out across the moor land and as the buzzards called their melancholy cry down to him and the winds ruffled his hair he knew he had taken the first steps on his journey.

So Yaan absorbed the layers of wisdom springing out from the cycles. All the animals of his land had their place on the circle acknowledging their corresponding characteristics. He found the wolves and the bears roaming the northern mountains. The salmon swimming their way across the western oceans and up the rivers to their ancient spawning grounds. In the South the deer roamed the leafy glades and the mystical Fire dragons swirled through the heat of the high Summer. In the East his beloved Eagles and Buzzards floated over his world, masters of the winds and breezes. He found the trees had their own entire language in the history of the land and the magicians who had worked with them, in turn informed the cycles as they spiralled up through her year. His own journey, the journey of his family and the journey of his ancestors; his place within this land would all have to be analysed in relation to the passage of time governing his existence on Arimathea. He would have to find out who he was in relation to his world and the flow of events that had led him to take this path. Then perhaps he could find out where it could take him in the future.

He learned he would have to embed himself in these cycles, recognise the wisdom when it was revealed and absorb it each time it was offered to him. To understand this world and his place on it he started to realise would take many years of dedication that would finally enable him to become continuous with those times and so the space he occupied on Arimathea. Each year he slowly pulled himself a little further away from the conditioning he had received from the machine world and closer to becoming a true spirit of Arimathea able to receive the visions she may in time offer him.

There was no time when he could say specifically he had left behind all he had been led to believe about his world. Perhaps his conditioning told him there would have to be some moment of blinding inspiration that would change the way he viewed his world forever. The ethic he had followed through his education to his professional qualifications was leading him to believe if he put enough work in and studied hard enough then he would be rewarded in a specific period of time. Perhaps the time frames he had imposed on his life told him he should be making break throughs, enhancing his standing in the academic community in which he moved, advance his career and progress his life plan. He found himself thinking these thoughts as again he sat out on the Moors and he smiled to himself. Still he was governed by all his culture had embedded into him. There seemed to be no end to the deceit with which it could fill his mind.

In these moments he would look up at the old tors, beyond the granite stones standing around him, unchanged now for millions of years since their molten rock had bubbled up from the depths of Arimathea. He began to realise he had to become more like them, deeply embedded in this land and static in their response to everything raging around them. He found over the years they were never the same when he looked up at them. They glistened with newly fallen rain or in bright starshine their form was organic almost as if finely sculptured additions to the bleak surrounding landscape. At dusk or dawn again, they would be transformed as rising or falling light from different directions, accentuated unseen contours, crevices or formations. But when the gloom of deep cloud or drifting mists enveloped them they were transformed again into dark brooding monsters perched on their hills watching over the millennia. He came to know their individual forms and configurations, individual rocky islands in the sea of marshy bog land, to journey to and savour, to rely on as beacons of reassurance when the landscape in which they stood was dimensionless and invisible.

Arimathea was old and her ways had slowly become evident upon her surface. He wanted to be part of her, share her mysteries but still he had not understood or truly accepted the nature of her being. Of course, he had had insights, moments of connection in which he had experienced those wonders. But no sooner had these moments passed his deceit had again told him he was nearer to his goal, told him to cling to it, to preserve and find a place for it in his latest lecture so he could shine in the world as a gifted enlightened human being who had thrown off the shackles of the machine that had shaped him and all those who were sitting listening to him, who had come to hear him and the revelations he had discovered.

He shuddered in these moments at his own naivety, as a man would shudder the morning after some drunken outburst or action under the influence of alcohol seeming so reasonable or natural the night before. However, the drunk would inevitably learn his lesson and eventually avoid such behaviour in the future or become dependent on it and let it destroy his or her life. Yaan then was learning what she expected of him. She had no interest in his salary or his house or his standing amongst his peers because those were the things that were tearing her apart. Slowly in those years as his life continued and happened around him; as disasters unravelled and tragedy struck as they will in a world sharing the opposing forces and the mystery of Light and Dark in equal measure, a truth started to dawn in him. Only as he started to understand what it meant he felt there was some possibility that one day he may be able to reach what amounted to now only a distant premonition. But like his other insights the significance was he felt the thought had passed through his being from the wider consciousness he was seeking.

She wanted him as pure as he could be; to come to her freely in Love. Not this day or that day or this hour of the day or when he felt lively or happy, or just when the star shone or when everything seemed to be going his way. She did not want him to have concern for her because he thought it would make him a better person or that he might gain some advantage in his machine world with the people surrounding him or in his career. She wanted him unconditionally to love her like a parent loves any one of his or her children. For then and only then could he understand what it was to be part of her; When her Love could flow through him continually, through every last detail of his life, and he could see that Love flowing through everything happening to him, in every triumph and disaster everything he saw and did, so every footstep and breath was some absorption of the wonder and beauty she had become. She had become the mystery in all her evolution. If he had decided to be part of her Life as opposed to her Death then it was the Love she possessed he would have to understand and how he could truly be part of such a Love. Only then could he decide how he would use what he had discovered.

So, he continued to live and breathe the wisdom he found all around him. His periods of doubt began to recede and the deceit tormenting him, troubled him less and less as he walked through the shining world now starting to appear all around him. He had not become angelic or a saint who was better or worse than his brothers and sisters who continued to walk around in their foggy bubbles. But he was expanding it seemed. He was suddenly hungry for experience of his world like never before. He filled his senses with every detail revealed to him that somehow he had missed in the years before; Colours, sounds, smells, even the textures and tastes he experienced had new significance, new meaning as the world around him became a vast and infinite continuation of Arimathea. He was unable to look or contemplate anything standing in isolation from the consciousness he was now experiencing.

On the occasions he entered the cities he could see the full extent of the dreadful deception his race had fallen under; now living in environments, filled with fumes and the faceless expression of the vast corporations controlling their lives they were told they were free. In reality, they were being dragged down by the enormous debts they had taken out to top up their diminishing salaries, no longer able to pay for the lifestyles they were told they needed to lead. These debts locked them even more tightly into their lives of agonising servitude. They were mostly exhausted and beyond disillusionment of the existence they were leading month after month, year after year. They had little interest in the harm being caused to their planet by a way of life now being adopted by or chased after by most of the human race. After all, how could it be any different?

With this new and disturbing perspective, he would return to the isolation of the moors where now she had begun to reveal herself in every gust of echoing wind and every perfect blade of quivering grass; greater complexity brought more of her wonder to him and so he sat enchanted by the streams as they gurgled through the weirs of ancient rock and watched the clouds send the starshine scurrying up and down the slopes of the hills leaving her visions to rest deep into his now fully receptive mind.

High on the tors he contemplated his world and all he wanted to know and returned to the stone circle where the traces of the peoples he had felt had become integrally bound into their environment and all it had contained. They had seen all this wonder; grown always as part of it, understood it, reflected its beauty in all they did and created. They had not been misled by the illusion their modern brothers and sisters had succumbed to and lived here innocently with the deer and the buzzards, using the abilities they had inherited as best they could to survive whatever their environment had in store for them. The human race had grown with abilities formed in minds to process a complex array of information; minds able to correlate and form complex models of their surrounding world on all the levels and dimensions and uniquely, through some twist of evolution solve the numerous problems it had presented.

Yaan looked down at his hands and thought about all they had come to create since his race's humble beginnings as hunter gatherer tribes slowly migrating and populating Arimathea. He knew from the continually growing fossil evidence for the development of the human race his own form had only emerged two hundred thousand years before after some four million years of evolution. At the end of that period some five thousand years before his own era, humans had started to set down their language in writing. Only in the last two hundred years had the human race started to change from a largely agricultural society into one which had become industrial and mechanised. So, for most of those four million years they had shared the natural world surviving as best they could alongside the other creatures inhabiting it. The complex mind and senses that had arisen in those time spans in response to the environmental conditions and the fluctuations that may have occurred was now compelled to deny its natural origins almost entirely.

In the light of his own discoveries about how his own psyche had been entirely over-ridden, he thought perhaps he was starting to understand the roots of the problem his world was facing. It now seemed hardly surprising the human race was desperate to find some means to replace the terrible loss it felt as it was denied the natural environments in which it had for so long been enveloped. No amount of education or programming or any luxury the mechanised world could offer could ever fill the need the human mind had for the sights, sounds and experience of the natural world in which they had evolved.

However now a dangerously high proportion of his race appeared to be in complete denial of these obvious facts and seemed intent on dragging the remainder into the illusion of increasingly mechanised civilisation. He started to wonder about what other abilities the human mind may have developed in its original state that now had withered and died as their profound connection with their natural environment had fallen away.

He remembered his fantasies about the moors and how close to the surface the old spirits had seemed. He thought he was starting to access some of those old genetic memories perhaps not buried that deeply considering the timescales they would have been predominant in every human mind. So much about this strangely beautiful mystical world that everyone wondered about was denied as the superstition of the uncivilised and uneducated mind; science had come to explain all it could quantify in its theorems and equations and left no room for the instincts and suspicions seeming to fit so naturally into the scheme of the world. Yet the deeper and more complex the science became the more and more it seemed those instincts and suspicions may have more basis in reality than just the fantasies of the unsophisticated mind.

It seemed finally he was lifting the veil clouding his understanding of the world. He returned regularly to the moors and the old stone circle where his realisations now overlapped with the deeper experience he was having. His meditations became clearer as he became increasingly able to remain undisturbed for longer periods by the demands in his life the illusion had put in his way. The genetic memories existing in his own and the consciousness of his race he believed were starting to surface.

He found himself wandering with an ancient people as they moved from place to place following the seasons. They moved through the land guided by the stories and myths carried by their tribe. Often they arrived at the old stone circles built by their ancestors. He felt the respect they held for these sacred places as they came to them on their journey; where again they could experience the wonder of enchanted atmosphere filling their minds so tuned to the sights, sounds and invisible energies of their world. There they would join with the oldest spirits; the old dragons who flew across the skies and swirled in the flooded rivers and glistened on the Starlit lakes, who lived in the largest, oldest ancient trees and whispered their wisdom through the forests; revealed their power in the storms as lightening flashed from the sky and as the winds howled across the lands or whipped up the seas sending crashing waves into the dark rocks and along the sandy beaches.

They saw them in the creatures with whom they shared their world, in their speed and strength, in their agility and their grace. They knew the dragon spirits as an inseparable energetic part of their world or even themselves. Often they would come to them in their dreams. Like the spectacular flight of a kingfisher down the course of a river or a hawk flashing through the forest, they would flash momentarily through their minds at the height of a dilemma; introduce an idea to give a new perspective or provide some resolution to an insoluble problem; bring a peaceful moment to an explosive or dangerous situation. They had always been open to the transformations the old dragons could bring, they had never known a time when they had not been there, slowly guiding and informing them as they battled to find their place in the world.

During one of his journeys he joined the spirit of a young man with whom he was able to share the experiences of a tribe on their journey through the land. They had been hunting and he had killed his first deer. This he knew would transform his standing in the eyes of the tribe, for another hunter who had gained the stealth and the skill to stalk and kill such an animal was cause for great celebration.

Yaan walked behind the lifeless animal as it was carried by two of his fellow tribesmen. He relived the moment as he had released the spear, carried by all the strength he had gained, all the lessons he had learned and memories he held which turned his seamless action into the deadly flight ending so precisely in the heart of this magnificent creature. It turned in the moment before it struck knowing his time was at an end, he would not forget the reflection in those eyes for it was the first of the many times he would see it. It was nowhere else to be seen. There was anger, defiance and disappointment but also the deer revealed some knowledge known only in that moment, transmitted from the eyes of the slain to the slayer. It was the knowledge of eternity that had under laid his life. It had been at the root of all the endless striving to preserve the precious life force it carried. Only the deer would have seen the eternity at the moment as it started its journey back into the vast and infinite ocean of the one soul. But there the mystery of his existence was revealed to him, as the life force left the eyes of the animal and it crashed unceremoniously to the ground with none of the grace or beauty it had held the moment before, in a tangle of limbs quivering from dying nerves and blood pumping from the heart that had driven it's life from the moment it had come into existence in the womb of its mother.

Here was the magic contained in all the life he saw around him. Yaan acknowledged, even he, who was actually living many thousands of years in the future, who lived in an era that had gained sophisticated knowledge of the anatomy of most creatures still saw death for what it was; an unexplained mystery. In all the arrogance of his race that boasted achievements in gaining a significant degree of knowledge about what was quantifiable and could be seen, the single wonder under lying everything still had not been explained.

If such knowledge was only the start of what could be known about their existence then his race had barely started on their journey to understanding about who or what they really were or could be. Yaan felt the awe now engendered in this young hunter as he followed his deer as the Star sank below the hills and the world darkened. The distant stars and their galaxies glistened with new wonder. These realisations brought on a euphoric daze in which he felt disconnected from all his actions. He floated through the landscape only dimly aware of the conversations happening around him. Occasionally the older hunters would check on him and seeing his state would remember what they themselves had experienced at this time and they would clap him vigorously on the back laughing and always congratulating him.

He watched in this state as they reached the old stone circle where he had been so often before. But how different the stones seemed today! Each stone reverberated with the aeons of their existence here, since they had formed from the cosmic debris fallen into the gravity of the star. The air was full of the souls of all his tribe and he walked from one to the other acknowledging the wonder they had become. He hugged his mother and his father and his brothers and sisters, thanking them for all they had ever done and been for him. He watched as the tribe built the fire and skilfully removed the complete hide from the deer and draped it over the stone in front of which he knew he would soon have to stand. Then he came to be standing in front of two strangers. They were taller than any of his brothers and sisters, looked different altogether with their smooth aquiline features; Yaan would have said they were from his own time by the fabric of their clothes. The young hunter had never looked into such startlingly blue green eyes. They had already been given wolf skins by his mother as a token of the tribes welcome. In his daze he questioned no further their place here, he acknowledged their presence with a warm greeting and continued his journey through his tribe for soon the ritual of his first kill was due to proceed. As the chant and the drumbeat started, the strange state he had drifted into and his normal existence started to merge and as the fire grew and the smell of the cooking deer filled the circle, the chanting grew in intensity.

The dragon came out of the flames or out of the light energy they had produced; spirit energy originally from the stars bound up in the dead wood of the trees as they had stood for decades in the Earth fed briefly by generations of their leaves that had fallen around them. The dragon light flowed out of the fire and around the tribe's people as they fell silent. Yaan saw the dragon as light but as a kind of light he had not seen before. As if there were some combination of the spectrum he had not been able to access or comprehend in his life in the future. The feeling he felt as it flowed around him was vaguely familiar but it was like nothing he had ever experienced before. It had the same resonance as a dream that had reoccurred at different times in his life.

The bloody hide of the deer was placed over his body as the dragon light surrounded him and as his brothers moved away, it flowed through his body, into his mind filling him with the vast infinity of space he could see above him and the trace of the recently departed deer stag's soul. He felt the weight of the heavy hide and the blood remaining on the inside of the skin running down his body. He felt the weight of the antlers bearing down on his skull stretching into the night sky and he felt the residual life force of the animal blending with his own. Again, his senses appeared to sharpen. His own memories of the landscapes he knew the deer would have frequented were enhanced and further expanded.

He could reach further into the distance amongst the trees and across the mountain slopes searching amongst the familiar fragrances and sounds for unusual signs indicating threat and danger. Even through the ground he could detect vibration he would not normally feel in relation to that environment and most importantly in which direction it was moving. He could feel the strength of the life force at the height of its power in the moment before his spear struck as a continuation of the dragon light now connecting him, further beyond the reaches of the mountains and the plains, further than he had ever travelled in his world across the oceans and into the freezing wastes of which he had heard only the stories passed by the wanderers whom they had encountered. Further even, deep into the Stars above where the knowledge of the dragons extended far out into the night sky.

This knowledge became strangely clear to him as each of the stars, at all stages of their life cycle span through their spiral galaxies towards the inevitable vortex at their centre, each shining a fractional part of the light burning through the dark emptiness of the universe. Those two powers strained in two different directions for the harmony they knew to exist at either end of the journey they were on. But the struggle between them had brought disharmony, rage, anger, greed, cruelty and pain as well as unimaginable beauty in the powerful love consciousness that had emerged. The emptiness drained the beauty wherever it could as if the death of everything and the end of the possibility of all progression and the potential of any kind of advancement in the future would prevent such horror emerging again to torment the spirit soul of the Universe. But the powers of light searched out the harmony in the future through all the wonder the dragons were able to coax out of life and the consciousness. The emptiness of oblivion had unleashed new horror as the powers of the dark fought the rise of the harmony at every opportunity. The dragons dreamed harder struggling towards the day when this crude solidity would merge with the ethereal spirit world to open up unimaginable depths of understanding and self- realisation for the Universal soul and all of its sentient occupants.

The young hunter recognised the battle raging on through the Stars as the battle for survival he and his fellow human beings had become part of. The pain they felt was how they recognised the ecstasy and the joy when it soon enough returned. It seemed his race had a further destiny in the battle perhaps in the far distant future and Yaan standing here from that future recognised the inspiration that had perhaps carried his race to where they now had come to. They both realised everything had come from this struggle.

Both the young hunter and Yaan himself decided from those moments they would pursue the harmony to wherever it would take them and find the dragon light whenever they could and bring it into the world. Perhaps this was where the dragons had sown the future destiny of their world; where the lines had been drawn up for the battles that would rage here in the name of this their ultimate dream.

Yaan returned to his own time with this insight into the lives of these early people and the experience of their world he had so craved. He decided as he had suspected, his own race and theirs were not so very different. In those early times they had developed a rugged powerful strength and insight that had carried them through the millennia as they interacted with the very nature of their world in their efforts to survive. There seemed little doubt to him they had come to know intimately the powers dwelling within their world perhaps in a similar way they had come to know the other creatures. As a result of these relationships undoubtedly they had developed into cunning predators able to survive the many upheavals they would experience in those early years. It was not hard for Yaan to see how they had developed into the creatures now dominating the planet of Arimathea.

Often he sat in the circle of stones on the moor contemplating the lives his ancestors would have led, knowing he would return to his house with its' continual supply of hot water on hand to ease away the aches and pains of his exertions out here in their world. The struggle against serious injury and disease commonplace for them had been almost eliminated in his time. But it had been eliminated as a result of the early survival strategies those early tribes had developed.

It was not hard to see how the predilection of the human race for comfort, warmth and a life free from pain had arisen. His tribe had sat around their fires in the thick furs they had cut from the animals they had killed and eaten. They would have made ingenious shelters to protect them from the worst of the weather and used plants they found around them to cure illness whenever they were able. It seemed priorities had really not changed so much. But recently the human race had been able to find more sophisticated and dangerously wasteful ways of solving the problems it had always faced.

He had returned from the moor that morning contemplating an invitation he had had for a lecture at a conference in Eremoya. This was definitely an encouraging development in his lecturing career. Careful! He smiled to himself. His expenses as well as a sizeable fee would be paid. He had been sent a written invitation but then almost immediately he had received a phone call from a young woman called Grace who had said she had seen one of his lectures and felt he would fit perfectly in amongst the other speakers she had invited. The conference was, she had said perhaps a little apologetically about trying to get to the bottom of what was really happening on Arimathea and whether there was anything at all that could be done. It seemed she had started a foundation and mercilessly pursued the wealthiest people she imagined might have an interest until they had agreed to fund such a gathering.

As things had turned out she had been able to offer sizeable fees and so had been able to attract some of the most eminent and brilliant minds from around the world who had been assessing the problems facing their planet. She had no idea what may come of it but was sure something would and please would he come and give one of his wonderful lectures. Yaan had chuckled at the enthusiasm crackling down the phone at him from the other side of the world. He told Grace he felt honoured to be asked and requested her to send all the details and he looked forward to meeting her and the other delegates. He was intrigued and in another part of his mind he had started to prepare a new lecture for this his international debut!

That morning he had decided he had the bones of what he would be able to bring to such a gathering. His lectures had always blended the knowledge of the civilisations he had gained with the philosophies he had learned and blended to entice his students into the mindset of those ancient worlds. They had not always been for the faint hearted, for the human race had in its ascendancy adopted some strange and brutal ideas to keep order and enslave the growing populations. He knew now there were people on Arimathea who had found a complexity in the existence of their world far beyond such primitive ideas. These were the people he hoped Grace would bring to her conference.

He had decided to turn on the TV to catch the International news before he started work. He made himself a cup of coffee strong enough to enable him to do little except turn his mind to conjuring the words to mesmerise his audience into the worlds of the distant past. He flicked the remote control expecting to see the carefully manipulated environment of an international news broadcasting studio and the face of a presenter delivering with carefully controlled emotion the latest global events. However, there was no sign of the studio today. Instead the picture on his screen was from an ocean in which were being filmed a gathering it seemed of many hundreds of dolphins, manta rays and whales cruising together across the sea.

Suspecting he had opened on the wrong channel he clicked again and again until it was obvious this was one of broadcast hijackings now becoming so common in the aftermath of a terrorist action. But this was different and quickly Yaan was being drawn in by the images as he realised what he was watching. The spectacular high definition photography was showing, what he imagined was an unprecedented event and slowly he sat back in awe. He was watching dolphins diving in and out of the wake of blue whales as their tail fins followed them back into the ocean and great mantas soaring into the air, gliding, before plunging back into the surf and the magnificent orcas with their unmistakeable black and white markings racing in amongst this multitude of sea creatures.

Yaan sat transfixed as the young monk turned the camera on himself and started to give his speech. As he saw Okino's face he muttered a series of expletives, spilt his coffee without noticing and sat up in his chair hardly daring to believe the face he was watching on a cruise ship filming this momentous oceanic event, he had last seen in his first kill meditation at the tribal ritual in the stone circle. He watched the rest of the broadcast struggling to make sense of what was happening to him or in his world.

Chapter Fifty.
Home.

Mariella had had little warning of the circumstances that had led her to be so dramatically lifted from the journey she was sharing with Okino. Her mother's health had not been good in the months running up to her departure but nothing had indicated she would go into such dramatic decline in the period she was away. Mariella had been compelled to make a decision and during those long months leading up to her departure, the shadow had often become an uneasy shiver at the back of her waking moments. There was always a possibility her mother's illness would escalate and she would need to travel back home as fast as possible. In the little contact she had made with her father everything had been fine. Her mother had been busy as usual with the larger community in which they had become involved since they had moved out of the city. Mariella always smiled as she thought of all her mother had done despite the resistance of the local population to the affluent lawyer's wife who had moved into one of the larger properties in the suburbs. She knew she was growing to be like her Mother. The affect the genes she had inherited from her mother and father could be clearly traced in the woman she was becoming. One of the many differences defining her individuality was of course the era into which she had grown.

Her mother and father had looked around their city and beyond and seen the injustice and suffering still being directed towards many of their more unfortunate fellows. So, her father had set out to be a lawyer and ultimately defend the rights of the people he felt were at the mercy of a society that showed little interest in them until they committed some desperate crime in their battle for survival. She knew he had defended some of the truly bad people who had come to live in his city. As she had started to understand what it was he did when he left the house in the mornings and came to see the people he was defending, she had asked him about why he had decided to help these bad and destructive people. They had been on one of their tours of a small town they had decided to visit. Sitting in the square watching the people going past conducting their business. He smiled and indicated,

"Look Mariella at any one of these people. Each one of them, I have come to believe some would not, was born as innocent and free and guiltless as the next. Everything that happened to them subsequently, possibly in the next two hours of their life made them into the person they became. You have, whether you acknowledge it as important or not, grown up in a family that has loved and supported you. How could any child grow up any other way you will ask? How could two parents treat their beautiful bundle of light and love with whom they had been blessed in any other way?"

He was silent for a moment as the memories of what he had heard and seen poured through his mind. He shook his head and looked up almost distraught. It had been the first time she had seen tears in his eyes.

"You would not believe the degradation children are subjected to. You will have heard some of the dreadful cases that come to light occasionally. But they do not highlight how badly a lot of our children are treated. I have sat in front of men who have murdered and robbed, controlled entire communities with fear and fed the narcotic addictions of entire neighbourhoods, supplied entire arsenals of weapons to more desperate souls than themselves to fuel wars they themselves have instigated. These things have shocked me. But the thing that has always shocked me more is how they were treated as children. No support, no love, beaten and often raped from an early age. They have grown up in a dark void where there was only pain and brutality. I, as a caring parent who has pandered to you and your brothers every whimper, encouraged and nurtured every sign and action that could awaken the potential to make you the beautiful people you have become, have been tormented by the pain these people have had in their lives.

This pain is ingrained through generations of families and in my profession supposedly upholding the law of this land I and a few of my colleagues have made it clear to the judges we have stood before that the terror these individuals have wrought in our towns and cities we have brought upon ourselves. We have allowed our communities to fragment to such a point that many of our children are growing up isolated from the support structures that would have nurtured these kids in the past….and don't ask me when it all started, my darling, I believe we are a strange aberration of a species,. We are so powerful and all our actions have enormous consequences, sometimes devastating and yet we are taught so little about this aspect of our lives. You will grow into your world Mariella, many of the influences you have you may not be aware of. Conversations long forgotten can change the paths long after they have ended. So, when you decide how you will act in the world you must be fully aware of the magic you are weaving."

She had been surprised when he had mentioned magic; although she had never thought of him as anything less than a wise old wizard who she was lucky enough to have as her father. So, she asked him if he had ever worked any magic in the world as far as he knew and he had smiled as he always did when he was about to say something amazing and said..

"Every time I stand in front of a jury or a judge and tell them what has happened in the life of the unfortunate creature standing before them and see them start to feel for him or her, despite the atrocity they have committed, I am working the magic every one of us can work in the world. It's Love Mariella, compassion for all we see around us no matter how much it upsets us or offends our privileged sensibilities. When there is compassion there is a possibility for healing and yes the individual may well be incarcerated for a long period of time. But if he can be helped to understand why he has become who he is then he will have a chance to get nearer to the beautiful innocent child spirit who came to live with us on this world. I believe that is magic in the true sense; transformation of the destructive and harmful into the productive and benevolent. In alchemical terms you would say, iron into gold or darkness into light."

When she had heard him tell her these things it was if she was suddenly walking through a different world. Slowly as she had grown he had explained to her about the world in clear uncomplicated terms which she or anyone could have understood. But he had not told her what to believe. It was as if his explanations were like the soil in which her own thoughts and ideas could germinate and grow. He never really told her what was wrong or right but always seemed to give her all the parameters in which she was operating. This, of course, she realised later was what made him such a brilliant lawyer. He understood the parameters in which the human race operated on Arimathea. Much of which he had learned from the books which lined his study but much of which he always maintained he had learned from sitting quietly and watching the world go by. This of course is where he had met his Ezme, her mother so the tale went.

They had been sitting in the park on parallel benches at lunch time in the Summer watching the world flowing past. The business executives cutting deals and employees eating their dinners and moaning about their bosses, the adoring mothers with their sweetly gurgling newly born or their noisily growing children, the park gardeners, the soil which they lovingly cared for ingrained in their weather beaten hands and the beautiful place which they continually made for everyone, the students and their books and their falling in love, the multi coloured, multi patterned pigeons scrapping for the crumbs at the feet of everyone and the trees and the fluffy white clouds all of which drifted past as if in exerts from some fabulous dream that could never be recreated or remembered but whose resonance and effect would last forever in minds barely registering the wisdom contained in those moments.

Aaron Keating had come to know this and now as he absorbed the connections and interconnections layered through this everyday urban scene, she had slowly come into focus. He to her and she to him. They both said they had known as that focus became more intense. Her mother had got up to walk away, back to her work at the very last minute having hoped her father was going to come over and pass the time of day but he hadn't and off she went. Her father had told her a form of panic had set in he had never experienced before or since and he pursued her out of the park until he was up beside her. He had said...

"Perhaps I will see you in the park tomorrow or if it is raining perhaps the next day....oh supposing it rains all week...look if it does rain all week and you are not there this time next week perhaps we will meet in the café next to the bowling green...now I am being presumptuous...."

Her mother famously grinned at him leapt on a bus and disappeared. Of course, they were both sitting on the same benches in the pouring rain the very next day and they had been inseparable ever since and had built their lives together. He slowly built his law firm in the backstreets of Straam guiding the petty criminals, junkies and the many other unfortunates who found themselves in an entanglement with the Eremoyan legal system through their own misdeeds or those of someone around them. They had liked him and his way of unravelling the entanglement and his reputation grew until the more sinister members of the community started to turn up at his door. The bigger the crime, the bigger the paycheque and his meteoric rise to being one of Straam's top defence lawyers soon meant the best and the brightest lawyers were beating a path to his door. However, the full horror of the human suffering being perpetrated amongst the people of Straam and the surrounding areas was becoming fully apparent to Aaron and his new wife.

As he worked in the legal system to stem the tide of corruption and terror now with such a considerable role in city life, Ezme became increasingly involved with the organisations growing up to support the victims caught up in the horror. She soon found resources were absurdly inadequate and became a tireless fundraiser to upgrade and expand facilities to support the growing tide of human beings, young and old who found themselves cast adrift from the support of families or even mainstream society in Straam. She became a dedicated volunteer in the facilities of the foundation she and Aaron had originated. Continually the effects of an early life of deprivation and lack of care were highlighted as they became inextricably linked with young and old from the darker side of the Straam society. At the same time their own children arrived. They had always been determined to make sure none of their commitments should interfere with the time they spent with them. Aaron and Ezme, then, had striven to give Mariella and Nick as much attention and care as they judged would enable them to grow into well-adjusted independent human beings who would be capable of making their way safely in the world in the difficult times in which they had chosen to arrive.

On the flight home high in the atmosphere of Arimathea, Mariella remembered one of the visits she had made with her mother. She had been very young perhaps seven or eight years old. One of the larger buildings the foundation supported served as a multi-purpose facility. There had been high security around the building and its grounds on the outskirts of the city. There were offices and interview rooms, living rooms and a restaurant where much of the daily administration and help for the continual stream of unfortunates would take place. There also had been a large residential unit where the people in the most fear of violence could be temporarily sheltered while the factors surrounding the threat could be rectified. This often took many weeks when particularly violent partners disappeared into the vast ghetto populations of Straam where even the police would rather not go.

Her mother had been talking to one of the support workers in particularly grave terms about an incident that had occurred that morning. Mariella had wandered away through the public area into one of the living rooms. It was a hot and humid day and the doors of the room had been thrown open. There was a boy and a younger girl of her own age sitting silently on one of the built-in sofa seats running along the walls then segmenting the large room into more personal spaces. She went over to them and said hello and asked if it would be all right if she sat and talked with them while her mother was busy. The boy looked up startled and the little girl did not move. He said with only the glimmer of a smile…

"Sure, that would be Ok!"

Mariella remembered thinking how different they looked from the friends she had at her school. They looked slightly ragged; their clothes looked considerably more worn than she normally would have seen but this was not really what made them look different. She knew they were children of her own age because their faces were those of children but there was something missing from their faces she would have associated with children of her age. In fact, it seemed there was something in their faces reminding her of much older people. As she observed them, she realised the youthful glow of energy and early life she so took for granted in her friends was missing from these children. They rarely moved and the excited vitality she nearly always encountered with children of her own age who would already be excitedly chattering about their day, or their homes or one of their pets or their favourite toy in a situation such as this, simply was not happening.

They seemed to be looking into an empty space that had formed in front of them. Mariella even then had sensed something terrible had happened to these children. She had heard on occasions the conversations her mother and father had been having about the things that could happen to children as a result of the lives being led in the city. But she had not suspected the effect could be so dramatic. They actually seemed to look grey; as if they had some terrible shock or been nearly frightened to death. Something had temporarily taken away their life force, even consumed it. She suddenly realised normally, by now, there would have been a mother checking up on her children. Mariella looked around the room and into the garden perhaps expecting to see a mother talking to another mother or a doctor or enjoying a few moments of starshine before hurrying back. But there was no one. These children were completely alone. Mariella shuddered, as here was a concept she had rarely contemplated in such depth.

Of course, she had been alone in the woods at the end of her garden where she had happily played in the imaginary world so often she would conjure up. But that was in the knowledge her world was carefully wrapped around her. She knew she could run back up to her mother or father at any point, everything was familiar and in place and enabled her to feel safe in the world she had invented; the wrap around world in which these children had felt their safety had clearly been taken away very recently, if it had ever existed. She had felt desperately sorry for these two children and something between them knew she did. She could not bring herself to ask them what had happened and in those moments, it did not seem to matter.

She got up from her place and sat between the two children, gathered up the silent, lifeless form of the little girl and held her silently. The girl responded by cuddling into Mariella. She took the hand of the boy to her lips and kissed it silently as she looked deeply into his sad brown eyes. He smiled weakly and leant into Mariella who then put her other arm around him. There they had sat with a strip of golden Starshine laying across the room, she remembered, like three lost souls in a vast universe a long way from home sharing for a few moments their confusion and their incredulity for the vulnerability underlying their lives so easily brought to rest by the closeness and the love they now were feeling.

Ezme had found Mariella huddled together with the two children. Mariella had asked her Mother what had happened to the children on the way home but she had said she was sorry but she would not tell her. She said only the centre would care for them and help them the best they could until they were ready to go to a new home. Mariella had wondered of course what had happened to them but as her safe and busy life continued the incident passed into the deeper recesses of her memory where it would only resurface at times when she felt particularly alone and she was able to find a strange comfort in the moments she had experienced with those children. However, from then on she had looked into the faces of every person she met to observe how much of the original childlike vitality was missing from the complexion in front of her. This became both a surprising, enlightening and sometimes a shocking gauge to the health and wellbeing of the person.

Surprising, because in some of the oldest of faces much of their vitality still twinkled out from bright eyes and in many of the fittest young adults she had met the vitality was sadly almost gone. She smiled to herself as she remembered when she had looked into the eyes of the dragon; almost as if all the eyes she had ever looked into and assessed had been preparation for that moment. There had been the origin of all life, the infinite glow that had brought life and consciousness to this world and possibly previous worlds for aeons. Now transferred and carried in the soul of every living thing, the strength of which could be detected in the eyes of every creature who possessed it. So easy then to imagine a soul, consciousness and life force, bundled up into the same package and transferred into a collection of infinitely dividing cells that would once again become a being who could again experience what it was like to be alive. To be alive like a mountain leopard or an eagle, a wolf or a whale, one of Okino's lizards or an Okino, consciousness infinitely split and divided and connected to all the souls who were here incarnate and living within the consciousness of Arimathea.

How absurd it was to contemplate the infinite consciousness when it was so much easier to focus on a small intimate part of it where it was shining out all its beauty in one moment; to illuminate some undiscovered unique part of its mystery. She was thinking now of Okino. She smiled as she thought of him arriving aboard the cruise liner in his dusty robes and then transformed in the evening suit she had chosen for him and how on those long days she had looked forward to walking into dinner with him, clean and sparkling in the dark blue evening dress she had chosen.

She looked out of the cabin window of the airliner into the cloudless night where the moon shone down onto the ocean somewhere in the distance below. She imagined she could see the boat steaming across the face of the world carrying Okino the monk with his clarity and purity still fresh from the rarefied atmosphere of the temple high in the mountains. How would he react to the world which he would soon encounter and how would it react to him? She had already missed him in the hours they had been apart. She was also missing the world from which he came and through which she had travelled and become a part. Here encapsulated in the technology of the pressurised cabin it was hard to acknowledge she had become involved with the Original magic of the world.

They had become so close in their journey with the horses. She smiled as she remembered the decision to abandon the idea of putting up two tents because they had been so tired and sore from riding. How hungry they had been and how ridiculously they had come to recount to each other the most memorable meals they had ever had; which had involved some of the best and some of the worst. How clear he was, even more so since sharing the spirit of the dragon. She wondered whether they had really separated, Okino now being as near as possible to the dragon once again incarnate on Arimathea. Ever since her own experience in the waterfall her own connections and empathy with Arimathea and her dragon had grown stronger and she shuddered to think how she would react to the world into which she was returning. Now travelling high in the atmosphere at well beyond the speed of sound she knew the shock and disorientation awaiting her was almost certainly underway.

For the moment she had relished the comfort and rarefied environment of the airliner and had drifted into a deep unsettled sleep as the in-flight movie unravelled. The soundtrack had become mixed with her own memories of the day into a jumble of unsettling scenarios. She had felt sick as the helicopter had risen into the air over Zedocha and heartbroken to leave Okino and her horses. She had felt vulnerable and dangerously unstable in the flight along the coast to the airport and now a strange montage of images and impressions from the journey streamed through her sleep.

She was playing in the gentle surf with the children from the centre enjoying the cool breeze as the star sank towards the horizon. The breeze had increased in intensity and so the waves became stronger. At first, she had relished the greater force of the waves colliding with her body but soon the strength of the wind had increased further and the force of the waves steadily increased until she found she was unable to stand comfortably. The children and everyone on the beach had disappeared. She struggled against the rip tide to return to the beach but was unable to make any progress. The beach floor became stony and unable to find any stability she had been knocked off her feet by a series of powerful waves. She had tumbled in the surf having lost all direction in a whirling of darkness and the dying glow of the Star. She had tumbled through the strange salty pebbly maelstrom until finally she was deposited up beyond the beach on the pavement of the road amongst the bright lights and mechanised chaos of a city. The surf ran away back to the sea stranding her in this terrifying new episode of her dream.

She struggled to her feet and made her way along the pavement into the town. Her bedraggled appearance that had caused many people to walk cautiously around her gradually changed until she was again dressed appropriately for her urban existence. She had walked into a café and her father had been there to greet her. She had felt safe again with him as she gave him the hug she had so looked forward to since leaving on her journey. Her brother was playing in the band at the back of the large room and her friends were amongst the audience. Their faces flashed past as she connected with each one fleetingly. But there was someone else in the room she needed to find and as usual time was running out. She thought she had seen Okino at the front and she made her way towards him. The music was loud, as loud as the helicopter taking off and there were tall dark faceless strangers smiling and showing her a way through the crowd. But there was no way through and soon she was again lost in this new sea of dark flashing light, intolerable sound and smell. As her panic set in she awoke with a start as the credits to the film ran down the screen. All the names looked strangely familiar and within minutes the captain was notifying the passengers they soon would be arriving at the city airport of Straam.

If she did not have her eyes closed for the rest of the journey, out of the plane through the airport and out into the passenger lounge she had certainly felt removed from the entire experience; Tumbling through the surf with the other passengers back into the midnight world until there he was standing in front of her looking down at his vagrant daughter. She had turned down all the suggestions of the men in black to change or wash or even let go of the large rucksack in which she had carried the essentials of her life for the time she had been travelling. So now she stood in front of the most eminent lawyer in Straam in her dusty blue robe and the turquoise jacket she had brought in Asima. He looked down into those deep blue eyes shining out of her weather-beaten face, wildly surrounded by long unkempt straggly dark hair and fell in love with her all over again.

"Welcome home my sweetheart"

Her dream became reality as he gathered her up in his arms and held her to him. How skinny she had become he thought but how strong. He knew in those first few moments this was not the naïve child who had left all those months before and he wondered how easy it would be for her to adjust back into the life she had left. She stood back from him and looked up into his face with a grin he could tell had the story of a lifetime to tell and he shuddered to think what it might be. However now she was safely home and all the prayers to whatever god he had been praying had been heard and answered and finally he was able to relax again.

Chapter Fifty-One.
The Mother.

Aaron drove them through the streets of Straam, quiet now in the soft morning light. The early shifts had started. The delivery vans, the street vendors and the street cleaners clearing up the rubbish discarded on the streets by late night revellers. How wide these streets had become since Mariella had seen them last and how few people occupied them. She remembered Okino's story of the goats who had run wild in his town. She wanted the goats to come out of a side road or see some chickens pecking in amongst the left-over fast food cartons. Of course, there were only the pigeons and she suspected in amongst the shuffling, the occasional rat. Where were the brightly coloured yaks wandering untouched in amongst the traffic. Her mind teemed with the juxtapositions she felt and she wanted to tell her father so much about what had happened to her and Okino. About Okino! But there was an awkward silence between them as if they had momentarily become strangers.

Eventually when she asked, he told her how her Mother's illness had taken a grip of more of her body. The doctor had said there would not be long for her to live which was why he had sent the urgent message. She had felt a sense of irony as she registered she had made her journey to in some way improve the health of her world and now she had returned to face the almost certain death of her own mother. She saw him looking over at her every now again as if he couldn't quite believe she had returned so quickly and touched his arm reassuringly and smiled at him…

"I think this is all going to take some time, dad. I have so much to tell you, some of which is still hard for me to believe."

"It's Ok, Mari, I'm just glad to have you back. It's been hard with your mother and you are going to have to be strong in these next few days. I know you will be. I can feel you have grown and you can tell me all about your adventure when you are ready. But for the moment just do your best to settle!"

They arrived in front of the steel gates at the beginning of the long drive. The gates opened silently and Aaron drove them down to their home. So much of what she would have to become used to relied on the enormous wealth in which she would again be enveloped. In this world much of what had become part of her everyday life in Jahalala simply did not exist here in the same way as she had become used to; people and animals had been everywhere and their lives had become an inseparable part of her journey through the landscape. There had been no gates or walls or certainly none high enough to stop a determined goat from jumping over. Many of the people she had met had given freely of everything and anything they could offer and always had time to stop and pass the time of day and welcome her into their houses.

Here the streets were full of a continual stream of vehicles being driven through them. The people in them remained anonymous and unseen behind carefully reflective and tinted glass. There was a string of questions just in these simple facts she would have to address, eventually answer for herself and come to terms with if she was to live here again. She shook her head smiling as if to shake away a disturbing image as the gates closed behind them. All she held precious about her life was here and she had yearned to see it all again and feel it all around her, yet now it seemed unreal and somehow fraudulent in the light of all she had seen and been exposed to. Many of these questions had been instrumental in sending her on her journey and the funds that had paid for it had also originated here.

For now, however her primary concern must be with her mother. So later in the morning when she had extricated herself from the robe and soaked in possibly the longest bath she had ever had she found herself at the door of her mother's room. She pushed the door gently open and went in. The room was in a part of the house which always received the afternoon Star light. It was bright and cool and Ezme sat propped by several cushions in her bed. She appeared to be sleeping. Mariella quietly walked over to her bedside and sat down in the chair placed for such visits. She took her hand now thinner and more delicate than she remembered and felt the fragile life it still contained. The strong vigorous woman who had given her and her brother life and fought so fervently for the rights of the children in Straam whose circumstances had become desperate was clearly now in a vulnerable state. She stirred in her sleep possibly realising someone had taken her hand. She opened her eyes to see her daughter at her side. Mariella felt her pulse quicken as she acknowledged her arrival. Her eyes opened further and a smile came over her face. Mariella saw those deep blue eyes sparkling out from the frail face. She tried to sit up further and Mariella stood up and bent down to embrace her.

"Mariella you have come home. I am so pleased to see you. Did you have an absolutely marvellous time? You look so well, so different, a little skinny but that is no bad thing for you. Oh, I have so many questions for you. I have thought so much about what you said to me before you went. Now look what has happened to me. I am so sorry you have had to rush home for me but I so wanted to see you."

"Don't be silly Mum. There was never any doubt in my mind when I knew you were as ill as you have become and we were on our way home anyway."

Mariella had said 'we' and Ezme had picked up on it immediately.

"You say 'we' were coming home…you mean you have found some half mad stray on your travels who you are bringing home to meet me!"

Mariella smiled down at her beloved mother whose primary aim in life had to firstly make her own children as happy as they possibly could be. Then she had set out to bring as much of this happiness to all the other traumatised and neglected children who she had come across in the seething machine world of Straam city.

"Yes, mother there is a beautiful boy on his way to see you. He is on the ship I would have been on had I not flown most of the way round the world to be here now!"

"Oh, Mariella they are always beautiful, but is he a sensible human being?"

Mariella laughed out loud as she applied the all-important 'sensible Human being' to Okino to see if it fitted. She remembered him at the waterfall in Asima his hands raised in reverence to the sinking Star.

"I think he is one of the most sensible human beings you are ever likely to meet!"

"Oh, I am glad Mariella, where did you meet him. Was he on his travels like you!"

"He was actually and we met in a town I was visiting in one of their markets. He had set out from his village where he is a priest to find out the reason for the pollution in their fishing lakes."

"So, he is a priest and you say you have been travelling together!"

"Well we have been travelling together but we are not *together* if you get my drift!"

"Oh, you young people are full of surprises. So, what kind of priest is he? Is it a religion I would know about.!"

"It is an Ancient Order and they have dedicated themselves to keeping alive the connection between us humans and the spirit of Arimathea."

"Oh, so he really is a sensible human being. Did he talk very much about how their connection was made possible?"

"He did mother and a lot more. The whole thing has been completely amazing! Would you like me to tell you all about it?"

"Of course, Mariella. I want to hear everything you have done, seen and heard. There may be something I need to know before I start on my own journey…you know this final journey. Do you think there is?"

"Oh yes I am sure there is in fact you may have some instrumental part to play in the next episode knowing the nature of this story so far!"

"How exciting but if I fall asleep, you'll have to finish it tomorrow, promise me!

"I promise."

So, Mariella started to tell her mother the story about how Okino and she had come to play their part in the further evolution of Arimathea with the dragons, a race of advanced spirit beings who had come from the stars to live within her. Ezme let Mariella's words flow deep into the place in her old soul she had kept guarded and pure for when this story finally arrived. As Mariella continued, she felt Arimathea was feeding into her thoughts and on occasion included some detail Okino had forgotten to tell her from his own flight with the dragon. Ezme listened intently, watching Mariella with a contented smile as she unravelled her story. For a time, she forgot the severity of her illness as she lived through all that had been revealed in Asima and when Mariella told her about their meal with Sherana and her magical bones Esme started to speak.

"She is right of course. The change in the flow of events has been awaited for many generations. Arimathea has come under such pressure and now I can see why. So much of our own life is about how or when we act or how and when we don't. We debate endlessly the action we could take, whether it will be too much or too little. If we act to the advantage of one group of people, another may lose out. Often, Mariella the decision to take action becomes so difficult and full of endless complication that we decide to do nothing and everything goes on as before. When we have acted and we see how everything changes, in our own lives or in all the lives we have affected, immediately or as the years go by, then we get a glimpse of the power we have. We can never accurately predict outcomes. There will be an infinity of connections having to adjust and the consequences may last for many years if not for ever.

Arimathea knew to unleash her dragon may have consequences she could not possibly foresee. But really, what was her alternative? Now she has set a path and freed him again into the world. He is a wise universal spirit who has been battling with the forces of Oblivion for as long as they have both been in existence. He will have known the risks involved and everything now in place comes from the risk he took all those many centuries ago. It seems he will have to take little action other than dream his light filled dreamscape into the consciousness, in the knowledge this new tide will start to wash away the hurt that has come to Arimathea!"

She paused and started again with a new enthusiasm…

"We are like her Mariella! Our children, even before they are born are guiding us to where they can again come into the world and thrive, become part of all this magnificence. They will be guiding you now and possibly your priest. Our lives are preparation for their lives and all the lives to come in the future. We are always laying the pathways. She has nurtured this beautiful world and all the creatures upon it as I have nurtured you and your brother and likewise she is guided by the future; all the children who have yet to bring their genius and their vision into her consciousness collected perhaps over many lifetimes, many incarnations.

This is why I have worked so hard with the children at the foundation. They arrive battered and bruised, sometimes the life has nearly literally been driven out of them through neglect or physical or mental cruelty. When joyful vitality has been taken from a child they can never enjoy the simple and profound beauty this world offers to all of us; it by passes them and all the benefits and unique skills they have brought are lost as their lives continue in the only way they know through violence, abuse and disrespect.

Arimathea and all she has become is nothing to them and so she becomes their battleground where they fight for control and superiority where they imagine their pain will eventually stop. Sometimes we can reverse the hurt. Sometimes the beautiful original spirit emerges again and can take his or her place in the world."

Mariella is quiet as her mother pauses again. She is clearly tired now. She senses a clarity originating from some deep reflection that had occurred in these last days of her life as perhaps she came to terms with the reality it was about to end. She knew, as the soft evening light flooded the room sending the wavering shadows of the trees across the furniture, walls and her bed, Arimathea was here with them.

"…and I like the idea of this new parallel world Merilon has dreamed. I think I would like to go there. So far Okino has not met anyone except Mithrael…I wonder how it all will come to be."

There is a knock at the door..

"Come in Aaron."

"I hope I'm not interrupting anything too important, ladies, but I think you might like to see this Mariella. I think it may have something to do with you."

He goes over to a TV screen placed on a chest of draws and switches it on. The picture appears. The high definition images and sounds of the gathering as it swarms through the ocean around the cruise ship dominate the room. Aaron switches the channel over and over again until it is clear it is all that can be reached.

"It seems it is one of those channel blocking stunts the terrorist organisations have been using to advertise their atrocities. But this seems very different…oh and Mariella perhaps you might recognise this fellow!"

Mariella instantly recognises Okino making his speech and points stunned at the screen and excitedly looks at her father and back to her mother.

"This is how it is starting to happen. You see, I leave him for two minutes and already he is broadcasting to the world!"

"Mariella, I'm trying to hear what he's saying!"

"Sorry mother"

"Arimathea is a fully sentient being and everything on her contributes in some way to her health and wellbeing. Her spirit… her soul dwells in every living thing and she experiences the beauty and the wonder she has grown here through the senses of all those lives.…Every one of us is our own world with infinite cells and molecules and atoms making and constructing, driving our world, allowing us to breath, allowing us to digest our food and ultimately reproduce, allowing us to experience our lives through the senses we have evolved…Arimathea is all of this and far more than we can possibly understand without the ability we have lost. We are drifting blindly through our lives cut off from the incredible miracle into which we have grown.

We have a privileged place on the web of life she supports. We do have the intelligence to understand our place here and that gives us a responsibility to the being of whom we are an integral part.…I think the time has come when we are going to start to find our abilities again and I think this is Arimathea showing us how beautiful and powerful she is. She will wake us up by finding her way into whatever part of us we have neglected…and when you see this, what is happening here, you can't help wondering whether there is something going on here we haven't yet discovered or accounted for in our scientific theories."

"…and this is being broadcast onto every channel throughout the whole of Arimathea. All those beautiful creatures coming together, there must be thousands…and such beautiful pictures! I am so proud of you Mariella!"

Chapter Fifty-two.

Dream Weaver.

The dragon had been moving through the consciousness of Arimathea exploring all she had become. Always feeling for the possibility of some deeper connection with the beings who had come to live there. He drifted into the natural places where the trees and animals immediately knew his presence. The animals as always in their struggle for existence would stop for a few moments and savour the sensation of his passing and the intensified feeling of well-being and peaceful harmony they felt rising from the ground as he moved through their territory. For these smaller creatures, fundamental activity was always filled with the danger of becoming a meal themselves. So, they would stop for a moment and feel the magic flow through their lives.

Even the tiniest shrew scuttling backwards and forwards along the paths she frequently used could feel the wonder and the magical diversity of Arimathea in those moments as he passed. Her mountain ranges the expanses of jungle were only abstract dream formulations. She had little understanding of how or why they had come to her. But in those moments, she felt linked strangely to her distant relations foraging in the fallen debris of a forest for the distant relations of the grubs and insects they had both come to know could sustain them.

Their journeys, on the landmasses as they had slid and pushed and shifted over the millennia, by chance, had taken them to very different areas of Arimathea and had demanded they find very different skills to survive. But survive they must at any cost. There was a feeling in even the simplest of life forms the life they had been given was precious. They strived continually to keep it and pass on the gift. When the magic faded the memory and the possibility remained and was held and passed on as he flowed through the world.

As they felt the magic of the dragon from below or as it passed through their life, the parameters within them became wider and the possibilities greater as perhaps the grass tasted sweeter or the water tasted fresher. A moment such as this could take the shrew down a very different route where she could chance on a new and more abundant food source hitherto undiscovered. This new source may involve some adaptation of her present skills but could start the family of shrews on a new journey into the future. Her discovery may result in many generations being able to widen entirely the parameters of their existence, improve their chances of keeping their precious life force and so their place in the consciousness. Again, the world would shift as adjustment to her newly found fortune rippled its way through the web of life. In this way life had always evolved on Arimathea.

Very few incarnated spirits had ever come to understand the true importance of the place they held within the consciousness of their world. It was mostly incalculable to any other being other than a dragon. In such a calculation, the experience of the vast expanses of time and space in which it existed and so how it was infinitely connected and so held infinite possibility was fundamental. However, for every being that had ever emerged from its' mother or an egg or the ground, an overriding urge immediately became apparent. The sparkling new creature fresh from the ethereal realms from where it had been called would have to master the skills that would keep it alive.

Each newly incarnated spirit would have to develop and master a comprehensive model of the world in which it now existed. This was in the form of an understanding gradually constructed in the powerful minds evolved to process the information needed to operate effectively in this complex reality. As this understanding and information was assessed, the perceptions and intuitions arising would also contribute to the model as it evolved in the mind of the being where it was growing. The survival of the individual and the survival of its species depended on the effectiveness of this understanding. As understanding became knowledge it became wisdom and was passed on from generation to generation.

As the model grew in scope and accuracy then the ability of the being to operate within the reality of the world increased dramatically. A further ability enabled each experience both beneficial and detrimental to be held as a memory. These memories provided the ability to remember past situations and imagine future scenarios in which the being could make assumptions about the near or distant future. This allowed assessment of every situation likely to arise. As insight and knowledge of all the influences and powers at work in the world were added to the model, a powerful new ability had arisen. The power of imagination had allowed the ability to dream. This became a powerful tool for the sentient being living within the consciousness. It could presume outcomes and make decisions to avoid danger and ultimately alter circumstances where danger or even discomfort could arise.

To alter the world so outcomes became entirely predictable, possible or even remotely possible became the most powerful ability available to a sentient being or spirit. It had originated with the original ethereal spirit when she arose as this universe was formed in the darkness and had eventually been carried by the dragons to Arimathea. It was the fundamental driver for the progress of evolution through the aeons. It was a distant notion, a sparkling way into the future, an unformed idea which would eventually arise and as it flowed in the consciousness it could influence all the energy circulating within it. Here the dragon had his edge over the dark forces of Oblivion for here a new dream could be born to reshape the world.

These times had not been typical for the dragon after his long absence. In the time before he had been stranded in the caves deep in the mountains his consciousness would have moved across the surface and passed through enormous distances, predominantly, he would have spent his time deep in the rocky caverns of Arimathea asleep and mixing his dreams into the energy of the crystals surrounding him. They in turn would have emanated through to the surface contained in their unique frequencies to be absorbed into the consciousness of Arimathea. For billions of years since he had merged with the spirit of Arimathea his dreams were of the most beautiful and stable worlds in which he had lived.

Not for a dragon the chaotic rush of conflicting events and images rushing through the mind of a dreaming creature. A dragon will remember a peaceful or memorable moment within a place where for a few moments he had felt the harmony the Great Spirit had dreamed at the beginning of this physical time. In a Star filled forest he would remember the glow of life surrounding him, the power of the majestic trees and the beauty of the dappled light falling all around him, the infinite tangle of shape and form, the beauty of the birds and their song as they inhabited the branches above and perhaps a path leading through into a mysterious glade beyond.

In his beloved mountains he would record for eternity, that could be a dragon's life, every Star beam filtered through a cloudy sky, the rise and fall of the hills and even the scents drifting over the landscape with the sounds of the breezes, filling and refreshing his mind. The light always gave the memory of a place so much of its' energy, all of its' colour, the warmth and love; a rainbow, as a rain shower approaches or recedes, the texture of the grass and the sparkling reflections on the water of a lake or a sea in the distance, the sounds of a brook or a stream as it tumbles down the mountainside soon to join the flood made by ten thousand of its' kind then to fling itself into space and to fall through endless rainbow spectres to the valley floor below and race across the world to the sea.

He remembered the summits where he had dwelt. Here he could see the true wonder stretched out before him. The clouds skimming across and swooping and rolling down the slopes, the flat of the land and how it buzzed and hummed with life, the width of the endless blue sky as it extended deep into space beyond refracted of its deep threatening darkness and how it glowed green at first in the dawn, then burning gold as it cracked the horizon or at Star set as a graceful flight of swans returned to the river, or the sounds of the surf and the gulls wheeling above the curve of a beach disappearing into the distance, the rattle of the pebbles or the gentle lap of the waves as they dissolved into the sands.

A river, drifting lazily through the star filled woods and fields, reflecting the light filled leaves as branches hung over the transparency of the surface where below the trout wavered silently waiting for the hapless fly amongst the wavering water plants. Then the darting flight of the kingfisher as he flashes through, proclaiming his iridescence, precisely, stealthily over the surface in his search for the silvery prey below. The breeze sounding through the trees and the wood pigeons chanting their gentle call to prayer as the world breathes and ripples and glows.

From the ice filled oceans of the frozen wastes to the drifting dunes of the star scorched desert regions, the tropical jungles filled with the towering ancient tree beings to the endless savannahs where a million creatures drift through their world in their annual migrations. All these and an infinity more he had collected his memories.

The dragon had dwelt in a thousand worlds where he had found or attempted to create the peace and stability for which he had always striven. Anything he can absorb to preserve a moment, he will drink into his dragon soul where it will reside until a time when he can revisit that place and dwell in its sublime memory. Again and again, he will dream his visions of peace and tranquillity over the endless aeons into some desperate exploding world, as it shifts and expands and groans and lurches from one era to the next with no continuity or purpose until slowly it responds to the love and soothing energy he has brought and dreamed into its boiling bubbling sphere. These are the dreams the dragon brings.

His problem now and so relatively recently in terms of the life time of Arimathea, was that the human beings had lost their connection with the consciousness of their world to such a great extent his dreams simply could not penetrate the layers of misguided reason they had built around themselves. However now it seemed Okino the monk through his deeper connection with the dragons and Arimathea had been able to penetrate the consciousness of the animal kingdoms. They had seen this as the reason for a great celebration resulting in the gathering of the dolphins, the whales and all the other creatures who had joined the gathering.

This single extraordinary gesture from the oceans had not been enough to entirely remove the solid and intransigent barriers around the human psyches. However, the images and the message Okino had sent from the cruise ship and Azeera had projected into the multitude of TV channels surrounding the world had aroused the natural curiosity of the humans. The dragon had come to understand how the human races' imaginative model of the world was now continually informed by the global information system. The ability for the entire planet to take part in an event or hear some piece of news on mass even at a similar time had become increasingly prevalent. He had also realised in this imaginative model, virtually anything was possible and the reality of what was fictitious or reality had become blurred over recent years. The result was their dream space was constantly fed and mixed with both the hyper reality of the shocking events constantly happening around Arimathea and the wild hyper reality fictitious dreamscape concoctions fed to them by the vast movie studio corporations' intent on keeping them as distant from the true hyper reality as was possible.

Any large corporation with an interest in keeping the mass consciousness of the human race diverted from the true hyper reality was almost certainly funding the fictitious hyper reality. For the most part what was being fed to the human inhabitants of Arimathea through their screens blended into a blur of information mostly satisfying their need to have their attention diverted away from the ever more frightening situation on their world.

The starkest of these hyper realities was there seemed very little they could do about the scale and pace at which the degradation of Arimathea was now taking place. Governments and their politicians were being funded by some of the worst and most corrupt offenders. They found their representatives were indirectly involved in money laundering, tax avoidance, and the worst kinds of global environmental pollution and destruction. They found, they themselves, were paying into corporations involved in some of the worst degradation when they paid for the food they were feeding their families or the fuel running their homes; they found when they bought their clothes or the luxury products filling their homes they were supporting the exploitation of vulnerable people and children where the laws for the rights of workers had yet to be fully developed.

Democracy the hallowed political system of the industrialised world giving its' people power to appoint their politicians, was being manipulated in the interest of short-term re-election strategies when now more than ever the planet needed long term planning.

The majority of the human race was struggling with the cost and the fear of disaster in their lives and the worry the powerful institutions and organisations who had the responsibility for the wellbeing of their world were completely out of control. In their greedy race to grow the power they were exerting throughout more and more of the world they were grasping more and more of its' wealth. Their breath-taking irresponsibility seemed beyond the control of any law as they registered their companies in countries where they could conceal their clandestine activities. They were unopposed and were even encouraged and the areas of Arimathea undamaged by their activities were rapidly disappearing. As a result, it seemed the stress their world was under was becoming ever greater and their own models seemed to be shakier and more uncertain almost daily.

The dragon however, in this growing darkness, noticed an encouraging change in the human dream state. It was in their daydreams they wondered of possibilities. In the idle moments when they relaxed from the frantic race of their day to day existence or even during the many monotonous tasks the industrialised world had made available for them, they dreamed of how their lives might be and how much happier they would become if some how they could change some aspect of their fragile monotonous lives. In these moments much of their life was held up to scrutiny.

Could they change the job they were doing or stop it all together? Could they change where they were living or leave the partner or spouse they were living with? Could they move to a different area maybe to another country where there was warmer weather and healing seas and everything would be less expensive. And really, was there any possibility any of these changes could reduce the feeling of emptiness gnawing deeply away in their psyche.

However, they could be challenged occasionally by the mysteries of life on their world and now they had been presented with such a mystery. All over Arimathea as children stared idly out of the windows of their classrooms and their mothers and fathers retreated into the imaginary world just behind the office or the factory reality, they were wondering about the ocean gathering they had watched unfolding that morning or the night before on their televisions. For this was a mystery unexplainable on so many levels and it was leaving so many unanswered loose ends the human mind could not help but wonder and hypothesise about how it had come to be. The more they wondered the deeper the mystery became and in the canteens and the coffee bars, as they met in the markets and in the streets of their towns and cities they started to talk. The dragon became aware of this increased activity in the human consciousness and had flowed for a while into the world to feel how deeply it was reaching.

As he flowed through an industrial complex on the outskirts of a sprawling city the operatives were leaving their workplaces on a production line where they had been packaging components for one of the large telecommunication corporations. They lifted the same parts off the moving line in front of them and put them in the boxes piled all around them for the three hours of each shift they worked. Most of the workers were working three shifts every day. They were entitled to half an hour in their canteen between each shift.

They had watched the ocean gathering in the canteen together between the afternoon shifts the day before. The noisy canteen had become quiet as everyone began to comprehend what was happening. They had talked little of what they had seen but now the dragon sensed a conversation was imminent. They chose their meals and settled down at the table they would generally use if it was available and started to eat. Often, they were silent and chose to watch whatever was on the screens unless the weekly company propaganda was being shown telling them how well or how badly they had been doing or which of the management had exceeded expectations and been promoted. Then someone would pull the plug out and they would sit in silence or they would gossip about their colleagues or debate a current news event. A girl in her mid-twenties clearly was itching to start some debate. One other woman and two men were ignoring her looking down at their newspapers. She started anyway.

"But why would they all gather together like that? Around a cruise liner. I mean has anyone seen anything like it before. Not just dolphins or whales…pods of dolphins coming together is common enough …sometimes up to a hundred or so, but this was different species of marine creatures all swimming along together!"

The two men lowered their newspapers and looked at her thought fully.

"Look its' bound to be a stunt by those maniac terrorists. They've realised we're getting bored with seeing the towns they keep blowing up and somebody had the crazy idea to get some special effect movie company to bring all those creatures together. You know what they can do these days in a special effects studio."

One of the other women had finished her lunch.

"No, this was not a fake. My other half managed to record some of it and I watched it again when I got home last night looking for the seams and the repetition. The movies where they have thousands of people in a battle scene always have a very clever and almost invisible repetition but it will be there. No, this was genuine and it was amazing. No one has an explanation because it is entirely unprecedented. The monk has something to do with it. There are legends about what those guys get up to in those remote mountain temples."

One of the men laughed.

"So, what are they getting up to? Sitting around up there for hours on end burning incense. They've got far too much time on their hands."

The young girl leaned closer to the man.

"So, what they just made temples in some of the most remote places in the world so they could avoid getting a job is that what you think? Absolutely ridiculous! There are people who have been up there. They have come back with stories about the monks who practice meditation techniques handed down for thousands of years. Why would they keep doing that for so long and hand the tradition on, down through the generations unless they were really getting something out of it."

The man sat up straight now clearly intent on being antagonistic to the girl and any ideas that she may have.

"So, what are they getting out of it. Come on you tell me and if you start talking about god or aliens I know you'll be talking rubbish. It's primitive superstition. We've learnt our lesson about all that stuff down here and where it all leads."

"I don't know exactly but there are things I've have seen that make me wonder. For instance, our cat, you won't see him around and you don't think about it but then you realise you haven't seen him all day and you just wonder where he is. Then almost immediately he will turn up. Not just once or twice or even at the same time of day, this has been happening day in and day out for years. There has to be some kind of telepathy they pick up on. He must be picking up on my thoughts perhaps down at the end of the garden or wherever he is. But there can be no doubt my thoughts are travelling from my head into his or the other way around. This has been happening for years there is absolutely no doubt, it simply cannot be coincidence."

"So, does he arrange parties with all the other cats in the neighbourhood like you seem to assume these whales have done?"

The older woman laughs mockingly…

"What she's saying is these creatures may be more complex than we can possibly imagine. They've been around for millions of years longer than us, living in the oceans. Why wouldn't they have evolved some very special communication skills to bring them together on mass if a situation should arise."

"…yeah and what about a flock of starlings flying in one massive three-dimensional organism as if there is one thought being shared by thousands of birds in the same moment….and bee colonies are incredibly organised.

They have up to 50,000 bees in each colony. Everything revolves around the queen bee and her ability to keep laying eggs, so the hive is continually rejuvenated. The worker bees, all female incidentally, have many different tasks looking after the queen and making sure she gets the honey with the greater concentration of pollen and honey. There are bees who are continually making and repairing the bees wax hive cells where the pollen and nectar are stored and where the queen will lay her eggs in the early summer after she has been fertilised by the male drone bees. Sometimes she will lay up to fifteen hundred eggs a day! She then fertilises the eggs destined to become female workers and possible queens and the unfertilised will become the male drones. When they have fertilised the queen, the male drones are driven out of the hive in the winter to starve when the honey supplies get low."

"Seems a bit harsh!" said one of the men.

"Yeah, only good for one thing and then driven out to starve when no longer needed. I think we could learn a lot from bees."

The women laughed and the men went back to reading their papers. The younger girl continued when the laughter has died down.

"Then there are workers who will be sealing the cells and looking after the pupae as they develop into the larval stage before they emerge to start their duties in the hive. They have different organs enabling them to do all the different tasks, so brood food glands, scent glands, wax glands, and pollen baskets. There are workers who are continually cleaning the hive and specific workers who remove the dead bees and take them well away from the hive to prevent any disease being transmitted back into the hive. There are workers who will be cooling the hive by continually fanning the air with their wings and the actual honey is made by fanning the nectar in the cells to reduce the concentration of water within it.

There are also workers who will be collecting water to bring into the hive where it evaporates and also aids cooling. Some workers collect the pollen and nectar from the foragers who have been out retrieving it from flowers, and pack it and seal it into cells. Foraging is the final task the workers will perform before they die. They travel to up to a hundred flowers to fill their pollen baskets before returning to the hive. There are others patrolling outside and at the entrance to the hive to prevent any foreign bees from entering by stinging and releasing pheromones if there is imminent danger. They know all the bees from their own hive by a specific pheromone scent emanating from the queen shared by the entire colony.

In a good year when there is enough honey left over from the winter and there are too many bees for the hive, a new queen will be prepared by the workers in a newly constructed enlarged cell with concentrated pollen and honey. As she is about to emerge, the old queen and about half the bees will swarm and fly away from the nest to find a new location where a new hive will be constructed and worker bees will be raised for the process to start all over again. The weird thing is they are not all buzzing around all the time. They spend a lot of time just standing or walking around before the next round of frantic activity as if they understand the need for rest and contemplation.

So that is how the bee population is maintained and there are good years and bad years but you can see the colony is an incredibly complex social structure and way beyond any explanation we have for how it all happens the way it does. There is marvellous unexplained animal behaviour throughout the world which infers intelligent consciousness far beyond the instincts we associate with them.

The young girl seems surprised by her knowledge and becomes quiet as her work colleagues stare admiringly over at her.

"You know all that about bees! They are certainly ingenious little creatures. I mean you see them flying about and then you go and buy a pot of honey but it is remarkable to hear about how it actually happens!"

"All I'm saying is we don't have all the answers about this world we share with all these creatures. Far from it and this looks like something drawing our attention to that…and I would say pretty effectively."

"But what do we need to know that they can tell us. Those dolphins might have some system of talking to each other we don't know about but it's not going to be any good to us because if you haven't noticed we're not dolphins!"

The other older man who has been listening quietly, now speaks.

"I tell you what and I don't know how it has happened or who is really responsible but we all take this world for granted far too much. I walk around sometimes and watch it all going on. All this, all that we have made all bolted together with steel and glass and even these little phones we carry around with us all put together with silicon and transmitting to satellites. So that is what we have done which we think is pretty clever because dolphins haven't got mobile phones or skyscrapers or built motorways. But then why would they because they don't need them and maybe they've got it all up here"

He taps at the temples of his head.

"..and I think we had it all at one stage which is why your cat can still pick up messages from you and I don't think we've entirely lost it because when I get into these states when I'm looking round at everything we have done, it is clever and we have made beautiful things but just go to the park and see how delicate trees and flowers are, and the swans swimming on the lake. They've all come about without any help from us….and if there was another conscious intelligence on this world, say the dolphins or the whales and they could see what a mess we are making of things wouldn't they sooner or later try to find some way to tell us. The cleverest thing we have done is to discover how amazing this world really is and how it all runs and lives and really all we need to do is enjoy it, which is probably what those monks are doing."

The young girl looks over at him as if with new respect.

"I like that, another conscious intelligence on our world. Suddenly I don't feel so vulnerable to the stupidity of the Human Race Gang. Perhaps there is a race of real grown-ups out there watching over things!"

The dragon continued on his journey. Seeds were being planted in the minds of the human beings as they noticed Arimathea revealing herself. In discussions and thoughts and idle daydreams their parameters were being widened, in many cases the bubbles around them were starting to break down. These seeds would rapidly start to grow in the fertile soil of the knowledge they were being given. These germs of ideas would soon grow into realisations about the true nature of their world and would lead them once again into the deeper realms of the dragon's dream.

Chapter Fifty-Three
Dreamscape

Okino was settled contemplating the ocean stretching out all around him. He had identified this position from his explorations of the ship as possibly the highest point where a person could sit and so enjoy stunning views over the surrounding ocean. However, he had not been able to find any access to what would have been called the crow's nest. He tentatively asked the captain about the access. He grinned and showed him the route to the bridge through the command centres where the passengers were not permitted to enter unless under strict supervision or on a scheduled guided tour of the boat.

Okino was able to make his way to the deck which in turn led to the mast. Then there was only a short climb to the small platform where the radio and satellite equipment could be serviced. To meditate at Star rise was everyday practice for a monk in the Order of the Dragon. But his discipline had slipped as the delights of being curled up in the warm yurt with Mariella had gradually worn away even his formidable resolve. But now with such an excellent position at his disposal that would have made even the most devout and disciplined monk a little bit envious he had resumed the practice. High above the hustle and bustle of the ship's early morning activity, he was able to contemplate the wonder of his existence with only the seagulls gliding effortlessly on the breeze above with their cries taking him deeper into the consciousness of his ancient world.

He had settled into his voyage on the Osira remarkably well despite becoming a celebrity amongst almost everyone after the broadcast had made the entire ship famous around Arimathea. This had made movement extremely difficult for the young monk who had been happy with the degree of anonymity with which he had arrived. It seemed everyone had a similar question for him and after an initial greeting now found it imperative to ask…

"What on Arimathea have you monks hidden away from the eyes of the world, been doing all these years in your remote monasteries?"

This question on the lips of much of the population of Arimathea was now regularly being asked by the passengers on the Osira. He had decided to speak to the Captain about his predicament and they decided he would give a short talk one afternoon. He hoped this might deflect some of the attention he was now receiving. The Captain himself had been curious from the start as to the appearance of the dusty monk who had had his first-class passage paid by one of the wealthier families in Straam. He had learned very little about the monk from their meetings, as he had found, like many of the passengers who had met him, he seemed very adept at letting them do the talking.

When the afternoon arrived the theatre usually used for the cabaret performances in the evenings was filled with curious passengers whose cruise had been carefully specified in their brochures to avoid any contractual wrangles due to any presumption of what might or might not happen. Their holiday therefore had contained few surprises so far, other than being accompanied across the ocean by many of the creatures inhabiting it for the best part of an entire evening.

There were those who had been disinterested as there had been in the general population as a whole. Remarkably they were in a minority. They were the rich and famous whose sense of themselves relied on the intensity of the spotlight directed upon them. However, as this new phenomenon began to grip the curiosity of the people of Arimathea the interest in their futile lives began to wane. Those who now awaited eagerly to hear the mysterious monk shed some light on his lifestyle may not have previously contemplated anything happening outside of their own countries could have any consequence for their world. But now it seemed there was and they were curious to hear more about it. Okino, however had worried continuously about how much he would be able to reveal and considered in hindsight, it may have been an easier option just to lock himself in his suite for the rest of the voyage.

Eventually he decided there was much he could tell the passengers about their lives in the monastery involving their practice being handed down through the generations and continually extending out into their community. He explained to the crowd, who he suspected wanted to hear of ancient magical practices and secret rites, about a way of life the Ancient order of the Dragon had held sacred and passed through the generations that had allowed a deep and continuous connection to the consciousness of their world. The meditation carried out in their temple unique in its relationship to the mountains where the atmosphere was as pure as could be found anywhere on Arimathea, although being a vital part was only the foundation for an entire process involving the entire community.

"When we meditate we become quiet, quiet in our bodies and most importantly quiet in our minds. Then we can become closer to the silence of the high mountains all around us. In this silence we have found the consciousness of our world Arimathea. We conduct much of our lives in this awareness. It is maintained in all the tasks of work and pleasure we perform throughout our day. So, as we tend to the gardens and our crops or our animals it is in contemplation and awareness of the consciousness in which all our lives are embedded. It is our belief and experience; everything is part of this consciousness. The more we acknowledge the depth of the connection the deeper the understanding of the knowledge becomes. Everything happening around us, all the actions we perform in our days, then is in harmony with the life of Arimathea.

We are closely connected to the people in our community and help it in any way we can by guiding and counselling them in all aspects of their lives with the wisdom retained in the temple by the generations who have gone before. We also work in the fields with everyone else when the need arises. It is still a dangerous and fragile environment for humans to live in. We live very carefully gently coaxing the life nurturing us out of our land. We have found through the generations, as have many of the mountain communities that if we live with an awareness that everything we do effects the outcome of our lives then there is a better chance we will survive: and so we have through all these hundreds possibly thousands of years. In the schools we teach the children to apply this principle to all they do. They learn to be quiet from an early age, to concentrate on what they are doing. Each child's potential and aspiration is considered so their individual skills are used with most effectiveness in the community. We teach them mathematics in relation to the fields they see their mothers and fathers working and all we know about the processes happening in amongst the rows of crops growing from the ground.

Each child grows into an adult who will find his or her place in the running and operations of the town which gives them their sense of worth, belonging and self-respect. This in turn, perhaps most importantly allows every member of the community to gain respect through the success of their role. It works pretty well in a small community and of course there can be difficulties when we find we have a bunch of children who all want to be bakers or builders so we are careful to make sure everyone can perform as many roles as possible. Bakers can be builders and builders who have to be the most flexible can generally put their hand to just about anything. We have learnt to be flexible and it seems to keep most people busy all the time. This makes for a harmonious community able to cope with the difficulties with which living in such a remote place constantly presents.

Through the centuries we have not drifted away from the natural forces acting upon us and our land. We and our entire community have grown closer to them with each new generation. The Ancient Order of The Dragon has always observed and held sacred the knowledge our community has developed. We record all we learn and the discoveries we make about what we see around us. Our knowledge of the consciousness and the energies contained within it has grown and with it the closeness of our connection to them.

Every aspect of our lives has become as close to harmonious with the life consciousness of our world as we have been able to make it. Only through experience handed on and by observing the outcomes of all we do in the context of our conscious lives have we continually attempted to make our lives become increasingly continuous with the higher energies we believe surround us. Then it seems they can act through us in everything we do. This depth of connection has now possibly become deep enough for us to begin to communicate throughout the consciousness and so to the other beings with whom we share our world."

As he had spoken these words he had realised fully the extent to which the entire community had become a part of this new breakthrough. He and all his fellow villagers had lived for many generations with the benefit of accumulated wisdom perhaps going far back to when the dragons had visited the world in their mortal form. He was the end product of the whole process. The rest of his race had plunged headlong into a period in which it had explored freely and entirely recklessly the potential their world was able to offer without concern for the damage it might cause. In isolation from this reckless advancement, the monks had been able to maintain and increase their ability to develop a connection with their world so if and when a time came for their entire race to engage with her consciousness the ability would be available. A strange evolution then had occurred and yet the outcome was still dangerously in the balance.

Okino was high in the crow's nest travelling into the breeze bringing its' warmth up from the lands in the south where soon he would arrive. The limitless expanse of the sky and ocean stretched in all directions around him. He smiled as he closed his eyes and felt the bright Starlight fill his being. The warm breeze wrapped around him and he stretched out his arms as if they were wings that could lift him weightlessly from the ship into the cloudless blue sky. As his solidity fell away he could feel precious flight feathers responding to the breeze. Instinctively he could adjust the pitch of each wing to hold him steady as he registered the fluctuations of the breeze. He sent out his call proclaiming through the parallel world into which he had crossed, his presence to all who might join him.

Merilon heard his call and flashed through the light and the boundaries separating them and merged with the eagle spirit floating through the worlds. Okino knew he had arrived and acknowledged their joining by dipping his wings taking them into a dive hurtling down towards the lands into which they now had crossed. The dragon proudly announced this was the dreamland he had formed. Okino dropped to a height where he could observe the landscapes now drifting below him. An immaculate parallel dream world overlapping and sharing the consciousness of Arimathea.

But as he glided over the fully-grown trees and dark flowing rivers it seemed as solid and as real as the one he had recently left. However, he knew from the experiences he had already received here this was no ordinary world. Even here high above the landscape the vision with which the dragons had filled this world seemed to radiate through the atmosphere. So, the river winding its' way lazily through the meadows became a continuous thread running through the years connecting generation after generation of the creatures living alongside it; an entire eco system containing those lives and all the wisdom surrounding their life and survival.

For the first time he was able to see small settlements in amongst the plains and hills where people were going about their business. He knew them to be the race who had built the stone temples. He was curious to meet these people. The dragon acknowledged and was delighted by his curiosity so they dropped down over one of the villages and the eagle landed on a stone chimney overlooking a patch of luxurious grass on which three sheep were grazing amongst a number of waist high stones arranged loosely in a circle. Men, women and children walked and worked amongst the dwellings with their low stone walls and thatched roofs. Okino's attention was drawn to a figure who sat cross legged on the edge of the stones with his dark tanned face raised into the Starshine. He was older than the other people and noticeably was wearing fine leather trousers and a jacket carefully sewn with leather cord and a beautiful feather head dress itself decorated with fine coloured beads. Okino wondered would he be able to talk to this person and the dragon gave his encouragement. The eagle flew down from the roof to a path beyond the houses and Okino took on his human form. He wandered casually into the stones and asked whether he could sit down next to the old Indian. The old Indian smiled up at him and indicated for him to sit down beside him.

"Have you travelled far, young man?" he asked Okino intently.

"Perhaps I have in one sense but in another I am precisely in the place I was this morning!"

"Oh, I understand. More of you are starting to arrive." He said knowingly.

"..and how have you come to be here on this beautiful day Sir?"

The old Indian smiled at Okino. He removed a long pipe from where it hung in his jacket.

"Do you smoke, young man?" …and without waiting for Okino's answer he preceded to quietly fill the pipe with some dried plant material which he took from his pouch while observing Okino. He lit the pipe, took a puff and handed it to Okino who grinned and himself took a puff and inhaled the dense smoke. It raced down the length of the pipe and flowed deep into his lungs where the plant's magic was released into his blood stream. It was carried to his mind where it mingled with his thoughts and visions. Again, the perception of his world was changing. The old Indian was no longer a stranger but someone he apparently had known for many, many years. The old Indian saw his astonishment as he handed back the pipe, he grinned himself and took another puff on his pipe.

"What is your name young man?"

"My name is Okino,"

"I am honoured to meet you, Okino, I am Running Bear."

"I am honoured to meet you, Running Bear."

"I was a chief of a noble people who lived on the plains of a vast open country. We were great hunters and warriors fearing neither our enemies nor the death they would bring upon us. I lived out my natural years though, the bravest of all warriors and greatest of hunters." He smiled and handed the pipe back to Okino."

"I think we have fought many battles together and shared many pipes in the lodges of our people."

Okino had vivid memories of skirmishes with neighbouring tribes and many aspects of a life he may have led with this tribe. He had had many strong sons and beautiful daughters who had also come to follow the buffalo across the great plains as the seasons changed from one year to the next.

"Now I have come to this place where there is everything I need for an honourable life. There are many of us here who have shared the blissful eternity of the Great Spirit. But certain of us have emerged to preside over this new world. It is somewhere in between your world and the one of the Great

Spirit. I can hunt but there is sadly little to fight over," he grins and accepts the pipe back from Okino.

"I have travelled here before, at the beginning with the Spirits who live in the hills. They have shown me the temples you and your people have built to channel their wisdom."

"There is much wisdom here, my son. In the legends of my people there was a land where the bravest and the wisest would go after the troubles of their mortal lives were over. It seems there are many wise souls who have come here to guide the ones who come from the troubled soul of the mortal world. Many have lost themselves and all that is important in the struggle of their existence. But now they have lost the ways to find their way back; the ways known by the old peoples of your world. However, there are those who are starting to find the ways through the veil existing between your world and this." The old chief looked over at Okino curious to hear his response.

"Have you met many of these people?"

The old chief nodded calmly and closed his eyes and raised his face to the Star.

"There was one who came. His name was Yaan as I remember. Through careful observation of the old ways he had found his way through to the old Wolf circle up in the hills. He lives in a part of your world where the boundaries are thin between the present and the past. In a place where the old peoples had a close relationship with the spirits in their lands. He had been with them and undertaken an old initiation which had allowed him knowledge into their tribal wisdom. He told me in his dreams he had been wandering again on the moors which he was accustomed to do. On this day he saw a hilltop in the far distance. He had felt there was a vision waiting for him there so he had decided to walk towards it. At first he was unable to see clearly the path in front of him. There were distractions in his mind. There were many other things constantly demanding his attention which seemed of greater importance than following the path. The more he persevered and searched the stronger the path became in front of him. He found himself wandering in an ancient forest, now unable to decide whether he was lost or not he found himself standing in a ring of ancient trees. Their branches had filled the space over the circle.

He said he had felt completely cocooned by the life flowing through the trees all around him. He told me a change had then become apparent. It had been winter and very quiet, the air cold and crisp with little sign of life. As he stood there the trees started to grow their leaves the air became warmer and the forest was full of the sounds of birds and the other animals. Now he could see a wide path leading out through the trees and up to the top of the hill he had first seen. He knew he had somehow passed over from one place or time into another. He had no way of knowing at this stage exactly what had happened.

When he came out of the forest the path led to the top of the hill and the old wolf circle. The wolf is a powerful hunter as you may understand; he has a strong family but is happy at times of his life to go alone through the world. They are inquisitive beasts, with great daring and little fear especially when the rest of their pack is depending on them in a hunting situation. They are highly revered by my people and there are many rituals to bring the power of their spirit into the new warriors of our tribe. The old wolf spirit directed him as he sat amongst the stones to travel to the mountains beyond and visit a temple there.

Time passes strangely here and the nature of the dream in which it exists can distort our memory so an experience can be complete without the normal flow of time having taken place. Perhaps you have experienced this in your dreams Okino. You maybe have the memories of an entire lifetime you could never possibly have lived out. Our solid and narrow ideas of time and our lives only allows us this one life, this one set of experiences. But it seems from these dreams there may be far more to our existence within multiple lives.

So Yaan made his way through the mountains and eventually found himself at the temple. He was grateful for the warmth of the fire burning in the hearth filling the space of the hall into which he had entered. As he warmed himself he remembered he had travelled long distances along many perilous mountain passes. He remembered days walking in the icy wastelands, through astonishing vistas as the Star shone down from cloudless skies but also storms had threatened to freeze the blood in his veins.

There had been people who had joined him, materialised, perhaps when his determination was starting to ebb away. They had inspired him to move forward by reassuring him of his ability. Sometimes they had referred to the times in his life when he had overcome enormous difficulty to become the person with the life he had attained. He had wanted to take risks. There had been steeper routes which would have taken perhaps days off his journey, but he had seen the faces of his mother and father, his wife, of their future children and their children pleading with him to stay safe and he had stomped off on the long route.

His doubt and fear of his capability to scale the long icy slopes as he climbed higher and higher had worn away at his resolve. At one point he had been unable to move, gripped in the sheer terror of the physical and mental task looming in front of him. These are the times my son when we find out who we truly are. There are no rehearsals, there is no wisdom or anyone who can tell us whether we can or cannot achieve what we need to accomplish in the next month, week or day. All we have is who we have become and the strength we can draw into ourselves even though there seems to be little left.

When he came to look around the hall he saw a number of large books laid out on the table in front of him and on other tables around the hall. He pulled one over, opened it up and examined the detailed script in front of him. To his astonishment he had started to read about a particular episode in his life. The morning he had met his wife he had originally decided he would not go to the lecture. He had planned a visit to an exhibition in the next city displaying artefacts excavated from the surrounding countryside. He was particularly determined to see the jewellery on show, convinced he would be able gain insight into the state of the artists mind all those millennia before. Even then it had been the people, how they had lived and perceived their world that had predominantly interested him. He felt sure they had the key to some of the frustration his own generation were feeling with their existence. He had left his house, got in his car to start the journey and it had failed to start. Nothing within his capability would persuade it to start so he abandoned the idea and decided to go to his college and the lecture on the bus.

Now in this dream he found it all had been recorded in this book. He leafed through the pages and found other episodes of his life as if somebody had been standing at his shoulder. Then a strange thought occurred to him looking at the books on the tables and lining the shelves of the hall. If these books were all about his life then he wondered how far they would go back. He started to find books of his early childhood and the last of the series on this table at the beginning appeared to describe the time and circumstances of his actual birth. But still there were many more books on the tables and shelves around the hall. So, intrigued he started to delve into the other books where he found details of the previous lives he had led. He was initially surprised and suddenly slightly sceptical about what appeared to be happening but as he read through the pages they seemed strangely familiar to him.

In his last life it seemed he had been a carpenter who had spent much of his life building the large ocean-going sailing ships that were carrying men and their trade to the distant lands of Arimathea. The descriptions of his skills in carving and jointing the large timbers brought about an eerie familiarity to come over him. But then he had always had a fascination with the intricacy and skill with which these vessels had been constructed and their ability to withstand the brutality of the most violent of Arimathea's ocean storms. The smell of newly cut Oak had always brought a mysterious resonance. He had been drawn to the coast and the old harbours where the boats would have been made. He had always been comfortable with the idea of making things from wood and had relished starting to make pieces of furniture when he first brought his house. The tools had felt familiar in his hands as they crafted the wood for parts of his new home.

He started to delve deeper into the timelines he had uncovered, past another birth in more painful circumstances it seemed to when he had been a farmer. He had been born into a farming family and so much of his life had been involved with the growing of crops and the rearing of all kinds of animals. This immediately explained his delight when faced with a field of ripened barley ready for harvest or a herd of cows grazing contentedly across a field of lush green grass. Perhaps for this reason he had immediately set about converting a section of his garden into a vegetable patch where he found he had an uncanny knack for being able to grow almost any seed, tuba or bulb he put in the ground. His interest in the weather and its diversity on the misty island had always been an obsession.

He delved further. He had been a soldier who had fought in a mass revolution against injustice and the cruel domination of the rulers of the world. He recognised the anger and the rage he and his fellow countrymen had felt when they came to realise how so much of their freedom had been taken from them over the generations as the power and greed of their rulers had increased; he recognised the revolutionary fervour described as he marched into battle against the loyalist forces and as they charged across the field to confront the professional soldiers of their king. He recognised the confusion and the fury with which they had fought and the dreadful scenes as his countrymen sliced and cut each other to death while the lords commanding their army watched on a distant hill; he remembered the thunder of the horses....

Further back still he had been a fisherman in a small settlement on an estuary living in what appeared to have been an abundant and peaceful time. He had knowledge of the seas around his home and how to sail and navigate his small fishing boat as he traded his fish with neighbouring communities. Deep emotion arose in him as the account told how he would see his wife and children waiting for him as he sailed up beside the little jetty he had built and how he would leap from his boat filled with fish to greet them and pull them all to him in the happiness and joy of his life there with them. He became fascinated by the insights into the character he had become influenced by the different lives he had led. Many of his skills and his response to the world it seemed came from the knowledge and instincts he had acquired previously in the rich weave of lives he had led. They clearly had resulted in this soul he had now become.

The common thread through all these lives he found was he had always become a teacher: Whether to his own children or to the apprentices who he had taken under his wing. He recognised the ease with which he was able to convey his thoughts and actions and the benefit of his experience to any who had an interest in the wisdom he had gained.

Perhaps this all had been preparation for the final account he was able to find or had been allowed to find. He opened the last book sitting on the shelf above him and opened it in front of him. In the account he was walking down a wide path leading through a dense forest towards a large timber roundhouse. Inside there was a circle of elders sitting around a fire. Smoke drifted up through an opening in the roof. They greeted Yaan and asked him to sit amongst them with fond familiarity and a discussion slowly started to take place.

It seemed it was at a time when large numbers of people were invading and settling in their land. There was great demand for fields as the increase of farming was taking place and so the forests were being cut down and burnt. One of the elders had had a vision. He had seen a time when the network of sacred groves spread across the country in the great forest would slowly be forgotten as it was destroyed. He had fore seen a time when the knowledge embedded in the ancient trees growing around these special places and the special atmosphere and energy flowing there would be lost for ever.

This was of great concern to the elders for it was in these places where the people had always been in contact and guided by the spirits of the forest and their land.

The wisdom of the great Oaks was threaded deeply into their culture providing stability and coherence within the natural world in which they lived. As they stood in peace and tranquillity with their roots deep in the Earth and their branches, bathed in Starlight, gently swaying in the winds, reaching for the stars, changing with the path of the Star in the day and the moon and the stars at night, providing shelter and stability and livelihood for the multitude of creatures living amongst them they provided the central metaphor for the mystery at the centre of their lives. For as they threw down their leaves in the icy grip of Winter they appeared to die. However, when the warm breezes of the Spring again drifted through the forest and their green gowns were replaced they appeared to have returned from their icy death to be reborn. Here was a certainty that did not necessarily follow through into all their lives. The world at its' core was redemptive, life conquered death and light conquered the darkness.

They talked, those elders, long into the night about those places and the trees surrounding them. They knew the trees had responded to the special places in the land but also the special places where the spirits flowed had responded to the ancient trees growing around them. They interacted in a special relationship entirely beneficial for the outlook of the people at all times of their lives. They had always been there for the community of humans who lived with them at the centre of their existence. If they were lost it would be difficult to imagine what the result might be.

But there was a tide that would be hard to turn. The land was fertile and more settlers were arriving every day. It was time to act for what they had in mind would take many long years of work and planning. Deeper into the early morning and after many pipes had been passed they agreed what they must do. In amongst the trees they would place circles of carefully prepared stones; embedded deep into the Earth so they could never be moved. Similar to those made by the old peoples out on the desolate moors. They would be placed to reflect the relationships the trees had had with their Star and the moon and the other stars so important to each place. As the ancient forest was lost and the time of the trees gradually fell away at least these special places in the land would not be forgotten. Then perhaps one day the trees would return to once again restore their wonder to those places and the world."

The old Indian became silent and began to fill his pipe. He lit it, inhaled deeply the thick aromatic smoke and handed it over to Okino.

"He has returned now as you must. I think perhaps I have kept you too long."

"Thank you Running Bear. May the Blessings of the stars be always upon you!"

"..and on you my son."

The eagle who had been waiting in a tree swooped down over Okino and whisked his spirit back into the bright blue skies where the seagulls were gliding on the winds of change circling Arimathea.

Chapter Fifty-four
Arrival.

Mariella had driven out from the suburbs to the docks on the harbour edge of Straam. It was the day the Ocean liner carrying Okino from the other side of the world would arrive in her city. She stood on the long quay straining her eyes out to the distant horizon for her first site of the ship. Still it was not visible. Even through her expensively coated sunglasses the glare of the hazy mist was making the fine line between sea and sky almost indefinable. She looked down at her watch. She had left earlier than she had needed to and the streets had been relatively clear by Straam's standards. So now she had to wait. But even if she had stayed at home she would have had to wait. She had been waiting for days. Eleven and a half days since she had left Okino and the horses watching forlorn and lost in the square of the Eremoyan embassy as she was whisked off to be at the bedside of her Mother.

Mariella shuddered in the horror of remembrance and guilt. Guilty she had forgotten momentarily in her excitement of seeing Okino her mother had died seven days earlier. Her passing had left both her father, her brother and herself lost and distraught. Their only consolation being she had died peacefully during her sleep in the night. They had wept in each other's arms almost constantly that day. Then sat silently in the garden in the easy chairs they had shared with her on the long summer days and evenings, staring out into the universe where they imagined she had already ascended into the paradise she had planned and demanded from her gods and goddesses leaving them there to carry on without her to help them through all this…all this life.

They had told all their stories and dissected infinitely the parts she had played in them, the lines she had had in them. How would they manage without her encouragement her beautiful dismissive attitude towards anyone or anything that had upset them or stood in their way without denigrating their fear or worry? How would they manage without her love for them? Mariella saw her father actually deflate as the realisation she had gone hit home. As he finally realised he would never look into those soft startling blue eyes again. She had gathered him up in her arms and he had wept again like she had never heard any one weep before; the uncontrolled emotion, of grief and loss cascading from a human being leaving nothing for him to hold onto except her as he fell. So, this was what it was like to lose your soul mate…and your mother.

So, they had all disintegrated together. Looking round expecting her to be there waiting for her to say something to get them moving, to sort them out; tell them to go to the shops to buy some food; eat some food, turn the TV on, ring some friends; anything but just sitting there wishing she hadn't died. But she had died and they had become hungry when all the food had run out and they had to start to make the little decisions that allowed life to go on. Find the keys to the car, go to the car, start the car and drive out to the shop; to surprisingly find the world going on as normal exactly as it had been the day when she had been there, when she was in the world with everyone else. How did they not know about this tragedy happening in their world without everything grinding to a halt? But it was going on and soon they had joined in again but with a crushing emptiness that left the food they cooked tasteless and everything going on around them futile and meaning less. They drifted through those days like ghosts from a world that had disappeared, leaving only an empty husk without the nourishment, the joy and the colour. Without Ezme. They fought back the tears but much of the time relented and again sat down and sobbed. They thought they felt her around them telling them it was fine and they would be fine and to pull themselves together. But it was only them knowing that that was exactly what she would be saying to them and for the first time they giggled through their tears as they realised this was how it was now and she had left them well prepared possibly for all eventualities in the precious time they had spent with her.

Slowly this new thought took grip and expanded in their minds to bring those ghosts to life again in a world full of all the love and wonder she had left for them. As these realisations took hold, the readjustment to their new lives began. Mariella remembered something beautiful was about to happen in her life. The one person perhaps within many light years of where she was standing who she knew would put back some stability where there was currently none was heading towards her town. Again, she strained her eyes into the misty distance and thought perhaps at that very moment a microscopic trace of the cruise liner did come into her view there on the dock.

The sky had darkened and the first drops of rain were starting to splatter down on the concrete around her. She had no idea how long it would take the ship to cruise from the distance where she had spotted it. She was resolved for a long wait. As the strength of the rain increased, she looked across to the terminal building for shelter and possibly something to entertain herself for the period ahead. The crowd she had anticipated had not yet formed entirely but was starting to accumulate. She assessed the group who stood in various huddled groups and decided they were mostly the children, predominantly middle aged, of their elderly parents who were also approaching on the ship. Now they also wanted shelter and inevitably they started to drift towards the smell of freshly brewing coffee and the comfortable chairs awaiting them in the terminal building. There was also another group who clearly were not there to greet passengers.

They were identified by large documentary style broadcasting cameras and electronic audio-visual equipment scattered around them. Others perhaps presenters and directors stood slightly apart from their technical crew talking while glancing around at their peers now disappearing towards the restaurant ignoring them with concentrated disinterest. Mariella wondered whether they were here to catch the first glimpses of Okino as he arrived in the city. In her grief, as she, her brother and her father had turned their backs on the world, she had not fully considered the amount of interest the rapacious media would almost certainly show in the young monk. His broadcast from the cruise liner had unleashed a tidal wave of discussion as the underlying anxiety surrounding the global environment and the plight of the creatures living within it rolled around Arimathea. Eventually the general opinion had been reached the creatures of the oceans had come together in solidarity to send a message to the human race. There seemed to be no other explanation for this unprecedented event. Endless debate as to what the message was had filled current affairs programmes. Leaders and politicians were only allowed limited airtime to justify the policies that had led to the dire state in which the natural world now found itself. The subsequent discussions came to little as everybody stood in their own corner firmly blaming everybody else.

This mood change in the general population of Arimathea could not be ignored and was carefully registered by the leaders and politicians and more importantly perhaps by those who supported and relied on them staying in power to enforce and pass the legislation enabling the degradation to continue quietly and uninterrupted as before. In boardrooms around the world of Arimathea deceitful strategies of appeasement were planned and drafted to public relations companies. However, the time when the airing of an advertising campaign showing corporate activity continuing harmoniously alongside pristine forests thick with biodiversity and seas teaming with abundance appeared to be over. Okino was heading into a maelstrom. Mariella shuddered when she thought of the young monk leading his horse through the streets of Zedocha in his dusty robes. It would be hard enough for him to cope in this strange future world without being at the centre of a global dispute between its people and their leaders. The cruise liner was now clearly visible on the horizon as Mariella retreated from the increasingly heavy rain into the embarkation terminal restaurant.

On the ship Okino was again in the crow's nest. He had sighted the city of Straam as a blur across the murky blue grey sea. Now his levels of anticipation and suspense had become almost unbearable. He had compared the intolerable speed and what appeared to be the negligible progress each day to the movement of the yaks through the interminable plains of the mountain landscapes of Jahallala. From day to day nothing had changed. The distant horizons of ocean had stretched out all around him until now. They were at last approaching Straam and he wondered how far it was. He knew if he sat and watched the city approaching this final part of his voyage would seem ridiculously protracted. He peered down towards the lower decks. There was a greater and intense level of activity as his fellow passengers came to realise fully they would be soon leaving the floating home that had absorbed and accommodated them so entirely. Soon they would be back in their homes with the memories they had gleaned from their expensive voyage around Arimathea. The fascinating places they had visited and the people they had met soon would fade and then be adapted to take their place in the library of memories each of those lives already contained. How many of the people from the lists of connecting information would ever be contacted as they settled back into the lives where family and a web of acquaintances gradually reassumed itself into their lives?

The voyage had been a release for a few moments from what their lives had become and now they were returning to those lives many with a sense of dread of what the future held for them in a world increasingly alien to them; where the life choices open to them had become narrower as the years flew by. These were not the faces Okino had seen in the glossy advertisements of the magazines that had made their way up to his village. They had had their time in the limelight and now had to make do with the shadows as a new younger generation shaped the world. They could not help thinking this reshaping seemed absurd and reckless until they smiled to themselves and remembered how defiant they had been of the generation they had left in their wake.

Okino sensed he was heading towards the heart of the accumulated defiance of many generations. Each had inherited a bigger tool kit in the shape of the knowledge accumulated in those previous years. Knowledge that had grown exponentially in those previous decades enabling a mechanised society separated on unprecedented levels from the world they inhabited. As the city approached Okino started to appreciate the concentration of power that had resulted from the reckless manipulation of this knowledge. The vast sky-scraping towers symbolising the success of the human race and their ability to dominate their environment slowly grew as the ship approached the city.

Okino thought he had prepared himself for the incredible spectacle now unravelling before him. Now this new world was taking shape fully in his own consciousness he had to acknowledge an array of entirely contradictory thoughts and feelings. From the moment he had set out from the monastery he knew these moments would come. A sense had always existed in his village of the world growing beyond their own remote village. It had seemed it had had nothing to do with them. It was another culture with different precedents, ideals and goals. When confronting these questions the village folk would look with pride at their humble village hewn from the mountain and the forests and thanked the spirits for the opportunities they had been given and assumed the opportunities other races had been given by the spirits were in response to their own separate destiny. There was little or no connection or correspondence to be made. This world beyond the mountains was difficult to comprehend when compared with the small part they themselves had come to occupy. It was assumed they would always exist separately from each other and so each would have negligible influence on the other. However, as soon as Okino had seen the dead and dying fish in the lakes the idea of an external influence from beyond their valley had suddenly become a stark reality.

As he watched the city of Straam looming out of the ocean before him, he realised he was seeing for the first time the raw power of the enormous forces weaving the history of his world and at its heart he could feel the dark emptiness which had driven its creation. He knew the dragon was close, sensed its excitement at being engaged again with the narrative that would move the story on to wherever it would eventually be. He felt the strength coming from his conviction the time was right for his influence to return to the world. All the debts had been paid and although he was more deeply aware of the boundaries he must not cross he felt there were new possibilities in his alliance with Okino.

The young priest had made a surprisingly intuitive connection and had developed a deep understanding which enabled him to make decisions remotely from the dragons influence; for as his spirit had flowed into the spaces almost undetectable between and amongst the universes and dimensions, he had been absorbed and become part of the dragon. They had shared notions and experience of their worlds as the forces of time and space had altered the paths of the future world. In the moments Okino had felt Mithraels' sword being driven through him and he had shared a death with Merilon, his life force had crossed over, somehow been blended with the eternity of the dragon.

Now, as the old conflict had resumed, a new creature had been born into the consciousness of Arimathea and now was emerging into a world eager to utilise those newly evolved abilities. Okino had felt increased ability to travel in the dragon's newly constructed world, in the layers of consciousness below his own. But now for the first time he felt the strength and potential of his merging with this supernatural power of his world. As he was confronted with the colossal power displayed by the skyscrapers rising before him, an excitement and a resolve was rising from deep within him as he contemplated all that may lay in store for him in the days ahead.

The rain now beat in against the plate glass windows of the arrival terminal. Mariella strained to see if the ship was any nearer but looked out on a world now blurred by the wind-blown rain and the glass. How quickly she thought, she had become separated again from those elemental forces. She had travelled for months and had become accustomed to the vagaries of the mountain weather. The plummeting temperatures of the nights, the blistering heat and the torrential downfalls had through necessity become part of her life which she had come to relish. She wondered how Okino was coping with the civilisation which would have been thrust upon him without her to guide him through it. She felt her long dark hair tied up and realised Okino would probably not recognise her. She pulled out the tie and shook out her hair as she walked hurriedly out of the entrance doors and out into the rain.

The raindrops, given added velocity by the wind stung and instantly covered her face with a cool layer of water. She turned and raised her face into the wind as it took hold of her hair and claimed it as its own. She closed her eyes and felt the wild world blowing through her, awakening her senses again from the sleep into which the life here seemed to almost immediately induce. She rubbed the water into the skin of her face and felt the water running down her neck over her skin under her clothes like the invading tendrils of an elemental creature who had come to claim her back from where she had strayed. As she felt herself drifting back into her wild world, she heard the vast engines of the approaching cruise liner. Almost immediately with this acknowledgement came the sound of the foghorns filling the bay, announcing the arrival of Okino in the city of Straam.

She watched as the immense ship was manoeuvred into its position beside the dock and securely fastened to the solid land from which for so long it had been independent. She watched as the docking process continued as disembarkation tunnels were raised and secured in place. High on the promenade decks she could see people hurrying to wherever they needed to be. She returned to the open space of the terminal building in anticipation of Okino appearing through the customs barriers. As so often when levels of anticipation were so high everything seemed to be happening interminably slowly in almost total silence. Members of the terminal staff continued the endless task of maintaining the terminal. One of the bins was being emptied and a cleaner shuffled a mop across the sparkling marble floor. The announcement board announced disembarkation would soon occur. Plants were watered; port officials came out of one set of doors and went into another causing a detonation clearly a fault with the closing device making everybody jump.

The younger children were becoming impatient but mostly were restrained. However, two had developed a game in which they chased each other, dodging in and out of the waiting crowd of adults and children. It was clearly irritating the parents who had made the effort to keep their fractious offspring quiet and under control. Mariella watched now intrigued as the game became more frantic and faster as the children became more excited until the inevitable did happen. One of the children dived in between two families, miscalculated the turn and the amount of friction he could rely on during the skid on the polished floor and crashed into one of the smaller outlying children.

Both crashed to the floor tumbling into a tangled heap. There was a moment of stunned silence. Then screams of agony echoed through the high open space of the terminal lounge. The outraged parents of the scuttled child hurried to her side while looking around for the parent of the offending child who appeared reluctant to show themselves immediately. The larger child got up while being shouted at quite viciously by the father of the screaming toddler at which point the parents unable to listen to their child being so denigrated by a total stranger rushed over to his defence.

An enormous row developed between the two sets of parents as insults and gestures became progressively more violent. When the capability of the offender's parents to raise such an 'animal' was questioned the line was clearly crossed. A wild flailing punch was thrown by the miscreant's father knocking the now hysterical child's father off his feet to where his child a few moments before had been lying. He jumped to his feet immediately and charged at his assailant and a full-scale fight broke out. Now each of their wives were screeching at each other while trying to wrestle their respective husbands away from the fracas. Four enormous security guards emerged from one of the sets of doors and attempted to separate the warring families without great success to start with and not before one of the security guards was punched by one of the wives. As the fight continued in a melee of whirling, writhing limbs and bodies and insults, passengers began to emerge from the customs area. Mariella smiled as she spotted Okino almost straight away. He would have been almost the first person off the boat. She had wondered what he would choose to wear to enter this new environment. As a result, he probably hadn't given it a second thought.

Then he was standing before her with an enormous grin on his face in his carefully laundered and now immaculate crimson robes. He put his hands together and made one of his small bows in front of Mariella. She slowly wrapped her arms around him and hugged him silently. He put his arms around her and pulled her to him. She had intended to hide her delicate emotional state at least until they were safely at home. She sank into him, into the presence she had so wanted to have close to her those last few days, into the beautiful strength of the clear understanding she had so wanted to access in her desperate confusion, into the love she had always felt when she was with him; even from the first moments they had met. She lost all her sense of resolve and silently started to release the emotion she thought she had had under control. Okino felt the change in her immediately. The capable self-assured young woman who he had watched disappear into the sky in Zedocha had buried herself deep in the recesses of her being.

He closed his eyes as he held her, felt out into the etheric spaces to bring through her the life healing energy of the goddess Arimathea and the infinite love which he knew had come to live there, brought it to her, brought it to this broken spirit in the hope it would touch her and sooth the distress he knew she was feeling. But as he felt the love flow through him and into her, he felt the emptiness he had first sensed out in the distant ocean when first he had seen Straam. But now it was nearer, almost on top of him. He shuddered as he remembered the unfathomable vortex they had released when the stone plinth across the top of the dragon hill had been destroyed. Now, although nowhere near as concentrated it was on a scale which he was unable to entirely comprehend, spreading out around him and into the far distance. He forced the sinister feeling out of his mind and concentrated on enveloping Mariella in all the sustaining planetary life force she needed if only for a brief respite from the agony she was clearly in.

She felt the love flood through her, transforming the hopeless spiralling descent into a floating platform of light where she could breathe and rest. It was gradually growing and pushing her upwards away from the pit of despair into which she was disappearing. She turned her face up and touched his face, kissed his lips gently and looked deep into his eyes. She thought she saw, perhaps imagined she had seen the green glow of the dragon flicker momentarily in the depths of his dark eyes.

"Welcome, my dearest Okino to our mad, bad town."

The fight had been brought under control and the two main combatants were being led through the doors to what lay beyond. Okino smiled as the energy he was holding faded away.

"I am glad to be here with you, Mariella."

Chapter Fifty-Five
Straam City

The narrow skies allowed only an eerie subdued light at street level in the canyons formed by the skyscrapers. Okino was as silent as he had ever been stalking through the mountains on the trail of the leopards. In his silence he was having to readjust his perception and much of the understanding he had of his world. In a small way on the cruise ship he decided he had begun to become accustomed to the new sense of scale he would experience on this part of his journey. Now however he was astonished by what he was seeing for the first time. Again, the magazines and the images they had offered him of this city had not prepared him for the stature of the buildings around him. As he became used to the idea of the skyscrapers as feats of engineering he realised they were also full of people.

Mariella had chosen mid-morning for their first walk in the city when the thousands of people who worked in Straam were safely behind their desks leaving the streets less busy than they would have been at the beginning or end of the working day. But for Okino the city was brimming full of humanity in a way he could never have imagined. There was little around him he had not seen before. There were buildings sitting alongside streets and people who walked alongside each other as they went about their daily tasks. There were fewer animals than he was accustomed to but they were here. He smiled as he watched the rock pigeons strutting along the cornice of a building. There was where the similarity ended.

The people walked here as anywhere in groups or alone consumed by their own thoughts. Occasionally they would exchange a greeting with an acquaintance or a total stranger who they had briefly and inexplicably connected with. As anywhere else the expressions on their faces did not betray the gravity of the thoughts they were processing. They carefully negotiated their way down the pavements avoiding collisions and confrontations, perhaps pausing occasionally to look into a shop window or drift into one of the numerous coffee bars. He assumed these were the lucky ones of whom the captain had talked, whose lifestyles were backed by solid jobs or investments paying successfully for everything that allowed them to be walking here. The dramatic towers serving as the backdrop to their lives, now so exciting to Okino, had long since become ordinary in minds consumed by the complexity of their existence. Okino soon began to realise how these buildings represented the economic forces operating within the city controlling all of the lives of the people now drifting past.

In the stories of the dragon, the priests of the alien religions had expressed the power of their gods by building their soaring ornate churches funded by the rich merchants eager to buy their way into the favour of these new more corruptible gods. The astounding feats of ingenuity that had sent the slender stonework soaring into the mediaeval skies were surely rivalled here by the sheer audacity of these massive towers. Many had footprints on some of the most expensive real estate on the planet. The sheer faces of glass rising into the sky reflecting clouds and glinting sunlight were undoubtedly impressive; however, the reasons why and how they had come to be, as with the towering churches reaching to a fabled heaven, may prove to be less awe inspiring.

He felt an expansion in his awareness as the Star moved out from the clouds now directly over the street and flooded it with light. This was where the dragon needed him to be and it seemed they were again seeing through the same eyes, processing all this information in the same mind. The scale and wonder of the city had momentarily seduced him but he began to see the monster lurking behind the illusion of stability and wellbeing here in the centre of what he already knew to be an enormous city. He turned to find Mariella quietly observing the street in her own dreamy state. She noticed his glance and smiled up at him.

They continued to walk silently on through the city of dreams. Along the pavements where the position of each slab had been carefully thought out, where the streetlights and the litter bins, the planters and the railings had all been carefully positioned for their function to be met and the ambience of the street maintained. Shop fronts beckoned out to him. Enticing him to lust after finely cut clothes, suits for him and expensively cut dresses for Mariella carefully placed on manikins of perfectly perhaps impossibly contoured models, breath taking jewellery embedded with coloured stones mined from the depths of Arimathea, the next shop, shoes and then cars or all the paraphernalia of the communications industry, televisions, hi fidelity music systems, telephones and all the latest gadgetry to further distract the restless city dwellers mind. Everything was here lavishly displayed to tempt him to enter the rarefied domain which it fronted where a further assault would be made by a carefully trained sales executive lurking in the trap like a predatory spider waiting for the victim to fly into her web.

As Okino looked deeper into the scene around him nothing had been left to chance. Everything had been considered, calculated and given a value. The streets were dominated by a continual procession of automobiles belonging to the motorists of Straam. Okino saw what seemed like an almost infinite variety of styles. As he observed more carefully he could see how the older styles had been superseded by more modern versions as designers had responded to newer trends making them bulkier or sleeker, more spacious or less. Every consideration had been given to making each vehicle part of its own era; but to give it its own identity with careful detail to make it stand out and have its own appeal.

Okino then started to notice another criteria layered over all the cars before him. Ultimately they were carefully manufactured boxes of steel and glass with four wheels connected to an engine. They enabled the owner freedom to travel unhindered by the reliance of any other mode of transport. However, Okino began to see there was more to this first assumption. Suddenly he could see all the careful detailing had little to do with the efficiency or function of the machine. As far as he could see all these vehicles were travelling at much the same pace. So not much faster than he and Mariella were walking. As he looked more carefully he became aware of the difference in the attention paid to the design and the finish lavished on each car. He could see almost immediately how each and every vehicle displayed at a glance how it had been conceived to reflect its owner. Like brightly coloured feathers on courting birds or the thick manes of dominant male lions everything about the status of the human race was on display here. The full implication of this hierarchy soon started to become apparent to Okino. Each car reflected the wealth and status of its driver. He assumed the correlation was broadly accurate but he presumed there would be some rich people driving old second-hand cars and some poorer people who had stolen brand new limousines. However here it seemed, broadly the social structure of Straam was laid out before him.

Once he had become accustomed to this idea, everywhere he looked the structure was apparent; not only in the cars on the street but on the people who were walking with him on the pavements. He started to notice this display of perceived wealth everywhere he looked. He could see it in the cut of their clothes and the shoes they were wearing. Everything they carried from their briefcases and handbags were a calculated display to everyone around them. Their sunglasses, even the dogs they were walking, every detail was signalling to their fellow citizens at what stage and what level they had attained in the economic hierarchy of the city. Or as Okino began to suspect what level they wanted people to think they had attained.

This phenomenon had not been so noticeable on the ship because there had appeared to be one stratum of people who presumably aspired to the same lifestyle. But here the structure was apparent everywhere. Okino soon found there was little correlation with this outward display of apparent wealth and the wellbeing of the soul inside. In his travels with Merilon he had gained a sensitivity enabling him to look through these outward facades. Although most displayed a bland, cool non-descript exterior, in amongst the coats and the shoes and the make-up, he sensed many, even those who appeared to be the wealthiest and who he would have assumed to have the least problems, seemed to be the most deeply troubled. He wondered if this prolific outward expression had arisen through the lack of communication taking place. They rarely stopped and suspended the activity of their day for a quick chat. These people were barely looking at each other. They certainly did not acknowledge his and Mariella's existence even though he was still wearing his robes.

Okino had often found even a brief look into someone's eyes could provide a fairly accurate insight into their state of mind. But now with this expansion in his own levels of perception there was far more he was able to detect in one of these brief encounters. He soon found, under exterior layers of cool sophistication there were a huge number of very worried and anxious people who had an array of problems connected with their complicated lifestyles. Many seemed to be predominantly worried about their financial situation in turn determining their place in the hierarchy. The nature of their society demanded they at least held their place but always be striving to be higher.

Everyone had their own set of problems it seemed. The unfortunate people who didn't have enough were consumed by the fear their lives were soon to collapse. Most were struggling to continually earn the amount they needed to keep afloat as the cost of their lives rose steadily beyond the rate of their incomes. Those seeming most self-assured displaying the highest wealth were either in such complicated financial webs of their own or their husband, wives or partners, they appeared to have entirely lost any sense of their own independence. They were lost in a maze of complex calculations involving the money they did or did not have. Complicated and tenuous investments and financial services maintaining their lifestyle had been mostly entrusted to people who they felt they couldn't trust. Okino was surprised to find higher levels of anxiety in these people than the people who knew moment to moment exactly the perilous financial situation they were in.

Buried deep in the tangle of highly charged emotions exasperated by insecurity and anxiety Okino found spirit souls long since retreated from the surface levels of their everyday consciousness. Disconnected and isolated from all that could nurture them they had become forgotten and neglected in all the confusion of life in the city. Now the shells of their people were being led through their lives leaving little time for anything except work and carefully planned time with their family and friends. The constraints on this personal time caused stress of its own as high expectations for those precious moments were unnaturally high. Every aspect of their lives was now informed by someone or something who could offer them a service or product to alleviate their anxiety for a few days or nights; until again the emptiness returned perhaps heightened when the purchase had now worsened their anxiety and fear.

As a result of this disparity between their waking consciousness and their spirit souls, Okino was detecting potential and actual chronic illness at alarming levels. He found bodily systems evolved to operate with energy generated at all levels of consciousness were under performing and at worst showing signs of malfunction as underperforming organs vital for the healthy working of the whole system were left under stimulated by lowered levels of hormone activity. Even though the people he was observing were probably some of the best nourished humans on Arimathea he found their overall well-being seemed precariously balanced. Many who seemed to be healthy and coping, appeared to be on the point where the slightest upset could cause an almost complete breakdown.

As this emptiness and confusion revealed itself to varying degrees in the people passing he started to register an even more sinister phenomenon. Many of these people were carrying high levels of synthetic chemicals flowing through their systems and into their neural networks. They were reacting with and prompting the underperforming systems of their bodies and minds that otherwise would have been regulated, activated or simply enabled by the natural processes inherent within a healthy body. Okino detected minds only holding their own in this environment because of the substances flowing through them. He sensed carefully researched and targeted chemicals in many areas of their bodies but particularly worrying was the sophistication of the chemicals being targeted toward and so flowing through their minds. In many of these minds Okino could find only the remnants of their original personality.

They drifted across his path almost entirely lost to the world, like shadowy ghosts operating in a miasma of synthetic chemical reaction and the intractable web of influences in the society surrounding them. There was a strange emptiness in these people which Okino had never experienced. Eyes were lifeless and actions seemed almost instinctual, as if a set of mechanical operations had taken over the normal and natural functions. These personalities were only moving towards their next prescription so they could bring what personality they had left to the surface again.

He wondered how the knowledge had been acquired to make these drugs and who could be making them. Did they really know the effect they were having on the people they were being given to? The implications were astounding as he looked out over the scene before him. The skyscrapers towering around him like enormous hives of metal and glass, packed full of people working away all with very specific tasks in a vast collective taking more and more of themselves away, their minds guided and manipulated so they could work more productively, earn and consume more effectively and so proliferate a system which was increasingly endangering its' own existence.

At the root of all this there was something incredibly predictable and natural. Creatures of many different species gathered together for protection and safety or perhaps near prolific feeding opportunities. Humans had settled on hills with good defensive positions, on the banks of rivers or on the shores of a sheltered bay. In these places they had flourished, traded, expanded and their ability to organise their ideas and thoughts and carry out strategies eventually had allowed these cities to develop. But there had been such power channelled here; A will and determination to grow beyond what could be thought as achievable or even possible on this world. The only consideration it seemed given to the natural forces when these buildings were considered was how to defy them. There was a joy in this defiance. Suddenly human beings had the upper hand over their world that had so terrified and dominated them for so long. They had understood the biology of diseases it had sent to kill them, systematically and without mercy. At the same time, they had mastered physics and chemistry allowing them to dominate and expand into their natural environments like never before unchallenged by the limitations that had previously held them back.

But as their dreams and aspirations had grown ever larger so had the need to mobilise a workforce disciplined and compliant enough to complete these new ambitious works. Okino knew from his own exploits in the mountains how much suffering the human spirit could endure in severe hardship. What he had never experienced was the pressure corporations and governments run by ruthless driven individuals could bring upon the majority of ordinary people to achieve their aims. He had arrived from a very different world and if he had not known better he would have immediately thought some supernatural force had initiated this extraordinary expansion. As he stood there in amongst the hives of steel and glass he began to wonder.

He had felt the power the dreams of the dragon had held in the world. How his will to grow and expand had slowly guided Arimathea's evolution. Through all her growing pains she had eventually arrived at a time and a place where all this could and had been achieved; but only when the influence of the dragon dreams had faded from the world. Had it been inevitable the human beings had come to disregard his guidance but adopted his power? Had the will for transformation he had brought from the stars become so deeply embedded in their consciousness, they had carried on creating, pushing to the limits, to find where or if the edges he had brought actually existed? Perhaps the minds that had conceived the engineering wonders now dominating Arimathea had decided there were no parameters and anything was possible.

The men who had found their way into a position where they had become responsible for the transformation of the world, it seemed had become intoxicated with the power it offered. The forces of creation had inadvertently landed in their lives and there would be little to persuade them they should not take full advantage of their inheritance. Had they come to think they had been given the power of their gods, as they unleashed a flood of universal creative power into their world? Had the lowly souls of the general population they had at their disposal to complete their visions for this new world become like the steel and glass, the nuts and bolts needed to construct their buildings, roads and railways, wire up their communication systems so their domination of Arimathea could finally become complete?

Now they appeared to have devised even more despicable means to pursue their seemingly unquenchable thirst for power. He looked down at Mariella quietly walking beside him. For the first time he fully understood the concerns for Arimathea which had taken her halfway around her world to find a group of human beings who had fully avoided the uninhibited growth of the machine world now existing in these cultures. She looked up at him as if she had heard the processes at work in the silence between them. She knew him well enough to know he would already have worked through his initial amazement and would be forming theories, possibly with Merilon sharing his thoughts, to the very roots of all that was happening here. Sure enough she saw the look of concern in his eyes as he scanned the high buildings around him.

She took hold of his arm and tugged at it affectionately.

"Look Okino, we have reached our first destination. Time for some coffee. You look far too deep in thought. You cannot expect to figure it all out on the first day."

For the last few days they had been living in the house belonging to Mariella's family on the outskirts of Straam. They had told their stories of those intervening days as they shared the luxury of the Keating residence. She found he had developed his love for strong coffee on the cruise ship. They had decided it was a harmless enough vice for the monk to adopt so Okino was initiated into the many ways and the large variety of machinery existing to sample the pleasures of the simple and miraculous coffee bean.

Mariella explained as much as she thought he needed to know about the society in which he was becoming involved. They had discussed at length their world and it's machinations on their trip through the mountains and down to Zedocha. But now Mariella was able to show him the global web of information at his disposal. Frequently they would be sitting in one of the spacious, brightly lit living rooms overlooking the expansive gardens deep in conversation when a question would arise. Invariably their discussions would take them deep into the web of connections which held and enabled life on Arimathea as they continued to delve into the problems of their world. A fact or a question about a place or statistic would be needed to illuminate some theory. Mariella had not tired of seeing Okino's amazement when the information emerged on the clear electronic screen before them; perhaps not only the fact but a film or an interview with a group who had also answered and already fully explored the question.

When they were not in the house surfing across the ocean of information accrued by the human race they would ride out into the surrounding countryside. The horses had had little problem acclimatising to the lush green fields of the temperate climate and the warm stables filled with fresh straw. They seemed considerably more lively on their new nutritious diet much to the consternation of Okino who had preferred them in their less frisky state. Into the landscapes they had ridden through the carefully managed fields and woodlands where Mariella showed Okino her favourite haunts from her childhood. Okino relished the tall slender trees allowed to live and grow, taller and wider for hundreds of years in the temperate climate untroubled by the ferocious winds and cold which had always limited the stature of the trees in his own land.

They stood one morning in a beautiful grove of tall beeches as the low autumn light flooded the scene before them. Okino gasped with delight as he absorbed the astounding beauty before him. The intense early morning light shone through the canopy and illuminated the delicate browning leaves and as it beamed through the larger gaps between the foliage filling the whole scene with a rippling slightly hazy golden glow.

"When I cross the plains with the mountain ranges as their backdrop I am awestruck by the majesty of those vast spaces. I can see the Star and the Moon in the same sky and the weather systems as they roll in from the ranges to the North or the warmer oceans to the South. I can watch the planet in all her moods as weather systems unfold and transform the atmosphere over the day or perhaps in a matter of hours; the sky and so the infinity of space is interacting with the land on which I am standing and I become joined again with our world and the cosmos beyond.

But when I stand in the forest I am in a very different drama. On a sensual level, it is as if I can feel the life force, the consciousness of Arimathea we share with the trees flowing all around me and through me, radiating out from all the solidity that has grown from her and it is blending with me so I feel unmistakeably part of her. No wonder the dragons felt so at home here. Here she is manifest all around us, breathing through us in this light filled layer of delicate life. Then, everywhere I look, enhancing this feeling of connection is the elegance and wonder which my old soul recognises and responds to with an enormous almost over whelming joy, as if I am transported back to the origin where the vision for a material existence was first encountered."

There was a fine delicate texture to the landscapes here. The rolling hills and their valleys had an intimacy which allowed the scene before him to be continually changing. At every turn, over every rise a new vista would reveal itself to them. After the vast expanses of his own land with its continuous backdrop of snow-capped mountains and fast flowing mountain rivers always filled with snow melt, Mariella's land seemed like the setting for an enchanting fairy tale. She rode through it on the horse that had carried her up the mountain passes into Jahallala and across the plains to Asima still deeply tanned from the strong Star shine as if she had been travelling the world continuously for a thousand years. Okino often couldn't help smiling when he watched her. He could not help the admiration he held for her and what she had become, all her opinions and ideas, the knowledge and understanding she had of the complex world she had grown up in.

He had been watching her, smiling in this way when she had been explaining the financial system of her country and how the global monetary systems and stock exchanges of individual countries were now connected into all the markets and economies of the world. He was wondering even then of the strange twists of fate that had brought him here to this place, with this girl to her home with its cushioned chairs and continuously carpeted rooms, filled with electronic gadgetry, paintings and sculptures. There were clocks everywhere. Time it seemed was continually and accurately given in every room.

Then he had come to meet and know Aaron Keating. He had greeted Okino warmly and made him feel instantly at home. He thanked him for looking after Mariella so well. Okino thought of the incident in the mountains with Azeera and the protection he had provided for his daughter on her journey. He faded in and out of the big house and they rarely saw him. He was clearly going to his office and although Mariella was concerned they had little contact in those first days. Then he joined them for dinner the night before their visit to Straam.

They had talked about all that had happened and ultimately about Okino's broadcast and its implications. He listened attentively sometimes asking for explanations. He was particularly curious about Merilon. For him along with almost the entire human race the dragon was a mythical creature who dwelt in legends and if they were to be believed in the consciousness of the world, in the land and the rivers, in the high mountains and the hills. Now through Okino and his monastery the dragon or whatever universal energy it had come to represent, had again found its' way from its subconscious layer into this layer of reality. He had sat back at this point and stared intensively into the fire he had lit earlier in the large hearth, as if accessing all his experience of the world and its parameters. Then he spoke thoughtfully.

"There have always been mystics who have suspected these beings have been here, flowing through the ground and the atmosphere around us. They have decided the beauty and complexity of the world is too elegantly conceived to have randomly appeared. All religions and faiths have their origins in legends and old folk tales based on the belief of a greater force, a creator spirit. But for this power to have revealed itself is a turning point in the evolution of this world."

Okino responded immediately.

"…I think we knew these powers before we began making this 'machine world'. Their memory is buried deep within us. They were never separate from us. Every living thing on this world is part of the consciousness that has evolved. They have always been a part of us but we have lost our ability to understand how they are working through us. Many quite basic things in our lives, our instincts, emotional responses, our creativity, our need to nurture our children and care for each other, our will to succeed are all tied up with these natural forces."

Aaron looked over at Okino,

"At any other time in my life I would have been sceptical about what you are telling me. But something is happening in this city making me wonder whether things are beginning to change in a very subtle, almost intangible way. In a sense when I'm working in the law I am always watching a kind of evolution, the evolution of how we treat each other and the world around us. New precedents can be set, slightly changing the way we conduct ourselves and our society. Something happened recently that has made me think about this more deeply.

A woman representing a group of people came to me about a situation that had arisen in her neighbourhood. She lived adjacent to a large piece of derelict waste ground. Or so it appeared to all who lived around it. There had been a factory which had been owned and run by a large employer in the area. As the way things are in the world it had gone out of business when the kitchen products it manufactured became less expensive to produce in an emerging economy on the other side of the world. A different story but part of the same really was there was also a downturn in the economy. The factory was outdated and was sold for scrap and the value of the land was now higher than it was actually worth. You'll get used to the economics of the madhouse if you stay here for any length of time Okino.

So, the land was mothballed as we say; Left frozen in time by the corporation who eventually inherited the asset from some tremendous debt. Left and forgotten about, as interests moved to other areas until eventually the value rose again. Forgotten by the world of finance and profit but not by the people who lived adjacent to it in a city where open space was rare and for the most part highly organised and unappealing to adventurous young minds.

So, over the years, fences fell into disrepair and children began to inhabit and play in it. The area was completely overgrown and dangerous piles of rubbish had been left there unregulated over the years. Inevitably one day some of the rubbish collapsed onto some kids who had decided it would be a good idea to explore inside the pile! One of the kids was really badly hurt and lost a lot of blood. They managed to get him to hospital in time but then after the incident all the families whose kids played on it got together and decided it would be easier to clear it up rather than trying to stop the kids from playing there.

They got rid of the rubbish and tidied the place up generally so that it was safe for the kids to play on. Over the years though they went further and converted a fraction of it into a public space that pretty much anyone could use. They raised money and built swings, climbing frames and a shelter on it for when it rained. The rest had been left to go wild. Paths had been made through to the open areas which had naturally formed over the years. The woman told me thirty turnings must have gone by and this place had become so knitted into the community no one could even remember when it had been waste ground.

Then of course one day a group of men turned up, threw all the kids and mothers off what now had become a small park, fenced it all off again and put a big notice up saying, "Private Property Keep Out." It turned out it had been sold again to a billionaire developer who quite literally had forgotten about it when he had wound up his business after a nervous breakdown. When he died and his estate was examined his family, keen to realise all his assets found the deeds to the piece of land tucked away in a safe. Which incidentally they had to get 'professionally' opened because the old man hadn't told the combination to a living soul. Now of course the neighbourhood had spent time and money on the space and the woman came to me to ask if there was any chance they had any rights to the land after occupying it for so long. It was an interesting case for me but in land law the person who has the deeds owns the land. The exception is that if you have occupied the land for a period of time you may be able to claim the land as your own. But this is very rare as so often the terms of the occupation are virtually always disputed. This case was no exception. The family's lawyers were therefore claiming it had not been continually occupied in the sense the law specified it should have been.

But there was something about this woman and her enthusiasm. These people had transformed this site which otherwise would have gone from bad to worse and become hazardous to the area. I decided to take the case as I felt there was an outside chance the judge would find in favour of the community and I made an appeal to the high court that the claim of legal possession should be reviewed. When the case came up in court I made the case to the judge, we were lucky to get him to be honest. I pleaded that because of the scarcity of land of this nature it was too valuable to be left unused for so long. I argued it was irresponsible for whoever owned it to leave it to deteriorate and quoted the case of the kid who was buried under the pile of rotting steel. I claimed nearly a generation of children had benefited from having the open space to play and roam in thanks to the initiative of the surrounding community. Although it had not been 'Occupied continually' in the conventional sense it had become occupied by that community with benefits which really could not be quantified.

Everyone prepared for the worst. Now the value of the land had risen the land could be sold and developed. However much to our surprise the judge ruled in our favour and legal possession was handed over to the community which of course now gave me even more work as an extremely complicated contract had to be devised which to tell you the truth kept a good proportion of my office busy for a number of weeks. The difficulty, and it underlies all of our law, is that land has to be owned by someone. The deed eventually named all the people in the community who had an interest in the land. It amounted to hundreds of people who all would have to agree if the land was ever to be sold or developed commercially.

So, you see things have moved on. A precedent has been set which says that land and its use is not necessarily only valued in hard currency and by the name on the deeds. In certain situations where a social benefit can be proved over a number of years the land could revert back to the people who have claimed it. It will rarely be used as landowners will become even more wary about allowing their land to fall into the wrong hands. But every now and again when a piece of land such as this falls off the radar it will be quoted. The precedent may slowly change the way we value the land on which we all live and depend. But for now, there has been a strange twist in the tale."

As Okino listened to the twist in Aaron's tale he sensed a pathway opening before him. In the same way as when he had sat on the Dragonhill and saw the path which had subsequently led him down to the encounter with Mithrael. Deep in Merilons' dream he had little idea of how he was to proceed but had come to trust and depend on the signposts as they emerged. Now he was in the same position. Here surrounded by all the luxury of the Keating home he had started to lose sight of the challenge he had been set by Arimathea. He had started to understand how all this comfort could easily hide the dangers continually lurking in the world. He could see how the temptation to relax, as if the problems facing Arimathea lay in the future could or would be dealt with by others more able or better placed; or that really they simply did not exist. He suspected this was at the root of an acceptable theory held by many people. Here it seemed was the greatest excuse to do nothing, to carry on as if nothing was happening. Freedom to act without responsibility or concern brought on by complete denial.

But now as he walked the streets of Straam he began to understand how deeply the people in this land of wealth and privilege were being manipulated or perhaps even denied the ability to make sensible judgements about what was actually happening on their world. Now the path into the heart of the darkness he had sensed as he approached Straam on the cruise liner was opening up to him.

Chapter Fifty-six.
Settlement.

Okino and Mariella had entered one of the many cafes set in between the shops and show rooms lining the central street in Straam. The atmosphere was immediately more intimate. The café was busy but certainly not overcrowded and there was a gentle hum of conversation mixed with the gurgling and the steaming of the coffee making machinery. Here it seemed as if some unspoken protocol of which Okino had not yet been informed had been lifted. Even those in deep conversation lifted their eyes to briefly acknowledge their entrance. Now Okino was being observed by eyes keen to assess a new customer. When there appeared to be no threat to their quiet retreat from the streets outside they resumed their conversations. Okino was becoming used to the searching looks as occasionally his robes demanded a second glance or more careful observation. Often the people who remembered his face from the broadcast were respectful enough not to invade his privacy; so recognition had so far not been a problem. These people seemed to appreciate only a respectful acknowledgement was needed. Okino could feel the flow of information to the dragon whom he knew to be close. He was interested in everything about the city and the perspective he could gain through Okino's fresh interpretations and analysis of all he was seeing, hearing and feeling. Filtered through Okino's own understanding of his race the insight they were gaining was enlightening and at the same time mystifying.

In so many ways they were not different from the species who for so long had learnt to live and survive in Arimathea's natural environment. In those early times their senses had become acute and their intelligence had made them able to respond to opportunities arising every day tuned into and able to adapt to her varying moods as their environments changed around them. They were doing exactly what any creature on Arimathea would be doing. When the Star came up they would wake and the days battle to eat, stay safe, reproduce and sleep would begin.

In all of these activities they would have been engaging with Arimathea in all her diversity. Some days she would be serene and calm to be marvelled at and worshipped, perhaps for entire seasons. But then she may turn into a dangerous and threatening adversary who needed to be out witted at every turn. In the struggle that had ensued many relationships had changed as humans developed different roles to deal with different areas of their existence. The complexity of their society and cultures had grown from those early adaptations. In a relatively short time here they were walking or driving through the streets of Straam with little or no concern for the environment surrounding them.

It seemed now their idea of themselves existed purely as a swirling mass of contradictory, confused and transitory thoughts about how they should be conducting their lives and relating to the world around them. Most of these ideas came from the influences of an ephemeral consumer world which continually reinvented itself to sell another set of stock; so clothes, cars, kitchens, living rooms and everything to go in them were continually being scrutinised upgraded in relation to fashions and market forces. The discontent and obsession with upgrading material things was now spreading to relationships and jobs and friendships. Lurking in the background of all this material worry was the far more seriously damaging question, "Am I good enough for him or her or this job?", "Are people looking at my house and my car, where my kids go to school and thinking, Is this the sort of person we want to spend our precious time with?"

Okino and the dragon found this continual worry was destabilising everything needing to be stable in the people of Straam city. Stability was not what the vast rolling economic force driving the city wanted at all. It needed change which often was described as vibrancy and growth. As the time spans of fashion, trends and crazes became progressively shorter so the confusion and the fear of falling out of the cycle became greater, the anxiety more acute and the drugs to cure it more accessible.

The original spirit who was born full of information inherited from thousands of previous generations ready to react to Starshine and Moonlight, to the intricate beauty and variety and rhythms of the natural world was now being deprived on almost every level of this birth right. The sights, the smells the sounds locating and informing instincts and perceptions recorded deep in the cellular structures of brain function and anatomy enabling the release of energies and impulses to delight and inspire were no longer available amongst the steel and glass and the tarmac and the dim eerie light in the depths of the concrete canyons.

Okino and Mariella walked to the back of the café where they recognised and were greeted by a group of young adults in their early twenties. They were sitting at a large table covered with empty plates and cardboard cups, the untidy remains of many recently consumed breakfasts. The faces, of the two boys and three girls were the brightest Okino had seen all day. One of the boys and one of the girls were clearly together as they appeared to be almost embedded into each. Their eyes were clear and lucid and clearly living an unconventional life in comparison to the people who had passed Okino on the street so far that morning. These young people did not have the scrubbed clean look about them which most of the occupants of Straam seemed to exhibit. Coming from a land where people had not yet become obsessed with this extreme cleanliness, these young people had a natural grubbiness to them Okino recognised and identified with. Their clothes did not appear to have been recently bought or cleaned instead seemed to have been repaired in places where they had worn with material from perhaps other garments. The garments spoke of practicality and living closer to the elements, but also were brightly coloured in places in contrast to the dull, dark colours the majority of their fellow city dwellers were wearing. They were clearly excited to be meeting Okino and Mariella, moving down their benches so the new arrivals could move in next to them and hurriedly tidying the assortment of plates and cups. Mariella immediately ordered coffee for everyone around the table. There was an expectant silence as the new coffees arrived and the first few sips were taken. Mariella smiled over at Okino before starting to speak.

"Well, thanks so much for coming to meet us at such short notice. I should apologise for my dad who told us about your situation. It sounded fascinating and there was something about it we felt we wanted to know more about and to be honest we are not sure what that is yet, we just had a gut feeling there was something going on in your lives, well Okino did actually, which was going to be important for his visit to this city."

"That's no problem we're pleased to come and meet you, we did eventually see your broadcast from the ocean liner and recognised the significance it might hold for our world." The rest agreed with the tall raggedly haired blond boy now sitting opposite Okino and Mariella.

"My name is Matt and this is my girlfriend Selina. …and these are my friends Jack, Erica and Aliya. I'm not sure how much you know about what has happened but we started this whole thing with the waste ground. I'm not sure if start is the right word. It has just developed in our lives as we have grown up.

"My dad told us about how the land came to be in possession of the community; all very interesting. Perhaps you could tell us how it all happened."

"So as I said this whole thing had been going on since early on in our lives. It was a bit of empty ground which by the time we were big enough to be roaming by ourselves was already pretty overgrown with brambles, small trees and wild shrubs. As far as we were concerned this was a jungle or whatever we wanted it to be. It was so large we rarely ventured to the furthest boundaries in those early days. There were still the piles of rubbish and burnt out cars then but we rarely went anywhere near them. Nature was rapidly reclaiming everything and as it blended with those old structures they all became just a little bit more fascinating and of course Jack here got trapped when a pile collapsed. That was when our parents started to take notice of what was happening under their noses. Up until then we were out playing and returned undamaged, happy and sleepy. They had little concern for the worlds we had constructed out there."

"…and when he says worlds," Jack interrupts. "he means worlds. That piece of waste ground could be transformed into any environment we were able to imagine. Some places were covered in thick concrete where the old warehouses and factory had been. The plants started to force their way through but these generally were the wide-open spaces, the deserts, the oceans or expanses of space between the worlds to which we could travel. Beyond these spaces the landscape around the buildings was totally overgrown but with the concrete and gravel paths running all the way through they became our highways to every corner of that piece of ground."

He looked over at Matt and grinned,

"We had three beautiful summers, we must have been ten or eleven years old and spent almost our entire lives there when we weren't at school. All the way through, along the paths, in different locations we constructed some sort of encampment. With whatever we could find on the site. We started this thing where we went around the neighbourhood taking peoples rubbish away. Not their garbage, just the stuff lying around we could utilise in the structure of the latest moon base or desert island out post. They became more and more elaborate as we collected evermore more materials from further and further afield in the small cart we had built for transportation.

Sometime around then the girls started to get interested. Sometimes they took part in the exploration but they were mainly interested in the constructions and the homes they could build inside them. Once we had finished one we were off to find a new site for the next one and had often plundered valued material particularly useful for roofs or walls and doors. Often however, at this point we started to face opposition from the girls if we wanted to dismantle one to take deeper into the dream. It was becoming more and more like a dream. So, we left them and just started new ones."

"It was amazing what they were doing,"

Selina interjected,

"..and as we started to inhabit and feel at home in them we wove a story around each of them which was reflected where and in the way they had been built. Jack said about the moon base…it was awesome. They drilled holes through the steel sheeting that had been lying around everywhere and bolted it together onto old poles and steel posts, anything they could drag round there….and we were just fascinated…by them and what they were doing out there…and these beautiful little places where we were all acting out these wild fantasies in this separate world which could be anything we wanted it to be. But not just in one of these places there was about five or six major constructions each one a backdrop to some amazing fantasy we had made up."

"Of course, pretty soon other like-minded kids, started to cotton on to what was going on. It just became the most amazing playground for all the kids in the neighbourhood. It was like another dimension which we could use for whatever purpose we chose. Different groups of kids settled in one particular camp and eventually we started to organise competitions. Just so much started to happen and I'm sure we were learning about the structure of community but deeper about a sense of this place and its' relationship to the rest of the city and the land around it.

When we lit a fire at the end of the day and the darkness closed in which we often did, we really could have been in any place we could dream for it. Whether we learnt or gained anything from those places I don't know but I'm sure we did step into other lives where there was stuff, knowledge we wouldn't otherwise have known. Do you have any idea what I am talking about?"

Matt looked over at Okino for reassurance. He had rarely told the story in such detail but now had felt compelled to talk to the monk about the strange world they had found or invented or had been revealed to them which they had been able to shape for themselves so innocently and independent of any adult interference. Okino smiled over at Mariella. There was no need for them to voice their recognition of the dream world the children had created. There were parallels with the dragon's dream so uncanny it was as if it had somehow seeped through some crack between the two dimensions into the minds of Jack and Matt as they had innocently played and constructed their worlds in the waste ground. Okino was now very curious about the nature of this ground. Waste ground now but what he wondered had this place been before the city of Straam arose around and over it.

"A lot of the insightful knowledge came from the stories we started to invent," Aliya had been quiet up until now listening carefully to all being said.

"The city was a continual presence. You could hear it and see it's light looming in the distance beyond. There was a continual low rhythmical throb if you listened carefully. We always wondered how the sounds of so many machines presumably all operating at different speeds with different sized engines could all unite into this one continuous throb. Most of the time you wouldn't notice it but it was always there night and day, lurking there like a huge monster prowling around on the outskirts of our world. It was so consumed in its own life and survival it had not yet noticed our land. We assured ourselves in our fantasy, the monster could not see this world because it could not recognise a place so unspoilt by the festering malaise of the city and all it had become. We were free from it here and hoped it would always leave us alone free from the terror we anticipated it might bring should it notice us."

Aliya smiled as she looked around at her friends, Okino and Mariella to make sure she had their full attention as she transported them back to the magic of the worlds they had conjured. They peered back over the table at her motionless and already fully immersed as she began to weave her magic once again through their minds.

"…. We began to weave the story of the folk who came to live in this hidden land. Originally they came out of the light. They had always been here but it was as if they came to life again through us. It had been their land but as the nature of it had fallen away so they had gone back into the light. Now the nature, the essence they had so relished and come here to experience had been allowed to return. We had found it and they had found us and when we were here we became them and they us. We began to experience the essence they had found here in the earliest of times when there was only a forest.

Although the imprint of the machine monster was all around, it was as if this place had forgotten it, moved on and left it to return to how it was meant to be. In the stories we described it as a world where magic had been allowed to return. The magic came again with the wild nature of the place as it was allowed to grow and flourish. So, there were wild brambles and bushes growing untended and the grass was uncut and unfertilised. Trees had grown in amongst the brambles and already were providing shade and further habitat for an array of songbirds. Wildflowers had appeared naturally and beautiful butterflies, many varieties of beetles and multi coloured insects of all descriptions had come to feed on them. They were captured in the bright Starlight and we became somehow enhanced as if we had been enriched by seeing them and the auras they seemed to project around them. It was like nothing we had ever experienced before.

They became the essence of the magic, these beautiful beings with unworldly colour covering their wings and their shining iridescent skins and shells. We returned here from our lives outside whenever we could, to find it again, entered our magical realm where these magical creatures lived their momentary lives where anything was possible and we lived in the story of this place as it rose again in the world.

Then there was the stream. Beyond our land it had been buried in drains which flowed down the streets but when the factory was made someone had discovered it and decided to free it from its gloomy underground journey. It emerged from a circular concrete pipe at the higher end of the site and flowed in a carefully constructed channel lined with pebbles and rocks through the gardens surrounding the factory. We dreamed it had come from a spring somewhere in the surrounding land. It brought dreams and the knowledge of the magic left by the people from a crystal cave where it rose under an enchanted hill.

A small pond had been made which was always clear and surrounded by plants. There were other beings living along its way. The ancient wise old frogs and dragonflies. No one knew how old they were or what knowledge of the old place they had. Also, miraculously we thought a small family of fish made their way up and down the stream and through the pond. The stream became central to the story surrounding our 'lost world'. Pure and fragile, the butterfly beings and their flower food were replenished here by the dancing sparkling light and the birdsong drifting through it, separated but amidst the stench and filth of the surrounding metropolis. Here the people could stay hidden, independent of the terrible slavery the monster inflicted on the unfortunate citizens of the surrounding lands.

Of course, they would eventually venture out into the city, tempted by the machinery and the things they could bring to their world they thought might improve it. But when these things from the dark place arrived they felt some of the magic fall away and the people felt the grip of the monster as if they could become enslaved by the power they contained. They were mostly discarded or removed from the world. If anyone became lost, folk would venture out to rescue them and become embroiled in the strange lives of the city people in an effort to find a way to bring back their missing friends....if they ventured out on some agreed quest they might be recognised, followed back and when the secret was released into the world there would be invasion. We often used magic at this point to repel the invaders or take away the memory of those who had seen what had lain so perfectly hidden.

We could cloak our world or surround it in dense mists so any who ventured into it became hopelessly lost. There were often tragic love affairs between the people who lived in the separate worlds. They could not be resolved until one or the other renounced their own world. Beings often surfaced from other dimensions sometimes bringing great riches in exchange for the purity we had nurtured to take back to their degraded world. The nature of our wealth often changed and quite often the water through which the fish had swum or the air through which the dragonflies had flown became the most precious things to be guarded and preserved at all cost.

The stream might become a spirit being living deep in the worlds below the planet surface and a wise race might come to seek the wisdom for their own failing civilisation. But they would become so obsessed by the essence they would decide to take the land for themselves. Of course, the stream would dry up and the wise race would rage and fight amongst themselves until they were all destroyed. Then the stream would again start to flow.

Some travellers did venture out successfully and came back with knowledge to ensure the safety of the land for ever. Tales such as these generally involved the hero making some dreadful self-sacrifice in the service of the lords who were controlled by the monster. Or they would craftily ensnare the lords in a plan of complete genius so those same lords became eternally indebted to them.

Solemn vows were often made to protect this land. The water of the stream so the essence of the spirit being, bound us in our brother and sisterhood. If drunk, it would give insight into supposedly insoluble problems. So, we became seers and mystics looking into the stars to find the truth in the problems we faced. Sometimes we were compelled to act but sometimes we were able to see a germ of truth in the heart of a situation and know the problem would eventually resolve itself. So when the invaders came in search of material treasure they found only the clear stream and butterflies and rarely would stay for long…. because they could not see the true nature of this world! Looking back, it was the Summer island we felt could go on for ever, uninterrupted and undiscovered by the monster continually lurking all around as long as we told our stories in which it was defeated."

"So, you came to believe the power of the land here was unassailable."

Mariella was intrigued by the idea of these children conjuring up a world of stability and magic for themselves which they could protect as long as they continued to weave beautiful stories around it. She had known those stories herself and eventually had set out across the world to see if any of them could be made to come true.

"So, do you think there was something you did or a time when all this started to change and the monster rediscovered the land and came to reclaim it?"

The young adults looked around at each there. Matt decided to speak for them all.

"It was a strange time. We eventually came to a stage when we were putting more time into the transition we would be expected to make into the adult world. So, we became more deeply involved in our education. We had come to see this as an extension of any one of our stories in which we went out to seek wisdom from a distant land. The site was in no way neglected as the kids playground was always in regular use. When they did come and put the fence around it we were all pretty shocked. The thought of it being built over after all the years it had almost returned to wild land seemed devastating to us. In fact the whole community could see something extremely valuable being unjustly taken away from us….and of course you know what happened when our parents decided to go and see your father, Mariella."

"I do. He was quite surprised by the outcome I think. He thinks it may set a new precedent in the way land law is dealt with. But we were interested…well Okino here felt he wanted to come and talk to you. We wanted to meet you and find out your take on what happened next!" Mariella turned to Okino who had been silently listening to the fascinating story being unravelled.

"I was interested because even as Mr Keating told us the story some of what you have subsequently told us was coming through to me…now you have told us you came to imagine this land to be perhaps sacred in some way. I am completely intrigued to hear from you what did happen next!"

Erica spoke now.

"I don't think any of us could tell you for certain whether the land was special because we were just kids inventing and imagining like kids do. It seemed like a magical time for us but how would we know if it would have been any different somewhere else. What I can tell you is that once the land had been secured by the community things did change. This piece of land had real value and it was in our ownership but all the people who had signed that document had to agree on what was going to happen there. There was no way everybody was going to agree to build a housing estate or a factory on it to realise the value. Although I think some would have.

No, it was going to have to be a resource to benefit the entire community and in the end what had been working so beautifully there? A beautiful space the kids could play in. Why change anything? We could make it safer by constructing the dens out of proper materials so they were not in danger of collapse. We could make them properly weatherproof and improve the landscapes around them so they did not turn to mud as soon as the rain came. So, a playground that could be used by the whole community even the adults on the occasions they felt like staying out with the kids in the long summer evenings. It was the only thing everybody could come anywhere near agreeing on so that is exactly what we did.

The community as a whole raised enough money to reproduce the dens we had constructed. But now they were built only in the spirit of those first constructions. We did drawings and decided exactly how they were going to be. These were now solid examples of a new architecture starting in response to so many of the environmental problems caused by the built environment. These were now beautiful cosy little dwellings with as many as three rooms. There was nothing in them so they could be inhabited temporarily for one or two nights by anyone who wanted the experience they offered. We did manage to get the water company to run water into everyone but that was really the only luxury. The solid landscaping was minimal but we made stone terraces outside the front doors and fire pits for cooking, all built solidly to last and able to be left without too much worry when they weren't being used."

After all the work had been done the waste ground was now more like a park. We were able to live in the lodges as they now have been named and carry on our lives independently. However, things started to change fairly rapidly. For most people the site beyond the small area where the climbing frames had been built really hadn't existed; where they did not go or even think about because as far as they were concerned it just wasn't there. But now the profile had been raised as it became accessible. As it came into view of the community suddenly it came into the view of the rest of the world. Once the council became involved by connecting up the water there was local news interest. The journalists came and pounced on it as a shining example of cooperation in a city community. After all it was a great resource which we all could be proud of. But to broadcast about free space in a city where people could barely move without stepping on each other and where there was a problem with vagrancy and homelessness was bound to be disastrous.

Sure enough as the profile was raised we started to notice more and more visits at night. Probably individuals to start with but the word soon started to spread through the homeless community. We could not have anticipated what would happen next but perhaps we should have done. It is well known there are groups of homeless people in this city. They band together in large numbers to make it more difficult for the Police to move them on. Numbers are increasing and the spaces these large groups can occupy are becoming rarer so when one does come to be known it doesn't take long for word to get around. Now they have come to our once forgotten land. The monster most definitely has invaded and with it came some very dangerous and unpredictable characters. They organise and offer some very vulnerable people an umbrella of protection. The cost of this protection is being compelled to spread the crime that brings so much chaos and misery deeper and deeper into the city."

"But first the gangs have to fight for dominance of this new space. So, you can imagine what it has been like. The really violent street fighters come first. They took over three of the lodges to start with and waited for the other gangs to arrive. They rarely use guns but there have been some pretty horrific injuries as the gangs have battled for supremacy. They fight at night. We just hear the shouting and the screaming. So now we have a war going on where for so long there had been just peace and quiet for kids.

They don't care about anyone or anything and to be honest the park has been turned back into a waste ground, but now with a settlement of some of the most desperate people in the city. The authorities are bound by another completely different set of land legislation. They have raided the place on several occasions but the gangs are back the next day. The community has looked into putting a high security fence all the way round but there is no certainty that a section of it won't be torn down and everyone will return. Then we've got what is effectively a prison ghetto in the centre of our community."

There was silence around the table. Okino and Mariella looked over at each other. They both sensed there was something about the dispute over this piece of ground and how it had been predicted in the stories the children had been telling each other that reflected so many of the problems Arimathea was facing. Okino also had an overwhelming feeling that somewhere in this situation there was a connection to the darkness he had felt when arriving in Straam. He had not been able to dislodge the memory from his consciousness and it had left an edge to his mood which he had battled to suppress both day and night since those moments. Now there was focus to the edge as if an unknown figure had emerged from a crowd as familiar. He needed to find out what or who the figure was. He said quietly.

"I think we should go there!"

Although she knew the trouble they could be heading into Mariella agreed and asked,

"Will you take us up there, to the forgotten land now discovered?"

The young adults look around warily at each other. Jack decided to speak....

"We will take you up there and give you whatever help we can."

Chapter Fifty-Seven
Future world

They walked out of the streets lined with the intimidating towers and the canyons they had formed in the commercial centre deeper into the city. As they walked the buildings became lower and the office style skyscrapers started to give way to earlier lower buildings now stained with a hundred years of the dark residue of fumes and pollutants which had drifted visibly and invisibly across the city. Now where land prices had decreased there were still older buildings that may have stood before even this generation of building had taken place.

Police stations, churches, administration buildings with lavish masonry details, unaffordable on the more modern buildings, boasted gargoyles and cornices, columns and pediments over entrances. They brought to mind an era when a building was a fine thing to bring into the world. In earlier times there had been a certain supernatural significance in its appearance and so it was imbued with protection from the wilder spirits of where it had been conjured. Builders of more modern buildings had neglected this practice without fully understanding its origin and the old spirits flowed around and through the new edifices.

Trees had started to appear in ragged gaps of greenery surrounded by iron fencing where people were taking a few minutes to enjoy a brief rest from their relentless lives. They stared up into the ancient trees to watch the pigeons or the squirrels scrambling amongst the highest branches. The birds waited expectantly as the visitors to their green island homes quietly ate sandwiches and cakes. They dived down and scrambled and squabbled over the crumbs when the diners had resumed their careers or their journeys into the light or the darkness.

Okino thought pigeons must be one of the most successful creatures on Arimathea. Here in Straam they were much the same as they had been in Aharri and Zedocha even in his home village of Lamai. Their extraordinarily diverse mixture of feather colour and symmetry always followed the structure of bodily pattern and seemed to be the work of a painter who had tried to give each creature as many features as was possible on one small scruffy bird.

Perhaps not as successful as the rats who could occasionally be glimpsed shuffling in a sack of garbage outside one of the many fast food shops now starting to appear. Occasionally he would notice a cat on a wall or a windowsill carefully observing the world, out of harm's way half dozing, half alert, ready to pounce and kill at any moment. Their distant cousins would be prowling in the mountains, rare, sleek and shy of human contact. Here their domesticated relations retained their wildness, a separateness and displayed similarities when they levelled their icy stares or flicked their tails defiantly or stretched in the Star shine full of rat or pigeon. The creatures around them would relax, until their appetite returned and the hunting game would start again.

The sign of the perpetual hunger of the occupants of Straam from the debris of takeaway food lay discarded everywhere. These streets were not pristinely cleansed or perhaps the habits of the street dwellers were different here. Certainly, they were different. If the pre-occupations, confusion and worry of living in the city were also here they were not as apparent. There was an undercurrent of conversation and banter, laughter mixing gently with the low rumble of the traffic. It moved no faster here than in the richer parts of the city.

Crucial conversations were conducted or frivolous exchanges underlying some more serious issue, but it was a signal saying, "I need to talk about this before I go insane with the worry of it." Boys arranged later meetings hoping to meet the girls who walked across the street from them pretending not to notice their interest. They'd be talking about their visits to the game or a late assignment, their crazy boss or an argument they had had with their wife or mistress. They spoke of drug deals or who had been arrested as a police vehicle nudged past flashing it's urgency to the stationery traffic, squeezing past the drivers who reluctantly pulled over perhaps sheltering whatever it was they were doing while idling in the city street waiting for something to shift somewhere in another part of town.

There were wilder looking dogs fending for themselves, sniffing at bags of garbage out side of the restaurants, sometimes surprised by a rat enjoying a scrap of discarded meat, or hissed at by a cat, they snarled or snapped as they passed their captive brothers, groomed and well fed on leads and chains, cleared up after by their owners that really did bear a resemblance to them. Okino had read this in a magazine and now was continually amused and always pointed out the similarities to Mariella. She laughed and fell more deeply in love with him.

Okino knew this was happening because of course since he had been here in Straam and they had been together again, the separation had only emphasised what was happening between them. Still he felt he needed to hold the clarity of the thoughts being passed between him and the dragon.

They watched self-consciously as couples walked past arm in arm clearly delighting in the intimacy they had found and shared and now could share with the world. They looked at each other shyly, as the lovers passed, like two leopards passing on a trail knowing they could be friends or lovers but surely it would upset the balance of the world and that wasn't why they had passed that day. But the thought would never go away now and when the moon was high enough and full enough one night they would meet on the hillside again and give in to the urge of all the world because a new generation beckoned, was straining to be released, to play their part, take their chance on the magical mystery tour, feel the spark, the light and it's magnificence filling them once again.

Everywhere on the streets there were signs of the struggle for existence. Across the street an argument broke out amongst two traders over the correct price for a sack of potatoes. Young men struggled around them under the loads of sacks bulging with fruit and vegetables being carried from one marketplace to the next. The concern in their faces showed the hope they would make some profit for their effort and worry they would not. Perhaps today would be the day and they would be able to buy just a little bit more tomorrow. Perhaps enough to save at the end of the week when the children were fed so at the end of the year they could buy a small truck to drive out to the fields themselves.

They had everything planned. Everyone who bustled through the street had a plan and was trying to push it through. Buying the vegetables, the radios, the watches, the shoes, the bicycles for as little as possible and selling for as much as possible. In the process they haggled and argued with each other, everyone full of the calculation in his mind goading and persuading, extrapolating and exaggerating the worth or the value, denigrating and underestimating, undermining, delving for a weakness to take advantage to sell or buy whether there was need or not. They had no concern for anything, only the calculation, the equation and the faces of their hungry children.

They joked and made light of this deadly serious game they were playing with each other always hoping they could help each other out with a higher price or a larger quantity for a lower price. But everyone had their own plan and it made business on these streets as tight and unforgiving as in the towers in the distance rising above the unkempt terraces where the stakes were higher but for all the same reasons. It was part of the plan, the aim to be there in a tower. They lived in envy of how they thought it would be, of the multi-million deals and the offices overlooking the park and the sleek sports cars and the beautiful companions who sat beside them. It was in their plan as they strived for those things, hoping they could be the one who did occasionally find the route from here to there; where they would wear the suits and sit in the restaurants into the afternoon drinking champagne and eating the eggs of exotic species because this would bring them not only the money but all the other things they strove for; admiration, respect and envy.

But most of all they yearned for power over their fellows who had ruled them. Whom they had had to depend on, who had taken advantage of their weakness, except their price because of who they were. So that when the deal was done so tightly again with all the advantage to them they had cursed them, had secretly wanted to humiliate them in front of their wives and children, sleep with their wives to see the shock and the pain in the betrayal and wished dreadful things upon them and their families and would have happily raised their houses to the ground if they thought they could have got away with it.

Then these men and women would come to them with their plan and their calculation nagging a way in the back of their minds like their entire world and everything in it depended on the decision made. Either way they would have the power. The power in the world which had continually eluded them. It had tantalised and frustrated them driven them almost to despair. All their life they had been subjected to this power and it had made them desperate and twisted and into someone they disliked and to some extent had become frightened of and were desperate to gratify.

All this simmering malevolence and hatred was underlying the busy streets as Okino and Mariella followed Matt and his friends deeper into the city. Now there were more often signs of where the system was failing as they began to see the people who had been unable to provide a living for themselves. Here were the stationary people, inactive and motionless. Or they moved slowly, shuffling possibly having abandoned the straight lines on which the people who still had their plans were able to progress along the streets. They wavered or staggered or had collapsed under the weight of the disillusionment and pain which had come upon them. The plan they had made or had been made for them now simply did not exist and they had stopped at the mercy of passers-by who may or may not give them money to buy themselves a meagre meal.

Many had chosen to cushion whatever terrors they had faced or were facing in their lives and minds with the lesser cousins of the champagne, the city bankers would be using to celebrate a deal enabling them to buy another yacht or beach mansion. High in the restaurants they would look down into the streets fully aware, because they would drive past them on their way back to their mansions in the country, their fellow humans down there had nowhere to go, no one to help them and had become so confused by the complexity of the maze outside and inside their heads in which one day they had found themselves they had simply stopped. Stopped planning, striving, caring, worrying about anything except drowning the pain which was ripping through their consciousness. They had stepped outside the tightness, given up on the struggle relinquished their place, their right not to be stepped over, to have no power, even over the dogs and the rats who crawled over them on the way to the bins they sat expectantly next to. They had given up on their race and lay or shuffled alongside them as if they had become another species somewhere between the dogs and the rats with whom they now shared the streets.

Here were the parts of town the captain had warned Okino about, told him to visit, but it did not shock him any the less. They walked on as the Star continued its journey across what remained of the sky to where the monks would be tending the herb gardens, delving deeper into the mysteries of the dragon while attempting to assist the people of Lamai with the problems and contradictions of their existence in the bright Starlight of the afternoon as darkness started to fall on the city of Straam.

Onward through the streets they advanced, along the brightly lit streets full of traffic now exiting the city for the suburbs. The harsh white electronic light cast their shadows crisply on the pavements as if they were followed by dark ghostly counterparts. The noise and continual flashing of headlights as they passed strained their ability to observe little beyond what was directly in front of them. They talked little, seeing few people. The mechanised environment surrounded them, had entirely engulfed them. There was nothing to remind them of her softness now the sky and the Star had finally fled the city. Only the long low metallic sheds of the warehouses and factories loomed in the darkness and the lights of the machines flashing past carrying their drivers to whatever domestic arrangement awaited behind the closed doors of the homes they would drive up to.

Slowly, the landscape began to change again, signs of life again appeared. Trees and hedges started to line the pavements as they emerged into the residential areas lying on the outskirts of the city. Individual houses and the small terraces appeared, set back from the road with driveways and front gardens and lights on. Occasionally the people could be seen inside as they again settled into their homes for the evening, their front rooms already flickering from the rapidly changing lights of the multi-media television sets that would provide the backdrop for the evening. Outside they passed with their dogs on leads or in their tightly fitting sports clothing as they ran intensely past, buried in thought or the sound in their earphones through the pools of light into the darkness beyond. Okino noticed a strange uniformity pervaded each of these streets as if around every corner he was reliving an experience that had ended in the previous street but was now starting up again.

When he looked more closely, he realised there were a limited number of styles for the houses continually being repeated. He wondered whether these people realised they were sharing identical houses with many other people as near as the next street. Perhaps they never thought beyond their own streets so really it didn't matter that each street was little more than a carefully manipulated real life set, a phoney backdrop acceptable to whoever it had to be acceptable; planners, company executives answerable to accountants and shareholders and repeating itself over and over again possibly in cities up and down the land. Okino found the reduction of the living experience to what amounted to an equation to satisfy the profit margins of the builders who brought these neighbourhoods into being, deeply unsettling. Here, more than ever he started to fully understand how the people of Straam's lives were being dictated to them. No wonder these people needed drugs to keep them sane.

Eventually they came to the park. Matt had entered on the side as yet uninhabited by the street gangs, although they could hear music being played loudly out in the open coming from the direction of the glow of a fire amongst the trees in the distance. They could hear intermittent shouting and screeching as arguments broke out punctuating the constant bass throb of loud dance music. Okino felt drawn to this gathering over in the trees.

From the moments Aaron had told him about this place he knew there was something here for him; Some revelation, some connection with everything that had happened. In the cold evening air with the sound of the distant throb of the city mingling with the sound of the strange electronic music he suddenly realised how far away from home he really was. He looked around for Mariella who was close at his side. She had sensed his disquiet and stayed close to him. She also sensed how close this all was to unravelling from something manageable into an unpredictable situation very quickly.

Particularly if Okino had to go and engage with whatever or whoever was sitting, standing or dancing around that fire.

She touched his arm and he felt her supportive intention flow through him and bring him back to where he needed to be. He had slipped into a feeling of vulnerability and insecurity in this strange town. He had little or no understanding about what could or might happen next and was wishing he had never left the monastery the day of the storm when he had met with Arimathea. But then everything he was and had ever been had taken him there and ultimately brought him here. He heard her words echoing faintly amongst the sounds of the city in the distance and the chaotic gathering and the low flying aircraft and the cursing of Jack as he found the last of the lodges had been briefly invaded; he heard her in the underlying breeze flowing across his face as if she had touched him to remind him she was there with him and all he had to do was to reach into the silence below all this noise. The temporary clamour of this transient age.

In a blink of her time it would be gone and peace would reign again across her lands and her oceans and the damage she had sustained would heal or it would not. He reached into the peace of those millennia she offered him, past and future, felt them resounding through him, felt again the ancient strength he had found in himself the night he had freed the dragon and subsequently as he had travelled through his dream to the place where he had emerged on the old dragon hill, looking down on the misty world as if it was her first day. But now here, after all that had happened he could hear the echoes, the stories of the world bound up in those ancient stones, bound up in the vibration of their fabric hewn from the solid mantle of Arimathea, embedded in the old trees and the hills surrounding them and the ancestral memories of all the creatures living amongst them and conjured for him and Mariella by the dragon, the alchemist of dreams and visions, the keeper of the ancient prophecy of life and fulfilment of its ultimate destiny.

In sacred light it had been born, lived and had been held by its receptors until again it could be released and heard by those who knew the sound of those old vibrations, before they finally faded from the world. And so it had been released. They had heard the old legend and how it all had come to be, now, as it was. He turned to Mariella smiled down at her and started to walk towards the fire. She walked resolutely at his side excited to again engage with the mystery in which she had become so fascinatingly involved.

Chapter Fifty-Eight
The Spaces in between.

Flames and sparks leapt randomly from the untidy pile of rubbish that had been collected and ignited in the fire pit outside one of the lodges deeper into the park. A long low continuous roofline ran from waist height over the timber and stone walls. The flames reflected, dancing in the small recessed windows. The double doors were flung open but there seemed to be little activity inside. All activity at this time was concentrated around the fire. They sat and stood talking or screeching in groups of two or three or individually. They may have numbered as many as thirty individuals. They were a strange and ragged bunch with very little in common other than it was difficult to see how they could have been involved in any of the activities happening on the streets during the day.

They wore layers of stout clothing that wrapped around them, moulded around them, possibly never removed, hair long and lank, tangled beards fell and joined with leather and thick high collared coats. Hair had been partially removed completely and replaced with expansive tattoos curving around skulls bleeding into eyes, sunk into lean dirty faces worn with age and nights of exposure to the polluted night air. Their collection of multi coloured, multi sized dogs lay nearest to the fire battling with worn studded boots for warmth and exposed to the flying debris. They yelped along with angry curses as another piece of molten material exploded haphazardly from the flames.

They drank from an assortment of bottles replenished from the back of a battered vehicle. It may once have been something bright and new and shiny, driven from the production line of an auto motive factory to fulfil someone's manufactured dream. Here was the origin of the loud music surrounding the gathering, filling it with rhythmical pace and tension also manufactured far from here in a pristine studio by artists and executives who may well have imagined such scenes as they levelled synthesisers and drum machines, mixed them with the language familiar to the desperate and disenfranchised and laced them with defiance and rage for the machine, setting the mood for such a scene. Lines and verses easily distinguishable easily latched onto identifying with hopelessness, filled with ridicule and insolence for all the authority, all the power reigning over them and chanting rebellion, mutiny and the revolution that one day would come.

So, the mood was tense and as potent with destruction as the liquids continually being consumed and substances smoked, thick acrid clouds blown towards the flames and over the animals who winced and fell deeper into their sleep. Bags of chemicals handed around and ingested without thought but soon adding to the wild and dangerous atmosphere, no one there at all in control but riding the chemical night train flat out into the warm summer night. Alive with the fire exploding in front of them and racing through their veins through cortex and into the old spirits who stood there defiantly outside the control of all their oppressors, preparing themselves, making themselves ready to go into the dark city and do their work.

Okino and Mariella stood in the shadows invisibly behind the swaying excited assembly as they laughed and cursed and argued, squabbled over drinks and smokes as they handed them round. Okino watched the quiet ones on the edges of the scraps and the horseplay as they stared into the flames only moving when the bottle or the smoke needed to be raised to their mouths, hoods raised possibly for some shelter and protection from the violence in the air, remembering, finding the paths through the chaos and disaster, going over the words, the crisis in all it's bizarre finality the mistakes made and the opportunity for resolution missed. Possibly for the hell of it, just to seal their fate once and for all. Winced as they came to the end scene, with the faces and the 'no more chances' and 'how could you let this happen, and the final acceptance as their lives drifted away and they walked away into the night and found themselves here.

Okino watched them and felt them shudder. These were the ones who had had a plan but it had slipped away through circumstance and they could not find their way back or had lost the will to continue the journey. Matt and Jack were beside them now. Jack handed Okino and Mariella cans of beer and as they broke the seals and the initial gush of liquid and pressurised air was released their presence was revealed. Heads turned curious for a moment to see who had joined the crowd. They registered Matt and Jack and somebody said "It's just the kids" and with no apparent reason for any further acknowledgement or interruption to their party they went back to their plans or conversations or arguments. Okino looked over at Jack who seemed relieved there had been no antagonism.

"Well these guys can be unpredictable!"

There were some spaces next to one of the quieter characters Okino had been observing. He had very little connection with rest of the gathering, silently staring into the fire and smiling or grimacing at some of the more outrageous comments drifting through the smoky air. Okino nudged Mariella and indicated towards the spaces as if perhaps they should sit down and join the circle around the fire. She followed him closely and they settled down on the log that for the moment had been vacated. Mariella moved closely next to Okino and lifted his arm around her shoulders keeping the hood of the coat she had bought almost two months before in Asima, pulled fully over her head. They sat quietly looking into the fire and after a few moments…

"Haven't seen you guys here before, did you come with the kids?"

Okino turned to see the quiet man he had been observing was looking over to him. A thick black beard covered much of his lower face but beneath the dark hood Okino could see inquiring eyes, tired and worn out but alert and genuinely interested in the couple who had come to sit beside him.

"In the last part of the journey we did come with Matt and Jack"

"The last part, so have you come a long way then?

"I have come a long way, almost half-way around this world as it happens."

"So where is halfway round the world for you."

"I have come from a small mountainous country called Jahallala where I am a Monk in a temple above a small town in the mountains called Lamai."

"Ah, ha ha, so I am visited by a priest"

He laughs and shakes his head,

- 501 -

"..not before time I might say. I am pleased you have come and found me here. Here look, my name is Brett," he offers his hand to Okino…

"I am Okino and this is my friend Mariella with whom I have been travelling, we're pleased to meet you."

Mariella only slightly adjusts her position to acknowledge Brett across Okino. She is slightly surprised by Brett's lucid nature but smiles to herself in the shadows as she realises Okino has probably picked precisely the right person to be talking to amongst the crowd around them.

"…and I'm pleased to meet you both. So that is quite a journey. How did you come across the ocean?"

"I came on a cruise liner, one of the big ones full of people travelling around Arimathea. I certainly had some interesting moments" Okino wondered if Brett had been near a television in the last few weeks and decided he probably had not.

"Aah the high life Okino, rob the temple roof fund did you?" He laughs. Okino laughs with him. Brett becomes quickly serious as he realises what he has said could easily have offended the monk.

"Sorry, only joking, Okino. I've heard there are some pretty serious individuals up in those temples in the mountains. Could do with a few more of you down here to be frank spreading that beautiful mysticism you guys get involved with! I don't know how long you've been here but to tell you the truth Okino on this side of the world everything is truly going to shit!

"I have only been here a week and a lot of the problems you have in this country are well known to us even in our extreme location. But experiencing the city for the first time, coming in contact with your people has been, well illuminating. You don't really feel the power of a skyscraper until you are standing at the foot of it looking at the sky reflected all the way up a hundred storeys. But then in the next streets there are people begging, not moving, while the city moves on around them, as if they weren't there, as if they were fulfilling some role in it."

Brett was quiet when he heard Okino's words and looked back deeper into the fire as if he could find some white heat there to invisibly destroy the memories searing through his troubled mind.

"There is so much that is surprising here. Perhaps that is at the root of it though. There is just so much; so much of everything!"

"…and everyone you see who hasn't stopped as you say, is trying to get their hands on as much of it as possible because they think it will set them free. They sell us this dream that it will set us free. But it only locks you in tighter Okino. The more of it you have the tighter you are bound in by those people at the top of those skyscrapers, in their office suites looking down on us scrambling around with the rats and the stray dogs in all the pollution made by the cars they have persuaded us we need, getting fat on the food they persuade us to eat which is unable to sustain us in the lifestyles they insist we should be leading. I know Okino, I went there into the land of dreams where everyone wants to be; Where you can have everything!"

Okino had sensed earlier this man had a story to tell. He looked around the fire at the other men and women knowing they would all have their own journey. How they came to be here with virtually nothing in a country where a man could amass enough wealth to buy his own island in a tropical paradise, have ships and planes and helicopters to get to it, have a crowd of people to look after it when he wasn't there, when he was here in his tower surfing the markets of the world generating more and more wealth. Now it seemed Brett was going to tell his story. How he came to be here.

"So, what happened then on your journey into this land of dreams?" Okino prompted him.

"I became a builder, nothing like those huge skyscrapers but in the end large multi-million Dezari schemes. I did what came naturally to me, went to college learnt how to build, came out and started doing little bits and pieces. I was lucky. Don't believe anyone who tells you they didn't have any luck on the way. But if you think about it someone has got to be at the right place at the right time.

So, people I did work for, this was when I was younger, started to give me opportunities. They would have a piece of land and they wanted to build a house or a warehouse or anything they could make a return on for their capital outlay when the job was done. So, I would build them as quickly and cheaply as they wanted within the accepted parameters. The faster, the cheaper, the less money would have to be borrowed to fund it and more profit made in the years to come. Unless of course they were going to live in it themselves.

So, I started building small houses, then bigger houses and office buildings and I started to build a company. I was lucky enough to find some really good people who I could trust who wanted the same things as I did and I paid them respectably for what they were doing and soon enough we were building a number of fairly large projects. The finance side of making these buildings was a very fine balance so really there is very little room for manoeuvre and budgets and deadlines were always looming but that is why you are there and to tell you the truth Okino, to be there was incredible.

To bring a building into the world, despite all the business and finance, can be a mystical experience. Every now and again I would get it, when everything was going smoothly, when everyone knew exactly what they were doing and had everything they needed to get on with it. Then you see what a remarkable race we are and how we have come to operate so effectively on this world, Okino. Of course, ultimately, we were all in it for the money. But when you see people working together all practicing the extraordinary skills they have managed to gain over the years to bring this new piece of the world into existence, see the determination and the will it demands from every single person in the team to make the project successful in all the ways it has to be was one of the truly remarkable experiences of my life.

To see it gradually forming, filling the empty space into which it was growing, on a carefully considered time path, where the skills of all the people who have become involved were carefully juggled, until, there it is. Did you ever have that experience where a new object has arrived and you sit and look at it and in some way it doesn't look completely solid yet. As if the energy hasn't quite fully occupied the space and causes all around it to shimmer as you try to focus on it. I saw this sometimes as I watched the frames being erected and then being covered with skins and filled with pumps and circuits until finally there it is exactly as someone conceived it, imagined it, brought it out of the thin air; a new part of the world where people will spend their lives.

They'll have good days and bad days, their lives will unravel there amongst the crudely formed columns and the slabs we have cast and disguised by covering them with soft fabrics and silky white paint. Those new spaces glow when the star shines through them with comfort and warmth and familiarity. When we inhabit them, start to move through them, it is like we have remade a part of our selves where we can be safe, be secure and free from fear. Before they fill with bosses and managers and machinery and all the hierarchy and stress of the modern work place, you can see these places, where you could live amongst all the soft glowing colours as if you were in some womb that would always protect you, let you grow, until you could be safely born ready and strong enough to face all that was in store for you.

I gathered a team of people around me who would go from one project to the next, getting better and better at what they did and the company became increasingly successful. As the years went by we all benefited. We had made it to the land where our houses could become bigger, our cars more expensive, our wives and children could have what they wanted, go to whatever schools we could choose for them, we became popular, sought after because we had the keys to the kingdom and there were always plenty of people who wanted the benefit of our trade, the contracts we could offer on the big building projects.

When it is like this Okino it is like you are floating through a dream, somewhere deep down you know it is unreal, but it is going on all around you so you accept it, come to relish it, start to feel nothing can touch you, you have become special, risen out of the general scramble and elevated yourself onto some different flow of existence. It has separated you out from the rest into some new stratosphere where you live with all the privileges and comforts money and the power brings to you and those around you. And how they love you for it…but then I was never completely convinced of that.

You have glimpses, see how tightly you are bound into the system. All the freedom, the money and the power it gives you is reliant on the money continually rolling in. There are always correlations you can see in whatever life you are leading; Cause and effect, today and tomorrow all very different places which have their own needs and I don't know how much you know about our economic system, Okino, but really it is pretty fragile, on much the same knife edge as much of the life on this planet. Whatever people tell you.

So gradually the illusion started to unravel. The bankers who were loaning the money for all these projects were generating it from ever riskier financial models. The safe traditional funds where our savings pensions and mortgages were held could only yield so much. As riskier more uncertain packages were created, they were bought and sold and it seems the banks were no longer opening the packages to see what was inside. When they eventually did open the boxes all was not as had been assumed and the new owners found them not to contain the value they had been sold.

Sounds like the oldest trick in the book it would seem but this is what was happening in the fantasy land we all had entered. Pretty soon the system started to go into melt down. The banks overnight started to withdraw funding from the investment bankers who were using these fantasy funds for leverage to get the enormous sums they now needed to borrow in a market now falsely expanded. Projects were stopped over night; sites were closed as the rich full streams of money were abruptly dammed further up-stream. Many of us were left high and dry despite the watertight contracts we all had entered into.

During this time, one of the outings we had come to enjoy was going to the races. There was an atmosphere amongst the sleek highly bred horses at the height of their fitness and stamina as they strutted around the paddocks and then tore around the courses, fitting for the time we were having. We knew in a sense we were gambling everyday as we promised ever riskier outcomes to our greedy clients in our continual struggle to prevent them seeking the services we offered elsewhere. But here the gamble was just about the thrill of watching a horse cross the line ahead of all the others when you had a stack of money on it. At that time it had no life repercussions because we only used the money we could afford to lose.

Here again, I found the mystery of all the world as I watched the horses parading in front of us. One of them would in the next half an hour be the winner and all you had to do was delve into the secret corridors of time to see which one it would be. No wonder the horse race has continued to fascinate since ancient times. Here we look into the mechanisms of time and space, the ancient art of seer ship, of prophecy and far sight was bound up in the performance of these dark mystical creatures. So we invented our systems: observed their posture, their mood, the energy they exuded, were they using energy now that they could be using on the track, what about their physicality, were they small and compact or large and powerful; examined the reaction in our thoughts as each passed through the cortex that unknowingly to us may have access to those time corridors and give us the clue to the outcome. I thought that may be the answer was in their eyes or how they moved or how they had run in their previous races. Sometimes it was one of these theories that had made you put your money on one particular horse.

It was easy to become convinced when you collected the multiple of money you had put in the hand of the bookie that you had found the secret. I had a remarkably good run. I had three good wins in a row. I was on the dangerous ground where everything can change fairly suddenly. The fantasy had mounted up all around me and become my reality. I had begun to think the normal rules didn't apply. Everything you now think to be solid and real is nothing of the kind. All the decisions I then made were in the wake of the illusion I had built around myself. When you are here on the other side, its' easy to see how this all came to be, how the universe, the mystery, God had set me up in this fantasy so I could be stripped right back down to the person I needed to be. So, it was then when reality decided to reveal itself and come thundering back into my life."

Brett indicated all around him to the desolation in which he now existed and looked over at Okino for the first time in his story. He stared from eyes deeply sunken into his young face. He had become old as the destruction of his fantasy world had taken place. He had explained perfectly to Okino and Mariella what had happened. Perhaps he had honed the story or perhaps he had been finally granted the space by the priest to finally face and tell it honestly. Mariella knew what had happened and leant forward to look into those tired eyes and said softly, understanding and forgiving him finally for the mistake he had made.

"So, you took all the money you had left and put it on a horse you were convinced would win!"

Brett nodded as tears began to stream from his eyes.

"I lost everything, not all in that moment but from that moment and have not been able to find my way back. I'm not sure I want to. Everyone has turned their backs on me, slammed the door on me."

In those moments Brett's anguish had truly surfaced possibly for the first time. In the space Okino had given him he had found the courage to delve down, to find and finally realise the deep damage he had sustained in the depths of his soul as his family, his partners and his employees had turned their backs on him when he could no longer supply the life style on which they had come to depend. The separation Okino had already found between souls here, deeply buried by the illusion of the lives they were leading had made it impossible for Brett to deal with the misfortune he had experienced. As far as he had been concerned, he had been the bad guy who had let everyone down, because he believed he had become the super hero everyone had depended on to keep their lives together; not because of circumstances or the crash but because he had failed as the special human being he thought he had become.

Okino felt the change as Brett was transformed by the revelation he had now received. Now slowly he would again be reunited with the soul that had come from the stars, the spirit who had been born into a world in need of his special ability, to travel through it, to find the reason he had been granted such a tremendous privilege and find again the path he had been granted and had become lost to him.

Brett had begun to surface once again for the first time since those early days when he had glimpsed the person he would eventually become. He was able, at last, to truly acknowledge the powers of the world he had courted and in which he had become totally enmeshed. He had realised how this illusion of success and power had become reversed and how it had affected him and thousands of others who had probably found themselves in the same position. He looked over at Okino in amazement with a grin now surfacing on the face that had become so tired, so neglected in his struggle to find his way back.

"How did you do that, Okino? You've hardly said ten words to me and yet suddenly everything makes sense again."

Okino smiled back at him.

"Maybe I just asked the right question to which you already had the right answer."

"I saw him do it to a Yak in the middle of the busiest most congested street you ever could imagine. One minute not going anywhere next minute setting off as if his or her life depended on it!"

Mariella had watched and listened as the monk had gently lead Brett out of his confusion as easily as if he had come to the temple in the high mountains with a dilemma about which crops he should plant. He had not provided any blindingly intelligent philosophy or teaching he had just listened and all he had become had allowed him to ask the right question.

"Yaks are easy to deal with on the whole. Their motivations have been ruthlessly exploited by my people for many, many generations and are easily manipulated. In the wild they have to travel long distances for very small amounts of food, so scarce in their mountain environments and if left on their own they become difficult to find after a few days. So, you see we allow them to do for us what they do very naturally for themselves."

"Hardly," Mariella had interrupted, laughing. "It is not natural for them to carry the huge weights you load them up with in their search for food.!"

Okino remembered the dream he had had under the pine tree the morning Mariella had gone to find the explosives and how he had led his horse back down to the ruins.

"Maybe one day the Yak will become the dominant species on Arimathea until such a day I fear they will be doing most of the carrying."

Okino noticed a sudden change in the atmosphere as a tall dark, broadly built figure pushed his way into the circle. He was greeted with good humour by the two men he had emerged between. They were pleased to see him and gradually as the rest of the gathering realised he had arrived they sent greetings across the fire to him. He acknowledged each of them smiling over to each in turn. He had long dark hair which emerged from the hood of the long dark coat partially covering his head. His face had a heavy stubble which had not become a fully-fledged beard and he wore leather boots and gloves. He had a large bag slung over his shoulder. He removed his gloves and held his bare hands out to the fire. He grinned at the heat he felt and looked around at the assembled crowd who for the most part had gone back to their previous conversations.

Okino observed the new arrival carefully and couldn't help thinking there was something very familiar about him. Okino noticed a large crow had landed in one of the trees behind the circle. It ruffled and adjusted its feathers as it looked down and called loudly twice over the fire. It was almost inaudible over the music, but the trace of the sound was amplified in his mind and reverberated deep into his memory. He was transported back into the hills where Samir had followed the call of the crow to the hills where he had met with Mithrael.

Okino shuddered as he remembered the encounter. Could this be Mithrael who subsequently in their fatal meeting after the storm had driven his sword mercilessly through Merilons' heart? He was surprised and a little shocked by this new turn of events and pulled his hood as unobtrusively and as far over his head as possible. But surely Mithrael would not recognise him and how had he come to be here at all?

"So, are you all ready to go out into the city and make money for us tonight?"

There were yelps and further screeching from the assembled crowd as they gave an enthusiastic acknowledgement. Mithrael then lowered the bag from his shoulder and put it on the ground in front of him. He unzipped it and removed two plastic packages which he handed on to the nearest people on the circle. This process was repeated until the hold all was emptied and all the bags had been distributed. Brett had been handed one of the bags. Okino was able to see the contents. There appeared to be a large number of small bright yellow capsules filling the bag. Brett looked up and saw Okino looking enquiringly over at him and the capsules. He spoke under his breath.

"It's what they call 'Sunshine' Okino. It's the latest party drug. This guy Zanda brings it round for us and we go out and sell it in the clubs all over town. He says it pays for us, our food and the shelters we have here, the protection we have from the other gangs and the police. But that only accounts for a small amount of what is made, this stuff is a national craze at the moment and to be fair it's pretty good! But I dread to think what the profits from this stuff might be funding."

The crowd started to leave the fire and moved off down one of the paths away from the fire. They followed Zanda onto a large bus parked on the side of the road. Okino looked questioningly at Mariella.

"How far are we going to go with this. This character Zanda…!"

"Get on the bus, Okino. Tell me whatever it is when we're on the way; seems like we're going to a party."

Once everyone had been installed Zanda set off back to the city in the ancient bus. Back through the suburbs where Okino noticed the angry looks of outraged residents on the streets as they registered the noise and the lurid graffiti distinguishing this machine from the city buses normally seen running through these quiet suburban streets. Somebody had opened one of the bags of Sunshine and was passing it through the bus. Okino suddenly realised how far he had come and when Brett who was sitting next to them across the aisle passed it over to them, Mariella took the bag from him and turned to Okino. She spoke quietly to him.

"So, what do you think Okino? You said you had something to tell me about Zanda."

"Yeah, just a little thing. I think he's Mithrael. Remember who nearly killed me and put Merilon out of his own game for a few centuries or however long it was. He's here now running drugs to the kids of this city. I remember one of the things he said. The human race will have to make up their own minds. He's not giving them much opportunity here, in this time."

"So, who is he and what is he doing here?"

"I think he is what we traditionally call one of the bad guys. But I think he is more dangerous than your average gangster. His deep connection with Arimathea and the crows destroyed the dragon's plan to help the human race better understand the nature of their existence here."

"I do remember. He said we would have to find out for ourselves whatever the consequences. But here he seems to be actively making things worse."

Mariella seemed genuinely puzzled by this new twist.

"This means he must have been alive for well over one thousand years."

Okino was thoughtful,

"I cannot believe he has just managed to become a drug runner in all that time. But here he is in the heart of the monster we have heard so much about, encouraging presumably its victims to further proliferate the misery amongst the people of Straam."

"It depends though, Okino, this is a dragon we are talking about. We have no idea what he is doing for the rest of the day or what he has been doing for all those centuries."

"We know them mainly as spirits who work in the light but maybe he decided after he killed Merilon it would be better for the great spirit if he worked for the transformative forces of the dark. Perhaps he became lost in his own life as the strange hybrid dragon human he had become and Oblivion just took advantage.

In planetary terms everything has to be acted out one way or the other. For all the creativity and wonder happening in the world there will always have be a destructive force trying to drag it all back to where it can begin again. These forces do not differentiate or worry about how it is achieved. They are just doing what they have always done."

"So, do you think he may have become deeply involved with the meteoric rise of the human race as the industrial era took hold?"

"He could well have been. They are powerful creatures. Maybe their motivations are not as clear as we imagined. I have been continually feeling something enormous similar to what you and I felt on the Dragon hill permeating this entire city. As if the dark emptiness we released has grown exponentially and has been driving the whole rise of the mechanised world while the other the dragons have been absent from the world. How he has become involved in that I dread to think!"

"So, this drug running set up may only be the tip of an enormous iceberg of destruction he is floating through the world; An iceberg floating silently in an ocean waiting to drift into the path of the cruise ship of humanity. We are all having such a good time on board we're forgetting about how difficult it can be to avoid icebergs."

"..and certainly how dangerous they can be. We never found out the full story about the sword I eventually removed from Merilon."

"He definitely has that dragon look about him…but the glow I saw in Merilon's eyes is not there…he is very human."

"I know, I thought the same thing when I saw him. Maybe there is another story still unrevealed…it could provide explanation for the remaining unsolved mysteries."

"Like where the sword came from!"

"…or why Mithrael became separated from the dragons in the first place."

"Perhaps he decided the only way he could fulfil his role as a dragon was to become completely human!"

Chapter Fifty-Nine.
Into the Heart.

The bus swung precariously through the suburbs and the party continued. It rapidly filled with the vapours produced by the many psychoactive substances the wild passengers had continued to consume. Okino and Mariella were unable to avoid the strange effects such a cocktail produced in such a confined space. Brett was unable to resist telling his fellow gang members the true identity of the monk and from where he had travelled. This unusual novelty brought instant attention and both he and Mariella were bombarded with questions about the legendary mysticism of those distant outreaches of the human race on Arimathea. Mariella stayed close and watched and listened as the monk told them about his world, his journeys through the mountain ranges and his experiences with the unfathomable natural forces that continually surrounded his people.

The icy winds and the wolves and the leopards, the yaks and goats, the snowstorms in the cruel mountain winters were very real in Okino's mind and in the reality of his existence, but in the expanded state of many of the minds who were now listening, they soon became an array of supernatural forces, the tribe and the monks continually had to interact and battle with. Here they decided was the root of the rumours and tales that had filtered back to their lives in the cities. They put themselves high in the mountains and in the temples excited by the direct contact they would have with their world. A world where they could deal directly, physically and philosophically with the problems surrounding them however harsh they might be. Where they lived now, the powers were remote and untouchable. Until Zanda had organised them they were helpless victims of the ebb and flow of the vast economic experiment being conducted and precariously upheld by the elite technocrats high in their towers.

As the chemicals in the air made their way into his mind up until now influenced only by fresh air and the wisdom gathered through their continual battle for survival, Okino came to see more clearly how a town such as his might be seen as the last outpost of humanity able to steer the lost human race back to where it needed to be. As these fundamental truths of their existence on Arimathea were extemporised into drug induced fantasies of superheroes and super villain spirit forces, Okino looked down the bus to see if Zanda was listening or was showing any kind of acknowledgement of what was happening. He noticed Zanda was intermittently adjusting his head when traffic conditions allowing his concentration to drift up the bus as if straining to hear what was being said.

As they were accepted into the company of this disenfranchised gang of would be wizards, warrior kings and queens, became bound into their sect, into their brother and sisterhood it became impossible or seemed churlish not to accept their hospitality. An initiation was offered when they were given two of the yellow 'Sunshine' pills. They sat innocently in the palm of his hand. Okino looked over at Mariella who still had her hood firmly covering her long dark hair. Into those deep turquoise eyes which he had come to trust and perhaps had been guided by before they had even met in the market of Aharri.

The strange trick Arimathea had played on him resonated from the cave and the fire and her words to here on this bus. They all became quiet. Was it her quiet again allowing him to understand the moment, the gravity of the choice he had to make? Turn towards the wolf's den in the height of the storm. Turn back and pick up the stone after he had seen the flash in the grass, push the ring he had found in the pool onto his finger, pull the sword out of the dragon lying in the snow of the winter wood deep in his dream and then follow Mariella to the ruins of Asima. She had always given him the choice. To go deeper down the rabbit hole, deeper into the mystery she had provided for him or turn back and return to where he would never know the final outcome. She had never given him any insight into that outcome and perhaps she had not known herself, he had had to make the decision to go forward, open up the next door. Now his doubt was almost overwhelming.

His mind seemed to be drifting away on some strange tide pulling it from where his focus could balance all the criteria he would normally assess to make his decision; only his instinct was left, his gut feeling. He had sensed the damage in the people he had seen in the streets of Straam that very day. He had shuddered at the deep emptiness of feeling and the lack of connection with almost everything within and beyond bodies and minds violated by these intrusive chemicals. But if this was at the root of the darkness he had felt, or even some external contributory factor allowing it to thrive and spread through one devastated soul at a time surely, he would have to know how it was working. He looked around at the faces staring down at him and into Mariella's eyes as he placed the pills onto his tongue. A can of beer was thrust into his hand and he took a long swig washing the pills down into his body. There was a huge cheer from the surrounding entourage and Mariella took her pill with a grin and gave him a quick kiss on the cheek.

"So, take me to the party, beautiful boy. I think it is time for you to see how we have a good time in the city!"

Music and laughter and the loud shouting conversations continued to fill the bus. It rose and fell and vibrated, thumped through the structure of the enclosed space as it wove its way onward. It was separated now from the glimpses Okino caught of the people who walked on the streets outside. He started to notice all the light around him, where it was intense and where it made shadows and where it was completely absent. The streetlamps streaked the world outside and he thought he could see all the colours in the white lights flashing past. There were pools of warmth and illumination, a group of people in a moment negotiating their world, frozen for ever in a pose or a stance never to be seen again but burnt there offering the joy, or the sadness or the frustration, anger, shock, exhilaration, concentration, compassion, blank expression without any contact. He was in a tube of frightening potential danger racing onward through this city he previously could never have imagined in his most surreal and fragmented nightmares.

But it was all right now; everything was finally going to be all right. The world was a beautiful self-regulating paradise governed by an eternally burning star giving life and love to all who could reach out and find it in the light surrounding them. Soon they would find it in the beautiful light pulsating through their minds evolved and conditioned to respond to it beneficially, progressively, so as they came to relish it and as they became more accustomed to it, understood it's nature, as it fell all around them, illuminating everything that had come to be as a result of it's being there.

And the glowing life force, the energy, the inexplicable higher state, it was always there in the light. In some layer of it, some echelon where it had come to dwell. No not dwell more like pervade or emanate like the scent of blossom on a spring breeze, perhaps it had drifted many miles, or even across an Ocean and you would notice when it wasn't there because the colour would fall out of the light, leaving it without the contours defining it. Like a face without a smile. If it hadn't been there it would be like when the Star goes behind a cloud and the warmth goes and an unsettling, chilling wind rushes in as the pressure drops, blows across your face and the joy would lessen, some unexplainable magic would be gone.

It holds radiant eternal moments you are able to capture in the depths of your soul. They shine through your firmament guiding your future travels in the beautiful light, filling you with love day after day, through the long dark nights of winter, in all your despair and the damage you have suffered from the ones who have not been bothered to find, or who have dismissed as irrelevant where your light is shining. The light is indivisible, has no end and wherever it falls there will be life and eventually understanding of it must arise because its ultimate destination is to know the true wonder of all it has come to be.

As these thoughts flowed through him, he felt a swell of well-being and happiness rising in his being and when he closed his eyes it was like he was sitting in the Star shine of a beautiful summer's day. He looked around at his new friends laughing and joking and saw through the rough exteriors to the innocent children they had grown from. They had applied this outlandish protection to shield them from the world they had found which had threatened and diminished them and their dreams. He realised all this experience was now the chemicals finding the pathways through his veins and into the areas of his mind where such feelings could be activated. For now, he would not worry about the implications of this for the survival of his world, because he could not, for here there was no threat, no approaching cataclysm there was just warmth and light shining through and into everything and everybody.

The streets became increasingly filled with crowds of young people on their way towards their chosen entertainment for the night. The destinations became obvious as a concentrated crowd was massing around an entrance or an orderly queue appeared to stretch down a street. Here the bus would stop and two of the entourage would leave the bus. They were instantly surrounded by young people thrusting their money in the form of a low denomination notes towards them. Each note was taken and calmly exchanged for one of the yellow 'Sunshine' pills. When the pills had been consumed, the single-minded efforts to get into the club were resumed and the bus continued its journey through the streets of Straam.

Okino sat with Mariella half within the party happening around him but mostly staring out of the window into the streets of Straam as they flew past. The streets were now lit by the vast lighting towers punctuating the pavements at regular intervals. The neon advertisement signs burning corporate logos into the minds of the people walking under them, reinforcing their power and their need to be identified with. Vast video screens stretching across the lower floors of the skyscrapers ran films of graphically manipulated models enjoying all the supposedly life enhancing products available in the shops below. Now illuminated from within and with the added height of the bus it was easier for Okino to see into the shop floors.

He had been to smaller shops and supermarkets with Mariella and had not ceased to be amazed at the amount of food in particular on offer to the inhabitants of Straam in their everyday lives. The late-night shoppers wearily making their way home from their work with the bags of food they had bought from the convenience stores, now had to dodge the random swerving and possibly perceived as disrespectful actions of the young people on the way to the clubs. They were shocked by the drunken swaggering and boisterous language of the boys and the girls who had virtually nothing covering any part of their bodies. They were sober and tired and were hoping their own children would not be taking the substances that appeared to be fuelling this discourteous behaviour but feared they probably were. Then they hoped they would not be exposed on their night out to the desperate forces they were told were at work in the underworld of the city in the clubs and the bars where they went but feared they probably would.

All through the day Okino had sensed this fear. It seemed to be an accepted part of life in the city and now he had heard Brett's story he knew how real it was; the monster lurking on the outskirts waiting to pounce in an unguarded moment or even worse actually stalking behind them continually, or embedded entirely in every aspect of their lives waiting for some circumstance of their own making or possibly beyond their control that could turn their lives upside down in a very short space of time and send it spiralling out of the little control they thought they had had.

So now Brett had become part of the underworld he himself would have feared and avoided when he walked the streets or his children were out in the clubs. The monster had struck, destroyed the life he had built for himself, his family and all the employees who had come to depend on him and in the process it had revealed the illusion in which he had been living.

And here was Mithrael again playing some ambiguous role. Was he continuing the intent he had when he had wrecked the plans of the dragons by bring the forces of darkness deeper into Arimathea? They had imagined they could set the human race on a path avoiding all of this but here was one of their own weaving it through her lost children. Meanwhile the inhabitants of Straam went on with their lives amongst the images flashing down from the screens above them, embedding the mantras of the illusion deeper and deeper into their tired minds and consciousness.

Zanda had turned the bus into a side street, parked it and turned off the engine. The people who had remained on the bus now started to dismount into the street below. Mariella and Okino followed. They were soon walking through a crowd of young revellers waiting to enter what appeared to be the largest of the venues so far. They could hear loud thumping music quite clearly out here on the street. Zanda led them up to the entrance where he talked confidently to the two large doormen. They appeared to be sharing a joke and smiled briefly before clapping Zanda on the back and pushing him between them into the club. Although eyed suspiciously by the doormen the rest of Zanda's crew with Okino and Mariella followed him in to jeers of frustration from the people waiting in the long queue.

Inside there was a vast hollowed out space stretching four storeys high. Okino could see balconies stretching off into the distance where people could be seen drinking, talking and observing the space below. He slipped easily through the people who had already entered and followed Zanda and the rest of the crew, who were instantly approached for 'Sunshine', to a long bar which was already two or three people deep. Zanda was able to walk straight through them up to the bar. He was clearly well known here and was either highly respected or highly feared. Somewhere in the distance there was a monstrous sound system filling this vast urban cavern with an eerie pounding electronic synthesised soundscape. Multiple searing coloured stray lasers flashed through the space above, bounced off reflective walls and ceilings and stroboscopic light flashed across faces and bodies slowing and distorting movement and time into separated and discontinuous episodes.

Okino felt an intense excitement rise out of the easy comfortable light filled state into which he had drifted on the bus. Mariella too had felt the change in the atmosphere and with a huge excited grin took Okino's hand and pulled him from his awestruck standstill contemplating his latest experience in what seemed to be the actual belly of the beast, through the crowd towards the music. As the music came nearer the volume seemed to increase exponentially and the crowds of people became denser and altogether less static. Now Okino knew what they had come for as he saw and heard and felt the sensations going on around him. The enormous sounds of the synthesised music now thunderous, soared and levelled with strange harmonics and counter beats, etheric lyrical chants cut through, above and under, chased away into the distance and came blasting back tenfold raising each time each minds capacity for exposure to extreme and joyful sensation.

All this convergence of sound was timed to be dramatically mixed into the laser show, continually flashing, stroboscopically through the drifting ice and smoke. The beat adapted and rose and fell assaulting his senses now heightened into a continual vast rapturous moment. He thought he would explode into the night, into the world, disappear into the lasers and the ice and the thumping sound, like the vast cruise ship sailing out of Zedocha into the moonlight onto the endless ocean of the Universe and into its' sheer throbbing rotational rhythmic exploding magnificence.

Although these sensations flooded his mind with an expanded elation, he became more and more aware that nothing here was real. His ability to live and be within his own consciousness would not allow the illusion of the synthetic drugs and the manufactured music to totally transport him as they had the revellers around him. Occasionally he would catch a glimpse of the minds that had given themselves over to the trance the music had initiated in them. They had no reason to resist. This is what they had come for; to be taken out of their lives and all the monotony and the servitude of their mind-numbing existences. Here the terrifying psychopathic ego maniacs who controlled them, who held them in fear all of their working days were far, far away forgotten in the waves of ecstasy now engulfing them. For these hours they forgot the stresses and strains of the struggle they undertook every day to hold their place in this city, relinquished control of their senses to the manipulators of this crashing, roaring, flashing, vibrating sonic environment where they would dance themselves beyond their exhaustion with a thousand other souls deep into the night and early morning.

As Okino had these thoughts and realised the club was just another extension of the illusion the entire city was under he heard a new sound calling through the clouds of dry ice surrounding him, the infinite sound that would always summon him to reverence, call him to look into the skies to see the spirit creature who was flying high above him. It was the unmistakeable call of the eagle. The incessant beat of the dance music was faded slowly out and the eagle called again, filling the space with its distant melancholy against the background of one ethereal chord it soared and echoed. Then a new rhythm started, the single electronic thud was replaced by the rhythm of many carefully orchestrated single drums. It was soon enhanced by a haunting chant of many different voices, punctuated again by the calls of the eagle. The chant and the drums gathered intensity and soon the children of the city were dancing again, with a new enthusiasm as they became enchanted by this new sound. They soon hooked into the chant and soon the vast space was filled with the pure and ancient sound of the drums accompanied by a throng of voices joined in the oldest form of human song. Okino caught Mariella's eye, she was looking back with an open-mouthed grin of astonishment on her face. She also had recognised the chant and Okino shouted into her ear...

"Have I lost it completely or is this the chant from our night in the dragon cloud stone circle?"

She laughed as she began to dance as she had danced when she had been wrapped in the wolf skin that night perhaps many thousands of years before and joined with the rest of the tribe to celebrate the first kill of the new hunter.

"Yes Okino, I do believe it is. How did you do that?"

He flung back his head, his arms held out and laughed in wonder, at all that was happening to him and then flung himself into the dance, surrendering now finally to these new rhythms which he recognised and pulled him out of the illusion back to the plains where the stars hung in their infinite dome reflected now in the thousands of crystal white lasers piercing the translucent layer of misty smoke now surrounding them. The rhythm was reaching the thunderous crescendo he remembered from the night when the dragon had emerged from the fire and surrounded the tribe's people.

Here in the heart of the city of Straam he felt an intense but gently shimmering light gradually moving through his consciousness, overwhelming the synthetic high of the drug he had taken, replacing it with the well-being and happiness he had always felt when he was in his mountains looking out over his world and the eagles were floating above him. He could see Mariella was having her own experience of the light and all around him he saw everyone had also crossed the etheric bridge into the light, into the sound with every and any part of their bodies that could move or shake rhythmically, into this new rapture the club had supplied for them.

There was no question or reason or excuse now or any meaningful explanation, so Okino and Mariella gave in to the bliss on offer to them here and started to bounce and sway and gyrate into the light with a thousand other souls and the soaring thunderous sound of the infinite Universe as it began to unravel all around them.

Chapter Sixty.
The Rising.

The dragon continued to merge his soul with the consciousness of Arimathea from which he had been separated for so long. In his explorations around the planet he had found the beauty and the wonder was still prevalent. The misery had increased as had the horror of destruction and decay. But now there was a new complexity the humans had brought to the world through their growing ingenuity and vision. The planet had always been evolving and this often meant added layers of complexity in the processes involved. But here was a new kind of evolution which he found intriguing. Their own creation of a mechanistic society denied so much of the world in which it existed, separated them from it but in reality had been drawn from it, was powered by it and as much as they felt they controlled it, the dragon knew they still were all very much dependent on it.

As he explored he was surprised to find a few isolated tribes of humans living as they had done for thousands of years; Still eking out a meagre life in some of the most inhospitable parts of the planet where the mechanistic world would not or could not live. In the deepest jungles and the widest savannah lands, the hottest deserts, they lived apart with the understanding and the wisdom that had sustained them in these most inhospitable of places for as long as anyone could remember. They lived as spirits in the spirit world of Arimathea. They saw everything around them and everything they attempted and achieved to be part of her ever-expanding knowledge of the greater universe. This knowledge had been passed to them by their elders through the myths and legends their tribes had carried.

The knowledge held that every tree, every plant, every breeze, every wisp of sand in the sand dunes or every ripple on a pool or wave on an ocean was a reflection of her. They found resonance with the spirit animals with whom they shared their world and saw them as further intermediaries between themselves and Arimathea. The results of their own actions and those of the people around them also were seen to be deeply embedded and a reflection of Arimathea. They had no doubt she was growing as they grew. She hurt as they hurt. They had no reason to think anything else. So, they did as little as they could to hurt or disrupt her processes and always considered the repercussions of their actions in their wider world. She was not separated from them, she and they were living and breathing intricately as part of her, like the animals and the trees and the winds and the rains as part of her growth. They learnt about her and their own journey as they watched this growth in everything they saw, felt and heard.

So, they grew with her. Were respectful of her in everything they did as if she was their mother who held them gently in her arms. They knew how sensitive she was and how perfect she had become as they watched and took part in the world around them. They knew how easily a life could become more difficult in the delicate balance she held. They had always dedicated their lives to her increasing well-being. Everything they did was with this in mind.

They saw if she was flourishing then it was more than likely they would be. In the winds and the storms which could bring such devastation they saw her awesome and unassailable power. This power was hers ultimately and they understood and respected it and realised it was also theirs to relish, wonder at and celebrate. But this way of life was under threat and could soon be lost forever if the greedy machine world eventually discovered there was something under their land it needed.

There were many who now lived in the shadow of the cities which were growing at a colossal rate in the lands around Arimathea. They farmed and maintained their traditions as they had done for generations. They used animals in the fields growing rice and corn where they could. The children were taught in the schools but often worked with their parents in the fields when they were strong enough to do so. This way of life was always under threat as the cities came closer and closer and often the land on which they had lived since anyone could remember was absorbed mercilessly into the outskirts of the advancing city. They were often evicted from their land and given accommodation in the huge tower blocks which were being built cheaply, to accommodate them. They were then given work operating machines in the factories constructed to make products and parts for the complex machines operating in more affluent areas of the world. They were given low wages so the products they made could be sold at prices to compete in the richer countries which demanded ever cheaper products for their own populations.

Taken from their villages and support networks they attempted to carry on the traditions they had held for so long. They were able to buy their own food and goods from traditional markets which had grown up in the cities; supplied by the rural populations who had not yet been absorbed by the process of urbanisation. So, the older generations although now living in the concrete jungles provided for them and enslaved by the voracious machine world were able to preserve some aspects and connections with their previous lives in the city.

Increasingly however the younger generations were tempted deeper into the city way of life. Here they were able to further embed themselves into the benefits they could see from fully embracing the machine age. If they were lucky they were offered training in the latest technologies enabling them to work in the better paid areas of the technology industry. They worked in enormous telephone call centres answering calls from distant lands from consumers who had problems with their broadband connection or their faulty washing machines or their lapsed car insurance. With computer skills they worked as programmers creating electronic computer games or operating on the web undermining the global markets for the services they could provide more efficiently to companies on the other side of the world who were always willing to undermine their own people to make their service more competitive.

As their earnings rose they were soon leaving behind the traditional ways. They followed the global trends and emulated the lifestyles they believed were being led by people in the richer countries. They wore the fashionable clothes sewn together by the children of countries in similar positions to their own and ate manufactured food from the supermarkets. They threw away the packaging without a thought as to where it would end up. They bought cars to drive across their already dangerously polluted cities to their airconditioned offices. They began to fly to other countries for their holidays into the already over-crowded polluted skies where they marvelled at the lives of the people who were living there. They absorbed their entertainment through the networks set up by the giant global corporations who immediately proceeded to fill their psyches with the fear and the yearning continually fed to the populations of the industrialised world to keep them buying into the material lifestyles they so aspired to. In this way the machine world was assimilating the old world into its evermore destructive ways.

The dragon found this tide of increasing expansion was flowing relentlessly around Arimathea. Their wonderings about how to make their lives easier, less painful and happier had continued to expand. They floated through the mass consciousness until they found the right person or group of people, at the right time, with the will and the means and the circumstances to manifest it in the world. Idea on idea, knowledge growing from and building upon knowledge. Passed on as it always had been, carefully and efficiently communicated, now held and stored in microchips, the new memory banks of the world. Information now too complex and too prolific for any human mind. All the irrelevant wisdom that had brought them here being slowly disregarded as they continued their quest to achieve complete independence from the world their ancestors had so struggled with.

In these affluent areas of Arimathea they could cure all manner of disease, mental or physical, with carefully targeted chemicals. They lived and worked in the skyscrapers of overcrowded cities and received their stories separately through the multi-media broadcasting channels directly into their homes. They traded and communicated through the web of electronics now encircling their world. They still ate animals and plants but now they were grown in farms remote from their cities and they had no connection with this or any of the processes sustaining them. They had become completely dependent on the electronic fuel driven machine world their knowledge had enabled them to build.

In their own evolution these machines had become almost fully automated, programmed in the super brain computers, to do not only the repetitive tasks but also more complex tasks people had previously performed. In fact, most of their lives had been taken over. Now most everyday tasks that would have taken up their time, would have in some way used their creativity or meant having a conversation or used some physical exertion so at the end of the day they had some sense they had achieved something, contributed to their world, made something, grown something, looked after something, seen some transformation as a result of what they had done. These fundamental, life assuring pleasures, their last connections with the beings they had grown into were rapidly disappearing for the people in the developed countries of Arimathea.

But many would never understand this new world growing around them. There was less for them to do because the computers were organising and making everything. If they had nothing to do how would they live? They saw their leaders were gaining more power and wealth as a result of the machines they had brought into the world. They started to realise what was happening to them and the dragon felt a new wondering was starting to surface and float through the consciousness of the human race.

"Perhaps we have got this wrong. Perhaps we have allowed all this technology to go too far. It seems to have fallen into the wrong hands. It is not helping us or making our lives better as we had been promised and perhaps we have been fooled again because it seems everything in our lives and our direct surroundings and the world beyond is deteriorating. For the moment we are managing but it is getting harder and many of us really aren't. There have been global economic crises but when they are over and we are deeper in debt as a result, everything goes on as before. There are conflicts across the world being caused by injustice and inequality any one of which could erupt into a serious war. Every year the storms are getting worse or some other part of the world has been hit by a drought or catastrophic flooding. There are fires burning out of control for longer. As a result, refugee camps are full of displaced hungry people fed by international charities unsupported by the corrupt governments who have caused the crisis that have put the there. Still the leaders of the world talk about growth and promises that our lives will get better! Has this all gone too far and is it not time we had a rethink?"

The dragon was falling back into his sleep deep in the caverns of the planet and joining his dream into the cathedrals of Arimathea's crystal frequencies. The creative power in the strength of the light was reflected in the astounding nature of the world he had found on his visit to the surface. Life had taken hold here on this planet like never before. There was so much happening. It seemed every possible area was developing and expanding. The extraordinary nature of all he had seen filled him with a new enthusiasm and determination. It had given him hope that a way to curb the powers of Oblivion could be found as he contemplated a developing evolutionary thread as strong as he had ever seen before.

The arrival of Okino the monk from the Dragon temple, with his ability to move through the layers of existence and the dimensions of space and time and to an extent channel his dragon powers through those dimensions surely had to be seen as a powerful new ally for the creative powers of light in the eternal struggle against Oblivion and its dark intention to return to the original silence. Also, Mariella, perhaps as strongly as anyone on her world had heard the call of Arimathea and had decided to respond and start her journey to find Okino and connect him into the story that had come to her.

Now they had moved together and talked together and allowed the legend to rise through them. They had been able to release the curse that had been held over their world. Now the effects of their journey and the discoveries they had made were already being felt across the surface of Arimathea. Since his broadcast from the cruise ship many more incidents of fascinatingly revealing animal behaviour had been noticed by a media ready to consolidate on the raised global interest in this new development. Perhaps this was the revelation for which everybody had been waiting. Their planet was alive and conscious in ways they could never have imagined and it was calling out to them. People were responding to the perceived cry for help from the animal kingdoms as they continued to hear about the relentless destruction of their world. The global aid organisations were receiving unprecedented sums for their conservation work and even politicians had sensed a movement in the nature of the debate and had started to adjust their policy announcements. In all of this the dragon sensed a convergence, a chain of events that had the possibility of sending reverberations deep into the future.

Now, however, unsurprisingly Okino and Mariella had been led to Mithrael where he was living in the heart of the city. Merilon had hoped he would not have to reveal how he had become central to the story but now the threads were converging so rapidly he had no alternative. Okino would have to endure the most harrowing and terrifying dream the dragon would ever have to send him.

Part Three
Spirits of the Desert.

Chapter Sixty-One
Mithrael the Dragon.

Mariella had called the taxi from the club in the early hours of the morning. The energy in the club had shown little sign of winding down as new streams of young people continued to arrive, possibly from closing venues nearby. When the tiredness had found its way through the stimulants and the exhilaration of dancing together with hundreds of energised young people to the powerful music, they wearily made their way up to one of the many bars in the balconies surrounding the hall. As they drank water thirstily they noticed Zanda on a table further up the balcony. There were a number of girls and another male at the table who were clearly not from his renegade community, a number of whom could still be seen peddling the yellow 'sunshine' pills. Zanda himself had left his long black leather coat at the door and had tied back his long dark hair. Judging by the clothes he was now wearing he was clearly not living rough. He laughed and joked with the girls who had wrapped various parts of their under clothed bodies into the close proximity of his own. He was completely immersed in their company.

Okino and Mariella were able to study him without too much fear of being caught in such close observation. Okino decided he did not look any older than the day he had encountered him when Merilon had been killed and yet that was almost certainly over a thousand years ago. Merilon had greeted him that night as 'brother' but nothing had so far confirmed he was the dragon who had been missing from the meeting in the mountains. The taxi arrived and as they were leaving Mariella and Okino walked past Zanda as they made their way out of the club. He looked up and caught Okino's eye as he walked past. Okino thought there may have been a glimmer of recognition. Mariella kept her head down and marched Okino firmly past so there could be no attempt at communication by either man.

The taxi carried them through the deserted streets back out into the countryside beyond the suburbs. They talked little but stayed close to each other as the events of the day played through each of their minds. Okino felt the intensity of the huge unanswered question whirling through all these thoughts. If Mithrael was not the missing dragon then who else could he possibly be? In his tired sleepy state and partially hypnotised by the passing of the streetlights he smiled and imagined he could feel Merilon in his thoughts. He wondered whether they could all meet early tomorrow for a chat in the beech woods away from this city and the monstrous forces of Oblivion. He had seen and heard plenty of evidence they were concentrated here. Held in the minds of the people of Straam… by whom… by the people at the top of the towers?

The taxi pulled up outside Mariella's house. Both half asleep they made their way quietly through the hall, up the stairs towards their bedrooms.

Mariella gave Okino one of her extended kisses and a long hug and pushed him affectionately into his room where he staggered a few steps before collapsing onto the luxurious bed. The stars he could see out of the window, tiny bursts of light, perhaps a galaxy a million light years away, took him finally out of the day and he fell exhausted into a deep sleep.

Okino drifted through the consciousness he shared with the universe in his dream into that distant galaxy. Across a swirling carpet of light made from a billion stars and their fragmented worlds growing apart, unknowing of each other, unable to bridge the fantastic distances now blending in a glistening spiral of light, he felt the flexing and eventually the distortion of the boundaries holding the fabrication of space and time as he hurtled across the vast expanse of space towards the centre, where he plunged into an abyss of spiralling light. There he evaporated in amongst the infinity of diaphanous honeycombed membranes holding time and everything that had ever happened flowing osmotically together eventually forming only one eternal all-encompassing moment; One moment in which the spark of life glowed through everything. In this moment Okino knew he could remember all that had ever come to be and where it had its place in the growth of all this moment had become.

Each word or smile or birth or death of any kind, every transaction and action, every act of creation or destruction and all the consequences were recorded and accessible in the surrounding glow. As if in the centre of an immense star library, he could feel the weight of the information, knowledge and wisdom stretching out endlessly around him. Each moment was accessible. Each moment could be analysed for the potential it held and its consequences could then be tracked and assessed.

Here he knew one day someone in some form would come and find the time containing Arimathea; to find out what had gone wrong or eventually had gone right. Now he was guided into that time. The time when Arimathea's environment had eventually settled from the mass of seething, raging hell fires welding her together and when in an atmosphere in amongst the soft skins of plants and trees, sentient life had eventually arisen.

Okino was on the edge of a woodland, hiding it seemed in amongst the shadows thrown by ancient trees. Before him was a scene of terrible devastation. Numerous piles of charred timber which had probably not long ago been the dwellings of a small village, still smouldered under the gloom of the leaden skies. Everything was intensely scorched as if a raging fire had been unleashed and exploded across the plain on which it stood. Only the stream running through glistened as it had before, but with a reddish hue …before what.

Okino walked into the burnt village. There was no sound, no birdsong, no breeze, as if the world was holding its breath. Almost immediately he started to find the remains of appallingly butchered men, women and children lying beside their animals where they had been cut down on the paths between their homes. Many of the men had been brutally tortured as they remained tied to upright posts with their heads and other limbs and entrails lying around them. Many charred corpses had remained, almost certainly imprisoned in their houses, as they were burned inside them. Okino caught flashes in his mind of the dreadful violence. The agonising screams of the terribly injured and terribly distressed as they watched helplessly while their loved ones were torn to pieces by dogs or cut to pieces by the savage blades of merciless invaders.

Okino saw tall, muscular invaders in demonic masks and animal furs bound around their bodies streaming up from the sea across the landscape in terrifying waves allowing nothing to live. They were covered in the blood and gore of their victims, raping girls and women, destroying as if in some ancient rite of war and destruction. They came with the anger and fury of some terrible vengeful god they had invented to satisfy their lust for the smell of blood and to completely erase life from the land so only they could be there. Erase all knowledge of the previous race, a gentle race who would shame their barbaric activity. Drain their blood into the ground they had harvested and loved in sacrifice to their gods who had now come to rule. Feed their flesh to the ravens and the crows who were allied to these gods of death and war so their spirits would protect them in this world and the next.

Okino fell to his knees in his dream and vomited onto the charred ground. But it did not help because he could not escape these scenes. He imagined them as his brothers and sisters and the mothers and fathers of his village as if some terrible force had overrun their mountain home and saw them there, grotesquely and brutally murdered crying out, begging them to spare their children as their conquerors sliced through their tender flesh, toughened tendon, sinew and bone, ripping out the life force, expelling it instantaneously, releasing it back without concern or any remorse for what had been lost to the world. A ghoulish spirit of death, unleashed in men by some terrible brew or herb they had distilled, perhaps with wives and children of their own, justified by their need for land or treasure or simply for senseless terrible extermination, had come to a peaceful land to take it for their own.

Okino staggered amongst the horror and came across a single distraught man. He was sitting on his haunches in front of a dismembered woman. He himself was covered in blood and he had the corpses of many of the invaders around him and an axe in one hand and a small golden object in the other. He was sobbing uncontrollably. Okino went over to him and put a hand on his shoulder. The man started and looked up through his long dark hair tangled in blood and tears in a few moments of silence, perhaps expecting to see his executioner. Okino recognised Mithrael immediately. His large stature even sitting here and his swarthy appearance were unmistakeable even in these moments of terrible grief. Okino sat next to him and put an arm around him, closed his eyes and summoned all the love he could imagine passing through him into Mithrael.

In the light of those moments at one with traumatised Mithrael, the deathly silence changed to birdsong. Okino opened his eyes and he was now in a woodland glade. At one end there was a crude dwelling. The walls were made of rough-hewn stone and there was a door made of broad timber planks. The roof rafters were narrowly spaced and crude slates could be seen at the eaves overhanging the wall. They soon were hidden by the layer of turf which had been placed on top now growing wildly with grasses and wildflowers. To the side there was a workshop open at the front but with a similar roof running into the dwelling. The two buildings formed a dog leg arrangement and the ground outlying both had been crudely but effectively paved. Inside the shelter Okino saw Mithrael was working. In the centre of the glade there was a large stone forge, fully alight. Intense heat radiated throughout the glade and sent shimmering waves of searing heat from a bowl of burning charcoal on which was placed a stone crucible. In the crucible glowed molten metal.

Mithrael came out of the shelter and glanced over at Okino on the edge of the clearing. He smiled as he put on a thick leather glove and grasped the metal tongs at the side of the forge, secured them around the crucible, lifted it and turned it carefully to check the consistency of the molten liquid.

"Greetings stranger. How do you come to be here in the depths of this wood at this time?"

Okino walked up to the forge where he could see what Mithrael was doing.

"I am in a dream, Mithrael. I am not sure why I have come here; perhaps sent by your brother, Merilon."

Mithrael looks up and studies Okino and grins.

"Oh yes, I thought I recognised you. It seems the fates have brought us together again.

"What time has Merilon brought me to now?"

Mithrael laughs loudly and the sound echoes out amongst the trees.

"This time now is for you; between everything that has happened and is happening. For some reason it is important for you to know. We have no secrets between each other because essentially we are one creature, different aspects of one spirit that on occasions make different choices, pursues different ends. There have been greater splits between us on other worlds. If you ever get to sit down with Alamistra ask her about the trouble she and the other female dragons caused on Reiminilia. Now that is quite some story.

Ultimately we are all working towards the dream of harmony whenever or wherever it may come to be. However, tyranny and subjugation have always been the ally of Oblivion; It has always existed and long before you humans instigated it upon this world. It arises it seems out of the tension between life and death and in the fear of all the mystery holds. Otherwise you are clever and inventive and also are capable of great compassion. But you have a ruthless streak which can surface when there is power at stake. It is so dangerous and causes so much pain. More than you can possibly imagine. I have watched it with Merilon and all the other dragons taking grip again and again. So, on this world they decided enough was enough and to prevent it's destruction."

Okino looked puzzled.

"So, when did you decide you would not be a part of that?"

Mithrael grinned again as he removed the crucible from the fire and carried it to a stout bench in the shelter where he poured the molten metal into a stone cast. The glowing liquid ran into the two halves of a cast clamped together to form a narrow aperture. Mithrael examined the result closely and seemed pleased.

"…When back there happened; the devastated village where you have just been. It is a long story but I'll make it as short as possible. We always have had the ability to become mortal and live on the surface but the time spans are so massive that once we embed ourselves into a world, we become so much a part of the fabric and consciousness it generally never occurs to us unless something very specific happens. We become deeply connected to the planet and so are able to feel everything happening within and around it.

So, time went on and for the most part through the millennia very little changed. But at this particular time, I had felt something. Eron, the island I was most connected to had a rich and ancient forest covering virtually all of its land. Over the centuries the people who lived there had developed a culture which had been founded on their connection with the trees. They had come to realise their fundamental importance in the transference of energy from the Star and the surrounding universe on and into the planet as their lifecycles continued.

I started to feel this relationship was changing. You must understand the nature of time for us is entirely different. We have existed over billions of turnings and so as a hundred turnings pass we detect little change happening to the surface of your world. But now I felt a sinister tremor which felt different from what I had felt before and it was coming from the forests. Maybe a warning to me from Arimathea. It suggested it would affect my own connection with the people of Eron.

So, I decided to awaken. I quietly transformed and over the next few turnings I gradually assimilated myself into the world. I lived in the forest like this. The people had made villages surrounded by fields. They were connected by trackways but this had made little impact on the forests so far. They had started trading with the lands over the sea and everything had been peaceful for as long as anyone could remember. Local kings and lords squabbled amongst themselves, but the island was often shrouded in a mist and so was protected from invaders. I settled near a village by the sea, made a house like this in the woods. Dragons as you know have knowledge of Fire and I set up my forge and started making things for them, nothing spectacular, everyday things they needed. I had decided this was what I wanted to do for a while, just be mortal, and really feel it and everything it entailed.

But also, something was worrying me about the trees. I retained very little of my dragon power and began to lose contact with my dragon soul in Arimathea but was aware of all the connections I still had and could use but on the whole I became human. I started to speak with the shamans about the forest and found they had the same concerns. They had seen a time when the forest would be cleared and the connection to the sacred groves and the dragons would be lost forever. It wasn't long before we realised what we would have to do.

In the wandering times they had intuitively found the places where our energy flowed close to surface of the lands. They were able to access the inspiration directly from our dreams in those early times and to mark these places they started to build stone circles. They learnt how to bury the stones and align them so the energy from the ground below mixed with the stars to enhance the connection they had found with us, Arimathea and beyond. They built them along the routes on which they travelled and they became significant gathering places for many different tribes on their migrations through the seasons. They were often located close to rivers or lakes and eventually many of them became surrounded by settlements as the transition from wandering to farming gradually took place.

In the forests however the sacred spaces were defined by the huge old trees that had always grown around them. There was no need for stones or alignment because the trees had grown naturally in the energy most conducive for their good health and they recorded perfectly the movements of the stars and the moon through their limbs lacing the skies above. Now it seemed these beautiful natural spaces and their unique connectivity may be threatened. So, I initiated a plan with the Shamans and the leaders of the settlements to build stone circles in the sacred groves so they would not be lost if the forests were cleared.

But the invasions became steadily more prolific and events on the island took a turn for the worse. I had built friendships with them, became part of their tribe although I stayed separate from them. After millions of years of peaceful dreaming I found their activity and continual noise was too tiring for me and I liked to be out here in the woods. But the friendships and our connections became deeper and then inevitably I fell in love with one of their women. It was an amazing time for me to be opened up to such intensity of emotion. We know about love because we know it to flow through everything, to be where everything originated but to feel the bond it can forge between two people was like nothing I have ever experienced in all the universes I have travelled.

The morning the invaders arrived I was out here. I heard the drums and started to make my way towards them expecting perhaps a visitation from another village. I heard the screams as I was walking through the woods and came to the village as it all was happening. These people were no longer warriors and they were quite literally being destroyed. I raised all the dragon power I had retained and fought like a deranged demon the like of which even the invaders had never seen and as you probably saw I killed as many as I could. But soon they had gone and I was left standing surrounded by death and agony. I found my lover, bloody and defiled with her throat cut.

So this was what it was like to be human; if the power of love we had felt between us was the ecstasy, the pain I now felt was unimaginable and indescribable and I lay amongst my friends for many days before some other people who had escaped from another village arrived and found me in the stench. We buried the entire tribe; some fifty people.

So now I had been initiated it seemed into the full range of human emotion including the rage I soon began to feel when I came to realise what had happened. I became involved in the construction of the defences being built around the villages and towns and with the gathering together of a force that could withstand these barbarian attacks at short notice. They settled in parts of the land they cleared and what was left of the population was slowly driven further inland. Eventually armies were raised and we did our best to punish the invaders. The bloody battles went on for many years backwards and forwards across the country until eventually we all lost the taste for war and started to get on again with living our lives with our new neighbours.

But now there were scars of the horrors that had happened. I could not forget; none of us could. The pain went on and on though we buried it as deep as we could, it was there in our dreams when we didn't expect it or with a word or a glance when we weren't expecting, the terror returned. Somewhere then, Okino, I started to have terrible insights into what was happening in the wider universe, in the great Mother Spirit who had yearned for this new state in which all this was taking place; not just here on those battlegrounds and now in our dreams and memories but that it was the nature of all life in this new state. For the promised ecstatic harmony in the far distant future to eventually arise, there would always have to be this suffering as life continually transformed and renewed itself. This continual pain would only be alleviated occasionally by unimaginable bliss, a reminder to us and her why we had started out on this journey.

This pain would be felt across the entire human and animal kingdoms until the harmony, the ultimate fusion between the spirit and solid existence, conscious of itself, was able finally to come to be. Before this all started, there had just been the endless light of pure sacred love flooding through eternity. But now she was feeling this agony through her spirit planet. I started to think that Oblivion must be some part of her yearning to return to the emptiness and the eternity of bliss. Because of my love for her I wanted to stop this relentless suffering as this experiment continued endlessly into the future. It all suddenly seemed so much more unlikely after what I had seen."

The sword had cooled and the molten metal solidified. Mithrael carefully released the newly forged sword from the two casts and placed it in a trough of water. It was black and the edges were ragged. It hissed angrily; steam was released as it stood in the water. Just high enough for Okino to see the strange runic symbols he remembered seeing on the sword he had removed from Merilon. So, here was its origin. Had he been here at its casting? Was the story of Mithraels horrifying experience bound up in its cooling? He wondered if Mithrael would tell him. He asked…

"Is this the sword that you embedded into Merilon resulting in his absence from the world and presumably all the other dragons for all that time?; The time that has brought Arimathea and all the incredible life evolving there to the brink of a new extinction."

Mithrael looked over at Okino. There was no humour now in his eye or any of the compassion he had previously felt. He was again the cold ruthless killer he and Merilon had met in the wood all those years before.

"No Okino, this is not the sword. I made several attempts before the actual sword that could separate Merilon from his beloved Arimathea came into the world! As I was taken from my love!

But this one horrifying event and all I had come to understand about this world and the human race came to guide my thoughts. It was that the human race would have to feel the suffering of Arimathea to allow a great surge of compassion to rise within their entire mass consciousness or certainly some vast majority of it, before any kind of peace could arise again with in the Great Mother. Of course, I had no idea how this could ever come to be in those days and so thought it ultimately impossible.

My motivation began to change and as the bitterness refused to subside, I forgot entirely who I was, who I had been. I was living here in this solid existence and everything else started to fade away.."

Okino started to understand what had been happening while the other dragons had been sleeping and Mithrael had lived as a human being having forgotten his dragon origin. But still everything he had seen did not entirely add up.

"So, you have lived as a human being down through all those centuries and in all that time you have only managed to become a low life drug dealer!"

Mithrael laughed loudly again as he removed the sword from the water in the stone trough. He examined it closely, this metal that had come from her body, feeling down the blade, imagining how it would shine when he had worked it, heating it again and again, in the white heat of the charcoal made from the fallen limbs of these ancient Oaks. So, the forces of the universe flowed: Energy moving endlessly from one state to the next.

"The years passed and even though I had become mostly human and had rarely visited my Dragon hill, I started to feel that soon I would have to sleep, possibly for a long time. A whisper told me what I had to do. I retreated into the distant hills and into the mountains where I found a deep cave in which I felt I would be able to sleep until my life force had been regenerated. Accustomed to sleeping for a million years it felt as if my one hundred and thirty-five years in the cave had lasted no more than a few days. I woke feeling strong with vague memories of why I had woken in this remote place. This became a pattern over the next one thousand years.

"When I awoke, I found a place where I could continue to practice my craft; the knowledge of the smith and their forge was always in demand through the centuries once it had been found. We used the fire of the Star to manipulate the beauty of the metals now being found and mined on Arimathea originally to make weapons or jewellery, things of immense value. But it was also the everyday things that gradually started to transform their lives and their world. Where would you start? Perhaps in the fields where we made the ploughs to loosen the earth and the scythes to cut the corn when it was grown: We made brackets to strengthen their carts to carry the grain to their markets and the ships that carried them across the seas to trade with their brothers in distant lands. This is the alchemy that has transformed the world, here amongst these burning embers; with their ability to dream, invent and make strategies they have brought their wonder into the world.

But I found, of course I had knowledge other men did not. I could make the metals stronger or lighter or gleam in special ways when the star caught them to send a flash of Light to an admiring or fearful eye. These swords became particularly sort after and the richest of the Lords and many of their Kings, would pay handsomely for a blade forged and honed in this forge. I had long forgotten where the knowledge I possessed had come from but as the price increased so did my wealth. Even as war became peace, they came out here and asked me to make them one of my swords. For this is where I have always lived, out in the woods amongst the trees and in the wildernesses away from their continual clatter and activity.

The revolution brought about by Merilon and the other dragons eventually began to sweep around the planet. I still felt the pain of losing my lover. I had carried it through from my previous life and my hatred for the human race had begun to grow. I knew the dragons were trying to end the malaise they saw growing amongst them but as my bitterness festered I only wanted to see it destroyed for ever to bring the peace back to the Great Spirit and the rest of Arimathea. Then I was visited by Samir and we began to orchestrate the downfall of Merilon and the other dragons. The dragons had taken a risk by defying the unwritten laws they had always followed. They had known the possible consequences of becoming mortal and guiding the course of history directly with the power they could wield in the physical world. But they had decided to take the risk. Now it would take some powerful magic to curtail the action they had decided to take. However, I was sure Oblivion would not allow such an advantage to be held for long. There were bound to be repercussions soon and I waited, curious to see what was to happen."

Mithrael paused at this point and for a moment seemed anguished as if there was some conflict within himself which he had not entirely resolved.

"You know as well as I do Okino, the universe is a strange and enormous expanse where energy of infinite description has become transformed into many, many conflicting energies and powers. Perhaps in your legends you would call them spirits. All of which may have interests far back in times beyond even the dragons can remember. We will all have some of that essence, unknown energy deeply embedded in us. But we cannot, no matter how deep we delve and analyse, be sure our motivations are not influenced by those interests that have been lost in the mists of time.

Somewhere in the conflict that ensues amongst all the ideas and the action we take, everything moves forward to somewhere; somewhere in the future."

Okino studied the uncertainty Mithrael had now revealed. He sensed perhaps he was not completely confident the action he took next had been entirely correct or even justified.

"There will always be conflict if we have to choose between two ways leading in different directions. How can we ever know if our actions brought about the necessary outcome? Sometimes we just have to make choices. Who or what guides us or to what ends cannot be known to us and so we have to live with those decisions?"

"Of course, you are right Okino and I have told you the nature of my conflict and how I was acting on the agony I was feeling for myself and the Great Mother Spirit. I also told you I had unexplained abilities, residue from the dragon I had once been. One of these and the most harmless until now, was my ability to travel through the labyrinths into the many parallel dimensions flowing deep into the Universe surrounding us. This has enabled us to travel through the endless emptiness of space on our journey through the eons. My journeys were harmless because I was careful not to exercise any influence on events that may cause ripples through into our own dimension. The labyrinth is a complex weave of inter reaction and connection and consequences are almost impossible to avoid however microscopic the actions taken. But dragons are builders of worlds and the complexity of reaction is what makes diversity and diversity increases the web in which the probability of increase and proliferation exist. In other words, we have always taken risks.

In one of my journeys, I had taken a route through the star fields and was exploring a distant galaxy, searching, for the beginnings of primitive worlds. These can so often provide some insight into the trouble, some complexity that has evolved on this world. There is rarely atmosphere or anything resembling an ecology but because I am travelling in light, below the problems of existing in actual matter a lack of atmosphere will never affect me and of course I have been doing this since time began; unlike the group of souls who I met on one of the worlds I discovered.

I was standing on a cliff edge under a crimson sky streaked with purple clouds looking over a gently undulating orange mirrored sea. It was spitting continuously globules of molten lava into the atmosphere above its surface. It hissed and steamed and lapped with glowing molten consistency on the rocky shore far below. There were islands possibly recently thrust from the unstable mantle below, fins and pointed prominences possibly more slender blocks now dissolved. The islands were encircled by platforms flowing into causeways running back into the hellish brew. Archways and slender bridges had formed between the islands and I inadvertently found myself working out a route over the bridges through this primitive and dramatic landscape. There was a canyon to one side of me. Here was the origin of the flowing molten currents and eddies rippling across the surface.

In the walls of the canyons were the beds of sediment laid over the planet's lifetime. Varying in thickness and colour and solidity as again the acid material had picked out the softer material to leave a relief of horizontal fins in the striations. Other planets loomed like great green spheres high in the crimson sky and threw a peculiar light down onto the sides of the canyon. The light was glinting as it rebounded from something extremely reflective embedded densely over the sides of the canyon.

This is where I saw them for the first time. There was a group of seven of them. Some were sitting resting, feet dangling over the rocky pavement forming the edge of the river below. Others were working at the soft face of the canyon wall, smashing into it with larger rocks. I positioned myself a little further down the river on the path and wandered down to where they were gathered. I watched them for a few moments before making myself known and decided they were trying to extract the shining material that seemed so prolific in the softer striations. It was diamond or something extremely similar and more in this one cliff face than ever would be discovered on Arimathea. I walked over to them and when they saw me, they started back in surprise and probably fear. They had not expected to see another human here and almost immediately signs of worry and stress had appeared when they realised someone else now knew about their discovery. There was some tension to begin with, but I managed to put their minds at ease, although I realised those minds were shattered even then.

We sat and talked about our circumstances and how we had come to be there. We both of course had fantastic stories and so were both as surprised it would seem as the other. There seemed no point in lies or pretence. We had both travelled thousands of light years from Arimathea so there would have to be some extraordinary method behind our journey. They told me they had been scientists, specifically physicists who had become more and more aware of the layered nature of time and space. They had found parallels with what they were discovering in the writings of the old shamans who talked of parallel worlds that could be accessed in deep trances and with the aid of natural substances occurring in the jungles in which they lived.

They pushed deeper and deeper into their theories substantiated with the laws they had uncovered and known only to themselves until eventually they found they could open the doors to the labyrinth through which they could speed themselves out across the Universe. We do it naturally, we always have. Go down below the molecules and the atoms and into the spaces between, evaporate into them. Now, they had found a way of separating their energy and projecting it into the empty spaces at sub molecular levels. However, the dragons had disrupted things in ways Oblivion could waste no time in compensating for. Doors I would say had quite literally been opened for them.

So here they were, having found potentially enough wealth to buy Arimathea. But they had a problem. They were completely lost and had no way of finding their way back. They had come here from some of the farthest reaches of the Universe, the dark places where even stars cannot be born and so where light has never been and where life or any kind of consciousness could never exist. I could see this had affected them deeply in perhaps ways they had not realised and I would have to get them back to Arimathea as soon as possible or they would certainly die as the darkness they had encountered gradually consumed their life force.

Now the impossibility of our meeting was starting to register and again I started to sense Oblivion may have forced these circumstances to resolve its' struggle with the dragons. As I assessed all the circumstances a dreadful thread started to emerge enabling me to link this all together into one ghastly strategy. I realised I may be able to separate the dragons from Arimathea's consciousness to bring nearer the crisis that would finally force the human beings to confront the nature of their world or face their death. I shuddered when I first realised how the powers of Oblivion had so effectively manipulated everything around me. They knew the power I still potentially had to transform and manipulate the circumstances they had offered. They had presented me with the means to come one step nearer to the ultimate peace, free from the agony of physical life, for the Great Mother Spirit.

I took the traveller scientists back to Arimathea to the time when the dragons were still in their council in the mountain and shared my thoughts with them. The dragon hills were being prepared by the rulers of the world who had been delighted to have a strategy for defeating the dragons. But now the scientist shamans convinced them they had the knowledge to completely solve their problem. They demanded their own kingdom: Although they did not plan to have a king. A land then taken from the continent of Tarilana. It lay in the centre of the large southern continent and was surrounded by high mountains which provided a beautiful, naturally defended and temperate land. The scientist shamans demanded to be separate from all the other nations of the planet in every way. No other country would have any jurisdiction in any matter over them, ever, and this was to be enshrined in the law of every nation. In short they would have complete independence. There was immediately a resistance to accepting these terms. A nation state unaccountable to the rest of the community with power they did not entirely understand filled them with foreboding. But the alternative was the rule of the dragons for as long as could be imagined. So, they accepted and the Independent nation state of Zinederland was born.

Then, in those dark nights before the dragons returned, with the knowledge I and the scientist shamans had acquired in our travels across the universe, high on Merilons' hill, I opened a pathway through the labyrinth from those farthest reaches of the universe to each of the Dragon hills and filled them with the unfathomable darkness existing there, infesting the channels of light they used to bring them from their caverns deep in Arimathea. I knew even the dragons would be powerless to penetrate such dark unfathomable emptiness. I cast the final sword on one of those nights with the darkness swirling in the air around me feeding the white heat of my forge in which the precious metals were smelted. Cast it in this stone mould. Then I turned and folded it through the night, hammering into it all the agony I had felt on the morning of the attack on my village and cast in these runes, the name of the dark energy from those distant worlds I had invoked in its' making. Now the human race would have to feel her pain, the pain they had made for her.

I found I had to sleep again after exerting such enormous effort. I still had little knowledge or concern where my abilities had come from, so consumed I had become with this hatred I continued on regardless. Again, I awoke in a distant cave but this time I was surrounded by gold and gemstones. I began travelling the land, eager to find ways to increase the incredible wealth I supposed I had accumulated in some other life.

Eron was at peace again. I saw how the two races who had fought each other so viciously had now mixed together as if it had always been so and now worked beside each other in the fields and the towns. The forest was thinning as more of the land was taken up for the growing of wheat and pasture for animals. Still they visited the old stone rings we had made on the sites of the old sacred groves.

I remembered the problem with wheat had always been the conversion of the hard little husks into the soft flower that would make the delicious bread which had become so important in their diet. However, the traditional watermills while making extraordinary profits from the farmers in the surrounding countryside were struggling to convert the amounts of grain being grown every year.

Windmills were starting to be built to supplement the watermills. I could see how, high on a hill where a strong breeze in the second half of the year was almost constant, a windmill could substantially multiply any investment put into its construction. So, it was I built three windmills high on the ridges looking over to the eastern seas. The fields in their lee were sheltered and well drained providing excellent conditions for the growing of large quantities of wheat. The windmills were a great success and within a few years they had paid for themselves and again I was increasing my wealth. They were also beautiful and much admired. Their great stone bases and their cleverly constructed timber towers and sails brought a new elegance to those hilltops.

When those great sails were turning and I could see a queue of carts unloading their grain into the timber barns standing next to them I felt my pain was beginning to lessen. Here we were thriving, working and cooperating together to feed the people in the towns and villages while they were able to progress their own lives and businesses. But humans are hardy and resilient and they will laugh and joke with their friends as they watch the grain pouring into the mill while they wonder if the weight of the flour being weighed will pay for their farm to continue in the next year after they have paid their expenses, fed their wives and children and paid the taxes and the duties to their Lords.

I continued to work the forge in a large piece of woodland I had managed to save from the axe by buying it outright from a farmer. There was a river running to one side of it and it had been well kept so I built my house in the centre and joined it with a track to the road that went to the town. It had tall ancient Oaks full of song birds, badgers and foxes. Often I would sit in the grove at the centre of the wood and they would wander through and I'd watch them flitting through the high branches and I found my pain was being lost in the beauty she was allowing me to share, as she wrapped herself around me, wanting me to love her, wanting to soothe the horror I had felt, tempting me back from the dark path I had laid into the future.

Swords were now less in demand and I continued making the everyday things that were continually needed. Although every now and again in the cover of darkness a noble youngster would come to my house and ask me to make him one of my swords. I saw the characteristics in them that would potentially bring the terror back to the land. They liked to appear strong and fearless but I knew they needed to prove themselves; to their fathers, to their potential wives and all their generation, but most of all to themselves. They had been raised by their fathers to fight and rule and now when they had been asked to keep an eye on how productive the fields were or getting the taxes in, they were bored and disgruntled and itching for a fight. I watched them slicing through the air with the swords I had made for them, imagining the limbs or heads they would sever. I knew from watching them that soon there would be a reason to fight again and the agony would return to the land; to the wives who had not cared whether they were strong enough to fight in a war but wanted them to love and come home to raise their children or to their mothers to whose hopeless lives they had brought meaning and joy beyond measure.

Sure enough an uprising would eventually break out and the senseless slaughter would begin again. Rebellions were frequent against the ruling lords but were often quelled as fast as they arose, brutally and without any mercy. Again, the hatred would increase amongst the people towards their rulers. It constantly simmered waiting for some flashpoint to throw the countryside into chaos again. In between these ineffectual revolutions there was a constant threat of invasion from their neighbours whose lands had become crowded or less productive or suddenly less attractive than those beyond their own borders. They would invade and if they had worked out a sensible strategy for their conquest they would, as the invaders had done before, assimilate the land and eventually merge into the general population. Things would change again as their culture was absorbed or became dominant.

Soon the horror of those invasions was again forgotten and life would resume. But the wars that started to change the plight of the average human were those in which the rulers themselves argued about the power and the jurisdiction they had in the land and ultimately over their people. A new leader would emerge with some new interpretation of the old or new religion and so would claim to be the rightful king. If this new interpretation increased the underlying discontent of the generally subjugated population then they would again rise up against the forces of their rulers.

The interpretation that always had caused the most anger was the claim they had been chosen by their god to hold and direct his power through the land. Disagreement frequently arose as to how this power should be disseminated. Particularly unpopular was the supreme power allowing the king to tax the general population to near starvation to fund his own ridiculous expeditionary conflicts in the name of his god in faraway lands. Also, when the king decided this supreme power sent by a god, gave him and his supporters the right to live in luxurious palaces when the average family was living in abject poverty. The feeling was generally this god and so his representative were not seeing the situation fairly. This divine right was starting to wear very thin and a number of successful and bloody rebellions took place in which entire populations rose up against their kings. The small armies they held and were retained by their supporters were ineffectual against these mass revolutions and kings started to be executed.

These revolutions marked a huge change in the way human society was organised. The power to organise what and how things would happen and who would pay for it was slowly handed over to representatives of the general population. As a legitimate taxation system started to evolve, wealth that normally would have been taken by the king could be amassed by anyone who had the nerve and the enterprise to devise some method to attain it, without having it instantly taken away by a power hungry despot with a spurious mandate from a fictional god.

It was during this new time I emerged from one of my hibernations. I had stored my own wealth in Zinederland where the construction of the new country had been well underway funded by the enormous wealth the shamans had amassed from the sale of the diamonds we had transported back through the labyrinth. They had made it into a beautiful place. Up until then the population had lived in a primitive rural economy with only minimal contact with the world beyond. Now their towns and villages and the houses they were living in had been upgraded and boasted the latest sanitation and provided infinitely superior accommodation.

The older people were able to work as they always had in the valleys and the high pastures with their animals if they wished but the younger people were now offered employment in the industry that had arisen through their unique new relationship with the world outside. The scientist shamans had indulged their fantasies and built beautiful castles on particularly startling sites. These were the public buildings where any of the population could go to use the public baths, halls and libraries that had been provided within them.

Unfortunately, the scientist shamans had died early deaths as I suspected they might after being driven out of their minds by the darkness that had grown and engulfed their consciousness. But not before they had founded an amazing country and established a society within the people of Zinederland who would guard the secrets and the wealth of their original success. As an original member of the conspiracy I had become a founder member which had brought me immense privilege and advantage in the world. My continual appearance with little or no sign of ageing meant the secrecy of my identity had to be sworn to be upheld by each new member who was admitted into the society.

The true wealth of Arimathea had now started to emerge as individuals who had amassed funds from their endeavours formed companies and organisations to trade around Arimathea. They were growing a crop in one country sailing it around the world to make a product cheaply, sailing it again to sell it on for vast profits in another part of the world, a continual flow of trade amassing value and so ultimately greater profit at every stage of its journey.

As the evolution of the global economy became more complex so the banking industry had started to become the new force across Arimathea. They funded the enterprises and held and then redistributed considerable amounts of money in the form of loans being generated by them. Most of these new enterprises eventually found their way to one of the many banks founded in Zinederland to store their own profits and borrow the sums they themselves could not guarantee. The transactions they had started to make were immune from the laws of the rest of the world and they would pay no tax on those profits. There was literally no limit to the amount of money to be generated and invested from this tiny land and the young people were mainly employed to count and organise the money. As the wealth of Zinederland increased it found itself with the ability to fund more and more of the transformative developments happening on Arimathea.

The vision of the scientist shamans had been uncanny. I often wondered whether on their travels they had managed to access the hallowed halls of the Time Lords. But they had never talked about it, would not, and it is a secret that had died with them.

So, you see Okino I have not just become a drug dealer. I just like doing that because it keeps me outdoors and in touch with the people who are struggling as a result of all this. In fact, as a founder member of Zinederland Incorporated I have become a fairly powerful individual, because guess where all the governments of the world come to when they want to borrow some money and they don't want anyone to know about it!"

Chapter Sixty-Two
High in the Tower.
The next morning high in the steel and glass tower on the forty-second floor of the Wade Corporation skyscraper Harri Wade sat at the end of his long boardroom table and watched silently as his executives took their

places. On each of these occasions they would have to justify the huge salary he was paying them in terms of the business they had brought or kept in the company. Many of them were younger than he would have liked but they were the strong ones and often the most ruthless, confidence and arrogance intact, as yet undamaged by catastrophic error or unforeseen misfortune. Something would eventually arise unexpectedly and bring them down, down where he would decide what to do with them, weigh them up, give them another chance or strip them of everything and have them thrown to the wolves waiting out on the sidewalks and in the bars they would visit to stop the pain, shut out the confusion and the embarrassment.

Then there were his seasoned campaigners. The older executives who had been through the pain and so had become a little less arrogant and slightly craftier; they knew the options in any given situation instead of the one the youngsters would always adopt. They knew the strategy of driving the hardest bargain, using the immense power of the corporation behind them to bring in their profit margin could come back to haunt them if the tables should ever be turned. But those margins had to be made and their strategies may seem less brutal as the customer was tempted and lulled into a sense that his life could only improve by what was on offer. Only to find once the deal was done, the contractual agreement into which they had entered was as tight and unrelenting as any vice.

They were grateful to him if he gave them another chance. He knew the pressure they were under. He had been under it all his life and it had brought him here to his tower overlooking the central avenue of Straam. But every night his fear was the same, as it always had been. All this unimaginable wealth he had accrued had never managed to subdue the fear he could lose his place here, amongst all this privilege which really meant nothing to him. He would then be returned to the merciless brutality in which he had spent much of his childhood and teenage years. These people he employed, they were the educated ones, the lucky ones from secure families who had nurtured and guided them successfully into their adult lives. He needed them to charm and speak intelligently to his clients, understand the vagaries of the economics and the complexities of the world in which he operated.

Ultimately, he needed them to turn up every-day and have the nerve to do what he expected of them. He had brought in the damaged ones before, helped them, given them a long leash to learn, to gain confidence but rarely had they responded. Any kind of pressure brought back the terror they had been through and they nearly always became self-destructive and unreliable. There were few as strong as him. But he knew they were out there in their own towers looking across at him, watching the financial indexes waiting for him to make a mistake, waiting to pounce if he should show any kind of vulnerability. For the moment this was his jungle and it had to stay that way.

His own terror had always stayed with him. The slamming of the door in the high rise flat and the click of the bolt as the key turned leaving him imprisoned again had resonated through his life. Then he would be alone for another day with only the long wave radio to keep him company. More often than not there had been little food and he had been hungry until his father had returned later that night having been drinking, perhaps with a strange woman and some paltry scraps of food.

He had lived his life through the voices that had come to him on the airwaves. The voices were his friends and his teachers. They explained to him about a world which he presumed must exist beyond the streets of the dank city which he could see from the tiny balcony. There were few people in their lives. His father had become isolated through the nature of his own relationship with the world and the terrible shadows and demons stalking through his own mind which he continually attempted to suppress with any substance he could lay his hands on.

Harri knew little of his business or how he obtained the money to fund this continual abuse. There were visits from a small band of men who Harri had presumed were his father's colleagues or partners in crime; men as dishevelled and brooding and silent with a similar air of terrifying danger with which he associated his own father. They would gather around the table in the spacious living room and drink and play cards. This was when his father had been as happy as he had ever seen him and some of the few times he could relax in his room with his radio on and drift off into some distant land where he was able to listen to a reporter or a journalist who had uncovered some fascinating story about an individual or a community and their place in the world and how they were able to maintain it or not.

Often the evenings would end in some terrible argument and perhaps violence and again his fear would rise. For if his father was angry or frustrated he would direct this anger towards his vulnerable and defenceless son on whom he would inflict terrible beatings. It was not the pain which upset Harri so much as the presumption that his father appeared to hate him so much. Often in these episodes his father would curse his missing mother for deserting them. He had little knowledge of her other than from these raging diatribes. But he longed for her to return; for her to batter down the door of the flat one day and take him to a new and beautiful life where he knew she lived in a white villa beside a sunny coast with blue seas and blue skies. Where he would go fishing with her kind husband and when they returned, they would cook their fish on the beach as the star sank into the sea. He would watch the falcons flash through the dusky skies pursuing the fat bugs and later at night the bats as they came out from their mysterious caves deeply eroded into the rocky coastlines. But she never came and he feared she never would for fear of crossing paths with the man whose mystery he imagined, she had fallen for and perhaps who she hoped she could heal with her love.

So, these Star kissed beaches and his angelic mother who would be kind and look after him were at the centre of his fantasy world and perhaps preserved Harri's young life through the terror of living with a drunken criminal. But it was not only the beauty existing in the world that came across the airwaves and began to furnish Harri's fantasy. There was a world that was being ravaged by wars and ever-expanding corporate forces. In the dramas and the documentaries he heard there were always people at the mercy of these larger forces over which they had no control; The soldiers fighting in the wars, the refugees who were forced from their homes, to live in refugee camps in a neighbouring land where they were resented for being there or the young men who were fighting for freedom. There were the miners in the deep opencast mines that left the gaping wounds in the surface of their world that could be seen from space and people who drove bulldozers through the rainforests, the people who flew the aeroplanes, drove the juggernauts, sailed the vast cargo ships around the world full of the products the restless, directionless populations were so desperate for. The people who looked after the pits the obsolescent products would be thrown into when their life was over.

There were the engineers, artists and designers who dreamt the products up. There were the film makers and the journalists who interpreted everything as they thought it was happening or how they wanted everybody to think it was happening and fed it back in whatever form the people who were paying for it saw fit. There were the communities on the edge of this world who had little knowledge about the technology which had transformed the world beyond their jungle or their ice cap or mountain. They were puzzled when they were suddenly visited by explorers who came with the film makers who wanted to tell their story to the world but gave them little but trinkets and their diseases.

Never far from all these stories were the police and the law enforcement trying bravely it seemed to hold back the tide of decay as the gangsters and the corporations continued to increase their grip and squeeze on the general population. Even here there was corruption on astounding levels. He heard about policemen at the highest levels who had been discovered taking beneficial career advancement to overlook some vital evidence in a corruption scandal involving corporations or governments. Perhaps they had arrested a politician who had appeared so good, so upstanding that thousands of people had voted for him or her but whose life had subsequently been proven to be a mire of corruption and deceit.

Every conceivable aspect of the web of human activity on Arimathea came to Harri through his radio and every time he heard one of these stories he put himself at the centre of it. All these people, their responsibilities to their job, their world, the suffering they caused or was brought down upon them and all the people who were influenced or affected as the story continued, registered in the mind of Harri Wade. But because he was already a victim, the people he became fascinated with most in his terrified world were the ruthless dictators and the powerful uncaring chief executives who cared only for the margins their businesses were producing. The gang leaders and the drug lords who were prepared to have entire sections of the community addicted to the drugs they were pedalling to fuel their outrageous lifestyles. He relished the ability he had in these his fantasy worlds to exert control over his fellow soldiers, the rest of his desert tribe, a network of gangs and all the criminals like his father that controlled a city of people who although entirely free, were stupid enough to be controlled and manipulated; almost like they wanted to be controlled, almost like they had given their permission.

These were the powerful people who would never wake up in fear of humiliation or a beating because they controlled their world as a result of their achievements and ultimately through the fear they could hold over those they controlled. So as he grew, regularly beaten by the fists of a viscous cowardly monster, somewhere in Harri's mind isolated in a world where there appeared to be little justice, he decided he would one day be in control of an army, of a corporation, he would be a drug lord, a dictator or the president of a continent or the entire world. It would be his prime motivation and nothing would stop him, it would drive him until the day he died. Then he would find his mother and live with her in the white villa on the beach, go fishing and watch the falcons and the bats as they swooped to devour the fat bugs who were and always had been at their mercy.

But first he needed to escape. Once he had made up his mind he sat in front of the door for the rest of the day. It was solid and well bolted and there was nothing in the flat he could use to batter it down. Eventually he decided he would have to get out when it was open. So, he waited and made his plans, gathered what belongings he had around him and one night waited for his father to return. As the door opened and his father staggered in he bolted around his legs and down the corridor to the stairs at the end. Before his father had worked out what had happened, he was half-way down the stairs to the ground floor and out onto the streets beyond.

So young Harri Wade made his way into the world. At the age of twelve with virtually no experience of the outside world other than what he had heard on his radio, he slipped into the darkness of the Summer's night, allowed it to envelop him and for the first time he became part of the world of which he had only heard tales and reports. The fear he felt of being alone and cold with nowhere to sleep greeted him with mild panic after the brief euphoria of his escape. However, he soon realised, the fear with which he had always lived had now disappeared without trace and suddenly this new fear when he looked more deeply felt much like freedom to him. Now beyond the walls and the bolted door he swore to himself that nothing would ever constrain him again.

He began to live in the shadows. He learned how to become invisible to the considerable threats which were all around him and in those early days like a wild animal who has been finally abandoned by its parents he was driven by his hunger. The sensation was nothing new to him. In his prison his father would eventually bring him food but out here he had to track it down for himself, find his own strategies, plan and calculate risk against the projected outcome, choose his moment. The city was full of food and all he needed; he just had to get his hands on it.

So, in those early days and years he haunted the open markets where all the food and clothing was easily accessible. Tantalisingly accessible. He learned to move invisibly amongst the crowds as they drifted amongst the food stalls, and when his hunger became worse than he could bare and when a stall holders attention was diverted in pursuance of a transaction he would quickly reach out his hand and take the food he was so desperate for. Then he would be gone, back into invisibility with the fruit or some raw vegetables and find a place back in the shadows where he could eat. Food had never tasted so good and would never again and when he was finished, he would start the process again.

On many occasions he was discovered and had to run for his life but he was fast and learned the backstreets and the alleyways in which he could soon disappear again. Money was the key and while he had none he was as vulnerable to a beating as he ever had been if he was caught. Occasionally he begged, sitting forlornly on the pavements watching for a kindly passer-by to part with some coins. Eventually in a day or a morning these donations may amount to a sum that would buy him a meal but soon he was uncomfortable with this. He was putting himself in a position of dependency and this was the last thing he wanted so he continued with his initial strategy of stealing, living rough and searching for the opportunity that would allow him to have money for himself.

There were many others with whom he shared the streets. There were the numerous adults many of whom were hopeless alcoholics or drug addicts. They were the most dangerous and gathered together in the waste grounds and parks on their self-destructive journeys into the oblivion they had chosen or had fallen into in despair or in a time when they had just stopped caring what happened to them. He soon learned from the other children, for there were also many, he was to avoid these places at all costs to avoid being enslaved by the desperate drug crazed junkies who would do virtually anything to get their fix of drugs every day.

Many of these children ganged together for their own safety. Gangs of various sizes had found old abandoned buildings where they could live safely in their numbers, careful to avoid the continual raids from the junkies. They were led or organised by older teenagers or young adults who often fought for supremacy. Younger children felt safer in these organised collectives and no longer robbed or stole for themselves but anything they stole during the day was pooled in the 'treasury' of the gang and food and necessities were then shared after the leader and his direct followers had taken their cut. Depending on how well the children were fed depended on how long the leaders stayed in power or however long it took for a new leader to emerge.

Harri watched the older teenagers carefully. They continually assessed the performance of their workforce, devising and planning new and different crimes and scams for the children to undertake. They could be kind and compassionate to the little kids but ruthless and merciless if they felt they had been betrayed. The kids on the whole wanted to be in the gangs for here they were safest and so would support their leaders and for the most part would do what they were told. But if the plans became too mad or dangerous then the trouble would start and there would be a challenge. Harri would never be big or strong enough or even crafty enough to challenge for the leadership of one of these gangs. He would need his own henchmen to support him in the battle that would ensue when the challenge finally came. He would have to fight these street kids who were tougher and more ruthless than possibly he could ever be. But certainly, in the future here was an eager workforce willing to follow any leader who could keep them happy and well fed. Even to form his own gang which he felt he probably could, would put him in competition with the established gangs and so war was inevitable either way if he wanted his own army.

But he felt no urge to stay in any of these places now and started to wander for days out in the countryside when he had stolen enough fruit or meat to make a journey to the next city. The emptiness in the surrounding country was strange to him at first but he came to relish the open skies and soft warm ground he could lay on, next to a fire and where he cooked the raw meat in the old pans he had also liberated from some unfortunate store holder who had given chase initially but had stopped when the pain in his chest had given him warning to relinquish those particular items to the great flow of the world. He had smiled to himself as he watched the wild skinny boy dodging his way through the crowd, as agile as any fox or rabbit being pursued by one of his hunting dogs.

Harri remembered many of the people from whom he had stolen. He knew they were in the same struggle as himself and he thought one day he would like to return to those markets and find them and if they were still selling their apples and potatoes, make an offer to repay them or buy the whole stall but leave them with it. It would not always be like this; robbing and pilfering. Sooner or later his luck would turn or run out and he would be caught and possibly held between the walls and the doors again. For now, he had to survive and perhaps they had stolen from someone at some time and perhaps that was how the world really worked.

It was on these journeys through the countryside he saw where all the produce in the markets was coming from. Here it was out in the summer fields and alone in the moonlight he was free to wander amongst the fruit and the vegetables waiting to be harvested in the light of the day. He could not go hungry out here but perhaps here was the opportunity he had been looking for. If he could get enough money to buy a quantity of the vegetables, he could find a market for himself. Immediately the draw backs came to mind. He had no vehicle to transport the quantities of vegetables he would need to make the kind of profit that he would need to buy the next batch. He needed something of high value he could carry relatively easily, to give a high return for his effort with virtually no out lay.

As he wandered, he thought of each and every one of the stalls he had seen in the markets and imagined and calculated how he would get himself into a position where he could have one of his own. With no money however his options seemed severely limited if non-existent. He watched the workers in the fields and contemplated asking the farmers for some work and then save some money. But as he watched the men and women in the fields working through the day perhaps for enough money to buy what he could plunder from the field that night when they had gone he smiled to himself and gave up on the idea.

Occasionally, he would come to one of the rivers flowing in the mountains. They would flow down into the woods and water meadows and through the towns which had grown beside them. He often found himself staying beside the rivers. In the summer he could swim in the cool clear waters which he found as exhilarating as anything he had ever done and so made him feel better despite his ongoing inability to find himself a sensible life. At some point he had managed to add some fishing line and some fishhooks to his odd collection of possessions. He had remembered a program he had heard about fishing on his radio and he had made himself a crude fishing rod.

One evening he had come to one of the rivers. He had climbed above the meadows and the fields in which the crops were growing, and where it flowed in amongst rocky pools and the trees over hung softly shadowing the waters below. The Star was hovering endlessly in the middle sky and the flies hovered in their multitudes over the gently rippling water. Then the fish had started to rise. As he watched he identified the places where the fish were jumping for the flies and quickly assembled his rod, plucked a struggling fly from the river and placed it carefully on the hook next to the downy feather that would keep his lure to the fish below floating across the surface of the water.

Carefully he floated the fly down to where he knew the fish was swimming. The first few times the fly floated down the river and nothing happened. Harri replaced the fly but still no bite and he began to think he may be wasting his time. However, as this thought passed through his mind the fish below caught a glimpse of the struggling fly and sped to the surface taking the fly and the hook as it flew into the dusky sky above. The hook embedded itself into the lip of the unfortunate creature who now sped off down the river only to find it was on the end of Harri's line. So, the struggle for survival between man and beast began again.

The fish dived backwards and forwards across the river loosening the line then pulling again until it eventually started to tire. Harri was able to slowly pull the fish in on the line until the point where there was no choice other than to jump into the river and grab the slippery fish and drag it still battling to escape back to the bank where he was able to throw it before himself scrambling out. The fish flipped and spun in desperation, gasping for oxygen filled water until Harry reluctantly killed the splendid creature with the hunting knife he had also stolen. He sat with the fish on the side of the bank, blood and burns from the line on his hands, looking at the magnificent creature he had caught. It was enormous and far bigger than he had imagined when he first saw it flying out of the river.

In fact, far too big for him to contemplate eating but certainly big enough to sell to the fishmongers down in the local town for what to him would be a fairly considerable amount of money. He wrapped the fish in a piece of his clothing and put it in one of the rocky pools at the edge of the river. He renewed the fly on the line and started the process once again hoping this time he would catch a fish small enough for him to cook over his fire and eat. In the excitement of this piece of good fortune he had forgotten how hungry he really was. He caught three more enormous fish.

The next day he took the fish down to the town and showed them to the fishmonger who eagerly parted with a large quantity of cash for them and displayed them in pride of place in his shop window. Harri was delighted and went to the local fishing shop and bought himself a proper fishing rod and returned to the bend in the river. He spent most of the summer, day after day, pulling the fish from the river. Their size was not always as magnificent as those first three but the fishmonger paid him by the weight and the more he caught the more cash the fishmonger would give him. He had found his opportunity and it occurred to Harri that it was almost as if he was mining the river. He just needed the equipment and he could pluck out the naturally occurring fish and if the value of the fish being extracted was more than what he was paying to get them out he was making money; until the fish ran out. Slowly during the summer as he successfully embarked on his first mining operation it dawned on him what he was going to do. But he would need more money, a lot more money.

In his journeys down to the fish mongers he had noticed an old refrigerated van in the back yard. It was slowly falling into disrepair and clearly had not been used for years. Harri had talked to the old fishmonger who had been moaning that buying fish out here away from the coast was becoming more of a problem. There was an unreliable service that only came once or twice a week and if he had had a busy few days he would have to close the shop because he had no stock. They agreed if he could bring the van back to life then perhaps between them they could start a new fish and seafood distribution network from the ports on the coast to all the towns in the surrounding countryside. Harri would use the money he had made from his fishing to renovate the van and they agreed percentages and made an agreement. By the time the van was ready to go into business he was old enough to drive on the roads of Arimathea. It had been five long years since he had escaped from his father but now he was on his way with a sensible business strategy to work with.

The strategy had paid off because here he was at the top of his own steel tower The Chief Executive Officer of one of the biggest corporations responsible for some of the largest mineral extraction projects across the face of Arimathea. Now his own board was assembling to discuss their latest mining venture. The long table was lined on each side with solemn men and women. There was one chair at the other end of the table which was still vacant. Harri looked nervously at his watch. The representative from the bank would arrive slightly later. There was a decision to be made in the next hour and he knew there would be a great deal of discussion and the bank had agreed to fund the project so…Harri started to speak..

"Ok, let's continue. Thanks for coming everybody. We have a decision to make. This is an important step for Wade International and we want to be sure we are going to make the right decision. So, Frank could you give us a run down on what has happened so far.."

"Yeah thanks Mr Wade. As you will know Wade International is in a very advantageous trading position at this moment in time. The world economy is such that our raw materials and the products we eventually turn them into are extremely competitive in the global marketplace. Labour costs, our transportation network, investment in the efficiency of the factories the marketing and distribution have made us a corporate family that many of the world's largest brands have been happy to join. I don't have to go into the list but there is a good chance that one in five of you will be driving a car that has been driven out of a factory that is ultimately owned by Wade..."

Harri interrupts..

"That's great Frank and it is important but we know it's a great company that's why we're all still working here after all this time and you've got three of those cars, which to be frank….hah, sorry I never get tired of that… is too many. So, tell us what has been happening, these guys need to get home for their dinner tonight."

"Yeah Sorry Mr Wade…So many of you may or may not be aware that a number of years ago, about a decade ago in fact, scientific reports became so pessimistic about the global climate situation a council of the leading industrial nations realised that if something was not done immediately there was a good chance that civilisation as we knew it could end in the next few decades. They had become convinced that efforts so far had been utterly inadequate and as more of the world became industrialised the use of fossil fuels was still steadily rising. At the same time the easily accessible supplies were running out. The cost of the more inaccessible supplies and the growing demand would make the price of fuel so expensive a global economic collapse was entirely possible. All the major economies of the world depend on cheap oil and nobody would be making any money and of course that means us. Add in the effects of desertification, flooding, the storms and the growing conflict over land we have already seen and they portrayed a pretty gloomy scenario.

So, a decision had to be made. There would have to be a concerted effort to change to pollution free energy production. Advances had been made with windmills and solar power and wave motion, hydro and wave motion but still our addiction to the burning stuff that comes out of the ground could not be dissipated. The only thing left was Nuclear energy. We all know the images, the scenarios and the risks of meltdown and the waste having to be stored for thousands of years. But unless we turn back the clock back fifty years to when we simply consumed about one tenth of what we are consuming now we are heading for a disaster. The situation seemed far too serious to be avoided any longer and the interested nations formed an international consortium. They eventually decided to fund the building of one hundred state of the art Nuclear power stations around Arimathea to come online within ten years.

However, building these new power stations with the levels of security and safety the nations agreed to, if this was all to go ahead has meant that the build time has been wildly underestimated. Not surprising since nothing like this has been attempted on a global basis before. Time has gone on and now they will be ready to be commissioned in the next year or so. Meanwhile over the years Wade and a number of other companies had been attempting to secure the contracts offered by this consortium to supply the fuel for these power stations.

Nuclear fuel, so Uranium is much rarer, almost non-existent compared with coal and gas and at the time the contracts were issued, mines able to supply the quantity necessary had been located in only three countries. Those supplies had been used extensively in the nuclear power stations already in existence. But then, knowing all this each of the companies bidding for the contracts would have to guarantee a supply for one hundred years when the contract was signed.

There was some whispering and sideway glances, nervous drinking of water and note taking. Frank allowed the inference of what he had said to sink in. He looked down the two rows of executives trying to find the one who would ask the question. All averted their eyes until his gaze fell upon a sleek auburn haired lady who held his stare with clear unwavering eyes. Then she spoke confidently.

"So, Frank reading between the lines I'd be very surprised to hear you brought us all here to tell us we haven't signed a contract to supply the Uranium for all these power stations! So, did you sign, without actually knowing whether we could, or even whether there was any more Uranium left on the planet"

There were gasps and more drinking of water and note taking.

"Looks like we've been rumbled Harri."

Harri looked down the table assessing each of the reactions of his executives. These were the tough ones. The ones he had brought with him through some tough times and he needed to be able to rely on them now. This was the nature of the risk he had always taken and had kept his company the leanest most competitive predator in the jungle. He looked back to Frank and gestured for him to continue. Frank did not waver..

"We signed because we had had continual research going on for years locating sources knowing this moment would eventually come! We had bought the best people, in fact we had most of the best people working for us but yes there was risk but that's what we do. You all know that."

"So, have we found the Uranium?"

…. Rose calmly out of the murmuring from one of the younger male executives who had been listening with little reaction to what he was hearing from his senior colleagues.

"The amount we would be supplying was always the concern. But having dealt with some of the more nefarious regimes in some fairly remote areas of the world, yes, we have located and have the rights to enough Uranium to fulfil the contract for possibly one of the most lucrative energy deals of this century, well of any century. We just need the money to start digging the mine. Which is why I am expecting a representative from the bank."

Everyone around the table seemed visibly relieved, nervously grinning across the table at their fellows but sensing there was more to come. The auburn haired lady spoke again..

"So, what is the catch? If it was straight forward and going ahead we wouldn't all be sitting here having this little softening up session. Come on Frank what is going on?"

Frank looked over at Harri who gestured again for him to continue.

"The catch is that this place is remote, South West Cayana semi desert near the deep Southern Ocean. There is nothing there, no one has ever shown any interest in it for that very reason; it's scrubland, interspersed with dramatic mountain ranges which attract some of the more extreme climbing fraternity, but the heat down there makes it generally pretty inhospitable to most of the human race."

He paused,

"..The exception however are the two tribes of indigenous Indians who are living down there in almost total isolation from the modern world. But these are not just any Indians. We have anthropologists who have been working down there who say they may be closely related to the earliest known human beings on this planet. There seems to be a high possibility their lifestyle hasn't changed much, even down to the animals they are hunting and the plants they are eating perhaps in the last one hundred thousand years. They move continually through the area as the seasons dictate following the migratory patterns of the animals across the land and the fish in the oceans. Now you may or may not know what a Uranium mine such as the one we are considering looks like and what it does to a landscape such as this but just in case you don't here is one of a similar size taken from a space satellite."

The image flashed up on the wall behind Harri. The size of the open cast mine was not entirely comprehensible until Frank pointed out the images of the microscopic hundred tonne lorries which were moving along the carefully terraced roads formed in the sides of the mine as it had been excavated deep into Arimathea. There were more gasps. This was not what the executives of Wade International wanted to hear or see. Now obvious signs of panic became manifest; contorted faces and heads in hands, more visible and vigorous shaking of heads and some extreme signs of perspiration.

Harri was watching for these signs of stress. He needed his team behind him in this new venture. He would need many of them to be involved in setting up such a complex operation and the hundreds of subcontracts that would be let to the companies who would become involved in actually extracting the Uranium from the ground and getting it to the power stations. Thousands of people would be involved ranging from some of the highest paid lawyers on the planet who would find their way through the maze of legislation that now governed such operations to the people who worked for the mining organisations who would physically remove the Uranium from the ground and then transport it to the processing facilities.

Processing nuclear fuel was not like bundling coal into a furnace or even similar to the relatively simple process of refining Oil. Each part of the process would have to be carefully organised so that Wade International could realise the staggering profits that could be made without any chance or even a whisper that anyone or anything was in danger. Except of course the two tribes who lived in the desert where the mine would interfere with just about every aspect of their lives. A way of life possibly untouched since the dawn of humanity and possibly long before it had even started to use fire now would be lost for ever so that the rest of the world could continue on its fuel hungry trajectory and wherever that would eventually lead. Harri knew all the arguments; all the 'issues'. But now he had convinced himself this was the right way to go and he had brought Wade International as an organisation to a place where it was capable of playing a crucial role at such a critical time for the life of Arimathea. He stood up to speak and everyone became still.

"I know what you're thinking and knowing most of you it is not direct concern for the plight of the Indians and the fact we are going to dig a crater and carve up their land with transport infrastructure ruining it for ever. Most of you will be concerned this will be fought out in the public domain in a way that rarely happens, it will effect share prices and future investments and so there will be risk to your personal lives, your careers and everything depending on them. So that is why I want you all to be sure this is the right course of action for Wade as certainly one of the biggest, if not the biggest corporation in the world.

We have a responsibility to the billions of people who will need this energy to see this through. Already there have been demonstrations and outraged statements by all the bleeding hearts who think they know what is best for this world….who have not fully considered the catastrophes that are ahead of us if we don't use this nuclear technology we have at our disposal. Every step in our evolution has brought some change some hardship to another set of people or another part of the world; but now they live in their cities, driving their cars to work and are interacting with the world through their phones and their computers. Do you really think they would want to go back to chasing an animal around all day and sitting in front of a fire at night in the dirt waiting for it to cook?

We'll build these people houses down on the coast, we'll buy them some fishing boats and teach them to fish and there will be some land down there that will be virtually untouched by the new infrastructure where they can build their old houses if that's what they want to do. We'll make their transition from the Stone Age as easy as we can and they will love us for it. When you think about what has happened to the rest of the world they are lucky to have been left in peace for so long. This is where I want you to be because the confidence you have in what we are doing will directly affect the success of what happens in the next few years. Wade International has secured the rights for this land to be mined so it is going to happen with you or without you. So, think about it and if you don't want to be involved in this next exciting phase I want you to tell me!"

There was a motionless silence around the table which was suddenly broken by a disturbance in the reception area outside the conference room. A sharply dressed woman looking harassed came through the door.

"I'm sorry Mr Wade there is a gentleman here who says he is from the bank!"

Almost immediately behind her a tall man with a long black leather coat and long dark hair burst into the room closely followed by two girls. They are all dressed as if they have been out all night and have come straight from a club.

"Hiya Harri, it's good to see you!"

Harri Wade was ashen faced and the executives watched in disbelief as the tall dark figure pulled out the chair at the end of the table and collapsed into it. The girls sat in the easy chairs carefully placed around a table at the back of the room flicked through the magazines before starting to roll up large quantities of processed plant material in oversized cigarette papers.

"Zanda, how nice of you to stop by!"

"Yeah, sorry I'm late Harri, but I've been out all night entertaining and being entertained you know how it is and well here I am now. I believe this is what you have been waiting for."

He pulls a large bound document from inside the depths of his coat and slides it down to the centre of the table where it comes to a standstill with fifteen sets of horrified eyes fixed upon it.

"So there it is Harri, all the money you need for the finance of your mine. As we agreed I just need each one of your signatures and then we can start digging that big hole down there."

One of the girls handed him the lighted joint. He sat back in the chair, put his boots up on the table, inhaled deeply and grinned...

"Nothing like a great plan coming together, eh Harri!?"

Chapter Sixty-three
Underlayer.

Yaan was on a ship sailing across the ocean on his journey from Eron to Eremoya. He had come out on deck to watch the Star set on the western horizon. In three days he would deliver his lecture to the ensemble of eminent speakers, global environmental theoreticians and anybody who had decided they wanted to be part of Grace's gathering to confront the problems facing Arimathea. She had described her concept as a conference in her phone call. Now it seemed her initial idea had expanded. As she had explored the idea of such an event, further opportunities had presented themselves to her. When he had visited the web site dedicated to the event it now seemed a music and arts festival had been added to the rigour of the intellectual discussion she had first presented to him. This had been a welcome development. A conference entirely devoted to the plight of the planet would have been a sobering if not depressing experience.

He had been determined to emphasise the many aspects of their civilisation in the lecture he had been asked to give. With Grace's change he had adapted his material and brought in audio visual material and transformed his lecture into a multi-media experience attempting to address the entire human condition in terms of its' emergence from the prehistoric plains of Arimathea. He had approached film makers and television companies in search of material depicting humanity at its best and worst and had been surprised at the cooperation he had received. Grace's conference had received global recognition and had already provoked discussion on what might be discussed at such an event and whether it really could make any difference to Arimathea's predicament.

Many of the media companies were glad to supply material for a credit at the event where some leading figures from the global music business had now agreed to appear. He had worked with directors and editors to coordinate the images projected onto the screens behind him to accentuate the points he was making in his address. It had been an exciting time for him and now he was excited to be heading for Southern Eremoya where Grace had chosen to locate her event. The pictures she had published showed a desert location; a wide flat plain surrounded by mountains rising out of the hazy distance with little or no civilisation nearby. Anyone who wanted to go to her event had been encouraged to travel by train from their city to the nearest town and walk the final stretch to the site. Yaan was particularly encouraged to see the plain was rich with the remains of an Indian settlement which included burial sites and to his complete delight a mysterious and pristine old stone circle.

At first, he had wondered why Grace had contacted him or how she had found him. He was not well known on the International stage. But as he had talked to her and seen the program evolve he had seen something at the heart of what she was doing. At some point he imagined she must have realised the importance of understanding the human race's earliest ancestors who would have lived in these wild places. Her choice of venue would link them directly into what was happening in the world today. He liked to think she may have heard one of his lectures or read one of his papers while looking into her theory.

He looked out across the ocean admiring the dramatic pink and purple light reflected on the waves from the Star set. He was excited to be on his way to see her and take part in the festival she had organised which now appeared to be dedicated to 'our humanity'; particularly in the light of what had been happening in the development of his own work, now so bound up in his quest to understand the early peoples of Arimathea and their motivations.

His journey had taken him deep into the dragon lands still deeply buried in amongst the layers of consciousness surrounding the world. He had come across a revelation which had immediately diverted his attention and research. Up until then he had concerned himself with delving into academic papers researched in the light of the discoveries made by archaeologists from excavated sites. There was information and evidence spread throughout the islands of Eron giving evidence of occupation by human beings and their ancestors thousands of years into the past. There was much to be gained from this research. But it was research that had been done. He could piece it together in different ways and come up with different theories but a clue that would give him some fresh insight into their lives had still alluded him.

On one of his journeys into the dream consciousness he had sat in a circle of shaman elders in a roundhouse deep in an ancient forest and discussed the invasion of marauding forces into their comparatively warm and fertile island. They had discussed the destruction of the forests in which they lived amongst the ancient trees with wisdom and lore which had inspired and underpinned their culture. They had conceived a plan to preserve at least the sacred places within the forests that had become the focus for their harmonious existence in the world. The dream aspect of this episode had unsettled him for a number of weeks. However, in that period there were a number of occurrences which appeared to make the dream more solid and its reality beyond doubt.

He immediately began to come across ancient trees everywhere he went. Even on his journeys into the cities and towns he found them around a corner, at the end of a street, through the parks as he walked across them. They were there as they had always been. But now he was compelled to pause for a while and admire or even sit if the weather permitted, beneath them. On more than one occasion somebody noticed his admiration, approached him and told him their story about the tree: how it or they had always been there to meet under, to shelter under and how they connected the coming and goings of the leaves with the weather and the passing of the seasons from one to another and there was something about it that was important to them.

"It is obvious and I hardly notice it,"

They would say but he realised they did and with the weather so predominantly noticeable on the misty island it was a connection with

Arimathea that had not been taken away and perhaps they hadn't even realised it was so important to them.

As each of these encounters occurred, his ability to accept this as information passed to him specifically at this time for a reason, slowly began to increase. Trees were still rooted, physically and metaphorically in the lives of the people around him. There were protests when some bureaucrat decided they had to be cut down because they had grown too large or if they were in the way of some new road scheme. The children of the bureaucrats climbed them and made their houses in them, defying any bailiff to drag them from their rickety platforms in the sky. They buried themselves under them and chained themselves to them, raised petitions with thousands of names from people in the area who walked past them every day and simply could not bear the thought of them not being there. The young shamans would come in the evenings and the early mornings and bless them and ask the spirits to protect them and to curse any bureaucrat who brought harm upon them, and when they came with their chainsaws and their bulldozers they lay down in front of them and screeched like demons for them to leave.

He fully accepted this may have been because his awareness was now fully focussed on the dream and it's meaning in his work. But after all this was taken into account these occurrences, his meetings and the trust in his developing intuitive instinct, convinced him to look deeper into the dream to see whether there was any factual evidence for the initiation of the plan he had witnessed; a long term plan to build a network of stone circles to mark the sacred groves as the ancient forests were destroyed.

So, he started this new research to ascertain whether there was any correlation between these two events. Again he went back to the research that had already been done. Any of these dates could have been spread over many hundreds of years. But he was looking for an overlap he felt sure he would recognise. If the forests had been cut down a thousand years before the stone circles had been built the theory would clearly be wrong. So he started to delve into the Archaeological records; many of which had to be retrieved from specific research establishments and universities in secure libraries where names had to be registered before access was granted. This aspect of his work had always puzzled Yaan. He had nothing to hide and the nature of the information could hardly be termed as dangerous or sensitive. He had come to terms with the fact this was how his society had come to work. The powers of the state whoever they now were, it seemed needed to know who was looking into what at any one time.

The dates for the first mass invasions were well documented and coincided with food shortages as populations increased in other parts of the continent. Fluctuations in the climate had been common in the history of Arimathea and had often resulted in migration. It had only become a problem when populations had started to increase and the early agriculture was unable to sustain larger populations. The dates of these earliest movements were conclusive in many of the accounts and research papers he referred to and seemed to point to a period from approximately six and a half thousand years previously.

By this time Eron was trading metals with the continent the invaders had likely originated from. This would indicate they had probably visited on trading missions and liked what they had seen. Evidence the majority of the ancient forest was intact at this point in time was not so easy to come by. The numbers of people living in the settlements up until that point made it unlikely they would have been able or had any need to clear the vast areas of forest remaining. So much of this chronological evidence relied on carbon dating of the human remains found at burial sites. Beyond the burial sites were the settlements where habitation had become easy to date from the compacted ground and any remains, stone or timber of the dwellings holding their long hidden secrets in the ground.

For thousands of years they had been protected by the fear of curses left by the wild idolatrous shamanic priests who may have been lurking amongst the grave goods, left to guide and secure their owners journey into the worlds beyond. More recent less superstitious generations had plundered their contents and now they lay stored in the glass cabinets of little museums up and down the land. If these robbers had been tormented for the remainder of their days by the disturbed spirits of their ancient ancestors there never had been any acknowledgment of their curses existence.

However, this was where Yaan had first become enchanted and began his studies of these ancient peoples. Immediately he had seen the intricately carved stonework, the worked bronze and silver and in the more secure museums gold artefacts, the mystery had grown in his mind. He had been chasing for the answers ever since. Somewhere in his education he had been led to believe these ancient people were little more than savages living a hand to mouth existence in abject poverty at the mercy of the cruel environment surrounding them. When he had seen these exquisite pieces of jewellery, of weaponry, of body armour, he found it hard to imagine how people in his own era could achieve such quality of workmanship. So, it was clear these people were considerably more advanced than he had been led to believe.

He had turned his research to the mysterious stone circles, stone rows, the old dolmens and strange isolated standing stones that consistently appeared across his land. They existed on the moors and out in the hills whose slopes had been too steep or too wild for the growing of crops. He found them hidden away on private estates preserved as they were, passed down through the generations and finally purchased by a preservation or conservation charity. He found their remains in and around isolated country churches. He discovered many of these temples to the alien gods had been built from the stones originally encircling the site.

On the moor where he had chosen to live he found their isolation made them more mysterious. He had learned to douse and followed the strange twisting energy lines across the boggy landscapes. As he found the alignments spreading out across the moor and the lore lying embedded in the direction and placement of the stones his fascination had deepened. Now his fascination, had led him deep into the memories contained within his land. Could the stone circles have been built to explain or even enhance a network of dragon light flowing through the land his ancient ancestors had always known had existed. As he delved through the carbon dating information for the surveyed stone circles and monuments, he was faced with the same conundrum always facing the historians trying to piece together a picture of people living in the distant past.

He found the building of the stone circles could have coincided with the felling of the forests. But he could not pinpoint such a time with any more accuracy than within a hundred years. So still he could not be certain the building was undertaken to preserve the sites of the old sacred groves so mercilessly cut down as the barbarian hordes populated the land. But they were definitely in the same time frame and although his conclusions would not stand up to rigorous academic scrutiny, which would after all only accept a handwritten and signed manifesto by a head shaman priest, the correlation was certainly compelling.

Yaan had moved back into a communal lounge area inside the ship. He was perhaps halfway through his journey. There was a movie playing but he had no interest tonight in the manufactured fantasy of the corporate film industry. It seemed as if there was a blockbuster quietly brewing in his own life. As the mystery deepened, his everyday life continued but now he remembered how even that had become encroached upon. Beth's and his financial situation had been fairly healthy. He had more well paid lectures and her teaching job at the University had put them beyond the panic zone in which they had spent much of their married life. So, he was surprised one morning when he received a phone call from the bank saying they had been unable to make a number of payments because there had not been enough money in his account.

It had been a long time since he had the sinking feeling associated with having no money and decided he would go straight into the bank to find out what had happened as there was a book he needed to be pick up from the bookshop. He felt sure there was nothing to worry about and continued to plan his trip to the lakes he had been contemplating. This would combine visits to some of the most beautiful and well preserved stone circles and burial sites with climbing and walking through some of the most spectacular mountain scenery in the land of Eron.

At the bank it had turned out there had been some mix up with the payment from his last lecture. The bank employee smartly dressed in her corporate uniform dealt with the problem calmly by ringing the bank where the payment had been missed. Everything was sorted out as Yaan contemplated the banking hall which in fairly recent times would have been buzzing with people, talking, exchanging gossip and making contact with each other but now was virtually empty and silent. He thanked the representative and was walking back out through the bank as a man came rushing through the entry doors. Yaan remembered when he had often come to the bank in the same state: looking a bit rough around the edges, tired and stressed. As he came nearer Yaan recognised the approaching face. They caught each other's eye and both exclaimed almost at the same time..

"Is that Paulo?"

"Is that Yaan? Whoa it's great to see you man. Must be bloody years since we've seen each other."

"Well yes it will be. Must have been those last days of University which if I remember where a bit blurry anyway?"

"...and you had just started to get things together with Beth after prowling round her all year."

"Hah...Yes my loyalties were a bit divided in those last days...we needed to celebrate all that hard work and the time we had spent digging around in libraries and fields in the middle of nowhere and then I finally had a chance at the girl who had been giving me the run around for months.!"

"She was alright though, I remember you staggering out of the union mostly held up by her in those last nights!"

"Yeah, she's a good lass and actually we have stayed together. In fact, it seems we will soon be having our first child."

"Congratulations, that is fantastic. Where are you guys living?"

"We're out on the edge of the moors, not far from here actually. Couldn't resist it. You don't live round here do you, mate?"

"No, I came down for a few days hiking on the moor for the same reason as you live down here. You just get so close to the ancient world out there. Look, my girlfriend is waiting in the car and I've got a bit of a mess to sort out here as it happens...I thought of you the other day. Are you still into all that pagan mysticism stuff you were always going on about...because I don't know if you heard but some county court bailiffs were clearing a big old castle up on the north coast and found a cellar full of relics. They reckon there were multiple treasure troves, ancient stuff from plundered burial mounds.

It seems the old fella who owned it died completely alone, hadn't been out for years and was the last person in the family. He left massive debts. Some pretty weird stuff going on if you ask me... car crashes...suicides.... like they got caught up in one of those old curses. Look I'll give you my card and write the site to visit on the web. I don't know where you've got with it all but... by the sounds of it they have found some interesting stuff up there. Great to see you Yaan, send my love to Beth and we'll catch up soon. Can't wait to hear what you've been up to."

Yaan had looked up the site where the find was fully explained and took details of all the agencies involved and in what area. It appeared to be not far away from where he was going anyway, so he planned a trip to see what he might be able to find out. He had taken a train and after arriving at four different stations each one progressively more primitive than the last he arrived at his destination somewhere deep in the countryside. A taxi dropped him at the gates of the enormous mansion. Yaan was surprised to see the high steel gates swinging open on rusty hinges. He asked the taxi to return in a couple of hours. Although he had not been confident the taxi driver would return as he sped back into the tight little lanes.

The house was a large formal mansion set in gardens now growing gradually ramshackle. The external openings of the building had been expertly sealed. Every window and door had been fitted with a steel shutter fixed into the reveals. Whatever was inside had obviously warranted a large investment to keep it safe in this remote location. He had walked up to the front where a flight of steps rose to the entrance at a half storey level. Columns supported the entrance canopy and as he stood looking out over the lake stretching out over to the mountains he wondered which of the rich and powerful had stood there contemplating their strategies and manipulations. For the moment whatever importance it had, had been sealed inside, more securely though, than one of the tombs from where the riches enclosed inside had been robbed.

Yaan sauntered dreamily through the assortment of buildings associated with such a house and towards the farm buildings. There were modern spacious steel constructed barns which may have housed cattle through the winter months. Now they were strangely deserted. Empty but haunted by the animals that had lived there; their shufflings and their munchings and their steamy breaths puffing into the cold winter air, their accusing stares from behind the steel bars confining them had long since disappeared. The pasture through which they would have roamed lay beyond. Pasture now grown wild; perhaps left for more than a year. The grass was thick and knee high, wet with condensation from the night before and although it was untrodden, Yaan was sure he could see some shadow, some trace of a path leading out and across to the woods on the other side of the field.

He decided to follow where he perceived the path to be and soon was soaked in dew as he battled his way through the long grass and across the field. Crows were perched in the trees, eerily calling down to him as he reached the edge of the wood. There was a sharp fall immediately inside the fence. Yaan could not see the bottom through the trees. Ordinarily at this point he may have returned to the buildings but now he decided to go on down the slope and into the wood. There was no sign at this point of any human passage or interference but again Yaan felt a way was being opened before him in his mind. He continued deeper into the wood. At the foot of the slope the trees had thinned in their attempt to compete with the trees on the steep slopes. He had found himself moving through a hidden valley echoing with birdsong and dim light strained down through the tall trees as they stretched up into the light.

He thought he had heard the soft rhythm of a drum imperceptibly filling and echoing around the spaces between the trees. He stood and listened for a few moments. The sound could have been part of the wood as if the noises of the creatures and the breezes in the trees were conspiring to become rhythmically one. It was difficult for Yaan to follow as there seemed to be no direction in particular it was coming from so he carried on down the valley. It became rocky and a stream appeared gently cascading down from what Yaan presumed was the lake above. The stream rippled across a pool surrounded by rocks and ferns on the valley floor. The sides of the valley had become rockier and the rhythm of the drum had become more pronounced and more identifiable. He looked deeply into the shady light ahead. He felt sure he should be able to now see the source of the drumming.

Small outcrops of rocks had changed into larger boulders and longer upright shards projected from the valley sides. He edged forward, wary now of who he was about to meet. Between one of these larger outcrops lodged in the side of the valley he noticed something looking far more regular than any of the other boulders. It had been carefully constructed from slabs of stone, now almost entirely covered with moss, lichens and ferns it was almost invisible. The walls rose perhaps to the height of at least two men carefully disguised amongst two outcrops of rock. A window, partly hidden by another boulder, had been formed with crudely dressed stone jambs and lintels, the stout shutters were open and there was an opening in one corner where a solid door lay half ajar. The wall was overhung by a roof of long heavy slates supported on heavy oak rafters. This was undoubtedly where the drumming was coming from.

Yaan made his way quietly towards the door and put his head tentatively through. The space was lit by the window conceived as part of its structure. The room was perhaps ten good paces across and six deep. There were stone flagstones laid across the floor to what appeared to be the stone face of another substantial rock feature.

In a large and beautifully carved chair sat a dark haired woman. She sat with the drum between her knees. She was still gently tapping at the soft hide with long slender fingers. Her hair was long and framed a face with well-defined aquiline features darkened by long exposure to Starlight. She was smiling openly and with great amusement over at the startled Yaan. She got up from the chair and walked towards him and took both his hands. She was taller than Yaan. He found himself looking up into green eyes the like of which he had never seen and that seemed to have a supernatural glow. She wore an old but in every other way immaculate dark coat over a long dress of dark green heavy cotton, shaped around the curves of her body then laced to a collar over her breastbone. She wore a symbol on a fine silver chain around her neck which Yaan did not recognise.

"Hello Yaan."

She looked deeply into his eyes; he felt her delving deeply into his soul and beyond. He felt as if she was scanning through all his memories, everything he knew and felt about his life and his world.

"Er, yeah hello."

The woman turned and took her place back in the seat.

"Take a seat, make yourself comfortable Yaan."

He pulled a chair out of the corner and sat down. He took a look around and noticed there were tables and shelves made from stout planks of

Oak carefully placed around the room. On them there were many different objects; many from even a first glance looked to Yaan to be very old. As he moved from place to place his fascination grew with what he was seeing. Some of the metallic items had been dusted off. A large carefully worked chalice with a long stem sparkled in a shaft of starlight from the high window. Then he saw a sword lying across a table, also glinting in the starlight from a lower window.

He looked over at the woman full of apprehension and questioning. With a movement of her startling green eyes she invited him to take a closer look. Yaan moved over to the table and examined the beautifully crafted sword. He spotted the rune marks towards the hilt but again like the symbol around the woman's neck he did not recognise them or their significance. He carefully clasped the handle of the sword and lifted it for closer examination. It was lighter than he had expected and as he ran a finger on the edge he realised it was razor sharp. He looked again over at the woman who was smiling over at him.

"So Yaan, do you know who I am?"

Yaan scanned his life, his memories, the dreams and visions he had received and been part of and which had become part of him and now had begun to guide him through his life. He could find nothing to explain this tall woman now sitting in front of him.

"I am afraid I have no idea!"

"I just needed to make sure there was no dream in which someone else may have revealed my identity."

"No, there are none I remember and I feel sure I would not have forgotten if we had met before!"

She laughed.

"Well Yaan. I am Alamistra and I am one of the creator spirits of this world or, what your race have called us at various times in their and our history, a dragon. I have brought you here because of the place you have come to in your understanding of what has happened in this world and because there is something that I need you to do for me."

"Do you mean the dreams I have had. Visiting the stone circle and my rite of passage…the visit to the castles and the plan of the old shamans I have been looking into. Is that what you mean?"

"It is Yaan. Specifically at this moment what you have discovered about the stone circles needs some embellishment…some explanation say…that you will never find out from anywhere but from one of us and it is important. Someone, somewhere will say it is interference but we have some catching up to do. When you meet Okino and Mariella you can ask them about that. But now we haven't much time!"

"Okino was the monk in the circle at my initiation and then in his video from the boat…you say I will meet him?"

"Yes, you will meet them soon and yes you will have a lot to talk about…but for now I need you to listen very carefully to what I am going to say."

She stood up and went over to the table where the chalice had fallen into shadow.

"I know you are here because of the discovery of the artefacts stored in the house. You will also know they were taken from burial sites in and around this area. You may or may not know this area has great importance for this island and these islands for the rest of the world."

"I have not come across this significance as yet, but please continue."

"The dragons have always held a particular part of this world as their own and we have always been especially aware of what is happening in our own lands. The human race was originally sensitive to our dreams as they flowed through their world and in this way we were able to maintain contact with them. The dragon who presided over this island, Eron, was Mithrael. He has been the restless one on this world. At first he decided to become human when he sensed the forests were threatened with destruction. They had always provided him with a unique connection with his land and her peoples. He discussed this with the shamans and they became determined to preserve the places in the forest as best they could".

Yaan immediately recognised a similarity with his own experience in his dream.

"I was at a meeting with some of those old shamans when they were discussing building stone circles to mark the old sacred groves in a round house deep in the forest. Perhaps Mithrael was there."

"I think almost certainly he would have been; they had become very close."

Alamistra then explained to Yaan how Mithrael had come so close to this human tribe but as a result came to oppose the dragon's plan to bring the human race closer to the consciousness after suffering the loss of his human wife.

"During his time with the tribe he passed on a great deal of the dragon knowledge about the consciousness from which all life had evolved, a little of which I am going to tell you now. These early peoples still had their ability to connect with the consciousness. This is the knowledge you have lost. It is the consciousness that supports you. Your civilisations now live as if you are in a vacuum only supported by what you yourselves create and surround yourselves with. All through the universe, the cycles of the stars and all the worlds supported by them are held in this supreme state; you have a basic understanding of this in your mathematics and physics, but it is infinitely deeper than you have dared to think or even can imagine.

It governs all your movements, all the processes of your body, all the processes of the world around you and allows all this to be. It came from the will to be somewhere in the future. It has brought about many evolutions. Early base matter is transformed into intelligence and the ability to comprehend and interact with a world. It originated, in this time, from the cataclysm at the beginning of this universe. Such was the detonation many surrounding previously stable dimensions collapsed in on each other. Subsequently when the residual energies emerged they found they had become conscious of their place in this new universe.

Every material thing is a weave of the interconnected aspects of the consciousness which arose and then merged with the original state of the One Love; the all-encompassing state of balance and progression, that survived from the last universe. In this new state energetic constituents searched each other out, wove and merged in an infinity of combinations into a process of fusion which allowed a progression to begin. Once this process started to flow through the chaos, it soon began to increase infinitely. The finest new state that came into being was Light; Light from the searing white heat of the stars now being formed.

The newly formed consciousness found it was able to merge with this light and searched for some form amongst all the chaos. The dragons eventually emerged, as the consciousness combined with the beautiful purity of light, into a new state of being, spirit. The dragon light consciousness soon found it could influence future states as the fusion of the energy continued to form this new universe.

The dragons found they held the memories of worlds and existences in the previous universe. They dreamed those memories into the fusion of energy making new infinite connections throughout as the elemental evolution began. These dreams became the foundation for all that slowly came to be. In this infinity of transformation, the consciousness continued to search for an ultimate state in which it could find expression and identity. So, in those eons of searching through the infinity of potential, the dragons eventually brought about the profusion and diversity that enabled the states of Love and Light to eventually become Life.

The exact moment, the place where sentient life began to arise is lost in those primordial swamps, where the turning point, the moment of pure clarity and possibility was eventually reached. Life progressively developed as a result of the memories flowing from the dragon dreams, through the continuing fusion and blending of energy to where we are here talking together. Everything we have become is bound up in the original yearning for expression; to see, feel and understand the results of this incredible journey and acknowledge our place in this extraordinary world so full of the wonderful diversity that has arisen.

Even in those original days there had been fear which you and we all still carry. This precious thing that had come to be perhaps against all odds would always have to be protected nurtured and held as sacred.

For this reason every living thing within the consciousness had to be aware of where and how it existed and have an idea of its place in the vastness surrounding it. There would always be a passing through temporal and physical states so the progression could continue; now it was governed by cycles as it travelled in a dimension enabling everything to live in the transformative Light but also to return to the Original darkness.

Here was where the tension providing so much of the suffering in this new state began to arise. As the new life became more complex so this aspect of the consciousness became more apparent. As human beings became as developed as you are now, many millions of turnings later they lived within the consciousness as the consciousness lived through them. There was no separation in those early times. They became aware of the tension and began to understand it was at the root of the struggle with which all life would have to engage in this state. Although their lives were hard and often short they were able to experience for the first time on this world the wonder and the enchantment of being sentient on such a magnificent and beautiful world.

They lived with the rhythms created by the turnings as they travelled through it, lived with the creatures with whom they shared their world, hunted and killed them as they also were hunted and killed. They lived, were animated, breathed, reproduced and eventually died and when skin and fur was pealed back they found they shared a similar physiology of bones, hearts and brains. They assumed they were the same spirits in different form and suspected the force or energy that animated them was the force that animated all they saw around them. They acknowledged the life force living in themselves was the same as lived in the animals and when they danced under the stars in the thunder of their drums having feasted on the flesh of the animal they had hunted, they celebrated the fabulous nature of the life of which they had become a part.

Because they could feel the consciousness within themselves and we were part of the consciousness we could appear to them, flow amongst them, deepening their understanding of who they were and what they had become. They lived side by side with us and everything around them they saw to be as a result of the consciousness flowing through the world.

When Mithrael decided to become human he taught them about the consciousness in terms of everyday objects they used in their lives. Each object became associated with an aspect of the consciousness as they were used and helped them in their lives. They were buried with them to help them on their journey to and in their next life.

Necklaces came to represent the whole interconnected existence they saw around them. The Rings they wore came to represent the cycles in which they were held. Their Swords always represented their ability to exist in the world in which they struggled and fought. Their Shield protected them in these struggles and their Cloak and clothes provided them with protection from the Elements which in turn they held sacred with special Stones seen to be the bones of the world by which they were supported in life and to which they would return to in death. Their bowls and cups held the most sacred element of their lives; the food they ate and the water they drank all of which came from the living world and sustained them in it.

Often they had skulls of the animals they had hunted representing the bond they felt with the spirit world. They kept a set of bones which they could look into and deduce the circumstances surrounding them at any particular time. As they looked into the depths of transparent crystals they found they gave them insight into their dreams and so what might happen in the future. Their Drums joined them in their rituals with the heartbeat and the rhythms of Arimathea. They often carried staves marked with symbols recording their names and those of their family which they also held sacred and represented their place in the world. They made the journey through their lives with their Staff. They often kept small Daggers concealed in their clothing and these came to represent the darker side they often needed to survive in a world where difficult decisions often had to be made. As the years went by and their abilities became more sophisticated the system of the sixteen aspects of the consciousness became integrated into many of their rituals and rites of passage.

They found them again and again when they opened up the tombs. The old man built this place. It has remained undiscovered. In it he has hidden these special relics found in the burial tomb in which the ashes of kings and generation after generation of people had been interred. They believed these objects would keep them in contact with the worlds they suspected existed beyond their lives, through the spirits of their kings, themselves sacred to the land. This they had learned from Mithrael through their contact with him even before he became a human, before he decided to turn against our plan…and this was how he found his way into the dreamscape, through this system we had initiated reflecting these aspects of the consciousness, where he confronted Merilon and turned him to stone for more than a thousand years."

She sat back in her chair carefully whirling the necklace of carefully carved stones around one of her long slender fingers and watched Yaan as he slowly let the incredible story in which he had become involved fall piece by piece into place. She leaned slightly forward closer to Yaan and spoke quietly and more intimately to him.

"So, you see these are the sacred relics of their lives. Now the things you make assisting you in your life have lost their sacred meaning. They are mass produced in vast numbers in mechanised impersonal factories. But each object enhancing and benefiting your continuation can become sacred to your life. They connect you every time you use them into the spirit as you continue in the world. If you are aware of the continuation they allow your experience of the consciousness to be enhanced."

Yaan listened to her words resonating through the Starlit space while he contemplated the beautifully crafted objects before him. He contemplated how every mouthful of food taken from these bowls, every blow struck with these weapons, how the cycles of the years and the stars and all that happened within their turnings shown so effectively in the continual metaphor of the ring and the necklaces and the beating rhythms of their drums gave meaning and connection to the dangerous, beautiful world by which they were surrounded.

Perhaps this was where the human worship or reverence for their material possessions had originated.

His gaze alighted upon something altogether different in the collection of relics. High on a shelf next to some well-preserved animal skulls he saw a small golden eagle. Its wings were outstretched. It was setting off from the perch where it had been settled. It shone brightly, sparkled in the starshine falling on and all around it, perfectly captured in the beginnings of its search for the prey that would sustain itself and the next generation who would also one day soar through the skies.

"…and the eagle. Do you know of its significance?"

"We think it was made by Mithrael. There would have been few who could have crafted such a beautiful object and known of the significance of Gold in such early times. We think perhaps he made it for his wife who was so tragically killed and perhaps he buried it in the tomb with her ashes to guide and be with her."

She was quiet again and watched him. He had become fixated by the eagle and thought perhaps he could see the life of the magnificent bird glowing from the shining metal."

Alamistra started to speak again.

"The eagle has represented in many cultures the creature coming nearest to the manifestation of the great spirit in the physical world. When it disappears into the Star shine high above it is thought to be symbolic of the dead person's soul passing through the boundaries of this dimension on its journey back into the great spirit. Almost as if it has become pure consciousness. It has represented for many people in its flight how spirit and consciousness mixes and flows through the world, infinitely searching for ways to find new forms of being in the ethereal light.

Everything you have made, everything you have dreamed has come from the original urge of the great spirit to exist in the physical universe. It works through your lives and the circumstances you have made to find new possibilities, new connections it can exploit to bring it closer, nearer to the dream of peaceful harmony it imagined. Now this time is so tantalisingly close. Many of your race have seen and felt the possibility that could exist for the entire world but there are so many damaged souls, so many spirits lost on their way through a world from which they have become separated, almost denied to them.

You have forgotten your ability to find the simple entry points all around you in every aspect of your lives; doorways to connect you to the Love in all of your beings. As you make your way through the world on any day you move under the open sky. In so many ways it can open you to those deeper layers of consciousness. All of your lives are governed by what is happening there, the movement of the Star and the clouds; the movement from day to night and night to day is at root of your existence.

Then everything that happens to you, all the people you meet and interact with, the animals you acknowledge and all the beautiful trees and plants you are surrounded by. All are gateways filling every moment with an opportunity to find your way into those deeper worlds of consciousness and Love within you. There you will find the peace you are striving for; that so alludes you. Your race has tragically replaced it with its' own version, its own narrative of how it all is.

However, you are starting to suspect striving for happiness through the dream of material wealth is only an illusion you have been brought under, made to enslave you in the mechanistic world. You accepted it because you thought it would lead to the peace you crave. But it has only led to a deeper craving for something in the future which is unattainable.

But now we have sensed a change. Circumstances in this last era while we have been asleep in our caves separated from the world, have taken you to a time where every one of you can know and understand what is happening on this world and you have started to understand the incredible nature of what has come to be and the tragedy that could unfold if it were ultimately neglected and eventually lost. The time has come Yaan, an acknowledgement is rising amongst your race that the great experiment which has brought so much astounding innovation to fruition must be thought of now in the context of the beautiful world which has given you so much of the wonder you have created."

Yaan looked around the room at the objects surrounding Alamistra in the light of what she had told him. Star light from the high windows fell onto her. She stood in a pool of light as if the Love had come to illustrate all she had explained by illuminating the extraordinary creature she had become. He felt awe and amazement for his life and his world.

All his explorations, all his delving into the spirit of his ancestors he had found on the Moors had been connecting him back into this original consciousness. As it had lived through them it had started to live through him as he found the ways to connect himself with those old memories lying dormant in his DNA that had travelled down from those early times. Now a dragon had come to him and confirmed all he needed to know about the origins of his race, their fortunes and their destiny to perhaps move closer to living in harmony with their world.

"So why have you brought me here to tell me all this."

"You know all these things but somewhere the sheer wonder of what has happened has been lost. Perhaps it could not be fully comprehended or wasn't meant to be until now. But now the time has come for the consciousness to again fully arise amongst the human race. You Yaan, have understood the nature of the plan the ancient shamans put in place with the help of Mithrael. I have told you the place consciousness holds in your race and how they have known it. The memory of that knowledge sleeps in their genetic memories. It must be awoken now so they can experience all the wonder as it flows through this world and most importantly, intricately through all of their lives.

You have understood how the network of Sacred places are connected and so flow together through the world. These objects represent the sixteen aspects of consciousness present in the dreamscape my brother and sister dragons are at this time dreaming and holding in a layer buried deep in the consciousness, too deep now for the people of Arimathea to reach. If you could hold these sacred relics and all they represent in your own consciousness and project them into the networks the old shamans created on Eron, the light in the networks will be strengthened, a stronger closer link for your race will rise from the dreamscape of the dragons. Take the eagle, Yaan. It will guide you to Mithrael. He will have to find his peace again if the problems of this world are to be resolved."

So now as he floated across the ocean of his world he remembered how he had carried out what Alamistra the dragon had asked of him. He had walked into the land of lakes and mountains. He had been haunted by the knowledge of the consciousness she had given him in the strange folly that had remained undiscovered as the rest of the property had been plundered to pay the debts of the old man. He had discovered breath taking scenery where the juxtaposition of mountains and lakes produced beauty, inspiring feelings of awe and wonder almost at every turn; where he had found tender nature living side by side with the vast unfathomable forces of weather and climate as they drove their way through and over the landscapes. Where he had found people equally amazed, equally in love with what they had found here. They had been moved in the same way by the beauty they had found in the heart of their land.

For this surely was what it was, the heart of the island of Eron. In her heart he had found a contentment, a deep stillness even amongst the turbulence of the winds and the changing cloudscapes, as the starlight raced across the surfaces of the choppy lakes and landed in the stillness of some perfect cove where anyone could dream to live in peace for ever. As he had climbed high onto those towering peaks and looked down to where the strange world he inhabited was carrying on now invisibly, he wondered at how vulnerable he felt here, how humble he must be to escape those heights to negotiate down the steep slopes again to the lands of green, the wonderland that lay down there separated from these strange cloaking mists and deceptive vistas.

Then eventually he had come to the stone circle in which he had planned to merge all Alamistra had told him back into the networks of his land. Surrounded by the mountains and a dramatic cloudscape, the star had climbed along the sloping side of the hill and freed itself to throw down it's dazzling light onto the stones. Their long tendril shadows stretched out across the dew covered grass so carefully cropped by unconcerned sheep. In the dawn at the Spring Equinox of the year where light and dark had become equal in day and night, he sat in quiet meditation remembering all that had happened to him in those previous years and in the history of his world.

Then as he felt the dragon light flow up from the ground within the stones he allowed all Alamistra had told him to flow into the light. As it flowed around him he imagined expansive possibilities coming to fruition on

Arimathea as the human race began to consider her in all their activities. He allowed these thoughts to mingle with the wonder and magnificence of the scenery and released them into the beams of Starshine, into the light reflected on the stones, into the warm ground, allowed them to radiate and roll like powerful waves through the markers of Solstices and Equinoxes, of Moonrises and Star rises, into the green hills beyond and out into his world. He thought he felt Arimathea breathing in these new possibilities as they flooded out into her consciousness and settled amongst all her sacred lands, where eventually they would be absorbed through the dreams of her anxious people.

Chapter Sixty-four
Preparations.

Grace was standing on the remote plain she had chosen for her festival conference. The star had not yet risen over the distant mountains but the clear crisp light of the early morning revealed the extent of the activity she had been responsible for bringing to this far flung and normally deserted expanse of Eremoya. She had wanted to be disconnected from the cities and the infrastructure on which they relied even though the consequences were she would have to bring everything out here. Everything a large collection of people would need to survive in the desert for three or four days. It would be an island filled only with the precious resources on which the Human race had come to rely. Visible tanks and containers would hold those resources for everyone to see. In the early stages of her plan she had been confronted and astounded by the quantities needed to host such an event; at a most basic level how much water each person would need on a daily basis not only on a personal level but to meet the standards of safety and hygiene legislated to stage such an event. Then there was the power for the stages and 'the village' as it had soon become known where people would eat and congregate during their stay; power that would need generators and generators out here would need fuel. All had been calculated by the team of consultants she had appointed to oversee the logistical side of this event. They would plan for every eventuality that may arise in such a location when bringing perhaps many thousands of people to such a remote location.

The results of their planning had started to appear in the past few days. A steady stream of articulated juggernauts had brought the deconstructed village to the location from the warehouses where it had been stored and in some cases from the factories where it had been made and dumped here untidily in this previously empty place. Since then Grace's workforce had delved into these piles of seemingly random objects and slowly the framework in which the dream she had conceived would take place, slowly started to take shape.

She stood in front of the tanks that would hold the fuel for the generators and the towers that would hold the hundreds of thousands of gallons of water to be consumed each day. A vast array of solar panels was being built and spread far into the distance across the flat terrain to allow the use of fossil fuel to be minimised. The insulated coverings of the tents to protect the audiences from the late Autumn star and any surprise storms heading in from the ocean were being hauled into position and now stood like a futuristic family of insect beings striding amongst the frantic activity of the creatures hurrying amongst them. Accommodation pods were craned into place for the guests who could not or would no longer tolerate the crude living conditions their audiences would endure.

Cooking facilities, restaurants and refrigeration units to contain the food needed to cater for the varying appetites of many different generations who would soon be arriving were carefully bolted together. Washing and toilet facilities even a small hospital was being built to ensure any medical emergency could be treated effectively and as quickly as possible on site; all this Grace had seen gradually evolving before her. Everyone seemed to know what they were doing and the part they were playing in this fragment of human endeavour. Each with their part in the plan they had made because she had decided something had to be done after her world had been blown apart by the stray bullet on her journey to work only a few months previously.

Nothing much of her previous life had been left intact. She had spent much of the first week drifting in and out of consciousness with no awareness about what had happened. She had been supported through this strange time by machines and a cocktail of drugs. The surgeons had kept her body functioning as she became used to her new liver. When she occasionally surfaced she had registered the faces of her friends and relatives. But she had not been certain whether they were part of a dream she had fallen into. She had remembered episodes but there was no coherent stream of events. Many had been with her friends or strange combinations of people in landscapes, townscapes, buildings and ruins. They were areas of her life she recognised but had only passed briefly through. They were often associated with previous trauma which long ago had been in the forefront of her consciousness. Now they rose again as her own consciousness desperately sought something to cling on to as this new trauma made its place in her body.

There were consequences in her life of which she had not been aware. These emerged on disconnected journeys which slipped incoherently from scenario to scenario. She would be in some backstreet cafeteria or next to a river or in some crowded piazza where a performance was being acted out for her. The actors were her family but they had been changed from her not being there. Many of these scenes often reflected the deep fears she had buried. There had been implications to her not speaking out or standing up for herself. She had allowed the situations and people around here to influence her decisions. After each of these episodes the world went on but she had been diminished and become less visible to those around her. Less considered when decisions were made. She had found herself in deserted landscapes where she was free of the criticism she felt and the influences making her take the paths she would not necessarily have taken and now she had been shot on the way to a job which she would not have taken. She had taken the wrong path. But maybe not.

There had been no choices or ways to escape or had she just missed them. In the dream however she knew she could wake up but she felt there was a process she was being led through. There was always a tall woman in the background, in the crowds just out of reach watching over her. As the dream fluctuated she provided stability and continuation. Perhaps she had been there to lead her back onto the path she was meant to be on. Even in the landscapes she had been in the distance, on a hill or on a distant shore. Grace had wanted to talk to her but if she moved towards her she had disappeared.

Eventually she had emerged out of her dream into the hospital and was told what had happened. Everything had been still and quiet except for the sounds of the heart monitor and the world in the distance going on without her. Immediately she felt the power of her dreams; how they had twisted and turned in such unlikely sequences. Where all the mundane and trivial had been removed to leave just concentrated life, rich and stark and full of the meaning she had missed before. She felt they had left her with a changed perception of her world. Perhaps orchestrated by the woman who had walked with her. When she finally awoke and saw her concerned and relieved family sitting around her bed, sleepless and panic stricken she understood something serious had happened and they had suffered more deeply than she herself.

She began to understand the nature of the dreams when she was told a bullet had ripped through her body. It had provoked a reaction in her mind to enable her to come to terms with the horror of what had happened. She had been shot and one of her major organs had been destroyed and now she had the liver of the person who had been killed in the same incident. It was not a movie where the person got up and went back to work the next day. This was trauma of deep consequence and only she knew how deep it had taken her so she could live again. She remembered she had been at the point of her death but something had held her back because there was more and her time had not come and although many deaths were untimely and tragic and cut people off in the prime of their lives, hers was not now and she had to continue with the trauma or even because of the trauma because these new depths had opened up some realisation about all her existence and the nature of it. So, it wasn't long before, in this new state of awareness, she began to see the ridiculous state the world to which she had been returned was in.

Then she had been projected into the limelight by the city media; The victim of the continuing violence rife in a city with an underworld catering for all the city dwellers darkest and most sinister habits. No one really knew who was in charge or who was benefiting. It was there and while everyone was getting on with their own lives and perhaps smoking some of the more exotic vegetation on offer or using some of the highly processed powders and potions for a party when they needed to shine and sparkle amongst their shiny sparkling peers then it wasn't a big priority for the cities media.

But if a respectable hardworking girl like Grace who could have been any one of their daughters was shot and nearly killed then a torrent of outrage flooded through the city and would be directed at all the disadvantaged souls who had fallen through the net of the city's flawed social systems. Of course, none of them had any knowledge the money being made was being laundered through their pension schemes or how they were hidden away in the offshore banks through which they diverted the funds they needed to remain invisible.

Grace became the opportunity for the focus to be diverted away from their shameful activities and towards the flood of anarchy and lawlessness overtaking their hitherto blameless society. Her face became known across the city and she was invited to talk about her experience at functions and dinners where the great and the good could be found huddling together invisible from the less fortunate city beyond. After her speech she often found herself talking to the rich and famous who were always at the top of the invitation list.

They were the millionaires and billionaires who had found themselves with an eye watering fortune by founding a corporation from the humble beginnings of a market stall or who had become household names by selling groceries or washing machines or had inherited an oilfield, an airline company or a publishing empire. She was surprised how ordinary they had seemed or in some cases unhappy, worried and defensive. But because she was who she was, she often found herself having very real and frank conversations with some of the most influential and sought after people in her country.

As she talked and they listened, the politicians flapped around transparently trying to manipulate a way into their favour and the funds they undoubtedly could bring to their ascent to power and they so obviously craved and were chasing. In these conversations on occasions she had found herself talking about her worries for the world as a whole beyond where she imagined a lot of the problems being encountered in their city originated.

One night she found herself sitting next to an elegant silver haired lady immaculately dressed in a dark beautifully cut suit. She had encouraged Grace when she stood up to go to the stage where she would speak. Grace was always far too nervous to engage with the people around her or eat or even stand up and often wondered before these ordeals why she had accepted another one of these invitations. Then she would remember the torrent of mail she had received from all the people in the city who had identified and felt inspired by what she had said. They told her repeatedly they felt as if their struggle had become too much to cope with day in and day out.

Grace had felt very humble. Her injury had brought about many difficulties in the past months but many of the stories she had heard were heart breaking and so she had decided to continue if and when a request was made for her story to be told. Now her latest ordeal was over and the applause had died down and she carefully sat down in her seat and took a long drink from the glass of water which had remained untouched and breathed out. The silver haired lady was watching her with a new respect as she finished the last of the strawberries and cream she had chosen for her desert. She recently had had her own tragedy and much of how Grace had explained her own recovery from the strange indefinable vulnerability of drifting weakness and despair had resonated with her deeply. Grace had felt her attention and turned to her and smiled.

"Please forgive me, it's just doing this takes everything I can summon up. Sometimes I feel the slightest thing could unnerve me and I would run out of the hall and never be seen again. Then I am up there and there are just the lights. I know you are all out here but I cannot see your faces and I want to run but then the lights remind me of the seconds I was awake in the operating theatre. A surgeon said there was someone looking after me and I remember being relieved it was him because he sounded like a nice clever man and I felt grateful he was there and I felt safe."

"You have nothing to apologise for my dear. We are all indebted for what you are saying. Let me introduce myself, Grace. I am Jane Warwick and you may or may or may not know of my recent loss but it is what you say about feeling safe that is touching so many people. I think so many of us don't feel safe for some reason and there is something about the way this world has turned out that is causing these feelings."

"I am very pleased to meet you Jane, and I'm sorry about your husband.."

"Oh, I'll tell you about that in a minute but look I want to hear about what you said up there.."

Grace looked around at all the people who ten minutes before had sat silently spell bound by her message. She wondered if it had sunk in at all or whether now as the drink started to flow business was progressing as normal.

"I didn't know what to talk about really when people first started asking me. Then I remembered the surgeon and I have to come back to him; there was before what he said to me and after. When I left hospital, everything had changed. My whole world changed by being in the wrong place at the wrong time when the bullet passed through me and that was just the start. It took me some time to work it out but I eventually realised what it was. Bullets and guns all that stuff didn't happen in my world it only happened in other people's worlds. But now it had happened in mine and it had changed everything. All the stuff which was nothing to do with me happening outside the bubble I had made around myself was now very much part of my life. My safety bubble, the wall I had built around myself whatever you like to call it had been taken down and suddenly I was connected into everything!

The only protection I ever had was that I was in a state of denial about what was happening all around me. Maybe it is enough dealing with your own life in this city, keeping yourself in a state of mind where you can get out of the comfort and security of your home and go to work; summon the strength to deal with everything coming your way. People are under appalling stress as their work situations become more and more difficult, others are living in terrible conditions as rents become higher and higher, my friends who I think are doing ok suddenly are having break downs and splitting with their partners, the city is awash with the crime that caused me to be shot. A crime, a tragic accident originating apparently in another country caused by the changing climate which took away the livelihood of the immigrant who accidentally shot me, whose liver is now keeping me alive. So no, I don't feel safe anymore. Perhaps we do not ever have the right to feel safe, really did we ever. Can we ever?"

"I'm not sure we ever felt we were completely safe, but I know exactly what you are saying. Perhaps in times gone by the danger on the whole was in your direct vicinity but even then tragedy could always arrive from a distant shore and from circumstances way out of our control. But I think we are encouraged by all these people.."

She waved her hand at the surrounding diners as they poured down their vintage champagne..

" I think we are encouraged to live in our bubbles as you put it. We don't know the full extent of what is going on and really how dangerous the situation on this world really is!"

"So why do they want me here talking about all this."

"Because people are waking up to it and I can assure you they will find a way of bending it to their advantage and make the people of the country and the city think they are on their side and they are doing everything they can to sort it out…"

"…When in fact they are doing exactly what they have always done and ignoring all the danger. So, everything is steadily getting worse and worse."

"You got it, darling!"

Grace looked around again and back to Jane who looked back with a smile of one who had revealed a secret that really everybody knows.

"So, what about you, Jane? Obviously your husband passing away so suddenly must have been a terrible shock?"

She looked around the room; clearly running through those previous months after her husband and soul mate had died. His death had brought a devastation and perhaps in the same way it had taken Grace to come to terms with the incident that had changed her life it was only in these past few days and perhaps as she had listened to what Grace had said she had really begun to understand what it had meant. She turned back to Grace. Grace felt her soft brown eyes engage with her as they had not done previously.

"Steve was a good man, Grace. He came from a family that had broken early on his life and he just started working. He was a trader. You probably met one yourself some time. He'd see an opportunity in some product, a lump of money he could move, a situation he could turn around to make a profit. Sometimes it was the actual product sometimes it was the gamble; the crop would come in and the money he made on the eventual sale would double or triple his outlay. The profit was everything of course like with all of these guys. That is what they are working for, to add to the pile they are making. I was not aware he ever did anything illegal or anything to put anyone in any danger but he worked too hard, my dear. I think he was always working, always looking for the next trade to add to his pile. Of course, the pile of money was his wall, his bubble as you put it. The more he made the better he liked it because in his own bubble, the one he had created to deal with the insecurity caused by the collapse of his family, he imagined the money meant he could not be touched by all the craziness he saw happening around him.

He was careful and I said he gambled but only when he was completely sure it would go his way and to be fair he did his homework thoroughly and in the years we were together he ended up trading companies as they were absorbed by corporations as if they were bags of potatoes and he did make an enormous amount of money….and yes we had a nice house and we did travel to much of Arimathea and saw what a beautiful amazing world it was.

But we saw the problems. He was well aware of them but it never occurred to him he could use some of his money to in some way alleviate it, even in a small way. The money he had made was for us and eventually the kids to keep us and them safe in the bubble he had made for us all, protect us from what he had become convinced was the reason his parents had split….that they never seemed to have enough money. Of course, life is never that simple and of course ironically it was the stress of maintaining and creating his bubble that eventually killed him. He died of a heart attack in the middle of some deal, it was of course going to be the last deal; they always were and I knew it never would be because this obsession would never leave him. It was like I think you said, it was how he dealt with his life, how he could live in his own skin."

"So, did he leave you and your children a colossal amount of money?"

"He did Grace, which is of course why I am invited to these functions. But it's funny Grace. Steve was always in control of the money and of course that was part of it. He talked to me about it and where we would go or how we would use it but there was always an understanding that it was for us and our direct family. He held it, Grace like he had some powerful creature chained up in a dungeon he could bring out to fight against anyone who dared to challenge him. Everybody wanted some of that power but he was ruthless the way he kept it. I have come to realise this, strangely only since I have been in control of the money he left to me. I am not sure Steve was conscious of all this or thought about the power it gave him other than it was the armour he used to protect us. But I have come to realise the nature of what it is;. pure and raw, enabling you to do whatever you like in a world where it can bring you anything you could possibly imagine.

In the grieving process I started thinking what was now left of Steve. Of course, I have a lifetime of memories with him but also inseparable from him is this enormous fortune he amassed. As I thought about him I thought about it and what it actually represented now his connection with it had gone. How did I relate to that power? I wondered if Steve's obsession with amassing all that potential had had anything to do with his illness. I began to come to terms with the whole notion of what it now represented to me. I went right back to the beginning because it must have come from somewhere; there wasn't just a pile of cash sitting on the planet somewhere and people just came and helped themselves to it. But in a sense that was exactly what it was, us and the planet and everything we could dig and transform from it, all the animals we could tame and trade, it all came from what we found around us and transferred amongst ourselves and at some point it became this huge pile of cash I was now in control of.

So, I came to the conclusion of course this power had come directly from the planet of Arimathea. Everything belongs to her because everything has come from her and in her care it very rarely stays in the same place for very long. It always flows whether water in her rivers, air around her weather systems or lifeblood in our veins. We use this power she has given us or we have discovered, but no longer acknowledge where it came from or maybe it hasn't been as important as it is now and we need to be considering her when we use her power in all the changes we are making to her. Then I saw the monk on the TV broadcasting from the ship and all the whales, the rays and dolphins all swimming together. I was so moved. I watched it again and again and I remembered what he said..

'Arimathea, this world is a fully sentient being and everything on her contributes in some way to her health and well-being. Her spirit... her soul dwells in every living thing and experiences the beauty and the wonder growing here through all of those lives.'

So, this is where I have come to Grace. I want to use the money Steve left to me to continue bringing this idea into the world. I want to speak up for Arimathea. I want her power that has come to me to carry on the momentum caused by the monk's broadcast and all the discussion that has subsequently happened to actually come to something or at least continue that momentum. I don't know how this could happen but when I heard what you said tonight, heard your passion for the world you have lost, I thought it is the world we are all losing, it is slipping away without us really noticing or even caring!"

They talked that night in wildly ridiculous and then more serious terms about how the human race could ever come to think of their planet as a being of which they were all a part of; who could be affected in some way by every thought, word and action taking place upon her, day in and day out. As they talked the more likely it seemed the monk was talking a truth that only now could be fully comprehended as the planet could be contemplated as one vast interconnected web of thought and information. It was not a huge leap to imagine if half of the people of the world went out and performed some act of kindness for the other, the planet would be transformed overnight. Then it followed it seemed that if just about everyone was indifferent to what was happening around them then nothing would ever change. So how could these polarities be reversed on Arimathea?

They came to an agreement the process may well have been started, judging by the unprecedented broadcast of the monk from the ocean liner and possibly in the wider community of the beings with whom they shared their world. So how could they continue to increase the momentum? Perhaps they were unqualified to answer such a question, but maybe if they brought as many of the people together in the same place who had a better idea of what actually had to be done then maybe an answer would be more forthcoming. In the coming week they talked again and the idea of a gathering with something of the qualities of both a serious conference and a celebratory music festival began to surface. At the very least, they imagined it would bring large numbers of the people interested in finding an answer to their question together in one place.

Two large additional juggernauts had arrived on the site out in the desert and slunk to a halt with the creaking and hissing of air brakes. Grace had been watching as a further workforce had materialised and now appeared to be disembowelling them. Two huge sleeves of colourful material were being dragged out of the containers and stretched across the ground in the early morning Starshine. As she felt the first warmth of the early morning Star on her face she remembered the dream she had had almost as she awoke that morning. It had been vivid and real in a way that dreams sometimes seem to reveal an alternative existence where one path splits into two and then continue running in parallel.

The dream had felt so real she could still taste the sea air gently blowing across the beach on which she had been standing. The beach curved away into the far distance and there was movement there. Dawn was slipping gently back into the world. The Star was already pinkly lighting the underside of the clouds slowly moving across the clouds above the sea's horizon. There was a profound stillness, even the gulls had become silent in their wheeling above her. Waves lapped gently at her feet, fizzing as they disappeared into the pristine stretches of sand they had left in their retreat. She looked again to the movement in the distance. There was a group of something. She strained deeper into the image…of white…moving steadily towards her. Now she looked to the Star, surely soon it would rise above the horizon; but then back to the movement on the beach.

Suddenly she could see what the movement was. There was a small group of white horses walking up the beach towards her. She realised in a moment their movement and the rising of the Star was inextricably linked. She watched the progression of the horses as the Star became nearer to its appearance over the edge of the world. The horses advanced purposefully until a beautiful mare who had led her extended family straight up to her, nuzzled

- 575 -

up to her pushing her softly with her great head. Grace saw into her eyes, evaporated into her eyes, entranced by the love and the intelligence of the being she found there.

Then the mare turned out towards the sea lowered her head, laid her ears gently back and half closed her eyes. Grace looked around at the other horses, who now all stood facing the horizon, heads lowered, ears back, where the first crack of light had appeared. She herself had turned and stood with the horses and experienced with them the rising of the Star; experienced light returning to their world. She stood in a profound state of peaceful awareness, her body glowing with the enlivening magic she knew had always been available to her but she had managed to ignore for all these years; with the horses who she now knew returned to this place or another place and performed this ritual every day of their lives. She had been deeply moved and woke with tears streaming down her face.

Two large cradle like structures had been removed from the juggernaut with another large piece of lifting machinery. They were gradually being moved into place at the foot of the two sleeves of material. Grace watched and listened as the gas burners were noisily ignited and started to blow hot air into the billowing sleeves. Then they started to take shape as hot air balloons; at first inflating along the ground and then gradually rising into the air to hover, straining at the tethers holding them to the ground.

Grace smiled to herself. The balloons each had a beautiful cartoon portrayal of Arimathea carefully incorporated into their design and now they floated, swaying gently in the early morning breezes beckoning to Grace whose task that morning, now awaited her. She could see two people carrying camera equipment had arrived and were already climbing into the cradle beneath one of the balloons. They were connecting up their equipment in preparation for their flight. Their director was talking to one of the sites organisers and he looked around and saw Grace standing, watching as everything unfolded before her. He was beckoning for her to come over. She smiled to herself and gently shook her head and started to make her way over to the balloons.

Chapter Sixty-five
The Summoning.

Grace had clambered into the basket of the balloon with the cameraman and the journalist. The hot air balloon was gently rising into the cool early morning air. Bursts of the ignited gas blasting from the burner occasionally shattered the silence, providing more buoyancy as the balloon rose higher and higher. Grace clung tightly to the rails provided around the basket. She resisted the urge to look down at this stage concentrating on looking out to the mountains in the distance. They had timed the ascent to perfection. The first rays of the rising Star were bursting through some of the lower valleys on the distant horizon. Here she was again as the Star rose into her world. Long shadows thrown by the peaks knifed across the desert floor towards the hive of activity where the infrastructure of her event now took the form of the untidy workings of some desert creature that had found its' way to the surface and now sought to protect itself in this new environment.

Up above the balloons began to float into the new rays of Starlight. The effect was dramatic. One side of the balloons with the beautiful graphics of Arimathea blazoned across them shone fully illuminating oceans and mountain ranges, land masses and the enhanced rivers flowing across the continents. The camera pointed out towards the Star rise with filters adjusted to allow enough light into the electronics to allow the magnificence of the scene now unravelling to be converted and beamed to a destination in the media networks of Arimathea. A team of producers and technicians would be waiting for the interview scheduled for the early morning news show. They spoke to the journalist through an earpiece. Grace did not hear what was said but the journalist who looked like he had been awake for days turned to Grace,

"How are you feeling Grace are you ready to do this…we're nearly ready to go. As you know we'll be feeding live into the studio."

The earpiece crackled again,

"…we got two minutes. So, collect your thoughts and breath deep. I'm sure you know what you want to say so I'll give the intro then it'll be over to you."

The wave of terror of which she had spoken to Jane about all those weeks before flooded through her being. Here though there was nowhere to run to. She had her emergency parachute and for a few split seconds she considered her escape from this latest exposure she had brought upon herself or had been brought upon her. She wished Jane could have been here with her to help explain what they had cooked up between them. Flashes of their conversations echoed through her thoughts as she grappled for themes and reasons, explanations for this stunt they had planned between them; to draw the attention of any one sitting at home eating their breakfast, drinking their coffee preparing for the onslaught of the day, listening with one ear open just in case there was something they needed to know, wanted to know about what was happening in their world.

Now this was happening. Jane had decided she had wanted to convert the power Steve had accumulated into an appeal, a plea, a desperate scream to the people of Arimathea. Here she floated above the mountains like an eagle, warm air under her wings searching the world below, aware of the Star and everything that had come into being because of its' proximity to this world. Everything she depended on and depended on her was down there; Her prey, her offspring, her mate, soaring over some distant peak also searching for the elixir of life that scuttled below amongst the scrub and the stones. Depended on it being there eventually, because it always was, sometimes just before it was too late but it would be there somewhere and they would all live another day.

But Grace knew, unlike the eagle that all the power her race had accumulated, enabling her to be here to feel all this, the true wonder of the world they had inherited had come at a terrible price for human and eagle. There was a further crackle in the journalist's earpiece...The cameraman counted down and then pointed at the journalist.

"As you can see I am high above the desert in these magnificent balloons created specifically for the event happening in the next few days down below us. I'm up here with Grace Evans who you may know from the publicity around her recent shooting in the Straam city. It seems the concern she has had for her city has transformed into a greater concern. She has told me it is the same concern. So anyway, the best person to explain what is happening here would be Grace herself. So, Grace how has this all come about since the terrible shooting incident in Straam."

The camera turned to Grace. Who looked back at it silently for a few moments.

"Good morning, everybody. I hope you are enjoying your breakfast." She looked back at the Journalist and then away from the camera out to the mountains in the distance; then she started talking into camera.

"...Beautiful isn't it!? The mountains and these amazing balloons; we have made them to fix an image in your head so you won't forget us. All carefully orchestrated up here just after dawn so I can grab your attention about what we are intending to do here in the next few weeks. If you know anything about what happened to me and my subsequent work in the spotlight of the Straam media you will be used to hearing me talk about how I know longer feel safe in the city; unsurprising perhaps since I was mistakenly shot in an argument between two drug dealers. Since then I have had a lot of feedback from many of you out there who have had similar feelings after experiencing some major trauma in your own lives. All this feedback has encouraged me to carry on with this work rather than disappearing back into my old life.

Many of the discussions I have had, have taken this strange feeling of feeling unsafe further than the context of the city in which I live into the wider world. Coincidentally, in recent months we have had some remarkable communications it would seem from the other beings, other species with whom we share this planet. We have made substantial changes to our world, their world which perhaps has provoked their response. There has been much discussion about what we must do. I have met people who share my concerns to such an extent we have decided to organise an event out here in the desert. It will be a celebration of our humanity on Arimathea and all we have achieved but it will also be a retrospective on where we have gone wrong. We hope we will have some insight into how we could make it better.

So, we will have a conference with some of the big names in the world of conservation and environmental science, politicians will be given their say, we have archaeologists, lawyers, doctors and architects. We have priests and shamans, and they'll bring the spirits of this entire world and the world's beyond. Of course, we have the poets and the artists; they will bring their unique perspective which often reflects the troubles of our world. We want to find out what is happening here at this time and why. We want to find out if there is anything we can do, that all of you out there can do for everyone who shares our beautiful world. We are going to have a party down here with some big acts and some big sound systems and with no one to upset its' going to be LOUD. So, get down here if you feel you want to get involved, play your part! It's time to change the world, well, well past that time actually, but this time we're going to go much, much further. I look forward to seeing you all!"

The people of Arimathea had been waiting for her announcement, her invitation. They had asked themselves and pleaded with their screens and radios as the signs and displays, the calls from the other ancient species with whom they shared their world seemed to plead with them to take action.

"What shall I do? What can I do when I am just one of billions on this world? What can I do as the huge mechanism of humanity rolls on every day chanting the silent and unsaid mantra to greed and profit? What can I do as the skies and the seas are filled with the pollution of its machinery, of its need for progress and growth, of its need for domination of not only of its own species but of all its wild and beautiful places and all the creatures who live amongst the tall trees growing there. How can I have a voice in this place where I am wrapped and cushioned in this illusion my society has become, where my words will not sound derogatory and obsolete?

This society that has evolved by looking past the beauty in these places and seeing the trees and the mountains not as the flesh and bones of a beautiful paradise but only as empty expanses devoid of life and soul to be exploited for their great riches. Here we continue our tragic search, for something we have lost but was always there. It was not in the profits generated from cutting down the trees and levelling the mountains but in the spirit wonder that was living there. Is it too late to change this way of looking at our world?"

This was the question so many of the people had asked or had wanted to ask long before they saw Graces plea through the electronic media of Arimathea. Long before they started to receive the dreams the dragons were sending from their crystal caves offering them the wonder they suspected laid all around them but dared not acknowledge in case when they had invested their emotion in such beauty it was again taken away from them. They had seen the devastating industrialisation of their world. Only as they had started to learn about and see the beauty of the vast forests that had become the lungs of the world, that had more creatures and plants in a grove of trees than other areas had in entire countries; they had also learnt about their destruction. They had learnt this was happening on an unimaginable scale and for a few seconds they might have imagined what it would be like to see an area of jungle being cut down and burnt, imagined what would happen to the life living in those areas. They had hoped the cute monkeys swung off into the forest and resumed their lives as normal in a new tree, next to a new river.

The alternatives were too distressing to think about because now they had seen the beautiful primates nursing their babies in their close knit communities. They had seen how closely the affection they lavished on their offspring so resembled how they had treated their own children and perhaps their family structures seemed closer, more supportive, more human! So they had buried their worry and the horror they felt, and if they had the luxury, forced it out from the protective bubble they had built around themselves. They had even allowed themselves to be persuaded by a sinister fashionable opinion that it did not matter because the human race needed to advance, could not stand still. They had not been the people who dared to speak out against the destruction, who were labelled as idealists who did not understand that it was only through this growth that everyone would eventually be able to share in the wealth it was creating.

These were the people now sitting hurriedly eating their breakfast fuelling up for another day working in and reinforcing the illusion of their machine culture who heard what Grace had said. Across the country of Eremoya the broadcast eventually was played in the homes of tens of millions of families once other networks, having seen the beauty of the pictures and knowing the popularity and interest Grace had attracted played it on their own news items later in the day. The empathy they had felt while watching the programmes about their world and all the wonder that abounded in it, lay buried deep in their subconscious. Many of them had dreamed in the early morning before they woke of a beautiful Star rise in their favourite place or some place they had imagined one day they would visit. Many had shared the experience with another species nearby, also clearly relishing the event. The magic of their dream had touched those buried places where they held their love and awe for Arimathea and many had awoken with a deeply profound sense of belonging to their world in a way they had rarely felt before. Many then decided they would go to Graces' event, to show their solidarity with the sentiment and her appeal. Many decided they would contribute in some way, take their skill or something they could offer in the spirit of awareness they now felt was rising irresistibly on Arimathea.

Chapter Sixty-six
The Crystal Cave of the Dragons mind.

Okino had taken to slipping out into the gardens of the Keating mansion before the Star had risen. This practice the monks had instilled in him in the year and a half he had spent in the monastery. They would meditate allowing the first rays of the newly risen Star to refresh and revitalise any tiredness or confusion remaining after the previous nights' sleep. Clarity of mind was the goal of the monks lifestyle. However, often unacknowledged dilemmas and confusions could arise in the dreamscapes of the monk demanding a response which often meant further and deeper soul searching. Deep in meditation, empty of all external influences he would allow landscapes and characters within those landscapes to surface hoping they could give some guidance into the nature of this trouble. So deeply attuned to themselves they had become, they presumed these characters were aspects of their deep subconscious which had been or remained difficult to access even after the rigorous training they had undergone. However, they acknowledged the depths of these internal realms, possibly influenced by genetic memories passed on to them by previous generations. They were resigned this work would almost certainly never be completed during one lifetime.

Reincarnation was an accepted and much explored area at the heart of the monks personal and communal life. Although like so much of their work in the other realms there was little scientific and so provable evidence for this phenomenon. Practically it seemed acceptable if physical and even personality traits could be handed from generation to generation then certainly any circumstances forming those personalities may well have also made the journey. The personality then, maintained some essence of those previous generations. It was believed in certain cases the actual person had again been reborn. They were the most holy of people who had transcended the normal bounds and cycles of rebirth. They would come again and again with the purity and clarity they had eventually achieved as a result of the lives they had led.

So this was the goal for every monk; to resolve the various information he had carried into his new life as best he could. They accepted their spirit carried the information in some form of inter dimensional energy and became conscious again in their new soul. Their spirit and so the experience of their lifetime would continue after the death of their physical body and be merged again into the great spirit. Here they would reside in the invisible realms where this spirit would await a new soul to continue the journey in the physical realms' lifetime after lifetime. Generations of monks had concluded this was the only logical explanation for the transition of spirit energy. It had become the accepted teaching and so collective wisdom as they continually explored the mystery of their existence in time and space.

As Okino sat quietly on the carefully mown lawn in front of the large stone fishpond it was his soul and all his spirit with whom he was once again becoming aligned. He had resumed his observation of the large golden fish endlessly patrolling the shallow depths of the pool; gently and hypnotically swaying onward amongst the lily pads and the white lotus flowers which sporadically covered the pool. He found it infinitely entertaining and felt insights arise and correspondences burst through his mind as he watched the slow, deliberate and flowing passage of the fish held in the clear invisibility of their watery home. They moved deliberately without pause with little to upset the course of their lives. They rarely collided or even needed sudden changes of direction to avoid collision.

He wondered whether they had worked out in the years they had been navigating these confined waters how their routes perhaps would never meet. What thoughts were they lost in, possibly unbroken for many years as they swam amongst the serenity of the snowy white Lotus flowers. What profound philosophies might be arising even being shared amongst these peaceful golden beings with their diaphanous fan tails and fins on their silent journeys and their endless and undisturbed meditations. In their journeys through this space could it be possible they were evolving their own state in isolation from the rest of their species. He smiled to himself. He had no way of knowing what the fish were thinking or whether they had anything beyond the next few feet of water on their mind and really wasn't he thinking about his life in the rarefied atmosphere of the monastery surrounded by the snowy mountain peaks of Jahallalah.

Then there were the squirrels diving through the Oak trees standing on the edges of the lawn. Their leaves were slowly yellowing now and gradually falling to Earth, as the autumn started to take hold and the length of the days shortened. They were not unlike the Oaks in his own valley through which he had walked in the early part of his journey. In the forest they were mostly considerably older and surrounded by their fallen limbs. The wood was being broken down and the nutrients returned to the soil. In the great flow of time they would again take their place in the life of the tree. He had seen squirrels briefly in the branches as they scurried through the thick canopy. But now it seemed he was watching an entire family chasing one another through the branches. They raced along the narrow limbs without any recognition they possessed fear in their small agile frames. The younger members of the family chased each other at speeds seemingly defying their ability to make sensible decisions about their routes through the canopy. Inevitably their path would regularly end with them hurling themselves from the flimsy end of one branch through the space between to grab onto an equally flimsy branch in the neighbouring tree. He smiled. As if they were leaping from one life to the next.

Yet they never fell. They seemed to defy their physicality as if they had forgotten they were still made of flesh and bone and had found themselves to exist only in the energy they could generate in their bodies. It seemed they knew, without question, this energy could carry them through any of the death defying antics they would need to perform in their chase, in their need for escape or to collect food from these trees in which so many generations of them would have lived. Okino acknowledged again the wonder of the evolution that had come to this world. The squirrels had become adapted to their environment like the wolves and the goats, the leopards and the eagles. This ability they had developed had enabled them to take their place living in amongst the trees.

The Oak trees generated excessive acorns; far more than were needed to ensure the survival of the wood or the next generation of trees. But they made energy enough for these small creatures to live and thrive amongst their solid boughs. In return the squirrels would forget where they had buried the surplus acorns and the next generation of Oak trees would be born and start to grow.

The wind gusted strongly. Starlight fell through an opening in the clouds as they raced across the sky. It fell on the pool illuminating the water. The golden fish appeared to have taken on an ethereal glow as they swayed on their endless voyages, the squirrels shrieked in delight as they tumbled amongst the ancient limbs and a new blizzard of leaves released from the Oak trees, fluttered down onto the lawns and amongst the ripples on the surface of the pond.

"All in a dream."

The phrase surfaced gently amongst Okino's thoughts. He knew Merilon to be close or possibly directly in contact with him from the depths of Arimathea where he had once again fallen into a deep sleep amongst the crystal caverns, filling their vibration and Arimathea's life force with his dreams. Had all of this, all he could see around him, all he had lived through and would live through been condensed or in some way guided by his dreams? Was it all a product or a bi product, a residue, a trace of the strange and beautiful amalgamation of knowledge Merilon had brought from his home in the stars? Had his dream initiated this voyage and allowed it to continue through this space and time in which it had occurred and carried all this life through the millennia, somehow given it the means, the knowledge to survive and become ever more beautiful and ever more sophisticated.

Again, the wind gusted and Mariella had appeared strangely and briefly illuminated in a ray of starshine at the end of the fishpond which had moments before, so effectively reflected the mechanisms of the universe into Okino's meditative state. She stood watching him for a few moments uncertain as to whether he was deeply embedded in one of his altered states, possibly in another time conversing with one of the dragons. In those moments he was able to see her without the connection they normally had.

His beautiful friend Mariella who had extracted him from his world in Jahallala and brought him here to where he sat amongst the fishponds and the manicured gardens he had seen in the magazines. She was a warm and sensual young woman who had encouraged him to expand into the being he had become in the previous months but who he knew could put him firmly in his place if such a situation should arise. In those moments he saw the aspect of the tough survivor, with a very specific responsibility to her world. She had become as close to Arimathea as he and Merilon and now it felt as if they were all walking through the world together. As she realised he was staring back at her she smiled, her face became animated again in the way he had become used to and she walked around to where he was sitting and sat down beside him.

"You have found my beautiful fish Okino. Have they been telling you all their secrets?"

Okino chuckled.

"As a matter of fact they have. You see the one just coming around here and the one over there just coming around the corner."

"Yes." Mariella prepared herself...

"They have managed to avoid speaking to each other for three centuries!"

"...That is extraordinary Okino because I don't think they have been in this pond more than one hundred turnings of our beloved Star!"

"Apparently, and it may take some more investigation and lengthy conversations, it is more complicated than that."

Mariella laughed.

"You wouldn't think so would you, the way they just swim around and around day after day.."

They laughed together in the light, and in each other's eyes, in the breeze and the falling leaves and the racing squirrels and the solidity of the Oaks; In the happiness they shared when they were together and she gave him one of her kisses and playfully pushed his shoulder.

"Look, I've come down here to disturb you for a reason!"

"You don't need a reason, always come and disturb me if you want to."

"Thank you, Okino. I will remember that when I haven't spoken to you for three days. But seriously there has been something on the TV this morning...there was a girl called Grace Evans who was shot in the street while I was away. She has become quite a celebrity and now she is organising an enormous conference type festival event out in the desert. She's managed to persuade some pretty clever people to go down there and talk and play and discuss how we can change everything...it should be good and I think we should go.."

"Yeah, definitely I think we should go. Sounds like things are really starting to move on a bit."

There was a silence between them for a few moments.

"Are you Ok, Okino!"

"Yeah I'm fine!"

"It's just you seem a little distant this morning. Have you been running around with that dragon again?"

Okino knew Arimathea was there in the gardens in the light filled silence allowing him, almost urging him to find the words he needed for the thoughts now arising.

"Everything just suddenly seems less clear cut."

"When was it ever? Life evolving from one phase to the next, it's rarely a smooth process and more often than not it gets a bit messy. Then it goes on in the new state. The process will always be the mystery. In the end we have to trust Arimathea to find her way into the future. She has trusted you to help her and that is exactly what you have done and things are happening. You have woken her dragon and perhaps there was a very good reason why they had to have a separation at such a crucial time of human development. Fabulous things have happened in that time…"

"I know, I know and you are right of course. But it's been meeting Mithrael and finding out that he is working so emphatically against all we have been working towards."

"He obviously lost his way as a result of his tragedy and part of the process I should imagine will be reuniting him with Merilon and the other dragons."

"But he is in so deep with his world banking operation and who knows how deep his drug running operation goes. It's difficult to see how he could just turn it all around even if Merilon did manage to persuade him to join their circle again."

Mariella laughed. She remembered when she had found Okino in Aharri confused and unsure about the dragon dreams he had been having and how she had seen and heard how he had travelled with Merilon to where the dragons had worked in their underlying dimensions and how they had been able to work out what had happened in those past centuries to bring about the changes gradually making themselves apparent in the world.

"Okino they are working again through the world as they always did. But I think everything has moved on. We have moved on in our understanding of the consciousness and what we can do. I think the dragons have moved on as a result of their own journey in the consciousness and with the elemental spirits."

"…and I agree perhaps that is why they needed to separate…"

"So, their dream can be brought into the world at this time now it is ready.. Arimathea is ready because she feels what is happening is endangering her life…the dragons are ready because they have a new connection with the consciousness and they can go back to what they do best. I think we are ready because we have so much more knowledge about the world. We have become sensitive and receptive to external forces continually trying to influence us. You've seen it now Okino, with the TV and all the advertising; Our society is continually making and peddling dreams to entice us deeper into its' illusion and we are continually absorbing them. I think the dragons invented a dream world a thousand years ago way ahead of its time."

"But people have always had dreams."

"Of course, but now we have all the stories and all the plotlines which have ever been told, available to us to retell and reinterpret. Still they have the same meanings but now we can make them as real as if they were happening in front of us, even to us. Their character and situation archetypes we understand perhaps in a way we never have before. So, we have superheroes working as everyday people, people who we can identify with, who have god like powers to fight crime and injustice within their fictional scenarios. We have ideal men and women as flawed or as damaged as they need to be to act out the times of our lives we struggle with. Then we can laugh or empathise with how it all turns out and we do feel better for the experience. We have the worst and most despicable kind of criminals and geniuses and we can be transported in a couple of hours to any place the producers want us to be.

Every character we see in films or on the TV is an amalgam in the story tellers mind. They delve into the old stories find the characters who have always inspired us or who have scared us to death and they transport us out of ourselves as they become real characters acting out real scenarios. The skill of the production and the ability of the technology to make these dreams has dramatically increased but also our ability has developed exponentially to transport ourselves out of this reality. They can take us anywhere we are prepared to go and the competition to find those new places is fierce because we will pay to go there.

We can leave all the grind and horror of our everyday existence behind and enter these fantasy worlds where all those old archetypes are used to trip the switches that excite us or thrill us or leave us horrified or breathlessly happy so we can face the real horror again the next day. More often than not light will triumph over dark, the good guys will win out in the end and that is what we need to feel, they need us to feel. Then we will go back to our struggle thinking it is worthwhile and we the good guys will one day get our reward, the pile of cash or the beautiful person who we assume will eventually arrive in the life we can only dream of."

Now Okino was chuckling as Mariella had become as impassioned as he had ever seen her.

"You've been thinking about this haven't you?"

"I have. Think about it, Merilon has the ability to put us in dreams which are tailor made for our own beneficial experience. He and Arimathea want us to come closer to them, understand our relationship with them before it is too late. The thing is I am pretty sure I had one of Merilons' dreams last night. But it was all my own experience, constructed from my own memories and I woke with this amazing feeling I had been given a look into some fabulous truth about our world."

"So, what was your dream, Mariella?"

"My dad used to take us all down to the coast on our holidays in the summer when we were very young. There was a little timber holiday home we used to stay in down by the beach and in my dream it was pretty much how I have remembered it or had chosen to remember it. The outside was timber planks painted blue and grey, the paint was a bit flaky and it had little windows and a porch on the front where there were all the stones and shells we had collected. Inside it was just boards on the floor which was always a bit sandy with a few Indian rugs and a strange collection of woven furniture.

I used to wake even before the Star came up but the room was always full of light it seemed and the smell of the sea. I was lying in my bed listening to the gulls and the sound of the surf in the distance wanting to go out into it and knowing I would soon but just lying there feeling the warmth and safety in the house and how close it was to the ocean and how wonderful that felt and how I felt knowing that Nick was in his bed next to me and my mum and dad were there and really life was as perfect as it ever could be.

Then I'm sliding out of bed and pulling on my clothes. Our little dog has noticed the movement and is waiting for me as I move through the front room through the door and out onto the sand dunes. I stretch and breathe great lung-fulls of the delicious sea air and the dog is bouncing around in front of me. The sea is out in the distance and I want to be down there and I start running down towards the edge of the ocean, across the pristine patterned sand and when I reach the surf without hesitation I bound straight into the waves gently rolling onto the shore.

The intensity of the cold water electrifies me and the splashing water surrounds me. I bend down, gather sea water in the cup of my hands and throw it into the air, over and over again. The Star is rising now and bounces light from the droplets of water surrounding me with a million stars holding their position surrounding me in this new light, it invades me, filling me with joy and happiness. I have never forgotten the feeling almost like it was my true arrival on Arimathea and that finally I had been woken up to her delights and no matter what happened from now these moments would always shine through to remind me of what it meant to be truly alive upon her.

Then I am standing there in the surf, the waves lapping just below my knees in the ocean, in all this blue and grey and green, glistening surfaces of beach and the sea rolling in over it, filling my footprints. I hear the gulls and the surf and the soft breeze is in my hair mixing it with the endless blue skies in front of my face and I feel I have moved, or grown just slightly away from where I had woken that morning as if I will experience my life in a deeper way from that point on. I walked down the beach with our dog splashing through the surf thinking perhaps all this has happened to him also but then I thought I had never seen him any other way. He was always just full of life and joy when he was out here.

We made our way down to the headland where there was a rocky out crop. The sea had left pools of clear salty water amongst the rocks eroded into the sculpted shapes left by millennia of the tides flowing across them. There were tiny valleys and canyons and I lay down in front of them as my clothes dried in the warming sun and watched the creatures they contained scuttling across their pristine sandy floors. I watched the tiny crabs with their intricate detail shuffling into the cover of overhanging precipices to await a transparent shrimp all eyes and waving antennae destined to fall prey to the monstrous grasp and the disproportionately large slicing claws. I moved from pool to pool watching these tiny worlds unfolding, entranced and transported by the minute precision and imagined it could be enormous and that I could walk around amongst the coloured stones glistening there, perhaps fallen as the remains of some outcrop long receded and washed away by the action of the ocean.

I had become lost for a while all those years ago in the purity of those moments unspoiled by the worries and fears I have since accumulated. But I have always remembered them as somehow sacred to my life and I awoke thinking in those moments we seem to formulate what will become important to us as we progress into our adult lives. We remember them deep in our subconscious as times when we were so comfortable and in tune with ourselves and our world we actually experienced love for the first time from something other than our parents and the other people around us. These are the moments we will always try and work our way back to and they form the fundamental relationship we need to survive on our world. Our Love for it."

"Do you think everyone has these precious memories to guide them through their lives. In your dream is a child who is loved and well cared for in a solid family?"

"No Okino I don't and I wonder what dreams they will have when they dream of their childhood. But perhaps there are sublime moments in every child's life even in their daydreams to guide them through whatever horror they have to go through!"

"I think we were both lucky."

They are both silent and contemplative. The episode of their young lives was predominantly of support and encouragement to expand and grow into the people they had needed to become in the moments they were now sharing.

"I wish you could have met my mother Okino. When I told her about You and Merilon in the days before she died she didn't seem surprised. She spoke as if Arimathea was speaking through her to me, but not someone else, it was most definitely her but as if she finally had come to an understanding of how things were after all those years of life, living it day by day experiencing it, seeing the results of action and reaction taking shape perhaps over the entire time she had lived. She worked with those deprived children, the damaged ones, tried to mend their minds give them those moments; moments filled with love for them to cherish. She slowly brought the light back into their eyes and showed them the world could be a beautiful place with people who would love them and that one day they would feel healed of all they had been through and although the memories would always be there they would understand they were because the people who inflicted such pain upon them knew only those ways, did not have those beautiful moments themselves. She wanted to break the chain of reaction in as many of the children who came into her foundation. It was her way, Okino, her way of changing the world."

Okino heard a change of intensity in Mariella's voice. He had been watching the hypnotic paths of the fish and listening to her calmly explaining her dream. He turned to her and saw the tears and her distraught face. He had almost forgotten she was in the process of grief for the death of her mother and now he offered an arm and she collapsed into him and quietly sobbed into his crimson robes. He thought of the old monks in the monastery who would often help the grieving villagers through this process. He tried to remember how they did this or what they had said. He could not think of anything and perhaps there was nothing he could say. So much of the grief was bound up with the relationship between those two people in the life they shared and where their relationship had ended. He knew Mariella and Ezme to have had a deeply loving and caring life together and he felt Mariella was wise enough to carry this now into the time she was facing without her mother. But now she had just lost the struggle to keep it all under control and wept uncontrollably, He felt her whole being shaking and convulsing in pain as if the strong woman had finally given way to the little girl on the beach who had felt so safe knowing that her mother was safely back in the house making her breakfast. He needed to bring her back. He squeezed her closer to him.

"I also had a dream Mariella. We have a kind of festival in the Springtime at the time of the Equinox when the last of the winter snow has finally receded. Winter is extreme up there and the change over to the longer days and warmth and growth is really special. It is something we always celebrate and the whole village takes part. Everybody gets up early before Star rise and makes their way down to the fish lakes. As the star rises over the mountains in the distance it is directly aligned with the river flowing down through the valley. But it's not just the people it is all the animals as well."

Okino notices the sobbing has eased slightly, he smiles and carries on relating his dream.

"In my dream I am riding one of the yaks. All the other children are also riding yaks; sometimes, with the smaller children two or three on one yak. The yaks have all their bells and brightly coloured blankets and tassels draped over them. They look resplendent and although I think they are acting as if it is just another day I think they are proud and seem to be behaving cooperatively. I can feel the gentle gait of the yak slowly making her way out from the cobbled street into the meadows, solid and dependable playing her part at the heart of our lives. My father is leading her, my mother walks beside him with her arm threaded through his. We are surrounded by the whole village: All our family and all our friends and neighbours. Everyone is dressed in their best clothes. Many have brought and are playing their brightly painted drums and pipes. The monks are with us too, in their crimson robes. They blow their horns and sing their mantras, filling the valley with their eerie haunting sound that echoes off into the far distance calling the spirits of the other worlds to join us in our celebration.

The older children and the people not involved with the instruments dance around each other to the rhythms of the drums and stringed instruments as the tempo gradually increases. Threading their way through all of this, all the goats and the chickens wander freely, the whole unruly happy crowd is herded on it seems by the unusual variety of dogs who have over the generations come to share our village and our lives. One of the yaks pulls a cart on which there is enough freshly baked bread to infuse the whole scene with it's wonderful smell and feed the entire village at the feast after the proceedings. The whole scene is one of complete and organised chaos moving on a gentle tide towards the centre of the valley. A cacophony of screeching, squawking, lowing, singing, banging and bellowing, chattering singing creatures, carefree for a few hours after the strain and worry of the long winter months.

I am smiling with the infectious happiness pervading the scene and as I look further out beyond the teeming crowd I think I caught sight of the family of wolves who have been prowling around the village out on the fringes. High in the sky above, the eagles are spiralling on the early morning air. Roused now by the noisy drums and the infectious celebrations of their human neighbours they peer down from their ethereal flight hungrily observing, ruthlessly calculating, and patiently waiting for their next opportunity to slaughter a chicken or a young goat. Even death is following us down into the valley, everyone is here gradually moving together now, through the meadows as we have moved together through the months and the years, each with their role, each with their story, everyone has survived and those who have not walk with us as if they have, because they could be on the fringes of this crowd unseen this year but like they had been for all those previous years when the chaos had been filled with their special song or screech or drumbeat, even their smile will always belong here, radiant unforgotten.

Then we are standing and gradually the humans at least know it is time for quiet. The goats and the chickens less so and the soft glow of the Star rise becomes an intense thread of brightness over the hills. The monks say their prayers asking the spirit of Arimathea to grant us her blessings and kindness with beneficial weather to grow our crops strong and healthy and to keep our children always safe. The bread is passed around and the monks bless all of us and all the animals for the coming year. Then the Star gradually rises above the mountains. It fills the scene with warm golden light and sends a sparkling stream of light snaking through the valley up the bends of the river into the lakes amongst which we are now standing. We are surrounded by the Star gleaming, sparkling and shining from every surface and liquid movement from which it can reflect. For a few moments we stand breathless in the magnificent splendour in which we find ourselves.

Then, out of the silence, from somewhere deeper than I can say, with one voice, a great roar of overwhelming joy erupts from all of us. Then the cacophony starts up again. Everyone is jumping and dancing and savouring the bread, kissing and hugging each other and taking blessings and giving blessings, shaking their large horned heads and sounding their bells, blowing their horns and banging their drums, saying their prayers, scratching at some itchy old fur or delving for some root in the dirt, or crowing or butting or chasing a brother or a sister. A great eruption of ecstatic life celebrating our life together and that Summer however brief is on its way. This was the dream I had and I awoke with the sound of its joyfulness ringing through my head."

Okino looks down to where Mariella is now still and silent. He carefully adjusts his hold on her shoulders and sees her eyes have closed and her rhythmic breathing tells him she has fallen asleep. He smiles to himself and resumes his vigil observing the constant circulations of Mariella's golden fish. He hopes all is well in Lamai high in the mountains of Jahallaala and remembers why he started out on the journey that has brought him so far from the little town across on the other side of his world.

Chapter Sixty-seven
Harri's Mine.

Later that morning Mariella and Okino were back in the house in Aaron's study overlooking the garden. Mariella was quiet and introspective but was enthusiastic when Okino announced he wanted to track down the corporation who had been responsible for the pollution of the river running into the lakes in the valley. The only clue he had was the name he had seen on the packaging of the chemicals at Haran's farm. He typed the letters carefully one at a time into the computers search engine.

WADE

Immediately the screen was filled with references to the name that had become so graphically imprinted on his mind during the long journey from the farm. It became obvious almost immediately that the word **WADE** represented an enormous corporation with its headquarters here in Straam, the capital city of Eremoya. Okino carefully began to study the information offered. He already had become used to operating the computers browser and soon was delving deep into the Wade Corporations global operation. Mariella sat in a chair next to him and together they picked their way into the maze of information, into the links offered through every screen.

Deeper and deeper they went down the rabbit hole. It was taking them to every corner of Arimathea where the Wade corporation conducted its business, held influence and transformed for its own advantage whatever and wherever it could. It held as the core of its work mining and manufacturing. These main areas then branched into food production and the provision of energy. There were pictures, supported by bland text, of workers in fields and looking over vast open cast mines; in factories they stood next to production lines where the latest models of family saloons and expensive sports cars were undergoing their final spray paint coats before further pictures of a family happily driving their new dream machine out of a car show room.

They drove to the supermarket where they filled their shopping trolleys with food and in turn loaded it into their cars. In each scene the Wade corporation's involvement was indicated and particularly stressed the care and consideration that had been made in supplying each of these products to give the best value to their customers for the optimum most competitive price. Then in their homes having feasted on the food they had bought they settled down in their living rooms warmed by energy supplied by Wade and in armchairs made in the Wade factories, watching programmes made or commissioned by Wade.

Each area seamlessly interlinked with the next, back into factories and the fields where the products were produced and grown, always populated by dedicated workers happily absorbed in their work. The pictures still and moving were slick and carefully orchestrated giving a concise narration of the journey many of the products and services took from where they originated to where they were finally bought and consumed. In these films and pictures the Star was always shining, environments in all cases were pristine and new, set against a backdrop of a thriving world to which the company was contributing successfully, useful and valuable products that people in all parts of the world were being employed to manufacture and were buying to use in their homes and their lives.

Okino and Mariella found the team of executives who were miraculously orchestrating this wonderful unprecedented global phenomenon and bringing its benefits to the people of Arimathea. Well groomed, smiling friendly looking people with startling attributes and credentials appeared one after the other, each with their responsibility and contributions to the success story endlessly listed. Finally, the chief executive officer of the Wade Corporation flashed onto the screen. Okino studied the face of Harri Wade. A man in his early fifties clearly who had carried authority, hair greying slightly looking out of keen intelligent steely blue eyes set in a lean and slightly thin looking face. Okino found a distance in the eyes he was looking into and a weariness caused by some fear perhaps buried deeper than Harri Wade himself would admit. But most startling was that Okino recognised this face.

"Mariella I recognise this face and I suspect you may as well."

"I do have a vague recollection of his face but he is quite a famous person so I may have seen his face on some programme or other.."

"No not on a programme, Mariella."

He leapt up and ran out of the room and disappeared into the house leaving Mariella staring at the space he had left and on the screen the image of the man who could have been the father of any of her friends, someone she would pass in the street without any suspicion he was the CEO of one of the most powerful global corporations on Arimathea. So, she wondered now how Okino had recognised him and where he had gone. She had never seen him move so fast and with such enthusiasm. She looked out across the garden out to the fishponds where she had found him meditating that morning. She thought of how easily he had calmed her with the account of his dream telling her and giving her further insight into the nature of the life he had led until very recently. How easily he had walked into this world of hers and started to understand it and delve into it, continuing in his quiet unassuming way, the mission Arimathea had granted to him. Now here was the man who was ultimately responsible for the tragedy unfolding in his community. He would not be an easy man to meet or even to find. She smiled to herself as she heard the clatter of Okino bounding down the stairs. No doubt it was being taken care of!

Okino appeared in the doorway. He was carrying one of the wolf skins which had come back with them on the night of their journey in the stone circle on the way to Asima. He held it out in front of Mariella.

"He was there in the circle that night, he was the chief who greeted us. Not in his grey suit and shaven with barely any hair but in skins and with long hair and a beard, younger and more muscular but those eyes, Mariella I remember them so clearly from when they greeted us and shook our hands."

Mariella looked again. Perhaps she had not looked so deeply. She remembered how surprised she had been to be so suddenly in such a strange new world but clearly in the same place and particularly still reeling after having such a profound experience with Arimathea.

"I don't Okino, I really don't. But if you think it was him I have no reason to doubt what you are saying. Perhaps last year I would have said you were completely insane but after all we have been through it seems almost as if it could only have been him."

Okino was sitting again staring intently at the screen.

"So, Mr Wade we will meet again, Under slightly different circumstances. I wonder if you will recognise me after ten thousand years."

Deeper into their search on the web they found less enthusiastic reports about the Wade corporation. It seemed Okino's problem was not an isolated one. They found reports from many different countries in which the company was mentioned in disputes about the exploitation of its workers in their factories. People in developing countries where there was little or no legislation governing worker's rights were being paid poor wages to work extremely long hours in factories where dangerous machinery was being used. Accident rates were high and in most cases they found compensation had never been paid.

Then whole factories had been closed down without warning. This often left a large proportion of the town who had come to depend on this investment from outside without the money they had come to depend on. Then the safety of the actual factories had been disputed on several occasions and linked with the leakage of contaminants into the surrounding landscapes. Wade had been linked with several incidents where the illegal draining of waste into the rivers and seas around the coasts had been suspected but never proved.

Environmental activists had been silenced as they had raised the profile of these exploitative activities in some of the most sensitive areas of Arimathea's shrinking and most beautiful wildernesses. However, they were often the poorest. Corrupt governments it seemed were eager to exchange the use of these areas for a share in the wealth the corporations could offer them. Wade it seemed had been involved in many such deals. If the valuable minerals needed for the continual expansion of the global machine economy were discovered in a rainforest or in a river valley or high in sacred mountains, the sums Wade could offer for the rights to mine still meant they could make extraordinary profits even after the delighted government had been paid off.

These in turn were the profits demanded by the pension funds and the shareholders who invested in these corporations to pay for their lifestyles and their retirements which were becoming longer and more profligate. So, the terrorism had started and continued as people desperate to save their planet from these vast unaccountable global organisations meeting the demands of the richer nations whose own resources were now in protected environments. Wade had been named in the aftermath of several of these attacks on city centres across Arimathea in some of the worst examples of exploitation and degradation. All of which had been denied or justified by some indignant spokesman who claimed only to be helping the afflicted country to rise from poverty and join the rest of the International community with all the benefits that came with it.

Now the circle it seemed was complete. They had met Azeera in the hills of his country and here on the screen in front of them was a man at the head of an organisation directly involved in the degradation that had driven such people to think terrorism was now the only justifiable response to what was happening to their world.

"It is time I went to meet Mr Wade."

Okino was as serious as Mariella had ever seen him. He had been clearly shocked by what he had seen and how little concern there appeared to be from the international community. The problem in the lakes was inconsequential compared to the pollution and destruction he had seen and now he was in a position to confront one of its main protagonists.

Mariella's long neglected sports car growled quietly and powerfully through the streets of Straam. Okino had decided he wanted to go straight to the steel tower in Straam where the Wade corporation had its headquarters. He saw no point in delaying the meeting any longer. He had no doubt Harri would be in his tower waiting for him to arrive. There was little to discuss so they had got straight into the slightly dusty car to make the journey out of the suburbs into the city.

Okino was quiet. He had been rehearsed the meeting in his head with this monster on many occasions. Now however it appeared it was not as simple as he had assumed. This man had been a chieftain, a leader or certainly an influential elder of a tribe who probably had had regular contact with the dragon in the days before the human race had lost their connection with the spirits of their world. There would be residual memory of those days and Harri had probably been sub consciously guided by the wisdom of those days. Okino knew this to be part of the mystery he himself had faced since the night in the forest before he had awoken Merilon.

He had sensed an older being than himself somewhere in his past who now had some ability to guide his thoughts with wisdom or understandings from that former time. He himself had understood this presence to be a positive influence. So, there may have been some upset in Harri's soul journey in some form between the time when he had previously met him in the circle. Then he had seemed a wise and a clever human being who was guiding his tribe through dangerous times perhaps because they were still able to stay connected to the dragon spirits of their land. It would be an interesting meeting.

"So, do you think they will let you walk in off the street in your robes, wander in and have a little chat with the boss of one of the biggest corporations on Arimathea: assuming they admit he is there."

Mariella knew it was something Okino hadn't thought of. Then Okino was surprised he hadn't thought of it. Then they laughed because somehow it seemed like an unimportant detail. The atmosphere around them was changing. Okino felt a merge developing between him and his immediate environment in the streets beyond. As he absorbed the light he felt the change to which he had become accustomed. He felt the familiar expansion of his perception as Merilon moved into his consciousness. Now he was not alarmed or worried and he didn't feel as different as he had in some of their previous encounters but he knew the dragon was there and would be present in the confrontation about to take place.

He watched the city and all the people taking part in their daily lives unaware of the place to which their world had come. A place where all they understood about it and a lot they didn't was under scrutiny by the powers which flowed through it: perhaps their growing fear in the consciousness had awakened Arimathea fully to the threat and their feeling of helplessness had provoked her into this latest action.

Okino and Mariella stood in front of the tower. It rose forty two stories into the skies of the city and loomed with the towers surrounding it over the monk and his companion. It was a short walk across the paved square through the fountains to the front entrance. Mariella squeezed Okino's hand and looked up at him. His face was set and determined. She knew the dragon had arrived. The gentle monk was given a deeper steely strength in his presence. They walked up to the plate glass doors and Okino smiled at her as he pushed through them. The entrance foyer rose high above them. The bank of five lifts that would take them to the upper floors were making their silent slithering ascent and descent continually on the back wall of the atrium. They crossed the polished marble floor and walked up to the reception desk where two immaculately dressed young women watched as Okino and Mariella approached. Okino came to the high frontage of the desk clad in the marble present throughout the atrium and made a priestly bow. The two young women smiled.

"I have come to see Harri Wade."

The two girls smiled again at each other and the one who Okino had addressed asked.

"..and your name Sir?"

"My name is Okino."

She looked down at her screen and examined the appointments for Harri Wade and then looked at her fellow receptionist in surprise then down at the screen again.

"Indeed, you have. Mr Wade has been expecting you. The second lift on the right will take you up to forty-second floor where you will be shown to his office."

Okino and Mariella walked towards the lifts and when they were out of hearing range of the receptionists Mariella talked quietly to Okino.

"'You were right we didn't need to worry. Look Okino, I think this is something you need to do by yourself. I will wait down here. I am quite interested in the comings and goings through here so I'll see you later.!"

"Yeah, Ok I'll see you later." Okino was far too focused now to disagree or argue with Mariella's decision to remain in the reception area and started to observe the glass cab of the lift make its descent to where he stood on the ground floor. Then it was Mariella's turn to watch Okino rapidly rising into the air above her as the glass lift quickly gathered momentum carrying Okino rapidly up to the forty second floor. The lift doors opened and Okino walked out into a smaller reception area. Another young woman greeted him and escorted him along a wide corridor and finally showed him to a large door with Harri Wade's name on a steel plate at eye level on the door. The young woman pushed open the door and ushered Okino in.

Harri was sitting on his long conference table adjacent the glass façade of his huge office overlooking the city of Straam. The table was strewn with paperwork and files. He was in his shirtsleeves; his tie was untidily loose around his neck. He had had a difficult night. There had been dreams. Vivid unsettling dreams. The content had been disturbing. He had been walking out of the city. The countryside around the city was in the distance. He knew in his mind there were hills and rivers and meadows filled with flowers. There were vistas into which he could stare for as long as he felt he needed to before he ran down into them, where he would be able to smell the subtle scent of the meadows or dive into the cool waters of the river. There was a small village where he lived with his family. They were waiting for him. They would not start their meal without him. The village was not far and he had spent most of his adult life making this journey with his cows or his sheep either to or from the market in the town, with the cart full of grain and his wife and children beside him.

He couldn't wait to be with them. See their smiling faces so full of love for him and sit with them again knowing they had become part of his life. He felt grateful and lucky and all he had to do was walk down the road through the fields and into their home. But instead of getting closer it seemed he was getting further away. People had emerged to tell him there were things he needed to do before he went home. Everything down there depended on those tasks being done and he would have to return or all would be lost and he would never see his family again. But he knew that if he did not go then they would not be there when he eventually arrived. Surely one or the other could wait until tomorrow. The dilemma deepened and deepened as he tried to find some solution. But there appeared not to be one and he felt the decision he had to make would rip him apart as soon as it was made. So how could he make it.

All the while around him the world surrounding him seemed to have cracks appearing in it. In the sky, in the road, in the spaces between the buildings, these cracks momentarily appeared allowing dazzling light to breakthrough from a surrounding dimension into this, his world, seeming finite, bounded by some invisible barrier in the distance around him.

Sometimes there were many cracks like portals which he knew if he could enter the dilemmas would disappear. But he didn't believe they were there and persuaded himself they were some anomaly of the light that afternoon, some reflection off the glass of the buildings or flashing from the cars speeding past unaware or unconcerned by the sight of a confused old man staggering along the road as all around him, his world, the life he had built, all the stability he had finally felt was slipping away and was starting to disintegrate. One day, but not today he would know what the cracks contained or where they led. This was the only certainty he had left.

He had woken in the middle of the night. Everything was as it should be. His wife lay beside him and everything was as he had left it before he went to sleep. He lay awake in the comfort of the bed and the security of his home disturbed by the nature of the dream. It had felt real and it had left residue which he had been feeling as he delved into the contract Zanda had left the day before.

He looked up to see the monk in his crimson robes standing before him. He momentarily struggled to remember why he was there or who had authorised his entry. Perhaps he had not woken and he was still in his dream and this monk was an envoy from the portals beyond. These were his last thoughts as Okino pulled out a chair and sat across the table from him surveying the paperwork set out haphazardly across the glass table.

"Good morning Harry. I hope you are not too busy but it is important I speak to you today. I have travelled a long way; halfway around the planet in fact."

"Who are you and how did you get in here?"

Okino smiled and picked up one of the opened documents and idly scanned the page for something he might recognise. The text was thick with legal jargon and although the dragon sensed the meaning this was not, for the moment, why he was here.

"My name is Okino. I have come from a village high in the mountains in the small country of Jahallalah. It is not like your country at all. We live very simply surviving only on what we can grow and trade in the neighbouring towns. We have had little contact with your world except from the people who have found their way to our monastery.

"So why have you made this journey?"

Harri was curious now. The anxiety he had felt since he had woken in the night had fallen away as he sat in the presence of this calm self-assured young man. It was rare for him to see such serenity sitting opposite him on this table. So often there was either blind terror or extreme calculation.

"We are lucky enough to have some lakes in our valley in which live the most beautiful fish. They are very precious to us and we treat the lakes and their existence with great respect. When we have a special occasion or the need for a celebration, we will catch one or a number of these fish and they will become part of the feast."

"You eat the fish."

"Yes, Harri we eat the fish. You could say they are a valuable source of protein and of course they are. We would say they have become an intricate part of our way of life where all sources of energy are fundamental for our survival and so they have become sacred to our existence. So, it follows it is of great concern to us when any disruption or harm comes to any of these sources of energy. When the fish began to show signs of disease, I started my journey up the valley following the river to see if I could find the source of this disease. I followed the river to an old disused farm higher in the valley. I found it had been re inhabited by the family who had originally owned and abandoned it. They were growing herbs which apparently would be useful in the struggle against the epidemic of ill health you have on this side of the world caused by overeating.

This in itself causes much consternation in my land. However, to meet the targets for growing the amounts needed for such a market the farmer in question had been using synthetic fertiliser. The bags of fertiliser he was using and that I saw stored in his barn had the name of your corporation on them, The **Wade** Corporation. So here I am to tell you your product has travelled all the way around this world and has polluted one of the most pristine environments on this planet to such an extent it is having an impact on a tradition going back hundreds perhaps a thousand years."

Harri looked over at the young monk in disbelief. He looked down at the contracts in front of him where the plight of an entire country was at stake. He looked out across the city through the towers surrounding his own as if he might be able to see or imagine the tiny village out in the distance.

"It's difficult to know what to say to you son, apart from growing the herbs in containers so the fertiliser doesn't leak out. Every product we sell and distribute is tested rigorously to standards dictated to us by international laws and organisations who can test scientifically the levels of these chemicals the soil can take. If some freak reaction happens way up on a mountainside with soil conditions no one has ever heard of then I'm absolutely certain we cannot be held liable for any damage caused. So look I've got some pretty weighty decisions to make here, so if you could just leave me to it I'd be grateful and perhaps write a letter to my legal department, I'll let them know to send you some compensation. Probably buy you enough fish to feed your village for a year."

"No Harri, I'm afraid it is not as easy as that. On my journey I have gained some special insight, let us say into the way the world is working or not working as it seems. More precisely how this planet is being torn to pieces by corporations such as yours. You probably know in detail what I am talking about. Is it all in there buried in amongst the figures, the profit and loss? How much money did your company make last year Harri, Ten billion, Twenty billion?

Okino and Merilon watch as the figures flash through Harry Wades mind.

"Wow, as much as that. So how much of that was taken from pristine rainforests in your mining operations. What was the cost to the creatures that lost their habitats, what was the cost to the bio diversity of this world as plants disappeared that may never have been discovered; Plants that may have been able to cure your mother or your children when they have some critical disease in the future."

"How dare you talk about my mother and my children. I've had enough of this I want you to leave now or I'll have you thrown out of this building."

Harri reaches for the phone and presses the intercom.

"Hilary, get security up here immediately I want this monk out of my building now!"

There is no answer only the buzzing of an engaged tone. Harry gets up and strides towards the door and angrily goes to push it open only for it to stay firmly shut. He pushes again then looks back at Okino surprised at how solidly the door has been locked. He returns to the opposite side of the table. Okino is again leafing through one of his legal documents for the Uranium mine. His anger is already turning to fear. He suspected this day would eventually arrive when some crazy managed to get through the security so fastidiously woven around him. He thought he would be out on one of the fishing trips he took out to the lakes or on the way to his in laws in the next state, But not here in his office. How had this all happened? Who was this person? He tried the phone again. Now it was completely dead.

"So, you see Harri, we are going to have a serious chat about what is going on with you and this company of yours. There is far too much taking going on and not enough giving back. Apart from the pollution caused by your smelting plants of course. The gases clogging up the atmosphere when you convert all the chemicals and ores you dig up from your mines into fertilisers and metals. Fertilisers we know are destroying the natural balance of the soil to grow the abundance of food your people are eating which is making them overweight; metals to make the cars that are adding even more pollution to the skies and making your people steadily more inactive.

All this pollution Harri, it is changing the nature of this world. You'll know about the countries on the edges of the deserts taking over their countries. Low lying islands being submerged under rising sea levels. Even in your own country the seasons are changing to such an extent that rainfall patterns have been disrupted. So that is weather systems being disrupted. So that is millions of people depending on the rain falling at the same time every year so you can grow the crops to feed them all; rain fall patterns calculated long before there were billions of tons of pollution flooding into the skies every year. Now all the trees able to absorb the pollution are being cut down and it is being absorbed into the Oceans. So yes, Harri that will mean your oceans will slowly be dying. Not just my few fish for which you obviously have no concern but all your fish as well. Have you any idea of the amount of people in the world depend on fish in their diet; So, with your wheat crops failing and the fish dying out that is an awful lot of starving people. We're not there yet but it is not very far away."

"Why are you coming to talk to me about this. You can't hold me responsible for this global catastrophe which is frankly little more than theoretical nonsense dreamt up by idealists who would like to see the global economy go back to the stone age. It just isn't going to happen."

"I am afraid it was your name on the bag that ended up in my valley and that is precisely what is going to happen if no attempt is made by the human race to curb their activity."

"But I'm not responsible I just do what I do in response to demand. I always have done and I think you'd be surprised to hear how this all started just so I could survive at one point. We all do what we have to do Okino. Who decides I can't do this or that today because my pollution is going to tip the planet into global catastrophe? Who wakes up and says I'm not going to drive my car or put my central heating on today because my action will eventually cause the rainfall to change and so we might all starve to death at some point? We need more cars not less; we need more food not less. Everybody wants more of everything. I just respond. I try to give people what they want, what they need to make their lives better and that of course means giving it to them at the right price, a price they can afford."

"…and the price depends on how much or how little you pay the workers in your factories. Then when their factory is no longer profitable you close it down. Whole communities go into collapse when they no longer have the money they have come to depend on. Have you any idea how it feels for someone to go home to tell his wife he has no money to feed their children."

"I go to these places and build the factories and give them the work they need."

"But then you take it away without thinking what you are doing. What they need is some stability, any kind of stability to raise their families in safety year after year. A few generations ago they had fields or jungles in which they lived but now the fields are being worked by a handful of men in machines and they are working to cut the jungles down. Where before they had a life now there are vast plains where cattle are being grazed to feed over fed populations in countries beyond their own. They don't see the benefits their governments told them they would receive. The benefits go to the people who can afford to live in the best parts of the city where the luxury homes and infra structure has been built by their governments eager to hold favour with the sections of the population who will vote for them in their elections; who will in turn benefit from the power that brings to them. Everyone is striving and battling to get to the levels in your society where the structures of power are maintained and where the crimes I have been talking about are being proliferated."

"This is not crime; no one is acting against any laws by supplying the goods and services people all around the world need to go about their lives."

"Not crime in your eyes or through the eyes of the people who are benefiting from it but what about the people who are seeing their lands ravaged by foreign corporations like yours who feel helpless as their politicians exceed to all your demands. What about the creatures whose habitats are being exterminated? After all we share this world with them. If they had laws would we not be guilty of destruction and neglect of their homes? You say there are no laws Harri; but what about the laws of the world? The laws evolved over the billions of years allowing the complexity of life that exists on this planet to come to fruition. The laws we have made allow our societies to thrive unhindered by what we have decided is detrimental to us reaching our ultimate potential. So, the laws of the world have come to do the same thing. The planet is always finding a way to move towards its greatest potential. We are bound up inextricably into the two sets of law, the first we make for the progression of our own interests but ultimately, we need to adhere to the interests of the planet which supports us.

We have not arrived yet, certainly at this time, where the two places can merge because it seems are own interests, or the interests of a certain section of the human race come higher on the list of priorities than the planets. Still we can breathe and still we can feed ourselves so the problem for the moment can be ignored. But there are parts of the human race who have recognised things will have to change before the laws governing the health of the planet are so compromised there will be a failure of her systems. Also, it is now widely believed we have had warnings and messages from other species who have seen fit to declare their presence as sentient beings with whom we share this world."

"You are talking as if you believe this planet is some kind of being with some kind of future destiny; a destiny we presumably are bound into with all these other species. It is a theory I have heard and frankly have paid little attention to. Clearly more nonsense spread by the Stone Age contingent."

"…and you are talking as if the Stone Age, presumably referring to the time in prehistory when we had none of the advantages we have now was a bad time for the human race!"

"Well of course it was and who would want to go back to all the poverty and disease-ridden life, dancing round naked in circles we so cleverly as a race have worked our way out of."

"..but there are places on this planet, in fact I have come from one where we don't have electricity or cars or TV and yet look here I am the same as you Harri and I think you will find that many of the foundations for the societies you and we all have adopted were set in place in those early times: times we may have actually known considerably more about the origins of our world than we do today."

"Now you are being ridiculous. I personally have seen the telescopes that are observing the beginnings of the Universe millions of light years away."

"..not because we could see the catastrophic explosion that brought all this into existence…but because we still had the senses that had taken millions of years to evolve and enabled us to survive quite literally wandering the world before we settled down and started farming. In the life of the evolution of our species it is not that long ago and much of the knowledge we gained is still bound up in who we all are. It is lying dormant in our subconscious and perhaps accessed far more than we would be prepared to acknowledge…Yes I'm afraid to say it Harri but you are not much different from the person you were in the stone age you apparently so despise."

Okino couldn't help but smile at the irony of what he had said.

"Yeah right, but now I'm the boss of a multi-national company in an unprecedented technological age that has come about as a result of the genius of the human race to understand and exploit the resources of this planet."

"Ok…so how have you done that, become this great leader with such an instinct and ability to grow your organisation with the authority to direct all the people you employ to successfully run this global company? Not everyone has the ability to do what you have done and I am curious to know how it all came about."

Harri looked over at the Monk. He had cleverly drawn him into a discussion he did not much want to have. He looked down at his watch expecting an hour to have passed since the monk came in. But it appeared his watch had stopped. Who was this boy he asked himself again? He had a calm authority which he recognised in the people he himself had come to respect; whom he knew ultimately he had to respect if he was to have any chance of negotiating a beneficial outcome for himself. He sensed the monk had some advantage he could not know about and now if he explained any aspect of his journey and how it had brought him here the advantage would in some way be revealed. But he no longer felt threatened or in danger and had started to feel something extraordinary and possibly to his advantage may be taking place.

He remembered the dreams he had had the night before where his world was quite literally cracking up around him. Now this calm almost angelic creature had walked into his office talking about the destiny of the planet as if he had walked out of those cracks through the portals from the world or worlds beyond. As he acknowledged all this a particular time in his life, in his journey came shining into his mind. It was as clear as if he were back there. It was the time, the turning point when all this had become possible and as he looked over at Okino he found he was excited about telling him how it had all happened.

"Ok Okino, monk from the Stone Age I will tell you the story about how this all came to be. I am not sure what is going on but I have a strange feeling it is not all bad and since it seems I have no choice at the moment I am going to go along with you."

Harri began telling Okino his story. About his early childhood and how he had escaped from his father to live on the streets with the gangs of children. He told him about how he had spent the summer fishing and how he had gone into business with the fishmonger and the fish distribution business. Okino laughed when he explained about the fish.

"I will compensate you for the fish, I was always going to because really that is how I survived and where it all started but it was where the idea of mining really took a grip on me. Suddenly everywhere I looked there was potential to use the world around me and turn it into profit and my advantage. I tried a few things alongside the fish business but one day I heard of a place down in the southern continent, out in the desert where there was a community of miners living almost completely underground in their tunnels. They were digging for a rare and beautiful gemstone called a Teorite.

This latest deposit had been found by chance out in the southern desert by a couple of rally drivers who had become lost on one of the races regularly organised across what is supposed to be some of the most challenging terrain in the world for humans to drive across. The gemstones were supposed to have originated from meteorite strikes at various times during Arimathea's long history. It seemed the rally drivers had strayed into one of the strike zones and miraculously carved one of the stones out of a cliff face deep in an ancient river gully as they sat waiting to be rescued. I had by this time saved a fair amount of money. I franchised out the fish distribution business and when I had secured a solid income from it I decided I wanted to try something different. I had become more and more fascinated by the idea of seeking out these strange stones possibly from some far flung part of the galaxy. They had become treasured by women all over the world and so their lovers desperate to buy and maintain their affections.

However, this would be no ordinary mine and the miners would not be ordinary men. But it seemed like an ideal opportunity and so I decided to go down there to see what I could find. I bought a large pickup truck and built in extra water and diesel tanks, filled it with supplies and set out on this new adventure. I stayed in hotels on the road to start with but became used to sleeping along the highway and often at night I would watch the skies and the moon next to my fire much like I had done in those early days when I had escaped from my dad. But now it was different I had money and this strange plan. I had no idea whether it would work, but I had a gut instinct that so far on this journey had served me well and under the stars on the lonely nights beside the road I imagined finding a large deposit of the beautiful meteorite stone that had crashed down onto our world in some distant age possibly before life had emerged here. I had no idea really what I was letting myself in for but as I say this dream was gnawing away at me and really, I had no choice but to see where it would take me.

The further South I drove the sparser the vegetation became and eventually I found myself driving across the desert. Down there it was so hot I found I could not drive during the day because the truck would start to overheat and if that broke and I couldn't fix it I knew I would be in a life-threatening situation. I laid up during the heat of the day and started to drive during the night towards where the place where the miners would be. I had picked up a crude road heading in the direction I had calculated I would find the mine and after a few days I saw a thin wisp of dark smoke on the horizon and decided it could only be my destination.

I arrived early next morning as the Star was creeping over the horizon. The desert was already shimmering from the heat. There was a small complex of large timber sheds with a large fuel tanker parked outside with a feed pipe leading straight in through the wall. Dark smoke drifted from a steel pipe and there was the sound of a large generator buzzing away somewhere inside. At that moment the place seemed totally deserted. There were large piles of spoil lying across the landscape in all directions. I was as nervous as I had ever been and was starting to doubt the feeling in my gut that had brought me here.

I wandered through the sheds wondering where everyone was, apprehensive now and feeling I was trespassing into someone else's domain in which I may or may not be entirely welcome. The place was strewn with rubbish and the detritus of an active colony of humans living out in the desert. Large oil cans, drifting newspaper, bottles, plastic and glass, the empty skins of stuff left to become a new landscape for which it was clear the humans who lived here had little time or concern. There were battered trucks similar and larger than mine looking as if they had been making journeys through the desert for many years. They were rugged and dusty with an indestructible air as if they had made some pact with the desert and had taken on some of its characteristics to blend with it so they could move through it untroubled by its rigours. Of course, this was the nature of the men who eventually emerged from the landscape around me. From the ground, from the sheds, maybe, I had not seen.

I watched the two miners walking towards me. These would be my companions. They were tall and a little underweight, they wore wide brimmed hats that may have had some shape at some time in their lives. Deeply tanned, their beards were clearly being kept at bay for some reason, they wore enormous leather boots and battered combat trousers and shirts with sleeves rolled up and like their vehicles they were caked in the grime and the dust of the desert. From those rugged faces shone blue eyes and grey eyes filled with a little suspicion now and perhaps some amusement as they stood before me and assessed this new arrival as they had done many times before. They made their appraisal and looked past me to the truck standing behind me as if it was my companion who would be staying also. It had only a thin covering of sand, the element ruling this parched world of heat and dust, it stood alone, vulnerable to the critical gaze of the miners, forged by this land in which they had chosen to adopt as their own, now wondering if these two characters in front of them had what it took to join them, become part of their clan.

As they ran me and my vehicle through their thoughts, they remembered all I would have to endure to make it worthwhile me staying. They were not an easy crowd to be with, isolated from civilisation, living a sparse mostly poverty-stricken life of self-denial where few of the comforts of modern life were on offer. They lived with the hope they would find the stones that would buy them all they now denied themselves out here in this unforgiving land. On occasions the frustration of all they endured would erupt if there was some dispute, some argument over who ate or drank this or that more than someone else. Mostly they went about their lives quietly in hope or despair.

There was no contract or stake to be bought or bargained for. If you could live and work here in this place then you were entitled to what you could find. Only the government had to be paid, the rent craftily negotiated before any knowledge of the gemstones had been leaked to the world. In the deed was mentioned a retreat as far away from the luxuries of the world as could be imagined and certainly it was that. Retreat from the hurt and destruction many of these characters were running from. Circumstances that had left a simmering destructive rage buried in the soul of its owner. They worked away silently in the depths of Arimathea in the dim light allowed by the generator unaware of the volcanic eruption that would be caused if all the factors were again initiated, all the buttons pushed.

In the silence, with the past behind them and the one strand ahead leading through the rock into the future. Pasts leading to this present. To this independent pioneering defiant present: Defiant of all that had been left behind with perhaps some guilt or regret or devastating loss or cruelty all kept in delicate balance as the mechanical chisels rang out breaking into the solidity ahead causing the choking dust and the carts rolling out with the spoil, eager eyes always searching for the turquoise sparkle that would take away the spectre of the grinding past and its frightening relentless companion, the present and replace it with the glowing light of comfort and pleasure, perhaps a new love, tenderness, caresses and warmth. All this I would find out for myself, but they knew as we stood there, watching me before all that transpired in the next years had happened to us. It was as hard a life as could be imagined and in those next few hours, I met the other men I would be sharing it with. There were eleven at the time. They greeted me with silence and smiles and open warmth and sincere commiserations I had decided to come here. Eventually I knew some would want to know what those reasons were; others I knew would never be concerned.

In the early days I learned about the mine and how I would operate alongside the other miners. They lived entirely underground. All the accommodation had been carved out of the sandstone below the sand covering of the desert above. Entry was through the gully where the original stone had been found into a communal space and smaller cave like rooms where there was a bed and whatever other furniture could be fitted in. They varied in size and had blankets only covering the crude openings. All the cooking was done communally in the central hall where there was a strange assortment of tables and chairs around them; there were armchairs and sofas enough for everyone to sit and talk together. The dust and sand of the desert was everywhere and little or no effort was made to keep it at bay. Refrigeration was obviously the largest problem. However, at some stage three large industrial refrigerator freezers had been bought and were run off the generators.

During this time, I also found out how these guys ran the mine. As I said there was nothing organised. The miners had their own tunnels which ran from the spine tunnels leading away from the central hall. More Teorite had been found in a specific direction so slowly the tunnels reflected the direction in which the gems were being found. The miners told me I would start a new tunnel parallel to the ones they were working. The ground through which we were mining was sandstone compressed over the millennia. The strata in which they were digging was where the meteorite had landed in the desert many millions of years before and where the biggest deposits had been found to date.

No one had any idea whether the majority had been found or if there was still an enormous find somewhere up ahead. The thinking generally was as long as the Teorite was still being found there was still a chance of the big find somewhere in the future. The gems were still being found regularly so everyone was still optimistic that sooner or later the bulk of the meteorite that had fallen on Arimathea would eventually be found.

At this point in time when a gemstone was found then the person who found it claimed the money for this find and then paid a proportion for the fuel, the food and the upkeep of the mine. This monetary arrangement was organised by Stu who assiduously kept track of all the finds, how much people had been paid and what they had paid towards the running of the mine. As long as you paid your share of the running you could stay, if not and this had obviously happened to a great number of people, you would have to leave.

I am sorry to tell you about all this but it is important in what eventually did happen. Nobody dared to talk about what would happen between them if there was a really big find although you would have thought it would have been fundamental. I felt this strange obstacle fixed in the minds of these men as I got to know them in the next few months. Often they would talk about this big find and assuming they would reap the benefits alone and had planned their future lives accordingly. Of course, there would be houses around Arimathea and yachts to cruise in between them. There would be cars and girls and travel to every exciting part of the planet. So, lives carefree and work free and mostly very expensive and actually as I very loosely calculated unsustainable after a year or two even if a fairly large lump of Teorite was found.

But these were the dreams keeping these men in their dark tunnels chiselling away at the sandstone month after month. Much the same reason people do a lottery and go to work every day all around the world. There was some imaginary light shining through the darkness of their hopeless lives that had already gone hideously wrong in their conventional existence. Now it was easier to stay in the darkness of the tunnels and the isolation of the mine than to face the consequences of what had transpired for whatever reason in their previous life.

So, I started my life at the end of one of the tunnels and eventually I did start to find the stones we were all there to find. I was on my way but of course it was only the start. As far as I could make out the stones were in a particular stratum of the rock where there was also layer of sediment which seemed to indicate some evidence of water flowing. Strangely no actual maps had been made to document the finds. This possibly had not been seen as necessary or may well have been beyond the organisational capacity of this particular group of human beings. So, as I hammered and chiselled away I started to think if the meteorite strike had been here the stones may at some time been washed away from it by the current of a stream or river. If the finds were mapped then we would start to get a better picture in which direction the centre of the strike was.

We often sat around drinking in the central hall and one night I decided to voice my theory. I had come to know most of the men by now. Many had off loaded their stories and had been grateful for someone to listen to them. I told them of the terror in my own childhood and my subsequent escape and gradually I became someone they were no longer suspicious of but someone who had been through similar if not worse distress as the rest of them and gradually as I worked and paid my way I started to earn their respect and was bonded unofficially it seemed but successfully into their clan. When the conversation about girls and yachts had come to a natural lull I started to tell them what I had been thinking. They listened carefully to what I had to say and after I had finished a strange silence ensued. Then Stu who kept the accounts spoke up…

"What you have suggested Harri, changes everything as you probably may or may not have realised," he said to me and his fellow miners.

"..because up until now we have worked for ourselves and what we find we benefit from and there is no contract in place that would mean anyone else would benefit from any other find than their own. If and I mean if we decided to start to make this map then we would be starting a whole different venture in which we all would have a stake, if the map we all have made enabled us to find the central meteorite. The advantage of course is that we would be more likely to find the meteorite and less likely to drive a tunnel straight past it. Also of course we will all benefit from the find because we will be splitting the find amongst each and every one of us. The benefit of this also is that if any one of us finds the stone then it will avoid the inevitable melt down in relations with the rest of us and all that would entail."

The silence continued and the drinking continued and the thinking started. The discussions went on well into the night before we all dispersed into our separate living accommodation. But I think something had changed in the discussions we had deep in our subterranean home in the desert, far away from the law courts and their costly lawyers and attorneys. I think we started to think of the possibility we could be a company rather than a group of individuals and that we could eventually benefit from such an alliance more successfully than if we went on like we were. Nothing was agreed and in fact it took a few days before we all came together again. In that time everyone decided the map had to be made and that an agreement would have to be drawn up between us. I think Okino in those moments Wade International was born and many of the miners who signed that agreement are still shareholders in this company and have become wealthy beyond anything they had dreamt of at the end of their dark tunnels in that god forsaken desert."

Harry now fully relaxed and excited got up from the table and walked over to the plate glass windows of his skyscraper and continued.

"We were all still on risky ground; or deep in this sandstone substrate I should say. Perhaps the meteorite was only big enough for only one of us to really live out our dreams. But now we were convinced, had convinced ourselves or allowed ourselves to be led deeper into our fantasy. Here now we had come together with a common destiny that enabled the dream to have even greater power. Suddenly it had all made sense. Here we were tunnelling blindly around underground like a bunch of demented desert rats all be it far less suited to their environment, rather than doing what we as human beings do best which was agree a common strategy amongst ourselves and work towards it. Here now everything was in place for us to fulfil what we all wanted to do, which somewhere we decided, was not just to make loads and loads of money but it was to sensibly join and engage with the world in a meaningful way again and possibly what we were starting to find was so important amongst ourselves, gain the respect of our fellow human beings.

So, we started the map. We detailed the position of all the tunnels we were working in and crudely measured all their levels. We positioned all the finds we could definitely remember we had made in the recent weeks and continued to position them for the next year. Still the work was hard but there was a new enthusiasm amongst the miners. We had become a team and I found I was with a naturally competitive bunch now a clear end had become more tangible. Almost immediately we could see the direction of the river's flow that had washed the stones down from their possible origin and so the tunnels changed course in that direction and even started to merge into wider galleries as concentrations became more apparent. But it was more than an entire turning of the Star before the pattern truly started to emerge.

In a few days we had an unprecedented seven finds. The stones were larger as if they could not have been carried or pushed as far as the smaller stones on the current. The map had shown us the stream may have been over one hundred paces across and had been deeper and shallower in places as would be expected. But when we plotted on these seven finds there was suddenly a sense of scale to the flow of the river and how it had deposited the stones there had not been before. We looked to where the flow was indicating on the map and of course there was only table. We found more paper and pieced it far enough across the table to where the flow of the river and the position of the stones we had found suggested the fallen fragment of the meteorite would be, where it had to be. The evidence we had made for ourselves was staggeringly clear. If we carried on in our present tunnels it would take us another year to reach it. So we decided to start to dig in the area where the map pointed to; where the bulk of the meteorite had landed and lain buried in the desert, where a river had once flowed, after circling the universe for possibly billions of years.

We sank the new shafts in a circle around where we had calculated the meteorite might be and tunnelled towards the centre. Almost immediately we were finding even larger lumps of the Teorite. But a mix of materials different from what we had been finding before. If this was the actual meteorite then now we were finding fragments of the thick iron casing that had carried and protected it as it fell through the atmosphere and that had shattered possibly mostly vaporised on impact and left what we were finding. All the way through the circle we found Teorite from the core that had washed down through the sediment with the iron and nickel crust. The blue stones smoothed by the scouring of the water over the millions of years since their arrival looked crude and unexciting. But as they came into our central hall one after the other we knew our new strategy had been overwhelmingly successful. These stones now were as large as a hand width across. It was an exciting time and we worked even harder tearing through the sandstone expecting to find something even bigger and even more valuable.

Then one morning a number of us were tearing through one of the walls when one of the miners hit something very solid. We chiselled our way deeper into the wall until we revealed what must have been almost a quarter of the surface of what had travelled out from the stars and landed here on Arimathea. The iron casing held a huge lump of Teorite core possibly measuring as much as one and a half paces across. The Teorite was encased in further iron and nickel deposits but it was so large we decided we would chisel off a fraction to reveal the stone beneath the murky covering. In those moments we knew we had uncovered something very special. Even in the dim lights of the generators the blue light flooded out from the fragment. We ran up out of the tunnels and stood in the desert twisting the stone in the Starlight.

The light experience known as rainbow was not entirely adequate to describe what we were seeing. There is not adequate language to describe the beauty we were seeing. But Star rises on different worlds refracted through nebula storms as the remains of exploding galaxies flashed through unexplained, undiscovered matter merging with spirit light was what I eventually came up with. And of course, it was proclaimed as one of the great geological mining sensations of the century and we sold most of it for an astronomical sum and founded this company. It is still being sold and resold at extraordinary prices. Here look, I kept that fragment, perhaps you would like to have a look."

Harri went over to some glass shelves at the back of his office and took a fragment of the highly polished Teorite carefully down and handed it to Okino. Okino held it gently in his two hands and looked down into it. A galaxy exploding was how Harry had described the flash amongst the debris of nebulas and spirit light. Okino twisted it as they would have first twisted it outside the mine. Harri's description of spirit matter drifted through it mixing with the multi coloured light emanating from the surrounding stars reflecting the dust of long since forgotten worlds was in an understated way fairly accurate. Okino was genuinely astounded. This was not what he had expected when he had planned his journey that morning; not only because of what he was seeing in front of him but because of what he had buried deep in the pocket of his robe. He reached in tentatively hoping it had survived the rigors of the journey from the plain in the faraway mountains of Jahallala. There it was, the familiar roughness. He pulled the stone out.

"It's strange Harry, your whole story because I have this."

He offered it for Harry to look at. Harry immediately fixed his eyes upon it, approached attentively and accepted it from Okino. Now it was Harry's turn to be astounded. He took the stone over to the glass curtain wall and held the stone up to the Star. He saw the drifting mists of colour and the flash Okino had just registered in his own fragment of what appeared to be part of the same meteorite.

"So, where did you find this?"

"Near the lakes where our fish were being poisoned on the day I set out on this journey."

Harry sat down again opposite Okino on the long boardroom table. He was watching Okino very carefully. He was in strange uncharted territory. In his business and in his life as a whole he liked to have the cold hard facts in front of him. He looked down for a moment at the thick document Zanda had given him. In amongst all the camouflage there would be some phrase, some sentence, some unnoticed clause that could finish him if he did not find it. He would find it though, as sure as he had found the Teorite out in the desert. It would be there in black and white and if he couldn't find it he would get his lawyers to find it. But here now in front of him was something different and it had come at this very specific time when he had this deal. This contract to sign. Something had spooked him about it in the dream and now this boy monk had arrived with his fragment of Teorite and he wanted to know more.

"I think it is about time you started telling me exactly what you have been up to on your journey, son!"

Chapter Sixty-Eight
War.

Down in the reception area Mariella was waiting patiently for Okino to emerge from his meeting with Harri Wade. She hadn't thought how long this may take and after some considerable time had passed, her interest in watching the executives who worked in or were visiting the Wade tower was starting to wane. She had drunk as much coffee as she was sensibly able and the magazines left on the low level glass tables glamorising the world of global finance and outlining it's remarkable contribution to the wellbeing of her world had made her wonder if she was living on the same planet as the people who had written these articles. But of course, that was why they were here. Perhaps she should have gone with Okino to see Harri Wade but every time this thought crossed her mind she remembered something had told her to stay down here with the smiling receptionists and the tropical plants which had never been in or near a jungle but seemed to be thriving in the bright, highly regulated atmosphere of this building in the heart of the metropolis.

In fact, they had grown high and strong in their large planters regularly topped up with the optimal amount of nutrients. Their leaves and foliage were regularly wiped with milky liquids so they could process effectively the artificial light from the powerful lamps high in the ceiling of the atrium and through the layers of glass designed to allow in as much light as was naturally healthy for plants and humans alike. These were the plants that would have been growing on the forest floor in the bed of mouldy and discarded vegetation where all manner of plant and creature competed mercilessly amongst the carefully ordered chaos of the jungle floor. Where each survival technique honed over millions of years by the tiniest scuttling insects to the largest predatory carnivores helped to control this complex dynamic habitat.

Somewhere amongst the parasitic mould devouring the brains of an eight million zombie ant colony and the footprints left by a silent leopard patrolling its spider and snake infested territory, Mariella felt Arimathea moving through the dimness. Then, out of the dimness and into the brightness of the city atrium. She surrounded the glowing green leaves, moved through their sugar converting processes and into the mechanically processed air. The soft green light drifted through Mariella's mind opening all the gateways to the pathways Arimathea had left imprinted in her soul. There she came to rest again looking out through Mariella's turquoise eyes onto her world where the steel and glass that defied her and had forgotten her despite all it owed to her. She felt the nervous change in Mariella as she acknowledged her presence. As she became aware of everything around her as it had happened or was happening both in the past and present as she realised and began to process the additional information flooding through her being.

She knew he was coming before he walked in. She gasped silently as the automatic doors slid silently open and he strode in as if this was his own building, his own world in which he had allowed the human race to exist as his tenant, a necessary component in his vision of how one day all things would come to be as he had ordained. Now he stalked up to the reception desk in an immaculate dark suit, his long dark hair tied neatly and falling down his back.

"I need to see Harri Wade immediately, it is really important. I've been phoning for an hour and no one will connect me through to his office."

Both girls sat up attentively and the nearest asked..

"..and your name Sir?"

"Zanda Borrowdale of the Ravensberg Banking Corporation."

The receptionist picked up the phone and talked to the personal assistant in Harri's office suite never taking her eyes off Zanda.

"I am afraid he is not taking any calls or accepting any visitors at the moment, Sir."

Zanda seemed on edge and impatient and turned his back on the reception desk to look out onto the street, thinking deeply, apparently weighing up the situation. Mariella wondered what Zanda was doing here and what business he had with Harri Wade. However, she read the situation immediately. Zanda would attempt to go up to Harri's office. Okino was in Harri's office and the last thing everyone needed at this point in time was a confrontation between two dragons, here in the centre of Straam city, forty-two stories up in a skyscraper. She leapt up from her comfortable leather chair and hurried over to where Zanda was still leaning on the reception desk trying to decide what Mariella and Arimathea already knew.

"Hi Zanda, how have you been? Haven't seen you for ages. What are you doing here? You are looking so smart. Is this your other life or something!?"

Zanda looked down at Mariella, jolted out of his thoughts and surprised by this uninhibited intervention into his space, into the bright turquoise of her beautiful eyes. Momentarily he forgot his problem as he raced through his memory trying to find where he had seen these eyes before. It is all Mariella needed to distract him. Impatiently Zanda asked.

"Do I know you? It seems I do but I have no specific memory I can pin down."

Mariella laughed, delved deeper into the dark eyes where she could see the remnants of the green glow which had been all but extinguished many centuries before. She had his attention and continued to hold it as she ruthlessly tempted him deeper into her sparkling oceans.

"Yeah well I have sorted myself out since I was running with your crew and you didn't pay me much attention then anyway, we spoke a few times but it was mainly instructions about how many pills you wanted me to sell that night."

"Look…What is your name, I haven't got much time.."

"You've got time enough Zanda, for a chat with me. Are you sure you don't recognise me?"

Mithrael looked deeper into the turquoise pools of light demanding his full attention. They provoked some impulse to race through the ancient corridors of his mind down through the centuries where eventually he hoped he would find those eyes staring back at him. But there were so many faces, so many memories. But this was no ordinary memory he was searching for. Something was stirring in the old spirit he had denied for so long. His spirit had to answer to whatever was calling him, the swirling essence was infiltrating the wider universal mind in which he had at one time dwelt and which now he dared not access for the fear of all it would reveal, the truth and the agony it would uncover.

"Come and sit with me for a while Zanda or should I say Mithrael."

Mariella knew the dragon was attempting to return to his universal awareness. Arimathea sensed him attempting to open the great doors that had remained so solidly and impenetrably closed to his dragon soul for so long. He began to sense the infinite light filled memory behind the yearning he was experiencing. Without understanding what had momentarily suspended the feeling of emptiness consuming his being he had wondered again, wondered what lay behind those doors. Mithrael followed her to the chairs around the table with the magazines and Mariella's empty coffee cartons. The street and all the people on it were out there beyond the tinted armoured glass filtering the starlight falling all around him but somehow dim now because all he could see were the endless unfathomable depth of her eyes; All the worry and the concern he had felt only moments before was evaporating under the enchantment taking hold of his entire being.

Around him the lobby, the building, the city was fading and being replaced by the open expanses around the summit of a hill. The land below shimmered in the distance. There were ancient stones encircling them giving solidity now and radiating the essence of those lands, her essence in the air all around him and before him, through him allowing him to remember who he was or had been. He started to push open those ancient doors to where lay the knowledge of all he had learnt on his journey from dragon to blacksmith and warrior, to farmer and miller and now the co-founder and owner of the bank of Zinederland. Now returned to his dragon self. High on his Dragon hill amongst the old stones he remembered who he was, his origin. He shuddered as he remembered what he had become. She was transformed now. An ancient raiment wrapped around her emblazoned with the symbols, creatures and misty visions of her world, of seas and drifting clouds and tumbling streams and waterfalls, fluctuating always changing, her dark hair blew out in the breeze and still her eyes shone from the delicately sunburnt face, both young and old, wise, frivolous and mischievous, she stood now in front of him looking out over the landscape before her.

"I think you became lost didn't you Mithrael!?"

"Maybe I did and maybe I didn't. There is not much which is cut and dry about this universe we have come to live in and you know and all the other dragons know it's difficult for us not to become involved. The deeper I get involved with this physical world the more I see how we should have stayed separate from it. But I have seen the consequences of what is happening as a result of the original dream for all the beings who are enduring it year after year. For us in the course of universal time it is happening in a blink of an eye. We have all become involved. How could we not. We are involved even if we stay deep in your heart dreaming out all the wonder. But the wonder was always overlaid with Oblivion. We made a pact with death and destruction and it has played a key role, acts through it so all this can progress. Despite this we have brought the beauty of light and love into this world and all the worlds in which we have dwelt. But the vastness of Oblivion will always be there nibbling away at the light whatever brilliant genius arises in the world, whether it is created by human or dragon.

As the process rolls on we are all, every molecule and atom deeply enravelled in the depths of its machinations. How can this be what the dream intended? There is no certainty it will ever end. The pain will go on and it has become so deeply embedded in the Humans, I'm not sure they can ever escape from the cycle of suffering and misery being embedded within their race. It seems their lives have become one long attempt to escape it!"

Arimathea turns to Mithrael, holds out her hands towards him and the surrounding landscapes and speaks to him gently and authoritatively.

"I have always been here for them and every living thing on this world, in all the darkness and in all the pain their lives bring to them. But you dwell so much on this suffering Mithrael. There is so much joy and love to be had in everything around them. How else could all this have survived and been proliferated through all these billions of years, if Life was not the most precious thing any creature could be in possession of? Why have they clung to it whatever the dire circumstances they found themselves in? It is because in those times I am there for them in the peace surrounding them. Their spirits come close to me and they know I will always be there for them. I can hold back the emptiness, the hopelessness of oblivion is inconsequential in the face of the love and wonder I offer. But I have not been alone as all this has come to be. We have made this beautiful world together, the love surrounding them, instilled in its fabric shines all around us. Look how beautiful it has become!"

"Yes, Arimathea it is very beautiful, but the price for the humans has become so high they are drowning in their misery and they are destroying their world in the process. Like all the creatures of this world they have struggled for survival. This instinct is embedded in them as deeply as any other creature; they are intelligent, with a will of their own and they can organise themselves to an incredible degree but they are governed by hormones and chemical reactions driving them to continue their species just like any other animal. They have competed continually and set themselves against their fellows in the struggles for the best land, optimum circumstances and the best partners with whom to have their children. These basic physical instincts, continually driving them cause them so much pain and confusion as they attempt to manipulate the world around them for their selfish ends.

Ultimately it has led to wars on unprecedented levels. Whole generations of children, husbands, fathers and lovers have been wiped out in the mechanised warfare that has arisen as one or other of their races has decided it wants more land or better land with better resources in which to raise its children and expand its activities. Savagery and barbarity has occurred on such a level that if they had been considered possible in the moments when all this was first conceived this experiment may never have been allowed to get underway.

These are beings capable of great sensitivity and compassion. Vast swaths of them retain memories of their children being blown to pieces or cut down by machine guns and left to die in bomb holes. They never recovered from this kind of loss. They concentrated on a future that could fill their emptiness; A future where they would not have to access those dark disturbing places of loss. They built this world of instant gratification so they could forget but where they feel they are powerless to change what they have become.

These were the places they used to feel all this, your beauty, our love that flows through the world. Now they are locked away. Gradually the wonder of this world has become no longer apparent. They have been left with an emptiness which cannot be filled, as their reliance on their own machine world becomes ever deeper. It is directly accessible to them. They do not have to access their consciousness or their intuition or their imagination to live there and progressively it has become controlled by the most ruthless of them. So you see Arimathea, this beautiful world means nothing to them anymore. All they see is a painful physical prison they have accidentally been born into where they are constrained by everything around them. But all they have learnt allows them to spread like a deadly virulent plague eating into the very life force of this world. This was not part of what this was all meant to be about and it should be ended. Any more interference from you and the other dragons is merely prolonging the agony for everything and everybody."

"Of course I have felt this pain Mithrael. Their pain and the destruction does not bode well for my survival. But there is a new tide coming in and you must be part of it. They are waking up from the sleep they have been in. The world they have made does cross over into ours in many ways and they are becoming aware of it as they find the threads binding them together and it is starting to free them from the influences of their oppressors. They have started to realise the problems of their world are becoming more extreme and are caused by the emptiness and the pursuit of these dreams of material happiness being continually sold to them.

New souls, the old souls are starting to return and they will find the old connections and will seek ways to make and proliferate them in this new world. Far from being over as I feel you assume, I think we are coming closer, as always to the fulfilment of the dream. So if you have any thoughts at any level or in any part of the dragon or human you have become to bring to an end the development of this world to end your own pain, remember this Mithrael; Under no circumstances will I allow this world to be destroyed. You must reunite with your dragon soul and return to us and if you have a problem with that then an alternative will have to be found!"

Mithrael felt a change in her voice and looked over at Arimathea. The beautiful face of the young woman had become harder, stern and authoritative; thunder rumbled in the distance, the skies above the hill and the surrounding countryside had darkened as the clouds rushed over leaving only a beam of starlight to illuminate her on the hill. Then as quickly as it had emerged the landscape around him started to fade and he was sitting in the reception of the Wade skyscraper staring over at Mariella who was grinning back at him. He felt shaken as he looked over into her turquoise eyes. He grasped quickly to remember what had just happened between them but the memories flew away as he attempted to chase them down. But there was something and it had left a lingering chill in his soul.

Up on the forty second floor Okino had finished telling Harri the story of his journey so far. Harri was sitting back in his chair staring over at Okino in amazement.

"So you see why I have become fascinated in how you became the leader of this global organisation. How you have come to this point in time to meet me here. I think you may be carrying knowledge in your subconscious about those times when you were leading your tribe as it roamed the world and when the dragons were still connecting with human beings. It would be a very good time for old souls such as yours to be returning with the knowledge they had back in those times."

"It is a wild story Okino and were it not for the dreams I have been having and how you have held my attention and the Teorite I would have said you were totally insane. Now I do not. But regrettably however I don't remember anything. Only that in the dream last night it felt as if there was something that I should remember and I think it could surface at any time. But it sounds from what you were saying it may need prompting out in one of these old stone circles. Perhaps I need to take a trip."

Okino was now studying the documents lying out in front of him across the boardroom table. He and Merilon delved into them searching for something to perhaps connect all the ends up.

"There is a gathering down in the desert organised by the girl who was shot, Grace…"

"Yes, I remember she was shot outside this building not so long ago."

"Deeper and deeper we go. Apparently she's organised it near an old Indian sacred site and there is a stone circle down there. Perhaps you should come down. It may open everything up so we can find out what is going on here. But all this out on the table, what is this?"

"Okino this is the biggest deal Wade has ever been involved in. In fact it is probably the biggest deal anyone has ever been involved in. I can't tell you it is so sensitive.."

"How sensitive…C'mon Harri… if we are going to get to the bottom of what is going on here you are going to have to tell me everything!"

Harri paused and again looked over at Okino. He felt a mixture of suspicion and awe for this person who now sat in front of him. As soon as he had seen the stone he knew he was way out of his depth and now having heard about Okino's journey, Arimathea and the dragons it seemed he really had drifted into some strange parallel universe possibly on the other side of the cracks he had seen in his dream. And there was something about this Uranium deal that had been unsettling him. So, he explained to Okino about the nuclear power stations and the contract he had entered into with the nations who had organised it to supply the Uranium.

"So this is the contract I will enter into with the Ravensberg bank to fund the actual building of the mine."

"So until this is signed then the actual mining operation to supply all these nuclear power stations will not begin?"

"That is correct."

"Don't sign it Harry. Whatever you do, do not sign this contract before you have visited the stone circle and found out why you are here. It's on in the next few days you'll have to find your own way there,"

Okino had felt a warning from Mariella possibly through Arimathea and Merilon that he must leave immediately.

"Harri I have to go now. It has been very interesting meeting you and I hope we will see you down in the desert in the next few days.

Harri got up from the table and offered Okino his hand and they shook on their new friendship or alliance or the meeting of the oldest souls in the world.

"It has been very illuminating meeting you Okino and I will get down to the gathering. It would do me good to get a rest from all this."

"Don't sign it Harri, whatever happens, don't sign the contract."

He gives Harri a quick formal bow, hurries out of the office and down the corridor past Harri's puzzled personal assistant and orders the lift. He watches the numbers climbing up to his floor with an unexplained and increasing sense of urgency. He slips quickly into the glass cab as soon as the doors open. It starts its rapid descent towards the lobby. As it emerges into the lobby space he looks down and is able to see the lift approaching from below. As it passes he watches aghast as Mithrael passes only paces away from him. He was looking directly out of the front of the ascending cab deep in thought.

Chapter Sixty-Nine.
Graceland.

The infrastructure of Grace's dream to allow an expanse of the Southern Desert to accommodate the people who felt they were able to respond to her appeal, was complete. The array of stellar panels stretching out across the desert gleamed in the early afternoon Starlight. Two young men were checking the connections amongst the silicon faces of the panels. A network of cables would transfer energy unused for powering the festival to where it would be stored in battery units during the day. In the evening this power would supply enough electricity to run one of the sound stages, the food stalls and the accommodation units well into the night. Annan and Kerval Ranisco had built the system they were working on based on the systems they had installed in other locations. This however was the largest and certainly had the highest profile and represented the pinnacle of their company's work as a supplier of Stellar power installations. They stood amongst the panels looking over the gleaming rows and grinned at each other.

"Who would have thought all his tinkering down in that old shed would have ended here with all this!"

"Yeah. It's a shame he's not here to see it. All those years believing, well knowing it would happen and meeting with disbelief and ridicule and now here we are."

They were talking about the history of the stellar power revolution on Arimathea and the pioneers who had worked for almost a generation inventing and improving ways to harness the power from the radiation of their Star. The old shed which held many memories of their father had been full of these early inventions. The earliest were long frames of glass tubes placed on the roof facing directly into the Star. Water was continually circulated during the day, heated to its' maximum temperature and stored in heavily insulated tanks. This reduced the amount of fuel needed to heat it up when it was needed for heating and hot water later in the day.

In the heat of the Summer and as the optimum size of tube was eventually reached little additional fuel had been needed for scalding hot water to supply showers and the washing up. They had been continually questioned as children and young adults as to the temperature of all these activities. Statistics reflecting the savings on conventional gas and electricity sources when a new system was being tested were enthusiastically quoted to them from an early age.

So it was not surprising they had become seduced by the wonders of this new, but obviously the oldest source of power, as a way of solving the problems associated with the use of fossil fuel. They had known from the despondency their father frequently displayed about the short sightedness of the human race who knew it was only a matter of time before they started to realise the sense in what he and his fellow converts had known for years and years. Meanwhile the atmosphere continued to be choked as he installed his latest systems in 'ineffectual numbers' as he described them in the locality of their neighbourhood and the nearby town. They remembered how he had shown them the letters describing the amazement of people he had persuaded to have one of these crude early systems.

"We have cut our energy bills significantly. This will pay for the system in (so many) years and so we literally will be spending less than half we were on the energy to heat our homes."

They knew all the sales pitches. Stellar power had been like a kind of religion in their family. They had often found themselves on doorsteps or at stellar power conventions trying to convince some potential disbelieving householder 'this all could be theirs' if they believed what they were telling them. But frequently in those early years they did not. Fossil fuel was abundant and cheap so why spend hard earned income on saving fractional amounts on saving it or the planet. But as their father had frequently told them this situation would not last and he frequently quoted how many million barrels of oil, tons of coal and gas were being mined out of Arimathea's reserves every day. He would tell them how much carbon dioxide that equated to gradually filling the inner atmosphere of their planet and trapping in fractionally more of the energy coming down from the Star every year.

He showed them the signs in the forests and on the heaths as they walked as a family on the weekends when he wasn't installing a stellar system or at a sales conference. The birds had arrived from the South too early or too late for the emergence of the insects they fed upon. Flowers came out too early and bees emerged to start foraging for their expanding communities as it became warmer. Then there were frosts or snow or torrential rain and so the bees drowned or died from cold and there was a bad year for apples and every other fruit because the trees didn't get fertilised. He had said it seemed the rest of the world couldn't see the links or didn't want to because they had so much invested in their destructive ways.

He had said the seasons were shifting and the weather systems had become disturbed as warming and cooling patterns across the planet's surface were changing. He taught them the signs to look for every year so they would start to notice the variations from year to year in the same way he had. As they grew into young adults and started to look at the world through their own eyes with the knowledge he had passed on to them they could see he was right. But the politicians and the corporations who sold the oil and gas said it was natural and the planet was always changing and any way what was the alternative.

So, he worked on in the tiny Stellar industry with all the others who had shared his passion and who knew eventually the planet would come to demand the systems they had advocated all those years. His two sons never saw him become disillusioned or despondent. But in his darker moments he had often said the human race had lost its way at some point and he often cursed the politicians and the leaders of the world. As he struggled to come to terms with the apathy he saw all around him, his boys turned into men.

He had given them little choice as to whether they would share his concerns or the belief in the systems he had advocated all his life because he always shared his enthusiasms with them and their mother. He had made it seem like it was the game he played in the world and although it seemed like he was losing the war, he won his battles over and over again as a new customer came to see the light and they all had celebrated those victories with him down through the years and came to know what he was fighting for. But eventually he had become worn out and retired and went to live by the sea with their mother in a house in which he did not have to pay any energy bills and his two boys started to run the business he had built up over the years.

The years flowed by and slowly things had started to change. The changes in the climate became undeniable as freak weather conditions and events became more extreme and more violent. Whole cites were wiped out in low lying areas next to the oceans by hurricanes and flooding and the deserts of the world continued their expansion. The wildlife continued to decline as the seasons slipped and changed. Everybody could see what was happening and scientific evidence became incontrovertible and so after years of debate and argument about whose fault it was or wasn't, legislation to reduce the gases started to be enforced by the council of the world's international community.

Soon it became almost impossible for the rich governments of the world not to subsidise stellar energy. In those early years the fledgling industry had prepared itself for the inevitable moment when the investment in the new technology would develop exponentially as the opportunity to share in the huge profits from this new industry was grasped by the greedy human race.

Kerval and Anaan then, were in the right place at the right time. They had embraced the new technology as did their industry as a whole. They had been waiting for this bonanza for a generation. Now they would not miss this opportunity as it suddenly started arriving down the telephones into their offices. In the same offices used to taking phone calls enquiring about systems for one or two houses a week, they were now taking enquiries from investors who wanted to cover entire fields with Stellar panels. The incentives on tax breaks and subsidies for selling stellar power back into the power grids of the world had become very hard to ignore as the penalties imposed by the International community for exceeding emission levels set by them became increasingly punitive.

The sons told their father who had read about how the boom was finally happening. He laughed and they all laughed as they walked down the beach with the dogs splashing about in the surf. He hoped it wouldn't be too late and said he would like one of the new state of the art stellar systems on his house. They told him he could have a new state of the art house if he wanted with the money they were now making. He thought for a moment, closed his eyes and felt the Star on his face and took a lungful of the fresh sea air and said he and their mother were happy enough where they were.

Now they were here. Grace had called their company in her investigations to find a way of making the festival as fossil fuel free as possible. She had eventually spoken to Anaan who had told her almost anything was possible with the right technical designs. He had supplied systems for festivals before but never on this scale. They had always been an addition to the main systems that would be run off the main power grid. Space to layout enough stellar panels to generate the type of power necessary and house a structure to contain what would amount to a small suburb of battery units to store the power for the night time activity had never been available.

Grace had said she thought this might have been the case at the outset. This was why they had decided the desert, where there was almost unlimited starshine and space, was probably the best place to hold the event. If this was the case, he had told her, if she had enough money he could design her a system to supply all the power she needed for day and night without a single molecule of pollution being added to the atmosphere.

Grace had laughed down the phone and told him to make a list of what he needed and how much it would cost because as far as she was concerned he was hired. They had met later in Straam when Anaan had decided upon the system he would supply her with. He had shown her what he proposed. She was amazed at the number of stellar panels that would be needed and delighted when he showed her what he had devised for the battery storage units. He had consulted an engineering company to design a construction with as small a footprint on the desert as possible. They had devised a frame into which all the necessary storage could be bolted into. The structure had been wrapped in stairways and gantries so access could be gained to all the necessary areas in such a way it had become a beautiful work of sculptural architecture rising out of the desert able to be seen far away across the flat landscape. It would be lit up at night from the power it contained to draw attention to the service it was providing and to celebrate the arrival of this new technology.

They had made their way down to the storage tower now soaring into the clear blue sky above them. It would be a few hours before the power stored during the day would be needed and they would continue to carefully monitor the levels being attained before the moment when it would all be turned on allowing the party in the cool desert evening to begin. They had decided to stay for the event as it was a unique system and while they trusted any one of their technicians to be able to fix any problems they had a feeling there just may be something they needed to be around for. This certainly seemed the case around the strange array of tents and temporary buildings that had sprung up in the desert. Since they had arrived two days before there had been a hive of activity as the construction of this small town had finally been completed.

A steady flow of people had started to arrive after their long march across the desert from the nearest town to where the trains had brought them from the surrounding cities. This was one of Graces' more onerous stipulations. There would be no vehicles parked on site and as the nearest town did not have parking facilities for thousands of cars the train would be the only option. A regular amount of comfortable refreshment points had been provided along the way. The whole strategy had been controversial and there had been criticism from groups of people who clearly would not be able to walk for what would be effectively most of one day across the desert. But Grace had been determined this was not going to be an event about solving the environmental problems of Arimathea while clearly adding to it by thousands of people driving their cars to it. This she had always felt would lay herself open to far more criticism from those opposed to any kind of action to solve or even confront the problems she intended to address.

Now as the evening was approaching the festival guests had started to arrive in greater numbers. In small groups during the afternoon but as the star lowered in the sky over the mountains in the distance a continual stream of souls made their way into Grace's festival complex. They wore the hats they had brought themselves or those provided at the comfort stations along the way and little else; they were looking hot and flustered, perhaps slightly shocked by the distance they had had to walk in the still strong autumnal Star shine. But now they had arrived they walked in awe around this new village out in the desert. Their march out here had been an act of faith in what Grace had told them and what she had represented. They had paid a fraction of the price they would normally expect to pay for such an event and so they had very little idea what to expect.

Now they wandered amongst the expansive tents cooled by giant fans whirling continuously high in the skeletal fabric covers. In one entire tent comfortable chairs and low tables filled the space. Here they were able to immediately relax and drink the chilled water which would always be available day or night. They walked down the tented street dedicated to an extensive selection of cafes and restaurants where they would be able to buy a wide variety of food representing many cultures from across the face Arimathea. Their senses were immediately assaulted by the powerful aromas of cooking spices and already the restaurants were filling to satisfy the voracious appetites resulting from the long walk from the train station.

They ate and chattered happily together already with a common bond; Grace's mad idea to make them walk across the desert to get there. A tiring end to a journey that perhaps had been hectic and perhaps the culmination of a complicated set of circumstances allowing them to eventually extricate themselves from their everyday lives to be here. They told each other of their compulsion to support Grace and her widely distributed appeal. Young and not so young had felt they needed to be here. They talked about the times they found themselves in; about the wider society and their personal experiences within it and as they talked together they found they had nearly all experienced dreams in the previous nights. They had woken filled with insight but strangely unsettled. Then when the broadcast had come on it slowly dawned on them during the next few days that making the decision to visit the festival was the only way they would settle their unease.

As they talked they found they had shared the same sense of isolation from the people around them as they worried about the plight of their beautiful world. They told how they had found confusion which had led to denial. It seemed convenient to deny the problem existed which in turn made it easy not to feel guilty about doing nothing at all; They knew the way of life everybody was enjoying and bound into was demanding ever more fuel and resources. Nobody really wanted to give up the lifestyle they had become used to. So how could there ever be any reversal in the demands of the increasingly affluent populations as they demanded better and more food and where health care through the ingenuity of the human race had improved dramatically allowing more people to live longer and healthier lives? They looked around them and saw their mothers and fathers, sisters, brothers and boyfriends, work colleagues and in fact virtually everyone owning a car and using aeroplanes to travel. Somehow their lives had become almost impossible to conduct without them and all the other trappings of modern life which they used without any consideration for the resources they were consuming.

As they found this common ground amongst themselves and discussed the insanity they felt was continually unravelling around them in their homes, in their workplaces and in the world in general they started to grow closer. In every conversation they explored the problems facing their world, sometimes inventing scenarios where a shift could take place or some wild idea that might change the pattern of consumption. Many of them had accepted and brought these ideas into their own lives and had stopped using cars or using so much heating in their homes and again they found common ground as they discussed the difficulties they had found as they tried to make changes in their own lives. They agreed such changes generally would demand an enormous shift in the mindset of the human population who had so successfully been sold and now demanded, many argued, the idea of luxury, ease and continual entertainment that ultimately would lead to fulfilled and happy lives.

If they did not find resolution, they found in their direct vicinity a new continuity with their own worries and misgivings. As they aired their suspicions and their fears about being manipulated by the global system and the insights they had made from standing outside it, they found strong new bonds forming through the sympathy and empathy they felt for their world. As the population of the festival increased and these conversations and many others continued from an origin Grace had instilled long before any of these people had met, an excitement seemed to be rising. The excitement was rising because they suddenly felt they were not alone and perhaps from expectation or relief that finally something might and could be done if enough people came together with similar concerns.

Okino and Mariella arrived in the early evening as this excitement was gathering momentum across the entire site. They had travelled from Straam after the meeting at the Wade skyscraper. They had gone to the train station where they had been surprised to find a growing crowd of people from the city who had decided to take up Graces invitation and make the journey out to the desert. They had found the festival atmosphere had started long before the actual site had been reached as the festival goers stood on the station weighed down by the enormous packs in which they carried all the paraphernalia they would need to live outside in the desert for the next few days.

Okino had noticed the bond forming between young and the not so young as they battled onto the train ill equipped for the amount of luggage now being brought onto it. The train company had been warned of the increase in passengers so had supplied additional trains with more carriages and they were now filling with the excited pilgrims. As a result, every seat, every storage bay and shelf was stuffed full of hopeful humanity. The young adults chattered loudly unafraid of who might hear their conversations. They wore the tatty brightly coloured clothing that had come to signify the movement Grace had inspired. It was a statement that had rejected the reserved sombre colours of the latest couture fashions for the bright vibrant colours of the natural world. Those parents, uncles and aunts who had also heard the call stood, sat or talked more quietly as they recognised their younger selves. The youthful enthusiasm reached a crescendo when the train finally crept out of the station.

Many of the passengers young and not so young had recognised Okino from the broadcast he had made. It had been continually played on the news channels for days on end as the debate it had inspired raged on in the global media. They were thrilled to meet him and were interested in the journey he had made from the remote monastery in Jahallala. They were pleased he was heading towards the festival and asked whether he was going to make any contribution to the debate.

"It is an interesting question but I have had no contact with Grace the organiser. But you will understand my journey has been full of the unexpected and I have a feeling many converging threads may come together at the place where we are now heading."

Okino had glanced casually out of the window as the outskirts of the city were flying past at a speed which had momentarily taken his breath away..

"… at what appears to be an enormous speed!"

His fellow passengers had laughed good naturedly at his surprise for something they had taken for granted and had experienced regularly all their lives. But this made them more curious about his life up in the distant mountains and they asked him how he was coping with their world. Mariella and Okino laughed.

"He's hopelessly addicted to coffee already and continually compares everything to the advertisements on which he based all his previous understanding of this side of the world and to be fair it has been very illuminating!"

"How can advertising have any greater significance than the lies keeping our society asleep in this illusion, when the products they promote are given almost mythical status in their attempts to make us buy them."

"Hah, but if you think like a monk who lives in a town where there is never that much to eat…and I hope you won't mind me saying this Okino.."

"Depends what it is.."

"It's about the fishponds!"

"Oh yeah…that's fine…"

"Oh, go on, you'll explain it better than me!"

Okino looked around at the little gathering that had gravitated around him, faces and minds hungry for knowledge or some insight into what was going to happen in these next few days. He had felt the dragon flowing through the enthusiasm on the station. He grinned briefly catching the glances of many of their expectant eyes..

"It was just, often the advertisements for cars, or clothes or expensive jewellery were set in the fabulous grounds of some beautiful estate. There was often a fishpond somewhere in the background, sometimes set in beautiful ornate stonework but often a natural pond with reeds, perhaps a little summer house on the side. Often these particular advertisements were brought to our attention if one was found in some new magazine that had found its way up the mountain. Then we would pour over it and discuss not the car or the beautiful people wearing the clothes or the jewellery, but what kind of fish they had in the pond. You see by assessing the size of the pond we could imagine the size and number of fish it could accommodate and so how many people it could feed and at what regularity!…"

Mariella stepped in..

"They have no interest in the stuff in the advertisement. They have no use for it in an environment where for a lot of the year they can't get out of their valley. But the fish in the ponds provide endless discussions!!"

"…and as luck would have it Mariella has a beautiful fish pond in her garden where I have become fascinated by the journeys of the fish in a way I have not been able to before…because clearly they are not associated with food in any way and I am well fed!"

"But we do keep a regular count of the fish to make sure he's not slipping into his old ways!"

Eventually the questions died down and the journey continued as the high speed train sped through the countryside and the towns where it stopped and picked up more people. This seemed to Okino the ideal way to travel through this new world he had come to. The train flew through the suburbs where people tended their gardens and then through fields where animals grazed and their young ran in a brief panic as the steel monster appeared from nowhere without any explanation or apparent reason. What would his own goats have thought of this intrusion into their otherwise silent world? Other than providing a further excuse for their seemingly natural instincts to cause havoc and mayhem.

Deeper through forest wilderness and deer grazing in the grassy spaces made between the trees and the tracks. Signs of human habitation became less and less as the landscapes became emptier. Through the darkness of the long tunnels burrowing through the hills and the mountains then out again beside a sea or a lake sparkling in Starshine and the boats of fishermen, their tranquil vigil disturbed momentarily by the hissing of air over the streamlined steel as it hurtled past. Perhaps they looked up and saw the train and the eager faces and their waves because sometimes they waved back in amusement.

Now they walked amongst the cafes and restaurants hungry and tired after their walk through the desert. Mariella threaded her arm through Okino's and they wandered closely as the Star was about to sink behind the mountains in the distance. They watched as the light in the street lowered and the golden light of the sinking Star flowed around and through the conversations, through the connections being made for the first time, through all the anticipation, through the light in wide open eyes as they passed their light, their understanding and love for the first time to a being they had never met before or who they had met again and now were able to rekindle some previous friendship or love affair in these increasingly magical surroundings.

In those dusky moments Grace was also wandering on her own through the streets she had imagined. She watched the people laughing, smiling, talking, meeting and acknowledging and uniting as individuals, as an entire community already coming to agreement, finding their fears and their joy together in only the first few hours here in the pure unpolluted golden light of the desert wilderness. If nothing else happened here in the next few days, she thought, all she had planned for during the last few months had been a success; just in these few moments again Arimathea had moved forward, deep in the consciousness of her world, of which she had had very little experience, only in those moments when she had nearly died and felt it pulling her back so she could be here and watch all this.

Now she experienced the same force solidly around her, holding her, showing her why it had all come to be. In those moments she knew what an amazing, breathtakingly beautiful place the Universe and her world had become. All this had unravelled in her life with all the strange impossibilities and improbabilities that had occurred so she could be standing here in the golden light deciding when was the right moment to radio over to Annan and Kerval to turn on the lights. It was hard to decide because the gathering dusk was so soft and this softness unlike any darkness was now enveloping them replacing the golden light with all the wonders that now would be revealed in the skies above. But she sensed the danger and switched on the small transmitter she held in her hand.

"Hey, Annan, are you there?"

The transmitter fizzed into life. It's little green light shockingly bright was all she could see and then..

"Yeah I'm here Grace, must be nearly time isn't it, to see if this is all going to work,"

She heard Kerval laughing in the background. She moved in the street so she could see the tower where the two engineers stood high on the gantry monitoring their system with all the computer technology they had combined into it.

"Definitely. Turn it all on guys and you better hope it works!"

Annan turned to his console and gently pressed the last key bringing the electronics he and his brother had carefully designed to life. Electronic charge made by the desert Starlight lying stored in the great batteries was released into the circuits running around the site. Into the strings of lights running along the streets and into the stages where amplifiers and monitors, synthesisers and the microphones purred into life as Starlight flowed into them. All was transformed and a howl of delight went up from the people whose eyes had become used to the soft darkness. A new night land had been revealed and their transportation from where they had woken that morning in the complex web of technology wrapped around them, was now complete.

A sound system rumbled into action somewhere in the complexity as sound engineers experimented with the technology they had been supplied to deliver the wide variety of sounds scheduled for the next few days. A low beat rumbled tentatively out from one of the systems and was soon followed by an orchestra of synthesised sound triumphantly wrapping itself into the deep base, breathing its way through the night air, filling it with harmonies and space defying melody, feeling its way into and electrifying every mind it found on its way. Grace watched as the children started to dance down the streets and faces young and old lit up as magic they rarely experienced in the lives they had left was revealed to them. Deep in forgotten recesses of their minds possibly dormant for many years were suddenly again freed to experience unbridled pleasure.

Then there was a face she recognised in front of her, in crimson robes with a dark haired girl on his arm. He stood grinning enormously, memorably from his tanned face and then with his hands raised in prayer, bobbed in front of her. The girl grinning also stood unassumingly at his side as the greeting took place. Grace searched through the faces she had met in those previous months, but instantaneously knew this was the monk she had seen on the broadcasts from the ocean cruiser; who had started the global debate amongst the chattering, sensation focused media about the nature of sentient life on the planet. Who had inspired Jane to create an event, this event to continue the momentum he had started.

Now she stood in front of him he looked little older than a boy except for those eyes in which she was rapidly losing herself. She remembered the girl and shifted her glance over to his companion. Her glance was instantly pulled into the startling blue or green eyes looking across at her. There was a familiarity between the two young women, some recognition that filled the space between them; both were searching for the time they had met or caught the others eyes across a crowded bar or street. But the memory was older and more intimate than a chance encounter. Mariella realised when it had been but before the thought could fully form Okino initiated the conversation between them.

"This is quite something Grace, you've done so well to get it all off the ground. The idea of walking out here I have to say was inspired. This festival really started way back in Straam as soon as we got on the train."

"Never mind me I just seem to have been caught up on…well on a series of waves really…one of which was undoubtedly started by you and your film from the cruise liner."

"Well it's funny you should say that because I feel pretty much the same about what has happened to me. Mariella here has organised everything but actually mostly things have just unravelled before us. We have actually done very little accept enjoy the ride."

"I am sure you are being modest…I mean for a start how did you manage to get a camera capable of broadcasting such quality material to affectively the whole planet from the middle of the biggest ocean on Arimathea. What you did is legendary and arguably has changed everything."

Okino and Mariella looked at each other as if to say "yes how did we do that" or "yes that was a pretty clever trick," then burst into laughter themselves again.

"It is a very long story Grace and not as traumatic as your own I gather. I hope you have fully recovered."

"Getting shot was frankly the easy bit. Look what it has got me into!"
She gestured around her.

"But it's amazing Grace and if there is anything I can do!"

Grace had been feeling the moment sneaking up on her. Here was the central character in her plot and now he had asked her whether there was anything he could do. There had been so many moments like this that had presented opportunities to her. She had missed very few and none she had regretted so far. Some had been hard and she had had to steel herself to raise the profile she had needed, talk to the people she needed to speak to; but this the final victory, the icing on the festival cake would be as easy as walking down a tropical beach into the warm surf and floating there for the rest of the day.

"Would you speak? I mean would you give us a…not a lecture but you know just tell us what has been happening with you…so that we, or something!"

It hadn't been as easy as she had thought. But Okino just grinned his grin and took both her hands and said…

"Of course, I will speak for you, to your festival and tell you what I think has been going on or something!"

"Well thank you very much. It is so good to meet you, it's Okino isn't it and.."

"Mariella. I've just been looking after him.. also a long story."

"So many long stories and at this time virtually no time to hear them because of course everything is going to get going now. So look, here is a pass into the backstage area, it's pretty much the nerve centre of the whole event and I will be there most of the time and there are other people you need to meet of course. So come by any time and you can tell me if you still feel you can stand in front of 20,000 people and bare your soul. Welcome and come and see me!"

Grace gave her own bow and apologising disappeared into the crowd. Mariella remembered her memory as Grace vanished. She had been the younger of the women in the stone circle who had offered the wolf skins to them when they arrived in the stone circle. She was almost certain; the connection was the closest she had made with anyone in the dream. She had felt even at the time as if somehow they had met before possibly as neighbours or even relatives who had come to live in different tribes. The wolf skins had been offered in a more profound sense than a mere loan for the evening. It had felt as if some gift had been returned or given to honour their arrival at the ceremony. As Okino and Mariella continued their walk down the street she pondered these thoughts. Okino had recognised Harri from the circle earlier. If he came to the gathering there would be four people at least who had been in the stone circle. Could there be more she wondered arriving at the gathering who had been there that night and how or why would they all be meeting together now. Okino suddenly became more animated sniffing the air as if he had scented a creature he wanted to pursue on the breeze.

"Can you smell that Mariella, I might be wrong but I think there is a large pot of vegetable curry somewhere nearby!"

They found the café restaurant from where the aroma Okino had caught was emanating and both ordered a portion and settled down to eat amongst the other festival goers.

"I think Grace was in the stone circle as well that night. She was one of the women who offered us the wolfskins."

Okino flashed back to the dream and immersed himself in all he had carried from the ceremony. Perhaps he had already focused on Harri. He remembered accepting the skins but there was no memory of the two women who had offered them. He also remembered the young hunter who had become central to the celebration and the ritual. The curry arrived and they began to eat hungrily and silently. These new developments were expanding through each of their minds and they realised the mystery was growing into even wider dimensions, certainly across time and the thousands of years between the ceremony in the circle and now across the face of this world and possibly beyond.

"This all could be so much more than just a festival in the desert." Mariella ventured.

"Did we ever imagine it would be?"

The music from the main stage was interrupted and an announcement for an introduction to the festival was due to start at any time. Mariella found a programme and looked up the person who was to make it.

"This guy is a lecturer in ancient Archaeology and Philosophy from the island of Eron. Yaan Fairweather. It says he's going to put all this into context, explain about what is going to happen and what we might hope to achieve! Then bands after that will go deep into the night it looks like."

"We better get going then. Wasn't Eron where Mithrael was originally the dragon before it all went wrong for him?"

They made their way towards the music emanating from the main stage to where the introduction was about to start. The stage was formed and covered by what appeared to be the two sides of a vast concave shell impressively cutting into the night sky. The main stage area was brightly lit and already covered with the paraphernalia of a large live performance. It was hung with lights and the newly arrived festival goers now refreshed and eager to absorb whatever had been prepared for them, watched as the technicians hurried about their work connecting and adjusting the mass of electrical audio equipment. Now they gathered under the clear starlit skies of the desert and waited for Yaan Fairweather to arrive on the stage. The program mentioned an audio visual performance and indeed on the large screen at the back of the stage a series of images had started to be projected. The now thickening crowd started to fall silent as they began to recognise the show had begun.

The first images were of Arimathea from far out in space taken by space probes. They had sent images back before disappearing out into deep space on their lonely electronic exploration of the Universe. In these early pictures Arimathea seemed as lonely as one of these probes, alone, floating through the darkness of space circling her Star with the other planets in the star system. Closer in, satellites operating at the edges of the gravitational influence of the planet had sent pictures with cloudy weather systems, deserts and forest regions clearly visible, and the predominant oceans surrounding the landmasses. Further in the edge of Arimathea's atmospheric sphere was clearly visible and was projected over the entire back of the stage. With this backdrop Yaan walked onto the stage.

"Good evening everybody and welcome to our festival to celebrate life on Arimathea. It's great to see you all here!".

A great howling cheer came up from the audience, greeting him and proclaiming to all around them and themselves they had arrived and were pleased to have arrived. Yaan was surprised at the wave of enthusiasm and the energy of all those before him. Many of his lectures were delivered in the studious atmospheres of the lecture theatres of universities and the hallowed halls of learned societies where he knew his ideas were not as popular as they might be here. He waited patiently for the excited cheers to die down.

"Most of you will have seen Graces announcements on the news channels so you will know to a certain extent what the next few days will be about. We obviously want you to have a good time but really and I hope this is why you have all come..."

He gestured up at the photograph behind him.

"...It's all about this place and this thin line around our world which separates us from the dark emptiness of space.

He paused as the magnificence of Arimathea shone from behind him. Then he started again.

"We still do not know if there is anywhere else in the Universe like it. The numbers are impressive and certainly point to the chances of another planet such as ours being high; If you think of millions of galaxies and millions of stars, surely out there, there must be a world like ours with an atmosphere and oceans and landmasses that make it all interact together to form forests and plains and deserts where over a few billion years, a world similar to our own has been able to come into being. But as yet we do not know where it is. I suggest with all the chance factors that have brought us to this point we should consider that there is a high probability there may not be. Each one of you may have contemplated this possibility. What I want you to briefly remember is how you reacted to that thought because that is what the next few days are about.

As you may know from the program, I have studied ancient races and so our early beginnings; really I suppose how we have come to this point. I originally thought and in fact went quite far down the route of preparing an audio visual rundown of the story so far. But I was compiling images we all know so well, images we live with constantly, making them dramatic with music to concentrate our minds to bring home the complexity of the problems on this world we have been born onto.

I decided not to continue with it. You will have seen those images and they may have stuck in your memory and you may well be playing them in the screen in your head at this very moment. You know the ones I mean. What do you think the predominant one is? I'll tell you because I've done this experiment before on a number of occasions. Its bulldozers pushing over burning trees in ancient rain forests; followed closely by pictures of open cast mines. Both these images may involve animals or other human beings being driven away from their homes. Closely after that there will be freeways full of traffic and industrial trawlers scouring the seas of fish.

These are in the library of images we have to explain what is happening on our world when we talk about our time. How we relate to the destruction. We think of cities and millions of people living and working together in those vast constructions we have made through our huge ingenuity and will. Environments in which we all have a role as if we are in some vast mega machine that employs organisms flowing through the subways and down motorways like rivers that must be in the right place at the right time every day to do whatever it is we need to do to keep it alive and functioning effectively. You older ones will know what I mean. Because you have passed the same people at a particular place, stood on the platform, met them coming out of the shops, seen them going past you at the end of your road at the same time for years. This is our actual experience and the archetypal images of our world blending together.

We know we're in it and that everything flows out from our acceptance of what we do every day when we get in our car and put fuel in it. When we go to the supermarket and buy cheap food or when we are just buying more stuff and throwing the old stuff away because it's not quite as shiny new as it was or does not fit in with the latest fashion. The chances are we have made some bargain with ourselves at some point, come to our own conclusion and then made some decision about how each one of our actions are affecting this!

Yaan points back to the biosphere picture behind him. The crowd is quiet.

"We think of ourselves in this mass but also ultimately we think of ourselves as individuals. But because we are one individual with one thought in a mass of people who we often suspect do not share what we believe or know to be true, we feel powerless and isolated. So, you might think tomorrow I won't drive my car to work or I will go to the local shop where I know the food is locally grown and I will get my stuff repaired instead of buying new stuff. But what is the point of that when nobody else is doing it. So the result of course is we all carry on and put the worry to the back of our minds or out of our minds so we don't have to deal with all the problems this causes us; so we can get back to our place in the machine every day.

Has all this come about because we are who we are as a species? We have always had to eat and sleep to continue our lives and we have been good at it; better than most and all this stuff we have made has come into being through the thoughts we have had and how we would like to see ourselves existing in this world. If you believe or understand there to be a consciousness on this world then all of this has come from Arimathea. At what point did we decide to separate ourselves from her consciousness or certainly our understanding of it. You may say we have always been manipulated by the more ruthless individuals amongst us who knowingly or unknowingly, initiated this separation which now serves the machine world they brought into being and ultimately control.

We are now gradually discovering we are not separate from the consciousness and are in fact playing a dominant role in all areas of its ecosystems. Sadly, this has been since we have discovered we have been doing great harm, damaging her almost beyond recognition. So now we have something serious we have to deal with and perhaps it is our greatest challenge, perhaps the greatest challenge any species will ever have and that of course is the survival of Arimathea.

So, the next few days is an experiment. We need you to talk and connect to each other. We've made it easy for this to happen. There are comfortable places to relax and chat in the restaurants and throughout one whole tent. So get to know each other and find the connections. They will be there and swap these ideas and all the other ideas you have had.

What is your experience of living on this world and how do you connect with it? Is it ordinary or does its complexity continually amaze you? If it is a continually astounding experience why doesn't everybody feel the same way? How do you really feel about the degradation? Do you think it is inevitable or is there something we can do about it? What would you be prepared to do to keep it and what do you do? What do you think at the moment when you decide whether you act or you don't act and what do you think is holding you back from making those decisions? Would you commit fully if you thought everyone else was also? Or is it just a practical thing of getting around and leading a life in a modern society. How could you reduce your footprint living in this modern society as you do and are there are ways you can influence the people around you without alienating yourself?

Hopefully then at the end of the week you will feel there are at least twenty, thirty or even forty thousand people who share your concerns and think in a similar way as you are going out into the world making decisions to change it.

Many of you may also be aware of deeper activity within your own consciousness, in your dreams and in the connections we have had from other species. We are hoping as you all become closer and this gathering gradually binds together into a mass consciousness here on this site then those connections will be deepened and spread more powerfully into the consciousness of Arimathea and all her people.

"The last thing I have to tell you is because we are operating on Stellar power alone it will not be power unlimited as you are used to. We can only maintain this stage and this sound system for certain periods of time. So certainly during the night there will be less than you are used to but it will allow you to have low level light around the site throughout most of the night. But we hope what you do experience is something you will never forget. So without any more from me and here to get this party really started are, all the way from the city of dreams... The Lost Indians!"

The enormous applause for Yaan as he left the stage was followed by a roar of delight and excitement as six musicians came on each carrying an enormous drum over their shoulders. They set the drums on the stands and stood silently behind them. Then they started to play. The huge sound system Grace and Annan had decided was the largest they could run to exploded into action. The primeval sound of the powerful amplified drums filled the warm evening air. The crowd now continually increasing, fed by the now well-trodden path across the desert responded instantly and became a rolling sea of bouncing humanity.

The rhythm levelled out as if it had become the heartbeat of the world in the centre of the desert. Two of the musicians left the drums. One picked up a guitar and the other stood behind a bank of keyboards. They began to play. Harmonics and ethereal stringed chords rose over the drums. The haunting guitar riffs penetrated deep into the night reaching into the stars increasingly visible in the clear desert air. As guitar and keyboards found their balance with the rhythm of the drums the band started their chant; A chant now familiar to everyone in the audience.

Okino suddenly realised what was happening and shouted over to Mariella....

"Wasn't this the chant we originally heard in the Stone circle outside Asima and which they played at the club we went to the other night?"

"yeah definitely...and I don't know what you thought but Yaan Fairweather looked very familiar as well."

"Do you think he was there as well?"

"I think he may well have been. I think he was the young hunter who was being initiated!"

The Lost Indians had become even more famous since they had released the recording they had made in the stone circle. It had gained rapid

- 633 -

popularity when the radio shows who picked up the most successful music playing in the clubs and dance venues started playing it regularly. So through the radio, media downloads and exposure in the clubs, the chants had become the music cultures latest and most familiar landscapes. Thousands of voices joined as one with the primeval drums and the eerie electronic sounds as they thundered out into the night, as if they could awaken everyone who was degrading their world and ruining it for all the generations who would inherit it in the future.

From the moment they had decided to join Grace in her crusade they had relished arriving in this moment. As they felt the power of what was happening they chanted even louder and jumped even higher as a wave of enthusiasm, joy and excited defiance surged through the crowd around them. There was nothing to interfere with the sound as it was amplified by the gigantic sound system. It washed over the stones and the vast expanses of sand, this ancient sound now magnified exponentially by the experience and wisdom, the yearning and the explorations of generations of musicians to get even closer to the mystery and the magnificence of their world. Now it penetrated deep into the layers of consciousness inhabited by all the creatures and spirits who dwelt there.

It travelled out into the atmosphere and out across the landscape of the desert, up through the valleys into the mountains, reverberating through the canyons and into the exit mouths of the mysterious rivers leading into the deep network of tunnels formed by the steady and forceful flow of the vast underground rivers flowing from the giant aquifers under the mountains, filled and emptied many millennia before when Arimathea had turned on an entirely different axis. The sound travelled down through the tunnels, echoed through and around the huge ancient caverns and down into the bedrock of the planet where vibrations and frequencies reached deep into the ancient fabric of Arimathea.

As the set continued and the celebrations reached deeper into the night the frequencies travelled deeper to where the dragons, the ancient spirits of the Universe slept in their crystal caves, remembering, wondering and dreaming out the harmony they had set out to find in the aeons before they had found and inhabited the fertile spirit of Arimathea. Now again they felt the sound which had originally called them to the surface of this world. They had developed a special sensitivity to all sensations reaching them through the layers of stratified rock where heat and pressure had formed the crystal caverns in the early years of her creation. They had returned now released from their exile in the mountains, where they were again able to exist in the vibrations of the crystal generators at the heart of their world. From here their spirit streams could flow up to the surface of Arimathea and into the mystery which had been able to come to life there. All their dreams and wonderings then could drift in the consciousness like a breeze through a forest on a summer's day.

The world they had found was now very different from the one they had left all those centuries before. It seemed as if an entirely new race had come to live on Arimathea. They predominantly lived barely tolerating or even acknowledging the natural world as if it was an alien place unimportant now, which they had left behind. They had shut themselves away from it at every opportunity in the vast concrete and glass hive cities where they had become oblivious and complacent. They had little concern for the skies or the Earth in which all their food was grown. They gave only passing thought to the effects of this neglect and the problems which were steadily growing as their denial became ever more entrenched. Travelling between one hive and the next in their increasingly sophisticated, rain free, wind free transportation and supplied with all their necessities by the machine corporations who in turn they worked for and continually supported, there was little opportunity for connection with the spirits who were impatient to demonstrate the danger inherent in the diminishing relationship with their ever more troubled world.

However, this world they denied was never far away and would not allow them to entirely dismiss it. They caught sight of it in the distance looking out from their trains or their automobiles as they sped from one place to the next on their busy schedules. If they did look and wonder about the forest or the hills out on the horizon, some memory may have surfaced deeply buried from this life or the one before. Perhaps they had visited those mountains or similar, their summits now enshrouded by a cloudy layer separating them from the high lands where their spirits had once roamed; on the plains and the lower slopes they had drifted in amongst the old trees towards the higher rocky slopes. Perhaps they had wondered if they would ever return; surely they should make the time; but when? Then some new thought would race in from their digitized quantum world to again divert their attention.

The thought was lost as they sped on towards whatever destiny lay ahead for them. But the thought had infiltrated the inconsequential and the trivial of the day. There the mysterious influences brooded unseen, unheard amongst their plans and ideas, observations, of their machine world as they travelled home or to some liaison and eventually to their beds exhausted, they were compelled to shut down their minds and bodies and surrender to their uncharted dreamland. In their unguided nocturnal journey, they came across the old memories and where they had lodged as the chaos faded all around them. There once again the dragons were able to release their magic.

In those wild remembered places, they found an unsuspected familiarity in everything around them. They wanted to run up and greet the old trees. Huddle between the great buttresses, in amongst the old roots as they dived into the ground. They felt a surprising comfort in the surrounding forest and all their sounds. In the myriad of life scuttling in amongst the debris; growing in spectacular forms and patterns on the fallen trees. Felt sadness for those venerable beings who having stood a hundred, two hundred turnings amongst their brothers and sisters were slowly draining back to feed their offspring as they had fed. Then, on the slopes of the hills they found the tumbling streams spoke some language they almost recognized and felt they could speak. Bubbling, sparkling fresh, telling of their journey from sea and sky over weirs and waterfalls and resting in crystal pools where they lay amongst the rounded symmetry of the infinitely coloured stones. They wanted to reach in and pick out the stones to wonder at the colours, possess something of this wonder.

Then, if they were guided to some peak where all the land was spread, shaded and speckled by the traveling water vapor creatures, they would marvel at the intricacy and how astoundingly beautiful it all was. They could see in the pattern the places they had been but now knew of the wonders living there, breathing, multiplying, dying and then bursting back into life under the spreading canopies. The lakes, the rippling seas shining with the mysterious mists drifting over cliffs and across the lands, making islands in the billowing clouds. Saw the raining coming in and felt its leading conquering legions as they spattered down upon their faces, where some drip running, gathering momentum ran down over open lips to be gently received, where it invaded purified senses with the essence of their world; with all they had touched and had been in the journey from the beginning to here. Exploding ten million atomic star bursts of delight into the neural network to leave an indescribable pleasure.

This plan, all to bring them here to release the wonder in this tiny silent droplet into this sleeping being, now awakened like never before, alive like never before in their world and in this consciousness like never before. Feeling the joy and the bliss but as if they had found again a long lost friend or fallen in love again with one who had been lost or denied.

Then they would wake and sleepily resume their life in the machine hive world. But there was a warm feeling, like something delicious had been there and although they didn't know what it was it had changed how they were seeing their world.

Now it was the dragon who had been awakened. It had become curious as to the origin of the new vibrations so successfully interpreting the complex rhythms fundamental to the formation and the diversity of life. There had been a new intelligence and insight into all the systems they had so enjoyed in the realms of consciousness. They had always travelled to experience the humans and their explorations in the same way as they had to experience a star filled forest or a lightning strike or a waterfall. The relationship between the early humans had been initiated as they discovered and started to reflect in their lives everything they saw and felt around them and as they experimented with ways of making a deeper connection with it. Now the fascination of the dragon was being awakened again as the celebration on the plains of Eremoya filtered down to the crystal caverns. It was the ancient call with the familiar ancient rhythms but with a new sophistication signalling an understanding surfacing in beings who had developed a deeper sense of the forces at work in their lives and in their world.

So, as they had done then, again they flowed up towards the surface, up towards this new vibrant expression of life. They flowed into the rhythms and the sounds, savouring these new sensations and delighting in this new interpretation of the wonder; suspended themselves in the joy of life pulsating out from the gathering of humans in the desert as it filled the night far away into the distance of the surrounding desert.

Fascinated with the power of their experience in the consciousness and curious as to the mechanism of its production they drifted into the electronics. Through the throbbing speaker systems deep into the complex circuitry of amplifiers and through the labyrinth of wires and cables to the source of the power held in the complex mix of chemicals. There it was carefully controlled and channelled to all the equipment reproducing and amplifying the inspiration converted by the skill of the musicians. In those moments, luxuriating in the concentrated Starlight, the dragon felt something he had not experienced on any world or in any thought or dream for a very long time. He felt the excitement of discovery, of walking into a new land where everything was fresh and undisturbed as if it had been looked on for the first time and he felt a new hopefulness and a surge of optimism for the first time since he had returned from his long sleep in the dark labyrinths. Deep in the heart of this system he felt where the energy generated by the nuclear fire of the distant star was held. The dragon luxuriated in it, expanded into and through the power as it fuelled the party in the cool desert night.

In those same moments Annan and Kerval were monitoring their system high on the tower. Everything was stable and their system was performing exactly as they had designed it to. They were standing high on one of the gantries enjoying the sights and sounds unravelling below them. They grinned at each other continually acknowledging to each other how important these moments were for them. After all the worry of the planning and the teething problems they had managed to overcome in the last few days it was all happening. The reality was even more astounding than they could have possibly imagined and they wondered if anyone, even Grace could have known this was going to turn out so well. She would be down there somewhere, chanting and dancing in the great seething mass of humanity as it delighted in the magic of technology when it was combined with pure unbridled human creativity.

Then the light went on bathing them and the surrounding gantry of the tower in sinister red light. They both looked at each other questioning, wanting answers and meeting only the same look of terror. They turned to the control panels embedded in their covered alcove in the side of the tower.

"I don't know what is happening here. But it appears we have a massive power surge and its far greater than anything the panels could possibly have put into the system!"

Annan was tapping into his keyboard to adjust whatever he could to re channel the new power.

"There's nothing I can do, it's kind of like the laws of physics have changed, everything is as it should be but we've just got more power than we should have."

They both watched the readouts as the numbers increased but no matter what they did to try to slow them they continued to rise.

"So this looks like good bye party night, in fact it looks like good bye just about everything for tonight."

"What on Arimathea can be happening; this just is not right at all!"

They watched the readouts continue to soar out of control for a few more moments.

"I'm surprised it's held out this long!"

They turned in trepidation to the scene before them. In those few seconds for the thousands of festival goers everything was still normal. Then there was a blinding flash of light from behind the stage area where the small substation channelled power to the various places it was needed. For a few moments there was total silence then there were screams of panic. The emergency generator came into action and the silence was filled with the racing mechanical engine. The emergency lights came on across the site giving an eerie half-light just enough for the crowd to see where they were and eventually where they would have to go. The light reflected in the huge cloud of white smoke that had arisen from behind the stage and was hovering over the crowd who now were attempting to see what was happening around them with lighters and any torches they were carrying which further illuminated the underside of the smoke now extending out across the entire area of the crowd.

Okino and Mariella stood silently as the festival goers around them reacted with a mixture of panic, amusement and disappointment. They wondered whether this was a temporary hitch that could be fixed but suspected it was something more and mostly stood patiently waiting for some announcement as to what had happened and what to do next. Their attention was gradually turned to the cloud of smoke as it drifted over them; probably because there was very little else to see but also because there were strange swirls and eddies starting to appear in the smoke.

"I don't know if it's just me Mariella but are there shapes of creatures appearing in that cloud?"

"Do you know I think you might be right? But now I'm looking at it more closely the whole cloud is starting to look more and more like a dragon!"

So again the dragon was released into the world and flowed above and around and through the minds of the mystified festival goers. It could feel their light and their life essence eager to learn and absorb, the combined aura of thousands of souls that only minutes before had chanted as one the holy word sounds found in the echoes of the deepest caverns by those ancient peoples as they had roamed and explored the new world they had inherited. Sounds of the flooding rivers, the howling winds and the crashing oceans as they circled through four billion turnings of the star, echoed in their thunder rhythms, a hundred life times or one beat in the heart of the spirit at the centre of their world mixing their dreams in amongst all the chaos, willing the peace they knew could reign across its surface so life could arise once more amongst the gentle grasses and the towering trees.

These stubborn wiry inquisitive creatures had eventually emerged amongst all the dust from the space debris and the meteorite ice storms that had come to flood and feed and cool the fiery atmosphere. They had seen in their wanderings the rhythms of the star and the great turnings and incorporated the knowledge into the heart of their lives in their struggle for survival. They had stood in peace when they had endured the danger of a day or a year or through a generation and looked with wonder at all they saw. They had chosen those rhythms, the natural progression of sound through time to concentrate the lifetimes they had experienced in the safety they had eventually made, away from the danger of all they had had to overcome to be there. They had learned how to celebrate in their families and their tribes and in their joy they had summoned up the spirits of their world from deep in their subterranean caves.

The dragon flowed amongst the humans in the smoky vapours of the overloaded electrical explosion. Many millennia had passed since the smoke and the warmth of their fires had mixed perhaps with the mists of the ancient marshlands and they had become visible, flowed through their minds so clear and untroubled, activating deep in the neural networks, in amongst the cells and mitochondria that had split and reformed and carried the knowledge through ten million generations to those very earliest of times when the decision had been made to allow the dream to be free. Flowed again into those cells where the memory had been waiting, forgotten amongst all the fabrication the human race had built so carefully around it.

In those moments the smoke enlivened and formed by the ancient spirits of Arimathea drifted through the crowds of young and old, wrapped itself in amongst the future generations of those early people; around the carefully tailored skin tight clothing and the quantum computer equipment they carried in their pockets and the bodies kept free from disease for so much of their lives by miraculous scientific discoveries; as they stood free protected by laws and governments and treaties that had allowed them to grow without having to fight and experience the terror of warfare and through minds full of knowledge of their world and all it had become like no previous generation; as they drifted sleepily across the site to wherever they were going to sleep that night. The dragon had made a unique and profound connection with them and so he chose to send a dream to everyone who had come to Grace's festival; a special insight into their life on Arimathea as they floated on their tiny world through the vast infinity of the stars.

Chapter Seventy
The Source.

In the strange light of the back-up generators the crowd made their way back to their tents now spreading across the desert like an immense multicellular organism intent on devouring the surface of the world. There was much discussion as to what had actually happened. Grace had made announcements as soon as she had realised why the show had come to such a dramatic end. The reason she gave was obvious to all who had experienced the dramatic end. There had been an unexplained surge of power which had resulted in a catastrophic electronic overload. Perhaps expected from a system untried for any length of time out on the very edge of what it had been designed to do. She assured everyone it all could be fixed and soon everything would be as planned and there was no reason to be alarmed. But for tonight the party was over. She said how much she regretted what had happened and every precaution was being taken so nothing like it happened again. As they stood and listened everyone accepted what she had said and really the set they had witnessed and been a part of had been of such extraordinary quality and as memorable as any could remember. So, they turned happily and wandered from the performance area, resigned to the plight of this first night.

However, they wondered, if this had been the first night what could possibly be in store for them in the next few days. It seemed everyone had dealt with the disappointment and the failure of the electronics. Underlying this resignation was a creeping suspicion amongst many who had seen the cloud as it had floated over them that there was something more mysterious going on. When Grace had talked to Annan and Kerval they had seemed strangely puzzled by the overload and had not been able to give her a satisfactory explanation for why it had happened. She had seen the cloud and the strange swirling images within it. She had been reminded of an ancient spirit from a myth from long ago, before the world in which she had grown had formed; of which she was frequently reminded in the twisting branches of old oak trees which often had the same prehistoric echoes. There was a mystery here and it was unsettling her. It was enough to have thousands of people out here in the desert with everything running smoothly within the normal parameters of existence. But if there were suddenly things happening that could not be explained then everything could become more complicated.

Okino and Mariella wandered back with the crowd into the makeshift community carefully organised amongst the temporary streets and walkways. They talked with the young and old alike who were also wondering about the strange circumstances and the feeling they had been left with as they walked away from the first set of the festival which had ended so strangely.

"I came because I felt there was something that would be completed here or even started. I suppose endings and beginnings have strange synchronicities. Many people I have spoken to have had the same feeling. They felt they were almost compelled to be here."

In the half-light, their conversation with the girl had arisen as they stood at a crossroads of streets while wondering in which direction they should head to find their tents. They made a choice and wandered on.

"I came with excitement and if I am honest great expectation. I have watched Grace and listened to what she has said. In a strange way she has started to talk about things people have dared not talk about. We feel controlled in so many aspects of our lives, the pressures she has talked about and we all have those residual fears don't you think, of being left out, that somehow the party is going on somewhere else and they play on those fears the people who bring these new trends into our lives.

But what happened tonight has convinced me. The party is most definitely going on here and at this moment in time I am very happy to be here. I feel as happy and contented and yes harmonious in myself as I ever have been. After being involved in those chants and the power of those drums, they seem to have awoken something buried very deep. It feels like another layer is being added to whatever has been happening, after the whales and the dolphins and the monk talking about the planet as if it was a being. What he said resonated with me when I heard it. When I went out I was looking at everything differently and the idea just kept on expanding. Wherever I looked something made me smile and I understood a little bit more about what he meant.

It was funny. Everywhere I went there were pigeons; pigeons looking for food or sitting up in trees making that contented sound they make or chasing each other around from tree to tree and across the roof tops. After seeing the whales and the dolphins I started to see the pigeons in a totally new light and this will make you laugh, as if they are another strange and magical race living amongst us with their own laws and rules. They think of us like we think of a rainstorm or a sunny day or a volcano erupting; something that has to be dealt with or avoided or perhaps made use of. We are just there for them. They do not judge us like we judge them, putting everything into categories of good things and bad things, they just are getting on the best they can living on Arimathea. I think we could learn a lot from them."

The girl becomes silent.

"By the way I'm Elisa. I work in a factory somewhere out there making components for phones and I have recently started to keep bees because I strangely discovered I knew a lot about them!"

Okino and Mariella smiled.

"We're pleased to meet you Elisa. I am Okino and this is my friend Mariella.!"

There is a short silence. Then an excited...

"Oh my goddess, you are the monk aren't you; I thought there was something familiar about you!"

"I am and for the record I have often thought the pigeon along with the yak is indeed a magical race."

"You're just saying that to be polite, you must think I'm mad talking about pigeons like that."

"Perhaps, but if you came to my land you would find we share our monastery with many pigeons and doves."

They walked on through the tents where people were forming into small groups sharing their thoughts of the day's events. Elisa eventually joined one of these discussions and Okino and Mariella having miraculously stumbled upon a familiar set of tents soon were able to find their own. They were both as weary as they ever had been wandering through the mountains and after a final look at the fabulous clarity of the desert sky, found their way into the tent and struggled into the sleeping bags they had hurriedly flung into the tent after their hike across the desert. Mariella wriggled up against Okino. He knew she was smiling and tempting him but there was still work to be done before they could ever be together. He looked up through the uncovered mesh in the roof of the tent into the Universe beyond and thought about the apparition that had appeared in the cloud of smoke after the explosion and its distant origins across the star fields above him. Merilon was here of that there was no doubt but to what purpose. As if to answer his question a thought passed through his mind...

"I wonder how old Harri got on with Mithrael. Do you think he will make it and surely Mithrael won't miss an opportunity to pedal some of his 'Sunshine' and I wonder how Grace will deal with him and his crew."

But there was only silence here in his own tent and mostly beyond as he and all those around him, exhausted by all they had been through that day, made the journey towards the dreamlands awaiting them.

Merilon moved through the consciousness of the human beings in their conversations and as they drifted off to sleep in their tents. He felt the excitement as their tired minds processed the information of the day in the last throws of wakefulness before again they surrendered themselves to their dreams. All that had happened to them in the last two weeks and beyond had come to a strange culmination as the electronics had exploded and darkness had fallen over the site. Their normal lives now ran alongside strange possibilities. Could their world really be changing? Now they were here, enticed by this hopeful possibility, so far they had not been disappointed. The inspirational opening speech Yaan had made outlining what they hoped might happen now mixed with the strange vision like apparitions that had appeared in the swirling cloud above them.

As they had talked and compared their experience and thoughts many of them had agreed the cloud had surprisingly taken on many different animal aspects. They remembered the deep expanses where the eyes would have been, a long snake like body but more muscular like a whale or a dolphin and its head an amalgamation of reptile, bear and cat and even horse with the horns of a deer. The wings between a flitting bat and a soaring eagle and always shimmering in and out of focus; changing from one moment to the next. Now these memories fresh in their minds mixed with their experience of the days and weeks before and into the sub conscious landscapes of the people they had become. There were few minds in which these new images sat easily. It was not what they had been prepared to see. This was a spirit creature of legend and myth, a poetic representation of a supernatural power that may or may not have existed in the world.

So long had the dragons been absent from the human minds there was only the tiniest remnant of recognition deep in the genetics that had come from the days when humans had accepted unquestioningly the existence of the spirit world. For in those days they had never known anything any different. Now these ancient memories mixed with the confusions they suffered in the lives they led; confusion that had resulted from the inconsistency and contradiction in their modern lives. The complexity and sophistication demanded of them as they lived in an ever more technological world was taking them further and further away from the biological creatures they actually were.

Their worlds now were guided by an entirely fabricated set of beliefs and creeds that had been evolved by the priests of the alien gods down through the centuries. Although they had long faded from prominence, and their beliefs for the most part discredited, the foundations of the law and the social systems they had invented to control the masses with fear still underlay the system in which all these minds struggled with their existence. Now mixed with the new creeds of the superhighway markets and the bankers, the human mind was as confused as it ever had been. Even here amongst some of these beings who had a better grip on what their world had become, the dragon found deep seated worry and fear for the future.

Further into the dream land where all was exposed the dragon found deep sadness, often despair manifest in strange circumstances as their dreams began to unfurl. Often in strange environments or landscapes these scenarios were rarely continuous. They fluctuated from one bizarre situation to the next, each deeper than the last and each involving greater exposure to an insecurity or distrust. Strange characters and situations continually arose as their minds attempted to bring them back to equilibrium ready for the next day's onslaught. They had evolved sophisticated minds capable of processing and creating so much information about their world. But now they floundered amongst the instincts and urges of the creatures that had to survive from day to day, dealing with the basic truths of their existence while the superficial illusion of their culture demanded they pursue ever more impossible dreams and aspirations to fuel the greed and insincerity at its root.

Each mind had attempted to develop its own coping strategies. The dragon knew the human race had been extremely successful at adapting to the many, sometimes catastrophic changes it had faced during its evolution. Now again they were attempting to adapt to this new environment. These modern humans were adrift in a world so entirely different from the lives they had been living as little as two or three hundred years before. But again they were developing strategies not only to survive, but develop in their cultures and their civilisations, in the vast cities and communities that sprawled out across even the most inhospitable lands and where they had thrived as the most successful creature ever to have inhabited Arimathea..

For many of the individuals who had made the decision to come to the desert, their personal strategies were enabling them to cope successfully with the world in which they had found themselves. Many, however, were not. Merilon sensed many of the sleeping minds were on the point of crisis in many aspects of their lives. They were simply unable to mend the damage being caused each day by the intolerable pressure they found themselves under from this new environment. Merilon knew very well every one of them had the ability to access the places in the deeper layers of their own consciousness to heal this damage. He also knew those places and the means to access them had long been forgotten leaving them with minds capable of processing phenomenal amounts of information but unable to keep a balanced perspective in their complicated lives.

He remembered the relief he had felt when he was recently reunited with his own soul and he wondered whether he should attempt to help the humans to connect deeply with their own souls buried under the layers of complexity and worry and so the knowledge of the solidity they had lost. After all he had been through since he last decided to defy Oblivion and help the human beings he assumed there would be consequences. Again, he was faced with the dilemma he had confronted all those centuries before. Then he had been awakened by the humans who had searched and found the power sleeping at the centre of their world. It had been a very different world and to interfere in the same way here in this time would be far more dangerous.

As before when the dragons met at their council in the mountains he concluded he could only do what he had always done. He decided he would send a dream. He would send one of his dragon dreams into the chaos of misinterpretation and confusion, worry, fear and guilt and all the other blind alleys the confused human psyche had taken their owners.

So Merilon conjured a dream, serene and filled with the peace that had filled the world when dragon and human had shared it together and transferred it into each of their sleeping memories. He projected into their minds a beautiful vision of his most beloved green hills where the high mountains beckoned with their ethereal delight far in the distance. They emerged into breezes amongst gently floating clouds and endless space glistening with rivers and lakes, travelling on an open path leading onward into the endless day higher and higher into the hills.

As they walked further and higher they became aware of a beautiful glow around them. It emanated from the ground below their feet and the rocks they passed. The clouds and sky and the light from the star endlessly filled this glow. But strangely the glow did not come from the Star. It was as if everything had emerged from this glow and once they had acknowledged it they knew, they also had come from it. It was like no other light they had experienced because the radiance did not come from the star. They understood even then, the world and the star and all the stars were contained within it. They travelled on and climbed onto the peaks and looked over the lands stretching out before them and they sat down on the grass and relaxed in the glow and stared astounded by the beauty before them.

As the beauty filled their minds so they were filled with the glow. Each mind was suffused by the glow, it worked its way into all the space and all the time that had been caught there in the memories of its owner illuminating everything as if it had been relived the very day before. But now they were filled with the footnotes of hindsight that had made those memories so crucial as the life journey proceeded. So each face and each situation was now fully informed by the years that had passed as it shone out of the glow where it had first been made and even now still existed.

In the glow now was the last few weeks, the decision to come to the festival and why it had become so important. Who had been there who had opposed or had encouraged the decision? How would this effect the future of their lives, would it be a turning point like so many others that were queuing like aeroplanes stacking up for a runway at a busy airport? But as the memories stretched back into the distance so the ending or the arrival here at the festival seemed inevitable. They had always been concerned for their world. In the glow they saw all their loved ones, everyone they had ever known living in the world as it progressively came under more and more pressure seemingly oblivious to what was happening.

They saw themselves as their lives slowly changed as they had grown, often with specific events shining through out of the glow. The glow it seemed had always been there even if there had been a disaster. If there had been a parting between employer, or a loved one, if there had been a dreadful accident that had changed a course of events, the glow had suffused everything and still everything seemed to come out of it. It was like concentrated Love. It softened everything, even the worst catastrophe. Everything came out of it because there was a need for its' presence in every moment and not it seemed because there was any specific destiny in the future but as if there was some vast equation in the glow which was continually calculating an answer, or a circumstance which meant the universe could continue into the next moment.

They knew now it had never been as simple as a string of events resulting from another string of events further back in time that now had become joined. They knew it was the glow and perhaps it would never be explained and really why should it be; why should everything have an explanation? Then as they sat in the glow they started to realise what had happened. Their race, the Human beings had evolved into such complex beings perhaps because they had been so inquisitive and so had always searched in desperation for explanations. They had always tried to find an explanation for everything no matter what theory or paradigm the proven information gave them. No matter how crude or ill-informed these theories may have been, they had held weight, become ingrained in their culture and guided the human race for hundreds of years and perhaps they still did.

As the festival goers followed their lives back into the glow and acknowledged each situation that had been instrumental in the course of their life, they became more and more convinced the turning point situations were only explainable in terms of the glow. However, at this stage of their development figuring it all out would be like a small rodent living on a savannah, at the mercy of every other flesh eating animal, trying to understand how a quantum computer worked.

They did however realise, sitting on their hills whatever process or equation was behind the glow somewhere in its all-encompassing influence it was, in some way, to do with them and the path they were taking through their lives. It had been about the opportunities offered to them and the choices they had made. They knew the moments and the times these moments had escaped them or they had grasped them because they were the most prominent memories and in those memories the glow seemed to be at its strongest and now it was illuminating all that had taken place, carrying them back down through the years of their life's journey.

They had continually built and rebuilt and clung on to and followed anything that shone some light into the gloomy worlds surrounding them. They travelled through betrayals and heartbreak, through their victories and defeats, failure and success, through their migration from childhood to adulthood, as they started their careers, fell in love and started their own families. Then as they watched their own children growing with their own disaster and happiness, they found they had drifted or had been carried down the years on the tides of emotion and the glow had been forming each and every one of them as sure as if it had been a sculptor who was chiselling away at a raw piece of stone that had been left in the world when they had been born once again, kicking and screaming into it.

At times they had thought they could not go on. Perhaps, at times when so much seemed to be stacked up against them, they had felt they just did not have the power to face the world again. But hadn't the glow been there and then when they had struggled on again hopefully towards the carefree easy days' paradise awaiting them when at last all their plans fell into place or their luck changed or their numbers came up. Then they would be fulfilled and happy. Meanwhile they made their way on whatever path they had found to take them into the future.

There were many who had realised the beauty of Arimathea had always been bound up in the glow. There was some unexplained remnant of something older than even time itself. It was continuous with their own lives and their psyche and it was why they had recognised what Okino had said. Their planet full of consciousness from which they and everything around them had evolved. This peaceful, all embracing, unexplained glow had always been present if they needed it to be, as if a guilty pleasure they had nurtured secretly, indulged themselves in amongst the mayhem they were experiencing elsewhere in their lives. If, while their peers were using drink or drugs to cope, then it was out here where they had found strength and perspective. In these hills and in the starlit woods and by the rivers, in the mystical peace separated entirely from the crazy human world which, day by day seemed to make less sense and drifted further away from the essence of pure joyful life they had discovered.

Now Merilon accessed this fondness and brought it to the surface in the glowing light as they sifted through the joy and the upset, softening it with the beauty they had experienced by a sea or a moment grabbed on a summers day in the park with their lover or their families when for a few moments there had been harmony and it had felt bigger than something that was happening to them because it felt too big for them to contain. Perhaps this deeper connection with their world had been more than just a background to allow them to cope but in some deeper sense had lead them through, perhaps they had been following it, allowing themselves to be guided by it with each of the decisions they had made. Many of them suspected and probably would not have denied the presence of some deeper or higher power behind the circumstance that had sent them down paths perhaps years before resulting in them being there, precisely where they needed to be. Many around them called it coincidence and it could have been but now they weren't so sure.

As they had watched the consistency down through the years, how the world was held so precisely in what could almost be a single moment undisturbed in its continual orbit, when it could be almost anything else, it all seemed to be so much more. Over the years they had acknowledged their suspicions and allowed them to grow as they saw their lives unfurl around them. Now they were able to find their way back through the strangeness and the wonder; to the places where there were no explanations and the mystery would always remain.

Back along the intense rollercoaster of their lives; the car crashes and the divorces, the births and deaths, back through the first loves and the last loves and the grind of everyday existence and all the pleasure they had found, all the habits and rituals that had held them there year after year, back through the battles with bosses and colleagues as they had tried successfully or unsuccessfully to assert themselves in the world of work. Back through all their education and the teachers and the merciless bullies, the terror of exams, passing and failing thinking that nothing could ever be so important again and having their parents there or not in those early years and their relationship with those mothers and fathers who had allowed the battles to happen or had endured them as this new human established itself in the world. Being alone, feeling alone for the first time. Right back to when they first remembered themselves being in the world and what that was like.

Again, terror and elation and did some of those coping mechanisms emerge in those early days as the company of peers was effortless or strained, perhaps lessons were easily understood or never completely grasped and was this where the confusion had first started to arise. Had what they would be, the strengths and weaknesses that would shape their lives emerged at that time. Had they been the creative ones, the gifted ones, the storytellers or the merchants, the healers or the peacemakers as the fights had broken out in playgrounds or had they been the fighters in the thick of the brawl; had they been the curious ones who would be the scientists or the thinkers who would break into new realms previously uncharted by their race. Or had they just felt lost with nothing much to cling onto while they saw their peers all racing forward into any one of these roles. Their only gift it seemed was they had seen and felt the world with absurd clarity which no one understood and there was seemingly no use as they struggled to find their place amongst the strong and the confident who walked easily through the machine world.

Then further back. How had it felt to be new in the world with no memory, no time played out or stretching back? Now they were in those earliest memories, who had been there, who had offered the words held sacred through all this life or scarred it or filled it with laughter and adventure and were any of them still here? What had happened in those early days? Perhaps isolated events, the holiest and the purest of all their memories held in the glow from those earliest of times when they were undamaged by all that would happen to them.

Memories became thinner and then there was nothing. Perhaps their mother had told them of the circumstances of their birth. But now there were only stories. But as they had chased those memories and lived through them in the dream the dragon had sent they had gone beyond those early memories because on the journey into the glow they had uncovered and discovered who they were. It had given them insight into the essence of who they had become, almost who they had been destined to become. They had seen how the struggles had become part of the shaping and the forming of the being who had merged back into the world, to be a part of it and at the same time form part of it, hold their part of the equation.

In those moments looking out over the hills into the expanses of the bright universe the star had become too bright, all the world around them too colourful and full of sensation and they had been compelled to close their eyes and in the shining glow in which they found themselves finally they were joined back into the soul; their soul, the soul of Arimathea and the dragons. The soul who had wanted them to return and the soul who needed them to be incarnated once again, who knew it was their time, who knew there was a place for them to be, a role for them to play and re-form to continue their journey; here they felt the perfection and the joy, the unlimited energy conjured to live a lifetime, guide a spirit once again emerging, into gentleness and the stillness, into the glow. Ultimately, the conception of the vast understanding needed to condense a soul into a moment from the all-encompassing eternal soul of the infinite Universe once again into a new life.

Chapter 71.
Harri's Dream Time.

A giant transporter plane was heading towards the Arralan desert where Grace had chosen to hold her festival. The four-propeller engines of the aircraft thundered over the moonlit clouds suspended in its flight amongst the stars to fly over the southernmost extremity of the country of Eremoya. Then out over the Southern Ocean heading towards the Barai archipelago of islands where it would deliver the fresh fruit and vegetables carefully packaged and stowed in the refrigerators of the cargo bay. The plane would then be loaded with fresh fish and the more exotic fruit the islands had themselves produced to fly back to Eremoya. There it would be distributed amongst Straam city's many expensive and exclusive restaurants. There was a small cabin directly connected into the flight deck able to deliver up to six passengers in relatively comfortable conditions to any one of the islands the plane might be visiting.

Harri had been running his fish distribution business for many years before he sold the franchise, took it back and resold it on several occasions. He would always deny his interest in the company was sentimental. However, he had always kept the bulk of the shares and so had always managed to keep a voice and play a major part in how the business had been developed over the years. Now once again he owned the company entirely. Every now and again he joined the flight to some of the more extreme and distant islands where the largely indigenous populations had never become involved in the industrial fishing practices taking place on the wider oceans of Arimathea. Harri had always enjoyed his involvement with the fishermen and women in these communities and had kept his interest in the business for this very reason.

Wade International had become a vast corporation dealing with extreme numbers. Harri watched the numbers from one day to the next as the sensitive intercontinental markets increased and decreased their demand for the raw materials his machines were continually and ever more efficiently extracting from the surface and deep below the planet. As the demand for everything from skyscrapers to family saloon cars continually fluctuated so did the profits of his company. He watched it all on the computer screens in his office and heard how production levels were falling or had been exceeded from the executives he had employed to oversee the corporation's effective performance.

Harri was endlessly fascinated by how all this had developed and unravelled in the world and relished the role he was still able to play. Even though the output of the company was entirely dictated by the numbers on the screens as they rose and fell, there were always decisions to make as to the best way forward. Strategies were continually developed and implemented as relationships became strained or the changing fortunes of the countries and the other organisations with which Wade was involved showed signs of economic difficulty. In turn this would put in jeopardy the margins of profit being made there. How long should it be given to turn around? Were there political circumstances responsible? If there had been a revolution, could their relationship work with the next government? If it looked like it would be difficult how much would it cost him to renegotiate or should he move to one of the rising star countries who were begging for him to mine their ores, make his cars or buy their crops?

His company was a global player. This excited him in the same way as when he had been running fish around in the van he had renovated all those years before. There were many of course who shared responsibility for the company but ultimately, he was head of this tribe: A global tribe which was wheeling and dealing and competing with all the other global tribes. They fought for the numbers on the screens and were ruthless in their machinations to see them grow. Market share was everything and the goal was always complete domination.

So, he liked to go to the islands and meet the fisherman, perhaps go for a drink with them and talk about how the fishing was and what sort of price he could expect to pay for their fish. He would pay them well and often helped their families or gave them money for their school or some other necessity. He did not have to justify it to himself or feel that it somehow was at odds with the rest of his business in which potentially he had the power to change the economic output of entire countries. He did it because it was something he needed to do to keep in contact with the kid who had been locked in a room for the early part of his life.

Now Harri was sitting in the small cabin just below the flight deck in one of his planes. As always, he had a lot to think about. The monk had come the morning after the cracking up sky dreams with his extraordinary revelations and his ability to suspend the movement of time. How had he done that?! There was definitely something he wasn't telling him. Then the meteorite and the fish, all overlapped into the Harri Wade story and had left him utterly bewildered. Then, almost immediately, Zanda had turned up and put pressure on him to sign the contract for the Uranium deal. He had come to know Zanda well over the years as he had done more business with his bank. But nothing put him on edge more than someone who had enormous power who was effectively threatening him with it.

Still he had not found a clause in the contract with which the bank would nail him. All his intuition, all the business acumen he had gathered, every instinct about human nature told him he was going to be nailed by this creature who had come to his office and put his boots on his Oak table and smoked some foul smelling plant material, presumably narcotic, in front of his entire board. This was abuse of power the like of which he had never witnessed and he had sat down with some of the most ruthless men on the planet.

As Zanda had sat in front of him, demanding, berating him for letting him down, accusing him of delaying the finalisation of the deal he compared this arrogant lout with the gentle monk who had been in his office only moments before. He played through his mind what he had said and played with the possibility of visiting the festival down in the desert. Zanda could see Harri was ignoring him as he had moved over to the glass walls of his office and was contemplating the distant horizon. He realised he was wasting his time. He had barked some ultimatum as he stormed out of the office. Harri had returned, relieved to his table and closed up the files of documentation for the deal with the bank remembering the words Okino had said.

"Don't sign it Harri. Whatever you do, do not sign this contract before you have visited the stone circle and found out whether there is something you need to know."

So here he was on the transporter plane soon to be flying over the desert site as the Star rose over the mountains. A condition for attending the festival was he couldn't drive out to the site but there was nothing to tell him he couldn't fly out here. The pilot shouted down from the cockpit.

"Any minute now Harri and we'll be over the drop zone. The wind will drop you on the stage if that is where you want to land. Make your way down there and I'll open her up. We are up at about ten thousand so you'll have a nice little drop. We timed it well, the Star is just starting to rise." Have a nice flight."

Harri grinned and did a final check on the straps that harnessed him into the compact parachute over the khaki jet pilot flight suit. He checked his altimeter and slipped the helmet over his head, buckled the chin strap and slipped the aviator goggles carefully over his eyes. He left the comfortable seat and made his way to the back of the aircraft through the crates and refrigerators full of the food for his friends out on the islands. As he arrived, the cargo door had started to open and soon revealed the desert expanse below punctuated by the ranges of mountains slicing through them, which from the perspective Harri now had, seemed rhythmical and remarkably well planned.

Then he was running and hurling himself out into the vast emptiness suddenly revealed as he left the aircraft. The roar of the four engines gradually receded as he plummeted downwards. Then the peace; only filled with the rushing of the air around his streamlined suit as he hurtled downwards. Now, with only the reference of Arimathea from horizon to horizon the sensation of suspension and so the illusion of flight, which had come to fascinate Harri so much in these last years, became possible. Floating above the world, which so often came to him assessed and quantified with numbers on his computer screen, he was reassured how wrong it was for his race to think of Arimathea as purely numbers calculated as percentages or algorithms. From here he saw the true magic of the world he lived on and had escaped into all those years ago.

He had heard of its beauty and diversity from the journalists who had also discovered the wonder for themselves and had dedicated their lives to telling the people who could only hear about it on their radios, of whose lives and circumstances they knew nothing about. He thought he would never tire of the sensation of freedom allowing him to twist and turn, float and dive in the vast blue of space all around him. Only in these moments between leaving the aeroplane and again touching down on Arimathea did he feel truly free of all that had happened to him.

He had tried everything as the wealth he had accumulated increased his ability to explore the deep recesses of his consciousness where all his fear lurked. As the techniques of another psychotherapist delved through the layers of trauma they only seemed to reinforce the horrors recurring in his mind. He just could not reconcile his previous life with this one he had made, where fear and insecurity had driven him to control so much of his world but denied him the peace he needed to enjoy all the advantage he had gained. Somewhere down there, there was someone who could turn it all around, return him to dependence and so imprisonment and Zanda was as near to that person as he had come across and it was upsetting him. It needed to be resolved. If the monk had some ability or knowledge to finally put his fear to rest then he was compelled as ever to seek it out.

Soon he was able to make out the insect like activity of Graceland. Its body gleamed and sparkled with tendrils and veins leading to its armoured body and organs. He felt excitement as he contemplated an environment so different from where he normally existed and prepared himself to see and meet whatever it was that was waiting for him. When his altimeter showed two thousand, he reached for the toggle to release the parachute and dramatically slow his descent. He often left this operation to the very last moment but today he needed to guide himself visually into where he wanted to be. The monk had said he should visit the stone circle. He released the parachute and it flowed out above him and inflated with the pressure of the downward forces filling all the seams and fabric and chords with the stresses calculated to slow and carry the weight of a human being safely back to the ground where he or she could safely resume their life.

Harri always thought of the numbers and the people who had calculated them as the parachute rapidly slowed his descent, as tension and solidity returned to his life. Then again, a deeper peacefulness as the rushing of the air stopped to be replaced with a gentle hissing of the fabric above him as he adjusted the canopy for his final descent. The orange orb of Arimathea's Star had now risen over the mountains and so into the atmosphere all around him, transforming again the desert below so he could now make out the expanse of tents and the sound stages.

He had examined the layout of the site carefully before he had left. But he was going to land as close to the stone circle as was possible and he searched now for the plain high in the valley between two prominent ridges of hills running into the higher mountains beyond. The Star would have risen at the higher end so at that very moment it would be completely illuminated and flooded with the early morning Starshine. As the slopes and contours of the mountain range came into view, Harry spotted the valley and adjusted his descent accordingly. As he descended through the early morning Starlight, he began to be able to make out the nature of the ground below. It seemed as parched and featureless as the surrounding desert. Then directly in his path he saw the stone circle, prominent and proudly standing in a flat sandy area at the widest part of the valley.

Harri landed lightly, perfectly in control only a few paces away from some of the outlying stones of the monument. He quickly gathered up the sophisticated fabric floating down behind him and carefully folded it into the backpack where he also had stored a minimal amount of water and enough food to maintain himself for the few hours before he made his way to the festival down the valley and out across the desert. He took a drink and walked across to where the stones stood. He noticed immediately the veins and strata of the rock and how they had weathered. They had been here for a considerable amount of time. In any other situation he would already be questioning what mineral they contained, where they had come from, was there more and could he mine and make profit out of it. These questions however were now far from his mind.

The monk had inferred that perhaps here lay answers to what had been troubling him for so long; Answers to his strange dreams; Answers to why Zanda was causing him so much anxiety or why he had come all the way round the world with his strange story to find him? What should he do now that he was here? Again, he was struck by the silence, the peacefulness all around him. Clearly, the festival had not woken up yet. There was a definite presence around each stone. They had been carefully placed it seemed and had a strange symmetry that connected them all together which in turn gave the space within a distinct quality. Harry grappled with the sensation being exerted over him by these old stones. Was is it his imagination or was the air very slightly shimmering or brighter around each of the stones? Was it how this place had such clarity, how the colours of the stones were so vivid and made him want to touch them as if he would be able to feel the shimmering air? Certainly, the stones were engaging with all his senses in a powerful almost intoxicating way.

Again, he looked out to the mountains beyond. Their mass and stature were enhanced now by the affect the stones were having on his ability to comprehend. He thought he heard an eagle call somewhere further up the valley and turned to look. There she was, circling high over the peaks. He wondered how he would seem to her from the place where she glided on the early morning desert thermals now gathering strength as the star warmed the sandy slopes and rock. The gathering heat and the exhilaration of spent adrenalin now made him feel suddenly weary, the stones and the ground wanted him near and seemed to be pulling him to them. He chose a stone that looked comfortable enough to support his back and lowered his body carefully down to where he could lean up against the stone.

However, much he tried to deny them, the aches and pains always came after the excitement had gone and he relaxed back into the body that had carried him through well over fifty turnings of Arimathea's star. There was always payback for the actions that would have tested a thirty-year old as if somehow he had used more energy than he had and his body just had to shut down for a few moments to compensate, allow itself to catch up. He looked out down the valley, reached for the water in his pack, and took a swig. He felt the liquid running coolly down his throat. He wanted it to enliven him. To purge him of this urge to sleep out here in the shimmering heat when there was so much to do, to understand, out here and down there at the festival where the monk would be meditating in this same Star light.

Harri awoke on the ground covered only in various sewn animal skins. He was amongst a small outcrop of rocks from which the upright stone circle surrounding him had probably at some point been carefully hewn. The slight rise was over-looking a plain where spiny trees and undergrowth spread over to where purple hills rose in the distance. He looked down at his hands and arms. He had dark skin and a long straggle of hair fell over his face. He brushed it away, surprised for a moment who he had now become, before losing all memory of who he had been.

He was in his early adulthood and acknowledged the vigour and energy he suddenly felt as he became fully awake. The Star had been risen for an hour and he could smell the sea somewhere in the near distance. There was no sign of any other human beings and he knew he was alone and had been for some days. Although the ground had been hard he had slept soundly and as he woke to the sound of the world going on around him he remembered he was on his walkabout; he had set out on the ordeal as a boy. His name was Tulla and he would return from his journey as a man. He had lost count of the days he had been wandering due to the strong hallucinogenic fungus his elders had ritually administered to him before he left.

He had come through the ancient dream lands of his people, following the dream time paths of his culture. They had been carefully taught to him so in his fifteen turnings they had become second nature to him. He knew how to find water and food out here as if he had been a snake or a cricket jumping from one source of nutrition to the next. Now he contemplated his predicament. He knew he could die and that of course was the point.

He needed to be strong enough to lead his life and possibly make decisions to carry the lives of his people through the tough conditions they had grown into. This ruthless rite of passage would test him and show not only the rest of his tribe he was strong enough to be dependable but prove to himself and give him the confidence he needed to survive and carry on his life in this land where he would eventually bring up his own family. Also, it was hoped he would find a vision to carry him forward through his life. The vision it was said by the dreamtime, had been carried in his soul from his previous life and that only by following the dream time paths could he find out who he truly was or would be.

He remembered the dreams he had followed in the previous days, as real and tangible, now as the heat and the dust beneath his feet. He had memorised the old legends and myths taught to him by the shamans and the places in which they had originated. They had become part of the everyday construct of his world.

He had followed the great eagle mother over the mountains on the winds she created to fly over and observe her world. The winds bringing the rains and the scent washing over the land bringing life and so her wisdom into all the hearts who understood her. Then he had followed the fastest of the spirit horses who had challenged the wind to a race across the plains and in the race had created and forged the time that from then on would be the marker of all the distance across the world. Then he had come across the great bear father as he wandered the rocky outcrops. He had followed him up into the hills to where he had stood when all the stars had begun to fall and where he had held up the heavens so from then on all men could find their way by the stars he held in place.

In the darkness, when the mighty Star had made his descent, in his nightmares he had fallen into the places where the darkest of all dreams originated. He felt the emptiness, the missing light had left and came to know how the monsters lurking in the dark shadows of his mind could bring on paralysing fear and foreboding; how if they spread untamed through his dreams they could become the scourge of his life. Also, he had followed the stars at night. The great Dragon constellation had appeared and had swooped down from where it watched, protecting the world, filling the darkness with the brightest of distant stars and galaxies where shone each one of his family and the members of his tribe who had encouraged him on his journey and wished him the strength and wisdom to return to them.

In the rivers, he had seen the oldest salmon spirits. It was told they had dreamt the rivers so they could always return to the sacred places they had found when they had first come to this world. There again in the silent pools, they would release the essence they had carried from the distant realms so life could resume again. To the ends of these rivers he had journeyed. He had found these ancient pools and swum in their light. He had listened to the calls of the shaman owl spirits whispering their knowledge of the tunnel paths across the plains and through the forests of the oldest of trees, into the ancient groves where the great stags fought their crashing tournaments in the dying light of the years. Where the one who became the victor, with the greatest strength and cunning would again father the future spirit of the wild world so it could continue on with the majestic lineage granted to it by the strongest, fastest and bravest of all the spirits of this world and those far, far beyond.

These spirits and many more had brought him now to this place where he had emerged from this dream. Where now he contemplated his next move. As he watched the world unfolding before him a wolf came trotting across the plain followed by two cubs, ragging and chasing and fighting unconcerned of any danger in her wake. She was clearly travelling to some pre-ordained place as the air of determination she displayed meant she was entirely undistracted by Harri under the tree in one of his previous incarnations. He watched her disappearing further into the distance before he decided he must follow her.

He leapt up and careful not to alert her, trotted off behind her and her boisterous offspring. She appeared to be heading towards the sea and the shoreline as the sound of the waves became louder. Over the rise of a hill, he saw the ocean glistening in the morning Starlight stretching away to a distant horizon. There was a gully falling down to the beach before him. He followed a stream down the stony, mossy slopes onto the beach below, down to the shoreline and walked in the surf along the sandy beach as the stiff breezes brought the waves slinking up the beach. In the far distance he could see a girl walking up and down the beach. His instinct was to run down and greet her, share some time with her and tell her the stories of his solitary adventure.

A cliff face had arisen where the sea had cut into the high plains and the rise of the hills over the expanse of time it had taken the mantle of rock to push itself out of the surface of the world. On closer examination it seemed there had been breaches in the seemingly impregnable face of rock where fissures had emerged and into which the sea had driven. As a result, a series of openings and archways had been bored through the protruding shoulders of the cliff face creating tall cave halls seemingly conceived and then carefully crafted by a race of master sculptors to create a fascination to draw in passers-by.

Tulla became entranced and made his way up the beach and warily into the great sculpted halls where he stood in amongst the echoing of the surf beyond and the dripping of the water from the ground above. The Star shine sliced in, glistened off walls as water trickled down over the mineral stained rocks. Pools of water carved by a million advancing and receding tides. Hard rib shelled creatures clinging, waiting for the waters to rise again. The glare from the sea and the intense light beyond bounced in from the rock pools onto the high walls causing them to shimmer as the wind tousled surfaces reflected onto the sheets of water draining down the walls.

Tulla peered deeper into the cave which appeared to be stretching far back into the rock face. He could see no discernible end to the cave as it disappeared into the darkness. He wanted to be out on the beach amongst the brightness and the lively surf. He wanted to walk down the length of the beach and meet the girl he had seen in the distance. But the depths of the cave were beckoning to him and he felt a flow from here into its centre as if all the many spirits who had been here were pulling him along with them, encouraging him to venture deeper into the dream. If all up until this point had been confronting him, educating him about the surface of his world and all living therein, it seemed certain now was the time for his lesson about what dwelt below.

He was apprehensive as he started his walk into the thick darkness. Light became progressively less available until he realised the light behind him had almost completely evaporated. Thankfully much of the effects of the fungus had worn off and so he was alone with all the fear locked into his psyche about the dark in which he was now being deeply enveloped. He examined the nature of this fear as he tentatively edged his way into the depths of the cave. The shamans who had taught him all that had brought him to this place, he suddenly realised had entirely neglected to prepare him for this experience.

He had no paths or spirits to follow, no smells or winds to indicate his way. There was just this darkness and now, apart from the occasional sound of running water or a drip landing explosively somewhere beyond him there was nothing for his senses to lock onto. He was utterly deprived of the stimulus that normally enabled him to continue through the world and yet he was compelled to continue along what seemed a gently descending slope deeper into the cave. What sort of creature would live down here he asked himself? He knew there may be bats hanging high in the vaults of the ceiling but larger predators he managed to persuade himself would be reluctant to travel so far into a cave in which they might endanger their own lives.

Who were the spirits who dwelt in this sub-terranean world? Were they the immortal remains of wandering spirts who had chosen to dwell on the border states of both life and death? Had they always felt accustomed to the cold darkness even in the warmth of life? Or had they been prevented from leaving these realms by some horrific and untimely dismissal from their lives? Now consumed and unable to escape the horror of this end, the trace they left disturbed the equilibrium so violently that any who had the misfortune to see or feel them would certainly themselves be filled with such psychotic terror they certainly would be unable to visit such a place again. He felt into the darkness for a trace of these lost souls. He could feel nothing other than the residual edge left by the powerful hallucinogen.

His primeval instincts told him he wanted to run. Turn tail and sprint as fast as he could away from this latest ordeal. He had to battle this urge as irrational panic surfacing amongst calm reason, which only moments before had persuaded him he was the most frightening being in this cave to the millions of bats that hung sleepily over his head. If he ran and frightened them everything could become quite alarming as they bolted on mass for the light. He edged his way forward deeper into the void on a precipice between blind terror and calm resolve.

As he started to become used to this new state and was wondering how deep the cave would continue down into Arimathea, he came to the end. His hands feeling into the darkness ahead of him came to cold damp solidity. Other than this there was no change. Still complete darkness behind and beyond. He felt along the solidity but there was nothing beyond and he was loathed to go too far either way from the route he had arrived on.

Tulla took a few paces back into the space from which he had come. He turned and stood and felt. Felt for anything, the procession of time or a gust of air even a squeak from one of the bats. But there was nothing. All he could feel was himself; his own being, the beating of his heart pumping his blood through his veins. He could feel his feet and where they made contact with the cave floor and how his weight was supported by the muscles all the way up through his legs, through his hips up into his torso, into his neck, into his head where all this was registering and where everything he had ever seen or felt had been registered in his memory. His memory was suddenly ablaze with the colour and the wonder of his world. He craved it and decided he would always relish it after the emptiness he had experienced down here in this place.

In the darkness, he felt his eyes finally losing grip on the part of his mind that created the images he normally would see. The cavern now contained a soft almost imperceptible glow. He couldn't see it in the way he normally saw light. It seemed as if it had been replaced by some other sense, perhaps forgotten or abandoned, it had surfaced again now his mind had been deprived of all others. As he became used to this new experience the glow started to increase in intensity. Then he started to become aware of the construction of the glow. It appeared to be an infinity of tiny particles of light each connected and contributing to the whole. It was continuous and made only slight delineation of the solid rock around him. He found he could expand his consciousness fully into this glow. He had always suspected this phenomenon within his own body but now he was able to feel out beyond these confines. As this feeling became more solid, he was able to feel different intensities and textures in the glow.

His ability to feel into the glow continued to intensify and he realised underneath there were further deeper layers. They appeared to be moving continuously through what appeared to be the membranous inner wall of the cavern. Now it seemed nothing was still. He was surrounded and engulfed with waves of light originating from far beyond the cavern. They carried images of the sea and the sky, of the breaking waves on the beach and the warmth of the Starshine but even deeper there were waves from powerful events far beyond the cavern which he sensed would carry on travelling through the light far across the world. These images came to him as if he was able to recall a memory, to savour it and relive some precious time. He felt himself immediately reacting beneficially to the most harmonious scenes from the beach outside but in amongst these there were scenes of suffering and degradation from far beyond washing over and through these scenes.

There were other waves moving through the glow; specific flows that appeared to be coming from the depths of the planet itself and from a specific destination. The waves from outside seemed wide and expansive and created new images for him. But the waves from below made him feel as if he was standing in the channel of a powerful river. There were strong and lesser currents, they spiralled and undulated, twisted and wound together and as they flowed through and around him his mind was flooded with many rich memories of his own life. Many of his favourite memories as well as many others buried deeper and long forgotten arose easily but now with specific details and given specific significance, they gave new insight into all that had happened to him.

He contemplated the mountains through which he had climbed and the rivers in which he had swum and all the fabulous things he had seen and done, the exhilaration he had felt. Then specific memories started to flash through his mind. He remembered his mother teaching him to cook and her smiling face as he had eaten the first food he had fully prepared. He remembered walking with his father to the river where they had fished all day. He had often told him stories of his own childhood and his own father and all they had done. He remembered running through the trees with his brother and sisters, throwing themselves down on the top of the hill, talking nonsense and watching a thunderstorm approaching, watching bolts of lightning and counting the time between the bolt and the thunder.

He recalled all his lessons with the old shaman and all the things he had learnt about the animals and the trees. They had often, quietly waited for the animals to emerge from the surrounding land and then quietly watched them unobserved going about their lives. He smiled as he remembered the shaman pulling up a clump of plants down near the river, pulling the vegetable from the roots, rinsing it, handing it to him, indicating to him to eat and the rich taste of the food and knowing that he would always be able to find food no matter what happened to him. He and his friends would try to sneak up on the old pigs skulking around the village, sometimes they would catch them but the pigs would scream and wriggle so much they would always have to let them go and they had laughed so hard they thought they would burst.

He had sat by the river with one of the girls from the village, they had watched the fish rising, and the birds diving to catch them as the river flowed by, the star glinted on the ripples, reflecting shimmering light onto her face and into her eyes. He had watched her thinking he would never see anything so beautiful again and now how he missed her and how when he returned, he would proudly tell her about all his adventures.

Then there were the times of the day when the Star would crack through the clouds on an overcast day, surrounding him with its special magic or illuminate some feature of the landscape in the distance as if it held some secret to be unearthed. Perhaps he had found some new place in the forest where the atmosphere spoke to him of this ancient world to which he knew he would return again and again, to immerse himself in its light and fragrance. Where he knew the animals of the forest would come to and amble through to share the magic they all knew to be there.

In all of these and many, many more scattered amongst all the life he must have forgotten, he had felt almost indescribable happiness and a sense of belonging to a magical world in which there was so much to learn and understand. In these moments, he had remembered feeling as if the universe had somehow conspired so he could be there to share this sublime place or time. All these people now shone through his mind. It was clear they had been guiding him, showing him through these ethereal landscapes with the benefit of their own experience and wisdom possibly handed on to them. Even the rain falling, or the biting winter wind had some place in the story, bringing him here so he could understand the true nature of this consciousness, this glowing light in the darkness, of which all these memories were held and had become an important part.

Again, he was in the cave surrounded by the glow emanating from the stone of the walls. Waves were rippling into the space around him. He could feel they were coming from the planet surface but also from deeper below in the planets core. Now images were coming faster. The beach outside was serving as a backdrop as further scenarios drifted through and surfaced in his mind of fabulous lands and creatures of which he had no knowledge or memory. Images that had drifted across the ocean from islands covered in nesting sea birds and their cacophony and the sheer abundance of their colony, intermingled with images from deeper in the oceans where whales and dolphins were swimming through the endless expanses living the lives they had led for thousands of turnings. They tenderly encouraged their offspring on through the spaces amongst the rich sounds of the ocean soundscapes constantly around them. Sharks silently cruising the oceans, searching endlessly for an opportunity to prolong their sinister lives.

There were images from across the land masses where vast forests stood. Bears and cougars wandered through the landscapes with their own offspring. Interacting with their world, scratching the trees and marking their territories as they searched for food. They stopped reverentially at the lakes and streams to drink. Looked up momentarily to the Star, felt its warmth as the life-giving water invigorated their bodies before carrying on their search through the forest. He saw the entire life cycles of birds and insects flashing through his mind as they lived amongst the trees. Colonies of ants streaming across the forest floor, new trees racing towards the canopy, climbing plants strung out between them, huge sluggish green rivers running amongst and under the trees where monstrous river creatures lurked continuing their mysterious lives breathing the oxygen rich water.

A clearing where his own kind were reconstructing a village, they were again to re-inhabit. They stripped large leathery leaves, small trees and saplings from the forest to reinforce the timbers that had rotted in the temporary houses. The houses had stood in the jungle since the last time they had been inhabited and now they had become as much a part of the landscape as any of the indigenous features. The Indian people interacted with the wildlife, the brightly coloured birds and the monkeys as they watched or continued their lives on the edges of the clearing. They called to them mimicking their exotic songs, offering them food encouraging them down into their space. Children ran around chasing the monkeys who had already been tempted down. A fire smouldering, a meal cooking, tended by women nursing the younger children. He felt the bond between them. The waves of love in the glow washed over him mingling with the sounds of the surf and the breeze in the trees. The wild call of a jaguar deeper in the jungle.

Then across a vast plain, the howl of wolves in the high mountains. A mountain leopard padding through a snowstorm. The snowy white owls sitting high in their trees. A glacier edging its' way down to the sea and the cliff face of ice as it met the edge of the Ocean. Fur clad native people pulling canoes and huge white bears tracking across the ice in search of food in sub-zero temperatures. A family of seals lounging around an opening in the ice. Far away a hurricane forming over an ocean, sinister dark clouds revolving, sucking up water, whirling onwards driven by fantastic pressures, it's power building, preparing to unleash its' havoc on the land. Tear a village down with its' occupants, wash it back down to the sea where it would drift and wash up on a distant shore. A desert island surrounded by coral reefs, a kaleidoscopic myriad of teeming colourful life.

Wind, ice and steamy heat, currents of streaming seas and pressure rising and falling interacting together all around the world. In a desert, a lizard scampers down a sand dune in the scorching heat, set against bright blue cloudless sky above. No rain here for a thousand years just occasionally moisture from a sea mist. On the edges the vegetation sparse enough before the giant elephants and giraffes arrive to strip what greenery has emerged from the ancient thorn trees, stood for hundreds of years, roots probing and tapping what little moisture they could find from deep in the soil.

A profusion of animal life on a lush savannah. Lions prey on everything, the millions as they move across the stormy landscape, forlorn in the rain as it sweeps over the hills. Filling the rivers where prehistoric predators wait to grab a desperate creature as it fills with the enlivening fluid, dragging it down to its' macabre underwater store. Giant birds soaring through the skies, descending to pick the bones of the lion's feast. Human beings, still vulnerable, living amongst the herds in the wilderness in this pristine living, breathing world, dying and being born in extraordinary quantities into a precarious life in the glow.

Wave upon wave, searing the true inescapable nature of Arimathea into his mind. A living conscious world full of complex processes and organisms, advancing and interacting together, feeding on each other, pushing it further into the future moment by moment, guided, inspired and motivated when needed by the waves from deep in the planet below constantly mixing into it, feeding and nourishing and filling the glow with ancient knowledge of when this had all happened before. The glow had become all this consciousness being shown to him. It had originated here in the molecular fabric of the world in the darkness of the rock deep below the starlit shores where again the young of the ancient race of turtles would emerge from sparkling crystal sands, scuttle to the edge of the sea to begin their life journey, then to swim in the current streams flowing around the oceans and then return here to continue their part in the ancient dream world of Arimathea.

All this had grown and had become embedded in the fabric of this world filling it with life and potential. Despite all the wonder he had seen he knew it had changed and been changed by him being there and would be changed again as he discovered and revealed more of its mysteries. He felt a deep understanding rising about how this energy was working through all he had seen, connecting it all together. All he would ever have to do to live successfully within it was to become at one with it, carefully assess each intervention he made so he would always benefit the flow of the circumstances he saw around him. He had experienced the waves and how the energies flowed through everything around him and how they might influence everything in the glow. Wonderful actions would always have wonderful consequences in this strange and magical world containing wonders beyond all his imagining. Of this he had no doubt.

Then he was on the beach walking towards the person he had seen earlier. He watched the girl carefully as he advanced towards her. She was looking deep into the stream running from a gully steadily eroded over the millennia by the continual flow of water from the interior of the hills beyond. She looked up suddenly as she noticed him coming towards her but unbothered by this intrusion went back to her observations.

She had long dark hair, her skin was lighter than his own but deeply burnt by exposure to the star. She wore a dress carefully fashioned with colourful material and fur that hung raggedly above her knees. She was filling a small bag with whatever she was searching for. Harri stood across the stream from her. He could easily have crossed. The strongly flowing stream would have only covered his calves but he stood across the stream wondering whether he should greet her or wait for an indication a communication would be appropriate. She glanced up at him and smiled and then went back to her observation. He felt her warmth and friendliness instantaneously transmitted to him from the silent momentary gesture. He stood now captivated, entranced by the girl who was the first person he had seen in many days. He did not know what to say. She glanced up at him again and looked at him curiously.

"Forgive me for saying but you look like you could be a long way from home!"

Tulla was surprised to hear the girl speak. Her friendly smile seemed to have allowed him to know so much about her already, this girl alone on the beach searching through the stream. He was fascinated by her and wanted to help in her search.

"I have travelled through many lands and seen many things."

He grimaced, immediately hating what he had said.

The girl smiled again.

"I saw you come out of the cave. Did you see anything in there?"

Tulla suddenly felt as if she knew there was a mystery in the cave but wondered how he could explain his experience to her. She smiled again as if she knew the conflict he was in.

"Don't worry about that now anyway. Look you can help me with my search!"

She had spoken knowingly as if she had read his thoughts and as if whatever had happened to him would help him in the searching of the stream.

"So, what is it you are looking for?"

She looked up at the sky and beckoned to him to come over to her side of the stream and once he was standing beside her she started to explain..

"You have to wait until the Star comes out again."

They waited for a few moments as the Star gradually emerged again from behind a cloud where it had been obscured while they had been speaking.

"Now look. See how the stones in the stream are illuminated, how there are so many different colours and how rich those colours seem when they are in the water.."

She reaches down and plucks out one of the stones. The water covering it glistened in the Starlight. Tulla saw the reds and greys and whites richly shining up at him. Then she picked up a similar stone from the beach which was no longer wet.

"You see these stones depend on the water for their shine. But look at these."

She reached into her bag and pulled out another stone and held it in her fist in front of him and then turned it over and opened her fist revealing the stone. But this was dry and shone with a surprising intensity.

"..But these beautiful yellow stones do not become dull when they are dry. I sometimes think they get even shinier…and look when you see them in the stream they glint in the starlight as if they are telling me where they are so I can rescue them."

Tulla looked carefully at the shining yellow stone in the palm of the girl's hand. There was a strange echo through the being he was here on the beach who had travelled on his spirit dream journey through the ancestral lands of his people and the being Harri Wade who he would eventually become.

"This is what I am looking for. You can help me if you like I nearly have enough."

"Enough for what.?"

She goes back to searching and indicated towards the stream for him to do the same and they resumed the search for the shining yellow stones.

"There is a man who has come to live near us. He lives alone outside the village. He is taller than the men in our village and there is something strange about his eyes. Well not strange really, just green, but all the people in the village are slightly afraid of him and do not have much to do with him. But he has helped us with things."

"What sort of things?"

"Oh, he is very good at making things. He knows a lot about plants and I know he has made people better and well he tells these amazing stories about the world as if there are parts of it completely different than this. But not many people want to be his friend and he seemed a bit lonely so I have become his friend. One day I showed him these shining yellow stones and he laughed for ages and told me he knew some magic that could turn the stones into whatever I would like. I thought for a few days about what I would like the stones turned into. There are people who carve little toy animals for the children out of wood so I asked him if he could make me a little pig. He said he would and gave him some of the stones. He wouldn't tell me anything about the magic and said that when I came back in a few days' time he would have the pig ready for me. When I went back, he had the pig. It was the most beautiful thing I had ever seen and so I keep it safe at home but he also made me this to wear around my neck from some of the left over stones."

She reached underneath her clothing and pulled out a small figure. Harry came closer to her and examined it. The tiny form was clearly serpentine with feathered wings. It had been exquisitely crafted and had tiny claws and the head seemed like it could be a wolf or a bear but had the antlers of a deer and was clearly the strange amalgamation of creatures Harri as Tulla had come to know in his childhood as a dragon.

"I asked him if I bought him more stones whether he could make me an eagle like the ones you see flying over the mountains but bigger than the pig which is small. So that is why I am collecting more stones. Look …I don't think you are trying; I've just seen one right under your nose."

She delved down into the water and pulled out another one of the yellow stones and proudly held it up in the Starlight. It was astoundingly beautiful with the water still glistening across its surface and the scenery around seemed to fade into a dreary backdrop to emphasise the stunning light seeming to emanate from the stone. In the nature of the light there seemed something of the glow he had felt in his experience of the cave. As he reached out to hold it for himself the girl opened the bag and dropped it in.

Harri felt himself looked at her indignantly and was instantly ashamed and to cover and hoping she hadn't noticed asked...

"Did you tell me your name, no I don't think you did, but I am Tulla."

"My name is Singing Moon."

"I am very pleased to meet you Singing Moon and I would very much like to meet your friend."

They walked away from the beach and into some woods. The trees had grown tall in their battle for the light and space. The wood was bright and airy and full of birdsong. Singing Moon followed a well-trodden path through the ferns growing prodigiously all around, running her hand over their feathery fronds and chatting happily about her tribe and how they lived here in the Summer next to the sea while the seas were warm and filled with fish migrating up the coast. As the winter came, they would move further inland away from the storms into the shelter of the mountains. The path led them into a clearing where there was a collection of large stones and where a fire was smouldering. Across the clearing was a small circular dwelling whose walls had been constructed with stones similar to those laying around the fire reminding Harry of the colours he had recently seen in the bottom of the stream. The roof had been carefully thatched and the timbers of its structure could be seen protruding out from the eaves. There was a small timber door hewn from crude planks hanging open as if who ever lived here was probably in the close vicinity.

"I wonder where he is? He's probably up in the trees. You see, look high in the trees up there."

Tulla followed Singing Moon's pointing finger through the branches of the trees up to where a platform had been constructed in amongst the branches of some of the highest trees. As he looked a figure appeared peering down through the branches.

"Is that you Singing Moon?" The figure shouted down.

"It is me Mithrael, can we come up?"

"Of course, the ladders are down."

Tulla and Singing Moon walked over to where the ladders were hanging down from high above and started to climb. They soon arrived on the platform through a small opening formed in the timbers strapped between the great limbs of the trees. There were rails all the way around, cut and expertly jointed into the main structure and there was a further shelter in one corner. There was clearly some work under way. There were wood shavings and chippings strewn across the surface of the platform in front of a stool.

"Hello Mithrael, this is my friend Tulla. I met him on the beach where I was searching for the shining stones. He has been in the cave."

Mithrael was a tall man; Taller than Tulla had ever seen. He had long dark hair a strong weather-beaten face with striking green eyes. He laughed openly and offered him a hand in a friendly greeting fixing a deep exploratory look into Tulla's eyes.

"So Tulla, what has brought you to me and my home here in the woods."

"I am on my dreaming journey. All the young men of my tribe have to undertake the journey when they come of age. We are sent to find a vision that will guide our lives and prove we are strong enough to hold responsibility and be strong and brave enough to join the hunters of our tribe."

"It is a worthy quest Tulla. Come and sit with me and Singing Moon. I think there are things we need to discuss."

There were now two more stools. Harri could not remember seeing them before but the thought only passed momentarily through his mind before his attention was again fully taken by Mithrael. Singing Moon had emerged from beneath the shelter with a wooden carving.

"Is this my eagle, Mithrael. Can you turn this into a shining eagle like my pig?"

"If it is what you imagined your eagle would be like and you have bought me enough of the shining stones I will turn it into a Golden Eagle for you."

He glanced smiling over at Tulla as he said the words. Singing Moon was flying it high over her imaginary mountains swooping it down over their heads and the carefully carved outstretched wings came dangerously close to green eyes and brown as the beautiful carving sped past to rise again

"Yes, Mithrael I would love you to make this into an eagle and that word, here are the shining stones. Do you think there are enough?"

She emptied her little pouch and the stones rattled out on the timber planks in front of him. He carefully assessed the stones before him.

"I think we have enough Singing Moon. What do you think Tulla?"

Again, he looked and again he searched and smiled as he appeared to find what he was looking for.

"I think there are probably enough of the shining stones to make a Golden Eagle of the size you have carved."

"Well that is excellent. Singing Moon you shall have your eagle before the new moon rises and throws her gentle light over the tides of the early morning sea."

"Oh, Mithrael I just can't wait so long. Surely you can make it faster than that."

Mithrael laughs, ruffles her hair and points over to some apples under the shelter and gestures to her to bring them over. Again, Harri does not remember seeing them. Singing Moon brings them over and offers one to him and Mithrael.

"So Tulla you have been in the cave. Did you find what you were looking for in there?"

Harri as Tulla looked over to Mithrael and bit into the large succulent apple. The sweetness was unlike anything he had ever tasted and it seemed to flood through his senses instantly energising his mind weary from his dream journey and the mushroom hallucinogen. He watched Singing Moon with the Eagle and remembered his climb high onto the mountain ridge to get nearer to the Mother Eagle as she beckoned him higher into her presence. Up into the glowing world and the breezes on which she glided, wrapped around him and sang their songs to him as they whispered over the rocks and through the grass and carried the clouds as they shifted into all the creatures and characters he had ever known.

He casts his thoughts out into the tree canopy surrounding him, into the star light and the translucence of the green filling the air and closed his eyes and listened to the songs of the birds filling the space around him for as far as he could hear. Each sonorous arrangement of notes became like one of the brilliant points of light in the dark universe he had experienced in the cave. Each tiny creature calling across a universe of sound filling the vast expanses of space with its infinite variety, its own special signature never heard before and never heard again.

"There are many echoes here. Perhaps the mushrooms I have eaten have sharpened these senses or distorted them so I feel intersections with other times, as if there are many layers here with you and Singing Moon and we could delve into them and see how everything will turn out. When I saw the shining stones there was a resonance the like of which I have never experienced and when you said 'Golden Eagle' I felt a shiver and then you smiled at me as if you knew what I was experiencing. I know sitting here now my journey has led me here to you and Singing Moon."

Mithrael smiled over at him and took a final bite of the apple before throwing the core out into the woodland where they heard it crunch to the ground in amongst the ferns and the multitude of tiny creatures who would descend on it and devour it and be thankful for the magical energy they derived from it. Mithrael picked up one of the shining stones and rolled it around in his hands

"If I am not mistaken you experienced the original consciousness in the cavern, the driving energy behind all evolution on this and every other world. There are two energies at work in consciousness. They work together in every being coming into existence. They come out of the energy dwelling deep in the heart. You may have heard the words 'Soul' and 'Spirit'. They are very different but are part of the same whole. You will have felt both in the cave. The soul, your soul is a container. It holds the history, the memory of your process, all which has gone before in your life and how it has been affected by everything that has happened to you.

It contains who you are, who you have become and why. Think of any of the memories you have retained. You probably had a few rise up in the cave. They have all contributed to the quality, the state of your soul. Your soul is like a vast lake which your spirit continually flows through, like a current from a stream or a river, it leaves the memories and the experience it is carrying in the elemental quality of the waters in the lake. If you are putting good things in, then your soul will mature and grow and will be of benefit to the world around you. Your spirit then will continue to flow with the benefit of its time in the lake of your soul.

Your spirit and your soul live together informing each other through each lifetime. It is your soul which processes all the actions and journeys of your spirit as you make your way through your life. All your joy and all your hurt is processed there and in time it is where you are healed. Eventually the hurt you feel will be absorbed into the soul of the world and however far it extends. This process can never end because energy cannot be destroyed. Everything in your soul is the result of the energy your spirit has expended in your growth as a being who has come into this existence. It goes on and on, transforming and changing as it comes in and out from the universal soul to where it will always return. Your spirit needs your soul to guide it and inform the person or creature it is destined to become because ultimately your soul is connected to the Universal soul which holds the original dream. The connection between them is crucial and fundamental to the success and direction of your life as part of the original dream. If you are in tune with the original dream of harmony within the great spirit you are in tune with the universe as a whole."

Mithrael becomes quiet as Tulla processes what he has told him.

"I felt everything that happened and everyone around me was influencing who I was becoming in the glow. I noticed it was mostly there at the special times when everything seemed to come together, it made the memories special, so they have lasted. I felt happy and content aware of my life and everything around me continuing."

"I think you have a beautiful soul Tulla, but you may have challenging lives ahead. They will test you and attempt to crack you open. It will be important for you to remember all you have seen here. Did Arimathea send you any further visions?"

"I saw strange lands and oceans inhabited by strange animals I have never seen before along with other human beings in very different landscapes to the ones I know. Were they all living as part of Arimathea?."

"It sounds as if you have had a remarkable vision for one so young, Tulla. And yes, they were all from this remarkable planet. Everything is driven by these two energies, Spirit and Soul and their connection within the greater Spirit consciousness as it flows through universal time. Your life and every life becomes part of the greater consciousness, nourishes and adds to the greater soul in its continuation and expansion, the development onwards into the next state. It cannot stay still, it can never just remain the same, it yearns for future expression and everything that could and will exist within it. Life and Death are its most powerful engine continually regenerating, in any way it can, the old dies, the new will adapt, learn new ways and becomes stronger, more capable, better able to carry the life force further into the distant mists of time. It just must go on. Now the human race has become one of its most powerful instruments with which it can pursue the journey into the future and has the ability and the capability to transform this world into the new state dreamed all those eons ago at its' conception.

Here is some history, Tulla. The consciousness eventually found a place in the burning mists born from a terrible conflagration at the beginning of this time. It found the bonds that could join it into the nuclear dust as it filled the universe. Then it drifted, searching through the darkness. Eventually it became embedded in the concentrated masses of burning stars as they formed in the spiralling vortexes of the new space time. These nuclear masses began in turn to form orbits pulling in the dust to form vast conglomerations that became planet worlds. When and if the warm glow of consciousness became embedded in the fabric of these new worlds as they were bathed in light from the burning Stars, a new creation spirit, a new soul and eventually Arimathea would be born..

The glow became embedded in minerals as they came together to form the world. It became particularly concentrated in these yellow stones Singing Moon has been finding. It is the golden glow of concentrated consciousness you are seeing and it is why Singing Moon and all her race will become so beguiled and intoxicated by these shining golden stones and come to value them so highly. It is because they share the consciousness, the shining glow, with all other minerals of this planet. It is the light in the darkness you felt in the cave. You and Shining Moon have come from that consciousness, that one universal soul.

It is the yearning you feel so strongly, the urge to live, transform and develop; send all you have learnt and experienced to be a guide in the future, to have a part there, take a role, as you do here in whatever you will come to be. Did you feel almost desperation to hold the stone she showed to you, take it for your own as if when you had it almost anything would be possible?"

"...I did feel it and I wanted it, I felt the possibility, it took me over and I was disappointed when Singing Moon put it in her pouch and then I was ashamed I had had such feelings."

"It is nothing for you to be ashamed of. But you see how Singing Moon is fascinated by them. How she searches for them and how she brings them to me to turn into beautiful things for her. Can you feel how it wants you and her to help it in its transformation and to take your part in the journey of its Spirit?"

"I know exactly what you are saying."

"Then imagine how it would be if men came here or to other places where people had found the shining stones and they developed the same yearning to possess them as you. But they had not been in the cave and experienced the fundamental magic that shines out of them. They have no one to explain to them their origin and why they have such a hold over them. So, they let the urge possess them, take them over and eventually when they find other men feel the same urge and they find they can exchange them for other things like food or weapons, they want to possess it in greater quantities.

Then one day one of these stones is in a wooden house when it catches fire. It becomes such an inferno that it melts the stone into a different form. They experiment as humans will and eventually, they are making beautiful things for themselves and anyone who sees these things made from the shining stones will exchange food or weapons, even their land to possess them. So, if you find enough of the shining stones, you can live without hunting or fighting because you can give men the shining stones to do it for you.

Imagine an idea like that between your village and the next if you had the shining stones and they did not. Imagine the power you would have over them. But as the shining stones become more widely used perhaps, they would come to have a common value against which all manner of goods could be obtained and traded. The land containing the shining stones would become highly sought after and men would go deeper and deeper into the ground to get them out. Certain people and countries would be so driven by their need to possess them they would amass vast quantities and so would have incredible power over the people and countries who had lesser amounts.

Eventually the people would become obsessed and enslaved by the idea of possessing more and more of the shining stones for the power they could have and the reason for their true power would never be known. The world would be transformed if such an idea took hold, Tulla. Men would have power over other men the like of which they never could have dreamed. Who knows where it could lead? Power can be a terrible thing in the hands of men who do not know what is behind such power. Do you understand what I am saying to you?'

'I think I do. I reached out for the stone and was overcome by a strange desire to possess it. All it's beautiful shining wonder. Almost as if the power of this world from which we all have emerged was shining enticingly from it…This magic has come from a time long ago. It is the shining consciousness which has made this world and it has become especially concentrated in these stones. You have asked me to imagine, if this became something of a phenomenon amongst men unaware of the source of this magic what kind of power these shining stones may have in the world.'

"You have listened to me well young Tulla and one day you will remember what I have told you."

Mithrael paused and looked out across the canopy of the wood in which he had made his home. The echoes were fading. Something had awoken him from his own dream in the caverns deep below. More and more they had summoned him, tempted him out with the intensity of their rhythms and their ability to connect with his kind and the spirits they had come to feel so keenly. They had sensed and had wanted to know the secrets their world held for them. Their dreams were mixing into the dreams of his own kind. Perhaps one day these new dreams would lead them to forget the dragons and he had become curious about the implications such a situation would have. He had felt a warning this unique connection they had formed was in jeopardy and he knew it would have consequences for the whole of Arimathea.

So, he had woken and emerged from his hill as a human into this fabulous world. Now he was becoming used to it and all it had to offer him and the idea of returning to his eternal sleep remembering and holding the harmony in the centre of the dream was seeming less and less appealing. But now his curiosity had turned to worry. He had seen and felt the nature of power on this world and how it was fundamental to the existence of all life here. The human race although still in its' infancy were starting to realise the potential of the power it possessed in the world it inhabited.

Also, he would always be dragon and the residue of the power he had would stay with him. If he forgot he was dragon but found himself with such powers wouldn't he be tempted to use them. This could endanger the world in unimaginable ways. He needed a failsafe. Somehow this boy was involved with or maybe even provoking these thoughts now rising through his consciousness, still connected however tenuously, to the spirit of the dragons sleeping at the centre of Arimathea.

"Also, Tulla or whoever you are, I need you to remember something else. I could explain the other story but for you to understand it would take longer than we have. I will tell you this only and you will have to believe me. I too have come from a distant place to be here with you today and you will have to trust me on this, we will meet again and I will need you to say some words to me. You will know when the time has come. Do not hesitate there may be important things at stake for the entire world. Will you do this for me?"

"I will do this for you."

"You must take this with you on your journey. It has the words you will have to say to me engraved on it. Take it wherever you go in your life and show it to as few people as you need to. When you come to the end of your life make sure it is in a safe place where it cannot fall into the wrong hands. Do not worry about it being lost it will be found when the time is right"

Mithrael then produces a long thin object wrapped in a dense material and gives it to Tulla. Tulla unravels the material and finds a finely crafted sword. The words are engraved along the length of the blade. Tulla reads out loud following the words down the gleaming blade.

"Arrak nayan sola tri Draganera amani" So what does this mean?"

"Dragon, it is time for you to return!"

Chapter 72
Revelations.

Okino was watching the swathe of coloured material as the inhabitants of the cocoons it contained emerged as if for the first time into the early morning light. They stood looking all around them, up to the mountains and over to where the enormous empty tents hovered over the sands as if expectantly waiting for their offspring to return from their mysterious night-time activity. They shook their heads, rearranged hair, scratched into scalps and other exposed parts of their bodies. In many cases it seemed the metamorphosis they had undergone had caused irritation to sensitive skin as the true and tiny inhabitants of these sandy plains, perhaps previously in some lengthy hibernatory stasis were now provided with new hosts. Subsequently they had found their way into these new havens of unimagined comfort to continue whatever life cycle it was they needed to complete. Okino himself had been afflicted by this unforeseen consequence of life in the desert and had removed a number of these creatures from various parts of his body before settling into the soft light rising over the mountains.

He had been exposed to the dragon spell as it had woven its way through the sleepy halls and landscapes of the weary festival goers' dreams. He too had been taken back to the origin of his life, to the original light as it gently flickered into existence in those first cells and began to rapidly multiply. In those moments he sensed the dragon had been there. He had been searching through the labyrinths for a way out from his prison, searching for a soul who could transcend all the boundaries between the dimensions in which he had become trapped and separated from his love, Arimathea.

At last, amongst this eternity of birth and transference, he had recognised this ancient soul, called out from the great mystery to once again act as the intermediary; to reconcile the world with all the anomaly and paradox that had arisen in its evolution, with survival instincts and mechanisms that had brought it so far, through the brutality and viciousness as it had battled for its place in the future, so carefully and recklessly programmed into every soul to be reborn whether in the icy seas or the baking savannahs.

Now perhaps he would be free again to continue his struggle with the darkness, against the darkness. He had felt it growing enveloping the life force, weakening Arimathea, sucking out little by little each of the tiny threads that held the dream together. The human race now lost in their unguided searching for the light could not see how as each of the threads were removed, the weave of the world was once again weakened. Each plant or creature, large or small driven to extinction or even losing its influence in the eco system in which it had come to exist, would weaken her again and everything they depended on. They had been unable to accept how tenuously their lives were held as their world spun in its orbit around the star bathed in its perfect light and how easily it could slowly drift away.

The dragon had recognised an understanding in the Okino soul, as it had formed in the first light of its new life perhaps conceived over many of his previous lifetimes, a true traveller. He would eventually know on the distant edges of his consciousness, it was he who could initiate a new era of enlightenment in the human race so they would struggle away from the old ways of instinct and law of the jungle, the selfish survival of the powerful over the weak. Not because he was a guru or a great religious leader, a great thinker or even a great scientist but because in these moments at the beginning of his life he had understood the nature of the consciousness into which he was again being reborn, unseparated from whales and sharks, from the lions and elephants roaming the plains and all the tiny burrowing insects searching for a way to continue. Not born alone, isolated, but into the vast eternity of life as it had come to be in all its extraordinary vibrancy.

He would have the ability to unleash these thoughts, these truths about the nature of existence into a world which was teetering towards annihilation. He would know all this and feel powerless to act but he had understood in those moments a new possibility had been released into the consciousness. From then on it would be present making its way into the world. He would be the catalyst and every moment he breathed the air of Arimathea and entered his thoughts into her consciousness a new possibility would be growing. But the dragon knew it would need light to grow, like a tree in the forest surrounded by the gloom made by its fully-grown neighbours it would need to be strong. Free again, he would be able to provide light enough to enable him to grow and hold his own amongst all his neighbours in the forest.

Okino smiled to himself as he watched the itching and the scratching of his fellow campers. All the shadows of his life, the suspicions that had driven him high into the mountain ranges where he had felt closer to where he needed to be; his fascination with the animals he had found and tracked and contemplated, his need to be with the monks in their gardens and their temple who he suspected could help him learn as much as he could about these shadows he had experienced, this and much more all now finally made perfect sense. He wanted to wake Mariella and find out what she had dreamt and tell her she had always been right and with all that had happened how could he have doubted himself.

He looked over to where their tent huddled in with their neighbours even though there was space enough for a city around the festival site. There was no sign of Mariella, so he continued his observation of the subtle changes in the mountains as the Star rose. On the edge between the flat sands and where the mountains started their ascent in the distance, a shimmering ripple of heat had started to form. Somewhere out there amongst the slopes of the valleys and their slippery scree was the stone circle. They had tried to find out what they could about it before they left. But they had found little and as with most of those old monuments there was little other than speculation as to its true origin.

Okino had suspected when he had seen the images of the stubbornly upright red stones it was probably one of the portals into the strange labyrinths of light that travelled through and around the planet, moving forwards and backwards in time as he and Mariella had experienced in the stone circle outside Asima. They connected to the streams of mysterious magical energy directed by the dragons in their caverns to the surface where any who were able and willing to listen could be guided slightly closer to The Great Universal Soul.

As he watched this blurred edge separating the two landscapes, he noticed a disturbance in the shimmering heat. Almost imperceptible at first, he took it for another feature coming into view as the heat expanded higher above the plains. As he watched there was regular movement as if a man was walking away from the mountains directly towards him. Inseparable at first from the haze in which it walked Okino strained to comprehend the mirage or otherwise now striding towards him. In a few further moments the figure left the haze and its features became distinguishable.

The phantom was now revealed as a tall man wearing a kaki flight suit and a cap. The slender outline reminded Okino of the silhouetted person he had seen recently outlined against the Straam skyline. It was Harri Wade emerging from the desert towards him. He watched him carefully as he walked steadily out of the haze. It seemed he had taken Okino's advice. It took some time before Harri eventually walked up to where Okino was sitting. Okino got up and offered both his hands to Harri in greeting. He was surprised to feel how pleased he was to see him. Up until the meeting in the office, he had very definitely been in Okino's mind, a major contributor to the senseless destruction taking place on his world. But since they had talked and he had recognised him from the stone circle his opinion had very definitely changed. It appeared he may well be an ally the dragon had guided him to, perhaps with an important role in this the latest struggle underway on Arimathea. He looked weary and sunburnt, but he greeted Okino with a grin and shook his hands vigorously. He had a gleam in his eyes, a sparkle Okino had not remembered seeing in the greying executive high in his skyscraper. His frame seemed sturdier and heavier, more in the world than the man who he had first met.

"You made it, Harri. I didn't see you arrive, so I assumed you had more important stuff to do."

"Yeah well, I didn't walk across the desert like the rest of you suckers!" he laughed and unhooked the back pack containing the parachute and flung it on the ground before Okino who was able to make out what it was from the graphics on the front. He laughed.

"You flew over and parachuted in!"

"I did son, because this, I came to the conclusion soon after you left, was probably the most important thing I have had to do for a very long time, perhaps ever!"

"It looks like you came from the mountains. Did you visit the old Indian circle up there?"

"I did, son."

He took off his cap and wiped the sweat from his brow

"..and very surprising it was to…look is there any where I can get a shower and some breakfast I've been through a lot in the last twelve hours and I could do with a drink. I ran out about an hour ago."

Okino reached down to his steel alloy water bottle and offered it to Harry who took it and drank deeply without further discussion.

"aah yeah that's better, now where is that shower?"

"You should head over to the main complex of tents…everything is over there. If you head over, I'll just wake my friend…"

He saw that Harri's attention had been distracted in those last few moments to something behind him. He turned to find Mariella carefully negotiating her way through the tents. She beamed over at them and came up beside Okino and took his arm.

"We are honoured Mr Wade, Okino has been telling me all about you. I am surprised you've managed to find time to come to our little gathering. I am Mariella and I'm pleased to meet you.!" She offered her hand to Harri who took it immediately and then she remembered in a flash when she had met him in the circle.

"Call me Harri, please, well, I need some time out. I'm not sure what is going on at the moment but I hope to find out very shortly. So where was that shower?"

As he turned Okino and Mariella saw the sword Harry was carrying strapped into its scabbard on his back.

"Erm Harri, the sword; perhaps you should leave it in the tent for now!"

A battered old coach was making its way through the town slightly faster than the residents would have been comfortable with. The indescribable sound of pounding highly manipulated grunge rock music was filling the wide main street possibly louder than any of the residents had ever heard music being played before. The occupants of the bus were as wild, as stoned and as drunk as any of the residents of this sleepy town knew human beings could be. They stood and stared, dumfounded, ready to run for their lives at the spectacle of the highly graffitied intercity bus go screeching into a full burning rubber skid and come to a halt outside their little supermarket.

They watched in terror as the creatures they presumed may have been distantly related to the human race, then poured out onto their street. They wheeled and staggered and fell, wriggling helplessly with raucous laughter, unable to right themselves as if overturned turtles kicking their feet at the universe. Those still standing kicked their fallen brothers contemptuously and fought with each other as they swigged further copious amounts of what could only be assumed from their state were very strong spirits.

A group amongst them who seemed less incapable from the vast amount of chemicals that clearly had been consumed on the bus made their way into the supermarket. They started to empty it of all the alcohol it had for sale and stowed it in the back of the bus. The shop assistants and the manager were flapping about, demanding money as they took the booze and as much food as would fit in next to the alcohol. The residents then watched as a taller and slightly more sober man extracted an enormous bundle of banknotes from his black coat and handed over a significant portion of it to the manager and then flung the rest up in to the air where it drifted on the breeze and gradually fell onto the street. The taller fellow climbed back into the bus and screeched it back into action and almost immediately brought it to a halt again. Other stranded occupants still in the street staggered back and where necessary dragged each other back onto the bus before it again screeched off, much to everyone's relief, out of the town. Then there was a rush for the banknotes which were now drifting across the street. Fights and arguments regretfully broke out as they were claimed.

Mithrael grinned watching the spectacle in his mirror as he careered off the road into the desert where a well-worn track led off into the sandy expanse ahead. Everything seemed solid enough as he had calculated and he continued to drive the old coach as fast as the desert would allow towards the festival in the distance. His renegade band continued their debauchery unabated, consuming the yellow 'Sunshine' miracle pills that he had had so carefully synthesised by a laboratory of some of the foremost underpaid scientists in the pharmaceutical industry. Normally they would have been developing ineffective headache pills for some vast corporation increasingly worried by litigation as the earlier effective pills in large quantities had become a favourite for suicides. Now they had synthesised this 'Sunshine' wonder drug for him.

Already declared illegal three times they had changed the chemical constituents at molecular level so although it was different as far as legislation was concerned as far as the user was concerned it provided exactly the same experience. As the town faded into the distance he watched this strange renegade crew who now had become the nearest he had to an actual family. They all had had their disasters and had been left stranded as if on some distant shore where an unfamiliar tide had left them gasping for the element in which they had swum so freely. They had been left there at the mercy of any who might chance to pass either to further abuse them or take pity on them and guide them back into the ocean to swim again. Around the fires in the waste grounds and the abandoned buildings similarly forgotten or rejected they had found solace amongst the others who had met with similar or worse situations as themselves.

They shared their brother and sisterhood battling with their demons together in their own post-apocalyptic nightmares which they had brought upon themselves or had been brought upon them by the circumstances of the world. The chaotic life they now led, loosely orchestrated by himself, for the most part existed beyond the world of civilisation where they had held responsibility in their work and for their families. The younger ones had perhaps never entered this world of privilege and opportunity, unable to find the means or the ability or the support needed to make the transition from child to adulthood. So now they rampaged on the fringes, using his craft to take advantage of the latent dissatisfaction and worry always simmering within the respectable society they had been unable to respond to.

Many of them had been exposed to much of the trouble existing there. They had been beaten or worse as children and failed to make headway at school. As adults they had been unable to form successful relationships and gradually started to fall through the net which held the 'society' together. But Mithrael had respect for them. They had nowhere left to fall, there were no more lies left to tell because here they were and it wasn't as if this was all pretence and next week they would all go back to their mansions in the hills and resume their normal successful lives with their wives or husbands and families.

Mithrael would often take them to the festivals where they could sell copious amounts of the 'Sunshine' drug. There was a crossover between the two worlds at these events. The young adults attending these events were the same generation who were attending the clubs in Straam where the new drug had been so successful. They were still young and rebellious enough to be suspicious of the lives being mapped out for them by the previous generation. At these events they could make the crossover for a few days into the chaotic freedom and mayhem they felt they were leaving behind.

Mithrael looked up into the mirror again and grinned as he watched this wild crew. These were the kings and queens of the mayhem. Although the kids might walk past them in the cities even if they were begging for some breakfast, here they were the gurus of the freedom they longed for and which was rapidly being taken away from them. They would come in imitation of their clothes, unshaved, unwashed for days before, so for those moments they could descend into a world where they could ditch the illusion, live as if they were in charge of their own destinies, not their parents or their bosses. And his gurus had the elixir to those hallowed halls, the miraculous yellow pills which made it all fall away without too many consequences if and when a normal life needed to be resumed. If… because Mithrael was not averse to nudging some unsuspecting soul, over the edge into the abyss. Another one saved he would think. One more who would avoid the misery of a shackled life as a battery in the machine, alone and terrified as the full price to be paid was realised and the bill landed thunderously into a life already heavily in debt. Mithrael drove on into the desert and the party went on relentlessly behind him.

Harri had not enjoyed a shower so much in years. The cool unheated water filled with sparkling Star shine flooding through the open air enclosures refreshed and reactivated his tired body. All he had learnt and experienced in his dream circulated through his mind making connections from the dream deep into the life he had been leading. After the shower he drifted out into the festival where more people were appearing and the smell of cooking lead him down one of the streets in search of some breakfast. The smells of freshly baked bread and coffee brewing led him to a small tent halfway down the street. It was comfortably laid out with the familiar low tables and a number of large armchairs carefully arranged so at least twenty people could sit comfortably while their food was cooking. There were a group of young men and women lounging in some chairs around one of the tables apparently already deep in conversation. They looked up when Harri entered the tent and greeted him in an open friendly manner and invited him to join them.

"That is very kind of you and yes I would be delighted to join you, there are a few things I will have to check."

He waved the communications device and they seemed to understand. He ordered coffee and fresh bread and sat in a chair next to their table. He flashed the device on. There were a number of messages from the day before and one from his wife hoping his jump had been successful. He messaged back that all had gone to plan and he was now enjoying his breakfast. The conversation started up again on the table and he relaxed glad not to be the centre of attention for the moment.

He checked how the stocks of Wade International were looking. It seemed they were slightly lower than the day before. He grimaced knowing that the markets would be waiting for his final decision on the Uranium mine. Every day he didn't make the decision the effects on the stocks would probably become worse. There was nothing he could do now. He was more unresolved than he ever had been about anything. The memory of the cave felt so real and Singing Moon and her shining stones. Then he had found the sword buried in the sand next to one of the stones as he had left the circle. The buckle of the belt had been exposed and glinted in the starshine as he had passed. He only had to scrape off a few handfuls of sand to expose the scabbard. Then he had removed the sword and had seen the same words as had been on the sword Mithrael had given him in the dream. He immediately was in no doubt these dreams had been carefully orchestrated from somewhere.

"…so it seems we all have had a similar dream after the bizarre circumstances of last night!"

…One of the young men had concluded. Harri immediately registered the conversation and looked around at the group he had been invited to sit with. There were two young men and three young women all in their mid-twenties. Their clothes were carefully and designedly scruffy and clean. Harri thought they could have come straight from the office where they worked.

"If we all had the same dream then it begs the question whether everyone on the site did."

The group looked expectantly over at Harri assuming he had heard the last lines of their conversation.

"…aaah.. no..erm…I didn't actually sleep here last night."

"Oh right!"

Said one of the young men.

"Sorry it just kinda looks like you did. Did you walk across the desert during the night then?"

"I arrived early this morning and since you asked I parachuted. Landed just north of here and then walked in."

There was a surprised silence. The group noticed in the light of what Harri had said he was wearing a flight suit. Gradually the silence was broken with grins and calls and hand signals of respect from the younger people. One of the girls turned to Harri.

"So, you probably don't know what has happened so far."

"I have friends here but we haven't spoken at length yet."

Harri listened carefully as the group of young men and women explained about the sudden explosion as the first act was reaching its phenomenal crescendo. Then they explained about the dreams.

"It seems we all went back to when we were actually conceived, right the way back through our lives, all the turning points, all the places and episodes that have bought us to where we are now."

Harri looked around at them, remembering again back to the cave where Tulla's simple life had come shining out of the darkness to him. Had he been Tulla? Was his spirit here now again listening at a place in a time when all the meaning behind these mysteries was about to be revealed.

"So now you have experienced those initial moments in your existence how does that make you feel in relation to all of this. Wasn't this conference about finding a way forward into the future without completely trashing our world?"

Again, there was silence. It had taken Harri to allow them to see the bigger picture. They all knew what it was but had not aired it yet. Possibly had not found the context in which to bring it all together. The girl who had addressed Harri earlier.

"Sorry what was your name?"

"Yeah I'm Harri very pleased to meet you all in the circumstances!"

"Hi Harri and I am Anna. But before you mentioned the event I'm not sure any of us had really combined the two ideas. But when I think of the profound enormity of those moments, I experienced in my dream in a way the problems we have on Arimathea fade into virtual insignificance. It seems we can experience all the magnificence of eternity and find our potential and our planets potential somewhere in the future. All we have to do is to make a few adjustments to our lifestyles."

There were a few chuckles from around the table.

"All we have to do!! Are you kidding? You know how this world is run. It is run by psychopathic maniacs who thrive on power. Whether actual physical power or the power they have over you and me, they offer their perverse incentives of material wealth if we go along with their own power crazed psychopathic dreams they in turn have been sold by previous generations who knowingly or unknowingly have brought us to the place where we now find ourselves. Do you think they are going to just give it all up without a fight?"

Harri felt a cold chill in his soul. He realised this young man was talking about him and everyone like him sitting in the towers in Straam checking their stocks and then acting accordingly through the day so the next morning they would see a rise or some rally or that they had stopped falling so fast. People like him who did not think of the people who would lose their jobs or die in an unsafe mine or the family of monkeys or graceful big cats who would have to flee in terror from the bulldozers just so he could see his stocks rise the next morning.

Now the world was waiting for his decision to start the mine. It would erase the way of life of an entire tribe perhaps uninterrupted since humans had first emerged. Then a deeper chill wind came whistling through. The land where Tulla had lived and travelled on his walkabout could certainly have been the country in which the mine was to be excavated. He would be wiping out his own ancestors. All this had been so carefully orchestrated he would be surprised if it was a coincidence. Then he thought of all the lore and understanding he had acquired on his journey. Understandings possibly which had guided the early human beings to where they existed today and which for the most part was slowly being wiped from the world. He looked up at the boys and girls sitting before him. They could be his own children who now would be driving to work carrying all the hopes and dreams they had acquired from his generation. He was ashamed and embarrassed and knew he would have to make his confession to them now. He sat up straight and almost shouted to the entire tent....

"I am one of those men. In the moments before you addressed me I was checking the stocks of the global corporation which I founded and am still the chief executive. I have a decision to make which is affecting the global markets and it is about power. The power you were talking about. I am one of the power crazed psychopaths!"

Harry reached into his pocket and flung the communications device out of the tent. Then he slowly put his head in his hands hiding his face from the startled looks of the young people around him. Suddenly he had been hit by the emotional wave that had been rolling through his life somewhere out on his distant Ocean. It smashed through him and he felt all the pain he had buried. The pain he had allowed no one to uncover which he had denied and covered up to everyone and mostly to himself. Now it was ripping through the hardened executive deep down into the small child behind the locked door in fear of another beating from the father he had loved so much.

He had become a monster, perhaps worse than his father if the vision he had had in the cave concerning the nature of the life force of Arimathea had any bearing on the events now unfolding. The series of events from the moments he had escaped to live on the streets to survive with all the other lost souls, like animals unguided and uncared for, responding only to the gnawing hunger in their stomachs, now unravelled through the years as he sat looking out of the tent into the blue desert skies. As his life had continued and even became more stable, he had never been able to shake off the feeling there was a beating around the corner. It lurked as unsubstantiated fear, deep in his unconscious. He denied it to himself and to all the therapists and the people who had loved him as if his childhood had been an episode that had happened to somebody else in another life and he had moved into this new life unaffected. Now he saw it had shaped every decision he had ever taken.

He had built a fortified castle around himself and all his dealings in the world, in case, whatever it was he felt was lurking out there suddenly appeared. Then it would find only the cold hard rock of his denial. It seemed so obvious. So often it had been pointed out to him but until this moment when the boy had described exactly what he had become, that it was he and all the other damaged men and women like him who were dragging the world towards an unprecedented disaster. Now he had suddenly understood and the phantom that had held him in fear for so many years was starting to drift away.

Okino and Mariella had been searching for Harri since they had been separated earlier on. Now in the daylight Okino had become more recognisable and wearing his robes he found he was unable to go very far without being stopped and asked questions about the broadcast from the cruise liner. He laughed and offered a blessing and said something like…

"There are probably strange unexplained happenings that have occurred in all of our lives, some perhaps we didn't even notice. These are the mechanisms of the great spirit operating amongst and through us. If these events are to become more effective in the world, we must become more aware of their meaning as they arrive."

This would either cause more debate or the questioner would wander on to ponder the words of the young monk who had become in a short space of time one of the most recognised people on the planet. So it was as they walked up one of the more deserted streets in their search for Harri, they saw his discarded communications device flying out of the tent and landing a few paces in front of them, flashing and sounding disconcertedly after being so suddenly discarded and violently separated from its owner. Mariella picked it up and they both peered into the tent to see Harri slouched in his chair his head leaning on one hand and an arm propped by one of the arms of the chair. They made their way into the tent through all the furniture and walked up to where Harri was sitting..

"Hey Harri, Everything all right. I think you might be needing this."

Mariella placed the phone on the table in front of him.

"Oh yeah everything is just fine. Oh, apart from the bit where my whole life is disintegrating around me!"

Okino laughed and collapsed in the chair next to him. Mariella went to the table at the back of the tent and ordered coffee and some of the tempting pastries now freshly made and tantalizingly displayed.

"So is that bad news for you but good news for the rest of the planet, Eh Harri."

The girl who had been doing her best to comfort Harri looked up horrified at Okino.

"I think he's having some sort of life changing episode. I don't think you could quite call it a breakdown but we were talking about the power hungry psychopaths who were running the world and he suddenly admitted to being one of them. Is he a friend of yours? He also said he jumped out of an aeroplane this morning to get here. I think he is generally in a delicate state."

Okino laughed again and looked over at the disconsolate Harri. Mariella arrived with the coffee and pastries and sat down across the table from them.

"Harri is having some sort of breakdown, Mariella."

"He certainly looks a bit depressed. What is the problem Harri? I suppose you must be missing being in control of half the world since you've been out here."

The girl still concerned was still looking over to where Harri was slouched.

"So, he is one of the power hungry psychopaths?"

Okino smiled over at her and she recognised who he was.

"You're that monk, aren't you?"

"I am "That monk". But my name as you may or may not know is Okino and I am a monk of the most Ancient Order of the Dragon, the monastery of which is halfway around this world in the mountainous region, mostly inaccessible, named Jahallalah. I started my journey on foot many months ago to find the reason why the fish in our lakes were being poisoned and if possible, rectify the situation. My journey has led me to this man."

He points to Harri.

"…and although he doesn't look like a power-hungry psychopath now, he and his fellow psychopaths are responsible for some of the more scary stuff happening on this planet. So, Harri, what is your problem this morning?"

Everyone looks at Harri and he looks up. He was following through the implications of his realisation as everyone caught up with the situation so far. He looks around at the questioning faces from the twenty-five year old demographic. They were probably all well-educated and starting out in their adult lives un-ladened by debt which soon they would be persuaded to take on to buy cars and houses and all the products they would need to live the lifestyles his and all the other advertising agencies would tell them they needed to function in their world, compete with their peers, rise up the ladder, follow the path dictated to them for a successful life. This is how he thought of the human race, had thought of the Human race. Until now.

He looked into each of their faces. Faces full of vitality with an underlying optimism for their lives. This is what he and his kind would exploit. Channel their energy newly emerging into the world and divert the incomes they would generate, relentlessly, ruthlessly as fast as possible into their enormous bank accounts so they could ravage and exploit another part of the world to provide what they were told they needed as cheaply as possible. He started to speak...

"I'm not entirely sure why all this is happening now but I have a fairly good idea. As I said I have a decision to make and in a strange way it affects all of us, the whole world, so it is entirely appropriate I should be going through this enormous soul searching process. I believe it started the night before this young man came into my office earlier in the week. When we make a decision, we need all the facts. The advantages and the disadvantages, the pros and cons. We gather information from the world as we see it or how we want to see it and of course there are also many influences we must be aware of.

But supposing the influences are wrong or misguided or come from a different time when our race had different ideas about the world. Supposing we went along with those old ideas because they were so deeply ingrained in our culture. If everything we were told and learnt and subsequently did was based on this information, then wouldn't we all be acting entirely wrongly.

Maybe an example off the top my head would be a child who has been brought up in a family of bank robbers. Generations of the family have always been bank robbers and criminals. This innocent child has grown up thinking bank robbery is a legitimate profession, after all it provides income and a way to operate in the world, most of his family's friends and associates of course are all bank robbers so really he doesn't have any alternative view of the world. So, he becomes a bank robber himself. It's easy, he and we all go along with what we see going on around us, year in, year out nobody seems to be getting hurt and the world goes on. It's what we do.

But supposing at some point the world changes and bank robbery is not as easy as it used to be. There are not huge piles of money in the banks anymore and security has tightened. He does a raid which goes badly wrong, he has a close escape and so he must start to look at what he is doing in an entirely different way. The kid, now a grown man living in his mansion down on the coast with his family supported by the successful heists of three generations has to look a little harder into the business he and his family have so successfully been involved in. In his research he finds out the hurt he is causing to the society he is living in. Bank employees get fired and the people who were in the bank when the robbery takes place live in emotional trauma throughout their lives. Insurance premiums go up for the banks because money has been lost and it must come off a balance sheet somewhere and ultimately if everyone started doing it the society would collapse very quickly

In amongst all our mad old ideas there is one undeniably truth. At some point we decided what was wrong and right and one of the big things was we don't take stuff off other people. It is fundamental to us all co-existing together and no matter how much we try to convince ourselves to the contrary some things are just plain wrong. Suddenly there are consequences for his actions for who he is as a human being. I have come to that point. I have operated in the world as only as I have known without fully appreciating the consequences. As a child I grew up in a dangerous world. I eventually escaped and then was prepared to do anything to avoid going back. The world had happened around me, it had made the horrifying situation I found myself in and I had to avoid going back to it at all costs.

But now I have been shown the true facts. The actions I used to operate in the world and protect myself have been guided by centuries of assumptions which were entirely misguided and perhaps dangerous to the survival of our species and Arimathea. Now things are totally out of control. I think we have all been robbing the bank of Arimathea for far too long. I am ashamed to say I have become one of the ring leaders.

I have been shown how this planet is alive in a way we could not possibly have imagined. It is like an incredible super-being from whom we have all been stealing and who up until now has, despite all this, shown us only more of her wonder. She supports everything we are and everything around us. I have now become convinced as we mine and excavate deeper and deeper into her surface extracting her minerals and fuel and destroying her natural habitats, we are gradually draining away the energy which maintains her life force. In other words, we are killing Arimathea."

Chapter 73
The System.

Now the site was waking fully from the silence Merilon's dream spell had laid across it. Grace's beautiful hot air balloons were being inflated. The intense roar of the flames ignited from the gas expelled at high pressure from the steel tanks, provided the backdrop for many of the other sounds emerging into the landscape. As the balloons began to fill, the bleary-eyed festivalgoers gathered around to watch the depictions of Arimathea and her Moon so lovingly reproduced across their surfaces expanding to their full wonder. As they hovered, still tethered with steel hawsers, the people on the ground orbited around them to admire the beauty of the work. The oceans and their creatures flowed around the landmasses where flourishing forests and jungles, baking deserts and the vast frozen expanses of the Arctic regions glistened in the early morning sunshine. Many in the light of all they had experienced the night before were moved to tears as their planet home onto which it seemed they had been so miraculously incarnated, floated in the blue infinity of space above them.

Around them the mechanics of the day's events were underway. There were sound checks on the system on the main stage which had so abruptly been silenced. Now it had been coaxed back into life by the puzzled stellar power engineers who had replaced the components so mysteriously overloaded the night before. Now again the batteries were filling with power from the clear desert Star shine to be diverted into cookers and kitchens where breakfasts were being ordered, into the circuits of the complex mixing decks which would carefully organise the impulses from voices and instruments alike and send them booming out across the desert from the stages to delight and enrapture the audiences who would gather in front of them.

Grace had awoken to the familiar sound of the balloons being inflated and somewhere in the distance the "1-2-3 testing…can you hear me all right, mate…" of a sound check getting underway. In her own dreams the happenings of the night before had faded into insignificance with the terrible dread she had felt as the realisation of a festival without power started to dawn upon her. The sound of the PA filled her with instant happiness and relief and she wriggled in the comfort of the bed carefully integrated into the metal pod that would be her home for the length of the festival. She lifted the blind over the window just enough to see the festival unravelling below her. She had thought very little of what may happen after all this had again died down. She had enjoyed the whole process of organising the festival project with Jane and more than once they had discussed the idea of the festival becoming something that moved around the country to different locations so the benefits of Steve's fortune would continue to be felt.

A show travelling the world ultimately they had thought. Travelling the world in her metal pod with all these wonderful talented people so dedicated to the search she and Jane had embarked upon. She was watching the balloons floating above the crowds who were gathering to watch their ascent. It had been more, so much more than a search… more like a quest so often brought on in ancient tales by a life changing experience. She had been in the wrong place at the wrong time, or so it had seemed. Now she had begun to think differently about the shooting. Meeting Jane at the conference had given her the confidence she had needed. Her new big sister had told her how she had been so inspired by what she had said in her speech at the dinner. She had told Grace the profound implications of her words, a reflection Grace had not expected.

Now they were searching or had become involved in some wider search, some yearning amongst the generations who found themselves on Arimathea in these troubled times. She remembered her meeting with the monk and the beautiful girl with whom he was travelling. She had not contemplated their meeting before now as the events of the previous night had filled her thoughts. What had he said?

"…but actually, mostly things have just unravelled before us. We have actually done very little accept enjoy the ride."

Here she felt everyone was on their own search, on their quest to find a way, any way forward from the confusion she had found so many of her fellow travellers were feeling. She would have to find the monk and find out what he thought was actually going on. But perhaps, and she had felt this as the fabulous music had thundered out into the night, the way was being made from here. All these people had heard her call and were out there instigating the conversations she had hoped they would be having. Sharing their own dreams. Listening to the talks from all the wise and clever people she had invited to tell them about what they knew and what the possibilities were. She remembered when she had heard Yaan talking about the theories he had had, so many of which, had been born out when he had re-examined the ancient history of his species. Now he would tell all his theories, perhaps never heard outside the privileged University campuses, to the people who needed to hear them, suggesting we all carried the twist and turns of our evolution, of our journey in our genetics, in every cell of our body. He believed if we found ways of accessing this information it would give us abilities to interact with our world in ways we could never have imagined.

She had walked out into her world and looked at it in a totally new light and she hoped everyone who heard the passion with which he spoke would also set out on the quest she had subsequently embarked on with Jane. Then they would listen to all the other learned people she had found who had had fresh new ideas in their own chosen professions about how the human race could find better ways to live on their world. They would talk and swap their own ideas with new confidence and maybe get together and who knows what might happen as the wave she and the monk had felt they were on, rolled around the world and gathered momentum in the consciousness of the human race.

These thoughts were drifting happily through her mind as she watched the balloons rising into the skies over the desert. The crowd below jumped and cheered and waved. A feed from a camera on board projected the image of the waving crowds below on a screen in front of them as they disappeared amongst the sprawling insect tents. Grace smiled again. Whatever the way forward there would have to be power. The advantages and the wonder they had all experienced, the gifts it had brought, would have to be part of this new way. She had been so intrigued and now sold on the use of power from the Star and here it was working, supporting all this equipment. But she knew at a cost. The human race had squandered the oil and the coal at its disposal. Now the cost of power would have to be re-evaluated and perhaps that was part of the new way. For a few moments as she surveyed the scene before her from the comfort of her pod, all seemed to have resumed as planned and she was looking forward to a day at the party with all the wonderful people who had chosen to come.

Then Mithrael arrived in his graffitied bus full of his renegade gang. He drove it into the space left by the balloons and was instantly surrounded by the security guards who Grace had employed to keep everyone safe. For a few moments there was a stillness as everyone who had been enjoying the balloons watched as this new spectacle unravelled before them. Was this the next part of the show? Grace's first reaction was of horror as now her carefully laid plan to keep this a vehicle free zone had been ignored. Then she realised this may be the least of her problems as the occupants started to disembark or tumble or crawl out of the bus. Her phone rang. She could see it was her security chief. She could see him looking over to the pods.

"I don't know if you are watching what's going on out here but we either have a problem or we don't depending on what you think we should do next. These guys are mostly pretty steamed up and could cause trouble whatever we do."

"I don't think there is much we can do and we certainly don't want to provoke them. Try and make sure they haven't got any weapons and we'll have to leave it at that for now and hope there aren't a fleet of similar buses behind them"

"Ok, we'll keep an eye on them, but I'm with you, it would be mad to try any kind of control tactic, that could all go very wrong!"

Grace watched intrigued as each of the gang was carefully and tactfully searched for any weapons they may be carrying. However, despite their intoxicated appearance all seemed to be good natured and the search of the fifty or so individuals went without any trouble. Through the entire episode she watched the individual she assumed was their leader. He had driven the bus onto the site and parked it where the maximum impact from his arrival would be achieved and now he stood watching the security guards as they checked through the grimy layers of his companions clothing.

He stood calmly and probably not as drunk as the rest as he assessed his new surroundings. He was tall and his black coat hung almost into the desert sand. His appearance was dishevelled and neglected, perhaps for the last few days but he did not display the ingrained filth of the rest of his crew. Then he turned suddenly and looked straight up towards her as if he had suddenly felt her looking down at him from her pod. He had dark wrap around star glasses but strangely she felt the intensity of the eyes behind them as they scanned into the mind of whoever was watching him. Had he recognised her? Because she felt he had, as if he knew she was one of the people he would encounter here and would eventually become involved in whatever he had come to do.

Her first assessment of Mithrael as she watched him was that he was a dangerous character and by his very presence the nature of her gathering had changed. But not because he may be a common thief or a drug dealer who had brought his crew to her festival to rob them or sell them the enormous supply of chemicals no doubt he had safely stored somewhere in his bus; but because the atmosphere had changed, it was thicker and there was an edge which had arrived with him and she felt a shiver of apprehension as she acknowledged it. The optimistic mood she had entertained only moments before had been transformed along with the atmosphere below. She watched as everyone silently drifted back into the surrounding infrastructure of the festival leaving only the empty bus where it had come to a standstill. And he was gone.

Okino had also felt the change. He knew Merilon was either here or he was deeply connected to him in which ever cavern deep in the heart of Arimathea he was currently sleeping. He wondered whether what had happened next had had anything to do with the proximity of the dragon. Harri had become very quiet as a result of his enormous emotional existential crisis. He apparently had undergone a complete reversal of his understanding of his place in the world. As a result, his life and all he had previously believed to be solid was rapidly being overturned as he applied this new outlook to all his dealings.

When the full implication of overseeing one of the largest corporations in the world combined with this new understanding had fully hit home, he had groaned as if this new weight exerted on him had suddenly become intolerable. Then he had groaned again even more deeply when he realised where his insane life had brought him, as if it would crush him entirely. He had to make the decision about the contract to start the mine. He got up from the arm chair and started to pace around the café much to the amusement now, of all who had gathered there for the pastries whose reputation was already spreading rapidly across the site through the electronic devices and the networks into which all the festival goers were regularly updating.

"…So, where do I go from here… I've got countries, governments, entire economies waiting on this one decision. Even before all this I knew it was dangerous but then it was just dangerous to me and my company. Now I know it has implications for everything; how we see ourselves and who we are as we go into the future, not to mention the danger in mining such potent material from our planet and putting it into machines to run for a hundred maybe two hundred years. Will we able to look after them for that long;

supposing the world goes to shit and we can't mend the coolers and something goes wrong with each one of them one by one…and what will we do with all that power, how much more of this world can we rip up and build over?

What if Arimathea is about to demand the bill for what we have already taken…and that is going to be a big bill and she isn't going to accept currency, what use will that be when there is no clean water or the crops aren't being pollinated? I've had people on my doorstep for years warning me about this approaching crisis. They've shouted and screamed at me trying to get me to realise.. but I've just ignored them, accusing them of being mad and just gone on playing the game…this deadly pointless game and getting everybody to play it with me.

I've been destroying this world for something that happened to me when I was a little kid…and people have been telling me that as well and guess what I ignored them too…and now there are some mighty big chickens coming home to roost because all of us, all of you have been tricked. We have not given you the full picture because perhaps we didn't know it fully and if we had done would any of us have done it any differently…it was just talk, all the threats, I know all the tricks of coercion, people making up scenarios to frighten me like I was frightening you to buy stuff I made you think you needed to keep up in the race, the race we invented, competing with each other, our noses pressed up against the windscreens of our narrow existences while we have been slowly destroying as far as we understand the most beautiful and marvellous thing that has ever come into existence, aaaarghh I feel as if I might burn for ever!!"

He then stormed out of the tent leaving his concerned audience to resume their breakfast and compare their experiences of the night before.

Mariella and Okino finished their breakfast and wandered out into the festival where gradually the day's events were starting to begin. They wondered briefly about Harri but quickly came to an agreement that if he was having a life changing crisis then here was as good a place as any to have it and it was probably not a moment too soon for the rest of the world. After all he had been clever enough to get himself into the situation in which he now found himself and probably would not waste a lot of time worrying about it before he started to turn everything around to get himself out.

He would be a powerful ally for Arimathea should he decide he was now sympathetic to her plight and wanted to make amends for the years of destruction and misery he had been causing. It seemed he had been sent a powerful dream on his visit to the circle. A dream as powerful perhaps as those experienced by everyone on the site the night before.

They drifted with the crowd of people who were now making their way towards the main stage to hear the first speaker of the day. Gentle acoustic music drifted through the air, guitars mixed with soulful voices and soft drums were setting the atmosphere for the first day's exploration into the state of the world. There was excited chatter and enthusiasm as they walked together, eager to find out how the proceedings would develop from the previous night. When a significant majority of the population of the festival had gathered, Grace came on to the stage to rapturous applause.

"Hi Everybody…I hope you had a peaceful night and were not to disappointed by the slight…well no, total malfunction at our first concert last night. I think we will have to put it down to teething problems. Anyway, we're all back up and running now as you can see and hear, so I hope you have an amazing thought-provoking day because we have some amazing people to come and share their knowledge with us. So, without wasting anymore of your time here is our first speaker today. She is as eminent a biologist as I could drag out here and she's going to share some thoughts with you and push you a little further down the rabbit hole. So please give a big welcome for Ursari Oran."

There was a great howl of applause and welcome as Ursari walked out onto the stage and Grace disappeared behind the bank of speakers and PA. Ursari started to speak as the picture of Arimathea appeared on the screen behind her.

"Thank you Grace and I thank you for such a wonderful welcome and it's great to see so many eager faces so early in the morning. So here we are out in the desert on this beautiful world. I was here last night and heard Yaan asking us to consider how we connected with and experienced Arimathea and of course this goes on from the fabulous speeches Grace has made in the city about how she managed to get shot and what that means for us all and our well-being and ultimately the collective well-being of our species. Being shot on the way to work is, I should imagine, about as traumatic as life can get and from the trauma she experienced, all she has done and all the people she has inspired has now resulted in this gathering.

There are many questions as a biologist arising from this set of circumstances. Ultimately, her experience has happened to her alone but then when you look at it in terms of our wider community it kind of happened to us all because subsequently she has raised questions about our safety and really how we are operating as a society in general. As a biologist I study systems like all you Engineer's out there. Structures like bridges or skyscrapers stand on their own but are subject to the forces of the planet. A huge system of calculations have been made to allow for the movement in the ground, the gravity which will always be wanting to tear it down, the wind will want to blow it over and the rain which will want to gradually reduce it to a pile of rust and dust from where it originally came.

In the same way each being, each one of you out there is an independent system that ultimately has to react and respond to any environment in which you find yourself. So here in the desert you may find yourself drinking more water and seeking the shade. Just as if we had decided to go the ice caps to hold this event you would be wrapping yourself in great bundles of insulated clothing to preserve your body heat. Your system, any system must act within the parameters within in which it was designed to operate. A skyscraper or your body will have to survive in whichever country it finds itself.

As bio-logical beings we will only survive if we consume enough water and enough nutrition to keep our system functioning. We have warning signs if we are not getting enough of what our system needs. We get thirsty and hungry. These are basic responses to our basic needs and the ones we are most often aware of. But there are many more systems acting within our bodies automatically without us knowing anything about them at all. All the functions of our organs, our blood stream, all our senses, how fast our heart is beating or how fast the oxygen in our blood is being delivered to our muscles when we increase our activity are all regulated and managed without us having to make any decisions. So, with the right nutrition, water and exercise our body will function like any animal or plant for the lifetime it has evolved to have.

If the system comes under threat, there are further systems which will instantly try to isolate and destroy the threat. If the threat is too powerful and our systems begin to degenerate for whatever reason we will die. Could be old age, our life force fading, I'll come onto that in a moment. We can disregard those systems toiling away day in and day out unnoticed with little or no thanks or respect or even with active abuse and that may well eventually result in an inability of those systems to perform. There will be warnings which we can choose to heed or ignore. It's how a system works or does not work. If cables on your suspension bridge start to snap the whole bridge won't come down immediately but it is telling you there is some stress hitherto unnoticed which is affecting the whole structure. You look into the whole structure to see what is causing those cables to snap and make the necessary adjustments. You probably have guessed where I am going with all this."

Ursari indicates up to the image of Arimathea floating amongst the stars behind her on the stage.

"We live as part of a vast and complex system, everything I have said applies to our planet. Take it to the next level. In the same way you have processes operating in each one of your cells toiling away oblivious to the vast system in which they live and serve, so you are an organism in the body of Arimathea. Yeah, even you really important people in the pods at the back there, and this is what is so great about these gatherings. All of you out there are fundamentally the same. Human organisms; each one of you living within human parameters within the planetary system. Ultimately, all you have to do is find your food and find your water and doing that you will keep all your systems functioning.

As we evolved, at some stage we found we needed to compete with each other. Almost certainly at first for resources to provide the nutrition and the water which may have come into short supply, to keep us alive. We were ingenious and became crafty, but also devious and if it came to it we would fight and subdue any rivals to obtain the resources we needed, much like any threat in any system. We had no idea about this system because we just needed to stay alive. Back then we had no need to know because we had no idea what we had become a part of. Thousands and thousands of generations on, we have of course come to want so much more than those simple needs and there is overwhelming evidence to suggest we have become so successful and our numbers have increased to such an extent we have become a threat to the larger organism."

She pauses. There is quiet across the audience in front of her and she points over to the balloon of Arimathea floating high over the desert above them. The audience turns and looks up.

"The question is and it is why we are here; Is there anything we can do now we know we are a part of this huge and beautiful organism? Are we doing it already by coming to this event and having the conversations no doubt you are all having? Is this Arimathea taking conscious steps to help herself? And if the quality of the biosphere continues to decline as a result of all the systems we have developed, could she decide to act more directly to reduce the threat we are now posing."

Again, she is quiet as the burners of the balloon fire up, suspended now over the audience, each of whom look up in delight and awe.

"Each one of those systems I talked about earlier has arisen in response to environmental phenomena. So, the gravity and the atmosphere on our world. Over billions of years all the processes have slowly evolved to bring you to the creature you have become. As a result, you are inseparable from this world. If you were put on another world where the atmosphere and gravity were different you would more than likely die instantly. We know physically we are bound up inextricably with this planet. But also we are conscious beings. Perhaps in the same way as we are physically part of a larger system then perhaps we are inseparable from a wider consciousness encapsulating this entire planet. Perhaps we have evolved with other animals who may or may not be more conscious than ourselves, or have a different kind of consciousness, so Arimathea could have some awareness or even become aware of herself.

For millions of years, any change to this world would come from generation after generation of slow adaptation. Now this world is covered with our cities and the results of our ingenuity and the dreams and ability we have to create and develop our world and our place upon it. We have travelled into space and left satellites in orbit there to bounce our conversations to the other side of the world. We have become the greatest single creative force on this world, really as a result of its own nature. In our excitement and enthusiasm, we have become destructive and created problems perhaps because we forgot the knowledge we once had about the true nature of our world.

Now we know we are inseparable from Arimathea we cannot ignore our threat to her. We know instinctively, however much we try to deny the problem, it is something we will have to sort out. But because we are all individuals this may seem overwhelming to us when we contemplate the immensity of the problem. However, although this threat and the consequences have arisen in her physical systems, the possibilities to overcome the threat may well be flowing through our own consciousness.

However seriously it is or it is not being taken, it is there and it is challenging us all to find new solutions to the way we live on this world. We do know what they are actually, but adjusting the enormous global financial system we have invented to support our development seems an impossible task because it relies almost entirely on people and organisations being in debt and the interest being paid to keep the machine endlessly crawling into the future. Ultimately we need to pay off our debts and start again.

But in our thoughts and dreams we may be searching for ways to solve this problem and because we have a global communication system we know these problems will be in the minds of the majority of the humans in our community. Some of those humans will be in a better place to act to solve the problem as one set of cells in our bodies will be responsible for the successful operation of our immune system and so the destruction of any invader. If, for a moment, we accept the idea of this consciousness. In the distant future it may seem like the denial of its existence was similar to when we were in denial of Arimathea's rotation around our Star. We may eventually discover all its organisms are informed by energies or ideas in the same way our cells are directed by electrical responses and communications from our brains and our central nervous system.

It follows then, that each one of you can respond to this new threat flowing through this consciousness, our combined consciousness. We all need to stop using so many resources, burning so much fuel and eating so many animals. But any one of you may have a greater role to play; an idea or a dream that has come to you, which only you have the ability to bring into the world with the people you know or the unique resources you have around you. As we all take responsibility, we can all become involved in the successful evolution of our world rather than the disease destroying it. This all may seem way too complex for us to grasp but that is no reason for it not to be true. The life force and consciousness are some of the last remaining mysteries we know about that could open doors for us into a whole new era. Perhaps it will mean we will not feel so alone or be more able to make decisions and act with greater compassion towards our wider community.

Our world Arimathea is the most remarkable thing we know about and a remarkable thing has happened here. We have taken it all for granted and mostly dismiss the privilege of living on her. We share it with every living thing on this world everyone as fabulous as the next. If we have not understood things in the past, we have put them down to magic or the power of the gods but so often we have proved with our continual delving and relentless searching there has been a logical explanation to many of these 'mysteries'. Who knows what understandings we will come to in the future about our world and the wider Universe? Perhaps consciousness really is about gods or magic but unlike the old ideas of gods from whom we were made to feel separate and at the mercy of, this new knowledge will give each one of us a unique role to play in the understanding and the continual evolution of such a being, so it can continue towards whatever destiny there is in store for her and us!"

Chapter 74
Meltdown.

Zanda stood silently in the crowd listening carefully to every word Ursari was saying. He looked around at the people absorbing her thoughts. She explained her knowledge simply so no one would get lost in complex scientific jargon, lose interest and wander off. She spoke clearly in terms they all understood and he recognised they were quiet, remarkably quiet and attentive he thought. He was thinking back through the years of his life, or his lives, to when he had heard such a speech or had such knowledge. He had a blurred sense of many of the lives between the long sleeps through which he had lived. The separations between his dreams and his conscious lives were generally easy to distinguish. In his dreams he had rested again and then travelled through the labyrinths of time and space in search of the ancient harmony from which all this had once sprung. It was perhaps deeper now than he could travel and perhaps had been lost forever. But he would continue his search into the past or into the future, for it contained the truth behind all this existence.

In the fraction of Universal time he continued with this search, Arimathea would continue with her evolution. Then in these short interludes from the life he had chosen on Arimathea he would find himself being awoken again. He would feel the call deep from within the world in which he had chosen to sleep, through the fabric and the densely packed cosmic debris accumulated from all parts of the multi dimensioned universe in which he had come to exist. The calls would drift softly to start with, through his dream but would soon become more insistent and slowly he would stir. He would awake, entirely human again, deep in the cave he had chosen, in a land so remote he would have to wander for weeks to reach any kind of civilisation. He left symbols and maps and the golden dragon was always around his neck, gleaming as it had been the first day he cast it. But he would often be as much as one hundred and fifty years into the future before he woke again. Every time he slept the world had changed again, to the point on this last awakening it seemed as if he had awoken on a different planet entirely.

The journey through the isolated mountain ranges where he had chosen to sleep rarely changed. If he had awoken in the depths of winter the large bear skin coat he generally slept in protected him from the worst ravages of the winter weather. As he made his way to the nearest village or town he had marked on his map he would begin to see the changes. Often these towns or villages had grown but occasionally whatever had held them there had moved on and the town had been deserted. He would make his way to one of the larger towns or cities where he would be able to exchange one of the gemstones he had brought from his previous life for whatever currency was now being used. He was always wary of the rate he was given. Then he would slowly decide how to resume his life in this new time in which he found himself. He rarely found this to be a problem and slowly he would begin to live mostly anonymously on the outskirts of the towns where he could again start his forge and make whatever he found to be needed by the neighbouring communities.

He shuddered as he remembered this, his latest emergence. He had stumbled through the mountain ranges in the worst storm he could ever remember. It seemed to go on for days. Thunder and lightning continually flashed around the peaks and snow fell thickly, blown by ferocious winds as they howled around the mountains and through the passes. At these times he hadn't eaten for all the time he had slept and the storm had made it impossible for him to find any kind of food. He had become weaker and weaker as the days went on. The storm had eventually ended. He had been surprised to hear what sounded like thunder continuing to rumble in the distance.

He thought no more about it and concentrated on finding food as he came down from the mountains. Now there were plants he could eat and he had stayed by a river for a few days resting and building up his strength. Still the echoes of thunder in the distance rumbled around the mountain peaks behind him. He was surprised and mystified as to why the thunder did not move. Eventually he had continued his journey, curious to see this storm which never ended and never seemed to move.

Again, the landscape started to change. He had come across dwellings, sometimes entire villages which had been quickly abandoned. Domestic animals had been left running wild around the houses and through the streets. Then the thunder had stopped and the land seemed dramatically quiet. He came across burnt out buildings which in some cases had been completely destroyed. He found the remains and the contents scattered in the vicinity and in some cases a great distance from the destroyed dwelling. These he knew to be signs of conflict but he was relieved to find the occupants had been able to leave before whatever force had done this had descended upon them

Everything started to look increasingly ravaged and eventually burnt. He stood aghast on a low hill looking out over the landscape he had entered. There was no vegetation or buildings. Where there were signs they had existed there were stumps of burnt out trees and further indistinguishable ruins. There was little grass in expanses of mud and earth, which now were covered in craters often full of water. Then he started to see the remains of what once had been human beings. They littered the landscape partly buried in the mud or floating in the craters. He stumbled in horror through the apocalyptic scene of complete and diabolical destruction.

There were lines of coiled jagged wire stretching into the distance where it seemed further young men, some almost complete had met their fate, but now hung tangled in the wire waiting for whoever would eventually collect their remains. Mithrael stood in amongst the carnage and the stench of death and wondered how far into the future he had awoken. What weapons had the human race developed that could cause such complete disintegration. He noticed there was a reddish hue to the ground on which he stood. He sank to his knees and vomited violently as he realised he was walking in the blood flowing from the humans who had died there.

Every step on his continuing journey across the battlefield revealed some further horror. Skulls separated from the bodies of their owners still registering looks of surprise, legs, severed spines, hands holding rifles, feet with boots half on and the contents of torsos scattered, broken and torn, smashed and mutilated, men and horses everywhere in amongst the remains of guns and trenches and drifting smoke. Then somewhere in the distance the thunder started up again. He started to hear whistling overhead. He had realised these were the shells being fired from one side of the battlefield to the other both of which were completely out of sight. He heard the explosions as the shells landed far off in the distance and looked around again at the carnage and realised what was happening.

The human race had taken warfare to entirely new level of barbarity and now were killing each other far away in the distance. But still there were foot soldiers who had had to march out over the land and capture it from their enemy. March out into this holocaust as their fellows were blown to pieces around them. How much deeper could the depravity of this race sink to. They had sent their children and these beautiful horses out here to what they must have known would have been certain death. He stood in utter despair as the thunder increased on both sides. Shells started to drop short on both sides. He watched the ground erupting where the shells landed and exploded sending shockwaves across the waste ground they had created, shaking the bodies hanging in the wire, and raining further body parts down all around him.

He vomited again as a shell landed and exploded far enough away to envelope him in a furnace of fire and earth. He was blown off his feet and could hear nothing but knew his beloved bearskin was on fire. It was strange how he had thought of how long he had worn that skin and how now it would be ruined. How he had worn it the last time he had seen Alamistra. How lovely she had looked. But the burning was eating into him and he had to act. In a final effort, Mithrael leapt up and ripped off the burning fur and jumped into a crater full of water which now he would share with another less fortunate than himself who had lost most of his skull and now floated in the foul water which mercifully had quickly extinguished the flames on the remainder of his clothing.

He deliriously drifted in and out of consciousness floating in the stinking water at the bottom of the shell hole. With tremendous effort he managed to crawl half out of the water and up the side of the crater. Then another wave of soldiers came staggering across the waste ground, there was smoke and more agonised screaming and the shells and bullets whistled overhead, thudded into the ground around him and perhaps he may have been hit by one because there was more pain and then darkness again. He woke again when the screams and the thunder had died down and there were other people clambering through the craters. He felt a soft warm hand on his neck and a shout...

"Here, over here there's one alive!"

There was movement and excruciating pain. Mithrael had heard a scream. But It must have belonged to someone else, some other being who had suffered terrible trauma and degradation because in here, in the glow he had felt warm and safe.

He had awoken again in what he had presumed was a hospital. Still there were terrible screams. There were young men and women hurrying amongst the broken bodies trying to calm the young boys in their final moments as they screamed for their mothers. Blood gushed from their horrific wounds onto the doctors and the nurses who desperately wrapped and sawed and stitched and injected the ones who had some chance of living through the next few hours. They worked oblivious it seemed to the horror in which they were involved. But there was terror here and Mithrael had felt it. Felt it on the battlefield and in the young people here struggling to hold the life in the bodies of those who had come into their care. Far away from home in a strange land.

Mithrael fell into a deep dream in amongst the chaos. In the dream all had been quiet. There was no blood, or discarded sawn off limbs, The nurses and doctors had clean white clothing and the patients were sleeping quietly. One of the nurses came over to him and saw he was awake. She took his hand and he recognised the face instantly. It was Singing Moon and it filled him with happiness to see her after so long. They had always been almost inseparable and when she had grown into a young woman, they had become lovers. The tragedy of her death at the merciless hands of the invaders that fateful morning had haunted his lives on Arimathea ever since. Now here she was in his dream. Surrounded by the Moonlight flooding in through the tall windows.

"Mithrael, my beloved. I am so sad to see you here like this; so injured by this terrible war. But I am pleased to see you are still alive. I loved you so much Mithrael and I know you can stop all this, all this terrible suffering. I know the power you hold. You are one of the infinite beings, who came from the stars and who preside over this world and you must do something to help us. I know you can, Mithrael, help us. We are drowning in this terror. We have nothing to care for these children who have been sent here by the devils in their castles back there, far away from this destruction. Thousand upon thousand of them are here, dying and there is nothing we can do. I can hardly bare all their screams. Please help us, Mithrael the dragon, or whoever you are. Help us!"

Mithrael looked around at the children, gathered here in the desert, they were mostly older than those he had shared the hospital with. His own crew were now mingling through the crowd. The sad bunch of unfortunates and misfits who he had rescued from themselves and the vicious society that still allowed them to sleep on the streets even after all the previous generations of young people had done to keep their privileged lifestyles safe from the marauding forces of Oblivion. Still they were enslaved by 'the devils in their castles' Singing Moon had called them. At least he had seen Singing Moon. He smiled as he watched them trying to peddle the 'Sunshine' pills to their contempories. They were not having much luck it would seem. Things must be changing. Kids turning drugs down at music festivals. They seemed to be arguing amongst each other good naturedly. He was glad the kids were turning down the drugs. It meant they were healing and thinking for themselves and rejecting the pain relief he was offering them. They could turn on their own minds. They didn't need him to do it for them.

"Hello Mithrael, Good to see you after all these Eons!"

Mithrael span round to where the voice had spoken his name.

"Well I'll be steered off course by the multiple Moons of Rigor 3, Alamistra how on Arimathea are you. It is so good to see you. I must have picked up you were here I was only just thinking about you.!"

"In a good way I hope!"

"Of course in a good way. Except I was at the bottom of a bomb crater thinking how amazing you looked when I last saw you!"

He turned to her and took her in his arms and they embraced affectionately and the unique energy held in these ancient spirit beings was once again shared between them. Mithrael had rarely been visited in such a way during his time as a human. When they had been forced to retreat to their caves as a result of his decision to betray them they had lost their ability to communicate with him entirely. As the energy flowed he was unable to deny the special kinship he felt with Alamistra and the rest of the dragons. Momentarily while his guard was down, he realised how much he had missed the bonds they held between each other.

His journey on Arimathea, flashed through his being. His mortality had brought him huge insight into life on this world but it suddenly felt inconsequential to the infinite life he had shared with the other dragons when they were whole and dreaming together. This feeling had surfaced unexpectedly but he suspected not unintentionally with the sudden appearance without any prior warning of Alamistra. As much as he might have denied her impact upon him, the feelings had arisen and he relished her warmth and the depth of feeling he had once again felt before she started to release him from her embrace. They stood staring deep into each other's eyes as the connection deepened again and their own personal memories of each other wound together and were again awakened through both of their beings.

They smiled as they registered the enormous love they had always shared and now had rediscovered. The speaker had left the stage and the balloons were drifting out over the desert. Music had resumed to entertain the crowds as they waited or drifted off towards some other venue to find some further nourishment elsewhere. The two dragons drifted themselves with the crowd.

"So, what has brought you here, Alamistra?"

Now he remembered his last thoughts had been of Singing Moon and her plea to him in his dream. Often he felt the dragons had infiltrated his life through their ability to speak to him through the people he had met and had become close to him. They had occasionally been in his dreams reminding him of who he was and perhaps of his responsibility even though at that time he had chosen to become mortal. They were the spirits of the Universe and they had become inseparable in whatever state they chose to live and however complete the separation had become.

"There was someone who I had to visit. I heard a call. Perhaps like yourself when you first came to the surface, I had felt a yearning for knowledge. This person had gained a specific and unique understanding and it was advantageous for us to give him the final chapter so he could complete what he had set out to do. Although, of course he did not know originally what he had set out to do. He just had an urge to discover more about his world and how he had come to be on it the way he was.

"Then I needed to come and see you Mithrael!"

Again she turned towards him and looked deep into his eyes further igniting the memories of the tremendous experience and knowledge they shared. Mithrael was startled. He had just become used to the level of memory they had been able to share a few moments before.

"You may or may not know the other dragons have been released from their exile and have been reunited with Arimathea. I myself have not returned completely for the moment because of what I have told you and because I needed to come and see you."

"So why is that Alamistra. Have you come for revenge? In the great scheme of things and all we have been through this was all pretty minor."

Alamistra laughed...

"...yeah well that remains to be seen. Maybe we were wrong, maybe you were wrong, but in the end we do what we do because of who we are. Revenge is an interesting idea and I'm sure we could think of something... but it's where you have come to with all of this we need to understand. Your experience now is so utterly unique and whether you choose to return to us now or in the future it will have to become integrated into our dream. It will further define the dreams with which we will fill the world. The human race has found its own way, destructive and belligerent though it is and what you have learnt will be invaluable."

Alamistra saw suspicion rising in Mithraels eyes.

"It sounded like you had been in some kind of war when you said the last time you had thought about me you were in the bottom of a bomb crater."

Mithrael was drifting deeper into his dragon spirit as Alamistra wove her spell deeper into him. Clearly this was why she had been sent and his human self with all its worries and concerns was becoming distant. He wanted to keep hold of Zanda for the moment but he became resigned to Alamistra's charms and after all the years of separation he was enjoying the company of one of his own kind.

"If you spend any amount of time with them sooner or later you will become embroiled in one of their wars. It seems they always can find something to fight about and increasingly with more deadly effect. The woman talking up there, I don't know how much you heard but she was talking about Arimathea as a system with great hordes of bacteria in a body continually trying to eradicate each other. They are becoming more effective at it and as things stand, they have the capability to destroy most of the life on this planet in a few hours. The final escalation has ironically saved them from the final holocaust as so far there has been no one crazy enough to instigate it. But really it's only a matter of time."

Alamistra looks over at the human dragon incredulously.

"Yeah well you can look at me like that, but this is a crazy world."

"So how did you get here from the bottom of the bomb crater?"

They had reached one of the tents and decided to relax on one of the armchairs provided, looking over the scene unfolding before them. The tent was buzzing with conversation inspired by Ursari's speech. Mithrael poured water from the refrigerated storage cylinders into the large cups provided and settled down next to Alamistra and started to tell her his tale.

"They found me in the bomb hole more dead than alive I would think. I was badly burned by the bomb and had been unconscious. But someone I knew in my first life here came to me in a dream and reminded me of who I was. You understand I have blurry memories of my dragon self. It is not straight forward like..

'I'm a dragon but I'm also human and I can use my dragon powers because I know what they are.'

It's more like a shadow in the back of my mind which I can never entirely grasp and every now and again something happens and I think,

"Well that wouldn't happen to a normal person."

When I had recovered and could finally walk around, all the horror of their first mechanised war was going on around me. Kids looking after kids who had been terribly blown apart by the weapons which were becoming progressively more terrible. I don't know if it was something that had been triggered by the bomb or whether it was Singing Moon who had somehow enabled this ability,"

"Singing Moon?!"

"Yeah, Singing Moon she was a woman I knew, I fell terribly in love with her and she was killed and it was the first time I felt what it was really like to be human and it has haunted me terribly and is very much part of this story!"

"...and one I will be interested in hearing at some stage!!"

"Don't be like that Alamistra I haven't seen you for several millennia and there were going to be other people let's face it"

Alamistra laughed and prompted him to continue...

"Anyway, so as I walked around amongst these terribly injured souls, I found I could see the light energy in everything. Light and life force in each of the poor men and boys who were there. I could see how it was flowing through them. How it flowed around them, from their minds and into the rest of their bodies. I knew the places I could divert the light to, to stop their pain and help their bodies to heal by increasing the light and allowing their life force to travel to the appropriate organs. I would just sit with them and hold their hands for an hour or so, calm them down and I was able to take away their pain. The screaming gradually started to stop. This went on and as I recovered and I was able to help more people this ability became quite well known. Eventually word found its way to the high command in the castle behind the front lines and I was summoned to see the general in the castle.

At this stage I haven't said but I had only just woken from a sleep and had no idea who I had become in my previous lives. This was the strange thing, I always had to find my way back to where I had been. This is another story and I will have to tell you this."

Mithrael explained about how he had met the Shamans out in the distant reaches of the Universe, how they had founded Zinederland and subsequently how he had become involved in their banking activities.

"So strangely this general recognised the golden dragon I originally cast for Singing Moon and had worn ever since she had been killed. It turned out he was one of the tight circle of people in Zinederland who had been initiated into the secret and how it had all been founded.

At the heart of the mystery there was a being who returned after many generations to re-establish his links with the original mystery into which he had been contractually bound. Once I had been taken back to Zinederland and my identity had been proven and celebrated amongst the inner circle, I once again took my place in the global banking corporation of Zinederland. But after the war of course. For the rest of the war I went back to the front lines to help ease the pain of the wounded.

Using my ability to see and feel the life force flowing around the body I started to work with pharmacologists. We developed new drugs that could travel to the places where they were needed to turn on or off the appropriate part of the wounded soldiers' brain to reduce their pain and increase their ability to heal. After the war I worked with the same scientists and formed a company to manufacture on mass the drugs we had developed in the hospitals on the frontline. There was terrible trauma and depression amongst the survivors and the families of the people who had lost their loved ones who never had been found. So, the idea of drugs to ease the general pain of their existence gradually started to become acceptable.

There was so much pain even after the agony of the war had subsided. The company I founded became my own personal success. The person you see here is the person who went back to the hospitals to help the kids escape their pain. They grow up in this world still run by the devils who sent them to that war. They enslave them in dull lives to service their vast money making operations that feed all their privilege and wealth. I made these 'Sunshine' pills which give them a great night out or wherever or whenever they want. It makes them feel like it's a beautiful day on Planet Earth where we spent all those blissful years. So long ago now. I named them after it's beautiful star, the Sun. They have to deal with how much they take but it's so mild compared to the trauma they are suffering in the service of the greed machine, I think it's probably worth it. But I notice some of them, well most of them are turning them down today, so something must be going on. I don't suppose it's anything to do with Merilon and the rest of the dragons'"?

Alamistra smiled enigmatically.

"So there really is something going on? Tell me about it later. So where was I. Oh yes. The greed machine. I have become caught up in this through my involvement with the bank of Zinederland. In a few generations this planet has become engulfed in a vast financial network. Everyone is dependent on everybody else but sadly not in a good way. Everybody owes somebody something else. They have to build this or buy that but because of the nature of the world and the way they have become, as their exploits and schemes have become ever larger they borrow the finance from somebody else and the loan pays interest into the future. Debt is traded from bank to bank. Every time a debt is organised or reorganised somebody makes money. Eventually there has to be someone who is securing the whole system. That somebody at this time, and since the idea was invented because of the wealth brought back by me and the shamans is the Bank of Zinederland. It has invested enormously in the great infrastructure projects of the industrial world and has grown phenomenally to such an extent that most countries are actually in debt to us. All the other banks lending money out to companies and corporations at some stage have become indebted to The Bank of Zinederland. I have simplified this but it is the basic reality. The Bank of Zinederland has the power to recall the debt owed by most countries around the world.

"But you wouldn't because the world would become bankrupt and fall into chaos and it would probably be the end of the human race."

"Well exactly! And that of course is not in our interest because our existence and our wealth and all our people depend on the interest being paid!"

"If this is mostly Mithrael the dragon talking to me now, how does your human persona deal with this kind of power? I mean that is an enormous amount of power for an organisation to have amassed and it seems like you have an enormously prominent role there. It seems everything has become very mixed up between your human and dragon personas. I could see how if your human side started to realise the power he could command as dragon he might find himself open to some of the very darkest aspects of Oblivion if for any reason he had decided a return to the origin might benefit the Great Spirit."

Mithrael looked at her darkly. Now he knew why she was here. He suddenly remembered the visit from Arimathea in Harri's office.

"Well yes Alamistra you may be right. But when you are human, power is everything and when you taste it and what it can bring to you on this world..."

"Tell me everything, Mithrael!!"

Mithrael was powerless now the female dragon had started to unravel how his life on Arimathea had brought this strange hybrid being to where he was.

"I met this character years ago called Harri Wade. He had started a mining company and he was a client of one of the banks we dealt with. Mining was something I had become involved with, mainly Gold mining, as it happened and he had a proposition involving one of our mining operations. We met and we get on very well. Harri was obsessed with Gold and I gave him the chance to take over the management of the mine. He was as ambitious and hungry as I had seen any other human and I was caught up in his enthusiasm and we became friends. One of the few real friends I have ever made.

He wanted it all. It was strange to me though. It was never something I had particularly pursued or even thought about. I had my human life; I was very wealthy but was never particularly extravagant and never craved the power it could bring. From the outset Harri clearly did. He wanted everything money could buy and as much power over his fellow human beings as he could have. He would have ruled a country and he often mused about what he would do if he was in my position in the Zinederland corporation.

He didn't talk much about his past but I felt something was driving him. As the years went by we did more and more business. He began to grow an enormous corporation and anything we leant him always provided good returns on our investment. There was a vast expansion of the operations the human race was undertaking. More and more capital was needed and with the percentages involved Harri was becoming an extremely wealthy man as his corporation started to become one of the largest on Arimathea. The world had literally become our oyster. The sheer wealth we could command had bought us the freedom of the planet in ways previously unimagined and we took advantage of it whenever we could.

We both had our own jets and would fly off to places like anybody else would go down to the shops or out for a Sunday afternoon walk. With the loyalty of the countries in the debt of Zinederland we were able to travel freely around the world. Harri wanted to experience everything the planet had to offer and we both agreed it was the unique privilege this enormous wealth could buy. So, we took great entourages out into the deserts and the polar regions, we went deep into the jungles and climbed up into the highest mountain ranges all with the best people and state of the art equipment our fortunes could buy.

Harri bought an enormous yacht where we would stay on our latest adventure. It had a helicopter so we rarely had to have any contact with local communities. Harry always had a thing about locked doors and keys and all the security stuff going on around hotels. He had become convinced he would be kidnapped by one of the wild terrorist groups who continually harassed his company about what he saw as his legitimate business deals and they saw as robbery, extortion and exploitation of their countries.

He liked being on his yacht where he could see everything and anything that was coming anywhere near him and on which he kept enough weapons to make things very unpleasant for anyone who even thought about putting a foot on his boat without his knowledge. Weapons supplied of course by the regimes who had borrowed money from me to buy and supply them to Harri. Which he didn't know about actually.

It was like Arimathea had become our back yard for a while and we watched the Star rise over just about every mystical monument and went to the source of every major river and watched them tumble over the highest waterfalls. All the ancient places which now made up this incredible world and their history, the atmospheres that had gathered as a result of all our dreaming for all the aeons since we came here, I was able to visit and experience. But although this world is limitless and the experience almost infinite there is something in the human spirit, which of course I had now taken on, which began to make it all seem a bit ordinary after a while.

I realised this was often the point where humans started to take drugs to enhance the experience yet again. We met the casualties along the way. But Harri rarely even drank alcohol and he was becoming restless with these frivolous games even though he was running the corporation in parallel to all this other activity. I think he had discovered this was not what he wanted from his wealth. What he really wanted was just more and more control. He told me once that if he did manage to control the entire planet he would have to find out what was going on in the rest of the universe just in case there was a chance somebody out there could invade and take it away from him. He started to give up our jaunts around the world and started to concentrate on ever bigger and bigger projects to continue the expansion of his corporation which already, through my own help, had already infiltrated most of the major and minor economies of the world.

However now the fears of global climate change started to seep through into the consciousness of the governments of the world and the carbon-based fuels became scarcer and more difficult to extract. Many reserves were in areas politically sensitive and under regimes who were now pleased to be able to command the price to the wealthy countries who had previously exploited them mercilessly and who now needed their treasured natural resources. Harri found his operations were becoming more expensive and eroding his profits as taxes were increased on the old fuels or capital was needed to install the new solar and wind infrastructure which was still a long way off from supplying all the vast energy demands of this now fuel hungry planet. So, Harri came to me with his plan.

"I think we should build a nuclear power station in as many countries of the world as we can to supply the power we need. Then we can control the cost of energy throughout the world."

At first I looked at him in disbelief and then I laughed out loud and waited for him to join in. But he didn't and he remained deadly serious. Zinederland would supply the money to build the power stations and he would mine the Uranium to power them. By the time everything was up and running the cost of energy would be so high that everyone would be queuing round the block to buy our energy. I watched him sitting there. This was what really excited him. His joke about wanting to control the world really wasn't a joke. He really did want to control the world. But in its strange megalomaniacal reasoning it did make sense. It was just the next step up in the economies of scale humanity had introduced to all their economics. Sooner or later everything would become too large and unwieldy and everything would have to be consolidated to provide a lower unit cost.

I had the accountants go into the figures and hired energy experts, in fact just about every kind of expert I could think of to find out whether Harri's plan for global domination could work. As the calculations and the forecasting continued it started to become apparent Harri's idea really did make sense. I became deeply enthused with the idea myself, and became more convinced that somehow the old scientist Shamans had been able to foresee their whole enterprise ending up here in some bizarre revenge on the world that had shunned ideas they knew could have changed the course of human history. The board of The Zinederland Banking Corporation was amazed at the audacity of this latest venture and unanimously backed it as did many of the countries who we approached to have one of the power stations. Those that didn't were reminded of the loans they still had outstanding with Zinederland."

Mithrael became quiet and looked over to Alamistra to gauge her reaction. She was watching the activity going on around her while processing all Mithrael her brother dragon had said. He had now spoken the plans out as dragon. He had not spoken about his own frustration with the human race and their obsessive determination to ignore the plight of their planet. However, as Alamistra turned her gaze over to Mithrael he was left in no doubt she had been able to fill in the gaps for herself. Her face had darkened and had become as grave as Mithrael had ever seen her. He was unprepared for the crashing thunder he saw in her eyes, unaccustomed as he now was to power of the ancient spirit before him after many hundreds of years of separation.

"It's an incredible story Mithrael. But look at what has happened on this world because you let your human emotions govern your decision to separate us from Arimathea. Maybe it will work through to where everything needs to be but at what cost. Now you have entirely lost your way and the confusion between your dragon spirit and your human persona is causing this conflict between your human motivations and the power your dragon has been able to come by or attract over the centuries. I think you should seriously consider what is happening to you and how vulnerable you have made Arimathea to the darkest powers of the universe who will be drawing closer to the power you have as we speak. They have always wanted to destroy this beautiful world! You must see that Mithrael. Your adventure has gone way too far and it really is time for it to end."

With this and before Mithrael could react in any way, Alamistra rose from her seat and silently disappeared out of the expansive tent and evaporated back into the crowds. She had tricked him and convincingly. He realised what she had done as the memory of their conversation and his dragon self started to fade. She had made him name the conflict in which he had become embedded. Before now he had not been able to fully understood how vulnerable the power of his dragon soul had become to the influence of the dark forces of the Universe who seemed to be propelling him deeper and deeper into the destructive plans he had allowed to become possible on Arimathea.

For a few moments he struggled to remain, clung desperately on to Mithrael and the terrible realisation Alamistra had allowed to surface. But he faded and Zanda found himself sitting in the tent sipping the cool clear water with a strange sense of panic. Again, the shadow was there and again he was unable to understand what had created the dark spectres haunting his mind. He suspected they were to do with the creature he had become who woke alone in mountain caves far from any civilisation with little or no memory of who or what he was. Again the mystery would slowly unravel and again he would take his place in this new world and he would stop worrying because he found most of the humans he met felt they didn't belong here or they were in the wrong body or they had been born in the wrong time with the wrong parents and any other number of strange imaginings and intuitions which could disturb the delicate human psyche.

He finished the water and walked back out into the festival to find the rest of his crew. He was aware he was having to actively push the feelings of dread and unease to the back of his mind. They refused to be banished into the shadows and his state of panic began to increase. All the dark truths surrounding the human race and all it had become were seeping out of the deep recesses of his being, where they had resided, stagnating for centuries, all the terrible things he had seen and become involved with. Now they were surfacing in his body, filling all his limbs and organs, flowing through his mind as if there had been some closed portal holding them there before the time when they could be released through him into the world. He realised he had no power over whatever process or power had taken control of his being.

As a result of the confusion Alamistra had revealed, his vulnerability had been entirely exposed and any defences were now swept aside by the vast emptiness of Oblivion. It flowed through him into everything and everyone around him. Suddenly he could see the crowd only as a vast, all-consuming plague ravaging the weakening body of Arimathea. Here at the festival in the desert was the perfect analogy for how they had swarmed over the planet.

They had brought all their noise and the infrastructure they needed to survive. They had already transformed this quiet and tranquil place into the equivalent of one of their cities consuming endlessly and pointlessly the enormous quantity of resources needed to keep them alive and interested from one minute to the next. They were unable to make decisions for themselves and were continually reliant on some invisible command structure to guide them through the day preventing them from starving to death or wandering out into the desert unable to find their way back. He began to verbalise these thoughts as he wandered aimlessly through the crowds.

"And why have you come here? To discuss the possibility of being able to survive on this world without tearing it to pieces into the distant future. Why do you or your species deserve to survive? Possibly the most intuitive and intelligent creature ever to have evolved has not realised you have to make some effort to look after the world that has given you everything you could possibly think of.

Did it never occur to you to think of ways you could make your lives less destructive and dangerous in your endless quest for self-gratification? What went wrong with you to such an extent you must continually indulge the idea you have of yourselves? What perversity has surfaced that has made you so misguided in your ordinary lives that you have some divine right to degrade this planet so badly. Yes, Ordinary. You heard the guy, you are all the same. But some strange twist in the evolution enables you to maintain the idea, the accumulation of more and more stuff can make you better than the man or woman next to you.

I would expect this kind of behaviour from a wild animal who has to attract a mate. But don't you think you should have risen above all that by now. You think you are so clever but actually you are really stupid because you know you are messing up their world as well as yours. You haven't got anything to show off about. You are the worst creature on this planet. You would know this if you accessed even the most basic level of understanding you have achieved. If you did you would start considering something in your short insignificant but indescribably wasteful lives more than what you are going to buy next. Perhaps think of some alternative to grinding through your agonisingly mundane lives interspersed with excessive shopping experiences. These seem to make you feel better for a day or two then it's back to the pills. Hardly surprising with all the rubbish you buy, soon forgotten and then thrown away and buried.

You continue to maintain the lies you have woven around your lives. The bigger and wider and the more fantastic the bullshit the better. But hey wake up, nobody cares about your lies because they have their own to maintain and worry about. This deception is endangering everything wonderful that has come to be here. You don't care about that either, you might say you do, because isn't that part of the lie. All this is Ok because we've put a solar panel on our house now or we've got a 'little' car. If you really did care, you would stop driving your cars down to the shops every day. Then you could walk to where you buy the rubbish you are putting into yourselves and your children making them fat and unhealthy. The food made or grown by people who are virtually enslaved in countries where the process consumes more clean water than they are able to drink.

If you cared, wouldn't you start to think about the issues that actually matter, like what kind of world your children are growing up in? Why wouldn't that be more important than anything. How can you look at your kids and all the resources you are using and think this is a sensible way to be operating? What will be left for them when the climate is broken and there is nothing for them to eat? What about the creatures you share the world with: you've enslaved them turning them into little more than products for your own consumption, whole species genetically manipulated, enslaved and endlessly slaughtered. Any you cannot eat, you hunt and kill for fun and wrap their fur around you and consume their body parts as if that could make you like them: if you are not eating or hunting them to death you are wiping out their habitats, cutting down all the woods and forests, polluting the seas where they live so you can continue to satisfy your ravenous greed.

What kind of misguided illusion have you have come under? Flying around the world in jets that use as much fuel as a small village in a year raining their exhaust down on the planet? What has made you think you can do all this? Destroy the entire world and all the beauty and wonder in it so you can feel better about yourselves when you park your car on your drive every night."

Zanda had stopped. He had opened a bottle of whisky and had been drinking from it intermittently and the alcohol was now flowing through his blood stream giving air to ever more audacious accusations He appeared to be pleading with the sky perhaps where he now thought the threat from humanity was coming from. His rant had become louder and an increasingly large crowd was gathering around him. He started to address them.

"And why can't you stop your disgusting warmongering. Why can't you just sit down and work out what will make everybody happy and do it. You are blowing this up and blowing that up and this lot of people because they have a different god from you or they want to do this or they don't want to do that. There just isn't enough space for you all to be just doing exactly what you want, or all have different gods, who say to eat this or don't eat that or who you can be with or who you can't.

The man said it; you've got to find a drink and a sandwich every day and be nice to each other. You haven't got much time to sort this out….you know how time flies on this planet ..if we are twenty years down the line and nothing has changed and that is not a long time you will be in serious trouble….and don't tell me it's not you or you…"

He's pointing into the crowd at the people in front of him…

"…because it is you, and you, allowing all this to happen. Day in and day out the processes that support you are all adding to the holocaust being stored up for this world…."

Zanda became silent staggering under the alcohol and the darkness which had consumed him. He fell to his knees in the desert sand laughing mockingly at the shocked faces all around him…

"But don't worry. It soon will be all over for the human race. Maybe a few more generations. This world just cannot take much more of this abuse. Arimathea cannot support you and your growing billions crawling all over her sucking out her life, polluting her systems. It will be painful like no other nightmare you ever had and it won't be like the comfy little fantasies your film studios have invented about how all this will come to an end… there will be nothing and all you will have to eat is yourselves and the strongest will eat the weakest and the diseased and then they will die too. I've seen it all before on other worlds where it has all happened before. I thought it could be different this time…"

"…and you've been planning that end haven't you Zanda or whoever you are. I can see it all now all these years you have been my friend, you've been drawing me deeper into this; I don't know, what do you call it in your perverse and distorted mind.."

Harri has stepped out of the crowd and is standing in front of Zanda. Zanda sits up on his heels taking another swig from the bottle of whisky. He laughs again when he sees who it is…

"Aaargh Harri I am surprised to see you here. Have you come to save the world from yourself? Have you signed the contract yet? We need to be getting that mine underway. It won't be long before the power stations are completed. We'll need to be supplying all these lovely people with their cheap power so they can continue with the rampaging abuse of their world. They'll all be very disappointed if they can't turn on their lights when all the gas and coal has run out."

"Oh yeah the mine. A few things have happened since the last time we met Zanda and I've decided I'm not going to get involved in the whole nuclear power thing and from what I've just heard not a moment too soon. The trouble is, it does make sense, it always has. All the economics and the whole idea of consolidation it all adds up. It adds up like every ground-breaking piece of development the human race has ever made add up. You know how it goes…

'We've invented this amazing new technology or process everybody, the world will benefit, nothing can possibly go wrong.'

So we've pushed and muscled our way into the future despite all the warnings from the wiser people amongst us, who perhaps were accused of wanting to keep the human race in the Stone Age, who thought this new technology or where we were taking it may cause us problems in the future. But we always have disregarded those people and gone on with everything because that is who we are. We were never going to hold back on progress when there was money to be made; it just wouldn't have been in the spirit of the human race. Or whatever race controls this planet and I'm not entirely sure who that is at the moment having seen a monk walk into my office and appear to stop time or certainly delay it."

"A monk you say. Are you sure he was a monk Harri?"

"Yeah definitely a monk, cropped hair, crimson robes…He's here somewhere, I saw him this morning. But what I'm saying is it's time we stopped. We have just got to start saying no to these things. We are seeing the effects of everything we have done and you said it yourself, Arimathea is on her knees.?"

"But this will help. We've been through all of this. Everybody benefits. Less gas goes into the atmosphere energy will eventually be cheaper and you have low cost energy to power your factories, so the cost of everything comes down."

"…and that is the point the cost will come down to make even more stuff. Digging up even more of Arimathea. Then there are the people down where the mine will be. They could be our last connection with our earliest ancestors and a way of life that started everything. All this!"

"They have built nearly one hundred nuclear power stations Harri. They need fuel and you agreed to supply it. You cannot just change your mind. You made the decision when you agreed to supply the fuel we're just agreeing the terms of the cost of the mine. In the end this is a decision effecting the future of Arimathea."

"I know what I agreed to and if you had read the contract you will remember I buried a little fail safe in for myself. Just in case, you understand, and if you haven't found it yet, it was basically…

"…If any new research comes to light proving the product would endanger the life or well-being in any of the areas surrounding the operations it shall be deemed to negate any agreement formerly made until proven otherwise.."

"There is no research, you're talking shit, Harri!"

"But I'm afraid there is. I commissioned my own report into the safety of the reactors you are using. There appears there is a possibility that after fifty years of use one of the safety valves could fail and compromise the whole system. It will be difficult to prove otherwise without testing the valve for fifty years.

So yes Zanda, you are right it does affect the future and I'm thinking of the future. The future when things are starting to wind down on this planet. The post-industrial era. It is on the way and nothing can prevent it. It can be like you say. A violent chaos or we can manage it. All this power they're making here, all from the star, no waste, no danger if it's not maintained. How long will one of these power stations remain safe? How long before they start melting down when the infrastructure collapses to such an extent they simply cannot be maintained. That is an awful lot of radiation flowing around the world. It does not bear thinking about the horror that may be unleashed across the face of this world.

I have the rights to that land and I can make the government there as rich as is needed to keep them on my side. I want those people to survive and I am going to start making solar panels and storage facilities in my factories. I have woken up Zanda. I want no part in this venture. It is the bridge too far and I'm afraid you will have to find somewhere else to buy your fuel."

"There is nowhere else, we scoured the planet for that amount of fuel, certainly not shallow enough to get out and make it all worthwhile!"

Zanda clambered to his feet and stood in front of Harry. He was wavering drunkenly, still clinging to the whisky bottle. His wrap-around Star glasses concealed the anxiety ripping through him after the revelations Harri had made to him. He had not been prepared for Harri's 'awakening' and these consequences. It was new conflict and unexpected confusion in the string of events that had already transpired in the last hour. Still the darkness and the threat from the human race to his beloved Arimathea hovered around him sucking out his light; still Alamistra's soft words, the resurrected feelings he had felt for her and her deception, now his friend Harri's betrayal undermining his plans for Zinederland churned through his thoughts. Deeper though, he knew he was held by the pact he had made with Oblivion as he had held Singing Moon's mutilated body amongst the smouldering ruins of her parents' house to wipe the human race from the face of Arimathea so the rest of life could thrive without the scourge of its existence.

At this point Zanda no longer had the capacity to process the energy being created by the consequences of his actions. Alamistra, by inference, had effectively woven his two personas together and now they were battling for supremacy. The dragon who had dreamed for aeons all his beautiful memories into the world struggled with the human being whose bitter experience had allowed the forces of Oblivion to guide him into a position of incredible power and continue with their destructive plans. He became very still for a few moments but then his body began to shiver. He no longer had the ability to hold closed the portal to the dark expanses where Oblivion dwelt in the labyrinth. The pathways he had opened to bring back the scientist shamans with their enormous wealth and which had kept the dragons separated from their souls was now opening. They had lain dormant since setting the human race on its path to destruction but now threatened to flow through Mithrael the dragon, unhindered into the world.

His whole body seemed to become engulfed in extreme cold. It delineated a zone of icy vapour around him. Across the vapour crackled static electricity which occasionally stung down into his body causing him considerable pain. His face became dark under the layer of frost and ice forming on his features. He began to shake uncontrollably and was barely able to stand upright and he staggered forward finally dropping the bottle of whisky. All his light, his life-force seemed to be leaving him. It was being sucked out relentlessly through his eyes and semi-congealed blood oozed from under his Star glasses leaving frozen crimson rivulets laced down over his cheeks and jaw.

The elemental changes continued to become wilder and more unpredictable as if a violent storm had been unleashed, sand from the desert was sucked into the isolated winds swirling around him and combined with small and violent flashes of lightening, igniting areas of fire which then licked around his body vaporising the ice forming over his clothes. The pain from the shifting temperature, ice and fire started to blister and soon in places the top layer of skin on his face and hands was removed and left his body below raw. The crowds around him drew back in horror as Zanda appeared to be going into a process of extreme disintegration. The fire then seemed to engulf him and finally he screeched out in pain and the anguish of what was happening to him. But as he screamed out, gradually the fire, the ice, the crackling electricity and the light that had been leaving and whirling around his body trying to find some point of re-entry seemed to find some equilibrium.

He began to stop shivering and became still again and stood as if adjusting to this new power. Energy appeared to be leaving the ground and the sky and it seemed to be flowing through him so the conflict could find a balance in its' new state. The ice and the fire shimmered around him, the vapour flowed down across his body and static randomly crackled down his arms and across his torso. His face, darkened now with congealed blood and the remains of his burnt skin, became calm as Zanda was transformed into this new state of being. The dragon and the human appeared to have combined into a new elemental creature, neither flesh or light, channelling energy from all around him into this new body. This new horrifying apparition Mithrael had become then roared out with such defiance, the ground, the sky and all of Arimathea around him seemed to shudder with dread as this new creature was born amongst the stars.

Chapter 75.
The Spirit Dimensions.

Okino and Mariella drifted through the crowds as they contemplated the next event. Occasionally someone would approach Okino to pay their respects and ask him about his life in the mountains. Then they might tell him briefly or at length about their own lives and how they felt so much concern for their world and how powerless they felt to change it. He listened carefully to what they had to say. Often he found himself indicating to the thousands of people around them.

"Did you ever think there would be so many people prepared to walk over the desert to come to this event…Everyone here has made the first step. We all will have to decide what we can do. There is no one who can make the decision for us."

They would disappear back into the crowds to continue their quest to find some inspiration, some wisdom to propel them into a new life. They hoped for a new age when the people of Arimathea would change their ways, throw off the shackles of the machines and begin to nurture the home they so miraculously had inherited. Then they wouldn't have to worry about their world and how their generation was leaving it for their children and grandchildren. They wanted an antidote, a saviour who would put everything right in a year or may be two. Even Okino knew this was not the kind of change that could happen in these kind of time spans. It could be instigated here but it would happen slowly and only if the entire human race decided to take on this new challenge and again came to understand the true nature of their world.

He was watching Grace up on the stage conferring with Yaan. He smiled as he remembered the night in the stone circle when it appeared they had been in some earlier era and lived together in a tribe. Now it seemed important for them all to be together in this time. They had travelled to be together in this future to share the knowledge and experience they had gained. Wisdom as energy travelling through the years to a new time to transform and change a new set of circumstances. How many more he wondered had also stood amongst those old stones and watched Yaan's initiation? How much knowledge did they have locked up from those previous lives needing to be unlocked? Now they were eager to find out what their role might be, find the key to the knowledge embedded deep in the memory of their soul, from perhaps many journeys in and out of this material world.

The dragons would carry them deeper into those invisible worlds in the coming months. Carry them into the lands where the old shamans lived high in the hills and deep in the cities. They would learn from them the ways of their world and the spirits with whom they shared it; would see how they meshed together. How each movement and each decision had consequence in lives that could change for ever with an ill-conceived action or word. How a smile or a curse could have instant and startling effect from the precise moment of its inception.

They would learn to consider again the forces of the Universe continually at work in their lives as they were taken to the streams and rivers or out into the forests where lived the most ancient of beings. They would watch the wild animals, perhaps become them in their trials of life. They would come to understand again the precious nature of each day they could once again live and breathe upon this world. They would learn about the flow of energy from one state to the next and how precious it always had been for every plant and animal as it enabled their life to go on.

Perhaps the greatest truth they would learn from these wise folks they would meet in the landscapes and the markets of the world the dragons had dreamed was how completely unique they were. All their lives they had been separated into an age group or a gender, a class or a cast type; they had been fitted into this band of people or that band of people. Then they had been expected to fulfil the criteria, the aims and the goals of the category in which they had been placed and if they didn't they were made to feel as if they were failing as human beings. Now unsurprisingly everyone felt as if they were failing.

The shamans would help them to find out who they really were. They would reassure them and tell them they had a unique place in the world. They would show them the gifts with which they were able to savour each and every moment they spent here. In the forest they would ask them out of all the trees, where is one which is the same. They would find even within the same species there was not one with the same configuration of branches.

"They have grown and experienced uniquely their environment and so have you." The shamans would say to them.

In time they would begin to see how Arimathea and they had arrived in this place. Like the tree which had stood in a wood for a thousand years and adapted as every new trial had come before it, Arimathea had accepted the challenge in the only way she was able as the forces in all their complexity and diversity had acted upon her. The consequences had been the struggle that had ensued in which Okino and Mariella had become embroiled. Okino put his arm around Mariella's shoulder and gave her an affectionate squeeze. She looked up at him and grinned..

"So, are you glad you came?"

"We have an old yak herder's expression in our village when everything is as it should be"

"Oh, and what is that…"

"Feels like five yaks are pulling in the same direction."

Mariella laughed..

"Whoa, must be pretty good then…"

"Yes, well moments when it is said are rare. Such is the temperament of the yak putting five together is rarely successful. They are most effective in ones and twos."

For a few moments Okino and Mariella settled into the blissful state they had often experienced on their journey together, just before the next part of the tale began to unravel. So, it was here, as they stood at the centre of Grace's dream, so beautifully considered, executed and administered. It was her defiant statement to the world. She and all the other people who had gathered here would not except the fate of Arimathea. There was a defiance here Okino had not been prepared for and he hoped the magic and enthusiasm being generated would become contagious in the rest of Arimathea's population.

As he thought how this might come to be, Mithraels' unworldly scream tore through the air, stopping conversations in mid-sentence and suddenly halting journeys across the site. The atmosphere then changed dramatically. Okino remembered the moments before he had entered the temple of swords, before he and Merilon had fought with Mithrael. Despite the warmth of the desert late in the year there was suddenly a chill in the air.

Thick dark clouds had gathered over the mountains and were rapidly moving over the plain to obscure the early morning Star. A gentle breeze which had suddenly stiffened seemed to grow in strength with every gust. The flags on the tents were starting to billow frantically and hats were held on nervously. Light was fading as an entire weather system now appeared to be revolving over the site. The resultant winds were now blowing hard enough to raise the sand from the desert floor. The festival site was rapidly becoming the centre of a vast tornado whose revolving speed was increasing rapidly. Festival goers ran across the site in panic, not knowing where to run to for protection. Mariella clung to Okino, her long dark hair blowing chaotically around the two of them.

"What has happened Okino, seems like the yaks have fallen out big time!"

"It certainly would appear so. There is nothing natural about this and I have a terrible feeling it's worse than the yaks going their separate ways. It reminds me of my dream when Mithrael killed Merilon. I wonder… the sword Harri arrived with, I never had a chance to ask where it came from. It doesn't seem the sort of thing he would have brought with him. Any way I think we should get it just in case!"

They ran back to the tent through the panicking crowds as the sand in the wind flew faster through the air stinging into exposed faces, arms and legs. Many of the tents had not been properly fixed down in hurried arrivals the day before. Now unattached they were scattering clothes and other belongings as they rolled across the site. They ran down the streets where others were frantically banging in pegs as their tents flapped relentlessly in the now ferocious winds. Visibility had become poor but eventually after running in vain down a number of the streets they eventually found their tent. Sand was already piling up around the edge and the zip had become buried. Mariella pushed the sand aside and Okino pulled the exposed zip to the top and dived inside. There was the sword safely buried in its' stout leather scabbard. He reached for it and grabbed at the handle. As he touched the handle to take it from the tent a blinding light flashed through his mind. Mariella saw him slump unconscious in the tent with one hand gripping the sword.

Okino found himself in front of one of the temple castles, it was surrounded by large Oak trees and a stream ran sparkling through the closely cropped grassland. A number of horses were tethered loosely to the trees and grazed calmly on the short grass. He could smell and hear the sound of surf in the distance and gulls flew overhead calling down their familiar greeting. The Star was high in the sky and he was walking on a sandy path leading up to the castle. He could see the large door was ajar at the top of a flight of steps.

As he approached the castle he decided the owners of the horses may well be inside and possibly waiting for him. He climbed the steps and pushed open the door. Inside three men and two women sat around a long table. They appeared to be closely examining documents and maps strewn over the table. There was a large spherical compass sitting on the maps. They looked up immediately as he entered and one of the men rose from the table and came over to greet him. He recognised the face but for the moment had no recollection from where. They were all tall and there was a familiar green glow from their eyes.

"Welcome Okino, we have been expecting you. We have met before briefly but you may not recognise us in such solid form. We were around the fire when you were alone in the ruins at Asima."

"So you are dragons."

"We are, I am Zaramir and this is Aralstir, Teron, Pirilinor and Karalla. Merilon will soon be arriving. Although during the last few months you have more often become the same being. We have brought you here to explain to you what is happening."

"So this is to do with the wind and the scream. I was in the tent and had reached for the sword Harri arrived with."

Aralstir beckoned over to him.

"Come Okino, we have something to show you."

Okino took a place at the table. Aralstir motioned a hand over the maps. Slowly a number of translucent spheres started to rise from the surface of the table and the maps covering it. They rose high enough so they could be observed at eye level. They were moving in a circular motion around some point at a point in their centre. The spheres were out of alignment. They overlapped and intersected and so moved in a continually changing mass as their relationship with each other finely adjusted moment by moment.

"Do you recognise what you are looking at Okino.."

"It does look familiar but in the same way as I recognised you when I came in, I have no idea where from."

"It is because you may have seen these charts and these forms before or Merilon has and you carry many of his memories buried deep in your subconscious."

Teron then rose from her chair and indicated to the spheres.

"You will have memories of the labyrinth from when Merilon was effectively cursed by Mithrael. These old maps and charts were produced many eons ago when the first whisperings of what is now happening first came to our knowledge. These old charts were created by another race of humans who lived on a similar world, in a time when they were accustomed to living with the effects of what you call spirit and the dimensions. In a similar way to your own race they made complex equations to explain the phenomena surrounding you.

Much of what is unexplained to you, but you suspect, is due to the layers of these dimensions overlaying and underlaying your world. This is where the spirit moves, invisible to you now, through your world. Each of these dimensions have made your world and the universe, which you see and don't see, into what it has become. These phenomena are all around you. The residue of your ability to understand them is still contained within your cellular make up, in a continual stream from those early days. It is why you feel you can understand your animals or have premonitions about what is going to happen in the near and distant future: why you think you can communicate telepathically between each other; why things start to change when they have been steady for so long. They are why your life and everything connected to it suddenly starts to go smoothly or chaotically wrong at the same time or when things seem to happen in perfect time for when they are meant to. They are how you feel so connected to some people and not to others; similarly, with areas of the planet where you live. You may go somewhere to which you have never visited but feel it could well have been your home. You have the residual ability to connect to anywhere on the planet through any number of these dimensions.

On the most fundamental level it is how this planet manages to stay in balance. Think of all the knowledge you have of this physical dimension you live in, the world you see and know about. Think of that as the physical world. So you could break that knowledge down into the physics, mathematics and biology and all the separate areas you know about the actual planet and the rest of the universe. Beyond what you know about all these areas there is an infinity of knowledge that you don't know. Think of each of these areas as a separate dimension. Even though you don't know all this information it doesn't mean it is not working all around you holding your world together, enabling you to exist and live in it. Occasionally some phenomena, subject to that invisible unknown mass of information will slip through into your world and will enable you to see or comprehend something you would not otherwise be able to.

These dimensions run parallel to your physical existence. They act within your consciousness and every aspect of your world. They are infinitely complex and your ability to understand them is bound up with the powerful naturally evolved intuition you originally developed but which has subsequently faded. You have had much explained to you about the course of events on this world. Much of what has happened is the result of the shifting of these dimensions. You have seen how the power of the dragons has waned. The fabric of time and space and all its inhabitants are subject to the rise and fall of their influence; they flow around us and through us illuminating and obscuring all we need to know."

Now Pirilinor stood up and started to speak indicating the direction of flow and intersections across the old maps.

"These charts were conceived and mapped out by the Shaman people on that other world over many centuries. They discovered ways to watch the influence of the dimensions wax and wane. Over time they were able to predict this moment would eventually arrive. They observed and learnt the rhythms of these forces as they operated on the world. As you know this dimension, the dimension in which you live, acts in cycles and the solidity you have discovered can be explained in your equations. In the same way as the physicality changes in your atmosphere as a result of Arimathea's changing position in relation to her Star, so the influence of the dimensions in the universe shift around her. They wax and wane as their position changes in relation to the forces of the infinite cosmos acting upon them. They drift apart and come back together. These changes can result in long periods of peaceful development or eras of great turmoil. They effect the entire complexity of influences on the planet itself. These charts tell of their heightened influence as they work in conjunction with each other in these days we are now experiencing."

She motioned her hand around the spheres. They continued to revolve as before but now they were gradually coming together. The intersections and anomalous shapes of the mass of light began to form into a perfectly formed sphere.

"The storm in which Mithrael is now engulfed is a direct result of the cycles of decay that have been in ascendancy in these last one hundred or so years. They have influenced Mithrael, as powerful a being as they have ever had at their disposal and acted upon him; guided him into such conflict with himself he has caused this vortex between the dimensions and so a direct channel for the forces of destruction into this world. All you have seen has been the result of a struggle between the dimensional forces acting through the minds of the human race to create the conditions where they can enter this dimension and rapidly accelerate and so precipitate the return to the original emptiness."

Okino had listened carefully. It all made perfect sense. He thought of Harri locked in his tiny flat harbouring thoughts of escape and subsequently driving himself into the place where no one could ever harm or lock him up again. How he, with Mithraels' accumulated wealth had orchestrated his enormous rise to power. How he himself and Mariella had been guided by Arimathea to awaken the dragons to strengthen the dimensional forces of light and creation.

"Now these dimensions have come together. They have become perfectly aligned over each other. This will last for only a fraction of Arimathea's turning around her Star. All the dimensions now will have an equal influence on everything happening in the world. The intensity with which you will feel the world will increase. It will seem as if everything is happening at once. As a result your ability to transform yourselves and the world around you, will escalate as the forces of light and creation flow more deeply through everything. But first the breech oblivion has been able to make as a result of the near proximity of all these dimensions will have to be healed."

The tall dragons looked over the table at Okino. He had a terrible feeling, with his hand on the sword Harri had carried out of the desert, what was going to be asked of him.

"So what do you need me to do?"

Karalla had remained seated while the other dragons had been speaking, now she spoke gravely.

"You and Merilon will have to merge as you have before and confront Mithrael at the heart of the vortex forming in the desert. The two of you will have to stop Mithrael becoming the channel which will allow Oblivion to flood this world with the horrors it is able to bring from the far flung regions and dimensions of the Universe. If you do not there will be a very different path for Arimathea and all who live upon her."

Okino looked down the table past Teron and saw Merilon sitting at the end of the table. He was grinning.

"So it's you and me kid, against the rest of the Universe."

Then he was standing next to Okino offering him his hand. Okino grasped it and felt the familiar flood of energy and life force filling his being.

He felt himself back in the tent drifting in semi consciousness.. Mariella was calling in the distance.

"Okino, wake up, are you all right…this is no time to sleep, wake up Okino."

Chapter 76.
Inside the Vortex

Okino and Mariella stumbled through the streets of flapping fabric tenuously anchored to the sand towards the centre of the spinning vortex. Anything not secured and tied down and was light enough to be blown along was on the move. When they reached the centre such was the force of the winds there appeared to be an almost a solid wall of flying sand. They stood with many other of the apprehensive festival goers in awe of this new phenomenon, apparently still gathering strength. The infrastructure Grace had planned so carefully, was standing solidly, miraculously resisting the forces of the winds being exerted on them.

Okino had slung the scabbard and the sword over his back and was preparing himself for what he might find inside. He felt the dragons had been holding something back in their explanation. Mariella assumed from Okino's brief description of this next stage into which he was carrying a sword there would be danger and possibly violence. The hilt of the sword shone strangely, glistening on Okino's back as if the time for which it had been brought into being had arrived.

She saw the shadow of the dragon had appeared across Okino's face and the familiar distance between them had arisen as she watched him concentrating on what may lay ahead. She herself felt Arimathea's anger as she contemplated what amounted to one of her systems being hijacked by whatever force was now driving the winds. She knew in those moments she would have to follow Okino into the vortex. It seemed there would be aspects of the ensuing confrontation only Arimathea would be able to deal with. She also steeled herself and when Okino turned to face her and started to tell her he was about to go in…

"I'm coming with you Okino. Arimathea feels certain she will be able to help you and Merilon with whatever might arise."

Okino looked immediately concerned but saw Mariella's face had also changed. The ancient soul of his world he had first seen in the snowstorm on the mountainside had returned. He smiles..

"I'm glad you are coming…it seems only right the two of us should be confronting this together after all we've been through to be here. Shall we..!"

"Definitely."

Okino took Mariella's hand and with gasps and looks of concern from the surrounding crowd, they walked into the swirling cloud of sand.

Immediately the density of the sand in the air made it hard for them to draw breath. They pulled their clothing up to allow some protection around their mouths. They had to close their eyes down to the narrowest of gaps to see their way forward but there was little they could see ahead. They had to put their heads down and push with all their weight into the ferocious currents of air. The wind pushed them relentlessly in every direction away from where they needed to be going and tore viciously around them in a melee of hissing and roaring sound. If they had been able to open their mouths to speak their words would have been lost in the eerie sound of the battering wind.

Deeper and deeper they forced their way on not knowing how much further they would have to go before they broke through into the calm centre of the tornado. Unable to communicate in any meaningful way they had to confront their fears alone. They both worried they were losing their sense of direction and now were wandering aimlessly perhaps in circles or back towards where they had entered. They had tried to keep the flow of the wind in the direction from which it had originally blown but felt sure the winds seemed to change direction. They both felt they had lost track of time as they moved through the cloud.

They started to become aware of layers of sparkling light, as if there were shining minerals in layers of sediment embedded in strata of the wind. These layers appeared to be changing the nature of the space around them… the idea of the desert started to fade until they felt they could have been anywhere they had previously visited on their journey so far. It made them feel even less certain about how this would turn out. Eventually the intensity of the currents around them seemed to fluctuate and at last after it seemed like they had been trudging through the wind for an eternity the density of the sandstorm appeared to be lessening and they were able to see clear space ahead. With immense relief they hurried onwards and eventually burst through into daylight.

Nothing could have prepared them for what now confronted them. They were standing on a promontory rock high on the side of a mountain range. It disappeared off into the far distance and the slopes all around them and as far as they could see were covered in dense tropical jungle. The atmosphere was hot and humid. In the far distance they could see a wide fast flowing river winding its way down through the trees and vegetation in the valley below. On the far side of the river there appeared to be a further outcrop of rock on which had been constructed a complex stone structure. Okino recognised the structure as similar to the temple castles he had experienced in his previous dreams. This insight was then confirmed by an affirmation from Merilon.

As they concentrated their gaze on the castle in the distance they could see, what appeared to be a cloud of dark matter spiralling down from the rotating thunder clouds above. They could hear above the sound of the cascading river below, the calls of thousands of crows, vultures and other scavenging birds wheeling on the currents of whatever was passing between the clouds and the castle below. Okino could now see where the forces of Oblivion had been able to access the new dimension the dragons had brought into being, almost certainly through Mithrael's terrible confusion, possibly without him even knowing. The jungle between where they now stood and the castle below seemed impassable. Okino turned to Mariella…

"It appears we have moved into the dimension the dragons have made. It seems as if one of their temples has been taken over by Mithrael. The crows, I imagine are being attracted by the forces of concentrated destruction. I would assume who or whatever is behind such a force is possibly planning the destruction of this entire dimension. As it collapses the catastrophic degradation may seep out through the connections made with the consciousness into our own dimension..

"What will happen then...look can you see the jungle is already starting to deteriorate around the castle…It looks like it's just dying Okino, more and more of it as we watch…will there be animals in there…"

"This is a spirit world, a complex dream construction now being infiltrated by something very powerful and very destructive, the ultimate nightmare,"

"…and that could then move through into our world through our dreams and we all could become a channel for it and everything would just start dying."

"It would appear that may well be true…but for now, we are still in the dream so Merilon and Arimathea will have powerful influence here. The battle with Mithrael will be right on the edge between the dream and the nightmare. We need to get down there as quickly as we can before the decay and death gathers too much momentum and becomes unstoppable!"

"But we'll have to clamber through all this jungle, it could take us hours!"

"Come on Mariella, we have the dragon and the spirit of Arimathea with us. They won't give up without significant effort. So, we'll just get going and pretty soon it will all start happening, trust me."

She looked into Okino's dark eyes now tinged unmistakeably with the luminous green of Merilon's life force and suddenly felt her own deep connection with the trees growing around her and their roots delving deep into the ground sucking out the nutrients and mixing with the starlight above. She felt out further to the spirits of the animals she could now feel roaming their paths through the maze of thick tangled vegetation, pathways soaring up through the tree canopies and over the rivers where huge trees had fallen to provide the bridges from one bank to the next.

She could hear the jungle for miles around and she searched for a familiar footfall; for a shadow creature invisible to all but her own who lived here undisturbed in the dragons dream waiting, ready to pass all she knew to any who passed her way. Mariella heard the soft growl as her thought passed through the soft cortex, felt her response and adjust her path as she herself clambered down the rock behind Okino and was confronted by a wall of impenetrable jungle. They were powerless here in the form they had become but Mariella put a hand on Okino's shoulder.

"I think help is on its way Okino. Do not waste your energy now."

He turned and looked at her. She had changed again. She had become part of the jungle, as if she had always lived there; her face and limbs, the colour of trees were strong and lithe, her eyes so full of the blue sky and the silent green of the river were sharp and strong, her hair long and beautifully tangled already had flowers growing through it. There was an infinity and the strength of elemental power reigning here and all the creatures of the forest shone from her. He and the dragon fell even more deeply in love with the creation spirit Merilon had sensed across the wastes of space all those eons before. Okino who had been adopted by her and been brought here to help her went over to her. He pulled her close to him, closer than they had ever been; all the energy and all their story, all their destiny, the strange entanglement of fate and circumstance winding its magic through the universe blended through them and brought them together into one fabulous spirit creature.

On the rock above where they had stood only moments before the leopard had arrived and stood looking down at the embracing couple. She did not hesitate for this was her fate also. She was here now to play her part in the story now unfolding between the forces of her world. She leapt down towards Okino and Mariella floating in their moment of ecstasy. She effortlessly combined the two spirits into her own as she flowed through them and landed on the wide trunk of a fallen tree. The vegetation had yet to close the gap around the trunk. For the moment it provided an entrance to the pathway she used every day to take her down to the river where she could drink or catch an unsuspecting fish idling, unsuspecting in the shallows.

Now she had become one with these two spirits. She knew the one who had called her. She was always there. In the Star light and the shadows. In the moon light on the waters of the river at night. Yes, she knew her and now she was carrying her and was feeling her wonder. The other spirit came from deeper in her world, had been in her thoughts; she recognised him from when she had some decision to make or dilemma to sort out, felt him when she was hunting, calming her, holding her back until the exact moment she needed to make her moves.

Now they were part of her. Feeling her every step and leap as she made her way down her forest pathway. Through the tunnels her family had used for generations, through the network of fallen trees and branches sometimes high over the clearings where the other animals congregated to eat the sweet grass or flowers growing there. Through the territories of the monkeys and the birds who called down their warnings to her as she entered; called to her to tell her they knew she was there. Tomorrow maybe, they would not, she thought. Quickly past the trees where the largest and deadliest of the snakes lived. Of all the creatures in the jungle she feared them most. As quick as lightening they could come, bring death out of nowhere, such was the brilliance of their camouflage and the potency of their poison the power of their suffocating bodies. They were to be avoided at all costs. There were shallow streams too, down which she could pass. She did not like to swim but she would if it meant avoiding the territory of a large snake. She was always stealthy, always on the lookout for an opportunity to fill the aching hunger. She would stop, freeze herself if she came upon a creature who had not become aware of her, all her senses would become alive and she would creep, balanced perfectly in absolute silence towards the moment.

Now she sensed the urgency. She had eaten that morning so she made her way quickly through the trees and down towards the river to where the fallen tree, the lianas and vines had woven their crossing over the fast flowing waters below.

It had taken Mariella and Okino a few moments to realise what had happened. Then to their delight they had found they were sharing the body of a fully-grown female leopard and she was carrying them through the jungle. For Okino who had shared the spirit of dragon, dolphin, fox and eagle during his journey now to be combined into the body of a Leopard and with Mariella was just about as good as his life could be and probably would be ever again. He had ceaselessly wondered what it might be like to have such senses, the poise and elegance of one of these magnificent creatures. He had been in awe of the mysterious snow leopards ever since he had known of their existence. Mariella had been infected by his enthusiasm and now they padded through the jungle relishing every sound and the sheer beauty of the leopards' movement as she effortlessly leapt and jumped and made her way down the paths of her home.

As they approached the river however the sounds started to change. The steady rhythmical calls of territorial claims and establishment became the shrieks and screeches of danger and panic. The leopard apprehensive now, approached and crossed the bridge. On the far bank she stopped and peered up at the stone castle before her. Okino and Mariella materialised from the solidity of the leopard and appeared standing beside her as she contemplated the castle. The surrounding area of jungle was fading rapidly. The vegetation was losing its vital green. Insects and small animals were streaming out across the ground back into the healthy jungle. Much of the vegetation around the base of the castle had already turned to fine dust and lay in a thick lifeless layer over the ground.

The leopard cowered, frightened, back towards the river and Mariella shuddered as she felt the edge of the cold and unexplainable emptiness approaching as it began to envelop them. Okino was looking up towards the top of the castle between the large circular turrets where the dark matter, sucking light and any visibility beyond the column out of the sky and fragmented clouds beyond. The crows continued to circle the column of dark energy adding their eerie screeching to the malevolence as it forced its way out of the dimension where it existed into the dragon's construction.

"Mithrael must be up there somewhere. I'll have to go up there if we are going to have any chance of stopping all this."

From where he was standing, he could see no sign of any entrance. He left Mariella and started to circle the perimeter of the castle. He could see only the higher windows, so he continued his search for an entrance. Merilon wanted to fly immediately to the top of the castle to confront Mithrael but Okino had felt a change in the atmosphere around him.

In a moment of calm Mariella had felt Arimathea looking through her eyes assessing all that was happening. The crows were now flying around the entire castle, swirling and diving and crying their incessant screech of defiance. She could see the light energy coming up through the bedrock where the stonemasons had so carefully connected the temple structure into the currents flowing up through the planet from the crystal caves. She could see the exposed stone structure glowing with the light flowing up from below. She wondered idly for a moment how it would feel to be in this structure so directly connected and engineered to surround anyone inside with the glow.

Then she saw how the dark matter was permeating into the stone walls, infusing itself into the spaces between the atoms and the molecules. Now completely enveloped, she saw the light from the glow start to flicker and very slightly dim. Suddenly she realised what was happening. The dark matter intended to enter directly through the stonework into the layer of consciousness the dragons had made, which eventually would be feeding into the dreams of the Arimatheans. It then would have access into the entire consciousness of her world. The implications were incalculable. Her systems and all her life force would be flooded with this sinister annihilating force.

Arimathea knew she was now under severe threat. There was a possibility this entity was attempting to consume and possibly drain the life force of the entire planet. The implications of this terrible scenario flashed through the mind of the being they had become. A planet slowly dying as its energy was gradually or even instantaneously drained by this Alien inter dimensional force or being. She knew exactly what she had to do.

Okino had returned from his search for an entrance. He found Mariella completely transformed. She stood with her eyes closed concentrating intensely with her hands outstretched towards the castle. She had become Arimathea. Her expression had strengthened with the wisdom of her age and the leopard had returned and stood strongly and defiantly beside her. The advance of the emptiness appeared to have stopped and the vegetation remaining behind her seemed to be gaining strength and was now growing towards the castle. Intrigued by this intervention, Okino and Merilon, stood beside her. As they felt the energy of the jungle enveloping them, they began to understand what Arimathea was doing. The growth of the vegetation was increasing explosively. Creepers, vines and lianas were visibly growing across the jungle floor across the perimeter of the emptiness in front of them towards the castle. Stems and leaves and tendrils shot out into the air and ground and sped towards the sheer stone walls where they started to climb.

Mariella opened her eyes and walked forward towards the castle; arms still outstretched as if she was directing her own assailing army. Up and over the walls they rapidly climbed, pushing destructive tendrils into the stonework so carefully constructed by the masons, advancing the decay normally brought on by millennia of gradual and incessant delving and intrusion. The spirit goddess of the world strengthened them immeasurably. Now in a position where she could channel her frustration and anger, she poured the elemental powers she was able to command into the destruction of the castle.

The enormous vines spiralled as if in direct opposition to the dark matter above them around the turrets of the castle, forcing themselves through windows and into any weakness they could find, forced them open, creating gaping cracks in the structure. The cracks ripped through the stonework joining with further fissures opening from below as the rock on which the construction was founded began itself to split. Large areas of wall started to fall, collapsing and exposing the heavy internal construction of walls and staircases as they wound into the towers; nothing could withstand the assault now being unleashed upon it. Great panels of constructed stonework crashed unceremoniously and chaotically to the ground where they were enveloped in the clouds of the fine dust billowing into the air.

At one point in the collapse, enough of the structure remained, standing between two of the towers to reveal Mithrael standing his own arms outstretched receiving the dark matter, channelling it down through his own psyche into the surrounding dimension. It seemed he had no concern for himself or the destruction of the castle, so locked into the process he had now become merely a lifeless conduit for all he had wished for; all he had striven for and worked towards in his many lives since the death of Shining Moon. Now he had no conscious understanding of what was happening to him or the devastation it might all eventually bring. Arimathea encouraged even further by the sight of her wayward dragon increased the power of the destructive forces.

The collapse of the castle increased in speed and violence as the last of the structure crashed into the ground. The pile of rubble it had become was rapidly being absorbed back to where it had been so painstakingly excised.

Only a billowing cloud of dust remained into which the dark matter was still being relentlessly channelled. The crows had flown higher, screeching their panic and dismay as the castle collapsed and now were flying down into the dust perhaps in search of Mithraels' corpse. The chaotic beating of thousands of black wings started to disperse the dust. Mithrael was revealed standing defiantly amongst what remained of the masonry. He was barely recognisable now as anything resembling a human being. He was covered in a thick layer of dust, his star glasses were still on but his coat was ragged and torn and his large black motorcycle boots remained firmly planted on the ground in amongst the rubble. He was grinning over at Okino and Merilon as he started to speak..

"So here we are again Merilon I see you are with the monk again. I just can't understand why you want to continue with all this. Nothing has changed, your precious human race is still wrecking their world and even more people are enduring the suffering. Why don't you just let it all go and all this can end once and for all."

Okino and Merilon took a step forward..

"Not a chance Mithrael. Even as we speak, new hope and life is being born. Have you no idea of the trauma you are planning on releasing into the psyche of the Universe if what you have planned is successful. It would take eons to heal and return to where it all began. Presumably that is what you intend. In such lengths of time this world could find a way from this point to the heart of the mystery several times over even if there was an apocalypse brought on by the humans. Perhaps you have yourself been misled by the aims of whatever force is guiding you."

"But then it will go on again and again. It can never stay the same, it has to go on through this process of pain and suffering and the endless yearning to find the answer to it all. We have no knowing it can ever be attained or if this meaningless struggle can ever really end."

"But then if it all goes back to the beginning, the urge will still be there. Eventually it will be compelled to start the search again. Whichever way we go from this point the result will eventually always be the same. Surely we have to give this generation a chance. They have come so far without us with their mad and destructive ways even though they have been disconnected from the dream. You said it the last time we met and perhaps you were right. Who knows where we would be now if you had not taken the course of action you chose? But they have found their own way and maybe it was their right and destiny, even ours. They have become infinitely connected to each other, with the knowledge they have gained they have understood in a global sense the consequences of the environment they have created. They have understood the incredible and true nature of this planet on which they have evolved and the extraordinary process they have become a part of.

There are many who are stuck in their old ways but even they are feeling the benefit of us being back in her centre, dreaming the old wisdom back into the world. Now with all they have been through and learnt and seen and dreamt for themselves they can understand what it is; like never before. When they first knew all this they never questioned it because they knew nothing else. In the same way as every child will go along with his or her parents while they are in charge. However, eventually the child will have to make its own way and defy all the old ways. But like their parents before them there are fundamentals which have to be maintained and they will realise them and in turn, they will be defied by their children in the same way. The human race is coming to such a point. They have gone off and had their wild party but they are starting to see the wreckage around them.."

"They cannot change Merilon. If you had experienced what I have, even since we last met, you would know what I mean. They are a cruel and selfish species who will send their own children to hideous deaths to protect their own interests. Not just to protect their families but to protect their wealth, their money and their power. No other species has come anywhere near how disgusting they have become and I think every last one of them should be destroyed so even if there is the smallest possibility something better, some time, may come out of it, it should happen and immediately. As for the suffering they will go through in the process, well, if you want my honest opinion, they deserve it for what they have put this world through."

Mithrael then grinned over at Okino and Merilon and resumed his attention to the dark matter which continued to spiral around him. He was bathing in the emptiness relishing the long awaited respite from the angst and the worry, the pity, the guilt and the yearning for something entirely unattainable. Soon he would be freed from the terrible pain of the loss he had felt which had never really left him.

Okino and Merilon knew the time had come. The direction in which the Universe was to flow had to be decided. Okino felt Merilon pulling the sword from the scabbard strapped across his back and his life force fully engaging with every muscle and sinew; every sparking synapse every impulse and instinct had now became entirely dragon. Mithrael must have heard the sword slithering out of the scabbard or caught a flash from the shining steel because he looked over at Merilon. He grinned and pulled out his own sword from under what was left of his battered coat. He bounded forward without any further warning and swung several powerful blows at Okino's body and head.

Merilon now was not fully accustomed to such aggression and was surprised by the vehemence of the attack. But he remembered what was at stake as he watched the dark matter out of the corner of his eye spiralling down from a distant universe containing unknown and possibly unfathomable horror. He struck back mercilessly as Mithrael raised his blade again thinking Merilon had again come easily to his slaughter. Merilon smashed through the defence he raised and delivered a strike which Mithrael managed to parry only a moment before it cut through his body. So Merilon had come for a fight. He would certainly get one now.

Mithrael channelled the full force behind him into the sword he was now wielding at Merilon. The sword seemed to take on a life of its own as it crashed time and time again into Merilon's defences. Both of these swords had been made in Mithrael's forge and had the strength of all his knowledge and experience of conflict bound into them. The steel met with such force it seemed this world shuddered and on each occasion with the enormous crash came a great spray of sparks arcing through the surrounding air.

Each dragon was searching, desperately to find a way through the others defences with increasing ferocity. Nether it seemed had any strength advantage or disadvantage and their determination one to exterminate the other held no brotherly feeling. Merilon however in the heat and the pressure of watching the precision of the blows directed towards him began to notice what was happening to Mithrael. He thought whatever force was acting through him had little or no interest in the creature it was now manipulating. Mithrael had become like a shell for its existence. Merilon, knew he alone stood in its way. It was the first time this power from wherever it had come had revealed itself. Instantly Merilon realised he was no longer fighting his brother dragon but the force of Oblivion which had gathered its strength across Arimathea in the past centuries.

The attack was unrelenting and clearly Mithrael or whoever was controlling him was not going to give up until Merilon and Okino were dead. Okino began to feel the strange dark fog he had felt in the tunnel under the Dragon hill starting to move across his mind. His will was being gradually ground down by the attack. He felt it was only a matter of time until his will to defend himself started to drift away giving Mithrael the chance he needed. The thought flowed through the combined mind of the dragon and the monk at the same moment. This was precisely what Oblivion was doing to Arimathea. It had created a continual onslaught always waiting for some weakness to emerge. When a weakness showed itself it was there to exploit it further and debilitate her just a little bit more.

The weakness now was the human race. They didn't care about their world and they were making it easy for Oblivion to erode her systems by weakening the web of life and choking the atmosphere. It was wearing her down until she would eventually give up the will to fight and everything would start to collapse in a chain of events no one could have actually foreseen or been categorically certain would happen. So the degradation went on. Bees dying in their billions. Still the chemicals known to be harming them being sprayed all over the crops. Whales being washed up on the shores with their stomachs so full of plastic they had no room to digest their food so they starved to death. Still plastic being thrown in the Oceans. Bird populations in collapse because their food was being killed by pesticides and herbicides. Still pesticides being used on fields. Fields the size of countries feeding their entire populations with one crop and then one year the rain fails to come. People starving to death. Still every other person on the planet driving to work every morning and flying around the world. Life on Arimathea slowly but surely falling away and…and what!! Here, this force in front of them slowly silently was making it happen. Closing the minds which should have been open.

Merilon realised he was thinking through all this while he was fighting an ever increasingly fierce onslaught. Mithrael was not giving up but Merilon had found the rhythm. It was in his nature to find these rhythms so he could effectively fill them with his dreams. These rhythms had always been the key to the steady evolution of a world. Day after day, year after year, for hundreds and thousands of years then something would change because probability had said it eventually would and everything moved on again. He had to know those rhythms so he could recognise when the potential for change could occur. Like when Rabir had found the waterfall in Asima. Then he could slow down time and concentrate on every moment, every feeling, make sure every second counted while the potential existed so the change he needed would inevitably happen.

Now he had slowed down the rate of the blows. In between the thunder blows of war and desolation there could be hours, days, years of peace in between, when crops could be grown, children sent to school, houses built and rebuilt, marriages and relationships embarked on, damage and trauma healed everyone moved forward until the next blow came rattling in and all was tenuous and uncertain again. But the rainbows would come and the fields would be replanted and all would be well. Evolution was all about the synchronicity of rhythm and timing.

In these spaces where time had slowed he realised the Leopard had been amongst his thoughts, in all his actions. This ultimate hunter predator had slowed down the world around her because she was so quick, she moved with invisible stealth and with casual invisible speed she struck. When she had caught her prey, the hardest part was over; now all she had to do was to decide how she was going to bring about the death and how long it would take.

So from this moment onwards although Mithrael fought fiercely and as well as any demon using all the dark force coursing through his body, his sword flashing, cutting and slicing into Merilon's defences, whirling and sidestepping and using every trick of sword play he had ever learnt from the greatest of the warriors who had bought his swords and tested them out in the bright woodland glades where they had been forged, he would never beat a leopard and a dragon.

Merilon even started to taunt him, cut off a lock of his long dark hair, knocked off his star glasses to reveal his sad empty eyes and tripped him so he fell awkwardly amongst the fallen masonry. Humiliated now, he jumped up quickly but Merilon again taunted him by slicing through a sleeve cutting through into his arm. First blood to Merilon. So strong he felt, and so slowly, teasingly and relentlessly in the dream of their construction he wore his brother dragon down. Merilon had slept for a thousand years and visited in his dreams the great spectacles of the cosmos, filled himself with the wonder and now felt at ease with it and himself. He knew in this battle his cause was right and he was strong; full of the light of stars and galaxies. He shone the strength of this light into the dark wastes of Oblivion and slowly the attack started to weaken.

Then for the first time he noticed the words engraved on the side of the sword. He searched for their meaning through the eons of his existence. Then he remembered. Only one other person on this world or any other and so the dragon standing before him could know the meaning of the words or would understand them when they were uttered to him. He wondered how they had been sent here and he realised Harri had brought the sword. As he toyed with his tired brother dragon, he smiled as he sidestepped and cut another swathe out of Mithrael's coat. What an extraordinary Universe it had become! Mithrael suddenly appeared to becoming heavier and his sword had become even slower in the arc from the inception of the blow to it's now feeble landing. Merilon remembered the words as he had done all those millennia before. So, as the bedraggled Mithrael, exhausted and entirely disillusioned from his monumental excursion into the psyche of the human race lowered his sword. Merilon spoke the words.

"Arrak nayan sola tri Draganera amani"

Mithrael stood with the sword resting on the ground. He looked at Merilon in disbelief possibly as he too remembered the origin of those words. He dropped his sword. His hands fell to his side and he raised his head to the sky and the dark clouds over head. Merilon smiled at him as he drove his sword through his body to where he knew it would cut through his enormous dragon heart.

Chapter 77

The Golden Eagle.

Zanda was lying in the extensively equipped temporary hospital Grace had brought to the site. His life had been in critical danger when Okino had dragged him from where he had fallen in the centre of the tornado. He had been barely alive but with expert analysis of everything that had been sucked out of his body the surgeon in charge had brought him back to the stable state in which he now was lying. The heart monitor sounded with steady regularity as Okino, Mariella and Grace stood at the side of his bed. His appearance had almost completely recovered and he was sleeping peacefully despite his lower legs and feet over sailing the standard human sized bed. All attempts to revive him had failed although all his vital signs said he should be able to wake. Grace was standing over him.

"So, who is this guy? We all spotted him when he drove the bus onto the site as the balloons took off. He and all his crew disappeared into the crowds and from what I gather were trying to sell drugs...which no-one appeared to be buying and then this weather arrives and you Okino disappear into it with a large sword on your back and came out without it and ..this!…I mean…what is going on?

The damage doesn't seem extensive but there are a lot of nervous people out there. It might be a good time to do your speech Okino, just to settle everybody down. Particularly as there appears to be a rumour people saw a dragon in the cloud of smoke made by the exploding sub-station last night."

Okino looked over at her on the other side of the bed. He looked down again at the enormous man lying there peacefully recovering. At least he had appeared only to have lost consciousness when the storm had passed and the sword driven through his heart had thankfully remained in the dimension where the fight had taken place. Inevitably Grace did want to know what was happening to hi-jack her festival. He looked over again at Mariella looking for some answer as to how they were going to explain Zanda was really one of sixteen dragons who had dreamt out the consciousness of Arimathea. He had become incarnate and had lived several lifetimes and had somehow become involved with one of the most powerful corporations on the planet. Okino was intermittently carrying the spirit of one of his brother dragons who were trying to prevent him from destroying the world because his human wife had been savagely killed more than twelve hundred turnings of the Star before. Mariella had appeared to understand his thought. Perhaps because it was the only question he really could be asking her at that moment in time.

"Yes Grace," she said. "I think we will need to have a little chat. Perhaps we should go and have a sit down, get you a stiff drink or maybe a few and then we can tell you what has happened!"

Up until this point the entire story had not been told and so once Grace had been considerably sedated, Okino and Mariella gave her the basic outline of what had happened, the culmination of which now appeared to be happening out here in the desert. Of course it took some time to explain everything had begun in a stone circle long before Mithrael had decided to become mortal when she, Harri, Yaan, all the drummers from the Lost Indians, Mariella and Okino had all taken part in a ceremony where Mithrael in his dragon form appeared to have visited the circle and united them all in whatever destiny they all had together in the future. He then became human and managed to set off a chain of events which resulted in the whole of the industrial and subsequently the technological era on Arimathea.

The dragons had lost their ability to dream the wisdom needed to regulate the evolution of all this because they had been separated from their dragon souls who were still embedded deep in the crystal caverns of Arimathea and everything had gone crazy. When they had finished there was a long silence as Grace allowed what she had been told, to find its way to a place in her mind where it could make some sense, any sense.

"So you think Mithrael, Zanda, this human dragon or whoever is lying here in my hospital had something to do with us all being there and then all being here so we can deal with whatever it is which is happening here now?

"It would appear so!" Mariella said almost apologetically.

"I think you should speak to Yaan he has done a lot of work into those times over in Eron and if that was where Mithrael originated and it was Yaan's initiation into the mysteries of their tribe he might remember something when he hears the story you've told me."

She extracts her phone from her pocket. She operates the screen and puts it up to her ear.

"Yeah Hi Yaan, how is it going out there?"

She puts the phone on speaker..

"It's Ok actually, we have the stage running again and one of the acts is just about to start. Everybody seems a little nervous but I think it will be all right."

"I'm very glad to hear it. Look Yaan I've got Okino here in the lounge. I'm trying to get to the bottom of what is happening here. Something has come up you might be able to help us with. I wonder if you could come over for a few minutes."

"I would be very glad to. I've been wanting to meet him and I'm sure there is stuff we need to talk about."

Grace and Mariella caught each other's eye as she put the phone down on the table. Grace began to speak to Mariella...

"I had a strange feeling we had met before when I met you last night in the street. I mean we could have seen each other by chance in Straam in a restaurant or anywhere and Okino I definitely remember from the Broadcast...but this is completely amazing I have to say."

Okino smiled over at her.

"I did say we've been on a bit of a ride."

Mariella observed..

"...and it is unresolved to an extent because Mithrael is lying unconscious over there perhaps somewhere between dragon and human and we are going to need to know how to get him back."

Grace had quickly come to accept the situation and added.

"Surely Merilon will know what to do."

"Mithrael needs to be returned into Arimathea to join again with his dragon soul of that I am certain. But it's how we can make it all happen. Merilon was asleep when all this was happening and I'm sure Yaan was the only person amongst us who had actual contact with Mithrael back then. There may be some detail he can remember to bring Mithrael back to consciousness so he can find his own way back."

A few moments later Yaan rushed into the tent and walked up to the table where they were all sitting. Okino rose to greet him,

"I am honoured to meet you, Yaan. I have gathered you are an ancient spirit who has been here on many occasions."

"...and I am honoured to meet you, my friend. I literally had been in a ceremony way back in the mists of time, an initiation where I had met you and Mariella and I came home to see you broadcasting from the ocean with the whales and dolphins. It was quite incredible!.

"Aah, so you remember me and Mariella. Do you remember Harri and Grace and what about the Lost Indians. They were all there."

"I didn't recognise them actually but as you probably know the initiation blew me away. Grace had rung me the day before and I had a strange feeling our destinies were tied into together when she asked me to come and help with all this. I remember you two as clear as it was yesterday!"

"Did you see Mithrael and did you recognise him. He is the key to all of this and I think you may have met him way back when you and your Shaman friends were initiating the building of the stone circle network."

Grace accessed her link to the closed circuit camera in the hospital and a picture of Mithrael flashed up on her phone. She showed it to Yaan. Okino watched the deep concentration on Yaan's face as he delved down into the memories of his journeys in the dragon's dimension where he had re visited the time when all this had been initiated. He saw the light come on in his mind as the string of thoughts and memories down through the years gradually started to link up to take Yaan down the path to where he had sat with the incarnated dragon who had been so enthusiastic about building the stone circle network.

"He was desperately afraid of what was happening in his land as the foreign invaders battled and fought his people. He knew Eron was a small island and her ancient forests were unique and held a deep connection to the spirit world in which he himself had dwelt. It was through the Ancient trees he had built such a strong bond with the Shaman peoples.

But the urgency he felt about the destruction of the forests and the loss of the old sites was not felt amongst the people. They saw only the vast effort and the huge resources needed for such an undertaking and they had been reluctant to get it all started for something that might happen in the distant future. After all the forests around them were vast and mostly impregnable.

He was so sure of what he had foreseen, he decided he would oversee himself the strategy of building as many circles within the sacred groves as possible. In the next years he set about the project which had become so important to him. He travelled the length and breadth of his land explaining all he had feared to his people. He told them this would all happen over long periods so they had plenty of time. But they needed to set up some legacy in their tribe or area to build the stone rings within the groves over the next generations or the magic they knew to be contained there would be lost forever. The people knew he was their dragon and listened carefully to him. In every village he visited he performed one of their ritual ceremonies in which the whole tribe was able to see the stone circles complete. Then they couldn't wait to start building.

Some say he did make those circles and the actual physicality was like those great stones being sucked into where he had placed them in those ceremonies. In this way he started it all. The tribes even became competitive amongst each other and the stones became larger and larger as the program continued down through the years. Vast stones were dragged across the land, floated up the rivers. The stones themselves were often said to hold magical properties with the ability to heal and transform the communities who built them.

But the raids continued down through the years. The invaders came more frequently and with greater ferocity as their own lands became unable to support their numbers. Eron was warm and damp and wherever they went they could grow their own food and they started to establish their settlements. They became merciless, killing everything in their path whereas before they had found some land and settled peacefully. Mithrael had fallen in Love and married one of the women. She was killed in one of the raids along with an entire village. Everyone, the chieftain, all his sons and daughters and wives, and all the families slaughtered and hideously butchered."

Yaan had his head in his hands clearly in pain.

"I started all this because I thought we had lost something in our technological societies. I felt there was something missing from our experience of the world. I wanted to find out what it was. I did find what we have lost but in a sense it is still here and we can find our connection with our planet again. But what I found back there and what I know to be still prevalent amongst the human race is the brutality we are capable of to our fellow beings."

Then Okino saw his light come on again and he looked around the table as if all the terror and darkness had been obliterated in one single shining thought.

"Once the carnage had stopped a few of us returned to the village and found Mithrael amongst all the dead being devoured by the Wolves and Crows. We had to fight them to get the corpses away. I swear I have never seen a man so destroyed as that dragon. I thought then he might never recover. Many were the same. But he took it really badly. We burnt the remains and interred them in the old burial mound of their ancestors along with their personal stuff, the things they had made. Mithrael had taught them all they made and created connected them back into the Great Spirit and the magic of their world because they had used them to enhance and continue their lives in ways they thought had become ordinary, but were really deeply magical as well. Mithrael had made, Singing Moon was her name, a Golden Eagle and he had found it with her body and he buried it in the mound with all the rest of their belongings.

A few thousand or so years later, as you know, it became fashionable amongst gentlemen archaeologists in the name of research into these ancient peoples to plunder these tombs and the contents were brought back into the world. The tomb where the remains of Mithrael's village had been buried was discovered by a particularly prolific robber. Most of these people had nothing to do with archaeology and were simply treasure hunters. Many of the tombs had only ornate clay pots and some rusty arrow heads and jewellery, rotted through their time in the ground.

They were looking for the special graves where the powerful and wealthy kings had been interred with all their most valuable objects. So when he found this tomb it was extremely rare to find such riches contained within it. But when he discovered this grave for some reason he decided he would not sell and cash in on his find. He hid all the stuff he found in a place where it would never be found. In another strange string of events I was taken to the place and I was shown it by one of the dragons. The Golden Eagle was in the collection. Alamistra noticed my interest and explained how Mithrael must have buried it with Singing Moon for her journey back into the Great Spirit."

Okino was beaming over at Yaan.

"Mithrael showed me the slaughter and I found him myself in the days before you arrived. I agree he was devastated. But he was holding the eagle. I am absolutely certain of it."

They were all quiet for a few moments. But it seemed the same thought arose in their minds at the same time. They looked around at each other wondering and hardly daring to ask...

"So where is the eagle now, Yaan." Grace asked nervously.

"Alamistra saw my interest and it may have been the reason she brought me there because she knew of my connection with Mithrael."

He looked around grinning at the anxious faces.

"She said I should take the eagle. So I did and I had a feeling it was important in all of this so I have brought it with me. It is back in my pod."

So the golden eagle Mithrael had made for Singing Moon was placed beside his bed; Amongst the computerised complexity of the bleeping machinery monitoring his weakened life force. It glowed there in the artificial light hovering in its flight across the ages reunited again with its' supernatural creator.

Chapter 78
Healer.

As the sword penetrated the heart of the Dragon all had become quiet. The storm had dissipated and rumbled off over the horizon back into the depths of the dimension from where it had originated. In a complex infinite Universe, the destruction of a world may never be fully understood however straightforward it may seem. Whatever immediate threats there had been to the continuation of Arimathea they had for the moment retreated and their origin may never be fully known. Only if the circumstances arose again and whatever consequences had been imagined came to fruition, would anyone know what had been avoided.

For now, this part of Mithrael's journey was almost over. Whether he had been entirely self-motivated by the circumstances which he had found on Arimathea or by those darker powers who now were retreating back to where he had found them, would be open to conjecture and debated by the dragons in the millennia to come. He would argue perhaps when they talked about fate and destiny, that he had let go of both of these constructs.

He had allowed himself mostly to be free of his dragonhood, the creator spirit who could dream worlds and who would always have the ability and so the temptation to manipulate some circumstance, perhaps only small but perhaps magnificent to change a path for his convenience and the dream he had initiated. He had allowed himself to become subject to the changing winds of fortune in the lives he had led amongst the tens of billions being lived out on Arimathea at any one time. He had met with all the wonder and the terror, the fear and sheer exhilaration, the heartbreak and the pain inevitably left by living such a life. He had met with successes and failures, with the love and the joy such times will bring and how those two forces must live together creating the energy for the magic and the mystery to find its way into the world. Mostly he had let go of his dragon knowledge so he could understand how the evolution of a world could only happen in this way. Ultimately he had used the powers of transformation which came so naturally to him, dragon or human. So, the course of the world had been changed and nothing would ever be the same again. Such is the perilous nature of dragon power as it flows on through the eons of time and space.

Now Merilon had said the words he himself had sent forward and it was time for him to return. But not before all he had experienced was assimilated back from the human into the dragon who he had to become again. But there would be no drifting lost through the labyrinths for him. The dragons were in the centre of the dream now and Alamistra had known when she spoke to him his nightmare was soon to be over. They had regained their stability. Their bond with Arimathea was complete and now they must concentrate on healing the damage Mithrael had sustained in his struggle as the humans had established themselves so independently on Arimathea.

It was considered too dangerous for Mithrael and the dimensions in which he was now existing to be subjected to any further conflict. To further encourage the forces which had concentrated and eventually taken advantage of his duality would be catastrophic. They would bring him back gently. They all would benefit from the powerful experience he had had as it was disseminated through the dream and after all, the dragons would need all the insight they could find if they were to overcome the entrenched forces of Oblivion still festering in the human structures as they attempted to secure Arimathea's progression into the future.

Mithrael woke where Okino and Merilon had driven the sword through his heart. He had collapsed amongst the rubble of the castle. He had immediately changed into the body of his original form. The stone dragon had laid in the jungle for over a hundred turnings in the dragon's dimension. A tall circle of trees had grown around the clearing formed by the expansive creature laying out across the jungle floor. The dragon was covered in vegetation and his wings and tail had become buried under the humus of the jungle floor.

Enough remained visible however, for the presence of the stone dragon to become well known to animal and human populations of the jungle and so was often visited.

The most nourishing and succulent fruit was always found in the surrounding trees. The appearance of the dragon to the local population of Indians living in the surrounding forest was something of a miracle and they regularly came to perform their rituals and ask for a blessing from the supernatural creature that had mysteriously arrived amongst the trees. The sword had remained firmly embedded in the dragon despite many efforts of the Indians to remove it. Mithrael had not experienced the passing of this time. He had simply slept in a dreamless sleep as the culminating horror and confusion of his lives as a human was slowly absorbed by the trees growing around him and then dissipated into the atmosphere as they naturally processed the nutrients and air around them. Slowly as he slept, he was able to return to his dragon spirit.

Then one morning he became aware, somewhere in the distance, he was in his stone dragon form laying in the jungle covered by the creepers as the scent of their flowers started to ignite his sleepy senses. He became aware of small agile creatures scampering playfully up and over his vast torso. As he became more aware in a more direct sense of everything around him, he realised there was a larger creature nearby. It was a female leopard and the creatures scampering over his body were her offspring. Immediately a memory was sparked. But the connection was lost as he was able to catch sight of the three small leopards careering and tumbling over each other in their playful battle. He knew he was smiling and he knew he was feeling their joy as he was able to watch these beautiful creatures and their mother vigilantly dozing, laid out across one of his wings.

He felt only the purity of his situation, laying in the jungle amongst the trees. Nothing more than pure consciousness floating in light and joy and amusement for the antics of the young leopards and the movement of the Star across the glade. Then suddenly without warning the leopards left and their youthful growls were replaced by the movement and conversation of human beings as they came into the clearing. They were the indigenous Indians adorned with little other than feathers and ornate tattoos over their arms, chests and faces. He was aware they were standing on the edge of the clearing looking down at him. A young man started to talk to the elder tribesmen.

"The leopards were in the dream, the three young ones and their mother laying across the wing. I was compelled to go over and pull the sword out of the dragon. It filled with green light and the whole dragon came back to life before me, it was wonderful, he looked at me as if he knew who I was. He had a universe, some eternity floating in there then he roared and flew off over the Jungle and I woke up."

"Well what are you waiting for? Go over and pull the sword out of the dragon."

The young man had expected slightly more excitement from his elders. Perhaps they were slightly annoyed, perhaps understandably, he had been sent the dream they had all been waiting for. He had been chosen to pull the sword out of the dragon. But hadn't he sat here all through his life amongst the trees wondering about the fate of the dragon before him. It had become a holy and sacred place for his tribe but it was he who had really absorbed this strange mystery and now he would become part of the mystery and its continuation. He walked gingerly over to the dragon and the sword, gleaming as it had when Mithrael had cast it all those turnings before with the strange symbols he did not understand cast into the blade. He stood before the sword and looked up into the sky through the trees, felt the Star shine on his face put his hands over the handle and gently pulled out the sword.

Mithrael felt the sword leaving his body. The light and the birdsong in the clearing gathered in intensity as he evaporated into. He watched the face of the boy holding the sword expectantly watching and waiting for whatever happened next in his dream. He saw the smiling faces of the elders and remembered thinking they had also had a dream as he drifted back into the light.

Then there were memories as he slipped back down through the years. Singing Moon walking down on the beach, waves lapping round her feet. Walking through a newly constructed town in Zinederland. The Shaman scientists and how he knew they were dying. Sailing across an Ocean in full sail on a tea clipper. Exploding shells, flashing swords and at the head of a hoard of blood thirsty warriors waiting to ambush an unsuspecting enemy. Wanting to kill them and eviscerate them. Hammering away at the forge in the woods. Sitting around fires with a workforce in the evening discussing the building of the vast circular stone henge they would build at the centre of the network. Walking the hills and watching Star rises and Star sets with Singing Moon and her happiness when he gave her the Golden Eagle. He felt his sadness again and the terror of the day she was killed. However now it seemed he had come to terms with this his worst nightmare which had so haunted him. He felt the trace of the gentle healing light flowing through him.

Images and more images everything he had retained and from which now he felt strangely detached. Meeting Harri and all that had transpired in their friendship and how his hatred of the human race had been reinforced at the bottom of the shell hole as he realised the horror they had brought to Arimathea was growing. The young monk in the wood had seemed to know nothing but Merilon had been there…all the beautiful and all the ugly. Still raw as if it had all been the day before and now all the feelings associated with them. Seeing Harri on his yacht firing two machine guns out over the ocean, grinning with a huge cigar in his mouth and laughing as he had not laughed in two hundred years of life. There had been girls, beautiful girls who he thought might take her place, but he had grown so much and he had known they just wanted his money and the banquets and all the distractions the money he had could buy.

Then there had been the Sacred sites where he had felt strange connections coming up through the ground and how he had wanted to dive down into it. Harri had found him one morning asleep in the sarcophagus of an ancient pyramid in the desert. Had he really spoken to the king of all the known world about why he had had the monument built and about the alien gods who had helped him build it? There really had been alien gods! They had known so much and the human race were little more than slightly advanced monkeys to them and so they had sent one of their own in disguise, so that one day they might come up to their level of understanding; gave them advanced philosophies about the nature of life and the universe. But the useless power grabbing human monkeys had just used it to exert even more power over their misfortunate populations and to legitimise even more war and mass control and mercilessly exploit them. Told them what to feel, what to do, and how to spend their money, live their lives to keep favour with the jealous god they invented to replace the kind envoy who had been sent.

So much confusion as they were manipulated misled and abused like pigs or sheep. Still all so raw every detail…but then there had been the farm and the windmills and he had been married. Despite all this he had been happy and for a while there had been no war. How they had hoped it would last and maybe this golden time could go on forever. All they had to worry about was the weather. But anything would grow on this land and their boys grew up strong and were soon chasing the girls and racing horses across the fields and the girls always wanted the wildest boys.

Then the rich boys would come and beg him to make them one of his swords and their strong wilful girls would want them and to go off with them to their castles and sometimes they did. Then there would be a child and their hearts would be broken because their fathers, the lords, had already arranged for them to marry the daughters of rich merchants to pay for the upkeep of their castles and the land so they could hold their power over people like them.

So much injustice, so much prejudice, so much bitterness festering between these people making their spirits heavy and intractable so nothing could satisfy except revenge. Chewing on a stalk of ripened corn in the fields leaning against sacks of grain, watching friends and family bundling up the last of the straw and loading the last of the wagons. Singing and dancing when it was all done. The windmills turning and turning in the breeze, grinding the grain into the bread he would eat tomorrow at the harvest festival with sweet honey from his beehives. The little bees buzzing across the world always tirelessly working to make their golden food.

Then he was waking again. A voice in the distance…

"Rael…Rael Smith it is time for you to wake. You'll need to have some breakfast before you go to the market. Jeremiah will be here any minute and here you are still sleeping like a teenager."

Mithrael started awake. He knew exactly where he was. In the bedroom of the old farmhouse where for a time he had been happy again. He remembered making the arrangement with Jeremiah. They both had lambs to take to the market. It would be a good day. There would be Ale and he would buy his wife a shawl with the money he made from selling the lambs. He got out of bed, the stiffness in his limbs lasting slightly longer in the mornings. Breakfast laid out for him all his family around him, kids all squabbling and arguing and his wife trying to quiet them down. But he just smiled today. Somehow it all felt different like the first warm breezes of the spring blowing the winter away. He wiped the remainder of the egg from his plate with the fresh bread made from the mill and tucked it into his mouth. He couldn't remember anything ever tasting so delicious. Three loud knocks on the door he got up and lifted the latch and pulled open the heavy oak door and let Jeremiah in. They were pleased to see each other. He pulled on his coat.

"See you at the market later my lover, I have a surprise for you."

He kisses her. He savours her warmth and her light.

"…and you lot behave yourselves or there'll be trouble mark my words!"

He grinned over at them and the familiar chorus.

"Yes, dad."

Walking down the lane with Jeremiah, all the lambs ahead of them together in the arrangement they had come to. They were fat and healthy and as always, he would be sad to see them go but they would all be back the next year. Strange that, the same characters year after year. It had always made them laugh.

"I been worried about you, Rael."

"Why's that then, Jeremiah."

"You been seeming distant as if you are far away. I know you're working hard and that with the mills going and keeping the farm paying… I'm still thinking about cutting the old wood down."

"Don't do it Jeremiah. You would never forgive yourself. I can help you out with your roof. We'll get up there and fix the bastard thing…two fine men such as us."

"That's good of you mate, but as I say I'm worried about you today. You don't get five minutes to yerself. Look, why don't I take the lambs in and you can walk up the hill to the old mound. Look at the fields all golden and ripe, those that haven't been cut yet. Everything's fine, just go up there. My old dad always said

"you gotta look after yer soul son. That's where you keep everything, all your memories, where it's all processed, where you make sense of it all. If you lose contact with your soul, son,…"

He'd say,

"You can't make no sense of nothing."

Reckon he was right. He'd say,

"Yer soul, it's connected into the soul of the world and it's in the golden light, especially across these fields when their ripe and ready for cutting."

It's the time, see, when it all comes together, all the work we put in, the weather we watch, the seeds we plant, all the agony we go through with those old ploughs and the work we put those horses through. It's what it's all about Rael, putting the food on the table, letting those kids grow up fit and arguing like. You know it, I know you know it but you gotta know it in your soul, mix it up with the golden light, the old man used to say, goes in good and solid like that so you can feel it glowing there inside of you. Then you don't forget it till next year."

"He was great your old dad and of course he was right."

He stretched into the sky.

"I'm going to take you up on your offer, Jeremiah. I haven't been up to the old mound for ages. And you're right it is a beautiful morning."

Walking up the hill along the old tracks. The star high now but lower over the ridge of the hill. The old mound silhouetted there. Some old warrior king, it was said, buried up there and perhaps his whole tribe over the generations installed in amongst the badger warrens and the fox dens. The breeze rippling the golden corn and yes such a holy feeling. Golden Star light on the golden life-giving corn. Growing out of the world, perhaps if Jeremiah's dad was right growing straight out of her soul, her life manifest again, they had managed to coax out of the ground with the magic she had taught them. No wonder it tasted so good with the eggs from his chickens and the honey from his bees, washed down with the milk from his cows. Here they were in tune with their world and all the joy she offered them. Still a goddess as far as he was concerned. He laughed. No male god would make bread taste as good as she could. He walked up onto the mound, paid his respects to the old warrior king and his wives and sons and daughters, careful to avoid the badger and the fox holes. Stood on the top and looked out over the land on which he had farmed all his life. He remembered what Jeremiahs dad had said
...

"You gotta know it in your soul and mix it all up with the golden light."

So he remembered carefully how it had all fitted together, the year before so he could get the harvest in and suddenly his life flashed before him, not just this life but also all the other shadows he knew were there but he had buried and dismissed for years now. But now they rose again, standing there in the early morning starlight, in the golden light, he felt the amazing wonder filling the life he had experienced as the light came from the mound deeper in the hill. He felt it come spiralling up through his feet. The light in his body and the golden Star light from the fields mixed together and for a few moments he felt the peace come over him, peace like he could not remember he had felt in his life like something had been missing but now he had become complete again. So he stood there remembering, laughing and crying and healing until it was time to continue on his journey.

Chapter 79

Ancestors.

Far away from the rest of the world, in the cooling autumn Star Shine Grace's festival, or the Festival of Grace was continuing despite the surprisingly eventful first day. The nature of the infinitely connected world wide web meant news of such dramatic events had inevitably leaked out through the communication devices most of the young people were carrying. But the news from the festival of the exploding PA and a tornado in the desert apparently appearing out of nowhere was barely acknowledged as it competed with the endless stream of absurdity and horror the owners of the appropriate technology were continually exposed to. However, for the thousands of people who had witnessed these events they had been anything but forgettable and they would be proudly narrated for many years to come.

They were relishing all the strange chaotic happenings they had witnessed. The stories and interpretations of these events raced around the site told by those who had first-hand knowledge and expanded by those who were relaying the stories they had heard. So the reality, extraordinary though it was, was being distorted in the telling in the light of the dreams and the expectations of all who had come to this festival.

The decision to come to any festival was often bound up with the need to escape mostly repetitive and entirely unstimulating lives in the service of the machine culture in which the majority of people now found themselves. If they felt the need to adopt a new persona they could. For a few days they could become somebody living an entirely different life to whatever degree they felt necessary to give them a break from the monotony and anxiety. There was a chance to meet new friends, even lovers, find new philosophies and share experiences, find the moments in the Starshine or in the pouring rain which could give some meaning to some part of their life. Many were making the transition from childhood to adulthood or suffering some life changing occurrence and had found themselves drifting on an uncertain sea and had come to find some wisdom to guide their lives into an endless and worrying future. Most had come for a brilliant and fabulous party where they could forget about what was happening in the disastrous world they appeared to have inherited from past generations.

But the Festival of Grace was different. The thousands of people who had come had wondered, whether, if the Human race decided to put their heads together the problems facing their world could be solved. At least they were curious to find out what the people who Grace had invited thought could be done even though they themselves were pessimistic. If Grace had carried out a survey this would probably have been the position most people would have admitted to. They assumed the problems on the planet were so severe and intractable there was very little anyone could really do to stop a catastrophe in the future.

Many who had heard Mithrael's drunken outburst before he had disappeared into the depths of the tornado, although angry he had assumed they were part of the oil guzzling consumer society he had so berated, were sympathetic to his view and now were concerned about his apparent disappearance into the hospital. However, in his strange metamorphosis from drunken drug dealer into a light filled elemental creature who appeared to have summoned the tornado, quite literally, a new dimension had been added to their expectations for the next few days. Added to the dreams they had all experienced and the emergence of the dragon in the smoke from the exploded PA, a powerful supernatural aspect to the proceedings appeared to be developing.

In their wildest imaginings they had suspected this would be the only way Arimathea could be saved from the greedy Human race and now they were pleased to have a front row seat for whatever was about to be unravelled before them out here in the desert. So, in the Starshine and separation they now increasingly felt amongst the whirl of stories and rumours, the journeys of the festival goers continued surrounded by the music and the possibilities they found and absorbed. As this feeling of separation from their world increased a new sense of freedom began to emerge and many of the boundaries with which they had been surrounded or surrounded themselves had started to fall away.

Elisa had struck up a conversation with Brett when he had offered her the Sunshine pills. She had recognised him as one of Zanda's crew. She had been watching the balloons take off and seen the arrival of the bus. She said she thought he looked too thin and said she would take him to one of the cafes and buy him some breakfast. In return she would have him tell her his story. Brett had grinned and said if she bought some pills then they wouldn't be worrying about the breakfast. Elisa laughed but most definitely did not want the pills and she would tell him why after he had told her his story.

She wanted to know who Zanda was and how he had become so entangled with him. Brett looked at her carefully now. She had seen him; through the unkempt appearance of his street life, his uncut hair and beard, the grime and the disarray into which he had fallen. She had looked past all that, straight down into where he had shut himself away and it had made him shiver. She was well dressed in the ragged way the kids were when they came to these festivals. But she was no kid and probably had a normal life living in a house, with a good job. Years ago, she might have arrived in his office to make some deal or to tell him the progress on one of his sites. She had deep soft brown eyes and he knew he could or would fall for her if he had not already. He knew where all that could take him and he felt the full bag of Sunshine in his pocket, little of which he had sold. He had no resolve, no resistance anymore to the tides of fortune on which he had been carried all these years. Now, perhaps, it seemed they had carried him to his own paradise island. So he went along with her to the café.

Elisa had been surprised to find how easily she had been able to connect with Brett. Although she would never shy away from conversation with any of the interesting characters by whom she was surrounded. Brett from his outward appearance and at first sight might seem a dangerous person to give any kind of idea she wanted to get to know him. But she had looked up into his eyes as they pleadingly tried to sell her the pills and had strangely been able to see through the grim exterior shell holding him together and into the lost soul hiding inside. They swapped names as they started to walk off towards the café street and she chattered on and he appeared to be listening politely probably she thought, as he contemplated the free meal he was about to be treated to.

But there was something more going on. She began to feel even more intensely the soul of the person walking beside her. Almost as if the shining being who inhabited this grimy unfortunate shell was now walking beside her. If she had believed in angels, she might have said she could see his wings and a golden shining man, self-assured and confident but now subdued and down beaten by all that had happened to him. She was silent for a moment and looked away at all the other boys and girls, men and women surrounding her. Perhaps there was a lighter and brighter aura around them. But it was definitely not something she was actually seeing. She may have said it was her imagination but then it was more than something she was creating for herself almost as if there was an underlying layer, she now had the ability to see. She looked back at Brett and from this underlying layer there seemed to be an angelic soul standing before her. She remembered her dream from the night before where she had gone back to where she had started her life. Where there had been just light and love and potential. Was she now able to see this original potential, this light in the ragged and what appeared to be the disastrous human being she was now walking beside?

They were walking past the showers. Grace had decided if she was to have a festival out in the desert there would have to be clean cool water and a never-ending supply of it for everybody to shower whenever they felt like it. She had worked from this idea and eventually had the shower block engineered to her exact specification. She had had vast water tanks constructed the size of several large swimming pools. The reservoir was cleverly and fully insulated so it could not warm up. It had strategically placed heat pumps cooling and filtering the water so when it was demanded by the showers below a deluge of clean cool water cascaded over the festival goer beneath who was standing on a carefully tiled and drained floor. The water then was completely recycled back into the reservoirs. In this process none of the water which had been brought across the desert in a long convoy of tankers would be wasted. This was showering on an industrial scale and it had soon caught on and was proving extremely popular in the relative heat of the desert.

Already however the areas dividing the boys and the girls were rapidly being disregarded as many of the taboos which governed the world from which they had come and now were becoming increasingly separated, started to fall away. So, as Brett and Elisa walked past the impressive shower block it became obvious both sexes were showering together. They heard screams of delight and hilarity and watched as discarded, soaking clothes came flying out from behind the screens pursued by screeching, naked male and female revellers. The scene was proving infectious to everybody walking past and other people were tearing their clothes off and diving with more ecstatic screeching into wherever there was space into what amounted to a good-sized waterfall out in the centre of the desert.

Elisa looked up at Brett and he looked down at her. She gently started to remove the battered leather jacket in which he was buried.

"Now come on Brett you must be so hot in this old leather jacket!"

"No, no I'm fine in it, just fine in fact just the right temperature."

"No, you're not, you are far too hot and if you are going to come and have breakfast with me, we're going to have to get you cleaned up."

She started more forcefully to remove his jacket. So, he thought, it really was his lucky day. She grinned up at him into the hypnotic light she was watching shining out from his eyes. She screeched in delight as he bundled her easily up over his shoulder, carried her into the stream of falling water cascading from the shower heads above. He put her down and they stood under the cascading water. Relishing it streaming over their faces and through their hair and soon there was nothing else to do but to remove their soaking clothes and stand in the bliss of the water falling over them with the slithers of early morning Starlight forcing their way under the great tanks above. They looked shyly around at each other and everybody else enjoying the sensation of being in this primal state with their fellow beings; A state in which in the lives they had left behind would have been entirely unacceptable. But here now with all they had experienced it was just beautiful and natural, cleansing and freeing and they all became closer. Elisa saw a man who had shaved and was starting to leave.

"Could I borrow your razor and soap."

He looked at Brett and smiled.

"Of course, you can!"

Elisa turned to Brett.

"Brett, would you mind if I shaved off your beard? I want to see what you look like without it."

Brett laughed. To have a beard had not been a conscious decision. He cut it as best he could when he had scissors and a mirror at his disposal but there was no attachment. It was just part of who he had become as his life had started to disintegrate.

"Yeah shave it off but be gentle it's been some time."

Elisa glanced quickly down, turned her attention to making the foam in her hand as she sensed there may have been some other meaning to what he had said. Brett stood with his back in the shower as she rubbed the foam into his beard. She found the razor was sharp, perhaps recently sharpened and so she started to carefully shave off the thick dark hair from Brett's face. He grimaced at the first cuts and she lessened the angle of the blade across his face. Slowly she revealed his cheeks and down around his jaw, across the top of his mouth, over and underneath his chin, carefully cutting around the contours of his face, shaking off the beard and foam to the tiled floor below where it floated off into the drain around the shower.

Brett stood with his eyes closed in the slither of star shine still entering the showers. He now felt uncertain and vulnerable, having put his trust in Elisa to perform such an intimate and personal task for him. But he soon relaxed and relished the tenderness and care she was showing to him. All he had been through surfaced in his mind. All the physicality and the terror, the danger of being on the streets, the cold and the uncertainty of what the next day or night might bring and all the guilt that had tormented him started to fall away. As his beard was removed and he was transformed, so he felt this disastrous period of his life was also being transformed into a surreal nightmare dream which he was now waking from. Immediately he realised he would not have denied all he had been through and it would be an important part of who he now would become; whoever that may be. For now it was falling away and it had all been worthwhile so he could be standing here in the desert with all this cool refreshing water streaming over his body and Elisa showing him tenderness he had not experienced for a very long time and then he thought possibly ever.

Elisa watched him carefully as she revealed his face. She collected his long hair, twisted it temporarily together and put it over his shoulders. His light she had seen seemed stronger and had become increasingly so as she had shaved his face and showed him the care, she was aware had become so unfamiliar to him. She pushed him back under the mainstream of water and he felt over the smooth flesh of his face. She had done well and he turned and smiled down at her as she again enjoyed her shower.

"Thank you, Elisa. It means a lot to me"

"That's Ok, I am honoured and now I think we should go and find some breakfast."

They left the showers put on their soaking clothes and walked out into the star shine, down the street towards the café areas. Elisa was quiet for a while, uncertain what was happening to her. She hooked her arm through Brett's enjoying the sights and sounds of the festival and the people around her as the strange circumstances of the previous day started to fall away. Everything now seemed lighter and less troubled. Not just because of what had happened had been forgotten or put aside but generally it seemed as if some shadow had been lifted and a new lighter atmosphere was gradually establishing itself. They chose a café and soon were eating their way through a selection of the now famous pastries, freshly baked bread and strawberry jam which was mostly strawberries and drinking strong black mountain coffee. Elisa soon found her inquisitiveness overcoming her again and asked Brett tentatively and only if he wanted to tell her, what had happened to him.

Brett told her about all that had happened. About his building company and his family. He told her about the bankruptcy and the horse racing and how he had lost everything in what seemed a blink of an eye. He told her about how he had realised the illusion he had fallen under and how he felt as if he had become somehow special. He told her how he had seen the world as it really was as he watched his life fall apart and all the ones he had loved turn away from him. He told her about Zanda and how he had first met him sitting round a fire on a piece of waste ground listening to similar stories as his own.

"He listened like no one I had ever met before. Not just listened but he absorbed everything, all you said like he wanted to be in your place so he knew what to do if he found himself there. He offered a hand to all the people around the fire. He told us we shouldn't worry. We were alive on a beautiful planet and although we felt we had been thrown out of our society we were in fact the lucky ones because now we had seen how things really were. He never told us much about himself but always bought the Sunshine pills for us to sell which enabled us to buy the basics to survive. He said it would help the kids we sold them to, to get through the monotony of the prison that had been built for them and eventually a time would come when it would help them to find a way to live in their world without being slaves.

He would disappear and reappear. We never knew much about him but we were always pleased to see him return. He was one of those people you just felt safe with; like you were when you were with your mum and dad. He always raised our spirits and made us laugh with the other disaster stories he had heard in his travels. We assumed he was linked to a charity of some kind but the drugs didn't really equate with that. So we stopped wondering as we had about everything that was happening to us and just got along the best we could. That is really all I know. But now all this has happened."

Elisa was gazing thoughtfully over his shoulder trying to piece everything she now knew together.

"I met the monk you know, wandering back to the tents the other night. I was rambling on about how I had had this idea that pigeons were some sort of super race living amongst us after I had seen his broadcast from the ocean. I felt I had known both of them for ever."

"A monk you say and a girl? Perhaps the same couple who I met around a fire back in Straam one night. Said he had come on a cruise liner. He was with a good looking, dark haired girl. Kept to herself to start with but they came with us to the clubs and we all had a great night together. He was another one who just listened come to think about it. But she realised what had happened, cracked me right open."

"Sounds like it could be the same couple. Well it's all very interesting and now we are all here. I hear he is giving a speech tonight before the bands. Not to be missed me thinks."

They finished their coffee and wandered off into the festival. Within a few minutes they had come to one of the stages where a man was beginning to deliver his presentation. There were pictures of a family of smiling people from a southern Savannah sitting outside their simple Adobe and timber dwelling. Their children were waving at the camera.

"This is Mr and Mrs Enabao and their three children outside their house on the southern Arawana savannah."

The house disappears and a frozen scene with a family wrapped in furs are standing outside their house made of seal skins and whalebones grinning widely and filling the screen at the back of the stage.

Brett turns to Elisa..

"This guy is an architect. You can tell them a mile off. I'd like to stay and hear what he has to say."

"…and no prizes for guessing where the majority of you or anyone would prefer to live."

There was a ripple of laughter through the crowd.

"I work as an architect, but I have travelled through much of Arimathea and visited many of her varied cultures. I have found human beings wherever they come from are very much alike. We have needs on a basic level which are very simple. We like to feel secure and safe. We want to be sheltered from the vagaries of the weather, so we want to feel dry and warm. We are social creatures, so we like to be near other people and we like to move around. When these needs are met and even when they are not, we reproduce and thrive as a species.

We have met these basic needs in many ways all around our world. There are peoples who still live in the same way as they have lived for thousands of years in surroundings like this out here in the desert and yet in other parts of the world we live in our mega cities. The humans who are living in each of these places are satisfying these basic needs. Yet one culture has virtually no impact on the planets ecosystems and the other is putting them under severe stress. We know which is which. Most of you I should imagine live in a city or a town where there is electricity and water at the flick of a switch and the turn of a tap. I don't need to spell out to you the difference between what your family consumes and the family who lives in the desert, the difference between their culture and our culture.

From an architect's point of view humans are spatial beings. We stand up in the world and see the far horizon and we feel the space around us. We live in three physical dimensions which adhere to the physical parameters of our world and the Universe. Within this physicality there are geometric systems. They are running through us and all of the physical world we ultimately are a part of and respond to. We know when things feel right because we have evolved with all this around us. Our aesthetics, so bound into all we create are really governed by this geometry. But the aesthetics of the desert will be different from the aesthetics of the forest and of course we have responded to the influences of the environment in which we have found ourselves.

Most of you will be living in an environment where the creatures you have evolved into find few of the sights and sounds which fed and stimulated your ancestor's senses for millions of years. We have attempted to find ways of making up the shortfall with all the wasteful distractions we have invented for ourselves and adapted, perhaps not as well as we might think to these new environments.

But we have made these adaptations because of those basic needs we need to meet for our lives to go on. Everything comes from there, however advanced we may think we have become. We live in a complex world full of complex systems and we have evolved into a creature which can see them operating all around us. The more we understand the complexity the more we realise there probably is no end to it. But we have created our own complexity to deal with the problems that have arisen for us. We have looked at the world and seen how it works and created our systems to work alongside it.

So, with our houses we have worked towards safe, comfortable environments which protect us from adverse climatic conditions where we can store our food and eat and where we can have beneficial relationships with our families. The extent to which these have been developed will always rely on resources and the part of the world on which we find ourselves. But there is not one house serving the needs of humanity. In fact, no one person's house will ever be the same. Into each of our houses we will bring our own personal universe. Then they will become our homes. They become our personal spaces in which we feel comfortable and secure. They are informed by the fabric of our lives and what has become important for us. So, someone who lives in an icy frozen environment will have a different house from someone who lives on the plains of a savannah. Their houses will depend on what is in abundance for them to build the shelter that meets their needs.

Here in a society which has an economy everything becomes more complicated. Our expectations for satisfying those needs have been entirely overtaken by the abilities we have individually developed to meet them and the complex social issues which dictate the levels of aspiration we now have.

We want to stay healthy and feel well so we can enjoy our lives to the full. Again, resources will dictate the level of care any one person receives across Arimathea. We have built healthcare facilities and hospitals. They are now able to cater for virtually every known illness or condition we can fall at the mercy of. There will be operating theatres removing and replacing organs and limbs and wards where the sick and recovering can be looked after. These are places where the concentrated understanding we have come to acquire is used for our overall well-being.

Then other special disciplines require other types of building. Libraries where we store the sum of all our understanding, gymnasiums where we exercise to keep ourselves fit and healthy, law courts where the laws of our lands are put into practice and continually evolve, offices where we work, shops, retail centres, supermarkets where we buy our food. All brought into the world for a specific reason to satisfy a need and connected into the infrastructure of our city or the town where it has been built. Perhaps it has replaced an older building that no longer could satisfy its original purpose. Time moves us forward and now we are evolving the world around us.

Although we are the same creatures who wandered the southern plains the processes we are inventing are becoming more and more sophisticated. Our buildings are sleeker and use less energy. The functions we perform within them have demanded constant temperatures and humidity. The electronics of our computers and communications equipment demand dry atmospheres above all else. As we have become more sophisticated so have they and as the technology to build them has improved we have remembered the need to connect with our world and we make them so they let in more light and air and so are more conducive to our well-being.

Somewhere along this path, I think perhaps we did lose our way. After so many years of being at the mercy of our world and its environment perhaps we did want to shut the door on it. Like some petulant child who could finally live free of its parents. But I think, I hope, we have started to grow up now; at least contemplated what it would be like now we are starting to understand the consequences of our wild selfish behaviour. Now we cannot ignore what is happening to our world. Deep down the ancient wanderers stored in our DNA, who came so close to her cannot sit by and watch their relations in the distant future destroy their world.

Intuitively deep in our subconscious we will be responding to all the dimensions and energies they felt and responded to. Perhaps in some way they haunt the world we have made. In those hospitals where we care for our sick and our law courts where we dispense our justice, in our houses where we retreat to at the end of the day to feel safe and warm, and to our churches where we still feel we need to perform our rituals in the silence they occasionally demand. We have built them, all these structures in response to the constants running through our world. They will have felt these as strongly as we feel them today. Perhaps their response to them has remained instilled in us. Perhaps here is where we hold the magic of our universe without acknowledging it.

We have used the ingenuity they developed to operate this magic and thrive on this world and brought us to where we are able to continue our journey. Just look around at the beautiful tents Grace has brought here and the balloons floating like worlds within worlds. I like to think those ancient peoples are here, within all of us willing us, guiding us to where we need to be. They are our conscience and perhaps connect continually with us across time through our genes but perhaps also through those dimensions they may have known so well. Invisible now, more like shadowy suspicions or illusive apparitions for us, but still possessing those ancient spirits and all their wisdom working through all we do in a timeless dream beckoning us into the future. I often wonder when I am bringing another building into the world whether they are working through me from those other dimensions.

It was after all they who started us off on this journey of discovery. For whatever reason they travelled across Arimathea in search of food or safety and ended up travelling to the four corners of this planet. Now we have invented machines to placate this urge and we can travel to wherever we want to go in very little time. But I think this travel has become more about the destination than the journey. When we set out on a journey on which we don't necessarily know how all the component parts are going to fit together we allow the wonder of the unexpected to take over. As soon as we take a step into the unknown and the unplanned, a string of events begins to open up before us.

The people we meet and the conversations we have will give insight into other ways of life and enrich and inform our own immeasurably. We experience new sights and sounds and sensations on which we can feast and add depth to the people we are always becoming. While we are dealing with the unexpected ecstatic or disastrous, we are growing, allowing experience to enrich our ability to live. As we journey into the unknown, we can witness how the rich tapestry of space and time brings everything into being through improbability and chance and how it can take us into realms we simply would not have contemplated.

I am convinced when we were making the journeys through the early wildernesses of our world, adapting continually to circumstances presented to us we were sowing the seeds for all we have subsequently achieved. Every day I walk from one building to the next and between there is planet, so sky and ground which is mostly concrete and tarmac, so I try to walk on the grass when I can and there are trees and birds in the trees and nothing is ever the same. We are not separate from the world of sky and earth, sea, wind and rain and as a designer of buildings I try to make them as transparent and as responsive to the characteristics and atmospheres surrounding them as well as including all the other specifications demanded of this new world I am creating.

We belong to this world Arimathea; we are an integral and important part of her; to integrate acknowledgment of her beauty and her fragility into everything we make and do should be right at the top of our list of what makes a building or anything successful. A significant part of this new adulthood should be nurturing a deeper awareness of the natural processes going on around us. We breath air and watch clouds rolling across the sky unaware or uncaring of how we are filling them with the gases causing so much harm. If suddenly those gases became black and caused us nausea then pretty soon they would be banned. But the companies who are selling us the fuel have made them invisible and the slow choking of our world goes on.

Without awareness you will not notice there are fewer birds arriving back from their migrations or the seasons are getting longer or shorter and the rainfall patterns have been disrupted. You won't notice the foliage of the trees are looking thinner each year or they are losing their leaves not because of the onset of autumn but because some bug from a land on the other side of the planet has found this new climatic condition suits its life cycle and there is a ready food supply in one particular species of tree.

This is the awareness we need to have. If we see the struggles she is having, as we would with anyone we love, we will start to have Empathy for her and start to understand what is happening. We have relinquished so much responsibility to the people in charge, the governments the corporations and the investment banks who decide what will happen in our world. To be fair over time they have taken control; told us what we must and must not do.

But now in this situation at last they are powerless without us. We need to start getting used to acting without them. They will not tell us to stop driving our cars or flying away on our holidays. They won't tell us to stop eating so many animals because their system, this system, our system in which we all live depends on all of those activities continuing. If politicians started telling us not to do these things, they know we wouldn't vote for them. They depend on the system as it is, as always, to enforce the power that protects the minority who care only for their own wealth.

Now we understand this, how the ruthless amongst us have always manipulated our world, we need to act on our own, every single one of us, become a citizen of Arimathea again, not be a slave to the system that is destroying her. We need to set out on our own journey again. We could all gradually move towards living more simply, nearer to those basic needs. I think this silent, bloodless revolution would take a few generations but gradually the system destroying our world would change. The demand for fuel and commodities would start to lessen as different parts of our lives became important.

The first and most obvious result of course would be that suddenly we would wake up to the senseless devastation happening across Arimathea. The remaining forests and all our natural habitats and the creatures in them would suddenly become valued above all else and the preservation and conservation of them and Arimathea would become paramount to all the governments of the world as we found ways of leading our lives without the necessity for their continual destruction.

These of course are my dreams and thoughts. But as I see it, it is the only sensible way we can start to live on this world without choking it to death with pollution and our discarded rubbish. Architects will give you what you want which is what they say about politicians. If you decide to come to me and tell me you want a house which causes no pollution, even your own house, I will tell you how you can do it. It may involve more woolly jumpers and blankets in the winter even when your house is fully insulated but it can be done. Life on Arimathea has always been about the preservation of energy. We have always had to make a continual assessment about how we get it and how we use it to stay alive. It will be for each and every one of us to start thinking more carefully about that equation as we consider how we want our world to be in the future.

We have always made decisions about how we wanted our lives to be. It is why we are in the mess we are now in. We have dreamed and calculated and planned and then we have made our dreams come true with little thought for our world. Now there must be one collective over riding dream to find ways for us all to live much simpler lives. Then perhaps life on

Arimathea will continue so generations in the future can be proud of what we decided to do."

There was a huge and extended round of applause for the architect as he walked off the stage and again people started to drift off to the next venue or settled down to wait for the next speaker or act. Elisa and Brett drifted towards the sound of someone singing with a guitar somewhere out in the smaller performance areas. Elisa was sifting through her mind what the Architect had said about dimensions and the how he thought we were possibly being guided by the ancient peoples.

She looked through the crowds out towards the mountains in the distance. She had noticed they were never the same. As the angle of the Star adjusted or the conditions in the atmosphere changed so the light was refracted over to the back of her retina in a different way. She led Brett out towards the edge of the crowds where they had an unobstructed view. There they were able to see the surface of the desert stretching to the foot of the mountains. It shimmered in the rising heat of the morning. Lines had become blurred and the whole scene had lost its clarity. The purple mountains rose as if over a strange transparent sea lapping over the shores of the desert and washing into the lower slopes of the hills in the distance. Out here she felt they could have been cut adrift from the rest of the world to evolve in a new time disconnected from the influences of the craziness carrying on there; just for a few days to develop some new thread which could feed into the polluted matrix and spread it's purity through its infected systems.

As she watched the undulations caused by the phenomena of rising heat and intense light, Elisa knew the intense pressure of heat and light on her brain had the potential to cause her to see mirages, so infamous for drawing the disorientated traveller farther away from the path and deeper into the featureless desert in search of water or company or both. She searched deeper into the shimmering light watching the waves rising and falling trying to identify the intense intuition she had had as the architect had said about being guided by the ancient peoples.

Then there they were. Walking through the desert shimmering in the heat but fully distinguishable in a procession with their children, laughing and chasing on the edges. The elders in their ceremonial attire and their head dresses and the warriors with their spears and weapons. The women in their carefully woven dresses and their long hair combed and shining in the light. Perhaps many generations moving transparently from another era or many only in the wavering light, heading out into the desert. They were following a continuation of the line they had all walked, out from the town the night before. As if they had not yet arrived and there was still a way to go to get to the true destination. She turned to Brett who had started talking to the couple standing next to them.

"Brett look, over there, can you see them in the haze walking out into the desert?"

Brett looked but he could not see anything. He looked over to Eliza smiling.

"Perhaps we should go and find you some shade and some water!"

She looked back, expecting to see them gone. But there they were. Silently moving in all their splendour and reverence on a path they had followed for perhaps thousands of years before their culture had been evaporated into, or by the craziness. Here they were, their trace now somehow ingrained in the memory of the desert. For perhaps only her to see. But that was enough. She had seen them, was seeing them and not because she had star stroke or she hadn't eaten or was hallucinating but because they were there and it suddenly seemed important she told someone; like Yaan Fair-weather or Zanda lying in the hospital. Yes, he must know. For some reason he would know whether it was important and what to do.

She started off towards the hospital. Brett followed her across the site puzzled by her strange behaviour. They reached the hospital doors and Elisa pushed her way in and walked up to the receptionist closely followed by Brett.

"I wonder if I could see Zanda, the big guy who is in here."

"…and you are?" The receptionist asked.

"Well..I'm…I just need to see him. I think it's about his coma or whatever state he is in."

Brett took over.

"He's my friend. I came with him. There was a group of us and we are all very concerned about how he is."

"Just wait a few moments."

The receptionist rang Grace who said she was near and would come over immediately. Elisa and Brett waited tensely in the hospital waiting area before Grace arrived with Yaan who she had asked to be there. Grace smiled calmly and reassuringly at the two young people.

"So you want to see Zanda and you came with his crew on the bus."

"I did but Elisa here said she needed to see him."

"I'm Elisa and this is Brett. This may seem strange but I've seen spirits walking out across the desert. A whole tribe, perhaps more than one. I thought I was hallucinating but I looked back and they were still there. They looked as if they were on some sort of ceremonial procession. I thought of you Mr. Fairweather and Zanda. I think they are something to do with him. I don't really know why."

"There were tribes here many years ago..."

Yaan was intrigued by what Elisa was telling him.

"There are remains and the circle up in the mountains. It was almost certainly a sacred site. It is why Grace chose this location for the festival. She had an idea of making a continuation with an indigenous culture, close to a stream of knowledge we all need to remember. If, you have seen them and I fully believe you have then it is justification for her suspicion. I just wonder where they were or are going. Most signs of settlement were around this area."

Grace smiled and touched Elisa's arm.

"To be honest we are all a little in the dark about what is going on with Zanda. But I think as Brett is in his party, I think you can both see him in the circumstances. He is still unconscious, but he should have awakened by now, so who knows. He is through there."

Elisa and Brett push their way through the swinging doors into the room where Zanda was lying. Elisa walked up to the side of the bed. She looked down to where the enormous man was lying. She saw the Golden Eagle sitting on the cupboard next to him and carefully picked it up. A flash of light goes through her mind. A stony beach and a stream, a woodland and she was up in the trees. The eagle was there and this man lying here. She tried to remember more but the dream came only fleetingly. Then Zanda stirred as if his life force had come back to him. He raised his hand and his eyes opened very slightly and he turned his head towards Elisa and softly asks.

"Singing Moon is that really you?"

Chapter Eighty.
Spirits.

Outside the hospital the Spirit tribes processing out into the desert were being seen by more and more people. They turned away from the stages and the performances and the discussions they were having to catch a glimpse of the extraordinary phenomena unravelling before them. If at first they could not see them they were encouraged to look deeper into the haze formed by the heat rising from the desert. Then gradually the spirit Indians came into view. The crowds of people young and old, stood aghast at what they appeared to be seeing. The Indian procession seemed to be walking out of thin air at one point in the heat haze, bringing the circumstances of the last few hours into focus. Many of them had had similar experiences to Elisa during the morning as the influence of the invisible conditioning their machine culture had brought upon their minds had started to fall away.

They had begun to feel the shining pure spirit they had found deep in their dream and started to see those spirits shining through from everyone around them. Now they could see the spirits of the Indians. Clearly whatever process was underway was in some way changing the nature of their collective reality or they were suddenly able to see deeper or more vividly into it. Clearly something fundamental was happening to change everything so dramatically. But no one it seemed had or was offering any explanation. So, in their new light filled existence the festival crowd decided for the most part they had come nearer to the spirit realms. It seemed to follow they would begin to see more spirits and the phenomena from other realms and dimensions which they now presumed, if they had not in their previous lives, were all around them.

Elisa had decided Mithrael was the only person on the festival site who would be able to answer these questions for her and now she stood over him in the hospital as the dragon was slowly coming back to full consciousness. He was now convinced Shining Moon had again resurfaced in his life. But had soon realised Elisa showed no recognition of him or any idea of the closeness they had shared all those years before. But she was curious and would not dismiss what he was saying entirely. She had been completely fascinated by him from the moment he had stepped off the bus. She had recognised his lonely other worldly nature and seen his strange transformation and wondered why it had all felt so familiar. From the moment she had picked up the eagle, Mithraels waking had undoubtedly started. Perhaps they had been close in some previous life. She would never have any way of knowing and it all seemed overwhelmingly problematic and complicated.

The result was an uneasy atmosphere in the sterile soul-less hospital compartment. Mithrael had woken calm and relaxed. His agitation and aggression had fallen away. He sat grinning on the side of the bed and was delighted to find his Star glasses on the cupboard beside his bed. They were still dusty from the heart of the tornado but were undamaged and he started to clean them carefully with the edge of one of the sheets. He was clearly fascinated with Elisa and watched her every move delving into her soft brown eyes if she looked his way, attempting to ignite some memory lying buried deep in her soul. All present knew she could well be Shining Moon because so many of the characters from those early years and the stories that had arisen were here. Elisa chose to ignore Mithraels' claim and resisted his attempts to reconnect them for the moment. She felt it was important to find out about the spirits walking across the desert.

"Where have these spirits come from. Are they many generations of spirits from the time their tribe lived on this land or have they surfaced in this place from other areas? Why have they come here at this specific time? Where are they going and what originally prompted them to be moving in such numbers across the desert and should we be following them?"

They all waited for his answer. He looked around at Grace, Yaan and Brett and finally looked up to Elisa.

"So many questions. You always were the inquisitive one. It's the monk you need to be talking to now. He will know. He and my brother Merilon they have taken up the flow. I have been on this world far too long. Well, for as long as it has taken to bring it to this point. It all could have ended badly, but it will be stronger for all that has happened as everything starts to unravel from here."

He laughed again and took Elisa's hand. She saw the peaceful good nature and the love for her in his eyes. She knew he had slept. Now he had awoken all his problems and dilemmas, all his worries, the horror and hopelessness he had felt living as a human separated from his dragon soul had now finally been dissipated and resolved. She knew he would not be here for much longer. He would return to his dreams for however long it would be before he was called again to wield the power he would always have on this world in response to the powers who in turn governed him.

She looked down at the eagle and knew he had made it for her. She knew they had lived in a beautiful land together down by the sea in peace with her people until… She looked down into the green glow of his eyes. She knew the terrible pain he had felt and the relief and happiness he was now feeling to be here with her. She took him in her arms and held him tightly. She knew the healing of Mithrael the dragon was nearly complete. He would carry the memory of his life, their life together and her terrible death in his vast cosmic memory for as long as his spirit could dream its way onward through space and time. Although the pain of the human reality he had allowed to take hold of his psyche would always be accounted for in his dreams, it would be gradually absorbed and expelled in the collective consciousness of his brothers and sisters. For now, however, he was happy to feel the special energy he had become so fond of around him and again flowing through him.

Grace, Yaan and Brett left the hospital room. They had felt the sudden cascade of emotion as Elisa had finally realised what was happening. They left them to their reunion and hurried back out into the festival to find Okino.

They found him sitting with Mariella beside him. She was drawing pictures in the sand while he was talking to a small group of boys and girls outside one of the cafes. Grace looked over at Yaan and grinned…

"No particular emergency really…"

"Just a tribe of ghost Indians emerging from some other dimension….at least they are walking away from the festival,"

"…and why is that," she said indignantly, "Have we not managed to provide enough to entertain them?"

Yaan smiled and settled down in the small group to listen to Okino. He acknowledged them with a smile of his own and continued talking.

"…there are wolves and leopards who live around our town and bears higher up in the mountain forests but we rarely see them. Everybody struggles up there really, busy making a living for themselves, trying to get through winter or preparing for winter I suppose."

"So why do you all stay up there? You could come down into the town or the city and not have to worry about the winter."

Okino looked over at the boy who had asked the question and smiled. He looked out into the far distance for a few moments and remembered the little community from which he had travelled so far. No one had asked him such a question and of course the answer was as long or as short as a priest from the little monastery chose to make it. How long did they have? He could tell them the whole story, not only his but of his tribe and their connection to Rabir and the dragons and how Arimathea had told him she had a task for him. He grinned…

"We stay on the mountain because it is where we belong. We stay there because although our life there is still tenuous and hard, we have mastered it to such an extent we have survived for many, many generations back as far as anyone can remember. The struggle brings meaning to every aspect of our life and our world because the struggle is so totally bound up with it. We prepare ourselves as best we can for the worst and when we get through again we have the most amazing celebrations. We have all struggled together in the face of the snows which have blocked us all in again or a harvest that has failed...but we have back-ups for back-ups and when we have all pulled together again and the warmth from the Star shines down on the rice padi and the first green shoots are emerging we all feel the joy together. We are, with all the mountain people in the surrounding country, an enormous family which have shared special bonds for many generations. There is a continual history and knowledge we have gathered together. I have heard on my journey what happens to such a family when it is split up and the knowledge is lost. Individuals have to fend for themselves in environments where everyone has become separated from their ancestral knowledge."

Yaan could not resist asking him a question which had bubbled up as he had listened to his answer...

"Is there any of the technology you think you could take up to your town which you could integrate into your life up there that would not affect or even benefit what you have just told us?"

Okino laughed and was quiet again. He smiled as he remembered when he had arrived hot and dusty on the cruise ship after trekking through the mountains with Mariella.

"Undoubtedly it would be the hot shower.....it is the single most miraculous thing I have found to be part of your modern life...and I am sure folk would come from miles around to use it and so we would always be rich in chickens and so the eggs they so beautifully provide.."

Everyone laughed and agreed unanimously...

Grace waited until the laughter and the chatter had again died down.

"Okino I think you should come and see what is happening. We hope you might have some explanation."

"I am afraid you will have to excuse me, my friends. I hope I will see you all again during the next few days."

He and Mariella followed Grace and Yaan across the site, to the outskirts of the crowds where people were gathering to watch the Indians who continued to emerge from the shimmering desert air. He watched silently for a few moments and then deep in thought and under his breath he said.

"Suranasala"

"Suranasala, Okino, what is Suranasala?" Grace asked tentatively.

Okino slowly turned his head towards her. He had a distant look as if he had connected into some vast thought or idea which was still rising in his mind as he listened and attempted to respond to the question Grace had asked.

"It's something I read in one of the old books in the monastery. Often the monks have a work, some idea, some philosophy they feel they need to look deeply into. It is their own work and is in addition to the work they do with the community. They write their work in manuscripts which are then stored in the library where any of the other monks can read them. It is the most fascinating place and full of the deepest and most profound thoughts they have come to in their lives in the monastery and serving the community.

Sometimes they are about old legends or stories they have heard about or come across in a dream which they have decided to delve into. Many of these legends often have some origin or meaning which has been lost in the mists of time. Suranasala is an old legend about a lost land whose actual existence is much debated. We meditate and search for meaning in all we see around us to expand the idea we have had. When we do this, we deepen our connection with Arimathea and know we are looking straight into the histories of this and many other worlds. This is how our tradition has continued, untarnished and uncorrupted.

Each piece of research completed in this spirit is respected as valid information about what ever area of existence it has uncovered. I remember the research and thoughts I read about Suranasala vividly as I am watching this…I think perhaps…You know, Grace when you asked me to speak to everybody. I think the time has come. I think I need to speak to everybody sometime this afternoon and not too late.!"

"Of course, Okino. We would be honoured. But if there any more surprises it would be great to know about them. All though of course if we knew what they were then they wouldn't be surprises would they!?"

She looked nervously over at Okino. Who now had fully returned from his thought and was beaming a radiant smile over at her.

"Grace, this can only be wonderful if what I am thinking and seeing is actually happening"

"I just hope it mainly involves all these people standing around in the desert, in this wonderful venue we have provided for them, eating and drinking and listening to inspirational people and music for the next few days!"

Okino smiled back at her mysteriously. Mariella looked up at him suspiciously. Mysterious generally meant there would probably be some involvement with dragons. Grace picked up on her suspicion…

"Perhaps you could tell us a little more about this hunch or idea you have had before you address the entire festival."

So Okino told Mariella, Grace and Yaan the Legend of Suranasala which he had learnt from one of the monks high in the mountains of Jahallaala. He transported them back to the steep slopes and the terraces where he had talked with the old monks looking over the snow-capped mountains. To the life of dedication which had allowed them to explore so deeply into the nature of their existence and all its possibilities. Now he had seen Straam and its skyscrapers and the vast and extraordinary community it had become. Its nature reflected the human dream that had emerged on this world. How the people of his race had gathered there together to share their skills and ingenuity to build such a community but how as they had become caught up in their dream they had come to disregard Arimathea, seeing her ultimately as their infinite playground to use and abuse as their ambition increased. If the legend of Suranasala was arising here now perhaps it would offer some of the knowledge lost to the human race and he managed to persuade Grace to allow him to tell it to the crowds gathered at her festival who he knew would be eager to listen.

Chapter Eighty-one
Suranasala.

Grace's smooth machinery of organisation rolled quickly into action. She announced to the crowds that Okino would be speaking later in the afternoon. There was little preparation time. When Grace had first asked him to speak, he had wondered what he would tell the people who had come so far and who had been listening to some very wise and clever people. They knew far more about the problems facing their culture and Arimathea and were better placed than he to suggest solutions. He had listened and been fascinated by these people and the different angles they had come at the same problem. It had made him realise there could not possibly be one solution for such a complex problem effecting all the people of Arimathea.

Now he had been reminded of a legend he had read about in the library. So he knew exactly what he was going to talk about. Later in the afternoon he took to the main stage much to the delight of all who were gathered there and to a rapturous and long applause. He grinned and bowed to them and was completely overwhelmed by the kindness and Love with which he was being shown. Mariella watched him from in the crowd with Yaan and Grace and was as moved and as happy as she had been since her mother had died. All this had come from him and Arimathea who had prompted her to make the journey to find him, bring him here and all he knew into her troubled world. It had responded to all the magic surrounding him with disbelief and scepticism. But the more they looked and the more they tried to explain within the narrow boundaries of what they understood they had found it hard to deny he had brought some previously unexplored or unexplained aspect of their world into the light. So now he began to speak…

"Thank you for your welcome. I am honoured of course to be here with every one of you and have enjoyed meeting so many of you and hearing your thoughts and really I did not know what I could say to you since you have been listening to so many amazing people. But now I have decided because again something extraordinary is happening here. As you may know I have come from a monastery high in the Northern mountains of Jahallaala. I have been told there are many mysteries which surround the existence and practices of my people but as you can see I am very much like you…we get along up in the hills the way we always have and there will be wisdom perhaps we have found which could illuminate your lives… as there is wisdom you have which could transform our lives.

But every one of us would have to choose to understand and accept each other's wisdom before we acted upon it. I could stand up here and tell you everything but really it is not our way. If I became friends with you all, over the years our friendship would develop and we would learn from each other all we knew as our lives went on. We would develop as human beings as our relationship developed and as our 'lives' happened around us. We are all learning as we go and we apply whatever we know to the next set of circumstances which arise. So here we are and I have become your friend hopefully and now it seems many generations of spirits are materialising where we have all chosen to be. I am reminded of two things and I want to tell them to you.

Every year like you but on an entirely different scale we grow our crops in the beautiful valley in which we live. We grow wheat and barley on the plains but on the steeper slopes descending rapidly at one end over many generations my people have made the rice padis. These as you may know are a series of level terraces built into the hillside with stone walls. They are filled with clay over which silt and sediment has washed over the years to form a fertile growing medium for the rice. There are hundreds of these terraces and responsibility is shared amongst all the families of our town as their ability to undertake their cultivation changes from year to year. It is an important crop for us so it is important each family is undertaking the right amount of cultivation.

The river runs through the valley and as the weather warms in the spring the snow which has fallen on the lower slopes during the winter starts to melt rapidly and the river rises to its fastest speeds and fullest levels. This is when we flood the rice padis. A weir is opened in the bank of the river. This sends the clear fresh ice melt water flooding down through the main channel. In turn this feeds into all the other channels which gradually feed all the hundreds of terraces where the rice is then planted and grown.

The flow of water in each channel can be carefully controlled by the manipulation of a complex system of less sophisticated weirs down through the entire system. Some are as simple as a few stones that need to be moved at the end of the process. So every terrace can receive the exact amount of water across it for the rice to grow. The adjustment as you can imagine will be continually happening during the growing season and the result hopefully is the rice has an ideal depth of water to grow in. The rice will always grow because the snow is always melting somewhere, whereas the success of the wheat and the barley can depend on the rainfall and the amount of starshine.

I have been reminded of this process as I have listened to you and all the speakers here. Each one of us it seems is like one of these intricate systems of rice padis. Our life force, our spirit essence flows into the padi at the beginning of our lives from the great river. During our lives we come to understand we have many aspects of ourselves, our terraces, which need to be nurtured and cared for. Each terrace has to have the right amount water, each terrace perhaps has different processes which are looking after it. Some of which we are aware and some of which we are not. But we have to be aware of the importance of the whole process and we have to learn each one of us, how to enable our own process to perform at its best.

We will find if we neglect a number of these terraces how quickly we will deteriorate and be unable to perform. So if we choose we can spend a lifetime adjusting the stones to allow a little more water here where the star shines all day but less there in the padi where there is less starshine. We make these adjustments continually and they will change through our lives as our needs change. Each terrace then has its own peculiarities and we learn them to our advantage or not to our detriment. The important thing about the padi is that the rich nutritious river water flows through it continually so the water on the terraces remains fresh. If all goes to plan the rice seeds sown will reach their full potential and we will all benefit from a plentiful harvest. If you nurture all your own terraces then you will have a healthy and productive life. Then the water will flow back into the river and continue on its journey down to the sea fresh and pure improving the quality of the water as it flows around the world.

I thought of all this when I saw the spirits walking into the desert and remembered an old legend told in our culture. It is the Legend of Suranasala. Remember the river full of clear fresh flood water racing down from the high mountains. Think of it as the spirit of the Universe when it existed in one infinite ethereal state. In the legend there was no separation just Pure Love and Consciousness. But this consciousness gradually became aware there could be more and was unable to resist an attempt to attain this further state. This consciousness eventually brought about the cataclysm and this material state we all have become was formed in the darkness which ensued.

But the original state had become infinitely divided in the cataclysm. In each division a part of the original spirit remains as each blade of rice is nurtured by a tiny fragment of the river as it continually sucks the water into it enabling it to grow. There are more blades of rice than you could possibly count and each will produce more grains with the potential to feed and grow more rice. The Universe is infinitely expansive and this has become its way. It must expand, we must expand but eventually our life force will fade and unexplained as the process is, we assume our spirit and our energy will return to the great river of spirit.

If you look at your world you will see everywhere the urge of spirit is to join together in as big and monumental numbers as possible to fulfil its aims. Look at the way we have gathered in our cites, look at the mass migrations of animals; vast numbers of creatures coming together and moving as one across the landscapes of our world. Great shoals of sea creatures swim through the oceans and vast flocks of birds move as if in one thought through the air. Colonies of ants and bees gather in their thousands guided it would seem by a single thought. As if they have asked, "How can we in this particular life form optimise our ability to survive and proliferate endlessly in the environment we find ourselves?" The ultimate example would be trees.

Anywhere where the climate has been optimal for their growth they have grown in their millions and formed the great forests of the world.

It would seem spirit is happiest and most fulfilled when it is coming nearer to its original state in a huge mass growing and living as one. It seems like a defiance of the material division that happened, as if some terrible mistake had been made and really spirit and now the life force, it has become, wants to be back in the one thought, the one consciousness it has arisen from. This is where the Legend of Suranasala has its' origins.

It was said in the legend there would be a time in the history of the planet when the nature of space and time and the dimensions which underlie them would allow all the spirits who had inhabited the world to once again form into the one consciousness and experience the bliss of the one Love from which all this emerged. In the legend there was a beautiful paradise high in a mountain valley, a profoundly holy place close to the energy flows and multiple dimensional layers and intersections. All the spirits of the teachers, holy men and women, the gurus and the masters and all the spirit and shaman tribes were guided in their dreams to make this the destination of the spirit journey on which they had embarked.

There they would be instructed by the gods and goddesses and the ascended spirit beings how they could blend their own spirits with the one consciousness and into all the dimensions through which it worked. They would move back into this physical dimension and eventually the ability they had gained would flow through all the peoples of the world. The limitations of physicality would fall away and their separation would end. This would fulfil the prophecy that the Great Spirit and all its' infinite parts would again be joined again as one in the Universal consciousness.

However, when they did eventually join in this ultimate state of being they found they had the knowledge and experience the consciousness had gained from all the other infinite states living in the consciousness. This enabled them to enter the mind of the Supreme being, the mystery or the Great Spirit. They found they had the knowledge to defeat the powers of darkness who were destroying their world; so the Great Spirit could to continue in its search to unlock the infinite potential promised in the original dream."

There was a deathly hush across the crowd. They were looking up at Okino enthralled by what he was telling them. He smiled broadly and continued.

"This of course is a legend which can host a whole cast of gods and goddesses as they guide the spirits towards their destination across great tracts of Universal time to the wisdom they need to find. Of course, they battle over the knowledge and are unable to agree on how best to use it or even decide what the true powers of darkness in the world really are! The legend can go on and on from one world to the next and of course it frequently does when told on the long dark winter nights high in the snow covered mountains of Jahallaala.

It is an ancient story, one of many handed down in our lands which expresses our feeling of separation and ultimately stems from the loneliness we feel in this world and from the feeling we could have shared the experience of being alive in a much deeper sense with our world had the separation not occurred.

The spirits heading into the desert and all I have experienced on my journey has reminded me how everything has rolled together to bring us all here and has opened my mind to some incredible possibilities which are vaguely laced through everything I have told you. I know many of you have had illuminating dreams perhaps life changing insights into who you are and seen some strange things you might not otherwise have believed could actually have happened. I think you started your journeys many years ago so you could be here and accept what you have seen and heard and all I am telling you. So now I welcome you all to the journey my friend Mariella and I have been on these past months!"

There was a huge roar from the crowd as he acknowledged and welcomed them into this new episode of his story. He looked down at Mariella who was jumping and cheering madly with the rest of the growing crowd.

"So I think we should follow the spirits out into the desert. They are clearly heading somewhere pretty special and if it is some version of Suranasala then I think we will be heading for a party none of us will ever forget…. So what do you think?"

The roar from the crowds below arose loud and thunderous from a great sea of waving and jumping people; clearly following the spirits out into the desert was meeting with overall approval. Okino grinned down at them put his hands together, bowed to them, offered them all a blessing and left the stage to a deafening crescendo.

Grace shuddered at what she had heard and what Okino had now instigated. However, she had become resigned as the events of last day had proved there seemed to be some further supernatural agenda running in parallel with her own being acted out here. She thought briefly whether there was anything she could do but remembered the crowd and their enthusiasm for Okino's suggestion and reluctantly decided she would have to except this new development. She smiled to herself as she thought there was little she could do anyway. After all she and Jane had talked about wanting to light a fire in the world and to continue the discussion which Okino had started. But then had they started the fire or had it already been set alight and had they just added some fuel by providing a venue for the blaze to catch hold?

She had been watching some of the videos being posted on the media web sites. There were a few of Okino dragging the enormous Zanda across the sand behind him, unconscious and battered as if he had been in some terrible fight. Okino thankfully no longer had the sword he had had when he disappeared into the tornado. There were clips of some of the speakers all of which could not have been better. But the one before the tornado of Zanda holding a bottle of whisky and berating the crowd for destroying Arimathea was not so good!.

She had wanted to achieve a platform for these people. She knew the world would be watching what was happening down here so a little bit of notoriety and intrigue could only help to concentrate interest amongst the news hungry millions who would be following her every move. In which case some footage of the crowds disappearing into the desert with the spirit tribes would certainly provoke further discussion. Again she shuddered as she considered this thought. On the other hand, the problems with the sound system seemed to have been rectified so in balance everything was running pretty smoothly and presumably not everyone would want to follow Okino out into the desert.

Later in the afternoon Grace was watching a considerable gathering of people starting to form. In the light of what he had said they had decided Okino's suggestion to follow the spirits into the desert was an opportunity too good to miss. They were waiting a few hundred paces away from where the Indians were still emerging. They carried extra water and food in their rucksacks and talked excitedly amongst themselves. Any who had them had brought their instruments. The famous headlining band, the Lost Indians had immediately picked up on the irony of the whole situation and had brought as many of their instruments as they could carry or get carried which would not need amplification. Their enormous drums were already thundering out their haunting rhythms.

Grace could not help but notice Mithrael had joined the crowd. He stood head and shoulders above everyone around him and seemed happy and relaxed, his renovated star glasses firmly back wrapped around his face. Elisa was standing close to him. He was talking seriously to Brett and the rest of his crew. They stood silently listening to him and she wondered what he was saying to them. Harri Wade had emerged from wherever he had been hiding. She had not met him yet but Okino had made it clear he had an integral part in the whole saga. He looked bedraggled, unshaven but also relaxed and was entertaining some young people probably with some frightening story about global domination or what he was going to be doing now he was considering giving it all up. That was a conversation she would like to be listening to. Yaan had come up beside her and stood silently with her watching the gathering crowd.

They caught glimpses of Okino and Mariella as they moved through the crowd talking and laughing. They were close, she thought, almost inseparable. There were a lot of photographs being taken of people with them. All of which would flow around the media networks of the world to further increase their fame. What would he do when all this was over? Could he go back to his little mountain town and become a monk again and tell the story in the long winter nights as if it was the Legend of Suranasala; which was something that had occurred to her. They didn't know the ending yet but she felt it was near. Or would he stay with Mariella?

"Are you going out there Grace?" Yaan asked her quietly.

"I thought carefully about it Yaan and have decided I will. I have a feeling there is something out there amazing about to happen and it would be one of those 'continually having to kick yourself to death for the rest of your life' things if you missed it. I really don't think there is any danger and like everyone I seem to have fallen head over heels under the spell of the monk."

Yaan laughed.

"Yeah he is quite a character. Like one of those ascended masters he was talking about. But not how you would have expected one to be before you met one. If you know what I mean?"

She turned to Yaan and looked at him smiling.

"I do know exactly what you mean, Yaan!"

It seemed the crowd was as large as it was going to be so Okino and Mariella went over to Mithrael and talked to him briefly and then they started walking through the crowd and then in parallel with the ghost Indians out into the emptiness of the desert before them.

They slowly moved onwards in two separate streams but soon began to move into one as the living became less apprehensive about the dead. As the two streams merged then so did the states they were in until there was no difference either could detect and they moved together perhaps less alive or less dead into a dimension where they now could interact. To begin with they moved quietly occasionally catching the eyes of those walking near to them, then smiling because of the nature of the situation and then laughing and then asking each other their names. Then they were curious about where they had come from and why they were walking here together into the desert. The Indians were less surprised than the festival goers because they knew the nature of the realms they were now walking between.

Yaan was still walking with Grace. They watched silently as this interaction was carrying on all around them. They were walking with a tall warrior spirit and his wife. Immediately there were many questions Yaan felt he needed to ask but as he considered what they actually were he realised there seemed no importance to the mechanics of what had or was happening. As he was wondering what he would say the Indian next to him started talking as if they had always been part of the same tribe.

"It is good we are walking together again, Talking Horse, I missed you in the lodge when you passed into the great mystery. But glorious your departure was and much celebrated was our victory that day. We missed your daring and skill at the hunt when again we caught up with the great buffalo herds."

"I was always with you, Howling Wolf, did you not know it was me who warned you to turn when the spear narrowly missed your head in battle later that year?"

Howling Wolf laughed aloud and gave Yaan a friendly thump on the shoulder.

"I am grateful to you, my brother. Of course, there is little we can know of the nature of the worlds beyond before we have passed entirely through them. But now perhaps we will learn more!'

Yaan knew of the life he had had with these people. He had a lifetime of memories it seemed. Grace had been with him as his wife.

"It is a time we always knew must happen. Just as the great buffalo herds join again to cover the plains as far as a man can see so the Great Spirit will always bring his people together as one to share their knowledge so all can benefit from what they have learnt. The eternal drum beat of her heart will always echo in the thunder of the rains and the crashing of the wave upon the shore. We have always heard her voice, Howling Wolf, as we have heard your own brothers and sisters in the frozen winter woods singing out their brotherhood as the moon rises through the silent trees."

"It is true, many lives we have led Talking Horse and much we have learnt. Now all our spirits can join again, guided as we have to this time. Each one of us with our story of the lives we have led, the spirits we have inhabited and the souls we have become in our journey through the stars."

Grace had been listening quietly as the two men talked.

"You talk of the mysteries of life and all we have become and our passing but no less important is the time of our birth and our coming into the world. These are the mysteries of your wives and your sisters for they alone are preparing all their lives to bring these new spirits into the world. We are the vessel of the spirit and it is in harmony we must be with her to allow her to work constructively through us. Then all who come here will find their place as quickly and easily so their time can begin again."

"It is true, Summer Breezes, a new spirit is a great gift we can bring to the world and although they will be guided on their path it is we who must bring them to the path. To come to this world from the eternal light is the greatest challenge we face, then to remember our connection, use it throughout our lives in all we do and when our time is passed, carry all we have learnt back into the Great Spirit. So all our light and all our dark is one again."

"This is the knowledge which has been lost to our world. The children grow up in confusion. Only if they are left alone to wander across the great plains and they hear the soft voice of their Mother Arimathea calling to them will they become open to her and accept her back into their eternal souls."

In another part of the crowd Harri was walking with Running Bear and they were having a similar conversation about the nature of their journey to this place...

"...but Running Bear you were a great leader. You left behind such a great understanding for our tribe and all we had become!"

"...and how were you not a wise chief, Rises with Eagles? To find the wisdom you found took enormous strength and allowed us to live in the peace that certainly brought our tribes to this place today.

But your greatest victory has been in this time. To find your way here through all the troubles you have had establishing yourself again in the world, become a great chieftain again and then most importantly to listen to her voice when she found you and make the changes you are making. The strongest and bravest of spirits are needed in the world to bring resolution to the challenges it faces. Only because of what you have lived through and brought about can the lost dragon return to reclaim his soul. However, now you have heard her voice, the power you have in this world is unprecedented. So be sure to be very careful how you use it!"

"Thank you for your kind words Running Bear. If only we could know these things while they are happening to us."

Running Bear laughs

"It is a Mystery, Rises with Eagles, and for good reason!"

So as the people who had chosen to come to the festival walked into the desert their mortal lives faded and they were able to talk with the spirits of their ancestors; of the lives they had shared and the lives they had led since they had parted. Each person with their own specific journey and so their place in the continuation of the dream. When the stories had all been told and their meanings had been illuminated and the Star had begun its' final descent towards the horizon on the Autumnal Equinox of the year the gathering of Spirits arrived where it had been ordained they would all meet to resolve the crisis their world was facing.

Chapter 82
The Chapel on the Hill.

The Indians knew they had arrived. They had been here on many occasions at the times it had again been necessary for them to meet since they had passed back into the Great Spirit. They knew from the slopes of the hills and the mountains in the distance. They knew from the stars in the sky above them. They had their names for the constellations which always returned over this place at this time. Their eagle mother spirit hovering over the peaks of The East, the solitary wolf running high over the hills in the North, The salmon rising in the valleys of the west and the stealthy leopard stalking over the plains in the South. These creatures filled their minds and their skies as if they were the dreams that had made them; there was nor ever had been any separation between the myths surrounding their own spirits and the spirits of these creatures with whom they had shared this land.

They had come to a place equidistant and harmoniously central to the hills and mountains all around them and the awestruck humans who had followed them gasped amongst themselves as the equilibrium in the surrounding space time took hold in their consciousness. When they had fully acknowledged and fully appreciated this astounding phenomenon they became quiet and strained to see what was happening. They realised they were standing on the edge of an indentation in the desert, as if a basin had been formed perfectly here in the centre of the plain. The effect meant now they could see down to where the Indians had gathered in a large circle in this bowl and how the thousands of people and spirits who had followed them here had formed a great gathering spreading out into the desert.

Mariella and Okino, Harry and Yaan, Grace and Elisa with Mithrael and all the drummers and musicians from the Lost Indians had been ushered into the circle by the spirit Indians. There were others who Okino did not recognise but he presumed they had also been in the circle all those millennia before and now had returned to witness and be a part of what now was to unravel out here in the desert. They stood in silence amongst the stars and the shadows of the hills as meteors slid down, across and into the atmosphere burning out in some distant sky. As the salmon started her descent back into the oceans of the stars beyond the hills and the moon rose cradled by the hills, the Indians signalled to the drummers to start the ancient rhythm.

Slowly, softly, relentlessly the power of the drums filled the warm night air, delicately accentuating the rhythms of Arimathea in the same way the ancient human beings had interpreted them all those many years before. Everyone felt the change in the air and the ground around them as the chant the Lost Indians had brought back from an earlier time began to spread from the centre and gather intensity in the surrounding crowd as if a loud harmonious murmur had been released from the sands on which they stood.

As the murmur increased and took hold, the land seemed to respond to this new caress and lightly trembled beneath the feet of all who were gathered there. The tremble slowly turned into deeper vibration and in amongst the murmur of the chant a deeper rumble came from the perimeter of the bowl. On specific points just above the rim of the basin, the ground started to move beneath their feet as if small platforms were slowly rising from the ground below. All who were standing on these places rapidly moved as the ground started to rise more rapidly. Then the nature of this movement was revealed. It could be seen to be happening at regular intervals indicated by the disturbances around the edge of the bowl.

Large upright stones were slowly pushing their way out of the ground and were rapidly rising above the crowd. Crudely but accurately formed from stone in the surrounding mountains they continued to rise until they were almost three times the height of the people surrounding them; there they stopped and stood bringing a new and dramatic effect to the basin. Twenty to twenty five paces apart there were fifty to sixty stones in a circle now looming over the crowd, casting long shadows from the bright full moon over the stunned gathering. This new event reduced the intensity of the chant for a while but as soon as the crowd realised the Indians had continued oblivious, they again began to concentrate on bringing the murmur up to its previous levels. The stones were concentrating the sound within the circle but also raising the intensity of the rhythms as they flowed out into the desert.

Okino noticed Mithrael becoming increasingly restless as the chant and the effect it was having on the surrounding atmosphere seemed to have been increased. There was a new intensity, a sharpness in the air and the moonlight. He remembered his fellow monks' research into the nature of the old stone circles and he cast his mind back to the old circle outside Asima. It had been a similar night but now he was in the presence of a circle of stones many, many times bigger and subsequently many times more powerful. They felt rigorously aligned into the land and with the stars from where they had absorbed and now perhaps were releasing energy from the planet and universal sources they had been gathering for perhaps thousands and thousands of turnings. Who had built such a monument and what magic had they used and cast over it so these stones had remained buried and undiscovered for so long? Or had the dragons crossed the entire festival gathering over one of the boundaries into their parallel dimension on the dusky walk across the desert.

These were his stars, the constellations he knew, even if they shone down from the night skies at different times of the year on his side of the world. The resonance in the air had increased dramatically since the appearance of the stones. Then he remembered his first encounter with the fifteen dragons around the pool in the mountains and how the nature of his dream had changed as the vibration in the air around him had increased. But he had been dreaming then and he was as certain as he ever had been he was not dreaming now. He looked over to Mariella. She grinned up at him which didn't prove anything so he asked her…

"I wonder what Merilon has in store for us now?"

She smiled up at Okino. She was as happy he thought as he had ever seen her.

"The beauty of this whole journey has been we have never known; like any journey worth taking for that matter."

She was right. When they had left themselves open to the dragon they had experienced new dimensions and realities relating to a deeper world they found they were sharing with powerful supernatural beings. They had the ability to shift perceptions and ideas of "reality" at will to give new insight into the nature of the state in which they existed. He smiled down at Mariella and relaxed again. She put her arm around his waist and pulled him close to her as Mithrael walked out into the centre of the circle.

He stopped in the centre and stood still and silently like one of the dark stones which had risen from the surrounding sand. He stared up into the stars. Okino knew he was looking for his way home. The place he had come from through the indeterminable periods of time in which he had travelled through the stars. He yearned for the peace he had rarely been able to find in the time he had spent as a human. Instead he had found only more questions he knew now could never be resolved by dragon or human or any combination of the two. The mystery ran as deep as it ever had. There were no answers it seemed only possibilities. In the struggles and the conflicts in which he had become involved he had become convinced he knew his place in it now. Hopefully this little world would survive and he vowed there, under the stars and amongst all the spirits he had come to know, to dream harder in the coming years for it to continue. He looked back at the faces around him, some in deep meditation, some in a state of extreme happiness. In many of the faces he could also see the glimmer of a new understanding. He saw the monk and his beautiful friend standing, watching him. He walked over to them and enveloped them both in the huge being he had become.

"Thank you, both of you for what you have done for me and this world. You have our blessing and we will not forget!"

He walked back into the centre of the circle. The Indians increased the tempo of the drums and the chant increased in intensity. As Okino felt the resonance around him again increase, he felt the light, saw the underlying glow coming out from where it mostly lay hidden in amongst the molecules and the atoms and the quarks and the parallel dimensions, where it held its place in amongst the flows of time and space and all that had been and eventually would be. He saw it flowing around this place in which they had gathered; he saw it gather in intensity as it flowed from each of the people and spirits who had gathered there, he saw it grow in strength as it absorbed their stories and the knowledge they had gained in their lives, the understanding and the resolve they had found to live successfully or unsuccessfully in the big beautiful consciousness that was Arimathea. He watched it as it flowed into the space the Indians had formed at the centre of the gathering and he watched as it spiralled towards and eventually began to envelop and transform for the last time Mithrael the dragon. Then, he and everyone standing within and around the vast stone circle were engulfed into and absorbed by a prolonged burst of intense glowing light.

Okino found himself back in the spirit consciousness around a high and pronounced hill which rose out of the flat land stretching out to hills in the distance. Remarkably, he found he was sharing the consciousness here with everyone who had been in the desert. It was night and the moon was also high in the sky in a similar place he remembered it in the desert. They were here, as one, in the breezes, amongst the old trees in the lands below and the calls of the owls and the other creatures of the night. Perhaps in the cries of the foxes shuffling through the bins of the town nestling in the shadow of the hill or deer sheltering in the Oak woods stretching out across the silent landscape. They glistened in the forming dew and the ruffled grass as water vapour condensed all around them and fell to the ground. No one questioned how they had come to be there because it seemed as if there had been no movement other than the falling away of all the constructions in their own minds where they had always dwelt. Up until this very moment they had never been able to question or even had the breadth of understanding to comprehend such a state could exist.

Now all the structure holding these edifices in place had fallen away leaving only the pure idea from which they had been raised. Constructions of emotion and instinct, of habit and indoctrination had given the edifice identity and safety which could be held on to and used as stature and protection to face the world in which they stood. They gave shape to the urges and ambitions to be this or that, or more or less. They previously had hidden so effectively what they now had become. In the world left behind there were calculations of mass and stress counterbalanced in gravity and atmosphere. Now they had become only the infinitely combined potential the dragon dream had promised when they had returned to their conception.

They were experiencing the pure source and their place in it, the original spirit energy that had become the consciousness and the cosmic womb in which the beautiful Arimathea and all worlds had been gestated. They were existing outside the turmoil it had taken to build such a world in a vast empty Universe. They knew why such suffering had been entirely necessary to forge such wonder out of the emptiness in which only the pure love of the glow had previously existed. In all that had happened, they had been guided to this time. Now they could understand and relish the extraordinary nature of what had been achieved; experience it all as one vast interconnected spirit being for the first time, divorced entirely from the pain and anguish which had been largely present in its making and since first it had been decided to make these moments come to fruition.

Mithrael was standing in front of an old chapel on top of the hill. The building was small, it had a traditional pitched roof and narrow ornate stone windows with a large door at one end and a tall tower at the other. It stood defiantly on top of the hill, silhouetted against the starry sky. It was old and well used and perhaps had seen many replacements and repairs over the centuries and had become part of the charm of the place in which it stood in observation, a sentinel for the surrounding countryside.

He looked around puzzled as if he had come to the wrong place. Again, he looked into the Stars and decided he was definitely where he needed to be. There could be no mistake because this was his hill, but since he had been here last everything had changed. How long had that been? He had lived on Arimathea for many centuries. He had lived in many different lands and he had not been back here for much of that time. Perhaps it had been built when the other dragon hills had been covered over or maybe on the excellent foundation Samir and the other kings of the world would have laid across its summit.

He walked over to the chapel, pushed open the substantial Oak door and went in. The interior was empty apart from a number of heavy wooden benches and some religious icons on a small altar. The moon sent rays of light piercing through narrow windows. He sat on one of the benches contemplating the moonlight piercing the tiny space. There was perhaps room for eleven or twelve people to gather. It had undoubtedly been used for prayer and worship of the alien gods. This is not what he had expected to find.

He felt into the trace left by the prayers and found confusion and unresolved belief and worry. There was the yearning and guilt he had so often found within the religions of the alien gods. The priests of their religions promised so much to their faithful but they had been bound up with onerous conditions. So, there was only ever disappointment and disillusion when their promises were discovered to be the remnants of the power games their rulers had once played to ensure their loyalty when they were needed to fight or provide the finances for another war. Dying on a battlefield in agony often cured them of their faith. But then of course it was too late. It was only then they had felt the true mystery which certainly existed in far greater intensity outside these stone tombs, in the wind and the rain, which they had been built to exclude.

He concentrated in the silence. What had they hoped to achieve by so completely cutting themselves off from all the beauty of the world outside? He contemplated the windows of coloured glass. The moonlight flowed through lighting the depictions of their writings and teachings, the fantasies they had invented to envelop simple unsophisticated minds into their sinister fabrication. He could hear their readings and proclamations echoing amongst the dense stone walls and he felt the fear rising in his people. He felt the frustration that had provoked the action of his brothers and sisters all those years before. But he told himself those times were long passed and the world had changed again. Deeper in the silence he stretched his thoughts out to where the tall stones would have stood. So what had happened to those magnificent monoliths his tribe had brought and placed so carefully on the summit of this hill? Again he felt into the silence and into the walls surrounding him and he began to hear the terrible answer to his question.

He heard the clamour of a large workforce. They had lit huge fires, burning the seasoned limbs of Oak trees around the bases of the stones. When they were hot enough and started to crack they drove Iron wedges into them sending the fissures up through the bed of the stones splitting and disintegrating them. When the stones had been broken sufficiently they were pulled to the ground with ropes and when they had landed with great thumps the men cheered and congratulated each other. Then they set about further cutting and shaping them into sizeable pieces they could easily lift and made huge piles of them on the side of the hill. In this way the magnificent circle of stones that had stood for thousands of years and been visited and admired by generations of his people, had brought them connection with their ancestors who had built them in respect to the magic and the mystery alive in their land, had been systematically reduced to little more than rubble. They had built this little building from its desecrated remains.

Then suddenly, he was filled with a terrible realisation. In the silence of the small chapel, alone, separated from the wind and the moonlit clouds and the soft ground and the calls of the owls, he saw how his revenge and his vendetta against the human race had resulted in this previous work to preserve the relationship with the land being put into jeopardy. The humans had come and found the stone they needed to block his passage back into the hill already in place. All they had to do then was rearrange it with the spell he himself had instructed the magicians to embed into the hill. He shuddered as the consequences of all that had come to be since those times, rushed through the small chapel the humans had built on his hill.

Of course, it had happened and time could not be reversed. It was the final quirk of fate, an irony he would always carry with him. In the quest to bring peace to the great Mother Spirit and Arimathea, the dragon of whom he had always been a part, even though he had lived as a human all these years had brought even greater turmoil and unrest. But what would have happened if they had left everything as it had been; if they had not sown the seeds of revolution in the human spirit when they did? Perhaps the human race would have become entirely dominated by the dark forces that clearly had had designs on Arimathea for whatever dreadful reasons and eventually left Arimathea as a charred or frozen world devoid of all life now or in the future.

They had made a decision to take their part in the mystery and it had unravelled into the time in which the world now found itself. There were still owls calling through the night and snow leopards were stalking silently through the mountains. They had a chance to turn it all around and wasn't that all any world could ever expect. He smiled to himself. Had this all been so they could gain an insight into the nature of the dream in which they had all become involved? Had it been to guide the human race back to where they needed to be or maybe this is what it took to bring the dragons to true enlightenment? Had it taken all these centuries and all that had had happened to them on this amazing world to understand the full breadth of the wonder in which they had become involved all those eons before? He had become caught up in these evolutionary impulses and subsequently the responses to them and been swept along like a fallen leaf in a hurricane. The tension between the dragons and their disagreement on the best course of action had not brought about an outcome they would have preferred.

The humans had been free to develop all their crazy amazing abilities and potential, unhampered by the concerns for the health and oblivious to the true nature of their world. Now perhaps they were starting to realise. Had it been necessary for them to go through so much to get here where they were starting to understand all they had inherited? They had come by a dangerous route and still there were some steep and treacherous paths for them to climb. But it seemed there was no pre-ordained path, no plan for the journey, it could not be manipulated or guided and the attempt they had made had soon been lost in the vastness of the infinite nature of the consciousness.

There was only the dream, forming and reforming as it expanded in all its infinite complexity into the future and now he needed to return to the only place in which he could truly play his part, sleeping amongst the crystal light deep in the warmth of his beloved Arimathea. In the silence from outside in the moonlit night he heard a flurry of honking and squawking, the beating of determined wings as an enormous flight of geese flew over the chapel.

They would be in the initial stages of their own journey, their return to the warmer lands as winter returned, where they would live in a gentle green valley beside a lake within the reflection of the mountains over which they had finally flown to reach it, shining in the Starlight magically all around them. There they would raise their young, preparing them for their own journey for when their time came, to fly on the winds relentlessly and endlessly circling their world.

Mithrael had been alone, as alone as he ever had been. He stood wearily in the chapel now. The barrier of tortured stone preventing him from returning to Arimathea. He felt out into the night where the geese were already disappearing over a distant horizon and to where he could feel all the spirits of the Indians and the people who had followed him into the desert in the consciousness surrounding the Moonlit hill. He felt out further, out to the dragons who were also willing him to return. He found he was able to channel as much power through the people and the dragons from the consciousness and the dream to make one final change, a change which would become vital for his return. He felt their approval and although he knew he was again tampering with the fabric of the world after his previous revelations he felt justified in what he felt he must do.

He drew in all the light and energy from the consciousness shining through the Moonlight and felt into fabric of the space and time around him. He found the tortured remains of the broken standing stones in the walls of the chapel and their chiselled fragments carefully laid over the top of the hill. He projected the light through each stone and pulled them together in the consciousness, in the time, in the moonlight and in all the powerful stories and precedents for change he and they had heard from all the people who had spoken. He brought it together, brought them all together in a vision of the Old Stone Circle on top of the hill as it had been before it had been destroyed. He asked them to concentrate on the vision he had given them. He asked them to concentrate on bringing it out of the consciousness through the portals of the labyrinth, where all dreams are initiated and back into physicality on the hill where it's trace still was held even all these centuries after it had been dismantled. The darkness from the distant galaxy it appeared had been almost completely disseminated. Perhaps it had lost its power when Okino had banished it from Merilon's hill or by the wind circling it continually, purifying and consoling each of the distressed and broken stones; perhaps the pilgrims who had come here in their reverence to sit in its splendid isolation away from the bustle of the world below, had driven it away bit by bit; perhaps it had been carried away by the geese who had passed over its roofs and tower, year after year tempting out the spirit he had embedded here to make its own return to those distant realms from whence it had come.

What was left shrank away, without any resistance to the intensity of the Love light being projected towards it. As a result of all this attention the fabric of the stones was able to find the original form into which they had been arranged on the hill with no further difficulty. The little chapel evaporated in spiralling swirls and eddies of light, in gentle fallings and transferences and in the light of the full Moon now at its spectacular zenith, the magnificent Stone Circle on the Dragon hill was slowly reformed.

Mithrael stood and walked silently amongst the tall stones, looking over each vista the spaces between the stones had created. He could feel the rivers of glowing energy flowing up from the dragons dreaming deep in their caverns below and out into the night and mixing with the consciousness and the energy from the stars. As he became immersed in this sensation he was able to remember with great clarity all he had experienced on his human adventure. His dreams and all the dreams of the dragons would always be informed by the knowledge he had gained of the intensity with which life was led here and how it had formed Arimathea. He smiled as the most memorable of those times began to surface. They were always embedded into a story; always connected into the people and the circumstances surrounding it and so into each of the stories of everyone who had become involved as their lives had become enmeshed together.

He knew how in this way the light or the emptiness of dark oblivion was passed on and on, infinitely through the vast web of interconnection this world and the consciousness surrounding it had become. The light always came out of the darkness and the dark could just as easily come out of the light. Some act of kindness could leap from story to story enriching all it touched as it rippled through the world. Alternatively, an act of selfish greed could stultify and discourage any who came in contact with its destructive force. Either could gather and stagnate and transform into something unnatural if the flow from one to the other was allowed to be lost. He knew he had become an instrument of these processes in the time he had spent here.

The stories he now remembered were a reflection of those processes as they had transformed the world. One or the other of those fundamental forces had gained or lost momentum as it flowed through the lives and the circumstances in which he had become involved. There had been many battles fought and won, love gained and lost. He had lived through times of peace and times of enormous turmoil. All these memories and experiences had been a fundamental vehicle for his own development and evolution. Where he had lost sight of the tension, allowed his own darkness to become prevalent and denied the ability of the love Light to heal and transform him, he had endangered Arimathea. She had felt his hurt, seen the danger and merely allowed the power she had to bring him back to who he was, standing here now. Perhaps a dragon being enveloped in and influenced by the dark emptiness stalking the Universe had been the only way to provoke the extreme powers of light to arise amongst the consciousness of Arimathea's inhabitants. Only then could the dragon rise and flow again through her and start her healing. As the world became more complex, the tension was becoming greater, more was at stake and its future success may well depend on how well this new force survived and how well and truthfully this story was told and listened to by the people of Arimathea. He would do all there was in his power to enable them to hear it.

With these thoughts finally settling in his mind he walked into the centre of the circle of tall stones. He raised his arms to the stars. In response, as if they had been waiting for his summons, tiny strands of starlight were sent from which ever distant galaxy they existed, down to where the dragon was standing. As they converged on his enormous form, he and the space between the stones became a blaze of starlight and his transition from human being to the ancient spirit of the legends of this and all worlds once again began. Each of the ancient spirit creatures appeared as he was engulfed in the light. The mighty bear towering again amongst the stones, the eagle on feathered wings of outstretched light, the salmon and the dolphin, the wolf and the leopard, the great stag and the gentle horse spirits all stood in the light filtering infinitely down from the stars. Finally, the dragon appeared, larger than any life and raising its mighty head, roared its defiance back out into the shivering Stars. Then he leapt into the sparkling air and hovered momentarily in the moonlight over the newly incarnated circle of magic stones, savouring these final moments and the sensation of being alive under the stars before diving back into the Dragon hill, there to be gloriously reunited with his dragon soul.

Chapter 83
Digital Cities.

In the desert circle risen from the sands, thousands of minds were experiencing the full wonder of being joined into the one planetary consciousness. They had access to every process, every idea which had ever arisen. They could understand the thoughts and actions of every conscious creature which had ever walked, crawled or flown over their world. Surrounding and within all these lives they felt the original peaceful glow underlying the existence which had drifted out of the stars and settled on their world. It underlay all the terror and the turmoil, the raging fires and the ferocious storms instrumental in her evolution. Arimathea had shifted and exploded her way through the millennia to this place where they could contemplate her existence. They knew how everything lived and died within the peace under the quiet skies of their Star. Now they had been enveloped in the gentle cycles of Moonlight shining through the darkness of the night.

They could follow every creature travelling again into their dreamtime. Out of the day and into the night. Every creature sifting through the strange wonder of their waking hours and unravelling all their confusion to wake in the peace of the soft morning light. Each day if only momentarily they could experience the peace the world could offer. Then again, the web they had woven rushed in and their day, their life would start again wherever they had left it.

This was the terror they felt next. As the terrifying angst and confusion of a billion and half of Arimathea's human inhabitants rose into Arimathea's consciousness. The unbearable scream ripping through the peace of the world, all their yearning, all their striving for the things they could never have, all the hurt they carried for the generations before, their own generations and they themselves, the agony being left in the wake of their misunderstanding, the terrible lies which had been told to them and which they lived out and would live out until their world was crushed under the weight of them. They were lost. More lost than ever with only a distant glimmer of understanding for how amazing it all could be.

They had for the most part de-mystified the fundamental processes governing their world. With these discoveries had come the truth about themselves. They knew there was no biological differences between the races of their world. They knew that men and women were only separated by the biology of their reproductive roles. At the root of many cultures was the premise that each person had as much right to a fulfilled and poverty free life as his brother or sister in any country of the world. This was even being extended to the rights of animals in some areas of Arimathea. As communications and the level of information available to every person, any injustice continuing in the world was likely to become exposed and placed under the scrutiny of the international community.

But still the injustice went on. The emptiness that had found its' way into human souls was still there; carried through the generations from the time it had first been initiated. Oblivion occupied the minds of human beings as powerfully as ever. It had made many of them cold and ruthless, robbed them of their humanity. Unaware of the dark energy that had gripped them they were driven by its urge to bring about the death of everything. They wasted and polluted with their machinery, destroyed the wonder, whether they knew it or not and left burning wastelands filled with the stench of death and hopelessness wherever they went.

Unaware how they were in service with all the others who had been infected by this destructive cause they had made their structures of power increasingly unassailable and more formidable. In their greed for wealth and power they had made any opposition or challenge ever more impossible. Most of the wealth was now hidden in the electronic networks and within the shores of rogue states who profited from their ability to hide from the rest of the world the proceeds of illegal activity and the taxes which otherwise would be accounted for in their country of origin.

With this knowledge the festival spirits had settled into the conscious psyche of the human race evolved as it had through the eons. Would it ever be possible to reduce the terrifying power which was so dominating their majority and ravaging and killing their planet? Would it ever be possible to banish the fear of separation and the fear of loss? Could their dreams one day be filled with feelings of belonging to a huge and wonderful family where no one would ever feel lonely or forgotten or excluded ever again? How could they reassure their brothers and sisters Arimathea was a plentiful planet and there were many opportunities awaiting them when this family came together to share her incredible gifts.

They merged the consciousness into the human communication networks where the fear and the imbalance were reflected in the economic structures to a greater or lesser extent of every country in the world. It was easy for them to find the islands of wealth and privilege built by the fear. It was easy to find the consequences in the tragedy and the poverty, material and psychic the human race was living in as a result. It was easy to feel the damage which had been done to the systems of Arimathea as this abuse had been proliferated.

Deeper and deeper they found they were able to explore within the systems of the financial networks. They could scrutinise every transaction from the enormous sums paid between the largest countries and corporations to each individual who used their bank accounts to pay their bills. In amongst the legitimate transactions was the true story of the power being wielded across Arimathea. The backhanders, the bribes, the ransoms and pay offs, the softeners and the incentives, the inducements and enticements being paid to governments and individuals who in turn had the ability to allow the will of the power crazed technocrats to further enslave and degrade Arimathea and all her inhabitants.

The newly united dragons felt the depth of this scrutiny. With their knowledge and understanding of the electronic systems many of the festival goers were able to delve deeper than even the dragons had been able to fathom on their early explorations of this new human dimension. The level of the injustice which had developed in the years since the lords had sat in their stone castles carrying out the will of their kings by extorting taxes from the families in their region, surprised even the dragons. They were finding fairly regularly that even a small percentage of one of the excessively rich individuals' wealth could enable the standard of living of a fairly large poverty-stricken country to rise to levels where all the inhabitants could drink water regularly and have a reasonable diet.

In many extreme cases the wealth of criminal dictators who were selling the resources of their own country was being supported by powerful global corporations. Often food grown with dwindling water supplies was being sold to other developed countries, while their own people remained hungry and thirsty. They were often supporting a large and well-armed militia who could be utilized if the general population decided everything had gone too far.

As they explored more deeply, they found the structures in the networks supporting these systems. There were clearly organisations and individuals who were benefitting from their complexity and so the inability of the authorities to track and police their activities. They found the information superhighways and where they led, ultimately to the vast digital cities which had been constructed to hold the ever-expanding amounts of information being generated and held.

These cities were in turn populated by the cyber forces which had been programmed to regulate and protect all who had interests there. Extensive fire walls protected from the rogue invasion of viruses. The most sinister and destructive of which had been introduced by the environmental revolutionaries who disagreed with the increasingly detrimental effect the city centre explosions were having on their cause. Now they were making viruses manufactured in some extreme corner of the network, remaining undetected until released. In theory they could rampage through the electronic web releasing hidden instructions bringing the systems of the world to a standstill. Many had tried but still the technology of the firewalls and the computing tech giants was keeping ahead of the unshaven genius hiding undetected in the frozen wastes Uritania.

However, there were more sophisticated programs patrolling the electronic web of the world. They were designed to search out these envoys of destruction and bring them to the attention of the security syndicates eager to protect the wealth now predominantly paying for their existence. Roaming the digital highways unobserved and equipped with sophisticated search mechanisms they could pick up the fallout from any irregular activity in the colossal cloud computers purring away in remote deserts where they remained invisible and hidden from attack.

Eventually they began to find, carefully hidden in the digital cities, the hidden citadels and the inner most sanctums behind the most sophisticated multiple fire walls. Here the unknown and incalculable wealth of the global corporations and the richest individuals on the planet was being held in the equivalent of the impregnable fortresses the dragon had rendered ineffective many centuries before. These new fortresses, the dragon realized were considerably more sophisticated than the crude old stone castles the lords had hidden themselves away in. In this new electronic network, he found millions of smaller constructions constantly directing their funds into these enormous fortresses. He found very little flowing back. A situation which he found almost identical to the one he had discovered before in the pre-industrial landscapes of Arimathea. Here the extraordinary power of the new rulers of the world was held in these technological landscapes. Access to these inner realms was carefully protected with codes and passwords held only by the most trusted individuals. Now an extraordinary possibility started to rise in the collective mind of the newly formed dragon sister and brotherhood.

The dragon was surprised by the complexity the humans had developed for themselves. They had learned from their world and the universe over successive generations and unlocked the mathematics lying beneath the natural structures and systems they saw around them. They had developed their own invisible dimension where they stored their information and processed their own thoughts and dreams and had turned them into any reality they could imagine. He had noticed the similarity with his own abilities when he had first seen the extent of Harri Wade's empire and how it had spread across Arimathea. They had proved they had the ability to dream worlds and certainly Harri had manipulated the companies he had made, bought and sold by adjusting their economic climates.

But the dragon had dreamed many entire worlds and now they were again complete, all his brothers and sisters had merged again into the one powerful being for the first time in well over a thousand turnings of the Star. Although the humans thought they had built infinite combinations into the pass codes and protocols protecting their growing empires, the dragon could clearly see through the matrix which they thought governed the infallibility of the system. The dragon sent an idea, a dream out into the consciousness. He hoped the dream would gather momentum, grow and be built upon, expand until every spirit who now resided there added their version to the dream. The dream would gain strength as each version was added, reinforcing the power of the initial idea.

The dragon lands dimension had come ever closer to the surface of the human dream state. It was reaching more and more people who were benefitting from travelling there. Their connection with Arimathea was kindled as they experienced the wonders being revealed to them. Spirits who had been called from the consciousness to colonise this new world guided them to the experience they would personally need to awaken them and bring them closer to her. They met these spirits and each other, they met the spirits of the animal kingdoms and received inspiration as they sat under the trees growing there. In every encounter the underlying state of the dream on Arimathea was revealed to them. They woke with the sole intent to guide their lives to a place where they could live closer to the peaceful glow of love and light.

A whisper from a tree, a call from a distant animal, a falling sunbeam in a glade, a ripple across a pool, a flame from a fire, a falling feather, a smile from a loved one, a mountain in the distance revealed; each of these occurrences was able to cut through the noise, the interference, the fear, the disillusion, the distress, the heartbreak to reveal the peaceful glow behind each and every one of these moments. They began to find the freedom to live again, saw the wonder shining out from everything. It wasn't complicated, they didn't need to study with anyone or pay anyone or climb to the top of a holy mountain. They just needed to feel the Peace and the Love flowing through the world. In time they found they could throw off the bonds their race had bound them into. When it had been revealed to them, they found it difficult to see how it had been kept from them for so long.

This was their inheritance. They felt the knowledge flooding back from those ancient days when they had wandered Arimathea with her and all who had come to exist upon her. Despite the fear their rulers continued to exert over them slowly they were able to guide their lives back to where they could live in the glow. Slowly it would become deeply ingrained into their day to day existence. The dragon knew the more people who came to it and lived in its ways the quicker and the more opportunity there would be for Arimathea to start her healing process. The lifeforce was still being ripped and drained from her. The riches belonging to all her people who had largely created it, through the drudgery and enslavement in which they had been held since the dragon had been absent from their dreams was held by their rulers. Held more tightly and more securely than ever in the digital fortresses.

The new dream was growing and gathering strength in the consciousness. In the crystal caverns the dragons dreamed harder and flooded the world with the dream of the dragon lands and each night more people came to see the wonder of living in the glow underlying the world. A critical mass would have to be reached when the number of people who had begun to live and reinforce the ancient glow of love light became high enough for the dream to be successfully held in the world. The festival goers' spirits with the help of Mithraels' detailed knowledge of the banking networks, learnt the intricacies of the structures in the digital world where the power was held. They learnt the abilities and scope of the patrolling viruses, how they travelled through the web of electronics surrounding Arimathea. How they could be in one place and yet all places in their singular task to seek out invaders.

Combined in the mind of the dragon they could map and hold this information in one thought at any moment at any point to determine the level of surveillance. They had begun to understand, extraordinary as this seemed to any one of them the entire complexity of this electronic world. As this understanding grew so the nature of the new dream was growing. Each spirit slowly came to understand how the dream would be released. They would guide it through the electronic superhighways with the specific information they had acquired from the depths of the networks controlling and reinforcing the machine world. The equations which held the entire structure together were being slightly changed as the knowledge crept through the quantum world making it slightly more vulnerable as the ghost was being prepared to be released into the machine; stretched as it was from the everyday threats of the hackers who roamed the superhighways and the digital cities searching for some opportunity to extricate the extreme wealth from behind the walls. They were narrowly avoiding and sometimes not, the continual search being carried out by the patrolling viruses released to pursue them; to find and annihilate the ability they had to enter and disrupt the shadowy underworld of manipulation under the thin veneer of corporate respectability.

At last, the dragon and the spirits who had come to Grace's festival were joined by enough people who had found their way into the dragon's dreamland and the critical mass was reached. The magical code they had been growing was released into the digital networks. Silently it swept through and under the layers of calculations containing the guardians, only as undetected impulses lost amongst the cascading rivers of information so necessary to keep the machine world running at the intensity the humans had built into the system. The code moved through each set of calculations which had become the life force of the web. In every action it left a small corruption. It radiated through as if a small sound had made an enormous explosion and had sent an infinite series of undetectable ripples into a shoreless ocean.

The ocean held the premise the human race had operated under from when they had first stopped wandering the planet and were first establishing their communities across the world. It had governed all their activity since those early times. It was that strong leaders would lead the rest of their tribe by whatever means they could get away with. Now it had been enshrined in their latest and most sinister method of controlling and manipulating their fellow beings who they thought of now as only the units and numbers to further their ambitions of reckless domination. The power they had built over many generations was stored in this web of electronics and so every calculation made to reinforce this web reflected and upheld the premise to hold and build on this power.

It had grown the enormous mountains of wealth with each and every new transaction. At the origin and always reinforcing this premise down through the years had been the emptiness of oblivion. It was ingrained in these networks, connected through the electronics to the minds who had invented and maintained it. It lurked unseen, spreading its malicious subliminal messages through the populations of Arimathea who progressively used the web in almost every aspect of their lives. It pervaded every aspect of its construction. It had become especially concentrated in the search for viruses as they patrolled, hunting the web for threats to its destructive mission on Arimathea. Here the final chapters of its strategy were being played out. Here it found it was being able to guide the human race and the cruel disruptive world it had made to its final demise more speedily than at any other time. However, the whole operation was ambitious and as with most human endeavours was held together by a wish and a prayer and unknown to the populations who depended on it was always on the edge of catastrophic failure.

The ability of the premise to be held in the electronic networks relied on the stability of the programming to counter the threats being continually made on it. The immensity of this task was overstretching even the giant tech corporations whose responsibility it was to keep the power structures of their masters safe. Now the dragon and the spirits who had joined him knew where the signs of stress were showing. As his magical code, containing the ancient geometry and symmetry that had formed and enabled the universe to continue for billions of years, invaded more and more of these systems the more vulnerable they became.

The systems dominating time and space of which the dragon was a master relied on the flowing of matter and spirit from one state to another. Nothing even in the deadest and most destroyed parts of the universe was ever held in stasis. Even over millions of years they were changing. This was the one unchangeable truth that governed everything. Nothing could ever stay the same. Humans had tried in so many ways to defy this truth as they built their mechanized world. They had decided that the planet would infinitely give her fabulous wealth up to them. They thought in their arrogance that they could waste it and destroy it, mistreat and slaughter everything that stood in their way. They took no heed of the warnings given by the brightest and the cleverest of their race who had always spoken out against this terrifyingly destructive orgy of greed and violence.

They did not notice or did not care about the darkening skies in their bunkers or the thickening clouds of dust and pollution in the atmosphere swirling around their dark towers. After all there was no force more powerful than they themselves with their mountains of wealth piling up in the banks of the world. The governments whose countries were reeling from the amount of money they were taking out of them were begging them to use their wealth to generate growth for their dwindling economies. Their people were turning on the governments holding them up to ridicule. So they piled money into their armies and their weapons which they hoped would hold the frantic anxious populations at bay with their restlessness and their wondering about where all the wealth of the world had actually gone.

As the rainforests disappeared faster and faster, more machinery continually appeared to ravage the natural world with ever more efficiency and convert it into more wealth for the monsters who had taken it over for themselves. There was more junk food and more mindless entertainment and the crushing fear continued to grow amongst the people that they would lose their hold and be unable to cope. They felt they were being made numb and subservient and given just enough to keep the machine monster alive.

The total disregard of the most ruthless of the Humans for their world was now coming to fruition. Unbeknown to them the bloodstreams of the monster they had created were filling with the magic which had existed long before the star had bathed their world in light. Relentlessly it flowed filling the electronics, moving through the chains of electrons leading to the high walls of the great citadels where the technological defences had been so concentrated. It was not surprising these tech companies had become so rich. They held the secrets of the wealth carefully hidden away from the desperate economies of Arimathea. The dragon had been startled at the callous nature of the humans who could watch their world deteriorate while holding so much potential to solve the problems they had caused. As he approached and began to engulf the systems surrounding the citadels, he found they were encircled by wastelands drained by the terrible construction which lay in their heart. The true horror of all he suspected was made clear to him as he saw and felt for the first time the enormous endeavour that had been put into fortifying these electronic fortresses. They could no longer disguise the scale of the invasion they had up until now kept completely undetected. The virus defenders were suddenly alerted and began to flood through the web to where they had detected an unprecedented global attack on their powerbases.

The dragon and the millions of old souls who had returned in such numbers when they had heard the call now surrounded the highly encrypted walls. The ancient power held in the enormous fortunes inside, which had been ripped from Arimathea's surface and used to enslave her people and used to further weaken her day by day, draining her of her life force, felt the ancient magic through the complex array of digital defences. Felt it beginning to eat through the numbers as it resolved each defensive riddle, each equation designed to hold out the raiding forces of the increasingly desperate world beyond.

But the walls were also being infiltrated by Oblivion. Adapting the numbers shifting the balance in the equations, cloaking the defences of the citadels with a new layer of impermeability. For the dragon everything seemed the same. He was allowed to continue to devour the continually adapting matrix but now he noticed an added defence had been added and he recognized with horror this new obstacle. His old adversary who had kept him trapped on the surface of Arimathea for all those centuries was here in the electronics. In the same way it had obstructed the channels through Arimathea it was now blocking his path into the heart of the darkness pervading Arimathea. He was feeling his energy and the energy behind the whole attack was being drained away and fed back into the defences of the citadel walls. The emptiness was growing moment by moment as Oblivion now fully alerted flooded into the web from the surrounding wastes of space. The dragon suddenly had no idea how long it would take him to tear through the fire walls and at what cost to himself and the other spirits who had joined him. Certainly, there was a chance they may become so drained they would be lost in the wastes of Oblivion. He was not prepared to risk their safety. He decided he would have to withdraw for the moment and find some new strategy.

He pulled back into the wastelands around the citadels. This new setback flashed through the one mind as they retreated to contemplate this new threat. Again, they felt the power of their alliance away from the frantic struggle with the reinforced firewalls. They started to re-energise themselves by remembering the peaceful glow of their lives on Arimathea. The power of the light and all that had arisen as a result of it flooded through the one mind. It reminded them all, dragon, spirits of the festival, the spirits who had now joined them from the dragon lands and the elemental spirits, what was now at stake. If they retreated now and left oblivion to continue its rampaging destruction of Arimathea she would certainly be lost forever. Such an alliance and these circumstances may be difficult to achieve again in the future. It was paramount a way was found through the walls into the heart of the citadels.

Okino, deep in the one mind felt the urgency. He remembered how this had all started. With the legend of Suranasala to which he had listened so often. How the wise people of the world had made their way to a hidden paradise in the mountains where they had learnt the wisdom to defeat the chaos that was rising in the world. Had the legend foreseen this time and these very moments and what was the wisdom with which they finally prevailed. They had each brought their own knowledge and they found they had in the one mind the ability to enter the mind of God. He felt the knowledge of the Spirits around him flowing through his own understanding. He thought deeper into the flow and found the individual currents of each of the people they had been, all the wonder they had experienced and held in their lives on Arimathea.

In each mind there was a world held in phenomenal detail. In each world there was the life force which had driven it. Every life different. Every life unique and holding an abundance of sublime light filled moments formed in reaction with the environment around them and which had gradually, in turn, formed their unique vision of the world. These were the lives the destructive force opposing them would have denied them by taking the world and the universe back to the original peace. There would be no past and no future.

They had been bought to the edge of time. Where everything was to be decided. Nothing or everything stretching into the future. Surely there was something here to combat what was in front of them, threatening to deny the destiny they were so close to. His thoughts were flooding through the one mind. Each spirit had begun to remember each of their light filled moments when, although unaware at the time, they had become more deeply connected into the glow. Okino smiled as the thought ran away from him and into the infinite mind to which he was now joined.

As they remembered each one of these beautiful timeless memories, they began to travel through their individual lives. There had been drudgery and confusion even pain when they had felt lost and alone but the doors had eventually been opened again into the glowing wonder. Then they remembered gleaming island after gleaming shining island, each one filled with belonging and the sublime light of the glow. It shone from the eyes of their loved ones, their parents and their friends, their lovers and their children; from the places they had loved and visited down through the years where they always had felt profound moments of alignment. They remembered the perfect timing of events which had changed everything, the spirits that had jolted them out of the sleep they had fallen into, even the animal spirits who had come to them and shown them a way of being in the glow they had not found amongst their human fellows. Each moment connecting them with something that was moving them deeper into the greater mystery of their lives. Rare moments when they had all known this life was far beyond anything they could ever really understand.

At these times, they had felt something so wonderful they had been left breathless and had felt emotion rising in them so powerfully they thought they would be unable to contain it and their tears had begun to flow. Emotion flowing, he thought. Held and still it was unable to move to enable to illuminate and inspire. Flowing out of the glow, they could feel it, almost see it in the air around them emanating from the eyes of the person in front of them, from the ground, from the trees, from the pavements and the buildings, out of the shimmering distance and the minute detail they could suddenly see glistening on the diaphanous wing of a beautiful creature that could have been huge and had landed here on them, touched them at a precise moment like it had been the hand of God reaching out to intensify, make real and mark undeniably the nature of what was happening to them.

These glistening wonderful moments always emerged into their lives like newly fledged creatures, breathing this elixir into them for the first time, flooding their minds, these limbs, as if they were taking their first flight, their first steps and were watching the world they had miraculously surfaced in again, after a gestation in the warmth of a womb or an egg or the chrysalis that had held them. They had not realized until now what they had become involved in. The sheer mind-blowing immensity they had become a tiny part of and how they contained everything that had made it.

They had become aware of all this wonder and then gone back to what had previously appeared to be their mundane existence. But now each moment if they chose to let it could be filled with the immensity of this discovery. If they chose to live in the glow. These moments could become closer and closer together. They were not rare and interspersed; they became more frequent and more apparent as they recognized the worlds carrying on around them. Shining with their own intensity. Everything shining with the light that had multiplied and multiplied over the eons and become the miracle in which they were taking part.

Okino found himself back in his life out in the back of his parents' house. It was early morning and he was feeding the chickens. He threw down the glistening golden corn he had seen growing and taken from the fields. The chickens pecked it up clucking peacefully, occasionally they looked up at him and he caught their eyes. Was he mistaken or could he see the same power he had seen in the eye of the dragon? It had been there all along and shining from the beautiful colours of their feathers. He went back into their house and found his mother. He loved her so much. She was folding some blankets and she asked him to help her and they performed the task like they always had done, like she had taught him to do. But now it felt like the Universe couldn't have gone on unless they had performed this everyday act together. He wandered around their house and contemplated each and every pot and pan, their brightly coloured crockery from which he had eaten all her delicious meals, each chair and the table around which they had all sat, each of their strange collection of pictures, the rugs on the floor, the stonework of the rooms, the timber on the handrails of the stairs worn by a million touches of his own and previous generations of his family, the thick glass with the imperfection which distorted the mountain in the distance. Timeless wonder shining from every object. How they had been made, how they had come to be here, who had used them and all that had happened in this room had all become part of them.

All those times and experiences bound into their fabric so when he acknowledged them they shone with all the thoughts and visions they had encouraged and held. He walked out to the front of his house and saw the people of his village going about their business. They talked and laughed as they met in the square. There were two yaks standing in the shade of the old pine tree, ears twitching and tails flicking away the flies relentlessly tormenting them. His friends were sitting round the old table playing their game. They waved over to him to join them. A flight of eight swifts screeched, diving and swooping through the shimmering air and four dogs lay dozing in the Starshine. One had three butterflies chasing each other, circling, spiralling above him. He lay still as they landed on his head absorbing the warmth and the light. He could see the monastery on the side of the mountain. An eagle wheeling in the blue sky high above. Prayer flags fluttered in the breeze. A long horn sounded in the distance vibrating the air with the ancient sound and mixed with the chattering of the smaller birds. The scent of fresh bread and jasmine was on the air. His heart was filled with happiness. He had come so far and he wanted to be home. All these worlds spinning through his own beautiful world and everything they had created going on and on. Everything shining in the light, everything moving on in the glow. Ordinary but profound beyond imagining from one moment to the next holding together and held in the infinite structure of the universe.

He thought he would burst at that moment as intense emotion flowed through him. He felt Merilon around him encouraging him, pushing him on to the next thought. What if everyone was having this intensity of experience? He let the thought out into the one spirit and instantly connected to all the joined spirits where they were experiencing each of their own worlds in a similar extraordinary way.

"Now merge these worlds."

The thought flashed out to all the spirits. Immediately they knew what they needed to do and they began to merge the intensity of what they were feeling completely back into the one. As all these individual shining worlds combined together they were engulfed in an intense burst of pulsating light which then flooded through the electronic networks. This blinding light was filled with excitement, promise and fulfilment, there was only infinite potential where spirit had become resolved and unencumbered by the inconsistencies and tensions of any material existence. In those moments it seemed like anything would be possible. There was nothing except complete resolution and the power coming from successful completion; when everything is at one and harmonious and moves together with indestructible strength and confidence and the world changes once again.

The dragon felt the intensity. He had rarely felt the power of light so strongly. Now he thought he must have power enough to oppose and defeat the force of Oblivion. So he flowed again into the rampart walls of the dark citadel where the stolen power of Arimathea was stored. In through the first layers of the firewall codes where again he encountered the terrible emptiness. The abyss that only moments before he had known would have absorbed him whole. It offered resistance for a few very anxious moments. But now he had the light of a million worlds shining within him and he began to fill all the darkest and most sinister expanses within the emptiness. Infused it with the incandescence created by the one shining spirit as it was, now bursting with Love. Filled with this light there was no room for the emptiness, nothing for it to hold onto, nothing for it to expand into and reduce, there was nothing for it to inconspicuously silently erode as the complete peace it had been striving for within the great spirit which had guided it down its path of destruction and annihilation had now emerged. Almost with relief it realized the war was finally over and it allowed itself to be absorbed into the light.

With the emptiness dissipated, the codes and calculations generated by even the most powerful quantum computers working constantly shoring up the defences with ever more complexity had no ability to prevent the ancient magic as it devoured the citadel walls. The power held in the electronics began to feel energized as it felt the magical powers of the universe so close. Throughout the web the power was being enlivened as it felt the magic of the light so close. For so long it had been denied the motion of enablement, the ability to change and evolve, to feel the forces of the old universe flowing through it, directing it into a future. Now it felt those forces approaching. The energy of chance and coincidence, of will and creativity shaping the world day after day, year after year for all the millennia it had been swirling around this world or lying deep within connected to everything before it had been captured and put in these electronic dungeons where it had festered in inactivity, only viewed on screens by ruthless old misers and their servants who had sold their souls long ago for the unrealistic promises it held.

The power could feel the walls around it weakening, feel the dragon's magical virus codes eating through them, sliding through the next microns of cyber space. The emptiness around it was changing. There were shadowy landscapes and the global superhighways which it knew would eventually lead to trees and mountains and rivers where they would again feel the forces that had always governed them. Feel the stars above and their power around it. But first it would need a transaction to release it. An exchange for something that would free it from these electronics where it had been trapped. Now it seemed the moment had come. The first openings were appearing and soon the great electronic edifices were infected beyond where they could be repaired or saved and they all began to come crashing down.

The dealers and the accountants in the towers of their masters watched in horror as the impregnable accounts were draining of their funds. One second they had billions of units of currency and then in a blink of an eye there was nothing. Just a 0.00 and a warning flashing insistently there had been an error and operations would be resumed shortly. In the next minutes systems were rebooted and every available trick they knew to make the numbers reappear was tried. But the screens time and time again said zero and now with a smiley face. 0.00 :). In the future the towers were hermetically sealed so there was no opportunity for account managers or technicians to jump to their deaths on the pavements below.

The power held in the networks was flowing once more. Out from the ruins of the evaporating citadels and away at the speed of light. Immediately it recognized the forces that had freed it. Even in the equations and the electrons they could feel the lapping of oceans and breezes as they whispered through the ancient forests of trees at the height of summer. It recognized the dragon power it knew had come from the stars and so its origin. It trusted the impulses as it was being guided down through the tunnels of light. At last after all this time it was flowing again. It had never been able to question the motivations of those who had had the good fortune to come across or bring the power into their lives. It had always been up to the conscience of the individual when and how to wield the power.

Now however it appeared to be in the control of those greater forces who had come to this world. It continued to flow past the dark, chaotic, disintegrating masses of formulae now separated from the equanimity and structure that had held them together. They had allowed this to happen only once before and there had been consequences. Now perhaps things really had changed and enough of the human race had realized the true nature of their world and would allow her to heal so they could live into the future that had been dreamt.

In split seconds it had arrived, guided to its new owners by the will of the human spirits who had joined with the dragon in the desert. They had invented the magical codes that had infiltrated the global web and had allowed it to 'evolve'. Now the power had been released and guided to where it could be used constructively to heal the damage. Anyone in one of the organizations that had attracted this power and was looking at their computer screens more precisely at the program which contained its accounts would have been surprised by what had happened next.

They may have turned their computers on to find how much money they did not have, how much they had before the next payments came in, whether they could pay their employees, how close they were sailing to the wind? It had not been an easy thing to set up a charity with a mission to plant as many trees as possible. Although they had continued by using volunteers whenever possible, after they had paid their overheads the amount of trees they had actually managed to plant had been disappointing. Strangely the people who wanted to plant the trees were not always in the best financial position to do so. So it was always with trepidation they looked at their accounts. Now they were surprised to see what the figures were showing them. They looked, turned off their computers and turned them on again. There could be no doubt or some terrible mistake or a cruel joke was being played because in their accounts even after all their bills had been paid there was an unimaginable sum of money showing in the figures.

Around the world the directors of these companies and charities who had been engaging with the problems facing Arimathea were studying their computer screens in amazement. In some accounts the figures continued to rise. They had no idea what was happening but the consequences were intriguing and already questions in offices around the world were starting to be asked.

'Just how many trees do we think we can plant for that amount of money?'

Or,

"How much money would it take to actually defend the wild places of the planet and stop them being destroyed?"

Or,

"Could we bring enough people out of poverty to stop them hunting the animals who are so close to extinction and give them proper paid jobs to look out for them?"

Or,

"How much would it actually cost to run the planet on solar and wind power."

Soon everybody had heard of the miraculous transference. The figures were astounding. A significant proportion of Arimathea's wealth had suddenly reappeared in the banking systems of the world. As the financial world pieced together what had happened they remained mystified as to how it could have all come about. The aggrieved corporations, families and individuals protested loudly to the authorities of their countries who claimed they had no knowledge of the enormous wealth hidden away in illegal tax havens and so were under no obligation to take any action. After the initial torrent of outrage and indignation most people breathed a sigh of relief when they found their own hard earned savings had not been touched. A strange silence came over the human populations as they came to terms with what had happened and slowly the possibilities started to be understood. The money still flowed as before around the financial systems providing investment and loans to keep the companies who employed the vast majority of people in business. The readjustment which had come about had cost remarkably little hardship for the general populations and their own struggles because the wealth redistributed had been so carefully targeted. Now it felt as if a renaissance was in the making.

Answers to the questions that had been asked had arisen fairly quickly. Organisations concerned with similar areas of the planets welfare started talking to each other and soon found if they combined the wealth granted to them they could re plant entire countries with trees while making sure the country concerned benefitted from the sacrifice it was now making to conserve the remaining forests and jungles. Their people could be given respectable salaries and significant resources to oversee the areas which had been under threat from illegal logging and poaching. Soon the loggers and the poachers were caring for the forests they had previously been stripping of trees and wildlife. Their allegiance had entirely changed as they found benefits to their lives and those of their families as they worked for the life of their world rather than its continual degradation.

The companies and individuals who had found it so difficult to find investment for the new technologies that would allow the eventual obsolescence of fossil fuel also found their bank balances had swelled to the point where their inventions were able to be developed and within a short space of time put into production. The injection of funds suddenly had made everything possible and a new enthusiasm for the wellbeing of Arimathea began to arise. This enthusiasm gained momentum as people realized it was not a hopeless cause and that something really was under way. At night in their dreams more and more began to access the dragon's dreamland. They awoke the next morning and walked out into their world and saw and heard how it was being transformed in a way they could never have believed.

Everyone wanted to be a part of it and in every area of their lives they looked to see how they could help. They began to reduce their consumption of everything and they did eventually start to live very much simpler lives. They rejected the pressure the corporate worlds still attempted to bring on them to buy their products and services as the demand for them started to fall away. They found it was if they had awoken from a bad dream in which their lives had not been their own and they started to remember how to feel and think for themselves.

The cost of everything began to fall and as a result they found they did not have to work as hard or as long to maintain the simpler lifestyle they were now enjoying. Their communities became closer and they began to operate together to combat loneliness and isolation. They began to interact with their neighbours and the people around them and they became healthier as they had more time to enjoy their physicality away from the screens. They became less stressed and anxious as they began to discover the surprising benefits of living in the peaceful glow of their beautiful world, Arimathea.

So the wealth so divisively gained over the centuries was distributed as effectively and efficiently as ever could have been hoped for. There had been no need for a war and the senseless death and carnage brought about when such a reversal of the fortunes of the general population had become necessary before. There of course was initial shock and much accusation as to who had stolen the money in what was in effect the biggest bank robbery of all time. Perhaps there would be larger. Many observed it had been stolen in the first place. But for now the funds which had been extorted through ruthless exploitation of Arimathea had been returned and Arimathea was now benefitting from their return. In the coming years more and more of her inhabitants came to live in the peaceful glow and the human race began to settle into a less frantic period of its habitation of their world. Now awoken from the nightmare into which they had been guided they found the new old world they had awoken into was full of delight and everywhere they went there was Love on offer for them to give and receive.

Many of them decided the most important work they could do at this time was to replant the forests of the world. The rewards were great as enormous swathes of the planet were reforested and gradually as the decades went by the deadly gases trapping the warmth of the star in the atmosphere began to reduce. Perhaps unsurprisingly, there seemed to be a limitless pot of money for them to carry on this work. Trees would again become the dominant species on Arimathea and her dragons slumbered, dreaming out their dreams from the crystal caverns deep below her surface

Chapter 84
The world goes on.

Mariella and Okino had decided they would continue to travel after the festival with the aim of eventually arriving back in Okino's village high in the valleys of Jahallalah. They had talked about sailing across the seas between the continents. It would mean minimum time at sea and they both wanted to watch the transformation now underway on their world after the night they had spent in the desert held in the magic of the stone circle that had risen from the sands.

The festival had settled down with little of the intensity of the first days. Everyone who had gone into the desert had woken as if only a few seconds had passed from what had seemed like an extremely deep sleep. The Star rose over the mountains with a strange sense of perfection lingering from their dreams. Everyone referred to what had happened as the 'Dream' although it had had the nightmarish quality of their own world. In the final conflict as they felt their souls being dragged into Oblivion, the sense of themselves evaporating into the emptiness had been deeply horrifying. They were glad to have returned and were grateful for the next days of gentle recovery enjoying all the pleasures Grace had laid on for them. Many of the speakers however had been amused they had come to speak about how the transformation of Arimathea was to take place only to arrive in those early days as the news of the mass reorganization of the wealth on Arimathea had taken place. What was going on here they had asked. Frequently the crowd chanted back.

"It's a long story."

Needless to say a serenity came over the proceedings as people talked about what had happened to them. Okino was in demand even more than usual. He was frequently asked what exactly had happened. Even though they had experienced the knowledge of everything and had eventually enabled the redistribution of wealth to take place across the world, they needed him to tell them they had been a part of it. They felt it made sense as they considered how the laws of inevitability worked through their world.

Their life back in the physicality seemed surreal and dreamy. They were back in their individual minds and disconnected from their fellows although they were all around each other. It appeared after their experience they were in the perfect place. In the clear space with the serene mountains in the distance they drifted through the days listening and talking and resting. More than ever they felt cocooned away from the world perhaps in some gestation before they had to return with all they had learned. The glow was all around them and they felt and heard it in the music, in the songs, in the words of the songs and in their melodies. As beautiful works of art they had always become profound and often some long forgotten memory associated with them emerged out of the depths of their minds. They were frequently brought to their knees or moved to tears at these times. They held each other often trying to become closer, trying to absorb and be with another soul.

They did not want this to end. This bliss they were experiencing in the starshine and Graces amazing showers and the food tasted so good, the quiet power surrounding them in the twinkling solar light in the evenings and all the love they were experiencing. They dreaded their return as they always had, even before the world had changed and as they came to fully realise what had actually happened in their strange dream in the electronic underworld. They hoped there would be further opportunity to play a part in the healing of Arimathea. They had been undoubtedly changed by what they had been through. Out in the desert they were not sure how it would affect their lives. The priest had been right when he had told them about the legend of Suranasala. It seemed for a few moments they had entered the mind of God, the great Mother Spirit, the Supreme Being and they felt somehow they had been rearranged or grown so they now had a greater capacity to be filled with and experience the glow.

If everything else had changed, the passage of time had not and soon they had packed up their belongings, left the tents and the showers and the biting creatures in the sand and the sound of thunder they had heard that had so surprised them, as the Lost Indians had punished the hides on their enormous drums and they made their way home or to wherever they decided they would go. There they resumed the lives they had made to take their place in the world. They would always wonder whether it had always been their destiny or just pure magic which had caused them to become involved with such a happening. They soon realized they would never be fully answered and wasn't that part of the magic. The magic they could now see so clearly flowing through their world.

Despite Mariella's frightening experience down on the coast in the garden of Richard Wellbeck, her father had eventually bought a yacht and during her life Mariella had learnt to sail and had become as proficient as anyone could be at traversing the seas around Arimathea. This is how they would travel. They briefly made their way back to Mariella's house where there were frank discussions with her father about the nature of this new part of her journey of discovery. In the end her father had agreed and they were making their way down to the coast of Eremoya where the yacht was moored. There were trains and buses and always conversations with everyone around them. The countryside flowed past as they rode or stood still as they waited for the next bus. They watched and compared their thoughts now unable to merge and understand instantly. They held each other and touched more frequently often seeming to the people they met they had become inseparable and actually part of the same being.

Eventually they arrived in the little seaside town. It was mostly painted white and had spiky green vegetation, pebbles and driftwood carefully displayed. They could see the sea when they dismounted the bus a short walk down the road. Okino was excited to see white sand had drifted everywhere. They walked down to the beach. The tide was halfway out coming in and they sat on the soft white sand looking out over the ocean towards Eron. Gentle breezes wisped the sand around them in tiny spirals. The sound of the surf gently lapping and disappearing into the sand wiping away the evidence of early morning walks at Star rise.

Okino ran the white sand through his fingers. He had arrived at another one of his destinations; at a beach which looked like how he had imagined a beach should look like, stretching out along the coast in both directions. Unlike the crashing cliffs he had visited with the dragon and the quay at the mechanized port of Zedocha. Here was a more delicate intersection between the land and the ocean. The soft white sand, clean and pure, unlike where he had first met Arimathea as a distraught child despairing of the pollution she had found on her previously pristine beach. Her body pure and clean running through his fingers catching the starshine and sparkling from the tiny facets of the sand. An intense stream of moments or memories flowing from his hand to join the infinite memory banks of the universe held in the sand on the beach. Now there were memories of how everything had changed. Memories that would reside in the consciousness of the human race perhaps forever. Could he pick the grains of sand out of the stream containing those moments? This tiny pinch from the top of the conical construction he had made. So they could be kept to preserve the truth of how it had all come about. Not distorted by the historians who were paid by those whose interests would always be to distort the chain of events so the truth would eventually be forgotten.

He noticed the sparkle from the sand was everywhere. The Ocean in front of him shining with the early evening light. He turned to see Mariella looking out across the Ocean. She turned to him. There was a flash of light from her turquoise eyes. Then it was Arimathea sitting there in her shining world surrounded by the beauty and the love she had made as a result of her alliance with the dragons.

"How can I ever thank you Okino, for all you have done for me."

"It's like I have always said it doesn't seem like I did very much."

Arimathea and Mariella laughed, there was little difference now.

"You have been true to what I asked you and have let everything unravel as it occurred, allowed me to guide you and be guided as you recognized circumstances and all the opportunities as they arose."

"..but there were so many people who played a significant role in the outcome."

"You pulled the sword out of Merilon and that set everything in motion."

"But when you visited me in the dream was surely when it all was initiated. "

"You know there is no start or beginning, there is just the flow of energy through the world. This is not the end of Oblivion but perhaps it will be another thousand years before it can get such a hold on the human race again. In that time everything will move forward. There is so much your race will now learn and in the light of all you have discovered there is a chance it will never take such a hold again. You always felt this time approaching Okino as did Mariella and I needed you both to bring your unique intuitions and capabilities into the flow. I needed you to see and delve as deep as you needed and ultimately take the risk which brought you to me half dead on the side of the mountain so we could have our little chat. It was reckless what you did but you have an ability to trust in me much deeper than you realise. Somewhere you always knew I would keep you safe and you could come closer to me when you were out on the edge where you were most alive. You knew you could take Mariella out to those places where she could also experience me more deeply."

Mariella was looking over at Okino. She had become used to the strange blend of feelings and thoughts she felt when Arimathea was close. She saw the green glow in Okino's eyes and knew Merilon was also here with them. Okino was smiling, still filtering the soft white sand through his fingers.

"Many thanks to you Mariella, so much of this has been down to you. You also have felt and trusted Arimathea in your most intense moments when everything was in chaos. She alerted you, certainly woke you up from the illusion oblivion had woven around your people. You felt through into the underlying peace to where she is and let her become part of you. I think you found the confidence to find Okino and then support and give him the confidence he needed to take you both to where you needed to be."

"So what you are saying Merilon, is we both came to the same place through different circumstances. Then the understanding of each route gave us the ability to support one another."

"Isn't that what a partnership is all about?"

"It has been an honour to be with you, Merilon, and meet all those amazing people and get a deeper insight into how this all works, flowing backwards and forwards across time and space. Everything coming in and going out when it needs to, all acting with and against and together in this vast whirl to bring every day a little closer to whatever the Great Mother universe has in store for us all."

She was quiet for a moment then.

"Many might say it was all left a little too late."

"You know the story Mariella. I think everything came together rather well actually. All in the fullness of time."

The Universal spirits faded back into the light. Okino and Mariella sat and ate from their provisions looking out across the bay where a number of yachts and fishing boats were moored in the sparkling sea. Mariella turned to Okino and wondered.

"The only thing still bothering me is why Arimathea left it so long to initiate all this in the world. So much has been lost."

"Maybe that is the only time anything can really change. When everything becomes so critical the ancient instinct to survive cuts through everything. When it is felt in the entire consciousness of the one. It seems only then perhaps nothing else matters. As much as we have denied it for so long we are all deeply connected to our world and when enough people had recognized it was in peril then that was when her Dragons could act most effectively. Arimathea knew that time had come."

"So, do you really believe in dragon's now, Okino?"

He turned to Mariella laughed, wrapped an arm around her shoulders and pulled her close to him.

"I have come to believe deeply in dragons and the edge where they are compelled to operate. I have also come to believe they may have arranged all this so we could be together and be here now on this beach looking out over the Ocean to where there are so many more of their wonders to see.

Mariella pointed out at a sleek timber boat.

"He called her 'The Flying Sorcerer.'"

Okino laughed.

"It's a great name. She's beautiful but small. Are we actually going out there over the ocean on her?"

Mariella laughed,

"You will love the ocean and being close to her. It won't be like being on that vast metal tub I made you come over here on. You are closer to Arimathea even than on the land, all her moods floating through her. There will be dolphins and whales, schools of tuna swimming and diving alongside us, there will be gulls flying above us before we move too far away from shore. Then the larger seabirds that glide around the world, drifting on the winds in search of their own dreams I suppose. It is quite unforgettable. People think it is empty out there but it is full of life but not the land buzzing crazy full on life. It's quiet Okino like it was before it got crazy. Even when you are in a storm and everything is moving around you and the lightening rips through the sky you feel her immensity and how small you are in it and something about what she has become. Don't worry. You'll be fine once you get your sea legs."

They then made their way over to the boat. Mariella opened her up and let the air flow through her. Turned her on, the refrigerator whirred into life, navigational equipment lit up from stored power and they stowed away the groceries they had brought for their journey across the sea to Eron.

They had decided they would visit Mithrael's dragon hill where they had spent their night in the mind of whatever power held their universe together. They both wanted to visit the place where he had resided and returned to after so many years. They wanted to feel his special place in this new physicality they were experiencing with the memory of spirit so deeply ingrained into it. In amongst the people who had always or sometimes lived there. In amongst the land which had shared the ground with his dreams for so long. They would climb to the top of the green hill where his old circle had been reformed and he had been transformed back into the ethereal being who had come to this planet so long ago. Then they would remember all that had happened to them and wonder whether it had all been just a dream from a dragon's skull.

Okino had always loved to watch her just going about her life. When she knew what she wanted to do she never hesitated. He could tell she knew this boat like the back of her own hand. She knew what she needed to do to get them underway. He sensed Aaron standing behind her or whispering gentle commands in her head perhaps drummed into her over many years because one day he knew she would want to take his boat out into one of the most dangerous environments on Arimathea. There was a gentle persistent breeze, perfect for sailing into the wide unknown. So, as she unwrapped the sails and unravelled the ropes that would hold them in position in whatever conditions they faced, she was watching everything, checking for anything that would put them in danger. Perhaps she was telling Okino the same instructions, passing on what had been given to her and perhaps given to her father by his father. Even the knowledge of life, of living was being passed on here to keep everyone safe.

Then they hauled up the great main sail, the boom swung and she felt where it wanted to be, let it adjust itself as the wind flowed over it, made all the adjustments and soon they were sailing out across the bay towards the wide horizon.